HEINRICH BÖLL

In 1972, **Heinrich Böll** became the first German to win the Nobel Prize for literature since Thomas Mann in 1929. Born in Cologne, in 1917, Böll was reared in a liberal Catholic, pacifist family. Drafted into the Wehrmacht, he served on the Russian and French fronts and was wounded four times before he found himself in an American prison camp. After the war he enrolled at the University of Cologne, but dropped out to write about his shattering experiences as a soldier. His first novel, *The Train Was on Time*, was published in 1949, and he went on to become one of the most prolific and important of post-war German writers. His best-known novels include *Billiards at Half-Past Nine* (1959), *The Clown* (1963), *Group Portrait with Lady* (1971), and *The Safety Net* (1979). In 1981 he published a memoir, *What's to Become of the Boy? or: Something to Do with Books*. Böll served for several years as the president of International P.E.N. and was a leading defender of the intellectual freedom of writers throughout the world. He died in June 1985.

The Essential
HEINRICH BÖLL

The
Collected Stories

HEINRICH
BÖLL

Translated by Leila Vennewitz
and Breon Mitchell

MELVILLEHOUSE
BROOKLYN, NEW YORK

The Collected Stories

All stories © Verlag Kiepenheuer &
Witsch GmbH & Co. KG, Cologne, Germany

With the exception of *The Mad Dog*, all stories are
translated by and © Leila Vennewitz
The Mad Dog is translated by and © Breon Mitchell

Melville House Publishing
145 Plymouth Street
Brooklyn, NY 11201
www.mhpbooks.com

ISBN: 978-1-61219-002-0

Printed in the United States of America

1 2 3 4 5 6 7 8 9 10

Library of Congress Cataloging-in-Publication Data

Böll, Heinrich, 1917-1985.
  [Short stories. English]
  The collected stories / translated from the German by Leila Vennewitz and
Breon Mitchell.
       p. cm.
  A new edition with previously translated stories compiled from various
sources, including several collections and individual periodicals.
  ISBN 978-1-61219-002-0
  1. Böll, Heinrich, 1917-1985--Translations into English. I. Vennewitz, Leila.
II. Title.
  PT2603.O394A2 2011
  833'.914--dc23
                                        2011038546

The Collected Stories brings together all of Heinrich Böll's shorter fiction published in English. With the exception of *The Mad Dog*, the stories and novellas in this volume are translated by Leila Vennewitz.

CONTENTS

CHILDREN ARE CIVILIANS TOO

The collection Children Are Civilians Too *was first published in German as* Wanderer, kommst du nach Spa... *by Friedrich Middelhauve Verlag in October 1950. An earlier translation by Mervyn Savill,* Traveller, If You Come to Spa..., *was published in English by Arco Publisher Limited in May 1956. The present translation was made from* 1947 bis 1951, *a larger collection of Böll's stories from the same period, and also includes* "Black Sheep," *first published in German in December 1951.*

ACROSS THE BRIDGE

The story I want to tell you has no particular point to it, and maybe it isn't really a story at all, but I must tell you about it. Ten years ago there was a kind of prelude, and a few days ago the circle was completed...

A few days ago I was in a train crossing the bridge that once, before the war, had been strong and wide, as strong as the iron of Bismarck's chest on all those monuments, as inflexible as the rules of bureaucracy: a wide, four-track railroad bridge over the Rhine, supported by a row of massive piers. Ten years ago I used to take the same train across that bridge three times a week: Mondays, Wednesdays, and Saturdays. In those prewar days I was an employee of the Reich Gun Dog and Retriever Association—a modest position; I was a kind of errand boy, really. I knew nothing about dogs, of course; I haven't had much education. Three times a week I would take the train from Königstadt, where our head office was, to Gründerheim, where we had a branch office. There I would pick up urgent correspondence, money, and "Pending Cases." The latter were in a large manila folder. Being only a messenger, of course, I never was told what was in the folder...

In the morning I would go straight from the house to the station and catch the eight o'clock train to Gründerheim. The journey took three-quarters of an hour. Even in those days, crossing the bridge scared me. All the technical assurances of well-informed people concerning the ample load capacity of the bridge were to no avail: I was just plain scared. The mere connection of train and bridge scared me; I am honest enough to admit it. The Rhine is very broad where we live. With a quaking heart I was invariably conscious of the slight swaying of the bridge, of the ominous rocking that continued for six hundred yards. At last came the reassuring, more muffled rattle as we regained the railroad embankment, and then came the vegetable plots, rows and rows of vegetable plots—and finally, just before Kahlenkatten, a house: it was

3

to this house that I clung, so to speak, with my eyes. This house stood on solid ground; my eyes would clutch at this house.

The exterior of the house was of reddish-brown stucco, it was very clean, the window frames and ledges all picked out in dark brown. Two floors, three windows upstairs and two down, in the middle the front door with three steps leading up to it. And invariably, if it was not raining too hard, a child would be sitting on these steps, a spindly little girl of about nine or ten holding a large, clean doll and frowning up at the train. Invariably my eyes would stumble over this child, to be brought up short by the window on the left, for each time I saw a woman in there, a bucket beside her, bent double, a scrubbing cloth in her hands, laboriously washing the floor. Invariably, even when it was raining cats and dogs, even when the child was not sitting there on the steps. The woman was always there: the thin nape of her neck betraying her as the mother of the little girl, and that movement to and fro, that typical scrubbing movement. Many a time I meant to notice the furniture, or the curtains, but my eyes were glued to this thin, eternally scrubbing woman, and before I could think about anything else the train had passed. Mondays, Wednesdays, and Saturdays, it must always have been about ten minutes past eight, for in those days the trains were nothing if not punctual. By the time the train had passed, I was left with a view of the clean rear of the house, silent and uncommunicative.

Needless to say, I began wondering about this woman and this house. All the other places we passed held little interest for me. Kahlen-katten—Bröderkotten—Suhlenheim—Gründerheim—there was nothing very interesting about these stations. My thoughts were always preoccupied with that house. Why does the woman wash and scrub three times a week? I wondered. The house didn't look at all as if there were dirty people living in it, or as if a great many visitors came and went. In fact it looked almost inhospitable, although it was clean. It was a clean and yet unwelcoming house.

But when I caught the eleven o'clock train from Gründerheim for the return trip and saw the rear of the house shortly before noon, just beyond Kahlenkatten, the woman would then be washing the panes of the end window on the right. Oddly enough, on Mondays and Saturdays she would be washing the end window on the right, and on Wednesdays the middle window. Chamois in hand, she rubbed and rubbed. Round her head she wore a scarf of a dull, reddish color. But on the way back I never saw the little girl, and now, approaching midday—it must have been a few minutes to twelve, for in those days the trains were nothing if not punctual—it was the front of the house that was silent and uncommunicative.

Although in telling my story I shall make every effort to describe only what I actually saw, presumably no one will object to the modest observation that, after three months, I permitted myself the mathematical combination that on Tuesdays, Thursdays, and Fridays the woman probably washed the other windows. This combination, modest though it was, gradually became an obsession. Sometimes, all the way from just before Kahlenkatten to Gründerheim, I would puzzle over which afternoons and mornings the other windows of the two floors were likely to get washed. In fact, I finally sat down with pencil and paper and devised a kind of cleaning timetable for myself. From what I had observed on the three mornings, I tried to figure out what was likely to get cleaned the other three afternoons and the remaining whole days. For I had the curiously fixed notion that the woman never did anything but wash and scrub. After all, I never saw her any other way, always bent double, so that I thought I could hear her labored breathing, at ten minutes past eight; and busily rubbing with the chamois, so that I thought I could see the tip of her tongue between her tightly drawn lips, shortly before twelve.

The story of this house preyed on my mind. I started daydreaming. This made me careless in my work. Yes, I became careless. I let my thoughts wander too often. One day I even forgot the "Pending Cases" folder. I drew down upon my head the wrath of the district manager of the Reich Gun Dog and Retriever Association. He sent for me; he was quivering with indignation. "Grabowski," he said to me, "I hear you forgot the 'Pending Cases.' Orders are orders, Grabowski." When I maintained a stubborn silence, the boss became more severe. "Messenger Grabowski, I'm warning you. The Reich Gun Dog and Retriever Association has no use for forgetful employees, you know. We can look elsewhere for qualified staff." He looked at me menacingly, but then he suddenly became human. "Have you got something on your mind?" I admitted in a low voice, "Yes." "What is it?" he asked kindly. I merely shook my head. "Can I help? Tell me what I can do."

"Give me a day off, sir," I asked diffidently, "that's all I ask." He nodded magnanimously. "Done! And don't take what I said too seriously. Anybody can make one mistake; we've always been quite satisfied with you..."

My heart leaped with joy. This interview took place on a Wednesday. And the following day, Thursday, was to be my day off. I had it all figured out. I caught the eight o'clock train, trembling more with impatience than with fear as we crossed the bridge: there she was, washing the front steps. I caught the next train back from Kahlenkatten and passed her house just about nine: top floor, middle window, front. I rode back and forth four times that day and had the whole Thursday timetable complete: front steps, middle window top floor front, middle window top floor back, attic, front room top. As I passed the house for the last time at six o'clock, I saw a little man's stooped figure digging humbly away in the garden. The child, holding the clean doll, was watching him like a jaileress. The woman was not in sight...

But all this happened ten years ago, before the war. A few days ago I crossed that bridge again by train. My God, how far away my thoughts had been when I got onto the train at Königstadt! I had forgotten the whole business. Our train was made up of boxcars, and as we approached the Rhine, a strange thing happened: one after another the boxcars ahead of us fell silent. It was quite extraordinary, as if the whole train of fifteen or twenty cars were a series of lights going out one after another. And we could hear a horrible, hollow rattle, a kind of windy rattle; and suddenly it sounded as if little hammers were being tapped against the floor of our boxcar, and we fell silent too, and there it was: nothing, nothing ... nothing; left and right there was nothing, a ghastly void ... in the distance the grassy banks of the Rhine ... boats ... water, but one didn't dare look too far out: just looking made one giddy. Nothing, nothing whatever! I could tell from the white face of a silent farmer's wife that she was praying; other people were lighting cigarettes with trembling hands; even the men playing cards in the corner had fallen silent...

Then we could hear the cars up front riding over solid ground again, and we all had the same thought: They've made it. If something happens to the train, maybe those people can jump out, but we were in the last car but one, and it was almost a foregone conclusion that we would plunge into the river. The conviction was there in our eyes and in our pale faces. The temporary bridge was no wider than the tracks; in fact, the tracks themselves were the bridge, and the side of the boxcar hung out over the bridge into space, and the bridge rocked as if it were about to tip us off into space...

But then all of a sudden there was a firmer rattle; we could hear it coming closer, quite distinctly, and then under our car too it became somehow deeper, more substantial, this rattle, we breathed again and dared to look out: there were vegetable plots! Oh, may God bless vegetable plots! And suddenly I realized where we were, and my heart throbbed queerly the closer we came to Kahlenkatten. For me there was but one question: would that house still be standing? And then I saw it, first from a distance through the delicate sparse green of a few trees in the vegetable plots, the red façade of the house, still very clean, coming closer and closer. I was gripped by an indefinable emotion. Everything, the past of ten years ago and everything that had happened since then, raged within me in a frenzied, uncontrollable turmoil. And then the house came right up close, with giant strides, and then I saw her, the woman: she was washing the front steps. No, it wasn't her—those legs were younger, a little heavier, but she had the same movements, those jerky, thrusting movements as she pushed the scrubbing cloth to and fro. My heart stood still, my heart marked time. Then the woman turned her face for just a moment, and instantly I recognized the little girl of ten years ago; that pinched, spidery, frowning face, and in the expression on her face something rather sour, something disagreeably sour like stale salad...

As my heart slowly started beating again, it struck me that today was in fact Thursday...

MY PAL WITH THE LONG HAIR

It was a funny thing: exactly five minutes before the raid started I had a feeling something was wrong... I looked warily round, then strolled along the Rhine toward the station, and it didn't surprise me at all to see the jeeps come dashing up full of red-capped military police who proceeded to surround the block, cordon it off, and begin their search. It all happened incredibly fast. I stood just outside the cordon and calmly lit a cigarette. Everything was done so quietly. Quantities of cigarettes landed on the ground. Too bad, I thought ... instinctively making a rough calculation as to the cash that must be lying around there. The truck rapidly filled up with the ones they had nabbed. Franz was among them ... he gestured to me from a distance in a resigned kind of way, as much as to say: Just my luck. One of the policemen turned round to look at me, so I left. But slowly, very slowly. Hell, let them pick me up too, I couldn't care less.

I was in no mood to go back to my room, so I continued my stroll toward the station. I flicked a pebble aside with my stick. The sun was warm, and a cool, soft breeze blew from the Rhine.

At the station buffet I gave Fritz, the waiter, the two hundred cigarettes and stuffed the money into my hip pocket. I had no more to sell now, just a packet for myself. In spite of the crowds jamming the place, I managed to find a seat and ordered a bowl of soup and some bread. Again I saw Fritz signaling me from across the room, but I didn't feel like getting up, so he came hurrying across to me, with little Mausbach, the contact man, in tow. They both seemed pretty excited. "Man, are you ever a cool customer!" muttered Fritz, and, shaking his head, he went off, leaving the field to little Mausbach.

Mausbach was all out of breath. "For God's sake, man," he stammered, "beat it! They've searched your room and found the dope... Oh my God!" He was almost choking. I patted him reassuringly on the shoulder and gave him twenty marks. "That's okay," I said, and off he trotted. But I suddenly had an idea and called him back. "Listen, Heini," I said, "d'you suppose you could find a safe place for my books and overcoat? They're in my room. I'll come by again in a couple of weeks, okay? You can keep the rest of my things." He nodded. I could trust him. I knew that.

Too bad, I thought again—eight thousand marks down the drain. Nowhere, nowhere could a fellow feel safe.

A few inquisitive glances came my way as I slowly sat down again and nonchalantly reached for my pocket. Then the buzzing of the crowds closed over me, and I knew that nowhere else could I have been as marvelously alone with my thoughts as here, surrounded by all these swarms of people milling around in the station buffet.

All at once I was aware that my gaze, as it more or less automatically circled the room without taking anything in, invariably halted at the same spot, as if attracted to it by some magnetic spell. Each time, as my gaze casually toured the room, there was that spot where my eye was caught for a second before sliding hastily over it. I awoke as if from a deep sleep and, now with seeing eyes, looked in that direction.

Two tables away from me sat a girl wearing a light-colored coat, a tan beret on her dark hair, reading a newspaper. I could see very little of her: her shoulders hunching slightly forward, a tiny portion of her nose, and her slender, motionless hands. And I could see her legs too, beautiful legs, slim and ... yes, clean. I don't know how long I stared at her; from time to time I caught sight of the narrow oval of her face as she turned a page. Suddenly she raised her head and for a moment looked me straight in the face with her large gray eyes, grave and detached, then resumed her reading.

That brief glance found its mark.

Patiently, yet conscious of my beating heart, I kept my eyes fixed on her until she finally finished the paper, leaned her arms on the table and, with a strangely despairing gesture, took a sip from her glass of beer.

Now I could see her whole face. A pale face, very pale, a small, fine-drawn mouth, and a straight, patrician nose ... but her eyes, those huge, grave, gray eyes! Like a mourning veil her black hair hung down in dark waves to her shoulders.

I don't know how long I stared at her, whether it was twenty minutes, an hour, or longer. Each time she ran her eyes over my face, her glance became more uneasy, more brief, but her face showed none of the indignation girls usually show on such occasions. Uneasiness, yes ... and fear.

God knows I didn't want to make her uneasy or afraid, but I couldn't take my eyes off her.

At last she got up abruptly, slung a worn haversack over her shoulder, and quickly left the buffet. I followed her. Without turning round she went up the steps toward the barrier. I kept her firmly, firmly within my line of vision as, with barely a pause, I hurriedly bought a platform ticket. She had a good head start on me, and I had to tuck my stick under my arm and try to run a little. I very nearly lost her in the dimly lit underpass leading up to the platform. I found her up at the top leaning against the remains of a bombed-out platform shelter. She was staring fixedly at the tracks. Not *once* did she turn round.

A chill wind from the Rhine was blowing right into the station. Evening came. A lot of people with packs and rucksacks, boxes and suitcases, stood about on the platform with harassed expressions. They turned their heads in dismay to where the wind was blowing from, and shivered. Ahead of them, dark blue and tranquil, yawned the great semicircle of the sky, punctured by the iron latticework of the station roof.

I limped slowly up and down, now and then glancing toward the girl to make sure she hadn't disappeared. But she was still there, still leaning straight-legged against the ruined wall, her eyes fixed on the flat, black trough in which the shining rails were embedded.

At last the train backed slowly into the station. While I was looking toward the engine, the girl had jumped onto the moving train and disappeared into a compartment. I lost sight of her for several minutes among all the knots of people jostling their way into the compartments, but before long I glimpsed the tan beret in the last car. I got in and sat down right opposite her, so close that our knees were almost touching. When she looked at me, very gravely and quietly, her brows slightly puckered, the expression in her great gray eyes told me that she knew I had been following her the whole time. Again and again my eyes fastened helplessly on her face as the train sped into the oncoming evening. My lips refused to utter a word. The fields sank from view, and the villages gradually became shrouded in the night. I felt cold. Where was I going to sleep tonight, I thought ... where would I ever be able to breathe easily again? Ah, if I could only bury my face in that black hair. That was all I asked, I asked for nothing more... I lit a cigarette. She cast a fleeting but oddly alert glance at the package. I merely held it out to her, saying huskily, "Help yourself," and felt as if my heart were going to jump out of my throat. She hesitated for a fraction of a second, and in spite of the darkness I saw her momentarily blush. Then she took one. She pulled deeply and hungrily on the cigarette as she smoked.

"You are very generous." Her voice was dark-toned and brusque. A few minutes later I heard the conductor in the next compartment, and as if at a signal we instantly threw ourselves back into our corners and pretended to be asleep. But I could see through my half-open lids that she was laughing. I watched the conductor as he shone his glaring flashlight onto the tickets and checked them. And the next moment the light was shining right into my face. I could feel from the way the light wavered that he was hesitating. Then the light fell on her. How pale she was, and how sad the white surface of her forehead.

A stout woman sitting beside me pulled at the conductor's sleeve and whispered something in his ear. I caught the words "American cigarettes ... black market ... no ticket ..." to which the conductor responded by giving me a spiteful jab in the ribs.

·There was silence in the compartment as I asked her quietly where she was going. She named a town. I bought two tickets for the place and paid the fine. The silence of the other passengers, after the conductor had gone, was icy and scornful. But her voice was strange, warm and yet mocking, as she asked, "So you're going there too?"

"Oh, I might as well get off there. I have friends there. I've got no permanent home ..."

"I see" was all she said. She leaned back in her corner, and in the close darkness I could only glimpse her face whenever a light outside rushed by.

It was pitch-dark by the time we got out. Dark and warm. And when we emerged from the station, the small town was already fast asleep. The little houses slept safe and sound beneath the gentle trees. "I'll go with you," I said hoarsely. "It's so dark you can't see a thing."

But suddenly she stopped. It was under a streetlight. She fixed me with a long, wide-eyed stare and said in a strained voice, "If only I knew where I was going." Her face moved slightly, like a scarf stirred by a breeze. No, we did not kiss ... We walked slowly out through the town and eventually crawled into a haystack. I had no friends here, of course: I was as much a stranger in this silent town as in any other. When it got chilly toward morning, I crept close beside her, and she covered me with part of her thin, skimpy coat. And so we warmed each other with our breath and our blood.

We have been together ever since—in these hard times.

THE MAN WITH THE KNIVES

Jupp held the knife by the tip of the blade, letting it joggle idly up and down; it was a long, tapering bread knife, obviously razor-sharp. With a sudden flick of the wrist he tossed the knife into the air. Up it went, whirring like a propeller; the shining blade glittered like a golden fish in a sheaf of lingering sunbeams, struck the ceiling, lost its spin, and plunged down straight at Jupp's head. In a flash Jupp had placed a wooden block on his head; the knife scored into the wood and remained embedded there, gently swaying. Jupp removed the block from his head, withdrew the knife, and flung it with a gesture of annoyance at the door, where it stuck, quivering, in the frame until it gradually stopped vibrating and fell to the floor. . .

"It makes me sick," said Jupp quietly. "I've been working on the logical assumption that people who've paid for their tickets really want to see a show where life and limb are at stake—like at the Roman circuses—they want to be convinced of at least the possibility of bloodshed, know what I mean?"

He picked up the knife and tossed it neatly against the top crossbar of the window, with such force that the panes rattled and threatened to fall out of the crumbling putty. This throw—confident and unerring—took me back to those hours of semidarkness in the past when he had thrown his pocketknife against the dugout post, from bottom to top and down again.

"I'll do anything," he went on, "to give the customers a thrill. I'll even cut off my ears, only it's hard to find anyone to stick them back on again. Here, I want to show you something."

He opened the door for me, and we went out into the hallway. A few shreds of wallpaper still clung to the walls where the glue was too stubborn for them to be ripped off and used for lighting the stove. After passing through a moldering bathroom, we emerged onto a kind of terrace, its concrete floor cracked and moss-covered.

Jupp pointed upward.

"The higher the knife goes, of course, the greater the effect. But I need some resistance up there for the thing to strike against and lose momentum so that it can come hurtling down straight at my useless skull. Look!" He pointed up to where the iron girders of a ruined balcony stuck out into the air.

"This is where I used to practice. For a whole year. Watch!" He sent the knife soaring upward. It rose with marvelous symmetry and evenness, seeming to climb as smoothly and effortlessly as a bird; then it struck one of the girders, shot down with breathtaking speed, and crashed into the wooden block. The impact itself must have been terrific. Jupp didn't bat an eyelid. The knife had buried itself a couple of inches in the wood.

"But that's fantastic!" I cried. "It's absolutely sensational, they'll have to like it—what an act!"

Jupp nonchalantly withdrew the knife from the wood, grasped it by the handle, and made a thrust in the air.

"Oh, they like it all right. They pay me twelve marks a night, and between the main acts they let me play around a bit with the knife. But the act's not elaborate enough. A man, a knife, a block of wood, don't you see? I ought to have a half-naked girl so I can send the knife spinning a hairsbreadth past her nose. That'd make the crowd go wild. But try and find that kind of a girl!"

He went ahead as we returned to his room. He placed the knife carefully on the table, the wooden block beside it, and rubbed his hands. We sat down on the crate beside the stove and were silent. Taking some bread out of my pocket, I said, "Be my guest."

"Thanks, I will, but let me make some coffee. Then you can come along and watch my performance."

He put some more wood in the stove and set the pot over the opening. "It's infuriating," he said. "Maybe I look too serious, a bit like a sergeant still, eh?"

"Nonsense, you never were a sergeant. D'you smile when they clap?"

"Of course—and bow too."

"I couldn't. I couldn't smile in a cemetery."

"That's a great mistake: a cemetery's the very place *to* smile."

"I don't get it."

"Because they aren't dead. They're none of them dead, see?"

"I see, all right, but I don't believe it."

"There's still a bit of the lieutenant about you after all. Well, in that case it just takes longer, of course. The point is, I'm only too glad if they enjoy it. They're burned out inside; I give them a bit of a thrill and get paid for it. Perhaps one of them, just one, will go home and not forget me. 'That man with the knife, for Christ's sake, he wasn't scared, and I'm scared all the time, for Christ's sake,' maybe that's what they'll say because they're all scared, all the time. They trail their fear behind them like a heavy shadow, and it makes me happy if they can forget about it and laugh a little. Isn't that reason enough to smile?"

I said nothing, my eyes on the water, waiting for it to boil. Jupp poured the boiling water onto the coffee in the brown enamel pot, and we took turns drinking from the pot and shared my bread. Outside, the mild dusk began to fall, flowing into the room like soft gray milk.

"What are *you* doing these days, by the way?" asked Jupp.

"Nothing ... just getting by."

"A hard way to make a living."

"Right—for this loaf of bread I had to collect a hundred bricks and clean them. Casual labor."

"Hm ... Want to see another of my tricks?"

In response to my nod he stood up, switched on the light, and went over to the wall, where he pushed aside a kind of rug, disclosing the rough outline of a man drawn in charcoal on the reddish color-wash: a strange lump protruded from what was supposed to be the head, probably signifying a hat. On closer inspection I saw that the man had been drawn on a skillfully camouflaged door. I watched expectantly as Jupp proceeded to pull out a handsome little brown leather suitcase from under the miserable affair that served as his bed and put it on the table. Before opening it, he came over and placed four cigarette butts in front of me. "Roll those into two thin ones," he said.

I moved my seat so that I could watch him as well as get a bit more of the gentle warmth from the stove. While I was carefully pulling the butts apart on the bread paper spread over my knees, Jupp had snapped open the lock of the suitcase and pulled out an odd-looking object: one of those flannel bags consisting of a series of pockets in which our mothers used to keep their table silver. He deftly untied the ribbon and let the bundle unroll across the table to reveal a dozen wood-handled knives, the kind that, in the days when our mothers danced the waltz, were known as "hunting cutlery."

I divided the tobacco shreds scrupulously in half onto the two cigarette papers and rolled them. "Here," I said.

"Here," Jupp said too, and "Thanks," bringing over the flannel bag for me to look at.

"This is all I managed to salvage from my parents' belongings. Almost everything was burned or lost in the rubble, and the rest stolen. When I got back from POW camp I was really on my beam ends, didn't own a thing in the world—until one day a dignified old lady, a friend of my mother's, tracked me down and brought along this nice suitcase. A few days before my mother was killed in an air raid she had left it with the old lady to be looked after, and it had survived. Funny, isn't it? But of course we know that when people panic they try to save the strangest things. Never the essential ones. So then at least I was the owner of the contents of this suitcase: the brown enamel pot, twelve forks, twelve knives and twelve spoons, and the long bread knife. I sold the spoons and forks, living off the proceeds for a year, and practiced with the knives, thirteen of them. Watch..."

I passed him the spill I had used to light my cigarette. Jupp stuck his cigarette to his lower lip, fastened the ribbon of the flannel bag to a button on the shoulder of his jacket, and let the flannel unroll along his arm like some exotic panoply of war. Then with incredible speed he whisked the knives out of their pockets, and before I could follow his movements he had thrown all twelve like lightning against the dim human outline, which reminded me of those sinister, shambling figures that came lurching at us toward the end of the war from every bill-board, every corner, harbingers of defeat and destruction. Two knives were sticking out of the man's hat, two over each shoulder, and the others, three a side, along the dangling arms...

"Fantastic!" I cried. "Fantastic! But you've got your act right there, with a bit of dramatizing."

"All I need is a man, better still a girl. But I know I'll never find anyone," he said with a sigh, plucking the knives out of the door and slipping them carefully back into their pockets. "The girls are too scared and the men want too much money. Can't blame them, of course; it's a risky business."

Once again he flung the knives back at the door in such a way as to split the entire black figure accurately down the middle with dazzling symmetry. The thirteenth knife, the big one, stuck like a deadly arrow just where the man's heart should have been.

Jupp took a final puff of the thin, tobacco-filled roll of paper and threw the scant remains behind the stove.

"Let's go," he said, "it's time we were off." He stuck his head out the window, muttered something about "damned rain," and added: "It's a few minutes to eight, I'm on at eight-thirty."

While he was packing the knives away in the suitcase I stood with my face by the open window. Decaying villas seemed to be whimpering softly in the rain, and from behind a wall of swaying poplars came the screech of the streetcar. But nowhere could I see a clock.

"How d'you know what time it is?"

"Instinct—that's part of my training."

I gaped at him. First he helped me on with my coat and then put on his windbreaker. My shoulder is slightly paralyzed and I can't move my arms beyond a certain radius, just far enough to clean bricks. We put on our caps and went out into the dingy corridor, and I was glad to hear at least some voices in the house, laughter, and a subdued murmuring.

"It's like this," said Jupp as we went down the stairs. "What I've tried to do is trace certain cosmic laws. Watch." He put the suitcase down on a stair and spread his arms, an Icarus poised for flight in the way the ancient Greeks used to show him. His matter-of-fact expression assumed a strangely cool and dreamlike quality, something between obsession and detachment, something magical, that I found quite spine-chilling. "Like this," he said softly. "I simply reach out into the atmosphere, I feel my hands getting longer and longer, reaching out into a dimension governed by different laws, they push through a ceiling, and beyond are strange, spell-binding tensions—I just take hold of them, that's all ... and then I seize their laws, snatch them away, part thief, part lover, and carry them off." He clenched his fists, drawing them close to his body. "Let's go," he said, and his expression was its usual matter-of-fact self. I followed him in a daze...

Outside, a chill rain was falling softly and steadily. We turned up our collars and withdrew shivering into ourselves. The mist of twilight was surging through the streets, already tinged with the bluish darkness of night. In several basements among the bombed-out villas a meager light was burning under the towering black weight of a great ruin. The street gradually became a muddy path where to left and right, in the opaque twilight, shacks loomed up in the scrawny gardens like junks afloat in a shallow backwater. We crossed the streetcar tracks, plunged into the maze of narrow streets on the city's outskirts, where among piles of rubble and garbage a few houses still stood intact in the dirt, until we emerged suddenly into a busy street. The tide of the crowds carried us along for a bit, until we turned a corner into a dark side street where a garish illuminated sign saying The Seven Mills was reflected in the glistening asphalt.

The foyer of the vaudeville theater was empty. The performance had already begun, and the buzzing of the audience penetrated the shabby red drapes.

With a laugh Jupp pointed to a photograph in a display case, where he was shown in cowboy costume between two coyly smiling dancers whose breasts were hung with sparkling tinsel. Beneath was the caption: The Man with the Knives.

"Come on," said Jupp, and before I grasped what was happening I found myself being dragged through a half-hidden door. We climbed a poorly lit staircase, narrow and winding, the smell of sweat and grease-paint indicating the nearness of the stage. Jupp was ahead—suddenly he halted in a turn of the stairs, put down the suitcase, and, gripping me by the shoulders, asked in a hushed voice, "Are you game?"

I had been expecting this question for so long that when it came its suddenness startled me. I must have looked nonplussed, for after a pause he said, "Well?"

I still hesitated, and suddenly we heard a great roar of laughter that seemed to come pouring out of the narrow passage and engulf us like a tidal wave; it was so overwhelming that I jumped and involuntarily shuddered.

"I'm scared," I whispered.

"So am I. Don't you trust me?"

"Sure I do ... but ... Let's go," I said hoarsely, pushing past him and adding, with the courage born of despair, "I've nothing to lose."

We emerged onto a narrow corridor with a number of rough ply-wood cubicles right and left. A few oddly garbed figures were scurrying about, and through an opening in the flimsy wings I could see a clown on the stage, his enormous mouth wide open; once again the roar of the crowd's laughter engulfed us, but Jupp pulled me through a door and shut it behind us. I looked around. The cubicle was tiny, practically bare. On the wall was a mirror, Jupp's cowboy costume hung on the single nail, and on a rickety chair lay an old deck of cards. Jupp moved with nervous haste; he took my wet coat from me, flung the cowboy suit onto the chair, hung up my coat, then his windbreaker. Over the top of the partition I could see an electric clock on a fake red Doric column, showing twenty-five after eight.

"Five minutes," muttered Jupp, slipping into his costume. "Shall we rehearse it?"

Just then someone knocked on the cubicle door and called, "You're on!"

Jupp buttoned up his shirt and stuck a ten-gallon hat on his head. With a forced laugh I cried, "D'you expect a condemned man to rehearse his own hanging?"

Jupp snatched up the suitcase and dragged me through the door. Outside stood a bald-headed man watching the clown going through his final motions on the stage. Jupp whispered something to the man that I didn't catch, the man glanced up with a start, looked at me, looked at Jupp, and shook his head vehemently. And again Jupp whispered something to him.

I couldn't have cared less. Let them impale me alive. I had a crippled shoulder, I had just finished a thin cigarette, tomorrow I would get three-quarters of a loaf for seventy-five bricks. But tomorrow... The applause almost blew down the wings. The clown, his face tired and contorted, staggered toward us through the opening in the wings, stood there for a few seconds looking morose, and then went back onto the stage, where he smiled graciously and bowed. The orchestra played a fanfare. Jupp was still whispering to the bald-headed man. Three times the clown came back into the wings and three times he went out onto the stage and bowed, smiling.

Then the orchestra struck up a march and, suitcase in hand, Jupp strode smartly out onto the stage. His appearance was greeted with subdued clapping. Weary-eyed I watched Jupp fasten the playing cards onto nails that were already in place and then impale each card with a knife, one by one, precisely in the center. The applause became more animated, but not enthusiastic. Then, to a muffled roll of drums, he performed his trick with the bread knife and the block of wood, and underneath all my indifference I was aware that the act really was a bit thin. Across from me, on the other side of the stage, a few scantily dressed girls stood watching... And suddenly the bald-headed man seized me by the shoulder, dragged me onto the stage, greeted Jupp with a grandiose sweep of the arm and, in the spurious voice of a policeman, said, "Good evening, Herr Borgalevsky."

"Good evening, Herr Erdmenger," replied Jupp, likewise in ceremonious tones.

"I've brought you a horsethief, a proper scoundrel, Herr Borgalevsky, for you to tickle a bit with your shiny knives before we hang him ... a real scoundrel..." I found his voice totally ridiculous, pathetically artificial, like paper flowers or the cheapest kind of greasepaint. I glanced at the audience, and from that moment on, faced by that glimmering, slavering, hydra-headed monster crouching there in the dark ready to spring, I simply switched off.

I didn't give a damn, I was dazzled by the glare of the spotlight, and in my threadbare suit and shabby shoes I probably made a pretty convincing horsethief.

"Oh, leave him here with me, Herr Erdmenger. I know how to deal with him."

"Splendid, let him have it, and don't spare the knives."

Jupp took hold of me by the collar while the grinning Erdmenger swaggered off the stage. Someone threw a rope onto the stage, and Jupp proceeded to tie me by the feet to a cardboard column that had a fake door, painted blue, propped up behind it. I was aware of something like an ecstasy of insensibility. To my right I heard the eerie stirring of the tense audience, and I realized Jupp had been right in speaking of its bloodlust. Its thirst quivered on the sickly, stale air, and the orchestra, with its facile drum roll, its muffled lasciviousness, heightened the effect of grisly tragicomedy in which real blood would flow, stage blood that had been paid for... I stared straight ahead, letting my body sag, the rope being so firmly tied that it held me upright. The drum roll became softer and softer as Jupp calmly pulled his knives out of the playing cards and slipped them back into their pockets, from time to time casting melodramatic glances my way as if to size me up. Then, having packed away all his knives, he turned to the audience and in the same odiously stagy voice announced, "Ladies and gentlemen, I am now about to outline this young man with knives, but I wish to demonstrate to you that I do not throw blunt knives." He produced a piece of string, and with perfect sangfroid removed one knife after another from its pocket, touched the string with each, cutting it into twelve pieces, and then replaced the knives one by one in their pockets.

While all this was going on I looked far beyond him, far beyond the wings, far beyond the half-naked girls, into another life, it seemed...

The tension in the audience was electrifying. Jupp came over to me, pretended to adjust the rope, and said softly into my ear, "Don't move a muscle, and trust me..."

This added delay nearly broke the tension, it was threatening to peter out, but he suddenly stretched out his arms, letting his hands flutter like hovering birds, and his face assumed that look of magical concentration that I had marveled at on the stairs. He appeared to be casting a spell over the audience too with this sorcerer's pose. I seemed to hear a strange, unearthly groan and realized that this was a warning signal for me.

Withdrawing my gaze from limitless horizons, I looked at Jupp, now standing opposite me so that our eyes were on a level; he raised his hand, moving it slowly toward a pocket, and again I realized that this was a signal for me. I stood completely still and closed my eyes...

It was a glorious feeling, lasting maybe two seconds, I'm not sure. Listening to the swish of the knives and the short sharp hiss of air as they plunged into the fake blue door, I felt as if I were walking along a very narrow plank over a bottomless abyss. I walked with perfect confidence, yet felt all the thrill of danger. I was afraid, yet absolutely certain that I would not fall; I was not counting, yet I opened my eyes at the very moment when the last knife pierced the door beside my right hand...

A storm of applause jerked me bolt upright. I opened my eyes properly to find myself looking into Jupp's white face: he had rushed over to me and was untying the rope with trembling hands. Then he pulled me into the center of the stage, right up to the very edge. He bowed, and I bowed; as the applause swelled he pointed to me and I to him; then he smiled at me, I smiled at him, and we both bowed smiling to the audience.

Back in the cubicle, not a word was said. Jupp threw the perforated playing cards onto the chair, took my coat off the nail and helped me on with it. Then he hung his cowboy costume back on the nail, pulled on his windbreaker, and we put on our caps. As I opened the door the little bald-headed man rushed up to us shouting, "I'm raising you to forty marks!" He handed Jupp some cash. I realized then that Jupp was my boss, and I smiled; he looked at me too and smiled.

Jupp took my arm, and side by side we walked down the narrow, poorly lit stairs that smelled of stale greasepaint. When we reached the foyer Jupp said with a laugh, "Now let's go and buy some cigarettes and bread..."

But it was not till an hour later that I realized I now had a proper profession, a profession where all I needed to do was stand still and dream a little. For twelve or twenty seconds. I was the man who has knives thrown at him...

RISE, MY LOVE, RISE

Her name on the rough-hewn cross was no longer legible; the cardboard coffin lid had already collapsed, and where a few weeks ago there had been a mound there was now a hollow in which soiled, rotting flowers and faded ribbons, mixed with fir needles and bare twigs, formed a nauseating pulp. Someone must have stolen the candle ends....

"Rise, my love," I whispered, "rise," and my tears mingled with the rain, the monotonous murmuring rain that had been falling for weeks.

I closed my eyes: I was afraid my wish might come true. In my mind's eye I distinctly saw the sagging cardboard lid that must now be lying on her breast, caving in beneath the wet piles of cold, greedy earth that were forcing their way past it into the coffin.

I bent down to remove the bedraggled flowers and ribbons from the sticky clay, and all at once I was aware of a shadow springing out of the ground behind me, with a sudden leap, as a flame sometimes flares up out of a banked fire.

I hastily crossed myself, threw down the flowers, and hurried to the exit. The opaque dusk was welling out of the narrow, shrub-bordered paths, and as I reached the main avenue I heard the sound of the bell summoning visitors from the cemetery. But I heard no footsteps approaching, saw no figure behind me, I just sensed that impalpable yet undeniable shadow at my heels....

I quickened my pace, clanged the rusty gate behind me, crossed the grassy roundabout at the intersection where an overturned streetcar lay exposing its bloated belly to the rain, the accursed gentleness of the rain drumming on the great metal box....

The rain had soaked through my shoes, but I was aware of neither cold nor damp, a hectic fever was driving the blood into the furthest extremities of my limbs, and through the fear that was breathing down my neck I was conscious of that strange gratification that comes from illness and grief....

23

Between rows of shacks, their chimneys emitting wisps of smoke, between ingeniously patched-up fences surrounding gray-black fields, past rotting telegraph poles that appeared to sway in the dusk, my route took me through what seemed to be infinite suburban regions of despair; stepping heedlessly into puddles, I walked faster and faster toward the city's distant, jagged silhouette looming up on the horizon, among the murky twilight clouds, like a labyrinth of misery.

Enormous black ruins sprang up left and right, strangely oppressive sounds assailed me from feebly lighted windows; more fields of black earth, more houses, ruined villas—and horror, as well as my fever, was eating its way deeper and deeper into my very bones as I experienced a nightmarish sensation: behind me it was almost dark, while ahead of me dusk was deepening in the familiar way; behind me night was falling, I was dragging the night after me, trailing it across the distant edge of the horizon, and wherever my foot touched the ground, darkness fell. Not that I saw any of this, but I knew: from the grave of my love, where I had invoked the shadow, I was dragging the relentlessly drooping sail of the night behind me.

The world seemed devoid of human life: a vast, muddy suburban plain, a low mountain range formed by the ruins of the city that had seemed so far away and was now, with unaccountable speed, suddenly so much closer. From time to time I halted, and I could sense the dark presence behind me, waiting, reining itself in, mocking me as it hesitated, and then driving me on with gentle, irresistible pressure.

And now I realized that the sweat was pouring down my whole body; it was an effort to walk, the weight I was dragging, the weight of the world, was heavy. Invisible ropes bound me to it, it to me, and now it was straining and tugging at me as a slipping load forces the exhausted mule inescapably into the abyss. I summoned all my strength to resist those invisible cords, my steps became short and unsteady, like a desperate animal I hurled myself into the strangling harness: my legs seemed to sink into the ground but I still had strength enough to keep my body upright, until I suddenly felt I could hold out no longer, that I was compelled to stop where I was, that the weight had the power to root me to the spot; and the next moment I felt I was losing my footing. I screamed and threw myself once more into the impalpable reins—I toppled forward onto my face, the bond was sundered, an unutterably exquisite freedom was behind me, and ahead was a shining expanse, and she was standing there, she who had been lying in that sordid grave under bedraggled flowers, and this time it was she who said to me, with a smile on her face: "Rise, my love, rise..." but I had already risen and was walking toward her....

THAT TIME WE WERE IN ODESSA

That time we were in Odessa it was very cold. Every morning we drove in great rattling trucks along cobbled streets to the airfield, where we waited, shivering, for the great gray birds that came lumbering across the tarmac; but the first two days, just as we were boarding, an order came through canceling the flight due to bad weather—the fog over the Black Sea was too thick or the clouds were too low—and we climbed onto the great rattling trucks again and drove along cobbled streets back to barracks.

The barracks were huge, dirty, and louse-ridden; we sat about on the floor or sprawled over the stained tables playing cards, or sang and waited for a chance to sneak into town. There were a lot of soldiers waiting there, and the city was off limits. The first two days we tried to slip out, but they caught us, and we were given KP duty and had to carry the heavy scalding coffee urns and unload the bread, while a paymaster, wearing a magnificent fur coat intended for the front lines, stood by counting to see that no one pinched a loaf, and to us it looked as though the paymaster was concerned less with paying than with counting. The sky was still cloudy and dark over Odessa, and the sentries sauntered up and down in front of the black, grimy barrack walls.

The third day we waited till it was quite dark and then simply walked to the gates; when the sentry stopped us we said "Seltchini Commando," and he let us through. There were three of us, Kurt, Erich, and myself, and we walked along very slowly. It was only four o'clock and already quite dark. All we had really wanted was to get outside those great, black, grimy walls, and now that we were outside we would almost rather have been inside again. We hadn't been in the army more than eight weeks and were very scared, but we also knew that if we had been inside again we would most certainly have wanted to get out, and then it would have been impossible, and it was only four o'clock, and we couldn't sleep because of the lice and the singing,

and also because we dreaded and at the same time hoped that the next morning might bring good flying weather, and they would fly us out to the Crimea, where we were supposed to die. We didn't want to die, and we didn't want to go to the Crimea, but neither did we want to spend the whole day cooped up in those grimy, black barracks that smelled of ersatz coffee and where they were forever unloading bread for the front and where paymasters in coats intended for the front lines stood around and counted to see that no one pinched a loaf.

I don't know what we wanted. We walked very slowly along that dark, uneven road on the outskirts of the city. Between unlighted, low houses, the night was contained by a few rotting fence posts, and somewhere beyond lay what seemed to be a wasteland, wasteland just like at home, where people believe a road is going to be built, where they dig sewers and fiddle around with surveying instruments, and nothing ever comes of it, and they toss out rubbish, cinders, and garbage, and grass grows again, coarse, wild grass, and rank weeds, and the sign saying "No Dumping" is hidden by all the rubbish they have dumped around it....

We walked along very slowly because it was still so early. In the darkness we met soldiers heading for the barracks, and there were others coming from the barracks who overtook us. We were scared of the patrols and would have liked to turn back, but we knew that once we were back in barracks we would really be desperate, and it was better to be scared than merely desperate inside those black, grimy barrack walls, where they were forever carrying coffee around and unloading bread for the front, forever unloading bread for the front, and where the paymasters got themselves up in fur coats while we shivered with cold.

Now and again a house to the left or right showed a dim yellow light, and we could hear shrill voices, high-pitched, foreign, scary. And suddenly in the darkness there was a brightly lit window, a lot of noise came from inside, and we heard soldiers' voices singing: "Ah, the sunshine of Mexico!"

We pushed open the door and went in: the air was warm and blue with smoke, and there were soldiers, eight or ten of them, some with women, and they were all drinking and singing, and one of the soldiers burst out laughing as we entered. We were young, and short, the shortest in the whole company; our uniforms were brand-new, the synthetic fibers pricked our arms and legs and the long underwear made our bare skin itch terribly, and the sweaters were brand-new and prickly too.

Kurt, the shortest, went ahead and picked a table; he was an apprentice in a leather factory, and he had told us where the hides came from, although that was a trade secret, and he had even told us the profit they made, although that was a really strict trade secret. We sat down beside him.

A very dark, fat woman, with a good-natured face, came out from behind the bar and asked us what we wanted to drink; since we heard that everything was very expensive in Odessa we first asked how much the wine was.

"Five marks in the carafe," she replied, and we ordered three carafes. We had lost a lot of money at cards and had divided up what we had left: each of us had ten marks. Some of the soldiers were eating too, roast meat, still steaming, on slices of white bread, and sausages smelling of garlic; we suddenly realized we were hungry, and when the woman brought the wine we asked the price of food. She told us the sausages were five marks and meat on bread eight; it was fresh pork, she said, but we ordered three sausages. Some of the soldiers were kissing the women or quite openly hugging them, and we didn't know where to look.

The sausages were hot and greasy, and the wine was very sour. When we had finished the sausages we didn't know what to do next. We had nothing more to say to each other; for two weeks we had lain side by side in the troop train and exchanged confidences. Kurt had been in a leather factory, Erich was from a farm, and I had come straight from school. We were still scared, but we weren't cold anymore....

The soldiers who had been kissing the women now buckled on their belts and went out with the women—three girls with round, friendly faces, giggling and twittering, but they went off now with six soldiers, I think it was six, five anyway. The only soldiers left were the drunk ones who had been singing: "Ah, the sunshine of Mexico!" One of them, who was standing at the bar, a tall, fair-haired corporal, turned round and laughed at us again; as I remember, we were sitting there at our table, very quiet and well-behaved, hands on knees, the way we did during instruction periods in barracks. The corporal then said something to the woman behind the bar and she brought us some clear schnapps in quite big glasses. "We must drink to him now," said Erich, nudging us with his knees, and I kept on calling "Corporal!" until he realized I meant him; then Erich nudged us again and we stood up and shouted in unison: "*Prost*, Corporal!" The other soldiers all roared with laughter, but the corporal raised his glass and called across to us: "*Prost*, grenadiers...."

The schnapps was sharp and bitter, but it warmed us, and we would have liked another.

The fair-haired corporal beckoned to Kurt, and Kurt went over to him and beckoned to us after a few words with the corporal. The corporal told us we were crazy not to have any money, we ought to sell something; and he asked us where we came from and where we were being sent, and we told him we were waiting at the barracks and were to be flown out to the Crimea. His face became serious, and he said nothing. Then I asked him what we could sell, and he said: anything.

We could flog anything here, he said, coats and caps, long underwear, watches, fountain pens.

We didn't want to sell our coats, we were too scared, it was against regulations, and besides we felt the cold very much, that time we were in Odessa. We emptied our pockets: Kurt had a fountain pen, I had a watch, and Erich a brand-new leather wallet he had won at a lottery back at barracks. The corporal took all three and asked the woman what she would give for them; she examined everything very minutely, said it was poor stuff, and offered two hundred and fifty marks, a hundred and eighty for the watch alone.

The corporal said that wasn't much, two hundred and fifty, but he also told us she wouldn't be likely to offer more, and if we had to fly to the Crimea next day maybe it didn't make any difference, we might as well take it.

Two of the soldiers who had been singing: "Ah, the sunshine of Mexico!" came over and tapped the corporal on the shoulders; he nodded to us and they all left together.

The woman had handed all the money to me, so I ordered for each of us two portions of roast pork on bread and a large schnapps, then we each had another two portions of roast pork and another schnapps. The meat was fresh and juicy, hot and almost sweet, the bread was soaked with fat, and we had another schnapps. Then the woman told us she had no more roast pork, only sausages, so we each had a sausage and ordered a beer to go with it, thick, dark beer, and we had another schnapps and ordered cakes, flat dry cakes made of ground nuts; then we had some more schnapps and were not drunk at all; we felt warm and snug and forgot all about our prickly long underwear and sweaters; and some more soldiers came in and we all sang: "Ah, the sunshine of Mexico! ... "

By six o'clock we had spent all our money, and still we weren't drunk; we went back to barracks because we had nothing else to sell. Along the dark, uneven road there were no more lights, and when we reached the gates the sentry told us to report to the guardhouse. The guardhouse was hot and dry, dirty, and smelled of tobacco, and the sergeant shouted at us and told us we needn't think we could get away with it. But that night we slept very well, and the next morning we again drove in the great rattling trucks along cobbled streets to the airfield, and it was cold there in Odessa, the weather was gloriously clear, and at last we were boarded onto the planes; and as they rose into the sky we suddenly knew that we would never come back, never....

"STRANGER, BEAR WORD TO
THE SPARTANS WE. . ."

After the truck stopped, the engine kept on throbbing for a while; somewhere outside a big gate was flung open. Light fell through the shattered
window into the truck, and I saw that the light in the roof was smashed
too; only its metal screw was left sticking out of the socket, with a
few quivering wires and shreds of glass. Then the engine stopped, and
outside a voice shouted, "The dead over here—got any dead in there?"

"For Chrissake," the driver called back, "don't you bother about
the blackout any more?"

"What the hell good is a blackout when the whole town's burning
like a torch?" shouted the other voice. "Well? Got any dead in there?"

"Dunno."

"The dead over here, d'you hear? And the others up the stairs into
the art room, right?"

"Okay, okay."

But I wasn't dead yet, I was one of the others, and they carried me
up the stairs. First came a long, dimly lit corridor, green oil paint on
the walls; bent, black, old-fashioned clotheshooks had been let into the
walls, and there were doors with little enamel plaques—VIA and VIB—
and between these doors, shining softly under glass in a black frame,
Feuerbach's *Medea* gazed into the distance; then came doors with VA
and VB, and between them hung a photograph of the boy plucking a
thorn from his foot, its marvelous russet sheen framed in brown.

The great central column at the foot of the stairs was there too,
and behind it, long and narrow, a beautiful plaster reproduction of the
Parthenon frieze, creamy yellow, genuine, antique, and everything was
all there just as it should be: the ancient Greek warrior, resplendent and
formidable, plumed like a cock; and there along the staircase wall—
yellow oil paint here—they all hung: from the Hohenzollern rulers
down to Hitler...

And over in the narrow passageway, where at last I could lie level on my stretcher for a few paces, there was the finest, biggest, most colorful picture of all: old Frederick the Great with his sky-blue uniform, lively eyes, and the great shining gold star on his chest.

Once again I was lying tilted on the stretcher and being carried past the racial paradigms, including the Nordic captain with the eagle eye and the stupid mouth, the Rhine maiden, a bit bony and severe, the East Prussian with his broad grin and bulbous nose, and the Alpine profile with lantern jaw and Adam's apple; then came another corridor, again I lay level on my stretcher for a few paces, and just before the stretcher bearers swung round onto the second staircase I caught a glimpse of it: the war memorial surmounted by the great gilded Iron Cross and the stone laurel wreath.

This all happened very quickly: I am not heavy, and the stretcher bearers were in a great hurry. Yet it might all be a hallucination, I was running a high fever and my whole body hurt—head, arms, and legs, and my heart was thumping like crazy. You see a lot of funny things when you're feverish.

But after the Nordic faces came all the other things: the three busts of Caesar, Cicero, and Marcus Aurelius, superb reproductions, standing sedately side by side against the wall, yellowed and genuine, antique and dignified, and then as we swung round the corner came the Hermes column, and way at the end of the corridor—painted pink here—way, way at the end of the corridor Zeus' big ugly mug hung over the entrance to the art room; but that was still a long way off. To the right, through the window, I could see fire reflected, the whole sky was red, and dense black clouds of smoke filed past in solemn procession... And again my eyes turned to the left and I saw the little plaques over the doors, IA and IB, and between the musty brown doors I saw just the tip of Nietzsche's nose and his mustache in a gilt frame because the other half of the picture had a sign stuck over it saying MINOR SURGERY.

I wonder, I thought fleetingly ... I wonder ... and there it was: the picture of Togoland, large, highly colored, flat as an old engraving, a thing of beauty, and in the foreground in front of the colonial houses, in front of the Africans and the soldier standing pointlessly around with his rifle, in the very foreground was the huge, lifelike bunch of bananas: one bunch on the left, one on the right, and on the middle banana in the right-hand bunch something had been scribbled, I could just make it out. I must have written it myself...

But just at that moment the door to the art room was flung open, and I floated in under Zeus' whiskers and shut my eyes. I didn't want to see any more. The art room smelled of iodine, excrement, bandages, and tobacco, and it was noisy. As they set me down I asked the stretcher bearers, "Light me a cigarette, will you, top left-hand pocket."

I could feel one of them fumbling in my pocket, a match hissed, and the lighted cigarette was stuck between my lips. I took a long pull. "Thanks," I said.

All this, I thought, doesn't prove a thing. Logically speaking, every high school has an art room, corridors with bent old clotheshooks let into green- and yellow-painted walls; logically speaking, the fact that *Medea* hangs between VIA and VIB and Nietzsche's mustache between Ia and Ib is no proof that I'm in my old school. No doubt there's some regulation requiring it to hang there. Rule for Prussian High Schools: *Medea* between VIA and VIB, *Boy with a Thorn* on that wall, Caesar, Marcus Aurelius, and Cicero in the corridor, and Nietzsche upstairs where they're already taking philosophy. Parthenon frieze, colored print of Togoland. *Boy with a Thorn* and Parthenon frieze are, after all, good old stand-bys, traditional school props, and no doubt I wasn't the only boy who had been moved to write on a banana "Long live Togoland." And the jokes, too, that boys tell each other in school are always the same. Besides, maybe I'm feverish, maybe I'm dreaming.

The pain had gone now. In the truck it had still been pretty bad; I had yelled every time they drove through the small potholes, the shell craters had been better: the truck rose and sank like a ship in a wave trough. But now the injection they had stuck in my arm somewhere in the dark seemed to be working: I had felt the needle boring through the skin and my leg lower down getting all hot.

It can't be true, I thought, the truck couldn't have driven that far: nearly twenty miles. Besides, I feel nothing. Apart from my eyes, nothing tells me I'm in my school, in my old school that I left only three months ago. Eight years in the same school is a pretty long time—is it possible that after eight years only your eyes recognize the place?

Behind my closed lids I saw it all again, reeling off like a film: downstairs corridor, painted green, up the stairs, painted yellow, war

memorial, corridor, up more stairs, Caesar, Cicero, Marcus Aurelius ...
Hermes, Nietzsche's mustache, Togoland, Zeus' ugly mug...

I spat out my cigarette and yelled. It always felt good to yell; but
you had to yell loud, it was a glorious feeling, I yelled like mad. When
someone bent over me, I still didn't open my eyes; I smelled someone's
breath, hot and fetid with tobacco and onions, and a quiet voice asked,
"What's the matter?"

"I want a drink," I said, "and another cigarette, top pocket."

Once more someone fumbled in my pocket, once more a match
hissed, and someone stuck a burning cigarette between my lips.

"Where are we?" I asked.

"In Bendorf."

"Thanks," I said, and drew on my cigarette.

So at least I really was in Bendorf, in my hometown, that is, and
unless I had an exceptionally high fever there seemed to be no doubt
that I was in a high school with a classics department; it was certainly a
school. Hadn't that voice downstairs shouted, "The others into the art
room"? I was one of the others, I was alive; the living were evidently
the others. The art room was there, then, and if I could hear properly
why shouldn't I be able to see properly, so that it was probably true that
I had recognized Caesar, Cicero, and Marcus Aurelius, and that could
only happen in a classics high school. I didn't think they stood those
fellows up against the wall in any other kind of school.

At last he brought me some water: again I smelled the tobacco-
and-onion breath and, without wanting to, I opened my eyes. They saw
a weary, elderly, unshaven face above a fireman's uniform, and an old
man's voice whispered, "Drink, lad!"

I drank; it was water, but water is glorious. I could taste the tin
mug against my lips, and it was wonderful to feel how much water was
still waiting to be drunk, but the fireman whisked the mug from my lips
and took off. I yelled, but he didn't turn round, just gave a weary shrug
of the shoulders and walked on. A man lying next to me said quietly,
"No use yelling, they haven't any more water. The town's burning, you
can see for yourself."

I could see it through the blackout curtains: there were flares and
booms behind the black material, red behind black like in a stove when
you throw on fresh coal. I could see it all right: the town was burning.

"What town is it?" I asked the man lying next to me.

"Bendorf," he said.

"Thanks."

I looked straight ahead at the row of windows, and sometimes at the ceiling. The ceiling was still in perfect condition, white and smooth, with a narrow antique stucco border; but all schools have antique stucco borders on their art-room ceilings, at least the good old traditional classics high schools. No doubt about that.

I had to accept the fact that I was in the art room of a classics high school in Bendorf. Bendorf has three of these schools: the Frederick the Great School, the Albertus School, and—perhaps I need hardly add—the last, the third, was the Adolf Hitler School. Hadn't old Frederick's picture on the staircase wall at the Frederick the Great School been the biggest, the most colorful and resplendent of all? I had gone to that school for eight years, but why couldn't the same picture hang in exactly the same place in other schools, so clear and noticeable that it couldn't fail to catch your eye whenever you went up the first flight of stairs?

Outside, I could hear the heavy artillery firing now. There was hardly any other sound; just occasionally you could hear flames consuming a house and somewhere in the dark a roof would cave in. The artillery was firing quietly and regularly, and I thought: Good old artillery! I know that's a terrible thing to think, but I thought it. God, how reassuring the artillery was, how soothing: dark and rugged, a gentle, almost refined organ sound, aristocratic somehow. To me there is something aristocratic about artillery, even when it's firing. It sounds so dignified, just like war in picture books... Then I thought of how many names there would be on the war memorial when they reconsecrated it and put an even bigger gilded Iron Cross on the top and an even bigger stone laurel wreath, and suddenly I realized that if I really was in my old school, my name would be on it too, engraved in stone, and in the school yearbook my name would be followed by "Went to the front straight from school and fell for..."

But I didn't know what for, and I didn't know yet whether I was in my old school. I felt I absolutely had to make sure. There had been nothing special about the war memorial, nothing unusual, it was like all the rest, a ready-made war memorial—in fact they got them from some central supply house...

I looked round the art room, but they had removed the pictures, and what can you tell from a few benches stacked up in a corner, and from the high, narrow windows, all close together to let in a lot of light because it was a studio? My heart told me nothing. Wouldn't it have told me something if I had been in this place before, where for eight solid years I had drawn vases and practiced lettering, slender, delicate, beautiful reproductions of Roman vases that the art teacher set on a pedestal up front, and all kinds of lettering, Round, Antique, Roman, Italic? I had loathed these lessons more than anything else in school; for hours on end I had suffered unutterable boredom, and I had never been any good at drawing vases or lettering. But where were my curses, where was my loathing, in the face of these dun-colored, monotonous walls? No voice spoke within me, and I mutely shook my head.

Over and over again I had erased, sharpened my pencil, erased ... nothing ...

I didn't know exactly how I had been wounded. I only knew I couldn't move my arms or my right leg, just the left one a little; I figured they had bandaged my arms so tightly to my body that I couldn't move them.

I spat the second cigarette into the aisle between the straw pallets and tried to move my arms, but it was so painful I had to yell; I kept on yelling; each time I tried it, it felt wonderful to yell. Besides, I was mad at not being able to move my arms.

Suddenly the doctor was standing in front of me. He had taken off his glasses and was peering at me. He said nothing; behind him stood the fireman who had brought me the water. He whispered something into the doctor's ear, and the doctor put on his glasses: I could distinctly see his large gray eyes with the faintly quivering pupils behind the thick lenses. He looked at me for a long time, so long that I had to look away, and he said softly, "Hold on, it'll be your turn in a minute..."

Then they picked up the man lying next to me and carried him behind the blackboard. My eyes followed them: they had taken the blackboard apart and set it up crossways and hung a sheet over the gap between wall and blackboard; a lamp was glaring behind it...

There was not a sound until the sheet was pushed aside and the man who had lain next to me was carried out; with tired, impassive faces the stretcher bearers carted him to the door.

I closed my eyes again and thought, I must find out how I've been wounded and whether I'm in my old school.

It all seemed so cold and remote, as if they had carried me through the museum of a city of the dead, through a world as irrelevant as it was unfamiliar, although my eyes, but only my eyes, recognized it; surely it couldn't be true that only three months ago I had sat in this room, drawn vases and practiced lettering, gone downstairs during breaks with my jam sandwich, past Nietzsche, Hermes, Togoland, Caesar, Cicero, Marcus Aurelius, taking my time as I walked to the lower corridor where *Medea* hung, then to the janitor, to Birgeler, for a glass of milk, milk in that dingy little room where you could risk a smoke although it was against the rules. They must be carrying the man who had lain next to me downstairs now, to where the dead were lying, maybe the dead were lying in Birgeler's gray little room that smelled of warm milk, dust, and Birgeler's cheap tobacco...

At last the stretcher bearers came back, and now they lifted me and carried me behind the blackboard. I was floating again, passing the door now, and as I floated past I could see that was right too: in the old days, when the school had been called St. Thomas's, a cross had hung over the door, and then they had removed the cross, but a fresh deep-yellow spot in the shape of a cross had stayed behind on the wall, hard and clear, more noticeable in a way than the fragile little old cross itself, the one they had removed; the outline of the cross remained distinct and beautiful on the faded wall. At the time they were so mad they repainted the whole wall, but it hadn't made any difference. The painter hadn't got quite the right color: the cross stayed, deep yellow and clear, although the whole wall was pink. They had been furious, but it was no good: the cross stayed, deep yellow and clear on the pink wall; they must have used up their budget for paint so there wasn't a thing they could do about it. The cross was still there, and if you looked closely you could even make out a slanting line over the right arm of the cross where for years the boxwood sprig had been, the one Birgeler the janitor had stuck behind it, in the days when it was still permitted to hang crosses in schools...

All this flashed through my mind during the brief second it took for me to be carried past the door to the place behind the blackboard where the glaring lamp shone.

I lay on the operating table and saw myself quite distinctly, but very small, dwarfed, up there in the clear glass of the lightbulb, tiny and white, a narrow, gauze-colored little bundle looking like an unusually diminutive embryo: so that was me up there.

The doctor turned away and stood beside a table sorting his instruments; the fireman, stocky and elderly, stood in front of the blackboard and smiled at me. His smile was tired and sad, and his unshaven, dirty face was the face of someone asleep. Beyond his shoulder, on the smudged reverse side of the blackboard, I saw something that, for the first time since being in this house of the dead, made me aware of my heart—somewhere in a secret chamber of my heart I experienced a profound and terrible shock, and my heart began to pound: the handwriting on the blackboard was mine. Up at the top, on the very top line. I know my handwriting: it is worse than catching sight of oneself in a mirror, much clearer, and there was not the slightest possibility of doubting the identity of my handwriting. All the rest hadn't proved a thing, neither *Medea* nor Nietzsche, neither the Alpine profile nor the banana from Togoland, not even the outline of the cross over the door: all that was the same in every school, but I don't believe they write on blackboards in other schools in my handwriting. It was still there, the Thermopylae inscription we had had to write, in that life of despair I had known only three months ago: "Stranger, bear word to the Spartans we..."

Oh, I know, the board had been too short, and the art teacher had bawled me out for not spacing properly, for starting off with letters that were too big, and shaking his head he had written underneath, in letters the same size, "Stranger, bear word to the Spartans we..."

Seven times I had had to write it: in Antique, Gothic, Cursive, Roman, Italic, Script, and Round. Seven times, plain for all to see: "Stranger, bear word to the Spartans we..."

The fireman, responding to a whispered summons from the doctor, had stepped aside, so now I saw the whole quotation, only slightly truncated because I had started off too big, had used up too many dots.

A prick in my left thigh made me jerk up, I tried to prop myself on my elbows, but couldn't. I looked down at my body, and then I saw: they had undone my bandages and I had no arms, no right leg, and I fell back instantly because I had no elbows to lean on. I screamed; the doctor and fireman looked at me in alarm, but the doctor merely shrugged his shoulders, keeping his thumb on the plunger of his hypo as he pressed it slowly and gently down. I tried to look at the blackboard again, but the fireman was standing right beside me now, obscuring it. He was holding down my shoulders, and I was conscious only of the scorched, grimy smell of his stained uniform, saw only his tired, sad face, and then I recognized him: it was Birgeler.

"Milk," I whispered...

DRINKING IN PETÖCKI

The soldier felt he was getting drunk at last. At the same moment it crossed his mind again, very clearly, that he hadn't a single pfennig in his pocket to pay the bill. His thoughts were as crystal-clear as his perception, he saw everything with the utmost clarity: the fat, shortsighted woman sitting in the shadows behind the bar, intent on her crocheting as she chatted quietly to a man with an unmistakably Magyar mustache—a true operetta face, straight from the *puszta*, while the woman looked stolid and rather German, somewhat too respectable and sedate for the soldier's image of a Hungarian woman. The language they were chatting in was as unintelligible as it was throaty, as passionate as it was strange and beautiful. The room was filled with a dense green twilight from the many close-planted chestnut trees along the avenue leading to the station: a wonderful dense twilight that reminded him of absinthe and made the room exquisitely intimate and cozy. The man with the fabulous mustache, half perched on a chair, looked relaxed and comfortable as he sprawled across the counter.

The soldier observed all this in great detail, at the same time aware that he would not have been able to walk to the counter without falling down. It'll have to settle a bit, he thought, then with a loud laugh shouted "Hey there!," raised his glass toward the woman, and said in German, *"Bitte schön!"* The woman slowly got up from her chair, put aside her crochet work equally slowly, and, carrying the carafe, came over to him with a smile, while the Hungarian also turned round and eyed the medals on the soldier's chest. The woman waddling toward him was as broad as she was tall, her face was kind, and she looked as if she had heart trouble; clumsy pince-nez, attached to a worn black string, balanced on her nose. Her feet seemed to hurt too; while she filled his glass she took the weight off one foot and leaned with one hand on the table. She said something in her dark-toned Hungarian that was doubtless the equivalent of *"Prost"* or "Your very good health," or perhaps even of some affectionate, motherly remark such as old women commonly bestow on soldiers.

The soldier lit a cigarette and drank deeply from his glass. Gradually the room began to revolve before his eyes; the fat proprietress hung somewhere at an angle in the air, the rusty old counter now stood on end, and the Hungarian, who was drinking sparingly, was cavorting about somewhere up near the ceiling like an acrobatic monkey. The next instant everything tilted the other way, the soldier gave a loud laugh, shouted *"Prost!"*, took another drink, then another, and lit a fresh cigarette.

The door opened and in came another Hungarian, fat and short, with a roguish onion face and a few dark hairs on his upper lip. He let out a gusty sigh, tossed his cap onto a table, and hoisted himself onto a chair by the counter. The woman poured him some beer...

The gentle chatter of the three at the counter was wonderful, like a quiet humming at the edge of another world. The soldier took another gulp of wine, put down his empty glass, and everything resumed its proper place.

The soldier felt almost happy as he raised his glass again, repeating with a laugh, *"Bitte schön!"*

The woman refilled his glass.

I've had almost ten glasses of wine, the soldier thought. I'll stop now, I'm so gloriously drunk that I feel almost happy. The green twilight thickened, the farther corners of the bar were already filled with impenetrable deep-blue shadows. What a crime, thought the soldier, that there are no lovers here. It would be a perfect spot for lovers, in this wonderful green-and-blue twilight. What a crime, he thought, as he pictured all those lovers somewhere out there in the world who had to sit around or chase around in the bright light, while here in the bar there was a place where they could talk, drink wine, and kiss...

Christ, thought the soldier, there ought to be music here now, and all these wonderful dark-green and dark-blue corners ought to be full of lovers—and I would sing a song. You bet I'd sing a song. I feel very happy, and I would sing those lovers a song, then I'd really quit thinking about the war; now I'm always thinking a little bit about this damn war. Then I'd quit thinking about it altogether.

He looked closely at his watch: seven-thirty. He still had twenty minutes. He drank long and deep of the dry, cool wine, and it was almost as if someone had given him stronger spectacles: now everything looked closer and clearer and very solid, and he felt himself becoming gloriously, beautifully, almost totally drunk. Now he saw that the two men at the counter were poor, either laborers or shepherds, in threadbare trousers, and that their faces were tired and terribly submissive in spite of the dashing mustache and the wily onion look...

Christ, thought the soldier, how horrible it was back there when I had to leave, so cold, and everything bright and full of snow, and we still had a few minutes left and nowhere was there a corner, a wonderful, dark, human corner where we could have kissed and embraced. Everything had been bright and cold...

"*Bitte schön!*" he shouted to the woman; then, as she approached, he looked at his watch: he still had ten minutes. When the woman started to fill his half-empty glass, he held his hand over it, shook his head with a smile, and rubbed thumb and forefinger together. "Pay," he said, "how many pengös?"

He very slowly took off his jacket, slipped off the handsome gray turtleneck sweater, and laid it beside him on the table in front of the watch. The men at the counter had stopped talking and were looking at him, the woman also seemed startled. Very carefully she wrote a "14" on the tabletop. The soldier placed his hand on her fat, warm forearm, held up the sweater with the other, and asked with a laugh, "How much?" Rubbing thumb and forefinger together again, he added, "Pengös."

The woman looked at him and shook her head, but he went on shrugging his shoulders and indicating that he had no money until she hesitantly picked up the sweater, turned it over, and carefully examined it, even sniffed it. She wrinkled her nose a little, then smiled and with a pencil quickly wrote a "30" next to the "14." The soldier let go of her warm arm, nodded, raised his glass, and took another drink.

As the woman went back to the counter and eagerly began talking to the men in her throaty voice, the soldier simply opened his mouth and sang. He sang "When the Drum Roll Sounds for Me," and suddenly realized he was singing well—singing well for the first time in his life; at the same time he realized he was drunker again, that everything was gently swaying. He took another look at his watch and saw he had three minutes in which to sing and be happy, and he started another song, "Innsbruck, I Must Leave You." Then with a smile he took the money the woman had placed in front of him and put it in his pocket...

It was quite silent now in the bar. The two men with the threadbare trousers and the tired faces had turned toward him, and the woman had stopped on her way back to the counter and was listening quietly and solemnly, like a child.

The soldier finished his wine, lit another cigarette, and knew he would walk unsteadily. But before he left he put some money on the counter and, with a *"Bitte schön,"* pointed to the two men. All three stared after him as he at last opened the door and went out into the avenue of chestnut trees leading to the station, the avenue that was full of exquisite dark-green, dark-blue shadows where a fellow could have put his arms around his girl and kissed her good-bye...

DEAR OLD RENÉE

Whenever you turned up at her place around ten or eleven in the morning, she looked a real fat slattern. Her round massive shoulders bulged beneath the shapeless flowered smock, battered curlers were stuck in her lifeless hair like lead sinkers caught in muddy weeds; her face was bloated, and breadcrumbs still clung to the neckline of her smock. She made no attempt to conceal her unlovely morning appearance, for she was at home to only a few select customers —usually only me—whom she knew to be concerned less with her feminine charms than with her excellent drinks. And her drinks were excellent at that, and high-priced too; in those days she still had a very fine cognac. Besides, she gave credit. In the evening she was a real charmer: well-corseted, her shoulders and breasts high and firm, some sexy stuff sprayed on her hair and her eyes made up, scarcely a man could resist her, and perhaps I was one of the few she was willing to receive in the mornings just because she knew I was always able to withstand her charms in the evenings.

In the morning, around ten or eleven, she was a mess. Her disposition was bad then too, she was given to moralizing and to delivering herself of sententious utterances. When I knocked or rang (she preferred me to knock, "It sounds so intimate," she used to say), I would hear her shuffling footsteps, the curtain behind the frosted-glass door would be pushed aside, and I could see her shadow. She would peer through the pattern of flowers on the glass pane, muttering: "Oh, it's you," and push back the bolt.

She was truly a repulsive sight, but it was the only decent tavern in the place, with its thirty-seven grimy houses and two run-down châteaux, and her drinks were first-rate; besides, she gave credit, and in addition to all this she was really very pleasant to talk to. And so the leaden morning hours would pass in no time. As a rule I stayed only until we could hear the distant voices of the company singing on its way back from drill, and it always gave you a funny feeling to hear the same old song, coming closer and closer, in the same old sluggish silence of that godforsaken hole.

"There it comes again," was her invariable comment, "that crappy war."

And together we would watch the company, the first lieutenant, the sergeants, the corporals, the privates, all marching past the frosted-glass windowpane looking tired and dispirited; we would stand watching the company through the pattern of flowers. Between the roses and tulips were whole strips of clear glass, and you could see the lot of them, row after row, face after face, all sullen and hungry and apathetic....

She knew nearly every one of them personally, in fact she knew them all. Even the teetotalers and the woman-haters, for it was the only decent tavern in the place, and even the most rabid ascetic sometimes has an urge to follow up a bowl of hot bad soup with a glass of lemonade, or in the evening possibly even a glass of wine, when he finds himself trapped in a godforsaken hole consisting of thirty-seven grimy houses and two rundown châteaux, a godforsaken hole that seems about to sink into the mud and to disintegrate in sloth and boredom....

But our company wasn't the only one she knew; she knew all the first companies of all the battalions of the regiment, for, according to some intricately devised plan, after a certain length of time every first company of every battalion was sent back to this dreary place for a six-week period of "rest and recuperation."

During our second period of rest and recuperation, which we spent in drill and boredom, she was starting to deteriorate. She was losing her self-respect. She usually slept now till eleven, served beer and lemonade at noon in her dressing gown, closed up the place again in the afternoon, because, with the company out drilling, the village was as empty as a drained cesspool—and didn't open up again till around seven in the evening, after dozing away the afternoon. She had also stopped bothering about her income. She would lend money to anyone, have a drink with anyone, let her massive body be persuaded to dance, bawling out the songs and finally, with the approaching sound of taps, giving way to paroxysms of sobbing.

On our second arrival in the village I immediately reported sick. I had chosen a disease that made it imperative for the medic to allow me to go to Amiens or Paris to consult a specialist. I was in a pretty good mood as I knocked on her door around ten-thirty. There was not a sound in the village, the empty streets were deep in mud. Then came the familiar shuffling of her slippers, the rustle of the curtain, and Renée's muttered exclamation: "Oh, it's you." A smile flitted across her face. "Oh, it's you!" she repeated as the door opened, "You fellows back again?"

"That's right," I said, throwing my cap onto a chair and following her. "Bring me the best in the house, will you?"

"The best in the house?" she asked, looking somewhat at a loss.

She wiped her fingers on her smock. "I'm sorry, I've been peeling potatoes." She held out her hand; it was still small and firm, a pretty hand. I sat down on a bar stool after bolting the door from the inside.

She was standing rather undecidedly behind the bar.

"The best in the house?" she asked, at a loss.

"Yes," I said, "and make it snappy."

"Hm," she muttered, "but it's a scandalous price."

"Who cares, I've got money."

"All right," she said, wiping her hands again. The tip of her tongue appeared between her bloodless lips, a token of her painful dilemma.

"D'you mind if I bring my potatoes in here to peel?"

"Of course not," I replied. "Get a move on, and have a drink with me."

When she had vanished beyond that narrow, scratched brown door to the kitchen, I looked round the room. Nothing had changed since last year. Over the bar hung the photograph of her alleged husband, a handsome marine with a black mustache, a color photo showing the fellow framed in a lifebelt bearing the word "*Patrie*." The fellow had cold eyes, a brutal chin, and a distinctly patriotic mouth. I didn't care for him. On either side hung a few pictures of flowers and lovers exchanging saccharine kisses. It was all exactly the same as a year ago. Possibly the furniture was a bit shabbier, but could it have got any shabbier? The bar stool I was perched on had one leg glued—I clearly recalled its being broken during a fight between Friedrich and Hans, a fight about an ugly girl called Lisette and this leg still showed the depressing trickle of glue, like a runny nose, that someone had forgotten to rub off with sandpaper.

"Cherry brandy," said Renée, a bottle in one hand and an enamel basin full of potatoes and peelings pinned to her side with her right arm.

"Any good?" I asked.

She smacked her lips. "The best there is, love, a real good one."

"Pour us a couple then, will you?"

She stood the bottle on the counter, let the basin slide onto a little stool behind the bar, and took two glasses from the shelf. Then she filled the shallow glasses with the red liquid.

"Prost, Renée," I said.

"Prost, my lad!"

"Now then—what's new?"

"Nothing," she sighed, deftly peeling her potatoes again. "A few more skedaddled without paying, some glasses got smashed. That nice Jacqueline's having another baby and doesn't know whose it is. The rain's been raining and the sun's been shining, I'm an old woman now and I'm clearing out."

"Clearing out, Renée?"

"Yes," she said without emotion. "Believe me, there's no fun in it any more. The boys have less and less money and get more and more cocky, drinks go down in quality and up in price. Prost, my lad!"

"Prost, Renée!"

We drank down the fiery red stuff, it was first-rate all right, and I immediately refilled our glasses.

"Prost!"

"Prost!"

"There," she said finally, throwing the last peeled potato into a saucepan of water, "that'll do for today. I'll just go and wash my hands so you don't have the smell of potatoes hanging around you. Potatoes smell horrible—don't you agree that potato peelings smell horrible?"

"Yes," I said.

"You're a good lad."

She vanished once more into the kitchen.

The cherry brandy was indeed excellent. A sweet fire of cherries flowed into me, and I forgot the lousy war.

"You like me better this way, eh?"

She was standing in the doorway, properly dressed now and wearing a cream-colored blouse, and you could smell that she had washed her hands with good soap.

"Prost!" I said.

"Prost!"

"So you're really clearing out—but you're not serious?"

"I am," she said, "I'm dead serious."

"Prost," I said, and started to fill the glasses.

"No," she said, "if you don't mind I'll have a lemonade, it's a bit early for me."

"All right, but go on."

"Well," she said, "I've had it." She looked at me, and in her eyes, those bleary, swollen eyes, there was a terrible fear. "D'you hear, my lad? I've had it. It's driving me crazy, this silence. Just listen." She gripped my arm so tightly that I was startled and really did listen. And it was uncanny: there wasn't a sound, and yet it wasn't silent either, there was an indescribable something in the air, a kind of bubbling: the sound of silence.

"D'you hear?" she asked, a note of triumph in her voice. "It sounds like a dunghill."

"A dunghill?" I said. "Prost!"

"That's right," she replied, swallowing some lemonade. "It's exactly like a dunghill, that sound. I'm from the country, you know, from a little place up north near Dieppe, and lying in bed in the evening I used to hear that sound quite distinctly: it was silent, and yet not silent, and later I found out what it was: it's the dunghill, that queer snapping and bubbling and slurping and sucking you hear when people think there's silence. That's when the dunghill is working, dunghills work all the time, and that's exactly the sound they make. Listen!" She gripped my arm tightly again, gazing at me intently, imploringly, out of those bleary, swollen eyes....

But I refilled my glass and said: "I see what you mean," and although I knew just what she meant and could also hear that curious, seemingly illogical sound of bubbling silence, I wasn't scared the way she was; I felt protected, although it was pretty depressing to be sitting here in this lousy hole, in this lousy war, drinking cherry brandy with a panicky tavernkeeper at eleven in the morning.

"Ssh," she said now, "Listen." Far away I could hear the rhythmic, monotonous singing of the company on its way back to the village.

But she put her hands over her ears.

"No," she cried, "not that! That's worse than anything. Every morning at the same minute that dreary singing, it's driving me crazy."

"Prost," I said with a laugh, filling my glass. "Snap out of it!"

"No," she cried again, "that's why I want to leave, it's killing me!"

She kept her hands over her ears while I smiled at her, went on drinking, and followed the singing as it came closer and closer, and it was true, it did sound ominous in the silence of the village. Now the tramp of boots was clearly audible, the barking voices of the corporals in the intervals between singing, and the shouting of the lieutenant who always mustered enough courage and strength to call out: "Come on, men, give us another song!"

"I can't take it any more," whispered Renée, on the verge of tears from sheer exhaustion and still doggedly holding her hands over her ears, "it's killing me, lying like this on the dunghill and listening to them singing...."

This time I stood alone by the window as they marched past, row after row, face after face, hungry and tired, an almost exalted grimness in their faces, yet still apathetic and sullen and somewhere in their eyes a spark of fear....

"Come on," I said to Renée, when the last of them had marched by and the singing had died away. I took her hands away from her ears. "Don't be so silly."

"No," she said obstinately, "I'm not silly, I'm quitting, I'm going to open a movie house somewhere, in Dieppe or Abbeville."

"And how about us, what's going to happen to us?"

"My niece is coming here," she said, looking at me, "a pretty young thing, she'll brighten up the place, I've made up my mind to hand it over to my niece."

"When?" I asked.

"Tomorrow."

"Not tomorrow?" I asked.

"Don't worry," she laughed, "I tell you, she's young and pretty. Look!" She took a photo out of the drawer, but the girl in the picture didn't appeal to me at all; she was young and pretty, but cold, and she had the self-same patriotic mouth as the man whose picture hung over the counter with his lifebelt. ...

"Prost," I said sadly, "tomorrow, then."

"Prost," she said, filling her own glass too.

The bottle was empty, and I felt as if I were rocking on the bar stool like a ship on the high seas, and yet my mind was clear.

"How much," I said.

"Three hundred," she said.

But as I was pulling out the bills she made a sudden gesture, saying, "No, don't, for old times' sake. You're the only one I cared for at all. Spend it all when my niece comes, if you feel like it. Tomorrow."

"Good-by," and she waved to me, and as I went out I saw her dipping her glasses into the chrome sink to rinse them, and I knew that the niece would never have such pretty hands, such small firm hands, as hers, for hands and mouth are almost the same, and it would be terrible if she had patriotic hands....

CHILDREN ARE CIVILIANS TOO

"No, you can't," said the sentry gruffly.

"Why?" I asked.

"Because it's against the rules."

"Why is it against the rules?"

"Because it is, chum, that's what; patients aren't allowed outside."

"But," I said with pride, "I'm one of the wounded."

The sentry gave me a scornful look. "I guess this is the first time you've been wounded, or you'd know that the wounded are patients too. Go on, get back in."

But I persisted. "Have a heart," I said, "I only want to buy cakes from that little girl."

I pointed outside to where a pretty little Russian girl was standing in the whirling snow peddling cakes.

"Get back inside, I tell you!"

The snow was falling softly into the huge puddles on the black schoolyard; the little girl stood there patiently, calling out over and over again, "*Khakes ... khakes ...*"

"My God," I told the sentry, "my mouth's watering, why don't you just let the child come inside?"

"Civilians aren't allowed inside."

"Good God, man," I said, "the child's just a child."

He gave me another scornful look. "I suppose children aren't civilians, eh?"

It was intolerable, the empty, dark street was wrapped in powdery snow, and the child stood there all alone, calling out "*Khakes...*" although no one passed.

I started to walk out anyway, but the sentry grabbed me by the sleeve and shouted furiously, "Get back, or I'll call the sergeant!"

"You're a damn fool," I snapped back at him.

"That's right," said the sentry with satisfaction. "Anyone who still has a sense of duty is considered a damn fool by you fellows."

I stood for another half minute in the whirling snow, watching the white flakes turn to mud; the whole schoolyard was full of puddles, and dotted about lay little white islands like icing sugar. Suddenly I saw the little girl wink at me and walk off in apparent unconcern down the street. I followed along the inner side of the wall.

"Damn it all," I thought, "am I really a patient?" And then I noticed a hole in the wall next to the urinal, and on the other side of the hole stood the little girl with the cakes. The sentry couldn't see us here. May the Führer bless your sense of duty, I thought.

The cakes looked marvelous: macaroons and cream slices, buttermilk twists and nut squares gleaming with oil. "How much?" I asked the child.

She smiled, lifted the basket toward me, and said in her piping voice, "Two marks fifty each."

"All the same price?"

"Yes," she nodded.

The snow fell on her fine blond hair, powdering her with fleeting silver dust; her smile was utterly bewitching. The dismal street behind her was empty, and the world seemed dead...

I took a buttermilk twist and bit into it. It was delicious, there was marzipan in it. Aha, I thought, that's why these cost as much as the others.

The little girl was smiling.

"Good?" she asked. "Good?"

I nodded. I didn't mind the cold, I had a thick bandage round my head that made me look very romantic. I tried a cream slice and let the delectable stuff melt slowly in my mouth. And again my mouth watered...

"Here," I whispered, "I'll take the lot, how many are there?"

She began counting, carefully, with a delicate, rather dirty little forefinger, while I devoured a nut square. It was very quiet, it seemed almost as if there were a soft, gentle weaving of snowflakes in the air. She counted very slowly, made one or two mistakes, and I stood there quite still, eating two more cakes. Then she raised her eyes to me suddenly, at such a startling angle that her pupils slanted upward and the whites of her eyes were the thin blue of skim milk. She twittered something at me in Russian, but I shrugged my shoulders with a smile, whereupon she bent down and with her dirty little finger wrote a 45 in the snow; I added my five, saying, "Let me have the basket too, will you?"

She nodded, carefully handing me the basket through the hole, and I passed a couple of hundred-mark bills through to her. We had money to burn; the Russians were paying seven hundred marks for a coat, and for three months we had seen nothing but mud and blood, a few whores, and money.

"Come back tomorrow, okay?" I whispered, but she was no longer listening. Quick as a wink she had slipped away, and when I stuck my head sadly through the gap in the wall, she had vanished, and I saw only the silent Russian street, dismal and empty; the snow seemed to be gradually entombing the flat-roofed houses. I stood there for a long time, like a sad-eyed animal looking out through a fence, and it was only when I felt my neck getting stiff that I pulled my head back inside the prison.

For the first time I noticed the revolting urinal stench from the corner, and all the nice little cakes were covered with a light sugar-icing of snow. With a sigh I picked up the basket and walked toward the building; I did not feel cold, I had that romantic-looking bandage round my head and could have stood for another hour in the snow. I left because I had to go someplace. A fellow has to go someplace, doesn't he? You can't stand around and let yourself be buried in snow. You have to go someplace, even when you're wounded in a strange, black, very dark country...

WHAT A RACKET

The Half-Woman, the "Woman with No Lower Half," turned out to be one of the most delightful persons I had ever met. She was wearing a charming sombrero-type straw hat, for, like any other modest house-wife, she was sitting in the sun on the little raised porch that had been attached to her trailer home. Below the porch her three children were playing a very original game known to them as "The Neanderthals." The two youngest, a boy and a girl, were obliged to be the Neanderthal couple, while the oldest, a fair-haired youngster of eight who during performances was the Fat Lady's son, took the part of the modern explorer who discovers the Neanderthal couple. Right at the moment he was doing his best to wrench his younger siblings' jawbones out of their sockets so he could take them back to his museum.

The Half-Woman stamped several times on the porch floor on account of the frenzied screams that were threatening to stifle our budding conversation.

The oldest boy's head appeared above the low railing, which was adorned with red geraniums, and he asked crossly, "Yes?"

"Stop that bullying," said his mother, a suppressed amusement in her gentle gray eyes. "Why don't you play Air-Raid Shelter or Bombed Out?"

The boy grumbled something that sounded like "Nuts!," disappeared below the railing, and shouted to the others, "Fire! The whole house is on fire!" Unfortunately I was unable to follow the further course of the game known as Bombed Out, for the Half-Woman was now eyeing me somewhat more closely. In the shade of her broad-brimmed hat, with the sun shining warm and red through it, she looked much too young to be the mother of three children and to fulfill the exacting demands, five times a day, of the role of Half-Woman.

"You are..." she said.

"Nothing," I said, "nothing at all. Consider me nothing but a nothing..."

"You are," she placidly continued, "a former black-market operator, I suppose."

"That's right," I said.

She shrugged her shoulders. "I can't really offer you anything. In any case, wherever we found a spot for you, you would have to work—work, do you know what I mean?"

"Ma'am," I replied, "possibly your idea of a black-market operator's life is a little on the rosy side. Speaking personally, I was, one might say, at the front."

"What?" She stamped her foot again on the porch floor, the children having set up a rather protracted and demented howling. Once again the boy's head appeared above the railing.

"Well?" he asked curtly.

"Play Refugees now," the woman said quietly. "You must flee from the burning city, understand?"

The boy's head vanished again, and the woman asked me, "What?" Oh, she hadn't lost the thread, not she.

"Right at the front," I said, "I was right in the front lines. Is that your idea of an easy way to make a living?"

"At the corner?"

"Well, at the station, actually; you know where I mean?"

"I do. And now?"

"I'd like some kind of a job. I'm not lazy, I assure you, ma'am, I'm not lazy."

"Excuse me," she said. Turning her delicate profile toward me, she called into the trailer, "Carlino, isn't the water boiling yet?"

"Hang on," called a bored voice. "I'm just making the coffee."

"Are you going to have some?"

"No."

"Then bring two cups, if you don't mind. You'll have a cup, won't you?"

I nodded. "And I'll invite you to a cigarette."

The screams below the porch now became so piercing that any further conversation would have been impossible. The Half-Woman leaned over the geranium box and called, "You must run for your lives, hurry, hurry—the Russians have reached the village!"

"My husband," she said, turning round, "isn't here at the moment, but when it comes to hiring I can..."

We were interrupted by Carlino—a slightly built, taciturn, swarthy fellow wearing a hairnet—emerging with cups and coffeepot. He looked at me suspiciously.

"Why won't you join us?" the woman asked him as he turned abruptly away.

"Not thirsty," he mumbled, disappearing inside the trailer.

"When it comes to hiring, I can act pretty well on my own. All the same, you would have to have some kind of skill. Nothing is nothing."

"Perhaps, ma'am," I said humbly, "I could grease wheels or take down the tents, drive the tractor, or be the Strong Man's knockabout."

"Driving the tractor is out," she said, "and there's quite an art to greasing wheels."

"Or operate the brakes," I continued, "on the gondola swings..."

She raised her eyebrows haughtily, for the first time giving me a slightly disdainful look. "Operating the brakes," she said coldly, "is a science, and it wouldn't surprise me if you broke all the customers' necks. Carlino is our brakeman."

"Or..." I was about to suggest diffidently, but a little dark-haired girl with a scar across her forehead came dashing up the half dozen steps that put me in mind of a gangplank.

Throwing herself into her mother's lap she sobbed indignantly, "I've got to die..."

"What?" asked the Half-Woman, aghast.

"I'm supposed to be the little refugee who freezes to death, and Freddi wants to sell my shoes and everything..."

"Well," said her mother, "if you will insist on playing Refugees..."

"But why always me?" said the child. "It's always me who has to die. I'm always the one who's got to die. When we play Bombs or War or Tightrope Walkers, it's always me that's got to die."

"Tell Freddi he's got to die; tell him I said it's his turn to die now." The little girl ran off.

"Or?" asked the Half-Woman. Oh, she didn't lose the thread that easily, not she.

"Or straighten nails, peel potatoes, ladle out soup, anything you say," I cried in despair. "Just give me a chance!"

She stubbed out her cigarette, poured us each another cup of coffee, and gave me a long, smiling look. Then she said, "I'll give you a chance.

You're good at figures, aren't you? You had to be, didn't you, in your former occupation, so"—she hesitated a second—"I'll make you cashier."

I had no words, I was literally speechless, I just got up and kissed
her small hand. We said no more. It was very quiet; all we could hear
was Carlino humming to himself inside the trailer, the way a man hums
when he is shaving. . .

AT THE BRIDGE

They have patched up my legs and given me a job I can do sitting down: I count the people crossing the new bridge. They get such a kick out of it, documenting their efficiency with figures; that senseless nothing made up of a few numbers goes to their heads, and all day long, all day long, my soundless mouth ticks away like clockwork, piling number on number, just so I can present them each evening with the triumph of a figure.

They beam delightedly when I hand over the result of my day's labors, the higher the figure the broader their smiles, and they have every reason to hug themselves when they climb into bed, for many thousands of pedestrians cross their new bridge every day...

But their statistics are wrong. I am sorry, but they are wrong. I am an untrustworthy soul, although I have no trouble giving an impression of sterling integrity.

Secretly it gives me pleasure to do them out of one pedestrian every so often, and then again, when I feel sorry for them, to throw in a few extra. I hold their happiness in the palm of my hand. When I am mad at the world, when I have smoked all my cigarettes, I just give them the average, sometimes less than the average; and when my spirits soar, when I am in a good mood, I pour out my generosity in a five-digit number. It makes them so happy! They positively snatch the sheet from my hand, their eyes light up, and they pat me on the back. How blissfully ignorant they are! And then they start multiplying, dividing, working out percentages, God knows what all. They figure out how many people crossed the bridge per minute today, and how many will have crossed the bridge in ten years. They are in love with the future-perfect tense, the future-perfect is their specialty—and yet I can't help being sorry that the whole thing is a fallacy.

When my little sweetheart crosses the bridge—which she does twice a day—my heart simply stops beating. The tireless ticking of my heart just comes to a halt until she has turned into the avenue and disappeared. And all the people who pass by during that time don't get counted. Those two minutes are mine, all mine, and nobody is going to take them away from me. And when she returns every evening from her ice-cream parlor, when she walks along on the far side, past my soundless mouth which must count, count, then my heart stops beating again, and I don't resume counting until she is out of sight. And all those who are lucky enough to file past my unseeing eyes during those minutes will not be immortalized in statistics: shadow-men and shadow-women, creatures of no account, they are barred from the parade of future-perfect statistics.

Needless to say, I love her. But she hasn't the slightest idea, and I would rather she didn't find out. I don't want her to suspect what havoc she wreaks in all those calculations, I want her to walk serenely off to her ice-cream parlor, unsuspecting and innocent with her long brown hair and slender feet, and to get lots of tips. I love her. It must surely be obvious that I love her.

Not long ago they checked up on me. My partner, who sits across the street and has to count the cars, gave me plenty of warning, and that day I was a lynx-eyed devil. I counted like crazy, no speedometer could do better. The chief statistician, no less, posted himself across the street for an hour, and then compared his tally with mine. I was only one short. My little sweetheart had walked past, and as long as I live I won't allow that adorable child to be whisked off into the future-perfect tense; they're not going to take my little sweetheart and multiply her and divide her and turn her into a meaningless percentage. It made my heart bleed to have to go on counting without turning round to watch her, and I am certainly grateful to my partner across the street who has to count the cars. It might have cost me my job, my very existence.

The chief statistician clapped me on the shoulder and said I was a good fellow, trustworthy and loyal. "To be out one in one hour," he said, "really makes no odds. We allow for a certain margin of error anyway. I'm going to apply for your transfer to horse-drawn vehicles."

Horse-drawn vehicles are, of course, a piece of cake. There's nothing to it. There are never more than a couple of dozen horse-drawn vehicles a day, and to tick over the next number in your brain once every half hour—what a cinch!

Horse-drawn vehicles would be terrific. Between four and eight they are not allowed across the bridge at all, and I could walk to the ice-cream parlor, feast my eyes on her or maybe walk her partway home, my little uncounted sweetheart...

PARTING

We were in that bleak, miserable mood that comes when you have already said good-bye but can't part because the train hasn't left yet. The station was like all stations, dirty and drafty, filled to its vaulted roof with vapory haze and noise, the noise of voices and railway coaches.

Charlotte was standing at the window of the long corridor, constantly jostled and shoved from behind, the object of much cursing, but during these final precious minutes, the last we would ever share, we needed more than just a wave from an overcrowded compartment...

"It was nice of you," I said, for the third time, "it really was nice of you to stop by on your way to the station."

"Don't be absurd, look how long we've known each other. Fifteen years."

"That's right, we're thirty now. Still ... you needn't have."

"Please. Yes, we're thirty now. As old as the Russian Revolution."

"As old as dirt and hunger..."

"A bit younger..."

"You're right: we're terribly young."

She laughed.

"Did you say something?" she asked nervously: she had been bumped from behind with a heavy suitcase.

"No, it was my leg."

"You must do something about it."

"Yes, I will do something about it, it really talks too much."

"Is it all right for you to stand so long?"

"Yes..." What I really wanted to tell her was that I loved her, but I couldn't find the words; for fifteen years I hadn't been able to find the words.

"What was that?"

"Nothing. Sweden, so you're going to Sweden."

"Yes, I feel a bit ashamed, this has become part of our life, really, the dirt and rags and ruins, and I feel a bit ashamed. I feel like a deserter..."

"Nonsense, that's where you belong. Be glad you're going to Sweden."

"Sometimes I am glad, you know, the food, that must be marvelous, and no ruins, no ruins at all. His letters sound so enthusiastic..."

The voice that always announces the train departures sounded out now one platform closer, and I held my breath, but it was not our platform. The voice was only announcing the arrival of an international train from Rotterdam to Basel, and as I looked at Charlotte's small, delicate face, I suddenly recalled the smell of soap and coffee, and I felt utterly wretched.

For a moment a desperate courage filled me, I wanted to drag this little person out of the window and keep her here, for she was mine, I loved her...

"What's the matter?"

"Nothing," I said, "be glad you're going to Sweden."

"I am. His vitality is fantastic, don't you agree? A prisoner of war for three years in Russia, that hair-raising escape, and now he's in Sweden lecturing on Rubens."

"Fantastic, it really is."

"You must get busy too, get your degree at least..."

"Oh, shut up!"

"What?" she asked, horrified. "What?" She had gone quite pale.

"Forgive me," I whispered, "I mean my leg. I talk to it sometimes..."

She didn't look in the least like Rubens, she looked more like Picasso, and I kept wondering why on earth he had married her. She wasn't even pretty, and I loved her.

It was quieter now on the platform; everyone had got onto the train, a few people stood around seeing their friends off. Any moment now the voice would say the train was leaving. Any moment might be the last...

"You really must do something, anything, you can't go on like this."

"No, I can't," I said.

She was the very opposite of Rubens—slim, long-legged, high-strung—and she was as old as the Russian Revolution, as old as the hunger and dirt in Europe, as old as the war.

"I can't believe it...Sweden...it's like a dream."

"It is all a dream."

"Do you think so?"

"Of course. Fifteen years. Thirty years ... another thirty years. Why bother about a degree? It's not worth the effort. Be quiet, damn you!"

"Are you talking to your leg?"

"Yes."

"What does it say?"

"Listen."

We were quite silent, we looked at one another and smiled, and we told one another without saying a word.

She smiled at me. "Do you understand now, is it all right?"

"Yes ... yes."

"Truly?"

"Yes, yes."

"You see," she went on softly, "it's not important to be together and all that. That's not what really matters, is it?"

The voice that announces the train departures was right above me now, official, distinct, and I winced, as if a great gray, impersonal whip had come swishing down under the vaulted roof.

"Good-bye!"

"Good-bye!"

Very slowly the train started to move, sliding away in the darkness under the great roof.

BREAKING THE NEWS

Do you know those dreadful little places where you keep wondering why the railroad ever built a station there; where infinity seems to have congealed over a handful of dirty houses and a dilapidated factory, with fields on all sides condemned to eternal sterility; where you are suddenly aware that they are without hope because there is not a tree, not even a steeple, in sight? The man with the red cap—at last, at last, he gives the signal for the train to pull out—vanishes beneath a signboard bearing an imposing name, and you feel he is paid just to sleep twelve hours a day under a blanket of boredom. A gray horizon is draped over bleak fields cultivated by no one.

Yet I was not the only person to get out: an old woman carrying a large brown-paper parcel stepped down from the next compartment, but by the time I had emerged from the grimy little station she had disappeared as if swallowed up by the ground, and for a moment I was at a loss, not knowing whom to ask for directions. The scattering of brick houses with their dead windows and yellowish-green curtains defied all idea of human habitation, and at right angles to this token street ran a black wall that seemed on the point of collapse. I walked toward this grim-looking wall, afraid to knock at one of the houses of the dead. Then I turned the corner, and next to the grubby, barely legible sign saying INN, I read the words MAIN STREET in clear, neat white lettering on a blue ground. A few more houses forming a crooked façade, crumbling plaster, and on the opposite side, long and windowless, the dingy factory wall like a barricade to the land of desolation. Following my instinct I turned left, but here the place suddenly came to an end; the wall continued for another ten yards or so, then came a leaden-gray field with a barely visible shimmer of green; somewhere the field merged with the gray, limitless horizon, and I had the terrible feeling that I was standing at the end of the world on the brink of a bottomless abyss, as if condemned to be dragged down into that silent, sinister, irresistible undertow of utter hopelessness.

On my left was a small, squat cottage, the kind workmen build in their spare time; I swayed, stumbled, toward it. Passing through a pitiful little gate with a leafless briar rose growing above it, I saw the number, and knew I had come to the right house.

The faded green shutters, their paint long washed away by the rain, were firmly closed, as if glued tight; the low roof—I could reach the gutter with my hand—had been patched with rusty corrugated sheets. The silence was absolute: it was the hour when twilight pauses for breath before welling up, gray and inexorable, over the edge of the horizon. I hesitated for a moment or two at the front door, wishing I had died in '45 when ... instead of standing here about to enter this house. Just as I was going to raise my hand to knock, I heard a cooing sound, a woman's laugh, from inside; that mysterious, indefinable laugh that, depending on our mood, can either soothe us or wring our hearts. Only a woman who was not alone could laugh like that; again I hesitated, and again the burning, rending desire rose up in me to plunge into the gray infinity of the falling twilight that now hung over the broad fields and was beckoning, beckoning me... and with my last ounce of strength I pounded on the door.

First silence, then whispers—and footsteps, soft, slippered footsteps; the door opened, and I saw a fair, pink-cheeked woman who immediately put me in mind of that kind of indescribable radiance that illumines the farthest corners of a shadowy Rembrandt. Golden-red she glowed like a lamp before my eyes in this eternity of gray and black.

With a low cry she stepped back, holding the door open with trembling hands, but when I had taken off my army cap and said, hoarsely, "Good evening," the rigid lines of fear slackened in that strangely shapeless face, and she smiled uneasily and said, "Yes." In the background a muscular male figure loomed up and melted into the obscurity of the narrow passage. "I'd like to see Frau Brink," I said in a low voice. "Yes," the woman repeated tonelessly, and nervously pushed open a door. The male figure disappeared in the gloom. I entered a small room, crammed with shabby furniture, where the odor of bad food and excellent cigars seemed to have settled permanently. Her white hand went up to the switch: now that the light fell on her she seemed pale and amorphous, almost corpselike, only her fair, reddish hair was alive and warm. Her hands still trembling, she clutched her dark-red dress to her heavy breasts although it was closely buttoned—almost as if she were afraid I might stab her. The look in her watery blue eyes was wary, alarmed, as if, certain that some terrible sentence was awaiting her, she were facing a judge. Even the cheap sentimental prints seemed to have been stuck on the walls like indictments.

"Don't be alarmed," I said, my voice tense, and instantly I knew that was the worst way I could possibly have chosen to begin, but before I could go on she said, in a strangely composed voice: "I know all about it, he's dead ... dead." I could only nod. I reached into my pocket to hand over his few belongings, but in the passage a furious voice shouted "Gitta!" She looked at me in despair, then flung open the door and called out shrilly, "For God's sake, can't you wait five minutes?" and banged the door shut again, and I could picture the man slinking off into a corner. Her eyes looked up defiantly, almost triumphantly, into mine.

I slowly placed the wedding ring, the watch, and the paybook with the well-thumbed photographs on the green plush tablecloth. Suddenly she started to sob, wild, terrible cries like an animal's. The outlines of her face dissolved, became soft and shapeless like a slug, and shining teardrops gushed out between her short fleshy fingers. She collapsed onto the sofa, leaning on the table with her right hand while with her left she fingered the pathetic little objects. Memory seemed to be lacerating her with a thousand swords. I knew then that the war would never be over, never, as long as somewhere a wound it had inflicted was still bleeding.

I threw aside everything—disgust, fear, and desolation—like a contemptible burden and placed my hand on the plump, heaving shoulder, and as she turned her astonished face toward me I saw for the first time a resemblance to that photo of a pretty, smiling girl that I had had to look at so many hundreds of times, in '45, when ...

"Where was it—please sit down—on the Russian front?" I could see she was liable to burst into tears again at any moment.

"No, in the West, in the prisoner-of-war camp—there were more than a hundred thousand of us..."

"And when?" Her gaze was wide and alert and extraordinarily alive, her whole face tense and young—as if her life depended on my reply. "In July '45," I said quietly.

She seemed to reflect for a moment, then she smiled—a pure and innocent smile, and I guessed why she was smiling.

Suddenly I felt as if the house were threatening to collapse about my ears, and I got up. Without a word she opened the door, she wanted to hold it open for me but I waited obstinately until she had gone ahead; and when she gave me her pudgy little hand she said, with a dry sob, "I knew it, I knew it, when I saw him off—it's almost three years ago now—when I saw him off at the station," and then she added almost in a whisper, "Don't despise me."

I felt a spasm of pain at these words—good God, surely I didn't look like a judge? And before she could stop me I had kissed her small, soft hand: it was the first time in my life I had ever kissed a woman's hand.

Outside darkness had fallen and, as if still under the spell of fear, I paused for a moment by the closed door. Then I heard her sobbing inside, loud, wild sobs, she was leaning against the front door with only the thickness of the wood between us, and at that moment I did indeed long for the house to collapse about her and bury her.

Then, slowly and very, very carefully—for I was afraid of sinking any moment into an abyss—I groped my way back to the station. Lights were twinkling in the houses of the dead, the tiny place seemed to have grown in all directions. I could even see small lamps beyond the black wall that seemed to be illuminating vast expanses of yard. Dusk had become dense and heavy, foggy, vaporous, and impenetrable.

In the drafty little waiting room there was only an elderly couple standing close together, shivering, in one corner. I waited a long time, my hands in my pockets, my cap pulled down over my ears, for there was a cold draft blowing in from the tracks, and night was falling lower, lower, like an enormous weight.

"If only there were a little more bread, and a bit of tobacco," muttered the man behind me. And I kept leaning forward to peer along the parallel lines of tracks as they converged in the distance between dim lights.

Suddenly the door was flung open, and the man with the red cap, his face a picture of eager devotion to duty, shouted out, as if he had to make his voice carry across the waiting room of a great railroad station: "Train for Cologne—ninety-five minutes late!"

At that moment I felt as if I had been taken prisoner for the rest of my life.

BETWEEN TRAINS IN X

As I awoke, I was filled with a sense of almost utter isolation; I seemed to be floating in darkness on sluggish waters, borne along by aimless currents. Like a corpse that is finally washed up by the waves to the pitiless surface, I eddied this way and that, gently swaying in a dark void. I could not feel my limbs, they had ceased to be a part of me, and my senses no longer functioned. There was nothing to see, nothing to hear, no smell to cling to; only the soft touch of the pillow under my head linked me with reality, my head was the only thing I was conscious of. My thoughts were crystal-clear, barely dimmed by the racking headache that comes from bad wine.

Not even her breath was audible; she slept as lightly as a child, and yet I knew she must be lying beside me. There would have been no point in reaching out my hands to grope for her face or her soft hair, I had no hands. Memory was but a memory of the mind, a bloodless structure that had left no trace on my body.

This was how I had often felt as I walked along the brink of reality with the assurance of the drunk making his way beside the narrow edge of a precipice, lurching with an unaccountable sense of balance toward a goal whose splendor is written on his mouth. I had walked along avenues lit only by sparse gray lamps, leaden lamps that seemed only to suggest reality the better to be able to deny it. With unseeing eyes I had submerged myself in somber streets crowded with people, knowing that I was alone, alone.

Alone with my head, and not even my whole head; nose, eyes, and ears were dead. Alone with only a brain that was straining to recapture memory, as a child builds apparently meaningless objects out of apparently meaningless sticks.

She must be lying beside me, although I had no physical consciousness of her.

The previous day I had left the train that continued south toward the Balkans as far as Athens while I had to change at this little station and wait for a train that was to take me closer to the Carpathian passes. As I stumbled across the platform, uncertain even of the name of the station, a drunken soldier came reeling toward me, a lone figure in his gray uniform among the Hungarians in their colored civilian clothes. He was shouting insults that burned themselves into my brain like the slap in the face whose stinging pain one remembers all one's life.

"Bunch of whores!" he shouted. "Swine, trash—I'm sick of the whole pack!" He was shouting all this into the very faces of the foolishly smiling Hungarians, while, carrying his heavy pack, he headed for the train I had just left.

Immediately a sinister steel-helmeted head called out from a train window, "Hey, you! You there!" The drunk drew his pistol, aimed at the steel helmet; people screamed. I made a dash for the soldier, put my arms around him, removed his weapon and hid it, keeping a firm grip on his flailing arms. The steel helmet shouted, people shouted, the drunk shouted, but the train moved off, and in most cases a moving train renders even a steel helmet powerless. I let go of the drunk, gave him back his pistol, and steered the dazed man to the exit.

The little place had a desolate look. The bystanders had quickly dispersed; the station square was empty. A tired and dirty railroad employee directed us to a tiny bar beneath some low trees on the other side of the dusty square.

We put down our packs, and I ordered wine, that bad wine which was responsible for my present misery. The soldier sat there mute and angry. I offered him cigarettes, we smoked, and I had a good look at him: he was wearing the usual decorations, he was young, about my age, his fair hair hanging loosely over a flat, broad forehead into dark eyes.

"The point is, chum," he said suddenly, "I'm sick of the whole business, see?"

I nodded.

"Sick to death of it, see? I'm getting out."

I looked at him.

"That's right," he said soberly, "I'm getting out, I'm heading for the puszta. I can handle horses, make a decent soup if I have to, they can kiss my ass for all I care. Want to come along?"

I shook my head.

"Scared, eh?... No?... Okay, anyway I'm getting out. So long."

He got up, left his pack on the floor, put some money on the table, nodded to me again, and went out.

I waited a long time. I didn't believe he had really quit, was really heading for the *puszta*. I kept an eye on his pack and waited, drank the bad wine, tried without success to strike up a conversation with the landlord, and stared at the square, across which, from time to time, wreathed in clouds of dust, dashed a cart drawn by thin horses.

After a while I had a steak, went on drinking the bad wine, and smoked cigars. The light was beginning to fade, now and then a cloud of dust would be wafted into the room through the open door; the landlord yawned or chatted with Hungarians as they drank their wine.

Darkness was coming on quickly; I shall never know all the things I was thinking about as I sat there and waited, drank wine, ate steak, watched the fat landlord, stared at the square, and puffed cigars...

My brain reproduced all this quite neutrally, spewing it out while I floated giddily around on those dark waters, in that hourless night, in a house I did not know, in a nameless street, beside a girl whose face I had never seen properly...

Later on I had hurried across to the station, found my train gone and the next one not due till the morning. I had paid my bill, left my pack lying beside the other one, and staggered out into the twilight of the little town. Gray, dark gray, flooded in on me from all sides, and only the sparse lamps gave the faces of passersby the look of living people.

Somewhere I drank a better wine, looked forlornly into the unsmiling face of a woman behind the bar, smelled something like vinegar through a kitchen door, paid, and disappeared again into the dusk.

This life, I thought, is not my life. I have to behave as if this were my life, but I'm no good at it. It was quite dark by now, and the mild sky of a summer evening hung over the town. Somewhere the war was going on, invisible, inaudible in these silent streets where the low houses slept beside low trees; somewhere in this absolute silence the war was going on. I was alone in this town, these people were not my people; these little trees had been unpacked from a box of toys and glued onto these soft, gray sidewalks, with the sky hovering overhead like a soundless dirigible that was about to crash...

Somewhere under a tree there was a face, faintly lit from within. Sad eyes under soft hair that must be light brown although it looked gray in the night; a pale skin with a round mouth that must be red although it too looked gray in the night.

"Come along," I said to the face.

I took hold of her arm, a human arm; the palms of our hands clung together; our fingers met and interlocked as we walked along in this unknown town and turned into an unknown street.

"Don't turn the light on," I said as we entered the room I was now lying in, floating unattached in the darkness.

I had felt a weeping face in the dark and plunged into abysses, down into abysses the way you tumble down a staircase, a dizzying staircase of velvet; on and on I plunged, down one abyss after another...

My memory told me all this had happened, and that I was now lying on this pillow, in this room, beside this girl, without being able to hear her breath; she sleeps as lightly as a child. My God, was my brain all that was left of me?

Often the pitch-black waters would seem to stand still, and hope would stir in me that I was going to wake up, feel my legs, hear again, smell, and not merely think; and even this modest hope was a lot, for it would gradually subside, the pitch-black waters would start eddying again, repossess my helpless corpse, and let it drift, timelessly, in total isolation.

My memory also told me that the night could not last forever. Day had to come some time. And it told me that I could drink, kiss, and weep, even pray, although you can't pray just with your brain. While I knew that I was awake, was lying awake in a Hungarian girl's bed, on her soft pillow in a dark, dark night, while I knew all this, I could not help also believing that I was dead...

It was like a dawn that comes very gently and slowly, so indescribably slowly as to be barely perceptible. First you think you're mistaken; when you're standing in a foxhole on a dark night you can't believe that that's really the dawn; that soft, soft pale strip beyond the invisible horizon; you think you must be mistaken, your tired eyes are oversensitive and are probably reflecting something from some secret reserves of light. But it actually is the dawn, growing stronger now. It actually is getting light, lighter, daylight is growing stronger, the gray patch out there beyond the horizon is slowly spreading, and now you know for certain: day has come.

I suddenly realized I was cold; my feet had slipped out from under the blanket, bare and cold, and the sense of chill was real. I sighed deeply, could feel my own breath as it touched my chin; I leaned over, groped for the blanket, covered my feet. I had hands again, I had feet again, and I could feel my own breath.

Then I reached down over the precipice to my left, fished up my trousers from the floor, and heard the sound of the matchbox in the pocket.

"Don't turn on the light, please," said her voice next to me now, and she sighed too.

"Cigarette?" I whispered.

"Yes," she said.

In the light of the match she was all yellow. A dark yellow mouth, round, black, anxious eyes, skin like fine, soft, yellow sand, and hair like dark honey.

It was hard to talk, to find something to say. We could both hear time trickling away, a wonderful dark flowing sound that swallowed up the seconds.

"What are you thinking about?" she asked all of a sudden. It was as if she had fired a shot, quietly and with such perfect accuracy that a dam burst inside me, and before I had time to take another look at her face in the light of the glowing cigarette tips I found myself speaking. "I was just thinking about who will be lying in this room seventy years from now, who will be sitting or lying on these six square feet of space, and how much he will know about you and me. Nothing," I went on, "he'll only know there was a war."

We each threw our cigarette ends onto the floor to the left of the bed; they fell soundlessly onto my trousers. I shook them off, and the two little glimmering dots lay side by side.

"And then I was thinking who had been here seventy years ago, or what. Maybe there was a field, maybe corn or onions grew here, six feet over my head, with the wind blowing across, and every morning this sad dawn came up over the horizon of the *puszta*. Or maybe there was already a house belonging to someone."

"Yes," she said softly, "seventy years ago there was a house here."

I was silent.

"Yes," she said, "I think it was seventy years ago that my grandfather built this house. That's when they must have put the railroad through here. He worked for the railroad and built this little house with his savings. And then he went to war, ages ago, you know, in 1914, and he was killed in Russia. And then there was my father; he had some land and also worked for the railroad. He died during this war."

"Killed?"

"No, he died. My mother had died before. And now my brother lives here with his wife and children. And seventy years from now my brother's great-grandsons will be living here."

"Maybe so," I said, "but they'll know nothing about you and me."

"No, not a soul will ever know that you were here with me."

I took hold of her small hand—it was soft, so soft—and held it close to my face.

In the square patch of window a dark-gray darkness showed now, lighter than the blackness of the night.

I suddenly felt her moving past me, without touching me, and I could hear the light tread of her bare feet on the floor; then I heard her dressing. Her movements and the sounds were so light; only when she reached behind her to do up the buttons of her blouse did I hear her breath come more strongly.

"You'd better get dressed," she said.

"Let me just lie here," I said.

"I don't want to put on the light."

"Don't put on the light, let me just lie here."

"But you must have something to eat before you go."

"I'm not going."

I could hear her pause as she put on her shoes and knew she was staring in astonishment into the darkness where I was lying.

"I see" was all she said, softly, and I couldn't tell whether she was surprised or alarmed.

When I turned my head to one side I could see her figure outlined in the dark-gray dawn light. She moved very quietly about the room, found kindling and paper, and took the box of matches from my trouser pocket.

These sounds reached me almost like the thin, anxious cries of a person standing on a riverbank and calling out to someone who is being driven by the current into a great body of water; and I knew then that if I did not get up, did not decide within the next minute or so to leave this gently heaving ship of isolation, I would die in this bed as if paralyzed, or be shot to death here on this pillow by the tireless myrmidons whose eyes miss nothing.

While I listened to her humming as she stood there by the stove gazing at the fire, its warm light growing with quiet wingbeats, I felt divided from her by more than a world. There she stood, somewhere on the periphery of my life, quietly humming and enjoying the growing fire; I understood all that, I could see it, smell the singeing of scorched paper, and yet nowhere could she have been further removed from me.

"Please get up, will you?" said the girl from across the room. "You must leave now." I heard her put a saucepan on the fire and begin to stir; it was a soothing sound, the gentle scraping of the wooden spoon, and the smell of browning flour filled the room.

I could see everything now. The room was very small. I was lying on a low wooden bed; next to it was a closet, brown, quite plain, that took up the whole wall as far as the door. Somewhere behind me there must be a table, chairs, and the little stove by the window. It was very quiet, and the early light still so opaque that it lay like shadows in the room.

"Please," she said in a low voice, "I have to go now."

"You have to go?"

"Yes, I have to go to work, and first you must leave, with me."

"Work?" I asked. "Why?"

"What a thing to ask!"

"But where?"

"On the railroad tracks."

"Railroad tracks?" I asked. "What do you do there?"

"We shovel stones and gravel so that nothing will happen to the trains."

"Nothing's going to happen to the trains," I said. "Where do you work? Toward Nagyvárad?"

"No, toward Szeged."

"That's good."

"Why?"

"Because then I won't have to pass you in the train."

She laughed softly. "So you're going to get up after all."

"Yes," I said. I shut my eyes again and let myself drop back into that swaying void whose breath was without smell and without trace, whose gentle rippling touched me like a quiet, barely perceptible waft of air; then I opened my eyes with a sigh and reached for my trousers, now lying neatly beside the bed on a chair.

"Yes," I repeated, and got out of bed.

She stood with her back to me while I went through the familiar motions, drew on my trousers, did up my shoes, and pulled on my gray tunic.

I stood there for a while, saying nothing, my cigarette cold between my lips, looking at her figure, small and slight and now outlined clearly against the window. Her hair was beautiful, soft as a quiet flame.

She turned round and smiled. "What are you thinking about now?" she asked.

For the first time I looked into her face. It was so simple that I could not take it in: round eyes, in which fear was fear, joy was joy.

"What are you thinking about now?" she asked again, and this time she was not smiling.

"Nothing," I said. "I can't think at all. I must go. There's no escape."

"Yes," she said, and nodded. "You must go. There's no escape."

"And you must stay."

"I must stay," she said.

"You have to shovel stones and gravel so that nothing will happen and the trains can safely go where things do happen."

"Yes," she said, "that's what I have to do."

We walked down a silent street leading to the station. All streets lead to stations, and from stations you go off to war. We stepped aside into a doorway and kissed, and I could feel, as my hands lay on her shoulders, I could feel as I stood there that she was mine. And she walked away with drooping shoulders without once looking round at me.

She is all alone in this town, and although my way lies along the same street, to the station, I cannot go with her. I must wait till she has disappeared round that corner, beyond the last tree in this little avenue now lying remorselessly in full daylight. I must wait, I can only follow her at a distance, and I shall never see her again. I have to catch that train, go off to that war...

I have no pack now as I walk to the station; all I have is my hands in my pockets and my last cigarette between my lips, and that I shall soon spit out. But it is easier to be carrying nothing when you are once more walking slowly but unsteadily toward the edge of an abyss over which, at a given second, you are going to plunge, down to where we shall meet again...

And it was comforting when the train pulled in on time, cheerfully puffing steam between tall heads of corn and pungent tomato plants.

REUNION WITH DRÜNG

The burning pain in my head let me pass smoothly into the reality of time and space from a dream in which dark figures in gray-green coats had been pounding my skull with hard fists. I was lying in a low room in a farmhouse, and the ceiling seemed to be sinking down on me out of the green dimness like the lid of a tomb. The few traces of light that made the room barely discernible were green: a soft, yellow-frosted green with a black door sharply outlined by a bright band of light, a steadily deepening green that became the color of old moss in the shadows above my face.

I awoke fully as a sudden, strangling nausea made me jerk upright, lean over, and vomit onto the invisible floor. The contents of my stomach seemed to drop into unplumbed depths, a bottomless well, before eventually penetrating my senses as liquid splashing on wood. I vomited again, bent painfully over the edge of the stretcher, and as I leaned back in relief the connection with the past became so clear that I at once remembered a roll of lemon drops, left over from last night's rations, that must still be in one of my pockets. My grimy fingers groped around in my greatcoat pockets, let a few loose cartridges fall clattering into the green abyss, and turned over every item—a pack of cigarettes, pipe, matches, handkerchief, a crumpled letter—and when I couldn't find what I was looking for in my coat pockets, I undid my belt, the buckle clanking as it struck the iron stretcher bar. I found the roll at last in one of my trouser pockets, ripped off the paper, and stuck one of the tart-flavored drops into my mouth.

At certain moments, when the pain flooded every level of my consciousness, relationships between time, space, and events would become confused again: the abyss on either side seemed to fall still further away, and the stretcher I was suspended on felt like a towering pedestal rising closer and closer toward the green ceiling. There were moments when I even thought I was dead, relegated to an agonizing limbo of uncertainty, and the door—outlined by its bright band—was like a gateway to light and enlightenment that some kindly hand must surely open; for at such moments I lay motionless as a statue, dead, and the only living thing was the burning pain spreading out from the wound in my head and associated with a sickening, all-pervading nausea.

Then the pain would ebb away again, as if someone were loosening a vise, and reality would become less brutal: the various shades of green were balm to my tormented eyes, the absolute silence soothing to my racked ears, and memory unwound within me like a roll of film in which I played no part. Everything seemed to lie in an infinitely remote past, whereas in fact not more than an hour could have gone by.

I tried to revive memories from my childhood, days spent in deserted parks instead of school, and these experiences seemed closer, and to involve me more directly, than what had happened an hour ago, although the pain in my head derived from these recent events and should have made me feel otherwise.

What had happened an hour ago I was now able to see very clearly, but distantly, as if I were looking from the edge of our globe into another world divided from ours by a vast abyss of glassy clarity. There I saw someone, who must be me, creeping over churned earth in nocturnal darkness, the lonely silhouette at intervals starkly illuminated by a distant tracer bullet. I watched this stranger, who must be me, struggling on visibly sore feet over the broken ground, often on all fours, then on his feet again, then back on all fours, up on his feet again, and finally heading for a dark valley where a group of similar dark figures stood gathered round a vehicle. In this spectral corner of the globe, where all was anguish and darkness, the stranger mutely took his place in a line of men whose mugs were being filled from metal cauldrons with coffee or soup by someone they did not know, had never seen, someone hidden by dense shadows, wordlessly ladling; the owner of a scared voice, also invisible, doled out bread, cigarettes, sausage, and candies into the waiting hands. And suddenly this mute, somber spectacle on the valley floor was luridly lit up by a red flame followed by screams, whimpering, and the terrified neighing of a wounded horse; more dusky red flames kept shooting up out of the ground, stench and noise filled the air; then the horse screamed—I heard it pull away and dash off, dragging the clattering field kitchen—and a fresh burst of fierce fire covered the figure that must be me.

And now here I was, lying on my stretcher, looking at the deepening shades of green in the dimness of this Russian farmhouse room where the only brightness was the light outlining the oblong of the door.

Meanwhile the nausea had subsided, the lemon drop had spread soothingly through the horrible muck filling my mouth; the vise of pain attacked less and less often, and I dug into my greatcoat pocket, pulled out cigarettes and matches, and struck a light. The flare revealed dark, damp walls, lit here and there by the flickering sulfur-yellow flame, and as I tossed aside the dying match I saw for the first time that I was not alone.

I saw beside me the gray, green-stained folds of a carelessly drawn-up blanket, saw the peak of a cap like an intense black shadow over a pale face; then the match went out.

At the same moment it occurred to me that there was nothing wrong with my hands or feet, so I kicked my blanket aside, sat up, and was startled to see how close I was to the ground: that apparently bottomless pit was scarcely more than knee-deep. I struck another match. My neighbor lay motionless, his face the color of crepuscular light filtering through thin green glass; but before I could get any closer to have a good look at his face under the shadow of his cap, the match went out again, and I remembered that in one of my pockets there must still be a candle end.

The vise of pain made another assault, and I just managed to stagger to the edge of my stretcher in the dark. I sat down, dropping my cigarette onto the floor, and since I now had my back to the door I could see only darkness, a green opaque darkness containing just enough shadows to give me the feeling it was revolving, while the pain in my head seemed to be the motor making it revolve; the more the pain in my head swelled, the more violently did these darknesses revolve like separate disks overlapping as they revolved, until once more everything came to a standstill.

As soon as the attack was over, I fingered my bandage. My head felt bulky and swollen; there was the hard, lumpy crust of clotted blood, and the ultrasensitive spot where the splinter must be. I knew now that the stranger over there was dead. There is a kind of silence and muteness going beyond sleep or unconsciousness, something infinitely icy, hostile, contemptuous, that in the darkness seemed doubly malevolent.

I finally found the candle end and lit it. The glow was yellow and soft; it seemed to spread slowly and diffidently before unfolding its flame to its utmost limits, and when the candle had achieved its full radius I saw the beaten earth floor, the bluish whitewashed walls, a bench, and the dead stove with a pile of ashes lying in front of its sagging door.

I stuck the candle onto the edge of my stretcher so that the center of its radiance fell on the dead man's face. I was not surprised to see Drüng. Rather, I was surprised at my own lack of surprise, for it should have been a great shock: I had not seen Drüng for five years, and even then so briefly that we had exchanged only the barest civilities. We had been classmates for nine years, but there had been such a deep antipathy—not animosity, merely indifference—between us that during those nine years we had spoken to each other for a total of scarcely an hour.

It was so unmistakably Drüng's spare face, his pointed nose, thrusting upward now, still and greenish, from the spare flatness of his face, his narrow-lidded eyes, always somewhat protruding, now closed by a stranger's hand; so unquestionably was it Drüng's face that there was really no need for me to confirm it by bending down and reaching in under the blanket folds for the label tied with string to one of his greatcoat buttons. On it I read by candlelight: "Drüng, Hubert, Corporal," the number of his regiment, and under the heading TYPE OF INJURY, "Multiple shell splinters, abdomen." Under this an academic hand had scrawled the word "Deceased."

So Drüng was really dead, or would I ever have doubted the hasty scrawl of an academic hand? Again I read the number of his regiment, one I had never heard of; then I took off Drüng's cap, whose black, sardonic shadow gave his face a cruel look, and there was that fairish, lackluster hair which at various times during those fluctuating nine years had been right in front of me.

I was sitting quite close to the candle as its flickering glow swung round the room, the strongest core of its yellow flame always centered on Drüng's face as its feebler offshoots roamed ceiling, walls, and floor. I was sitting so close to Drüng that my breath brushed the ashen skin on which a stubble of beard proliferated, unsightly and reddish-brown, and suddenly for the first time I saw Drüng's mouth. During our daily encounters over so many years, the rest of his appearance had become so familiar that I would have recognized him in a crowd—although probably unconsciously—but now I realized I had never really looked at his mouth. It was as if I had never seen it before: fine-drawn, narrow-lipped, pain still clinging to its pinched corners, a pain so alive that I thought I must be mistaken. This mouth seemed, even now, to be still fighting back the pent-up cries of pain to keep them from gushing out in a red spurt that would drown the world.

Beside me flickered the warm breath of the candle as it flared up, died down, then slowly fanned out, over and over again. I was looking at Drüng's face now without seeing him. I saw him alive, a sickly, shy fourth-grader, heavy satchel on thin shoulders, shivering as he waited for the school doors to open. Then he would rush past the burly janitor and, still wearing his overcoat, plant himself beside the stove, stand-ing guard over it with a defensive look in his eyes. Drüng had always felt the cold, he was of poor physique, poor in every way, the son of a widow whose husband had been killed in the war. He had been ten at the time, and he stayed like that for nine years, shivering, of poor physique, poor in every way, the son of a widow whose husband had been killed in the war. Never once did he have time for those foolish things that memory alone makes memorable, while we often look back on humorless obsession with duty as a foolish thing; never once did he talk back to the teacher, for nine years he remained well behaved, hard-working, always "of average ability." At fourteen he developed acne, at sixteen his skin was smooth again, at eighteen he had acne again, and he always felt the cold, even in summer, for he was of poor physique, poor in every way, the son of a widow whose husband had been killed in the war. He had a few friends, also of average ability, with whom he worked hard and was well behaved. I hardly ever spoke to him, or he to me. Occasionally, as is to be expected over a period of nine years, he had sat in front of me, his lackluster, fairish hair had been in front of me, quite close, and he had always prompted me—now for the first time I realized he had always prompted me, faithfully and reliably; and when he didn't know the answer, he had his own special way of obstinately shrugging his shoulders.

I had been crying for some time, and the candle was now casting its wider light around the room, sighing gently so that the barren little room seemed to rock like the cabin of a ship on the high seas. For some time—without being conscious of it—I had felt the tears running down my face, warm and soothing on my cheeks, and lower down, on my chin, cold drops that I automatically wiped away with my hand like a tearful child. But now that I remembered how he had always loyally prompted me, with never a word of thanks, faithfully and reliably, with none of the spitefulness of others who put too high a price on their knowledge to give it away—now I sobbed aloud, and the tears dripped through my matted beard into my muddy fingers.

And then I remembered about Drüng's father. During history lessons, when the teachers told us in edifying tones about World War I—assuming the topic fell within the curriculum and that Verdun fell within the topic—then all eyes would turn toward Drüng, and at such times Drüng acquired a special, fleeting glory, for it was not often that we had history, or that World War I fell within the curriculum, and still less often was it permitted or appropriate to talk about Verdun...

The candle was hissing now, hot wax bubbling in the cardboard holder; then the unsupported wick toppled over into the melted remains—but suddenly the room was filled with light and I was ashamed of my tears, a light that was cold and naked and gave the drab room a spurious clarity and cleanliness...

It was not until I felt myself grasped by the shoulders that I realized the door had opened and two people had been sent to carry me into the operating room. I shot another glance at Drüng, lying there with pinched lips; then they had laid me back on the stretcher and were carrying me out.

The doctor looked tired and irritable. He watched without interest as the stretcher bearers placed me on a table under a glaring lamp; the rest of the room was shrouded in ruddy darkness. The doctor came closer, and I could see him more clearly: his coarse skin was sallow, with purple shadows, and his thick black hair covered his head like a cap. As he read the label attached to my chest, I noticed the cigarette smell on his breath, and I could see the whitish rolls of fat on his neck and the mask of weary despair over his face.

"Dina," he called softly, "take it off."

He stepped back, and from the ruddy darkness emerged a woman's figure in a white smock; her hair was all wrapped up in a pale-green cloth, and now that she was close, leaning over me and carefully cutting the bandage over my forehead, I saw from the serene, pale oval of her kindly face that she must be blond. I was still crying, and through my tears her face appeared melting and blurred, and her great soft light-brown eyes seemed to be weeping too, while the doctor seemed hard and dry even through my tears.

With a sudden movement she tore the hard, bloody rag from my wound; I screamed and let the tears flow on. The doctor stood scowling at the edge of the circle of light, the smoke from his cigarette reaching us in sharp blue puffs. Dina's face was quiet while she bent over me, touching my head with her fingers as she began to sponge my clotted hair.

"Shave it!" said the doctor brusquely, tossing his cigarette butt angrily onto the floor.

Now the vise of pain renewed its attacks as the Russian nurse began to shave the filthy, matted hair around the gaping wound. Once again the disks started revolving and eerily overlapping. I had moments of unconsciousness, then I would come to again, and during those waking seconds I could feel the tears flowing more and more freely, running down my cheeks and collecting between shirt and collar, compulsively, as if a well had been drilled.

"Don't cry, damn it!" shouted the doctor from time to time, and because I neither could nor would stop, he shouted, "You ought to be ashamed of yourself!" But I was not ashamed, I was aware only of Dina now and again resting her hands in a caress on my neck, and I knew it was futile to try and explain to the doctor why I had to cry. What did I know of him or he of me, of filth and lice, Drüng's face, and nine school years that came punctually to an end when the war broke out?

"Damn it," he shouted, "for God's sake, shut up!"

Then he suddenly came closer, his face looming unbelievably huge, fiercely stern, as he approached, and for one second I felt the first boring of the knife, then saw nothing more and gave only one shrill scream.

They had closed the door behind me, turned the key, and I found myself back in the first room. My candle was still flickering, sending its fleeting light over everything it encountered. I walked very slowly. I was scared; it was all so quiet, and I felt no more pain. Never before had I been so entirely without pain, so empty. I recognized my stretcher by the rumpled blankets, looked at the candle, still burning just as I had left it. The wick was floating in liquid wax, one tiny tip sticking up just enough for it to burn, and any moment now it would be submerged. I patted my pockets apprehensively, but they were empty. I ran back to the door, rattled the handle, shouted, rattled, shouted. Surely they couldn't leave us in the dark! But outside no one seemed to hear; and when I went back, the candle was still burning, the wick was still floating, a tiny piece was still sticking up just enough for it to burn and produce an irregular, flickering light; this piece of wick seemed to have got smaller; in another second we would be in the dark.

"Drüng," I called, scared, "Drüng!"

"Yes?" came his voice. "What's the matter?"

I felt my heart stand still, and all about me there was no sound save the appallingly quiet consuming of this candle end, on the verge of going out.

"Yes?" he asked again. "What's the matter?"

I stepped to the left, bent down, and looked at him: he was lying there laughing. He was laughing very softly and painfully, and there was gentleness too in his smile. He had thrown back the blankets, and through a great hole in his stomach I could see the green canvas of the stretcher. He was lying there quite quietly, and seemed to be waiting. I looked at him for a long time, the laughing mouth, the hole in his stomach, the hair: it was Drüng.

"Well, what's the matter?" he asked again.

"The candle," I whispered, looking into the light. It was still burning; I saw its radiance as, yellow and fitful, forever expiring and forever burning again, it illumined the whole room. I heard Drüng sit up, the stretcher creaked softly, the corner of a blanket was pushed aside, and now I was looking at him again.

"Don't be scared," he shook his head and went on, "The light won't go out, it'll burn forever and ever, I know it will."

But the next instant his pale face seemed to disintegrate still further; trembling, he grasped my arm, I could feel his thin, hard fingers. "Look," he said in a frightened whisper, "now it's going out."

But the anchorless wick was still floating in the cardboard holder, it was still not quite submerged.

"No," I said, "it should have gone out long ago—there wasn't enough to last even two minutes."

"Oh, Christ!" he shouted, his face distorted, and he slammed his hand down onto the light, jarring the stretcher so that the iron clanged, and for one second we were enveloped in greenish darkness, but when he lifted his trembling hand the wick was still floating, it was still light, and through the hole in Drüng's stomach I was looking at a pale-yellow spot on the wall behind him.

"It's no use," he said, lying back on his stretcher, "you'd better lie down too, we'll just have to wait."

I pushed my stretcher right up close to his so that the iron bars were touching, and as I lay down the light was between us, flickering and unsteady, always certain and always uncertain, for it ought to have gone out long ago, but it did not go out; and sometimes we raised our heads at the same time and looked at one another in fear when the convulsive flame seemed to become shorter; and before our despairing eyes was the dark oblong of the door, surrounded by a bright band of shining light...

...and so we lay there waiting, filled with fear and hope, shivering and yet warmed by the panic that seized our limbs when the flame threatened to go out and our green faces met over the cardboard holder as it stood in the midst of those moving lights that flowed around us like soundless wraiths, and suddenly we saw that the light must have gone out, for the wick was submerged, no tip stuck out over the waxen surface now, and yet it was still light—until our amazed eyes saw the figure of Dina, who had come in to us through the locked door, and we knew it was all right to smile now, and we took her outstretched hands and followed her...

THE RATION RUNNERS

In the dark vault of the sky the stars hung like muted dots of leaden silver. Suddenly what had seemed to be random constellations began to move: the gleaming dots approached each other, grouping themselves into a pointed arch whose symmetrical curves were held together at their apex by a star that outshone all the rest. Scarcely had I taken in this minor miracle when at the lower end of each arching curve a star detached itself, and the two dots slid slowly downward to sink out of sight in the unending blackness. Fear stirred and gradually spread within me, for now, two by two, left and right, they proceeded to sink into the blackness, and from time to time I seemed to hear a hiss as their light went out. And so they all fell, one star after another, each pair gleaming softly as they sank together, until only the largest star of all remained up there, the one that had held the pointed arch together. It seemed to waver, tremble, and hesitate ... then it sank too, slowly and solemnly, with an oppressive solemnity; and as it approached the blackness beneath, my fear swelled like some terrible travail, and at the very moment when the great star reached the bottom and, despite my fear, I waited with bated breath for total blackness to cover the vaulted sky, at that very moment the darkness exploded with an appalling detonation...

...I woke up, I could still feel the air quivering from the real blast that had woken me. Part of the earth wall in front of our foxhole now rested on my head and shoulders, and the breath of the grenade still smoldered in the black and silent air. I brushed off the dirt, and as I leaned forward to pull the groundsheet over my head and light a cigarette, I could tell from Hans's yawn that he had been asleep too and was now awake; he held out his forearm to show me the phosphorescent dial of his watch, saying softly, "Punctual as the devil himself, on the dot of two. You'd better get going now." Our heads met under the groundsheet. As I held the match over Hans's pipe, I glanced at his thin face: it betrayed no emotion whatsoever.

We smoked in silence. In the dark there was no sound save the innocuous rumble of tractors bringing up ammunition. Silence and darkness seemed to have become one, lying like some enormous weight on the backs of our necks...

When I had finished my cigarette, Hans repeated softly, "You'd better get going, and don't forget to take him with you, he's lying up there by the old flak emplacement." And when I had clambered out of my hole, he added, "There's only half of him, you know, in a groundsheet."

I crossed the torn-up earth, groping my way with my hands, until I reached the path that over the months had been trodden by dispatch runners and ration runners. I had slung my rifle over my shoulders and tucked the old cloth bag securely into one pocket. After a couple of hundred yards I could already make out darker patches in the darkness: trees, the remains of houses, and finally what was left of the shelled hut of the old flak emplacement. I listened nervously, hoping to hear the voices of the others, but even when I got closer and could clearly see the dark square pit where the antiaircraft gun had stood, I still couldn't hear anything. Then I did see them, the others, squatting on old ammunition cases like great mute birds in the night, and it struck me as unspeakably depressing that they were not exchanging a single word. At their feet lay a bundle wrapped in a groundsheet, just like those bundles we used to lug off with the rest of our equipment from the uniform stores to sort the hideous camphor-reeking stuff in our dorms and try it on for size. It was strange that on this night, in the midst of the reality of war, I should recall our old barracks life more concretely and vividly than ever before, and I shuddered to think that the fellow lying there in the groundsheet, a formless mass, had once been yelled at like the rest of us when he was issued the same kind of bundle from the uniform stores. "Evening," I said in a whisper, and I got an indistinct murmur in reply.

I squatted down beside the others on the nearest pile of twenty-millimeter cardboard shell cases: they had been lying around here for months, some of them still full, just as they had been abandoned by the flak in its confused and hurried flight.

No one moved. We all sat there, our hands in our pockets, waiting and brooding, and each one of us must have glanced from time to time at the mute, dark bundle at our feet. At last the platoon dispatch runner got up, saying, "Shall we go?"

Instead of replying, we all rose; it was so futile to go on squatting there, it didn't make things any better for us. What difference did it make, after all, whether we squatted here or up front in our holes? And besides, we had heard there was a chocolate issue today, maybe even some schnapps, reason enough to get to the chow line as fast as possible.

"First group, how many?"

"Five," answered a subdued voice.

"Second?"

"Six."

"And third?"

"Four," I answered.

"There are two of us," counted the dispatch runner in an undertone. "Okay, let's call it twenty-one, shall we? I hear it's hash."

"Okay."

The dispatch runner was the first to go over to the bundle; we watched him bend down, then he said, "We'll each take one corner; it's a young sapper, half a sapper."

We bent down too, and each of us grasped a corner of the groundsheet; then the dispatch runner said, "Let's go," and we lifted the bundle and trudged off toward the outskirts of the village…

Every dead man is as heavy as the whole earth, but this half-a-dead-man was as heavy as the world. It was as if he had absorbed the sum of all the pain and all the burdens of the entire universe. We panted and groaned and, by tacit consent, set down our load after a couple of dozen yards.

And the distances became shorter and shorter, the half-a-sapper became heavier and heavier, as if he were absorbing more and more burdens. It seemed as if the earth's weak crust must collapse beneath this weight, and when in our exhaustion we lowered our bundle to the ground, I felt as if we would never manage to lift the dead man up again. At the same time I had the feeling the bundle was growing beyond all measurable limits. The three at the other corners seemed infinitely far away, so far that if I called they couldn't possibly hear me. And I was growing too, my hands became enormous, my head assumed nightmarish proportions, but the dead man, the corpse-bundle, was puffing up like some monstrous tube, as if it would never stop drinking in the blood of all battlefields of all wars.

All the laws of gravity and dimension were suspended and extended into infinity; so-called reality was inflated by the dim and shadowy laws of another reality, one that made a mockery of them.

The half-a-sapper swelled and swelled like a monstrous sponge saturating itself with leaden blood. Cold sweat broke out over my body, mingling with that foul dirt that had accumulated over it during the long weeks. I could smell myself, and I smelled like a corpse...

As I trudged on and on, carrying the sapper, obeying that strange urge that compelled us each to take hold of one corner again at a certain instant; as we went on and on, always a dozen yards or so at a time, lugging the burden of the world toward the outskirts of the village, I almost lost consciousness under the impact of an appalling fear that flowed from that steadily growing bundle and filled my veins like poison. I saw no more, I heard nothing, and yet I was aware of every detail of what happened...

I had not heard the grenade being fired or the whine of its approach; the explosion ripped apart the whole fine mesh of dreamlike, semiconscious agony. With empty hands I stared into space, while far away, somewhere along a slope, the echo of the explosion reverberated like peals of laughter; in front, behind, on both sides, I could hear that strange, laughing echo, as if I were caught in a valley between high mountains, and the sound reached my ears like the tinny jangle of those patriotic songs that used to crawl up and down the barracks walls. With an almost disembodied curiosity I waited expectantly for pain to make itself felt somewhere on my body, or for the sensation of warm, flowing blood. Nothing, nothing at all. But suddenly I realized that my feet were standing half over an empty space, that the front half of each foot was teetering over a void, and when I looked down, with the casual curiosity of someone just waking up, I saw, blacker than the surrounding blackness, a great crater at my feet...

I stepped gamely forward into the crater, but I did not fall, I did not sink; on and on I walked, always on marvelously soft ground beneath the absolute darkness of the vaulted sky. I kept wondering, as I walked along, whether I should report twenty-one, seventeen, or fourteen to the quartermaster sergeant ... until the great yellow shining star rose before me and planted itself firmly in the vault of the sky; then the other stars, softly gleaming, found their places, two by two, forming a closed

triangle. I knew then that I had reached a different destination and that
what I really had to report was four and a half, and as I smiled and said
over to myself: Four and a half—a great kindly voice spoke: Five!

REUNION IN THE AVENUE

Sometimes, when it got really quiet, when the hoarse growl of the machine guns had died down and that hideous harsh sound of grenade launchers had ceased, when over the lines there hovered an indefinable something that our fathers might have called peace: during those hours we would interrupt our lice picking or our shallow sleep, and Lieutenant Hecker's long hands would finger the catch of the ammunition case that was let into the wall of our dugout and known to us as our bar. He would tug at the leather strap, making the prong of the clasp snap out of its hole and disclose our property in all its glory: on the left the Lieutenant's bottle, on the right mine, and in the middle, jointly owned, our most treasured possession, saved up for the hours when it got really quiet...

Between the gray-white bottles of potato schnapps stood two bottles of genuine French cognac, the finest we had ever tasted. In some manner that defied explanation, passing through untold opportunities for pilfering and the very heart of the jungle of corruption, genuine Hennessy would turn up at intervals in our front-line dugouts, where we were fighting dirt, lice, and despair. The youngsters, with the craving of pallid children for sweet things, shuddered at the mere mention of schnapps, so we gave them chocolate and candy in exchange for their share of this golden elixir, and seldom, I imagine, was any barter concluded with greater satisfaction to both parties.

"Come on," Hecker used to say, after buttoning on a clean collar—if one was available—and running his hand voluptuously over his freshly shaved chin. I would slowly get to my feet and emerge from the shadowy depths of our dugout, lethargically brush the wisps of straw from my uniform, and confine myself to the only ritual for which I could still summon enough energy: comb my hair, and slowly, with a dedication bordering on the unnatural, wash my hands in Hecker's shaving water—some coffee dregs in a tin can. Meanwhile Hecker,

patiently waiting for me to clean my nails, would first set up an ammunition case between us as a kind of table, then take out his handkerchief
and wipe our two schnapps glasses: thick, solid affairs that we guarded
as carefully as our tobacco. By the time he had dug the big pack of
cigarettes out from the inner recesses of his pocket, I had completed my
preparations.

It was usually in the afternoon, we had pushed aside the blanket
hanging in front of our dugout, and sometimes a bit of modest sunshine
warmed our feet...

Our eyes met, we touched glasses, drank, and smoked. Our silence
had a quality of solemn rapture. The only evidence of the enemy
was the sound of a sniper's bullet striking the ground, with scrupu-
lous punctuality and at regular intervals, just in front of the beams
shoring up the earth bank at the entrance to our dugout. With a small,
rather endearing "flup," the bullet would whir into the crumbling
earth. It often reminded me of the modest, barely audible scurrying
of a field mouse across a path on a quiet afternoon. There was something soothing about this sound, for it reassured us that this delectable
hour now about to begin was not a dream, not an illusion, but part of
our real life.

Only after the fourth or fifth glass would we start to talk. Beneath
the exhausted rubble of our hearts, this miraculous potion awakened something strangely precious that our fathers might have called
nostalgia.

About the war, the present, we had said all we had to say. Too
often and too intimately had we seen the bared teeth in its hideous
face, too often had its nauseating breath set our hearts quivering as
we listened on dark nights to the wounded pleading in two languages
between the lines. We loathed it too deeply to be able to believe in the
cant sent up like soap bubbles by the riffraff on both sides to invest it
with the virtues of a "mission."

Nor could the future serve as a topic. The future was a black tunnel full of sharp corners that we were going to bump into, and we lived
in dread of it, for the appalling existence we led as soldiers who had to
wish for the war to be lost had hollowed out our hearts.

We talked about the past; about those meager rudiments of what
our fathers might have called life. About that all too brief span of human

memories caught between the rotting corpse of the Weimar Republic and that bloated monster of a state whose pay we had to pocket.

"Picture a little café," said Hecker, "under some trees, maybe, in the fall. The smell of moisture and decaying leaves in the air, and you're translating a poem by Verlaine. You're wearing very light shoes, and later, when dusk falls in opaque clouds, you scuff your way home— know what I mean? You scuff your feet through the wet leaves and look into the faces of the girls coming toward you..." He filled our glasses, his hands as quiet as those of a kindly doctor operating on a child, we touched glasses and drank... "Maybe one of the girls smiles at you, you smile back, and you both go on your way without turning round. That little smile you exchanged will never die, never, I tell you... It may be your signal of recognition when you meet again in another life ... an absurd little smile..."

A marvelously youthful light came into his eyes, he looked at me and laughed, and I smiled too, grasped the bottle and poured. We drank three or four glasses, one after another, and no tobacco ever tasted finer than the one that blended with the exquisite aroma of the cognac.

At intervals the sniper's bullet would remind us that time was dripping remorselessly away; and behind our pleasure and our enjoyment of the hour there was again that inexorable threat to our existence that could wipe us out with a bursting shell, a sentry's warning cry, or a command to attack or retreat. We began to drink faster, our conversation grew more distraught, the gentle contentment in our eyes was joined by passion and hatred; and when, as was inevitable, the bottom of the bottle became visible, Hecker would become unutterably sad, his eyes would turn toward me like blurred disks, and in a low, almost incoherent voice he would begin whispering: "That girl, you know, lived at the end of an avenue, and the last time I was on leave..."

That was the signal for me to cut him short. "Lieutenant," I would say, coldly and severely, "be quiet, d'you hear?" He had told me himself, "When I start talking about a girl who lived at the end of an avenue, it's time for you to tell me to shut up, d'you understand? You must, you must!"

And I obeyed this command, although it went against the grain, for when I reminded him, Hecker would stop in his tracks, the light in his eyes would go out, they would become hard and sober, and around his mouth the old creases of bitterness would reappear...

On that particular day, however, the one I am talking about, everything was unusual. We had been issued underwear, brand-new underwear, and a fresh supply of cognac. I had shaved and even gone so far as to wash my feet in the tin can; in fact, I practically took a bath, for they had even sent us new socks, socks with white borders that were still really white.

Hecker was leaning back on our pallet, smoking and watching me wash. It was absolutely silent outside, but this silence was evil and numbing, a threatening silence, and I could tell from Hecker's hands when he lit a fresh cigarette from the old one that he was on edge and afraid: we were all afraid, everyone who was still human was afraid.

Suddenly we heard the faint scurrying sound the sniper's bullet always made in the earth bank, and with this gentle sound the silence ceased to be unnerving. With one breath we both laughed out loud; Hecker jumped to his feet, stamped around a bit, and shouted like a child, "Hooray, hooray, now let's get drunk, drunk in honor of our friend who always fires at the same place and always at the wrong place!"

He unfastened the catch, slapped me on the shoulder, and waited patiently until I had pulled my boots on again and seated myself in readiness for our drinking session. Hecker spread a clean handkerchief over the case and drew two light-brown cigars of impressive length from his breast pocket.

"You can't beat that," he said as he laughed, "cognac and a good cigar!" We touched glasses, drank, and smoked with slow, rapturous enjoyment.

"How about you talking for a change?" cried Hecker. "Come on, tell me something about yourself," he said, giving me a serious look. "You know something? You've never told me a thing, you've always let me rattle on."

"There's not much to tell," I observed in a low voice, and then I looked at him, poured some more cognac, waited, and then we drank together, and it was marvelous to feel the cool, superbly warming drink flowing into us in a stream of dark gold. "You see," I began diffidently, "I'm younger than you and a bit older. I was hopeless in school, so I had to quit and learn a trade, they apprenticed me to a cabinetmaker. That was pretty hard to take at first, but in time, after a year or so, I began to enjoy the work. There's something tremendously satisfying about working with wood. You make yourself a drawing on some nice white paper, get your wood ready, clean, fine-grained planks, and then you plane them with loving care while the smell of wood rises into your nostrils. I believe I would have made quite a good cabinetmaker, but at nineteen I was called up, and I've never recovered from the first shock I got after passing through the barracks gates, not even now, after six years, that's why I don't talk much... With you fellows it's a bit different..." I blushed, it was the longest speech I had ever made in my life.

Hecker looked at me reflectively. "I see," he said. "I like the sound of that: cabinetmaker."

"But haven't you ever had a girl?" he suddenly resumed, raising his voice, and I knew at once that I would soon have to cut him short again. "Never ever? Haven't you ever leaned your head on a soft shoulder and smelled her hair... never?" This time it was he who refilled our glasses, and with these two drinks the bottle was empty. Hecker glanced round with a look of terrible sadness. "No walls here to smash a bottle against, eh? Wait a minute," he shouted suddenly with a wild laugh, "our friend must have something too, let's have him smash it."

He stepped forward and placed the bottle on the spot where the sniper's bullets always struck the earth, and before I could stop him he had taken the next bottle out of our bar, opened it, and filled our glasses. We touched glasses, and at the same moment a gentle "ping" sounded from outside on the bank: we looked up in alarm and saw how for an instant the bottle stood steady, almost rigid, but the next instant its top half slid off, leaving the bottom half still standing. The chunk of broken glass rolled into the ditch almost to our feet, and all I remember is being frightened, frightened from the moment the bottle was shattered...

At the same time I was seized by a profound indifference while I helped Hecker empty the second bottle as fast as he filled our glasses. Yes, fear and at the same time indifference. Hecker was frightened too, I could tell; our agonized eyes avoided each other, and that day I couldn't summon the strength to interrupt him when he started talking about the girl...

"You know," he said urgently, looking beyond me, "she lived at the end of an avenue, and the last time I was on leave it was in the fall, real fall weather, late afternoon, and I can't begin to describe how beautiful the avenue was." A wild, rapturous, yet somehow frenzied happiness leaped into his eyes, and if only for the sake of that happiness I was glad I had not interrupted him; as he went on talking he worked his hands like a person trying to give shape to something without knowing how, and I could feel him searching for the right expressions to describe the avenue to me. I filled our glasses, we drank up, I filled them again, we tossed them back...

"The avenue," he said huskily, almost stammering, "the avenue was all golden—I'm not kidding, it really was, black trees with gold, and a grayish blue shimmer in the gold—I was in ecstasy as I walked slowly along under the trees as far as that house, I felt as if that fantastic beauty had spun a web around me, and I drank in the intoxicating transience of our human happiness. Do you know what I mean? That magical certainty moved me inexpressibly ... and ... and..."

Hecker was silent for a while, evidently searching for words again; I poured out some more cognac, we touched glasses, and drank: at that precise instant the bottom half of the bottle on the bank was shattered too, and with maddening deliberation the pieces of glass rolled one after another into the ditch.

I was startled to see Hecker jump to his feet, lean down, and thrust the blanket aside. I held on to his sleeve, and I knew now why I had been frightened all along. "Let go!" he shouted. "Let go ... I'm going— I'm going to the avenue..." Outside, I stood next to him, holding the bottle. "I'm going," whispered Hecker, "I'm going all the way along it, right to the end where the house is! There's a brown iron gate in front of it, and she lives upstairs, and..." I ducked hurriedly as a bullet whistled past me into the bank, landing just where the bottle had stood.

Hecker was whispering incoherent, rambling words, on his face a look of serene happiness, mild and gentle now, and there might still have been time to call him back as he had ordered me to. From his ramblings I could distinguish only the same words, repeated over and over, "I'm going—don't try to stop me, I'm going to the house where my girl lives..."

I felt a real coward, crouching there on the ground holding the bottle of cognac, and guilty at being sober, cruelly sober, while Hecker wore an expression of unutterably sweet, serene drunkenness. He was staring straight ahead at the enemy lines between black sunflower stalks and shelled farmhouses; I watched him narrowly as he smoked a cigarette.

"Lieutenant," I called softly, holding out the bottle, "come and have a drink," and when I tried to stand up I realized I was drunk too, and I cursed myself to the very depths of my being for not having called him back soon enough, for now it was obviously too late. He hadn't heard me call, and just as I was about to open my mouth to call him again, at least to entice him back out of danger with the bottle, I heard the clear, high-pitched "ping" of an exploding bullet. With appalling suddenness Hecker turned round, gave me one brief and blissful smile, placed his cigarette on the bank, and collapsed, falling slowly, slowly backward. An icy hand gripped my heart, the bottle slid from my grasp, and I watched in shock and dismay as the cognac, gently gurgling, flowed out and formed a little puddle. Once again it was very quiet, and the silence was menacing...

At last I found the courage to raise my eyes and look into Hecker's face: his cheeks had caved in, his eyes were black and rigid, yet his face still bore a hint of that smile which had blossomed there as he whispered those frenzied words. I knew he was dead. But all of a sudden I started shouting, shouting like a madman. I leaned over the bank, oblivious to all caution, and shouted to the next dugout, "Heini! Help! Heini, Hecker's dead!" and without waiting for an answer I sank sobbing to the ground, seized by unspeakable horror, for Hecker's head had raised itself a little, barely perceptibly, but visibly, and blood was welling out of it and a ghastly yellowish-white substance that could only be his brains; it flowed on and on, and frozen with terror I could only think: Where can all this blood be coming from, just from his head? The whole floor of our dugout was covered with blood, the clayey soil didn't absorb it, and the blood reached the spot where I knelt beside the empty bottle...

I was alone in the world with Hecker's blood, for Heini didn't answer and the gentle swish of the sniper's bullet was no longer audible...

Suddenly, however, the silence was rent by an explosion, I scrambled to my feet, and at the same moment something struck me in the back, although strangely enough I felt no pain. I sank forward with my head on Hecker's chest, and while noise sprang to life around me, the frantic barking of the machine gun from Heini's dugout and the sickening impact of the grenade launchers that we called pipe organs,

I became quite calm: for mingling with Hecker's dark blood that still covered the bottom of the dugout was a lighter, miraculously light blood that I knew was warm and my own; and I sank down and down until I found myself, smiling happily, at the entrance to that avenue which Hecker hadn't known how to describe, because the trees were bare, solitude and desolation were nesting among wan shadows, and hope died in my heart, while far off, at an immense distance, I could see Hecker's beckoning figure outlined against a soft golden light...

IN THE DARKNESS

Light the candle," said a voice.

There was no sound, only that exasperating, aimless rustle of someone trying to get to sleep.

"Light the candle, I say," came the voice again, on a sharper note this time.

The sounds at last became distinguishable as someone moving, throwing aside the blanket, and sitting up; this was apparent from the breathing, which now came from above. The straw rustled too.

"Well?" said the voice.

"The lieutenant said we weren't to light the candle except on orders, in an emergency," said a younger, diffident voice.

"Light the candle, I say, you little pipsqueak," the older voice shouted back.

He sat up now too, their heads were on the same level in the dark, their breathing was parallel.

The one who had first spoken irritably followed the movements of the other, who had tucked the candle away somewhere in his pack. His breathing relaxed when he eventually heard the sound of the matchbox.

The match flared up and there was light: a sparse yellow light.

Their eyes met. Invariably, as soon as there was enough light, their eyes met. Yet they knew one another so well, much too well. They almost hated each other, so familiar was each to each; they knew one another's very smell, the smell of every pore, so to speak, but still their eyes met, those of the older man and the younger. The younger one was pale and slight with a nondescript face, and the older one was pale and slight and unshaven with a nondescript face.

"Now, listen," said the older man, calmer now, "when are you ever going to learn that you don't do everything the lieutenants tell you?"

"He'll..." the younger one tried to begin.

"He won't do a thing," said the older one, in a sharper tone again and lighting a cigarette from the candle. "He'll keep his trap shut, and if he doesn't, and I don't happen to be around, then tell him to wait till I get back, it was me who lit the candle, understand? Do you understand?"

"Yessir."

"To hell with that Yessir crap, just Yes when you're talking to me. And undo your belt," he was shouting again now, "take that damn crappy belt off when you go to sleep."

The younger man looked at him nervously and took off his belt, placing it beside him in the straw.

"Roll your coat up into a pillow. That's right. Okay ... and now go to sleep, I'll wake you when it's time for you to die ... "

The younger man rolled onto his side and tried to sleep. All that was visible was the young brown hair, matted and untidy, a very thin neck, and the empty shoulders of his uniform tunic. The candle flickered gently, letting its meager light swing back and forth in the dark dugout like a great yellow butterfly uncertain where to settle.

The older man stayed as he was, knees drawn up, puffing out cigarette smoke at the ground in front of him. The ground was dark brown, here and there white blade marks showed where the spade had cut through a root or, a little closer to the surface, a tuber. The roof consisted of a few planks with a groundsheet thrown over them, and in the spaces between the planks the groundsheet sagged a little because the earth lying on top of it was heavy, heavy and wet. Outside, it was raining. The soft swish of steadily falling water sounded indescribably persistent, and the older man, still staring fixedly at the ground, now noticed a thin trickle of water oozing into the dugout under the roof. The tiny stream backed up slightly on encountering some loose earth, then flowed on past the obstacle until it reached the next one, which was the man's feet, and the ever-growing tide flowed all around the man's feet until his black boots lay in the water just like a peninsula. The man spat his cigarette butt into the puddle and lit another from the candle. In doing so he took the candle down from the edge of the dugout and placed it beside him on an ammunition case. The half where the younger man was lying was almost in darkness, reached now by the swaying light in brief spasms only, and these gradually subsided.

"Go to sleep, damn you," said the older man. "D'you hear? Go to sleep!"

"Yessir … yes," came the faint voice, obviously wider awake than before, when it had been dark.

"Hold on," said the older man, less harshly again. "A couple more cigarettes and then I'll put it out, and at least we'll drown in the dark."

He went on smoking, sometimes turning his head to the left, where the boy was lying, but he spat the second butt into the steadily growing puddle, lit the third, and still he could tell from the breathing beside him that the kid couldn't sleep.

He then took the spade, thrust it into the soft earth, and made a little mud wall behind the blanket forming the entrance. Behind this wall he heaped up a second layer of earth. With a spadeful of earth he covered the puddle at his feet. Outside, there was no sound save the gentle swish of the rain; little by little, the earth lying on top of the groundsheet had evidently become saturated, for water was now beginning to drip from above too.

"Oh, shit," muttered the older man. "Are you asleep?"

"No."

The man spat the third cigarette butt over the mud wall and blew out the candle. He pulled up his blanket again, worked his feet into a comfortable position, and lay back with a sigh. It was quite silent and quite dark, and again the only sound was that aimless rustle of someone trying to get to sleep, and the swish of the rain, very gentle.

"Willi's been wounded," the boy's voice said suddenly, after a few minutes' silence. The voice was more awake than ever, in fact not even sleepy.

"What d'you mean?" asked the man in reply.

"Just that—wounded," came the younger voice, with something like triumph in it, pleased that it knew some important piece of news which the older voice obviously knew nothing about. "Wounded while he was shitting."

"You're nuts," said the man; then he gave another sigh and went on, "That's what I call a real break; I never heard of such luck. One day you come back from leave and the next day you get wounded while you're shitting. Is it serious?"

"No," said the boy with a laugh, "though actually it's not minor either. A bullet fracture, but in the arm."

"A bullet fracture in the arm! You come back from leave and while you're shitting you get wounded, a bullet fracture in the arm! What a break... How did it happen?"

"When they went for water last evening," came the younger voice, quite animated now. "When they went for water, they were going down the hill at the back, carrying their water cans, and Willi told Sergeant Schubert, 'I've got to shit, Sergeant!' 'Nothing doing,' said the sergeant. But Willi couldn't hold on any longer so he just ran off, pulled down his pants, and bang! A grenade. And they actually had to pull up his pants for him. His left arm was wounded, and his right arm was holding it, so he ran off like that to get it bandaged, with his pants around his ankles. They all laughed, everyone laughed, even Sergeant Schubert laughed." He added the last few words almost apologetically, as if to excuse his own laughter, because he was laughing now...

But the older man wasn't laughing.

"Light!" he said with an oath. "Here, give me the matches, let's have some light!" He struck a match, cursing as it flared up. "At least I want some light, even if I don't get wounded. At least let's have some light, the least they can do is give us enough candles if they want to play war. Light! Light!" He was shouting again as he lit another cigarette.

The younger voice had sat up again and was poking around with a spoon in a greasy can held on his knees.

And there they sat, crouching side by side, without a word, in the yellow light.

The man smoked aggressively, and the boy was already looking somewhat greasy: his childish face smeared, bread crumbs sticking to his matted hair around most of his hairline.

The boy then proceeded to scrape out the grease can with a piece of bread.

All of a sudden there was silence: the rain had stopped. Neither of them moved, they looked at each other, the man with the cigarette in his hand, the boy holding the bread in his trembling fingers. It was uncannily quiet, they took a few breaths, and then heard rain still dripping somewhere from the groundsheet.

"Hell," said the older man. "D'you suppose the sentry's still there? I can't hear a thing."

The boy put the bread into his mouth and threw the can into the straw beside him.

"I don't know," said the boy. "They're going to let us know when it's our turn to relieve."

The older man got up quickly. He blew out the light, jammed on his steel helmet, and thrust aside the blanket. What came through the opening was not light. Just cool damp darkness. The man pinched out his cigarette and stuck his head outside.

"Hell," he muttered outside, "not a thing. Hey!" he called softly. Then his dark head reappeared inside, and he asked, "Where's the next dugout?"

The boy groped his way to his feet and stood next to the other man in the opening.

"Quiet!" said the man suddenly, in a sharp, low tone. "Something's crawling around out there."

They peered ahead. It was true: in the silent darkness there was a sound of someone crawling, and all of a sudden an unearthly snapping sound that made them both jump. It sounded as if someone had flung a live cat against the wall: the sound of breaking bones.

"Hell," muttered the older man, "there's something funny going on. Where's the sentry?"

"Over there," said the boy, groping in the dark for the other man's hand and lifting it toward the right. "Over there," he repeated. "That's where the dugout is too."

"Wait here," said the older man, "and better get your rifle, just in case."

Once again they heard that sickening snapping sound, then silence, and someone crawling.

The older man crept forward through the mud, occasionally halting and quietly listening, until after a few yards he finally heard a muffled voice; then he saw a faint gleam of light from the ground, felt around till he found the entrance, and called, "Hey, chum!"

The voice stopped, the light went out, a blanket was pushed aside, and a man's dark head came up out of the ground.

"What's up?"

"Where's the sentry?"

"Over there—right here."

"Where?"

"Hey there, Neuer!... Hey there!"

No answer: the crawling sound had stopped, all sound had stopped, there was only darkness out there, silent darkness. "God damn it, that's queer," said the voice of the man who had come up out of the ground. "Hey there!... That's funny, he was standing right here by the dugout, only a few feet away." He pulled himself up over the edge and stood beside the man who had called him.

"There was someone crawling around out there," said the man who had come across from the other dugout. "I know there was. The bastard's quiet now."

"Better have a look," said the man who had come up out of the ground. "Shall we take a look?"

"Hm, there certainly ought to be a sentry here."

"You fellows are next."

"I know, but..."

"Ssh!"

Once again they could hear someone crawling out there, perhaps twenty feet away.

"God damn it," said the man who had come up out of the ground, "you're right."

"Maybe someone still alive from last night, trying to crawl away."

"Or new ones."

"But what about the sentry, for God's sake?"

"Shall we go?"

"Okay."

Both men instantly dropped to the ground and started to move forward, crawling through the mud. From down there, from a worm's-eye view, everything looked different. Every minutest elevation in the soil became a mountain range behind which, far off, something strange was visible: a slightly lighter darkness, the sky. Pistol in hand, they crawled on, yard by yard through the mud.

"God damn it," whispered the man who had come up out of the ground, "a Russki from last night."

His companion also soon bumped into a corpse, a mute, leaden bundle. Suddenly they were silent, holding their breath: there was that cracking sound again, quite close, as if someone had been given a terrific wallop on the jaw. Then they heard someone panting.

"Hey," called the man who had come up out of the ground, "who's there?"

The call silenced all sound, the very air seemed to hold its breath, until a quavering voice spoke, "It's me…"

"God damn it, what the hell are you doing out there, you old asshole, driving us all nuts?" shouted the man who had come up out of the ground.

"I'm looking for something," came the voice again.

The two men had got to their feet and now walked over to the spot where the voice was coming from the ground.

"I'm looking for a pair of shoes," said the voice, but now they were standing next to him. Their eyes had become accustomed to the dark, and they could see corpses lying all around, ten or a dozen, lying there like logs, black and motionless, and the sentry was squatting beside one of these logs, fumbling around its feet.

"Your job's to stick to your post," said the man who had come up out of the ground.

The other man, the one who had summoned him out of the ground, dropped like a stone and bent over the dead man's face. The man who had been squatting suddenly covered his face with his hands and began whimpering like a cowed animal.

"Oh, no," said the man who had summoned the other out of the ground, adding in an undertone, "I guess you need teeth too, eh? Gold teeth, eh?"

"What's that?" asked the man who had come up out of the ground, while at his feet the cringing figure whimpered louder than ever.

"Oh, no," said the first man again, and the weight of the world seemed to be lying on his breast.

"Teeth?" asked the man who had come up out of the ground, whereupon he threw himself down beside the cringing figure and ripped a cloth bag from his hand.

"Oh, no!" the cringing figure cried too, and every extremity of human terror was expressed in this cry.

The man who had summoned the other out of the ground turned away, for the man who had come up out of the ground had placed his pistol against the cringing figure's head, and he pressed the trigger.

"Teeth," he muttered, as the sound of the shot died away. "Gold teeth."

They walked slowly back, stepping very carefully as long as they were in the area where the dead lay.

"You fellows are on now," said the man who had come up out of the ground, before vanishing into the ground again.

"Right," was all the other man said, and he too crawled slowly back through the mud before vanishing into the ground again.

He could tell at once that the boy was still awake; there was that aimless rustle of someone trying to get to sleep.

"Light the candle," he said quietly.

The yellow flame leaped up again, feebly illumining the little hole.

"What happened?" asked the boy in alarm, catching sight of the older man's face.

"The sentry's gone; you'll have to replace him."

"Yes," said the youngster. "Give me the watch, will you, so I can wake the others."

"Here."

The older man squatted down on his straw and lit a cigarette, watching thoughtfully as the boy buckled on his belt, pulled on his coat, defused a hand grenade, and then wearily checked his machine pistol for ammunition.

"Right," said the boy finally. "So long, now."

"So long," said the man, and he blew out the candle and lay in total darkness all alone in the ground...

BROOMMAKERS

Our math teacher was as good-natured as he was hot-tempered. He used to come charging into the classroom—hands in pockets—spew his cigarette butt into the cuspidor to the left of the wastepaper basket, take the dais by storm and, standing by his desk, call out my name as he asked some question or other to which I never knew the answer, no matter what it was.

After I had floundered my way to a halt, he would walk over to me, very slowly, accompanied by the tittering of the whole class, and cuff me over the head—my long-suffering head—in his rough good-natured way, muttering, "You boneheaded broommaker, you."

It became a kind of ritual, the thought of which made me tremble throughout my school days, the more so since my knowledge of science, far from growing with increased demands, seemed to diminish. But, having duly cuffed me, he would leave me in peace, leave me to my meandering daydreams, for to try and teach me math was a completely hopeless proposition. I dragged my F after me all through those years like the heavy ball chained to a convict's feet.

What impressed me about him was that he never had a book or notes with him, not even a slip of paper: he performed his occult arts with casual ease, tossing stupendous formulas onto the blackboard with something of a tightrope walker's absolute mastery. The one thing he could not draw was circles. He was too impatient. He would wind a string around a long piece of chalk, pick the imaginary center, and swing the chalk round with such gusto that it would snap and, with a whining screech, go bounding across the blackboard—dash-dot, dot-dash. He never managed to make the beginning and end meet, and the result was an unsightly gaping outline, truly an unacknowledged symbol of Creation rent asunder. And that sound of the squeaking, screeching, chattering chalk piled further agony on my already tortured brain: I would stir from my daydreams, look up, and the minute he caught sight of me he would rush over, pull me up by the ears, and order me to draw his circles for him. For this was an art, springing from some slumbering, innate law within me, that I mastered to near perfection. What an exquisite feeling it was, to play with the chalk for half a second. It was a minor ecstasy, the world around me would drop away, and I was filled with a profound happiness that made up for all the agony ... but even from this sweet oblivion I would be roused by a rough, although this time respectful, tug at my hair, and with the laughter of the entire class in my ears I would slink back to my seat like a whipped dog, incapable now of reentering my dreamworld, to wait in perpetual agony for the bell to ring...

It was a long time since those early days, a long time since my dreams had become more disturbing, a long time since he had dropped the *du* when calling me "a boneheaded broommaker," and there were long months of torment during which there were no circles to be drawn and I was condemned to hopeless attempts to clamber over the brittle girders of algebraical bridges, still dragging my F behind me, the familiar ritual still being performed. But then when we had to volunteer for officer training a brief test was improvised, simple but nonetheless a test, and my expression of utter wretchedness as I faced the stern examining board may have softened the math teacher's heart, for he was so skillful in putting words into my mouth that I actually passed. Later on, however, as we shook hands with the teachers on leaving, he advised me to forego the use of my mathematical knowledge and to be sure to avoid joining a technical unit. "Infantry," he whispered, "join the infantry, that's the place for all ... broommakers," and for the last time, with a gesture that concealed his affection, he made as if to cuff me over the head—my now well-seasoned head.

Scarcely two months later, at the Odessa airfield, I was sitting crouched over my pack, in deep mud, watching a real broommaker, the first I had ever seen.

Winter had come early, and over the nearby city the sky hung gray and comfortless between the horizons. Dingy tall buildings were visible among outlying gardens and black fences. In the distance, where the Black Sea must be, the sky was even darker, almost blue-black, as if twilight and evening came from the east. Somewhere in the background the trundling monsters were being refueled alongside cavernous hangars, after which they trundled back and, standing there in horrible complacency, were loaded up with men, gray, tired, despairing soldiers whose eyes were devoid of all emotion but fear—for the Crimea had long since been encircled...

Our platoon must have been one of the last; no one spoke, and in spite of our long greatcoats we were shivering. Some of the men were eating in desperation, others were smoking, and because this was prohibited they covered their pipes with their palms and blew the smoke out in slow, thin puffs.

I had plenty of time to watch the broommaker as he sat a little way off beside a garden fence. He was wearing one of those rakish-looking Russian hats, and in his bearded face the short stocky brown pipe was as broad and long as his nose. But there were peace and simplicity in his quietly working hands as they picked up the bunches of furze twigs, cut them, tied them with wire, and fastened the finished bundles in the holes of the broom handle.

I had turned over onto my stomach, lying almost flat on my pack, and all I saw was the looming silhouette of this quiet, humble man, working steadily and unhurriedly away at his brooms. Never in my life have I envied anyone as much as that broommaker, neither the top student, nor Schimski the math brain, nor the best football player on the school team, nor even Hegenbach, whose brother had the Knight's Cross; not one of those had I ever envied as I envied that broommaker, sitting by a fence on the outskirts of Odessa and serenely smoking his pipe.

I longed secretly to catch the man's eye, for I fancied it would be comforting to look directly into that face, but I was suddenly jerked up by my coat, shouted at, and jammed into the droning aircraft, and once we had taken off and were flying high above the distracting jumble of gardens and roads and churches, it would have been impossible to try to make out the broommaker.

First I squatted on my pack, but then I slipped down behind it onto the floor and, stupefied by the oppressive silence of my fellow victims, was listening to the unearthly drone of the aircraft, while the constant vibration began to make my head quiver as it leaned against the metal wall. The darkness of the narrow fuselage was relieved only by a somewhat lighter darkness up front, where the pilot sat, and this pale reflection threw an eerie light on the mute, dim figures squatting left and right and all around me on their packs.

But suddenly a strange noise tore across the sky, so real and familiar that I sat bolt upright: it was as if the hand of a giant math teacher were drawing a massive hunk of chalk in an arc across the limitless expanse of dark sky, and the noise exactly matched the familiar one I had heard two months before, the same leap and chatter of protesting chalk.

Arc after arc was drawn across the sky by the hand of the colossus, but now, instead of being only white and dark gray, it was red on blue and purple on black, and the flashing streaks faded without completing their circles, chattered, screeched, and died away.

I suffered not for the terrified, frenzied groans of my fellow victims, or the shouting of the lieutenant vainly ordering the men to be quiet and stay where they were, or even the agonized face of the pilot. I suffered merely for those eternally uncompleted circles that flared up over the sky, in a fury of haste and hate, and never ever returned to their starting point, those botched circles whose ends never met to achieve the perfect beauty of the circle. They tormented me along with the chattering, screeching, leaping wrath of the giant hand, the hand I dreaded would grab me by the hair and cuff me brutally over the head.

Then came the real shock. I suddenly realized that this sky-splitting fury was in fact a noise: close to my head I heard a strange hiss as of a baleful, swiftly descending hand, felt a moist, hot pain, jumped up with a cry, and reached out toward the sky where just then another searing yellow flash blazed up; with my right hand I held on tight to this flailing yellow snake, letting it spin its angry circle, confident that I would be able to complete the circle, for this was the one and only art I had been born to master. So I held it, guided it, the flailing, raging, jerking, chattering snake, held on to it while my breath came hot and my twitching mouth hurt and the moist pain in my head seemed to increase, and as I brought the points together, drawing the glorious round arc of the circle and gazing at it with pride, the spaces between the dots and dashes closed and an immense, hissing short circuit filled the entire circle with light and fire until the whole sky was burning, and the abrupt momentum of the plunging aircraft rent the world in two. All I could see was light and fire, and the mutilated tail of the machine, a jagged tail like the black stump of a broom fit to carry a witch riding off to her sabbath...

MY EXPENSIVE LEG

They're giving me a chance now. They sent me a postcard telling me to come down to the Department, and I went. They were very nice to me at the Department. They took out my file card and said, "Hm." I also said, "Hm."

"Which leg?" asked the official.

"The right."

"The whole leg?"

"The whole leg."

"Hm," he went again. He proceeded to shuffle through various papers. I was allowed to sit down.

Finally the man found what seemed to be the right paper. He said, "I think I have something here for you. Very nice too. A job you can sit down at. Shoeshine stand in a public convenience on Republic Square. How about that?"

"I can't shine shoes; that's one thing people have always noticed about me, my inability to shine shoes."

"You can learn," he said. "One can learn anything. A German can do anything. You can take a free course if you like."

"Hm," I went.

"You'll take the job?"

"No," I said, "I won't. I want a higher pension."

"You must be out of your mind," he replied, his tone mild and good-humored.

"I'm not out of my mind, no one can give me back my leg, I'm not even allowed to sell cigarettes anymore, they're already making that difficult for me."

The man leaned all the way back in his chair and drew a deep breath. "My dear fellow," he said, launching into a lecture, "your leg's a damned expensive leg. I see that you're twenty-nine years of age, your heart is sound, in fact apart from your leg you're as fit as a fiddle. You'll live to be seventy. Figure it out for yourself, seventy marks a month, twelve times a year, that's forty-one times twelve times seventy. Figure it out for yourself, not counting interest, and don't imagine your leg's unique. What's more, you're not the only one who'll probably live to a ripe old age. And then you want a higher pension! I'm sorry, but you must be out of your mind."

"I think, sir," I said, also leaning back and drawing a deep breath, "I think that you grossly underestimate my leg. My leg is much more expensive, it is a very expensive leg indeed. It so happens that my head is as sound as my heart. Let me explain."

"I'm a very busy man."

"I'll explain!" I said. "You will see that my leg has saved the lives of a great number of people who today are drawing nice fat pensions.

"What happened was this: I was lying all by myself somewhere up front. My job was to spot them when they came so that the others would have time to clear out. The staffs in the rear were packing up, and while they didn't want to clear out too soon they also didn't want to leave it too long. At first there were two of us, but they shot the other fellow, he's not costing you a cent now. It's true he was married, but his wife is in good health and able to work, you don't need to worry. He was a real bargain. He'd only been a soldier for a month, all he cost was a postcard and a few bread rations. There's a good soldier for you, at least he let himself be killed off. But now there I was, all by myself, scared stiff, and it was cold, and I wanted to clear out too, in fact I was just going to clear out when—"

"I'm really very busy," said the man, beginning to search for a pencil.

"No, listen," I said, "this is where it gets interesting. Just as I was going to clear out, this business of my leg happened. And because I had to go on lying there anyway, I thought I might as well pass the word, so I passed the word, and they all took off, one after another, in descending order of rank, first the divisional staff, then the regimental, then the battalion, and so on, one after another. The silly part was, you see, they were in such a hurry they forgot to take me along! It was really too silly for words, because if I hadn't lost my leg they would all be dead, the general, the colonel, the major, and so on down, and you wouldn't have to pay them any pensions. Now just figure out what my leg is costing you. The general is fifty-two, the colonel forty-eight, and the major fifty, all of them hale and hearty, their heads as well as their hearts, and with the military life they lead they'll live to be at least eighty, like Hindenburg. Figure it out for yourself: a hundred and sixty times twelve times thirty, we'll call it an average of thirty, shall we? My leg's become a damned expensive leg, one of the most expensive legs I can think of, d'you see what I mean?"

"You really must be out of your mind," said the man.

"No," I replied, "I'm not. Unfortunately my heart is as sound as my head, and it's a pity I wasn't killed too, a couple of minutes before that business of my leg happened. We would have saved a lot of money."

"Are you going to take that job?" asked the man.

"No," I said, and left.

LOHENGRIN'S DEATH

Going up the stairs, the men carrying the stretcher slowed down a bit. They were both feeling resentful; they had been on duty for over an hour and so far nobody had given them a cigarette for a tip. Besides, one of them was the ambulance driver, and drivers are not actually required to carry stretchers. But the hospital hadn't sent anyone down to help, and they couldn't very well leave the boy lying there in the ambulance; they still had an emergency pneumonia to pick up and a suicide who had been cut down at the last minute. They were feeling resentful, and suddenly they were carrying the stretcher along less slowly again: the corridor was poorly lit, and of course it smelled of hospital.

"I wonder why they cut him down?" muttered one of the men, referring to the suicide; he was the one behind, and the one in front growled over his shoulder, "Yeah, why would they do that?" But because he had turned round as he spoke, he collided with the doorpost, and the figure lying on the stretcher woke up and emitted shrill, terrible screams; they were the screams of a child.

"Easy now, easy," said the doctor, a young intern with fair hair and a tense face. He looked at the time: eight o'clock, his relief should have been here long ago. For over an hour he had been waiting for Dr. Lohmeyer: they might have arrested him, anyone could be arrested any time these days. The young doctor automatically fingered his stethoscope, his eyes fixed on the boy on the stretcher, and now for the first time he noticed the stretcher bearers standing impatiently by the door. "What's the matter, what are you waiting for?" he asked irritably.

"The stretcher," said the driver. "Can't you move him onto something else? We've got work to do."

"Oh, of course—over here!" The doctor pointed to the leather couch. At that moment the night nurse appeared, her expression unemotional but serious. She took hold of the boy by the shoulders, and one of the stretcher bearers, not the driver, grabbed him by the legs.

The boy screamed like one demented, and the doctor said hastily, "Take it easy now, it's not that bad..."

The stretcher bearers were still standing there, waiting. The doctor's look of annoyance evoked a further response from one of them. "The blanket," he said stonily. The blanket wasn't his at all, a woman at the scene of the accident had let him have it, saying they couldn't drive the boy like that to the hospital with those shattered legs of his. But the stretcher bearer figured the hospital would keep it, and the hospital had plenty of blankets, and the blanket certainly wouldn't be returned to the woman, and it didn't belong to the boy any more than it did to the hospital, and the hospital had plenty. His wife would clean up the blanket all right, and blankets were worth a lot of money these days.

The child was still screaming. They had unwrapped the blanket from around his legs and passed it quickly to the driver. Doctor and nurse exchanged glances. The boy was an appalling sight: the whole lower part of his body was bathed in blood, his cotton shorts were mere shreds, and the shreds had coagulated with the blood into a revolting pulp. His feet were bare, and he screamed without pause, screamed with terrible persistence and regularity.

"Quick," whispered the doctor, "a hypo. Nurse, hurry, please!" The nurse's movements were skillful and swift, but the doctor kept whispering, "Hurry, hurry!" His mouth hung slack in his tense face. The boy kept up his incessant screaming, but the nurse was preparing the hypo as fast as she could.

The doctor felt the boy's pulse, his pale face twitching with exhaustion. "Be quiet," he whispered a few times distractedly, "be *quiet*!" But the child screamed as if he had been born for the sole purpose of screaming. At last the nurse brought the hypo, and the doctor swiftly and skillfully gave the injection.

With a sigh he drew the needle out of the tough, leathery skin, and just then the door opened and a nun burst into the room, but when she saw the accident case and the doctor she closed her mouth, which she had opened, and approached slowly and quietly. She gave the doctor and the pale lay sister a friendly nod and placed her hand on the child's forehead. The boy opened his eyes and looked straight up, in surprise, at the black figure standing behind him. It seemed almost as if the pressure of the cool hand on his brow were quieting him down, but the injection was already taking effect. The doctor was still holding the syringe, and he gave another deep sigh, for it was quiet now, blissfully quiet, so quiet that they could all hear their own breathing. They did not speak.

The boy was evidently out of pain now; he was looking quietly and interestedly around the room.

"How much?" the doctor asked the night nurse in a low voice.

"Ten," she replied, in the same tone.

The doctor shrugged his shoulders. "Quite a bit. We'll see what happens. Would you give us a hand, Sister Lioba?"

"Of course," the nun replied promptly, seeming to rouse herself from a deep reverie. It was very quiet. The nun held the boy by the head and shoulders, the night nurse took his legs, and together they pulled off the blood-soaked tatters. The blood, as they now saw, was mixed with something black. Everything was black, the boy's feet were caked with coal dust, his hands too, there was nothing but blood, shreds of cloth, and coal dust, thick oily coal dust.

"Obviously," murmured the doctor, "you fell off a moving train while pinching coal, eh?"

"Yes," said the boy in a cracked voice, "obviously."

His eyes were wide open, and there was a strange happiness in them. The injection must have been gloriously effective. The nun pulled his shirt all the way up, arranging it in a roll on the boy's chest, under his chin. His chest was scrawny, ludicrously scrawny like the breast of an elderly goose. Alongside the collarbones strangely deep shadows filled the hollows, great cavities where she could have hidden the whole of her broad white hand. Now they could see his legs too, as much of them as was still intact. They were skinny, and seemed to be fine-boned and shapely. The doctor nodded to the women, saying, "Double fracture of both legs, I imagine. We'll need an X-ray."

The night nurse wiped his legs clean with alcohol, and now they didn't look quite so bad. But the child was so appallingly thin. The doctor shook his head as he applied the bandage. He started worrying again about Lohmeyer: maybe they'd got him after all, and even if he kept his mouth shut it was still very awkward to let him take the rap for that Strophanthin business and get off scot-free himself, while if things had gone well he would have had a share in the profits. Hell, it must be eight-thirty, it was ominously quiet now, not a sound from the street. He had finished his bandaging, and the nun pulled the boy's shirt down again over his loins. Then she went to the closet, took out a white blanket, and spread it over the boy.

Her hands on the boy's forehead again, she said to the doctor as he was washing his hands, "What I really came about was the little Schranz girl, doctor, but I didn't want to worry you while you were treating this boy."

The doctor paused in his drying, made a slight grimace, and the cigarette hanging from his lower lip quivered.

"Well," he asked, "what about the Schranz child?" The pallor in his face was almost yellow now.

"I'm afraid that little heart is giving up, just giving up; it looks like the end."

The doctor took the cigarette between his fingers again and hung the towel on the nail beside the wash bowl.

"Hell," he cried helplessly, "what am I supposed to do? There's nothing I can do!"

The nun kept her hand on the boy's forehead. The night nurse dropped the blood-soaked rags into the garbage pail; its chrome lid cast flickering lights against the wall.

The doctor stood there thinking, his eyes lowered. Suddenly he raised his head, gave one more look at the boy, and dashed to the door. "I'll have a look at her."

"Do you need me?" the night nurse called out after him. He put his head in again, saying, "No, you stay here. Get the boy ready for X-rays and see if you can take down his history."

The boy was still very quiet, and the night nurse came and stood by the leather couch.

"Has your mother been told?" asked the nun.

"She's dead."

The nurse did not dare ask about his father.

"Whom should we notify?"

"My older brother, only he's not home right now. But the kids ought to be told, they're all alone now."

"What kids?"

"Hans and Adolf. They're waiting for me to come and make supper."

"And where does your older brother work?"

The boy was silent, and the nun did not pursue the question.

"Would you mind taking it down, nurse?"

The night nurse nodded and went over to the little white table which was covered with medicine bottles and test tubes. She pulled the ink toward her, dipped the pen in it, and smoothed out the sheet of white paper with her left hand.

"What's your name?" the nun asked the boy.

"Becker."

"Religion?"

"None. I was never baptized."

The nun winced; the night nurse's expression remained impassive.

"When were you born?"

"In 1933 ... September 10."

"Still going to school, I suppose?"

"Yes."

"And his first name!" the night nurse whispered to the nun.

"Oh, yes ... and your first name?"

"Grini."

"What?" The two women looked at each other and smiled.

"Grini," said the boy, slowly and peevishly, as anyone does who has an unusual first name.

"With an 'i'?" asked the night nurse.

"That's right, with two i's," and he repeated once more, "Grini."

His real name was Lohengrin. He had been born in 1933, just when the first photographs of Hitler at the Bayreuth Wagner Festival started flooding all the illustrated weeklies. But his mother had always called him Grini.

The doctor rushed suddenly into the room, his eyes blurred with exhaustion, his wispy fair hair hanging down into his young, deeply lined face.

"Come along, both of you, and be quick about it. I'm going to try a transfusion; hurry up!"

The nun's eyes went to the boy.

"That's all right," cried the doctor, "you can leave him alone for a moment."

The night nurse was already at the door.

"Will you lie there quietly like a good boy, Grini?" asked the nun.
"Yes," he answered.

But as soon as they had all left the room he let the tears flow
unchecked. It was as if the nun's hand on his brow had held them back.
He was crying not with pain but with happiness. And yet with pain and
fear too. It was only when he thought about the kids that he cried with
pain, and he tried not to think about them because he wanted to cry
with happiness. Never in his life had he had such a wonderful feeling
as now, after the injection. It flowed right through him like some wonderful, gently warmed milk, making him feel dizzy and yet awake, and
there was a delicious taste on his tongue, more delicious than anything
he had ever tasted, but he couldn't help it, he kept thinking about the
kids. Hubert wouldn't be back before tomorrow morning, and Father,
of course, wouldn't be home for another three weeks, and Mother ...
and right now the kids were waiting all alone, and he knew very well
that they listened for every step, every tiny sound on the stairs, and
there were so many, many sounds on the stairs, and the kids were disappointed so many, many times. There wasn't much hope that Frau
Grossmann would bother about them: she never had, why should she
today. She never had, and after all she couldn't know that he ... that he
had had an accident. Hans might try to comfort Adolf, but Hans was
so frail himself and the least thing made him cry. Maybe Adolf would
comfort Hans, but Adolf was only five whereas Hans was eight; it was
really more likely that Hans would comfort Adolf. But Hans was so
terribly frail and Adolf much stronger. Probably they would both cry,
for when it got close to seven o'clock they would tire of playing because
they were hungry and knew he would be home at seven-thirty to give
them something to eat. And they wouldn't dare take any of the bread;
no, they would never dare do that again—he had forbidden them too
strictly since those few times when they had eaten it all up, every bit,
the whole week's rations. It wouldn't matter if they took some of the
potatoes, but of course they didn't know that. If only he had told them
it was all right to take some of the potatoes. Hans was already quite
good at boiling them; but they wouldn't dare, he had punished them
too severely, in fact he had even had to hit them, for it just wouldn't
do for them to eat up all the bread; it just wouldn't do. But now he
would have been glad if he hadn't punished them, for then they would

take some of the bread and at least they wouldn't be hungry. So instead
they were sitting there waiting, and at every sound on the stairs they
were jumping up excitedly and thrusting their pale faces through the
crack of the door, the way he had seen them so often, so often, a thousand times maybe. Oh, he always saw their faces first, and they were
glad to see him. Yes, even after he had hit them, they were glad to see
him; they had understood, he knew that. And now every sound was a
disappointment, and they would be scared. Hans trembled at the very
sight of a policeman; maybe they'd make such a noise crying that Frau
Grossmann would be angry, for she liked peace and quiet of an evening,
and then maybe they would go on crying, and Frau Grossmann would
come and see what was the matter and take pity on them—she wasn't
so bad, Frau Grossmann. But Hans would never go on his own to Frau
Grossmann; he was so dreadfully scared of her, Hans was scared of
everything...

If only they would take some of the potatoes at least!

Now that he had begun thinking about the kids, he was crying
with pain. He tried holding his hand in front of his eyes so as not to
see the kids, but he felt his hand getting wet, and he cried even more.
He tried to figure out the time. It must be nine o'clock, maybe ten, that
was terrible. He had never got home later than seven-thirty, but today
the train had been closely watched and they had had to keep a sharp
lookout, those Luxembourgers were so trigger-happy. Maybe during
the war they hadn't been able to shoot much and they just enjoyed
shooting; but they didn't get him, oh no, they'd never got him, he'd
always given them the slip. Anthracite, people would pay seventy to
eighty marks for anthracite and think nothing of it—and he was supposed to miss a chance like that? But those Luxembourgers had never
got him; he'd managed to cope with the Russians, with the Yanks, and
the Tommies, and the Belgians, was he going to let himself get caught
by the Luxembourgers of all people, those clowns? He had slipped past
them, up onto the train, filled his sack, tossed it down, and then thrown
down whatever he still had time to lay hands on. But then, crash, the
train had stopped with a sudden jolt, and he knew nothing except that
he had been in the most frightful agony until he knew nothing whatever, and then there had been the pain again when he woke up in the
doorway and saw the white room. And then they had given him the

injection. Now he was crying with happiness again. The kids had gone; this happiness was glorious, he had never known such bliss. His tears seemed to be bliss itself, bliss was flowing out of him, and yet it didn't get any smaller, this flickering, exquisite, circling thing in his chest, this funny lump that welled up out of him in tears, didn't get any smaller...

Suddenly he heard the Luxembourgers shooting. They had machine pistols, and it made a horrible racket in the cool spring evening; there was a smell of fields, smoke from the station, coal, and even a bit of real spring. Two shots barked into the sky, which was dark gray, and the echo of them returned to him a thousand times over, and there was a prickling in his chest like pins and needles. Those damned Luxembourgers weren't going to get him, they weren't going to shoot him to bits! The coal he was lying on was hard and sharp; it was anthracite, and they paid eighty marks, up to eighty marks a hundredweight for it. Should he get the kids some chocolate? No, it wouldn't be enough, for chocolate they wanted forty marks, sometimes forty-five. He couldn't carry away that much: God, he'd have to lug a whole hundredweight for two bars of chocolate; and those Luxembourgers were crazy nuts, now they'd started shooting again, and his bare feet were cold and the sharp anthracite hurt them, and they were black and dirty, he could feel it. The shots were tearing great holes in the sky, but surely they couldn't shoot the sky to bits, or maybe the Luxembourgers could shoot the sky to bits...

Would he have to tell the nurse where his father was and where Hubert went at night? They hadn't asked him, and it was better not to answer unless you were asked. They'd told him in school ... damn those Luxembourgers ... and the kids ... the Luxembourgers ought to stop shooting; he had to get to the kids ... they must be crazy, completely out of their minds, those Luxembourgers. Hell, no, he wasn't going to tell the nurse where their father was and where their brother went at night, and maybe the kids would take some of the bread after all ... or some of the potatoes ... or maybe Frau Grossmann would notice there was something wrong: for there was something wrong; it was funny, there was always something wrong. The principal would bawl him out at school too. The injection had been wonderful, he could feel the prick, and suddenly there was that bliss! That pale-faced nurse had filled the needle with bliss, and he'd heard them all right; he'd heard that she had filled the needle with too much bliss, much too much bliss, he was no fool. Grini with two i's ... nonsense, he's dead ... no, missing. This bliss was glorious, one day he'd buy the bliss in the needle for the kids; you could buy anything ... bread ... whole mountains of bread...

Hell, with two i's, don't these people know a good German name when they hear it...?

"None," he shouted suddenly, "I was never baptized!"

Maybe their mother was still alive after all? No, the Luxembourgers had shot her; no, the Russians ... no, who knows, maybe the Nazis had shot her, she had got so terribly mad at them ... no, the Yanks ... for God's sake, what did it matter if the kids ate the bread, ate the bread ... a whole mountain of bread, that's what he'd buy the kids ... bread piled up to the sky ... a whole boxcar full of bread ... full of anthracite; and bliss in the needle.

With two i's, damn it!

The nun hurried over to him, felt at once for his pulse, and looked round in alarm. Dear God, ought she to call the doctor? But she couldn't leave the delirious child alone now. The little Schranz girl was dead, gone, thank God, that child with the Russian face! Why didn't the doctor come. She ran round behind the leather couch...

"None," shouted the child, "I was never baptized!"

His pulse was getting wilder and wilder every moment. Sweat stood out on the nun's forehead. "Doctor, doctor!" she called, but she knew quite well that no sound penetrated the padded door.

The child was now whimpering pitifully.

"Bread ... a whole mountain of bread for the kids ... chocolate ... anthracite ... the Luxembourgers, those swine, they oughtn't to shoot, damn it, the potatoes, sure you can take some of the potatoes ... go ahead, take some! Frau Grossmann ... Father ... Mother ... Hubert ... through the crack in the door, through the crack in the door."

The nun was weeping with anguish; she dared not leave. The child was beginning to thrash about and she held on to him by the shoulders. The leather couch was so horribly slippery. The little Schranz girl was dead, that little heart was in Heaven. God have mercy on her; dear God, mercy ... she was innocent, a little angel, an ugly little Russian angel ... but now she was pretty...

"None," shouted the boy, trying to flail around with his arms. "I was never baptized!"

The nun looked up in dismay. She ran to the sink, keeping an anxious eye on the boy, but there was no glass; she ran back, stroked the feverish forehead. Then she went over to the little white table and picked up a test tube. The test tube was soon full, it doesn't take much water to fill a test tube...

"Bliss," whispered the child, "fill the needle with lots of bliss, all you've got, for the kids too..."

The nun crossed herself solemnly, deliberately, then sprinkled the water from the test tube over the boy's forehead, saying through her tears, "I baptize thee..." But the boy, suddenly sobered by the cold water, jerked up his head so violently that the tube fell from the nun's hand and smashed on the floor. The boy looked at the startled nun with a little smile and said feebly, "Baptize ... yes..." Then he dropped back so abruptly that his head fell on the leather couch with a dull thud, and now his face looked narrow and old, frighteningly yellow, as he lay there motionless, his fingers spread to grasp...

"Has he been X-rayed yet?" cried the doctor, chuckling as he came into the room with Dr. Lohmeyer. The nun merely shook her head. The doctor stepped closer, felt automatically for his stethoscope, but dropped it and looked at Lohmeyer. Lohmeyer removed his hat. Lohengrin was dead...

BUSINESS IS BUSINESS

My black marketeer is an honest citizen these days; it was a long time since I had seen him, months in fact, and today I came across him in quite a different part of the city, at a busy intersection. He has a wooden booth there now, all done up in the best white paint; a handsome corrugated iron roof, solid and brand-new, shields him from rain and cold, and he sells cigarettes and all-day suckers, quite legally. At first I was pleased; it is always nice, after all, to see someone find his way back to normal life. For when we first met, things were going badly for him, and we were depressed. We still went around in our old army caps, and whenever I came by some cash I used to go and see him, and we would have a chat, about being hungry, about the war; and now and again, when I didn't have any money, he would give me a cigarette, or I would take along some bread-ration coupons, as I happened to be clearing rubble for a baker at the time.

He seemed to be doing all right now. He looked the picture of health. His cheeks had that firmness that comes only from a regular intake of fats, his expression was self-confident, and I watched him bawl out a grubby little girl and send her packing because she was short five pfennigs for an all-day sucker. And all the time he kept feeling around in his mouth with his tongue as if he were forever trying to pry shreds of meat from between his teeth.

Business was brisk; they were buying a lot of cigarettes from him, and all-day suckers as well.

Maybe I shouldn't have—I went up to him and said, "Ernst," intending to have a word with him.

He was very surprised, gave me an odd look, and said, "What's that?" I could see he recognized me but that he wasn't too keen on being recognized.

I was silent. I behaved as if I had never said "Ernst" to him, bought some cigarettes, since I happened to have some cash, and left. I watched him a while longer; my streetcar wasn't in sight yet, and I didn't feel in the least like going home. At home I'm always being pestered by people wanting money—my landlady asking for the rent, and the man with the electricity bill. Besides, I'm not allowed to smoke at home; my landlady always manages to smell it, she gets mad and I'm told that I seem to have money for tobacco but none for the rent. It's a sin, you see, for the poor to smoke or drink. I know it's a sin, that's why I do it secretly, I smoke outdoors, and just occasionally when I'm lying awake and everything is quiet, when I know that by morning the smell will have disappeared, then I smoke in my room too.

The terrible thing is that I have no profession. For you have to have a profession. That's what they tell you. There was a time when they used to say it was unnecessary, all we needed was soldiers. But now they say you have to have a profession. Just like that. They say you are lazy when you don't have a profession. But that's not so. I'm not lazy, but the jobs they give me are jobs I don't want to do. Clearing rubble and carrying rocks, and things like that. After two hours I'm soaked with sweat, everything becomes a blur, and when I go to the doctors they tell me there's nothing wrong. Maybe it's nerves. Nowadays they talk a lot about nerves. But I believe it's a sin for the poor to have nerves. To be poor and to have nerves, that seems to be more than they can stand. But my nerves are all shot, I can tell you that; I was a soldier too long. Nine years, I think. Maybe more, I'm not sure. Once upon a time I would have been glad to have a profession, I wanted very much to go into business. But once upon a time—what's the use of talking about it? Now I don't even feel like going into business anymore. What I like to do best is lie on my bed and daydream. I figure out how many hundreds of thousands of man-hours they need to build a bridge or a big house and then I think that in a single minute they can smash both the bridge and the house. So what's the point of working? To my mind there's no sense in working. I think that's what drives me crazy when I have to carry rocks or clear rubble so they can build another café.

A minute ago I was saying it was nerves, but I think that's the real reason: it's all so senseless.

Actually I don't care what they think. But it's terrible never to have any money. You've simply got to have money. You can't get along without it. There's a meter, and you have a lamp, naturally you need light sometimes, you switch it on, and right away the money's pouring out of the light bulb. Even when you don't need any light, you have to pay rent for the meter. That's the whole trouble: rent. It seems you've got to have a room. At first I lived in a cellar, it wasn't too bad down there—I had a stove and used to steal briquettes; but they unearthed me, they came from the newspaper, took my picture, wrote an article to go with the picture:

"Returning Veteran Lives in Poverty." I had to move, that's all there was to it. The man from the housing office said it was a matter of prestige for him and I had to take the room. Sometimes, of course, I make some money. Obviously. I run errands, deliver briquettes and stack them up nice and neatly in a corner of someone's cellar. I am very good at stacking briquettes, and I don't charge much either. Needless to say, I don't earn much; it's never enough for the rent, sometimes it's enough for the electricity, a few cigarettes and bread...

I was thinking of all this as I stood at the corner.

My black marketeer, who is now an honest citizen, threw me a suspicious look from time to time. That bastard knows perfectly well who I am, people do know each other, after all, when they've spoken to one another almost every day for two years. Maybe he thought I was going to steal something. I'm not as dumb as all that, to steal something at a busy spot with streetcars stopping every minute and even a cop standing at the corner. I steal things in quite different places: naturally I steal things sometimes, things like coal. Wood too. The other day I even stole a loaf in a bakery. You wouldn't believe how quick and easy it was. I just took the loaf and walked out, I walked along quite calmly, as far as the next corner, then I started to run. I've lost the nerve I used to have, that's all.

I certainly wouldn't steal anything at a corner like that, although sometimes it's easy, but I've lost my nerve. Several streetcars stopped, including my own, and I could see Ernst looking sidelong at me when mine came up. That bastard still remembers which is my streetcar!

But I threw away the butt of my first cigarette, lit another, and stayed where I was. I've progressed that far, at least, that I throw away butts. Yet over there someone was creeping around picking up butts, and you have to think of the other fellow. There are still some people who pick up cigarette butts. They aren't always the same ones. In the

POW camp I had seen colonels doing it, but this one wasn't a colonel. I watched him. He had his own system, like a spider lurking in its web he had his headquarters somewhere in a pile of rubble, and whenever a streetcar stopped or started up he would emerge and walk unhurriedly along the curb collecting the butts. I would have liked to go up to him and speak to him; I feel we are two of a kind. But I know it's no use; those fellows never say anything.

I don't know what was the matter with me, but that day I just didn't want to go home. The very word: home... I was past caring now, I let one more streetcar go by and lit another cigarette. I don't know what's wrong with us. Maybe some professor will find out one day and write an article about it in the paper; they have an explanation for everything. I only wish I still had the nerve to steal things, like I did in the war. In those days I used to be quick and easy. In those days, during the war, when there was anything to be stolen, it was we who had to go out and steal it; they used to say: Don't worry, he knows how to do it, and off we would go to steal something. The others just helped eat and drink up the stuff, send it home and all that, but they didn't steal anything. Their nerves were in perfect shape, and they managed to keep their copybooks clean.

And when we came home they got out of the war as if they were getting out of a streetcar that happened to slow down just where they lived, and they jumped off without paying the fare. They turned aside, went indoors, and lo and behold: the dresser was still standing, there was a little dust on the bookshelves, your wife had potatoes stored in the cellar, and some preserves; you embraced her a bit, as was right and proper, and next morning you went off to find out whether your job was still open: the job was still open. Everything was fine, your medical insurance was still okay, you had yourself de-Nazified a bit—the way you go to the barber to get rid of that tiresome beard—you chatted about decorations, wounds, acts of heroism, and came to the conclusion you were a pretty fine fellow after all: you had simply done your duty. There were weekly streetcar passes again, the best sign that everything was back to normal.

Meanwhile the rest of us stayed on the streetcar and waited to see if somewhere there would be a stop that seemed familiar enough for us to risk getting off: it never came. Some people went on a bit farther, but they jumped off somewhere too, trying to look as if they had reached their destination.

But we went on and on. The fare went up automatically, and we had to pay for our bulky, heavy baggage as well: for the leaden mass of nothingness that we had to lug around with us. First one inspector got on, then another, and we would shrug our shoulders and show them our empty pockets. They couldn't throw us off, the streetcar was going too fast—"and we were human beings after all"—but they wrote down our names, over and over again they wrote down our names, the streetcar went faster and faster; the smart ones jumped off quickly, anywhere; fewer and fewer of us stayed on, and fewer and fewer of us had the guts or the desire to get off. At the back of our minds, we meant to leave our baggage on the streetcar, to let the Lost and Found auction it off as soon as we reached the terminus; but the terminus never came, the fare went up and up, the streetcar went faster and faster, the inspectors got more and more skeptical—we are a highly suspect lot.

I threw away the butt of my third cigarette and walked slowly across to the streetcar stop; I wanted to go home now. I felt dizzy: one shouldn't smoke so much on an empty stomach, I know that. I quit looking over to where my former black marketeer was now carrying on a legitimate business. I really have no right to be angry; he made it, he jumped off, probably at the right moment, but I don't know whether it's all right for him to bawl out kids who are short five pfennigs for an all-day sucker. Maybe that's all part of legitimate business; I wouldn't know.

Just before my streetcar arrived, the bum walked unhurriedly along the curb again, in front of the ranks of waiting people, to collect butts. They don't like to see that, I know. They would rather it wasn't that way, but that's the way it is...

I didn't look at Ernst again until I was on the streetcar, but he glanced away and shouted, "Chocolate, candy, cigarettes, all ration-free!" I don't know what's wrong, but I must say I liked him better before, when he didn't need to send anyone away who was short five pfennigs; but now of course he has a proper business, and business is business.

ON THE HOOK

I know it's stupid. I ought to stop going there; it's so senseless, yet going there is what keeps me alive. A single minute of hope and twenty-three hours and fifty-nine minutes of despair. That's what keeps me alive. It's not much; there's precious little substance to it. I ought to stop going there. It's killing me, that's what: it's killing me. But I've got to go, I've got to, I've got to...

The train she's supposed to arrive on is always the same one, the 1:20 p.m. The train always pulls in on time—I keep a sharp eye on everything, they can't fool me.

The man with the baton is always ready for me when I turn up; when he comes out of his little signal house—I've already heard the signal bell ringing inside it—as I say, when he comes out, I go over to him, he knows me by this time: he puts on a sympathetic expression, sympathetic and a bit scared. Yes, the man with the baton is scared; maybe he thinks I'll go for him one day. I might at that, one of these days, I might beat him up, kill him, and dump his body between the tracks to be run over by the 1:20. You see, that man with the baton—I don't trust him. I don't know whether his pity is an act or not; maybe it's just an act. He's scared all right, that's genuine enough, and he has good reason to be: one day I'll beat his brains out with his own baton. I don't trust him; maybe he's in cahoots with them. After all, he does have a phone in his signal house—all he has to do is crank the handle and call them up— those railroad jokers get through in a second. Maybe he lifts the receiver, phones the last-but-one station, and tells them, "Take her off the train, arrest her; don't let her get back on... What?...That's right, the woman with the brown hair and the little green hat; yes, that's the one, hold on to her"—then he laughs—"that's right, that nut's here again; we'll let him wait for nothing again. Be sure you hold on to her, now."

He hangs up and laughs; then he comes out, puts on his pitying expression when he sees me shuffling over to him, and says, as he always does even before I ask him, "Right on time again, sir, same as usual!"

This not knowing whether I can trust him is driving me crazy. Perhaps he grins the moment he turns his back on me. He always does turn his back on me and acts as if he had something important to do, like on the platform; he walks up and down, waves people back from the edge of the platform, finds all sorts of things to do that are quite superfluous, for the people step back from the edge anyway as soon as they see him coming. He's just putting on a show, pretending to be busy, and perhaps he grins the moment he turns his back. Once I wanted to test him—I darted round in front of him and looked him straight in the face. But there was nothing there to confirm my suspicions: only fear...

All the same, I don't trust him, those fellows have more self-control than our sort; they're capable of anything. It's a kind of clique that's got strength and security, while we—the ones who wait—have nothing. We live on a razor's edge, balancing from one minute of hope to the next minute of hope. For twenty-three hours and fifty-nine minutes we balance on the razor's edge; one minute's respite is all we get. They have us on a tight rein, those fellows, those jokers with their batons, those stinkers, they call each other up, exchange a couple of words, and our life is down the drain again, down the drain again for twenty-three hours and fifty-nine minutes. They're the ones who run the show, those bastards...

His pity is an act, I'm quite sure of that now. When I really think about it, I have to acknowledge that he's double-crossing me. They're all crooks. They're holding on to her; I know she meant to come, she told me so in a letter: "I love you, and I'm coming on the 1:20 p.m." Arriving 1:20 p.m., she wrote; that was three months ago, three months and four days exactly. They're keeping her back, they don't want us to meet, they begrudge me the chance of ever having more than one minute's hope, let alone joy. They're preventing our rendezvous; somewhere or other they're sitting and laughing, they're all in it together. They laugh and call each other up, and that stinker with the baton gets paid, and well paid too, for telling me day after day, in that mealy-mouthed way of his, "Right on time again, sir, same as usual!" Even the "sir" is an insult. No one ever calls me "sir," I'm a poor down-and-out bastard who lives on one minute of hope a day. That's all. No one ever calls me "sir," shit on his "sir." They can do it to me backwards but they've got to let her go, let her get back on that train; they've got to give her to me, she's mine; didn't she send me a telegram, "I love you, arriving there 1:20 p.m."? "There" means where I live. That's what telegrams are like: you write "there," and you mean the town where the other person lives. "Arriving there 1:20 p.m." ...

Today I'm going to do him in. I'm about ready to blow my top. My patience is exhausted, my strength too. I'm at the end of my tether. If I see him today, he's had it. It's been going on too long. Besides, I've no more money. No more money for the streetcar. I've already sold everything I own. For three months and four days I've been living off capital. I've sold the lot, even the tablecloth. I can't kid myself anymore—today there's nothing left. There's just enough for one streetcar ride. Not even enough for the return trip, I'll have to walk back ... or ... or ...

In any case that bastard with the baton will be lying down there between the tracks, a bloody mess, and the 1:20 will run over him, he'll be wiped out, just as I'll be wiped out this afternoon at 1:20 ... or ... Christ!

It's really too much when you don't even have money for the return trip; they make things too hard for a man. The clique sticks together; they control hope, they control paradise, consolation. They've got their talons round everything. We're only allowed to nibble at it, for a single minute a day. For twenty-three hours and fifty-nine minutes we have to hanker after it, lie in wait for it; they even refuse to dole out the artificial paradises. And they don't even need them; I wonder why they hang on to everything? Is it just for the sake of the money? Why don't they ever give a man money for booze or smokes, why do they put such a terrible price on consolation? They keep us dangling on the hook, and every time we bite, every time we let ourselves be pulled up to the surface, every time we breathe light, beauty, joy for one minute, some bastard laughs, slackens the line, and there we are back in the dark...

They make things too hard for us; today I'm going to get my revenge. I'm going to take that stinker with the baton, that outpost of security, and dump him between the tracks. Maybe that'll give them a fright, sitting back there by their phones—Christ, if only a fellow could frighten them, just once! But you haven't a chance, that's the trouble. They hold on to everything: bread, wine, tobacco, they've got the lot, and they've got her too: "Arriving there 1:20 p.m." No date. That's the trouble: she never writes the date.

They're jealous because I might have kissed her. No, no, no, we have to perish, suffocate, despair utterly, go without consolation, sell everything we own, and when we've nothing left we have to ...

For that's the terrible part about it—the minute is shrinking. I've noticed it the last few days: the minute is shrinking. I think it may be only thirty seconds now, perhaps much less, I don't even dare work out how much really is left. Yesterday, anyway, I noticed it was less. Up till then, whenever the train came in sight round the curve, black and snorting against the city's spreading horizon, I was always conscious of being happy. She's coming, I used to think, she's got through, she's coming! I would go on thinking that the whole time, till the train came to a halt, the people got slowly out—the platform gradually emptied ... and ... nothing...

No, then I wasn't thinking that anymore. I must try above all to be honest with myself. When the first people got out and she wasn't among them, I wasn't thinking that anymore, it was all over. That happiness—it wasn't that it stopped sooner, it began later. That's how it was. One must be honest and objective about it. It began later, that's how it was. It used to begin when the train came in sight, black and snorting against the city's spreading horizon; yesterday it didn't begin until the train had come to a halt. When it had stopped moving altogether, when it was just standing there, that's when I began to hope; and when it was standing there, the doors were already opening ... and she didn't come...

Now I'm wondering whether that lasted even thirty seconds. I haven't the nerve to be quite honest and say: It's only one second ... and ... twenty-three hours, fifty-nine minutes, and fifty-nine seconds of black darkness...

I haven't the nerve; I can scarcely bring myself to go back there; it would be too horrible if not even this second were left. Are they going to take that away from me too?

It's too little. There are limits. A certain amount of substance is needed by even the lowliest of creatures, even the lowliest of creatures needs at least one second a day. They mustn't take this one second away from me; they're making it too short.

Their callousness is assuming terrible forms. Now I don't even have the money for the return trip. Not even for the fare straight there and back, let alone transfer, as I have to. I'm short exactly a nickel. Their callousness is cruel. They've even stopped buying. They don't even want to buy things now. Until now they've always been screaming to buy things. But now their greed has become so appalling that they're sitting on their money and devouring it. I really do believe they devour their money. I wonder what for? What do they want? They've got bread, wine, tobacco, they've got money, everything, they've got their fat women—what else do they want? Why have they stopped shelling out? No money, not an ounce of bread, no tobacco, not a drop of schnapps ... nothing ... nothing. They're forcing me to extreme measures.

I shall have to take up the struggle. I'm going to finish off that outpost of theirs, that bastard with his baton and his pitying expression, he screws me every time he talks to them on the phone! He's in cahoots with them, I know that now for certain, because yesterday I listened in on him! That bastard's double-crossing me, I'm sure of that now. I went much earlier yesterday, much earlier, he couldn't have known I was there; I ducked down under the window and waited, and sure enough!— he cranked the handle, the bell tinkled, and I heard his voice. "Super-intendent," he said, "Superintendent, something's got to be done about it. The fellow can't be allowed to go on like that. After all, the security of a civil servant is at stake! Superintendent," his voice implored—that bastard really was scared stiff. "That's right, Platform 4b."

Very well, so now I've got proof. Now they'll take drastic meas-ures. Now they're really going to finish me off. Now it's a fight to the finish. At least the position is clear. I'm glad of that. I shall fight like a lion. I'll run down the whole lot of them, herd them all together, and toss them in front of the 1:20...

Not one thing are they willing to let me keep. They're driving me to desperation; they want to rob me of my last second. And they've even stopped buying. Not even watches—till now they've always been keen on watches. All I got for my books was three pounds of tea—two hundred pretty nice books at that. I imagine they were pretty nice. I used to be very interested in literature. But three pounds of tea for two hundred books—what a lousy deal; the bread I got for the sheets and pillow slips was hardly worth mentioning, my mother's jewelry gave me enough to live on for a month, and you need such a tremendous amount when you live on a razor's edge. Three months and four days is a long time; a fellow needs too much.

As a last resort there's always Father's watch. The watch has a certain value. No one can deny that the watch has a certain value; perhaps it's enough for the return trip; perhaps the conductor has a kind heart and will let me ride back in exchange for the watch; perhaps, perhaps I shall need two tickets for the return trip: Christ!

It's twelve-thirty and I must get ready. That doesn't involve much, nothing at all really. I just have to get out of bed, that's all there is to getting ready. The room is bare, I've sold everything. A fellow has to live, after all. The landlady has taken the mattress for a month's rent. She's a good sort, a really good sort, one of the best I've ever met. A good woman. A fellow can doss down perfectly well on the wire springs. No one knows how well you can sleep on wire springs, if you sleep at all, that is; I never sleep, I live on capital, I live on one second's hope, on the second when the doors open and no one comes...

I must pull myself together; the battle's about to begin. It's a quarter to one, the streetcar passes at ten to; that'll get me to the station on the dot of quarter past, onto the platform by eighteen past; when that joker with the baton comes out of his signal house, I'll be just in time to let him tell me, "Right on time again, sir, same as usual!"

The bastard really does say "sir" to me; everyone else he just bawls out, shouting, "Hey you there—get back from the edge of the platform!" To me he says "sir"! That just shows: it's all a big fake, a horrible big fake. When you look at them, you're tempted to think they're hungry too, that they're all out of tea or tobacco or booze; the expression on their faces is enough to make you almost want to sell your last shirt for them.

A fellow could cry for years over the big fake they put on. I must try to cry; it must be wonderful to cry, a substitute for wine, tobacco, bread, and maybe even a substitute for when the single solitary second is extinct and all I have left is twenty-four naked, entire hours of despair.

I can't cry in the streetcar, of course; I must pull myself together, I really must pull myself together. They mustn't notice anything; and at the station I'll have to watch out. I'm sure they have people hidden somewhere. "After all, the security of a civil servant is at stake ... Platform 4b." I'll have to be damn careful. It makes me nervous the way the conductress keeps looking at me. She asks several times, "Tickets?" looking only at me. And I really have one; I could pull it out and hold it under her nose, she gave it to me herself, but she's forgotten already. "Tickets?" she asks three times, looking at me. I blush, I really do have one; she moves on, and everyone thinks: He hasn't got one, he's cheating the transit company. And all the time I've given up my last twenty pfennigs, I've even got a transfer...

I must watch out like hell; I very nearly ran through the barrier, like I always do; but they might be standing around anyplace. As I was just about to dash through, I realized I didn't have a platform ticket, or a nickel. It's seventeen minutes past, in three minutes the train will be in, I'm going crazy. "Take this watch," I said. The man looks insulted. "For God's sake, take this watch." He pushes me back. Their excellencies the ticket holders are staring. There's no help for it: I have to go back; it's seventeen and a half minutes past.

"A watch!" I shout. "A watch for a nickel! An honest watch, not a stolen one, a watch that belonged to my father!" Everyone takes me for a nut or a criminal. Not one of those bastards will take my watch. Perhaps they'll call the police. I must find the bums. The bums will help me at least. The bums are all down below. It's eighteen minutes past, I'm going crazy. Am I to miss the train today of all days, the very day she's going to arrive? "Arriving there 1:20 p.m."

"Hey, buddy," I say to the first bum I see, "give me a nickel for this watch, but quick, quick," I say.

He stares too—even he stares. "Listen, buddy," I tell him, "I've got one more minute, understand?"

He understands—he misunderstands, of course, but at least he tries to understand, at least it's something to be misunderstood. At least it's a kind of understanding. The others understand nothing.

He gives me a mark; he's generous. "Listen, buddy," I say, "I need a nickel, get it? Not a mark, understand?"

He misunderstands again, but it's so good to be at least misunderstood; if I get out of this alive I'll hug you, buddy.

He gives me a nickel as well, that's how the bums are, they give a bit extra and at least they misunderstand.

I manage to race up the steps at nineteen and a half minutes past one. But I still have to be on the alert, I have to watch out like crazy.

There comes the train, black and snorting against the city's gray horizon. My heart is silent at the sight of it, but I am in time, that's the main thing. In spite of everything, I've managed to get here in time.

I keep well away from the joker with the baton. He is surrounded by people, and suddenly he's caught sight of me, he calls out, he's scared, he waves to the clique hiding in his signal house, waves to them to catch me. They dash out, they've almost got me, but I laugh in their faces, I laugh in their faces, for the train has pulled in and before they get to me she is in my arms, my girl, and all I own in the world is my girl and a platform ticket, my girl and a punched platform ticket...

MY SAD FACE

While I was standing on the dock watching the seagulls, my sad face attracted the attention of a policeman on his rounds. I was completely absorbed in the sight of the hovering birds as they shot up and swooped down in a vain search for something edible: the harbor was deserted, the water greenish and thick with foul oil, and on its crusty film floated all kinds of discarded junk. Not a vessel was to be seen, the cranes had rusted, the freight sheds collapsed; not even rats seemed to inhabit the black ruins along the wharf, silence reigned. It was years since all connection with the outside world had been cut off.

I had my eye on one particular seagull and was observing its flight. Uneasy as a swallow sensing thunder in the air, it usually stayed hovering just above the surface of the water, occasionally, with a shrill cry, risking an upward sweep to unite with its circling fellows. Had I been free to express a wish, I would have chosen a loaf of bread to feed to the gulls, crumbling it to pieces to provide a white fixed point for the random flutterings, to set a goal at which the birds could aim, to tauten this shrill flurry of crisscross hovering and circling by hurling a piece of bread into the mesh as if to pull together a bunch of strings. But I was as hungry as they were, and tired, yet happy in spite of my sadness because it felt good to be standing there, my hands in my pockets, watching the gulls and drinking in sadness.

Suddenly I felt an official hand on my shoulder, and a voice said, "Come along now!" The hand tugged at my shoulder, trying to pull me round, but I did not budge, shook it off, and said quietly, "You're nuts."

"Comrade," the still-invisible one told me, "I'm warning you."

"Sir," I retorted.

"What d'you mean, 'sir'?" he shouted angrily. "We're all comrades."

With that he stepped round beside me and looked at me, forcing me to bring back my contentedly roving gaze and direct it at his simple, honest face: he was as solemn as a buffalo that for twenty years has had nothing to eat but duty.

"On what grounds..." I began.

"Sufficient grounds," he said. "Your sad face."

I laughed.

"Don't laugh!" His rage was genuine. I had first thought he was bored, with no unlicensed whore, no staggering sailor, no thief or fugitive to arrest, but now I saw he meant it: he intended to arrest me.

"Come along now!"

"Why?" I asked quietly.

Before I realized what was happening, I found my left wrist enclosed in a thin chain, and instantly I knew that once again I had had it. I turned toward the swerving gulls for a last look, glanced at the calm gray sky, and tried with a sudden twist to plunge into the water, for it seemed more desirable to drown alone in that scummy dishwater than to be strangled by the sergeants in a backyard or to be locked up again. But the policeman suddenly jerked me so close to him that all hope of wrenching myself free was gone.

"Why?" I asked again.

"There's a law that you have to be happy."

"I am happy!" I cried.

"Your sad face..." He shook his head.

"But this law is new," I told him.

"It's thirty-six hours old, and I'm sure you know that every law comes into force twenty-four hours after it has been proclaimed."

"But I've never heard of it!"

"That won't save you. It was proclaimed yesterday, over all the loudspeakers, in all the papers, and anyone"—here he looked at me scornfully—"anyone who doesn't share in the blessings of press or radio was informed by leaflets scattered from the air over every street in the country. So we'll soon find out where you've been spending the last thirty-six hours, comrade."

He dragged me away. For the first time I noticed that it was cold and I had no coat; for the first time I became really aware of my hunger growling at the entrance to my stomach; for the first time I realized that I was also dirty, unshaved, and in rags, and that there were laws demanding that every comrade be clean, shaved, happy, and well fed.

He pushed me in front of him like a scarecrow that has been found guilty of stealing and is compelled to abandon the place of its dreams at the edge of the field. The streets were empty, the police station was not far off, and, although I had known they would soon find a reason for arresting me, my heart was heavy, for he took me through the places of my childhood which I had intended to visit after looking at the harbor: public gardens that had been full of bushes, in glorious confusion, overgrown paths—all this was now leveled, orderly, neat, arranged in squares for the patriotic groups obliged to drill and march here on Mondays, Wednesdays, and Saturdays. Only the sky was as it used to be, the air the same as in the old days, when my heart had been full of dreams.

Here and there as we walked along I saw the government sign displayed on the walls of a number of love-barracks, indicating whose turn it was to participate in these hygienic pleasures on Wednesdays; certain taverns also were evidently authorized to hang out the drinking sign, a beer glass cut out of tin and striped diagonally with the national colors: light brown, dark brown, light brown. Joy was doubtless already filling the hearts of those whose names appeared in the official list of Wednesday drinkers and who would thus partake of the Wednesday beer.

All the people we passed were stamped with the unmistakable mark of earnest zeal, encased in an aura of tireless activity probably intensified by the sight of the policeman. They all quickened their pace, assumed expressions of perfect devotion to duty, and the women coming out of the goods depots did their best to register that joy which was expected of them, for they were required to show joy and cheerful gaiety over the duties of the housewife, whose task it was to refresh the state worker every evening with a wholesome meal.

But all these people skillfully avoided us in such a way that no one was forced to cross our path directly. Where there were signs of life on the street, they disappeared twenty paces ahead of us, each trying to dash into a goods depot or vanish round a corner, and quite a few may have slipped into a strange house and waited nervously behind the door until the sound of our footsteps had died away.

Only once, just as we were crossing an intersection, we came face to face with an elderly man, I just caught a glimpse of his schoolteacher's badge. There was no time for him to avoid us, and he strove, after first saluting the policeman in the prescribed manner (by slapping his own head three times with the flat of his hand as a sign of total abasement)—he strove, as I say, to do his duty by spitting three times into my face and bestowing upon me the compulsory epithet of "filthy traitor." His aim was good, but the day had been hot, his throat must have been dry, for I received only a few tiny, rather ineffectual flecks, which—contrary to regulations—I tried involuntarily to wipe away with my sleeve, whereupon the policeman kicked me in the backside and struck me with his fist in the small of my back, adding in a flat voice, "Phase One," meaning: first and mildest form of punishment administerable by every policeman.

The schoolteacher had hurriedly gone on his way. Everyone else managed to avoid us; except for just one woman, who happened to be taking the prescribed stroll in the fresh air in front of a love-barracks prior to the evening's pleasures, a pale, puffy blonde who blew me a furtive kiss, and I smiled gratefully while the policeman tried to pretend he hadn't noticed. They are required to permit these women liberties that for any other comrade would unquestionably result in severe punishment; for, since they contribute substantially to the general working morale, they are tacitly considered to be outside the law, a concession whose far-reaching consequences have been branded as a sign of incipient liberalization by Professor Bleigoeth, Ph.D., D.Litt., the political philosopher, in the obligatory (political) *Journal of Philosophy*. I had read this the previous day on my way to the capital when, in a farm outhouse, I came across a few sheets of the magazine that a student—probably the farmer's son—had embellished with some very witty comments.

Fortunately we now reached the police station, for at that moment the sirens sounded, a sign that the streets were about to be flooded with thousands of people wearing expressions of restrained joy (it being required at closing time to show restraint in one's expression of joy, otherwise it might look as though work were a burden; whereas rejoicing was to prevail when work began—rejoicing and singing), and all these thousands would have been compelled to spit at me. However, the siren indicated ten minutes before closing time, every worker being required to devote ten minutes to a thorough washing of his person, in accordance with the motto of the head of state: Joy and Soap.

The entrance to the local police station, a squat concrete box, was guarded by two sentries who, as I passed them, gave me the benefit of the customary "physical punitive measures," striking me hard across the temple with their rifles and cracking the muzzles of their pistols down on my collarbone, in accordance with the preamble to State Law No. I: "Every police officer is required, when confronted by any apprehended [meaning arrested] person, to demonstrate violence *per se*, with the exception of the officer performing the arrest, the latter being privileged to participate in the pleasure of carrying out the necessary physical punitive measures during the interrogation." The actual State Law No. I runs as follows: "Every police officer *may* punish anyone: he *must* punish anyone who has committed a crime. For all comrades there is no such thing as exemption from punishment, only the possibility of exemption from punishment."

We now proceeded down a long, bare corridor provided with a great many large windows. Then a door opened automatically, the sentries having already announced our arrival, and in those days, when everything was joy, obedience, and order and everyone did his best to use up the mandatory pound of soap a day—in those days the arrival of an apprehended (arrested) comrade was naturally an event.

We entered an almost empty room containing nothing but a desk with a telephone and two chairs. I was required to remain standing in the middle of the room; the policeman took off his helmet and sat down.

At first there was silence; nothing happened. They always do it like that—that's the worst part. I could feel my face collapsing by degrees, I was tired and hungry, and by now even the last vestiges of that joy of sadness had vanished, for I knew I had had it.

After a few seconds a tall, pale-faced, silent man entered the room wearing the light-brown uniform of the preliminary interrogator. He sat down without a word and looked at me.

"Status?"

"Ordinary comrade."

"Date of birth?"

"1/1/1," I said.

"Last occupation?"

"Convict."

The two men exchanged glances.

"When and where discharged?"

"Yesterday, Building 12, Cell 13."

"Where to?"

"The capital."

"Certificate."

I produced the discharge certificate from my pocket and handed it to him. He clipped it to the green card on which he had begun to enter my particulars.

"Your former crime?"

"Happy face."

The two men exchanged glances.

"Explain," said the interrogator.

"At that time," I said, "my happy face attracted the attention of a police officer on a day when general mourning had been decreed. It was the anniversary of the Leader's death."

"Length of sentence?"

"Five."

"Conduct?"

"Bad."

"Reason?"

"Deficient in work enthusiasm."

"That's all."

With that the preliminary interrogator rose, walked over to me, and neatly knocked out my three front center teeth—a sign that I was to be branded as a lapsed criminal, an intensified measure I had not counted on. The preliminary interrogator then left the room, and a fat fellow in a dark-brown uniform came in: the interrogator.

I was beaten by all of them: by the interrogator, the chief interrogator, the supreme interrogator, the examiner, and the concluding examiner. In addition, the policeman carried out all the physical punitive measures demanded by law, and on account of my sad face they sentenced me to ten years, just as five years earlier they had sentenced me to five years on account of my happy face.

I must now try to make my face register nothing at all, if I can manage to survive the next ten years of Joy and Soap...

CANDLES FOR THE MADONNA

My stay here was a brief one. I had an appointment in the late afternoon with the representative of a firm that was toying with the idea of taking over a product which has been causing us something of a headache: candles. We put all our money into the manufacture of tremendous stocks on the assumption that the electricity shortage would continue indefinitely. We have worked very hard, been thrifty and honest, and when I say "we" I mean my wife and myself. We are producers, wholesalers, retailers; we combine every stage in the holy estate of commerce: we are agents, workmen, traveling salesmen, manufacturers.

But we put our money on the wrong horse. There is not much demand for candles these days. Electricity rationing has been abolished, even most basements now have electric light again; and at the very moment when our hard work, our efforts, all our struggles, seemed about to bear fruit—the production of a large quantity of candles—at that precise moment the demand dried up.

Our attempts to do business with those religious enterprises dealing in what are known as devotional supplies came to nothing. These firms had hoarded candles in abundance—better ones than ours, incidentally, the fancy kind, with green, red, blue, and yellow ribbons, embroidered with little golden stars, winding around them, like Aesculapius' snake—and enhancing both their reverent and aesthetic appeal. They also come in various lengths and sizes, whereas ours are all identical and of simple design: about ten inches long, smooth, yellow, quite plain, their only asset the beauty of simplicity.

We were forced to admit that we had miscalculated; compared with the splendid products displayed by the devotional-supply houses, our candles look humble indeed, and nobody buys anything humble-looking. Nor has our willingness to reduce our price resulted in any increase in sales. On the other hand, of course, we lack the money to plan new designs, let alone manufacture them, since the income we derive from the limited sale of the stock we have produced is barely enough to cover our living expenses and steadily mounting costs. I have, for instance, to make longer and longer trips in order to call on genuinely or apparently interested parties, I have to keep on reducing our price, and we know we have no alternative but to unload the substantial stocks still on our hands and find some other means of making a living.

I had come to this town in response to a letter from a wholesaler who had intimated that he would take a considerable quantity off my hands at an acceptable price. I was foolish enough to believe him, came all the way here, and was now calling on this fellow. He had a magnificent apartment, luxurious, spacious, furnished in great style, and the large office where he received me was crammed with samples of all the various products that make money for his type of business. Arranged on long shelves were plaster saints, statuettes of Joseph, Virgin Marys, bleeding Sacred Hearts, mild-eyed, fair-haired penitents whose plaster pedestals bore the name, in a variety of languages and embossed lettering (choice of gold or red), Madeleine, Maddalena, Magdalena, Magdalene; Nativity scenes (complete or sectional), oxen, asses, Infant Jesuses in wax or plaster, shepherds, and angels of all ages: tots, youths, children, graybeards; plaster palm leaves adorned with gold or silver Hallelujahs, holy-water stoups of stainless steel, plaster, copper, pottery, some in good taste, some in bad.

The man himself—a jovial, red-faced fellow—asked me to sit down, affected some initial interest, and offered me a cigar. He wanted to know how we happened to get into this particular branch of manufacturing, and after I had explained that we had inherited nothing from the war but a huge pile of stearin which my wife had salvaged from four blazing trucks in front of our bombed-out house and which no one had since claimed as their property, after I had smoked about a quarter of my cigar, he suddenly said, without any preamble, "I'm sorry I had you come here, but I've changed my mind." Perhaps my sudden loss of color did strike him as odd after all. "Yes," he went on, "I really am sorry about it, but after considering all the angles I've come to the conclusion that your product won't sell. It won't sell! Believe me, I know! Sorry!" He smiled, shrugged his shoulders, and held out his hand. I put down the half-smoked cigar and left.

By this time it was dark, and I was a total stranger in the town. Although, in spite of everything, I was aware of a certain relief, I had the terrible feeling that I was not only poor, deceived, the victim of a misguided idea, but also ridiculous. It would seem that I was unfit for the so-called battle of life, for the career of manufacturer and dealer. Our candles would not sell even for a pittance, they weren't good enough to hold their own in the field of devotionalist competition, and we probably wouldn't even be able to give them away, whereas other, inferior candles were being bought. I would never discover the secret of business success, although, with my wife, I had hit upon the secret of making candles.

I lugged my heavy sample case to the streetcar stop and waited a long time. The darkness was soft and clear, it was summer. Streetlights were on at the crossings, people were strolling about in the evening, it was quiet; I was standing beside a big circular traffic island fringed by dark, empty office buildings. Behind me was a little park; I heard the sound of running water, and on turning round I saw a great marble woman standing there, with thin jets of water spouting from her rigid breasts into a copper basin. I felt chilly and realized I was tired. At last the streetcar arrived; soft music poured from brightly lit cafés, but the station was in an empty, quiet part of town. All I could glean from the big blackboard there was the departure time of a train which would get me only halfway home and which, if I took it, would cost me a whole night of waiting room, grime, and a bowl of repulsive soup at the station in a little place with no hotel. I turned away, went outside again, and counted my money by the light of a gas lamp: nine marks, return ticket, and a few pfennigs. Some cars were standing there that looked as if they had been waiting there forever, and little trees, cropped like new recruits. Dear little trees, I thought, nice little trees, obedient little trees. Doctors' white nameplates showed up against a few unlighted houses, and through a café window I looked in on a gathering of empty chairs for whose benefit a writhing violinist was producing sobs that might have moved stones but hardly a human being. At last, in a lane skirting the bulk of a dark church, I came upon a painted green sign: ROOMS. I stepped inside.

Behind me I could hear the streetcar on its return trip to the better-lit, more populated part of town. The hall was empty, and I turned to the right into a little room containing four tables and twelve chairs;

to the left, bottles of beer and lemonade stood in metal display stands on a built-in counter. Everything looked clean and plain. Green hessian, divided by narrow strips of brown wood, had been tacked to the walls with rosette-shaped copper nails. The chairs were green too, upholstered in some soft, velvety material. Pale-yellow curtains had been drawn closely across the windows, and behind the counter a serving hatch opened into a kitchen. I put down my suitcase, drew a chair toward me, and sat down. I was very tired.

How quiet it was here, even quieter than the station which, strangely enough, was some distance from the business center, a gloomy, cavernous place filled with the muffled sounds of an invisible bustle: bustle behind closed wickets, bustle behind wooden barriers.

I was hungry too, and I found the utter futility of this journey very depressing. I was glad of the few minutes to myself in this quiet, unpretentious room. I would have liked to smoke but found I had no cigarettes, and now I regretted having abandoned the cigar in the wholesale devotionalist's office. Although I might well be depressed at having gone on yet another wild-goose chase, I was aware of a growing sense of relief that I couldn't quite define or account for, but perhaps in my heart I rejoiced at my final expulsion from the devotional-supply trade.

I had not been idle after the war. I had helped clear away ruins, remove rubble, scrape bricks clean, build walls, haul sand, shift lime; I had submitted applications—many, many applications—thumbed through books, carefully watched over my pile of stearin. On my own, with no help from those who might have given me the benefit of their experience, I had found out how to make candles, beautiful, simple, good-quality candles, tinted a soft yellow that gave them the luster of melting beeswax. I had done everything to get on my feet, as they say: to find some way of earning a living, and although I ought to have been sad, the very futility of my efforts was now filling me with a joy such as I had never known.

I had not been ungenerous. I had given away candles to people living in cramped unlighted holes, and whenever there had been a chance of profiteering, I had avoided it. I had gone hungry and devoted myself single-mindedly toward this method of making a living; but although I might have expected a reward for what one might call my integrity, I almost rejoiced to find myself evidently unworthy of any reward.

The thought also crossed my mind that perhaps we would have done better after all to manufacture shoe polish, as someone had advised us, to mix other ingredients with the basic material, to get hold of some formulas, acquire a stock of cardboard containers, and fill them up.

In the midst of my musings the landlady entered the room, a slight, elderly woman. Her dress was green, the green of the beer and lemonade bottles on the counter. "Good evening," she said pleasantly. I returned her greeting, and she asked, "What can I do for you?"

"I would like a room, if you have one."

"Certainly," she said. "What price had you in mind?"

"The cheapest."

"That would be three marks fifty."

"Fine," I said, relieved. "And perhaps something to eat?"

"Certainly."

"Bread, some cheese and butter, and"—I ran my eyes over the bottles on the counter—"perhaps some wine."

"Certainly," she said, "a bottle?"

"No, no! A glass and—how much will that come to?"

She had gone behind the counter and was already pushing back the hook to open the serving hatch, but she paused to ask, "All together?"

"Yes, please, all together."

She reached under the counter, took out pad and pencil, and again it was very quiet while she slowly wrote and added up. Despite the reserve in her manner, her whole presence, as she stood there, radiated a reassuring kindness. And she endeared herself to me still further by apparently making several mistakes in her addition. She slowly wrote down the items, frowned as she added them up, shook her head, crossed them out, rewrote everything, added up again, this time without frowning, and in gray pencil wrote the result at the bottom, finally saying in her soft voice, "Six-twenty—no, six, I beg your pardon."

I smiled. "That's fine. And have you any cigars?"

"Certainly." She reached under the counter again and held out a box. I took two and thanked her. The woman quietly gave the order through to the kitchen and left the room.

Scarcely had she gone when the door opened and in walked a young man, of slight build, unshaven, wearing a light-colored raincoat; behind him was a girl in a brown coat, hatless. The couple approached quietly, almost diffidently, and with a brief "Good evening" turned toward the counter. The boy was carrying the girl's shabby leather bag, and although he was obviously at pains to appear undaunted and to display the bravado of a man who regularly spends the night with his girl in a hotel, I could see his lower lip trembling and tiny beads of sweat on the stubble of his beard. The couple stood there like customers awaiting their turn in a store. The fact that they were hatless and that the bag was their only luggage made them look like refugees who had arrived at some transit camp. The girl was beautiful, her skin alive, warm, and slightly flushed, and her heavy brown hair hanging loosely over her shoulders seemed almost too heavy for her slender feet; she nervously moved her black dusty shoes, shifting her weight from one foot to the other more often than was necessary; the young man kept brushing back a few strands of hair as they fell over his forehead, and his small round mouth expressed a painful but at the same time elated determination. I could see they were deliberately avoiding each other's eyes, and they did not speak to one another, while I for my part was glad to be busily occupied with my cigar, to be able to clip it, light it, look critically at the tip, relight it, and start smoking. Every second of waiting must be agony, I knew; for the girl, no matter how unabashed and happy she might look, continued to shift her weight as she tugged at her coat, while the boy continued to pass his hand over his forehead although there were no more strands of hair to brush back. At last the woman reappeared, quietly said "Good evening," and placed the bottle of wine on the counter.

I jumped up at once, saying, "Allow me!" She looked at me in surprise, then set down the glass, handed me the corkscrew, and asked the young man, "What can I do for you?" As I put the cigar between my lips and twisted the corkscrew into the cork, I heard the young man ask, "Can you let us have two rooms?"

"Two?" asked the landlady. Just then I pulled out the cork and from the corner of my eye saw the girl flush, while the boy bit hard on his lower lip and, barely opening his mouth, said, "Yes, two."

"Oh, thank you," the landlady said, filling the glass and passing it to me. I went back to my table, began to sip the gentle wine, and could only hope that the inevitable ritual would not be dragged out even further by the arrival of my supper. But the entries in the register, the filling out of forms, and the producing of gray-blue identity cards, all took less time than I had expected; and at one point, when the boy opened the leather bag to get out the identity cards, I saw that it contained greasy paper bags, a crumpled hat, some packets of cigarettes, a beret, and a shabby old red wallet.

During all this time the girl tried to look poised and confident; with an air of nonchalance she surveyed the bottles of lemonade, the green of the hessian wall covering, and the rosette-shaped nails, but the flush never left her cheeks, and when everything was finally settled they took their keys and hurried upstairs without saying good night. A few minutes later my supper was passed through the hatch; the landlady brought me my plate, and when our eyes met she did not smile, as I had thought she would, but looked gravely past me and said, "I hope you enjoy your supper, sir."

"Thank you," I replied. She remained standing beside me.

I slowly began my meal, helping myself to bread, butter, and cheese. She still did not move. "Smile," I said.

And she did smile, but then she sighed, saying, "There's nothing I can do about it."

"Do you wish there were?"

"Oh, yes," she said fervently, sitting herself down beside me, "indeed I do. I'd like to do something about a lot of things. But if he asks for two rooms... If he had asked for one, now..." She paused.

"What then?" I asked.

"What then?" she mimicked angrily. "I would have thrown him out."

"What for?" I said wearily, putting the last piece of bread in my mouth. She said nothing. What for, I thought, what for? Doesn't the world belong to lovers, weren't the nights mild enough, weren't other doors open, dirtier ones perhaps, but doors one could close behind one? I looked into my empty glass and smiled...

The landlady had risen, fetched her big book and a pile of forms, and sat down beside me again.

She watched me as I filled everything out. I paused at the column "Occupation," raised my eyes, and looked into her smiling face. "Why do you hesitate?" she asked calmly. "Have you no occupation?"

"I don't know."

"You don't know?"

"I don't know whether I am a workman, a salesman, a manufacturer, unemployed, or only an agent ... but whose agent?" Whereupon I quickly wrote down "Agent" and gave her back the book. For
a moment I considered offering her candles—twenty, if she liked, for a
glass of wine, or ten for a cigar. I don't know why I didn't; perhaps I
was just too tired, or too lazy, but the next morning I was glad I hadn't.
I relit my dead cigar and got to my feet. The woman had shut the book,
laying the forms between the pages, and was yawning.

"Would you like coffee in the morning?" she asked.

"No, thank you, I have to catch an early train. Good night."

"Good night," she said.

But next morning I slept late. The passage, which I had glimpsed
the previous evening—carpeted in dark red—had remained silent
throughout the night. The room was quiet too. The unaccustomed wine
had made me sleepy but also happy. The window was open, and all I
could see against the quiet, deep-blue summer sky was the dark roof of
the church opposite; farther to the right I could see the colorful reflection of the town lights, hear the noise of the livelier district. I took my
cigar with me as I got into bed so that I could read the newspaper, but
fell asleep at once...

It was after eight when I woke up. The train I had meant to catch
had already left, and I was sorry I had not asked to be woken. I washed,
decided to go out for a shave, and went downstairs. The little green
room was now light and cheerful, the sun shining in through the thin
curtains, and I was surprised to see tables set for breakfast, with breadcrumbs, empty jam dishes, and coffeepots. I felt as if I were the only
guest in this silent house. I paid my bill to a friendly maid and left.

Outside, I hesitated. The cool shadow of the church surrounded
me. The lane was narrow and clean; to the right a baker had opened his
shop, loaves and rolls shone pale brown and yellow in the glass cases,
and farther on, jugs of milk stood at a door to which a thin, blue-white
trail of milkdrops led. The other side of the street was entirely taken
up by a high black wall built of great square blocks of stone; through
a big arched gateway I saw green lawn and walked in. I was standing
in a monastery garden. An old, flat-roofed building, its stone window
frames touchingly whitewashed, stood in the middle of a green lawn,
stone tombs in the shade of weeping willows. A monk was padding

along a flagged path toward the church. In passing, he gave me a nod of greeting. I nodded back, and when he entered the church, I followed him, without knowing why.

The church was empty. It was old, devoid of decoration, and when by force of habit I dipped my hand in the stoup and bent my knee toward the altar, I saw that the candles must have just gone out: a thin black ribbon of smoke was rising from them into the clear air. There was no one in sight; Mass seemed to be over for this morning. My eyes involuntarily followed the black figure as it bobbed an awkward genuflection in front of the tabernacle and vanished into a side aisle. I went closer and came to a sudden halt. I found myself looking at a confessional. The young girl of the previous evening was kneeling in a pew in front of it, her face hidden in her hands, while at the edge of the nave, showing no apparent interest, stood the young man, the leather bag in one hand, the other hanging slackly by his side, his eyes on the altar...

In the midst of this silence I could hear my heart beating, louder, stronger, strangely unquiet, and I could feel the boy looking at me: our eyes met, he recognized me and flushed. The girl was still kneeling there, her face in her hands, a thin, faint thread of smoke still rising from the candles. I sat down in a pew, placed my hat beside me, and put my suitcase on the ground. I felt as if I were waking up for the first time, as if until now I had seen everything with my eyes only, a detached spectator—church, garden, street, girl, man—it had all been like a stage set that I had brushed by as an outsider, but now, looking at the altar, I longed for the young man to go and confess too. I wondered when I had last gone to confession, found it hard to keep track of the years, roughly it would be about seven, but as I went on thinking about it, I realized something much worse: I couldn't put my finger on any sin. No matter how honestly I tried, I couldn't think of any sin worth confessing, and this made me very sad. I felt unclean, full of things that needed to be washed away, but nowhere was there actually anything that in coarse, rough, sharp, clear terms could have been called sin. My heart beat louder than ever. Last night I had not envied the young couple, but now I did envy that ardent kneeling figure, still hiding her face in her hands, waiting. The young man stood completely motionless and detached.

I was like a pail of water that has remained exposed to the air
for a long time. It looks clean, a casual glance reveals nothing in
it: nobody has thrown stones, dirt, or garbage into it, it has been
standing in the hallway or basement of a well-kept, respectable house;
the bottom appears to be immaculate; all is clear and still, yet, when
you dip your hand into the water, there runs through your fingers an
intangible repulsive fine dirt that seems to be without shape, without form, almost without dimension. You just know it is there. And
on reaching deeper into this immaculate pail, you find at the bottom
a thick indisputable layer of this fine disgusting formless muck to
which you cannot put a name; a dense, leaden sediment made
up of these infinitesimal particles of dirt abstracted from the air of
respectability.

I could not pray; I could only hear my heart beating and wait for
the girl to go into the confessional. At last she raised her hands, laid her
face against them for an instant, stood up, and entered the wooden box.

The young man kept his place. He stood there aloof, having no
part in it, unshaven, pale, his face still expressing a mild yet insistent
determination. When the girl emerged, he suddenly put down the bag
and stepped into the confessional.

I still could not pray, no voice spoke to me or in me, nothing
moved, only my heart was beating, and I could not curb my impatience:
I stood up, left my suitcase where it was, and crossed over to the side
aisle, where I stood beside a pew. In the front pew the young woman
was kneeling before an old stone Madonna standing on a bare, disused
altar. The Virgin's face was coarse-featured but smiling, a piece of her
nose was missing, the blue paint of her robe had flaked off, and the gold
stars on it were now no more than lighter spots; her scepter was broken,
and of the Child in her arms only the back of the head and part of the
feet were still visible. The center part, the torso, had fallen out, and she
was smilingly holding this fragment in her arms. A poor monastic order,
evidently, that owned this church.

"Oh, if I could only pray!" I prayed. I felt hard, useless, unclean,
unrepentant; I couldn't even produce one sin; the only thing I possessed
was my pounding heart and the knowledge that I was unclean...

The young man brushing past me from behind roused me from my
thoughts, and I stepped into the confessional.

By the time I had been dismissed with the sign of the cross, the young couple had left the church. The monk pushed aside the purple curtain of the confessional, opened the little door, and padded slowly past me; once again he genuflected awkwardly before the altar.

I waited until I had seen him disappear, then quickly crossed the nave, also genuflecting, carried my suitcase back to the side aisle, and opened it. There they all lay, tied in bundles by my wife's loving hands, slim, yellow, unadorned, and I looked at the cold, bare stone plinth on which the Madonna stood and regretted for the first time that my suitcase was not heavier. I ripped open the first bundle and struck a match...

Warming each candle in the flame of another, I stuck them all firmly onto the cold plinth, which quickly allowed the soft wax to harden; on they all went, until the whole surface was covered with restless flickering lights and my suitcase was empty. I left it where it was, seized my hat, genuflected once more, and left: it was as if I were running away.

And now at last, as I walked slowly toward the station, I recalled all my sins, and my heart was lighter than it had been for a long time...

BLACK SHEEP

It would seem that I have been singled out to ensure that the chain of black sheep is not broken in my generation. Somebody has to be the black sheep, and it happens to be me. Nobody would ever have thought it of me, but there it is: I am the one. Wise members of our family maintain that Uncle Otto's influence on me was not good. Uncle Otto was the black sheep of the previous generation, and my godfather. It had to be somebody, and he was the one. Needless to say, he was chosen as my godfather before it became apparent that he would come to a bad end; and it was the same with me—I became godfather to a little boy who, ever since I have been regarded as black, is being kept at a safe distance from me by his anxious family. As a matter of fact, they ought to be grateful to us, for a family without a black sheep is not a typical family.

My friendship with Uncle Otto began at an early age. He used to visit us often, bringing more candies than my father thought good for us, and he would talk and talk until he finally ended up cadging a loan.

Uncle Otto knew what he was talking about. There was not a subject in which he was not well versed: sociology, literature, music, architecture, anything at all—and he knew his subject, he really did. Even specialists in their field enjoyed talking to him; they found him stimulating, intelligent, an uncommonly nice fellow, until the shock of the attendant attempt to cadge a loan sobered them up. For that was the outrageous thing about it: he did not confine his marauding to the members of the family but laid his artful traps wherever a favorable prospect seemed to present itself.

Everyone used to say he could "cash in" on his knowledge—as the older generation put it—but he didn't cash in on it, he cashed in on the nerves of his relatives.

He alone knew the secret of managing to give the impression that on this particular day he would not do it. But he did do it. Regularly, relentlessly. I fancy he could not bring himself to pass up an opportunity. His conversation was so fascinating, so full of genuine enthusiasm, clearly conceived, brilliantly witty, devastating for his opponents, uplifting for his friends: he could converse far too well on any topic for anyone to have dreamed that he would...! But he did. He knew all about infant care, although he had never had any children; he would involve young mothers in irresistibly fascinating discussions on diet for this or that ailment, suggest types of baby powder, write out ointment prescriptions, decide the quantity and quality of what they were given to drink. He even knew how to hold them: a squalling infant, when put into his arms, would quiet down immediately. He radiated a kind of magic. And he was equally at home analyzing Beethoven's Ninth Symphony, composing legal opinions, citing from memory some law that happened to be under discussion...

But, regardless of time and topic, as the conversation approached its end and the moment of parting drew inexorably nearer—usually in the entrance hall, with the front door already half shut—he would thrust his pale face with its lively dark eyes once more through the door and, right into the apprehension of the tensely waiting relatives, remark quite casually to the head of that particular family, "By the way, I wonder if you could...?"

The amounts he demanded fluctuated between one mark and fifty marks. Fifty was the uppermost limit: over the decades it had become an unwritten law that he was never to ask for more. "Just to tide me over!" he would add. To tide him over—this was his favorite phrase. He would then come in again, replace his hat on the hall stand, unwind his muffler, and launch into an explanation of why he needed the money. He always had plans, infallible plans. He never needed it directly for himself: its sole purpose was to place his livelihood at last on a firm footing. His plans varied from a soft-drink stand, which he was confident would yield a regular steady income, to the founding of a political party which would preserve Europe from its decline and fall.

The words "By the way, I wonder if you could..." were apt, as the years went by, to scare the wits out of our family; there were wives, aunts, great-aunts, even nieces, whom the sound of "just to tide me over" would bring to the verge of fainting.

Uncle Otto—I assume him to have been in the best of humors as he sprinted down the stairs—then took himself off to the nearest bar to mull over his plans. He would mull over them to the tune of one schnapps or three bottles of wine, depending on the size of the loan he had been able to raise.

I will no longer conceal the fact that he drank. He drank, yet no one had ever seen him drunk. Moreover, he evidently felt a need to drink alone. To offer him alcohol in the hope of dodging the request for a loan was so much wasted effort. An entire barrel of wine would not have deterred him, at the very last minute, when he was on the point of leaving, from thrusting his head once more through the door and asking, "By the way, I wonder if you could—just to tide me over...?"

But his worst trait I have so far kept to myself: sometimes he would repay a loan. Every so often he appeared to earn money in one way or another: as a former law student he occasionally, I believe, dispensed legal advice. At such times he would turn up, take a bill from his pocket, smooth it out with wistful tenderness, and say, "You were kind enough to help me out—here are your five marks!" Whereupon he would leave very quickly and return after a maximum of two days to ask for a sum slightly in excess of the one he had repaid. He alone knew the secret of managing to reach the age of almost sixty without ever having what is commonly called a regular occupation. Nor was his death in any way due to some illness he might have contracted as a result of his drinking. He was as fit as a fiddle, his heart was perfectly sound, and he slept like a healthy innocent babe full of his mother's milk that sleeps away the hours till the next meal. No, he died very suddenly: he lost his life in an accident, and what happened after his death remains the greatest mystery of all.

Uncle Otto, as I say, was killed in an accident. He was run over by a truck and trailer in heavy downtown traffic, and luckily it was an honest man who picked him up, called the police, and notified the family. In his pockets they found a wallet containing a medallion of the Virgin Mary, a weekly pass good for two more streetcar rides, and twenty-four thousand marks in cash plus the carbon copy of a receipt he had had to sign for the lottery office, and he cannot have been in possession of the money for more than a minute, probably less, because the truck ran over him scarcely fifty yards from the lottery office. What followed was rather humiliating for the family. His room bore the stamp of poverty: table, chair, bed, and closet, a few books, and a large notebook, and in this notebook an accurate list of all those to whom he owed money, including an entry for a loan that had brought him in four marks the previous evening. Also a very brief will naming me his heir.

As his executor, it was my father's job to pay the outstanding debts. Indeed, Uncle Otto's list of creditors filled an entire quarto-sized notebook, his first entry going back to the years when he had suddenly broken off his legal career to devote himself to other plans, the mulling over of which had cost him so much time and so much money. His debts totaled nearly fifteen thousand marks, the number of his creditors over seven hundred, ranging from a streetcar conductor who had advanced him thirty pfennigs for a transfer to my father, who had all together two thousand marks coming to him, probably because Uncle Otto had always found him such a soft touch.

Strangely enough, I happened to come of age on the very day of the funeral and was therefore entitled to enter upon my inheritance of ten thousand marks, so I immediately broke off my university career to devote myself to other plans. In spite of my parents' tears, I left home to move into Uncle Otto's room. It held a great attraction for me, and I am still living there, although my hair is now no longer as thick as it used to be. The contents of the room have neither increased nor decreased. Today I know that I made many mistakes in those early years. It was ridiculous to attempt to become a musician, let alone a composer; I have no talents in that direction. Today I know this, but I paid for the knowledge with three years of useless study and the inevitability of acquiring a reputation for loafing, besides which it used up my whole inheritance, but that's a long time ago.

I have forgotten the sequence of my plans: there were too many of them. Besides, the periods of time needed for me to recognize their futility became shorter and shorter. I finally reached the point where one plan managed to last just three days, a life span that even for a plan is too short. The life span of my plans dwindled so rapidly that they eventually became mere lightning flashes of ideas that I could not explain to anyone because they were not clear even to me. When I think that I devoted myself for three whole months to the science of physiognomy until I finally decided in the course of a single afternoon to become a painter, a gardener, a mechanic, and a sailor, and that I fell asleep thinking I was born to be a teacher and woke up firmly convinced that a career in the customs service was what I was cut out for...!

In short, I had neither Uncle Otto's charm nor his relatively great endurance. I am not a talker either: I sit silent among other people; I bore them and blurt out my attempts to extract money from them so abruptly into the silence that they sound like extortions. Only with children do I get along well. This is at least one favorable attribute that I seem to have inherited from Uncle Otto. Babies quiet down the minute I take them in my arms, and when they look at me they smile, insofar as they can smile at all, although it is said that my face scares people. Unkind people have advised me to found the profession of male kindergarten teacher as its first exponent and to put an end to my eternal planning by bringing at least this plan to fruition. But I never shall. I think this is what makes us so impossible: the fact that we cannot cash in on our real talents—or, to adopt the modern jargon, exploit them financially.

One thing is certain, though: if I am a black sheep—and personally I am by no means convinced of this—but if I am one, it is of a different kind from Uncle Otto. I lack his light touch, his charm; besides, my debts weigh heavily on me, while obviously his scarcely bothered him at all. And I did a terrible thing: I capitulated—I asked for a job. I implored the family to help me, to find me a job, to pull strings for me, so that for once, just once, I might be assured of tangible compensation in return for the performance of clearly defined duties. And they were successful. After I had sent off my petitions, given written and verbal form to my pleas, my urgent, imploring appeals, I was horrified to find they had been taken seriously and borne fruit, and I did something which no black sheep had ever done before: I did not flinch, did not turn it down, I accepted the position they had managed to find for me. I sacrificed something that I ought never to have sacrificed: my freedom!

Each evening when I came home I could have kicked myself for letting yet another day of my life go by that had brought me nothing but fatigue, rage, and just enough money to enable me to keep on working, if one can call what I was doing work: sorting bills alphabetically, punching holes in them, and fastening them into a brand-new file where they patiently submitted to the fate of never being paid; or writing the kind of circulars that travel ineffectually out into the world and amount to nothing but a superfluous burden for the mailman; and sometimes making out bills that now and then were actually paid in cash. I had to deal with salesmen who strove in vain to palm off the rubbish manufactured by our boss. Our boss: that bustling blockhead who is forever in a hurry and never does a thing, who persistently chatters away the precious hours of the day—an existence of stultifying stupidity—who never dares admit the extent of his debts, who cheats his way from one bluff to the next, a balloon-artist who starts blowing up one balloon the very moment another one bursts, leaving behind a repulsive rubber rag that a second earlier still had sheen, life, and bounce.

Our office was right alongside the factory, where a staff of a dozen or so manufactured the kind of furniture that, once bought, is an annoyance for the rest of one's life unless one decides after three days to chop it up into kindling: occasional tables, sewing cabinets, midget chests of drawers, arty little "hand-painted" chairs that collapse under the weight of three-year-old children, little stands for vases or flowerpots, shoddy bric-a-brac that ostensibly owes its existence to the art of the cabinetmaker whereas in fact an inferior workman, using cheap paint purporting to be enamel, produces a semblance of attractiveness intended to justify the prices.

So this was how I spent my days, one after another—nearly two weeks in all—in the office of this unintelligent man who not only took himself seriously but considered himself an artist, for now and again—it happened only once while I was there—he was to be seen standing at the drawing board, shuffling pencils and paper and designing some wobbly object or other, a flower stand or a new portable bar, yet another source of annoyance for future generations.

The appalling futility of his devices never seemed to enter his head. When he had finished designing one of these gadgets—as I say, it happened only once while I was working for him—he would dash off in his car to rest up from his creative labors, a respite that lasted a week after he had worked for only fifteen minutes. The drawing was tossed in front of the foreman, who would spread it out on his bench, study it with furrowed brow, and proceed to check the lumber supplies in order to get production under way. For days I could watch the new creations piling up behind the dusty windows of the workshop—he called it a factory: wall shelves or radio stands that were hardly worth the glue being wasted on them.

The only objects of any use were those turned out by the workmen without the boss's knowledge, when they could be quite certain of his absence for a few days: little stools or jewel cases of pleasing sturdiness and simplicity—great-grandchildren will straddle them or hoard their treasures in them; sensible laundry racks on which the shirts of many a future generation will flutter. What was endearing and serviceable was thus produced illegally.

But the really memorable personality I came across during this interlude of business life was the streetcar conductor who invalidated each day for me with his punch. He would take the slip of paper, my weekly pass, push it into the open maw of his punch, and an invisible supply of ink would blot out half an inch of it—one day out of my life, one precious day that had brought me nothing but fatigue, rage, and just enough money to continue in this futile pursuit. A godlike authority was vested in this man wearing the unpretentious uniform of the city transit system, the man who evening after evening wielded sufficient power to declare thousands of human days null and void.

To this day I feel annoyed with myself for not giving notice before I was practically forced to give notice; for not telling the boss where to get off before I was practically forced to tell him. But one day my landlady brought a sinister-looking individual along to my office who introduced himself as a lottery-office operator and announced that I was now the owner of a fortune of fifty thousand marks, provided that I was such and such a person and that I was the holder of a certain lottery ticket. Well, I was such and such a person and I was the holder of the lottery ticket. I quit my job on the spot, without giving notice, taking it upon myself to abandon the bills unpunched, unsorted, and there was nothing left for me to do but go home, collect the cash, and, by way of money orders, acquaint my relatives with the new state of affairs.

It was evidently expected of me to die soon or become the victim of an accident. But for the time being no automobile appears to have been singled out to deprive me of my life, and my heart is as sound as a bell, although I do not spurn the bottle. So after paying my debts, I find myself the possessor of a fortune of nearly thirty thousand marks, tax-free, and a sought-after uncle who has suddenly regained access to his godchild. But then children love me anyway, as I have said, and now I am allowed to play with them, buy them balls, ice cream, sundaes; I am allowed to buy whole gigantic clusters of balloons, and to populate the roundabouts and swings with the merry little throng.

While my sister has promptly bought her son, my godchild, a lottery ticket, I now spend my time wondering, musing for hours, about who among this new generation is going to be my successor; which of these thriving, romping, lovely children begotten by my brothers and sisters will be the black sheep of the next generation? For we are a typical family, and always will be. Who will be a good boy up to that point at which he ceases to be a good boy? Who will suddenly wish to devote himself to other plans, infallible, better plans? I would like to know, I would like to warn him, for we too have learned by experience; our calling also has its rules of the game, which I could pass on to him, my successor, still unknown, still playing with the gang like a wolf in sheep's clothing...

But I have a foreboding that I shan't live long enough to recognize him and initiate him into our secrets. He will come forward, reveal his true colors, when I die and it is his turn to take over. With flushed cheeks he will confront his parents and tell them he is fed up; and secretly I can only hope that when that time comes, there will still be some of my money left, because I have changed my will and left the balance of my fortune to the one who shows the first incontrovertible signs of being earmarked as my successor...

The main thing is that he shouldn't let them down.

AND WHERE WERE YOU, ADAM?

And Where Were You, Adam? *was first published in German as* Wo warst du, Adam? *by Friedrich Middelhauve Verlag in November 1951. This translation was first published by McGraw-Hill in 1970 as part of* Adam and The Train. *An earlier English translation by Mervyn Savill,* Adam, where art thou?, *was published by Criterion Books in 1955.*

AND WHERE WERE YOU, ADAM?

First came a face, large, yellow, tragic, moving past their lines; that was the general. The general looked tired. The face with puffy blue shadows under the malaria-yellow eyes, the slack, thin-lipped mouth of a man dogged by bad luck, moved hurriedly past the thousand men. The general started off at the right-hand corner of the dusty hollow square, looked sadly into each face, rounded the corners carelessly, with no dash or precision, and it was there for all to see: his chest bore plenty of medals, it sparkled with silver and gold, but his neck was empty, no decoration hung there. And although they knew that the Knight's Cross around a general's neck didn't mean a lot, it was discouraging to see him without even that much. That skinny yellow neck, unadorned, was a reminder of lost battles, bungled retreats, of rebukes, the unpleasant, scathing rebukes exchanged among senior officers, of sarcastic telephone conversations, transferred chiefs of staff, and a tired, elderly man who seemed without hope as he took off his tunic in the evening and, with his thin legs, his malaria-racked body, sat down on the edge of his bed to drink schnapps. Each of the three times three hundred and thirty-three men into whose faces he looked was aware of a strange feeling: sorrow, pity, fear, and a secret fury. Fury at this war, which had already gone on far too long, far too long for a general's neck to be still without its rightful decoration. The general raised his hand to his shabby cap—at least he saluted smartly—and on reaching the left-hand corner of the hollow square he made a somewhat brisker turn, walked to the middle of the open side, and stood still while the swarm of officers grouped itself around him, casually yet methodically; and it was embarrassing to see him standing there, with no decoration around his neck, while the Knight's Crosses of others, lower in rank, could be seen sparkling in the sun.

For a moment it looked as if he were going to say something, but he merely touched his cap again in an abrupt salute and turned so unexpectedly on his heel that the startled swarm of officers stepped back to let him pass. And everyone watched the short, spare figure get into the car, the officers saluted once again, and a swirling white cloud of dust announced that the general was driving west, where the sun was already quite low on the horizon, not far from those flat white roofs over there where the front did not exist.

Then they marched, three times one hundred and eleven men, to another part of the city, southward, past cafés of scruffy elegance, past movie houses and churches, through slums where dogs and chickens lay dozing in doorways, with slatternly, pretty, white-breasted women leaning on windowsills, where from dirty taverns came the monotonous, strangely stirring sound of drinking men singing. Streetcars screeched by at reckless speed—and then they came to a district where all was quiet. Here were villas surrounded by green gardens, army vehicles stood parked in front of stone gateways, and they marched through one of these stone gateways, entered meticulously tended grounds, and once again formed a hollow square, a smaller one this time, three times one hundred and eleven men.

Their packs were set down behind them, in rows, rifles were stacked, and when the men were standing at attention again, tired and hungry, thirsty, fuming and fed up with this damned war, when they were standing at attention again a thin, aristocratic face moved past their lines: that was the colonel, pale, hard-eyed, with tight lips and a long nose. They all took it for granted that the collar under this face should be adorned with the Knight's Cross. But this face was not to their liking either. The colonel took the corners at right angles, with a slow, firm tread, without omitting a single pair of eyes, and when he finally swung into the open side, a few officers in his wake, they all knew he was about to say something, and they all had the same thought, how thirsty they were, how badly they needed something to drink and eat, or to sleep or smoke a cigarette.

"Fellow soldiers!" came the high-pitched, clear voice. "Fellow soldiers, I bid you welcome! I haven't much to say to you, just this: it's up to us to chase those spineless creatures right back to their steppes. Understand?"

The voice paused, and the silence during this pause was embarrassing, almost deathly, and they all saw that by now the sun was red, dark red, and the deathly red reflection seemed to be caught in the Knight's Cross at the colonel's neck, concentrated in those four shining bars of the cross, and they saw for the first time that the cross was surmounted with oak leaves, which they called cabbage.

The colonel wore cabbage at his neck.

"Do you understand?" shouted the taut voice, cracking now.

"Yessir," a few of the men called out, but the voices were hoarse, tired, listless.

"Do you understand, I say!" the voice shouted again, now so strident that it seemed to soar into the sky, swiftly, far too swiftly, like some demented lark trying to pluck a star with its beak.

"Yessir," a few more called out, but not many, and those who did were also tired, hoarse, listless, and nothing in this man's voice could quench their thirst, satisfy their hunger, their craving for a cigarette.

The colonel lashed the air furiously with his cane, they heard something that sounded like "rabble," and he strode rapidly off to the rear, followed by his adjutant, a tall young first lieutenant, who was much too tall, and much too young, for them not to feel sorry for him.

The sun still hung over the horizon, just above the rooftops, a glowing iron egg that seemed to be rolling down over the flat white roofs, and the sky was burned gray, almost white; the sparse leaves hung limply from the trees as they marched on, eastward now at last, through the suburbs, past shacks, over cobbles, past the huts of rag-and-bone men, past a totally incongruous group of modern, dirty apartment blocks, past garbage dumps, through gardens where rotting melons lay on the ground and overripe tomatoes hung from tall stalks, covered with dust, stalks that were much too tall and had an unfamiliar look about them. The cornfields looked odd too, with their thick corncobs being pecked at by flocks of black birds that flew up lethargically at the approach of the men's weary tread, clouds of birds that hovered undecidedly in the air, then settled down to resume their pecking.

Now there were only three times thirty-five men, a weary, dust-coated platoon, with sore feet and sweating faces, led by a first lieutenant whose face plainly showed that he was fed to the teeth. As soon as he took command, they knew what kind of man he was. All he had done was look at them and, tired as they were, and thirsty, thirsty, they could read it in his eyes. "It's a lot of shit," said his expression, "just a lot of shit, but we can't do a thing about it." And then came his voice, with studied indifference, contemptuous of all regulation commands: "Let's go."

Next they halted at a grimy school standing among half-withered trees. The foul black puddles, with flies buzzing and darting above them, looked as if they had been standing there for months between rough cobbles and a chalk-scribbled urinal that gave out a nauseating stench, acrid and unmistakable.

"Halt," said the first lieutenant. He went into the schoolhouse, and his walk, elegant and languid, was that of a man who was fed to the teeth.

This time there was no need to form a hollow square, and the captain who walked past them did not even salute; he wore no belt, a straw was stuck between his teeth, and from the look of his plump face with its black eyebrows he appeared to be easygoing. He merely nodded, went "Hm," stopped in front of them, and said: "We haven't got much time, boys. I'll send along the sergeant major and have you assigned to your companies right away." But they had already looked past his round healthy face and seen the ammunitions trucks standing ready loaded, and on the ledges of the soiled open windows lay piles of battle packs, neat olive-drab bundles, beside them the belts and the rest of the gear, haversacks, cartridge pouches, spades, gas masks.

When they set off they were only eight times three men, and they marched back through the cornfields as far as the ugly modern apartment blocks, then turned east again until they reached the sparse woods in the midst of which stood a few houses that looked something like an artist's colony: flat-roofed bungalow affairs with picture windows. There were wicker chairs in the gardens, and when the men halted and about-faced they saw that the sun was behind the roofs now, that its glow filled the whole dome of the sky with a red that was just a shade too pale, like badly painted blood—and behind them, in the east, it was already deep twilight and warm. Soldiers were squatting in the shadow outside the bungalows, there were some rifle-pyramids, ten or so, and they noticed that the men had already buckled on their belts: the steel helmets hooked to their belts shone with a ruddy gleam.

The first lieutenant, coming out now from one of the bungalows, did not walk past them at all. He stopped at once in front of them, and they saw he had only one decoration, a little black one that wasn't really a decoration at all, an insignificant medal stamped out of black tin, a sign that he had shed blood for the Fatherland. The lieutenant's face was tired and sad, and now when he looked at them he looked first at their decorations, then into their faces, and said, "Good," and after a brief pause, with a glance at his watch, "You're tired, I realize that, but it can't be helped—we have to leave in fifteen minutes."

Then he looked at the sergeant major beside him and said, "No point in taking down particulars—just collect the paybooks and put them in with the baggage. Assign the men quickly so they've time for a drink of water. And don't forget to fill up your canteens while you're about it!" he called to the three times eight men.

The sergeant major standing beside him looked irritable and conceited. He had four times as many decorations as the lieutenant, and with a nod he shouted, "Come on now, let's have those paybooks!"

He placed the pile on a wobbly garden table and began sorting them, and while the paybooks were being counted and divided up the men all had the same thought: the journey had been tiring, a bloody bore, but it hadn't been serious. And the general, the colonel, the captain, even the first lieutenant, were all far away, they couldn't do anything to them now. But these fellows here, they owned them, this sergeant major who saluted and clicked his heels the way they all used to four years ago, and that bull of a sergeant who at this point emerged from the rear, threw away his cigarette, and adjusted his belt—these were the fellows who owned them, until they were captured or lay around somewhere wounded—or dead.

Of the thousand men only one was left, and he stood facing the sergeant major, looking helplessly around because there was no one beside, behind, or in front of him; and when he looked at the sergeant major again he realized he was thirsty, very thirsty, and that of those fifteen minutes at least eight had already gone by.

The sergeant major had picked up his paybook from the table and opened it; he looked at the first page, raised his eyes, and asked, "Feinhals?"

"Yessir."

"And you're an architect—you can draw?"

"Yessir."

"Headquarters platoon, we can use him, sir," said the sergeant major, turning to the first lieutenant.

"Good," said the first lieutenant, looking over toward the city, and Feinhals followed his gaze, and now he could see what was evidently fascinating the officer: the sun was lying on the ground, at the end of a street, between two houses; it looked very odd, just lying there on the ground like a flattened, shining apple between two dirty Rumanian houses at the edge of town, an apple growing dimmer by the second, almost as if lying in its own shadow.

"Good," repeated the first lieutenant, and Feinhals didn't know whether he really meant the sun or was just saying the word mechanically. It occurred to Feinhals that he had been on the move for four years now, and four years ago the postcard had said he was being called up for a few weeks' maneuvers. But suddenly the war had started.

"Go and get yourself a drink," the sergeant major told Feinhals. Feinhals ran over to join the others and found the water supply right away: a rusted iron pipe with a leaky garden faucet among some scrawny pine trees, and the water ran out in a stream no thicker than half the size of a little finger, but even worse was the fact that about ten men were standing there, shoving, cursing, and pushing away each other's mess bowls.

The sight of the trickling water drove Feinhals almost frantic. He grabbed the mess bowl from his haversack, forced his way through the others, and suddenly felt a surge of boundless strength. He squeezed his mess bowl in between the others, between all those shifting metal apertures, no longer knowing which was his; his eyes followed his arm, saw that his was the one with the darker enamel; he thrust it forward, and felt something that made him tremble: it was getting heavy. He was past knowing which was more wonderful: to drink, or to feel his mess bowl getting heavier. Suddenly, feeling his hands lose their strength, he jerked it back, his very veins trembling with weakness, and while behind him voices shouted, "Fall in—let's go!" he sat down, held the mess bowl between his knees because he lacked the strength to lift it, and bent over it like a dog over its bowl, his shaking fingers pressing it gently down so that the lower edge dipped and the water level touched his lips, and when he actually felt his upper lip getting wet and he began to sip, the word danced before his eyes in a kaleidoscope of colors, "Water, terwa, aterw," with insane clarity he saw it written in his mind's eye: water. Strength flowed back into his hands, he could lift the bowl and drink.

Someone jerked him upright and gave him a shove, and he saw the company lined up, headed by the first lieutenant, who was shouting, "Let's go, let's go!" and he swung his rifle over his shoulder and slipped into the space up front indicated by a wave of the sergeant major's hand.

Off they marched, into the darkness, and he moved without wanting to: what he really wanted was to drop, but he marched on, without wanting to, the weight of his body forcing him to straighten his knees, and when he straightened his knees his sore feet propelled themselves forward, carrying along great slabs of pain that were much too big for his feet; his feet were too small for this pain; and when he propelled his feet forward the whole bulk of his backside, shoulders, arms, and head started moving again, forcing him to straighten his knees, and when he straightened his knees his sore feet propelled themselves forward...

Three hours later he was lying exhausted somewhere on sparse steppe grass, his eyes following a vague shape that was crawling away in the gray darkness; the shape had brought him two greasy pieces of paper, some bread, a roll of lemon drops, and six cigarettes, and it had said, "D'you know the password?"

"No."

"Victory. That's the password: victory."

And he repeated softly, "Victory. That's the password: victory," and the word tasted like tepid water on his tongue.

He peeled the paper off the roll and stuck a lemon drop in his mouth; when he felt the thin, acid, synthetic flavor in his mouth, the saliva came pouring out of his glands, and he washed down the first wave of this sweet-tasting bitterness—and at that moment he heard the shells: they had been rumbling around for hours over some distant line, and now they were flying across it, sputtering, hissing, rattling like badly nailed crates, and bursting behind them. The second lot landed not far ahead of them: fountains of sand showed up like disintegrating mushrooms against the bright darkness of the eastern sky, and he noticed that it was dark now behind him and a bit lighter in front. The third lot he never heard: right in amongst them, sledgehammers seemed to be smashing up plywood sheets, crashing, splintering, close, dangerous.

Dust and powder fumes were drifting along near the ground, and when he had thrown himself over and lay pressed against the earth, his head thrust into a hollow in the mound he had heaped up, he heard the command being passed along, "Get set to advance!" Coming from the right, the whisper hissed past them like a burning fuse, quiet and dangerous, and as he was about to adjust his battle pack, to tighten it, there was a crash right next to him, and it felt as if someone had knocked away his hand and was tugging violently at his upper arm. His whole left arm was bathed in moist warmth, and he raised his face from the ground and shouted, "I've been hit!" but didn't even hear himself shouting, all he heard was a quiet voice saying, "Horse Droppings."

Far, far away, as if separated from him by thick panes of glass, very close and yet far away, "Horse Droppings," said the voice; quiet, well-bred, far away, subdued, "Horse Droppings, Captain Bauer speaking, yessir." Not a sound, then came the voice, "I can hear you, Colonel." Pause, not a sound, only a kind of bubbling in the distance, a gentle hissing and sputtering as if something were boiling over. Then he realized he had closed his eyes, so he opened them: he saw the captain's head, and now he could also hear the voice more distinctly; the head was framed in a dark, dirty window opening, and the captain's face was tired, unshaven and ill-tempered, his eyes were screwed tight, and he said three times in succession, with barely a pause between each: "Yes, Colonel"—"Yes, Colonel"—"Yes, Colonel."

Then the captain put on his steel helmet, and his broad, good-natured face and dark head looked quite ridiculous now as he said to someone beside him, "Hell—there's a breakthrough at Horse Droppings 3, Sharp-shooter 4, I'll have to go forward." Another voice shouted into the building, "Dispatch rider, report to the captain," and it carried on like an echo, reverberating around inside the building and getting fainter and fainter, "Dispatch rider, report to the captain—dispatch rider, report to the captain!"

Next he heard the rattle of a motor and followed the dry rasping sound as it came closer; he saw the motorcycle slowly turn a corner, slackening speed until it stopped in front of him, throbbing, covered with dust, and the driver, his face tired and apathetic, remained seated on the pulsing machine and shouted toward the window, "Motorcycle for the captain reporting!" And the captain came out, walking slowly, legs wide apart, a cigar in his mouth, the steel helmet giving him the look of a sinister squat mushroom. He climbed without enthusiasm into the sidecar, said "Let's go," and the machine bounced and rattled off, at high speed, veiled in dust, in the direction of the seething confusion up front.

Feinhals wondered if he had ever been so happy in his life. He felt almost no pain; his left arm, lying beside him like a tight bundle, stiff and bloody, damp and unfamiliar, felt faintly uncomfortable, that was all. Everything else was all right; he could raise each leg separately, wriggle his feet in his boots, lift his head, and he could smoke as he lay there, facing him was the sun as it hung a hand's breadth above the gray cloud of dust in the east. All noise was somehow remote and subdued, his head felt as if wrapped in a layer of cotton, and it occurred to him that he had had nothing to eat for almost twenty-four hours except an acid, synthetic lemon drop, and nothing to drink except a little water, rusty and tepid and tasting of sand.

When he felt himself being lifted up and carried away, he closed his eyes again, but he could see it all, it was so familiar, it had all happened to him somewhere else: they carried him past the exhaust fumes of a throbbing vehicle into the hot, gasoline-reeking interior, the stretcher scraped against the metal rails, and then the engine started up and the noise outside retreated farther and farther, almost imperceptibly, just as the evening before it had come imperceptibly closer. A few isolated shells burst in the suburbs, regularly, quietly, and just as he felt himself dropping off to sleep he thought: How nice, it was all over so quickly this time, so quickly... All it had meant was a little thirst, sore feet, and a little fear.

When the ambulance stopped with a jerk, he awoke from his half-sleep. Doors were flung open, once again the stretchers scraped against the metal rails, and he was carried into a cool white corridor where it was very quiet. The stretchers stood in rows like lounge chairs on a narrow deck, and next to him he saw a head of thick black hair, lying quietly, and on the stretcher beyond that a bald head, moving restlessly from side to side, and up at the end, on the first stretcher, a white head, heavily bandaged, completely covered, ugly and much too narrow, and from this bundle of gauze came a voice, piercing, shrill, clear, harsh as it rose to the ceiling, helpless yet insolent, the voice of the colonel, and the voice cried, "Champagne!"

"Piss," said the bald head calmly, "drink your own piss." Someone behind laughed, quietly and cautiously.

"Champagne," cried the voice in fury, "chilled champagne!"

"Shut up," said the bald head calmly, "why don't you shut up?"

"Champagne," whimpered the voice, "I want some champagne"; and the white head sank back, it was lying flat now, and from between thick layers of gauze rose a thin pointed nose, and the voice became even shriller and shouted: "A girl—get me a girl…"

"Do it to yourself," retorted the bald head.

At last the white head was carried through a door, and there was silence.

In the silence they could hear only the isolated shells bursting in distant parts of the city, muffled far-off explosions thrumming softly away at the edge of the war. And when the white head of the colonel, now lying silently on one side, was carried out and the bald head was carried in, the sound of a car could be heard approaching outside: the muted sound of a whining engine came closer, quickly and almost threateningly, and now it was so close it seemed about to ram the cool white building. Then suddenly silence fell, outside a voice shouted something, and when they turned their heads, startled out of their peaceful, dozing weariness, they saw the general walking slowly past the stretchers and wordlessly placing packs of cigarettes on the men's laps. The silence became more and more oppressive the nearer the little man's footsteps approached from behind, and at last Feinhals saw the general's face quite close: yellow, large and sad, with snow-white eyebrows, dark traces of dust around the thin mouth, and written in this face was the message that this battle, too, had been lost.

II

He heard a voice saying "Bressen—Bressen, look at me," and he knew this was the voice of Kleewitz, the divisional medical officer, who must have been sent here to find out when he would be going back. But he wouldn't be going back, he never wanted to be reminded again of that regiment—and he didn't look at Kleewitz. He looked fixedly at the picture hanging way over to the right, almost in the dark corner: a flock of sheep, painted gray and green, and in the middle of them a shepherd in a blue cloak playing a flute.

He thought about things no one else on earth would have dreamed of, things he liked thinking about, repulsive though they were. He wasn't sure whether he heard Kleewitz's voice; he did hear it, of course, but he didn't want to admit it, and he looked at the shepherd playing his flute instead of turning his head and saying, "Kleewitz, how nice of you to come."

Next he heard the shuffle of papers, and he assumed they were studying his medical history. He looked at the back of the shepherd's neck and recalled how for a time he had been a nodder at a hotel, in a very high-class restaurant. At noon, when the local businessmen came for lunch, he would walk through the restaurant, very erect, and bow, and it was funny how quickly and accurately he had grasped the required nuances: whether he gave a short bow or a deep one, whether he merely nodded and, if so, how he nodded, and sometimes he would just move his head very briefly, more of an opening and closing of his eyes really, that gave the impression he was moving his head. He found status differences so easy to recognize—like army ranks, that hierarchy of braided and flat, starred and unstarred, shoulder loops, all the way down to the great mass of people with their more or less undecorated shoulders.

In this restaurant the scale of bowing was relatively simple: it was all a matter of bankroll, of the size of the bill. He wasn't even especially obliging, he almost never smiled, and his face—despite his efforts to look as impassive as possible—his face never lost that expression of severity and vigilance. A feeling crept over everyone he looked at, not so much of being honored as of being guilty; all felt themselves observed, inspected, and he soon discovered that there were certain people who became confused, so confused that they unthinkingly applied their knives to their potatoes the moment his glance rested on them and who nervously fingered their wallets as soon as he had passed. The only thing that surprised him was that they kept coming back, even this kind. Back they came and submitted to being nodded at, to that uncomfortable scrutiny that goes with a high-class restaurant. His thin, aristocratic face and a knack of wearing clothes well brought him in quite a decent income; besides, he ate there for nothing. But while he tried to assume a certain air of haughtiness, he was in fact often quite nervous. There were days when he could feel the sweat gathering and breaking out all over his body so that he could hardly breathe. And the owner was a coarse fellow, good-natured, vain about his success but awkward in manner; late at night, when the place was gradually emptying and he could think about going home, the owner would sometimes dig his stubby fingers into the cigar box and, despite his protests, stuff three or four cigars into the top pocket of Bressen's jacket. "Go on," the owner would mumble with his diffident smile, "take them—they're good cigars." And he would take them. He smoked them in the evening with Velten, with whom he shared a small furnished apartment, and Velten never failed to be surprised at the quality of the cigars. "Bressen," Velten would say, "I must say, Bressen, you smoke an excellent weed." He would make no comment and no pretense at refusing when Velten brought home an especially good bottle. Velten traveled for a wine merchant, and when business was good he would take home a bottle of champagne.

"Champagne," he said out loud to himself, "chilled champagne."

"That's all he ever says," said the ward medical officer standing beside him.

"Are you referring to the colonel?" asked Kleewitz coldly.

"That's right, Colonel Bressen. The only thing the colonel ever says: Champagne—chilled champagne. And sometimes he talks about women—girls."

He had loathed having to take his meals at the restaurant. In a grubby back room off a worn tablecloth, served by the ungracious cook who paid absolutely no attention to his fondness for desserts—and in his nose, throat, and mouth that sickening stale reek of cooking, greasy and disgusting—and that constant coming and going of the owner, the way he would plump himself down beside him for a few seconds, cigar in mouth, pour himself a schnapps, and sit there silently knocking back the stuff.

Later on he had given lessons in social etiquette. The town he lived in was very suitable for this kind of instruction, containing as it did a great many rich people who didn't even know that fish was eaten differently from meat, who had literally eaten with their fingers all their lives, and who now had cars, villas, and women—people who could no longer bear to be the kind of people they really were. He taught them how to perform adequately on the slippery ice of social obligations; he

went to their homes, discussed menus, taught them how to handle servants, and stayed for dinner—he had to teach them every gesture, watch
them like a hawk, correct them, and he tried to show them how to open
a bottle of champagne without assistance.

"Champagne," he said out loud to himself, "chilled champagne."

"Oh, for God's sake," cried Kleewitz, "Bressen, look at me!" But
he had no intention of looking at Kleewitz; he never wanted to be
reminded of it again, the regiment that had disintegrated in his hands
like dry tinder; Horse Droppings, Sharpshooter, Sugarloaf—under the
command of his staff known as Hunting Lodge—all finished! And
shortly after that he heard Kleewitz leave.

He was glad to be able to detach his gaze at last from the flock
of sheep and the stupid shepherd; it was hanging a bit too far over to
the right and he was getting a crick in his neck. The second picture
hung almost directly opposite him, and he was compelled to look at it,
although that one didn't appeal to him either: it showed Crown Prince
Michael talking to a Rumanian peasant, flanked by Marshal Antonescu and the queen. The stance of the Rumanian peasant was alarming. He was standing with his feet too close and too firmly together,
and he seemed about to tip forward and throw the gift in his hands
at the young king's feet. Bressen couldn't quite make out what the gift
was—salt or bread or a hunk of goat cheese—but the young king was
smiling at the peasant. Bressen had long ceased to see these things; he
was thankful to have found a spot to stare at without worrying about
getting a crick in his neck.

What had amazed him so during those etiquette lessons—what he
hadn't known and had long tried to ignore—was that such things could
actually be learned, this little performance: how to handle a knife and
fork correctly. It often shocked him to see these fellows and their wom-
enfolk treating him after three months with formal courtesy, as if he
were a competent instructor of limited scope, and smile as they handed
him a check. There were some, of course, who never made it—their fingers were too clumsy, they were incapable of cutting the rind off a piece
of cheese without picking up the whole slice, or of holding a wineglass
properly by the stem—and then there was a third category who never
learned but who couldn't have cared less—as well as those he never
met but heard about, who considered it a waste of time to consult him.

His sole consolation during this period was the opportunity for an occasional affair with their wives—there was no risk attached to these little adventures, which didn't disappoint him although they seemed to put the women off him. He had many affairs during this time—with all kinds of women—but not a single one had ever come to him or gone out with him a second time, although he usually ordered champagne.

"Champagne," he said out loud to himself, "chilled champagne."

He said it when he was alone too—it felt better that way—and for a moment he thought about the war, this war, just for an instant, until he heard two more people entering the room. He went on staring at that indefinable hunk that the Rumanian peasant was holding out to young King Michael—and for a moment he caught a glimpse, between himself and the picture, of the pink hand of the senior medical officer as the latter leaned over and took the chart down from its hook.

"Champagne," said Bressen in a loud voice, "champagne and a girl."

"Colonel Bressen," said the senior medical officer, urgently but softly. "Colonel Bressen!" There was a brief silence, and the senior medical officer said to the person beside him, "Mark his tag HOME HOSPITALIZATION, and transfer him to Vienna—needless to say the division will be very sorry to have to get along without Colonel Bressen, but..."

"Right, sir," said the ward medical officer. Bressen heard nothing more, although they must be standing beside him because he had not heard the door. Then came the rustling of those damned papers again, they must be rereading his medical history. Not a word was said.

Later on certain people had recalled that there were things he really could teach and which there was some point in teaching: the new army regulations, already familiar to him because he received the new issues regularly. He was put in charge of training the Stahlhelm and Youth Groups in his area, and he clearly remembered this honor having coincided with that period in his life when he had discovered an inordinate craving for sweet things and a decline in his interest in affairs with women. His notion of keeping a horse had proved a good one, although it meant scrimping a bit, for now on maneuver days he could ride out onto the heath early in the morning, hold discussions with subordinates, go through the drill plan—and best of all he could get to know the men in a way that was hardly possible while they were on duty: veterans and strangely clear-headed yet naïve young men who now and again had gone so far as to risk openly contradicting him. What saddened him was a certain amount of official secrecy that prevented him from riding back to town at the head of the troops—but while on duty it was almost like the old days: he was thoroughly familiar with combat duty at battalion level, and he had no cause to find fault with the new regulations, which had made good use of wartime experience without aiming at anything in the way of an actual revolution in methods. The things he had always encouraged and considered of prime importance were: route marches, standing at attention, about-turns executed with maximum precision—and those were red-letter days when he felt sufficiently strong and confident to risk something that even in peacetime and with well-disciplined troops had been risky: battalion maneuvers.

But the secrecy was soon dropped, before long there were daily maneuvers, and it didn't feel very different when one day he was made a real major again, in command of a real battalion.

For a moment he was not sure whether he was actually turning or whether this turning was already one of those things beyond the edge of his consciousness, but turning he was, and he was aware that he was turning, and it was depressing to find that so far nothing had occurred beyond the edge of his consciousness: he was being turned. They had lifted him up and swung him carefully out of his bed onto a stretcher. At first his head fell back, for a moment he was staring at the ceiling, but then a pillow was pushed under his head and his gaze fell precisely on the third picture hanging in his room. This was a picture he had never seen, it hung near the door, and at first he was glad to be able to look at it, since otherwise he would have had to look straight at the two doctors, between whom the picture was now hanging. The senior medical officer seemed to have left the room. The ward medical officer was talking to another, younger medical officer he had never seen before; he saw the short, plump ward MO read some passages from his medical history to his colleague in a low voice and explain something to him. Bressen couldn't understand what they were saying, not because he couldn't hear—it bothered him very much that so far he had not been able to close his ears—no, it was just that they were too far away and whispering. From the corridor he could hear everything: people calling out, cries of the wounded, and the throbbing hum of motors outside.

He saw the back of the stretcher bearer standing in front of him, and now the one standing behind him said, "Let's go."

"The bags," said the front stretcher bearer. "Major," he called across to the ward MO, "someone'll have to carry out those bags."

"Get hold of a few fellows."

The two stretcher bearers went out into the corridor.

Without moving his head, Bressen carefully studied the third picture between the two doctors' heads: this picture was incredible, he couldn't understand how it had ever got here. He didn't know whether they were in a school or a convent, but as for there being Catholics in Rumania, he had never heard of such a thing. In Germany there were some, he had heard about those—but in Rumania! And now here was a picture of the Virgin Mary. It annoyed him to be forced to look at this picture, but he had no option, he was forced to stare at her, that woman in the sky-blue cloak whose face he found disconcertingly grave; she stood poised on a globe, looking up to Heaven, which consisted of snow-white clouds, and around her hands was twisted a string of brown wooden beads. He gently shook his head and thought: What a repulsive picture, and suddenly he noticed the two doctors watching him. They looked at him, then at the picture, followed his gaze, and slowly returned to him. It wasn't easy to stare between those two heads—those four eyes that were looking into his—at the picture which he found so repulsive. He couldn't think of anything to take his mind off it; he tried to let his thoughts slip back to those years which a moment ago had been so easy to recall, years when he felt that the things which had once been his world were slowly becoming a world again: the association with staff officers, barracks gossip, adjutants, orderlies. He found himself unable to think about them. He was hemmed in by those eight inches left free by the two heads, and in those eight inches hung the picture—but it was a relief to see this space become larger because now they were approaching him, separating, and standing one on either side of him.

Now he couldn't see them at all, just their white smocks at the periphery of his vision. He heard exactly what they were saying.

"So you don't think it has anything to do with this injury?"

"Definitely not," said the ward MO; he opened the medical history again, papers rustled. "Definitely not. It's only a trifling scalp wound—very minor. Healed in five days. Nothing—not a trace of the usual symptoms of concussion, not a thing. I can only assume it was shock—or...." He broke off.

"What were you going to say?"

"I'm not going to stick my neck out."

"Go on—tell me."

It was annoying that both the doctors should remain silent, they seemed to be exchanging some kind of signals—then the younger one burst out laughing. Bressen hadn't heard a word spoken. Then both doctors laughed. He was glad when the two soldiers came in accompanied by a third with his arm in a sling.

"Feinhals," the ward medical officer told him, "take the briefcase out to the ambulance. The heavy bags will be sent on later," he called to the stretcher bearers.

"Are you serious?" asked the other doctor.

"Absolutely."

Bressen felt himself being lifted up and carried off; the picture of the Virgin slipped away to his left, the wall came closer, then the window frame outside in the corridor, again he was swung—he looked into the long corridor, one more swing, and he closed his eyes: outside the sun was dazzlingly bright. He was relieved when the ambulance door closed behind him.

III

There were a great many sergeants in the German army—with enough stars to decorate the sky of some thick-witted underworld—and a great many sergeants called Schneider, and of these quite a number who had been christened Alois, but at this particular time only one of these sergeants called Alois Schneider was stationed in the Hungarian village of Szokarhely; Szokarhely was a compact little place, half village, half resort. It was summer.

Schneider's office was a narrow room papered in yellow; on the door outside hung a pink cardboard sign on which was printed in black India ink: DISCHARGES, SGT. SCHNEIDER.

The desk was so placed that Schneider sat with his back to the window, and when he had nothing to do he would get up, turn around, and look out onto the narrow dusty road leading on the left to the village, and on the right, between cornfields and apricot orchards, out into the *puszta*.

Schneider had almost nothing to do. Only a few seriously wounded men still remained in the hospital; all those fit to be moved had been loaded into ambulances and taken away—and the rest, the walking wounded, had been discharged, loaded onto trucks, and taken to the redeployment center at the front. Schneider could look out of the window for hours on end: outside, the air was close, muggy, and the best remedy for this climate was pale-yellow apricot schnapps mixed with soda water. The schnapps was mildly tart, as well as cheap, pure, and good, and it was very pleasant to sit by the window, look out at the sky or onto the road, and get drunk. Intoxication was a long time coming, Schneider had to fight hard for it; it was necessary—even in the morning—to consume a considerable quantity of schnapps in order to reach a state in which boredom and futility became bearable. Schneider had a system: in the first glass he took only a dash of schnapps, in the second a bit more, the third was 50:50, the fourth he drank neat, the fifth 50:50 again, the sixth was as strong as the second, and the seventh as weak as the first. He drank only seven glasses—by about ten-thirty he was through with this ritual and had reached a state he called raging soberness, a cold fire consumed him, and he was armed to cope with the boredom and futility of the day. The first discharge cases usually turned up shortly before eleven, most of them around eleven-fifteen, and that still gave him almost an hour to look out onto the road, where from time to time a cart, drawn by lean horses and churning up a lot of dust, would race past on its way to the village; or he could catch flies, conduct ingenious dialogues with imaginary superiors—sarcastic, terse—or maybe sort out the rubber stamps on his desk, straighten the papers.

About this time—around ten-thirty—Schmitz was standing in the room containing the two patients on whom he had operated that morning: on the left, Lieutenant Moll, aged twenty-one, looking like an old woman, his peaked face seemed to be grinning under the anesthetic. Clouds of flies swarmed over the bandages on his hands, squatted drowsily on the blood-soaked gauze around his head. Schmitz fanned them away—it was hopeless, he shook his head and drew the white sheet as far as he could over the sleeping man's head. He began pulling on the clean white smock he wore on his rounds, buttoned it slowly, and looked at the other patient, Captain Bauer, who seemed to be gradually coming out of the anesthetic, mumbling indistinctly, his eyes closed; he tried to move but couldn't, he was strapped down, even his head had been firmly tied to the bars at the head of the bed—only his lips moved, and now and again it looked for a moment as if he were about to open his eyelids—and he would start mumbling again. Schmitz dug his hands into the pockets of his smock and waited—the room was shadowy, the air fetid, there was a slight smell of cow dung, and even with closed doors and windows there were swarms of flies; at one time cattle had been kept in the basement beneath.

The captain's sporadic, inarticulate mumbling appeared to be taking shape; now he was opening his mouth at regular intervals and seemed to be uttering one single word, which Schmitz could not under-stand—an oddly fascinating mixture of *E* and *O* and throaty sounds—then all of a sudden the captain opened his eyes. "Bauer," cried Schmitz, but he knew it was no use. He stepped closer and waved his hands in front of the captain's eyes—there was no reflex. Schmitz held his hand close to the captain's eyes, so close that he could feel the man's eye-brows on his palm: nothing—the captain merely went on repeating his incomprehensible word at regular intervals. He was looking inside him-self, and no one knew what was inside. Suddenly he uttered the word very distinctly, sharply articulated as if he had learned it by heart—then again. Schmitz held his ear close to the captain's mouth. "Byelyogorshe," said the captain. Schmitz listened intently, he had never heard the word and had no idea what it meant, but he liked the sound of it, it was beau-tiful, he thought—mysterious and beautiful. Outside all was quiet—he could hear the captain's breathing, he looked into his eyes and with bated breath waited each time for the word: "Byelyogorshe." Schmitz looked at his watch, following the second hand—how slowly that tiny finger seemed to crawl across the watch face—fifty seconds: "Byelyo-gorshe." It seemed to take forever for the next fifty seconds to pass. Outside, trucks were driving into the courtyard. Someone called out in the corridor. Schmitz remembered that the senior MO had sent a mes-sage asking him to do his rounds for him, another truck drove into the yard. "Byelyogorshe," said the captain; Schmitz waited once more—the door opened, a sergeant appeared, Schmitz signaled impatiently to him to keep quiet, stared at the little second hand, and sighed as it touched the thirty. "Byelyogorshe," said the captain.

"What is it?" Schmitz asked the sergeant.

"Time to make the rounds," said the sergeant.

"I'm coming," said Schmitz. He pulled his sleeve down over his watch when the second hand came to twenty and the captain's lips had just closed—he stared at the man's mouth, waited, and drew back his sleeve when the lips began to move. "Byelyogorshe": the second hand stood exactly at ten.

Schmitz walked slowly out of the room.

That day there were no discharge cases. Schneider waited until eleven-fifteen, then went out to get some cigarettes. In the corridor he stopped by the window. Outside, the senior MO's car was being washed. Thursday, Schneider thought. Thursday was the day for washing the senior MO's car.

The building was in the form of a square open toward the rear, toward the railway. In the north wing was Surgery, in the center Administration and X-ray, in the south wing kitchen and staff quarters, and at the far end a suite of six rooms occupied by the administrator. This complex had once housed an agricultural college. At the rear, in the large grounds running straight across the open side, were shower rooms, stables, and model plantations, neatly defined beds containing all kinds of plants. The grounds and orchards went all the way down to the railway, and sometimes the administrator's wife could be seen riding there with her small son, a six-year-old straddling a pony and yelling. The administrator's wife was young and pretty, and whenever she had been playing with her son at the end of the grounds she would call in at the administration office and complain about the unexploded shell lying down there by the cesspool, in her view extremely dangerous. She was invariably assured that something would be done about it, but nothing ever was.

Schneider stood by the window watching the senior MO's driver painstakingly performing his duties; although he had been driving and looking after this car for two years, he was obeying the rules and had spread the lube chart out on a crate, had put on his fatigues, and stood surrounded by pails and oilcans. The senior MO's car was uphol-stered in red leather, and very low-slung. Thursday, thought Schnei-der, Thursday again. In the calendar of routines, Thursday was the day for washing the senior MO's car. He greeted the fair-haired nurse hur-rying past him and walked a few steps to the canteen door, but the door was locked.

Two trucks drove into the yard and parked well away from the MO's car. Schneider continued to look out of the window: at that moment the girl who brought the fruit drove into the yard. She held the reins herself, seated on an upturned crate, and drove her little cart carefully between the vehicles toward the kitchen. Her name was Szarka, and every Wednesday she brought fruit and vegetables from one of the nearby villages. People came with fruit and vegetables every day, the paymaster had a number of suppliers, but on Wednesdays only Szarka came. Schneider was quite sure about this: many a time he had inter-rupted his work on a Wednesday about ten-thirty, gone over to the window, and stood there waiting until the dust cloud stirred up by her little cart at the side of the avenue leading to the station came in sight, and he always waited until she came closer, until he could make out the little horse through the dust cloud, then the cartwheels, and finally the girl with the pretty oval face and the smile around her mouth. Schneider lighted his last cigarette and sat down on the windowsill. Today I'm going to speak to her, he thought, and at the same instant he thought of how every Wednesday he thought, Today I'm going to speak to her, and that he never had. But today he would for sure. There was something about Szarka that he had felt only in the women here, in these girls from the *puszta*, girls who were always shown in mov-ies as hot-blooded, capering ninnies. Szarka was cool, cool and of an almost impalpable tenderness; she behaved tenderly toward her horse, toward the fruit in her baskets: apricots and tomatoes, plums and pears, cucumbers and paprikas. Her gaily painted little cart slipped in between the greasy oilcans and crates, stopped at the kitchen, and she tapped her whip on the window.

Generally at this hour of the day all was quiet indoors. The MO was making his rounds, spreading a mood of anxious solemnity, everything was tidy, and an indefinable tension could be felt in the corridors. But today there was a restless hubbub, everywhere doors were being banged, people were calling out. Schneider was somehow aware of this at the edge of his consciousness; he smoked his last cigarette and watched Szarka negotiating with the mess sergeant. Normally she negotiated with the paymaster, who tried to pinch her behind—but Pratzki, the mess sergeant, was a slightly built, practical fellow, a bit high-strung, who was an excellent cook and reputed to have no use for women. Szarka seemed to be urging him, gesticulating, mostly the gesture for paying, but the cook merely shrugged his shoulders and pointed to the main building, to the very spot where Schneider was sitting. The girl turned and looked almost straight at Schneider; he jumped off the windowsill and heard his name being called in the corridor: "Schneider, Schneider!" There was a moment's silence, and again someone shouted, "Sergeant Schneider!" Schneider gave one more glance outside: Szarka took her little horse by the bridle and led it toward the main building; the MO's driver was standing in a large puddle folding up his lube chart. Schneider walked slowly toward the office, thinking of many things before he reached it: that he must speak to the girl today, whatever happened, that the MO's car couldn't be washed on a Wednesday—and that it was out of the question for Szarka to come on a Thursday.

He was met by the retinue accompanying the medical officer on his rounds. It emerged from the big ward, now almost empty; white smocks, a few nurses, the ward sergeant, the orderlies, a mute procession led not by the senior MO but by Schmitz, a noncommissioned medical officer, a man who was seldom heard to speak. Schmitz was short and plump and nondescript-looking, but his eyes were cool and gray, and sometimes, when he lowered the lids for an instant, he seemed about to say something, but he never did. The retinue dispersed as Schneider reached the office; he saw Schmitz approaching, held open the door for him, and the two men walked into the room together.

The sergeant major had his ear to the receiver. His broad face wore a look of annoyance. He was just saying, "No, sir," then the senior MO's voice was audible through the receiver, the sergeant major looked at Schneider and the noncommissioned MO, gestured to the latter to take a seat, and smiled as he looked at Schneider. Then he said, "Yes, sir; very well, sir," and replaced the receiver.

"What's up?" asked Schmitz. "I take it we're getting out of here." He opened the newspaper lying in front of him, flipped it shut again immediately, and looked over the shoulder of Feinhals, who was sitting beside him. Schmitz regarded the sergeant major coolly. He had seen that Feinhals was preparing a map of the surrounding area. SZOKAR-HELY BASE was printed across the top.

"Yes," said the sergeant major, "we've orders to redeploy." He was trying to remain calm, but there was a nasty glint in his eyes as he looked at Schneider. And his hands were trembling. He glanced at the crates, painted army-gray, stacked along the walls; with their lids open they could be used as lockers or desks. He still did not offer Schneider a chair.

"Give me a cigarette, Feinhals, till I can get some more," said Schneider. Feinhals got up, opened the blue pack, and held it out to Schneider. Schmitz took one too. Schneider stood leaning against the wall, smoking.

"I know," he said into the silence. "I'll be with the rear unit. It used to be the advance unit."

The sergeant major flushed. The sound of a typewriter came from the next room. The telephone rang, the sergeant major lifted the receiver, gave his name, and said, "Very well, sir—I'll have them sent over for signature."

He replaced the receiver. "Feinhals," he said, "go over and see if the order of the day is ready." Schmitz and Schneider exchanged glances. Schmitz looked at the desk and opened the newspaper again. HIGH TREASON TRIAL BEGINS, he read. He flipped the paper shut again immediately.

Feinhals returned with the clerk from the next room. The clerk was a pale, fair-haired noncom with fingers stained from smoking.

"Otten," Schneider called out to him, "will you be opening up the canteen again?"

"Just a moment, if you don't mind," said the sergeant major, furious. "I've got more important things to do right now." He drummed on the desk with his fingers while the clerk sorted the sets of paper. He turned the typed sheets facedown and pulled out the carbons. There were three sets, each consisting of two typed pages and four carbon copies. The typed sheets appeared to contain nothing but names. Schneider thought about the girl. Probably she was with the paymaster now, getting her money. He stepped closer to the window to get a better view of the gate.

"Don't forget," he said to Otten, "to leave us some cigarettes."

"Shut up!" shouted the sergeant major.

He handed the papers to Feinhals, saying, "Take these over to the senior MO for signature." Feinhals clipped them together and left the room.

The sergeant major turned to Schmitz and Schneider, but Schneider was looking out of the window. It was almost noon, and the road was empty; opposite was a large field where a market was held on Wednesdays: the littered stalls stood abandoned in the sunshine. So it *is* Wednesday, he thought, turning toward the sergeant major, who had a carbon copy of the order of the day in his hand. Feinhals had returned and was standing by the door.

"...will remain here," the sergeant major was saying. "Feinhals has a sketch map of the place. This time everything's to be done in battle order. A formality, as you know, Schneider," he added. "You'd better round up a few men and have the weapons brought in from the infectious ward. The other wards have already been notified."

"Weapons?" asked Schneider. "Is that a formality too?"

The sergeant major flushed again. Schmitz took another cigarette from Feinhals's pack. "I'd like to see the list of wounded. Will the senior MO be leading the advance unit?"

"Yes," said the sergeant major, "he's the one that drew up the list."

"I'd like to see it," said Schmitz.

Once more the sergeant major flushed. Then he reached into the drawer and handed Schmitz the list. Schmitz read it through carefully, saying each name quietly over to himself; there was silence in the room, no one said anything, they were all looking at the man reading the list. Outside in the corridor there was a commotion. They all jumped as Schmitz suddenly cried out; "Lieutenant Moll and Captain Bauer, for Christ's sake!" He flung the list onto the desk and looked at the sergeant major. "Any medical student knows that no patient is fit to travel an hour and a half after a serious operation." He picked up the list from the desk and rapped the paper with his fingers. "I might just as well put a bullet through their heads as load them into an ambulance." He looked at Schneider, then at Feinhals, then at the sergeant major and

Otten. "They must have known yesterday that we were clearing out today—why wasn't the operation postponed, eh?"

"Orders only arrived this morning, an hour ago," said the sergeant major.

"Orders! Orders!" exclaimed Schmitz. He threw the list onto the desk, saying to Schneider, "Come on, let's get out of here." When they were outside he said, "You weren't listening just then—I'm in charge of the rear unit—we'll talk about it later." He walked rapidly toward the senior MO's office, and Schneider strolled away to his room.

He paused at each window on the way, looking out to make sure Szarka's cart was still standing in front of the gate. By now the courtyard was jammed with trucks and ambulances, and in the middle stood the MO's car. They had already begun loading, and Schneider noticed that outside the kitchen the baskets of fruit were also being loaded, and the MO's driver was lugging a gray metal trunk across the yard.

The corridors were crowded. In his room Schneider walked quickly to the locker, poured the rest of the apricot schnapps into a glass, and added some soda water, and as he drank it he could hear the first motor starting up outside. Glass in hand, he went out into the corridor and stood by the window: he had heard right away that the first motor to start up was the MO's; it was a good motor, Schneider knew nothing about such things, but he could tell by the sound that it was a good motor. Just then the MO crossed the courtyard, he wasn't carrying any baggage, and his field cap was slightly askew. He looked pretty much as usual; only his face, otherwise rather distinguished, pale, with faint pinkish overtones, was scarlet. The MO was a good-looking man, tall and spare, an excellent horseman who mounted his horse every morning at six, whip in hand, and rode off into the *puszta* at a steady canter, a dwindling figure vanishing into that flat landscape that seemed to consist only of horizon. But now his face was scarlet, and only once had Schneider seen the MO's face scarlet, and that was when Schmitz had carried out with success an operation that the MO had not wanted to tackle. Now Schmitz was walking beside the MO; Schmitz was quite calm, whereas the MO was waving his arms ... but now Schneider had seen the girl coming toward him along the corridor. She seemed to be confused by all the commotion and looking for someone who was not involved in the general exodus. She said something in Hungarian that he did not understand, then he pointed to his room and beckoned her over. Outside, the first vehicle, the MO's, was moving off, and the column slowly followed...

Evidently the girl took him for a deputy of the paymaster's. She did not sit down on the chair he offered, and when he perched on the edge of the desk she continued to stand facing him, trying to make him understand what she wanted and gesturing vigorously as she spoke. It was a relief to be able to look at her without having to listen to her, for it was hopeless to try and understand what she was saying. But he let her talk just so that he could look at her. She seemed rather thin, perhaps she was too young, very young, much younger than he had thought—her breasts were small, the beauty of her small face was perfect, and he waited almost breathlessly for the moments when her long eyelashes lay on the brown cheeks—very brief moments in which her small mouth remained closed, round and red, the lips slightly too narrow. He studied her very carefully and had to admit that he was a bit disappointed—but she was charming, and all of a sudden he raised his hands defensively and shook his head. She stopped speaking at once, looking at him suspiciously; he said softly, "I'd like to kiss you, do you understand?" By this time he no longer knew whether he really did want to kiss her, and it embarrassed him to see her blush, to see the color slowly spreading over that dark skin, and he realized she hadn't understood a single word but knew what he meant. She took a step back as he slowly approached her, and he could see from the scared look in her eyes and from the thin neck with its wildly pulsing vein that she was three months too young. He stopped, shook his head, and said in a low voice: "Forgive me—forget it—understand?" But the look in her eyes became more scared than ever, and he was afraid she was going to scream. This time she seemed to understand even less. With a sigh he stepped up to her, took hold of her small hands, and as he lifted them to his mouth he saw they were dirty, they smelled of earth and leather, leeks and onions, and he brushed them with his lips and tried to smile. She looked at him in growing bewilderment, until he patted her on the shoulder, saying, "Come along, we'll go and see you get your money." Not until he held up his hand and made the unmistakable gesture of paying did she give a little smile and follow him out into the corridor.

In the corridor they ran into Schmitz and Otten.

"Where are you going?" asked Schmitz.

"To see the paymaster," said Schneider. "The girl wants her money."

"The paymaster's gone," said Schmitz. "He left yesterday evening, for Szolnok; from there he's going to join up with the advance unit." He lowered his lids for a moment, then looked at the men. No one said a word. The girl glanced from one to the other. "Otten," said Schmitz, "round up the rear unit, I need a few men for unloading, no one seemed to think of leaving any food for us."

"And the girl?" asked Schneider.

Schmitz shrugged his shoulders. "I can't give her any money."

"Should she come back tomorrow morning?"

Schmitz looked at the girl. She smiled at him.

"No," he said, "it had better be this afternoon."

Otten ran along the corridor, shouting, "Rear unit fall in!"

Schmitz went out into the courtyard and stood beside the truck, while Schneider accompanied the girl to her cart. He tried to explain to her that she should come back in the afternoon, but she kept vigorously shaking her head until he realized she was not going to leave without her money. He continued to stand beside her, watched her climb onto the cart, turn her crate up, and take out a brown-paper parcel. Then she hung the feedbag over the horse's nose and unwrapped the parcel: part of a loaf of bread, a large flat meat patty, and a leek. Her wine was in a squat green bottle. She was smiling at him now, and suddenly, in the midst of chewing, she said "Nagyvárad," and struck the air several times with her fist, horizontally away from her body, making a solemn face as she did so. Schneider imagined she was demonstrating a fistfight which someone had lost, or maybe—he thought—she was trying to show that she felt she had been cheated. He didn't know what "Nagyvárad" meant. Hungarian was a very difficult language, it didn't even have a word for tobacco.

The girl shook her head. "Nagyvárad, Nagyvárad," she repeated vehemently several times, striking the air again with her fist, horizontally away from her chest. She shook her head and laughed, chewing hard, and took a quick gulp of wine. "Oh!" she went, "Nagyvárad— Russ," again the boxing gesture, this time prolonged and in a wide arc: "Russ—Russ." She pointed to the southeast and imitated the noise of tanks approaching: "Bru-bru-bru..."

Suddenly Schneider nodded, and she laughed out loud, but broke off in the middle and assumed a very grave expression. Schneider realized that Nagyvárad must be a town, and the boxing gesture was now quite clear. He looked across to the men standing by the truck and unloading. Schmitz was standing up front beside the driver and signing something. Schneider called out to him, "When you have a moment, sir, would you mind coming over here?" Schmitz nodded.

The girl had finished her meal. She carefully wrapped up the bread and the remains of the leek and stuck the cork back in the bottle.

"Would you like some water for the horse?" asked Schneider. She looked at him questioningly.

"Water," he said, "for the horse." He leaned slightly forward and tried to imitate a horse drinking.

"Oh," she cried, "oh, yo!" Her eyes held a strange look, of curiosity somehow, curiosity and tenderness.

Across the yard the truck moved off, and Schmitz walked over.

Their eyes followed the truck; outside, another column stood waiting for the entrance to become free.

"What is it?" asked Schmitz.

"She's talking about a breakthrough near a town beginning with Nagy."

Schmitz nodded. "Nagyvárad," he said, "I know."

"You know?"

"I heard it last night over the radio."

"Is it far from here?"

Schmitz looked thoughtfully at the long column of trucks driving into the yard. "Far," he said with a sigh, "far doesn't mean a thing in this war—must be about sixty miles. Maybe we should give the girl her money in cigarettes—right now."

Schneider looked at Schmitz and felt himself blushing. "Hold on a minute," he said, "I'd like her to stay for a bit."

"Suit yourself," said Schmitz, walking slowly off toward the south wing.

As he entered the patients' room, the captain said in a low, hollow tone: "Byelyogorshe." Schmitz knew it was pointless to look at his watch; that rhythm was more precise than any watch could ever be, and while he sat on the edge of the bed, the medical history in his hand, almost lulled to sleep by that ever-recurring word, he tried to figure out how such a rhythm could come about—what mechanism, what clock-work, in that appallingly patched-up, sliced-up skull, was releasing that monotonous litany? And what happened in those fifty seconds when the man said nothing, merely breathed? Schmitz knew almost noth-ing about him: born March 1895 in Wuppertal; rank: captain; service: army; civilian occupation: businessman; religion: Lutheran; residence, troop unit, wounds, illnesses, type of injury. Nor was there anything particularly striking about this man's life: his school record was not good, he had been a very mediocre student, somewhat unreliable; he had only had to repeat a year once, and on graduating he had even had a B in geography, English, and Phys. Ed. He had had no love for the war; without wanting to, he had been made a lieutenant in 1915. He drank a bit, but not excessively—and later, when he was married, he could never bring himself to deceive his wife, however simple and entic-ing it might sometimes have been to arrange an affair. He just couldn't bring himself to do it.

Schmitz knew that everything in the medical history was virtually irrelevant as long as he didn't know why the man said "Byelyogorshe" and what it meant to him—and Schmitz knew that he would never know, yet he would have happily sat there forever, waiting for that word.

Outside it was very quiet. He listened tensely and expectantly to the silence into which from time to time that word dropped. But the silence was stronger, oppressively strong, and slowly, almost reluctantly, Schmitz got up and went out of the room.

After Schmitz had left them, the girl looked at Schneider and seemed embarrassed. She made a hurried gesture of drinking. "Oh, of course," he said, "the water." He went toward the building to get some water. At the entrance he had to jump back: an elegant red car drove past him, quietly but a little too fast and, carefully avoiding the parked ambu-lances, swung toward the rear, where the administrator had his quarters.

On coming back with the pail of water, Schneider had to jump aside again. Horns were sounding, the column was getting under way. In the first truck sat the sergeant major, the others followed slowly. The sergeant major did not look at Schneider. Schneider let the long line of trucks pass and stepped into the courtyard, now oppressively empty and quiet. He set the pail down in front of the horse and looked at the girl; she pointed to Schmitz, just then emerging from the south wing. Schmitz walked past them out through the entrance, and they slowly followed. They stood side by side watching the column move off in the direction of the station. "The two from the infectious ward actually did bring along some weapons," Schmitz said quietly.

"Ah, yes," exclaimed Schneider, "I'd forgotten about that."

Schmitz shook his head. "We won't be needing them—on the contrary. Come on, let's go." He paused beside the girl. "I think we'd better give her the cigarettes now, eh? Just in case?"

Schneider nodded. "Didn't they leave us a truck? How are we supposed to get away?"

"One truck's supposed to be coming back," said Schmitz. "The MO promised me."

The two men exchanged glances.

"There come some refugees," said Schmitz, pointing toward the village: a weary group was approaching. The refugees trudged slowly past without looking at them. They were tired and sad and did not look at either the soldiers or the girl.

"They've come a long way," said Schmitz. "Look how tired the horses are. It's useless to run away; at that speed they'll never escape the war."

A car horn blew behind them, sharp and impatient, insolent. They moved slowly apart, Schneider toward the girl. The administrator's car was pushing its way out; it was forced to stop, almost hitting a refugee cart. They could see the occupants quite distinctly, they were sitting right in front of their noses, it was like being in the front row at the movies, painfully close to the screen. In front, at the wheel, sat the administrator, his sharp, rather weak profile motionless; beside him on the seat was a pile of suitcases and blankets, firmly fastened with ropes so they would not topple over on him during the drive. Behind him sat his wife, her beautiful profile as motionless as his; both seemed bent on looking neither right nor left. She was holding the baby on her lap, their six-year-old boy was beside her. He was the only one looking out; his lively face was pressed to the glass, and he smiled at the soldiers. It was two minutes before the car could go on—the horses were tired, and somewhere farther along, the trek had stalled. They could see the man at the wheel grow tense: he was sweating, he blinked rapidly, and his wife whispered something to him from the back seat. There was scarcely a sound, only the refugees calling out wearily along the trek, and a child crying; but suddenly from the courtyard behind them came shouts, hoarse yells, and they looked back. At that instant a stone struck the car, but it only smacked into the folded tent; the second stone knocked a dent in the saucepan tied to the top as if for a family outing. The man who was yelling and running up to them was the janitor; he occupied two rooms in the bathhouse at the far end of the grounds. He was quite close now, standing right in the entrance, but he had run out of stones. As he bent down, cursing, the snag in the trek sorted itself out, and the car, hooting imperiously, got under way. A flowerpot swished through the air but landed only where a second ago the car had been standing, on the swept pavement of blue chips. The clay pot shattered, the fragments rolled apart, forming an oddly symmetrical circle around the lump of soil, which first seemed to retain its shape but then suddenly crumbled apart, releasing the roots of a geranium whose blossoms, red and innocent, remained upright in the center.

The janitor stood between the soldiers. He was not cursing now, he was weeping, the tears clearly visible on his grimy cheeks, and his posture was both touching and horrifying: leaning forward, fists clenched, his grubby old jacket flapping about his hollow chest. He jumped when a woman's voice screamed behind him in the courtyard, then he turned and walked slowly back, weeping. Szarka followed him, drawing away when Schneider put out his hand toward her. She took hold of her horse, led it outside, climbed onto the cart, and picked up the reins.

"I'll go and get the cigarettes," cried Schmitz. "Don't let her leave—I'll be right back." Schneider held the horse firmly by the bridle, the girl brought the whip down on his hand; it hurt, but he hung on. He looked back and was surprised to see Schmitz running. He wouldn't have thought Schmitz would ever run. The girl raised her whip again, but instead of bringing it down on his hand she placed it beside her on the seat, and Schneider was amazed to see her suddenly smile: it was the smile he had often seen on her, tender and cool, and he went up to the cart and carefully lifted her down from her upturned crate. She called out something to the horse, and when Schneider put his arms around her, he saw that she was still a bit nervous, but she did not resist, she just looked uneasily about her. It was dark in the entrance; Schneider kissed her carefully on the cheeks, on the nose, and pushed back her smooth black hair to kiss the nape of her neck. He was startled to hear Schmitz throw the cigarettes into the cart. The girl's head shot up, her eyes went to the red packages. Schmitz did not look at Schneider but turned on his heel and went back into the courtyard. The girl was blushing, she looked at Schneider but deliberately past his eyes, and all at once she called out to the horse, a crisp, short word, and jerked the reins. Schneider moved aside. He waited until she was fifty paces away, then called her name into the silence—she hesitated, did not turn around, raised the whip over her head in a farewell gesture, and drove on. Schneider walked slowly back into the courtyard.

The seven men of the rear unit were sitting over a meal outside what had been the kitchen; there was a pail of soup on the table in the courtyard, and beside it thick slices of bread and meat. Schneider heard muffled blows coming from inside the building. He raised his eyebrows at the men.

"The janitor's breaking down the door to the administrator's quarters," said Feinhals, adding a moment later, "At least he might have left the door open; there's no point in destroying it."

Schmitz entered the building with four soldiers to collect all the material for loading. Schneider stayed behind with Feinhals and Otten.

"I've been given a nice job," said Otten.

Feinhals was drinking red schnapps out of an enamel mug; he passed a few packs of cigarettes to Schneider. "Thanks," said Schneider.

"I've been given the job," said Otten, "of throwing the machine gun and the machine pistol and the rest of the junk into the cesspool, down there where the dud shell's lying. You can give me a hand, Feinhals."

"Okay," said Feinhals. With his soup spoon he was slowly drawing patterns on the table from a soup puddle that ran broad and brown from the center to the edge.

"Let's go, then," said Otten.

Shortly after this Schneider fell asleep, bent over the lid of his mess bowl. His cigarette went on burning. It was lying at the edge of the table; the fine ash ate its way slowly out of the cigarette paper, the burning tip crept on, burning a narrow black trail in the table as far as the edge of the cigarette, and four minutes later only a slender gray stick of ash was left, stuck to the table. This little gray stick lay there a long time, almost an hour, until Schneider woke up and brushed it off with his arm without ever having seen it. He woke up just as the truck was driving into the yard. Almost simultaneously with the sound of the truck they heard the first tanks. Schneider leaped to his feet. The others, who were standing around smoking, were on the point of laughing, but stopped short of it: that distant rumble spoke for itself.

"How about that," said Schmitz, "the truck really did turn up. Feinhals, go up into the attic, maybe you can see something from there."

Feinhals walked over to the south wing. The janitor was leaning on a window sill in the administrator's quarters, watching the men. His wife could be heard moving about inside, there was a faint tinkle, she appeared to be counting glasses.

"Let's load the stuff," said Schmitz. The driver gestured impatiently; he looked very tired. "Balls," he said, "climb in and leave the crap behind." He picked up a pack from the table, ripped it open, and lit a cigarette.

"Start loading," said Schmitz. "We've got to wait anyway till Feinhals gets back."

The driver shrugged his shoulders, sat down at the table, and ladled some soup from the pail into Schneider's mess bowl.

The rest of the men loaded the truck with everything that had been left behind in the building: a few beds, an officer's barrack box, his name printed on it in black paint, LT. GRECK, a stove, and a pile of soldiers' packs, knapsacks, kit bags, and a few rifles; then a pile of underwear: bundled shirts, underpants, socks, and some fur-lined vests.

Feinhals called down from the attic, "I can't see a thing. There's a row of poplars in the village blocking my view. Can you hear them? I can, quite clearly."

"Yes," called Schmitz, "we can hear them. Come on down."

"Okay," said Feinhals. His head vanished from the skylight.

"Someone ought to go down to the railroad embankment," said Schmitz, "he'd be sure to see them from there."

"It's no use," said the truck driver, "they're not in sight yet."

"How can you tell?"

"By listening. I can hear they're not in sight yet. Besides, they're coming from two directions."

He pointed toward the southwest, and his gesture seemed to conjure up the rumble over there too: he was right, they could hear it now.

"Hell," said Schmitz. "What do we do now?"

"Get going," said the driver. He stepped aside and, shaking his head, looked on as the others finished off the job of loading the table onto the truck, as well as the bench he had been sitting on.

Feinhals came out of the building. "One of the patients is yelling," he said.

"I'll go," said Schmitz. "You fellows get going."

They stood there, hesitating. Then they slowly followed him, all except the driver. Schmitz turned around, saying quietly, "Get going, I tell you, I have to stay behind anyway, with the patients." Again they hesitated, then promptly followed him again.

"Damn it all," Schmitz called back to them, "get going, I tell you. You need to get a head start on this damned plain."

This time they halted and did not follow. Only Schneider walked slowly after him as he disappeared into the building. The rest moved slowly toward the truck. Feinhals hesitated a moment. It was a brief pause, then he entered the building and came face to face with Schneider.

"D'you need something?" Schneider asked. "Everything's already on the truck."

"Unload some bread, and some margarine—and cigarettes." The door to the sickroom opened. Feinhals looked in and exclaimed, "My God, the captain."

"D'you know him?" asked Schmitz.

"Yes," said Feinhals, "I once spent half a day in his battalion."

"Where?"

"I don't know what the place was called."

"Get out of here, you two," cried Schmitz, "and quit fooling around."

Feinhals said, "Be seeing you," and left.

"What made you stay behind?" asked Schmitz, but he did not seem to expect a reply, and Schneider gave none. They both stood listening to the noise of the departing truck, the motor sounding hollow as the truck drove through the entrance; then it was outside on the road to the station—and even beyond the station they could still hear it, until it gradually became very faint.

The rumbling of the tanks had stopped. They heard firing.

"Heavy flak," said Schmitz. "We really should go down to the embankment."

"I'll go," said Schneider. Inside the room the captain said "Byelyogorshe." He said it almost without emphasis, yet with a certain pleasure. His face was dark, with a dense black growth of beard, his head was firmly bandaged. Schneider looked at Schmitz. "Hopeless," he said. "If he gets better, comes through this, well..." He shrugged his shoulders.

"Byelyogorshe," said the captain. Then he started to cry. He cried soundlessly, without the least alteration in his expression, but even through his tears he said, "Byelyogorshe."

"There's a court-martial proceeding against him," said Schmitz. "He was thrown off a motorcycle and wasn't wearing a steel helmet. He was a captain."

"I'll just run down to the embankment," said Schneider, "maybe I can see something from there. If any more troops come back, I'll join them ... so ... "

Schmitz nodded.

"Byelyogorshe," said the captain.

When Schneider came out into the courtyard, he saw that at the far end the janitor had run up a flag in the administrator's quarters, a pathetic red rag with a clumsy yellow sickle and white hammer stitched to it. Now the rumbling in the southeast was also becoming more distinct again. The firing seemed to have ceased. He walked slowly past the planted beds, only stopping when he reached the cesspool. Beside the cesspool lay the dud shell. It had been lying there for months. Months ago, SS units that had been dug in along the railroad tracks had been fighting Hungarian rebels holed up in the school, but it had been only a very brief skirmish: the traces of firing had almost disappeared from the façade. Only the dud had remained where it was, a rusty piece of iron, the length of an arm and tapering to a round point, scarcely noticeable. It looked almost like a piece of rotting wood. In the high grass it was hardly visible, but the administrator's wife had made numerous protests against its existence, and reports had been submitted that never received a reply.

Schneider's pace slackened a little while he had to pass the dud. In the grass he saw the footprints of Otten and Feinhals, who had thrown the machine gun into the cesspool, but the surface of the cesspool was smooth again, a green, greasy smoothness. Schneider continued on past the beds, through the tree farm, across the meadow, and climbed up onto the railroad embankment. Those four or five feet seemed to raise him to an immense height above the ground. He looked beyond the village out onto the broad plain to the left of the tracks and saw nothing. But the sound had become more distinct. He listened carefully for any firing. Nothing. The rumbling came from exactly the same direction as the tracks. Schneider sat down and waited. The village was absolutely silent; it lay there as if dead, with its trees, the little houses, the square church tower. It looked very small because to the left of the embankment there was not a single house. Schneider began to smoke.

Indoors, Schmitz was sitting beside the man who said "Byelyogorshe." Over and over again. His tears had dried up. The man stared straight ahead with his dark eyes and repeated "Byelyogorshe," like a beautiful melody, Schmitz thought—anyway, he could have listened forever to this one word. The other patient was asleep.

The man who kept saying "Byelyogorshe" was called Bauer, Captain Bauer. He had previously been a textile agent, and before that a student, but before he became a student he had been a lieutenant, for almost four years, and later, as a textile agent, things had not been easy for him. It all depended on whether people had money, and people hardly ever did have money. At least, not the people who might have bought his sweaters. Expensive sweaters always sold well, so did cheap ones, but his particular line, the medium-priced range, were always very hard to sell... He hadn't managed to pick up an agency for cheap sweaters, or for expensive ones—those were the good agencies, and good agencies went to the people who didn't need them. Fifteen years he had spent as an agent for those slow-selling sweaters; the first twelve years had been a loathsome, never-ending, horrible struggle, chasing from store to store, from building to building, the kind of life that wore a man down. It had put years on his wife. When he first met her she had been twenty-three and he twenty-six—he was still a student, fond of a drink, while she was a slender, fair-haired girl who couldn't drink any wine at all. But she had never uttered a cross word to him, a quiet woman who had held her tongue even when he sacrificed his university career to sell sweaters. He had often been surprised himself at his own stamina—to have been selling those sweaters for twelve years!—and at his wife's calm acceptance of everything. Then for three years things had gone a bit better, and suddenly, after fifteen years, the whole situation had changed: he acquired the agency for both the expensive and the cheap sweaters and kept the agency for the medium-priced range. Business had been booming, and now others were doing the legwork for him. He could spend all his time at home, telephoning and signing; he had a warehouseman, a bookkeeper, and a stenographer. Now he had money, but now his wife—who was never really well and had had five miscarriages in quick succession—had cancer. It had finally been confirmed. And besides, these halcyon days had lasted only four months—until the war broke out.

"Byelyogorshe," said the captain.

Schmitz looked at him; he would have liked to know what the man was thinking about. He felt an ungovernable curiosity to know the whole man, that large and rather hollow face, deathly pale under its stubble, those staring eyes that seemed to say "Byelyogorshe"—for now his mouth barely moved. Then the man started crying again, his tears running soundlessly down his cheeks. He was no hero, and it had been pretty rough to have the lieutenant colonel shout into the phone telling him to find out what his bunch were doing, that something was wrong at Horse Droppings, and to have to drive up to the front line with that steel helmet on his head, knowing what a fool he looked in it. He was no hero, he had never said he was, in fact he knew he wasn't. And when he was close to the front line he had taken off the steel helmet because he didn't want to look like a fool when he got to the front and had to start shouting. He held the steel helmet in his hand and thought: What the hell, why not take a chance, and the closer he got to that stupid mess up front, the less scared he was. Hell, they all knew there wasn't a thing he could do, that anyone could do, because they had too few guns and no tanks. So why start shouting like an idiot? Every officer knew that too many tanks and too many guns had been ordered back to cover staff quarters. Shit, he thought, unaware that he was being brave. And then he was thrown off the machine and his whole skull was ripped open, and the only thing left inside him was the word "Byelyogorshe."

That was all. It seemed to be enough to keep him talking for the whole of the rest of his life, it was a world for him, a world that no one knew or ever would know.

He had no idea, of course, that a court-martial had been instituted against him on grounds of self-mutilation because he had removed his steel helmet while under fire and, what was more, while on a motorcycle. He had no idea of this—and he never would have. The drawing up of the paper bearing his name and serial number, and all the other documents, had been so much wasted effort—he would never find out about them, they would never reach him now. He merely said, every fifty seconds, "Byelyogorshe."

Schmitz never took his eyes off him. He would willingly have gone out of his mind himself to know what was going on inside this man's mind. And at the same time he envied him.

He jumped when Schneider opened the door. "What is it?" asked Schmitz.

"They're coming," said Schneider. "They're here. No more of our troops managed to get through."

Schmitz had heard nothing. Now he heard them. They were there. To the left they were already in the village. Now he understood what the driver had meant: "I can hear they're not in sight yet." Now you could hear they were in sight—clearly in sight.

"The flag," said Schmitz, "we should have hung out the flag with the red cross—it would have been worth a try."

"We still can."

"Here it is," said Schmitz. He pulled it out from under his pack on the table. Schneider took it.

"Coming?" he asked.

They left. Schneider stuck his head out the window and pulled it back in again immediately. His face was white.

"They're right there," he said, "by the embankment."

"I'll go and meet them," said Schmitz.

Schneider shook his head. He raised the flag high above his head and went out through the door. He swung round to the right and made straight for the embankment. It was very quiet, even the tanks were quiet as they stood parked at the edge of the village. The school was the last building before the station. It was in that direction that their gun barrels were pointing, but Schneider didn't see them. He didn't see the tanks at all, he saw nothing. He felt ridiculous, holding the flag like that in front of himself as if he were in a parade, and he could feel that his blood was fear. Just plain fear. He walked stiffly, straight ahead, almost like a puppet, holding the flag in front of himself. He walked slowly until he stumbled. That woke him up. He had stumbled over a wire connecting the vinestocks in a model plantation. Now he saw everything. There were two tanks, they were parked behind the embankment, and the one in front was slowly veering its turret to aim at him. Then, when he had passed the trees, he saw there were more. They were standing behind and beside one another in formation across the field, and the red stars painted on them seemed repulsive and very alien to him. He had never seen them before. Next came the cesspool. Now he had only to pass the beds, cross the tree farm, climb up the embankment—but at the cesspool he hesitated; he was suddenly scared again, worse than before. Before he hadn't realized; he had thought his blood was turning to ice, he hadn't realized it was fear. Now his blood was like fire, and he saw nothing but red—nothing else—gigantic red stars that struck terror into him. Just then he stepped on the dud, and the dud exploded.

At first nothing happened. In the silence the explosion was staggeringly loud. The Russians knew only that the shell had not come from them, and that the man with the flag had suddenly vanished in a cloud of dust. Shortly after that they started pounding away at the building in a frenzy. They swung all their gun barrels around, redeployed themselves for firing, fired first into the south wing, then into the central building and the north wing, where the janitor's tiny flag hung limply from the window. It fell into the dirt that crumbled down from the building—and finally they fired again into the south wing, this time long and furiously; they had not fired their guns for a long time, and they sawed through the thin façade until the building toppled forward. It was not until later that they noticed there had not been a single shot from the other side.

IV

Only two big patches of color were left: one green, a cucumber ven-dor's great mound, the other pinkish-yellow, apricots. In the middle of the market square stood the swingboats. They were there permanently. Their colors had faded, their blue and red as dingy and dirty as the colors of a venerable old ship anchored in the harbor and patiently waiting to be scrapped. The swingboats hung down stiffly, not one was moving, and smoke curled up from the chimney of the trailer parked alongside them.

The patches of color were slowly breaking up: the dark and light greens of the intertwined mosaic of cucumbers dwindled rapidly; Greck could see from a long way off that two people were busy breaking it up. The apricots took longer, much longer: a woman, all by herself, was picking the apricots up one by one and carefully placing them in baskets. Cucumbers were evidently not as fragile as apricots. Greck slowed his pace. Deny it, he thought, simply deny everything. That's the only thing to do if they find out. The only thing. Life was worth a denial, after all. But they wouldn't find out, he was sure of that. It did surprise him, though, to find that there were so many Jews still around here.

The paving between the low trees and little houses was uneven, but he did not notice it. He was pretty scared, and he had the feeling: The faster I get away from there, the less chance there is of attracting attention, and most likely I won't have to deny anything. But I must hurry. He was walking faster again now, hurrying along. He had almost reached the square; the cart with the cucumbers was already passing him, and beyond it there was still that woman painstakingly packing away her apricots. Her pile had not yet been reduced by half.

Greck saw the swingboats. Never in his life had he gone for a ride on a swingboat. Such pleasures had not been for him; they were forbidden in his family, first because he was never really well, and then because that was no way to behave, in public, swinging through the air like some silly monkey. And he had never done anything that was forbidden—today had been the first time, and right off something so terrible, almost the worst thing you could do, something that automati-cally cost you your life.

Greck could feel the panic in his throat, and he lurched quickly, reeling in the sunshine, across the empty square toward the swingboats. Smoke was puffing more vigorously now from the trailer's chimney. They must have put some more coal on, he thought: no, wood. He didn't know what they put on stoves in Hungary. And he didn't care. He knocked on the trailer door: a man appeared, naked to the waist, he was blond, unshaven, and big-boned, his face had something almost Dutch about it; only the nose was strikingly narrow, and he had very dark eyes.

"What is it?" he asked in German. Greck could feel the sweat trickling into his mouth; he licked his lips, wiped the palm of his hand across his face, and said, "The swings, I'd like to go for a ride."

The man in the doorway screwed up his eyes, then nodded. He ran his tongue over his teeth. Behind him appeared his wife; she was in her petticoat, sweat was dripping down her face, and the dark-red shoulder straps were sweat-stained. In one hand she was holding a wooden spoon, in the other arm a child. The child was dirty. The woman was very dark, somber, Greck thought. There was definitely something sinister about these people. Perhaps they were suspicious of him. Greck no longer wanted a ride on the swingboats, but the man, whose tongue had finally settled down, said, "Well, if you really want to—in this heat—at midday."

He came down the steps; Greck moved aside and followed him the few paces to the swingboats.

"How much?" he asked feebly. They'll think I'm nuts, he thought. The sweat was driving him crazy. He wiped his sleeve across his face and climbed the wooden steps to the iron framework. The man released a brake, one of the swingboats in the middle swayed gently to and fro.

"I guess," said the man, "you'd better not go too high, or I'll have to stay here and watch. It's the law."

Greck found his German repulsive. It was an odd mixture of softness and impudence, as if he were uttering an entirely foreign language with German words.

"I won't," Greck said. "You can go... How much?"

The man shrugged his shoulders. "Give me one pengö," he said. Greck gave him his last pengö and carefully climbed in.

The little boat was wider than he had thought. He felt quite safe and began to use the technique he had so often been able to watch but

not use. He held on to the iron stanchions, unclasped his fingers to wipe
off the sweat, then straightened his knee, bent it, straightened it, and
was amazed to feel the swingboat move. It was very simple, all you had
to do was make sure the bending of your knee did not interfere with
the rhythmic movement set up by the swing: you had to increase the
rhythm by throwing your weight back, with straight legs, as the boat
swung forward, and by letting yourself fall forward as the boat swung
back. Greck saw that the man was still standing beside him, and he
shouted, "What's the matter? You don't have to stay." The man shook
his head, and Greck ceased to pay attention to him. All of a sudden he
knew he had been missing something vital in his life: riding a swingboat. It was glorious. The sweat dried on his forehead, and the gentle
coolness of the rocking motion even dried the sweat on his body: the
air blew through him, fresh and exquisite, with every swing, and furthermore the world was changed. One minute it consisted merely of a
few dirty planks with broad grooves running along them, and on the
downward swing he had the whole sky to himself. "Watch out!" cried
the man down below. "Hold tight!" Greck could feel the man putting
on the brake: a gentle jolt that severely hampered his swinging.

"Leave me alone!" he shouted. But the man shook his head. Greck
quickly swung himself up again. This was the glorious part: to stand
parallel to the earth as the little boat swung back—to see those dirty
planks that signified the world—and then, plunging forward again, to
kick your feet into the sky, to see it overhead as if you were lying in
a meadow, only this way you were closer to the sky, infinitely closer.
Everything in between was insignificant. On his left the woman was
carefully packing away her apricots; her pile never seemed to get any
less. On the right stood that fat blond fellow who had to obey the law
and slow him down; a few chickens waddled across his field of vision,
over there was a road. His cap flew off his head.

Deny it, he thought, as he calmed down, simply deny it; they won't
believe it if I deny it. I don't do things like that. No one would believe
I could do a thing like that. I've got a good reputation. I know they
don't think much of me because I've got chronic indigestion, but they
like me in their way, and no one would believe I could do a thing like
that. He was both proud and timid, and it was a glorious feeling to
find he had the courage to go on this swingboat. He would write to

his mother about it. No, better not. Mama didn't understand about things like that. Whatever life may bring, always behave with dignity! was her motto. She would never understand how her son, an attorney, Lieutenant Greck, could take a ride in a swingboat, in the middle of a broiling hot day in a dirty Hungarian market square, in full view of anyone—anyone at all—who happened to be passing by. No, no—he could picture her shaking her head, a woman without humor; he knew that and it was no use trying to fight it. And that other thing: oh, God! Although he didn't want to, he couldn't help thinking about it, how he had undressed in the Jewish tailor's back room: a stuffy little hole with scraps of patching material lying around, half-finished suits with buckram tacked onto them, and a repulsively large bowl of cucumber salad with drowning flies floating around in it—he could feel fluid rising into his mouth, and he knew he was turning pale, disgusting fluid in his mouth—but he could still see himself, taking off his pants and revealing his second pair, taking the money, and the toothless old man's grin following him as he hurried out of the shop.

Suddenly the world began to spin around him. "Stop!" he yelled. "Stop!" The man down below jammed on the brake, he felt it, the hard rhythmic jolting. Then the swing came to a standstill; he knew he looked ridiculous and pathetic, and he carefully stepped out, walked behind the framework, and spat: his stomach had settled down but he still had that disgusting taste in his mouth. He felt giddy, sat down on a step, and closed his eyes; the rhythm of the ride was still in his eyes, he could feel his eyeballs twitching, he had to spit again. It took quite a while for the movement of his eyeballs to calm down.

He rose and picked up his cap from the ground. The man was standing beside him, looked at him impassively; then his wife appeared. Greck was surprised to see how small she was. A tiny, swarthy little thing with a gaunt face. She was holding a mug. The blond fellow took the mug from her and held it out to Greck. "Drink," he said without emotion. Greck shook his head. "Drink," said the man, "it will do you good."

Greck took the mug; the stuff tasted very bitter, but it helped. The couple smiled, they smiled mechanically because they were used to smiling at this kind of thing, not because they cared for him or pitied him.

"Thanks very much," he said. He felt in his pocket for coins, there were none left, only that terrible great hundred-pengö bill, and he shrugged his shoulders helplessly. He could feel himself flushing. "Okay," said the man, "that's okay." *"Heil Hitler,"* said Greck. The man merely nodded.

Greck did not look back. The sweat was beginning to flow again. It seemed to come boiling out of his pores. Across the square was a tavern. He longed for a wash.

Inside the tavern the air was oddly chilly yet stuffy. The room was almost empty. Greck noticed that the man standing behind the bar looked first at his medals. The man's gaze was cool, not unfriendly, but cool. In the corner to the left sat a young couple with dirty dishes on the table in front of them and a carafe of wine, there was a beer bottle on the table too. Greck sat down in the corner to the right so he could look out on the street. He felt a sense of relief. His watch showed one o'clock, and he didn't have to be back until six. The man came out from behind the bar and walked slowly over to him. Greck wondered what he should drink. He really didn't want anything. Just a wash. He wasn't one for alcohol; besides, it didn't agree with him. Not for nothing had his mother warned him against it, just as she had against riding swingboats. Once again the innkeeper, now facing him, looked first at the left side of his chest.

"Afternoon," said the man. "What can I get you?"

"Some coffee," said Greck, "d'you have any coffee?" The man nodded. The nod said everything: it said that the glance to the left side of Greck's chest and the word "coffee" had told everything. "And a schnapps," said Greck. But it seemed to be too late.

"What kind?" asked the man.

"Apricot," said Greck.

The fellow went off. He was fat. His pants made fat rolls across his backside, and he was wearing slippers. Sloppy—like everything else here, thought Greck. He looked across at the young lovers. Swarms of flies were perched on the dirty plates with remains of food, chop bones, little mounds of vegetables, and wilted lettuce in earthenware bowls. Disgusting, thought Greck.

A soldier came in, looked nervously around, saluted Greck across the room, and walked over to the bar. The soldier had no medals at all. And yet there was a warmth in the innkeeper's eyes that annoyed Greck. Maybe, he thought, because I'm an officer they expect me to have more medals, splendid gold and silver affairs, these knuckleheads here in Hungary. Maybe I look as though I ought to be wearing medals: I'm tall and slim, blond. Hell, he thought, what a revolting business. He looked out the window.

The woman with the apricots was almost through now, and all of a sudden he knew what he really wanted to eat: some fruit. Oh, that would do him good! His mother had always given him plenty of fruit when it was in season and cheap, and it had done him a lot of good. Fruit was cheap here, and he had money, and wanted to eat some fruit. He hesitated at the thought of the money; his thoughts hesitated. Sweat broke out heavily again. Nothing would happen, and if something did: deny it, deny it, just deny everything. Nobody was going to believe some dirty Jew that he, Greck, had sold him his pants. Nobody would believe it if he denied it, and even if they identified the pants as his, he could say they had been stolen or something. But nobody was going to go to all that trouble. And anyway, why should they find out in his particular case? The affair had opened his eyes in a flash: everyone sold something, damn it all. Everyone. He knew now what happened to the gasoline that the tanks were short of, what became of the warm winter clothing—and they were his own pants, after all, that he had sold, the ones that had been made for him, at his own expense, at Grunk's, the tailor in Coelsde.

Where were all those pengös supposed to come from? Nobody's pay was enough for the kind of extravagances that cocky little lieutenant managed to afford, the one who shared his room and ate cream pastries in the afternoon and drank real whisky in the evening, had all the women he wanted, and turned up his nose at anything but a particular brand of cigarette that by this time cost a lot of money.

What the hell, he thought, I've been a fool, I've been a fool all along. Always respectable and law-abiding, while everyone else—everyone else has been having himself a good time. What the hell.

The innkeeper brought the coffee and the apricot schnapps. "Anything to eat?" he asked.

"No, thanks," said Greck.

The coffee smelled unfamiliar. He tried it: it was mild, with an odd mildness. Some quite pleasant substitute. The schnapps was sharp and burning but felt good. He sipped it slowly, drop by drop. That was it: he must take alcohol like medicine, that was it.

The apricot patch outside on the square had gone. Greck jumped up and ran to the door. "Just a minute," he called to the innkeeper.

The old woman was slowly driving her cart across the square; now she was level with the swingboats, and she speeded up her horse to a comfortable trot. Greck stopped her as she turned into the street. She pulled in the reins. He looked at her face: a broad-boned, elderly woman with handsome features, her face suntanned and sturdy. Greck went up to the cart.

"Fruit," he said, "give me some apricots, please." She looked at him with a smile. Somehow her smile had no warmth. Then she glanced at her baskets and asked, "Bag?" Greck shook his head. Her voice was warm and deep. He watched while she climbed around her seat onto the cart; her legs were surprisingly sturdy. Noticeably so. Greck's mouth watered at the sight of the fruit: it was magnificent. He thought of home. Apricots, he thought, those times when Mama had been able to get apricots! And here, here they got taken back from market. Cucumbers too. He took an apricot from the cart and ate it: it was tart yet at the same time sweet, already a shade too soft and warm, but he enjoyed it. "Very good," he said.

The woman smiled at him again. She took some loose pieces of paper and deftly made a kind of bag into which she very carefully laid the apricots. The way she looked at him struck him as odd. "Enough?" she asked. He nodded. She folded over the ends of paper, tucked them in, and handed him the package. He took his hundred-pengö bill out of his pocket. "Here," he said. Her eyes opened wide, and she said, "Oh, oh," then shook her head. But she took the bill, and for an instant she held on to his hand, clasping it up by the wrist although there was no need to, up by the wrist, for the merest second; then she took the bill, stuck it between her lips, and rummaged around under her skirt to pull out her purse. "No," cried Greck, "no, no, put it away." He looked anxiously around. That great red bill was horribly conspicuous. The street was busy, even a streetcar was passing. "Put it away," he cried, "put it away!" He tore it out of her mouth. She bit her lip, whether with anger or amusement he couldn't tell.

Furious, he dug out a second apricot, sank his teeth into it, and waited. The sweat was standing in thick beads on his forehead. He was having a hard time holding the apricots together in the loose bag. It

seemed to him that the old woman was deliberately taking her time—
he even considered running away, but she would probably set up a
terrible hue and cry and everyone would come running. The Hungarians were allies, not enemies. He sighed and waited. Across the street a
soldier emerged from the tavern, not the one who had just gone in. This
one had medals on his chest: three—as well as insignia on his sleeve. He
saluted Greck, and Greck nodded in response. Again a streetcar passed,
on the other side this time, people walked by, many people, and behind
him, behind that dilapidated board fence, the swingboat calliope softly
began to drone. The old woman smoothed out one bill after another
until it looked as though her purse held no more. Then came the coins.
Patiently she stacked up little nickel piles beside her on the seat. Then
she carefully took the bill from him and handed him first the bills, then
the nickel piles. "Ninety-eight," she said. He turned to go, but she suddenly laid her hand on his forearm: her hand was broad and warm and
quite dry, and her face came closer. "Girl?" she asked in a whisper, smiling at him. "Pretty girl, eh?"

"No, no," he said hastily, "thanks all the same."

She darted her hand under her skirt, drew out a scrap of paper,
and quickly passed it to him. "There," she said. "There." He added it
to the bills, she gave a flick to the reins, and he walked back across the
street carefully carrying his loose package.

The table in front of the young couple had still not been cleared. He
couldn't understand these people: flies clustered in hordes on the plates,
the rims of the glasses, and this young man was gesturing animatedly as
he spoke in a low insistent voice to the girl. The innkeeper came toward
Greck. "Can I have a wash?" asked Greck. The innkeeper stared at him.
"A wash," said Greck impatiently. "A wash, for God's sake." Infuriated
at the man's obtuseness, he rubbed his hands together. The innkeeper
gave a sudden nod, turned, and beckoned Greck to follow him.

Greck followed, paused to let the innkeeper hold back the dark-
green curtain for him—the fellow's expression seemed to have changed.
It looked as if he were asking something. They walked along a short narrow passage, and the innkeeper opened a door. "Here you are," he said.
Greck went in. The cleanliness of the washroom surprised him. The
washbasins were neatly cemented to the wall, the doors were painted
white. Beside the washbasin hung a towel. The innkeeper brought a

cake of green army soap. "Here you are," he repeated. Greck felt at a loss. The innkeeper left. Greck sniffed the towel, it seemed clean. Then he quickly removed his tunic, washed his neck and face all over, and ran water over his arms. He hesitated a moment, then put on his tunic again and slowly washed his hands. The soldier he had seen before came in, the one with no medals. Greck stepped aside so the soldier could get to the urinal. He buttoned his tunic, picked up the soap, and left. At the bar he gave the innkeeper the soap, said "Thanks," and sat down again.

The innkeeper's expression was stony. Greck wondered what was keeping the soldier. The young couple in the corner had gone. The table had still not been cleared, a jumble of dirty dishes. Greck drank the rest of his cold coffee and sipped the apricot schnapps. Then he began to eat his fruit.

He felt an insane craving for this juicy, fleshy stuff and ate six apricots in quick succession—and suddenly he felt nauseated: the apricots were too warm. He took another sip of schnapps; the schnapps was also too warm. The innkeeper stood behind the bar, smoking and somnolent. Another soldier came in. The innkeeper seemed to know him, and the two men whispered together. The soldier drank beer; he had one medal, the Cross of Merit. The soldier who had just been to the toilet came back, paid at the bar, and left. At the door he saluted. Greck returned the salute, and then the soldier who had just arrived went to the toilet. Outside, the swingboat calliope was droning away. The sound, wild yet sluggish, filled Greck with melancholy. He would never forget that ride. Too bad it had turned his stomach. Outside, things had begun to liven up a bit: across the square there was an ice-cream parlor, people were crowding in front of it. The tobacco shop next door to it was empty. The soiled green curtain in the corner was pushed aside, and out came a girl. At once the innkeeper's eyes went to Greck. The girl looked at him too. He could only just make her out; she seemed to be wearing a red dress, in that dense, greenish light the color looked nondescript, and the only thing he could see clearly was her heavily made-up face, very white, the mouth painted startlingly red. He could not see the expression on her face, he thought she was smiling a little, but he could be wrong; he could hardly see her. She was holding some money, holding the bill out straight, like a child, the way she would have held a flower or a stick.

The innkeeper gave her a bottle of wine and some cigarettes, without switching his gaze from Greck. He did not look at the girl at all, not a word passed between them.

Greck took the crumpled bills from his pocket and picked out the scrap of paper the old woman had given him. He placed it on the table and put the money back in his pocket. He was acutely conscious of the innkeeper's gaze and looked up. There was no doubt about it now, the girl was smiling at him; there she stood, holding the green bottle, her fingers curved around a few loose cigarettes, little white sticks that matched her face. All he was aware of in the darkness were her startling white face, the dark mouth, and the piercingly white cigarettes in her hand. She gave a brief smile, then moved aside the curtain and left.

The innkeeper was now gazing fixedly at Greck. His expression was stony, with something menacing about it. Greck was scared of him. That's how murderers look, he thought, and he would have welcomed the chance to leave quickly. Outside, the calliope was droning away, the streetcar squealed past, and sadness filled him, an alien and solemn sadness. The repulsive apricots, soft and warm, lay in front of him on the table, and flies were sticking to his cup. He did not wave them away. All at once he got up and called, "The bill, please," raising his voice to give himself courage. The innkeeper hurried over. Greck took some money from his pocket. He watched the flies now slowly gathering on the apricots, black sticky dots on that repulsive pink; the thought of having eaten them almost turned his stomach.

"Three pengös," said the innkeeper. Greck handed him the money. The innkeeper glanced at the schnapps glass, still half full, then at Greck's chest, at the scrap of paper lying on the table, and he picked it up at the very instant Greck reached for it. The innkeeper grinned, his big fat pale face looked repulsive. The innkeeper read the address on the paper: it was his own. He grinned, more hideously than ever. Sweat broke out over Greck's body again.

"Do you still need this paper?" asked the innkeeper.

"No," said Greck. "Good-bye." It occurred to him he had to say "Heil Hitler," and in the doorway he added "Heil Hitler!" The innkeeper did not respond. Turning round, Greck saw the man toss the remains of the schnapps onto the floor. The apricots shone warm and pink, like rose-pink wounds in a dark body... Greck was glad to be out on the street, and he hurried off. He was ashamed to go back to the hospital before his leave was up, the cocky little lieutenant would laugh at him. But what he really wanted was to go back right now and lie down on his bed. He felt like having a decent meal, but when he actually thought of food he remembered the apricots, repulsively pink, and his nausea increased. He thought of the woman he had gone to at noon, straight from the hospital. Her mechanical kisses on his neck suddenly hurt, and he knew why he had found the apricots so repulsive: they were the same color as her underwear, she had sweated a bit, and her body had been warm. It was a stupid idea to go to a woman in the middle of the day in this heat. But he had been following the advice of his father, who had told him he must be sure and have a woman at least once a month. This woman hadn't been bad, a sturdy little person who would probably have been delightful in the evening. She had taken the last of his money off him and known right away what he was up to as soon as she saw he was wearing two pairs of pants. She had laughed and given him the name of the Jewish tailor where he could sell them.

He slowed down. He felt sick to his stomach. He knew it: he should have had a proper meal. Now it was too late, he wouldn't be able to eat a thing. Everything disgusted him: the woman, the dirty Jew, even the swingboats, though that had been a novelty, but they disgusted him too, and the fruit, the innkeeper, the soldier—the lot. He had liked the girl. He had liked her very much. But it wouldn't do to have a woman twice in one day. She had looked very lovely, standing there in the dark in that green corner with her white face, but close up she was sure to be sweaty and smelly too. These girls probably couldn't help being sweaty, they didn't have the money to smell nice in the middle of the day in this heat.

He was passing a restaurant. Chairs stood on the street among tubs of stiff green plants. He sat down in a corner and ordered some soda water. "With ice," he called after the waiter. The waiter nodded. A couple at the next table were talking Rumanian.

Greck was now thirty-three and had been suffering from chronic indigestion ever since he was sixteen. Fortunately, his father was a doctor, not a good doctor but the only one in the small town, and they were reasonably well off. But his mother was thrifty. In the summer they used to go to health resorts, or south to the Alps, and often to the coast, and during the winter, when they stayed home, they ate poorly. The only time they ate well was when guests came, but they had few guests. In their small town the center for all social gatherings was the inn, and he was not allowed to go with his parents to the inn. When guests came, wine was served, but by the time he reached the age when he could have drunk wine, he was already suffering from chronic indigestion. They had always eaten a lot of potato salad. He didn't know exactly how often it had actually been, whether three or four times a week, but some days he had the feeling that as a boy he had eaten nothing but potato salad. A doctor once told him, years later, that his symptoms almost bordered on those of malnutrition, and that potato salad was poison to his system.

Word soon got around his hometown that he was sick, and indeed, you could see he was, and the girls more or less ignored him. His father wasn't that well off, not enough to compensate for his ill health. In school he didn't shine either. On finishing high school, in 1931, he was allowed to choose a graduation gift, and he chose a trip. He soon got off the train, in Hagen took a room in a hotel, and spent the evening feverishly roaming the town, but he couldn't find a prostitute in Hagen, and left the next day for Frankfurt, where he stayed a week. At the end of a week he had run out of money and took the train home. On the train he thought he would die. At home he was received with shocked surprise; he had had enough money for a three-week trip. His father looked at him, his mother wept, and there was a terrible scene with his old man, who forced him to take off his clothes and be examined. It was a Saturday afternoon, he had never forgotten it; outside, all was quiet in those clean streets, so medieval and idyllic, warm and deep, the bells rang for a long, long time, and he stood facing his father and had to submit to having his body tapped by the old man's fingers. In the surgery. He hated that fat face and the breath that always smelled slightly of beer, and he made up his mind to commit suicide. His father's hands kept tapping his body, that gray head of thick hair moving for a long time below his chest. "You're crazy," said his father on finally raising his head, and he grinned softly. "You're crazy. A woman once or twice a month is plenty for you." He knew his old man was right.

That evening he sat with Mama drinking weak tea. She didn't say a word, but all at once she began to cry. He laid aside the newspaper and went to his room.

Two weeks later he went to Marburg, to the university. He followed his father's advice to the letter, much as he hated him. After five years he graduated in law. In 1937 he did his first tour of military duty, in 1938 his second, and in 1939, after he'd spent two years in the district attorney's office, the war broke out, and he was sent to the front as a second lieutenant. He disliked the war. The war made new demands on him. It was no longer enough to be a qualified attorney, to have a good position with chances of promotion. Now they all looked at his chest when he came home. His chest was but meagerly decorated. In her letters Mama told him to take care of himself and at the same time made hints that felt like pinpricks.

"The Beckers' boy Hugo has been home on leave. He has the Iron Cross, First Class. Not bad for a boy who never got through high school, who couldn't even make it as a butcher's apprentice. I hear they're even going to make him an officer. Sounds incredible to me. Wesendonk has been badly wounded, they say he's going to lose his leg." Even that was something, to lose a leg.

He told the waiter to bring him some more soda water. The soda water made him feel better. It was ice-cold. He longed to be able to wipe out everything he had done, that silly business with the Jew, and that stupid idea of buying a bit of fruit on a busy street with a hundred-pengö bill. The thought of that scene made him sweat again. Suddenly he felt his stomach beginning to rebel. He kept his seat and looked around for the toilet. Everyone in the restaurant was sitting quietly chatting. Not a soul moved. He looked anxiously around until his eyes fell on a green curtain beside the counter; he got slowly to his feet and walked stiffly toward the green curtain. On the way he had to salute, a captain was sitting there with a woman; his salute was brief and smart, and he was glad to reach the green curtain.

By four o'clock he was already back at the hospital. The cocky little lieutenant was sitting there with his bags packed. He was wearing his black tank uniform, numerous decorations shone on his chest. Greck knew exactly which ones they were. There were five of them. The lieutenant was drinking wine and eating slices of bread and meat. He called to Greck as he entered, "Your barrack box has arrived."

"Good," said Greck. He walked over to his bed and dragged the box by the handle over to the window.

"By the way," said the lieutenant, "they had to leave your battalion commander behind at Szokarhely. Schmitz stayed with him. He wasn't fit to be moved, that captain of yours."

"Too bad," said Greck. He began to open his box.

"I'd leave it shut if I were you," said the lieutenant, "we have to move on, the lot of us, you too."

"Me too?"

"That's right," the lieutenant laughed, then his childlike face became solemn. "They're soon going to be organizing stomach commandos."

Greck could feel his stomach protesting again. He breathed heavily at the sight of the meat lying there right in front of his eyes in all its clarity. Those gritty specks of fat in the canned meat looked to him like fly eggs. He walked rapidly to the window to get some air. Outside, a cart was driving by loaded with apricots. Greck vomited—he felt an incredible sense of relief.

"*Bon appétit!*" cried the little lieutenant.

V

Feinhals had gone into town to buy pins, cardboard, and India ink, but all he had managed to get was the cardboard, deep-pink cardboard, the kind the sergeant major liked for making placards. On his way back from town, it started to rain. The rain was warm. Feinhals tried to push the thick roll under his tunic, but the roll was too long and too thick, and when he noticed the wrapping paper beginning to get wet at the edges and the pink of the cardboard coming through, he walked faster. At a street corner, he had to wait. Tanks were clumsily rounding the curve, slowly swinging first their gun barrels and then their rear ends as they continued on toward the southeast. People stood quietly watching the tanks. Feinhals walked on. The rain was coming down solidly now, dripping from the trees, and when he turned into the street leading to his clearing station, there were already large puddles on the black ground.

On the door hung the big white sign on which he had printed in pale-red pencil: "Hospital Clearing Station—Szentgyörgy." Soon a better sign would hang there, sturdy, deep pink, printed in script with India ink. Plain for all to see. At this hour there was no one about. Feinhals rang the bell, inside the porter pressed the switch for the latch; he nodded to the porter as he passed his little cubicle, and entered the corridor. In the corridor a machine pistol and a rifle were hanging on coat hooks. Beside each door was a little glass peephole with a thermometer hanging behind it. Everything was clean, and it was very peaceful, and Feinhals walked very quietly. Behind the first door he could hear the sergeant major on the telephone. In the corridor hung photographs of schoolmistresses and a large colored view of Szentgyörgy.

Feinhals turned to the right, went out through a door, and was in the schoolyard. The schoolyard was surrounded by big trees, and beyond its walls clustered tall buildings. Feinhals looked at a window on the fourth floor: the window was open. He walked quickly back into the building and up the stairs.

On the landings hung the photographs of former graduating classes. A whole row of big brown-and-gilt frames surrounding waist-length photos of girls: thick oval pieces of cardboard, each with a picture of a girl. The first frame showed the class of '18; 1918 seemed to have been the first graduating year. The girls were wearing stiff white blouses and smiling sadly. Feinhals had looked at them often, every day for almost a week. Surrounded by the girls' pictures was one of a very dark, severe-looking lady wearing pince-nez; she must be the headmistress. From 1918 to 1932 it was the same lady—in those fourteen years she did not seem to have changed. It was always the same photo; most likely she always took the same one to the photographer and had him stick it in the center. Feinhals paused in front of the class of '28. Here his eyes were drawn to a girl because of her figure: her name was Maria Kartök, she wore her hair in bangs low on her forehead, almost to her eyebrows, and her face was confident and pretty. Feinhals smiled. He had now reached the second landing and walked on up to the class of '32. He had also graduated in 1932. He looked at each girl in turn, they must have been nineteen at the time, his own age then, and now they were thirty-two: in this class there was another girl wearing bangs, only halfway down her forehead, and her face was confident and of a certain severe tenderness. Her name was Ilona Kartök and she was very like her sister, only she seemed slighter and less vain. The stiff blouse suited her well, and she was the only girl in the frame who was not smiling.

Feinhals stood there for a few seconds, smiled again, and continued slowly on up to the fourth floor. He was sweating but had no free hand to take off his cap, so he walked on.

At one end of the landing a statue of the Virgin Mary stood in a niche in the wall. It was made of plaster, a vase of fresh flowers had been placed in front of it; that morning there had been tulips in the vase, now there were yellow and red roses, tight, barely opened buds. Feinhals halted and looked along the corridor. Seen as a whole, that corridor full of girls' pictures looked monotonous: all those girls looked like butterflies, innumerable butterflies with slightly darker heads, preserved and collected in large frames. It seemed to be always the same ones, only the large, dark, center one changed from time to time. It changed in 1932, in 1940, and in 1944. Way up on the left, at the end of the third landing, hung the year of '44, girls in stiff white blouses, smiling and unhappy, and in the middle a dark elderly lady who was also smiling and also seemed unhappy. As he passed, Feinhals glanced at the year of '42; there was a Kartök in that one too, called Szorna, but there was nothing striking about her: she wore her hair like all the others, her face was round and touching. When he got to the top, to the corridor that was as silent as the rest of the house, he heard trucks driving up outside. He threw his stuff on the windowsill, opened a window, and looked out. The sergeant major was standing down on the street facing a column of trucks, their motors still running. Soldiers with bandages jumped down onto the road, and at the rear, from a large red furniture van, came a whole group of soldiers with their packs. The street quickly filled up. The sergeant major shouted, "Here—over here—everyone into the corridor—and wait there." A straggling gray procession moved slowly in through the doors. Across the street, windows were flung open, heads looked out, and people gathered at the corner.

Some of the women were crying.

Feinhals shut the window. The building was still quiet—the first sounds were just rising faintly from the corridor below; he walked slowly to the end of the corridor, where he kicked once at a door, and a woman's voice inside said, "Yes?" He felt himself blushing as he pressed down the latch with his elbow. He did not see her right away; the room was full of stuffed animals, wide shelves held rolled maps, and neatly galvanized glass-topped cases displaying rock specimens, and on the wall hung a colored print of embroidery samples and a numbered series of illustrations showing all the stages of infant care.

"Hello there," cried Feinhals.

"Yes?" she called. He went toward the window where a narrow aisle opened up between cabinets and map stands. She was sitting at a little table. Her face was rounder than downstairs in the picture, the severity seemed to have grown softer and the tenderness more pronounced. She was shy yet amused when he said "Good afternoon," and she nodded to him. He threw the big paper roll on the windowsill, then the parcel he had been carrying in his left hand, tossed his cap down beside them, and wiped the sweat off his face.

"I need your help, Ilona," he said. "I'd appreciate it if you could let me have some India ink."

She stood up, closing the book lying in front of her.

"India ink," she said. "India ink, I don't know what that is."

"I thought you were a teacher!"

She laughed.

"India ink," he said, "is a kind of drawing ink. Well, then—d'you know what a lettering pen is?"

"I can imagine," she said with a smile. "A pen for writing fancy lettering—yes, I know what that is."

"D'you think you could lend me one?"

"I believe so." She gestured toward the cupboard behind him, but he saw that she would never come out from the corner behind the table.

He had discovered her three days earlier in this room and had spent hours with her every day, but she had never come close: she seemed scared of him. She was very devout, very innocent and intelligent, he had already had long talks with her, and he could feel that she was drawn to him—but she had never come close, close enough for him to suddenly put his arms around her and kiss her. He had had long talks with her, hung around her for hours, and a few times they had discussed religion, but he would have liked to kiss her; only she never came close.

He frowned and shrugged his shoulders. "Just one word," he said hoarsely. "You've only to say one word, and I'll never come into your room again."

Her expression became serious. She lowered her lids, pursed her lips, looked up again: "I don't know," she said softly, "whether I'd like that—besides, it wouldn't make any difference, would it?"

"No," he said. She nodded.

He walked back to the aisle leading to the door and said, "I don't understand how anyone can become a teacher in a school they've gone to for nine years."

"Why not?" she said. "I always liked school, and I still do."

"Isn't there any school now?"

"Oh, yes—we've combined with another one."

"And it's your job to stay here and keep an eye on things, I know. Very smart of your headmistress to leave the prettiest teacher behind in the building," he saw her blush, "as well as the most reliable, I know..." He glanced around at the teaching aids. "D'you have a map of Europe in here?"

"Of course," she said.

"And some pins?" She looked at him in surprise and nodded.

"Be a nice girl," he said, "and let me have the map of Europe and a few pins." He unbuttoned his left pocket, fished out a small wax-paper envelope, and shook the contents carefully into his hand: little red cardboard flags; he picked one up and showed it to her. "Come on," he cried, "we're going to play General Staff, it's a great game." He saw her hesitate. "Come on," he cried, "I promise I won't touch you."

She came slowly out and walked over to the rack that held the maps. He looked down into the yard as she passed him, then turned around and helped her set up the stand she was dragging out from somewhere. She fastened in the map, undid the cord, and slowly cranked up the stand. He stood beside her holding the little red flags. "Good God," he muttered, "are we like animals, that all you girls are so scared of us?"

"Yes," she said in a low voice, looking at him; he could tell she was still scared. "Like wolves," she said, breathing hard. "Wolves that are liable to start talking about love any minute. Disturbing kind of people. Please," she said very softly, "don't do that."

"Don't do what?"

"Talk about love," she said very softly.

"Not for the present, I promise." He was peering at the map and did not notice the sidelong smile she gave him.

"The pins, please," he said without turning his head. He stood impatiently facing the map, staring at the brightly colored, irregular shapes, and passed his hand over them. The main front from East Prussia's eastern corner ran down almost dead straight as far as Nagyvárad, except in the middle, near Lvov, where there was a bulge, but no one had any exact information.

He glanced impatiently across at her; she was rummaging in the big drawer of a heavy walnut closet: towels, sheets, diapers, a large naked doll—then she hurried back, holding out a big tin full of pins. His fingers groped around in it, hastily picking out the ones with red or blue heads. She watched closely as he inserted the pins in the little cardboard flags and carefully stuck them into the map.

They looked at each other; outside in the corridor there was noise, doors banging, boots tramping, the voices of the sergeant major and soldiers.

"What's happening?" she asked in alarm.

"Nothing," he said calmly. "The first patients have arrived."

He planted a flag down at the bottom where there was a large dot—Nagyvárad—ran his hand gently across Yugoslavia, and carefully stuck a flag on Belgrade, then farther along on Rome, and was surprised to see how close Paris was to the German frontier. With his left hand resting on Paris, he slowly ran his right hand all the way across to Stalingrad. The distance between Stalingrad and Nagyvárad was greater than between Paris and Nagyvárad. He shrugged his shoulders and carefully stuck little flags in the spaces between the marked points.

"Oh," she cried—he turned to her, she looked tense, excited; her face seemed to have narrowed, it was smooth and brown, and on those pretty cheeks the down was visible almost up to her dark eyes. She still wore bangs, but shorter than downstairs in the picture. She was breathing hard. "Isn't it a great game?" he asked softly.

"Yes," she said, "terrible—it's all so—you say it—so—like a relief map."

"Three-dimensional, you mean," he said.

"That's it!" she cried. "It's all three-dimensional—it's like looking into a room."

The noise in the corridor had died down, the doors seemed to be closed, but Feinhals suddenly heard his name quite clearly. "Feinhals," shouted the sergeant major. "Where the hell are you?"

Ilona looked at him with raised eyebrows.

"Are they calling you?"

"Yes."

"You'd better go," she said in a low voice. "Please, I don't want them to find you here."

"How long will you be here?"

"Till seven."

"Wait for me—I'll be back."

She nodded, her cheeks fiery red, and stood facing him until he stepped aside to let her into her corner.

"There's some cake in that parcel on the windowsill," he said. "It's for you." He opened the door, looked out, and hurried into the corridor.

He walked slowly downstairs, although he could hear the sergeant major calling "Feinhals" on the third-floor corridor. He smiled at Szorna as he passed the class of '42, but the light was already fading and he could not make out Ilona's face; the big frame hung in the middle of the wall, and the shadows were closing in. And at the bottom of the stairs stood the sergeant major, who shouted, "For Christ's sake, where the hell have you been? I've been looking for you for an hour."

"I had to go into town, remember? I bought some cardboard for the placards."

"I know, I know, but you've been back half an hour. Let's go." He took Feinhals by the arm and walked down to the lower floor with him. The sound of singing came from the rooms, and the Russian nurses were hurrying along the corridor with trays.

The sergeant major had been very easy on Feinhals ever since the latter had returned from Szokarhely; he was easy on everyone and at the same time very much on edge since being given the job of organizing a hospital clearing station. The sergeant major was worried about things Feinhals could not know of. During the last few weeks something had happened in this army of which Feinhals could not be aware and the consequences of which he could not judge. But the sergeant major lived on these things, by them and them only, and the fact that they were no longer working worried him very much. Until recently, the possibility of a transfer or an unwelcome posting had been relatively remote; every order was circumvented before it even got to the unit. The authority that drew up the order was the first to circumvent it, and confidential phone calls informed the units to which the order was transmitted of the means of circumventing it—and as orders and regulations became more and more threatening, so the means of bypassing them became more and more simple, and in fact no one acted on them except to secure the removal of undesirable people. As a last resort: a medical examination or a phone call—and things went back to normal.

But all this had changed. Phone calls were no good now, because the people you had been used to talking to no longer existed, or existed someplace where they couldn't be reached—and the ones you did talk to now didn't know you and had no incentive to help you because they knew you in turn wouldn't be able to help them. The threads were confused or tangled, and the only thing left to do was to save your own skin from one day to the next. Until now the war had taken place over the telephone, but now the war had begun to dominate the telephone. Authorities, code names, superior officers changed every day, and it might happen that you were assigned to a division which the next day consisted only of a general, three staff officers, and a few clerks...

On reaching the bottom the sergeant major let go of Feinhals's arm and opened the door himself. Otten was sitting at the table smoking. The table had a distinct black scorch mark from a cigarette. Otten was reading a newspaper.

"Well, it's about time," he said, laying aside the paper.

The sergeant major looked at Feinhals, Feinhals looked at Otten.

"I can't do a thing about it," said the sergeant major with a shrug. "I have to transfer all those under forty who aren't on the permanent staff or who no longer qualify as patients. Honestly—I can't do a thing about it. You'll have to go."

"Where to?" asked Feinhals.

"To the redeployment center at the front—and what's more, 'forthwith,'" said Otten. He passed the marching orders to Feinhals. Feinhals read them through.

"'Forthwith,'" said Feinhals. "'Forthwith'—nothing sensible ever happened 'forthwith.'" The marching orders still in his hand, he said, "Do we both have to appear on the same marching orders—I mean, together...?"

The sergeant major gave him a close look. "What d'you mean? Now, don't go making a fool of yourself," he said in a low voice.

"What's the time?" asked Feinhals.

"Just on seven," said Otten. He stood up, he had already buckled on his belt and placed his pack on the table.

The sergeant major sat down at the table, pulled open the drawer, and looked at Otten. "Suit yourselves," he said. "Once you fellows are on your way, it's no longer up to me." He shrugged his shoulders.

"Okay, then, I'll make out one for each of you."

"I'll get my stuff," said Feinhals.

When he saw Ilona upstairs, he stopped in the corridor and watched her shut the door, then rattle the latch and nod. She had on her hat and coat and was carrying the parcel of cake. She was wearing a green coat and a brown beret, and he thought she looked even prettier than in her red sleeveless jacket. She was short, a shade too buxom maybe, but when he saw her face, the line of her neck, he felt something he had never felt before at the sight of a woman: he loved her and wanted to possess her. She gave the latch one more rattle, to make sure the door was really locked, and then walked slowly along the corridor. He watched her tensely and noticed that she smiled yet was startled to find him suddenly in front of her.

"I thought you were going to wait for me," he said.

"I'd forgotten I had to leave in a hurry. I was going to leave a message downstairs that I'd be back in an hour."

"Did you really mean to come back?"

"Yes," she said. She looked at him and smiled.

"I'll come with you," he said. "Wait for me. I'll only be a minute."

"You can't come with me. Don't." She shook her head wearily. "I promise I'll be back."

"Where are you going?"

She was silent, glanced around, but the corridor was empty; it was dinnertime, and subdued noises came from the rooms. Then she looked at him again. "To the ghetto," she said. "I have to go to the ghetto with my mother." She looked at him expectantly, but he merely asked, "What are you going to do there?"

"It's being evacuated today. Our relatives are there. We're taking some things to them. The cake too." She looked at the parcel she was carrying, and held it out to him. "You don't mind my giving it away, do you?"

"Your relatives," he said, taking her arm. "Come on—let's go." He walked down the stairs beside her, grasping her arm. "Your relatives are Jews? Your mother?"

She nodded. "And me," she said, "all of us." She stopped. "Just a moment." She freed her arm, took the flowers out of the vase in front of the Virgin Mary's statue, and carefully removed the faded ones. "Will you promise to put fresh water in the vase? I won't be here tomorrow. I have to be at school. Promise—and maybe some flowers too?"

"I can't. I have to leave tonight. Otherwise..."

"Otherwise you would?"

He nodded. "I'd do anything to please you."

"Only to please me?" she said.

He smiled. "I don't know—I'd do it anyway, I think, but it would never have occurred to me to do it. Just a minute!" he exclaimed.

They had reached the third-floor corridor. He ran along it to his room and quickly stuffed a few oddments into his bag. Then he put on his belt and ran out. She had walked slowly on ahead, and he caught up with her in front of the photos of the class of '32. She looked thoughtful.

"What is it?" he asked.

"Nothing," she said softly. "I would so much like to be sentimental—I can't. This picture doesn't move me, it means absolutely nothing to me. Let's go."

She promised to wait for him by the entrance, and he ran quickly into the office to pick up his marching orders. Otten had already left. The sergeant major grasped Feinhals by the sleeve. "Don't go making a fool of yourself," he said, "and good luck."

"Thanks," said Feinhals, and hurried out of the building.

She was waiting for him at the street corner. He took her arm and walked slowly beside her into town. It had stopped raining, but the air was still moist, with a sweet smell, and they walked along very quiet side streets that ran almost parallel to the main streets but were very quiet, past small houses with little low trees in front of them.

"How come you don't live in the ghetto?" he asked.

"Because of my father. He was an officer in the last war and got a lot of medals and lost both legs. But yesterday he sent his medals back to the garrison commander, and his artificial legs—a big brown-paper parcel. Please, let me go on alone now," she urged.

"Why?"

"I want to walk home alone."

"I'll go with you."

"It's no use. You'll be seen, someone from my family will see you," she looked at him, "and then they won't let me come anymore."

"You'll be back?"

"Yes," she said quietly. "For sure. I promise."

"Give me a kiss," he said.

She blushed and stood still. The street was empty and silent. Over the wall beside them hung branches of faded pink hawthorn.

"Why should we kiss?" she asked in a low voice; she looked at him sadly, and he was afraid she was going to cry. "I'm scared of love."

"Why?" he asked softly.

"Because there's no such thing—or only for a few moments."

"We won't have much more than a few moments," he said softly. He set his bag down on the ground, took the parcel from her, and put his arms around her. He kissed her on the neck, behind the ears, and felt her mouth on his cheek. "Don't go away," he whispered in her ear, "don't go away. It's not right to go away when there's a war on. Stay here." She shook her head. "I can't," she said, "my mother gets scared to death if I'm late." She kissed him once more on the cheek and was surprised to find she didn't mind—she liked it very much. "Here," she said. She turned his head as it rested against her shoulder and kissed him on the corner of the mouth. She now felt really glad that she would soon be with him again.

She kissed him once more on the corner of the mouth and looked at him for a moment. She used to think it must be wonderful to have a husband and children; she had always thought of both of them at the same time, but now she wasn't thinking of children—no, she hadn't been thinking of children when she kissed him and realized she would see him again soon. It made her sad, yet the thought pleased her. "There!" she whispered "I really must go..."

He looked over her shoulder along the street; it was empty and silent, and the noise from the next street seemed very remote. The little trees had been carefully pollarded. Ilona's hand was groping for his neck, and he could tell that this hand was very small, firm, and slender. "Stay here," he said, "or let me go with you. Never mind what happens. It won't work out—you don't know what war is—you don't know the people who make it. It's not right to separate even for a minute unless you have to."

"I have to," she said. "Try to understand."

"Then let me go with you."

"No, no," she pleaded. "I can't do that to my father, don't you understand?"

"I understand," he said, kissing her neck. "I understand everything, much too much. But I love you, and I want you to stay. Please stay."

She freed herself, looked at him, and said, "Don't ask me to. Please."

"I won't," he said softly. "Off you go. Where shall I wait?"

"Walk on a bit with me, I'll show you a little café where you can wait."

He tried to walk slowly, but she pulled him along, and he was surprised when they suddenly crossed a busy street. She pointed to a little narrow building, saying, "Wait there for me."

"Will you be back?"

"Yes," she said with a smile, "I promise—as soon as I can. I love you."

She threw her arms around his neck and kissed him on the mouth. Then she hurried off; he didn't want to watch her go so he walked toward the little café.

As he entered, he felt very miserable, very empty, as if he had missed something. He knew there was no point in waiting, yet at the same time he knew he had to wait. He must give God this chance of making everything turn out as it should, as it might have, although there was no doubt in his mind that everything had already turned out differently: she wouldn't be back. Something would happen to prevent her from coming back—perhaps it was asking too much to love a Jewish girl while this war was on and to hope she would come back. He didn't even know her address, and he must go through the motions of hope by waiting for her here, although he had no hope. He might have run after her, maybe, and forced her to stay—but you couldn't force people, you could only kill people, that was the only thing you could force on them. You couldn't force anyone to live, or to love, it was useless; the only thing that had any real power over them was death. And now he had to wait, although he knew it was useless. Moreover, he knew he would wait for longer than an hour, longer than tonight, because this was the only thing that linked them together: this little café her finger had pointed out, and the only certainty was that she had not lied. She would come, right away and very quickly, as quickly as she could, if she had the power to decide…

From the clock over the counter he saw it was twenty to eight. He didn't feel like anything to eat or drink so he ordered some soda water when the proprietress came over, and when he saw she was disappointed, he ordered a carafe of wine. Near the door sat a Hungarian soldier with his girl, and in the middle a fat fellow with a sallow face and a pitch-black cigar in his mouth. He quickly finished the carafe of wine so as to reassure the proprietress, and ordered another. The woman gave him a friendly smile; she was middle-aged, thin and blonde.

There were moments when he even thought she would come. Then he imagined where he would go with her: they would take a room somewhere, and before they went through the bedroom door he would tell her she was his wife. The room was dark, the bed in it old and brown and wide; there was a religious picture hanging on the wall, and a chest of drawers with a blue china basin containing lukewarm water, and the window looked out onto an orchard. That room existed, he knew it did, he had only to go into town and look for it and he would find it, that room, wherever it was he would find it, that very room, in a cheap hotel, in an inn, in a pension; that room existed, the room which for one moment had been destined to receive them tonight—but they would never enter that room. With painful clarity he saw the soiled rug beside the bed and the little window opening onto the orchard, the brown paint had peeled off the window frame; it was a lovely room with its big, brown, wide bed they had almost lain in together. But now that room would stay empty.

All the same, there were moments when he believed it wasn't decided yet. If she hadn't been Jewish—it was very hard to love a Jewish girl while this war was on, but he did love her, he loved her very much, enough to want to sleep with her and talk to her, for hours and very often and over and over again—and he knew there weren't many women you could sleep with and talk to for hours. With her it would have been possible—a lot of things would have been possible with her.

He ordered another carafe of wine. He had not yet opened the bottle of soda water. The fellow with the pitch-black cigar left, and now he was alone in the café with the middle-aged blonde proprietress, who had a skinny neck, and the Hungarian soldier with his girl. He drank some wine and tried to think of something else. He thought about his home, but he had hardly ever been there. Since leaving school he had hardly been home at all; besides, at home he was scared—the little town lay between railroad and river, in a great loop, as it were; the roads leading to it and through it were treeless, asphalted, and in summer there was only the musty, airless shade of the fruit trees. It didn't cool off even in the evening. He had usually gone home in the fall and helped with the harvest because he enjoyed that: those great orchards full of fruit, great trucks full, so many trucks full of pears and apples and plums being driven along the Rhine to the cities. Home was beautiful in the fall, and he got along well with his mother and dad, and it made no difference to him when his sister got married to some fruit grower or other—but home was beautiful in the fall. In winter the little place lay once again flat and deserted between river and railroad in the cold, and the heavy, cloying smell from the jam factory would drift in thick clouds across the plain and take your breath away. No, he was always glad to get away again. His job was building houses and schools, factories and apartment houses for a large firm, and army barracks...

But there was no point in trying to think about these things. Now he had to think of having forgotten to ask Ilona for her address—just in case. But he could get it from the building superintendent at the school, or from her headmistress, and there was no reason, after all, why he couldn't make inquiries, look for her, talk to her, perhaps go and see her. But all that belonged to those pointless things you had to do to give God a chance, you just had to do them, and sometimes it turned out that there was some point to them after all. The moment you admitted there might be some point to them, that they might come off—the moment you had to admit that, you were lost. And you had to keep on doing them. Search and wait—that was all there was to hope for, and that was terrible. He didn't know what they did with the Hungarian Jews. He had heard there had been a dispute over this between the Hungarian and German governments, but you could never tell what the Germans would do. And he had forgotten to ask Ilona for her address. The most important thing to do in wartime, exchange addresses, was the one thing they had forgotten, and for her it was still more important to have an address. But this was all pointless: she would never come back.

He preferred thinking about the room they would have shared together...

He saw it was close on nine: the hour had long since passed. The clock hand moved very slowly while you were looking at it, but as soon as you took your eyes off it, even for a moment, it seemed to jump. It was nine o'clock, and he had been waiting here for almost an hour and a half; he had to go on waiting, or he could hurry over to the school and ask the building superintendent for her address, and go there. He ordered another carafe of wine and saw that the proprietress was satisfied.

At five after nine the military police checked the café, an officer with a corporal, and at first they merely glanced inside and turned to leave—he saw them very distinctly because he had begun to stare at the door. There was something wonderful about staring at the door: the door was hope, but all he saw was this officer in his steel helmet and the corporal behind him, just looking in and then turning to leave, until the officer caught sight of him and walked slowly over to him. He knew the game was up: these people had the only effective means, they had death at their beck and call, death obeyed them instantly. And to be dead meant not to be able to do anything in this world anymore, and he still had plans for doing something in this world: he wanted to wait for Ilona, to look for her and to love her—even though he knew it was pointless, he wanted to, because there was just a chance it might work out. These men in their steel helmets held death in the palm of their hand, death was in their little pistols, their unsmiling faces, and even if these two men didn't want to call upon death, there were thousands standing behind them who were only too glad to give death a chance, with gallows and machine pistols—death was at their beck and call. The officer looked at him, said nothing, just held out his hand. The officer was tired, couldn't have cared less, really; he did his job mechanically, probably it bored him, but he did it, and he did it consistently and seriously. Feinhals handed over his paybook and marching

orders. The corporal made a sign to Feinhals to stand up. With a shrug
Feinhals stood up. He noticed that the proprietress was trembling and
the Hungarian soldier looked alarmed.

"Come along," said the officer quietly.

"I haven't paid yet," said Feinhals.

"Pay at the counter."

Feinhals buckled on his belt, picked up his bag, and walked
between the two men to the counter. The proprietress took the money,
and the corporal went ahead and opened the door. Feinhals went out.
He knew they couldn't do anything to him; still, he might have been
scared, yet he wasn't. Outside it was dark, lights were showing in stores
and restaurants, and everything looked very nice and summery. On the
street outside the café stood a large red furniture van: the door at the
back had been opened, part of it had been let down and rested on the
rough paving like a ramp. People were standing about on the street
and watching uneasily: in front of the opening stood a guard holding a
machine pistol.

"Get in," said the officer. Feinhals climbed up the ramp into the
van; in the darkness he saw a lot of heads, weapons—but no one inside
said a word. When he was all the way in, he noticed the van was full.

VI

The red furniture van drove slowly through the town; it was securely
locked, the padded doors bolted, and on its sides was painted in black
lettering GÖROS BROS., BUDAPEST. FORWARDING AGENTS. The
van did not stop again. Through the opening in the roof a man's head
looked out, carefully noting the surroundings, from time to time bending down apparently to call out something. The man saw lighted cafés,
ice-cream parlors, people in summer clothes, but suddenly his eye was
caught by a green furniture van that was trying vainly to overtake
them on the wide boulevard. The driver of the green van was a man in
army uniform, beside him sat a second man in army uniform holding a
machine pistol on his knees, but the opening in the roof of the green van
had been secured with barbed wire. The driver of the green van honked
impatiently behind the red van as the latter lumbered through the town.

Not until they reached a major intersection and the street widened and opened out could the green van overtake; it nipped quickly past, and the man looking out of the opening noticed that the green van turned into a wide street evidently going north whereas the red van drove south, almost due south. The face of the man in the opening grew more and more serious. He was short and slight, and his face had a wizened look, and when the red van had driven on a bit farther, he bent his head and shouted down into the van, "I'm pretty sure we're driving out of town, the houses aren't so close together now." From below came a muffled murmur in reply, and the red van was driving faster now, faster than one would have given it credit for. The road was empty and dark, and between the close branches of the trees the air hung moist and heavy and sweet, and the man in the roof opening bent down and shouted, "No more houses, highway now—going south."

The howls from below grew louder, but the van drove even faster. The man in the opening was tired, he had a long train trip behind him, and he was standing on the shoulders of two men of different heights, which made him even more tired, and he was ready to quit, but he was the shortest and slightest of the men in the van, and they had picked him to see what was going on outside.

Now came a long stretch where he saw nothing. A very long stretch, it seemed to him—and when the men down below pulled at his leg and wanted to know what was going on, he said nothing was going on, all he could see was the trees bordering the highway and the dark fields. Then he saw two soldiers with a motorcycle standing by the roadside, the soldiers were shining their flashlight back and forth across a map. They glanced up as the big furniture van passed. Then the man in the opening saw nothing again for a while, until they passed a stationary tank column. One tank seemed to have broken down, someone was lying on his stomach underneath it and someone else was shining a carbide lamp over it. Farmhouses slid past them very quickly, dark farmhouses, and a truck column overtook them on the left, driving very fast; soldiers were sitting on the trucks. From behind the trucks came a small gray car flying a commandant's pennant. The commandant's car was driving even faster than the trucks. Some soldiers, infantrymen, were sitting hunched up beside a barn; some were lying on the ground smoking. Next they went through a village, and shortly after the village

the man in the opening heard firing for the first time. It was a heavy
battery located to the right of the road; great barrels pointed steep and
black into the dark-blue sky. Bloody fire flashed from the gun muzzles,
casting a soft ruddy sheen on the wall of a barn. The man recoiled, he
had never heard firing before, and he was scared. He was a sick man,
a very sick man, with some chronic stomach ailment, his name was
Sergeant Finck, and he was the commissary at a big hospital near Linz,
on the Danube, and he had had misgivings ever since the head of the
hospital had sent him to Hungary to pick up some genuine Tokay wine,
Tokay and liqueurs and as much champagne as he could lay hands
on. Imagine going to Hungary for champagne. Still: he, Finck, was the
only man at the hospital who could be trusted to tell a genuine Tokay
from a phony one, and, after all, in Tokay there must be some genuine
Tokay wine. The old man, Colonel Ginzler, was very partial to
genuine Tokay, but it was probably mostly because of his drinking pal
and skat companion, that Colonel Bressen whom you involuntarily
called von Bressen because he looked so distinguished with his narrow unsmiling face and the unusual decoration around his neck. Finck
owned an inn back home, and he knew people, and he knew the old
man was just showing off, sending him off like that to pick up fifty
bottles of genuine Tokay—some bet or other which that colonel had
probably goaded him into.

Finck had been to Tokay, where he had picked up fifty bottles
of Tokay wine, and genuine at that, much to his surprise—he was an
innkeeper, an innkeeper in a wine town, he had his own vineyards too,
and he knew his wines. And he didn't trust the Tokay he had bought
as genuine in Tokay, a suitcase and a wicker basket full. He had managed to bring along the suitcase, it was down there in the van, but he
hadn't been able to bring the wicker basket. There had been no time
at Szentgyörgy, they had been herded straight from the train into the
furniture van; it had been no good protesting, saying he was ill, the
whole platform had been cordoned off, it was no good even trying, they
were marched straight into the furniture van parked outside the station.
Some of the men started to mutiny and shout, but the guards seemed
to be deaf and dumb.

Finck was nervous about his Tokay—the old man was touchy
about wine and even touchier about what he called his honor. He

was pretty certain to have given that colonel his word or some such thing that he would drink Tokay with him on Sunday. Most likely he had even named the hour. But now it was Thursday, probably Friday morning—it must be getting on for midnight at least—and now they were driving south, quite fast, and there wasn't the faintest chance of being able to deliver the wine on Sunday. Finck was scared, scared of the old man and scared of the colonel. He didn't like that colonel. He knew something about him that he never had and never could tell anyone, because no one would believe it, something disgusting that Finck wouldn't have thought possible. Finck had seen it for himself, quite distinctly—and he knew how important it was for him that the colonel shouldn't know he had seen it. He had to go along to the colonel's room several times a day, with something to eat or drink or some books. And the colonel was someone you handled with great care. One evening he had gone into the colonel's room without knocking, and there in the semidarkness he had seen it, that ghastly expression on the elderly white face—it took Finck's appetite away for the rest of that evening. When a young fellow was caught doing something like that back home they poured cold water over him right away, and it worked...

Down below, the men were pulling at his leg again, and he shouted down to them that he had seen cannon, cannon firing, and the yelling down below grew louder. The flashes from the gun muzzles they had driven past were fading away behind them, and the sound of the shells being fired, which at first had seemed horribly close, now seemed as far away as the sound of the shells landing, while the van was steadily approaching the area where the shells were landing. They drove past more tanks, stationary columns; then came more guns, these seemed to be smaller, they were standing next to a draw well, and the flames from their muzzles lit up the sinister gallows-outline of the well in sharp flashes. Again there was nothing for a while, until they passed some more columns, then nothing again—and then Finck heard the firing of machine guns. The van was heading straight for the area toward which the machine guns were firing.

And suddenly they stopped in a village. Finck clambered down inside and got out with the others. In the village all was confusion; there were trucks standing around all over the place, people yelling, soldiers running across the road, and the firing of the machine guns grew louder and louder. Feinhals walked behind the little sergeant who had been standing in the roof opening and was now carrying his heavy suitcase; he was so short and walked so doubled up that the butt of his rifle dragged along the ground. Feinhals fastened his bag to the carrying strap and took a stride forward to catch up with the little sergeant. "I'll give you a hand," he said. "What have you got in there anyway?"

"Wine," said the little man, gasping. "Wine for our hospital administrator."

"Leave it here, for God's sake," said Feinhals. "How can you lug a suitcase full of wine up to the front?"

The little man shook his head obstinately. He was so exhausted he could hardly walk, his knees were wobbling, and he shook his head sadly and nodded his thanks as Feinhals reached for the handle. The suitcase seemed fantastically heavy to Feinhals.

The machine gun on the right had stopped firing, the tanks were firing into the village now. From behind them came the crash of splitting timbers, and a gentle reflection from a fire threw a soft light over the muddy, rutted road.

"Throw the thing away, man," said Feinhals. "You must be out of your mind."

The sergeant did not answer; he seemed to grip the handle even tighter. Behind them another house started burning.

Suddenly the second lieutenant walking ahead of them halted and called out, "Get close to the house!" They ran right up to the wall of the house in front of which they had stopped. The little sergeant lurched against it and sat down on his suitcase. Now the machine gun on the left had also stopped firing. The officer went indoors and came out at once with a first lieutenant. Feinhals recognized him. They had to line up, and Feinhals knew the first lieutenant was trying to make out their decorations in the reddish twilight: on his own chest he now had one more, a proper one now, at least the ribbon for it, adorning his chest in black, white, and red. Thank God, thought Feinhals, he had that medal at least. The first lieutenant looked at them for a moment, smiling, then said, "Very nice," smiled again, and repeated, "Very nice, eh?" to the second lieutenant standing behind him. But the second lieutenant said nothing. They could see him distinctly now. He was short and pale, no longer very young, it seemed, and his face was grimy and unsmiling. He didn't have a single medal on his chest.

"Brecht," the first lieutenant told him, "take two men as reinforcement. And some bazookas. We'll send the others to Undolf—four, I guess. I'll keep the rest here."

"Two," said Brecht. "Yessir, two men, and some bazookas."

"Right," said the first lieutenant. "You know where to find those things?"

"Yessir."

"Report back in half an hour, please."

"Yessir," said the second lieutenant.

Feinhals and Finck were the first in line, and the second lieutenant tapped them on the chest, saying, "Come along," then turned on his heel and marched off. They had to hurry to keep up with him. The little sergeant snatched up his suitcase, Feinhals helped him, and they hurried off as fast as they could behind the little second lieutenant. Beyond the house they turned to the right into a narrow lane that seemed to lead out into the country between hedges and meadows. Ahead of them all was quiet, but behind them that tank was still firing regularly into the village, and the small battery, the last one they had driven past, was still firing to the right, roughly in the direction in which they were heading.

Feinhals suddenly dropped to the ground and shouted to the others, "Watch out!" There was a tinkle as they let go of the suitcase, and the second lieutenant up front also dropped to the ground. From up ahead, from the direction in which they had been marching, grenade launchers were firing into the village, they were firing in rapid succession now, there seemed to be a great many of them; splinters whizzed through the air, smacked against house walls, bigger fragments droned past them not far away.

"Get up," shouted the second lieutenant. "Carry on."

"Hold it!" cried Feinhals. He had heard that brittle clack again, a delicate, almost cheerful sound, and he was scared. There was a great crash as the grenade struck Finck's suitcase—the lid of the suitcase flew off with a fierce hiss and hit a tree twenty yards away, broken glass tore through the air like a swarm of demented birds, Feinhals could feel the wine splashing onto the back of his neck. He ducked in alarm: he hadn't heard these being fired, but there was an explosion ahead of them, on the field above a low earth bank. A haystack standing out black against the reddish background fell apart and started to smolder; it began to glow in the middle like tinder, then blazed up as it burst into flames.

The second lieutenant came crawling back down the hollow. "What the hell's going on here?" he whispered to Feinhals.

"He had wine in the suitcase," whispered Feinhals. "Hey there," he called softly across to Finck—a dark lump lying crouched beside the suitcase. Nothing stirred. "Hell," said the second lieutenant under his breath, "surely he's not..."

Feinhals crawled the two paces over to Finck, bumped his head against Finck's foot, propped himself up on his elbows, and pulled himself closer. The light from the burning haystack did not reach this hollow, it was dark in this shallow depression while the field at the side of the lane was already bathed in reddish light. "Hey there," said Feinhals quietly. He smelled the strong sweet fumes from a wine puddle, drew back his hands because he had thrust them into broken glass, and, beginning with the shoes, groped carefully up the man's legs, surprised to find how short this sergeant was; his legs were short, his body skinny. "Hey there," he called softly, "hey there, pal," but Finck did not answer. The second lieutenant had crawled over and said, "What's up?" Feinhals groped farther along until he touched blood—that wasn't wine— he drew back his hand and said quietly, "I think he's dead. A big wound in the back, soaked with blood; d'you have a flashlight?"

"Perhaps we could..."

"Or lift him up there onto the field..."

"Wine," said the second lieutenant, "a suitcase full of wine ... What did he want that for?"

"For a commissariat, I think."

Finck was not heavy. They carried him, walking doubled up, across the path, rolled him over the grass bank until he was lying flat, dark and flat in the light. His back was black with blood. Feinhals turned him over carefully—he saw the face for the first time; it was frail, very frail, thin, still slightly damp with sweat, the thick black hair clinging to the forehead.

"My God," said Feinhals.

"What is it?"

"He got one right in the chest. A splinter as big as your fist."

"In the chest?"

"That's right—he must have been kneeling over his suitcase."

"Contrary to regulations," said the second lieutenant, but his own joke seemed to turn sour on him. "Get his paybook and identity tag..."

Feinhals carefully unbuttoned the blood-soaked tunic, felt for the neck until his fingers closed on a bloodied piece of metal. He found the paybook right away too; it was in the left-hand breast pocket and seemed clean.

"Hell," the second lieutenant said behind him, "the suitcase is heavy—it still is." He had dragged it across the path and was also pulling Finck's rifle along by its strap. "Did you get the things?"

"Yes," said Feinhals.

"Let's get out of here." The second lieutenant dragged the suitcase along by one corner until the hollow came to an end and the ground was flat again, then he whispered to Feinhals, "Get behind that wall on the left," and crawled ahead. "Push the suitcase after me." Feinhals pushed the suitcase after him and crawled slowly up the little rise. Behind the wall, which ran at right angles to their path, they could stand upright, and now they looked at each other. The glow from the burning haystack was bright enough for them to see one another distinctly, and they stared at each other for a moment. "What's your name?" asked the officer.

"Feinhals."

"Mine's Brecht," said the second lieutenant. He smiled awkwardly. "I must admit I've got a hell of a thirst." He bent down over the suitcase, drew it onto the strip of thick grass, and carefully tipped out the contents. There was a gentle clinking and burbling. "Look at that," he said, picking up a small, undamaged bottle. "Tokay." The label was smeared with blood and wet with wine. Feinhals watched the officer carefully push aside the broken glass—five or six bottles seemed to be still intact. Brecht got out his pocketknife and opened one. He drank. "Marvelous," he said as he put down the bottle. "Want some?"

"Thanks," said Feinhals. He took the bottle and drank a mouthful; he found it too sweet, handed the bottle back, and repeated, "Thanks."

The grenade launchers were firing again into the village, farther away now, and suddenly a machine gun fired quite close in front of them. "Thank God," said Brecht. "I was beginning to think those had gone too."

He finished the bottle and let it roll down into the hollow. "We have to get past this wall on the left."

The haystack was in full blaze now, but at the very bottom only a glow was left. Sparks showered.

"You look pretty sensible," said the officer.

Feinhals was silent.

"What I mean is," said Brecht as he started to open the second bottle, "what I mean is, sensible enough to know that this war's a load of shit."

Feinhals was silent.

"By that I mean," went on Brecht, "that when you win a war it isn't a load of shit, and this war—so it seems to me—is a very, very bad war."

"Yes," said Feinhals. "It's a very, very bad war." The heavy firing of the machine gun at such close quarters was getting on his nerves.

"Where's the machine gun?" he asked quietly.

"Over there, where this wall comes to an end—it's a farm—we're in front of it now—the machine gun's behind it..."

The machine gun fired a few more short sharp rounds, then stopped. Next a Russian machine gun fired, then they heard rifle shots, and again the German and Russian machine guns fired together. And suddenly there was silence.

"Shit," said Brecht.

The haystack began to collapse, the flames were no longer beating so high, there was a gentle crackling, and darkness fell lower. The second lieutenant held out a bottle to Feinhals. Feinhals shook his head. "No, thanks, it's too sweet for me," he said.

"Have you been with the infantry long?" asked Brecht.

"Yes," said Feinhals, "four years."

"My God," said Brecht. "The stupid thing is that I don't know much about the infantry—practically speaking, that is, and I'd be a fool to say I did. I've had two years' training as a night fighter—just finished it—and my training cost the government a few nice single-family homes, all so that I can get blown to pieces in the infantry and lay down my life to get to Valhalla. What a load of shit, eh?" He took another drink. Feinhals was silent.

"What does one do, actually, when the enemy is superior?" the second lieutenant persevered. "Two days ago we were fifteen miles away, and we kept hearing we weren't going to budge. But we did budge. I know the rules too well. The rules say: The German soldier does not yield, he would rather be killed—something like that, but I'm not blind and I'm not deaf. I ask you," he said solemnly, "what do we do?"

"Clear out, I guess," said Feinhals.

"Great," said the second lieutenant. "Clear out. Great—clear out." He laughed softly. "There's something missing in our fine Prussian regulations: there's no provision for retreat in our training, that's why we have to be so smart when we do retreat. I believe our regulations are the only ones that say nothing about retreat, only 'delaying tactics,' and these jokers aren't going to let themselves be delayed any longer. Let's go," he said. He stuffed two bottles into his pockets. "Off to this lovely war again. My God," he added, "the poor bugger lugged that wine all the way here—the poor bugger..."

Feinhals followed slowly. As they turned the corner of the wall, they heard men running toward them. The footsteps were clearly audible, close now. The second lieutenant jumped back behind the wall, tucked his machine pistol under his arm, and whispered to Feinhals: "Here's your chance to earn eighteen pfennigs' worth of tin for your chest." But Feinhals noticed he was trembling. "Hell," whispered the second lieutenant, "this is serious, this is war."

The footsteps came closer, the men were no longer running.

"Don't worry," said Feinhals quietly, "those aren't Russians."

Brecht was silent.

"I wonder why they were running—and making all that racket..."

Brecht was silent.

"They're your men," said Feinhals. The footsteps sounded quite close now.

Although they could tell from the silhouettes that the men wearing steel helmets and rounding the corner were Germans, the second lieutenant called softly, "Halt, password." The men were startled; Feinhals saw them hesitate and flinch. "Shit," said one of them. "The password's shit."

"Tannenberg," said another voice.

"What the hell are you doing here?" said Brecht. "Get in behind that wall. One of you stand at the corner and listen."

Feinhals was surprised to see how many there were. He tried to count them in the dark, there seemed to be six or seven. They sat down

on the grassy strip. "That's wine," said the second lieutenant; he groped
for the bottles and passed them across. "Split it up between you."

"Prinz," he said, "Corporal Prinz, what's going on?"

Prinz was the one standing at the corner. Feinhals saw his medals
glinting in the dark as he turned.

"Lieutenant," said Prinz, "this is just nonsense. They've already
overtaken us left and right, and surely you're not trying to tell me that
here of all places, right next to this dirty farm, here of all places where
our machine gun happens to be standing, the front is supposed to be
held. Lieutenant, the front is several hundred miles wide and has been
slipping for quite a while now—and I don't believe these hundred and
fifty yards have been destined to produce a Knight's Cross—it's time we
cleared out; if we don't we'll be caught in the middle, and not a soul's
going to give a damn..."

"The front's got to be held somewhere. Are you all there?"

"Yes," said Prinz, "we're all here—and I don't think a front can be
held by convalescents and men just back from sick leave. Incidentally,
young Genzki's been wounded—he got a bullet through his arm. Genzki," he called softly, "where are you?"

A slight figure detached itself from the wall.

"All right," said the second lieutenant, "you can go back. Feinhals,
you go with him, the first-aid post is right where your bus stopped.
Report to the old man that I've moved the machine gun back thirty
yards—and bring some bazookas back with you. Send another man
along with them, Prinz."

"Wecke," said Prinz, "you go. Did you come with the furniture van
too?" he asked Feinhals.

"Yes."

"So did we."

"Go on," said the second lieutenant, "get a move on; hand in the
paybook to the old man..."

"Someone killed?" asked Prinz.

"Yes," said the second lieutenant impatiently. "Go on, get a move on."

Feinhals walked slowly to the village with the two men. Now several
tanks were firing into it from the south and east. Ahead of them, where the
main road entered the village to the left, they heard deafening explosions,
men yelling, and they stood still for a moment and exchanged glances.

"Great," said the short fellow with the wounded arm.

They hurried on, but when they emerged from the hollow a voice called, "Password?"

"Tannenberg," they growled.

"Brecht? Combat unit Brecht?"

"Yes," called Feinhals.

"Go back! Everyone back into the village; assemble on the main road!"

"Run back to the others," Wecke told Feinhals. "You go."

Feinhals ran down the hollow, up the other side, and called from halfway up, "Hey, Lieutenant Brecht!"

"What is it?"

"We've all got to go back—back to the village—and assemble on the main road."

They all walked slowly back together.

The red furniture van had almost filled up again. Feinhals slowly climbed the ramp, sat down just inside, leaned back, and tried to sleep. The deafening explosions seemed somewhat ridiculous to him now that he could hear it was German tanks trying to keep the road open. They were banging away much too much, there was altogether more banging in this war than necessary, but no doubt it was all part of this war. Everyone was in now except for a major handing out decorations and the few men to whom he was handing them. A corporal, a sergeant, and three privates were standing facing the little gray-haired major, who, his head bare, was hurriedly presenting the crosses and documents. From time to time he would call, "First Lieutenant Greck—First Lieutenant Greck!" Finally he shouted, "Brecht, where's Lieutenant Brecht?" From the depths of the van Brecht called, "Here, sir!" moved slowly forward, touched his hand to his cap, and, standing on the ramp, reported, "Second Lieutenant Brecht, Major."

"Where's your company commander?" asked the major. Although not furious, the major did look annoyed. The soldiers he had decorated walked slowly up the ramp and squeezed past Brecht into the van.

The major stood all by himself on the village street holding an Iron Cross First Class, and Brecht, his face expressing complete blankness, said, "No idea, Major. A few minutes ago Lieutenant Greck ordered me to lead the company to the assembly point, he had to," Brecht stopped and wavered, "Lieutenant Greck was suffering from severe indigestion..."

"Greck!" shouted the major in the direction of the village. "Greck!" He turned away, shaking his head, and said to Brecht: "Your company fought very well indeed—but we have to get out..."

A second German tank banged away from the street in front of them toward the right, and the small battery behind seemed to have veered round; it was firing in the same direction as the tanks. In the village many houses were burning now—and the church, which stood in the center of the village and was taller than any of the houses, was filled with a ruddy glow. The motor of the furniture van began to throb. The major stood irresolutely at the roadside and shouted to the van driver, "Get started."

Feinhals opened the paybook and read, "Finck, Gustav, sergeant; civilian occupation: innkeeper; place of residence: Heidesheim..."

Heidesheim, thought Feinhals, with a shock. Heidesheim was two miles from his home, and he knew the inn with the sign, painted brown, FINCK'S WINESHOP & HOTEL, ESTAB. 1710. He had often driven past but never gone in—then the door was slammed in his face, and the red furniture van drove off.

Again and again Greck tried to stand up and run to the end of the village where they were waiting for him, but he couldn't. As soon as he straightened himself, a griping pain like a corkscrew in his stomach forced him to double up, and he felt the urge to defecate—he was squatting beside the low wall surrounding the cesspool, his stool came in driblets, barely a tablespoonful at a time, while the pressure in his racked abdomen was enormous; he could not sit properly, the only bearable position was squatting, completely doubled up, and getting some slight relief when the stool left his bowels in small quantities—at such moments his hopes would rise, hopes that the cramps might be over, but they were only over for that moment. This griping pain was so paralyzing that he couldn't walk, he couldn't even have crawled slowly; the only way he could have propelled himself would have been to tip forward and drag himself painfully along by his hands, but even then he wouldn't have got there in time. It was another three hundred yards to the departure point, and now and again through the noise of the firing he would hear Major Krenz calling his name—but by this time he hardly cared: he had stomach cramps, intense, violent stomach cramps. He held on to the wall, his naked bottom shivering, and in his bowels that grinding pain would form and re-form, like some slowly accumulating explosive that surely must be devastating in effect but, when it did come, was always minimal, kept accumulating, kept promising to bring final release while never releasing more than a tiny morsel of stool...

Tears ran down his face; he no longer thought of anything connected with the war, although all around him shells were bursting and he could distinctly hear the trucks driving away from the village. Even the tanks withdrew onto the highway and moved off, firing, toward the town; he could hear it all, very graphically, and in his mind's eye he had a clear picture of the village being surrounded. But the pain in his stomach was bigger, closer, more important, monstrous. He thought about this pain that wouldn't let up, that paralyzed him—and in a frenzied, grinning procession, all the doctors he had ever consulted for his agonizing condition passed in front of him, headed by his repulsive father. They surrounded him, those useless creatures who had never had the guts to tell him straight out that his illness was due simply to constant malnutrition in his youth.

A shell landed in the cesspool, a wave splashed over him, soaking him with that disgusting liquid; he could taste it on his lips, and he sobbed more bitterly than ever, until he noticed that the farmhouse was in the tanks' direct line of fire. Shells were whining right past his ears, over his head, incredibly hard round balls that caused a great rush of air. Glass tinkled behind him, timbers shattered, and inside the house a woman screamed, chunks of plaster and splinters of wood flew all around him. He tipped forward, ducked behind the wall surrounding the cesspool, and carefully buttoned his pants. Although his bowels were still convulsively releasing tiny amounts of that terrible pain, he crawled slowly down the steep little stone path to get away from the immediate vicinity of the farmhouse. His pants were fastened, but he could crawl no farther, the pain was paralyzing him. He lay where he was, and for a few seconds his whole life spun round him—a kaleidoscope of unspeakably monotonous pain and humiliation. Only his tears seemed important and real to him as they flowed freely down his face into the muck, that muck he had tasted on his lips—straw, excrement, mud, and hay. He was still sobbing when a shell hit the center beam of a barn roof, and the great wooden structure with its bales of pressed straw collapsed and buried him.

VII

The green furniture van had an excellent engine. The two men up front in the cab, who took turns driving, did not talk much, but when they did, they spoke almost exclusively about the engine. "Isn't she a beaut," they would say from time to time, shaking their heads in amazement and listening spellbound to that powerful, dark, regular throbbing with never a false or disquieting note to it. The night was warm and dark, and the road, as they drove steadily northward, was sometimes choked with army vehicles or horse-drawn carts, and every now and again they had to jam on the brakes because they suddenly came face to face with marching columns and almost drove into that strange formless mass of dark figures whose faces were lit up by their headlights. The roads were narrow, too narrow to allow furniture vans, tanks, and marching columns to pass, but the farther north they drove the emptier became the road, and for a long time there was nothing to stop them driving the green van as fast as it would go; the cones of their headlights lit up trees and houses, sometimes, in a curve, shooting into a field and making the tall corn or tomato plants stand out sharp and clear. Finally the road became quite empty, the men were yawning now, and they stopped somewhere in a village on a side road for a rest; they opened their packs, gulped the hot, very strong coffee from their canteens, opened flat round cans of chocolate, and calmly made themselves sandwiches, opening their cans of butter, sniffing the contents, and spreading the butter thickly on the bread before covering it with slabs of sausage, the sausage red and ingrained with peppercorns. The men took their time over their meal. Their gray, tired faces revived, and one—the man now sitting on the left and the first to finish—lit a cigarette and drew a letter from his pocket; he unfolded it and took a snapshot out of the folds: it showed a charming little girl playing with a rabbit in a meadow. Holding the picture out to the man beside him, he said, "How d'you like that—cute, eh? My kid," he laughed, "a home-leave kid." The other man went on chewing as he answered, staring at the picture and mumbling, "Cute—home-leave kid, eh? How old is she?"

"Three."

"Haven't you got a picture of your wife?"

"Sure." The man on the left took out his wallet—but suddenly paused, saying, "Listen to that, they must have gone nuts." From the interior of the green van came a deep, angry mumbling and the shrill screams of a woman.

"Go and make them shut up," said the man behind the wheel.

The other man opened the cab door and looked out onto the village street. It was warm and dark outside, and the houses were unlit; there was a smell of manure, a very strong smell of cow dung, and in one of the houses a dog barked. The man got out, cursing under his breath at the deep soft mud of the village street, and walked slowly around the van. From outside, the mumbling was only faintly audible, more like a gentle buzzing inside a box, but now two dogs were barking in the village, then three, and suddenly a light went on in a window somewhere, and a man's silhouette became visible. The driver—his name was Schröder—couldn't be bothered to open the heavy padded doors at the rear, it didn't seem worth the effort, so he took his machine pistol and banged the steel butt a few times against the side of the van; there was silence at once. Then Schröder jumped up onto the tire to see if the barbed wire was still securely in place over the closed opening in the roof. The barbed wire was still securely in place.

He climbed back into the cab. Plorin had finished his meal; he was drinking coffee now and smoking, and the picture of the three-year-old girl with the rabbit was lying in front of him. "Cute kid all right," he said, raising his head for a moment. "You're not saying anything—don't you have a picture of your wife?"

"Sure." Schröder took out his wallet again, opened it, and removed a well-thumbed snapshot: it was of a woman, short, grown a little stout, wearing a fur coat. The woman was smiling inanely, her face was rather haggard and tired, and the black shoes with the heels that were much too high looked as though they hurt. Her thick hair, heavy and brownish, had been permed. "Good-looking girl," said Plorin. "Let's get going."

"Right," said Schröder, "start her up." He gave another glance outside; by this time a lot of dogs were barking in the village, and a lot of windows showed lights, and people were calling out to each other in the darkness.

"Let's go," he said, slamming the door. "Start her up."

Plorin turned the key in the ignition, the motor started at once; he let it idle for a few seconds, then pressed down the gas pedal, and the green furniture van maneuvered itself slowly onto the highway. "She's a beaut all right," said Plorin, "a real beaut."

The noise of the engine filled the whole cab, their ears were full of the steady hum, but after a short distance that deep murmur from the inside of the van became audible again. "Let's have a song," Plorin said to Schröder.

Schröder sang. He sang lustily, lifting up his voice, not very beautifully and not altogether accurately, but with real feeling. The emotional parts he sang with special fervor, and in some parts his voice was so emotional it sounded as if he were about to cry, but he did not cry. One song he seemed especially fond of was "Heidemarie," it was clearly his favorite. For a whole hour he sang at the top of his voice, and after an hour the two men changed places, and now Plorin sang.

"Good thing the old man can't hear us singing," said Plorin with a laugh. Schröder laughed too, and Plorin resumed his singing. He sang almost the same songs as Schröder, but he seemed to like "Gray Columns on the March" best, this was the one he sang most often; he sang it slowly, he sang it fast, and the especially moving parts, the ones stressing the misery and nobility of a hero's life, he sang very slowly and dramatically and sometimes several times in a row. Schröder, now at the wheel, stared fixedly at the road, driving the van at top speed, and softly whistled an accompaniment. They heard nothing more now from the inside of the green van.

It was getting chilly up front; they wrapped blankets around their legs, and from time to time, as they drove, they gulped coffee from their flasks. They had stopped singing, but inside the green van it was silent. Everything was silent, for that matter. Outside, everything was asleep; the highway was empty and wet—it must have been raining here—and the villages they drove through looked dead. They were caught briefly by the headlights in the darkness, a house or two, sometimes a church on the main road—for an instant they would leap up out of the darkness and then were left behind.

About four in the morning they stopped for a second breather. They were both tired by this time, their faces gray and drawn and grimy, and they hardly spoke; the hour's drive still ahead of them seemed endless. They made only a brief halt by the roadside, wiped their faces with schnapps, listlessly ate up their sandwiches, and swilled down the rest of the coffee. They finished the chocolate from their flat càns and lit cigarettes. Somewhat refreshed they drove on, and Schröder, now at the wheel again, whistled softly to himself, while Plorin, wrapped in a blanket, slept. Not a sound came from the inside of the green van.

A light rain started to fall, and dawn was breaking as they turned off the main road, wound their way through the narrow streets of a village out into the open country, and began driving slowly through a forest. Ground mist was rising, and when the van emerged from the forest there was a meadow, with army huts on it, then another little forest and a meadow, and the van stopped and impatiently sounded its horn in front of a big gate consisting of beams and barbed wire. The gate was flanked by a black-white-and-red sentrybox and a tall watchtower on which a man in a steel helmet was standing beside a machine gun. The gate was opened by the sentry, who grinned as he looked into the cab, and the green van drove slowly into the fenced enclosure.

The driver nudged his neighbor. "We're here," he said. They opened the cab doors and got out with their packs.

Birds were twittering in the forest; the sun came up in the east and shone on the green trees. Soft mist covered everything.

Schröder and Plorin walked wearily toward a hut behind the watch-tower. As they climbed the few steps to the door, they saw a whole column of trucks parked on the camp road ready to leave. It was quiet in the camp; nothing moved but the smoke that came pouring out of the crematorium chimney.

The SS lieutenant was sitting crouched over a table and had fallen asleep. As he woke up with a start, the two men gave him a tired grin, saying, "Here we are."

He got up, stretched, and said with a yawn, "That's good." He sleepily lit a cigarette, ran his fingers through his hair, put on a cap, straightened his belt, and glanced into the mirror as he flicked the grains of sleep from the corners of his eyes. "How many are there?" he asked.

"Sixty-seven," said Schröder, tossing a sheaf of papers onto the table.

"Is that the lot?"

"Yes—that's the lot," said Schröder. "What's new?"

"We're clearing out—tonight."

"Is that definite?"

"Yes—it's getting too hot around here."

"Where to?"

"Toward 'Greater Germany—Subdivision Austria'!" The SS lieutenant laughed. "Go and get some sleep," he said. "It's going to be another tough night; we're off tonight at seven sharp."

"And the camp?" asked Plorin.

The SS lieutenant took off his cap, carefully combed his hair, and with his right hand arranged his forelock. He was a handsome fellow, brown-haired and slim. He sighed.

"The camp," he said, "there's no more camp now—by tonight there'll be no more camp. It's empty."

"Empty?" asked Plorin; he had sat down and was slowly rubbing his sleeve along his machine pistol, which had got damp.

"Empty," repeated the SS lieutenant; he grinned faintly, shrugged his shoulders. "The camp's empty, I tell you—isn't that enough?"

"Have they been taken away?" asked Schröder, already at the door.

"Damn it all," said the SS lieutenant, "leave me alone, can't you? I said empty, not taken away—except for the choir." He grinned. "We all know the old man's crazy about his choir. Mark my words, he'll be taking that along again..."

"Hm," said each of the two men, and then again, "Hm..." And Schröder added, "The old man's completely nuts about his singing." All three laughed.

"Okay, then, we'll be off now," said Plorin. "I'll leave the van where it is, I'm all in."

"Never mind the van," said the SS lieutenant. "Willi can drive it away."

"Okay, then—we're off." The two drivers left.

The SS lieutenant nodded, walked to the window, and looked out at the green furniture van parked on the camp road, just where the waiting column began. The camp was quite silent. It was another hour before the green van was opened, when SS Captain Filskeit arrived at the camp. Filskeit had black hair, he was of medium height, and his pale and intelligent face radiated an aura of chastity. He was strict, a stickler for order, and would tolerate no deviation. His actions were governed solely by regulations. When the sentry saluted, he nodded, glanced at the green furniture van, and stepped into the guardroom. The SS lieutenant saluted.

"How many?" asked Filskeit.

"Sixty-seven, sir."

"Good," said Filskeit. "I'll expect them in an hour for choir practice." He nodded casually, left the guardroom, and walked across the camp ground. The camp was square, a quadrangle consisting of four times four huts with a small gap on the south side for the gate. At the corners were watchtowers. In the center were the cookhouse, the latrine hut; in one corner of the camp, next to the southeast watchtower, was the bath hut, and next to the bath hut, the crematorium. The camp was completely silent except for one of the sentries—the one on the northeast watchtower—who was singing something softly to himself; apart from that the silence was unbroken. Wispy blue smoke was rising from the cookhouse, and from the crematorium came dense black smoke, fortunately drifting south; the crematorium had been belching dense clouds of smoke for a long time. Filskeit gave a quick look around, nodded, and went to his office, which was next to the kitchen. He threw his cap on the table and nodded in satisfaction: everything was in order. He might have smiled at the thought, but Filskeit never smiled. To him life was very serious, his army career even more so, but the most serious thing of all was art.

SS Captain Filskeit loved art, music. Some people found his pale, intelligent face handsome, but the angular, oversize chin dragged down the finer part of his face and gave his intelligent features an expression of brutality that was as shocking as it was surprising.

Filskeit had once studied music, but he loved music too much to be able to summon that grain of realism that the professional must have, so he went to work for a bank and remained a passionate amateur of music. His hobby was choral singing.

He was a hardworking and ambitious individual, very reliable, and he soon advanced to the post of department head in the bank. But his real passion was music, choral singing. At first all-male choirs.

At one time, in the distant past, he had been choirmaster of the Concordia Choral Society, he had been twenty-eight, but that was fifteen years ago—and, although a layman, he had been elected choirmaster. It would have been impossible to find a professional musician who would have furthered the society's aims more passionately or more meticulously. It was fascinating to watch his pale, faintly twitching face and his slender hands as he conducted. The members were afraid of him because he was so meticulous, no wrong note escaped his hearing, he flew into a rage whenever someone was guilty of sloppiness, and there had come a time when these decent, worthy singers had enough of his strictness, his tireless energy, and chose another choirmaster. At the same time he had been conductor of the church choir in his parish, although the liturgy did not appeal to him. But in those days he had seized every opportunity of getting his hands on a choir. The parish priest was popularly known as "the saint," a gentle, rather foolish man who could sometimes look very severe: white-haired and old, he knew nothing about music. But he invariably attended choir practice, and sometimes he would smile gently, and Filskeit hated that smile: it was the smile of love, a compassionate, poignant love. And sometimes the priest's face would take on a look of severity, and Filskeit could feel his aversion to the liturgy mounting simultaneously with his hatred of that smile. That smile of "the saint" seemed to say: Futile—futile—but I love you. He did not want to be loved, and his hatred of those anthems and that priest's smile steadily increased, and when the Concordia dismissed him, he left the church choir. He would often think of that smile, that elusive severity, and that "Jewish" look of love, as he called it, which seemed to him both down-to-earth and loving, and his breast was devoured by hate and torment...

His successor was a schoolteacher who enjoyed his beer and a good cigar and liked listening to dirty stories. Filskeit had loathed all these things: he neither smoked nor drank, and he was not interested in women.

Not long after, attracted by the idea of racism, corresponding as it did to his secret ideals, he joined the Hitler Youth, where he rapidly advanced to the position of regional choirmaster, organized choirs, including "speaking choirs," and discovered his real love: mixed choral singing. At home—he had an austerely furnished barrack-like room in a Düsseldorf suburb—he devoted his time to choral literature and to every work on racism that he could get hold of. The result of this long and intensive study was an article of his own, which he entitled "The Interrelationship of Choir and Race." He submitted it to a state music academy which returned it to him with the addition of some sarcastic marginal notes. It was not until later that Filskeit found out that the head of this academy was a Jew called Neumann.

In 1933 he gave up banking for good in order to devote himself entirely to his musical assignments within the Party. His article was approved by a music school and, after some condensing, printed in a professional journal. He held the rank of unit leader in the Hitler Youth but his duties also embraced the SA and the SS, his specialty being speaking choirs, male choirs, and mixed choral singing. His qualities of leadership were undisputed. When war broke out he resisted being classified as indispensable, applied several times for admission to the SS Death's Head units, and was rejected twice because he had black hair, was too short, and patently belonged to the stocky, "pyknic" type. No one knew that he often stood for hours in despair in front of the mirror at home and saw what it was impossible not to see: he was not a member of that race which he so ardently admired and to which Lohengrin had belonged.

But the third time he applied, the Death's Head units accepted him because of the excellent references he submitted from all the Party organizations.

During the early war years he suffered greatly as a result of his musical reputation: instead of being sent to the front, he was assigned to training courses, later becoming a course director and then a director of a course for course directors; he directed the choral training of whole SS armies, and one of his supreme achievements was a choir of legionaries which, while representing thirteen different countries and eighteen different languages, sang a chorus from *Tannhäuser* in perfect vocal harmony. Later he was awarded the Cross of Merit First Class, one of the rarest military decorations; but not until he volunteered for the twentieth time for military service was he assigned to a military training course and finally got to the front: in 1943 he was given a small concentration camp in Germany, and at last, in 1944, was made commandant of a ghetto in Hungary. Later, when that ghetto had to be evacuated because the Russians were getting close, he was given this little camp in the north.

It was a matter of pride with him to carry out all orders to the letter. He had quickly discovered the enormous latent fund of musical talent among the prisoners—he was surprised to find this among Jews—and he applied the selective principle by ordering each new arrival to undergo a singing test and by recording each one's vocal capacity on an index card, with marks ranging from zero to ten. Very few were given ten—those were assigned immediately to the camp choir—and those who got zero had little prospect of remaining alive for more than two days. When required to supply batches of prisoners for removal, he chose them in such a way as to retain a nucleus of good male and female voices so that his choir always remained complete. This choir, which he conducted with a strictness harking back to the days of the Concordia Choral Society, was his pride and joy. With this choir he could have beaten any competition, but unfortunately the only audience it ever had were the dying prisoners and the guard personnel.

But orders were even more sacred to him than music, and he had recently received a number of orders that had weakened his choir: the ghettos and camps in Hungary were being evacuated, and because the large camps to which he had formerly sent Jews no longer existed, and his small camp had no railroad connection, he had to kill them all in his camp. But even now there were still sufficient work parties—for cookhouse and crematorium and bath hut—to preserve at least the very best of the voices.

Filskeit did not like killing. He had never killed anyone himself, and that was one of his frustrations: he was incapable of it. He realized that it was necessary, and admired the orders, which he saw were strictly carried out; the important thing, after all, was not whether one liked carrying out orders but to realize their necessity, to respect them, and to see that they were carried out...

Filskeit went to the window and looked out. Two trucks had driven up behind the green furniture van, the drivers had just got down and were walking wearily up the steps to the guardroom.

SS Lieutenant Blauert came through the gate with five men and opened the big heavy padded doors of the furniture van. The people inside screamed—the daylight hurt their eyes—their screams were long and piercing, and the ones who jumped down staggered to where Blauert pointed.

The first was a dark-haired young woman wearing a green coat; she was dirty, and her dress seemed to be torn; she was anxiously trying to keep her coat closed with her hands, and a girl of twelve or thirteen was clinging to her arm. Neither had any baggage.

The people who staggered out of the van lined up on the assembly square, and Filskeit counted them under his breath as he watched the roll call proceed: there were sixty-one men, women, and children, varying greatly in dress, behavior, and age. Nothing more emerged from the green van—six had apparently died. The green van moved slowly off and halted by the crematorium. Filskeit nodded in satisfaction: six corpses were unloaded and hauled off into the building.

The baggage of the van's occupants was stacked up in front of the guardroom. The two trucks were also unloaded. Filskeit counted the rows of five as they slowly filled up: twenty-nine rows of five. SS Lieutenant Blauert shouted through the megaphone, "Attention, everyone! You are at present in a transit camp. You will not remain here long. You will proceed one by one to the prisoners' registration section, then to the office of the camp commandant, to whom you will submit for a personal test. This will be followed by a bath and delousing, after which there will be hot coffee for all. Anyone offering the slightest resistance will be instantly shot." He pointed to the watchtowers, whose machine guns had now been swiveled round to aim at the assembly square, and to the five men standing behind him with cocked machine pistols.

Filskeit paced impatiently up and down behind his window. He had noticed a few fair-haired Jews. There were many fair-haired Jews in Hungary. He liked them even less than the dark ones, although there were specimens among them that might have embellished any illustrated work on the Nordic race.

He watched the first woman, the one in the green coat and the torn dress, enter the registration hut, and he sat down, placing his cocked pistol beside him on the table. In a few minutes she would be here to sing for him.

For ten hours Ilona had been waiting for fear. But fear did not come. In these ten hours she had had to experience and submit to many things: disgust and horror, hunger and thirst, gasping for air, despair when the light struck her, and a strangely cool kind of happiness when, for minutes or quarters of an hour, she managed to be alone—but she had waited in vain for fear. Fear did not come. This world in which she had been living for ten hours was spectral, as spectral as reality—as spectral as the things she had heard about. But hearing about them had frightened her more than now finding herself in the midst of them. She had very few desires left: one of these desires was to be alone so that she could really pray.

She had pictured her life quite differently. Up to now its course had been orderly, satisfying, according to plan, pretty well exactly as she had pictured it—even when her plans had turned out to be mistaken—but this was something she had not expected. She had counted on being spared this.

If all went well, she would be dead in half an hour. She was lucky, she was the first. She knew very well what kind of bath huts those were that that creature had spoken of, she knew she had to face ten minutes of death throes, but even this, because it still seemed so remote, did not frighten her. In the van, too, she had had to endure many things that touched her personally but did not penetrate. Someone had tried to rape her, a fellow whose sexual craving she had smelled in the dark and whom she now tried in vain to identify. Someone else had shielded her from him, an elderly man who had whispered to her later that he had been arrested because of a pair of pants, because of one pair of pants that he had bought from an officer; but now she couldn't recognize that man either. The other fellow had felt for her breasts in the dark, torn her dress, and kissed the nape of her neck—but luckily the other man had come between them. Even the cake had been knocked out of her hand, the little parcel, the only thing she had taken with her—it had fallen to the floor, and in the dark, groping around on the floor, she had managed to get hold of only a few broken pieces ingrained with grit and icing. She had eaten them with Maria—some of the cake had been squashed in her coat pocket—but hours later, when she drew small sticky lumps out of her pocket, they tasted wonderful; she gave some to the child and ate some herself, and it tasted wonderful, this squashed gritty cake which she scraped to the last crumb from her pocket. Some people had committed suicide, they bled to death almost without a sound, emitting odd gasps and groans in the corner, until those next to them slipped in the flowing blood and screamed hysterically. But they stopped screaming when the guard banged on the side of the van. It had sounded ominous and terrible, that banging, it couldn't have been done by a human being, they had long ceased to be among human beings...

She was also waiting in vain for remorse; it had been senseless to leave that soldier, whom she liked very much, whose name she did not even know, absolutely senseless. Her parents' apartment was already empty; the only person she found there was her sister's confused and terrified child, young Maria, who had come home from school and found the apartment empty. Her parents and grandparents had already gone—neighbors told her they had been picked up at midday. And it had been senseless for her and Maria to run to the ghetto to look for her parents and grandparents: as always, they reached the ghetto by way of the back room of a hairdresser's and ran through the empty streets, arriving just in time to be shoved into that furniture van which had been standing there, waiting to leave, and in which they hoped to find their relatives. They found neither parents nor grandparents; they were not in that van. Ilona was amazed that none of the neighbors had thought of hurrying over to the school to warn her, but even Maria had not thought of it. Still, it would probably have made no difference if someone had warned her... In the van someone had stuck a lighted cigarette between her lips, later she found out it had been the man who was picked up because of the pants. It was the first cigarette she had ever smoked, and she found it very refreshing and very soothing. She did not know her benefactor's name, none of them revealed their identity, neither that panting, lecherous fellow nor her benefactor, and when a match flared up all the faces looked alike: terrible faces full of fear and hatred.

But there had also been long stretches when she could pray. At the convent she had learned by heart all the prayers, all the litanies, and long sections of the liturgy for high holidays, and she was glad now that she knew them. Praying filled her with a cool serenity. She did not pray to be given something, or to be spared something, not for a quick painless death or for her life; she simply prayed, and she was glad when she could lean against the padded rear door and that at least her back was alone. At first she had stood the other way around, with her back to the press of bodies, and when she became tired and started to droop, tipping over backward, her body must have aroused that raging lust in the man she fell against, a lust that frightened but did not offend her—almost the opposite, she had a feeling of being somehow part of him, of this stranger...

She was glad to be standing free, at least with her back alone
against the padding intended for the protection of good furniture. She
held Maria close to her body and was glad the child was asleep. She
tried to pray as devoutly as she always did but found she couldn't; all
she could manage was a cool rational meditation. She had pictured
her life quite differently: she had passed her teacher-training finals at
twenty-three, then she had entered the convent—her relatives were
disappointed but approved her decision. She had spent a whole year
at the convent, it had been a very happy time, and if she had actually become a nun, she would now be a teaching sister in Argentina,
in some very beautiful convent no doubt; but she had not become a
nun, because the desire to marry and have children was so strong in
her that even after a year it had not been subdued—and she had gone
back into the world. She became a very successful teacher, and she
enjoyed it; she loved her two subjects, German and Music, and was
fond of the children, she could hardly imagine anything more beautiful than a children's choir. She was very successful with the children's
choir she organized at school, and the choral works sung by the children, those Latin choral works which they rehearsed for feast days, had
a truly angelic neutrality—it was a free and inward joy from which
the children sang, sang words they did not understand and which
were beautiful. Life seemed beautiful to her—for long periods, almost
always. What troubled her was this desire for tenderness and children,
it troubled her because she found nobody; there were many men who
became interested in her, some even confessed their love, and she let
some of them kiss her, but she was waiting for something she could
not have described, she did not call it love—there were many kinds
of love—she would have preferred to call it surprise, and she had
believed she was experiencing this sense of surprise when the soldier
whose name she did not know stood beside her facing the map and stuck
in the little flags. She knew he was in love with her. The last two days he
had been spending hours chatting with her, and she found him very nice,
although his uniform worried and alarmed her a little, but suddenly, in
those few minutes while she stood next to him and he seemed to have
forgotten her, his grave, poignant face, and his hands as they explored
the map of Europe, had surprised her, she had a sense of joy and could
have sung. He was the first man whose kiss she had ever returned...

She walked slowly up the steps to the hut, pulling Maria along; she glanced up astonished when the guard jabbed the muzzle of his machine pistol into her side and shouted, "Faster—faster." She walked faster. Inside sat three clerks at tables; big stacks of index cards lay in front of them, the cards as big as cigar-box lids. She was pushed toward the first table, Maria toward the second, and toward the third table came an old man, in rags and unshaven, who gave her a fleeting smile. She smiled back; that must be her benefactor.

She gave her name, her occupation, her date of birth, and her religion, and was surprised when the clerk asked her age. "Twenty-three," she said.

Another half hour, she thought. Maybe she would still have a chance to be alone for a bit after all. She was astonished at the casual atmosphere in this place given over to the administration of death. Everything was done mechanically, somewhat irritably, impatiently: these people were doing their job with the same lack of enthusiasm they would have brought to any other clerical work, they were merely doing their duty, a duty which they found tiresome but did anyway. No one did anything to her; she was still waiting for fear, the fear she had been dreading. She had been very scared when she left the convent, very scared as she walked to the streetcar carrying her suitcase, clasping her money in her moist fingers. The world had seemed alien and ugly, this world to which she had longed to return so as to have a husband and children—a series of joys which she could not find in the convent and which now, walking to the streetcar, she no longer hoped to find; but she was very ashamed, ashamed of this fear...

As she walked over to the second hut, she scanned the rows of waiting people for familiar faces but found none. She went up the steps; when she hesitated at the door, the guard waved her impatiently inside, and she went in, pulling Maria along: that seemed to be the wrong thing to do, and she had her second encounter with brutality when the guard wrenched the child from her and, when the child struggled, pulled her by the hair. She heard Maria scream, and walked into the room holding her registration card. There was only one man in the room, and he was in the uniform of an officer; he was wearing a very impressive, narrow silver decoration in the shape of a cross on his chest. His face looked pale and haggard, and when he raised his head to look at her, she was shocked at his massive chin, which almost disfigured him. He mutely held out his hand, she gave him the card and waited. Still no fear. The man read the card, looked at her, and said quietly, "Sing something."

She hesitated. "Go on," he said impatiently, "sing something— never mind what..."

She looked at him and opened her mouth. She sang the All Saints' Litany in a version which she had recently discovered and set aside to practice with the children. While she sang, she watched the man very intently, and suddenly she knew what fear was when he stood up and looked at her.

She continued to sing while the face in front of her became contorted like some horrible growth in a state of convulsion. She sang beautifully, and she did not know she was smiling, despite the slowly mounting fear now caught in her throat and waiting to be spewed out ...

As soon as she started to sing, silence fell, outside as well. Filskeit stared at her. She was beautiful—a woman—he had never had a woman—his life had been spent in stifling chastity—much of it, when he was alone, in front of the mirror, in which he vainly sought beauty and nobility and racial perfection—here it was, beauty and nobility and racial perfection, combined with something that completely paralyzed him: faith. He did not realize he was letting her sing on, even beyond the antiphony—perhaps he was dreaming—and in her gaze, although he saw she was trembling—in her gaze was something almost like love—or was it scorn—*"Fili, Redemptor mundi, Deus,"* she sang—he had never heard a woman sing like that.

"Spiritus Sancte, Deus"—her voice was powerful, warm, and of incredible clarity. He must be dreaming—now she would sing: *Sancta Trinitas, unus Deus*—he still remembered it—and she sang it:

"Sancta Trinitas"—Catholic Jews? he thought—I must be going mad. He ran to the window and flung it open: outside they were all standing there, listening, not a soul moved. Filskeit could feel himself twitching, he tried to shout, but from his throat came only a hoarse toneless rasp, and from outside came that breathless hush while the woman went on singing:

"Sancta Dei Genitrix"... With trembling fingers he picked up his pistol, turned around, and fired blindly at the woman, who slumped to

the floor and began to scream. Now he had found his voice again, once hers had stopped singing. "Wipe them out!" he screamed. "Wipe out the whole damn lot—and the choir too—bring out the choir—bring it outside—" He emptied the entire magazine into the woman, who was lying on the floor and in her agony spewing out her fear...

Outside, the slaughter began.

VIII

The widow Suchan had been watching the war for the past three years. It had all begun with the arrival of German soldiers and army vehicles, and cavalry; they had crossed the bridge that dusty autumn and headed toward the passes leading over to the Polish side. It had had the genuine look of war, grimy soldiers, weary officers and horses, motorcycles chasing back and forth, a whole afternoon of war, with a few intermissions: a fine spectacle, you might say. The soldiers had marched across the bridge, with the trucks driving up ahead and motorcycles fore and aft, and the widow Suchan had never seen them again.

After that things had quieted down a bit, except for a German army truck turning up now and again; it would drive across the bridge and disappear into the forest, and she could hear the sound of its engine for a long time in the silence as it drove up the mountain on the other side, laboriously wheezing, groaning, with a few intermissions—for a long time—until it had evidently disappeared over the ridge. She pictured the trucks driving past her native village, where she had spent her childhood, the summers on the pastures and the winters at the spinning wheel—very high up, all by herself in summertime on those barren stony meadows. She had often leaned over the ridge for hours to see if anything was moving up or down the road. But in those days there were no cars here yet; occasionally there would be a cart, usually it was Gypsies or Jews going across to the Polish side. It was not until much later, long after she had left, that the railroad had been built crossing the bridge near Szarny and running along the very same valley she used to look down on from those upland pastures. She had not been up there for a long time, almost ten years, and she listened for the trucks as long as she could—and she could still hear them even after they had vanished over the ridge and were driving along the mountain road, and maybe now it was her nephew's boys who were looking down at the German army vehicles toiling along.

But they did not come often. The truck came regularly every two months, and between times there were not many vehicles—occasionally one carrying soldiers who stopped in for a beer before having to drive up into the mountains, and in the evening it would come down carrying the other soldiers who stopped in for a beer before driving down into the plain. But there were not many soldiers up there; the truck came only three times altogether, for, six months after the war had passed by her on its way into the mountains, the bridge leading behind her house across the river was blown up. It happened at night, and she would never forget the blast and the shriek she let out, the neighbors calling from across the street, and the steady screaming of her daughter Maria, who was then twenty-eight and getting more and more peculiar. The windowpanes were smashed, the cows lowed in the stable, and the dog barked the whole night through. When daylight came, they saw what had happened: the bridge had gone, the concrete piers were still standing, catwalk, roadway, railings, had all been neatly blown away, and the rusty girders lay down below in the river, sticking out here and there. That very morning a German officer had arrived with five soldiers; they searched all of Berczaba, first her house, every room, the stables, and even Maria's bed, with Maria still in it—she had been lying there whimpering in her room since the blast during the night. Next they went through the Temanns' house across the street: every room, every bale of hay and straw in the barn; and even Brachy's house was searched although no one had lived in it for three years and it was slowly falling to pieces. The Brachys had gone to work in Bratislava, and so far no one had turned up who wanted to buy the house and farm.

The Germans had been furious, but they hadn't found a thing. They had hauled out the boat from her shed and rowed across the river to Tzenkoshik, the little village that lay just where the road started to climb: you could see the church spire beyond the forest from her attic window. But in Tzenkoshik they hadn't found a thing either, nor in Tesarzy—although, of course, they probably didn't know that the two Svortchik boys had disappeared after the bridge was blown up.

To her mind, it was ridiculous to blow up the bridge: the German truck crossed it only about every two months, and between times, very occasionally, a car would turn up carrying soldiers, and the bridge served no one but the farmers who owned pastureland and forests on the other side. It certainly couldn't matter to the Germans if once every two months they had to make half an hour's detour as far as Szarny, only three miles away, where the railroad bridge crossed the river.

It took a few days for her to grasp what the destruction of the bridge meant to her. At first a lot of inquisitive people had shown up, they would have a schnapps or a beer at her place and want to be told the whole story, but then Berczaba became quiet, very quiet; the farmers and hired hands who had to go into the forest or up to the pastures on the other side stopped coming, so did the people who used to drive to Tzenkoshik on Sundays, the couples out for a stroll in the woods, and even the soldiers, and the only thing she sold in two weeks was a beer to Temann from across the street, that skinflint who made his own schnapps. It was very depressing to think that in future all she was going to sell was a glass of beer to that stingy Temann—everyone knew how stingy he was.

But this very quiet period lasted only three weeks. One day a gray, high-speed little army car arrived with three officers who inspected the ruined bridge, paced up and down the bank for half an hour, field glasses in hand, stared out over the countryside, first from the Temanns', then went up into her attic and stared out over the countryside from up there, and drove off, without having so much as a single schnapps at her place.

And two days later a slow cloud of dust moved from Tesarzy toward Berczaba: it was some tired soldiers, seven of them plus a corporal, who tried to explain that they were to live, sleep, and eat at her place. At first she was scared, but then she realized what a good thing it was for her, and she hurried upstairs to Maria, who was still in bed.

The soldiers seemed in no hurry, they waited patiently—men, no longer young, who filled their pipes, drank beer, unloaded their packs, and made themselves comfortable. They waited patiently until she had emptied out three little rooms upstairs: the hired hand's room, empty for the past three years because she could no longer afford hired help; the little room which her husband had once said was for visitors or guests, but there were never any visitors, and guests never came; and her bedroom, the one she had shared with her husband. She herself moved in with Maria, into the latter's room. Later, when she came downstairs, the corporal began to explain that the village council would have to pay her a lot of kronen for this, and that she was to cook for the soldiers and would be paid for this too.

The soldiers were the best customers she had ever had. Those eight men consumed more in a month than all the people together who used to cross the bridge separately. The soldiers appeared to have plenty of money and any amount of time. Their duties seemed ridiculous to her: two of them always had to cover a certain route together—along the riverbank, then across in the boat, back again, along another stretch of riverbank—they were relieved every two hours; and up in the attic sat one man who scanned the countryside through his field glasses and was relieved every three hours. They made themselves comfortable up there in the attic, they had widened the dormer window by removing a few tiles, covering it with a sheet of metal at night, and there they sat all day long in an old armchair, with cushions on it, that stood perched on a table. There one of the men would sit all day long, staring up into the mountains, into the forest, at the riverbank, sometimes also back toward Tesarzy, and the others loafed around and were bored. She was horrified when she found out how much the soldiers got paid for this, and their families at home got paid too. One of them was a school-teacher, and he worked out for her exactly how much his wife got, but it was so much that she couldn't believe it. It was too much, what that schoolteacher's wife got paid for her husband to lounge around here, eat goulash, vegetables, and potatoes, drink coffee, eat bread and sausage—they even got tobacco every day. When he wasn't eating, he was lounging around in her bar leisurely drinking his beer and reading, he read all the time, he seemed to have a whole pack full of books, and when he wasn't eating or reading, he was lounging up there in the attic with his field glasses, of no use to anyone, staring at the forests and meadows or watching the farmers in the fields. This soldier was very nice to her, his name was Becker; but she didn't care for him because all he did was read, just drink beer and read and lounge around the place.

But that was all a long time ago. Those first soldiers hadn't stayed long, four months, then others had come who had stayed for six months, then others again for almost a year, and then they were relieved regularly every six months, and some would come back who had been there before, and they all did the same thing, for three years: loaf around, drink beer, play cards, and lounge about up there in the attic or over in the meadow, and stroll uselessly around in the forest with their rifles on their backs. She was paid a lot of money for housing the soldiers and cooking for them. Others came too; the bar had become a living room for the soldiers.

The sergeant who had been quartered with her for the past four months was called Peter, she didn't know his surname; he was heavy-set, walked like a farmer, even had a mustache, and the sight of him often reminded her of her husband, Wenzel Suchan, who had not returned from another war: soldiers had crossed the bridge then too, covered with dust, on foot and on horseback, with mud-caked baggage trains, soldiers who never came back—it was years before they came back, and she couldn't tell whether they were the same ones who had gone up the other side so long ago. She had been young, twenty-two, a pretty woman, when Wenzel Suchan brought her down from the mountain and made her his wife: she felt very rich, very lucky, to be the wife of an innkeeper who kept a hired hand to work in the fields, and a horse, and she loved the twenty-six-year-old Wenzel Suchan with his deliberate walk and his mustache. Wenzel had been a corporal with a rifle brigade in Bratislava, and shortly after the unfamiliar, dusty soldiers had made their way through the forest up the hill, past her native village, Wenzel Suchan had gone to Bratislava again, as a corporal with a rifle brigade, and they had sent him south to a country called Rumania, to the mountains; from there he had written her three postcards saying he was fine, and on the last postcard he told her he had been made a sergeant. After that she heard nothing for four weeks, then she got a letter from Vienna saying he had been killed.

Soon after that Maria was born, Maria who was now pregnant by that sergeant called Peter who looked like Wenzel Suchan. In her memory Wenzel lived on as a young man, twenty-six years old, and this sergeant who was called Peter and was forty-five—seven years younger than herself—seemed very old to her. Many a night she had lain awake waiting for Maria, and Maria had not come until dawn, slipping bare-foot into the room and getting quickly into bed just before the cocks began to crow. Many a night she had waited and prayed, and she had

put many more flowers before the Virgin Mary's picture downstairs
than she used to, but Maria had become pregnant, and the sergeant
came to see her, embarrassed, awkward as a peasant, and explained that
he would marry Maria when the war was over.

Well, there was nothing she could do about it, and she continued
to put lots of flowers before the Virgin Mary's picture downstairs in
the passageway, and waited. Things became quiet in Berczaba, much
quieter it seemed to her, although nothing had changed: the soldiers
lounged around in the bar, wrote letters, played cards, drank schnapps
and beer, and some of them had started up a trade in things that were
not obtainable here: pocketknives, razor blades, scissors—wonderful
scissors—and socks. They took money for them, or exchanged the
money for butter and eggs, because they had more leisure than money
to spend on drinks during this leisure. Now there was another one
who read all day and even had a whole case of books driven over by
truck from Tesarzy station. He was a professor, he also spent half the
day in the attic staring through his field glasses at the mountains, into
the forest, at the riverbank, and sometimes back toward Tesarzy, or
watching the farmers at work in the fields, and he also told her his wife
received money, large sums of money, so and so many thousand kronen
a month—and she didn't believe him either, it was too much, a crazy
sum, he must be lying, his wife couldn't be paid all that for her husband
to sit around here reading books and writing half the day and often
half the night, and then a few hours a day sitting up there in the attic
with the field glasses. One of the men used to sketch. In fine weather
he would sit outdoors by the river, sketching the mountains there was
such a fine view of from here, the river, the remains of the bridge. He
sketched her too a few times, and she admired the pictures very much
and hung one of them in the bar.

They had been stationed here for three years now, these soldiers,
always eight men, doing nothing. They strolled along the river, crossed
over in her boat, strolled through the woods as far as Tzenkoshik, came
back, crossed the river again, walked past along the bank, then partway
down to Tesarzy, and were relieved. They ate well, slept a lot, and had
plenty of money, and she often thought that maybe Wenzel Suchan
had been taken away, all those years ago, to do nothing in another
country—Wenzel, whom she badly needed, who could work and liked

to work. They had most likely taken him away to do nothing in that country called Rumania, to wait around doing nothing until he was killed by a bullet. But these soldiers under her roof didn't get hit by bullets: as long as they had been here they had only fired their rifles a few times. Each time there was great excitement, and each time it had turned out to be a mistake—usually they had shot at game that was moving in the forest and hadn't halted when challenged, but even that didn't happen very often, only four or five times in these three years, and once they had shot at a woman who had come down the river at night from Tzenkoshik and then run through the forest to get a doctor in Tesarzy for her child, they had shot at this woman too, but luckily they hadn't hit her, and afterward they had helped her into the boat and even rowed her across—and the professor, who hadn't gone to bed yet and was sitting in the bar reading and writing, the professor had gone with her to Tesarzy. But in these three years they hadn't found a single partisan. Everybody knew there were none left here now that the Svortchik boys had gone; even in Szarny, where the big railroad bridge was, no partisans were ever seen...

Although she was making money from the war, it was bitter for her to imagine that Wenzel Suchan had probably done nothing in that country called Rumania, that he hadn't been able to do anything. Most likely that's what war meant, men doing nothing and going to other countries so no one could see them at it. Anyway, she found it both disgusting and ridiculous to watch these men doing nothing for three years but steal time, and getting well paid to shoot once a year, at night, by mistake, at game or some poor woman who was trying to fetch a doctor for her child; disgusting and ridiculous for these men to have to loaf around while she had so much to do she didn't know which way to turn. She had to cook, look after the cows and pigs and chickens, and many of the soldiers even paid her to clean their boots, darn their socks, and wash their underclothes; she had so much to do that she had to take on a hired hand again, a man from Tesarzy, for Maria had been doing nothing ever since she got pregnant. She treated this sergeant as if he were her husband: slept in his room, got him his breakfast, kept his clothes clean, and sometimes scolded him.

But one day, after almost exactly three years, a very high-ranking officer turned up, with red stripes down his pants and a gold-braided collar—she heard later that he was a real general—this high-ranking officer arrived with a few others in a very fast car from Tesarzy. His face was all yellow, he looked sad, and in front of her house he bawled out Sergeant Peter because Peter hadn't been wearing his belt and pistol when he came out to report—and the officer stood there, furious, and waited. She saw him stamping his foot, his face seemed to shrink and get even yellower, and he barked at another officer standing beside him and saluting with a trembling hand, a gray-haired, tired-looking man of over sixty whom she knew because sometimes he would ride down from Tesarzy on his bicycle and chat in a very nice friendly way with the sergeant and the soldiers in the bar—and then later, wheeling his bicycle and accompanied by the professor, walk slowly back to Tesarzy. At last Peter came out, wearing his belt and pistol, and walked with the men to the river. They crossed over in the boat, walked through the forest, returned, and stood for a long time beside the bridge. Then they went up into the attic, and finally the officers drove off again, and Peter stood outside the house with two soldiers; they raised their arms in salute and stayed that way for a long time, until the car was almost back in Tesarzy. Then Peter went into the house again, furious, threw his cap onto the table, and the only thing he said to Maria was "Looks like they're going to rebuild the bridge."

And two days later another vehicle, a truck, came dashing up from Tesarzy, and out of this truck jumped seven young soldiers and a young officer who strode into the house and spent half an hour with the sergeant in his room. Maria tried to join in this conversation, walking right into the room, but the young officer waved her out, and she went in again, and again the young officer impatiently waved her out; she stayed at the top of the stairs, crying, and had to look on while the old soldiers collected their packs and the young ones moved into their rooms. She waited for half an hour, crying, flew into a rage when the professor patted her on the shoulder, and clung shrieking and sobbing to Peter when he finally came out of the room carrying his pack and with a very red face tried to calm her down, to comfort her—she clung to him until he had climbed into the truck. Then, still weeping, she stood on the steps and watched the truck dash off toward Tesarzy. She knew he would never be back, although he had promised her he would....

Feinhals arrived in Berczaba two days before the rebuilding of the bridge began. The tiny hamlet consisted of a tavern and two houses, one of which was abandoned and falling into decay, and when he got out with the others, the whole place was enveloped in the bitter smoke from the potato fires smoldering in the fields. It was quiet and peaceful, nowhere any sign of war...

It was only during the return trip in the red furniture van that he was found to have a splinter in his leg, a glass splinter, as the operation revealed, a minute fragment of a bottle of Tokay, and there had been an odd and embarrassing negotiation because he might have been in line for the silver medal for wounds except that the senior medical officer did not award silver medals for wounds caused by glass splinters, and for a few days the suspicion of self-mutilation hung over him, until Lieutenant Brecht, whom he named as a witness, sent in his report. The wound healed quickly, although he drank a lot of schnapps, and after a month he was sent to some redeployment center that packed him off to Berczaba. He waited downstairs in the tavern until the room Gress had chosen for them became free. He drank some wine, thought about Ilona, and heard the noise in the house made by the men getting ready to leave. The old soldiers were hunting for their belongings; the landlady stood behind the counter dourly taking in the scene, a middle-aged woman, quite pretty, still quite pretty, and in the passageway beyond her another woman was bawling her head off.

Then he heard the woman wailing and sobbing more lustily than ever, and heard the truck take off for the village they had just come from. Gress appeared and took him up to his room. The room was low, the plaster flaking off in places, black beams supported the ceiling, and it smelled stuffy; the air outside was close, and the window gave onto a garden: a grassy plot with old fruit trees, flowerbeds along the sides, stables, and at the end, outside a shed, a boat on blocks, its paint peeling off. It was quiet outside. To the left across the hedge he could see the bridge, rusty iron girders stuck out of the water, and the concrete piers were overgrown with moss. The little river seemed to be some forty or fifty yards wide.

So now he was sharing a room with Gress. He had met him yesterday at the redeployment center and decided not to say one word more than necessary to him. Gress had four decorations on his chest, and he liked telling tales—never stopped, in fact—about the Polish, Rumanian, French, and Russian girls he claimed to have left behind, all with broken hearts. Feinhals didn't feel like listening, it was a nuisance as well as a bore, embarrassing too, and Gress seemed to be one of those men who believed people would listen to them because they had decorations on their chest, more decorations than most.

Feinhals himself had only one decoration, a single medal, and he was a born listener because he never said anything, or hardly ever, and asked for no explanations. He was glad to learn that he and Gress were to take turns manning the observation post: this would mean he would be rid of him during the daytime at least... He lay down on the bed the minute Gress announced his intention of breaking the heart of a Slovak girl, any Slovak girl.

He was tired, and every night when he lay down to sleep somewhere, he hoped to dream about Ilona, but he never did. He would recapture every word he had exchanged with her, think about her very hard, but when he fell asleep she did not come. Often he felt, before falling asleep, that he needed only to turn over to feel her arm, but she was not there beside him, she was a long way away, and it was useless to turn over. He was a long time falling asleep because he was thinking so hard about her and imagining the room that had been intended to receive them—and when he did drop off, he slept badly, and in the morning he had forgotten what he had dreamed about. He had not dreamed about Ilona.

He prayed in bed at night too, and thought about the talks he used to have with her before they had to leave; she had invariably blushed, and she seemed embarrassed by his presence in the room, among stuffed animals, rock specimens, maps, and health charts. But maybe it had only embarrassed her to talk about religion—she had always gone fiery red—it seemed to distress her to state her beliefs, and she stated her belief in faith, hope, and charity, and was shocked when he said he couldn't go to church because the faces and sermons of most priests were more than he could stand. "We have to pray to console God," she had said...

He never thought she would let herself be kissed, but he had kissed her, and she him, and he knew she would have gone with him to that room he now saw so often in his mind's eye: none too clean, water still standing in the bluish wash basin, the wide brown bed, and the view into the neglected orchard where windfalls lay decaying under the trees. He always pictured himself lying in bed with her and talking, but he never dreamed about it...

Next morning the regular routine began. He sat perched up there in the armchair on the wobbly table, in the fusty attic of this house, looking with the field glasses out through the dormer window into the mountains, into the forest, scanning the riverbank and sometimes back toward the hamlet they had driven over from in the truck. He couldn't find any partisans—maybe the farmers in the fields were partisans, only you couldn't tell this with field glasses. It was so quiet that it hurt, and he felt as though he had been perched up here for years, and he raised the field glasses, adjusting the screw, and looked out across the forest, past the yellow church spire, into the mountains. The air was very clear, and way up there among craggy rocks he could see a herd of goats; the animals were scattered like tiny white hard-edged cloudlets, very white against that gray, soft-green background, and he could feel himself capturing the silenc through the field glasses, and the loneliness too. The animals moved very slowly, very seldom—as if they were being pulled along on short strings. With the field glasses he could see them as he would have donewith the naked eye at two or three miles; they seemed very far away, infinitely far away, silent and lonely, those animals; he could not see the goatherd. It was a shock to put down the glasses and find he could no longer see them, not a trace of them, although he gazed intently beyond the church spire up at the mountain. Not even their whiteness was visible; they must be a long way off. He picked up the glasses again and looked at the white goats, whose loneliness he could feel—but the sound of commands being given down in the garden startled him, and he lowered the glasses, looked first without them into the garden and watched the men drilling. Lieutenant Mück himself was in command. Feinhals lifted the glasses to his eyes, adjusted the lenses, and studied Mück closely; he had known him only two days, but he had already seen that Mück took matters seriously. His fine, dark profile was like a mask, deadly serious, the hands behind his back did not move, and the muscles of the thin neck twitched. Mück did not look well, his complexion was pasty, almost gray, the lips were bloodless and barely moved when they uttered "Left turn," "Right turn," and "About turn." At the moment Feinhals could see only Mück's profile, that deadly serious, rigid half of his face, the lips that barely moved, the sorrowful left eye that seemed to be looking not at the drilling soldiers but far away, somewhere—maybe back into the past. Then he looked at Gress: his face was swollen, he looked in some way upset.

When—again without the glasses—he looked down into the garden where the soldiers were doing left turns, right turns, and about turns on that lush, wonderful expanse of grass, he saw a woman hanging out the washing on a line strung between the stables. It must be the daughter who had been crying and carrying on in the passageway yesterday. She looked grave, somber—so somber that she was not pretty but beautiful, a fine-drawn, very dark face with tightly pressed lips. She did not even glance at the four soldiers and the lieutenant.

When he went up to the attic next morning, just before eight, he felt as if he had been there for months, years almost. The silence and loneliness seemed quite natural: the gentle mooing of the cows in the stable and the smell of the potato fires still hanging in the air, a few fires were still smoldering, and when he adjusted the glasses, aiming them at a point far off in the distance in line with the tip of the yellow church spire, all they captured in the lenses was loneliness. Up there it was empty—a gray, soft-green surface dotted with black rocks...

Mück had gone with the four soldiers to the riverbank to practice sighting. The sound of his brief, sad commands came softly across, too faint to disturb the silence—they enhanced it almost; and downstairs in the kitchen the young woman was singing a halting Slovak folk song. The old woman had gone into the field with the hired hand to dig potatoes. Across the street in the other farmhouse it was quiet too. Although he scanned the mountains for quite a time, his eyes saw nothing but silent, lonely expanses, steep rocks, except to the right where a train's white vapor came puffing out of the forest and quickly drifted apart; through the field glasses the vapor looked like dust settling over the treetops. There was not a sound to be heard except for Mück's brief commands at the riverbank and the young woman's haunting song from downstairs...

Then they returned from the riverbank, and he could hear them singing. It was sad to hear those four men singing, a pathetic, ragged, very thin quartet singing "Gray Columns on the March." He could also hear Mück's "left, right—left, right"; Mück seemed to be desperately battling the loneliness, but it was no use. The silence was stronger than his commands, stronger than the singing.

As they halted outside the house, he heard the first truck arriving from the hamlet they had left the day before yesterday. He quickly trained his glasses on the road: a cloud of dust was rapidly approaching, he could make out the cab and something large and bulky showing above the roof.

"What's up?" they called to him from the street.

"A truck," he said, keeping the lenses on the approaching vehicle, and at that moment he heard the young woman come out of the house. She spoke to the soldiers and called something up to him. He could not make out what she was saying, but he called down, "The driver's a civilian; there's a Brownshirt sitting next to him, seems to be someone from the Party; on the back of the truck there's a cement mixer!"

"A cement mixer?" they called up.

"Yes!" he said.

Now those down below could also make out the cab of the truck; and the man in brown, and the cement mixer, and they could see another truck approaching from the village, a smaller cloud of dust, then another and another, a whole column heading from the village toward the remains of the bridge. By the time the first truck halted just before the approach to the bridge, the second truck was already so close that they could make out the cab and the load of that one too: hut prefabs. But now they all ran up to the first truck, including Maria, all except the lieutenant, as the truck door opened and a man in brown jumped out. The man was bareheaded, suntanned, with a frank, attractive face. "*Heil Hitler*, boys," he shouted. "Is this Berczaba?"

"Yes," said the soldiers. They took their hands uncertainly out of their pockets. The man had a major's shoulder loops on his brown tunic. They did not know how to address him.

He called into the cab, "We're here, switch off the motor!" Looking beyond the soldiers at the lieutenant, he paused for a moment, advanced a few steps. The lieutenant also advanced a few steps; then the man stopped and waited, and Lieutenant Mück walked the rest of the way quite fast until he stood facing the man in brown. First Mück's hand went to his cap, then his arm went up for the *Heil Hitler* salute, and he said, "Mück!" and the man in brown also raised his arm, then held his hand out to Mück, shook hands, and said, "I'm Deussen—in charge of construction—we're going to rebuild the bridge here."

The lieutenant looked at the soldiers, the soldiers looked at Maria, Maria ran into the house, and Deussen bounced jauntily away to direct the approaching vehicles.

Deussen went about everything with great determination, great vigor, but with something obliging and friendly in his manner. He asked the widow Suchan to show him the kitchen, smiled, pursed his lips, said nothing, went across to the abandoned house, inspected it very thoroughly, and when he emerged he was smiling, and within minutes two trucks loaded with prefabs were on their way back to Tesarzy. He set up his own quarters at the Temanns', appeared shortly thereafter leaning on the windowsill smoking and watching the unloading of the trucks. There was another young man in brown with the trucks, wearing a sergeant's shoulder patches. Now and again Deussen would call something out to him from the window. Meanwhile all the trucks had arrived, ten of them, and the place was a hive of workmen, iron girders, beams, sacks of cement, and an hour later a little motorboat came down the river from Szarny. A third man in brown got out of the boat, and two pretty, suntanned Slovak women who were greeted gaily by the workmen.

Feinhals watched it all very closely. First the big kitchen stove was carried into the dilapidated house, then the following were unloaded: complete iron railings, rivets, screws, creosoted beams, survey instruments, and kitchen supplies. By eleven the Slovak women were already peeling potatoes, and by noon all the stuff had been unloaded, even a shed for the cement had been assembled, and three more trucks arrived from the village to strew gravel on the approach to the bridge. When he went downstairs for lunch, Gress having relieved him, he saw that a sign had been nailed over the bar entrance saying CANTEEN.

For the next few days he continued to watch the building activities very closely and was astonished at the precision with which everything had been planned: nothing was done needlessly, no material lay farther away than necessary from the point at which it was to be used. Feinhals had been on many construction sites in his time, and in charge of several construction jobs, but he was astonished to see how neatly and deftly this one was carried out. After only three days the bridge piers had been carefully filled with concrete, and while they were still pouring the last pier the erection of the heavy iron girders was already under way on the first one. By the fourth day a catwalk across the bridge had already been completed, and after a week he saw trucks driving up on the other side of the river carrying bridge sections, heavy vehicles that Deussen used simultaneously as ramp and base for erecting the final girder sections. Now that the catwalk was finished, everything went much faster, and Feinhals spent less time looking up to the mountains or into the forest. He observed the building of the bridge very closely, and even when he had to drill with the other men he usually watched the workmen: he loved this work.

In the evenings, when dusk was falling and the attic observation post was not manned, he would sit in the garden listening to a young Russian called Stalin—Stalin Gadlenko—playing the balalaika. Indoors there was singing, drinking, even dancing, although dancing was prohibited, but Deussen seemed to close his eyes to all that. He was in very good spirits: he had been given two weeks to build the bridge, and if the work continued at this rate, he would be through in twelve days. He saved a lot of gas because he could buy all the cooking supplies from Temann and the widow Suchan without sending a truck out all over the countryside, and he saw to it that the workmen were issued cigarettes, were well fed, and felt at ease; he knew this was better than exerting authority which, although it induced fear, actually inhibited the work. He had already built a number of bridges, most of which had meanwhile been blown up again; but for a time at least they had served their purpose, and he had never had any trouble meeting his deadlines.

The widow Suchan was pleased: the bridge would be there again, it would still be there even when the war was over, and if it was there the soldiers would probably stay and people from the villages would start coming back too. The workmen also seemed content. Every third day a snappy little light-brown car would drive down from Tesarzy and screech to a halt outside the tavern, and from the car would emerge a man in brown who looked old and tired and wore a captain's shoulder loops, and the workmen were rounded up and paid; they were paid plenty, enough to be able to buy socks from the soldiers, and shirts, and to spend the evening drinking and dancing with the pretty Slovak women who worked in the kitchen.

On the tenth day Feinhals saw that the bridge was finished: the railing was in place, the framework for the roadway completed, and he watched cement and girders being loaded and driven away, as well as the shed that had housed the cement. Half the workmen went back too, and one of the kitchen women, and Berczaba quieted down somewhat. All that was left now were fifteen workmen, Deussen and the young man in brown with the sergeant's shoulder patches, and one woman in the kitchen, at whom Feinhals looked very often. She spent the whole morning sitting by the window peeling potatoes, singing to herself, and she would pound the meat and clean the vegetables and was very pretty. When she smiled, he felt a pang, and through the field glasses he could plainly see her mouth on the other side of the street, and her fine dark eyebrows and white teeth. She always sang softly to herself—and that evening he went into the bar and danced with her. He danced a lot with her, and he saw her dark eyes close up, felt her firm white arms under his hands, and was rather disappointed to find that she smelled of cooking—it was close and smoky in the bar. She was the only woman, except for Maria, who sat at the counter and didn't dance. That night he dreamed about this Slovak woman whose name he didn't know; he had a very vivid dream about her, although after getting into bed he had again thought for a long time and very hard about Ilona.

Next day he didn't look across at her through his field glasses, although he could hear her singing, softly humming; he looked up to the mountains and was pleased to be able to pick out a herd of goats again, now they were to the right of the church spire, white specks moving jerkily against a gray, soft-green background.

Suddenly he put down the field glasses: he had heard a shot, the echo of a distant explosion coming down from the mountains. There it was again, very distinct, not loud, very far away. The workmen on the bridge paused, the Slovak woman broke off her singing, and Lieutenant Mück came running up to the attic in a state of agitation, wrenched the field glasses out of his hands, and looked up to the mountains. He looked up to the mountains for a very long time, but there were no more explosions, and Mück handed the glasses back to him, murmuring, "Keep watching now—keep watching," and ran back into the yard where he was supervising the men cleaning their weapons.

That afternoon seemed quieter than previous ones, although the sounds remained the same: the workmen on the bridge sawing creosoted beams, joining and screwing them together; the voice of the old woman scolding her daughter downstairs in the kitchen and getting no reply; and the gentle humming of the Slovak woman sitting by the open window as she prepared supper for the workmen—big yellow potatoes were frying in the pan, and an earthenware bowl of tomatoes shone in the dusk. Feinhals trained his glasses on the mountains, on the forest, scanned the riverbank; all was quiet on the other side, nothing moved. The two sentries had disappeared into the forest, and he aimed the glasses at the workmen on the bridge. They were already halfway through their work, the black, solid beams of the roadway were gradually meeting, and when he swung the glasses around, he could look down on the road at all the remaining material being loaded: tools and girders, beds, chairs, and the kitchen stove, and soon after that the truck with eight workmen aboard drove off toward Tesarzy. The Slovak woman leaned on the windowsill and waved them good-bye, the place seemed quieter, even the motorboat went off up the river in the late afternoon, and in the roadway over the bridge there was only one bit missing—three or four beams. There was a gap of about six feet when the men knocked off work. Feinhals saw them leave their tools lying on the bridge. The truck returned from Tesarzy, stopped outside the kitchen, and unloaded a small basket of fruit and a few bottles, and shortly before Feinhals was relieved, there came again the echo of muffled explosions from above: it resounded from the mountains like stage thunder, artificially multiplied, reverberating, dying away, three times—four times—then there was silence. And again Lieutenant Mück came running upstairs and looked through the field glasses, his face twitching. Swinging them from left to right he scanned the rocks, the ridges, put down the glasses with a shake of his head, wrote a message on a piece of paper, and within a few minutes Gress was pedaling off to Tesarzy on Deussen's bicycle.

After Gress had left, Feinhals distinctly heard sounds of a machine-gun duel from the mountains. The hard, hollow rasp of a Russian machine gun contrasting with the high-pitched, nervous barking of a German one that grated like a frenzied hornet—the shots came so fast they seemed to skid. The skirmish was brief; only a few rounds were exchanged; then hand grenades burst, three or four, and again the noise was multiplied. Over and over again, until they died away, they sent their echo down into the plain. Somehow it seemed ridiculous to Feinhals: the war, wherever it showed up, was associated with completely unnecessary noise. This time Mück didn't come upstairs, he stood on the bridge and stared at the mountains; one more isolated shot came from above, from a rifle apparently, the echo sounding as thin as the noise of a rolling stone; then all was quiet until dusk fell. Feinhals replaced the sheet of metal on the roof and slowly went downstairs.

Gress was not back yet, and down in the bar Mück was anxiously holding forth about increased alertness for the night. There he stood, his face deadly serious, his fingers fumbling nervously with his two decorations; he had hung his loaded machine pistol around his neck and his steel helmet from his belt.

Before Gress got back, a gray car arrived from Tesarzy and out of it got a stout, red-faced captain and a spare, stern-looking first lieutenant, both of whom walked across the bridge with Mück. Feinhals stood in front of the house and watched them. It looked as though the three figures had disappeared for good, but they soon came back; the car turned. Across the street Deussen was looking out of the window, and on the ground floor of the workmen's quarters the men were sitting in the semidarkness around a rough table, tomatoes and potatoes on their plates. In the corner of the room stood the Slovak woman, one hand on hip, in the other a cigarette—the flourish of her arm as she brought the cigarette to her lips seemed to Feinhals a shade too elaborate. Then, as the motor of the gray car started up, she came closer, leaned on the windowsill smoking her cigarette, and smiled at Feinhals. He looked intently at her face, forgetting to salute the two departing officers: the woman was wearing a dark bodice, and the white of her breast shone heartshaped below her brown face. Mück walked past Feinhals on his way into the house and said, "Bring the machine gun over here." Feinhals now saw that where the officers' car had been parked, a black, slender machine gun was lying on the road beside some ammunition cases. He slowly crossed the road and brought back the machine gun, then crossed over a second time and brought back the ammunition cases. The Slovak woman was still leaning on the windowsill; she flicked off the glowing end of her cigarette and stuck the rest into her apron pocket. She was still looking at Feinhals but no longer smiling—she looked sad, her mouth was a poignant pale red. Then all at once she pursed her lips a little, turned, and began to clear the table. The workmen came out of the house and walked toward the bridge.

They were still working on it when Feinhals walked across the bridge half an hour later with the machine gun. They were putting the last beam in place in the dark. Deussen himself screwed in the very last rivet. He had one of the men hold a carbide lamp for him, and to Feinhals it looked as though he were holding the spanner like the handle of a barrel organ, as though he were boring into a great dark box that produced no sound. Feinhals put down the machine gun, said "Just a moment" to Gress, and went back once more. He had heard the motor being started up in the truck standing outside the workmen's quarters; he walked back to the ramp and watched the rest of the household objects being loaded. There was not much left: a stove, a few chairs, a basket of potatoes, crockery, and the workmen's own things. The workmen walked back from the bridge and all got into the truck. They were carrying bottles of schnapps and drinking from them. The last person to get in was the Slovak woman. She was wearing a red kerchief around her head and had very little to carry: a bundle wrapped up in a blue cloth. Feinhals hesitated a moment as he watched her get in the truck, then walked quickly back. Deussen was the last to come off the bridge; he was holding the spanner and went slowly into Temann's house.

They spent half the night crouching there with the brand-new machine gun behind the little wall that bordered the ramp, listening into the night. The silence was unbroken. Now and again the patrol emerged from the forest; they would exchange a few desultory words and then go on crouching there mutely, their eyes fixed on the narrow road leading into the forest. But nothing came. Up in the mountains the silence was unbroken too. Just before midnight, when they were relieved, they went indoors and fell asleep at once. It was almost morning when they heard a noise and got up. Gress waited to put on his boots, but Feinhals stood barefoot at the window and looked across to the other side: a crowd of people were standing over there, arguing with the lieutenant, who evidently did not want to let them cross the bridge. They had apparently come down from the mountains and from the village whose church spire was visible beyond the forest, a long file of people with carts and bundles that seemed to extend even beyond the point where the forest began. Their shrill voices were full of fear, and Feinhals saw the widow Suchan, in slippers, throw a coat over her shoulders and walk across the bridge. She stopped beside the lieutenant and talked for a long time to the crowd, then started to argue with the lieutenant. Deussen arrived too; he walked slowly across, cigarette between his lips, and also spoke to the lieutenant, then to the landlady, then to the crowd—until at last the file of refugees on the other side started to move in the direction of Szarny. There were many carts piled high with children and crates, chickens in baskets, a long file that could proceed only at a snail's pace. Deussen returned with the landlady and, shaking his head, tried to explain something to her.

Feinhals dressed slowly and lay down again on the bed. He tried to sleep, but Gress was fussing about as he shaved and whistling softly to himself, and a few minutes later they heard two vehicles approaching. At first it sounded as though they were driving side by side, then one seemed to overtake the other; one was hardly audible yet as the other drove up to the door. Feinhals got up and went downstairs: it was the brown car that had sometimes brought the captain with the workmen's pay. He was standing across the street outside Temann's house, and just then Deussen walked toward the bridge with a man in brown who was also wearing a major's shoulder loops. But now the second car arrived too. This car was gray and caked with dirt and mud-splashed, and there seemed to be something wrong with it; it drew up in front of the tavern, and a cheery little lieutenant jumped out and called to Feinhals, "Start packing, it's getting sticky here. Where's the old man?" Feinhals noticed that the little lieutenant was wearing a sapper's shoulder patches. He pointed toward the bridge, saying, "Over there."

"Thanks," said the lieutenant. He called to the soldier in the car, "Get everything ready," and ran quickly toward the bridge. Feinhals followed. The man in the brown uniform with the major's shoulder loops inspected the bridge minutely, had Deussen show him everything, nodded appreciatively, even shook his head appreciatively, and walked slowly back with Deussen. Deussen emerged at once from Temann's house with his pack, spanner in hand, and the brown car drove quickly off.

Mück returned with the two machine gunners, the sapper lieutenant, and an artillery noncom without a weapon, dirty and harassed in appearance: sweat was running down the man's face, he had no pack either, not even a cap, and kept pointing excitedly into the forest, and beyond the forest up into the mountains. Now Feinhals could hear: vehicles were coming slowly down the road. The little sapper lieutenant ran over to his car shouting, "Hurry, hurry!" The soldier came running up with gray metal boxes, brown cardboard packages, and a bundle of wires. The lieutenant looked at his watch. "Seven," he said, "we've got ten minutes." He glanced at Mück. "It's to be blown up at exactly ten past. The counterattack's been called off."

Feinhals slowly mounted the stairs, collected his things in his room, picked up his rifle, placed everything outside the door of the house, and walked back inside. The two women, still not dressed, ran distractedly along the passages, snatching random objects from the rooms and screaming at one another. Feinhals looked at the Virgin Mary: the flowers had wilted. He carefully picked out the wilted stalks, rearranged the remaining fresh flowers, and looked at his watch. It was eight minutes past, and across on the other side the sound of the approaching vehicles could be heard more clearly now, they must have already passed the village and be in the forest. Outside, everyone stood ready to leave. Lieutenant Mück had a message pad in his hand and was taking down the particulars of the harassed artillery noncom, who was sitting exhausted on the bench.

"Schniewind," said the noncom, "Arthur Schniewind ... we're with 912." Mück nodded and slipped the message pad into his leather satchel. At that moment the little sapper lieutenant came running back with the soldier, shouting, "Take cover—take cover!" They all threw themselves onto the road, as close as they could to the house, the front of which stood at an angle to the bridge ramp. The sapper lieutenant looked at his watch— then the bridge blew up. There was not much of a crash, nothing whizzed through the air; there was a rending sound, then an explosion like a few hand grenades, and they heard the heavy roadway smacking into the water. They waited another moment or two until the little lieutenant said, "That's it." They stood up and looked at the bridge: the concrete piers were still standing, the catwalk and roadway had been neatly blown away, only across on the other side one section of the railing still hung in the air.

The approaching vehicles sounded quite close by now, then suddenly there was silence: they must have stopped in the forest.

The little sapper lieutenant had got into his car and, cranking down a window, called out to Mück, "What are you waiting for? You've got no orders to wait here."

He saluted briefly and drove off in his dirty little car.

"Fall in!" shouted Lieutenant Mück. They lined up on the road, Mück stood there and looked at the two houses, but in the two houses nothing stirred. All they could hear was a woman weeping, but it sounded like the old woman.

"Forward march!" shouted Mück, "forward march, march at ease." He strode ahead, deadly serious and sad—he seemed to be gazing somewhere far away, or back into the past, somewhere.

IX

Feinhals was surprised at the size of Finck's premises. All he had seen from the front was this narrow old building with the sign saying FINCK'S WINESHOP & HOTEL, ESTAB. 1710, some rather dilapidated-looking steps leading into the bar, a window on the left, two on the right of the door, and, next to the farthest window on the right the entrance to the courtyard, which was like every other winegrower's entrance: a sagging gateway, painted green, just wide enough for a cart to drive through.

But now, on opening the front door, he found himself looking through the passage into a large, neatly paved courtyard, its four sides formed by sturdy buildings. Around the second floor ran a balcony enclosed by a wooden railing, and through another gateway a second courtyard was visible, with sheds in it, and on the right a single-story building, obviously a reception hall. He took it all in carefully, listened, and paused suddenly at the sight of the two American sentries: they were guarding the second gateway, walking past each other like caged animals who have discovered a certain rhythm that enables them to pass. One was wearing glasses and his lips moved continuously; and the other was smoking a cigarette; they had pushed their steel helmets to the backs of their heads and looked pretty tired.

Feinhals tried the latch of the left-hand door, onto which someone had stuck a piece of paper marked PRIVATE, then the latch of the righthand door, which bore a sign saying BAR. Both doors were locked. He stood there waiting while he watched the sentries steadily pacing up and down. In the silence there was only the occasional shot to be heard; the opposing sides seemed to be exchanging shells like balls not meant to be taken seriously, just a token that the war was still on; they rose like alarm signals that burst somewhere, exploded, and announced in the silence, "War, this is war. Look out: war!" Their echo was only faintly audible. But after listening for a few minutes to this harmless noise, Feinhals realized he had been mistaken: the shells were coming from the American side only, none from the German side. It was not an exchange of fire, it was a purely one-sided discharge of explosions occurring at regular intervals and producing a multiple, slightly menacing echo on the other side of the little river.

Feinhals stepped forward, slowly, into the dark corner of the passage, where it led on the left into the cellar and on the right to a little door with a cardboard notice nailed to it saying KITCHEN. He knocked at the kitchen door, heard a faint "Come in, please," and pressed down the latch. Four faces looked at him, and he was shocked by the resemblance of two of the faces to that lifeless, exhausted face that he had seen, dimly lit by the ruddy reflection from the fire, on that far-off grassy slope outside a Hungarian village. The old man by the window smoking a pipe resembled that face very much; he was thin and old, with a tired wisdom in his eyes. The second face whose resemblance startled him was that of a boy of about six, playing with a toy wagon as he squatted on the floor and raised his eyes to him. The child also was thin, he also looked old, tired, and wise; his dark eyes looked at Feinhals, then the boy lowered his incurious gaze and listlessly pushed the wagon across the floor.

The two women sat at the table peeling potatoes. One was old, but her healthy face was broad and brown, and it was clear that she had been a handsome woman. The one beside her looked faded and aging, although she was obviously younger than she appeared: she looked tired and dispirited, the movements of her hands were apathetic. Wisps of blond hair fell over her pale forehead, whereas the older woman wore her hair combed tightly back.

"Good morning," said Feinhals.

"Good morning," they replied.

Feinhals closed the door behind him and hesitated, he cleared his throat and could feel the sweat breaking out on him, a fine sweat that made his shirt cling to his armpits and back. The younger of the two women sitting at the table looked at him, and he noticed she had the same delicate white hands as the boy, who was squatting on the floor and calmly guiding his wagon around some chipped tiles. In the small room there was a stale smell of innumerable meals. Frying pans and saucepans hung all around the walls.

The two women glanced at the man by the window who was looking out into the courtyard. He pointed to a chair, saying, "Please sit down."

Feinhals sat down beside the older woman and said, "My name's Feinhals—I'm from Weidesheim—I'm trying to get home."

Both the women looked up, the old man showed more interest. "Feinhals," he said, "from Weidesheim. Jacob Feinhals's son?"

"Yes. How are things in Weidesheim?"

The old man shrugged his shoulders, puffed out a cloud of smoke, and said, "Not too bad—they're waiting for the Americans to occupy the place, but they haven't done so yet. They've been here for three weeks, but they won't go the mile and a half to Weidesheim. The Germans aren't there either, it's a no-man's-land, nobody's interested in it, the location's not good..."

"You can hear the Germans firing into it sometimes," the young woman said, "but not very often."

"That's right, you can hear them," said the old man; he looked keenly at Feinhals. "Where have you come from now?"

"From the other side—I waited over there for three weeks, for the Americans to come."

"Directly across from here?"

"No—farther south—near Grinzheim."

"Grinzheim, eh? That's where you crossed over?"

"Yes, last night."

"And changed into civilian clothes?"

Feinhals shook his head. "No," he said, "I was wearing civilians over there—they're discharging a good many soldiers now."

The old man laughed softly and looked at the young woman. "D'you hear that, Trude," he said, "they're discharging a good many soldiers now. Oh, what can one do but laugh..."

The women had finished peeling potatoes; the young woman picked up the bowl, went to the sink in the corner, and shook the potatoes into a sieve. She turned on the water and began listlessly washing the potatoes.

The older woman touched Feinhals's arm. He turned toward her.

"Are they discharging very many?" she asked.

"Yes, they are," said Feinhals. "Some units are discharging every-one—on condition that they assemble in the Ruhr. But I didn't go to the Ruhr."

The woman at the sink began to cry. She cried soundlessly, barely moving her thin shoulders.

"Or cry," said the old man by the window, "laugh or cry." He looked at Feinhals. "Her husband was killed—my son." He pointed his pipe at the woman standing at the sink, crying as she slowly and care-fully washed the potatoes. "In Hungary," said the old man, "last fall."

"He was supposed to be discharged last summer," said the old woman sitting next to Feinhals. "They were just about to do so several times; he was a sick man, very sick, but I suppose they didn't want to let him go. He was running the canteen." She shook her head, and her eyes went to the younger woman at the sink. The younger woman shook the washed potatoes carefully into a clean saucepan and filled it with water. She was still crying, very quietly, almost without a sound, and she placed the pan on the stove and went over to the corner to get her handkerchief from the pocket of a smock.

Feinhals knew his expression must have changed. He had not often thought of Finck, only now and again and for brief moments, but now it all came back to him so vividly that the scene was clearer in his mind's eye than when he had seen it in reality: that incredibly heavy suitcase the shell had suddenly exploded into, the way the suitcase lid had whirled up and how the wine had splashed in the dark onto the path and the back of his neck, how the broken glass had tinkled—and how small and skinny the man had felt as his hand had groped along the body until it reached the great bloody wound and he had drawn back his hand...

He watched the child playing on the floor. With his thin white fin-gers he calmly pulled the wagon around the chipped tiles—little pieces of kindling lay there being loaded, unloaded, loaded, unloaded. The boy looked very frail and had the same listless movements as his mother, now seated at the table holding her handkerchief to her face. Feinhals looked around the room in distress and wondered whether he ought to tell them, but he lowered his head again and decided to tell them later. He would tell the old man about it. Right now he didn't want to talk about it; in any case, it didn't seem to occur to them to wonder how Finck had got from his field hospital all the way to Hungary. The old woman touched his arm again. "What is it?" she asked quietly. "Are you hungry? Don't you feel well?"

"No, I'm all right," said Feinhals, "thanks very much." With her penetrating gaze still on him he repeated, "No, I'm all right, really, thanks just the same."

"How about a glass of wine," asked the old man from the window, "or a schnapps?"

"Yes," said Feinhals, "a schnapps would be fine."

"Trude," said the old man, "get the gentleman a schnapps."

The young woman stood up and went into the next room. "We're rather cramped," the old woman told Feinhals. "All we have is this kitchen and the bar, but we hear they're moving on soon; they've got a lot of tanks here, and the prisoners are going to be taken away."

"Do you have prisoners here in the house?"

"Yes," said the old man, "there are some over there in the hall. They're all high-ranking officers being interrogated here. As soon as they've been interrogated, they get taken away. One of them's even a general. Look, over there!"

Feinhals went to the window, and the old man pointed past the sentries and through the gateway into the second courtyard, to the windows of the hall that were covered with barbed wire.

"There," said the old man, "another of them's being taken off for interrogation."

Feinhals recognized the general at once: he looked better, more relaxed, and he was wearing the Knight's Cross at his neck now; he even seemed to be smiling gently as he walked quietly and docilely ahead of the two sentries, who had the barrels of their machine pistols trained on him. Almost all the yellow had left the general's face, and he no longer looked tired either; his face was harmonious, quiet, cultivated, and humane, that very gentle smile made his face beautiful. He passed through the gateway, walked calmly across the yard, and preceded the two sentries up the steps.

"That was the general," said Finck. "They've got colonels in there too, and majors, all staff officers, close to thirty of them."

The young woman returned from the bar carrying glasses and the bottle of schnapps. She placed one glass on the windowsill in front of Finck and the other on the table in front of Feinhals's place. Feinhals remained standing at the window. From there he could see out across the second courtyard as far as the street leading past the rear of the building. Two sentries with machine pistols were standing there too, and across the street from where the sentries stood Feinhals now recognized the window of the coffin shop, and he knew this was the street where the high school was. The coffin was still in the window: polished black with silver fittings and a black cloth with silver tassels. Maybe it was the same coffin that had been there thirteen years ago, when he had gone to high school.

"*Prost,*" said the old man, raising his glass.

Feinhals went quickly to the table, picked up his glass, said "Thanks" to the young woman and "*Prost*" to the old man, and drank. The schnapps was good. "When d'you imagine would be a good time for me to try and get home?"

"You have to be sure and get through at a place where there are no Americans—by the Kerpel would be best—do you know the Kerpel?"

"Yes," said Feinhals. "Aren't there any there?"

"No, none. People often come across to get bread at night—women, they all come through the Kerpel..."

"During the day they do sometimes fire into it," said the young woman.

"Yes," said the old man, "during the day they do sometimes fire into it..."

"Thanks," said Feinhals, "thanks very much," and finished his schnapps.

The old man stood up. "I'm driving up the hill," he said. "You'd better come along. From up there you have a good view of everything, even your father's house..."

"Right," said Feinhals, "I'll come along."

He looked at the women seated at the table cleaning vegetables, carefully removing the leaves from two cabbages, inspecting the leaves, shredding them, and throwing them into a sieve.

The child looked up, suddenly abandoning the wagon, and asked, "May I come too?"

"Yes," said Finck, "come along." He put his pipe down on the windowsill.

"Now it's the next one's turn," he called. "Look."

Feinhals hurried to the window: the colonel was dragging his feet now, his gaunt face looked ill, and his collar, with the decorations dangling from it, was much too big for him. He hardly raised his knees, his arms hung limp. "A disgrace," muttered Finck, "a disgrace." He took his hat from the peg and put it on.

"Good-bye," said Feinhals.

"Good-bye," said the women.

"We'll be back for dinner," said Finck.

Private Berchem did not like the war. He had been a waiter and bartender in a nightclub, and until the end of 1944 he had managed to avoid being called up, and during the war he had learned a lot of things in this nightclub, things that had been confirmed for him once and for all in nearly fifteen hundred war-nights. He had always known that most men can't take as much alcohol as they think, and that most men spend a great part of their lives persuading themselves that they are real devils when it comes to drinking, and that they also try to convince the women they bring along of the same thing. But there were very few men who really knew how to drink, whom it was a pleasure to watch drinking. And even in wartime there were still precious few of those around.

Most people made the mistake of assuming that a piece of shiny metal on the chest or at the neck could change the man who wore it. They seemed to believe that a stupid fellow could become intelligent and a weakling strong if at some prominent spot on his uniform he were hung with a decoration, which he might very possibly have earned. But Berchem had realized this wasn't so: if it *was* possible to change a man by way of a decoration, then it could only be for the worse. But most of these men he had seen only one night, and he hadn't known them before, and all he knew was that most of them couldn't take alcohol, although they all thought they could and told convincing tales of how much they had drunk at one session at such and such a time and at such and such a place. It wasn't a pretty sight when they got drunk, and this nightclub, where he had spent fifteen hundred war-nights as a waiter, was not very closely checked for black-market goods: after all, there had to be someplace where heroes could get something to drink and smoke and eat, and his boss was twenty-eight, as fit as a fiddle, and even by December 1944 he still hadn't joined up. Nor was the boss bothered by the bombs, although they were gradually destroying the whole town. The boss had a villa out in the country, among trees, it even had an air-raid shelter, and sometimes he got a kick out of inviting a few heroes, the ones who were the best company, to a private drinking party, and he would load them into his car and entertain them in his villa outside the town.

Throughout fifteen hundred war-nights Berchem had kept a careful eye on what went on, and he had often had to listen too, although he found that boring. He didn't know how many assaults and encirclements he was familiar with from hearsay. For a time he had considered writing it all down, but there were too many assaults, too many encirclements, and there were too many heroes who wore no decorations and felt obliged to tell you that actually they deserved them because— he had listened to so many of these "because" stories, and he was fed up with the war. But some told the truth when they were drunk, and he also heard the truth from many heroes and barmaids from France and Poland, Hungary and Rumania. He had always got along well with barmaids. Most of them could handle their liquor, and he had a soft spot for women you could have a drink with.

But now he was lying in a barn in a place called Auelberg, with a pair of field glasses, an exercise book and a few pencils, and a wristwatch, and it was his job to write down everything he observed in a place called Weidesheim a hundred and fifty yards away on the other side of the little river. There was not much to see in Weidesheim: half the front of the place consisted of the wall of the jam factory, and the jam factory had closed down. Sometimes people crossed the street, once in a while; they would go off in the direction of Heidesheim and were soon out of sight in the narrow lanes. People climbed up to their vineyards and their orchards, and he could see them working up there, beyond Weidesheim, but he did not have to write anything down in his exercise book that happened beyond Weidesheim. The cannon for which he was acting as observer here got only seven shells a day, and these shells had to be fired somehow or other, otherwise the cannon wouldn't get any at all, and the seven shells weren't enough for a duel with the Americans who were occupying Heidesheim—it was useless, in fact forbidden, to fire at the Americans, because they returned every shot with a hundred of their own, they were very touchy. So no purpose was achieved by Berchem entering in his little book: "10:30 American vehicle from Heidesheim stopped at house next to entrance to jam factory. Car parked in front of jam factory. Returned 11:15." This car came every day and parked for nearly an hour a hundred and fifty yards away from him, but it was useless for him to enter it in his book: this car was never fired at. Every day an American soldier would get out of the car, remain in the house almost always for an hour, and then drive off again.

Berchem's first gunnery officer had been a lieutenant called Gracht, and he was said to be a clergyman. Berchem had not had much to do with clergymen, but he found this one very nice. Gracht had always directed his seven shells into the mouth of the river, which was to the left of Heidesheim, a sandy, swampy little delta known to the local inhabitants as the Kerpel, where only reeds grew. His shells certainly wouldn't harm anyone there, and Berchem had thereupon begun to enter in his little book, several times a day: "Noticeable activity at river mouth." The lieutenant had made no comment and continued to direct his seven shells into the swamp. But two days ago the command up there had changed; now it was a sergeant major called Schniewind, who took his seven shells very seriously. Schniewind also did not fire at the American car that was always parked outside the jam factory, what he had his eye on was the white flags: obviously the inhabitants of Weidesheim were still counting daily on the Americans occupying their village, but the Americans did not occupy the village. Its position was very unfavorable, in a loop, very exposed, whereas Heidesheim was hardly exposed at all, and the Americans were clearly not planning to advance. At other points they had already marched a hundred and twenty miles into Germany, they had almost reached the center of the country, but here in Heidesheim they had been stationary for the last three weeks, and for every shell that struck Heidesheim they had returned more than a hundred, but nobody was firing at Heidesheim now. The seven shells were intended for Weidesheim and its environs, and Sergeant Major Schniewind had decided to punish the people of Weidesheim for their lack of patriotic feeling. A white flag was something he could not stomach.

Nevertheless, that day Berchem entered in his little book as usual: "9:00 a.m. noticeable activity at river mouth." And he made the same entry at 10:15—and again at 11:45 he wrote: "American vehicle from H. to W. jam factory." At noon he left his post for a few minutes to go and pick up his lunch. As he was about to climb down the ladder, Schniewind called to him from below, "Hold on up there for a moment." Berchem crawled back to the barn window and picked up the field glasses. Schniewind took the glasses from him, threw himself on his stomach in the prescribed combat-ready position, and squinted through the lenses. Berchem looked sidelong at him: Schniewind was one of those people who can't take alcohol but persuade themselves and manage to convince others that they can take a great deal. There was something not quite genuine about the keenness with which he lay there on his stomach staring at the desolate, lifeless village of Weidesheim, and Berchem noticed that the star on his shoulder patch was still quite new, like the piece of braid encircling his shoulder patch with a perfect horseshoe. Schniewind passed the field glasses back to Berchem, saying, "The bastards, those goddamn bastards with their white flags—give me your book." Berchem handed it to him. Schniewind leafed through it. "What a load of crap," he said. "I can't think what you fellows imagine is going on in that swampy river mouth of yours, there's nothing but frogs there. Give me those." He snatched the field glasses from Berchem and trained them on the river mouth. Berchem noticed a slight trace of saliva around Schniewind's mouth and a very fine thread of saliva hanging down. "Nothing," muttered Schniewind, "not a single solitary thing in that river mouth—nothing's moving—what crap." He ripped a page from the exercise book, took a pencil stub from his pocket, and, still looking out the window, wrote something on the paper. "Bastards," he muttered, "those bastards." Whereupon he turned away, without saluting, and climbed down the ladder. Berchem followed him one minute later to go pick up his lunch.

From up here, looking down from the vineyard, there was a good view over the whole area, and Feinhals realized why Weidesheim had not been occupied by either Germans or Americans: it wasn't worth it. Fifteen houses, and a jam factory that had closed down. The railroad station was at Heidesheim, and across the river, Auelberg station was occupied by Germans: Weidesheim lay in a dead loop. Between Weidesheim and the hills, in a hollow, lay Heidesheim, and he could see solid rows of parked tanks on every open space of any size: in the schoolyard, alongside the church, in the market square, and on the big parking lot by the Hotel zum Stern—wherever you looked, tanks and vehicles that were not even camouflaged. In the valley the trees were already in blossom, slopes and meadows were covered with blossoming treetops, white, pink, and blue-white, and the air was mild: it was spring. From up here he could see the Finck premises lying like a fissure, the two square courtyards between the narrow streets; he could even make out the four sentries, and in the yard of the coffin shop he saw a man working at a big creamy-yellow box, slightly slanting, that was evidently to be a coffin—the freshly planed wood stood out clearly, shining pinkish-yellow, and the carpenter's wife was sitting on a bench in the sun, near her husband, cleaning vegetables.

The streets were busy with women shoppers and soldiers, and just then a crowd of schoolchildren came out of the school building at the end of the village. But in Weidesheim the silence was complete. The houses looked as if they were hiding among the great treetops, but he knew every house in the place, and saw at first glance that the Berg and Hoppenrath houses were damaged but that his father's was undamaged; there it stood, broad and yellow beside the main road with its comfortable façade, and the white flag hanging from his parents' bedroom on the second floor was extra large, larger than the white flags he could see hanging from the windows of other houses. The linden trees were already green. But not a soul was in sight, and the white flags hung stiff and dead in the windless air. The big courtyard of the jam factory was empty too, rusty pails lay around untidily in heaps, the sheds had been locked. Suddenly he saw an American car approaching from Heidesheim station and driving quite fast through meadows and orchards toward Weidesheim. Now and again the car would vanish beneath the white treetops, then reappear, finally emerging onto the main street of Weidesheim and pulling up at the entrance to the jam factory.

"For God's sake," Feinhals said quietly to Finck, pointing to the car. "What's that?"

Finck, sitting beside him on the bench outside the toolshed, calmly shook his head. "Nothing," he said, "nothing of any importance; that's Fräulein Merzbach's lover—he drives over every day."

"An American?"

"Of course," said Finck. "She's scared to come to him over here because sometimes the Germans fire into the village—so he goes to her."

Feinhals smiled. He knew Fräulein Merzbach well. She was a few years younger than himself, and at the time he left home, she had been fourteen, a skinny, restless teenager who played the piano much too much and badly—he could recall many a Sunday afternoon when she had been playing downstairs in the living room of the manager's apartment while he sat reading in the garden next door, and when her playing stopped her thin pale face would appear at the window, and she would look out into the gardens, sad and discontented. Then for a few minutes it would be quiet, until she went back to the piano to continue her playing. She must be twenty-seven now, and somehow he was pleased that she had a lover.

He thought about how he would soon be down there, at home, right next door to the Merzbachs, and that at noon tomorrow he would probably see this American. Maybe he could speak to him, and maybe there would be a chance of getting hold of some papers through him—he was sure to be an officer. It wasn't likely Fräulein Merzbach would have a private for a lover.

He also thought about his little apartment in town, which he knew no longer existed. The people there had written him that the house was no longer standing, and he tried to imagine it, but he couldn't imagine it, although he had seen many houses that no longer existed. But that his apartment should no longer exist was something he couldn't imagine. He hadn't even gone there when he was granted leave to check the damage; he couldn't see why he should go there just to see that there was nothing left. The last time he had been there, in 1943, the house had still been standing; he had nailed cardboard across the broken windows and had gone to the nightclub a few doors away. There he had sat for three hours, until his train left, and he had chatted for a while with the waiter, who was very nice, a quiet, matter-of-fact type, still young, who had sold him cigarettes for forty pfennigs and a bottle of French cognac for sixty-five marks. That was cheap, and the waiter had even told him his name—he had forgotten it now—and had recommended a woman whose attraction lay in her apparently genuine German respectability. Her name was Grete, and everyone called her Ma, and the waiter had said she was a very nice person to have a drink with and a chat. He had spent three hours chatting with Grete, who really did seem to be respectable; she told him about her old home in Schleswig-Holstein and tried to cheer him up about the war. It had really been very nice at that nightclub, although after midnight a few drunk officers and men had insisted on doing the goose step.

He was glad to be going home and to be able to stay there now. He would stay a long time, doing nothing until he could see what was what. There would certainly be plenty of work after the war, but he didn't intend to work much. He didn't feel like it—he didn't want to do anything, maybe help a bit with the harvest, without getting involved, like the summer vacationers who don't mind putting their hand to a pitchfork once in a while. Maybe later on he would start rebuilding a few houses in the neighborhood, if he could get the contracts. His gaze swept over Heidesheim: much of it had been destroyed, a whole row of houses next to the station as well as the station itself. A freight train was still standing there, its engine shot to pieces beside the tracks; lumber was being loaded from one freight car onto an American truck, and the fresh planks stood out as clearly as the coffin in the carpenter's garden that had been lighter and brighter than the blossoms on the trees, its creamy yellow shining brightly up at him...

He wondered which way to go. Finck had explained that American sentries were posted along the railroad tracks, where they had dug themselves in, and they didn't bother individuals going out to work in the fields. But if he wanted to make quite sure, he could crawl through the canal in which the silted-up river was caught for a few hundred yards; you could duck as you went through it, and many people who for some reason or other wanted to get to the other side had used it—and at the end of the canal was the dense underbrush of the Kerpel reaching all the way to the gardens of Weidesheim. Once he was in the gardens, nobody could see him, and there he knew every step of the way. Or he might carry a hoe or a spade on his shoulder. Finck assured him that many people came across every day from Weidesheim to work in the vineyards and orchards.

All he wanted was peace and quiet: to lie at home in bed, to know that no one could bother him, to think about Ilona, perhaps to dream about her. Later on he would start working, sooner or later—but first he wanted to sleep as long as he liked and be spoiled by his mother; she would be very happy if he came to stay for a long time. And most likely there would be tobacco or cigarettes at home, and at last he would have a chance to catch up on his reading. Fräulein Merzbach could almost certainly play the piano better by this time. He realized how happy he had been in those days, when he could sit in the garden reading and having to listen to Fräulein Merzbach play the piano badly; he had been happy, although he hadn't known it at the time. Now he knew it. Once he had dreamed of building houses such as nobody had ever built, but later he had built houses that were almost exactly the same as the ones other people built. He had become a very mediocre architect, and he knew it, but still it was nice to understand one's craft and build simple, good houses that sometimes turned out to be quite pleasing when they were finished. The important thing was not to take oneself too seriously—that was all. The way home seemed very long now, although it couldn't be much more than half an hour; he felt very tired and lazy, and he would have liked to drive the rest of the way very quickly by car, drive home, get into bed, and go to sleep. It seemed such an effort to have to walk the route he soon must walk: right through the American front line. There might be trouble, and he didn't want any more trouble; he was tired, and it all seemed such an effort.

He removed his cap and folded his hands when the noonday bell struck. Finck and the little boy did the same; and the carpenter down there in the yard, working away at the coffin, put down his tool, and his wife laid aside the vegetable basket and stood with folded hands in the yard. People no longer seemed ashamed of praying in public, and he found it somehow repugnant, in himself too. At one time he used to pray—Ilona had prayed too, a very devout, intelligent woman, who was even beautiful, and so intelligent that she couldn't be confounded in her faith even by the priests. Now as he prayed he caught himself

praying for something, as a matter of habit almost, although there was
nothing he wanted: Ilona was dead, what was there to pray for? But
he prayed for her return—from somewhere or other, for his safe homecoming, although this was now almost accomplished. He suspected all
these people of praying for something, for the fulfillment of some wish
or other, but Ilona had told him, "We have to pray to console God,"
she had read that somewhere and found it worth remembering, and as
he stood there with folded hands he made up his mind that he would
only pray properly when he could cease to pray for anything. When
that happened he would go to church too, although he found it hard to
bear the faces of most priests and their sermons, but he would do it to
console God—maybe to console God for the faces and sermons of the
priests. He smiled, unclasped his hands, and put on his cap... "Look,"
said Finck, "now they're being taken away." He pointed down toward
Heidesheim, and Feinhals saw that a truck was standing outside the
coffinmaker's house, a truck that was slowly filling up with officers
from Finck's little reception hall: even from up here their decorations
stood out clearly. Then the truck disappeared rapidly along the tree-
lined road toward the west, to where the war was over...

"People are saying they'll be advancing soon," said Finck. "D'you
see all the tanks?"

"I hope they take Weidesheim pretty soon," said Feinhals.

Finck nodded. "It won't be long now—will you come over and
see us?"

"Yes," said Feinhals, "I'll come and see you often."

"I'd like that very much," said Finck. "Have some tobacco?"

"Thanks," said Feinhals; he filled a pipe, Finck held out a match,
and for a while they gazed down onto the blossoming plain, Finck's
hand resting on his grandson's head.

"I'll be off now," said Feinhals suddenly. "I must go, I want to get
home..."

"Go ahead," said Finck, "it's quite all right, there's no danger."

Feinhals shook hands with him. "Thank you very much," he said,
and looked at him. "Thank you very much—I hope I can come over and
see you soon." He shook hands with the boy too, and the child looked
at him thoughtfully and a bit suspiciously out of his dark, narrow-
lidded eyes.

"You'd better take along the hoe," said Finck.

"Thanks, I will," said Feinhals, taking the hoe from Finck.

For a while as he walked down the hill it seemed as if he were heading straight for the coffin being made down there in the yard, he was walking straight for it, he watched the yellow shining box grow bigger and more distinct, as if through the lenses of field glasses, until he swung to the right past the village; there he was swallowed up by the stream of schoolchildren just leaving the school, he stayed among a group of children as far as the town gate and was alone as he quietly crossed the road to the underpass. He didn't want to crawl through the canal, it was too much of an effort. To walk through the trackless, marshy Kerpel was also too much of an effort—and besides, it would just make him conspicuous if he entered the village first from the right and then from the left. He took the direct path that led across meadows and orchards and was completely calm when a hundred yards ahead he saw someone walking along carrying a hoe.

The Americans had posted only a couple of sentries at the underpass. The two men had taken off their steel helmets and were smoking as they stared with bored expressions at the blossoming gardens between Heidesheim and Weidesheim; they paid no attention to Feinhals, they had been here for three weeks now, and for the last two weeks nothing had been fired at Heidesheim. Feinhals walked calmly past them, nodded, they casually nodded back.

Only ten more minutes now: straight through the gardens, then around to the left between the Heusers and the Hoppenraths, down the main road a bit, and he would be home. He might meet someone he knew on the way, but he met no one; it was perfectly quiet except for the distant sounds of rumbling trucks, but at this hour no one seemed to think of firing. Right now there were not even the regular sounds of shells exploding that had seemed like warning signals.

He thought with a certain bitterness of Ilona: somehow he felt she had shirked things, she was dead, and to die was perhaps the easiest—she should have been with him now, and he felt she might have been with him. But she seemed to have known that it was better not to become very old and build one's life on a love that was real only for a few moments while there was another, everlasting love. She seemed to have known many things, more than he did, and he felt cheated

because he would soon be home, where he would live, read, not work
too hard if he could avoid it, and pray, to console God, not to ask Him
for something He couldn't give, because He loved you: money or success, or something that helped you to muddle along through life. Most
people muddled along through life somehow, he would have to too, for
he wouldn't be building houses that could only be built by him—any
mediocre architect could build them...

He smiled as he passed the Hoppenraths' garden: they still hadn't
sprayed their trees with that white stuff his father claimed was indispensable. He was always having rows with old Hoppenrath about
it, but old Hoppenrath still hadn't got that white stuff on his trees.
It wasn't far now to his parents' house—on the left was the Heusers'
house, on the right the Hoppenraths', and he had only to walk through
this narrow lane, then to the left down the main road a bit. The Heusers had the white stuff on their trees. He smiled. He distinctly heard
the shell being fired from the other side, and he threw himself to the
ground—instantly—and tried to go on smiling, but he couldn't help
flinching when the shell landed in the Hoppenraths' garden. It burst in
a treetop, and a gentle dense rain of white blossoms fell onto the grass.
The second shell seemed to land farther along, more toward the Bäum-
ers' house, almost directly opposite his father's, the third and fourth
landed at the same level but more to the left, they sounded as if they
were of medium caliber. He got slowly to his feet as the fifth also fell
over there—and then there was nothing more. He listened for a while,
heard no more firing, and quickly walked on. Dogs were barking all
over the village, and he could hear the chickens and ducks frantically
flapping their wings in Heuser's barn—from some barns came the muffled lowing of cows too, and he thought: Pointless, how pointless. But
maybe they were firing at the American car, which he hadn't heard driving back yet; no, as he turned the corner of the main road he saw the car
had already left—the street was quite empty—and the muffled lowing
of the cows and the barking of the dogs accompanied him for the few
steps he still had to take.

The white flag hanging from his father's house was the only one
in the whole street, and he now saw that it was very large—it must be
one of his mother's huge tablecloths, the kind she took out of the closet
on special occasions. He smiled again, but suddenly threw himself to

the ground and knew it was too late. Pointless, he thought, how utterly pointless. The sixth shell struck the gable of his parents' house. Stones fell, plaster crumbled onto the street, and he heard his mother scream down in the basement. He crawled quickly toward the house, heard the seventh shell being fired, and screamed even before it landed, he screamed very loud, for several seconds, and suddenly he knew that dying was not that easy—he screamed at the top of his voice until the shell struck him, and he rolled in death onto the threshold of the house. The flagpole had snapped, and the white cloth fell over him.

ENTER AND EXIT:
A NOVELLA IN TWO PARTS

Enter and Exit *is a translation of Böll's* Als der Krieg ausbrach—Als der Krieg zu Ende war, *originally published by Insel-Verlag in 1962. This translation was first published by McGraw-Hill in 1965.*

WHEN THE WAR BROKE OUT

I was leaning out of the window, my arms resting on the sill. I had rolled up my shirt sleeves and was looking beyond the main gate and guard-room across to the divisional headquarters telephone exchange, waiting for my friend Leo to give me the prearranged signal: come to the window, take off his cap, and put it on again. Whenever I got the chance I would lean out of the window, my arms on the sill; whenever I got the chance I would call a girl in Cologne and my mother—at army expense—and when Leo came to the window, took off his cap, and put it on again, I would run down to the barrack square and wait in the public callbox till the phone rang.

The other telephone operators sat there bareheaded, in their under-shirts, and when they leaned forward to plug in or unplug, or to push up a flap, their identity disks would dangle out of their undershirts and fall back again when they straightened up. Leo was the only one wearing a cap, just so he could take it off to give me the signal. He had a heavy, pink face, very fair hair, and came from Oldenburg. The first expression you noticed on his face was guilelessness; the second was incredible guilelessness, and no one paid enough attention to Leo to notice more than those two expressions; he looked as uninteresting as the boys whose faces appear on advertisements for cheese.

It was hot, afternoon; the alert that had been going on for days had become stale, transforming all time as it passed into stillborn Sunday hours. The barrack square lay there blind and empty, and I was glad I could at least keep my head out of the camaraderie of my room-mates. Over there the operators were plugging and unplugging, pushing up flaps, wiping off sweat, and Leo was sitting there among them, his cap on his thick fair hair.

All of a sudden I noticed the rhythm of plugging and unplugging had altered; arm movements were no longer routine, mechanical, they became hesitant, and Leo threw his arms up over his head three times:

a signal we had not arranged but from which I could tell that something out of the ordinary had happened. Then I saw an operator take his steel helmet from the switchboard and put it on; he looked ridiculous, sitting there sweating in his undershirt, his identity disk dangling, his steel helmet on his head—but I couldn't laugh at him; I realized that putting on a steel helmet meant something like "ready for action," and I was scared.

The ones who had been dozing on their beds behind me in the room got up, lit cigarettes, and formed the two customary groups: three pro-bationary teachers, who were still hoping to be discharged as being "essential to the nation's educational system," resumed their discussion of Ernst Jünger; the other two, an orderly and an office clerk, began discussing the female form; they didn't tell dirty stories, they didn't laugh, they discussed it just as two exceptionally boring geography teachers might have discussed the conceivably interesting topography of the Ruhr valley. Neither subject interested me. Psychologists, those interested in psychology, and those about to complete an adult educa-tion course in psychology may be interested to learn that my desire to call the girl in Cologne became more urgent than in previous weeks; I went to my locker, took out my cap, put it on, and leaned out of the window, my arms on the sill, wearing my cap: the signal for Leo that I had to speak to him at once. To show he understood, he waved to me, and I put on my tunic, went out of the room, down the stairs, and stood at the entrance to headquarters, waiting for Leo.

It was hotter than ever, quieter than ever, the barrack squares were even emptier, and nothing has ever approximated my idea of hell as closely as hot, silent, empty barrack squares. Leo came very quickly; he was also wearing his steel helmet now, and was displaying one of his other five expressions that I knew: dangerous for everything he didn't like. This was the face he sat at the switchboard with when he was on even-ing or night duty, listened in on secret official calls, told me what they were about, suddenly jerked out plugs, cut off secret official calls so as to put through an urgent secret call to Cologne for me to talk to the girl; then it would be my turn to work the switchboard, and Leo would first call his girl in Oldenburg, then his father; meanwhile Leo would cut thick slices from the ham his mother had sent him, cut these into cubes, and we would eat cubes of ham. When things were slack, Leo would teach me the art of recognizing the caller's rank from the way the flaps fell; at first I thought it was enough to be able to tell the rank simply by the force with which the flap fell—corporal, sergeant, etc.— but Leo could tell exactly whether it was an officious corporal or a tired colonel demanding a line; from the way the flap fell, he could even distinguish between angry captains and annoyed lieutenants—nuances that are very hard to tell apart, and as the evening went on, his other expressions made their appearance: fixed hatred; primordial malice. With these faces he would suddenly become pedantic, articulate his "Are you still talking?," his "Yessirs," with great care, and with unnerving rapidity switch plugs so as to turn an official call about boots into one about boots and ammunition, and the other call about ammunition into one about ammunition and boots, or the private conversation of a sergeant major with his wife might be suddenly interrupted by a lieutenant's voice saying, "I insist the man be punished, I absolutely insist." With lightning speed Leo would then switch the plugs over so that the boot partners were talking about boots again and the others about ammunition, and the sergeant major's wife could resume discussion of her stomach trouble with her husband. When the ham was all gone, Leo's relief had arrived, and we were walking across the silent barrack square to our room, Leo's face would wear its final expression: foolish, innocent in a way that had nothing to do with childlike innocence.

Any other time I would have laughed at Leo, standing there wearing his steel helmet, that symbol of inflated importance. He looked past me, across the first, the second barrack square, to the stables; his expressions alternated from three to five, from five to four, and with his final expression he said, "It's war, war, war—they finally made it." I said nothing, and he said, "I guess you want to talk to her?"

"Yes," I said.

"I've already talked to mine," he said. "She's not pregnant. I don't know whether to be glad or not. What d'you think?"

"You can be glad," I said. "I don't think it's a good idea to have kids in wartime."

"General mobilization," he said, "state of alert, this place is soon going to be swarming—and it'll be a long while before you and I can go off on our bikes again." (When we were off duty we used to ride our bikes out into the country, onto the moors, the farmers' wives used to fix us fried eggs and thick slices of bread and butter.) "The first joke of the war has already happened," said Leo. "In view of my special skills and services in connection with the telephone system, I have been made a corporal. Now go over to the public callbox, and if it doesn't ring in three minutes I'll demote myself for incompetence."

In the callbox I leaned against the Münster Area phone book, lit a cigarette, and looked out through a gap in the frosted glass across the barrack square; the only person I could see was a sergeant major's wife, in Block 4, I think. She was watering her geraniums from a yellow jug; I waited, looked at my wristwatch: one minute, two, and I was startled when it actually rang, and even more startled when I immediately heard the voice of the girl in Cologne: "Maybach's Furniture Company." And I said, "Marie, it's war, it's war"—and she said, "No." I said, "Yes, it is." Then there was silence for half a minute, and she said, "Shall I come?," and before I could say spontaneously, instinctively, "Yes, please do," the voice of what was probably a fairly senior officer shouted, "We need ammunition, and we need it urgently." The girl said, "Are you still there?" The officer yelled, "Goddamn it!" Meanwhile I had had time to wonder about what it was in the girl's voice that had sounded unfamiliar, ominous almost: her voice had sounded like marriage, and I suddenly knew I didn't feel like marrying her. I said, "We're probably pulling out tonight." The officer yelled, "Goddamn it, Goddamn it!" (evidently he couldn't think of anything better to say), the girl said, "I could catch the four o'clock train and be there just before seven," and I said, more quickly than was polite, "It's too late, Marie, too late"—then all I heard was the officer, who seemed to be on the verge of apoplexy. He screamed, "Well, do we get the ammunition or don't we?" And I said in a steely voice (I had learned that from Leo), "No, no, you don't get any ammunition, even if it chokes you." Then I hung up.

It was still daylight when we loaded boots from railway cars onto trucks, but by the time we were loading boots from trucks onto railway cars it was dark, and it was still dark when we loaded boots from railway cars onto trucks again; then it was daylight again, and we loaded bales of hay from trucks onto railway cars, and it was still daylight, and we were still loading bales of hay from trucks onto railway cars; but then it was dark again, and for exactly twice as long as we had loaded bales of hay from trucks onto railway cars, we loaded bales of hay from railway cars onto trucks. At one point a field kitchen arrived, in full combat rig. We were given large helpings of goulash and small helpings of potatoes, and we were given real coffee and cigarettes which we didn't have to pay for; that must have been at night, for I remember hearing a voice say: Real coffee and cigarettes for free, the surest sign of war. I don't remember the face belonging to this voice. It was daylight again when we marched back to barracks, and as we turned into the street leading past the barracks, we met the first battalion going off. It was headed by a marching band playing "Must I Then," followed by the first company, then their armored vehicles, then the second, third, and finally the fourth with the heavy machine guns. On not one face, not one single face, did I see the least sign of enthusiasm. Of course, there were some people standing on the sidewalks, some girls too, but not once did I see anybody stick a bunch of flowers onto a soldier's rifle; there was not even the merest trace of a sign of enthusiasm in the air.

Leo's bed was untouched. I opened his locker (a degree of familiarity with Leo which the probationary teachers, shaking their heads, called "going too far"). Everything was in its place: the photo of the girl in Oldenburg, she was standing, leaning against her bicycle, in front of a birch tree; photos of Leo's parents; their farmhouse. Next to the ham there was a message: "Transferred to area headquarters. In touch with you soon. Take all the ham, I've taken what I need. Leo." I didn't take any of the ham, and closed the locker; I was not hungry, and the rations for two days had been stacked up on the table: bread, cans of liver sausage, butter, cheese, jam, and cigarettes. One of the probationary teachers, the one I liked least, announced that he had been promoted to Pfc and appointed room senior for the period of Leo's absence; he began to distribute the rations. It took a very long time; the only thing I was interested in was the cigarettes, and these he left to the last because he was a nonsmoker. When I finally got the cigarettes, I tore open the pack, lay down on the bed in my clothes, and smoked; I watched the others eating. They spread liver sausage an inch thick on the bread and discussed the "excellent quality of the butter," then they drew the blackout blinds and lay down on their beds. It was very hot, but I didn't feel like undressing. The sun shone into the room through a few cracks, and in one of these strips of light sat the newly promoted Pfc sewing on his Pfc's chevron. It isn't so easy to sew on a Pfc's chevron: it has to be placed at a certain prescribed distance from the seam of the sleeve; moreover, the two open sides of the chevron must be absolutely straight. The probationary teacher had to take off the chevron several times; he sat there for at least two hours, unpicking it, sewing it back on, and he did not appear to be running out of patience. Outside, the band came marching by every forty minutes, and I heard the "Must I Then" from Block 7, Block 2, from Block 9, then from over by the stables—it would come closer, get very loud, then softer again; it took almost exactly three "Must I Thens" for the Pfc to sew on his chevron, and it still wasn't quite straight. By that time I had smoked the last of my cigarettes and fell asleep.

That afternoon we didn't have to load either boots from trucks onto railway cars or bales of hay from railway cars onto trucks; we had to help the quartermaster sergeant. He considered himself a genius at organization; he had requisitioned as many assistants as there were items of clothing and equipment on his list, except that for the groundsheets he needed two; he also required a clerk. The two men with the groundsheets went ahead and laid them out, flicking the corners nice and straight, neatly on the cement floor of the stable. As soon as the groundsheets had been spread out, the first man started off by laying two neckties on each groundsheet; the second man, two handkerchiefs; I came next with the mess kits. While all the articles for which, as the sergeant said, size was not a factor were being distributed, he was preparing, with the aid of the more intelligent members of the detachment, the objects for which size was a factor: tunics, boots, trousers, and so on. He had a whole pile of paybooks lying there. He selected the tunics, trousers, and boots according to measurements and weight, and he insisted everything would fit, "unless the bastards have got too fat as civilians." It all had to be done at great speed, in one continuous operation, and it was done at great speed, in one continuous operation, and when everything had been spread out the reservists came in, were conducted to their ground-sheets, tied the ends together, hoisted their bundles onto their backs, and went to their rooms to put on their uniforms. Only occasionally did something have to be exchanged, and then it was always because someone had got too fat as a civilian. It was also only occasionally that something was missing: a shoe-cleaning brush or a spoon or fork, and it always turned out that someone else had two shoe-cleaning brushes or two spoons or forks, a fact which confirmed the sergeant's theory that we did not work mechanically enough, that we were "still using our brains too much." I didn't use my brain at all, with the result that no one was short a mess kit. While the first man of each company being equipped was hoisting his bundle onto his shoulder, the first of our own lot had to start spreading out the next groundsheet. Everything went smoothly. Meanwhile the newly promoted Pfc sat at the table and wrote everything down in the paybooks; most of the time he had only to enter a one in the paybook, except with the neckties, socks, handker-chiefs, undershirts, and underpants, where he had to write a two.

In spite of everything, though, there were occasionally some dead minutes, as the quartermaster sergeant called them, and we were allowed to use these to fortify ourselves; we would sit on the bunks in the grooms' quarters and eat bread and liver sausage, sometimes bread and cheese or bread and jam, and when the sergeant had a few dead minutes himself he would come over and give us a lecture about the difference between rank and appointment. He found it tremendously interesting that he himself was a quartermaster sergeant—"that's my appointment"—and yet had the rank of a corporal, "that's my rank." In this way, so he said, there was no reason, for example, why a Pfc should not act as a quartermaster sergeant, indeed even an ordinary private might; he found the theme endlessly fascinating and kept on concoct-ing new examples, some of which betokened a well-nigh treasonable imagination. "It can actually happen, for instance," he said, "that a Pfc is put in command of a company, of a battalion even."

For ten hours I laid mess kits on groundsheets, slept for six hours, and again for ten hours laid mess kits on groundsheets; then I slept another six hours and still had heard nothing from Leo. When the third ten hours of laying out mess kits began, the Pfc started entering a two wherever there should have been a one, and a one wherever there should have been a two. He was relieved of his post, and now had to lay out neckties, and the second probationary teacher was appointed clerk. I stayed with the mess kits during the third ten hours too. The sergeant said he thought I had done surprisingly well.

During the dead minutes, while we were sitting on the bunks eating bread and cheese, bread and jam, bread and liver sausage, strange rumors were beginning to be peddled around. A story was being told about a rather well-known retired general who received orders by phone to go to a small island in the North Sea where he was to assume a top-secret, extremely important command. The general had taken his uniform out of the closet, kissed his wife, children, and grandchildren goodbye, given his favorite horse a farewell pat, and taken the train to some station on the North Sea, and from there hired a motorboat to the island in question. He had been foolish enough to send back the motorboat before ascertaining the nature of his command; he was cut off by the rising tide and—so the story went—had forced the farmer on the island at pistol point to risk his life and row him back to the mainland. By afternoon there was already a variation to the tale: some sort of a struggle had taken place in the boat between the general and the farmer, they had both been swept overboard and drowned. What I couldn't stand was that this story—and a number of others—was considered criminal all right, but funny as well, while to me they seemed neither one nor the other. I couldn't accept the grim accusation of sabotage, which was being used like some kind of moral tuning fork, nor could I join in the laughter or grin with the others. The war seemed to deprive what was funny of its funny side.

At any other time the "Must I Thens" that ran through my dreams, my sleep, and my few waking moments, the countless men who got off the streetcars and came hurrying into the barracks with their cardboard boxes and went out again an hour later with "Must I Then"; even the speeches we sometimes listened to with half an ear, speeches in which the words "united effort" were always occurring—all this I would have found funny, but everything which would have been funny before was not funny anymore, and I could no longer laugh or smile at all the things which would have seemed laughable; not even the sergeant, and not even the Pfc, whose chevron was still not quite straight and who sometimes laid out three neckties on the groundsheet instead of two.

It was still hot, still August, and the fact that three times sixteen hours are only forty-eight, two days and two nights, was something I didn't realize until I woke up about eleven on Sunday and for the first time since Leo had been transferred was able to lean out of the window, my arms on the sill. The probationary teachers, wearing their walking-out dress, were ready for church, and looked at me in a challenging kind of way, but all I said was "Go ahead, I'll follow you," and it was obvious that they were glad to be able to go without me for once. Whenever we had gone to church they had looked at me as if they would like to excommunicate me, because something or other about me or my uniform was not quite up to scratch in their eyes: the way my boots were cleaned, the way I had tied my tie, my belt or my haircut; they were indignant not as fellow soldiers (which, objectively speaking, I agree would have been justified), but as Catholics. They would rather I had not made it so unmistakably clear that we were actually going to one and the same church; it embarrassed them, but there wasn't a thing they could do about it, because my paybook is marked RC.

This Sunday there was no mistaking how glad they were to be able to go without me. I had only to watch them marching off to town, past the barracks, clean, upright, and brisk. Sometimes, when I felt bouts of pity for them, I was glad for their sakes that Leo was a Protestant: I think they simply couldn't have borne it if Leo had been a Catholic too.

The office clerk and the orderly were still asleep; we didn't have to be at the stable again till three that afternoon. I stood leaning out of the window for a while, till it was time to go, so as to get to church just in time to miss the sermon. Then, while I was dressing, I opened Leo's locker again: to my surprise it was empty, except for a piece of paper and a big chunk of ham. Leo had locked the cupboard again to be sure I would find the message and the ham. On the paper was written "This is it—I'm being sent to Poland—did you get my message?" I put the paper in my pocket, turned the key in the locker, and finished dressing; I was in a daze as I walked into town and entered the church, and even the glances of the three probationary teachers, who turned round to look at me and then back to the altar again, shaking their heads, failed to rouse me completely. Probably they wanted to make sure quickly whether I hadn't come in *after* the Elevation of the Host so they could apply for my excommunication; but I really had arrived *before* the Elevation, so there was nothing they could do; besides, I wanted to remain a Catholic. I thought of Leo and was scared, I thought too of the girl in Cologne and had a twinge of conscience, but I was sure her voice had sounded like marriage. To annoy my roommates, I undid my collar while I was still in church.

After mass I stood outside leaning against the church wall in a shady corner between the vestry and the door, took off my cap, lit a cigarette, and watched the faithful as they left the church and walked past me. I wondered how I could get hold of a girl with whom I could go for a walk, have a cup of coffee, and maybe go to a movie; I still had three hours before I had to lay out mess kits on groundsheets again. It would be nice if the girl were not too silly and reasonably pretty. I also thought about dinner at the barracks, which I was missing now, and that perhaps I ought to have told the office clerk he could have my chop and dessert.

I smoked two cigarettes while I stood there, watching the faithful standing about in twos and threes, then separating again, and just as I was lighting the third cigarette from the second a shadow fell across me from one side, and when I looked to the right I saw that the person casting the shadow was even blacker than the shadow itself: it was the chaplain who had read Mass. He looked very kind, not old, thirty perhaps, fair and just a shade too well fed. First he looked at my open collar, then at my boots, then at my bare head, and finally at my cap, which I had put next to me on a ledge from where it had slipped off onto the paving; last of all he looked at my cigarette, then into my face, and I had the feeling that he didn't like anything he saw there. "What's the matter?" he finally asked. "Are you in trouble?" And hardly had I nodded in reply to this question, when he said, "Do you wish to confess?" Damn it, I thought, all they ever think of is confession, and only a certain part of that even. "No," I said, "I don't wish to confess." "Well, then," he said, "what's on your mind?" He might just as well have been asking about my stomach as my mind. He was obviously very impatient, looked at my cap, and I felt he was annoyed that I hadn't picked it up yet. I would have liked to turn his impatience into patience, but after all it wasn't I who had spoken to him, but he who had spoken to me, so I asked—to my annoyance, somewhat falteringly—whether he knew of some nice girl who would go for a walk with me, have a cup of coffee, and maybe go to a movie in the evening; she didn't have to be a beauty queen, but she must be reasonably pretty, and if possible not from a good family, as these girls are usually so silly. I could give him the address of a chaplain in Cologne where he could make inquiries, call up if necessary, to satisfy himself I was from a good Catholic home. I talked a lot, toward the end a bit more coherently, and noticed how his face altered: at first it was almost kind, it had almost looked benign, that was in the early stage when he took me for a highly interesting, possibly even fascinating case of feeble-mindedness and found me psychologically quite amusing. The transitions from kind to almost benign, from almost benign to amused were hard to distinguish, but then all of a sudden—the moment I mentioned the physical attributes the girl was to have—he went purple with rage. I was scared, for my mother had once told me it is a sign of danger when overweight people suddenly go purple in the face. Then he began to shout at me, and shouting has always put me on edge. He shouted that I looked a mess, with my "field tunic" undone, my boots unpolished, my cap lying next to me "in the dirt, yes, in the dirt," and how undisciplined I was, smoking one cigarette after another, and whether perhaps I couldn't tell the difference between a Catholic priest and a pimp. With my nerves strung up as they were, I had stopped being scared of him, I was just plain angry. I asked him what my tie, my boots, my cap, had to do with him, whether he thought maybe he had to do my corporal's job, and "Anyway," I said, "you fellows tell us all the time to come to you with our troubles, and when someone really tells you his troubles, you get mad." "You fellows, eh?" he said, gasping with rage. "Since when are we on such familiar terms?" "We're not on any terms at all," I said. I picked up my cap, put it on without looking at it, and left, walking straight across the church square. He called after me to at least do up my tie, and I shouldn't be so stubborn; I very nearly turned round and shouted that *he* was the stubborn one, but then I remembered my mother telling me it was all right to be frank with a priest but you should try to avoid being impertinent—and so, without looking back, I went on into town. I left my tie dangling and thought about Catholics; there was a war on, but the first thing they looked at was your tie, then your boots. They said you should tell them your troubles, and when you did, they got mad.

I walked slowly through town, on the lookout for a café where I wouldn't have to salute anyone: this stupid saluting spoiled all cafés for me. I looked at all the girls I passed, I turned round to look at them, at their legs even, but there wasn't one whose voice would not have sounded like marriage. I was desperate. I thought of Leo, of the girl in Cologne, I was on the point of sending her a telegram; I was almost prepared to risk getting married just to be alone with a girl. I stopped in front of the window of a photographer's studio, so I could think about Leo in peace. I was scared for him. I saw my reflection in the shop window—my tie undone and my black boots unpolished. I raised my hands to button up my collar, but then it seemed too much trouble, and I dropped my hands again. The photographs in the studio window were very depressing. They were almost all of soldiers in walking-out dress; some had even had their pictures taken wearing their steel helmets, and I was wondering whether the ones in steel helmets were more depressing than the ones in peaked caps when a sergeant came out of the shop carrying a framed photograph: the photo was fairly large, at least twenty-four by thirty, the frame was painted silver, and the picture showed the sergeant in walking-out dress and steel helmet. He was quite young, not much older than I was, twenty-one at most; he was just about to walk past me, he hesitated, stopped, and I was wondering whether to raise my hand and salute him, when he said, "Forget it—but if I were you I'd do up your collar, and your tunic too. The next guy might be tougher than I am." Then he laughed and went off, and ever since then I have preferred (relatively, of course) the ones who have their pictures taken in steel helmets to the ones who have their pictures taken in peak caps.

Leo would have been just the person to stand with me in front of the photo studio and look at the pictures; there were also some bridal couples, first communicants, and students wearing colored ribbons and fancy fobs over their stomachs, and I stood there wondering why they didn't wear ribbons in their hair; some of them wouldn't have looked bad in them at all. I needed company and had none.

Probably the chaplain thought I was suffering from lust, or that I was an anticlerical Nazi; but I was neither suffering from lust nor was I anticlerical or a Nazi. I simply needed company, and not male company either, and that was so simple that it was terribly complicated; of course there were loose women in town as well as prostitutes (it was a Catholic town), but the loose women and the prostitutes were always offended if you weren't suffering from lust.

I stood for a long time in front of the photo studio. To this day I still always look at photo studios in strange cities; they are all much the same, and all equally depressing, although not everywhere do you find students with colored ribbons. It was nearly one o'clock when I finally left, on the lookout for a café where I didn't have to salute anyone, but in all the cafés they were sitting around in their uniforms, and I ended up by going to a movie anyway, to the first show at one-fifteen. All I remember was the newsreel: some very ignoble-looking Poles were maltreating some very noble-looking Germans. It was so empty in the movie that I could risk smoking during the show; it was hot that last Sunday in August 1939.

When I got back to barracks, it was way past three. For some reason the order to put down groundsheets at three o'clock and spread out mess kits and neckties on them had been countermanded; I came in just in time to change, have some bread and liver sausage, lean out of the window for a few minutes, listen to snatches of the discussion about Ernst Jünger and the other one about the female form. Both discussions had become more serious, more boring; the orderly and the office clerk were now weaving Latin expressions into their remarks, and that made the whole thing even more repulsive than it was in the first place.

At four we were called out, and I had imagined we would be loading boots from trucks onto railway cars again or from railway cars
onto trucks, but this time we loaded cases of soap powder, which were
stacked up in the gym, onto trucks, and from the trucks we unloaded
them at the parcel post office, where they were stacked up again. The
cases were not heavy, the addresses were typewritten. We formed a
chain, and so one case after another passed through my hands; we did
this the whole of Sunday afternoon right through till late at night, and
there were scarcely any dead minutes when we could have had a bite
to eat. As soon as a truck was fully loaded, we drove to the main post
office, formed a chain again, and unloaded the cases. Sometimes we
overtook a "Must I Then" column, or met one coming the other way; by
this time they had three bands, and it was all going much faster. It was
late, after midnight, when we had driven off with the last of the cases,
and my hands remembered the number of mess kits and decided there
was very little difference between cases of soap powder and mess kits.

I was very tired and wanted to throw myself on the bed fully dressed,
but once again there was a great stack of bread and cans of liver sausage,
jam and butter, on the table, and the others insisted it be distributed; all
I wanted was the cigarettes, and I had to wait till everything had been
divided up exactly, for of course the Pfc left the cigarettes to the last
again. He took an abnormally long time about it, perhaps to teach me
moderation and discipline and to convey his contempt for my craving;
when I finally got the cigarettes, I lay down on the bed in my clothes
and smoked and watched them spreading their bread with liver sausage,
listened to them praising the excellent quality of the butter, and arguing
mildly as to whether the jam was made of strawberries, apples, and apricots, or of strawberries and apples only. They went on eating for a long
time, and I couldn't fall asleep. Then I heard footsteps coming along the
passage and knew they were for me: I was afraid and yet relieved, and
the strange thing was that they all, the office clerk, the orderly, and the
three probationary teachers who were sitting round the table, stopped
their chewing and looked at me as the footsteps drew closer. Now the
Pfc found it necessary to shout at me: he got up and yelled, calling me
by my surname, "Damn it, take your boots off when you lie down."

There are certain things one refuses to believe, and I still don't believe it, although my ears remember quite well that all of a sudden he called me by my surname; I would have preferred it if we had used surnames all along, but coming so suddenly like that it sounded so funny that, for the first time since the war started, I had to laugh. Meanwhile the door had been flung open and the company clerk was standing by my bed; he was pretty excited, so much so that he didn't bawl me out, although he was a corporal, for lying on the bed with my boots and clothes on, smoking. He said, "You there, in twenty minutes in full marching order in Block 4, understand?" I said "Yes" and got up. He added, "Report to the sergeant major over there," and again I said "Yes" and began to clear out my locker. I hadn't realized the company clerk was still in the room. I was just putting the picture of the girl in my trouser pocket when I heard him say, "I have some bad news, it's going to be tough on you, but it should make you proud too; the first man from this regiment to be killed in action was your roommate, Corporal Leo Siemers."

I had turned round during the last half of this sentence, and they were all looking at me now, including the corporal. I had gone quite pale, and I didn't know whether to be furious or silent. Then I said in a low voice, "But war hasn't been declared yet, he can't have been killed—and he wouldn't have been killed," and I shouted suddenly, "Leo wouldn't get killed, not him ... you know he wouldn't." No one said anything, not even the corporal, and while I cleared out my locker and crammed all the stuff we were told to take with us into my pack, I heard him leave the room. I piled up all the things on the stool so I didn't have to turn around; I couldn't hear a sound from the others, I couldn't even hear them chewing. I packed all my stuff very quickly; the bread, liver sausage, cheese, and butter I left in the locker and turned the key. When I had to turn around, I saw they had managed to get into bed without a sound; I threw my locker key onto the office clerk's bed, saying, "Clear out everything that's still in there, it's all yours." I didn't care for him much, but I liked him best of the five. Later on I was sorry I hadn't left without saying a word, but I was not yet twenty. I slammed the door, took my rifle from the rack outside, went down the stairs, and saw from the clock over the office door downstairs that it was nearly three in the morning. It was quiet and still warm that last Monday of August 1939. I threw Leo's locker key somewhere onto the barrack square as I went across to Block 4. They were all there, the band was already moving into position at the head of the company, and some officer who had given the "united effort" speech was walking across the square; he took off his cap, wiped the sweat from his forehead, and put his cap on again. He reminded me of a streetcar conductor who takes a short break at the terminus.

The sergeant major came up to me and said, "Are you the man from staff headquarters?" and I said "Yes." He nodded; he looked pale and very young, somewhat at a loss; I looked past him toward the dark, scarcely distinguishable mass. All I could make out was the gleaming trumpets of the band. "You wouldn't happen to be a telephone opera-tor?" asked the sergeant major. "We're short one here." "As a matter of fact I am," I said quickly and with an enthusiasm that seemed to surprise him, for he looked at me doubtfully. "Yes, I'm one," I said, "I've had practical training as a telephone operator." "Good," he said, "you're just the man I need. Slip in somewhere there at the end, we'll arrange everything en route." I went over toward the right, where the dark gray was getting a little lighter; as I got closer, I even recognized some faces. I took my place at the end of the company. Someone shouted, "Right turn—forward march!" and I had hardly lifted my foot when they started playing their "Must I Then."

WHEN THE WAR WAS OVER

It was just getting light when we reached the German border: to our left, a broad river, to our right a forest; even from its edges you could tell how deep it was. Silence fell in the boxcar; the train passed slowly over patched-up rails, past shelled houses, splintered telegraph poles. The little guy sitting next to me took off his glasses and polished them carefully.

"Christ," he whispered to me, "d'you have the slightest idea where we are?"

"Yes," I said, "the river you've just seen is known here as the Rhine, the forest you see over there on the right is called the Reich Forest—and we'll soon be getting into Cleves."

"D'you come from around here?"

"No, I don't." He was a nuisance; all night long he had driven me crazy with his high-pitched schoolboy's voice. He had told me how he had secretly read Brecht, Tucholsky, and Walter Benjamin, as well as Proust and Karl Kraus; that he wanted to study sociology, and theology too, and help create a new order for Germany, and when we stopped at Nimwegen at daybreak and someone said we were just coming to the German border, he nervously asked us all if there was anyone who would trade some thread for two cigarette butts, and when no one said anything, I offered to rip off my collar tabs, known—I believe—as insignia, and turn them into dark-green thread. I took off my tunic and watched him carefully pick the things off with a bit of metal, unravel them, and then actually start using the thread to sew on his ensign's piping around his shoulder straps. I asked him whether I might attribute this sewing job to the influence of Brecht, Tucholsky, Benjamin, or Karl Kraus, or was it perhaps the subconscious influence of Jünger that made him restore his rank with Tom Thumb's weapon. He had flushed and said he was through with Jünger, he had written him off; now, as we approached Cleves, he stopped sewing and sat down on the floor beside me, still holding Tom Thumb's weapon.

"Cleves doesn't convey anything to me," he said, "not a thing. How about you?"

"Oh yes," I said, "Lohengrin, Swan margarine, and Anne of Cleves, one of Henry the Eighth's wives."

"That's right," he said, "Lohengrin—although at home we always ate Sanella. Don't you want the butts?"

"No," I said, "take them home for your father. I hope he'll punch you in the nose when you arrive with that piping on your shoulder."

"You don't understand," he said. "Prussia, Kleist, Frankfurt-on-the-Oder, Potsdam, Prince of Homburg, Berlin."

"Well," I said, "I believe it was quite a while ago that Prussia took Cleves—and somewhere over there on the other side of the Rhine there is a little town called Wesel."

"Oh, of course," he said, "that's right, Schill."

"The Prussians never really established themselves beyond the Rhine," I said, "they only had two bridgeheads: Bonn and Koblenz."

"Prussia," he said.

"Blomberg," I said. "Need any more thread?" He flushed and was silent.

The train slowed down, everyone crowded round the open sliding door and looked at Cleves. English guards on the platform, casual and tough, bored yet alert: we were still prisoners. In the street a sign: "To Cologne." Lohengrin's castle up there among the autumn trees. October on the Lower Rhine, Dutch sky; my cousins in Xanten, aunts in Kevelaer; the broad dialect and the smugglers' whispering in the taverns; St. Martin's Day processions, gingerbread men, Breughelesque carnival, and everywhere the smell, even where there was none, of honey cakes.

"I wish you'd try to understand," said the little guy beside me.

"Leave me alone," I said; although he wasn't a man yet, no doubt he soon would be, and that was why I hated him. He was offended and sat back on his heels to add the final stitches to his braid; I didn't even feel sorry for him: clumsily, his thumb smeared with blood, he pushed the needle through the blue cloth of his air force tunic. His glasses were so misted over I couldn't make out whether he was crying or whether it just looked like it. I was close to tears myself: in two hours, three at most, we would be in Cologne, and from there it was not far to the one I had married, the one whose voice had never sounded like marriage.

The woman emerged suddenly from behind the freight shed, and before the guards knew what was happening, she was standing by our boxcar and unwrapping a blue cloth from what I first took to be a baby: a loaf of bread. She handed it to me, and I took it; it was heavy, I swayed for a moment and almost fell forward out of the train as it started moving. The bread was dark, still warm, and I wanted to call out "Thank you, thank you," but the words seemed ridiculous, and the train was moving faster now, so I stayed there on my knees with the heavy loaf in my arms. To this day all I know about the woman is that she was wearing a dark headscarf and was no longer young.

When I got up, clasping the loaf, it was quieter than ever in the boxcar; they were all looking at the bread, and under their stares it got heavier and heavier. I knew those eyes, I knew the mouths that belonged to those eyes, and for months I had been wondering where the borderline runs between hatred and contempt, and I hadn't found the borderline; for a while I had divided them up into sewers-on and non-sewers-on, when we had been transferred from an American camp (where the wearing of rank insignia was prohibited) to an English one (where the wearing of rank insignia was permitted), and I had felt a certain fellow feeling with the non-sewers-on till I found out they didn't even have any ranks whose insignia they could have sewn on. One of them, Egelhecht, had even tried to drum up a kind of court of honor that was to deny me the quality of being German (and I had wished that this court, which never convened, had actually had the power to deny me this quality). What they didn't know was that I hated them, Nazis and non-Nazis, not because of their sewing and their political views but because they were men, men of the same species as those I had had to spend the last six years with; the words "man" and "stupid" had become almost identical for me.

In the background Egelhecht's voice said, "The first German bread—and he of all people is the one to get it."

He sounded as if he was almost sobbing. I wasn't far off it myself either, but they would never understand that it wasn't just because of the bread, or because by now we had crossed the German border, it was mainly because, for the first time in eight months, I had for one moment felt a woman's hand on my arm.

"No doubt," said Egelhecht in a low voice, "you will even deny the bread the quality of being German."

"Yes, indeed," I said, "I shall employ a typical intellectual's trick and ask myself whether the flour this bread is made of doesn't perhaps come from Holland, England, or America. Here you are," I said. "Divide it up if you like."

Most of them I hated, many I didn't care about one way or the other, and Tom Thumb, who was now the last to join the ranks of the sewers-on, was beginning to be a nuisance; yet I felt it was the right thing to do, to share this loaf with them, I was sure it hadn't been meant only for me.

Egelhecht made his way slowly toward me: he was tall and thin, like me, and he was twenty-six, like me; for three months he had tried to make me see that a nationalist wasn't a Nazi, that the words "honor," "loyalty," "fatherland," "decency," could never lose their value—and I had always countered his impressive array of words with just five: Wilhelm II, Papen, Hindenburg, Blomberg, Keitel. It had infuriated him that I never mentioned Hitler, not even that May I when the sentry ran through the camp blaring through a megaphone, "Hitler's dead, Hitler's dead!"

"Go ahead," I said, "divide up the bread."

"Number off," said Egelhecht. I handed him the loaf, he took off his coat, laid it on the floor of the boxcar with the lining uppermost, smoothed the lining, and placed the bread on it, while the others numbered off around us. "Thirty-two," said Tom Thumb, then there was a silence. "Thirty-two," said Egelhecht, looking at me, for it was up to me to say thirty-three; but I didn't say it. I turned away and looked out at the highway with the old trees: Napoleon's poplars, Napoleon's elms, like the ones I had rested under with my brother when we rode from Weeze to the Dutch border on our bikes to buy chocolate and cigarettes cheap.

I could sense that those behind me were terribly offended; I saw the yellow road signs: "To Kalkar," "To Xanten," "To Geldern," heard behind me the sounds of Egelhecht's tin knife, felt the offendedness swelling like a thick cloud. They were always being offended for some reason or other. They were offended if an English guard offered them a cigarette, and they were offended if he did not; they were offended when I cursed Hitler, and Egelhecht was mortally offended when I did not curse Hitler; Tom Thumb had secretly read Benjamin and Brecht, Proust, Tucholsky, and Karl Kraus, and when we crossed the German border he was sewing on his ensign's piping. I took the cigarette out of my pocket I had got in exchange for my staff Pfc chevron, turned around, and sat down beside Tom Thumb. I watched Egelhecht dividing up the loaf: first he cut it in half, then the halves in quarters, then each quarter again in eight parts. This way there would be a nice fat chunk for each man, a dark cube of bread which I figured would weigh about two to three ounces.

Egelhecht was just quartering the last eighth, and each man, every one of them, knew that the ones who got the center pieces would get at least a quarter to a half ounce extra, because the loaf bulged in the middle and Egelhecht had cut the slices all the same thickness. But then he cut off the bulge of the two center slices and said, "Thirty-three— the youngest starts." Tom Thumb glanced at me, blushed, bent down, took a piece of bread, and put it directly into his mouth. Everything went smoothly till Bouvier, who had almost driven me crazy with his planes he was always talking about, had taken his piece of bread; now it should have been my turn, followed by Egelhecht, but I didn't move. I would have liked to light my cigarette, but I had no matches and nobody offered me one. Those who already had their bread were scared and stopped chewing; the ones who hadn't got their bread yet had no idea what was happening, but they understood: I didn't want to share the loaf with them. They were offended, while the others (who already had their bread) were merely embarrassed. I tried to look outside: at Napoleon's poplars, Napoleon's elms, at the tree-lined road with its gaps, with Dutch sky caught in the gaps, but my attempt to look unconcerned was not successful. I was scared of the fight that was bound to start now; I wasn't much good in a fight, and even if I had been it wouldn't have helped, they would have beaten me up the way they did in the camp near Brussels when I had said I would rather be a dead Jew than a live German. I took the cigarette out of my mouth, partly because it felt ridiculous, partly because I wanted to get it through the fight intact, and I looked at Tom Thumb, who, his face scarlet, was squatting on his heels beside me. Then Gugeler, whose turn it would have been after Egelhecht, took his piece of bread, put it directly into his mouth, and the others took theirs. There were three pieces left when the man came toward me whom I scarcely knew—he had not joined our tent till we were in the camp near Brussels. He was already old, nearly fifty, short, with a dark, scarred face, and whenever we began to quarrel he wouldn't say a word, he used to leave the tent and run along beside the barbed-wire fence like someone to whom this kind of trotting up and down is familiar. I didn't even know his first name; he wore some sort of faded tropical uniform, and civilian shoes. He came from the far end of the boxcar straight toward me, stopped in front of me, and said in a surprisingly gentle voice, "Take the bread"—and when I didn't, he shook his head and said, "You fellows have one hell of a talent for turning everything into a symbolic event. It's just bread, that's all, and the woman gave it to you, the woman—here you are." He picked up a piece of bread, pressed it into my right hand, which was hanging down helplessly, and squeezed my hand around it. His eyes were quite dark, not black, and his face wore the look of many prisons. I nodded, got my hand muscles moving so as to hold on to the bread; a deep sigh went through the car; Egelhecht took his bread, then the old man in the tropical uniform. "Damn it all," said the old fellow, "I've been away from Germany for twelve years. You're a crazy bunch, but I'm just beginning to understand you." Before I could put the bread into my mouth the train stopped, and we got out.

Open country, turnip fields, no trees; a few Belgian guards with the lion of Flanders on their caps and collars ran along beside the train calling, "All out, everybody out!"

Tom Thumb remained beside me; he polished his glasses, looked at the station sign, and said, "Weeze—does this also convey something to you?"

"Yes," I said, "it lies north of Kevelaer and west of Xanten."

"Oh yes," he said, "Kevelaer—Heinrich Heine."

"And Xanten—Siegfried, in case you've forgotten."

Aunt Helen, I thought. Weeze. Why hadn't we gone straight through to Cologne? There wasn't much left of Weeze other than a spattering of red bricks showing through the treetops. Aunt Helen had owned a fairsized shop in Weeze, a regular village store, and every morning she used to slip some money into our pockets so we could go boating on the river Niers or ride over to Kevelaer on our bikes; the sermons on Sunday in church, roundly berating the smugglers and adulterers.

"Let's go," said the Belgian guard. "Get a move on, or don't you want to get home?"

I went into the camp. First we had to file past an English officer who gave us a twenty-mark bill, for which we had to sign a receipt. Next we had to go to the doctor; he was a German, young, and grinned at us; he waited till twelve or fifteen of us were in the room, then said, "Anyone who is so sick that he can't go home today need only raise his hand." A few of us laughed at this terribly witty remark; then we filed past his table one by one, had our release papers stamped, and went out by the other door. I waited for a few moments by the open door and heard him say, "Anyone who is so sick that—," then moved on, heard the laughter when I was already at the far end of the corridor, and went to the next check point. This was an English corporal, standing out in the open next to an uncovered latrine. The corporal said, "Show me your paybooks and any papers you still have." He said this in German, and when they pulled out their paybooks, he pointed to the latrine and told them to throw the books into it, adding, "Down the hatch!" and then most of them laughed at this witticism. It had struck me anyway that Germans suddenly seemed to have a sense of humor, so long as it was foreign humor: in camp even Egelhecht had laughed at the American captain who had pointed to the barbed-wire entanglement and said, "Don't take it so hard, boys, now you're free at last."

The English corporal asked me too about my papers, but all I had was my release; I had sold my paybook to an American for two cigarettes. So I said, "No papers"—and that made him as angry as the American corporal had been when I had answered his question, "Hitler Youth, SA, or Party?" with "No." He had yelled at me and put me on KP, he had sworn at me and accused my grandmother of various sexual offenses the nature of which, due to my insufficient knowledge of the American language, I was unable to ascertain. It made them furious when something didn't fit into their stereotyped categories. The English corporal went purple with rage, stood up, and began to frisk me, and he didn't have to search long before he had found my diary. It was thick, cut from paper bags, stapled together, and in it I had written down everything that had happened to me from the middle of April till the end of September: from being taken prisoner by the American sergeant Stevenson to the final entry I had made in the train as we went through dismal Antwerp and I read on walls "*Vive le Roi!*" There were more than a hundred paper-bag pages, closely written, and the furious corporal took it from me, threw it into the latrine, and said, "Didn't I ask you for your papers?" Then I was allowed to go.

We stood crowded around the camp gate waiting for the Belgian trucks which were supposed to take us to Bonn. Bonn? Why Bonn, of all places? Someone said Cologne was closed off because it was contaminated by corpses, and someone else said we would have to clear away rubble for thirty or forty years, rubble, ruins, "and they aren't even going to give us trucks, we'll have to carry away the rubble in baskets." Luckily there was no one near me who I had shared a tent or sat in the boxcar with. The drivel coming from mouths I did not know was a shade less disgusting than if it had come from mouths I knew. Someone ahead of me said, "But then he didn't mind taking the loaf of bread from the Jew," and another voice said, "Yes, they're the kind of people who are going to set the tone." Someone nudged me from behind and asked, "Four ounces of bread for a cigarette, how about it, eh?" and from behind he thrust his hand in front of my face, and I saw it was one of the pieces of bread Egelhecht had divided up in the train. I shook my head. Someone else said, "The Belgians are selling cigarettes at ten marks apiece." To me that seemed very cheap: in camp the Germans had sold cigarettes for a hundred and twenty marks apiece. "Cigarettes, anyone?" "Yes," I said, and put my twenty-mark bill into an anonymous hand.

Everyone was trading with everyone else. It was the only thing that seriously interested them. For two thousand marks and a threadbare uniform someone got a civilian suit, the deal was concluded, and clothes were changed somewhere in the waiting crowd, and suddenly I heard someone call out, "But of *course* the underpants go with the suit—and the tie too." Someone sold his wristwatch for three thousand marks. The chief article of trade was soap. Those who had been in American camps had a lot of soap—twenty cakes, some of them—for they had been given soap every week but never any water to wash in, and the ones who had been in the English camps had no soap at all. The green and pink cakes of soap went back and forth. Some of the men had discovered their artistic aspirations and shaped the soap into little dogs, cats, and gnomes, and now it turned out that the artistic aspirations had lowered the exchange value. Unsculptured soap rated higher than sculptured, a loss of weight being suspected in the latter.

The anonymous hand into which I had placed the twenty-mark bill actually reappeared and pressed two cigarettes into my left hand, and I was almost touched by so much honesty (but I was almost touched only till I found out that the Belgians were selling cigarettes for five marks; a hundred-percent profit was evidently regarded as a fair markup, especially among "comrades"). We stood there for about two hours, jammed together, and all I remember is hands: trading hands, passing soap from right to left, from left to right, money from left to right and again from right to left; it was as if I had fallen into a snakepit; hands from all sides moved every which way, passing goods and money over my shoulders and over my head in every direction.

Tom Thumb had managed to get close to me again. He sat beside me on the floor of the Belgian truck driving to Kevelaer, through Kevelaer, to Krefeld, around Krefeld to Neuss; there was silence over the fields, in the towns, we saw hardly a soul and only a few animals, and the dark autumn sky hung low. On my left sat Tom Thumb, on my right the Belgian guard, and we looked out over the tailboard at the road I knew so well: my brother and I had often ridden our bicycles along it. Tom Thumb kept trying to justify himself, but I cut him off every time, and he kept trying to be clever; there was no stopping him. "But Neuss," he said, "that can't remind you of anything. What on earth could Neuss remind anybody of?"

"Novesia Chocolate," I said, "sauerkraut, and Quirinus, but I don't suppose you ever heard of the Thebaic Legion."

"No, I haven't," he said, and blushed again.

I asked the Belgian guard if it was true that Cologne was closed off, contaminated by corpses, and he said, "No—but it's a mess all right; is that where you're from?"

"Yes," I said.

"Be prepared for the worst ... do you have any soap left?"

"Yes, I have," I said.

"Here," he said, pulling a pack of tobacco out of his pocket. He opened it and held out the pale-yellow, fresh, fine-cut tobacco for me to smell. "It's yours for two cakes of soap—fair enough?"

I nodded, felt around in my coat pocket for the soap, gave him two cakes, and put the tobacco in my pocket. He gave me his submachine gun to hold while he hid the soap in his pockets; he sighed as I handed it back to him. "These lousy things," he said, "we'll have to go on carrying them around for a while yet. You fellows aren't half as badly off as you think. What are you crying about?"

I pointed toward the right: the Rhine. We were approaching Dormagen. I saw that Tom Thumb was about to open his mouth and said quickly, "For God's sake shut up, can't you? Shut up." He had probably wanted to ask me whether the Rhine reminded me of anything. Thank God he was deeply offended now and said no more till we got to Bonn.

In Cologne there were actually some houses still standing; somewhere I even saw a moving streetcar, some people too, women even: one of them waved to us. From the Neuss-Strasse we turned into the Ring avenues and drove along them, and I was waiting all the time for the tears, but they didn't come; even the insurance buildings on the avenue were in ruins, and all I could see of the Hohenstaufen Baths was a few pale-blue tiles. I was hoping all the time the truck would turn off somewhere to the right, for we had lived on the Carolingian Ring; but the truck did not turn. It drove down the Rings—Barbarossa Square, Saxon Ring, Salian Ring—and I tried not to look, and I wouldn't have looked if the truck convoy had not got into a traffic jam up front at Clovis Square and we hadn't stopped in front of the house we used to live in, so I did look.

The term "totally destroyed" is misleading: only in rare cases is it possible to destroy a house totally. It has to be hit three or four times and, to make certain, it should then burn down; the house we used to live in was actually, according to official terminology, totally destroyed, but not in the technical sense. That is to say, I could still recognize it; the front door and the doorbells, and I submit that a house where it is still possible to recognize the front door and the doorbells has not, in the strict technical sense, been totally destroyed. But of the house we used to live in there was more to be recognized than the doorbells and the front door. Two rooms in the basement were almost intact, on the mezzanine, absurdly enough, even three: a fragment of wall was supporting the third room that would probably not have passed a spirit-level test; our apartment on the second floor had only one room intact, but it was gaping open in front, toward the street; above this, a high, narrow gable reared up, bare, with empty window sockets. However, the interesting thing was that two men were moving around in our living room as if their feet were on familiar ground; one of the men took a picture down from the wall, the Terborch print my father had been so fond of, walked to the front, carrying the picture, and showed it to a third man who was standing down below in front of the house. This third man shook his head like someone who is not interested in an object being auctioned, and the man up above walked back with the Terborch and hung it up again on the wall; he even straightened the picture—I was touched by this mark of neatness—stepped back to make sure the picture was really hanging straight, then nodded in a satisfied way. Meanwhile the second man took the other picture off the wall: an engraving of Lochner's painting of the cathedral, but this one also did not appear to please the third man standing down below. Finally the first man, the one who had hung the Terborch back on the wall, came to the front, formed a megaphone with his hands, and shouted, "Piano in sight!" and the man below laughed, nodded, likewise formed a megaphone with hands, and shouted, "I'll get the straps." I could not see the piano, but I knew where it stood: on the right in the corner I couldn't see into and where the man with the Lochner picture was just disappearing.

"Whereabouts in Cologne did you live?" asked the Belgian guard.

"Oh, somewhere over there," I said, gesturing vaguely in the direction of the western suburbs.

"Thank God, now we're moving again," said the guard. He picked up his submachine gun, which he had placed on the floor of the truck, and straightened his cap. The lion of Flanders on the front of his cap was rather dirty. As we turned into Clovis Square, I could see why there had been a traffic jam: some kind of raid seemed to be going on. English

military police cars were all over the place, and civilians were standing
in them with their hands up, surrounded by a sizable crowd, quiet yet
tense. A surprisingly large number of people in such a silent, ruined city.

"That's the black market," said the Belgian guard. "Once in a while
they come and clean it up."

Before we were even out of Cologne, while we were still on the Bonn-
Strasse, I fell asleep and I dreamed of my mother's coffee mill: the coffee mill was being let down on a strap by the man who had offered the
Terborch without success, but the man below rejected the coffee mill;
the other man drew it up again, opened the hall door, and tried to screw
the coffee mill back where it had hung before, immediately to the left
of the kitchen door, but now there was no wall there for him to screw
it onto, and still the man kept on trying (this mark of tidiness touched
me even in my dream). He searched with the forefinger of his right hand
for the pegs, couldn't find them, and raised his fist threateningly to the
gray autumn sky which offered no support for the coffee mill. Finally
he gave up, tied the strap around the mill again, went to the front, let
down the coffee mill, and offered it to the third man, who again rejected
it, and the other man pulled it up again, untied the strap, and hid the
coffee mill under his jacket as if it were a valuable object; then he began
to wind up the strap, rolled it into a coil, and threw it down into the
third man's face. All this time I was worried about what could have
happened to the man who had offered the Lochner without success, but
I couldn't see him anywhere; something was preventing me from looking into the corner where the piano was, my father's desk, and I was
upset at the thought that he might be reading my father's diaries. Now
the man with the coffee mill was standing by the living-room door trying to screw the coffee mill onto the door panel; he seemed absolutely
determined to give the coffee mill a permanent resting place, and I was
beginning to like him, even before I discovered he was one of our many
friends whom my mother had comforted while they sat on the chair
beneath the coffee mill, one of those who had been killed right at the
beginning of the war in an air raid.

Before we got to Bonn, the Belgian guard woke me up. "Come on,"
he said, "rub your eyes, freedom is at hand," and I straightened up and

thought of all the people who had sat on the chair beneath my mother's coffee mill: truant schoolboys whom she helped to overcome their fear of exams, Nazis whom she tried to enlighten, non-Nazis whom she tried to fortify—they had all sat on the chair beneath the coffee mill, had received comfort and censure, defense and respite. Bitter words had destroyed their ideals and gentle words had offered them those things which would outlive the times: mercy to the weak, comfort to the persecuted.

The old cemetery, the market square, the university. Bonn. Through the Koblenz Gate and into the park. "So long," said the Belgian guard, and Tom Thumb with his tired child's face said, "Drop me a line some time."

"All right," I said, "I'll send you my complete Tucholsky."

"Wonderful," he said, "and your Kleist too?"

"No," I said, "only the ones I have duplicates of."

On the other side of the barricade through which we were finally released, a man was standing between two big laundry baskets; in one he had a lot of apples, in the other a few cakes of soap. He shouted, "Vitamins, my friends, one apple—one cake of soap!" And I could feel my mouth watering. I had quite forgotten what apples looked like; I gave him a cake of soap, was handed an apple, and bit into it at once. I stood there watching the others come out; there was no need for him to call out now: it was a wordless exchange. He would take an apple out of the basket, be handed a cake of soap, and throw the soap into the empty basket; there was a dull thud when the soap landed. Not everyone took an apple, not everyone had any soap, but the transaction was as swift as in a self-service store, and by the time I had just finished my apple, he already had his soap basket half full. The whole thing took place swiftly and smoothly and without a word; even the ones who were very economical and very calculating couldn't resist the sight of the apples, and I began to feel sorry for them. Home was welcoming its homecomers so warmly with vitamins.

It took me a long time to find a phone in Bonn; finally a girl in the post office told me that the only people to get phones were doctors and priests, and even then only those who hadn't been Nazis. "They're

scared stiff of the Nazi Werewolf underground," she said. "I s'pose you
wouldn't have a cigarette for me?" I took my pack of tobacco out of my
pocket and said, "Shall I roll one for you?," but she said no, she could
do it herself, and I watched her take a cigarette paper out of her coat
pocket and quickly and deftly roll herself a firm cigarette. "Who do you
want to call?" she said, and I said, "My wife," and she laughed and said
I didn't look married at all. I also rolled myself a cigarette and asked
her whether there was any chance of selling some soap: I needed money,
train fare, and didn't have a pfennig. "Soap," she said, "let's have a
look." I felt around in my coat lining and pulled out some soap, and
she snatched it out of my hand, sniffed it, and said, "Real Palmolive!
That's worth—worth—I'll give you fifty marks for it." I looked at her in
amazement, and she said, "Yes, I know, you can get as much as eighty
for it, but I can't afford that." I didn't want to take the fifty marks, but
she insisted, she thrust the note into my coat pocket and ran out of
the post office; she was quite pretty, with that hungry prettiness which
lends a girl's voice a certain sharpness.

What struck me most of all, in the post office and as I walked
slowly on through Bonn, was the fact that nowhere was there a student
wearing colored ribbons; and the smells: everyone smelled terrible, all
the rooms smelled terrible, and I could see why the girl was so crazy
about the soap. I went to the station, tried to find out how I could get
to Oberkerschenbach (that was where the one I married lived), but
nobody could tell me; all I knew was that it was a little place somewhere in the Eifel district not too far from Bonn. There weren't any
maps anywhere either, where I could have looked it up; no doubt they
had been banned on account of the Nazi Werewolves. I always like to
know where a place is, and it bothered me that I knew nothing definite
about this place Oberkerschenbach and couldn't find out anything definite. In my mind I went over all the Bonn addresses I knew, but there
wasn't a single doctor or a single priest among them; finally I remembered a professor of theology I had called on with a friend just before
the war. He had had some sort of trouble with Rome and the Index, and
we had gone to see him simply to give him our moral support; I couldn't
remember the name of the street, but I knew where it was, and I walked
along the Poppelsdorf Avenue, turned left, then left again, found the
house, and was relieved to read the name on the door.

The professor came to the door himself. He had aged a great deal, he was thin and bent, his hair quite white. I said, "You won't remember me, Professor. I came to see you some years ago when you had that stink with Rome and the Index—can I speak to you for a moment?" He laughed when I said stink, and said, "Of course," when I had finished, and I followed him into his study; I noticed it no longer smelled of tobacco, otherwise it was still just the same, with all the books, files, and house plants. I told the professor I had heard that the only people who got phones were priests and doctors, and I simply had to call my wife. He heard me out—a very rare thing—then said that, although he was a priest, he was not one of those who had a phone, for "You see," he said, "I am not a pastor." "Perhaps you're a Werewolf," I said. I offered him some tobacco, and I felt sorry for him when I saw how he looked at my tobacco; I am always sorry for old people who have to go without something they like. His hands trembled as he filled his pipe, and they did not tremble just because he was old. When he had at last got it lit—I had no matches and couldn't help him—he told me that doctors and priests were not the only people with phones. "These nightclubs they're opening up everywhere for the soldiers," they had them too, and I might try in one of these nightclubs; there was one just around the corner. He wept when I put a few pipefuls of tobacco on his desk as I left, and he asked me as his tears fell whether I knew what I was doing, and I said, yes, I knew, and I suggested he accept the few pipefuls of tobacco as a belated tribute to the courage he had shown toward Rome all those years ago. I would have liked to give him some soap as well, I still had five or six pieces in my coat lining, but I was afraid his heart would burst with joy; he was so old and frail.

"Nightclub" was a nice way of putting it, but I didn't mind that so much as the English sentry at the door of this nightclub. He was very young and eyed me severely as I stopped beside him. He pointed to the notice prohibiting Germans from entering this nightclub, but I told him my sister worked there, I had just returned to my beloved fatherland, and my sister had the house key. He asked me what my sister's name was, and it seemed safest to give the most German of all German girls' names, so I said, "Gretchen." Oh yes, he said, that was the blond one, and let me go in. Instead of bothering to describe the interior, I refer the reader to the pertinent "Fräulein literature" and to movies and TV. I won't even bother to describe Gretchen (see above). The main thing was that Gretchen was surprisingly quick on the uptake and, in exchange for a cake of Palmolive, was willing to make a phone call to the priest's house in Kerschenbach (which I hoped existed) and have the one I had married called to the phone. Gretchen spoke fluent English on the phone and told me her boyfriend would try to do it through the army exchange, it would be quicker. While we were waiting, I offered her some tobacco, but she had something better; I tried to pay her the agreed fee of a cake of soap in advance, but she said no, she didn't want it after all, she would rather not take anything, and when I insisted on paying she began to cry and confided that one of her brothers was a prisoner of war, the other one dead, and I felt sorry for her, for it is not pleasant when girls like Gretchen cry. She even let on that she was a Catholic, and just as she was about to get her first communion picture out of a drawer the phone rang, and Gretchen lifted the receiver and said "Reverend," but I had already heard that it was not a man's voice. "Just a moment," Gretchen said, and handed me the receiver. I was so excited I couldn't hold the receiver; in fact, I dropped it, fortunately onto Gretchen's lap. She picked it up, held it against my ear, and I said, "Hello—is that you?"

"Yes," she said. "Darling, where are you?"

"I'm in Bonn," I said. "The war's over—for me."

"My God," she said, "I can't believe it. No—it's not true."

"It is true," I said, "it is—did you get my postcard?"

"No," she said, "what postcard?"

"When we were taken prisoner, we were allowed to write one postcard."

"No," she said, "for the last eight months I haven't had the slightest idea where you were."

"Those bastards," I said, "those dirty bastards. Listen, just tell me where Kerschenbach is."

"I"—she was crying so hard she couldn't speak, I heard her sobbing and gulping till at last she was able to whisper—"at the station in Bonn, I'll meet you," then I could no longer hear her, someone said something in English that I didn't understand.

Gretchen put the receiver to her ear, listened a moment, shook her head, and replaced it. I looked at her and knew I couldn't offer her the soap now. I couldn't even say "Thank you," the words seemed ridiculous. I lifted my arms helplessly and went out.

I walked back to the station, in my ear the woman's voice which had never sounded like marriage.

18 STORIES

18 Stories *was published in English by McGraw-Hill in 1966. Most of these stories were collected in German as part of* Erzählungen, Hörspiele, Aufsätze *(Stories, Radio Plays, Essays), published by Kiepenheuer & Witsch in 1961.*

LIKE A BAD DREAM

That evening we had invited the Zumpens over for dinner, nice people; it was through my father-in-law that we had got to know them. Ever since we have been married he has helped me to meet people who can be useful to me in business, and Zumpen can be useful: he is chairman of a committee which places contracts for large housing projects, and I have married into the excavating business.

I was tense that evening, but Bertha, my wife, reassured me. "The fact," she said, "that he's coming at all is promising. Just try to get the conversation round to the contract. You know it's tomorrow they're going to be awarded."

I stood looking through the net curtains of the glass front door, waiting for Zumpen. I smoked, ground the cigarette butts under my foot, and shoved them under the mat. Next I took up a position at the bathroom window and stood there wondering why Zumpen had accepted the invitation; he couldn't be that interested in having dinner with us, and the fact that the big contract I was involved in was going to be awarded tomorrow must have made the whole thing as embarrassing to him as it was to me.

I thought about the contract too: it was a big one, I would make twenty thousand marks on the deal, and I wanted the money.

Bertha had decided what I was to wear: a dark jacket, trousers a shade lighter, and a conservative tie. That's the kind of thing she learned at home, and at boarding school from the nuns. Also what to offer guests: when to pass the cognac, and when the vermouth, how to arrange dessert. It is comforting to have a wife who knows all about such things.

But Bertha was tense too: as she put her hands on my shoulders, they touched my neck, and I felt her thumbs damp and cold against it.

"It's going to be all right," she said. "You'll get the contract."

"Christ," I said, "it means twenty thousand marks to me, and you know how we need the money."

"One should never," she said gently, "mention Christ's name in connection with money."

A dark car drew up in front of our house, a make I didn't recognize, but it looked Italian. "Take it easy," Bertha whispered, "wait till they've rung, let them stand there for a couple of seconds, then walk slowly to the door and open it."

I watched Herr and Frau Zumpen come up the steps: he is slender and tall, with graying temples, the kind of man who fifty years ago would have been known as a "ladies' man"; Frau Zumpen is one of those thin, dark women who always make me think of lemons. I could tell from Zumpen's face that it was a frightful bore for him to have dinner with us.

Then the doorbell rang, and I waited one second, two seconds, walked slowly to the door and opened it.

"Well," I said, "how nice of you to come!"

Cognac glasses in hand, we went from room to room in our apartment, which the Zumpens wanted to see. Bertha stayed in the kitchen to squeeze some mayonnaise out of a tube onto the appetizers; she does this very nicely: hearts, loops, little houses. The Zumpens complimented us on our apartment. They exchanged smiles when they saw the big desk in my study; at that moment it seemed a bit too big even to me.

Zumpen admired a small rococo cabinet, a wedding present from my grandmother, and a baroque Madonna in our bedroom.

By the time we got back to the dining room, Bertha had dinner on the table. She had done this very nicely too; it was all so attractive yet so natural, and dinner was pleasant and relaxed. We talked about movies and books, about the recent elections, and Zumpen praised the assortment of cheeses, and Frau Zumpen praised the coffee and the pastries. Then we showed the Zumpens our honeymoon pictures: photographs of the Breton coast, Spanish donkeys, and street scenes from Casablanca.

After that we had some more cognac, and when I stood up to get the box with the photos of the time when we were engaged, Bertha gave me a sign, so I didn't get the box. For two minutes there was absolute silence, because we had nothing more to talk about, and we all thought about the contract; I thought of the twenty thousand marks, and it struck me that I could deduct the bottle of cognac from my income tax.

Zumpen looked at his watch and said, "Too bad, it's ten o'clock; we have to go. It's been such a pleasant evening!" And Frau Zumpen said, "It was really delightful, and I hope you'll come to us one evening."

"We would love to," Bertha said, and we stood around for another half minute, all thinking again about the contract, and I felt Zumpen was waiting for me to take him aside and bring up the subject. But I didn't. Zumpen kissed Bertha's hand, and I went ahead, opened the doors, and held the car door open for Frau Zumpen down below.

"Why," said Bertha gently, "didn't you mention the contract to him? You know it's going to be awarded tomorrow."

"Well," I said, "I didn't know how to bring the conversation round to it."

"Now, look," she said in a quiet voice, "you could have used any excuse to ask him into your study, that's where you should have talked to him. You must have noticed how interested he is in art. You ought to have said: I have an eighteenth-century crucifix in there you might like to have a look at, and then..."

I said nothing, and she sighed and tied on her apron. I followed her into the kitchen; we put the rest of the appetizers back in the refrigerator, and I crawled about on the floor looking for the top of the mayonnaise tube. I put away the remains of the cognac, counted the cigars: Zumpen had smoked only one. I emptied the ashtrays, ate another pastry, and looked to see if there was any coffee left in the pot. When I went back to the kitchen, Bertha was standing there with the car key in her hand.

"What's up?" I asked.

"We have to go over there, of course," she said.

"Over where?"

"To the Zumpens'," she said, "where do you think?"

"It's nearly half past ten."

"I don't care if it's midnight," Bertha said, "all I know is, there's twenty thousand marks involved. Don't imagine they're squeamish."

She went into the bathroom to get ready, and I stood behind her watching her wipe her mouth and draw in new outlines, and for the first time I noticed how wide and primitive that mouth is. When she tightened the knot of my tie I could have kissed her, the way I always used to when she fixed my tie, but I didn't.

Downtown the cafés and restaurants were brightly lit. People were sitting outside on the terraces, and the light from the streetlamps was caught in the silver ice-cream dishes and ice buckets. Bertha gave me an encouraging look; but she stayed in the car when we stopped in front of the Zumpens' house, and I pressed the bell at once and was surprised how quickly the door was opened. Frau Zumpen did not seem surprised to see me; she had on some black lounging pajamas with loose full trousers embroidered with yellow flowers, and this made me think more than ever of lemons.

"I beg your pardon," I said. "I would like to speak to your husband."

"He's gone out again," she said. "He'll be back in half an hour."

In the hall I saw a lot of Madonnas, Gothic and baroque, even rococo Madonnas, if there is such a thing.

"I see," I said. "Well, then, if you don't mind, I'll come back in half an hour."

Bertha had bought an evening paper; she was reading it and smoking, and when I sat down beside her, she said, "I think you could have talked about it to her too."

"But how did you know he wasn't there?"

"Because I know he is at the Gaffel Club playing chess, as he does every Wednesday evening at this time."

"You might have told me that earlier."

"Please try to understand," said Bertha, folding the newspaper. "I am trying to help you, I want you to find out for yourself how to deal with such things. All we had to do was call up Father and he would have settled the whole thing for you with one phone call, but I want you to get the contract on your own."

"All right," I said, "then what'll we do: wait here half an hour, or go up right away and have a talk with her?"

"We'd better go up right away," said Bertha.

We got out of the car and went up in the elevator together. "Life," said Bertha, "consists of making compromises and concessions."

Frau Zumpen was no more surprised now than she had been earlier, when I had come alone. She greeted us, and we followed her into her husband's study. Frau Zumpen brought some cognac, poured it out, and before I could say anything about the contract she pushed a yellow folder toward me: "Fir Tree Haven Housing Project," I read, and looked up in alarm at Frau Zumpen, at Bertha, but they both smiled, and Frau Zumpen said, "Open the folder," and I opened it; inside was another one, pink, and on this I read: "Fir Tree Haven Housing Project—Excavation Work." I opened this too, saw my estimate lying there on top of the pile; along the upper edge someone had written in red: "Lowest bid."

I could feel myself flushing with pleasure, my heart thumping, and I thought of the twenty thousand marks.

"Christ," I said softly, and closed the file, and this time Bertha forgot to rebuke me.

"*Prost,*" said Frau Zumpen with a smile. "Let's drink to it, then."

We drank, and I stood up and said, "It may seem rude of me, but perhaps you'll understand that I would like to go home now."

"I understand perfectly," said Frau Zumpen. "There's just one small item to be taken care of." She took the file, leafed through it, and said, "Your price per square yard is thirty pfennigs below that of the next-lowest bidder. I suggest you raise your price by fifteen pfennigs: that way you'll still be the lowest and you'll have made an extra four thousand five hundred marks. Come on, do it now!" Bertha took her pen out of her purse and offered it to me, but I was in too much of a turmoil to write; I gave the file to Bertha and watched her alter the price with a steady hand, rewrite the total, and hand the file back to Frau Zumpen.

"And now," said Frau Zumpen, "just one more little thing. Get out your checkbook and write a check for three thousand marks; it must be a cash check and endorsed by you."

She had said this to me, but it was Bertha who pulled our checkbook out of her purse and made out the check.

"It won't be covered," I said in a low voice.

"When the contract is awarded, there will be an advance, and then it will be covered," said Frau Zumpen.

Perhaps I failed to grasp what was happening at the time. As we went down in the elevator, Bertha said she was happy, but I said nothing.

Bertha chose a different way home. We drove through quiet residential districts, I saw lights in open windows, people sitting on balconies drinking wine; it was a clear, warm night.

"I suppose the check was for Zumpen?" was all I said, softly, and Bertha replied, just as softly, "Of course."

HEINRICH BÖLL

I looked at Bertha's small brown hands on the steering wheel, so confident and quiet—hands, I thought, that sign checks and squeeze mayonnaise tubes—and I looked higher, at her mouth, and still felt no desire to kiss it.

That evening I did not help Bertha put the car away in the garage, nor did I help her with the dishes. I poured myself a large cognac, went up to my study, and sat down at my desk, which was much too big for me. I was wondering about something. I got up, went into the bedroom, and looked at the baroque Madonna, but even there I couldn't put my finger on the thing I was wondering about.

The ringing of the phone interrupted my thoughts; I lifted the receiver and was not surprised to hear Zumpen's voice.

"Your wife," he said, "made a slight mistake. She raised the price by twenty-five pfennigs instead of fifteen."

I thought for a moment and then said, "That wasn't a mistake, she did it with my consent."

He was silent for a second or two, then said with a laugh, "So you had already discussed the various possibilities?"

"Yes," I said.

"All right, then, make out another check for a thousand."

"Five hundred," I said, and I thought: It's like a bad dream—that's what it's like.

"Eight hundred," he said, and I said with a laugh, "Six hundred," and I knew, although I had no experience to go on, that he would now say seven hundred and fifty, and when he did I said "Yes" and hung up.

It was not yet midnight when I went downstairs and over to the car to give Zumpen the check; he was alone and laughed as I reached in to hand him the folded check.

When I walked slowly back into the house, there was no sign of Bertha; she didn't appear when I went back into my study; she didn't appear when I went downstairs again for a glass of milk from the refrigerator, and I knew what she was thinking; she was thinking: He has to get over it, and I have to leave him alone; this is something he has to understand.

But I never did understand. It is beyond understanding.

THE THROWER-AWAY

For the last few weeks I have been trying to avoid people who might ask me what I do for a living. If I really had to put a name to my occupation, I would be forced to utter a word that would alarm people. So I prefer the abstract method of putting down my confession on paper.

Until recently I would have been prepared at any time to make an oral confession. I almost insisted. I called myself an inventor, a scholar, even a student, and, in the melodramatic mood of incipient intoxication, an unrecognized genius. I basked in the cheerful fame which a frayed collar can radiate; arrogantly, as if it were mine by right, I exacted reluctant credit from suspicious shopkeepers who watched margarine, ersatz coffee, and cheap tobacco disappear into my pockets; I reveled in my unkempt appearance, and at breakfast, lunch, and dinner I drank the nectar of bohemian life: the bliss of knowing one is not conforming.

But for the past few weeks I have been boarding the streetcar every morning just before seven-thirty at the corner of the Roonstrasse; like everyone else I meekly hold out my season ticket to the conductor. I have on a gray double-breasted suit, a striped shirt, a dark-green tie, I carry my sandwiches in a flat aluminum box and hold the morning paper, lightly rolled, in my hand. I look like a citizen who has managed to avoid introspection. After the third stop I get up to offer my seat to one of the elderly working women who have got on at the housing settlement. Having sacrificed my seat on the altar of social compassion, I continue to read the newspaper standing up, now and again letting myself be heard in the capacity of arbitrator when morning irritation is inclined to make people unjust. I correct the worst political and historical errors (by explaining, for instance, that there is a certain difference between SA and USA); as soon as anyone puts a cigarette to his lips, I discreetly hold my lighter in front of his nose and, with the aid of the tiny but dependable flame, light his morning cigarette for him. Thus I complete the picture of a well-groomed fellow citizen who is still young enough for people to say he "has nice manners."

I seem to have been successful in donning the mask that makes it impossible to ask me about my occupation. I am evidently taken for an educated businessman dealing in attractively packaged and agreeably smelling articles such as coffee, tea, or spices, or in valuable small objects which are pleasing to the eye such as jewelry or watches; a man who practices his profession in a nice old-fashioned office with dark oil paintings of merchant forebears hanging on the walls, who phones his wife about ten, who knows how to imbue his apparently impassive voice with that hint of tenderness which betrays affection and concern. Since I also participate in the usual jokes and do not refrain from laughing when every morning at the Lohengrinstrasse the clerk from City Hall shouts out "When does the next swan leave?," since I do not withhold my comments concerning either the events of the day or the results of the football pools, I am obviously regarded as someone who, although prosperous (as can be seen from his suit material), has an attitude toward life that is deeply rooted in the principles of democracy. An air of integrity encases me the way the glass coffin encased Snow White.

When a passing truck provides the streetcar window with a background for a moment, I check up on the expression on my face: isn't it perhaps rather too pensive, almost verging on the sorrowful? I assiduously erase the remnants of brooding and do my best to give my face the expression I want it to wear: neither reserved nor familiar, neither superficial nor profound.

My camouflage seems to be successful, for when I get out at the Marienplatz and dive into the maze of streets in the Old Town, where there is no lack of nice old-fashioned offices, where notaries and lawyers abound, no one suspects that I pass through a rear entrance into the UBIA building—a firm that can boast of supporting three hundred fifty people and of insuring the lives of four hundred thousand. The commissionaire greets me with a smile at the delivery entrance, I walk past him, go down to the basement, and start in on my work, which has to be completed by the time the employees come pouring into the offices at eight-thirty. The activity that I pursue every morning between eight and eight-thirty in the basement of this respected establishment is devoted entirely to destruction. I throw away.

It took me years to invent my profession, to endow it with mathematical plausibility. I wrote treatises; graphs and charts covered—and still cover—the walls of my apartment. For years I climbed along abscissas and up ordinates, wallowed in theories, and savored the glacial ecstasy of solving formulas. Yet since practicing my profession and seeing my theories come to life, I am filled with a sense of sadness such as may come over a general who finds himself obliged to descend from the heights of strategy to the plains of tactics.

I enter my workroom, exchange my jacket for a gray smock, and immediately set to work. I open the mailbags which the commissionaire has already picked up earlier from the main post office, and I empty them into the two wooden bins which, constructed according to my design, hang to the right and left on the wall over my worktable. This way I only need to stretch out my hands, somewhat like a swimmer, and begin swiftly to sort the mail.

First I separate the circulars from the letters, a purely routine job, since a glance at the postage suffices. At this stage a knowledge of the postal tariff renders hesitation unnecessary. After years of practice I am able to complete this phase within half an hour, and by this time it is half past eight and I can hear the footsteps of the employees pouring into the offices overhead. I ring for the commissionaire, who takes the sorted letters to the various departments. It never fails to sadden me, the sight of the commissionaire carrying off in a metal tray the size of a briefcase the remains of what had once filled three mailbags. I might feel triumphant, for this, the vindication of my theory of throwing away, has for years been the objective of my private research; but, strangely enough, I do not feel triumphant. To have been right is by no means always a reason for rejoicing.

After the departure of the commissionaire there remains the task of examining the huge pile of printed matter to make sure it contains no letter masquerading behind the wrong postage, no bill mailed as a circular. This work is almost always superfluous, for the probity of the mailing public is nothing short of astounding. I must admit that here my calculations were incorrect: I had overestimated the number of postal defrauders.

Rarely has a postcard, a letter, or a bill sent as printed matter escaped my notice; about half past nine I ring for the commissionaire, who takes the remaining objects of my careful scrutiny to the departments.

The time has now come when I require some refreshment. The commissionaire's wife brings me my coffee, I take my sandwich out of the flat aluminum box, sit down for my break, and chat with the commissionaire's wife about her children. Is Alfred doing somewhat better in arithmetic? Has Gertrude been able to catch up in spelling? Alfred is not doing any better in arithmetic, whereas Gertrude has been able to catch up in spelling. Have the tomatoes ripened properly, are the rabbits plump, and was the experiment with the melons successful? The tomatoes have not ripened properly, but the rabbits are plump, while the experiment with the melons is still undecided. Serious problems, such as whether one should stock up on potatoes or not, matters of education, such as whether one should enlighten one's children or be enlightened by them, are the subjects of our intense consideration.

Just before eleven the commissionaire's wife leaves, and usually she asks me to let her have some travel folders. She is collecting them, and I smile at her enthusiasm, for I have retained tender memories of travel folders. As a child I also collected travel folders, I used to fish them out of my father's wastepaper basket. Even as a boy it bothered me that my father would take mail from the mailman and throw it into the wastepaper basket without looking at it. This action wounded my innate propensity for economy: there was something that had been designed, set up, printed, put in an envelope, and stamped, that had passed through the mysterious channels by which the postal service actually causes our mail to arrive at our addresses; it was weighted with the sweat of the draftsman, the writer, the printer, the office boy who had stuck on the stamps; on various levels and in various tariffs it had cost money. All this only to end—without being deemed worthy of so much as a glance—in a wastepaper basket?

At the age of eleven I had already adopted the habit of taking out of the wastepaper basket, as soon as my father had left for the office, whatever had been thrown away. I would study it, sort it, and put it away in a chest which I used to keep toys in. Thus by the time I was twelve I already possessed an imposing collection of wine-merchants' catalogs, as well as prospectuses on naturopathy and natural history. My collection of travel folders assumed the dimensions of a geographical encyclopedia—Dalmatia was as familiar to me as the Norwegian fjords, Scotland as close as Zakopane, the forests of Bohemia soothed me while the waves of the Atlantic disquieted me—hinges were offered me, houses and buttons, political parties asked for my vote, charities for my money; lotteries promised me riches, religious sects poverty. I leave it to the reader's imagination to picture what my collection was like when at the age of seventeen, suddenly bored with it all, I offered my collection to a junk dealer who paid me seven marks and sixty pfennigs for it.

Having finished school, I embarked in my father's footsteps and set my foot on the first rung of the civil service ladder. With the seven marks and sixty pfennigs I bought a package of squared paper and three colored crayons, and my attempt to gain a foothold in the civil service turned into a laborious detour, for a happy thrower-away was slumbering in me while I filled the role of an unhappy junior clerk. All my free time was devoted to intricate calculations.

Stopwatch, pencil, slide rule, graph paper, these were the props of my obsession; I calculated how long it took to open a circular of small, medium, or large size, with or without pictures, give it a quick glance, satisfy oneself of its uselessness, and then throw it in the wastepaper basket, a process requiring a minimum of five seconds and a maximum of twenty-five. If the circular is at all attractive, either the text or the pictures, several minutes, often a quarter of an hour, must be allowed for this. By conducting bogus negotiations with printing firms, I also worked out the minimum production costs for circulars. Indefatigably I checked the results of my studies and adjusted them (it did not occur to me until two years later that the time of the cleaning women who have to empty the wastepaper baskets had to be included in my calculations); I applied the results of my research to firms with ten, twenty, a hundred or more employees; and I arrived at results that an expert on economics would not have hesitated to describe as alarming.

Obeying my sense of loyalty, I began by offering my results to my superiors; although I had reckoned with the possibility of ingratitude, I was nevertheless shocked at the extent of that ingratitude. I was accused of neglecting my duties, suspected of nihilism, pronounced "a mental case," and discharged. To the great sorrow of my kind parents, I abandoned my promising career, began new ones, broke these off too, forsook the warmth of the parental hearth, and, as I have already said, eked out my existence as an unrecognized genius. I took pleasure in the humiliation of vainly peddling my invention, and spent years in a blissful state of being antisocial, so consistently that my punch card in the central files, which had long ago been punched with the symbol for "mental case," was now stamped with the confidential symbol for "antisocial."

In view of these circumstances, it can readily be imagined what a shock it was when the obviousness of my results at last became obvious to someone else—the manager of UBIA—how deeply humiliated I was to have to wear a dark-green tie, yet I must continue to go around in disguise as I am terrified of being found out. I try anxiously to give my face the proper expression when I laugh at the Lohengrin joke, since there is no greater vanity than that of the wags who populate the streetcar every morning. Sometimes too I am afraid the streetcar may be full of people who the previous day have done work I am about to destroy that very morning: printers, typesetters, draftsmen, writers who compose the wording of advertisements, commercial artists, envelope stuffers, packers, apprentices of all kinds. From eight to eight-thirty every morning I ruthlessly destroy the products of respected paper mills, worthy printing establishments, brilliant commercial artists, the texts of talented writers; coated paper, glossy paper, copperplate, I take it all, just as it comes from the mailbag, and without the faintest sentimentality tie it up into handy bundles for the wastepaper dealer. In the space of one hour I destroy the output of two hundred man-hours and save UBIA a further one hundred hours, so that altogether (here I must lapse into my own jargon) I achieve a concentrate of 1:300.

When the commissionaire's wife leaves with the empty coffeepot and the travel folders, I knock off. I wash my hands, exchange my smock for my jacket, pick up the morning paper, and leave the UBIA building by the rear entrance. I stroll through the town and wonder how I can escape from tactics and get back into strategy. What intoxicated me as a formula I find disappointing, since it can be performed so easily. Strategy translated into action can be carried out by hacks. I shall probably establish schools for throwers-away. I may possibly also attempt to have throwers-away placed in post offices, perhaps even in printing establishments; an enormous amount of energy, valuable commodities, and intelligence could be utilized, as well as postage saved; it might even be feasible to conceive, compose, and set brochures up in type but not print them. These are all problems still requiring a lot of study.

However, the mere throwing away of mail as such has almost ceased to interest me; any improvements on that level can be worked out by means of the basic formula. For a long time now I have been devoting my attention to calculations concerning wrapping paper and the process of wrapping: this is virgin territory, where nothing has been done, here one can strive to spare humanity those unprofitable efforts under the burden of which it is groaning. Every day billions of throwing-away movements are made, energies are dissipated which, could they but be utilized, would suffice to change the face of the earth. It would be a great advantage if one were permitted to undertake experiments in department stores; should one dispense with the wrapping process altogether, or should one post an expert thrower-away right next to the wrapping table who unwraps what has just been wrapped and immediately ties the wrapping paper into bundles for the wastepaper dealer? These are problems meriting some thought. In any case it has struck me that in many shops the customers implore the clerk not to wrap the purchased article, but that they have to submit to having it wrapped. Clinics for nervous diseases are rapidly filling with patients who complain of an attack of nerves whenever they unwrap a bottle of perfume or a box of chocolates, or open a pack of cigarettes, and at the moment I am making an intensive study of a young man from my neighborhood who earned his living as a book reviewer but at times was unable to practice his profession because he found it impossible to undo the twisted wire tied around the parcel, and even when he did find himself equal to this physical exertion, he was incapable of penetrating the massive layer of gummed paper with which the corrugated paper is stuck together. The man appears deeply disturbed and has now gone over to reviewing the books unread and placing the parcels on his bookshelves without unwrapping them. I leave it to the reader's imagination to depict for himself the effect of such a case on our intellectual life.

While walking through the town between eleven and one, I observe all sorts of details: I spend some time unobtrusively in the department stores, hovering around the wrapping tables; I stand in front of tobacco shops and pharmacies and note down minor statistics; now and again I even purchase something, so as to allow the senseless procedure to be performed on myself and to discover how much effort is required actually to take possession of the article one wishes to own.

So between eleven and one in my impeccable suit I complete the picture of a man who is sufficiently prosperous to afford a bit of leisure—who at about one o'clock enters a sophisticated little restaurant, casually chooses the most expensive meal, and scribbles some hieroglyphics on his beer coaster which could equally well be stock quotations or flights of poetry; who knows how to praise or decry the quality of the meat with arguments which betray the connoisseur to even the most blasé waiter; who, when it comes to choosing dessert, hesitates with a knowing air between cake, ice cream, and cheese; and who finishes off his scribblings with a flourish which proves that they were stock quotations after all.

Shocked at the results of my calculations, I leave the little restaurant. My expression becomes more and more thoughtful while I search for a small café where I can pass the time till three o'clock and read the evening paper. At three I reenter the UBIA building by the rear door to take care of the afternoon mail, which consists almost exclusively of circulars. It is a matter of scarcely fifteen minutes to pick out the ten or twelve letters; I don't even have to wash my hands after this; I just brush them off, take the letters to the commissionaire, leave the building, and at the Marienplatz board the streetcar, glad that on the way home I do not need to laugh at the Lohengrin joke. When the dark tarpaulin of a passing truck makes a background for the streetcar window, I can see my face. It is relaxed; that is to say, pensive, almost brooding, and I relish the fact that I do not have to put on any other face, for at this hour none of my morning fellow travelers has finished work. I get out at the Roonstrasse, buy some fresh rolls, a piece of cheese or sausage, some ground coffee, and walk up to my little apartment, the walls of which are hung with graphs and charts, with hectic curves: between the abscissas and ordinates I capture the lines of a fever going up and up; not a single one of my curves goes down, not a single one of my formulas has the power to soothe me. I groan under the burden of my vision of economics, and while the water is boiling for the coffee I place my slide rule, my notes, pencil, and paper in readiness.

My apartment is sparsely furnished, it looks more like a laboratory. I drink my coffee standing up and hastily swallow a sandwich, the epicure I was at noon is now a thing of the past. Wash hands, light a cigarette, then I set my stopwatch and unwrap the nerve tonic I bought that morning on my stroll through the town—outer wrapping paper, cellophane covering, carton, inside wrapping paper, directions for use secured by a rubber band: thirty-seven seconds. The nervous energy consumed in unwrapping exceeds the nervous energy which the tonic promises to impart to me, but there may be subjective reasons for this which I shall disregard in my calculations. One thing is certain: the wrapping is worth more than the contents, and the cost of the twenty-five yellow tablets is out of all proportion to their value. But these are considerations verging on the moral aspect, and I would prefer to keep away from morality altogether. My field of speculation is one of pure economics.

Numerous articles are waiting to be unwrapped by me, many slips of paper are waiting to be evaluated; green, red, blue ink, everything is ready. It is usually late by the time I get to bed, and as I fall asleep I am haunted by my formulas, whole worlds of useless paper roll over me; some formulas explode like dynamite, the noise of the explosion sounds like a burst of laughter: it is my own, my laughter at the Lohengrin joke originating in my fear of the clerk from City Hall. Perhaps he has access to the punch-card file, has picked out my card, discovered that it contains not only the symbol for "mental case" but the second, more dangerous one for "antisocial." There is nothing more difficult to fill than a tiny hole like that in a punch card; perhaps my laughter at the Lohengrin joke is the price I have to pay for my anonymity. I would not like to admit face to face what I find easier to do in writing: that I am a thrower-away.

THE BALEK SCALES

Where my grandfather came from, most of the people lived by working in the flax sheds. For five generations they had been breathing in the dust which rose from the crushed flax stalks, letting themselves be killed off by slow degrees, a race of long-suffering, cheerful people who ate goat cheese, potatoes, and now and then a rabbit; in the evening they would sit at home spinning and knitting; they sang, drank mint tea, and were happy. During the day they would carry the flax stalks to the antiquated machines, with no protection from the dust and at the mercy of the heat which came pouring out of the drying kilns. Each cottage contained only one bed, standing against the wall like a closet and reserved for the parents, while the children slept all round the room on benches. In the morning the room would be filled with the odor of thin soup; on Sundays there was stew, and on feast days the children's faces would light up with pleasure as they watched the black acorn coffee turning paler and paler from the milk their smiling mother poured into their coffee mugs.

Since the parents went off early to the flax sheds, the housework was left to the children: they would sweep the room, tidy up, wash the dishes and peel the potatoes, precious pale-yellow fruit whose thin peel had to be produced afterward to dispel any suspicion of extravagance or carelessness.

As soon as the children were out of school, they had to go off into the woods and, depending on the season, gather mushrooms and herbs: woodruff and thyme, caraway, mint and foxglove, and in summer, when they had brought in the hay from their meager fields, they gathered hayflowers. A pound of hayflowers was worth one pfennig, and they were sold by the apothecaries in town for twenty pfennigs a pound to high-strung ladies. The mushrooms were highly prized: they fetched twenty pfennigs a pound and were sold in the shops in town for one mark twenty. The children would crawl deep into the green darkness of the forest during the autumn, when dampness drove the mushrooms out of the soil, and almost every family had its own places where it gathered mushrooms, places which were handed down in whispers from generation to generation.

The woods belonged to the Baleks, as well as the flax sheds, and in my grandfather's village the Baleks had a château, and the wife of the head of the family had a little room next to the dairy where mushrooms, herbs, and hayflowers were weighed and paid for. There on the table stood the great Balek scales, an old-fashioned, ornate bronze-gilt contraption, which my grandfather's grandparents had already faced when they were children, their grubby hands holding their little baskets of mushrooms, their paper bags of hayflowers, breathlessly watching the number of weights Frau Balek had to throw on the scale before the swinging pointer came to rest exactly over the black line, that thin line of justice which had to be redrawn every year. Then Frau Balek would take the big book covered in brown leather, write down the weight, and pay out the money: pfennigs or ten-pfennig pieces and very, very occasionally a mark. And when my grandfather was a child there was a big glass jar of lemon drops standing there, the kind that cost one mark a pound, and when Frau Balek—whichever one happened to be presiding over the little room—was in a good mood, she would put her hand into this jar and give each child a lemon drop, and the children's faces would light up with pleasure, the way they used to when on feast days their mother poured milk into their coffee mugs, milk that made the coffee turn paler and paler until it was as pale as the flaxen pigtails of the little girls.

One of the laws imposed by the Baleks on the village was that no one was permitted to have any scales in the house. The law was so ancient that nobody gave a thought as to when and how it had arisen, and it had to be obeyed, for anyone who broke it was dismissed from the flax sheds, he could not sell his mushrooms or his thyme or his hayflowers, and the power of the Baleks was so far-reaching that no one in the neighboring villages would give him work either, or buy his forest herbs. But since the days when my grandfather's parents had gone out as small children to gather mushrooms and sell them in order that they might season the meat of the rich people of Prague or be baked into game pies, it had never occurred to anyone to break this law: flour could be measured in cups, eggs could be counted, what they had spun could be measured by the yard, and besides, the old-fashioned bronze-gilt, ornate Balek scales did not look as if there was anything wrong with them, and five generations had entrusted the swinging black pointer with what they had gone out as eager children to gather from the woods.

True, there were some among these quiet people who flouted the law, poachers bent on making more money in one night than they could earn in a whole month in the flax sheds, but even these people apparently never thought of buying scales or making their own. My grandfather was the first person bold enough to test the justice of the Baleks, the family who lived in the château and drove two carriages, who always maintained one boy from the village while he studied theology at the seminary in Prague, the family with whom the priest played taroc every Wednesday, on whom the local reeve, in his carriage emblazoned with the imperial coat-of-arms, made an annual New Year's Day call and on whom the emperor conferred a title on the first day of the year 1900.

My grandfather was hardworking and smart: he crawled farther into the woods than the children of his clan had crawled before him, penetrating as far as the thicket where, according to legend, Bilgan the Giant was supposed to dwell, guarding a treasure. But my grandfather was not afraid of Bilgan: he worked his way deep into the thicket, even when he was quite little, and brought out great quantities of mushrooms; he even found truffles, for which Frau Balek paid thirty pfennigs a pound. Everything my grandfather took to the Baleks he entered on the back of a torn-off calendar page: every pound of mushrooms, every ounce of thyme, and on the right-hand side, in his childish handwriting, he entered the amount he received for each item; he scrawled in every pfennig, from the age of seven to the age of twelve; by the time he was twelve, the year 1900 had arrived, and because the Baleks had been raised to the aristocracy by the emperor, they gave every family in the village a quarter of a pound of real coffee, the Brazilian kind; there was also free beer and tobacco for the men, and at the château there was a great banquet; many carriages stood in the avenue of poplars leading from the entrance gates to the château.

But the day before the banquet the coffee was distributed in the little room which had housed the Balek scales for almost a hundred years, and the Balek family was now called Balek von Bilgan because, according to legend, Bilgan the Giant used to have a great castle on the site of the present Balek estate.

My grandfather often used to tell me how he went there after school to fetch the coffee for four families: the Cechs, the Weidlers, the Vohlas, and his own, the Brüchers. It was the afternoon of New Year's Eve: there were the front rooms to be decorated, the baking to be done, and the families did not want to spare four boys and have each of them go all the way to the château to bring back a quarter of a pound of coffee.

And so my grandfather sat on the narrow wooden bench in the little room while Gertrud the maid counted out the wrapped four-ounce packages of coffee, four of them, and he looked at the scales and saw that the pound weight was still lying on the left-hand scale; Frau Balek von Bilgan was busy with preparations for the banquet. And when Gertrud was about to put her hand into the jar with the lemon drops to give my grandfather one, she discovered it was empty: it was refilled once a year, and held one pound of the kind that cost a mark.

Gertrud laughed and said, "Wait here while I get the new lot," and my grandfather waited with the four four-ounce packages which had been wrapped and sealed in the factory, facing the scales on which someone had left the pound weight, and my grandfather took the four packages of coffee, put them on the empty scale, and his heart thudded as he watched the black finger of justice come to rest on the left of the black line: the scale with the pound weight stayed down, and the pound of coffee remained up in the air; his heart thudded more than if he had been lying behind a bush in the forest waiting for Bilgan the Giant, and he felt in his pocket for the pebbles he always carried with him so he could use his catapult to shoot the sparrows which pecked away at his mother's cabbage plants—he had to put three, four, five pebbles beside the packages of coffee before the scale with the pound weight rose and the pointer at last came to rest over the black line. My grandfather took the coffee from the scale; wrapped the five pebbles in his kerchief, and when Gertrud came back with the big pound bag of lemon drops which had to last for another whole year in order to make the children's faces light up with pleasure, when Gertrud let the lemon drops rattle into the glass jar, the pale little fellow was still standing there, and nothing seemed to have changed. My grandfather took only three of the packages; then Gertrud looked in startled surprise at the white-faced child who threw the lemon drop onto the floor, ground it under his heel, and said, "I want to see Frau Balek."

"Balek von Bilgan, if you please," said Gertrud.

"All right, Frau Balek von Bilgan," but Gertrud only laughed at him, and he walked back to the village in the dark, took the Cechs, the Weidlers, and the Vohlas their coffee, and said he had to go and see the priest.

Instead he went out into the dark night with his five pebbles in his kerchief. He had to walk a long way before he found someone who had scales, who was permitted to have them; no one in the villages of Blaugau and Bernau had any, he knew that, and he went straight through them till, after two hours' walking, he reached the little town of Dielheim, where Honig the apothecary lived. From Honig's house came the smell of fresh pancakes, and Honig's breath, when he opened the door to the half-frozen boy, already smelled of punch, there was a moist cigar between his narrow lips, and he clasped the boy's cold hands firmly for a moment, saying, "What's the matter, has your father's lung got worse?"

"No, I haven't come for medicine, I wanted..." My grandfather undid his kerchief, took out the five pebbles, held them out to Honig, and said, "I wanted to have these weighed." He glanced anxiously into Honig's face, but when Honig said nothing and did not get angry, or even ask him anything, my grandfather said, "It is the amount that is short of justice," and now, as he went into the warm room, my grandfather realized how wet his feet were. The snow had soaked through his cheap shoes, and in the forest the branches had showered him with snow which was now melting, and he was tired and hungry and suddenly began to cry because he thought of the quantities of mushrooms, the herbs, the flowers, which had been weighed on the scales that were short five pebbles' worth of justice. And when Honig, shaking his head and holding the five pebbles, called his wife, my grandfather thought of the generations of his parents, his grandparents, who had all had to have their mushrooms, their flowers, weighed on the scales, and he was overwhelmed by a great wave of injustice, and began to sob louder than ever, and, without waiting to be asked, he sat down on a chair, ignoring the pancakes, the cup of hot coffee which nice plump Frau Honig put in

front of him, and did not stop crying till Honig himself came out from
the shop at the back and, rattling the pebbles in his hand, said in a low
voice to his wife, "Two ounces, exactly."

My grandfather walked the two hours home through the forest,
got a beating at home, said nothing, not a single word, when he was
asked about the coffee, spent the whole evening doing sums on the
piece of paper on which he had written down everything he had sold to
Frau Balek, and when midnight struck, and the cannon could be heard
from the château, and the whole village rang with shouting and laughter and the noise of rattles, when the family kissed and embraced all
round, he said into the New Year silence, "The Baleks owe me eighteen
marks and thirty-two pfennigs." And again he thought of all the children there were in the village, of his brother Fritz, who had gathered
so many mushrooms, of his sister Ludmilla; he thought of the many
hundreds of children who had all gathered mushrooms for the Baleks,
and herbs and flowers, and this time he did not cry but told his parents
and brothers and sisters of his discovery.

When the Baleks von Bilgan went to High Mass on New Year's
Day, their new coat-of-arms—a giant crouching under a fir tree—
already emblazoned in blue and gold on their carriage, they saw the
hard, pale faces of the people all staring at them. They had expected
garlands in the village, a song in their honor, cheers and hurrahs, but
the village was completely deserted as they drove through it, and in
church the pale faces of the people were turned toward them, mute
and hostile, and when the priest mounted the pulpit to deliver his New
Year's sermon, he sensed the chill in those otherwise quiet and peaceful
faces, and he stumbled painfully through his sermon and went back
to the altar drenched in sweat. And as the Baleks von Bilgan left the
church after Mass, they walked through a lane of mute, pale faces. But
young Frau Balek von Bilgan stopped in front of the children's pews,
sought out my grandfather's face, pale little Franz Brücher, and asked
him, right there in the church, "Why didn't you take the coffee for your
mother?" And my grandfather stood up and said, "Because you owe me
as much money as five pounds of coffee would cost." And he pulled the
five pebbles from his pocket, held them out to the young woman, and
said, "This much, two ounces, is short in every pound of your justice";
and before the woman could say anything the men and women in the

church lifted up their voices and sang: "The justice of this earth, O Lord, hath put Thee to death…"

While the Baleks were at church, Wilhelm Vohla, the poacher, had broken into the little room, stolen the scales and the big fat leather-bound book in which had been entered every pound of mushrooms, every pound of hayflowers, everything bought by the Baleks in the village, and all afternoon of that New Year's Day the men of the village sat in my great-grandparents' front room and calculated, calculated one-eighth of everything that had been bought—but when they had calculated many thousands of talers and had still not come to an end, the reeve's gendarmes arrived, made their way into my great-grandfather's front room, shooting and stabbing as they came, and removed the scales and the book by force. My grandfather's little sister Ludmilla lost her life, a few men were wounded, and one of the gendarmes was stabbed to death by Wilhelm Vohla the poacher.

Our village was not the only one to rebel: Blaugau and Bernau did too, and for almost a week no work was done in the flax sheds. But a great many gendarmes appeared, and the men and women were threatened with prison, and the Baleks forced the priest to display the scales publicly in the school and demonstrate that the finger of justice swung to and fro accurately. And the men and women went back to the flax sheds—but no one went to the school to watch the priest: he stood there all alone, helpless and forlorn with his weights, scales, and packages of coffee.

And the children went back to gathering mushrooms, to gathering thyme, flowers, and foxglove; but every Sunday, as soon as the Baleks entered the church, the hymn was struck up: "The justice of this earth, O Lord, hath put Thee to death," until the reeve ordered it proclaimed in every village that the singing of this hymn was forbidden.

My grandfather's parents had to leave the village, and the new grave of their little daughter; they became basket weavers, but did not stay long anywhere because it pained them to see how everywhere the finger of justice swung falsely. They walked along behind their cart, which crept slowly over the country roads, taking their thin goat with them, and passers-by could sometimes hear a voice from the cart singing, "The justice of this earth, O Lord, hath put Thee to death." And those who wanted to listen could hear the tale of the Baleks von Bilgan, whose justice lacked an eighth part. But there were few who listened.

MY UNCLE FRED

My Uncle Fred is the only person who makes my memories of the years after 1945 bearable. He came home from the war one summer afternoon, in nondescript clothes, wearing his sole possession, a tin can, on a string around his neck, and supporting the trifling weight of a few cigarette butts which he had carefully saved in a little box. He embraced my mother, kissed my sister and me, mumbled something about "Bread, sleep, tobacco," and curled himself up on our family sofa, so that I remember him as being a man who was considerably longer than our sofa, a fact which obliged him either to keep his legs drawn up or to let them simply hang over the end. Both alternatives moved him to rail bitterly against our grandparents' generation, to which we owed the acquisition of this valuable piece of furniture. He called these worthy people stuffy, constipated owls, despised their taste for the bilious pink of the upholstery, but let none of this stop him from indulging in frequent and prolonged sleep.

I for my part was performing a thankless task in our blameless family: I was fourteen at the time, and the sole contact with that memorable institution which we called the black market. My father had been killed in the war, my mother received a tiny pension, with the result that I had the almost daily job of peddling scraps of salvaged belongings or swapping them for bread, coal, and tobacco. In those days coal was the cause of considerable violation of property rights, which today we would have to bluntly call stealing. So most days saw me going out to steal or peddle, and my mother, though she realized the need for these disreputable doings, always had tears in her eyes as she watched me go off about my complicated affairs. It was my responsibility, for instance, to turn a pillow into bread, a Dresden cup into a semolina, or three volumes of Gustav Freytag into two ounces of coffee, tasks to which I devoted myself with a certain amount of sporting enthusiasm but not entirely without a sense of humiliation and fear. For values—which is what grown-ups called them at the time—had shifted substantially, and now and then I was exposed to the unfounded suspicion of dishonesty because the value of a peddled article did not correspond in the least to the one my mother thought appropriate. It was, I must say, no pleasant task to act as broker between two different worlds of values, worlds which since then seem to have converged.

Uncle Fred's arrival led us all to expect some stalwart masculine aid. But he began by disappointing us. From the very first day I was seriously worried about his appetite, and when I made no bones about telling my mother this, she suggested I let him "find his feet." It took almost eight weeks for him to find his feet. Despite his abuse of the unsatisfactory sofa, he slept there without much trouble and spent the day dozing or describing to us in a martyred voice what position he preferred to sleep in.

I think his favorite position was that of a sprinter just before the start. He loved to lie on his back after lunch, his legs drawn up, voluptuously crumbling a large piece of bread into his mouth, and then roll himself a cigarette and sleep away the day till suppertime. He was a very tall, pale man, and there was a circular scar on his chin which gave his face somewhat the look of a damaged marble statue. Although his appetite for food and sleep continued to worry me, I liked him very much. He was the only one with whom I could at least theorize about the black market without getting into an argument. He obviously knew all about the conflict between the two worlds of values.

Although we urged him to talk to us about the war, he never did; he said it wasn't worth discussing. The only thing he would do sometimes was tell us about his induction, which seemed to have consisted chiefly of a person in uniform ordering Uncle Fred in a loud voice to urinate into a test tube, an order with which Uncle Fred was not immediately able to comply, the result being that his military career was doomed from the start. He maintained that the German Reich's keen interest in his urine had filled him with considerable distrust, a distrust which he found ominously confirmed during six years of war.

He had been a bookkeeper before the war, and when the first four weeks on our sofa had gone by, my mother suggested in her gentle sisterly way that he make inquiries about his old firm. He warily passed this suggestion on to me, but all I could discover was a pile of rubble about twenty feet high, which I located in a ruined part of the city after an hour's laborious pilgrimage. Uncle Fred was much reassured by my news.

He leaned back in his chair, rolled himself a cigarette, nodded triumphantly toward my mother, and asked her to get out his old things. In one corner of our bedroom there was a carefully nailed-down crate, which we opened with hammer and pliers amid much speculation. Out of it came: twenty novels of medium size and mediocre quality, a gold pocket watch, dusty but undamaged, two pairs of suspenders, some notebooks, his Chamber of Commerce diploma, and a savings book showing a balance of twelve hundred marks. The savings book was given to me to collect the money, as well as the rest of the stuff to be peddled, including the Chamber of Commerce diploma—although this found no takers, Uncle Fred's name being inscribed on it in black India ink.

This meant that for the next four weeks we were free from worry about bread, tobacco, and coal, which was a great relief to me, especially as all the schools opened wide their doors again and I was required to complete my education.

To this day, long after my education has been completed, I have fond memories of the soups we used to get, mainly because we obtained these supplementary meals almost without a struggle, and they therefore lent a happy and contemporary note to the whole educational system.

But the outstanding event during this period was the fact that Uncle Fred finally took the initiative a good eight weeks after his safe return.

One morning in late summer he rose from his sofa, shaved so meticulously that we became apprehensive, asked for some clean underwear, borrowed my bicycle, and disappeared.

His return late that night was accompanied by a great deal of noise and a penetrating smell of wine; the smell of wine emanated from my uncle's mouth, the noise was traceable to half a dozen galvanized buckets which he had tied together with some stout rope. Our confusion did not subside till we discovered he had decided to revive the flower trade in our ravaged town. My mother, full of suspicion toward the new world of values, scorned the idea, claiming that no one would want to buy flowers. But she was wrong.

It was a memorable morning when we helped Uncle Fred take the freshly filled buckets to the streetcar stop where he set himself up in business. And I still vividly remember the sight of those red and yellow tulips, the moist carnations; nor shall I ever forget how impressive he looked as he stood there in the midst of the gray figures and piles of rubble and started calling out, "Flowers, fresh flowers—no coupons required!" I don't have to describe how his business flourished: it was a meteoric success. In a matter of four weeks he owned three dozen galvanized buckets, was the proprietor of two branches, and a month later he was paying taxes. The whole town wore a different air to me: flower stalls appeared at one street corner after another, it was impossible to keep pace with the demand; more and more buckets were procured, booths were set up, and handcarts hastily thrown together.

At any rate, we were kept supplied not only with fresh flowers but with bread and coal, and I was able to retire from the brokerage business, a fact which helped greatly to improve my moral standards. For many years now, Uncle Fred has been a man of substance: his branches are still thriving, he owns a car, he looks on me as his heir, and I have been told to study commerce so I can look after the tax end of the business even before I enter on my inheritance.

When I look at him today, a solid figure behind the wheel of his red automobile, I find it strange to recall that there was really a time in my life when his appetite caused me sleepless nights.

DANIEL THE JUST

As long as it was dark, the woman lying beside him could not see his face, and this made everything easier to bear. She had been talking away at him for an hour, and it did not take much effort to keep on saying "Yes," or "Yes, of course," or "Yes, that's right." The woman lying beside him was his wife, but when he thought of her he always thought: the woman. She was actually quite beautiful, and there were people who envied him his wife, and he might have had cause to be jealous—but he was not jealous. He was glad the darkness hid the sight of her face from him and allowed him to relax his own face; there was nothing more exhausting than to put on a face and wear it all day, as long as daylight lasted, and the face he showed in the daytime was a put-on face.

"If Uli doesn't make it," she said, "I can't bear to think what will happen. It would finish Marie, you know what she's gone through, don't you?"

"Yes, of course," he said, "I know."

"She's had to eat dry bread, she—really, I don't know how she could stand it—she's slept for weeks in beds without sheets, and when Uli was born, Erich was still listed as missing. If the boy doesn't get through his entrance exam—I just don't know what will happen. Don't you agree?"

"Yes, I agree," he said.

"Make sure you see the boy before he goes into the classroom where the exam's being given—say something to encourage him. You'll do what you can, won't you?"

"Yes, I will," he said.

One day in spring, thirty years ago, he too had come to town to take the entrance exam: that evening the red light of the sun had fallen over the street where his aunt lived, and to the eleven-year-old boy it seemed as if someone were spilling liquid fire over the roofs, and hundreds of windows caught this red light like molten metal.

Later, while they were sitting at supper, the windows were filled with greenish darkness for that half hour when women hesitate before turning on the light. His aunt hesitated too, and when she touched the switch she seemed to be giving the signal to hundreds and hundreds of women: suddenly yellow light from all the windows pierced the green darkness; the lights hung in the night like brittle fruits with long yellow spikes.

"Do you think you'll make it?" asked his aunt, and his uncle, who was sitting by the window holding the newspaper, shook his head as if the question were an insult.

His aunt proceeded to make up a bed for him on the bench in the kitchen, using a quilt for a mattress; his uncle let him have his blanket and his aunt one of their pillows. "You'll soon have your own bedding here," said his aunt, "and now sleep well. Good night."

"Good night," he said, and his aunt turned out the light and went into the bedroom.

His uncle stayed behind and tried to pretend he was looking for something; his hands groped across the boy's face toward the window sill, and the hands, which smelled of wood stain and shellac, groped back across his face; his uncle's shyness hung like lead in the air, and without saying what he wanted to say, he disappeared into the bedroom.

I'll make it all right, thought the boy when he was alone, and in his mind's eye he saw his mother, who at this moment was sitting at home by the fire knitting, from time to time letting her hands fall into her lap and sending up a prayer to one of her favorite saints: Judas Thaddeus—or was Don Bosco the proper saint for him, the farm boy who had come to town to try to get into high school?

"There are some things which simply shouldn't be allowed to happen," said the woman beside him, and as she seemed to be waiting for a reply, he wearily said "Yes," and noticed to his despair that it was already getting light; day was coming and bringing him the hardest of all his duties: that of putting on his face.

No, he thought, enough things happen which shouldn't be allowed to happen. All those years ago, in the darkness on the kitchen bench, he had been so confident: he thought of the math problem, of the essay, and he was sure everything would be all right. The essay theme would almost certainly be "A Strange Experience," and he knew exactly what he was going to describe: the visit to the institution where Uncle Thomas was confined. Green-and-white-striped chairs in the consulting room, and Uncle Thomas who—no matter what anyone said to him—always replied in the same words, "If only there were justice in this world."

"I've knitted you a lovely red pullover," said his mother, "you were always so fond of red."

"If only there were justice in this world."

They talked about the weather, about the cows and a little about politics, and Thomas always said the same thing, "If only there were justice in this world."

And later, when they walked back along the green-painted corridor, he saw at the window a thin man with narrow drooping shoulders gazing mutely out into the garden.

Just before they went out through the gate, a pleasant-looking man with a kindly smile came up to them and said, "Madame, please do not forget to address me as Your Majesty," and his mother said softly to the man, "Your Majesty." And when they were standing at the streetcar stop, he had looked across once more to the green house lying hidden among the trees, and seen the man with the drooping shoulders standing at the window, and a laugh rang out through the garden that sounded like tin being cut with blunt scissors.

"Your coffee's getting cold," said the woman who was his wife, "and do try and eat something at least."

He raised the coffee cup to his lips and ate something.

"I know," said the woman, laying her hand on his shoulder, "I know you're worrying about that justice of yours again, but can you call it unjust to lend a helping hand to a child? You're fond of Uli, aren't you?"

"Yes," he said, and this yes was sincere: he was fond of Uli. The boy was sensitive, friendly, and in his way intelligent, but it would be torture for him to go to high school: with a lot of extra coaching, spurred on by an ambitious mother, by dint of great effort and much intercession, he would never be more than a mediocre student. He would always have to carry the burden of a life, of demands, with which he could not cope.

"Promise me you'll do something for Uli, won't you?"

"Yes," he said, "I'll do something for him," and he kissed his wife's beautiful face and left the house. He walked slowly along, put a cigarette between his lips, dropped his put-on face, and enjoyed the relaxation of feeling his own face on his skin. He looked at it in the window of a fur shop; between a gray sealskin and a leopard skin, he saw his face on the black velvet draping the display: the pale, rather puffy face of a man in his mid-forties—the face of a skeptic, a cynic perhaps, the cigarette smoke wreathed in white coils around the pale puffy face. His friend Alfred, who had died the year before, used to say, "You have never got over certain feelings of hostility—and everything you do is influenced much too much by your emotions."

Alfred had meant well; in fact what he had had in mind was right, but you can't define a person with words, and for him the word "hostility" was one of the most facile, one of the most convenient.

Thirty years ago, on the bench in his aunt's kitchen, he had thought: No one will write an essay like that; no one can have had such a strange experience, and before he fell asleep he thought about other things: he was going to sleep on this bench for nine years, do his homework at this table for nine years, and throughout this eternity his mother would sit at home by the fire knitting and sending up prayers to heaven. In the next room he could hear his uncle and aunt talking, and the only word he could make out from the murmuring was his name: Daniel. So they were talking about him, and although he could not make out the words, he knew they were speaking kindly about him. They were fond of him, they had no children themselves. Then all of a sudden fear shot through him: In two years, he thought in panic, this bench will already be too short for me—where will I sleep then? For a few minutes this idea really scared him, but then he thought: Two years, what an eternity that is, such a lot of darkness, day after day it would turn into light; and quite suddenly he slipped into that little portion of darkness which lay ahead of him—the night before the exam—and in his dreams he was pursued by the picture hanging on the wall between the buffet and the window: grim-faced men standing in front of a factory gate, one holding a tattered red flag in his hand, and in his dream the boy could clearly read the words which in the semidarkness he had been barely able to make out: ON STRIKE.

He took leave of his face as it hung there pale and intense between the sealskin and the leopard skin in the shop window, as if drawn with a silver pencil on black cloth; he took leave reluctantly, for he saw the child he had once been, behind this face.

"'On Strike,'" the school superintendent had said to him thirteen years later, "'On Strike'—do you consider that a suitable essay theme to give seventeen-year-olds?" He had not given it, and by that time, in 1934, the picture had long since disappeared from his uncle's kitchen wall. It was still possible to visit Uncle Thomas in the institution, to sit on one of the green-striped chairs, smoke cigarettes, and listen to Thomas, who seemed to be replying to a litany which only he could hear. Thomas sat there listening—but he was not listening to what the visitors were saying to him, he was listening to the dirge of an invisible choir as it stood hidden in the wings of the world's stage chanting a litany to which there was but one response, Thomas's response, "If only there were justice in this world."

The man who always stood at the window looking out into the garden had one day been able—so thin had he become—to squeeze through the bars and fall headlong into the garden: his metallic laugh came crashing down with him. But His Majesty was still alive, and Heemke never failed to go up to him and whisper with a smile, "Your Majesty." "Types like that go on forever," the keeper said to him. "It'll take a lot to finish him off."

But seven years later His Majesty was no longer alive, and Thomas was dead too: they had been murdered, and the choir standing hidden in the wings of the world's stage chanting its litany waited in vain for the response which only Thomas could give.

Heemke turned into the street where the school was, and he was startled to see all the candidates. They were standing around with mothers, with fathers, and over them all lay that spurious, hectic cheerfulness which descends like a sickness on people before an examination: desperate cheerfulness lay like makeup on the faces of the mothers, desperate indifference on those of the fathers.

His eye, however, was caught by a boy sitting alone and apart from the rest on the doorstep of a bombed house. Heemke stopped and felt fear rising in him like moisture in a sponge: I must watch out, he thought, if I'm not careful, I'll end up sitting in Uncle Thomas's place, and maybe I'll be saying the same words. The child sitting on the doorstep reminded him of himself thirty years ago, so intensely that he felt the thirty years falling away from him like dust being blown off a statue.

Noise, laughter—the sun shone on damp roofs from which the snow had melted, and only in the shadows of the ruins was the snow still lying.

His uncle had brought him here much too early, all those years ago; they had taken the streetcar over the bridge, had not exchanged a single word, and while he was looking at the boy's black stockings he thought: Shyness is a disease that deserves to be cured the way whooping cough is cured. His uncle's shyness, coupled with his own, had caught him by the throat. Mute, his red scarf round his neck, the Thermos flask in his right coat pocket, his uncle had stood beside him in the empty street, had suddenly muttered something about "go to work," and was gone. He had sat down on a doorstep. Vegetable carts rumbled over the cobbles, a baker's boy walked past with his basket of rolls, and a girl carrying a milk jug went from house to house, leaving a little blue-white spot of milk behind on every doorstep. He had been very impressed by the houses, houses in which no one seemed to be living, and today he could still see traces among the ruins of the yellow paint that had so impressed him at the time.

"Good morning, Principal," said someone walking by; he nodded briefly, and he knew that inside his colleague would say, "The old man's off his head again."

I have three alternatives, he thought. I can turn into that child sitting over there on the doorstep, I can go on being the man with the pale, puffy face, or I can become Uncle Thomas. The alternative with the least appeal was to go on being himself: the heavy burden of carrying his put-on face. There was also not much to be said for turning into the child: books he had loved, had hated, gobbled up, devoured at the kitchen table, and every week the battle for paper, for exercise books which he filled with notes, problems, draft essays; every week thirty pfennigs which he had to fight for, till it occurred to his teacher to let him tear the blank pages out of old exercise books stored in the school basement. But he also tore out the pages where only one side had been written on, and at home he sewed them with black cotton into thick notebooks—and now he sent flowers every year for the teacher's grave in the village.

No one, he thought, ever knew what it cost me, not a living soul, except perhaps Alfred, but Alfred always fell back on one very silly

word, "hostility." It is useless to talk about it, to explain it to anyone—
the last person to understand would be the one with the beautiful face
who lies beside me in bed.

He hesitated a few moments longer, while the past lay upon him:
what appealed to him most was to take over Uncle Thomas's role and
spend his days reciting the one solitary response to the litany which the
choir was chanting in the wings.

No, he didn't want to be that child again, it was too hard—what
boy wears black stockings these days? The middle alternative was
the one, to go on being the man with the pale, puffy face, and he had
always chosen the middle alternative. He walked over to the boy and
as his shadow fell across him, the child raised his eyes and gave him a
startled look. "What's your name?" asked Heemke.

The boy got hastily to his feet and from his blushing face came the
answer, "Wierzok."

"Spell it for me, please," said Heemke, reaching in his pocket for
his notebook, and the child slowly spelled "W-i-e-r-z-o-k."

"And where do you come from?"

"From Wollersheim," said the child.

Thank God, thought Heemke, he's not from my village and doesn't
bear my name—he's not a child of one of my many cousins.

"And where are you going to live here in town?"

"At my aunt's," said Wierzok.

"That's fine," said Heemke. "It's going to be all right with the exam.
I expect you've always had good marks and a good report from your
teacher, haven't you?"

"Yes, I've always had good marks."

"Don't worry," said Heemke, "it'll be all right, you will..." He
stopped, because what Alfred would have called emotion and hostility were strangling him. "Mind you don't catch a chill on those cold
stones," he said in a low voice, turned on his heel and entered the school
through the janitor's premises, so as to avoid Uli and Uli's mother. Concealed behind the curtain of the hall window, he looked out once more
at the children and their parents waiting outside and, as happened every
year on this day, he was swept by a feeling of despondency: it seemed
to him that in the faces of those ten-year-old boys he could read a
bleak future. They were pressing at the school gates like cattle at the

stable door. Among these seventy youngsters, two or three would be better than mediocre, and all the rest would simply form a background. Alfred's cynicism has penetrated me deeply, he thought, and he looked despairingly over to the Wierzok boy, who had sat down again and, his head bowed, seemed to be brooding.

When I did that I got a bad cold, thought Heemke. This boy will get through, and if I, if I—if I what?

Hostility and emotion, Alfred my friend, these are not the words to express what I feel.

He entered the common room, greeted the other teachers who had been waiting for him, and said to the janitor who helped him off with his coat, "Have the children come in now."

He could tell from the faces of the other teachers how strange his behavior had been. Perhaps, he thought, I was standing out there on the street for half an hour watching the Wierzok boy, and he glanced nervously at his watch: but it was only four minutes past eight.

"Gentlemen," he said aloud, "bear in mind that for many of these children, the test they are about to undergo is more crucial and decisive than university finals will be for some of them twelve years from now." They waited for more, and those who knew him were waiting for the word he was so fond of using whenever he could, the word "justice." But he said no more, merely turned to one of the teachers and quietly asked, "What is the essay theme for the candidates?"

"'A Strange Experience.'"

Heemke stayed behind as the room emptied.

Those childish fears of his, that in two years the kitchen bench would be too short for him, had been superfluous, for he had not passed the exam, although the essay theme had been "A Strange Experience." Right up to the moment when they had been let into the school he had clung to his confidence, but as soon as he entered the school, his confidence had melted away.

When he came to write the essay, he tried in vain to grasp hold of Uncle Thomas. Thomas was suddenly very close, too close for him to be able to write an essay about him; he wrote down the title, "A Strange Experience," and underneath he wrote, "If only there were justice in this world," but as he wrote "justice" what he really meant was "vengeance."

It had taken him more than ten years not to think of vengeance whenever he thought of justice.

The worst of those ten years had been the year after he failed his entrance exam: the people he had left behind when he embarked on what merely seemed to promise a better life could be just as unsympathetic as those who were completely unaware, completely ignorant, and whom a phone call from his father saved from becoming involved in months of pain and effort. A smile from his mother, a clasp of the hand on Sunday after Mass, and a hasty word or two: that was the justice of this world—and the other, the thing he had always wanted but had never achieved, was what Uncle Thomas had so desperately longed for. The desire to achieve that had earned him the nickname "Daniel the Just." He was roused by the door opening, and the janitor ushered in Uli's mother.

"Marie," he said, "what—why…"

"Daniel," she said, "I," but he interrupted her, "I've got no time now, no, not even a second," he said fiercely, and he left his room and went up to the second floor: up here the sounds of the waiting mothers were muted. He went to the window overlooking the playground, put a cigarette between his lips but forgot to light it. It has taken me thirty years to get over it and arrive at a knowledge of what it is I want. I have eliminated vengeance from my idea of justice; I make a good living, I put on my grim face, and most people believe this means I have reached my goal; but I have not reached my goal. I have only just begun—but now I can take off my grim face, as you put away a hat you no longer need. I shall wear a different face, perhaps my own…

He would spare Wierzok this year; he did not want to make any child go through what he had gone through, any child at all, least of all this one—whom he had met as if it were himself.

THE POSTCARD

None of my friends can understand the care with which I preserve a scrap of paper that has no value whatever. It merely keeps alive the memory of a certain day in my life, and to it I owe a reputation for sentimentality which is considered unworthy of my social position: I am the assistant manager of a textile firm. But I protest the accusation of sentimentality and am continually trying to invest this scrap of paper with some documentary value. It is a tiny, rectangular piece of ordinary paper, the size, but not the shape, of a stamp—it is narrower and longer than a stamp—and although it originated in the post office it has not the slightest collector's value. It has a bright red border and is divided by another red line into two rectangles of different sizes; in the smaller of these rectangles there is a big black R, in the larger one, in black print, DÜSSELDORF and a number—the number 634. That is all, and the bit of paper is yellow and thin with age, and now that I have described it minutely I have decided to throw it away: an ordinary registration sticker, such as every post office slaps on every day by the dozen.

And yet this scrap of paper reminds me of a day in my life which is truly unforgettable, although many attempts have been made to erase it from my memory. But my memory functions too well.

First of all, when I think of that day, I smell vanilla custard, a warm, sweet cloud creeping under my bedroom door and reminding me of my mother's goodness: I had asked her to make some vanilla ice cream for my first day of vacation, and when I woke up I could smell it.

It was half past ten. I lit a cigarette, pushed up my pillow, and considered how I would spend the afternoon. I decided to go swimming; after lunch I would take the streetcar to the beach, have a bit of a swim, read, smoke, and wait for one of the girls at the office, who had promised to come down to the beach after five.

In the kitchen my mother was pounding meat, and when she stopped for a moment I could hear her humming a tune. It was a hymn.

I felt very happy. The previous day I had passed my test, I had a good job in a textile factory, a job with opportunities for advancement—but now I was on vacation, two weeks' vacation, and it was summertime. It was hot outside, but in those days I still loved hot weather: through the slits in the shutters I could see the heat haze, I could see the green of the trees in front of our house, I could hear the streetcar. And I was looking forward to breakfast. Then I heard my mother coming to listen at my door; she crossed the hall and stopped by my door; it was silent for a moment in our apartment, and I was just about to call "Mother" when the bell rang downstairs. My mother went to our front door, and I heard the funny high-pitched purring of the buzzer down below; it buzzed four, five, six times, while my mother was talking on the landing to Frau Kurz, who lived in the next apartment. Then I heard a man's voice, and I knew at once it was the mailman, although I had only seen him a few times. The mailman came into our entrance hall, Mother said, "What?" and he said, "Here—sign here, please." It was very quiet for a moment, the mailman said "Thanks," my mother closed the door after him, and I heard her go back into the kitchen.

Shortly after that I got up and went into the bathroom. I shaved, had a leisurely wash, and when I turned off the faucet I could hear my mother grinding the coffee. It was like Sunday, except that I had not been to church.

Nobody will believe it, but my heart suddenly felt heavy. I don't know why, but it was heavy. I could no longer hear the coffee mill. I dried myself off, put on my shirt and trousers, socks and shoes, combed my hair, and went into the living room. There were flowers on the table, pale pink carnations, it all looked fresh and neat, and on my plate lay a red pack of cigarettes.

Then Mother came in from the kitchen carrying the coffeepot and I saw at once she had been crying. In one hand she was holding the coffeepot, in the other a little pile of mail, and her eyes were red. I went over to her, took the pot from her, kissed her cheek, and said, "Good morning." She looked at me, said, "Good morning, did you sleep well?" and tried to smile, but did not succeed.

We sat down, my mother poured the coffee, and I opened the red pack lying on my plate and lit a cigarette. I had suddenly lost my appetite. I stirred milk and sugar into my coffee, tried to look at Mother, but each time I quickly lowered my eyes. "Was there any mail?" I asked, a senseless question, since Mother's small red hand was resting on the little pile on top of which lay the newspaper.

"Yes," she said, pushing the pile toward me. I opened the newspaper while my mother began to butter some bread for me. The front page bore the headline "Outrages Continue Against Germans in the Polish Corridor!" There had been headlines like that for weeks on the front pages of the papers. Reports of "rifle fire along the Polish border and refugees escaping from the sphere of Polish harassment and fleeing to the Reich." I put the paper aside. Next I read the brochure of a wine merchant who used to supply us sometimes when Father was still alive. Various types of Riesling were being offered at exceptionally low prices. I put the brochure aside too.

Meanwhile my mother had finished buttering the slice of bread for me. She put it on my plate, saying, "Please eat something!" She burst into violent sobs. I could not bring myself to look at her. I can't look at anyone who is really suffering—but now for the first time I realized it must have something to do with the mail. It must be the mail. I stubbed out my cigarette, took a bite of the bread and butter, and picked up the next letter, and as I did so I saw there was a postcard lying underneath. But I had not noticed the registration sticker, that tiny scrap of paper I still possess and to which I owe a reputation for sentimentality. So I read the letter first. The letter was from Uncle Eddy. Uncle Eddy wrote that at last, after many years as an assistant instructor, he was now a full-fledged teacher, but it had meant being transferred to a little one-horse town; financially speaking, he was hardly any better off than before, since he was now being paid at the local scale. And his kids had had whooping cough, and the way things were going made him feel sick to his stomach, he didn't have to tell us why. No, he didn't, and it made us feel sick too. It made a lot of people feel sick.

When I reached for the postcard, I saw it had gone. My mother had picked it up, she was holding it up and looking at it, and I kept my eyes on my half-eaten slice of bread, stirred my coffee, and waited.

I shall never forget it. Only once had my mother ever cried so terribly, when my father died; and then I had not dared to look at her either. A nameless diffidence had prevented me from comforting her.

I tried to bite into the bread, but my throat closed up, for I suddenly realized that what was upsetting Mother so much could only be something to do with me. Mother said something I didn't catch and handed me the postcard, and it was then I saw the registration sticker: that red-bordered rectangle, divided by a red line into two other rectangles, of which the smaller one contained a big black R and the bigger one the word "DÜSSELDORF" and the number 634. Otherwise the postcard was quite normal. It was addressed to me and on the back were the words "Mr. Bruno Schneider: You are required to report to the Schlieffen Barracks in Adenbrück on August 5, 1939, for an eight-week period of military training." "Bruno Schneider," the date, and "Adenbrück" were typed, everything else was printed, and at the bottom was a vague scrawl and the printed word "Major."

Today I know that the scrawl was superfluous. A machine for printing majors' signatures would do the job just as well. The only thing that mattered was the little sticker on the front for which my mother had had to sign a receipt.

I put my hand on her arm and said, "Now, look, Mother, it's only eight weeks." And my mother said, "I know."

"Only eight weeks," I said, and I knew I was lying, and my mother dried her tears, said, "Yes, of course"; we were both lying, without knowing why we were lying, but we were and we knew we were.

I was just picking up my bread and butter again when it struck me that today was the fourth and that on the following day at ten o'clock I had to be over two hundred miles away to the east. I felt myself going pale, put down the bread and got up, ignoring my mother. I went to my room. I stood at my desk, opened the drawer, closed it again. I looked round, felt something had happened and didn't know what. The room was no longer mine. That was all. Today I know, but that day I did meaningless things to reassure myself that the room still belonged to me. It was useless to rummage around in the box containing my letters, or to straighten my books. Before I knew what I was doing, I had begun to pack my briefcase: shirt, pants, towel, and socks, and I went into the bathroom to get my shaving things. My mother was still sitting at the breakfast table. She had stopped crying. My half-eaten slice of bread was still on my plate, there was still some coffee in my cup, and I said to my mother, "I'm going over to the Giesselbachs' to phone about my train."

When I came back from the Giesselbachs' it was just striking twelve noon. Our entrance hall smelled of roast pork and cauliflower, and my mother had begun to break up ice in a bag to put into our little ice-cream machine.

My train was leaving at eight that evening, and I would be in Adenbrück next morning about six. It was only fifteen minutes' walk to the station, but I left the house at three o'clock. I lied to my mother, who did not know how long it took to get to Adenbrück.

Those last three hours I spent in the house seem, on looking back, worse and longer than the whole time I spent away, and that was a long time. I don't know what we did. We had no appetite for dinner. My mother soon took back the roast, the cauliflower, the potatoes, and the vanilla ice cream to the kitchen. Then we drank the breakfast coffee which had been kept warm under a yellow cozy, and I smoked cigarettes, and now and again we exchanged a few words. "Eight weeks," I said, and my mother said, "Yes—yes, of course," and she didn't cry anymore. For three hours we lied to each other, till I couldn't stand it any longer. My mother blessed me, kissed me on both cheeks, and as I closed the front door behind me, I knew she was crying.

I walked to the station. The station was bustling with activity. It was vacation time: happy suntanned people were milling around. I had a beer in the waiting room, and about half past three decided to call up the girl from the office whom I had arranged to meet at the beach.

While I was dialing the number, and the perforated nickel dial kept clicking back into place—five times—I almost regretted it, but I dialed the sixth figure, and when her voice asked, "Who is it?" I was silent for a moment, then said slowly, "Bruno" and "Can you come? I have to go off—I've been drafted."

"Right now?" she asked.

"Yes."

She thought it over for a moment, and through the phone I could hear the voices of the others, who were apparently collecting money to buy some ice cream.

"All right," she said, "I'll come. Are you at the station?"

"Yes," I said.

She arrived at the station very quickly, and to this day I don't know, although she has been my wife now for ten years, to this day I don't know whether I ought to regret that phone call. After all, she kept my job open for me with the firm, she revived my defunct ambition when I came home, and she is actually the one I have to thank for the fact that those opportunities for advancement have now become reality.

But I didn't stay as long as I could have with her either. We went to the movies, and in the cinema, which was empty, dark, and very hot, I kissed her, though I didn't feel much like it.

I kept on kissing her, and I went to the station at six o'clock, although I need not have gone till eight. On the platform I kissed her again and boarded the first eastbound train. Ever since then I have not been able to look at a beach without a pang: the sun, the water, the cheerfulness of the people seem all wrong, and I prefer to stroll alone through the town on a rainy day and go to a movie where I don't have to kiss anybody. My opportunities for advancement with the firm are not yet exhausted. I might become a director, and I probably will, according to the law of paradoxical inertia. For people are convinced I am loyal to the firm and will do a great deal for it. But I am not loyal to it and I haven't the slightest intention of doing anything for it...

Lost in thought I have often contemplated that registration sticker, which gave such a sudden twist to my life. And when the tests are held in summer and our young employees come to me afterward with beaming faces to be congratulated, it is my job to make a little speech in which the words "opportunities for advancement" play a traditional role.

UNEXPECTED GUESTS

I have nothing against animals; on the contrary, I like them, and I enjoy caressing our dog's coat in the evening while the cat sits on my lap. It gives me pleasure to watch the children feeding the tortoise in the corner of the living room. I have even grown fond of the baby hippopotamus we keep in our bathtub, and the rabbits running around loose in our apartment have long ceased to worry me. Besides, I am used to coming home in the evening and finding an unexpected visitor: a cheeping baby chick, or a stray dog my wife has taken in. For my wife is a good woman, she never turns anyone away from the door, neither man nor beast, and for many years now our children's evening prayers have wound up with the words: O Lord, please send us beggars and animals.

What is really worse is that my wife cannot say no to hawkers and peddlers, with the result that things accumulate in our home which I regard as superfluous—soap, razor blades, brushes, and darning wool—and lying around in drawers are documents which cause me some concern: an assortment of insurance policies and purchase agreements. My sons are insured for their education, my daughters for their trousseaux, but we cannot feed them with either darning wool or soap until they get married or graduate, and it is only in exceptional cases that razor blades are beneficial to the human system.

It will be readily understood, therefore, that now and again I show signs of slight impatience, although generally speaking I am known to be a quiet man. I often catch myself looking enviously at the rabbits who have made themselves at home under the table, munching away peacefully at their carrots, and the stupid gaze of the hippopotamus, who is hastening the accumulation of silt in our bathtub, causes me at times to stick out my tongue at him. And the tortoise stoically eating its way through lettuce leaves has not the slightest notion of the anxieties that swell my breast: the longing for some fresh, fragrant coffee, for tobacco, bread, and eggs, and the comforting warmth engendered by a schnapps in the throats of careworn men. My sole comfort at such times is Billy, our dog, who, like me, is yawning with hunger. If, on top of all this, unexpected guests arrive—men unshaven like myself, or mothers with babies who get fed warm milk and moistened zwieback— I have to get a grip on myself if I am to keep my temper. But I do keep it, because by this time it is practically the only thing I have left.

There are days when the mere sight of freshly boiled, snowy pota- toes makes my mouth water; for—although I confess this reluctantly and with deep embarrassment—it is a long time since we have enjoyed "good home cooking." Our only meals are improvised ones of which we partake from time to time, standing up, surrounded by animals and human guests.

Fortunately it will be a while before my wife can buy useless arti- cles again, for we have no more cash, my wages have been attached for an indefinite period, and I myself am reduced to spending the evenings going around the distant suburbs, in clothing that makes me unrecog- nizable, selling razor blades, soap, and buttons far below cost; for our situation has become grave. Nevertheless, we own several hundred- weight of soap, thousands of razor blades, and buttons of every descrip- tion, and toward midnight I stagger into the house and go through my pockets for money; my children, my animals, my wife stand around me with shining eyes, for I have usually bought some things on the way home: bread, apples, lard, coffee, and potatoes—the latter, by the way, in great demand among the children as well as the animals—and during the nocturnal hours we gather together for a cheerful meal. Contented animals, contented children are all about me, my wife smiles at me, and we leave the living-room door open so the hippopotamus will not feel left out, his joyful grunts resounding from the bathroom. At that point my wife usually confesses to me that she has an extra guest hidden in the storeroom, who is only brought out when my nerves have been for- tified by food: shy, unshaven men, rubbing their hands, take their place at table, women squeeze in between our children on the bench, milk is warmed up for crying babies. In this way I also make the acquaintance of animals that are new to me: seagulls, foxes, and pigs, although once it was a small dromedary.

"Isn't it cute?" asked my wife, and I was obliged to say yes, it was, while I anxiously watched the tireless munching of this duffel-colored creature which looked at us out of slate-gray eyes. Fortunately the dromedary only stayed a week, and business was brisk: word had got round of the quality of my merchandise, my reduced prices, and now and again I was even able to sell shoelaces and brushes, articles otherwise not much in demand. As a result, we experienced a period of false prosperity, and my wife, completely blind to the economic facts, produced a remark that worried me, "Things are looking up!" But I saw our stocks of soap shrinking, the razor blades dwindling, and even the supply of brushes and darning wool was no longer substantial.

Just about this time, when I could have used some spiritual sustenance, our house was shaken one evening, while we were all sitting peacefully together, by a tremor resembling a fair-sized earthquake: the pictures rattled, the table rocked, and a ring of fried sausage rolled off my plate. I was about to jump up and see what the matter was when I noticed suppressed laughter on the faces of my children. "What's going on here?" I shouted, and for the first time in all my checkered experience I was really beside myself.

"Wilfred," said my wife quietly, and put down her fork, "it's only Wally." She began to cry, and against her tears I have no defense, for she has borne me seven children.

"Who is Wally?" I asked wearily, and at that moment the house was rocked by another tremor. "Wally," said my youngest daughter, "is the elephant we've got in the basement."

I must admit I was at a loss, which is not really surprising. The largest animal we had housed so far had been the dromedary, and I considered an elephant too big for our apartment.

My wife and children, not in the least at a loss, supplied the facts: the animal had been brought to us for safekeeping by a bankrupt circus owner. Sliding down the chute which we otherwise use for our coal, it had had no trouble entering the basement. "He rolled himself up into a ball," said my oldest son, "really an intelligent animal." I did not doubt it, accepted the fact of Wally's presence, and was led down in triumph into the basement. The animal was not as large as all that; he waggled his ears and seemed quite at home with us, especially as he had a bale of hay at his disposal. "Isn't he cute?" asked my wife, but I refused to agree. Cute did not seem to be the right word. Anyway, the family appeared disappointed at the limited extent of my enthusiasm, and my wife said, as we left the basement, "How cruel you are, do you want him to be put up for auction?"

"What d'you mean, auction," I said, "and why cruel? Besides, it's against the law to conceal bankruptcy assets."

"I don't care," said my wife. "Nothing must happen to the animal."

In the middle of the night we were awakened by the circus owner, a diffident, dark-haired man, who asked us whether we had room for one more animal. "It's my sole possession, all I have left in the world. Only for a night. How is the elephant, by the way?"

"He's fine," said my wife, "only I'm a bit worried about his bowels."

"That'll soon settle down," said the circus owner. "It's just the new surroundings. Animals are so sensitive. How about it, then: will you take the cat too—just for the night?" He looked at me, and my wife nudged me and said, "Don't be so unkind."

"Unkind," I said, "no, I certainly don't want to be that. If you like, you can put the cat in the kitchen."

"I've got it outside in the car," said the man.

I left my wife to look after the cat and crawled back into bed. My wife was a bit pale when she came to bed, and she seemed to be trembling. "Are you cold?" I asked.

"Yes," she said, "I've got such funny chills."

"You're just tired."

"Maybe," said my wife, but she gave me a queer look as she said it. We slept quietly, but in my dreams I still saw that queer look of my wife's, and a strange compulsion made me wake up earlier than usual. I decided to shave for once.

Lying under our kitchen table was a medium-sized lion; he was sleeping peacefully, only his tail moved gently and made a sound like someone playing with a very light ball.

I carefully lathered my face and tried not to make any noise, but when I turned my chin to the right to shave my left cheek I saw that the lion had his eyes open and was watching me. They really do look like cats, I thought. What the lion was thinking I don't know; he went on watching me, and I shaved, without cutting myself, but I must admit it is a strange feeling to shave with a lion looking on. My experience of handling wild beasts was practically nonexistent, so I confined myself to looking sternly at the lion, then I dried my face and went back to the bedroom. My wife was already awake, she was just about to say something, but I cut her short and exclaimed, "What's the use of talking about it!" My wife began to cry, and I put my hand on her head and said, "It's unusual, to say the least, you must admit that."

"What isn't unusual?" said my wife, and I had no answer.

Meanwhile the rabbits had awakened, the children were making a racket in the bathroom, the hippopotamus—his name was Gottlieb— was already trumpeting away, Billy was stretching and yawning; only the tortoise was still asleep, but it sleeps most of the time anyway.

I let the rabbits into the kitchen, where their feed box is kept under the cupboard; the rabbits sniffed at the lion, the lion at the rabbits, and my children—uninhibited and used to animals as they are—were already in the kitchen. I almost had the feeling the lion was smiling; my third-youngest son immediately found a name for him: Bombilus. And Bombilus he remained.

A few days later someone came to take away the elephant and the lion. I must confess I saw the last of the elephant without regret; he seemed silly to me, while the lion's quiet, friendly dignity had endeared him to me. I felt a pang at Bombilus's departure. I had grown so used to him; he was really the first animal to enjoy my wholehearted affection.

THE DEATH OF ELSA BASKOLEIT

The basement of the house we used to live in was rented to a shopkeeper called Baskoleit; there were always orange crates standing around in the passages, it smelled of rotten fruit that Baskoleit put out for the garbage trucks, and from beyond the dim light of the frosted glass panel we could often hear his voice, with its broad East Prussian dialect, complaining about the bad times. But in his heart of hearts Baskoleit was a cheerful man: we knew, as surely as only children can know, that his grumbling was a game, even the way he used to swear at us, and he would often come up the three or four steps leading from the basement to the street with his pockets full of apples and oranges which he tossed to us like rubber balls.

But the interesting thing about Baskoleit was his daughter Elsa, of whom we knew that she wanted to be a dancer. Perhaps she already was one. In any case, she practiced a great deal, she practiced downstairs in the basement room with the yellow walls next to Baskoleit's kitchen: a slender girl with fair hair who stood on the tips of her toes, dressed in green tights, pale, hovering for minutes like a swan, whirling around, leaping, or doing handsprings. I could watch her from my bedroom window when it got dark; in the yellow rectangle of the window frame, her thin, green-clad body, her pale strained face, and her fair head that sometimes, when she jumped, touched the naked light bulb, which began to swing and for the space of a few seconds expanded the yellow circle of light on the gray courtyard. There were some people who shouted across the courtyard, "Whore!," and I didn't know what a whore was; there were others who shouted, "It's disgusting!," and although I thought I knew what disgusting was, I couldn't believe it had anything to do with Elsa. Then Baskoleit's window would be flung open, and in the steam of the kitchen his big bald head would loom up, and with the light that fell from the open kitchen window into the courtyard he would pour out into the dark courtyard a torrent of oaths of which I didn't understand a single one. At any rate, Elsa's window was soon provided with a curtain, heavy green plush, which let out hardly any light at all, but every evening I would gaze at the faintly glowing rectangle and see her, although I couldn't see her: Elsa Baskoleit in her light-green tights, thin and fair-haired, hovering for seconds on end under the naked light bulb.

But before long we moved away, I got older, found out what a whore was, thought I knew what disgusting was, saw dancers, but liked none of them as well as Elsa Baskoleit, of whom I never heard again. We moved to another town, war came, a long war, and I thought no more of Elsa Baskoleit, I didn't even think of her when we moved back to the old town. I tried my hand at all sorts of jobs, till I became a truck driver for a wholesale vegetable dealer: handling a truck was the only thing I was good at. Each morning I was given a list, cases of apples and oranges, baskets of plums, and drove into town.

One day, while I was standing on the ramp where my truck was being loaded and checking what the warehouseman was loading on the truck against my list, the bookkeeper emerged from his cubbyhole, which is plastered with banana posters, and asked the warehouseman, "Can we supply Baskoleit?"

"Has he ordered something? Purple grapes?"

"Yes." The bookkeeper removed the pencil from behind his ear and looked at the warehouseman in surprise.

"Once in a while," said the warehouseman, "he orders something—purple grapes, I don't know why—but we can't supply him. Get a move on!" he shouted to the helpers in their gray smocks. The bookkeeper went back to his cubbyhole, and I ceased to check whether they were really loading the stuff that was on my list. I saw the rectangular, brightly lit frame of the basement window, I saw Elsa Baskoleit dancing, thin and pale, dressed in bright green, and that morning I took a different route from the one I was supposed to take.

Of the lampposts we had played beside, only one was still standing, and even this one was minus its head, most of the houses were in ruins, and my truck jolted through deep potholes. There was only one child in the street, which used to swarm with children: a pale, dark-haired boy sitting on a bit of broken wall and drawing lines in the whitish dust. He looked up as I drove by, but then let his head droop again. I stopped in front of Baskoleit's house and got out.

His small windows were dusty, pyramids of packages had collapsed, and the green cardboard was black with dirt. I looked up at the patched housewall, hesitatingly opened the door, and stepped slowly down into the shop: there was an acrid smell of damp soup mix, which was stuck together in lumps in a cardboard box by the door, but then I saw Baskoleit's back, saw his gray hair below his cap, and could sense how he disliked having to fill a bottle with vinegar from a big barrel. He evidently didn't know how to manage the spigot properly, the sour fluid ran over his fingers, and down on the floor a puddle had formed, a rotting, sour-smelling place in the wood, which squeaked under his feet. A thin woman in a rust-brown coat was standing by the counter, watching him with indifference. At last he seemed to have filled the bottle, he put in the cork, and once again I said what I had already said at the door, quietly said, "Good morning," but no one answered. Baskoleit put the bottle on the counter. His face was pale and unshaven, and he looked at the woman now and said, "My daughter has died—Elsa—"

"I know," said the woman hoarsely, "I've known that for five years. I need some scouring powder too."

"My daughter has died," said Baskoleit. He looked at the woman as if it had just happened, looked at her helplessly, but the woman said, "The loose kind—a pound." And Baskoleit pulled out a black barrel from under the counter, poked around in it with a metal scoop, and with his trembling hands conveyed some yellowish lumps into a gray paper bag.

"My daughter has died," he said. The woman said nothing, and I looked around. All I could see was some dusty packages of noodles, the vinegar barrel, which had a dripping tap, and the scouring powder and an enamel sign showing a grinning fair-haired boy eating a brand of chocolate that hasn't existed for years. The woman put the bottle into her shopping bag, stuffed the scouring powder in next to it, threw a few coins onto the counter, and as she turned round and walked past me she tapped her forehead briefly with her finger and smiled at me.

I thought of a lot of things, thought of the days when I had been so small that my nose was still below the edge of the counter, but now I could look without effort over the glass showcase bearing the name of a biscuit company and now containing only dusty packets of breadcrumbs; for a few seconds I seemed to shrink, I felt my nose below the dirty edge of the counter, felt the pfennigs for candies in my hand, I saw Elsa Baskoleit dancing, heard people shouting across the courtyard, "Whore!" and "It's disgusting!" till I was roused by Baskoleit's voice.

"My daughter has died." He said it mechanically, almost without emotion, he was standing by the showcase now, looking out into the street.

"Yes," I said.

"She is dead," he said.

"Yes," I said. He turned his back to me, his hands in the pockets of his gray smock, which was stained.

"She loved grapes—the purple kind—but now she's dead." He did not say, "What would you like?" or "May I help you?," he stood near the dripping vinegar barrel beside the showcase, saying, "My daughter has died" or "She is dead," without looking at me.

I seemed to stand there for an eternity, oblivious and forgotten, while around me time trickled away. It was only when another woman came into the shop that I could rouse myself. She was short and plump, and held her shopping bag against her stomach, and Baskoleit turned to her and said, "My daughter has died," the woman said, "Yes," began suddenly to cry, and said, "Some scouring powder, please, a pound of the loose kind," and Baskoleit went behind the counter and poked around in the barrel with the metal scoop. The woman was still crying when I left.

The pale, dark-haired boy who had been sitting on the bit of broken wall was standing on the running board of my truck, looking closely at the dashboard. He reached in through the open window and raised the right, then the left indicator. The boy jumped when I suddenly stood behind him, but I grabbed him, looked into his pale frightened face, took an apple from one of the cases on my truck, and gave it to the boy. He looked at me in amazement when I let him go, in such amazement that I was startled, and I took another apple, and another, stuffed them into his pocket, shoved them under his jacket, a lot of apples, before I got in and drove off.

A CASE FOR KOP

When Lasnov got back from the station, he brought a message that a case had arrived for Kop. Every day Lasnov met the train from Odessa and tried to make deals with the soldiers. During the first year he had paid for socks, saccharine, salt, matches, and lighter flints with butter and oil—and had enjoyed the generous margins that are always involved in bartering; later on the rates had become more established, and there was tough bargaining over this money that kept on decreasing in value as the fortunes of war declined. There was no more butter to trade, and no oil, and for a long time now none of those juicy hunks of bacon for which in the beginning you could get a French double-bed mattress. Trade had become acute, sour and exasperating, ever since the soldiers had begun to despise their own money. They laughed when Lasnov ran along beside the train with his bundles of notes, calling through the open windows in an agitated, singsong voice, "I pay top prices for everything. Top prices for everything."

Only occasionally did a novice turn up who let himself be talked out of a coat or an undervest, carried away by the sight of the bank notes. And the days were now few and far between when Lasnov had to negotiate so long over a more valuable article—a pistol, a watch, or a telescope—that he was obliged to bribe the stationmaster to keep the train waiting till Lasnov had finished his business. In the early days each minute had cost only a mark, but the greedy stationmaster, a heavy drinker, had long since raised the cost of one minute to six marks.

On this particular morning there had been no business at all. A gendarme paced up and down alongside the waiting train, compared his wristwatch with the stationmaster's pocketwatch, and shouted at the ragged boy who ran along by the train looking for cigarette ends. But the soldiers had stopped throwing away cigarette ends a long time ago: they would carefully scrape off the black ash and hoard their remnants of tobacco like jewels in their tobacco tins; they were no longer generous with bread either, and when the boy could not find any bits of tobacco and ran along by the train waving his arms and chanting most impressively in a howling singsong voice, "Bread, bread, bread, comrades!", all he got was a kick from the gendarme. When the train pulled out, he pressed himself against the wall, and a paper bag rolled to his feet. In it were a slice of bread and an apple. The boy grinned as Lasnov passed him on his way to the waiting room. The waiting room was empty and cold. Lasnov left the station and stood outside, hesitating. He felt as if the train had yet to arrive; it had all been over too quickly, correctly, punctually, but he could hear the rusty creak: the signal arm was slipping back into Stop.

Lasnov jumped when someone put a hand on his shoulder. The hand was too light for the stationmaster's; it was the boy's, and he was holding out the apple he had bitten into and mumbling, "It's so sour, the apple—but what'll you give me for this?" From his left pocket he pulled out a red toothbrush and held it out to Lasnov. Lasnov opened his mouth and involuntarily drew his forefinger across his strong teeth, which felt slightly furry; he shut his mouth, took the toothbrush from the boy, and studied it; its red handle was transparent, the bristles were white and firm.

"A nice Christmas present for your wife," said the boy. "She has such lovely white teeth."

"You monkey," Lasnov said softly, "what are you doing looking at my wife's teeth?"

"Or for your kids," said the boy. "You can look through it—like this." He took the toothbrush from Lasnov, held it up to his eyes, looked at Lasnov, the station, the trees, the dilapidated sugar factory, and gave the brush back to him. "You try," he said, "it looks nice." Lasnov took the brush and held it up to his eyes. On the inside of the handle the refractions were broken: the station looked like a long, long barn, the trees like broken-off brooms, the boy's face was distorted into a squat grimace, the apple he was holding up to his face looked like a red sponge. Lasnov handed the toothbrush back to the boy. "Yes," he said, "not bad at all."

"Ten," said the boy.

"Two."

"No," whimpered the boy, "no, it's so pretty." Lasnov turned away.

"Give me five at least."

"All right," said Lasnov, "here's five." He took the toothbrush and gave the boy the money. The boy ran back into the waiting room, and Lasnov saw him carefully and systematically going through the ashes of the stove with a stick, looking for cigarette ends; a gray cloud of dust rose up, and the boy murmured something to himself in his singsong voice which Lasnov was unable to make out.

The stationmaster came up just when Lasnov had decided to roll a cigarette and was checking his tobacco supply in the palm of his hand, separating the dust from the shreds of tobacco. "Well, now," said the stationmaster, "that looks like enough for two." He took some, without asking permission, and the two men stood smoking at the station corner, looking out into the street where booths, stalls, and dirty tents were being set up. Everything was gray, brown, or dirt-colored; there wasn't a spot of color even on the children's carrousel.

"Someone," said the stationmaster, "once gave my kids some coloring books; on one page you could see the finished pictures, in color, and on the opposite page the outlines where you had to put in the colors. But I didn't have any paints, or any crayons either, and the kids filled it all in with pencil—I always have to think of that when I look at this marketplace. I guess they ran out of colors, all they had was pencil—gray, dirty, dark..."

"Yes," said Lasnov, "there's no business at all; the only thing to eat is Rukhev's corn cakes, but you know how he makes those."

"Raw corncobs pressed together, I know," said the stationmaster, "then smeared with dark-colored oil to make you think they've been cooked in oil."

"Well," said Lasnov, "I'll see if I can't do something anyway."

"If you see Kop, tell him a case has arrived for him."

"A case? What's in it?"

"I don't know. It's from Odessa. I'll send the boy over to Kop with my handcart. Will you let him know?"

"Sure," said Lasnov.

As he strolled through the square, he kept looking over to the station to see if the boy was coming with the case. And he told everyone that a case had come for Kop from Odessa. The rumor spread quickly through the market, got ahead of Lasnov, and, as he slowly approached Kop's stall, came back to him on the other side of the street.

When he reached the children's carrousel, the owner was just harnessing the horse. The horse's face was thin and dark, ennobled by hunger: it reminded Lasnov of the nun of Novgorod whom he had once seen as a child. Her face had also been thin and dark, ennobled by abstinence; you could look at her in a dark-green tent at fairs, and it had cost nothing to go in; people were merely asked, when they left the tent, to make a donation.

The carrousel owner came up to Lasnov, leaned over, and whispered, "Have you heard about the case that's supposed to have come for Kop?"

"No," said Lasnov.

"They say it's got toys in it, cars you can wind up."

"No," said Lasnov, "I heard it was toothbrushes."

"No, no," said the carrousel owner, "toys."

Lasnov stroked the horse's nose affectionately, went wearily on, and thought bitterly of the deals he used to be able to make. He had bought and sold so much clothing that he could have outfitted a whole army, and now he had sunk so low that this kid had talked him into buying a toothbrush. He had sold butter and bacon and barrels of oil, and at Christmas time he had always had a stall with candy canes for the kids; the colors of the candy canes had been as piercing as the joys and sufferings of the poor—red like the love that was celebrated in doorways or beside the factory wall while the bittersweet smell of molasses came wafting over the wall; yellow like the flames in a drunk man's brain, or pale green like the pain you felt when you woke up in the morning and looked at the face of your sleeping wife, a child's face, whose sole protection from life was those frail pink lids, fragile little covers which she had to open as soon as the children began to cry. But this year there weren't even any candy canes, and they would spend Christmas sitting at home, sipping thin soup, and taking turns looking through the handle of the toothbrush.

Next to the carrousel a woman had put two old chairs side by side and opened a shop on them: she had two mattresses to sell with the words "Magasin du Louvre" still visible on them, a well-thumbed book entitled *Left and Right of the Railroad Tracks—From Gelsenkirchen to Essen*, an English magazine dating from 1938, and a little tin that had once contained a typewriter ribbon.

THE COLLECTED STORIES

"Some lovely things," said the old woman when Lasnov stopped beside her.

"Very nice," he said, and was about to move on when the woman pounced on him, drew him by the sleeve, and whispered, "A case has come for Kop from Odessa. With things for Christmas."

"Has it?" he said. "What things?"

"Candy, all colored, and rubber animals that squeak. It's going to be such fun."

"Sure," said Lasnov, "it's going to be fun."

When he finally reached Kop's stall, Kop had just begun to unload his stuff and spread it out: pokers, saucepans, stoves, rusty nails which he always found himself and hammered straight. Nearly everyone had gathered around Kop's stall; they stood there speechless with excitement, looking along the street. As Lasnov went up to him, Kop was just unpacking a firescreen with a design of gold flowers and a Chinese woman.

"I've got a message for you," said Lasnov, "a case has arrived for you. The boy who's always hanging around the station is going to bring it over."

Kop looked at him with a sigh and said quietly, "Now I'm getting it from you too."

"What d'you mean, me too?" said Lasnov. "I've come straight here from the station to give you the message."

Kop ducked nervously. He was well dressed and wore an immaculate gray fur cap; he always carried a stick, with which he made dents in the ground as he walked along, and as a sole reminder of his better days he kept a cigarette dangling nonchalantly from his lips, a cigarette that was rarely alight because he rarely had money for tobacco. Twenty-seven years ago, when Lasnov came back to the village as a deserter with the news of the revolution, Kop had been an ensign in command of the railway station, and when Lasnov had entered the station at the head of the Soldiers' Council to arrest him, Kop had been prepared to allow a movement of his lips, the angle of his cigarette, to cost him his life; in any case, they all looked at the corner of his mouth, and he realized they might shoot him, but he did not remove the cigarette from his lips when Lasnov approached him. However, Lasnov had merely slapped his face. The cigarette had fallen out of his mouth, and without it he looked like a boy who has forgotten his homework. They had left him in peace; first he had been a teacher, then a dealer, but still whenever he saw Lasnov he was afraid Lasnov would knock the cigarette out of his mouth. He raised his head apprehensively, straightened the firescreen, and said, "If you only knew how many people have told me that already."

"A firescreen," said a woman, "if only one had enough heat to shield oneself from it with a firescreen." Kop looked at her contemptuously. "You have no sense of beauty."

"No," said the woman with a laugh, "I'm beautiful myself, and look at all the nice kids I've got." She ran her hand lightly over the heads of the four children grouped around her. "You don't..." She looked up quickly as her children suddenly ran off toward the station, following the other children, toward the boy who was bringing Kop's case on the stationmaster's handcart.

Everyone hurried away from their stalls, the children jumped down off the carrousel.

"My God," whispered Kop to Lasnov, the only one who had stayed behind, "I could almost wish the case hadn't come. They'll tear me to pieces."

"Don't you know what's in it?"

"No idea," said Kop, "I only know it must be made of tin."

"There's a lot of things can be made of tin—cans, toys, spoons."

"Music boxes—the kind you turn with a handle."

"Yes—just imagine."

Kop and Lasnov helped the boy lift the case down off the cart; the case was white, made of fresh, smooth boards, and it was nearly as high as the table on which Kop had spread out his rusty nails, pokers, and scissors.

Everyone fell silent as Kop thrust an old poker under the lid of the case and slowly raised it up; you could hear the faint creak of the nails. Lasnov wondered where all the people had suddenly sprung from: he was startled when the boy suddenly said, "I know what's inside."

No one asked, they all looked at him in suspense, and the boy looked silently at the tense faces. He broke out in a sweat and said in a low voice, "Nothing—there's nothing inside."

If he had said that one second earlier, they would have fallen on him and beaten him up in their disappointment, but now Kop had just taken the lid off and was groping around in the shavings; he removed a whole layer of shavings, then another, then screwed-up paper—then he held up both hands filled with the things he had found in the center of the case. "Tweezers," a woman cried out, but they weren't.

"No," said the woman who had called herself beautiful, "no, they're..."

"What are they?" said a little boy.

"Sugar tongs, that's what they are," said the carrousel owner in a dry voice; then he suddenly let out a wild laugh, threw up his arms, and ran back to his carrousel, still roaring with laughter.

"So they are," said Kop, "they're sugar tongs—dozens of them." He threw the tongs he was holding back into the case and groped around in it, but although they could not see his face, they all knew he was not smiling. He ran his hands through the clinking metal tongs the way misers in paintings finger their treasures.

"Isn't that just like them?" said one woman. "Sugar tongs... I really believe if there was such a thing as sugar I could manage to pick it up in my fingers, eh?"

"I had a grandmother," said Lasnov, "who always picked sugar up in her fingers—but then she was a dirty peasant woman."

"I think I could bring myself to do that too."

"You always were a pig anyhow, picking sugar up in your fingers. Ugh."

"You could use them," said Lasnov, "to fish tomatoes out of jars."

"Provided you had any tomatoes," said the woman who had called herself beautiful. Lasnov looked at her closely. She really was beautiful; she had plentiful fair hair, a straight nose, and fine dark eyes.

"You could also use them," said Lasnov, "for pickles."

"If you had any," said the woman.

"You could use them to pinch yourself in the behind."

"If you still had one," said the woman coldly. Her expression was becoming more and more angry and beautiful.

"You could pick up coal with them too."

"If you had any."

"You could use them as a cigarette holder."

"If you had anything to smoke."

Whenever Lasnov spoke, they all turned toward him, and as soon as he had finished they all turned toward the woman, and the more ridiculous the sugar tongs became in this dialogue, the more empty and miserable became the faces of the children and their parents. I must make them laugh, thought Lasnov. I was afraid there would be tooth-brushes in the case, but sugar tongs are really even worse. He blushed under the woman's triumphant gaze and said loudly, "You could use them to serve boiled fish."

"If you had any," said the woman.

"The children could play with them," said Lasnov in a low voice.

"If you...," began the woman, then she suddenly laughed out loud, and everyone else laughed too, for children were something they all had plenty of.

"All right," said Lasnov to Kop. "I'll take three. How much are they?"

"Twelve," said Kop.

"Twelve," said Lasnov and threw the money down on Kop's table. "It's a real bargain."

"It's really not expensive," said Kop shyly.

Ten minutes later all the children were running about the square with their sugar tongs glittering like silver; they sat on the carrou-sel, pinched their noses with them, brandished them in front of the grown-ups.

The boy who had brought the case over had been given one too. He sat on the steps in front of the station and hammered his sugar tongs flat. Now at last, he thought, I've got something I can use to get in between the cracks of the floorboards. Of course he had never thought of this. He had tried with pokers, scissors, and bits of wire, but he had never been able to manage it. He was sure he would be able to now he had this tool.

Kop counted his money, stacked it, and placed it carefully in his wallet. He looked at Lasnov, who was standing beside him, gloomily watching the activity in the square.

"You could do me a favor," said Kop.

"What favor?" said Lasnov absent-mindedly, without looking at Kop.

"Slap my face," said Kop, "hard enough for the cigarette to fall out."

Lasnov, still without looking at Kop, shook his head thoughtfully.

"Do that," said Kop, "please do. Don't you remember?"

"I remember," said Lasnov, "but I don't feel like doing it again."

"Are you sure?"

"Yes," said Lasnov, "I'm sure. I've never thought of doing it again."

"Damn it," said Kop, "and here I've been dreading it for twenty-seven years."

"You didn't have to," said Lasnov. He walked back to the station shaking his head. There's still a chance, he thought, that they'll run a special, a leave train or one for the wounded; specials didn't come very often, but just the same there might still be one today. He thoughtfully fingered the toothbrush and the three sugar tongs in his coat pocket. There have been times, he thought, when three special trains have arrived in one day.

He leaned against the lamppost in front of the station and scraped the last of his tobacco into a little heap...

THIS IS TIBTEN!

Soulless people cannot understand why I take such pains and humble pride in performing duties which they regard as beneath my dignity. My occupation may not correspond to my level of education, nor was it foretold by my fairy godmother at my christening, but I enjoy my work, and it provides me with a living: I tell people where they are. Passengers who in the evening at their own railway stations board trains that carry them to distant places, and who then during the night wake up at our station, peer out, confused, into the darkness, not knowing whether they have gone beyond their destination or have not yet reached it, or are possibly even at their destination (for our town contains a variety of tourist attractions and draws many visitors)—I tell all these people where they are. I switch on the loudspeaker as soon as a train arrives and the wheels of the locomotive have come to a standstill, and I say diffidently into the night, "This is Tibten! You are now in Tibten! Passengers wishing to visit the tomb of Tiburtius must alight here!," and the echo comes back to me from the platforms, right into my cubbyhole: a dark voice out of the darkness which seems to be announcing something doubtful, although actually it is speaking the plain truth.

A number of passengers then hurriedly descend onto the dimly lit platform, carrying their suitcases, for Tibten is their destination, and I watch them go down the stairs, reappear on Platform I, and hand over their tickets to the sleepy ticket collector at the barrier. Very few people arrive on business at night—businessmen intending to fill their companies' requirements at the Tibten lead mines. The visitors are mostly tourists attracted by the tomb of Tiburtius, a young Roman boy who committed suicide eighteen hundred years ago for the sake of a Tibten beauty. "He was but a lad," is inscribed on his tombstone, which can be admired in our local museum, "yet Love was his undoing." He came here from Rome to purchase lead for his father, who was an army contractor.

Certainly I would not have had to attend five universities and obtain two doctorates in order to be able to call out night after night into the darkness, "This is Tibten! You are now in Tibten!" And yet my work fills me with satisfaction. I speak my lines softly, so that those who are asleep do not wake up but those who are awake will not fail to hear it, and I make my voice sound just enticing enough for those who are dozing to rouse themselves and wonder whether they had not meant to go to Tibten.

In the latter part of the morning, therefore, when I wake up and look out of the window, I can see the passengers who succumbed to the spell of my voice making their way through our little town, armed with the brochures which our travel bureau so generously distributes all over the world. At breakfast they have already read that the wear and tear of centuries has reduced the Latin Tiburtinum to its present form of Tibten, and they proceed to the local museum, where they admire the tombstone erected eighteen hundred years ago to the Roman Werther. A boy's profile has been chiseled out of reddish sandstone, his hands outstretched in vain toward a girl. "He was but a lad, yet Love was his undoing. . ." His youthfulness is also attested to by the objects which were found in his grave: little figures made of some ivory-colored substance, two elephants, a horse, and a mastiff, which—as Brusler claims in his *Theory of the Tomb of Tiburtius*—were said to have been used in a kind of chess game. I doubt this theory, however. I am sure that to Tiburtius these objects were simply toys. The little ivory objects look exactly like the ones we get as a premium when we buy half a pound of margarine, and they served the same purpose: they were for children to play with. . . Possibly it behooves me to refer here to the excellent novel written by our local author, Volker von Volkersen, entitled *Tiburtius: A Roman Destiny That Found Fulfillment in Our Town*. But I regard Volkersen's book as misleading, because he also supports Brusler's theory as to the purpose of the toys.

I myself—at this point I must at last make a confession—am in possession of the original figures contained in Tiburtius' grave; I stole them from the museum and replaced them with the ones I obtain as a premium with half a pound of margarine: two elephants, a horse, and a mastiff. They are as white as Tiburtius' animals, they are the same size, the same weight, and—what seems to me most important of all—they serve the same purpose.

So tourists come from all over the world to admire the tomb of Tiburtius and his toys. Posters saying "Come to Tibten" hang in the waiting rooms of the Anglo-Saxon world, and when at night I speak my lines—"This is Tibten! You are in Tibten! Passengers wishing to visit the tomb of Tiburtius must alight here!"—I lure out of the trains the people who at their own railway stations succumbed to the spell of our posters. To be sure, they look at the sandstone slab, the authenticity of which is unquestioned. They look at the touching profile of a Roman boy for whom Love was his undoing and who drowned himself in a flooded shaft of the lead mines. And then the visitors' eyes move to the little animals: two elephants, a horse, and a mastiff—and this is just where they could study the wisdom of the world, but they do not. Ladies from our own and other countries, deeply moved, pile roses onto the tomb of this young lad. Poems are written; even my animals, the horse and the mastiff (I had to use up two pounds of margarine to acquire them!), have already become the subject of lyrical endeavors. "Thou didst play, even as we play, with mastiff and horse..." goes one line in the verses written by a not unknown poet. So there they lie, free gifts from the Klüsshenn Margarine Company, on red velvet under heavy glass in our local museum: witnesses to my consumption of margarine. Often, before I go on shift in the afternoon, I visit the museum for a minute and study them. They look genuine, slightly yellowed, and are completely indistinguishable from the ones lying in my drawer, for I threw in the originals among those I got with Klüsshenn's margarine, and I try in vain to separate them again.

Deep in thought, I then go off to work, hang up my cap on the hook, take off my coat, place my sandwiches in the drawer, arrange my cigarette papers, tobacco, and newspaper, and, when a train arrives, speak the lines it is my job to speak: "This is Tibten! You are now in Tibten! Passengers wishing to visit the tomb of Tiburtius must alight here!" I speak them softly, so that those who are asleep do not wake up, and those who are awake will not fail to hear me, and I make my voice sound just enticing enough for those who are dozing to rouse themselves and wonder whether they had not meant to go to Tibten.

And I cannot understand why anyone regards this work as beneath my dignity...

AND THERE WAS THE EVENING
AND THE MORNING...

It was not until noon that he thought of leaving his Christmas presents for Anna in the baggage room at the station; he was glad he had thought of it, for it meant he didn't have to go home immediately. Ever since Anna had stopped speaking to him, he was afraid of going home; her silence bore down on him like a tombstone the minute he entered the apartment. He used to look forward to going home, for two years after his wedding day: he loved having supper with Anna, talking to her, and then going to bed; best of all he loved the hour between going to bed and falling asleep. Anna fell asleep earlier than he did because nowadays she was always tired—and he would lie there in the darkness beside her, he could hear her breathing, and from the far end of the street the headlights of cars now and again threw rays of light onto the ceiling, light that curved down as the cars reached the rise in the street, bands of pale yellow light that made his sleeping wife's profile leap up for a second against the wall; then darkness would fall once more over the room, and all that remained was delicate whorls: the pattern of the curtains drawn on the ceiling by the gas lamp in the street. This was the hour he loved more than any hour of the day, because he could feel the day falling away from him, and he would slide down into sleep as into a bath.

Now he strolled hesitatingly past the baggage counter and saw his box still there at the back, between the red suitcase and the demijohn. The open elevator coming down from the platform was empty, white with snow: it descended like a piece of paper into the gray concrete of the baggage room, and the man who had been operating it walked over and said to the clerk, "Now it really feels like Christmas. It's nice when there's snow for the kids, eh?" The clerk nodded, silently impaled baggage checks on his spike, counted the money in his drawer and looked suspiciously across to Brenig, who had taken his claim check out of his pocket but folded it up and put it back again. This was the third time he had come, the third time he had taken the claim check out and put it back in his pocket again. The clerk's suspicious glances made him uncomfortable; he strolled over to the exit and stood looking out onto the empty station square. He loved the snow, loved the cold; as a boy it had intoxicated him to breathe in the cold clear air, and now he threw away his cigarette and held his face against the wind, which was driving light, profuse snowflakes toward the station. Brenig kept his eyes open, for he liked it when the flakes got caught in his eyelashes, new ones constantly replacing the old, which melted and ran down his cheeks in little drops. A girl walked quickly past him, and he saw how her green hat became white with snow while she hurried across the square, but it was only when she was standing at the streetcar stop that he recognized the little red suitcase she was carrying as the one which had stood next to his box in the baggage room.

It was a mistake to get married, thought Brenig; they congratulate you, send you flowers, have stupid telegrams delivered to your door, and then they leave you alone. They ask whether you have thought of everything: of things for the kitchen, from salt shaker to stove, and finally they make sure you even have plenty of soup seasoning on the shelf. They estimate whether you can support a family, but what it means to *be* a family is something nobody tells you. They send flowers, twenty bouquets, and it smells like a funeral; then they throw rice and leave you alone.

A man walked past him, and he could tell the man was drunk, he was singing "Oh Come All Ye Faithful," but Brenig did not shift the angle of his head, so that it was a moment or two before he noticed that the man was carrying a demijohn in his right hand and he knew the box with his Christmas presents for his wife was now standing all by itself on the top shelf of the baggage room. It contained an umbrella, two books, and a big piano made of mocha chocolate: the white keys were of marzipan, the black ones of dark brittle. The chocolate piano was as big as an encyclopedia, and the girl in the store had said the chocolate would keep for six months.

Maybe I was too young to get married, he thought, maybe I should have waited until Anna became less serious and I became more serious, but actually he knew he was serious enough and that Anna's seriousness was just right. That was what he loved about her. For the sake of the hour before falling asleep he had given up movies and dancing, and hadn't even bothered to meet his friends. At night, when he was lying in bed, he was filled with devoutness, with peace, and he would often repeat the sentence to himself, although he wasn't quite certain of the exact wording: "And God made the earth and the moon, to rule over the day and over the night, to divide the light from the darkness, and God saw that it was good, and there was the evening and the morning." He had meant to look it up in Anna's Bible again to see just how it went, but he always forgot. For God to have created day and night seemed to him every bit as wonderful as the creation of flowers, beasts, and man.

He loved this hour before falling asleep more than anything else. But now that Anna had stopped speaking to him, her silence lay on him like a weight. If she had only said, "It's colder today," or "It's going to rain," it would have put an end to his misery—if she had only said, "Yes," or "No, no," or something sillier still, he would be happy, and he would no longer dread going home. But for the space of a few seconds her face would turn to stone, and at these moments he suddenly knew what she would look like as an old woman; he was seized with fear, suddenly saw himself thrust thirty years forward into the future as onto a stony plain, saw himself old too, with the kind of face he had seen on some men: deeply lined with bitterness, strained with suppressed suffering, and tinged to the very nostrils with the pale yellow of gall. Masks scattered throughout the everyday world like death's-heads ...

Sometimes, although he had only known her for three years, he also knew what she had looked like as a child. He could picture her as a ten-year-old girl, dreaming over a book under the lamplight, grave, her eyes dark under her light lashes, her eyelids flickering above the printed page, her lips parted... Often, when he was sitting opposite her at table, her face would change like the pictures that change when you shake them, and he suddenly knew that she had sat there exactly like that as a child, carefully breaking up her potatoes with her fork and slowly dribbling the gravy over them... The snow had almost stuck his eyelashes together, but he could just make out the Number 4 gliding up over the snow as if on sleds.

Maybe I should phone her, he thought, have her come to the phone at Menders'; she'd have to speak to me then. The Number 4 would be followed immediately by the 7, the last streetcar that evening, but by this time he was bitterly cold and he walked slowly across the square, saw the brightly lit blue 7 in the distance, stood undecided by the phone booth, and looked in a store window where the window dressers were exchanging Santa Clauses and angels for other dummies: ladies in décolletage, their bare shoulders sprinkled with confetti, their wrists festooned with paper streamers. Their escorts, male dummies with graying temples, were being hurriedly placed on bar stools, champagne corks scattered on the floor; one dummy was having its wings and curls taken off, and Brenig was surprised how quickly an angel could be turned into a bartender. Mustache, dark wig, and a sign swiftly nailed to the wall, saying NEW YEAR'S EVE WITHOUT CHAMPAGNE?

Here Christmas was over before it had begun. Maybe, he thought, Anna is too young, she was only twenty-one, and while he contemplated his reflection in the store window he noticed the snow had covered his hair like a little crown—the way he used to see it on fenceposts—and it struck him that old people were wrong to talk about the gaiety of youth: when you were young, everything was serious and difficult, and nobody helped you, and he was suddenly surprised that he did not hate Anna for her silence, that he didn't wish he had married someone else. The whole vocabulary that people offered you was meaningless: forgiveness, divorce, a fresh start, time the Great Healer—these words were all useless. You had to work it out for yourself, because you were different from other people, and because Anna was different from other people's wives.

The window dressers were deftly nailing masks onto the walls, stringing crackers on a cord: the last Number 7 had left long ago, and the box with his presents for Anna was standing all by itself up there on the shelf.

I am twenty-five, he thought, and because of a lie, one little lie, a stupid lie such as millions of men tell every week or every month, I have to endure this punishment; with my eyes staring into the stony future I have to look at Anna crouching like a sphinx on the edge of the stony desert, and at myself, my face yellowed with bitterness, an old man. Oh, yes, there would always be plenty of soup seasoning on the kitchen shelf, the salt shaker would always be in its proper place, and he would have been a department head for years and well able to support his family: a stony clan, and never again would he lie in bed and in the hour before falling asleep rejoice in the creation of evening, and offer thanks to God for having created rest from the labors of the day, and he would send the same stupid telegrams to young people when they got married as he had been sent himself...

Other women would have laughed over such a stupid lie about his salary, other women knew that all men lie to their wives: maybe it was a kind of instinctive self-defense, against which they invented their own lies, but Anna's face had turned to stone. There were books about marriage, and he had looked up in these books what you could do when something went wrong with your marriage, but none of the books said anything about a woman who had turned to stone. The books told you how to have children and how not to have children, and they contained a lot of big fine words, but the little words were missing.

The window dressers had finished their work: streamers were hanging over wires that were fastened out of sight, and he saw one of the men disappearing at the back of the store with two angels under his arm, while the second man emptied a bag of confetti over the dummy's bare shoulders and gave a final pat to the sign saying NEW YEAR'S EVE WITHOUT CHAMPAGNE?

Brenig brushed the snow from his hair, walked back across the square to the station, and when he had taken the claim check from his pocket and smoothed it out for the fourth time, ran quickly, as if he hadn't a second to lose. But the baggage room was closed, and there was a sign hanging in front of the grille: "WILL OPEN TEN MINUTES BEFORE ARRIVAL OR DEPARTURE OF A TRAIN." Brenig laughed, he laughed for the first time since noon and looked at his box, lying up there on the shelf behind bars as if it were in prison. The departure board was right next to the counter, and he saw the next train would not be arriving for another hour. I can't wait that long, he thought, and at this time of night I won't even be able to get flowers or chocolate, not even a little book, and the last Number 7 has gone. For the first time in his life he thought of taking a taxi, and he felt very grown-up and at the same time a bit foolish as he ran across the square to the taxi rank.

He sat in the back of the cab, clasping his money: ten marks, the last of his cash, which he had set aside to buy something special for Anna. But he hadn't found anything special, and now he was sitting there clasping his money and watching the meter jump up at short intervals—very short intervals, it seemed to him—ten pfennings at a time, and every time the meter clicked it felt like a stab in the heart, although it only showed 2.80 marks. Here I am coming home, with no flowers, no presents, hungry, tired, and stupid, and it occurred to him that he could almost certainly have got some chocolate in the waiting room at the station.

The streets were empty, the cab drove almost soundlessly through the snow, and in the lighted windows Brenig could see the Christmas trees glowing in the houses. Christmas, the way he had known it as a child and the way he had felt today, seemed very far away: the important things, the things that mattered, happened independently of the calendar, and in the stony desert Christmas would be like any other day of the year and Easter like a rainy day in November: thirty, forty torn-off calendars, metal holders with shreds of paper, that's all that would be left if you didn't watch out.

He was roused by the driver saying "Here we are..." Then he was relieved to see that the meter had stopped at 3.40 marks. He waited impatiently for his change from five marks, and he felt a surge of relief when he saw a light upstairs in the room where Anna's bed stood next to his. He made up his mind never to forget this moment of relief, and as he got out his house key and put it in the door, he experienced that silly feeling again that he had had when he got into the taxi: he felt grown-up, yet at the same time a bit foolish.

In the kitchen the Christmas tree was standing on the table, with presents spread out for him: socks, cigarettes, a new fountain pen, and a gay, colorful calendar which he would be able to hang over his desk in the office. The milk was already in the saucepan on the stove, he had only to light the gas, and there were sandwiches ready for him on the plate—but that was how it had been every evening, even since Anna had stopped speaking to him, and the setting up of the Christmas tree and the laying out of the presents was like the preparing of the sandwiches, a duty; Anna would always do her duty. He didn't feel like the milk, and the appetizing sandwiches didn't appeal to him either. He went into the little hall and noticed at once that Anna had turned out the light. But the door to the bedroom was open, and without much hope he called softly into the dark rectangle, "Anna, are you asleep?" He waited, for a

long time it seemed, as if his question were falling into a deep well, and
the dark silence in the dark rectangle of the bedroom door contained
everything that was in store for him in thirty, forty years—and when
Anna said "No," he thought he must have heard wrong, perhaps it was
an illusion, and he went on hurriedly in a louder voice, "I've done such
a stupid thing. I checked my presents for you at the station, and when I
wanted to pick them up the baggage room was closed, and I didn't want
to hang around. Are you angry?"

This time he was sure he had really heard her "No," but he could
also hear that this "No" did not come from the corner of the room
where their beds had been. Evidently Anna had moved her bed under
the window. "It's an umbrella," he said, "two books and a little piano
made of chocolate; it's as big as an encyclopedia, the keys are made of
marzipan and brittle." He stopped, listened for a reply, nothing came
from the dark rectangle, but when he asked, "Are you pleased?" the
"Yes" came quicker than the two "No's" had done...

He turned out the light in the kitchen, undressed in the dark, and
got into bed. Through the curtains he could see the Christmas trees in
the building across the street, and downstairs there was singing, but he
had regained his hour, he had two "No's" and a "Yes," and when a car
came up the street, the headlights made Anna's profile leap up out of
the darkness for him...

THE ADVENTURE

Fink walked over to the side entrance of the church. Right and left of the cracked asphalt were tiny triangular garden plots bordered with black iron railings: sour, gray-black earth and two box shrubs with leaves as tough and desiccated as leather. Leaning his shoulder against the brown padded door, he opened it and found himself in a musty entrance with another padded door ahead. This one he punched open with his fist, and before entering the church he glanced at a notice on a plywood board which read: "Third Order of St. Francis—Announcements...."

The church was filled with a greenish half-light, and on a wall painted a nondescript color Fink saw a white placard showing a hand, done in black, pointing straight down. Above the stiff, exaggeratedly long forefinger were the words: Confessional Bell. Underneath, in brown holders, were bell-pushes of dark ivory, and name plates. He did not bother to decipher the names but pressed one of the buttons at random, and it seemed to him that this act represented something irrevocable, final. Then he listened—not a sound.

He dipped his finger into a pink plaster stoup in the form of a shell; in the dim light it resembled a great artificial palate with a few bits chipped out of it. Slowly he crossed himself and entered the center nave. On either side he saw two dark confessionals, their red curtains drawn shut, and he now noticed that bomb damage had caused the stucco roof between the gothic columns to crumble away: the ugly masonry of yellow brick was laid bare, somehow it reminded him of an old-fashioned public bathhouse. What was once the main entrance had been walled up with rough stones, and squashed in among them was a crooked old window frame from which the white paint had flaked off.

Fink knelt down in the center nave and tried to pray, but over his folded hands he had to keep watching the four confessionals and peering into the dimness so as not to miss the priest who might suddenly appear from somewhere. He would probably come from the sacristy, up front, where in the semi-darkness Fink could make out a brass bell with a red velvet rope next to the perpetual light. Toward the middle the church got lighter, and he now saw that the whole center nave had been repaired: the ruined, jagged walls supported temporary, almost flat rafters boarded up with grimy old planks— some of the planks were dark with floor varnish—and the saints against the columns were all minus their heads, a helpless, pathetic double rank of strange plaster figures with their heads knocked off and their emblems torn from their grasp, somber truncated torsos which seemed to be holding out their mutilated hands to him in supplication.

Fink tried to summon feelings of remorse and contrition, but without success; he found it hard to concentrate, and from within him there arose a welter of stumbling, spasmodic, imploring prayers, interspersed with memories and the ever-recurring desire to get all this over with quickly and leave, get out and away from this town.

He could already sense it: the thing he wanted to confess was starting to become a memory, to acquire luster; imperceptibly it was emerging from the level of the sordid daily grind, and it seemed to him that one day, soon—he would somehow rise above it and look down: a beautiful, sinful adventure, while in reality—and this he knew too—he had simply followed the rules of the game out of a sort of politeness, rules so depressingly casual and so grimly serious that he had been appalled. Even before it happened, he had been seized with disgust, but he had joined in the game, persuading himself that after all it was nothing but a mechanical act, dictated by nature, while in his heart he knew that the arrow, already quivering in the bow, was going to be released, and would strike him unerringly in that invisible something for which he could find no other name than soul.

He sighed, and began to feel impatient; in his mind's eye the images—those which were gradually acquiring a golden patina, and the real ones—were hovering beside, above, below one another, occasionally merging for an instant, and his gaze traveled in agonizing suspense past the headless saints against their columns to that velvet rope beside the bell.

It occurred to him that possibly the bell was not even working, or that the priest whose name he had not bothered to read was not there. He was not familiar with this form of confession; in the old days they used to make jokes about it. He was just about to get up and go over to the bell-pushes again when he saw in the motionless background of the empty church a dark figure which emerged from the sacristy, genuflected before the altar, and crossed over to the confessionals on the right-hand side. His tense gaze followed the monk; he was tall and slight, and the circle of hair left by the tonsure was thick and black.

Fink quickly tried once more to summon a sense of remorse and contrition, he silently intoned the formulas he had known by heart for twenty years, and stood up. As he stepped into the aisle he stumbled; somewhere in the red and white tiles with their pattern of lilies there must be a damaged place; he steadied himself against a prayer stool and heard the priest switch off the tiny light and pull the curtain aside. As he knelt down in the airless, dark and very uncomfortable little space and made out the pale ear behind the grille, he felt his heart pounding in his throat; he was too agitated to speak.

"Praise be to Jesus Christ," said a colorless, detached voice.

He forced out a "For ever and ever Amen" and was silent. The sweat was pouring down his back, making his shirt cling to his skin, closely and relentlessly, as if it had been soaked in water; there seemed to be no room left to breathe. The priest cleared his throat.

"I have committed adultery," stammered Fink, and he knew that with that he had said about all he was capable of saying.

"Are you married?"

"No."

"But the woman is?"

"Yes."

"How many times?" The question brought him instantly to his senses. Everything that had been swimming in front of his vision, this large white ear, which looked enormous to him, and the grille—of a strange, crisp brown like the latticework on an apple pie—all this he now saw quite clearly, in all its reality, and he looked into the drooping sleeve of the priest's propped-up arm, a dark cavity between the monk's habit and the pale skin covered with light hairs.

"Once," and a deep involuntary sigh escaped him.

"When?" The questions came tersely, rapidly, impersonally, like a doctor's during an examination.

"Today," he said. Actually it had already receded far into the past for him, but the word brought it back again before his eyes, like a camera zooming toward its object to fix it for ever. One was compelled to look closely at something one did not want to look at closely.

"Avoid seeing this woman."

Now for the first time Fink realized he would be seeing her again; a pretty little housewife with a firm neck and wearing a red housecoat, with eyes which were both boring and sad, and he pictured her with such intensity that he almost missed the priest's question.

"Do you love her?"

He could not say no; to say yes seemed even more monstrous. He thought about it, while the sweat accumulated hot and burning above his eyebrows. "No," he said quickly, adding: "It will be very difficult to avoid seeing her."

The priest was silent, and for a moment Fink saw the lowered lids jerk up, a pair of very quiet gray eyes.

"I am a salesman for a firm that makes prefabricated houses," he said, "and the—the lady has ordered a house from us."

"And you have that territory?"

"Yes." He thought of how he would have to negotiate with her, present plans, discuss estimates, advise on details—countless details which, if one wanted to, could be dragged out for months.

"You must see that you are transferred."

Fink was silent.

The voice became more forceful. "You must do all you can not to see her again. Habit is strong, very strong. You have the sincere desire and resolve not to see the woman again?"

"Yes," said Fink at once, and he knew that for the first time he was really speaking the truth.

"Try; do everything in your power. Think of the Bible message: If thy left hand offend thee, cut it off. Accept the possibility of material loss." He was silent for a moment. "I know it is not easy, but Hell doesn't make things easy for us."

His voice had lost its personal quality again when he said: "Anything else?"

Fink was startled. He was not familiar with this kind of confession, although by this time he realized it was serious, extremely serious, more

serious than that regular mechanical hygiene he underwent at home
every three months with the chaplain.

"Anything else?" asked the voice impatiently. "When did you last
confess?"

"Eight weeks ago."

"And go to Mass?"

"Four."

In a monotonous voice the priest began to intone the Commandments, the way he did with the penitents he was accustomed to, people
who scarcely knew the Creed, whose religious vocabulary consisted
of Our Father and Hail Mary. Fink was feeling uncomfortable, he
wanted to leave.

"No," he said each time quietly, as far as the fifth Commandment.
The priest left out the sixth.

"Stealing," said the priest without emotion, "and lying, the seventh
and eighth Commandments."

Fink felt his color rising, it surged hot into his ears. For God's sake,
he wasn't a thief.

"Have you told a lie?"

Fink said nothing. Never before had anyone asked him whether he
had told a lie. In any case it seemed to him he had never confessed before.
These crude formulas struck him like hammer blows, and while he was
thinking he had never confessed before, he muttered: "Oh well, the houses,
our houses are not quite the way they look in the catalogue—I mean,
they—people are often disappointed when they actually see them...."

The priest could not suppress an "Aha." He said: "We must be
honest about that too, although ..." he groped for words, "although it
seems impossible. But it is a lie to sell something of whose value one is
not convinced." He cleared his throat again, and Fink saw the propped-
up arm disappear as the priest began to whisper: "Now we will take it
all together and fervently beseech Our Lord Jesus Christ to obtain our
forgiveness. He died on the Cross to free us from our sins, and each one
of our sins nails Him once more to the Cross. Summon remorse and
contrition within yourself again, and as a penance recite one decade of
the Sorrowful Mystery."

The priest sat up straight in the center of the confessional, murmuring with closed eyes, then he suddenly turned his face toward Fink

again, pronounced the *Absolvo te* in a clear voice, and made the sign of the Cross over him.

"Praise be to Jesus Christ—"

"For ever and ever Amen!" said Fink.

He was stiff all over, and he felt as if hours had gone by. He sat down in a pew and pulled out his handkerchief, and as he began to dry the sweat off he noticed the priest disappearing again into the sacristy.

Fink was tired. He tried to pray, but the words tumbled back inside him like a heavy fall of rock, and while he fought against sleep he saw through half-closed lids that in the dark corner next to the side door candles were now burning in front of the altar of the Mother of God: the cheap paraffin tapers flickered restlessly, consuming themselves in feverish haste, and their shimmer swung the silhouette of a small, old woman onto the wall of the center nave, in gigantic and outlandish detail: single hairs protruding from her forehead stood out hard and black on the wall, a childlike nose and the tired slackness of her lips moving silently: a fleeting memorial, towering above the truncated plaster figures and seeming to grow out beyond the edge of the roof.

MURKE'S COLLECTED SILENCES

Every morning, after entering Broadcasting House, Murke performed an existential exercise. Here in this building the elevator was the kind known as a paternoster—open cages carried on a conveyor belt, like beads on a rosary, moving slowly and continuously from bottom to top, across the top of the elevator shaft, down to the bottom again, so that passengers could step on and off at any floor. Murke would jump onto the paternoster but, instead of getting off at the second floor, where his office was, he would let himself be carried on up, past the third, fourth, fifth floors; he was seized with panic every time the cage rose above the level of the fifth floor and ground its way up into the empty space where oily chains, greasy rods, and groaning machinery pulled and pushed the elevator from an upward into a downward direction; Murke would stare in terror at the bare brick walls, and sigh with relief as the elevator passed through the lock, dropped into place, and began its slow descent, past the fifth, fourth, third floors. Murke knew his fears were unfounded: obviously nothing would ever happen, nothing could ever happen, and even if it did, it could be nothing worse than finding himself up there at the top when the elevator stopped moving and being shut in for an hour or two at the most. He was never without a book in his pocket, and cigarettes; yet as long as the building had been standing, for three years, the elevator had never once failed. On certain days it was inspected, days when Murke had to forgo those four and a half seconds of panic, and on these days he was irritable and restless, like people who had gone without breakfast. He needed this panic, the way other people need their coffee, their oatmeal, or their fruit juice.

So when he stepped off the elevator at the second floor, the home of the Cultural Department, he felt lighthearted and relaxed, as lighthearted and relaxed as anyone who loves and understands his work. He would unlock the door to his office, walk slowly over to his armchair, sit down, and light a cigarette. He was always first on the job. He was young, intelligent, and had a pleasant manner, and even his arrogance, which occasionally flashed out for a moment—even that was forgiven him, since it was known he had majored in psychology and graduated cum laude.

For two days now, Murke had been obliged to go without his panic-breakfast: unusual circumstances had required him to get to Broadcasting House at 8:00 a.m., dash off to a studio, and begin work right away, for he had been told by the director of broadcasting to go over the two talks on "The Nature of Art" which the great Bur-Malottke had taped and to cut them according to Bur-Malottke's instructions. Bur-Malottke, who had converted to Catholicism during the religious fervor of 1945, had suddenly, "overnight," as he put it, "felt religious qualms," he had "suddenly felt he might be blamed for contributing to the religious overtones in radio," and he had decided to omit God, who occurred frequently in both his half-hour talks on "The Nature of Art," and replace Him with a formula more in keeping with the mental outlook he had professed before 1945. Bur-Malottke had suggested to the producer that the word "God" be replaced by the formula "that higher Being Whom we revere," but he had refused to retape the talks, requesting instead that God be cut out of the tapes and replaced by "that higher Being Whom we revere." Bur-Malottke was a friend of the director, but this friendship was not the reason for the director's willingness to oblige him: Bur-Malottke was a man one simply did not contradict. He was the author of numerous books of a belletristic-philosophical-religious and art-historical nature, he was on the editorial staff of three periodicals and two newspapers, and closely connected with the largest publishing house. He had agreed to come to Broadcasting House for fifteen minutes on Wednesday and tape the words "that higher Being Whom we revere" as often as "God" was mentioned in his talks: the rest was up to the technical experts.

It had not been easy for the director to find someone whom he could ask to do the job; he thought of Murke, but the suddenness with which he thought of Murke made him suspicious—he was a dynamic, robust individual—so he spent five minutes going over the problem in his mind, considered Schwendling, Humkoke, Fräulein Broldin, but he ended up with Murke. The director did not like Murke; he had, of course, taken him on as soon as his name had been put forward, the way a zoo director, whose real love is the rabbits and the deer, naturally accepts wild animals too for the simple reason that a zoo must contain wild animals—but what the director really loved was rabbits and deer, and for him Murke was an intellectual wild animal. In the end his dynamic personality triumphed, and he instructed Murke to cut Bur-Malottke's talks. The talks were to be given on Thursday and Friday, and Bur-Malottke's misgivings had come to him on Sunday night—one might just as well commit suicide as contradict Bur-Malottke, and the director was much too dynamic to think of suicide.

So Murke spent Monday afternoon and Tuesday morning listening three times to the two half-hour talks on "The Nature of Art"; he had cut out "God," and in the short breaks which he took, during which he silently smoked a cigarette with the technician, reflected on the dynamic personality of the director and the inferior Being Whom Bur-Malottke revered. He had never read a line of Bur-Malottke, never heard one of his talks before. Monday night he had dreamed of a staircase as tall and steep as the Eiffel Tower; he had climbed it but soon noticed that the stairs were slippery with soap, and the director stood down below and called out, "Go on, Murke, go on ... show us what you can do—go on!" Tuesday night the dream had been similar: he had been at a fairground, strolled casually over to the roller coaster, paid his thirty pfennigs to a man whose face seemed familiar, and as he got on the roller coaster he saw that it was at least ten miles long, he knew there was no going back, and realized that the man who had taken his thirty pfennigs had been the director. Both mornings, after these dreams, he had not needed the harmless panic-breakfast up there in the empty space above the paternoster.

Now it was Wednesday. He was smiling as he entered the building, got into the paternoster, let himself be carried up as far as the sixth floor—four and a half seconds of panic, the grinding of the chains, the bare brick walls—he rode down as far as the fourth floor, got out, and walked toward the studio where he had an appointment with Bur-Malottke. It was two minutes to ten as he sat down in his green chair, waved to the technician, and lit his cigarette. His breathing was quiet, he took a piece of paper out of his breast pocket and glanced at the clock. Bur-Malottke was always on time, at least he had a reputation for being punctual; and as the second hand completed the sixtieth minute of the tenth hour, the minute hand slipped onto the twelve, the hour hand onto the ten, the door opened and in walked Bur-Malottke. Murke got up, and with a pleasant smile walked over to Bur-Malottke and introduced himself. Bur-Malottke shook hands, smiled, and said, "Well, let's get started!" Murke picked up the sheet of paper from the table, put his cigarette between his lips, and, reading from the list, said to Bur-Malottke:

"In the two talks, God occurs precisely twenty-seven times—so I must ask you to repeat twenty-seven times the words we are to splice. We would appreciate it if we might ask you to repeat them thirty-five times, so as to have a certain reserve when it comes to splicing."

"Granted," said Bur-Malottke with a smile, and sat down.

"There is one difficulty, however," said Murke: "where God occurs in the genitive, such as 'God's will,' 'God's love,' 'God's purpose,' He must be replaced by the noun in question followed by the words 'of that higher Being Whom we revere.' I must ask you, therefore, to repeat the words 'the will' twice, 'the love' twice, and 'the purpose' three times, followed each time by 'of that higher Being Whom we revere,' giving us a total of seven genitives. Then there is one spot where you use the vocative and say 'O God'—here I suggest you substitute 'O Thou higher Being Whom we revere.' Everywhere else only the nominative case applies."

It was clear that Bur-Malottke had not thought of these complications; he began to sweat, the grammatical transposition bothered him. Murke went on. "In all," he said, in his pleasant, friendly manner, "the twenty-seven sentences will require one minute and twenty seconds of radio time, whereas the twenty-seven times 'God' occurs require only twenty seconds. In other words, in order to take care of your alterations we shall have to cut half a minute from each talk."

Bur-Malottke sweated more heavily than ever; inwardly he cursed his sudden misgivings and asked, "I suppose you've already done the cutting, have you?"

"Yes, I have," said Murke, pulling a flat metal box out of his pocket; he opened it and held it out to Bur-Malottke. It contained some darkish sound-tape scraps, and Murke said softly, "'God' twenty-seven times, spoken by you. Would you care to have them?"

"No, I would not," said Bur-Malottke, furious. "I'll speak to the director about the two half minutes. What comes after my talks in the program?"

"Tomorrow," said Murke, "your talk is followed by the regular program 'Neighborly News,' edited by Grehm."

"Damn," said Bur-Malottke, "it's no use asking Grehm for a favor."

"And the day after tomorrow," said Murke, "your talk is followed by 'Let's Go Dancing.'"

"Oh, God, that's Huglieme," groaned Bur-Malottke. "Never yet has Light Entertainment given way to Culture by as much as a fifth of a minute."

"No," said Murke, "it never has, at least"—and his youthful face took on an expression of irreproachable modesty—"at least not since I've been working here."

"Very well," said Bur-Malottke and glanced at the clock, "we'll be through here in ten minutes, I take it, and then I'll have a word with the director about that minute. Let's go. Can you leave me your list?"

"Of course," said Murke. "I know the figures by heart."

The technician put down his newspaper as Murke entered the little glass booth. The technician was smiling. On Monday and Tuesday, during the six hours they listened to Bur-Malottke's talks and did their cutting, Murke and the technician had not exchanged a single personal word; now and again they exchanged glances, and when they stopped for a breather, the technician had passed his cigarettes to Murke and the next day Murke passed his to the technician. Now, when Murke saw the technician smiling, he thought: If there is such a thing as friendship in this world, then this man is my friend. He laid the metal box with the snippets from Bur-Malottke's talk on the table and said quietly, "Here we go." He plugged into the studio and said into the microphone, "I'm sure we can dispense with the run-through, Professor. We might as well start right away—would you please begin with the nominatives?"

Bur-Malottke nodded, Murke switched off his own microphone, pressed the button which turned on the green light in the studio, and heard Bur-Malottke's solemn, carefully articulated voice intoning, "That higher Being Whom we revere—that higher Being..."

Bur-Malottke pursed his lips toward the muzzle of the mike as if he wanted to kiss it, sweat ran down his face, and through the glass Murke observed with cold detachment the agony that Bur-Malottke was enduring; then he suddenly switched Bur-Malottke off, stopped the moving tape that was recording Bur-Malottke's words, and feasted his eyes on the spectacle of Bur-Malottke behind the glass, soundless, like a fat, handsome fish. He switched on his microphone and his voice came quietly into the studio, "I'm sorry, but our tape was defective, and I must ask you to begin again at the beginning, with the nominatives." Bur-Malottke swore, but his curses were silent ones which only he could hear, for Murke had disconnected him and did not switch him on again until he had begun to say, "That higher Being..." Murke was too young, considered himself too civilized, to approve of the word "hate." But here, behind the glass pane, while Bur-Malottke repeated his genitives, he suddenly knew the meaning of hatred: he hated this great fat, handsome creature, whose books—two million three hundred and fifty thousand copies of them—lay around in libraries, bookstores, bookshelves, and bookcases, and not for one second did he dream of suppressing this hatred. When Bur-Malottke had repeated two genitives, Murke switched on his own mike and said quietly, "Excuse me for interrupting you: the nominatives were excellent, so was the first genitive, but would you mind doing the second genitive again? Rather gentler in tone, rather more relaxed—I'll play it back to you." And although Bur-Malottke shook his head violently, he signaled to the technician to play back the tape in the studio. They saw Bur-Malottke give a start, sweat more profusely than ever, then hold his hands over his ears until the tape came to an end. He said something, swore, but Murke and the technician could not hear him; they had disconnected him. Coldly Murke waited until he could read from Bur-Malottke's lips that he had begun again with the higher Being, he turned on the mike and the tape, and Bur-Malottke continued with the genitives.

When he was through, he screwed up Murke's list into a ball, rose from his chair, drenched in sweat and fuming, and made for the door; but Murke's quiet, pleasant young voice called him back. Murke said, "But, Professor, you've forgotten the vocative." Bur-Malottke looked at him, his eyes blazing with hate, and said into the mike, "O Thou higher Being Whom we revere!"

As he turned to leave, Murke's voice called him back once more. Murke said, "I'm sorry, Professor, but, spoken like that, the words are useless."

"For God's sake," whispered the technician, "watch it!" Bur-Malottke was standing stock-still by the door, his back to the glass booth, as if transfixed by Murke's voice.

Something had happened to him that had never happened to him before: he was helpless, and this young voice, so pleasant, so remarkably intelligent, tortured him as nothing had ever tortured him before. Murke went on, "I can, of course, paste it into the talk the way it is, but I must point out to you, Professor, that it will have the wrong effect."

Bur-Malottke turned, walked back to the microphone, and said in low and solemn tones, "O Thou higher Being Whom we revere."

Without turning to look at Murke, he left the studio. It was exactly quarter past ten, and in the doorway he collided with a young, pretty woman carrying some sheet music. The girl, a vivacious redhead, walked briskly to the microphone, adjusted it, and moved the table to one side so she could stand directly in front of the mike.

In the booth Murke chatted for half a minute with Huglieme, who was in charge of Light Entertainment. Pointing to the metal container, Huglieme said, "Do you still need that?" And Murke said, "Yes, I do." In the studio the redhead was singing, "Take my lips, just as they are, they're so lovely." Huglieme switched on his microphone and said quietly, "D'you mind keeping your trap shut for another twenty seconds, I'm not quite ready." The girl laughed, made a face, and said, "Okay, pansy dear." Murke said to the technician, "I'll be back at eleven; we can cut it up then and splice it all together."

"Will we have to hear it through again after that?" asked the technician. "No," said Murke, "I wouldn't listen to it again for a million marks."

The technician nodded, inserted the tape for the red-haired singer, and Murke left.

He put a cigarette between his lips, did not light it, and walked along the rear corridor toward the second paternoster, the one on the south side leading down to the coffeeshop. The rugs, the corridors, the furniture, and the pictures, everything irritated him. The rugs were impressive, the corridors were impressive, the furniture was impressive, and the pictures were in excellent taste, but he suddenly felt a desire to take the sentimental picture of the Sacred Heart which his mother had sent him and see it somewhere here on the wall. He stopped, looked round, listened, took the picture from his pocket, and stuck it between the wallpaper and the frame of the door to the assistant drama producer's office. The tawdry little print was highly colored, and beneath the picture of the Sacred Heart were the words: "I prayed for you at St. James's Church."

Murke continued along the corridor, got into the paternoster, and was carried down. On this side of the building the Schrumsnot ashtrays, which had won a Good Design Award, had already been installed. They hung next to the illuminated red figures indicating the floor: a red four, a Schrumsnot ashtray, a red three, a Schrumsnot ashtray, a red two, a Schrumsnot ashtray. They were handsome ashtrays, scallop-shaped, made of beaten copper, the copper base an exotic marine plant, nodular seaweed—and each ashtray had cost two hundred and fifty-eight marks and seventy-seven pfennigs. They were so handsome that Murke could never bring himself to soil them with cigarette ash, let alone anything as sordid as a butt. Other smokers all seemed to have had the same feeling—empty packs, butts, and ash littered the floor under the handsome ashtrays. Apparently no one had the courage to use them as ashtrays; they were copper, burnished, forever empty.

Murke saw the fifth ashtray next to the illuminated red zero rising toward him; the air was getting warmer, there was a smell of food. Murke jumped off and stumbled into the coffeeshop. Three freelance colleagues were sitting at a table in the corner. The table was covered with used plates, cups, and saucers.

The three men were the joint authors of a radio series, "The Lung, A Human Organ"; they had collected their fee together, breakfasted together, were having a drink together, and were now throwing dice for the expense voucher. One of them, Wendrich, Murke knew well, but just then Wendrich shouted "Art!"—"Art," he shouted again, "art, art!" and Murke felt a spasm, like the frog when Galvani discovered electricity. The last two days Murke had heard the word "art" too often, from Bur-Malottke's lips; it occurred exactly one hundred and thirty-four times in the two talks, and he had heard the talks three times, which meant he had heard the word "art" four hundred and two times, too often to feel any desire to discuss it. He squeezed past the counter toward a booth in the far corner and was relieved to find it empty. He sat down, lit his cigarette, and when Wulla, the waitress, came, he said, "Apple juice, please," and was glad when Wulla went off again at once. He closed his eyes tight, but found himself listening willy-nilly to the conversation of the free-lance writers over in the corner, who seemed to be having a heated argument about art; each time one of them shouted "Art," Murke winced. It's like being whipped, he thought.

When she brought him the apple juice, Wulla looked at him in concern. She was tall and strongly built, but not fat; she had a healthy, cheerful face. As she poured the apple juice from the jug into the glass, she said, "You ought to take a vacation, sir, and quit smoking."

She used to call herself Wilfriede-Ulla, but later, for the sake of simplicity, she combined the names into Wulla. She especially admired the people from the Cultural Department.

"Lay off, will you?" said Murke. "Please!"

"And you ought to take some nice ordinary girl to the movies one night," said Wulla.

"I'll do that this evening," said Murke, "I promise you."

"It doesn't have to be one of those dolls," said Wulla, "just some nice, quiet, ordinary girl, with a kind heart. There are still some of those around."

"Yes," said Murke, "I know they're still around, as a matter of fact I know one." Well, that's fine then, thought Wulla, and went over to the freelancers, one of whom had ordered three drinks and three coffees. Poor fellows, thought Wulla, art will be the death of them yet. She had a soft spot for the freelancers and was always trying to persuade them to economize. The minute they have any money, she thought, they blow it; she went up to the counter and, shaking her head, passed on the order for the three drinks and the three coffees.

Murke drank some of the apple juice, stubbed out his cigarette in the ashtray, and thought with apprehension of the hours from eleven to one when he had to cut up Bur-Malottke's sentences and paste them into the right places in the talks. At two o'clock the director wanted both talks played back to him in his studio. Murke thought about soap, about staircases, steep stairs, and roller coasters, he thought about the dynamic personality of the director, he thought about Bur-Malottke, and was startled by the sight of Schwendling coming into the coffeeshop.

Schwendling had on a shirt of large red and black checks and made a beeline for the booth where Murke was hiding. Schwendling was humming the tune which was very popular just then: "Take my lips, just as they are, they're so lovely..." He stopped short when he saw Murke, and said, "Hello, you here? I thought you were busy carving up that crap of Bur-Malottke's."

"I'm going back at eleven," said Murke.

"Wulla, let's have some beer," shouted Schwendling over to the counter, "a pint. Well," he said to Murke, "you deserve extra time off for that, it must be a filthy job. The old man told me all about it."

Murke said nothing, and Schwendling went on, "Have you heard the latest about Muckwitz?"

Murke, not interested, first shook his head, then for politeness's sake asked, "What's he been up to?"

Wulla brought the beer. Schwendling swallowed some, paused for effect, and announced, "Muckwitz is doing a feature about the Steppes."

Murke laughed and said, "What's Fenn doing?"

"Fenn," said Schwendling, "Fenn's doing a feature about the Tundra."

"And Weggucht?"

"Weggucht is doing a feature about me, and after that I'm going to do a feature about him, you know the old saying: 'You feature me, I'll feature you...'"

Just then one of the freelancers jumped up and shouted across the room, "Art—art—that's the only thing that matters!"

Murke ducked, like a soldier when he hears the mortars being fired from the enemy trenches. He swallowed another mouthful of apple juice and winced again when a voice over the loudspeaker said, "Herr Murke is wanted in Studio 13—Herr Murke is wanted in Studio 13." He looked at his watch; it was only half-past ten, but the voice went on relentlessly, "Herr Murke is wanted in Studio 13—Herr Murke is wanted in Studio 13." The loudspeaker hung above the counter, immediately below the motto the director had had painted on the wall: "DISCIPLINE ABOVE ALL."

"Well," said Schwendling, "that's it, you'd better go."

"Yes," said Murke, "that's it."

He got up, put money for the apple juice on the table, pressed past the freelancers' table, got into the paternoster outside, and was carried up once more past the five Schrumsnot ashtrays. He saw his Sacred Heart picture still sticking in the assistant producer's doorframe and thought: Thank God, now there's at least one corny picture in this place.

He opened the door of the studio booth, saw the technician sitting alone and relaxed in front of three cardboard boxes, and asked wearily, "What's up?"

"They were ready sooner than expected, and we've got an extra half hour in hand," said the technician. "I thought you'd be glad of the extra time."

"I certainly am," said Murke. "I've got an appointment at one. Let's get on with it, then. What's the idea of the boxes?"

"Well," said the technician, "for each grammatical case I've got one box—the nominatives in the first, the genitives in the second, and in that one"—he pointed to the little box on the right with the words "Pure Chocolate" on it—"in that one I have the two vocatives, the good one in the right-hand corner, the bad one in the left."

"That's terrific," said Murke. "So you've already cut up the crap."

"That's right," said the technician, "and if you've made a note of the order in which the cases have to be spliced, it won't take us more than an hour. Did you write it down?"

"Yes, I did," said Murke. He pulled a piece of paper from his pocket with the numbers one to twenty-seven; each number was followed by a grammatical case.

Murke sat down, held out his cigarette pack to the technician; they both smoked while the technician laid the cut tapes with Bur-Malottke's talks on the roll.

"In the first cut," said Murke, "we have to stick in a nominative."

The technician put his hand into the first box, picked up one of the snippets, and stuck it into the space.

"Next comes a genitive," said Murke.

They worked swiftly, and Murke was relieved that it all went so fast.

"Now," he said, "comes the vocative; we'll take the bad one, of course."

The technician laughed and stuck Bur-Malottke's bad vocative into the tape.

"Next," he said, "next!"

"Genitive," said Murke.

The director conscientiously read every letter from a listener. The one he was reading at this particular moment went as follows:

Dear Radio,

I am sure you can have no more faithful listener than myself. I am an old woman, a little old lady of seventy-seven, and I have been listening to you every day for thirty years. I have never been sparing with my praise. Perhaps you remember my letter about the program "The Seven Souls of Kaweida the Cow." It was a lovely program—but now I have to be angry with you! The way the canine soul is being neglected in radio is gradually becoming a disgrace. And you call that humanism. I am sure Hitler had his bad points: if one is to believe all one hears, he was a dreadful man, but one thing he did have: a real affection for dogs, and he did a lot for them. When are dogs going to come into their own again in German radio? The way you tried to do it in the program "Like Cat and Dog" is certainly not the right one: it was an insult to every canine soul. If my little Lohengrin could only talk, he'd tell you! And the way he barked, poor darling, all through your terrible program, it almost made me die of shame. I pay my two marks a month like any other listener and stand on my rights and demand to know: When are dogs going to come into their own again in German radio?

With kind regards—in spite of my being so cross with you,

Sincerely yours,

Jadwiga Herchen

(retired)

P.S. In case none of those cynics of yours who run your programs should be capable of doing justice to the canine soul, I suggest

you make use of my modest attempts, which are enclosed herewith. I do not wish to accept any fee. You may send it direct to
the SPCA. Enclosed: 35 manuscripts.

> Yours,
> J.H.

The director sighed. He looked for the scripts, but his secretary
had evidently filed them away. The director filled his pipe, lit it, ran his
tongue over his dynamic lips, lifted the receiver, and asked to be put
through to Krochy. Krochy had a tiny office with a tiny desk, although
in the best of taste, upstairs in Culture and was in charge of a section as
narrow as his desk: Animals in the World of Culture.

"Krochy speaking," he said diffidently into the telephone.

"Say, Krochy," said the director, "when was the last time we had a
program about dogs?"

"Dogs, sir?" said Krochy. "I don't believe we ever have, at least not
since I've been here."

"And how long have you been here, Krochy?" And upstairs in his
office Krochy trembled, because the director's voice was so gentle; he
knew it boded no good when that voice became gentle.

"I've been here ten years now, sir," said Krochy.

"It's a disgrace," said the director, "that you've never had a program about dogs; after all, that's your department. What was the title
of your last program?"

"The title of my last program was—" stammered Krochy.

"You don't have to repeat every sentence," said the director, "we're
not in the army."

"'Owls in the Ruins,'" said Krochy timidly.

"Within the next three weeks," said the director, gentle again now,
"I would like to hear a program about the canine soul."

"Certainly, sir," said Krochy. He heard the click as the director put
down the receiver, sighed deeply, and said, "Oh, God!"

The director picked up the next letter.

At this moment Bur-Malottke entered the room. He was always at
liberty to enter unannounced, and he made frequent use of this liberty.
He was still sweating as he sank wearily into a chair opposite the director and said, "Well, good morning."

"Good morning," said the director, pushing the letter aside. "What can I do for you?"

"Could you give me one minute?"

"Bur-Malottke," said the director, with a generous, dynamic gesture, "does not have to ask me for one minute; hours, days, are at your disposal."

"No," said Bur-Malottke, "I don't mean an ordinary minute. I mean one minute of radio time. Due to the changes, my talk has become one minute longer."

The director grew serious, like a satrap distributing provinces. "I hope," he said sourly, "it's not a political minute."

"No," said Bur-Malottke, "it's half a minute of 'Neighborly News' and half a minute of Light Entertainment."

"Thank God for that," said the director. "I've got a credit of seventy-nine seconds with Light Entertainment and eighty-three seconds with 'Neighborly News.' I'll be glad to let someone like Bur-Malottke have one minute."

"I am overcome," said Bur-Malottke.

"Is there anything else I can do for you?" asked the director.

"I would appreciate it," said Bur-Malottke, "if we could gradually start correcting all the tapes I have made since 1945. One day," he said—he passed his hand over his forehead and gazed wistfully at the genuine Kokoschka above the director's desk—"one day I shall"—he faltered, for the news he was about to break to the director was too painful for posterity—"one day I shall... die," and he paused again, giving the director a chance to look gravely shocked and raise his hand in protest, "and I cannot bear the thought that after my death, tapes may be run off on which I say things I no longer believe in. Particularly in some of my political utterances, during the fervor of 1945, I let myself be persuaded to make statements which today fill me with serious misgivings and which I can only account for on the basis of that spirit of youthfulness that has always distinguished my work. My written works are already in process of being corrected, and I would like to ask you to give me the opportunity of correcting my spoken works as well."

The director was silent; he cleared his throat slightly, and little shining beads of sweat appeared on his forehead. It occurred to him that Bur-Malottke had spoken for at least an hour every month since

1945, and he made a swift calculation while Bur-Malottke went on talking: twelve times ten hours meant one hundred and twenty hours of spoken Bur-Malottke.

"Pedantry," Bur-Malottke was saying, "is something that only impure spirits regard as unworthy of genius; we know, of course"— and the director felt flattered to be ranked by the We among the pure spirits—"that the true geniuses, the great geniuses, were pedants. Himmelsheim once had a whole printed edition of his *Seelon* rebound at his own expense because he felt that three or four sentences in the central portion of the work were no longer appropriate. The idea that some of my talks might be broadcast which no longer correspond to my convictions when I depart this earthly life—I find such an idea intolerable. How do you propose we go about it?"

The beads of sweat on the director's forehead had become larger. "First of all," he said in a subdued voice, "an exact list would have to be made of all your broadcast talks, and then we would have to check in the archives to see if all the tapes were still there."

"I should hope," said Bur-Malottke, "that none of the tapes has been erased without notifying me. I have not been notified, therefore no tapes have been erased."

"I will see to everything," said the director.

"Please do," said Bur-Malottke curtly, and rose from his chair. "Goodbye."

"Goodbye," said the director as he accompanied Bur-Malottke to the door.

The freelancers in the coffeeshop had decided to order lunch. They had had some more drinks, they were still talking about art, their conversation was quieter now but no less intense. They all jumped to their feet when Wanderburn suddenly came in. Wanderburn was a tall, despondent-looking writer with dark hair, an attractive face somewhat etched by the stigma of fame. On this particular morning he had not shaved, which made him look even more attractive. He walked over to the table where the three men were sitting, sank exhausted into a chair, and said, "For God's sake, give me a drink. I always have the feeling in this building that I'm dying of thirst."

They passed him a drink, a glass that was still standing on the table, and the remains of a bottle of soda water. Wanderburn swallowed the drink, put down his glass, looked at each of the three men in turn, and said, "I must warn you about the radio business, about this pile of junk—this immaculate, shiny, slippery pile of junk. I'm warning you. It'll destroy us all." His warning was sincere and impressed the three young men very much; but the three young men did not know that Wanderburn had just come from the accounting department, where he had picked up a nice fat fee for a quick job of editing the Book of Job.

"They cut us," said Wanderburn, "they consume our substance, splice us together again, and it'll be more than any of us can stand."

He finished the soda water, put the glass down on the table, and, his coat flapping despondently about him, strode to the door.

On the dot of noon Murke finished the splicing. They had just stuck in the last snippet, a genitive, when Murke got up. He already had his hand on the doorknob when the technician said, "I wish I could afford a sensitive and expensive conscience like that. What'll we do with the box?" He pointed to the flat tin lying on the shelf next to the cardboard boxes containing the new tapes.

"Just leave it there," said Murke.

"What for?"

"We might need it again."

"D'you think he might get pangs of conscience all over again?"

"He might," said Murke. "We'd better wait and see. So long." He walked to the front paternoster, rode down to the second floor, and for the first time that day entered his office. His secretary had gone to lunch; Murke's boss, Humkoke, was sitting by the phone reading a book. He smiled at Murke, got up, and said, "Well, I see you survived. Is this your book? Did you put it on the desk?" He held it out for Murke to read the title, and Murke said, "Yes, that's mine." The book had a jacket of green, gray, and orange and was called *Batley's Lyrics of the Gutter*; it was about a young English writer a hundred years ago who had drawn up a catalog of London slang.

"It's a marvelous book," said Murke.

"Yes," said Humkoke, "it is marvelous, but you never learn."

Murke eyed him questioningly.

"You never learn that one doesn't leave marvelous books lying around when Wanderburn is liable to turn up, and Wanderburn is always liable to turn up. He saw it at once, of course, opened it, read it for five minutes, and what's the result?"

Murke said nothing.

"The result," said Humkoke, "is two hour-long broadcasts by Wanderburn on 'Lyrics of the Gutter.' One day this fellow will do a feature about his own grandmother, and the worst of it is that one of his grandmothers was one of mine too. Please, Murke, try to remember: never leave marvelous books around when Wanderburn is liable to turn up, and, I repeat, he's always liable to turn up. That's all, you can go now, you've got the afternoon off, and I'm sure you've earned it. Is the stuff ready? Did you hear it through again?"

"It's all done," said Murke, "but I can't hear the talks through again, I simply can't."

"'I simply can't' is a very childish thing to say," said Humkoke.

"If I have to hear the word 'art' one more time today, I'll become hysterical," said Murke.

"You already are," said Humkoke, "and I must say you've every reason to be. Three hours of Bur-Malottke—that's too much for anybody, even the toughest of us, and you're not even tough." He threw the book on the table, took a step toward Murke, and said, "When I was your age I once had to cut three minutes out of a four-hour speech of Hitler's, and I had to listen to the speech three times before I was considered worthy of suggesting which three minutes should be cut. When I began listening to the tape for the first time I was still a Nazi, but by the time I had heard the speech for the third time I wasn't a Nazi anymore. It was a drastic cure—a terrible one, but very effective."

"You forget," said Murke quietly, "that I had already been cured of Bur-Malottke before I had to listen to his tapes."

"You really are a vicious beast!" said Humkoke with a laugh. "That'll do for now. The director is going to hear it through again at two. Just see that you're available in case anything goes wrong."

"I'll be home from two to three," said Murke.

"One more thing," said Humkoke, pulling out a yellow biscuit tin from a shelf next to Murke's desk. "What's this scrap you've got here?"

Murke colored. "It's..." he stammered, "I collect a certain kind of leftovers."

"What kind of leftovers?" asked Humkoke.

"Silences," said Murke. "I collect silences."

Humkoke raised his eyebrows, and Murke went on, "When I have to cut tapes, in the places where the speakers sometimes pause for a moment—or sigh, or take a breath, or there is absolute silence—I don't throw that away, I collect it. Incidentally, there wasn't a single second of silence in Bur-Malottke's tapes."

Humkoke laughed. "Of course not, he would never be silent. And what do you do with the scrap?"

"I splice it together and play back the tape when I'm at home in the evening. There's not much yet, I only have three minutes so far—but then people aren't silent very often."

"You know, don't you, that it's against regulations to take home sections of tape?"

"Even silences?" asked Murke.

Humkoke laughed and said, "For God's sake, get out!" And Murke left.

When the director entered his studio a few minutes after two, the Bur-Malottke tape had just been turned on:

> ... and wherever, however, why ever, and whenever we begin to discuss the Nature of Art, we must first look to that higher Being Whom we revere, we must bow in awe before that higher Being Whom we revere, and we must accept Art as a gift from that higher Being Whom we revere. Art...

No, thought the director, I really can't ask anyone to listen to Bur-Malottke for a hundred and twenty hours. No, he thought, there are some things one simply cannot do, things I wouldn't want to wish even on Murke. He returned to his office and switched on the loudspeaker just in time to hear Bur-Malottke say, "O Thou higher Being Whom we revere..." No, thought the director, no, no.

Murke lay on his chesterfield at home smoking. Next to him on a chair was a cup of tea, and Murke was gazing at the white ceiling of the room. Sitting at his desk was a very pretty blonde who was staring out of the window at the street. Between Murke and the girl, on a low coffee table, stood a tape recorder, recording. Not a word was spoken, not a sound was made. The girl was pretty and silent enough for a photographer's model.

"I can't stand it," said the girl suddenly. "I can't stand it, it's inhuman, what you want me to do. There are some men who expect a girl to do immoral things, but it seems to me that what you are asking me to do is even more immoral than the things other men expect a girl to do."

Murke sighed. "Oh, hell," he said, "Rina dear, now I've got to cut all that out; do be sensible, be a good girl, and put just five more minutes' silence on the tape."

"Put silence," said the girl, with what thirty years ago would have been called a pout. "Put silence, that's another of your inventions. I wouldn't mind putting words onto a tape—but putting silence..."

Murke had got up and switched off the tape recorder. "Oh, Rina," he said, "if you only knew how precious your silence is to me. In the evening, when I'm tired, when I'm sitting here alone, I play back your silence. Do be a dear and put just three more minutes' silence on the tape for me and save me the cutting; you know how I feel about cutting."

"Oh, all right," said the girl, "but give me a cigarette at least."

Murke smiled, gave her a cigarette, and said, "This way I have your silence in the original and on tape, that's terrific." He switched the tape on again, and they sat facing one another in silence till the telephone rang. Murke got up, shrugged helplessly, and lifted the receiver.

"Well," said Humkoke, "the tapes ran off smoothly, the boss couldn't find a thing wrong with them... You can go to the movies now. And think about snow."

"What snow?" asked Murke, looking out onto the street, which lay basking in brilliant summer sunshine.

"Come on, now," said Humkoke, "you know we have to start thinking about the winter programs. I need songs about snow, stories about snow—we can't fool around for the rest of our lives with Schubert and Stifter. No one seems to have any idea how badly we need snow songs and snow stories. Just imagine if we have a long hard winter with lots of snow and freezing temperatures: where are we going to get our snow programs from? Try to think of something snowy."

"All right," said Murke, "I'll try to think of something." Humkoke had hung up.

"Come along," he said to the girl, "we can go to the movies."

"May I speak again now?" said the girl.

"Yes," said Murke, "speak!"

It was just at this time that the assistant drama producer had finished listening again to the one-act play scheduled for that evening. He liked it, only the ending did not satisfy him. He was sitting in the glass booth in Studio 13 next to the technician, chewing a match and studying the script.

> (*Sound effects of a large empty church*)
> ATHEIST (*in a loud clear voice*): Who will remember me when I have become the prey of worms?
> (*Silence*)
> ATHEIST (*his voice a shade louder*): Who will wait for me when I have turned into dust?
> (*Silence*)
> ATHEIST (*louder still*): And who will remember me when I have turned into leaves?
> (*Silence*)

There were twelve such questions called out by the atheist into the church, and each question was followed by—? Silence.

The assistant producer removed the chewed match from his lips, replaced it with a fresh one, and looked at the technician, a question in his eyes.

"Yes," said the technician, "if you ask me, I think there's a bit too much silence in it."

"That's what I thought," said the assistant producer; "the author thinks so too and he's given me leave to change it. There should just be a voice saying 'God'—but it ought to be a voice without church sound effects, it would have to be spoken somehow in a different acoustical environment. Have you any idea where I can get hold of a voice like that at this hour?"

The technician smiled, picked up the metal container which was still lying on the shelf. "Here you are," he said, "here's a voice saying 'God' without any sound effects."

The assistant producer was so surprised he almost swallowed the match, choked a little, and got it up into the front of his mouth again. "It's quite all right," the technician said with a smile. "We had to cut it out of a talk, twenty-seven times."

"I don't need it that often, just twelve times," said the assistant producer.

"It's a simple matter, of course," said the technician, "to cut out the silence and stick in 'God' twelve times—if you'll take the responsibility."

"You're a godsend," said the assistant producer, "and I'll be responsible. Come on, let's get started." He gazed happily at the tiny, lusterless tape snippets in Murke's tin box. "You really are a godsend," he said. "Come on, let's go!"

The technician smiled, for he was looking forward to being able to present Murke with the snippets of silence: it was a lot of silence, all together nearly a minute; it was more silence than he had ever been able to give Murke, and he liked the young man.

"Okay," he said with a smile, "here we go."

The assistant producer put his hand in his jacket pocket, took out a pack of cigarettes; in doing so he touched a crumpled piece of paper. He smoothed it out and passed it to the technician. "Funny, isn't it, the corny stuff you can come across in this place? I found this stuck in my door."

The technician took the picture, looked at it, and said, "Yes, it's funny," and he read out the words under the picture:

"I prayed for you at St. James's Church."

BONN DIARY

Monday

Unfortunately I arrived too late to go out again or pay any calls; it was 2330 hours when I got to the hotel, and I was tired. So I had to be satisfied with looking out of the hotel window at the city lying there scintillating with life—bubbling, throbbing, boiling over, one might say: there are vital forces hidden there just waiting to be released. The city is still not all it might be. I smoked a cigar, abandoning myself wholly to this fascinating electric energy; I wondered whether I should phone Inna, finally resigned myself with a sigh and had one more look through my important files. Toward midnight I went to bed: I always find it hard to go to bed here. This city is not conducive to sleep.

Night jottings

Strange dream, very strange: I was walking through a forest of monuments, straight rows of them; in little clearings there were miniature parks, each with a monument in the center; all the monuments were alike, hundreds, thousands of them: a man standing "at ease," an officer to judge by the creases in his soft boots, yet the chest, face and pedestal of each monument were covered with a cloth—suddenly all the monuments were unveiled simultaneously, and I realized, without any particular surprise, that *I* was the man standing on the pedestal; I shifted my position on the pedestal, smiled, and now that the covering had dropped off I could read my name thousands of times over: *Erich von Machorka-Muff.* I laughed, and the laugh echoed back to me a thousand times from my own mouth.

Tuesday

Filled with a deep sense of happiness, I fell asleep again, woke refreshed, and laughed as I looked at myself in the mirror: it is only here in the capital that one has dreams like that. Before I had finished shaving, the first call from Inna. (That's what I call my old friend Inniga von Schekel-Pehnunz, a member of the new nobility but an old family: her father, Ernst von Schekel, was raised to the aristocracy by Wilhelm II only two days before the latter abdicated, but I have no qualms about regarding Inna as a friend of equal rank.)

On the phone Inna was—as always—sweet, managed to squeeze in some gossip and in her own way gave me to understand that the project which was the main reason for my visit to the capital was coming along very well. "The corn is ripe," she said softly, and then, barely pausing: "The baby's being christened today." She hung up quickly, to prevent me from asking questions in my impatience. Deep in thought I went down to the breakfast room: had she really meant the laying of the foundation stone? My frank, forthright soldierly nature still has difficulty understanding Inna's cryptic remarks.

Again in the breakfast room this abundance of virile faces, most of them well-bred: I passed the time by imagining which man would be suitable for which post, an old habit of mine; before I had even shelled my egg I had already found first-rate material for two regimental staffs and one divisional staff, and there were still some candidates left over for the general staff; playing games in my head, so to speak—just the thing for a veteran observer of human nature like myself. The memory of my dream enhanced my pleasant mood: strange, to walk through a forest of monuments and to see oneself on every pedestal. I wonder whether the psychologists have really plumbed all the depths of the self?

I ordered my coffee to be brought to the lobby, smoked a cigar and observed the time with a smile: 0956 hours—would Heffling be punctual? I had not seen him for six years, we had corresponded occasionally (the usual exchange of post cards one has with inferiors in the ranks).

I actually found myself feeling nervous about Heffling's punctuality; the trouble with me is, I am inclined to regard everything as symptomatic: Heffling's punctuality became for me the punctuality *per se* of the ranks. I remembered with a touch of emotion what my old divisional chief, Welk von Schnomm, used to say: "Macho, you are and always will be an idealist." (Memo: renew the standing order for upkeep of Schnomm's grave.)

Am I an idealist? I fell into a reverie, until Heffling's voice roused me: I looked first at the time—two minutes after ten (I have always allowed him this microscopic reserve of privilege)—then at him: how fat the fellow's got, grossly fat around the neck, hair getting thin, but still that phallic sparkle in his eyes, and his "Present, Colonel!" sounded just like old times. "Heffling!" I cried, slapping him on the shoulder and ordering a double schnapps for him. He stood at attention as he took the drink from the waiter's tray; I drew him by the sleeve over to the corner, and we were soon deep in reminiscences: "Remember the time at Schwichi-Schwaloche, the ninth...?"

It is heart-warming to observe how powerless the vagaries of fashion are to corrode the wholesome spirit of the people: the home-spun virtues, the hearty male laugh, and the never-failing readiness to share a good dirty story, are still to be found. While Heffling was telling me some variations of the familiar subject in an undertone, I noticed Murcks-Maloche had entered the lobby and—without speaking to me, as arranged—had disappeared into the rear of the restaurant. By a glance at my wristwatch I indicated to Heffling that I was pressed for time, and with the sound instincts of the simple man he understood immediately that he had to leave. "Come and see us some time, Colonel, my wife would be delighted." Laughing and joking we walked side by side to the porter's desk, and I promised Heffling I would come and see him. Perhaps an opportunity would offer for a little adventure with his wife; every now and again I feel the urge to partake of the husky eroti-cism of the lower classes, and one never knows what arrows Cupid may be holding in store in his quiver.

I sat down beside Murcks, ordered some Hennessy and, as soon as the waiter had gone, said in my straightforward fashion:

"Well, fire away."

"Yes, we've made it." He laid his hand on mine and whispered: "I'm so glad, Macho, so glad."

"I'm pleased too," I said warmly, "that one of the dreams of my youth has come to pass. And in a democracy too."

"A democracy in which we have the majority of Parliament on our side is a great deal better than a dictatorship."

I felt constrained to stand up; I was filled with solemn pride; historic moments have always moved me deeply.

"Murcks," I said, choking back the tears, "is it really true then?"

"It's true, Macho," he said.

"It's all settled?"

"It's all settled—you're to give the dedication address today. The first course of instruction is starting right away. Those enrolled are still being put up in hotels, till the project can be officially declared open."

"Will the public—will it swallow it?"

"It'll swallow it—the public will swallow anything," said Murcks.

"On your feet, Murcks," I said, "let's drink a toast, let's drink to the spirit to which this building is dedicated: to the spirit of military memories."

We clinked glasses and drank.

I was too moved to undertake any serious business that morning; I went restlessly up to my room, from there to the lobby, wandered through this enchanting city, after Murcks had driven off to the Ministry. Although I was in civilians, I had the impression of a sword dangling at my side; there are some sensations which are really only appropriate when one is in uniform. Once again, while I was strolling through the city, looking forward to my tête-à-tête with Inna, uplifted by the certainty that my plan had become reality—once again I had every reason to recall one of Schnomm's expressions: "Macho, Macho," he used to say, "you've always got your head in the clouds." He had said it when there were only thirteen men left in my regiment and I had four of those men shot for mutiny.

In honor of the occasion I permitted myself an apéritif at a café not far from the station; I looked through some newspapers, glanced at a few editorials on defense policy, and tried to imagine what Schnomm—if he were still alive—would have said had he read the articles. "Those Christians—" he would have said, "who would have thought it of them!"

At last it was time to go to the hotel and change for my rendezvous with Inna: her signal on the car horn—a Beethoven motif—made me look out of the window; she waved up at me from her lemon-yellow car: lemon-yellow hair, lemon-yellow dress, black gloves. With a sigh, after blowing her a kiss, I went to the mirror, tied my tie, and went downstairs; Inna would be the right wife for me, but she has been divorced seven times and, not unnaturally, is skeptical about the institution of marriage; besides, we are separated by a deep gulf in background and outlook: she comes from a strict Protestant family, I from a strict Catholic one—all the same, numbers link us together symbolically: she has been divorced seven times, I have been wounded seven times. Inna!! I still can't quite get used to being kissed on the street....

Inna woke me at 1617 hours: she had some strong tea and ginger biscuits ready, and we quickly went once more through the files on Hürlanger-Hiss, the unforgotten field marshal to whose memory we planned to dedicate the building.

While I was examining the Hürlanger files once more, my arm around Inna's shoulder, lost in daydreams of her gift of love, I heard the band music: melancholy overtook me, for, like all the other experiences of this day, to listen to this music in civilian clothes was truly an ordeal.

The band music and Inna's nearness diverted my attention from the files; however, Inna had filled me in verbally so that I was fully equipped to give my speech. The doorbell rang as Inna was pouring out my second cup of tea; I jumped, but Inna smiled reassuringly. "An important guest," she said, returning from the hall, "a guest whom we cannot possibly receive in here." There was a twinkle in her eye as she gestured toward the rumpled bed in all its delightful disarray of love. "Come along," she said. I got out of bed, followed her in a kind of daze, and was genuinely surprised to find myself face to face in her living room with the Minister of Defense. His frank, rugged countenance was shining. "General von Machorka-Muff," he said, with a beaming smile, "welcome to the capital!"

I could not believe my ears. With a twinkle in his eye the Minister handed me my commission.

I think, looking back, I must have swayed for a moment and suppressed a few tears; but actually I am not quite sure what was going on inside me; all I remember is hearing myself say: "But Your Excellency—the uniform—half an hour before the ceremony starts...." With a twinkle in his eye—what an admirable man he is, what sterling qualities!—he glanced at Inna, Inna twinkled back at him, drew aside a chintz curtain dividing off one corner of the room, and there it was, there hung my uniform, with all my decorations on it.... Events, emotions followed so thick and fast that looking back all I can do is give their sequence in note-form:

We offered the Minister some refreshment and he had a glass of beer while I changed in Inna's room.

Drive to the building site, which I was viewing for the first time: I was extraordinarily moved by the sight of this piece of land on which my pet project is to become reality: the Academy for Military Memoirs, where every veteran from the rank of major up is to be given the opportunity of committing his reminiscences to paper, through conversations with old comrades and cooperation with the Ministry's Department of Military History; my own feeling is that a six-week course should suffice, but Parliament is willing to subsidize a three-month course. I was also thinking of having a few healthy working-class girls housed in a special wing, to sweeten the evening leisure hours of the comrades who are plagued with memories. I have gone to a great deal of trouble to find appropriate inscriptions. The main wing is to bear in gold lettering the inscription: MEMORIA DEXTERA EST; while over the girls' wing, which will also contain the bathrooms, will be the words: BALNEUM ET AMOR MARTIS DECOR. However, on the way there the Minister hinted that I should not mention this part of my plan just yet; he was afraid—perhaps rightly so—of opposition from some of his fellow members of Parliament, although—as he put it with a chuckle—no one could complain of lack of liberalization!

There were flags all around the building site, the band was playing: *I used to have a comrade,* as I walked beside the Minister toward the platform. Since with his usual modesty the Minister declined to open proceedings, I stepped up at once onto the dais, surveyed the row of assembled comrades, and, encouraged by a wink from Inna, began to speak:

"Your Excellency, comrades! This building, which is to bear the name Hürlanger-Hiss Academy for Military Memoirs, needs no justification. But a justification is required for the name Hürlanger-Hiss, a name which for many years—to this very day, I would say—has been regarded as dishonored. You all know the disgrace attaching to this name: when the army of Field Marshal Emil von Hürlanger-Hiss was obliged to retreat at Schwichi-Schwaloche, Hürlanger-Hiss could report a loss of only 8,500 men. According to the calculations of Tapir's specialists in retreat—Tapir, as you know, was our private name for Hitler—his army should, with the proper fighting spirit, have had a loss of 12,300 men. You are also aware, Your Excellency and comrades, of the insulting treatment to which Hürlanger-Hiss was subjected: he was transferred in disgrace to Biarritz, where he died of lobster poisoning. For years—a total of fourteen years—this dishonor has attached to his name. All the data on Hürlanger's army fell into the hands of Tapir's underlings, later into the hands of the Allies, but today, today," I cried, pausing so as to let my next words sink in, "today it can be taken as a proven fact, and I am prepared to make the material public, it can be taken as proven fact that our great Field Marshal's army suffered losses at Schwichi-Schwaloche of a total of 14,700 men: it can therefore be assumed beyond any doubt that his army fought with unexampled courage, and his name is now cleared of all blemish."

While I let the deafening applause pour over me and modestly diverted the ovation from myself to the Minister, I had a chance to observe from the faces of my comrades that they too were surprised by this information; how discreetly Inna had carried on her research!

To the strains of *See'st thou the dawn in eastern skies* I took the trowel and stone from the mason and set the cornerstone in place; it contained a photograph of Hürlanger-Hiss together with one of his shoulder-straps.

At the head of my comrades I marched from the building site to the villa, "The Golden Shekel," which Inna's family has put at our disposal until the academy has been completed. Here we had a brisk round of drinks, a word of thanks from the Minister, and a telegram from the Chancellor was read out, before the social hour began.

The social hour was opened by a concerto for seven drums, played by seven former generals; with the consent of the composer, a captain with musical aspirations, it was announced that it would be known as

the Hürlanger-Hiss Memorial Septet. The social hour was an unquali-
fied success: songs were sung, stories told, confidences exchanged, old
quarrels forgotten.

Wednesday

We had just an hour to get ready for the church service; in relaxed
marching order we made our way just before 0730 hours to the cathedral. Inna stood beside me in church, and I felt encouraged when she
whispered that she recognized a colonel as her second husband, a
lieutenant-colonel as her fifth, and a captain as her sixth. "And your
eighth," I whispered in her ear, "will be a general." My mind was made
up; Inna blushed; she did not hesitate when after it was over I took her
into the vestry to introduce her to the prelate who had conducted the
service. "Indeed, my dear child," the priest said, after we had discussed
the church's position, "since none of your former marriages was solem-
nized in church, there is no obstacle to you and General von Machorka-
Muff having a church wedding."

It was under these auspices that we had breakfast, in a gay mood,
à deux; Inna was elated, I had never seen her quite like that. "I always
feel like this," she said, "when I am a bride." I ordered champagne.

We decided to keep our engagement a secret for the time being, but
as a little celebration we drove up to the Petersberg, a lovely hill a few
miles outside Bonn, where Inna's cousin, whose maiden name was Pelf,
had invited us for lunch. Inna's cousin was adorable.

The afternoon and evening were devoted entirely to love, the night
to sleep.

Thursday

I still can't quite get used to the idea that I am living and working
here; it must be a dream! Gave my first lecture this morning: "Reminis-
cence as a Historical Duty."

Annoying interlude at midday. Murcks-Maloche came to see me
at the villa on behalf of the Minister to report that the opposition had
expressed itself dissatisfied with our academy project.

"Opposition?" I asked, "what's that?"

Murcks enlightened me. I was astounded. "Let's get this straight," I said impatiently, "do we have the majority or don't we?"

"We do," said Murcks.

"Well then," I said. Opposition—a strange word, I don't like it at all; it is such a grim reminder of times that I thought were over and done with.

Inna, when I told her at teatime about my annoyance, consoled me.

"Erich," she said, putting her little hand on my arm, "no one has ever opposed our family."

ACTION WILL BE TAKEN

An Action-Packed Story

Probably one of the strangest interludes in my life was the time I spent as an employee in Alfred Wunsiedel's factory. By nature I am inclined more to pensiveness and inactivity than to work, but now and again prolonged financial difficulties compel me—for pensiveness is no more profitable than inactivity—to take on a so-called job. Finding myself once again at a low ebb of this kind, I put myself in the hands of the employment office and was sent with seven other fellow-sufferers to Wunsiedel's factory, where we were to undergo an aptitude test.

The exterior of the factory was enough to arouse my suspicions: the factory was built entirely of glass brick, and my aversion to well-lit buildings and well-lit rooms is as strong as my aversion to work. I became even more suspicious when we were immediately served breakfast in the well-lit, cheerful coffee shop: pretty waitresses brought us eggs, coffee and toast, orange juice was served in tastefully designed jugs, goldfish pressed their bored faces against the sides of pale-green aquariums. The waitresses were so cheerful that they appeared to be bursting with good cheer. Only a strong effort of will— so it seemed to me—restrained them from singing away all day long. They were as crammed with unsung songs as chickens with unlaid eggs.

Right away I realized something that my fellow-sufferers evidently failed to realize: that this breakfast was already part of the test; so I chewed away reverently, with the full appreciation of a person who knows he is supplying his body with valuable elements. I did something which normally no power on earth can make me do: I drank orange juice on an empty stomach, left the coffee and egg untouched, as well as most of the toast, got up, and paced up and down in the coffee shop, pregnant with action.

As a result I was the first to be ushered into the room where the questionnaires were spread out on attractive tables. The walls were done in a shade of green that would have summoned the word "delightful" to the lips of interior decoration enthusiasts. The room appeared to be empty, and yet I was so sure of being observed that I behaved as someone pregnant with action behaves when he believes himself unobserved: I ripped my pen impatiently from my pocket, unscrewed the top, sat down at the nearest table and pulled the questionnaire toward me, the way irritable customers snatch at the bill in a restaurant.

Question No. 1: Do you consider it right for a human being to possess only two arms, two legs, eyes, and ears?

Here for the first time I reaped the harvest of my pensive nature and wrote without hesitation: "Even four arms, legs and ears would not be adequate for my driving energy. Human beings are very poorly equipped."

Question No. 2: How many telephones can you handle at one time?

Here again the answer was as easy as simple arithmetic: "When there are only seven telephones," I wrote, "I get impatient; there have to be nine before I feel I am working to capacity."

Question No. 3: How do you spend your free time?

My answer: "I no longer acknowledge the term free time—on my fifteenth birthday I eliminated it from my vocabulary, for in the beginning was the act."

I got the job. Even with nine telephones I really didn't feel I was working to capacity. I shouted into the mouthpieces: "Take immediate action!" or: "Do something!—We must have some action—Action will be taken—Action has been taken—Action should be taken." But as a rule—for I felt this was in keeping with the tone of the place—I used the imperative.

Of considerable interest were the noon-hour breaks, when we consumed nutritious foods in an atmosphere of silent good cheer. Wunsiedel's factory was swarming with people who were obsessed with telling you the story of their lives, as indeed vigorous personalities are fond of doing. The story of their lives is more important to them than their lives, you have only to press a button, and immediately it is covered with spewed-out exploits.

Wunsiedel had a right-hand man called Broschek, who had in turn made a name for himself by supporting seven children and a paralyzed wife by working night-shifts in his student days, and successfully carrying on four business agencies, besides which he had passed two examinations with honors in two years. When asked by reporters: "When do you sleep, Mr. Broscheck?" he had replied: "It's a crime to sleep!"

Wunsiedel's secretary had supported a paralyzed husband and four children by knitting, at the same time graduating in psychology and German history as well as breeding shepherd dogs, and she had become famous as a night-club singer where she was known as *Vamp Number Seven.*

Wunsiedel himself was one of those people who every morning, as they open their eyes, make up their minds to act. "I must act," they think as they briskly tie their bathrobe belts around them. "I must act," they think as they shave, triumphantly watching their beard hairs being washed away with the lather: these hirsute vestiges are the first daily sacrifices to their driving energy. The more intimate functions also give these people a sense of satisfaction: water swishes, paper is used. Action has been taken. Bread gets eaten, eggs are decapitated.

With Wunsiedel, the most trivial activity looked like action: the way he put on his hat, the way—quivering with energy—he buttoned up his overcoat, the kiss he gave his wife, everything was action.

When he arrived at his office he greeted his secretary with a cry of "Let's have some action!" And in ringing tones she would call back: "Action will be taken!" Wunsiedel then went from department to department, calling out his cheerful: "Let's have some action!" Everyone would answer: "Action will be taken!" And I would call back to him too, with a radiant smile, when he looked into my office: "Action will be taken!"

Within a week I had increased the number of telephones on my desk to eleven, within two weeks to thirteen, and every morning on the streetcar I enjoyed thinking up new imperatives, or chasing the words *take action* through various tenses and modulations: for two whole days I kept saying the same sentence over and over again because I thought it sounded so marvelous: "Action ought to have been taken;" for another two days it was: "Such action ought not to have been taken."

So I was really beginning to feel I was working to capacity when there actually was some action. One Tuesday morning—I had hardly settled down at my desk— Wunsiedel rushed into my office crying his "Let's have some action!" But an inexplicable something in his face made me hesitate to reply, in a cheerful gay voice as the rules dictated: "Action will be taken!" I must have paused too long, for Wunsiedel, who seldom raised his voice, shouted at me: "Answer! Answer, you know the rules!" And I answered, under my breath, reluctantly, like a child who is forced to say: I am a naughty child. It was only by a great effort that I managed to bring out the sentence: "Action will be taken," and hardly had I uttered it when there really was some action: Wunsiedel dropped to the floor. As he fell he rolled over onto his side and lay right across the open doorway. I knew at once, and I confirmed it when I went slowly around my desk and approached the body on the floor: he was dead.

Shaking my head I stepped over Wunsiedel, walked slowly along the corridor to Broschek's office, and entered without knocking. Broschek was sitting at his desk, a telephone receiver in each hand, between his teeth a ballpoint pen with which he was making notes on a writing pad, while with his bare feet he was operating a knitting machine under the desk. In this way he helps to clothe his family. "We've had some action," I said in a low voice.

Broschek spat out the ballpoint pen, put down the two receivers, reluctantly detached his toes from the knitting machine.

"What action?" he asked.

"Wunsiedel is dead," I said.

"No," said Broschek.

"Yes," I said, "come and have a look!"

"No," said Broschek, "that's impossible," but he put on his slippers and followed me along the corridor.

"No," he said, when we stood beside Wunsiedel's corpse, "no, no!" I did not contradict him. I carefully turned Wunsiedel over onto his back, closed his eyes, and looked at him pensively.

I felt something like tenderness for him, and realized for the first time that I had never hated him. On his face was that expression which one sees on children who obstinately refuse to give up their faith in Santa Claus, even though the arguments of their playmates sound so convincing.

"No," said Broschek, "no."

"We must take action," I said quietly to Broschek.

"Yes," said Broschek, "we must take action."

Action was taken: Wunsiedel was buried, and I was delegated to carry a wreath of artificial roses behind his coffin, for I am equipped with not only a penchant for pensiveness and inactivity but also a face and figure that go extremely well with dark suits. Apparently as I walked along behind Wunsiedel's coffin carrying the wreath of artificial roses I looked superb. I received an offer from a fashionable firm of funeral directors to join their staff as a professional mourner. "You are a born mourner," said the manager, "your outfit would be provided by the firm. Your face—simply superb!"

I handed in my notice to Broschek, explaining that I had never really felt I was working to capacity there; that, in spite of the thirteen telephones, some of my talents were going to waste. As soon as my first professional appearance as a mourner was over I knew: This is where I belong, this is what I am cut out for.

Pensively I stand behind the coffin in the funeral chapel, holding a simple bouquet, while the organ plays Handel's *Largo*, a piece that does not receive nearly the respect it deserves. The cemetery café is my regular haunt; there I spend the intervals between my professional engagements, although sometimes I walk behind coffins which I have not been engaged to follow, I pay for flowers out of my own pocket and join the welfare worker who walks behind the coffin of some homeless person. From time to time I also visit Wunsiedel's grave, for after all I owe it to him that I discovered my true vocation, a vocation in which pensiveness is essential and inactivity my duty.

It was not till much later that I realized I had never bothered to find out what was being produced in Wunsiedel's factory. I expect it was soap.

THE LAUGHER

When someone asks me what business I am in, I am seized with embarrassment: I blush and stammer, I who am otherwise known as a man of poise. I envy people who can say: I am a bricklayer. I envy barbers, bookkeepers and writers the simplicity of their avowal, for all these professions speak for themselves and need no lengthy explanation, while I am constrained to reply to such questions: I am a laugher. An admission of this kind demands another, since I have to answer the second question: "Is that how you make your living?" truthfully with "Yes." I actually do make a living at my laughing, and a good one too, for my laughing is— commercially speaking—much in demand. I am a good laugher, experienced, no one else laughs as well as I do, no one else has such command of the fine points of my art. For a long time, in order to avoid tiresome explanations, I called myself an actor, but my talents in the field of mime and elocution are so meager that I felt this designation to be too far from the truth: I love the truth, and the truth is: I am a laugher. I am neither a clown nor a comedian. I do not make people gay, I portray gaiety: I laugh like a Roman emperor, or like a sensitive schoolboy, I am as much at home in the laughter of the seventeenth century as in that of the nineteenth, and when occasion demands I laugh my way through all the centuries, all classes of society, all categories of age: it is simply a skill which I have acquired, like the skill of being able to repair shoes. In my breast I harbor the laughter of America, the laughter of Africa, white, red, yellow laughter—and for the right fee I let it peal out in accordance with the director's requirements.

I have become indispensable; I laugh on records, I laugh on tape, and television directors treat me with respect. I laugh mournfully, moderately, hysterically; I laugh like a streetcar conductor or like a helper in the grocery business; laughter in the morning, laughter in the evening, nocturnal laughter and the laughter of twilight. In short: wherever and however laughter is required—I do it.

It need hardly be pointed out that a profession of this kind is tiring, especially as I have also—this is my specialty—mastered the art of infectious laughter; this has also made me indispensable to third- and fourth-rate comedians, who are scared—and with good reason— that their audiences will miss their punch lines, so I spend most evenings in night clubs as a kind of discreet claque, my job being to laugh infectiously during the weaker parts of the program. It has to be carefully timed: my hearty, boisterous laughter must not come too soon, but neither must it come too late, it must come just at the right spot: at the pre-arranged moment I burst out laughing, the whole audience roars with me, and the joke is saved.

But as for me, I drag myself exhausted to the checkroom, put on my overcoat, happy that I can go off duty at last. At home I usually find telegrams waiting for me: "Urgently require your laughter. Recording Tuesday," and a few hours later I am sitting in an overheated express train bemoaning my fate.

I need scarcely say that when I am off duty or on vacation I have little inclination to laugh: the cowhand is glad when he can forget the cow, the bricklayer when he can forget the mortar, and carpenters usually have doors at home which don't work or drawers which are hard to open. Confectioners like sour pickles, butchers like marzipan, and the baker prefers sausage to bread; bullfighters raise pigeons for a hobby, boxers turn pale when their children have nose-bleeds: I find all this quite natural, for I never laugh off duty. I am a very solemn person, and people consider me—perhaps rightly so—a pessimist.

During the first years of our married life, my wife would often say to me: "Do laugh!" but since then she has come to realize that I cannot grant her this wish. I am happy when I am free to relax my tense face muscles, my frayed spirit, in profound solemnity. Indeed, even other people's laughter gets on my nerves, since it reminds me too much of my profession. So our marriage is a quiet, peaceful one, because my wife has also forgotten how to laugh: now and again I catch her smiling, and I smile too. We converse in low tones, for I detest the noise of the night clubs, the noise that sometimes fills the recording studios. People who do not know me think I am taciturn. Perhaps I am, because I have to open my mouth so often to laugh.

I go through life with an impassive expression, from time to time permitting myself a gentle smile, and I often wonder whether I have ever laughed. I think not. My brothers and sisters have always known me for a serious boy.

So I laugh in many different ways, but my own laughter I have never heard.

IN THE VALLEY OF THE
THUNDERING HOOFS

I

The boy had not noticed that it was his turn. He was staring at the tiles on the floor dividing the side nave from the center nave: they were red and white, shaped like honeycomb cells, the red ones were speckled with white, the white with red; he could no longer distinguish the white from the red, the tiles ran together, and the dark lines of the cement joins became blurred, the floor swam before his eyes like a gravel path of red and white chips; the red dazzled, the white dazzled, the joins lay indistinctly over them like a soiled net.

"It's your turn," whispered a young woman next to him; he shook his head, made a vague gesture with his thumb toward the confessional, and the woman went ahead of him; for a moment the smell of lavender became stronger; then he heard murmuring, the scuffing sound of her shoes on the wooden step as she knelt down.

Sins, he thought, death, sins; and the intensity with which he suddenly desired the woman was torture. He had not even seen her face; a faint smell of lavender, a young voice, the sound of her high heels, light yet crisp, as she walked the four steps to the confessional; this rhythm of the heels, crisp yet light, was but a fragment of the eternal refrain that seethed in his ears for days and nights on end. In the evening he would lie awake, beside the open window, and hear them walking along outside on the cobblestones, on the asphalt sidewalk: shoes, heels, crisp, light, unsuspecting; he could hear voices, whispering, laughter under the chestnut trees. There were too many of them, and they were too beautiful. Some of them opened their handbags; in the streetcar, at the movie box office, on the store counter, they would leave their handbags lying open in cars, and he could see inside: lipsticks, handkerchiefs, loose change, crumpled bus tickets, packs of cigarettes, compacts. His eyes were still moving in torment back and forth over the tiles: this was a thorny path, and never-ending.

"It's your turn, you know," said a voice beside him, and he looked up. A little girl, red-cheeked and with black hair. He smiled at the child and waved her on too with his thumb. Her flat child's shoes had no rhythm. Whispering over there to the right. What had he confessed, when he was her age? I stole some cookies. I told lies. Disobedient. Didn't do my homework. I stole from the sugar jar, cake crumbs, wineglasses with the dregs from grown-ups' parties. Cigarette butts. I stole some cookies.

"It's your turn." This time he waved mechanically. Men's shoes. Whispering and the obtrusiveness of that faint no-smell smell.

Once again his glance fell on the red and white chips of the aisle. His naked eyes hurt as acutely as his naked feet would have hurt on a rough gravel path. The feet of my eyes, he thought, wander round their mouths as if round red lakes. The hands of my eyes wander over their skin.

Sins, death, and the insolent unobtrusiveness of that no-smell smell. If only there were someone who smelled of onions, of stew, laundry soap, or engines, of pipe tobacco, lime blossom, or road dust, of the fierce sweat of summer toil, but they all smelled unobtrusive; they smelled of nothing.

He raised his eyes and looked across the aisle, letting his glance rest where those who had received absolution were kneeling and saying their prayers of penance. Over there it smelled of Saturday, of peace, bathwater, poppyseed rolls, of new tennis balls, like the ones his sisters bought on Saturdays with their pocket money; it smelled of the clear, pure oil Father cleaned his pistol with on Saturdays. It was black, his pistol, shining, unused for ten years, an immaculate souvenir of the war, discreet, useless; it merely served Father's memory, summoned a glow to his face when he took it apart and cleaned it; the glow of an erstwhile mastery over death, which a light touch on a spring could move out of the pale, gleaming magazine into the barrel. Once a week on Saturday, before he went to the club, this ritual of taking apart, caressing, oiling the black sections, which lay spread out on the blue cloth like those of a dissected animal: the rump, the great metal tongue of the trigger, the smaller innards, joints, and screws. He was permitted to look on, he would stand there spellbound, speechless before his father's enraptured face; he was witnessing the celebration of the cult of an instrument that so frankly and terrifyingly resembled his sex; the seed of death was thrust out of the magazine. Father checked that too, to see whether the magazine springs were still working. They were still working, and the safety catch held back the seed of death in the barrel; with the thumb, with a tiny delicate movement, it could be released, but Father never released it; delicately his fingers fitted the separate parts together again before hiding the pistol under some old checkbooks and ledger sheets.

"It's your turn." He gestured again. Whispers. Whispered replies. The obtrusive smell of nothing.

Here on this side of the aisle it smelled of damnation, sins, the sticky banality of the other days of the week, the worst of which was Sunday: boredom, while the coffee percolator hummed on the terrace. Boredom in church, in the outdoor restaurant, in the boathouse, movie, or café, boredom up at the vineyards where the progress of the Zischbrunner Mönchsgarten vines was inspected, slender fingers smoothly and expertly feeling the grapes; boredom which seemed to offer no escape except sin. It was visible everywhere: green, red, brown leather of handbags. Over there in the center nave he saw the rust-colored coat of the woman he had allowed to go ahead of him. He saw her profile, the delicate nose, the light-brown skin, the dark mouth, saw her wedding ring, the high heels, those fragile instruments which harbored the deadly refrain; he listened to them going away, a long, long walk on hard asphalt, then on rough cobblestones, the crisp yet firm staccato of sin. Death, he thought, mortal sin.

Now she was actually leaving: she snapped her handbag shut, stood up, genuflected, crossed herself, and her legs passed on the rhythm to her shoes, her shoes to her heels, her heels to the tiles.

The aisle seemed to him like a river which he would never cross: he would stand forever on the banks of sin. Only four steps separated him from the voice which could release and bind, only six to the center nave, where Saturday reigned, peace, absolution—but he took only two steps as far as the aisle, slowly at first, then he ran as if fleeing from a burning house.

As he pushed open the padded door, light and heat hit him too suddenly; for a few seconds he was dazzled, his left hand struck the doorpost, the prayer book fell to the floor, he felt a jab of pain on the back of his hand, bent down, picked up the book, let the door swing back, and stopped for a moment in the porch to smooth out the crumpled page of the prayer book. "Utter repentance," he read, before shutting the book; he put it into his trouser pocket, rubbed his smarting left hand with his right, and cautiously opened the door by pushing against it with his knee. The woman was no longer in sight, the forecourt was empty, dust lay on the dark-green leaves of the chestnuts; near the lamppost stood a white ice-cream cart, from the lamppost hook hung a gray sack containing evening papers. The ice-cream man was sitting on the curb reading the evening paper, the newspaper vendor was perched on one of the shafts of the ice-cream cart licking an ice-cream cone. A passing streetcar was almost empty: there was only a boy standing on the back platform, letting his green swimming trunks flap in the air.

Slowly Paul pushed open the door, went down the steps; within a few seconds he was sweating, it was too hot and too dazzling, and he longed for darkness.

There were some days when he hated everything except himself, but today was like most days, when he hated only himself and loved everything: the open windows in the houses around the square; white curtains, the clink of coffee cups, men's laughter, blue cigar smoke puffed out by someone he could not see; thick blue clouds came out of the window over the savings bank; whiter than fresh snow was the cream on a piece of cake which a girl standing at the window next door to the pharmacy was holding; white, too, was the ring of cream around her mouth.

The clock over the savings bank showed half past five.

Paul hesitated a moment when he reached the ice-cream cart, a moment too long, so that the ice-cream man got up from the curb, folded the evening paper, and Paul could read the first line on the front page: "Khrushchev," and in the second line, "open grave"; as he walked on, the man unfolded the paper and with a shake of his head sat down again on the curb.

When Paul had passed the corner by the savings bank and turned the next corner, he could hear a voice down on the riverbank announcing the next regatta race: men's four—Ubia, Rhenus, Zischbrunn 67. It seemed to Paul that he could smell and hear the river, which was a quarter of a mile away: oil and algae, the bitter smoke of the tugs, the slapping of the waves as the paddle steamers moved downstream, the hooting of long-drawn-out sirens in the evening; lanterns in outdoor cafés, chairs so red they seemed to burn like flames in the shrubberies.

He heard the starting gun, shouts, voices chanting, at first clearly in time with the beat of the oars: "Zischbrunn, Rhe-nuss, U-bja," and then all mixed up: "Rhebrunn, Zisch-nuss, Bja-Zisch-U-nuss."

Quarter past seven, thought Paul, till quarter past seven the town will stay as deserted as it is now. There were parked cars all the way to here, empty, hot, smelling of oil and sun, parked under trees, on both sides of the street, in driveways. As he turned the next corner and had a view of the river and the hills, he saw the parked cars up on the slopes, in the schoolyard, they were even parked in the entrances to the vineyards. In the silent streets through which he was walking they were parked on both sides, they heightened the impression of loneliness. He felt a pang at the glittering beauty of the cars, shining elegance from which the owners seemed to protect themselves with hideous mascots: grotesque monkey faces, grinning hedgehogs, distorted zebras with bared teeth, dwarfs leering malevolently above tawny beards.

The chanting became clearer, the shouts louder, then the announcer's voice proclaimed the victory of the Zischbrunn four. Applause, fanfare, then the song: "Zischbrunn, high on the slopes, caressed by the river, nourished by wine, pampered by lovely women..." Trumpets puffed out the tedious tune like soap bubbles into the air.

As he passed through a gateway it was suddenly quiet. In this courtyard behind the Griffduhnes' house the sounds from the river were muted: filtered through the trees, caught by old sheds, swallowed up by walls, the announcer's voice was subdued: "Ladies' pairs." The starting gun sounded like the pop from a toy pistol, the chanting like school choir practice behind walls.

Now his sisters were thrusting their oars into the water, their broad faces serious, beads of sweat forming on their upper lips, their yellow headbands turning dark; now their mother was adjusting the binoculars, elbowing away Father's hands, which were trying to snatch the binoculars. "Zisch-Zisch-Brunn-Brunn" roared one chorus that drowned out the others, now and again a feeble syllable: "U-nuss, Rhe-bja," then a roaring that here in the courtyard sounded as if it came from a muffled radio. The Zischbrunn pair had won: now the sisters' faces relaxed, they tore off the sweat-darkened headbands, paddled calmly toward the judges' boat, waved to their parents. "Zisch-Zisch," shouted their friends. "Hurrah for Zisch!"

Over their tennis balls, thought Paul, red blood over the white fleecy balls.

"Griff," he called softly, "are you up there?"

"Yes," replied a languid voice, "come on up!"

The wooden staircase was saturated with summer heat; it smelled of tar, of ropes that had not been sold for the past twenty years. Griff's grandfather had owned all these sheds, buildings, and walls. Griff's father owned scarcely a tenth of them, and "As for me," Griff always said, "all I'll ever own will be the pigeon loft where Dad used to keep pigeons. You can stretch out comfortably in it, and I shall stay up there and contemplate my big right toe—but even the pigeon loft will only be mine because nobody wants it anymore."

The walls upstairs were covered with old photographs. They were dark red, mahogany almost, the white had gone cloudy and yellow: picnics of the nineties, regattas of the twenties, lieutenants of the forties; young girls who had died thirty years ago as grandmothers looked soulfully across the passage at their life partners: wine merchants, rope chandlers, shipyard owners, whose Victorian melancholy had been captured and preserved by Daguerre's early disciples; a student of the year 1910 solemnly contemplated his son, an ensign who had frozen to death near Lake Peipus in Russia. Old furniture cluttered up the passage, and there was a stylish bookcase containing fruit jars, empty ones with limp red rubber rings rolled up on the bottom, full ones whose contents were only visible here and there through the dust; dark plum jam, or cherries of anemic red, pallid as the lips of sickly young girls.

Griffduhne was lying on the bed, naked from the waist up. His white, narrow chest contrasted alarmingly with his red cheeks: he looked like a poppy whose stalk has already withered. An unbleached linen sheet hung in front of the window, there were spots on it as if it were being X-rayed by the sun; the sunlight, filtered down to a yellow dusk, penetrated the room. Schoolbooks lay on the floor, a pair of slacks hung over the bedside table, Griff's shirt over the wash basin; a green corduroy jacket hung on a nail on the wall between the crucifix and photos of Italy: donkeys, steep cliffs, cardinals. An open jar of plum jam with a kitchen spoon sticking in it stood on the floor beside the bed.

"So they're rowing again; rowing, paddling, water sports—those are their problems. Dancing, tennis, wine harvest festivals, graduation parties. Songs. Is the town hall going to have gold, silver, or copper columns? Don't tell me, Paul," he said, lowering his voice, "that you were actually down there?"

"I was."

"Well?"

"Nothing. I left again. I couldn't stand it. It's so pointless. How about you?"

"I haven't been for ages. What's the use? I've been thinking about what's the right height for our age: I'm too tall for fourteen, so they say, you're too short for fourteen. D'you know anyone who is just the right height?"

"Plokamm is the right height."

"Huh—d'you want to be like him?"

"No."

"You see," said Griff, "there are..." He hesitated, broke off, as he watched Paul's eyes looking intently and uneasily around the room. "What's up? Are you looking for something?"

"Yes," said Paul, "where have you put it?"

"The pistol?"

"Yes, let me have it." Over the box with the new tennis balls is where I'll do it, he thought. "Come on," he said loudly, "hand it over."

"Wait," said Griff, shaking his head. Embarrassed, he took the spoon out of the plum jam, then stuck it back in the jar, folded his hands. "No, let's smoke instead. There's lots of time before quarter past seven. Rowing, paddling, maybe it'll be even later. Outdoor reception. Lanterns. Prize-giving ceremony. Your sisters won the pairs. Zisch, zisch zisch..." he went under his breath.

"Show me the pistol."

"Hell, why should I?" Griff sat up, seized the jar, and threw it against the wall: broken glass flew, the spoon struck the edge of the bookshelf, from there it did a somersault in front of the bed. The jam splashed onto a book that said *Algebra I*, some of it ran in a viscous blue across the yellow of the wall, dying it a kind of green. Without moving, without saying a word, the boys looked at the wall. When the noise of the crash had died away, and the last of the pulp had trickled down, they looked at each other in amazement: the shattering of the glass had left them unmoved.

"No," said Paul, "that's no good. The pistol's better, or maybe fire, a blaze or water—the pistol's best. Kill."

"But who?" asked the boy on the bed; he leaned over, picked up the spoon, licked it, and placed it tenderly on the bedside table.

"But who?"

"Me," said Paul hoarsely, "tennis balls."

"Tennis balls?"

"Oh, nothing. Give it to me. Now."

"Right," said Griff. He stripped off the sheet, jumped out of bed, kicked the broken glass aside, and took a narrow brown cardboard box from the bookshelf. The box was not much bigger than a pack of cigarettes.

"What?" said Paul. "Is that it? In there?"

"Yes," said Griff, "that's it."

"And that's what you fired eight shots at a tin can with, at a distance of thirty yards, and got seven hits?"

"That's right, seven," said Griff uncertainly. "Don't you want to look at it even?"

"No, I don't," said Paul; he looked angrily at the box, which smelled of sawdust, of the stuff blanks were packed in. "No, I don't, I don't want to look at it. Show me the ammunition."

Griff bent down. From his long, pale back the vertebrae stood out, disappeared again, and this time he quickly opened the box, which was as big as a matchbox. Paul took one of the copper cartridges, held it between two fingertips, as if to see how long it was, turned it this way and that, shook his head as he contemplated the round, blue head of the bullet. "No," he said, "that's no good. My dad has one—I'll get my dad's."

"But it's locked up," said Griff.

"I'll get hold of it. As long as I do it before half past seven. He always cleans it then, before he goes to the club. He takes it apart: it's a big one, black and smooth, heavy, and the bullets are big like this"—he showed how big with his fingers—"and..." He was silent, and sighed: over the tennis balls, he was thinking.

"Do you really want to shoot yourself, properly?"

"Maybe," said Paul. The feet of my eyes are sore, the hands of my eyes are sick, he thought. "Hell, you know how it is."

Griff's face suddenly turned dark and stiff; he swallowed, went to the door, only a few steps away; there he stopped.

"You're my friend," he said, "or aren't you?"

"Sure."

"Then go and get a jar too and throw it against the wall. Will you?"

"Why?"

"My mother," said Griff, "my mother told me she wants to have a look at my room when she gets back from the regatta, she wants to see whether I've improved. Tidied up and all that. She got mad at my report. Let her look at my room, then—are you going to get the jar now?"

Paul nodded, went out into the passage, and heard Griff call out, "Take the golden plum jam, if there's any left. Something yellow would look good, better than this purplish mess." Paul wiped off some of the jars outside in the semidarkness till he found a yellow one. They won't understand, he thought, nobody will understand, but I have to do it. He went back to the room, raised his right hand, and threw the jar against the wall.

"It's no good," he said quietly, while they both regarded the effect of the throw, "it's not what I want."

"What is it you want?"

"I want to destroy something," said Paul, "but not jars, or trees, or houses—and I don't want your mother to get mad, or mine; I love my mother, yours too—there's no sense to it."

Griff fell back onto the bed, covered his face with his hands, and murmured, "Kuffang has gone to that girl."

"The Prohlig girl?"

"Yes."

"I've been with her too."

"You have?"

"Yes. She's not serious. Giggles around there in the passage—stupid, she's stupid. She doesn't know it's a sin."

"Kuffang says it's great."

"No, I tell you, it's not great. Kuffang's stupid too, you know he's stupid."

"I know he is, but what are you going to do?"

"Nothing with girls—they giggle. I've tried it. They're not serious—they just giggle." He went across to the wall and smeared his forefinger through the big splash of golden plum jam.

"No," he said without turning round, "I'm going to get my dad's pistol."

Over the tennis balls, he thought. They're as white as washed lambs. The blood over the lambs.

"Women," he whispered, "not girls."

The filtered noise of the regatta came faintly into the room. Men's eights. Zischbrunn. This time Rhenus won. The jam dried slowly on the wooden wall, became as hard as cow dung, flies buzzed around the room, there was a sweetish smell, flies crawled over the schoolbooks, the clothes, flew greedily from one spot, from one pool, to another, too greedy to stay long on one pool. The two boys did not move. Griff lay on the bed, staring at the ceiling and smoking. Paul perched on the edge of the bed, bent forward like an old man; deep within him, over him, on him, lay a burden to which he couldn't put a name, a dark, heavy burden. Suddenly he stood up, ran out into the passage, snatched up one of the fruit jars, came back into the room, raised the jar—but he did not throw it; he stood there with the jar in his raised hand. Slowly his arm dropped, the boy put down the jar, on a paper bag which was lying neatly folded on the bookshelf. "Fürst Slacks," it said on the paper bag, "Fürst Slacks Are the Only Slacks."

"No," he said, "I'll go and get it."

Griff puffed his cigarette smoke at the flies, then aimed the butt at one of the pools. Flies flew up, settled hesitantly around the smoking butt, which sank slowly into the jam and fizzled out.

"Tomorrow evening," he said, "I'll be in Lübeck, at my uncle's; we'll go fishing, we'll sail and swim in the Baltic; and you, tomorrow you'll be in the Valley of the Thundering Hoofs." Tomorrow, thought Paul, who did not move, tomorrow I shall be dead. Blood over the tennis balls, dark red like in the fleece of the lamb; the Lamb will drink my blood. O Lamb. I shall never see my sisters' little laurel wreath, "Winners of the Ladies' Pairs," black on gold; they'll hang it up there between the photos of holidays in Zalligkofen, between withered bunches of flowers and pictures of cats; next to the framed graduation diploma hanging over Rosa's bed, next to the certificate for long-distance swimming hanging over Franziska's bed; between the colored prints of their patron saints, Rosa of Lima, Franziska Romana; next to the other laurel wreath, "Winners of the Ladies' Doubles"; under the crucifix. The dark-red blood will cling stiffly to the fuzz of the tennis balls, the blood of their brother, who preferred death to sin.

"I must see it one day, the Valley of the Thundering Hoofs," Griff was saying, "I must sit up there where you always sit, I must hear them, the horses charging up to the pass, galloping down to the lake, I must hear their hoofs thundering in the narrow gorge—their whinnying cries streaming out over the mountaintops—like—like a thin fluid."

Paul looked disdainfully at Griff, who had sat up and was excitedly describing something he had never seen: horses, many horses, charging up over the pass, galloping with thundering hoofs down into the valley. But there had only been *one* horse there, and only *once*: a colt, which had raced out of the paddock and cantered down to the lake, and the sound of its hoofs had not been like thunder, just a clatter, and it was such a long time ago, three years, maybe four.

"So you," he said quietly, "are going fishing; you'll go sailing and swimming, and stroll up the little streams, in wading boots, and catch fish with your hands."

"That's right," said Griff sleepily, "my uncle catches fish with his hands, even salmon, yes…" He sank back onto the bed with a sigh. His uncle in Lübeck had never caught a fish, not even with a rod or a net, and he, Griff, doubted whether there were any salmon at all up there on the Baltic and in the little streams. Uncle was just the owner of a small cannery; in old sheds in the backyard the fish were slit open, cleaned, salted or pickled; preserved in oil or tomato sauce; they were pressed into cans by an ancient machine which threw itself with a grunt like a tired anvil onto the tiny cans and shut the fish up in tinplate. Lumps of damp salt lay around in the yard, fish bones and skin, scales and entrails; seagulls screamed, and light-red blood splashed onto the white arms of the women workers and ran down their arms in watery trickles.

"Salmon," said Griff, "are smooth, silvery and pink, they're strong, much too beautiful to eat; when you hold them in your hand, you can feel their strong muscles."

Paul shuddered: they had once had some canned salmon for Christmas, a putty-colored mass swimming in pink fluid, full of bits of fish bone.

"And you can catch them in the air when they jump," said Griff; he sat up, knelt on the bed, threw up his hands, fingers spread wide, brought them together till they looked as if they were about to strangle something; the rigid hands, the motionless face of the boy, it all seemed to belong to someone who worshiped a stern god. The soft yellow light bathed the rigid boyish hands, lent the flushed face a dark, brownish tinge—"Like that," Griff whispered, snatched with his hands at the fish that wasn't there, and suddenly dropped his hands, letting them hang limp, inert, by his sides. "Come on," he said, jumped off the bed, picked up the box with the pistol from the bookshelf, opened it before Paul could turn away, and held out the open bottom half of the box containing the pistol. "Look at it now," he said, "just have a look at it." The pistol looked rather pathetic: only the firmness of the material distinguished it from a toy pistol; it was even flatter, but the solidity of the nickel gave it some glamour and a degree of seriousness. Griffduhne threw the open box containing the pistol into Paul's lap, took the closed glass jar from the bookshelf, unscrewed the lid, separated the perished rubber ring from the edge, lifted the pistol out of the box, dropped it slowly into the jam; the boys watched while the level of the jam rose slightly, scarcely beyond the narrowing of the neck. Griff put the rubber ring back around the edge, screwed on the lid, and replaced the jar on the bookshelf.

"Come on," he said, and his face was stern and dark again. "Come on, we'll go and get your dad's pistol."

"You can't come with me," said Paul. "I have to climb in through a window because they didn't give me a key—I have to get in at the back. They would notice; they didn't give me a key because they thought I was going to the regatta."

"Rowing," said Griff, "water sports, that's all they ever think about." He was silent, and they both listened for sounds from the river: they could hear the cries of the ice-cream vendors, music, fanfares, a steamer hooting.

"Intermission," said Griff. "Plenty of time still. All right, go by yourself, but promise me you'll come back with the pistol. Will you promise?"

"I promise."

"Shake."

They shook hands: they were warm and dry, and each wished the other's hand had been firmer.

"How long will you be?"

"Twenty minutes," said Paul. "I've thought it out so many times but never done it—with the screwdriver. It'll take me twenty minutes."

"Right," said Griff; he reached across the bed and took his watch from the bedside table drawer. "It's ten to six; you'll be back at quarter past."

"Quarter past," said Paul. He paused in the doorway, looked at the great splashes on the wall: yellow and purplish. Swarms of flies were sticking to the splashes, but neither of the boys moved a finger to drive them away. Laughter drifted up from the riverbank: the water clowns had begun to add zest to the intermission. An "Ah" rose up like a great soft sigh; the boys looked up at the sheet over the window as if they expected it to billow out, but it hung limp, yellowish, the dirt spots were darker now, the sun had moved farther westward.

"Water skiing," said Griff, "the women from the face-cream factory." An "Oh" came up from the river, a sigh, and again the sheet did not billow out.

"The only one," said Griff quietly, "the only one who looks like a woman is the Mirzov girl." Paul did not move. "My mother," Griff said, "found the piece of paper with those things about the Mirzov girl on it—and her picture."

"Good God," said Paul, "d'you mean to say you had one too?"

"Yes," said Griff, "I spent all my pocket money on it—I—I don't know why I did it. I didn't even read what was on the paper, I stuck it in my report envelope, and my mother found it. D'you know what was on it?"

"No," said Paul, "I don't, I bet it's all lies, and I don't want to know about it. Everything Kuffang does is a lie. I'm off now—"

"Right," said Griff firmly, "hurry up and get the pistol, and come back. You promised. Go on, go."

"Okay," said Paul, "I'm going." He waited a moment, listening to the sounds from the river: he could hear laughter, fanfare. "Funny I never thought of the Mirzov girl..." And he said again, "Okay," and went.

II

Cutouts might be like that, she thought, miniatures or colored medallions: the images were sharply punched, round and clear, a whole series of them. She was looking at it from a distance of twelve hundred yards, magnified twelve times through binoculars. The church with the savings bank and pharmacy, in the center of the gray square an ice-cream cart: the first picture, detached and unreal. A section of the riverbank, above it, in a semicircle of horizon, green water with boats on it, colored pennants: the second picture, the second miniature. The series could be added to at will: hills with woods and a monument; over there—what were their names?—Rhenania and Germania, torch-bearing, stalwart female figures with stern faces, on bronze pedestals, facing each other; vineyards, with green vines—hatred welled up in her, salty, bitter and satisfying. She hated wine; they were always talking about wine, and everything they did, sang, or believed was associated ritually with wine: puffy faces, mouths emitting sour breath, hoarse gaiety, belching, shrill women, the bloated stupidity of the men who thought they resembled this—what was he called?—Bacchus. She hung on to this picture for a long time: I'll certainly stick this little picture in my album of memories, a round picture of a green vineyard with vines. Perhaps, she thought, I might be able to believe in You, their God, if it were not wine which turns into Your blood for them, is wasted for them, poured out for those useless idiots. My memory will be a clear one, as acid as the grapes taste at this time of year when you pick one the size of a pea. All the pictures were small, distinct, and ready to be stuck in; vignettes of sky blue, grass green, river green, banner red, blending with the sounds which formed the background to the pictures, as in a movie, spoken words, dubbed-in music: chanting, hurrahs, shouts of victory, fanfare, laughter, and the little white boats, as tiny as the feathers of young birds, as light too, and as quickly blown away, the white feathers scudding airily across the green water. When they reached the rim of the binoculars the noise swelled slightly. That's how I shall remember it all: just a little album of miniatures. A tiny twist of the binoculars, and already everything was blurred, red with green, blue with gray; another twist of the screw, and all that was left was a round patch of mist in which noise sounded like

cries for help from a group of lost mountain climbers, like the shouts
of the search party.

She swung the binoculars up and down, trailed them slowly across
the sky, punching out circles of blue; just as her mother did when she
was baking, punching the uniform yellow dough with the cookie cutters, that was how she punched out the uniform blue sky: round sky-
cookies, blue, a great quantity of them. But where I am going there
will be blue sky too, so why stick these miniatures into the album?
That'll do. Slowly she let the binoculars sweep downward. Careful, she
thought, I'm falling, and she felt slightly giddy as she flew from the blue
of the sky onto the trees in the avenue, covering more than a mile in
less than a second; past the trees, over the gray tiles of the next house.
She looked into a room: a powder compact, a Madonna, a mirror, a
single black shoe, a man's, on the polished floor; she flew on to the living room: a samovar, a Madonna, a large family photo, the brass strip
along the carpet and the russet, warm gleam of mahogany. She stopped,
but her giddiness persisted in subsiding waves. Then she saw the open
box with the snow-white tennis balls in the hall—how ugly those balls
are, she thought, the way women's breasts sometimes look on statues I
don't like; the terrace: a garden umbrella, a table with a cloth and dirty
cups and saucers, an empty wine bottle still with its white foil cap. Oh,
Father, she thought, how wonderful to be going to you, and how wonderful that you don't drink wine, only schnapps.

Melting tar was dripping from the garage roof in a few places.
Then she jumped as Paul's face—eighty feet away, such a long way off,
but in the binoculars only six feet—came directly toward her. His pale
face looked as if he were on the verge of doing something desperate: he
was blinking into the sun, his arms, fists clenched, were hanging down
limply as if he were holding something, but he wasn't holding anything;
his fists were empty, squeezed tight. He turned the corner of the garage,
sweating, his breath labored, jumped up onto the terrace. The cups and
saucers clinked on the table; he rattled at the door, took two steps to the
left, swung himself up onto the window sill, and jumped into the room.
The samovar gave off a silvery chime as Paul bumped into the buffet:
inside, the rims of the glasses passed on the vibration to each other; they
were still faintly twittering as the boy ran on, across the brass strip in
the doorway. When he came to the tennis balls, he paused, bent down,

but did not touch them; he stood there for a long time, stretched out his hands again, almost as if in benediction or tenderness, suddenly pulled a little book out of his pocket, threw it on the floor, picked it up, kissed it, and placed it on the shelf under the hall mirror. Then all she could see was his legs as he ran upstairs, and in the center of this miniature was the carton with the tennis balls.

She sighed, lowered the binoculars, letting her eyes linger on the pattern of the carpet; it was rust red, with a black pattern of innumerable squares all joined together in labyrinths; toward the middle of each labyrinth the red got thinner and thinner, the black wider and wider, almost dazzling in its purity.

His bedroom was in the front of the house, facing the street. She remembered it from the days when he had still been allowed to play with her—it must be a year or two ago now; she had been allowed to play with him till he had begun to stare at her breasts with such a strange persistence that it interfered with their game, and she had asked: What are you looking at, do you want to see it? And he had nodded as if in a dream; she had undone her blouse, and she did not realize it was wrong till it was already too late. She saw it was wrong, not from his eyes but from the eyes of his mother, who had been in the room all the time, who came over now and screamed, while the darkness in her eyes turned to stone. That scream, that's also something I have to preserve on one of the phonograph records of my memory; that's what the screams must have sounded like at the witch burnings the man used to describe, the one who came to have discussions with Mother; he looked like a monk who no longer believes in God. And her mother looked like a nun who no longer believed in her God: home again in this place called Zischbrunn, after years of bitter disillusionment, salty error, preserved in the faith she had had and lost in something called Communism, floating in the brine of the memory of the man who was called Mirzov, drank schnapps, and had never possessed the faith which she had lost; her mother's words were as salty as her heart.

Scream across the carpet pattern, broken game on the floor: models of houses his father had been the sales agent for twenty years ago, little houses such as had not been built for twenty years; old pneumatic mail tubes from the bank, samples of rope which the other boy—that's right, Griff was his name—had contributed; corks of various sizes, various shapes; Griff had not been there that afternoon. All broken by that scream, which was to hang over her in future like a curse: she was the girl who had done what one must never do.

As she sighed, her glance lingered on the rust-red carpet, watching the sparkling threshold for his brown shoes to reappear.

Languidly she swung the binoculars back to the table: under the garden umbrella on the terrace, a basket of fruit, dark brown wicker-work full of orange peel, the wine bottle with the label "Zischbrun-ner Mönchsgarten"; one still life after another, with an undercurrent of noise from the regatta; dirty plates with remains of ice cream; the folded evening paper on which she could make out the second word in the headline, "Khrushchev," and in the second line, "open grave"; some cigarettes with brown filter tips, others white, stubbed out in the ashtray, a brochure from a refrigerator firm—but they had had one for ages!—a box of matches; russet mahogany, like fire in old paintings; the samovar gleaming on the buffet, silver and bright, unused for years, shining like some strange trophy. Teawagon with salt cellar and mus-tard pot, the big family photograph: the children sitting at table with their parents at a restaurant out in the country, in the background the pond with swans, then the waitress bringing the tray with two mugs of beer and three bottles of lemonade; in the foreground, the family seated at the table: on the right, in profile, their father, holding a fork level with his chest, a piece of meat skewered on it, noodles festooned round the meat; on the left their mother, a crumpled serviette in her left hand, a spoon in her right; in the middle the children, their heads below the edge of the waitress's tray: ice-cream dishes reached to their chins, patches of light, filtered through the leaves, lay on their cheeks; in the middle, framed by the curly heads of his sisters, the one who had stood for such a long time by the tennis balls and had then run upstairs: his brown shoes had still not returned across the brass strip.

The tennis balls again, on their right the clothes closet, straw hats, an umbrella, a linen bag with the handle of a shoebrush sticking out of it; in the mirror the large picture that hung in the hall on the left, of a woman picking grapes, with eyes like grapes, a mouth like a grape.

Tired of looking, she put down the binoculars. Her eyes plunged across the lost distance, smarted; she closed them. Red and black circles danced behind her closed lids, she opened them again, was startled to see Paul coming through the door. He was carrying something which sparkled in the sun, and this time he did not pause when he came to the tennis balls. Now that she saw his face without the binoculars—detached from her collection of miniatures—now she was certain he was going to do something desperate. Once more the samovar chimed, once more the glasses inside the buffet passed along the vibration, twittering like women exchanging secrets; Paul knelt down on the carpet in the corner by the window. All she could see of him was his right elbow, moving back and forth like a piston, regularly disappearing in a forward drilling movement—she ransacked her memory for a clue as to where she had seen this movement, she imitated the drilling pumping movement and then she knew: he was holding a screwdriver. The red-and-yellow-checked shirt came, went, was still—Paul jerked back a little; she saw his profile, raised the binoculars to her eyes, was startled at the sudden nearness, and looked into the open drawer. It contained bundles of blue checkbooks, neatly tied with white string, and some ledger sheets, bound through the holes with blue string. Paul hastily stacked up the bundles beside him on the carpet, clutched something to his chest, something wrapped in a blue cloth, put it down on the floor, replaced the checkbooks and ledger sheets in the drawer, and again all she could see, while the bundle in the blue cloth lay beside him, was the pumping, drilling movement of his elbow.

She cried out when he unwrapped the cloth: black, smooth, glistening with oil, the pistol lay in the hand that was much too small for it. It was as if the girl had shot her cry through the binoculars at him; he turned, she lowered the binoculars, screwed up her smarting eyes, and called out, "Paul! Paul!"

He held the pistol close to his chest as he climbed slowly out of the window onto the terrace.

"Paul," she called, "come over here, through the garden."

He put the pistol in his pocket, shaded his eyes with his hand, walked slowly down the steps, across the lawn, scuffed across the gravel by the fountain, dropped his hand when he suddenly found himself in the shadow of the summerhouse.

"Oh," he said, "it's you."

"Didn't you recognize my voice?"

"No—what d'you want?"

"I'm going away," she said.

"I'm going away too," he said. "So what? Everyone's going away, almost. I'm leaving tomorrow for Zalligkofen."

"No," she said, "I'm leaving for good, I'm going to my father's in Vienna..." and she thought: Vienna, that has something to do with wine too, in songs anyway.

"Vienna," he said, "down there ... and you're staying there?"

"Yes."

The look in his eyes, raised almost vertically to her, motionless, trancelike, frightened her: I am not your Jerusalem, she thought, no, I'm not, and yet your eyes have the look the eyes of pilgrims must have when they see the towers of their Holy City.

"I—" she said softly. "I saw everything."

He smiled. "Come on down," he said, "come on."

"I can't," she said, "my mother's locked me in. I'm not allowed out till the train leaves, but..." She suddenly stopped, her breathing was labored, shallow, excitement was choking her, and she said what she had not meant to say, "But why don't you come up here?"

I am not your Jerusalem, she thought. No, no. He did not lower his eyes as he asked, "How can I get up there?"

"If you climb up onto the roof of the summerhouse, I'll give you a hand and help you up onto the veranda."

"I—there's someone waiting for me." But he was already testing the trellis to see if it would hold; it had been recently nailed and painted, dense dark vine leaves were growing up the trellis, which formed a kind of ladder. The pistol swung heavily against his thighs; as he pulled himself up by the weathervane, he remembered Griff, lying in his room back there, flies buzzing round him, with pale chest and red cheeks, and Paul thought of the little flat nickel pistol: I must ask Griff whether nickel oxidizes. If it does, he'll have to stop them eating out of the jar.

The girl's hands were larger and firmer than Griff's hands, larger and firmer than his own too: he felt this and was ashamed when she helped him climb from the ridge of the summerhouse roof onto the veranda balustrade.

He brushed the dirt off his hands and said, without looking at the girl, "It's funny that I'm really up here."

"I'm glad you're here. I've been locked in since three." He looked warily over to her, at her hand, which was holding her coat together over her chest.

"Why've you got your coat on?"

"You know why."

"Because of that?"

"Yes."

He took a step toward her. "I expect you're glad to be going away?"

"Yes, I am."

"There was a boy in school this morning," he said in a low voice, "selling pieces of paper with things about you written on them, and a picture of you."

"I know," she said, "and he said I get part of the money he gets for the pieces of paper, and that he has seen me the way he drew me. None of it's true."

"I know it isn't," he said. "He's called Kuffang; he's stupid and tells lies, everyone knows that."

"But they believe him when he tells them *that*."

"Yes," he said, "it's strange, they do believe that."

She pulled her coat tighter around her chest. "That's why I have to leave so suddenly, quickly, before they all get back from the regatta—for a long time now they've given me no peace. You make a show of your body, they say; they say it when I wear a dress with a low neck, and they say it when I wear a dress with a high neck— and a sweater. They go crazy then—but I have to wear something, don't I?"

He watched her without emotion as she went on talking. He was thinking: Funny that I never thought of her, not once. Her hair was blond, her eyes seemed blond too, they were the color of freshly planed beechwood—blond and slightly moist.

"I don't make a show of my body at all," she said, "I just have it."

He nodded, pushed the pistol up a bit with his right hand, as it was lying heavy against his thigh. "Yes," he said, and she was afraid: he had that dream face again. You would have thought he was blind, that other time, those empty, dark eyes had seemed to fall upon her and yet past her in an unpredictable refraction, and now again he looked as if he were blind.

"The man," she went on hurriedly, "who sometimes comes to have discussions with my mother, the old man with white hair, do you know him?" There was silence, the noise from the river was too far off to disturb this silence—"Do you know him?" she asked impatiently.

"Of course I know him," he said; "that's old Dulges."

"Yes, that's the one—he's looked at me like that sometimes and said: Three hundred years ago they would have burned you as a witch. A woman's hair crackling, and the cry from a thousand unfeeling souls unable to tolerate beauty."

"Why did you make me come up?" he asked. "To tell me that?"

"Yes," she said, "and because I saw what you were doing."

He pulled the pistol out of his pocket, held it up, and waited with a smile for her to scream, but she did not scream.

"What are you going to do with it?"

"I don't know, shoot at something."

"At what?"

"Maybe at me."

"Why?"

"Why?" he said. "Why? Sins, death. Mortal sin. Do you understand that?" Slowly, without touching her, he made his way past her, in through the open kitchen door, and leaned with a sigh against the cupboard; the picture was still there on the wall, the one he had not seen for so long, the one he thought about sometimes: factory chimneys, with red smoke rising up from them, smoke pouring out and joining together in the sky to form a blood-red cloud. The girl was standing in the doorway, turned toward him. There were shadows across her face, and she looked like a woman. "Come inside," he said, "they might see us; that would be bad for you, you know."

"In an hour," she said, "I shall be sitting in the train. Here—here's my ticket—it's not a return." She held up the buff ticket, he nodded, and she put the ticket back in her coat pocket. "I shall take off my coat and be wearing a sweater, a sweater, d'you understand?"

He nodded again. "An hour's a long time. Do you know what sin is? Death. Mortal sin?"

"Once," she said, "the pharmacist wanted to—and the teacher too, your history teacher."

"Drönsch?"

"Yes, him. I know what they want, but I don't know what their words mean. I know what sin is too, but I don't understand it any more than I understand what the boys sometimes call out after me when I come home alone, in the dark; they call out after me from doorways, from windows, from cars sometimes, they called out things after me which I knew the meaning of but which I didn't understand. Do you know?"

"Yes."

"What is it?" she said. "Does it bother you terribly?"

"Yes," he said, "terribly."

"Even now?"

"Yes," he said, "doesn't it bother you?"

"No," she said, "it doesn't bother me. It just makes me unhappy that it's there and that other people want something—that they call out after me. Please tell me, why are you thinking of shooting yourself? Because of that?"

"Yes," he said, "simply because of that. Do you know what it means when it says in the Bible: Whatsoever thou shalt bind on earth shall be bound in heaven?"

"Yes, I know what that means; sometimes I stayed behind in class when they had religion."

"Well, then," he said, "maybe you also know what sin is. Death."

"I do," she said. "Do you really believe all that?"

"Yes."

"Everything?"

"Everything."

"You know I don't believe it. But I do know that the worst sin of all is to shoot yourself—at least, that's what I heard," she said, raising her voice, "with my own ears," she pulled her ear with her left hand, with her right she was still clutching her coat, "with my own ears I heard the priest say: We must not throw away the gift of life and toss it at God's feet."

"Gift of life," he said bitterly, "and God has no feet."

"Hasn't He?" she said quietly. "Hasn't He any feet, didn't they pierce them?"

He was silent, then flushed and said in a low voice, "I know."

"Yes," she said, "if you really believe everything, the way you say you do, then you have to believe that too. Do you believe that?"

"What?"

"That we mustn't throw away the gift of life?"

"Oh, I don't know," he said, and held the pistol straight up in the air.

"Come on," she said softly, "put it away. It looks so silly. Please put it away."

He placed the pistol in his right pocket, put his hand into his left pocket, and took out the three cartridge clips. The metal clips lay without luster on the palm of his hand. "That should do," he said.

"Shoot at something else," she said, "for instance, at"—she turned round and looked back at his own home, through the open window—"at the tennis balls," she said.

A deep flush enveloped him like darkness, his hands went limp, the clips fell from his hand. "How did you know...?" he whispered.

"Know what?"

He bent down, picked up the clips from the floor, pushed one cartridge, which had dropped out, carefully back into the clip; he looked through the window at the house standing in full view in the sunshine: the tennis balls were lying back there white and hard in their carton.

Here, in this kitchen, it smelled of bath water, soap, of peace and fresh bread, of cake; red apples were lying on the table, a newspaper, and half a cucumber, its cut surface pale, green, and watery; closer to the peel the cucumber flesh was darker and firmer.

"I also know," said the girl, "what they used to do to fight sin. I've heard about it."

"Who?"

"Those saints of yours. The priest told us about it: they whipped themselves, they fasted and prayed, not one killed himself." She turned toward the boy, afraid again: No, no, I'm not your Jerusalem.

"They weren't fourteen," said the boy, "or fifteen."

"Some of them must have been," she said.

"No," he said, "no, it's not true, most of them weren't converted till after they'd sinned." He came closer, pushing himself along the window sill toward her.

"That's a lie," she said, "some of them didn't sin first at all—I don't believe any of that—if anything, I believe in the Mother of God."

"If *anything*," he said scornfully, "but She was the Mother of *God*."

He looked the girl full in the face, turned aside, and said in an undertone: "Forgive me … yes, yes, I have tried. Prayed."

"And fasted?"

"Oh, fasting," he said. "I don't care what I eat."

"That's not fasting. And whipping. I would do that, I would whip myself, if I believed."

"Doesn't it bother you really?" he whispered.

"No," she said, "it doesn't bother me, to *do* something, to see something, to say something—but it does bother you, doesn't it?"

"Yes, it does."

"What a pity," she said, "that you're so Catholic."

"Why a pity?"

"Otherwise I'd show you my breasts. I would like so much to show them to you—to you. Everyone talks about them, the boys call out things after me, but no one has ever seen them yet."

"No one?"

"No," she said, "no one."

"Show it to me," he said.

"It won't be the same as it was last time, you know when I mean."

"I know," he said.

"Was it terrible for you?"

"Only because Mother was so terrible. She was absolutely furious and told everyone about it. It wasn't so terrible for me. I would have forgotten all about it. Come here," he said.

Her hair felt smooth and hard; that surprised him, he had thought it would be soft, but it was the way he imagined spun glass.

"Not here," she said. She pushed him along in front of her, slowly, for he did not let go of her head, he kept his eyes on her face while they moved, as if in some strange dance step invented by themselves, away from the open veranda door across the kitchen; he seemed to be standing on her feet, she seemed to be lifting him with every step.

She opened the kitchen door, pushed him slowly across the hall, opened the door to her room.

"Here," she said, "in my room, not out there."

"Mirzova," he whispered.

"Why do you call me that? My name is Mirzov, and Katharina."

HEINRICH BÖLL

"Everyone calls you that, and I can't think of you any other way. Show it to me now." He blushed, because again he had said "it" and not "them."

"It makes me sad," she said, "that for you it's a sin."

"I want to see it," he said.

"Not a soul—" she said. "You're not to talk to a soul about it."

"I won't."

"Promise?"

"I promise—but there's one person I must tell."

"Who's that?"

"Think for a moment," he said softly, "think for a minute, you should know all about that." She bit her lip, still clutching her coat tightly around her chest, looked thoughtfully at him, and said, "Of course, you can tell him, but no one else."

"All right," he said, "now show it to me."

If she laughs or giggles, he thought, I'll shoot; but she did not laugh: she was so serious she was trembling, her hands fluttered as she tried to undo the buttons, her fingers were ice-cold and stiff.

"Come here," he said gently, "I'll do it." His hands were calm, his fear lay deeper than hers; down in his ankles was where he felt it, they were like rubber and he thought he was going to fall over. He undid the buttons with his right hand, passed his left hand over the girl's hair, as if to comfort her.

Her tears came quite suddenly, silently, without warning, without fuss. They simply ran down her cheeks.

"Why are you crying?"

"I'm scared," she said, "aren't you?"

"Yes, I am," he said. "I'm scared too." He was so nervous he almost tore off the last button, and he took a deep breath when he saw Mirzova's breasts; he had been scared because he was afraid of being disgusted, afraid of the moment when politeness would force him to pretend, so as to hide this disgust, but he was not disgusted and there was no need to hide anything. He sighed again. As suddenly as they had begun, the girl's tears stopped flowing. She held her breath as she looked at him: the least movement of his face, the expression in his eyes, she took in every detail, and she already knew that in years to come she would be grateful to him, because he had been the one to undo the buttons.

He looked at them closely, did not touch her, just shook his head, and laughter rose up in him.

"What is it?" she asked, "may I laugh too?"

"Go ahead, laugh," he said, and she laughed.

"It's beautiful," he said, and again he was ashamed because he had said "it" instead of "they," but he could not bring himself to say "they."

"Do it up again," she said.

"No," he said, "you do it up, but leave it for a moment." It was very quiet, the sun pierced the yellow curtains, which had dark-green stripes. Dark stripes also lay across the faces of the children. You can't have a woman, thought the boy, at fourteen.

"Let me do it up," said the girl.

"All right," he said, "do it up." But he held her hands back for a moment, and the girl looked at him and laughed aloud.

"Why are you laughing now?"

"I'm so happy, aren't you?"

"Yes, I am," he said, "I'm happy because it's so beautiful."

He let go her hands, stepped back, and turned aside as she buttoned up her blouse.

He walked round the table, looked at the open suitcase lying on the bed; sweaters lay piled one on top of the other, underwear had been sorted into little heaps, the bed had already been stripped, the suitcase was lying on the blue mattress ticking.

"So you're really leaving?" he asked.

"Yes."

He moved on, looked into the open clothes closet: nothing but empty coat hangers, a red hair ribbon dangling from one of them. He shut the closet doors, glanced over to the bookshelf above her bed: empty except for some used blotting paper, and a brochure standing at an angle against the wall: "All About Winegrowing."

When he looked around, her coat was lying on the floor. He picked it up, threw it on the table, and ran out.

She was standing in the kitchen doorway, holding the binoculars. She winced when he laid his hand on her shoulder, lowered her binoculars, and gave him a frightened look.

"Please go," she said. "You must go now."

"Let me see it just once more."

"No, the regatta will be over soon, my mother's coming to take me to the train. You know what'll happen if anyone sees you here."

He said nothing, leaving his hand on her shoulder. She ran away quickly, round to the other side of the table, took a knife out of the drawer, cut off a piece of the cucumber, took a bite, put down the knife. "Please," she said, "if you stare at me like that much longer, you'll look like the pharmacist or that fellow Drönsch."

"Shut up," he said. She looked at him in astonishment as he suddenly came over to her, grasped her by the shoulder; she brought her hand up over his arm and put the piece of cucumber in her mouth, and smiled. "Don't you understand," she said. "I was so happy."

He looked at the floor, let go her shoulder, went to the veranda, jumped onto the balustrade, and called out, "Give me a hand." She laughed, ran over to him, put down the piece of cucumber, and held on to him with both hands, bracing herself against the wall while she slowly lowered him onto the roof of the summerhouse.

"I bet someone has seen us," he said.

"Probably," she said. "Can I let go?"

"Not yet. When are you coming back from Vienna?"

"Soon," she said. "D'you want me to come soon?" He already had both feet on the roof and said, "You can let go now." But she did not let go, she laughed. "I'll come back. When d'you want me to come?"

"When I can look at it again."

"That might be a long time."

"How long?"

"I don't know," she said, looking at him thoughtfully. "First you looked as if you were dreaming, then all of a sudden you looked almost like the pharmacist; I don't want you to look like that and commit mortal sins and be bound."

"Let go now," he said, "or pull me up again."

She laughed, let go his hands, picked up the piece of cucumber from the balustrade, and bit into it.

"I've got to shoot at something," he said.

"Don't shoot at anything living," she said. "Shoot at tennis balls or at—at jam jars."

"What made you think of jam jars?"

"I don't know," she said. "I could imagine it might be fun to shoot at jam jars. It's bound to make a noise, and splash all over the place—wait a minute," she said hurriedly as he turned away and started to climb down; he turned back and looked at her gravely. "And, you know," she said softly, "you could stand at the railroad crossing, by the water tower, and fire into the air when my train goes by. I'll be looking out of the window and waving."

"Good," he said. "I'll do that, when does your train go?"

"Ten past seven," she said, "at seven-thirteen it passes the crossing."

"Then I'd better get going," he said. "Goodbye. You'll be back?"

"I'll be back," she said, "for sure." And she bit her lip and repeated under her breath, "I'll be back."

She watched him as he clung to the weathervane, till his feet had reached the trellis. He ran across the lawn, onto the terrace, climbed into the house; she saw him cross the brass strip again, pick up the carton of tennis balls, turn back; she heard the gravel crunching under his feet as, with the carton under his arm, he ran past the garage and out onto the street.

I hope he doesn't forget to turn round and wave, she thought. There he was, waving, at the corner of the garage, he pulled the pistol out of his pocket, pressed the barrel against the carton, and waved once more before he ran round the corner and disappeared.

Up she went with the binoculars again, punching out circles of blue, medallions of sky; Rhenania and Germania, riverbank with regatta pennants, round horizon of river green with shreds of banner red.

My hair would crackle, she thought, it crackled even when he touched it. And in Vienna there's wine too.

Vineyard: pale-green, sour grapes, leaves which those fat slobs tied around their bald heads to make them look like Bacchus.

She looked for the streets, the ones she could see into with the binoculars. The streets were all deserted, all she could see was the parked cars; the ice-cream cart was still there, she could not find the boy. I'll be—she thought with a smile, while she swept the binoculars toward the river again—I'll be your Jerusalem after all.

She did not turn round as her mother opened the front door and entered the hall. A quarter to seven already, she thought. I hope he makes it to the crossing by thirteen minutes after. She heard the suitcase being snapped shut and the tiny key being turned in the lock, heard the firm footsteps, and she winced as the coat fell over her shoulders: her mother's hands remained lying on her shoulders.

"Have you got the money?"

"Yes."

"Your ticket?"

"Yes."

"The sandwiches?"

"Yes."

"Did you pack your suitcase properly?"

"Yes."

"You haven't forgotten anything?"

"No."

"The address in Vienna?"

"Yes."

"The phone number?"

"Yes."

The brief pause was dark, frightening, her mother's hands slid down her shoulders, over her forearms. "I felt it was better not to be here during your last hours. It's easier that way, I know it is. I've said goodbye so many times—and I did right to lock you in, you know."

"You did right, I know."

"Then come along now..." She turned round. It was terrible to see her mother crying, it was almost as if a monument were crying: her mother was still beautiful, but it was a dark beauty, haggard. Her past hung over her like a black halo. Strange words echoed in the legend of Mother's life: Moscow—Communism—a Red nun, a Russian called Mirzov; her faith lost, escape, and the dogmas of the lost faith continuing to twist and turn in her brain. It was like a loom whose spools go on turning although there is no more yarn: gorgeous patterns woven into a void, only the sound remained, the mechanism. All she needed was an opposite pole: Dulges, the city fathers, the priest, the schoolteachers, the nuns; and if you shut your eyes you could imagine prayer wheels, the prayer wheels of the unbelieving, the restless wind-driven rattle known as discussion. Occasionally, very rarely, her mother had looked the way she looked now: when she had been drinking wine, and people would say: Ah yes, in spite of everything, she's still a true daughter of Zischbrunn.

It was a good thing her mother was smoking; trickling down toward the cigarette, wreathed in smoke, her tears looked less serious, more like pretended tears, but tears were the last thing her mother would pretend.

"I'll pay them back for this," she said. "I hate to see you go. To have to give in to them."

"Why don't you come too?"

"No, no—you'll be back, a year or two and you'll be back. Never do what they think you've been doing. Never, and now come along."

She slipped her arms into the sleeves of her coat, buttoned it up, felt for her ticket, for her purse, ran into her bedroom, but her mother shook her head as she went to pick up her suitcase. "Never mind that," she said, "and hurry—there's not much time."

Heat hung in the staircase, wine fumes rose from the cellar, where the pharmacist had been bottling wine: an acrid smell that seemed to go with the hazy magenta of the wallpaper. The narrow lanes: the dark windows, doorways, from which things had been called out after her, things she did not understand. Hurry. The noise from the riverbank was louder now, car engines were being started up: the regatta was over. Hurry.

The ticket collector called her mother by her first name, "Okay, Kate, never mind about a platform ticket." A drunk staggered along the dark underpass, bawling out a tune, and hurled a full bottle of wine against the damp black wall; there was a crash of breaking glass, and once again the smell of wine rose to her nostrils. The train was already in, her mother pushed the suitcase into the corridor. "Never do what they think you've been doing, never."

How sensible to make the goodbyes so short; there was only one minute left, it was long, longer than the whole afternoon. "I expect you'd have liked to take the binoculars along. Shall I send them on to you?"

"Yes, would you, please? Oh, Mother."

"What is it?"

"I hardly know him."

"Oh, he's nice, and he's looking forward to having you—and he never believed in the gods I believed in."

"And he doesn't drink wine?"

"He doesn't care for it—and he's got money, he's in business."

"What kind of business?"

"I don't know exactly: clothing, or something. You'll like him."

No kiss. Monuments must not be kissed, even when they weep. Without a backward glance her mother disappeared into the underpass: a pillar of salt, a monument to unhappiness, preserved in the bitter brine of her mistakes. That evening she would start up the prayer wheel, give a monologue while Dulges sat in the kitchen: "Aren't tears actually a remnant of bourgeois sentiment? Can there be tears in the classless society?"

Past the school, the swimming pool, under the little bridge, the long, long wall of the vineyards, the woods—and at the railroad crossing by the water tower she saw the two boys, heard the bang, saw the black pistol in Paul's hand, and shouted, "Jerusalem, Jerusalem!" and she shouted it again although she could no longer see the boys. She wiped away her tears with her sleeve, picked up her suitcase, and stumbled along the corridor. I won't take off my coat yet, she thought, not just yet.

III

"What was it she called out?" asked Griff.

"Couldn't you hear?"

"No, could you? What was it?"

"Jerusalem," said Paul quietly. "Jerusalem. She shouted it again when the train had already gone by. Let's go." He looked disappointedly at the pistol, which he held in his lowered hand, his thumb on the safety catch. He had thought it would make more of a bang, that it would smoke; he had counted on it smoking. With a smoking pistol in his hand, that's how he had wanted to stand beside the train; but the pistol did not smoke, it was not even hot, he moved his forefinger carefully along the barrel, withdrew it. "Let's go," he said. Jerusalem, he thought, I could hear it quite plainly, but I don't know what it means.

They left the path that ran parallel to the railway tracks, Griff hugging under his arm the jar of jam he had brought from home, Paul carrying the pistol in his lowered hand; in the greenish light they turned to face each other.

"Are you really going to do it?"

"No," said Paul, "no, we must..." He blushed, turned his face away. "Did you put the balls on the tree trunk?"

"Yes," said Griff, "they kept rolling off, but then I found a groove in the bark."

"How far apart?"

"Four or five inches, like you said—listen," he said, lowering his voice and coming to a halt, "I can't go home, I can't. To that room. You do see, don't you, that I can't go back to that room." He moved the jam jar to his other hand, and held Paul, who wanted to go on, by the sleeve. "I just can't."

"No," said Paul, "I wouldn't go back to that room either."

"My mother would force me to clean it up. I can't, I tell you—wipe up the floor, clean the walls, the books, and everything. She would be standing there watching."

"No, you can't do that. Let's go!"

"What shall I do?"

"We'll see. Let's shoot first—come along..." They walked on, from time to time turning their green faces toward one another, Griff nervously, Paul smiling.

"You've got to shoot me," said Griff, "you've got to, I tell you."

"You're crazy," said Paul; he bit his lip, raised the pistol, aimed at Griff, and Griff ducked, whimpered softly, and Paul said, "You see, you'd scream, and I haven't even moved the safety catch."

He shaded his eyes with his left hand when they reached the clearing, blinked across to the tennis balls which were lying in a row on a fallen tree: three were still spotless, white and fluffy, like the fleece of the Lamb, the others were muddy from falling on the damp ground.

"Go over there," said Paul, "put the jar between the third and fourth ball." Griff walked unsteadily across the clearing, placed the jar behind the balls so that it stood at an angle and threatened to topple over.

"There's not enough room. I can't put it in between."

"Out of my way," said Paul, "I'm going to shoot. Stand over here by me."

He waited until Griff was standing beside him in the shade, raised the pistol, took aim, pressed the trigger, and, frightened by the echo of the first bullet, he banged away till the magazine was empty—the echo of the last two shots came back clearly out of the forest long after he had stopped firing. The tennis balls were still there, not even the jam jar had been hit. It was quite silent, there was just a slight smell of powder—the boy was still standing there, the raised pistol in his hand, he stood there as if he would stay there forever. He was pale. The chill of disappointment flowed into his veins, and his ears rang with the clear echo that was no longer there: clear, staccato barking reverberated in his memory. He closed his eyes, opened them again: the tennis balls were still there, and not even the jam jar had been hit.

He pulled back his arm as if from a great distance, stroked his fingers along the barrel: at least it was a little hot. Paul ripped out the empty clip with his thumbnail, slid a new one in, and pushed the safety catch back.

"Here," he said quietly, "it's your turn."

He handed the pistol to Griff, showed him how to release the safety catch, stepped back, and thought, while he stood in the shade trying to swallow his disappointment: I hope you don't miss, at least; I hope you don't miss. Griff threw up his arm with the pistol, then lowered it slowly toward the target—he's read about that, thought Paul, read that somewhere, it looks as though he had read it—and Griff fired stutteringly. Once—then silence; there were the balls, and the jar was still standing there; then three times—and three times the echo yapped back at the two boys. The dark tree trunk lay there as peaceful as some strange still life, with its six tennis balls and the jar of plum jam.

Only an echo; there was a faint smell of powder, and, shaking his head, Griff handed the pistol back to Paul.

"I've got an extra shot coming to me," said Paul, "the one I fired in the air—that leaves two for each of us, and one left over."

This time he aimed carefully, but he knew he would miss, and he did miss: the echo of his shot came back to him thin and forlorn, the echo penetrated him like a red dot, circled around inside him, flew out of him again, and he was calm as he handed Griff the pistol.

Griff shook his head. "The targets are too small, we must pick bigger ones. How about the station clock or the Rapier Beer sign?"

"Where d'you mean?"

"At the corner, across from the station, where Drönsch lives."

"Or a windowpane, or the samovar we have at home. We've *got* to hit something. Is it really true that you fired eight times with your pistol and got seven hits? A tin can at thirty yards?"

"No," said Griff, "I didn't shoot at all, I've never shot before." He went over to the tree trunk, kicked the balls, and the jam jar, with his right foot; the balls rolled into the grass, the jar slipped off and fell over onto the soft ground in the shade of the tree trunk where no grass grew. Griff snatched up the jar and was about to throw it against the tree, but Paul held back his arm, took the jar from him, and put it on the ground. "Please, don't," he said, "don't—I can't bear to see it. Leave it where it is, let grass grow over it, lots of grass..."

And he pictured the grass growing till the jar was completely covered; animals would sniff at it, mushrooms would grow in a dense colony, and years later he would go for a walk in the forest and find it: the pistol covered with rust, the jam decayed into a moldy, spongy scum. He took the jar, set it in a hollow at the edge of the clearing, and kicked some loose earth over it. "Leave it," he said softly. "Leave the balls too—we haven't hit a thing."

"Lies," said Griff, "all lies."

"Yes, all lies," said Paul, but while he was fastening the safety catch and putting the pistol in his pocket he said under his breath, "Jerusalem, Jerusalem."

"How did you know she was leaving?"

"I met her mother on my way over to you."

"But she'll be back, won't she?"

"No, she won't be back."

Griff returned to the clearing and kicked the balls; two of them rolled white and silent into the shady forest. "Come over here," he said. "Look at this—we aimed much too high."

Paul walked slowly across, saw the ragged blackberry bush, bullet holes in a fir tree, fresh resin, a snapped branch.

"Come on," he said. "Let's shoot at the Rapier Beer sign, it's as big as a cartwheel."

"I'm not going back into town," said Griff, "never again. I'm going to Lübeck. I've got the ticket right here. I'm not coming back."

They walked slowly back the way they had come, past the railroad crossing, past the long vineyard wall, past the school. The parked cars had long since left, the sound of music drifted up from the town. They climbed up onto the two pillars of the churchyard gates, sat ten feet apart at the same level, and smoked.

"Prize-giving ceremony," said Griff. "A ball. Vine leaves round their foreheads. Down there you can see the Rapier Beer sign on the wall of Drönsch's house."

"I'll hit it," said Paul. "Aren't you coming?"

"No, I'll stay here. I'm going to sit here and wait till you've shot it down. Then I'll walk slowly over to Dreschenbrunn, get on the train there, and go to Lübeck. I'll go for a swim, a long swim in the salt water, and I hope it'll be stormy, with high waves and lots of salt water."

They smoked silently, looked at each other now and then, smiled, listened to the sounds coming up from the town, which were getting louder and louder.

"Did the hoofs really thunder?" asked Griff.

"No," said Paul, "they didn't. It was only one horse, and his hoofs just clattered—how about the salmon?"

"I've never seen one." They exchanged smiles and were silent for a while.

"Now my dad's standing in front of the cupboard," Paul said then, "with his shirt sleeves rolled up, my mother's spreading the tablecloth; now he's unlocking the drawer; perhaps he can see the scratch I made when the screwdriver slipped; but he doesn't see it, it's dark now over there in the corner; he's opening the drawer, he stops in surprise, for the checkbooks and ledger sheets aren't lying the way he left them—he's got the wind up, he's calling out to my mother, he's throwing all the stuff on the floor, rummaging around in the drawer—now, right now—at this very moment." He looked at the church clock, whose big hand was just slipping onto the ten while the small one stood motionless below the eight. "At one time," said Paul, "he was champion pistol-cleaner in his division; in three minutes he could take a pistol apart, clean it, and put it together again—and at home I always had to stand beside him and check the time with a stop watch: it never took him more than three minutes."

He threw his cigarette butt onto the path, stared at the church clock. "At exactly ten to eight he was always through with the job, then he would wash his hands and still be at the club on the stroke of eight." Paul jumped down from the pillar, held his hand up to Griff, and said, "When'll I see you again?"

"Not for a long time," said Griff, "but one day I'll be back. I'll go to work for my uncle, canning fish, slitting them open. The girls are always laughing, and in the evening they go to the movies, maybe—they don't giggle, that's for sure. They've got such white arms and look so cute. They used to stuff chocolate in my mouth when I was little, but now I'm not so little anymore. I can't—" he said quietly. "You do see, don't you, that I can't go back to that room. She would stand beside me till it was all cleaned up. Have you got any money?"

"Sure, I've got all my vacation money already. Do you want some?"

"Yes, let me have some. I'll send it back to you, later on."

Paul opened his wallet, counted out the coins, opened the flap for the bills. "All my money for Zalligkofen. I can let you have eighteen marks. D'you want it?"

"Yes," said Griff; he took the bill, the coins, stuck it all in his trouser pocket. "I'll wait here," he said, "till I can hear and see that you've shot down the Rapier Beer sign; fire quickly and empty the whole magazine. When I can hear it, and see it, I'll go over to Dreschenbrunn and get on the next train. But don't tell anyone you know where I've gone."

"I won't," said Paul. He ran off, kicking stones aside as he ran, letting out a shrill cry so as to hear the wild echo of his voice as he ran through the underpass; he did not slow down until he was passing the railway yard and approaching Drönsch's house; he gradually slackened speed, turned round but could not see the churchyard gates yet, only the big black cross in the middle of the churchyard and the white gravestones above the cross. The closer he came to the station, the more rows of graves he could see below the cross: two rows, three, five, then the gates, and Griff was still sitting there. Paul crossed the station square, slowly; his heart was thumping, but he knew it was not fear, it was more like joy, and he would have liked to fire off the whole magazine into the air and shout "Jerusalem"; he felt almost sorry for the big round Rapier Beer sign, on which two crossed swords seemed to protect a mug overflowing with foaming beer.

I must hit it, he thought before taking the pistol out of his pocket, I must. He walked past the houses, stepped back into the doorway of a butcher's shop, and nearly trod on the hands of a woman who was washing the tiled entrance. "Watch it, can't you?" she said out of the semidarkness. "Beat it!"

"Excuse me," he said, and took up a position outside the entrance. The soapsuds ran between his feet across the asphalt into the gutter. This is the best place, he thought, it's hanging directly in front of me, round, like a big moon, and I'm bound to hit it. He took the pistol out of his pocket, released the safety catch, and smiled before he raised it and took aim. He no longer felt something had to be destroyed, and yet he had to shoot: there were some things that had to be done, and if he didn't shoot, Griff wouldn't go to Lübeck, wouldn't see the white arms of the cute girls, and would never go with one of them to the movies. He thought: God, I hope I'm not too far away—I *must* hit it, I *must*; but he had already hit it: the crash of the falling glass was almost louder than the noise of the shots. First a round piece broke out of the sign— the beer mug; then the swords fell, he saw the plaster of the house wall jump out in little clouds of dust, saw the metal ring that had held the glass sign, splinters of glass were clinging to the edge like a fringe.

Drowning out everything else were the screams of the woman; she had rushed out of the passageway and then ran back and went on screaming inside in the dark. Men were shouting too, a few people came out of the station; a great many rushed out of the tavern. A window was opened, and for a moment Drönsch's face appeared up above. But no one came near him because he was still holding the pistol. He looked up toward the churchyard: Griff had gone.

An eternity passed before someone came and took the pistol from him. He had time to think of many things: Now, he thought, Father has been yelling all over the house for the past ten minutes, putting the blame on Mother—Mother, who found out ages ago that I climbed up to Katharina's room; everyone knows about it, and nobody will understand why I did it and why I did this, shot at the lighted sign. Maybe it would have been better if I had shot into Drönsch's window. And he thought: Maybe I ought to go and confess, but they won't let me; it was eight o'clock, and after eight you couldn't confess. The Lamb has not drunk my blood, he thought, O Lamb.

There are only a few pieces of broken glass, and I have seen Katharina's breasts. She'll come back. And for once Father has good reason to clean his pistol.

He even had time to think of Griff, now on his way to Dreschen-brunn, over the slopes, past the vineyards, and he thought of the tennis balls and the jar of jam, which he already imagined completely overgrown.

A lot of people were standing around him at some distance. Drönsch was leaning out of the window on his arms, his pipe in his mouth. Never will I look like that, he thought, never. Drönsch was always talking about Admiral Tirpitz. "Tirpitz was the victim of injustice. One day history will see that justice is done to Tirpitz. Objective scholars are at work to find out the truth about Tirpitz." Tirpitz? Oh well.

From behind, he thought, I might have known they would come from behind. Just before the policeman grabbed hold of him, he smelled his uniform: its first smell was of cleaning fluid, its second, furnace fumes, its third...

"Where do you live, you young punk?" asked the policeman.

"Where do I live?" He looked at the policeman. He knew him, and the policeman must know him too: he always brought round the renewal for Father's gun license, a friendly soul, always refused a cigar three times before he accepted it. Even now he was not unfriendly, and his grasp was not tight.

"That's right, where do you live?"

"I live in the Valley of the Thundering Hoofs," said Paul.

"That's not true," shouted the woman who had been scrubbing the passageway, "I know him, he's the son—"

"All right, all right," said the policeman, "I know. Come along," he said, "I'll take you home."

"I live in Jerusalem," said Paul.

"Now stop that," said the policeman. "Come along with me."

"All right," said Paul, "I'll stop."

The people were silent as he walked down the dark street just ahead of the policeman. He looked like a blind man: his eyes fixed on a certain point, and yet he seemed to be looking past everything. He saw only one thing: the policeman's folded evening paper. And in the first line he could read "Khrushchev" and in the second "open grave."

"Hell," he said to the policeman, "you know where I live."

"Of course I do," said the policeman. "Come along!"

THE SEVENTH TRUNK

For thirty-two years I have been trying to finish writing a story, the beginning of which I read in the *Bockelmunden Parish News* but the promised continuation of which I never got to see, since, for unknown reasons (probably political—it was in 1933) this modest publication ceased to appear. The name of the author of this story is engraved on my memory: he was called Jacob Maria Hermes, and for thirty-two years I have tried in vain to find other writings by him; no encyclopedia, no authors' society index, not even the Bockelmunden parish register, still extant, lists his name, and it looks as though I must finally accept the fact that the name of Jacob Maria Hermes was a pseudonym. The last editor of the *Bockelmunden Parish News* was Vice-Principal Ferdinand Schmitz (retired), but by the time I had finally tracked him down I was unduly delayed by prewar, wartime, and postwar events, and when at last in 1947 I trod my native soil again, I found that Ferdinand Schmitz had just died at the age of eighty-eight.

I freely admit that I invited myself to his funeral, not only to do final honor to a man under whose editorship at least half of *the* most masterly short story I had ever read had been published; and not only because I hoped to find out more about Jacob Maria Hermes from his relatives—but also because in 1947 attendance at a country funeral meant the promise of a decent meal. Bockelmunden is a pretty village: old trees, shady slopes, half-timbered farmhouses. On this summer's day, tables had been set up in the yard of one of the farms, there was home-slaughtered meat from the Schmitz family storerooms, there was beer, cabbage, fruit, later on cakes and coffee—all served by two pretty waitresses from Nellessen's inn; the church choir sang the hymn that is *de rigueur* on the occasion of schoolteachers' funerals, "With wisdom and honor hast thou mastered the school." Trumpets sounded, club banners were unfurled (illegally, for this was still prohibited at that time); when the jokes grew broader, the atmosphere—as it is so nicely put—became more relaxed, I sat down beside each person there and asked them all in turn if they knew anything about the editorial estate of the deceased. The answers were unanimous and shattering: in five, six, or seven cartons (the information varied only as to quantity), the entire archives, the entire correspondence of the *Bockelmunden Parish News* had been burned during the final days of the war "as a result of enemy action."

Having eaten my fill and drunk a little too much, yet without obtaining any precise information on Jacob Maria Hermes, I returned home with that sense of disappointment familiar to anyone who has ever tried to catch two butterflies with one net but has only managed to catch the vastly inferior butterfly while the other, the gorgeous shimmering one, flew away.

Nothing daunted, I tried for the next eighteen years to do what I had been trying to do for the previous fourteen years: finish writing the best short story I had ever read —and all attempts were in vain for the simple reason: I couldn't get the seventh trunk open!

I regret having to expatiate a little here; not thirty-two but thirty-five years ago I fished out of the bargain barrel in a secondhand bookstore in the Old Town of Cologne a pamphlet entitled "The Secret of the Seventh Trunk, or, How to Write Short Prose." This remarkable publication consisted of only a few pages; the author was called Heinrich Knecht and described himself as "temporarily conscripted into service with the Deutz Cuirassiers." The pamphlet had been published in 1913 by "Ulrich Nellessen, Publisher and Printer, corner of Teutoburg and Maternus Street." Underneath, in small print, was the remark: "The author may also be reached at this address in his (very limited) free time."

I could, of course, hardly suppose that in 1939 anyone would still be serving in the Cuirassiers as he had been in 1913, for, although I did not (and still do not) know what a Cuirassier is, I did know that that part of the Republic in which I was living had been spared the presence of the Army (not forever, unfortunately, as it turned out five years later for the first time, and twenty-five years later for the second)—but there was a slight chance that the printer and publisher were still to be found at this corner, and somehow I am quite touched at the thought of that thirteen-year-old boy immediately mounting his bicycle and racing from a westerly part of the city to that southerly one to discover that the two streets do not form a corner at all. To this day I admire the persistence with which I rode from the northern entrance of Römer Park, where at that time the built-up right-hand side of Maternus Street came to an end, to the Teutoburg Street, which had (and still has) the impudence to end shortly before the western entrance to Römer Park— from there to the office of the Tourist Association where with a pencil I furtively extended the right side of Maternus Street and the left side of Teutoburg Street on the city map hanging there, to discover that, if these two streets formed a corner, they would do so in the middle of the Rhine. So Heinrich Knecht, the old so-and-so, provided he was halfway honest, must have lived roughly fifty yards north of Marker 686 in a caisson at the bottom of the Rhine and have swum every morning a mile and a half down-river to report for duty at his Cuirassiers' barracks. *Today* I am no longer so certain that he really did not live there, perhaps still does: a deserter from the Cuirassiers, the color of the river, with a green beard, consoled by naiads—little knowing that for deserters times are still bad. *At the time* I was simply so shattered by all this hocus-pocus that I bought the first three cigarettes in my life with my last nickel; I enjoyed the first cigarette, and since then I have been a fairly heavy smoker. Needless to say, there was no trace either of the Nellessen printing shop. I did not even attempt to find Knecht— perhaps I ought to have got hold of a boat, dived in fifty yards north of Marker 686, and taken hold of Heinrich Knecht by his green beard. The thought never occurred to me at the time— *today* it is too late: I have smoked too many cigarettes since then to risk a dive, and Knecht is to blame for that.

I need hardly mention that I soon knew Knecht's treatise by heart; I carried it with me, on my person, in war and peace; during the war I lost it, it was in a haversack that also contained (I beg forgiveness of all militant atheists!) a New Testament, a volume of poems by Trakl, the half-story by Hermes, four blank furlough certificates, two spare pay-books, a company stamp, some bread, some *ersatz* spread, a package of fine-cut, and some cigarette paper. Cause of loss: enemy action.

Today, enriched, saturated almost, by literary insight and hind-sight, and a little more perspicacious too, I have, of course, no dif-ficulty in realizing that Knecht and Hermes must have known about each other, that both names were perhaps pseudonyms for Ferdinand Schmitz—that the name Nellessen linking the two should have put me on the track.

These are unpleasant, embarrassing assumptions, terrible consequences of an education that was forced upon me, betrayal of that earnest, flushed boy riding his bicycle right across Cologne that summer's day to find a street corner that did not exist. It was not until much later, actually only now that I am writing it down, that I realized that names, all names, are but sounding brass: Knecht, Hermes, Nellessen, Schmitz—and the only thing that matters is: someone actually wrote this half of a short story, actually wrote "The Seventh Trunk," so when I am asked to acknowledge who encouraged me to write, who influenced me, here are the names: Jacob Maria Hermes and Heinrich Knecht. Unfortunately I cannot reproduce the Hermes short story word for word, so I will merely relate what happened in it. The central character was a nine-year-old girl who, in a school playground surrounded by maple trees, was persuaded, duped, perhaps even forced, by a nun who in a nice way was not quite right in the head to join a brotherhood whose members undertook to attend Holy Mass on Sundays, "reverently," not once but twice. There was only one weak sentence in the story, and I can recall it—the weaknesses of one's fellow writers are always what one remembers best—word for word. The sentence goes: "Sister Adelheid suddenly became aware of her senselessness." First of all I am firmly convinced that there was a typographical error here, that instead of senselessness it should have been sensualness (in my own case it has happened three times that printers, typesetters, and proofreaders have made senselessness out of sensualness); secondly: an outright psychological statement of this kind was utterly out of keeping with Hermes' prose style, which was as dry as immortelles. In the preceding sentence a spot of cocoa on the little girl's blue blouse had been mentioned. He must have meant sensualness. I swear with even greater emphasis: a man of the stature of a Jacob Maria Hermes does not regard nuns as senseless, and nuns who become aware of their senselessness simply do not belong in his repertoire, especially as three paragraphs further on, in a prose as arid as the steppes, he let the little girl become fourteen years old without having her suffer complexes, conflicts, or convulsions, although usually she went only once to church, on many Sundays not at all, and only on a single occasion twice. Nowadays one does not have to even get wind of ecclesiastical wrath, one has only to be an ardent TV-viewer, to know that both terms, senselessness and sensualness, as applied to a nun, will find their way directly into the Church Council chamber and out again. For some Council fathers would immediately attack the term senselessness as applied by a nun in an internal monologue to her own existence; others would defend it; and needless to say it would not be the attackers but the defenders who would cause an author considerable trouble, for he would have to point to a printer's error, send them a notarized copy of his manuscript, and still they would interpret his allusion to a typographical error as cowardice and maintain that he was "attacking progress from the rear."

It stands to reason that it was not Hermes' intention to attack anything or anyone from the rear, or to turn his back on anyone or anything. I am so indebted to him that, in his place, I bare my breast to reactionaries and avant-gardists alike, because I know very well: a short story which speaks of a brotherhood whose members undertake to attend Mass not once but twice on Sundays—prose of this kind is highly suspect to both parties.

For thirty-two years now I have been carrying the end of this story around with me, and what rejoices me as a contemporary but inhibits me as an author is the fact that I know (no: I sense) that this woman is still alive, and perhaps this is why the seventh trunk will not spring open.

This is precisely the place where I must finally explain about Knecht's seventh trunk. Before doing so I must quickly, in a few sentences, deal with the numerous works of which none ranks equally with Knecht's but of which many are worthy of considerable note. It seems to me there are so many handbooks on how to write a short story that I am often surprised that not more good ones are written. For instance: the directions given in every creative writing course, teaching every beginner, clearly and to the point, with a minimum of fuss, how to make a story so attractive and so convenient that it poses not the slightest difficulty for the Sunday supplement copy editor—i.e., has a maximum length of one hundred column-length lines, in other words roughly the size (comparatively speaking, of course) of the smallest transistor in the world. And there are many more directions than those I have mentioned: one has only to read them *and then just simply* (these four expansion words contain the entire secret of short-story writing), and then just simply write it down, except—except that Knecht's very last injunction states: "And from the final trunk, the seventh one, the finished short prose, lively as a mouse, must jump out the moment the trunk springs open." This last sentence has always reminded me of a superstition that one of my great-grandmothers —she must have been called Nellessen, which would make her the third in the conspiracy—used to tell us about. All one had to do, according to my great-grandmother, was take a few stale crusts of bread, and some rags, and tie them securely inside a cardboard or wooden box, open the box after at most six weeks, and live mice would come jumping out.

The moral of this would therefore be quite simple: one need only know Heinrich Knecht, read *half* a story by Jacob Maria Hermes, and have had a superstitious great-grandmother, and all one would have to do would be *to just simply* write down one's first short story. Of course one needs some *subject matter,* only a little really: a nine-year-old girl with cocoa spots on her blue blouse, a few nuns, who in a nice way are not quite right in the head, a school playground, a few maple trees, and seven trunks. Before any youthful readers bent on writing short stories go dashing off to acquire some trunks, I must quickly explain that the term "trunk" is of course variable: the seventh "trunk" can be one of those exquisitely designed little cases in which one keeps electric razors, it can be a carton for fifty cigarettes, an empty make-up kit might do too; what is important is what Knecht regards as indispensable: the "trunks" must get smaller and smaller; the first one sometimes has to be enormous. Where, for example, is an author in the first stage, the "preparation of subject matter," as Knecht calls it, to put a railway station, or a school, a bridge over the Rhine, or a whole block of tenements? He has to rent an abandoned factory site until—and it may take years—he needs only the color of the bridge, only the smell of the school, and these he must put into the second trunk, although in this second trunk a horse, a truck, a barracks, and an abbey may be waiting, of which, as soon as it is the third trunk's turn, he will keep only a hair, a squeak, the echo of a command, and a response, while in the third trunk an old blanket, cigarette butts, empty bottles, and a few pawn tickets are waiting. Pawn tickets were evidently Knecht's favorite documents, for I recall a sentence of his: "Why, O Scribe, carry large objects around with

you, when there are institutions which not only relieve you of having to
store these objects but even give you money for them, money that you
do not need to pay back if, after the due date, you are no longer interested in the object? Make use, therefore, of the institutions which help
you to lighten your baggage." It does not take long to tell all the rest, for
all the rest consists of: and so on. Needless to say—I am most anxious
to avoid any misunderstanding—needless to say, the fifth or sixth trunk
can be some little container the size of a matchbox, and the seventh
can be an old biscuit tin; all that matters is that the seventh trunk must
be closed, if only by a plain rubber band, and it must spring open by
itself. Only one question remains unresolved, and it will probably cause
youthful readers some anxiety: what does one do with living people
where they are needed for short prose? One can neither—and possibly
for twenty years, for it can take a good short story that long to wait for
its awakening in the seventh trunk—so, one cannot shut living people
up for that long, nor can one leave them at the pawnbroker's; what is
one to do with them? Answer: they are not needed: one can pull out a
hair, secretly remove a shoelace from a shoe, or brush a lipstick across
a piece of cigarette paper; that is enough, for—here I must earnestly
remind readers of my great-grandmother Nellessen: the point is not to
put life into the case or box, the point is that life has to be created in it
and jump out of its own accord. And so on—*and then just simply write*
the whole thing *down*.

A SOLDIER'S LEGACY

Written in 1949, A Soldier's Legacy *was published in Germany as* Das Vermächtnis *by Lamuv Verlag in 1982. This English translation was published in 1985 by Knopf.*

A SOLDIER'S LEGACY

I

Today, my dear sir, I saw a young man whose name I'm sure is familiar to you; it is Schnecker. He has been living—as far as I know—for a number of years in your neighborhood, and he was a schoolmate of your brother's, who was reported missing during the war. But that's not all. Today I also learned that for five years you have been waiting in vain to discover what actually happened to your brother, after you were informed, by way of that sinister official lie, that he had been "reported missing." Well, Schnecker could have corrected that lie. There are only two people in the world who could have told you with certainty: one is Schnecker, the other is myself. I have kept silent. After reading my report you will understand why I could not come forward and tell you what actually happened.

Forgive me if I must now inform you of something that cannot be glossed over. Your brother is dead.

Actually, when I ran across Schnecker on the terrace of an outdoor café, he appeared to be in the best of spirits. He was sitting under one of those colorful umbrellas that are surrounded by planters full of big red geraniums, where customers relax in the shade as they observe the passing scene from behind their sunglasses. Schnecker was in the company of a young lady.

The young lady was pretty, her manner lighthearted and natural. On an impulse, I stepped onto the terrace, sat down at the next table so I could overhear them, and ordered some ice cream.

The shock I felt was intensified by the fact that Schnecker hadn't changed. He was a bit plumper, seemed younger rather than older, and showed those first signs of the incipient bull neck that invariably begins to manifest itself in certain better-class Germans when they reach thirty-two and are old enough to take an active part in their father's political party. After I had thanked the waiter and seated myself so as to miss nothing, I overheard Schnecker say, "And Winnie?"

"She's married, didn't you know? She's happy—deliriously happy, in fact."

Schnecker laughed. "We'll be, too," he said gently, covering the girl's hand with his own. The way she turned her large, soft, slightly stupid eyes up at him made her look as though she would melt with happiness, leaving behind some kind of sugary mess on the graceful little terrace chair.

"Cigarette?" asked Schnecker, offering her his open case. She took one, and they smoked as they applied themselves to their ice creams. Beyond the terrace, a constant stream of perspiring, thinly clad people made their way to or from the summer clearance sales. Their faces revealed a strain similar to what one used to see, only a year ago, on the trains carrying people out into the countryside to scrounge for potatoes—fear, fatigue, greed. Deeply disturbed, I toyed with my ice cream; my cigarette didn't taste good anymore.

"Come to think of it," Schnecker began again, "we have every reason to celebrate today!"

"Yes, today's a red-letter day!" said the girl.

"You're right."

"Of course I'm right! The way you got through it all! So quickly and confidently and the only one to make it with honors. But tell me"—she giggled—"are they actually going to put a doctoral cap on your head?"

"No, my dear, but listen." He paused to swallow a spoonful of ice cream. "I suggest we drive out there right away, enjoy ourselves, then change and drive to the Cosmo for a little intimate celebration, before the official stuff gets under way..."

This time she placed her hand on his.

I suddenly felt so nauseated that I had to get up and do something. I left some money on the table, far too much and more than I could possibly afford. But I just didn't care. I staggered outside and let myself drift along with the perspiring, prattling crowd until I turned off onto a quiet, rubble-strewn street that was bathed in the shadow of still-standing façades. I sat down at random on what was left of a wall. The peace of rubble is the peace of graveyards...

It is time, I think, for me to introduce myself. My name is Wenk, and I was a dispatch runner for your brother, First Lieutenant Schelling. I have already told you that he is dead. You could have found that out long ago. You needed only to enter the house of your neighbor and look closely into his eyes, those eyes that will induce such a charming, rhapsodic girl to have him father their two planned children. Oh, that sweet young thing, how she will weep when the priest joins their hands while a Bach fugue resounds from the organ, played not by the regular organist, who is much too pedestrian and inartistic, but by a specially hired musician. Don't fail to attend the wedding. Don't forget to try the cake, the wine and cigars, and make sure your mother offers appropriate congratulations and sends a gift that matches the degree of friendship. This union, from which new Schneckers will spring, must be properly celebrated. I don't know what kind of wedding presents match that degree of friendship in your circles: with us it might be an electric iron, or a punch bowl that would be used once every three years or never.

Enough of this chatter! I'm just trying to put off something I find it hard to write about because it sounds too improbable in the context of this incipiently bull-necked fledgling doctor of laws. But let me tell you: Schnecker is your brother's murderer. There it is. There you have it. And I mean it not in any figurative or allegorical sense, but baldly and simply, the way I've said it: Schnecker is your brother's murderer...

You are a young man. About twenty, I would guess. I have taken the liberty of spending a few afternoons snooping around outside your house and Schnecker's, but I'm sure you won't remember that nondescript individual standing under an elderberry tree, wearing sunglasses and smoking a cigarette, a sort of amateur detective of fate who, in return for a pension of thirty marks graciously doled out to him every month at the post office, feels obliged to render the Fatherland a small service.

Well, you're twenty, I would guess. I saw you hurrying off with your book-filled briefcase at regular hours and fancied I could read something in your expression that I can only interpret as dread of your finals. Don't worry, you'll get through all right. Don't take it too seriously. We were still priding ourselves on getting a B in geography and math when we were forced to look at men who had just been neatly shot in the stomach by a machine-gun salvo. Believe me, they all looked alike, those who had a B in Latin and those who had never heard of Latin. They looked ugly; there was nothing, absolutely nothing uplifting about them. They were all alike—Poles, Germans, and Frenchmen, heroes and cowards. That's all I can tell you. They belonged to the earth, and the earth no longer belonged to them. That's all...

But before I tell you how Schnecker killed your brother, I must introduce myself in greater detail. I'm not exactly a confidence-inspiring person. Most of my time is spent lying on the bed smoking cigarettes. The venetian blinds are kept closed, letting in just enough light for me to tell which side of the cigarette paper is gummed. Next to the bed is my chair, on it a great heap of loose yellow tobacco. I occupy myself by rolling a new cigarette when the butt between my lips has become damp and no longer draws. The tobacco makes my throat burn; I flick the butts out the window, and whenever I lean out I can see great quantities of them floating in the roof gutter—burst, yellowish objects like bloated maggots—from some of them the tobacco has seeped out and is floating in the greenish soupy liquid filling the gutter that slopes away from the drain. Sometimes, when this scum has grown too thick, I borrow the broom belonging to my landlord's cleaning woman and sweep all the sludge toward the drain, where with a low gurgling sound it disappears...

I am very seldom persuaded to undertake any kind of activity. My one great concern is how to get hold of tobacco, which I pay for by selling my books. Even this activity is strenuous enough. Fortunately, I am fairly well informed as to the value of the books, although I must say I lack the patience to insist on getting their true value. So I reluctantly drag myself off to those dingy little secondhand bookstores that smell of the decay which only piles of books produce: dry, musty, moldy. Skinny yellow hands, whose movements remind me of the silent, repulsive haste of raccoons, assess my spiritual property according to its material value. I rarely haggle, only when the offer seems unreasonably low; otherwise I merely nod and remain adamant when the usurer thrusts his pitiful face toward me as he counts out the money, hoping to persuade me at the last moment to accept less. I have resigned myself to the fact that I can no more cope with these people than I could with the war.

II

I first met Schnecker in the summer of 1943. I had been ordered to leave an interpreter unit stationed in Paris and report to a coastal division where I was once again to partake of the joys of "real" infantry service. Leaving the last railroad station behind me, I had reached a sleepy little place that seemed to consist of long, low walls surrounding lush grass. There, in the northwestern corner of Normandy, parallel to the coast, runs a strip of land that breathes the brooding isolation of heath and marsh: here and there a few tiny hamlets, some abandoned, ruined farms, shallow streams meandering sluggishly toward the swampy arms of the Somme or petering out underground.

From the station I had laboriously asked my way to battalion headquarters. There, predictably, I had been kept waiting a considerable time before being directed to one of the companies. The clerk, a corporal, suggested I wait for the mail orderly of my future unit and go along with him. But since that would have meant a four-hour wait outside this desolate château, I asked the corporal how to get there, saluted, and left.

As I was shouldering my pack in the dark corridor, an officer passed by, a tall slim fellow who, in spite of his youth, was wearing the insignia of a captain. I performed the infamous "salute by standing at attention": he looked at me as if I were made of glass and, without so much as a nod, walked on. It was Schnecker.

Only half a second had passed, but in that half second I felt all the humiliation forced upon us by the uniform. Every second I wore that uniform I hated it, but now I was so choked by disgust I actually felt a bitter taste on my tongue. I hurried after the officer, who was walking toward the orderly room, and planted myself in front of him, thus preventing him from reaching the door handle. I stood at attention again and said, "I request the captain to acknowledge my salute." My loathing filled me with voluptuous pleasure. He looked at me as if I had gone out of my mind.

"What was that?" he asked huskily.

I repeated my words in an even tone, saluted again, looked at him, saluted again.

The battle was fought only between our eyes. He was fuming, ready to tear me to pieces, but from the ends of my coolly vibrating hair right down to my toes I was filled with a crystalline hatred. He suddenly raised his hand to his cap; I stood aside, opened the door for him, and walked away.

I passed quickly through the lethargic, sleeping village, took, as directed, the third turning on the left toward the coast, and soon found myself in a completely uninhabited area. Noonday heat quivered over the meadows; the road was dusty and stony; there were occasional little groups of trees, lots of bushes, no fields that I could see. I took advantage of the little shade there was and walked on for half an hour; then I suddenly stopped, looked up, and realized that all that time I had been staring unseeingly ahead of me. I was tired and suddenly felt quite exhausted. The roadside was covered with lush grass, but just as I was about to sit down I noticed, scarcely a hundred yards away, a larger group of trees that seemed to indicate a building. In the sultry heat the cows had sought the shade of the bushes. I walked along the flagstone path and stopped outside the building: it was very dilapidated, surrounded by tangled growth. The windows were blind, and above the door was a weathered sign, almost illegible, on which I could just make out the letters "auran" of the word "Restaurant."

The door was open. I walked into a stale-smelling passageway and opened a brown door on the right. The room was empty. I put down my pack, threw cap and belt onto a chair, pulled out my big handkerchief, and began to wipe the sweat off my face as I looked around.

In taverns like this, one automatically expects a sour old witch of a woman, mustached, dirty, who can offer only some lukewarm stuff. I was very surprised when a young girl, who was not only pretty but clean, came in and greeted me briefly but without hostility with the usual "Good morning, sir."

I returned her greeting and looked at her much too long. She was very lovely. Her brown eyes were large, slightly veiled, and seemed always to look away. Her reddish-brown hair fell loosely over her shoulders and was tied above her forehead with a blue ribbon. Her hands gave off a smell of milk and udders; her fingers were still spread, slightly curled...

"What would you like?" she asked.

I wanted to say "You!" but with a gesture stopped myself and said quietly, "Something to drink; something cold perhaps."

She closed her eyes and seemed to be letting my unspoken word sink into her. Then she raised her lids again and said mockingly, "Wine or lemonade?"

"Water," I said.

"I wouldn't recommend it, sir," she said. "Our water is as foul as the Somme."

"All right," I said, "wine, then; white, if you have some."

She nodded, turned, and disappeared.

The place was furnished like most country taverns in France. It used to be customary to dismiss them as being fusty, tasteless, uninviting. True, they did contain a lot of kitsch, both old and modern, but for me every one of those taverns held something of the elusive appeal of Cézanne's cardplayers.

The girl's pale face loomed up behind the glass panel, almost like the face of a drowning person rising to the surface once more before sinking for the last time. Quickly I jumped up and opened the door for her. In her right hand she was balancing a bottle of wine and a glass, in her left a soda-water siphon. To my astonishment the siphon, which I took from her, was cool. I commented on it, and while she set down glass and bottle she explained that they always kept the siphons in the well. As she spoke she avoided looking at me and murmured, "If you need anything, just call." She was about to leave.

I said very softly, "Tell me one thing: Are you always here? Are you the owner's daughter?"

Now for the first time she turned and looked at me. I had the impression she was smiling.

"Yes," she said, "I'm always here."

"Well, then, I'd like to pay. I'll take the rest of the bottle along, if I may—who knows whether there's anything available out there?" I pointed toward the coast.

"There are some taverns there too," she said indifferently, shrugging her shoulders, "but if you like..."

She went to the counter, and it seemed to me she did so merely in order to avoid touching my hand, for in taverns like that the money isn't paid formally at a cash register but simply passes from hand to hand. She gave me my change and said coolly, "Goodbye, sir." I was alone. It was good to know that she had said: I'm always here. I sat down, stretched out my legs, ate, drank, and smoked. After finishing half the bottle, I stood up, adjusted my pack, called in the direction of the door leading to the rear, "Goodbye!" and left.

The road was uneven and tiring; there wasn't a soul in sight, just meadows with streams trickling away into them, shrubs, clumps of willows, until finally in the distance I made out a straight row of trees that seemed to indicate the coast road. I took another breather, smoked a cigarette under that dull gray sky, and then walked toward the pale, bluish silhouette of the row of trees...

III

I promise not to become too garrulous. Nothing of what I am telling you is irrelevant if you happen to be interested in your brother's fate, in the part played by Schnecker and, to some extent, in my person. I can no longer keep silent. Fear and dread have taken hold of me since I have had to cast a brief but enlightening glance behind the rosy façade of the German "restoration" and "restitution," a glance into Schnecker's face. The face of an average person.

I forgot to tell you that I don't care for the sun. There are times when I believe I hate it. If I were to worship any of the idols of ancient or primitive peoples, I would choose to join those somber-minded tribes who offer tribute to the sun as a devil rather than those who venerate it as a god. I don't hate the light—I love light shining in the darkness—but that harsh summer sun, sheer light, that is something cruel.

The highway I soon reached was flanked only on the right by a row of trees whose shadow fell on open country, a meadow covered by lush, shoulder-high grass. It was only later that I discovered that all the meadows on both sides of the road were mined; left and right, grass and flowers grew with a luxuriance I had never seen before. A few fir saplings were dotted about. For three years no hand had been able to mow or care for those meadows, and no cattle had been able to browse in them.

Somewhere up ahead I had caught sight of a building at what seemed to be an intersection in the shady forest; but that bright sunshine not only dazzled me, it induced in me an almost demoralizing physical pain. The distance seemed endless, although it couldn't have been more than three hundred yards. After five minutes I reached the building. Another tavern. Scattered about the fir forest were attractive little modern houses, and along the road some other houses. At the intersection stood a little signpost that said BLANCHÈRES. The tavern bore a newly painted sign saying BUVETTE À L'ORIENT. I stepped inside and right away, without looking around, put down my pack and began to wipe the sweat off my face again.

As I gradually came to from my exhaustion, I found myself looking into a terrible face, which was smiling at me. I am sure you don't know about those creatures that live on the other, the seldom described side of war. Our patriotic literature has no room for reality.

The broad face was heavily coated with powder, the large, pale-blue eyes were bleary, below the eyes were terrible bags. It was the Blanchères tavern's landlady. She, too, played a major role in your brother's life: she washed his laundry, which was so important to him, and she washed it thoroughly and was cheap.

"Hello, soldier," she said to me in a surprisingly deep voice. "Have a seat," she added.

"Good afternoon, madame," I said.

"Oh," she cried, "I'm not madame, I'm mademoiselle!"

"Good afternoon, mademoiselle," I said.

"What'll you have?"

I had sat down on one of the chairs near the door.

"Beer, please, if you have any."

So far I had seen only her head, and automatically assumed her to be fat. It was a shock, when she now approached me, armed with a bottle of beer and a glass, to see that she was as skinny as an old hen, frighteningly ugly.

"*Santé!*" she said, without moving away. "You're new here?"

"Yes," I said, "I'm on my way to company headquarters."

"Oh, with that heavy pack?"

"Yes."

"Then wait a bit." She looked up at an old-fashioned clock hanging over the bar. "Just wait; the orderly from over in Larnton will be here any minute." She pointed down the road that led off to the left, whereas according to my instructions I should have walked straight on for another half mile or so. "He comes at four and has a bicycle. He'll take your pack. He's a nice fellow. You're joining the infantry, aren't you?"

"Yes," I said. I was surprised at how well informed she was. I looked at the clock: it was a few minutes to four.

Her eyes were almost bursting with curiosity. The main occupation of such creatures is to collect tidbits of news. They are just as garrulous and observant as their sisters of the other kind: the devout churchgoers. She continued the conversation as promptly as a skilled journalist embarking on an interview.

"Your sergeant is a good man," she said; "the CO is a swine. You'll see. And that one down there"—she pointed, presumably to a base—"is an angel. He is," she added firmly, as if I had been about to contradict her.

"Oh?" I merely said, dryly.

"Where've you come from?" she went on with hardly a break, the curiosity in her eyes now coupled with a kind of impertinence.

"From Paris."

"Ah," she cried again in her rough voice. "Where love reigns supreme!" I said nothing.

"Almost all of them nice fellows, your company," she prattled on. "In fact, the infantry's fine anyplace. Poor and fine, that's what I always say..."

All this time my eyes had been fixed on the road, which looked to me like a haven of peace and shade. It was bordered by dense pine forests that were flecked with pale, sandy patches heralding the proximity of the dunes. On either side of the road, at irregular intervals, stood charming little houses, but it was a while before I noticed that this whole area too was marked off by mine fences and mine warnings. So that explained this graveyard silence.

"How about giving me one?" she suddenly asked, looking at my pack of cigarettes.

"Oh, excuse me!" I said.

"You're certainly generous with your tobacco—let's see what you're like in a couple of weeks!" I had said nothing although she had taken two cigarettes. "Tobacco is as scarce as hen's teeth hereabouts." To my relief I at last saw a cyclist in uniform rapidly approaching out of the shadowy depths of the avenue. He was carrying his rifle in the regulation manner, with its strap across his chest.

"Ah," she cried, "there he is! Willi!"

She stepped outside and waved to the approaching soldier, whose face I could now plainly see. He was a pale, middle-aged man; his fair mustache, narrow and sparse, looked as if it was stuck onto his upper lip. He was wearing his cap, too, like a new recruit, and there was something eager about his expression.

He dismounted, propped his bicycle outside the door, and came in.

"Hello there," he said.

"Hello," I answered.

Willi looked enviously at the girl's cigarette, then at me, climbed onto a bar stool, and asked, "Did you manage to get some more cigarettes on the black market?"

"No," she said, "I'm supposed to get some tomorrow, cheap, seven francs each."

"What about that one?"

She pointed the lighted cigarette at me. I had already fished out my pack and was offering it to Willi. He gave me a surprised look, laughed shortly, and said, "Thanks a lot—you must've come straight from home, but then they don't have that much there either..."

"No," I said, "but are you that short here?"

"I'll say we are," he said. "You'll find out. We wait every day with our tongues hanging out for our three rationed cigarettes, but they're gone in an hour, then the butts, and then another twenty-three hours' craving."

"Want a drink?" asked the girl.

"Yes, please, Cadette, a beer."

"Here's to you," he said. "To your cigarettes, buddy..."

I paid when he did, seeing that he had quickly downed his beer and wanted to be off; I stepped up to the counter beside him as he put on his cap again. "D'you think you could take my stuff along?" I asked.

Assuming a rather ponderous expression, he looked first at my pack and bag and then said, "Mind you, it's a pretty wobbly old bike, an old rattletrap, but okay"—he made a great show of squaring his shoulders—"I wouldn't let a fellow soldier kill himself for nothing. So you're joining our outfit?"

"Yes," I said, "third company."

"Right, third, that's us. Okay, let's get your stuff loaded."

Feeling very envious, I watched him sail off. Fortunately the road was shady. On the left was dense forest, starting at Cadette's house and bordering the road, and to the right side of the smooth asphalt road stood a few houses, apparently still occupied. Next to one of them some soldiers' washing was hanging on a line: shirts, underpants, and the kind of socks—gray with horizontal white stripes—that are scattered over half the world. I hurried along, for, in addition to some nervousness about my new duties, I also felt a certain curiosity. There was always something exciting about a transfer. I still hadn't caught sight of the sea, but on the map shown me by the sergeant at battalion headquarters, the dot indicating the company's orderly room had been very close to that stirring dot-and-dash line marked "Main Battle Line—High Tide Line." I was impatient to see the sea again after three years.

Five minutes later the forest came to an end. On both sides of the road, those lush meadows again, and at last, beyond a gentle rise, I saw the house beside a sandy path. It looked quite charming, like a rich man's comfortable weekend cottage. To the right of the road was another tavern, a kind of summer café built of wood with a covered veranda; in the background, more buildings; then, for the first time since noon I saw sergeants' stars again among corporals' braid—a bunch of soldiers standing around a field kitchen—and all romantic notions of a lovely summer on the Atlantic coast vanished. I saluted a few sergeants who were standing by a shed watching the food distribution, and finally I reached the orderly room.

After walking up a few steps, the first thing I saw was my pack lying on the floor. There was a pervasive, musty smell of heat and dry timbers. I heard voices, among them Willi's calling out "Here!" someplace where mail was evidently being distributed. I entered the room that had a sign saying FIELD POST OFFICE NO.—. Well, that was the number I was to see so often on the postcards I later accepted here for your brother and took to Larnton. For you too that number must be unforgettable.

After completing the ritual of saluting at the door, I immediately heard a voice speaking in a Saxonian accent. I looked in that direction and saw a first lieutenant whose curly coal-black hair was cut in a rather fancy style, and my first impression was that the little red ribbon of his Iron Cross set off his glossy hair to a T. He looked about forty, and he too had a mustache, a black one, and at the sight of that black mustache it crossed my mind how magnificently that black in turn set off the silver of his Assault Medal.

"Aha," said this person on catching sight of me, not as if he were bawling me out but rather in a reproachful, schoolmasterly tone, and indeed half an hour later I learned that he was a schoolteacher. At the same time I became aware of the not unfriendly face of a first sergeant, still young, and the impassive countenance of a clerk who looked pleasant enough.

So, "Aha," said this person, "here we have the lord and master who feels too weak to carry his pack for a distance of half a mile—right?"

With his last words he opened his eyes wide, giving them a theatrical glint, and looked at me challengingly.

"Sir!" I said, standing to attention. "I could see no point in letting my comrade ride an empty bicycle while I carried the pack that I had already lugged all the way from Crutelles."

"All the way from Crutelles!" he repeated sarcastically. The topkick burst out laughing.

"Don't laugh, Fischer," the first lieutenant snapped at him. "These goddamn intellectual bastards who've been on special assignment for years are a cheeky bunch." Then he turned to me. "So you, a Pfc, take the liberty of thinking, using your head, if I have understood you properly—hm?"

I had become so accustomed to quasi-civilian manners that I almost nodded and said, "That's right." I suppressed it and uttered the regulation "Yessir."

"I see. And weren't you taught the opposite, that you're not supposed to use your head—hm?"

"No," I replied, "in my last unit I was sometimes required to use my head."

"Well!" he said, surprised, and for a moment he looked like a boxer on the receiving end of a well-placed blow. But suddenly he bellowed,

"There'll be none of that here, d'you hear me? No more thinking, understand? No more using your head, get it?"

"Yessir," I said.

"And what's more, remember that a soldier never allows himself to
be separated from his pack." He turned his cheap, fiery gaze away from
me, toward the topkick, and asked brusquely, "Where'll we put him?"
The topkick pulled a list out of a drawer, and the first lieutenant turned
his Storm Trooper eyes back to me (I later found out that he really
had been a platoon leader with the Storm Troopers in his hometown).
"What training have you had?" he asked me. "I mean military, of course."

"Rifleman," I said, "sir, and telephone operator."

"Balls," he said furiously, "we have enough telephone operators,
never enough riflemen."

"It's Larnton's turn for replacements," said the topkick.

"Good. We'll send him to Herr Schelling. Anything else? Tomorrow's schedule is clear, ammunition to be taken to the base for live
firing. Okay?"

"Yessir," said the topkick.

I flung open the door, stood at attention, and stepped aside for the
schoolteacher. He did not deign to look my way again.

"For Chrissake!" cried the topkick when the sound of footsteps
outside had died away. "I could've hugged you when I heard you were
from the Rhineland!"

He shook my hand; I looked into his face and felt glad. He pointed
to the clerk, who was watching us with a smile.

"Schmidt," he said, "at least Schmidt's from Berlin. We do have a
few fellows from Berlin, but otherwise they're a bunch of yokels."

I handed him the envelope containing my papers, which I had
closed and sealed myself. The clerk opened it, read and sorted the
papers, the topkick asked me how things were at home, when I had last
seen Cologne, his home town, and when I'd been on leave.

Soon after that he left for supper, and I was alone with the pleasant clerk. I asked him about the general atmosphere, the daily routine,
exchanged a few mutual, skeptical observations about the war and the
company commander, and fifteen minutes later I found myself walking
back along the same road. Again I stopped by Cadette's, again I had a
beer and gave her a cigarette.

Then I walked down that avenue that had so fascinated me. I still hadn't caught sight of the sea—from the orderly room it had been hidden by the forest; besides, I had been looking at the first lieutenant's pale-gray uniform.

But it was bound to come soon now. The road ran like a narrow ribbon between the minefields, and I felt as if I were running straight into a trap. On both sides stood attractive little houses, their gardens run wild; then the road opened up, and on the left there appeared a fair-sized, completely pillaged building that looked like a school. At last I saw the pale strip of beach... There was hardly any water to be seen, the coast being so flat at that point that at low tide the sea receded for more than half a mile. In the distance—indescribably far away, it seemed—I saw a pale, broad tongue, the narrow wave of foam that the sea pushes ahead or drags behind itself, and beyond that an equally narrow strip of gray: the water. And otherwise only sand, sand, and the pale sky that was also burned gray. I felt an uprush of disappointment at having landed in a dry infinity, for when I pulled back my gaze from the distance into which it had plunged, all I saw close by, too, was sand, dunes sparsely covered with grass, and among them the ruins of houses that had obviously been dynamited—and more sand...

And nowhere was there the bunker I had expected to find. Fortunately a soldier with a rifle was standing on a dune next to a spiked barrier across the road; a concrete path led up to him. I followed it. The steel helmet and the muzzle of the rifle grew bigger and more distinct, and on reaching the top I discovered a strange little colony. It looked almost like a fishing village where the nets are hung up to dry in the evening. These were camouflage nets covering guns and barracks, and the wooden huts were part of the famous Atlantic Wall in the summer of 1943 at a strategically vulnerable point. I walked toward the sentry, and when I asked him where I could find Lieutenant Schelling, he pointed with a bored expression to a hut slightly higher up, but before I had reached it, he called after me, "By the way, it's *First* Lieutenant, bud; don't get it wrong!"

"What?" I asked.

"He's a first lieutenant—not that he cares, but that's what he is. You might as well know."

I was amazed to find a first lieutenant heading a platoon. In 1943, officers were pretty thin on the ground, and it seemed extraordinary to me that this tiny base, which could, if necessary, have been in the charge of a sergeant, should be under the command of a first lieutenant.

The first person I saw as I entered the hut was Willi. He was alone, reading a letter.

"Ah," he exclaimed, "they've sent you to us!"

"Yes."

Willi laid the letter aside, pushing it under a telephone: he had opened the window, and there was a breeze from the sea.

"Let's see," said Willi, "if the first lieutenant is available." He knocked on the door, someone called out—reluctantly, it seemed to me—"Come in!" Willi opened the door and into the darkened room announced my arrival. A croaky voice said, "Very well—show him in." I stepped inside and closed the door behind me.

The window was covered by a blanket, and I could vaguely make out a bed with a long, gray figure lying on it, a cupboard, a table, and a few unidentifiable pictures on the walls.

I felt enormously heartened by the way this man immediately stood up as I entered. That may seem trivial to you, but, believe me, when one's been a soldier in this army for many years, always having to deal with so-called superiors, one develops an infallible instinct for the forms of human relationships. If you knew how many of your friends—I need only think of my own, or take any pleasant young man who you're sure would never hurt a fly—if you knew how he used to behave toward so-called inferiors, I believe you would blush with shame on his behalf...

Your brother was the first officer I ran across in five years of whom I can claim that he moved with complete confidence on the narrow borderline of simultaneous authority and humility, as befits a superior. No doubt you're familiar with the other kind, those pipsqueak lieutenants: totally ignorant, brainless, and not even competent in their military, let alone soldierly, craft, sustained solely by the authority of their two shoulder straps and, last but not least, of their elegant boots. And you may grasp the extent of the uniform's demonic power from the fact that this huge army relied exclusively on this idiotic perversion of values, for even before 1943, the original illusory conception had proven as void and insubstantial as a wizened toy balloon lying trampled on a fairground.

Try to imagine any one of your brother's many contemporaries or classmates—leaving aside Schnecker—any one of them, I say, a nice kind man whose behavior is invariably decent and blameless, and I tell you: in the barracks he's a swine! And that army carted its barracks all across Europe...

That's how X and Y were: X, who today stifles his bitterness over his temporarily obsolete career with American cigarettes and vague political aspirations, meanwhile getting together regularly with his former comrades to reminisce about how they used to "show them a thing or two"; and Y, who is grimly preparing himself to become a district attorney or a high-school teacher—either of which occupations offers enough scope for bullying creatures even more defenseless than soldiers: children and the poor.

IV

Your brother, as I said, got up from his bed for me. I need hardly describe him to you: tall and slim, with a slight stoop at that time, his blue eyes full of sadness, his uniform bare of any decorations. He was about my age, twenty-five or -six, and, although it may seem ridiculous to you, a first lieutenant's star on that figure seemed to me fraught with ominous significance. A first lieutenant on that tiny base in the dunes, with a garrison of twenty-five men, the commander of a bastion which at that stage of the war could well have been entrusted to a sergeant: there must be some story behind that.

He repeated my name in his rather husky voice.

"You will remain here," he said after looking me briefly in the eyes. "I need an orderly; my present one is going on leave tomorrow. Do you understand?"

"Yessir," I said.

"Good. Please have yourself briefed. You will share telephone duty with the stretcher bearer. In addition, you will be required to make two bicycle trips a day to company headquarters. And then"—he was silent for a moment and looked at me again—"you will have noticed on the way here that we are in a mousetrap, and no one is allowed to leave it other than on duty without my knowledge. There's no such thing as time off. Do you understand?"

"Yessir," I said.

"Good. Please have the orderly explain all practical matters to you."

His eyes met mine again. I took this for a silent dismissal, saluted, and left.

On this front of the Atlantic coast, my dear sir, a very special kind of warfare was being carried on, the war against boredom. Try to imagine a front extending from Norway to the Bay of Biscay and facing no opponent other than the sea. And this front was equipped like any other where each day saw wounded and dead, men screaming and dying, men horrifyingly mute. But here everything was completely frozen. Night after night, thousands of soldiers stood on guard waiting for an enemy who never came and whose coming some of them positively craved. Year after year, night after night, thousands stood there facing the sea, that monster which is eternally the same, eternally the same, comes and goes, comes and goes, is always smiling, always smiling with a serenity fit to induce a man to plunge headlong into it. An eternal smile; the sea, even when storm-tossed, always had something like laughter about it, wild laughter devoid of mockery, but still laughter. The sea was laughing at us, that was it. There stood the guns, mortars, machine guns; rifles by the hundred thousand lay there on parapets or were lugged back and forth by plodding sentries. Nothing. Year after year the same. Every evening a password to be memorized plus the various flare signals, hand grenades placed in readiness—hand grenades against the sea! During the day, instruction in the use of guns, mortars, machine guns, and other weapons, and drill on the road behind the dunes, year after year. Year after year. During the day, almost eight hours' duty, and at night at least four hours' sentry duty. The never-ending battle against the sand that relentlessly penetrated the farthest, most inaccessible crack of every weapon and never failed to be discovered by some bored corporal's eye. And somewhere beyond the horizon, far, far, incredibly far away, there was an enemy in whom it was impossible to believe—far, far away, an enemy from whom the sea seemed to have learned its laughter. All that lay like a pall of apathy over even the most idyllic little bays, driving us to drink.

Some of the men had been at it since 1940. But even those who had known it only for a few months were beginning to show signs of despair. Despair is the hope of the flesh, my dear sir. There is a kind of despair that, even if it exists only in the mind, is a wild, sensual pleasure. Despair has something of the substance of a movie. One drinks it, it is sweet, sweet, so sweet that one wants to drink up a whole sea of it, but the more one drinks the thirstier one becomes, the more convinced that this thirst is unquenchable, that perhaps here on earth one is already in hell, for hell might somehow be that perpetual thirst. Despair is terrible, despair is the hope of the flesh, and one might feel tempted to pray: Lead us not into despair.

Even a person like your brother, who was always assured of the consolations of his faith, whose strength was such that he could have spent his whole life walking along a knife edge, ultimately to leap from its utmost point into eternal bliss—even a person like your brother was feeling the gnawings of this despair when I arrived. During the first few days I was there, I observed in the melancholy expression of his eyes a vague something that almost reminded me of a person about to go berserk. Often, while he was on the phone talking to that schoolmaster, there was a quiver in his voice as if he were at breaking point, about to cry out: Nitwit, nitwit, nitwit! Incorrigible nitwit!

Well, I was as weak as he was strong. And I was no longer accustomed to any kind of hardship. I had brought off the seemingly impossible: in the uniform of an ordinary soldier I had managed to lead a life to my own liking. My firsthand experience of the war dated from 1940, when I had felt the urge for closer acquaintance after spending two years in barracks undergoing training as an infantryman. After those six weeks of campaign, I had had enough of war. Dust and dirt and heat, permanently painful, burning feet, blood, and a lot of hysteria, and, to crown it all, the worst part: helping those repulsive banners of the Nazis to invade the garden that was France. Not for me. Just four days before the Armistice I was wounded in southern France, on the border of Burgundy. I recovered, hung around for months in a military hospital, and, by bluffing a bit with my school French, contrived to have myself transferred to Paris. In those days a wounded soldier was still a hero.

Having succeeded in getting to Paris, I made the most of my illness in order, as we used to say, to maintain the position.

To some extent I had been looking forward to this new tour of duty on the coast, the way one always starts out looking forward to something new. But after a few days I was on the brink of despair.

The futility was appalling. There stood the men every morning with their machine guns or mortars, drilling, drilling, in the sand dunes, practicing the movements they had ceased to master because they had been practicing them for too long. They were personally acquainted with almost every grain of sand. And every morning the same, every night the same, and always only the one enemy, the sea; all around them, minefields, empty buildings. And not even enough to eat. Not even enough to eat to keep up their strength. Food is an essential part of war. Every sensible officer knows that. The waging of war knows no romanticism; there is no place anywhere for so-called ideas or emotions. A soldier who is permanently hungry is capable of the worst, and he is fully justified in obtaining whatever food he can. The rations were simply ridiculous, my dear sir. I know you aren't aware of that. How often have I carried postcards from the men that said, "Alive and well, thanks for the parcel. Heinrich."

Picture, if you can, a man who spends eight hours a day on duty plus four hours a night on sentry duty, living on a pound of bread, two spoonfuls of jam, an ounce of margarine and, at midday, a quart of soup made from water and cauliflower in which, for a hundred and fifty men, a quarter of a skeleton of a scrawny cow has been boiled after being stripped by the mess cook of its last vestiges of meat and fat. Maybe you think that's a lot. It's nothing when a man is fighting boredom.

Well, we found ways to help ourselves. We kept back ammunition and exchanged it for bread with overfed marines and gunners who could find the time to go rabbit-hunting. In that area the navy had its own farms, and at night, whenever we were off duty, we would sneak out onto the potato fields, eluding the sentries who were guarding the crops with cocked rifles, and in the darkness we would grub around in the soil, like wild boar, to fill up our sacks. And don't believe we had any romantic notions about exposing ourselves to the risk of being shot at, for the sentries did fire whenever they caught sight of us.

So you can add hunger to boredom, and just remember that your brother fought for three years on this front.

On the morning of the third day, as I awoke, the stale air fell like lead into my lungs. The room was full of smoke; the stretcher bearer had, as always, fallen asleep at the phone, his stupid head lying in a flattened tin can that we used for an ashtray. Naturally, as the latest arrival, I occupied the less desirable of the two bunks, the upper one, and, not yet used to the low ceiling, I would absent-mindedly sit up every morning and bump my head painfully against the ceiling. I looked at my watch: it was six-thirty. So once again he was an hour late for his wake-up duty.

The soldiers were stubborn, fighting tooth and nail for every minute of sleep. And they had every right, for they never had a single night of unbroken sleep, and what can be more ghastly than to be wrenched night after night out of profound sleep?

The night sentries were allowed to go off duty at 6:00 a.m., unless it happened to be high tide, which always meant an intensified state of alert. If they wanted, they could grab some extra sleep until seven-thirty before getting ready to go on duty again. In order not to leave the coast totally unguarded during the next two hours, a single so-called day sentry was posted for the entire base. This sentry had to stand on higher ground, was equipped with an alarm signal, and had to leave his post at 8:00 a.m. to take part in the day's regular duties. It was the orderly's job to wake that sentry. And you can take my word for it that not a single one of the night sentries, even if he happened to be lying in the bunk next to the day sentry, would have lifted a finger to wake him. It was the orderly's job, and if the orderly failed to do so, too bad: then the base was left unguarded, and the Tommies or the Yanks could come if they ever had a mind to do so.

So the base was left unguarded. During the first three days I took all this fairly seriously. I really did think the British were coming, and when I woke up in the morning around that hour—which was unquestionably the most favorable for a potential attack—I had a vision of landing barges gliding silently up onto the beach, their troops leaping from the bow ... and Hurrah!

So I jumped up, poked the stretcher bearer in the ribs, and said, "Get up, you have to wake the sentry!"

That stretcher bearer was one of the stupidest fellows I have ever met. He was middle-aged, forty-two years old, with crinkly hair and a thick, impenetrable skull and tiny, drink-sodden eyes. He was almost always asleep, and not only could he hardly write German—in his mouth even the spoken language became a very limited means of communication.

"Ah," he said, rubbing his eyes, "I sleeping, I goddamn sleeping, first time happen."

"Okay," I said, "first time happen, but get going now, it's time." He fumbled for a slip of paper lying under the telephone, held it up close to his eyes, and silently committed the name to memory. Then he put on his cap to leave, but I knew that he often woke up the wrong man— more than once we had barely saved him from being beaten up by his victim—so I took the slip and repeated aloud, "Pellerig, Bunker 4, first bunk left of the door, lower."

"What?" He heaved himself around. "I thinking Brunswick."

"No," I said. "Brunswick has to go to the orderly room, he's going on leave."

"Okay." He left.

I lit a cigarette, ran my fingers through my hair, and stepped out the door. It was wonderful outside. A cool, gentle wind came from the sea, whose foamy, lapping tongue had halted quite close to our hut, at the foot of a sand dune. It was high tide, the water was blue-gray, and there was a genuine smell of the sea. I stared at that endless surface, that grandiose plain of water, watched the seagulls, and shielded my eyes with my hand so as to savor the solitude. Perhaps I could make out a coast-guard vessel; it was always a pleasure to see the ocean enlivened by some rare vessel. The weather was overcast, the sun, behind me, lay wrapped up in a thick gray cloud. To the north, the view was hidden by the same pine forest that stretched from Cadette's tavern all the way to the coast. I had been told that one could see the mouth of the Somme by walking to the edge of the forest. I decided to give it a try that afternoon during a free half hour. So somewhere to the northwest was England ... one could sail across the sea, and suddenly an island would appear—England...

I kept my eye on Kandick, the stretcher bearer, and made sure he went into the correct bunker. Everything was silent; soft vaporous banks of morning fog lay above the dunes and huts. It was the only truly peaceful hour of the day here.

Suddenly a voice behind me said, "Good morning." I turned, stood at attention, and saluted.

Your brother made a wry face. "Let's not have any of that, please." I had been embarrassed too, but somehow or other I had to respond to his greeting, and I had already spent too long in the prison of my uniform to allow myself the liberty of a simple "Good morning," as one summer visitor to another. He noticed my embarrassment. "I know, that's what you were taught. But it's not appropriate here, and there's no need, is there? If you like, you can say 'Good morning' to me. I'd be sorry if I'd offended you, but I think we understand each other..."

I looked aside. "The point is," he went on, "I know that you find it repugnant—so do I."

He took out a cigarette and lit it from mine, then sat down on a little bench outside the entrance to our bunker. Those first minutes in the morning, when one stepped outside, saw the sea, felt the wind and the glorious air, when everything was still silent—those first minutes were beautiful. But the specter of daily duty was too real, too deeply ingrained in our memory, for us to be able to linger over our pleasure. Monotony is the most effective weapon of modern warfare.

"You know," he began again, "I'm told there are parents who greet their sleepy children in the morning with a snappy '*Heil Hitler.*' There really are such people, just imagine." His expression was somber. "Can you imagine anything more sickening?"

As I already told you, my despair had become greater after three days than that of your brother after three years. I am a weak person, I had no prop, no religion, only a very vague, ephemeral dream of a certain beauty and order. And yet on that particular morning we two were, I believe, on the same level with our despair. For three years he had swum alone against that sluggish tide of monotony and horror, I had leaped into that mire only three days before, and, filled with the same fear, we were both struggling against being swallowed up by it. We were each like a swimmer who, believing himself alone and lost in a vast body of water, suddenly looks around and finds someone at his side.

I looked at him. That remark about the Hitler salute was so daring that it put him completely at my mercy, at a time when one could be sentenced to death for even dreaming about lèse-majesté.

I said, "Sir, I believe we share the same opinion."

At that moment, Kandick's thick skull surfaced above the edge of the dune.

Your brother stood up to return to his hut because he wished to avoid rebuking Kandick for the five hundredth time for oversleeping.

I felt happy.

Until that evening we had no further conversation. I took over the phone while he and Kandick went on duty. That meant he went from one emplacement to the next, attended drill, while Kandick, on the alert for any possible injury during weapons practice, slept near the latrine—a portable outhouse standing somewhat higher up.

At 11:00 a.m. Kandick relieved me again; I had to go to company headquarters before they went off duty. In Pochelet—the hamlet where the orderly room was—I was handed instructions to go to battalion headquarters, where I was to be interrogated by a judicial officer about an incident that had taken place while I was still in Paris. I gulped down my meal in order to reach Crutelles punctually by twelve-thirty. Fortunately the sun wasn't shining. While pedaling at top speed past that lonely tavern, I cast a desperate glance into the empty garden.

The interrogation took place in a small room at battalion headquarters, conducted by a bilious second lieutenant who was a law graduate and due to be promoted to lieutenant in our regiment.

I had to watch my step very closely. I was supposed to give evidence about a comrade at my Paris headquarters who, as transpired during the liquidation of the unit, had for years been trading in blank forms for French identity documents. How much money had he spent, how many women had he had, and what purchases had he made; had anything aroused my suspicions? In answering all these questions with a quaking conscience, I tried to spare the accused as much as possible, feigning ignorance. Actually I was in extreme danger myself. I too had forged documents in order to acquire cigarettes; I had placed horse-racing bets and won, and in dingy bars I had exchanged German money for French.

For almost an hour he squeezed me from every angle, but each time I sidestepped skillfully into the inviolable naïveté of a simple mind, with the result that he got nothing out of me. He had to let me go.

"Damn it," he muttered through his teeth, "it's like wading through mud; you just don't get anywhere."

I rode back very slowly; by this time it was almost two o'clock.

Three days earlier I had come past that tavern at almost the same hour. I dismounted, threw the bike against the house wall, and tried the door. It was locked.

I was aghast. Hadn't she said "I'm always here"?

But, then, what does "always" mean? What do all those words mean that we utter so thoughtlessly? I rattled the doorknob, shouted—no response. I walked around the house, climbed over a small locked gate into the yard, rattled all the doorknobs, walked into the stable, stared into the calm eyes of the cows. I called and called—there was no one about. I climbed back over the gate, walked around the entire property, but there was nothing to be seen except for those sweltering meadows with their reed-choked rivulets ... a few sleepy cows ... not a living soul...

When would I have another chance to get out of the mousetrap? When would circumstances ever be so favorable again? Already I was making plans to sneak off at night or to invent stories that would justify another trip to battalion headquarters. My God, I simply *had* to see her!

In a fit of jealousy, I hated every stone of that bumpy courtyard where, within half an hour, her feet might be treading again; full of jealousy I hated the doorknobs she would touch with her hands that smelled of milk. I hated the whole house, and that fierce hatred was almost identical with the hope of seeing her again. The hope of the flesh is despair.

While I desperately pedaled off on my bicycle, I concocted an infallible plan for seeing her again. Our plans are always infallible. I would report sick; then I would have to go to battalion headquarters, and once I was in Crutelles, there would be nothing to stop me from seeing her again.

But there was something else in store for me.

V

I began by deciding to get drunk at Cadette's.

Just as the ultima ratio of the Christian is prayer, so my last resort was drink.

Any kind of narcotic holds an irresistible attraction for me. Maybe I should have become a chemist, providing mankind with new drugs of oblivion, though I know I'd never have had the will power to study the subject in depth and face possible failures in my experiments; I am not only weak, I am also impatient. Everything has to happen immediately: I couldn't wait to see that girl and put my arms around her...

Every soldier demands the solace of instant forgetfulness. Let this be your explanation for the apparently inexplicable and, for civilians, shockingly direct link between soldiers and prostitutes. The prostitute supplies instant gratification.

Every soldier permanently faces death, swaying on a gently teetering or perilously bouncing springboard that is ready to hurl him off.

While I was cycling back, the certainty that I would never see her again filled me with true despair. Never again to see that pale face, never again those compelling eyes and that darkly gleaming auburn hair above the pale-olive skin...

I decided to get drunk at Cadette's.

A soldier's goodbye is always, as it were, a goodbye forever. Think of that massive, insane load of pain hauled across Europe by those leave trains! Oh, if only those filthy corridors could speak, those grimy windowpanes scream! If only those railroad stations, those ghastly railroad stations—if only they would at last cry out with the pain and despair they have seen! There would be no more war. But with twenty pails of whitewash one of those terrible railroad halls has been restored to a forum for cheerful idiots: six brushes and a few raptly whistling painters on scaffolding, and life goes on. Life goes on. People go on living because of their weak memory. They walk through the same barrier through which they once passed full of the fear of death; but today, only a few years later, they are laughing, on their way to help in the erection of some Potemkin façade.

Oh, if only the fallen could speak, those who were hauled away in some train or other to their death, their faces gray and sad, their pockets full of jam sandwiches. If the dead could speak, there would be no more war. But look at me: the only survivors are the glib ones, those who weaseled their way through, who were smart; there wasn't a trap in Europe that could catch them.

Oh, if only there were nothing but infantrymen, all that shouting about war or no war would be superfluous. There would be no more war. All those surviving heroes, those specialists for whom war was a game, a game that had the attraction of being a little bit risky: all those glib ones praise war and, in the boredom of their bourgeois monotony, long for the "good old days." ...Oh, if only there were nothing but infantrymen! There used to be no need to spell out that war was despicable. Everyone knew it was gruesome, a pestilence, a horror. Just take a look today at those sentimental idiots stretching out their fancy little boots under the desks in their boring offices.

Oh, to get drunk, drunk ...

I finished two bottles before that terrible mollusk face behind the bar ceased to disgust me. Only then did my loosened tongue give me the courage to tell her straight out that even her sweetest of sweet smiles would not seduce me. She confined herself to bringing me more bottles, carefully sorting out my butts, and sometimes throwing in a good-natured word of comfort that I couldn't take amiss.

I daresay you don't know that strange feeling of sitting on a bar stool and realizing one's consciousness is gradually growing confused. There one sits, without moving, staring into space, yet filled with adventurous life. This vibrating immobility of the drunk can only be compared to the contained confidence of a tightrope walker, swinging high up between two towers in infinity. If one were to see that man only as far down as his feet, one would think, What a cautious fellow, how slowly and cautiously he is walking! Yet in reality the man on the tightrope is being quite *un*-cautious.

The secret of blissful drunkenness is a balanced imbalance.

Take this paradox any way you like. One pours wine into one's mouth, feels it pass the critical gateway of the palate, and at first everything flows into a silent underground reservoir that must be filled—until suddenly a kind of barometer starts to rise. Invisibly and quite involuntarily, something takes shape that resembles a U-shaped tube connecting the mind to the body; happiness and well-being increase as the levels of both sides of the tube approach each other. Body and mind are brought into balance—it is a constant interplay—like tightrope walking ... an exquisite test of one's own equilibrium. Incredibly clear insights transfix one but leave nothing behind. How sad! But no doubt their lack of substance corresponds to their indeterminate origin.

I was also perfectly aware that Cadette was cheating me (all publicans live off drunks). Several times, after wiping away the figure indicating the bottles I had consumed, she wrote down a higher one. I said nothing. Part of that condition is a sublime sense of total indifference to material things. There is no doubt that love and drunkenness, even under the most sordid circumstances, have something sublime about them even in their final stages. So I let Cadette do as she pleased, partly because of that indifference but also from inertia. I couldn't be bothered to open my mouth merely to start a conversation, let alone an argument, with that repulsive mask. She watched me tensely, like a spider lying in wait for the fly's last drop of blood...

Later one never remembers how one got home. Yet, with that deadly accuracy known only to the drunk, one has taken the safest and most direct route back.

Naturally the body has its revenge by allowing the barometer of well-being to drop far below zero. Four hours of sleep would have been enough for me, but Kandick was nothing if not petty. I had telephone duty, and I had to sit it out, even though he spent the next two hours slumped beside me. There he sat, laboriously scrawling a letter to his wife, now and then giving me a gloating poke in the ribs. Those fellows see to it that regulations are complied with!

Your brother had gone off to a staff meeting. He did not return, as I later found out, until almost eight o'clock, by which time I was asleep and Kandick had gone to bed. Your brother then sat beside me from eight until nearly midnight. I slept like a dead man; not even the shrill ringing of the phone right beside my ear wakened me. Sleep after wine is almost as delicious as the wine itself: that sinking into a blue well, into bottomless depths, with a wistful fear in one's heart, until one has sunk all the way down into a sediment of dark semiconsciousness. The man drunk on wine unconsciously performs strange embryonic gestures in his sleep; it is like a thrusting against the womb, and the awakening is like a birth: pain coupled with bliss ... I seemed to be clinging firmly to something, something that I wanted to pull toward me, but now it was pulling me. When I awoke, I found myself looking into your brother's smiling face and holding one of his tunic buttons in my hand.

Well, of course it was embarrassing; I didn't know where to look. But he caught my eye and asked, "Is your head reasonably clear?"

"Completely," I said, and it really was.

He stood up and looked over to the bunk where Kandick was

sleeping, gently snoring. Sitting down again, he began in a low voice, "Listen, I implore you: don't drink! If you start drinking, you'll be done for. If after only three days you need this phony, short-lived consolation, you'll be finished in a month. Find your consolation in staying sober, I beg you." He fell silent. Because of the blackout, the window had to be kept closed, the door too; the air smelled stale. An uncanny silence hung heavily over the room. I stood up, turned off the light without asking, and opened door and window: a breath of mild, cool air came in, free and fresh.

"Hell," he continued, "I hate lecturing anyone. It reeks of moralism, and, no matter what, there's always that holier-than-thou echo: I'm different—me, *I'm* not like that—look at me! I implore you, come to your senses." Then he suddenly asked, his tone vehement and brusque, "What are you looking for in booze?" Startled, I had to search for words, and the only thing I could think of was the threadbare platitude, "Oblivion and happiness."

"Happiness?" he repeated. "Happiness? We weren't born to be happy. We were born to suffer, and to know why we suffer. Our suffering is the only thing we will have to show for our lives. Good deeds can be performed only by a few saints, not by us ... and as for prayer ... perhaps you don't understand that—or perhaps better than I ... do you?" I was silent. Something prevented me from telling him about the girl; besides, this was my first experience of such melodramatic statements, and I was taken aback. I could only long for dawn never to come again.

"And if you can't understand that we weren't born to be happy, you will at least understand that we weren't born to forget. Oblivion and happiness! We were born to remember. Not to forget but to remember—that's what we're here for."

He spoke in a very low voice, but rarely have words had such an unforgettable impact on me. Kandick was asleep; outside in the dark the tide was rolling back, down the barely perceptible slope of the beach.

I couldn't think of any reply.

"You won't drop off again now, will you?" he finally asked quietly.

"I won't," I said.

"Good night."

"Good night."

He stood up, cautiously opened the door to his room, and I was alone. Quietly and steadily the tide rolled back, quietly and imperturbably Kandick went on snoring.

My first thought, after your brother had closed the door behind him, was: I will see her again! I can't forget that...

Every awakening was terrible, sir. Any consolation one imagined to have been gained the previous night had dissolved in the light of day, and none of the ocean's beauty, no freshness of wind or quiet gurgling of water, was of any help.

Several days passed in a strange, uneasy calm. I performed my duties methodically, and time went on like an unchanging ribbon drawn across a turbulent background. Whenever I was on telephone duty in the evening, your brother would sit beside me. Kandick had started operating a canteen in the cellar of a dynamited house behind the dunes.

In our conversations we never mentioned a name, never identified by name or title an institution or person of that foundering Reich. We played games with the language, we were like two kids playing ball, bouncing it—depending on energy or mood—fourteen times or seven times against the wall and, the moment we felt our strength giving out, quickly returning the ball to our playmate.

"Any person," your brother might say, "who is incapable of recognizing his own inadequacy is a nincompoop and essentially stupid. A vain genius is no longer a genius. Anyone who isn't aware that he is part of an unknown plan is stupid. There is no such thing as a stupid genius—ergo, he's no longer a genius. Which only leaves the inglorious possibility of being a genius of stupidity—or of crime. Do you follow me?"

"I do," I said, "and think of a blockhead who considers himself a genius, and every day he is confirmed in this by the hoarse roaring of the crowds—say, eighty million—confirming that he is a genius, and a universal genius at that—artist, statesman, strategist—all to an unprecedented degree. Every day they roar that at him. He is perfection personified. Anyone attempting to claim, for instance, 'I am like X,' would be avenged more drastically than if he were to say, 'I am like God.' Don't you agree?"

"Of course. To demand that such a person come to his senses is almost impossible. But how to render him harmless?"

"There's only one way," I said. "He must be assassinated." ·

"Okay. Assassinated. But then come the problems. How to get at him, what route to choose? You see..."

For several days that was how we discussed all the institutions of that damnable regime, reducing them to zero, blowing them up like soap bubbles, letting them collapse again, then gathering up all that was left to have a good look at whatever remained of substance.

In this way a few days passed quickly enough. One evening about five I had, as usual, ridden off to company headquarters. It was always a relief to get out of the mousetrap. I cycled slowly along that wonderful avenue leading from the beach, between the mined houses, past Cadette's tavern and onto the highway. I was always glad to see people—women, civilians. My God, the pleasure the sight of a woman can give a soldier when he spends all his time with men, with men only, their smell, their garrulousness, their dirt, all their dry gruffness. I always looked forward to those trips. And how lucky I was compared to all those others who, if they were lucky, were allowed to leave the base once a month. Of course, escapes were dreamed up with a recklessness explicable only by a desperate longing for the world— secret paths through the minefields, sudden desertion of one's post, but for most of them that world existed only in Cadette's dubious consolations.

So I always took my time, maybe stopping for a beer or a glass of wine on the way, picking up mail and passwords in the orderly room, and pedaling back just as leisurely.

By now it was September; the heat hadn't abated very much. In the evenings it lay like sultry clouds on the sandy patches among the pine groves. A hot, stifling monotony pervaded the huts, most of them wooden barracks that soaked up the heat.

That day the company commander was in a good mood. Normally he would keep pestering me about petty details: the shine on my boots or belt, the cleanliness of my bicycle. That he was in a good mood was something I noticed as soon as I came in. His eyes were shining. I was soon to learn the cause. Beautifully shaven, tanned, he was wearing a light summer tunic and carelessly flapping his cap at the flies drumming

on the windowpanes of the orderly room. The topkick seemed ill at
ease; the orderly was wearing his expression of Olympian indifference.
That fellow Schmidt could express everything by way of indifference:
contempt, friendship, pleasure, hatred.

"I leave it to you, Fischer my friend, to see how you manage it. In
any event, it's time something was done to improve the company's food
supplies. The ground has been laid, the practical details are up to you.
Heil Hitler! I'm looking forward to that roast!"

As he walked past me, I flung open the door and stood at attention.
Before leaving the room, he paused and said to me, "I'm very satisfied with you—a pleasant surprise, I must say!" I almost bowed before
that handsome schoolmaster. He stalked out: a fine figure of a man,
endowed with everything—good looks, a splendid physique, and all the
decorations appropriate to evening wear neatly displayed on his chest.

"Goddamn it," exclaimed the topkick, throwing down his pen.
"When he smells food there's no holding him."

The orderly laughed. "He says the calf's brain is for him, he's been
hoping for some for quite a while."

"I'd rather see the brain of an old sow in his belly," cried the topkick. Then he looked at me and, his eyes lighting up, exclaimed, "Say!
You can speak French, can't you?"

"Yes," I said.

"Can you handle cattle?"

"No."

He laughed. "Never mind. Listen: tonight at 0200 hours we're
supposed to fetch a cow from a farmer two miles from here—d'you
think you can manage that?"

I shrugged. "If I can have a horse and cart, some money, and two
men to help."

"Done!" cried the topkick. "And the next Cross of Merit to be
handed out in this bunch is yours."

He took the map out of the drawer; I bent over his desk and asked
him to show me the place. It was a tiny hamlet, two miles northeast,
toward the Somme. I was to meet the cart at the crossroads at 0200
hours, but I was also to ride over there this evening to give the farmer
exact instructions. I was delighted with the assignment. Any opportunity to taste a little unscheduled freedom was more than welcome.

Besides, I thought it might lead me to a cheap source of butter, for Cadette charged exorbitant prices for everything, and my money was slowly running out.

VI

Your brother was also in very good spirits that evening. During the briefing he had hinted that there was shortly to be some addition to the rations. As we went back to the bunker, I asked him, "So you know about it?" I imagined he had been referring to the scheme to buy a cow.

"No," he said in surprise. I explained my assignment. He was delighted. "Why, that's terrific! Then you'll have no trouble carrying out my plan at the same time. I was thinking of buying a sheep for our base."

I had planned to leave as soon as possible, but first there was a meeting I had to attend. We had come to the conclusion that, by extending the sentry's shift by only half an hour every night, we could ensure that each man on the base would get one night of unbroken sleep at least once every two weeks. With a garrison of twenty-eight men, this amounted to a gain of fourteen hours' extra sleep per day: i.e., for each man one night without sentry duty. I had volunteered to draw up the schedule; since we had to note down the individual sentries at each strongpoint every night in a sentry log, we were familiar with the technique of devising a sentry schedule. A meeting of all the NCOs— three corporals and a lance corporal—had been called. They brought along the results of a poll taken among their men: the plan had been rejected—the men suspected duplicity. In particular, a certain Töpfer, one of the older soldiers in the lance corporal's group, had asked what would happen if someone were suddenly transferred: if he had been doing his extra half hour for a number of days, who was going to make up for his lost sleep to him?

Your brother listened calmly, then shrugged his shoulders. "Obviously I can't force anybody. But try to explain to the men that, no matter what, *we* wouldn't benefit at all. Maybe then they'll agree." He looked at each of the four in turn. "Oh well, perhaps the men are right. Sentry duty is as ancient as playing soldiers, and sentry hours are just as ancient. And you can be sure that if it were possible to demand more from a soldier under normal circumstances, it would be demanded. Still, it might be worth a try." He paused for a moment, then said, "Okay, nothing doing, gentlemen. That'll be all. And you, Nolte," he said, turning to the youngest corporal, "please have the gap in the mine fence repaired this evening, preferably with old wire so it won't show, right?"

Nolte blushed; we all saluted and left.

I followed your brother into his room. He opened the window, beckoned me to his side, and pointed toward the south, where the beach was mined down to the high-tide line—a broad stretch of coast reaching as far as the next company's sector. A wonderful, still intact children's summer camp was located there in a dense minefield close to the beach. Perhaps there had been a reluctance to blow it up because it was such a valuable piece of property. I looked in that direction but was taken aback by his question: "Haven't you noticed anything about the outgoing mail the last couple of days?"

"Yes," I said in surprise. "It contained a tremendous number of small parcels."

"Right!" he went on with a laugh. "All unawares, you have been transporting, bit by bit, that children's summer camp to Dresden, Leipzig, Glauchau, and Schneiwitzenmühl or wherever. That's right!" he said, in response to my look of amazement. "For the last few days Nolte's group has been systematically looting over there during their off-duty hours. Now Frieger's group has got into the act, and soon there's going to be a glorious free-for-all, and today or tomorrow the entire base will be sneaking through the dunes on stocking feet to make sure they're not being done out of their share."

"For God's sake!" I cried. "What about the mines?"

"That's the least of their worries; there's no danger there, although they might bump into each other. But Nolte, that ingenious fellow, has ferreted out a sapper corporal from the regiment at Geneu, a man who originally helped lay the mines, so they have an accurate chart. Besides, mines that have had three years to rust through aren't that dangerous anymore. I only hope Nolte got the hint. Shortly before you arrived here, one of my corporals was court-martialed for snipping through mine fences with a wire cutter: the cows smelled the high, lush grass and, naturally, in they went. Result: two badly injured cows that had to be slaughtered on the spot." He gave another laugh. "Let's hope Nolte is sensible—I'd find it very difficult to report anything. The embarrassing thing is, you see, that I have nothing against looting."

He lit a cigarette, then slowly and happily blew the smoke out through the window; he seemed altogether very cheerful and relaxed that evening. "Listen," he said. "The way I feel, it's simply part of a soldier's job. You can't expect a soldier to behave like a chaplain on a summer vacation. Every occupation has its game rules. These laborers, shoemakers, electricians, they've been turned into soldiers, these good men have been made ferocious, proud, after having first been tamed. See what I mean?"

I saw nothing.

"Okay, then, let me explain. We stick these good men into uniform and destroy what the Prussians like to call gutlessness: a sense of human dignity and the glorious freedom of a civilian. Okay. So much for that. The barracks have—it is assumed—fulfilled their objective. Then the men are sent out to kill or get killed, and this activity makes them a bit wild—even here, where there's no killing. And especially when these heroes don't get enough to eat. But then they are confronted with regulations that demand more tameness from them than from a civilian, more respectability, dignity, self-sacrifice than they have ever in their lives possessed. They are forbidden to loot while at the same time they are allowed to go hungry. There you have a typical German incongruity. They rant and rave in their speeches, they want to reform the world, they call that 'revolution,' yet they're so scared for their good reputation that they wet their pants when a few soldiers happen to smash some windowpanes and grab a sausage or a couple of shirts. Do you follow me?"

I could only nod, astonished at this new, reckless frankness.

"On we go, then!" he exclaimed. "I can't wait to get this off my chest. All right, you can't have a slaughterhouse without a lot of blood, and a person who can't stand that should stop eating meat. And looting is, in my opinion, the inalienable right of every soldier. The point is not that looting should be prohibited but that we shouldn't turn these men into soldiers. The whole idiotic nonsense begins with the ill-conceived, romantic notion of a 'people's army.' Damn it all, soldiering is a profession, and it can be learned. And if they are forced—and they *are* all forced, all these good men—we shouldn't be surprised if maybe they do turn into soldiers. Well," he said as he walked over to his bed, "I hope you take my hints to heart and manage the job in such a way that I don't see anything. Now, off you go, and don't forget that sheep."

I left and got onto my bike.

The map given me by the topkick proved reliable. Beyond the crossing that led to the orderly room, I had to continue straight ahead for some distance and then make a right turn. Here some of the paths were already dangerous. They led past swampy patches sweltering away in the heat, saturated with silence. Twice I crossed a little stream, and after five minutes' pedaling I admit I felt a certain uneasiness at not having seen the slightest sign of human habitation. But immediately after passing a clump of trees I saw a solitary house. The way I read the map, that must be the spot marked "Daval." Almost every farmhouse in the world is entered from the rear, and as I turned into the yard I saw a very peaceful scene: a dark-haired woman sitting with a basket in front of her, shelling peas, a youth of about fourteen helping her, and the farmer sitting beside them smoking his pipe. I had interrupted their chat. Their laughter died away when I silently rounded the corner and stopped on the sandy ground. The woman let out a little scream; the man turned toward me without a word, and the youth looked curiously at the insignia on my sleeve.

"Good evening," I said. "Excuse me, but is this Daval?"

They exchanged glances. I had the impression they were expecting a confiscation or something of the kind, so I said, "I have to get to Tulby."

"Over there," said the man, pointing his pipe in an easterly direction.

"Is this Daval, then?"

"Yes," he said curtly.

"Do you know Monsieur Preter?"

"Yes," came the curt reply again, "he's her uncle." He pointed his pipe at his wife.

"Oh, I see," I said.

The woman glanced up briefly, and she struck me as being less hostile than the man. The farmer stared at me unabashedly. "Monsieur," I said to him, "couldn't you sell us a sheep?"

"Who wants to buy?" he asked frostily.

I tried to explain and mentioned a price of about thirty marks.

The husband and wife exchanged smiles; then the man said, "I suppose you mean twice that much, if—and I say, if," he drawled, "*if* I were to sell one."

"Perhaps we could talk about it."

"This year," he said shortly, "the weather's been too dry. I can't sell you a sheep. Not enough fodder for the animals."

"All the more reason," I said.

"What do you mean?"

"Well, if you haven't enough fodder, we'll slaughter one, and you'll have one less mouth to feed."

He laughed, no longer quite so hostile.

I felt like sitting down with them and helping with the peas; it was a wonderful evening, but standing there in that hated uniform, leaning on the crossbar of my bike, my cap in my hand, I felt very homeless.

"Well, what about it?" I asked.

"You're a very stubborn fellow."

"We're hungry."

His apathetic eyes lit up a bit. "You're hungry?" he asked, almost like a child. "Doesn't your company feed you, then?"

I was genuinely ashamed and blushed.

"Okay," I said impatiently, "yes or no?"

"Claire"—he turned toward his wife—"what do you think?"

I knew I had won. The woman hesitated, without looking up. "At that price..." she said.

He stood up. "Follow me."

We went into the house.

I struck a deal with him and agreed that we would come for the sheep that night. I left the equivalent of forty-five marks in francs with him. It was hard to leave the house. I stood there for a while after coming back from the stable, slowly finished my cigarette, and looked at the sky as it hung, a soft and rosy gray, over the sea. It was very quiet; there was only the distant croaking of frogs and the soft, almost musical sound of the peas as they hopped out of their shells into the tin bowl and sometimes bounced off the edge with a light ping.

I was also aware of the gentle hiss of the man's pipe as he sucked on it; and, although that icy hostility between us had been replaced by a certain good will, I could feel that I was not only intruding but unwelcome.

So I threw my butt onto the flagstones, hastily ground it out, said "Good night," and got back onto my bike. I soon reached the neighboring farm, situated in a dense little wood, one of those silent, dilapidated places often to be found thereabouts. The terrible part about those farms is that they look deserted whereas there are actually people living in them. What's missing is something of the atmosphere that is part and parcel of rural life: everything is pervaded by a kind of idleness that to us seems totally unrural, an air of decadence, of almost literary melancholy that, in the context of a farm, seems quite horrifying.

The farmer and his wife were sitting in the dark kitchen, and the first thing I saw was the glow of a cigarette.

"Good evening," I said, instinctively keeping my voice low. "I've come about the cow."

"Cow?" a woman's voice repeated slowly and sarcastically.

"That's right," a man's hoarse voice replied, equally sarcastically, more to the woman than to me. "They want to buy a cow, but..."

"I thought the deal was all settled," I broke in.

"Settled!" repeated that disagreeable male voice; I couldn't make out the face that went with it. "Nothing is settled, *nothing* has been settled, d'you get me?"

I was silent. Since nobody offered me a chair, I sat down on a stool by the window and began to smoke.

"Settled!" resumed that voice, this time a little less confidently.

"I was told," I remarked, "that the purchase had been completed. The cow's supposed to be picked up tonight."

"*Merde!*" shouted the voice. "That's what I'd call rushing things! Nothing doing—in Paris people are paying twenty-five francs for a pound of meat, and you expect me to sell two hundred pounds for twenty-five hundred francs! I'm not crazy, not by a long shot..."

"All right," I said evenly. "Put a rope around your cow's neck and take it to Paris. There you might even get forty francs a pound."

I could tell that the couple had both lifted their heads and were looking at me, but what bothered me was that I could see nothing except a pair of flashing knitting needles and the suggestion of a pale cloth cap; the cigarette had been spat out.

"After all," I said quietly, "nobody's forcing you to sell the cow, are they?"

The answer was a hostile silence.

These deals were a kind of legal black market, an infringement of a law that we had instituted ourselves and whose enforcement we should really have been safeguarding; but, as I already told you, soldiers who are permanently hungry don't give a damn about such laws. Needless to say, my question was ridiculous, since I was putting it as the delegate of an enemy company, even though, legally speaking, it was the farmer's duty to refuse the deal.

"No," came the sarcastic voice, "nobody's ever forced us, no indeed."

"Very well," I said as I stood up. "We'll be here tonight at two o'clock. I have part of the money with me." I opened my wallet and took from it three crisp, brand-new thousand-franc bills.

"Here you are," I said curtly.

There are few farmers who can resist the sight of real money. The couple were on their feet in a flash; the woman rushed to the light switch and turned it on. Now for the first time I could see them both, and immediately saw how they leaned their heads toward the money. They were old, gray-haired, with pinched faces, and for a moment I thought they were brother and sister, then I saw their worn wedding rings. The man couldn't resist; he took the bills from my hand and with a repulsive tenderness snapped them between his fingers.

We soldiers, sir, have a terrible contempt for money. Money alone is nothing. Its only value is what one can get for it at any given moment: wine, women, or tobacco. Money is no more than a means. To save it or hoard it seems to us absurd.

The deal was closed. The woman also offered me some butter and eggs; I left the house with a pound of butter, ten eggs, and a very special acquisition: a bottle of thick cream.

It was almost dark outside; a shadowy gloom hung over the meadows and bushes. Cautiously I rode back.

I was filled with a weary disgust. With complete clarity I could see everything that lay ahead: I would reach the highway, have a beer at Cadette's, then sit for four hours at the phone fighting sleep. I would smoke, although nothing tasted good; try to write a letter, without success; hear Kandick's snoring. And after two hours I would be left with nothing but fatigue, hopeless fatigue, and I would keep looking at my watch to see whether it wasn't time to waken Kandick. That's how it would be for the next four or five weeks; then we would be relieved, and in some godforsaken little place eight miles from the coast we would be drilled. I wouldn't even have any money left for booze, I'd have nothing to smoke, and after those six weeks I would once again be sitting in some other bunker night after night, at that phone that never rang, waiting for the moment when I would be allowed to sink into a leaden sleep.

At 2:00 a.m. I would be collecting the cow and the sheep, then sitting at the phone again from seven to eleven, riding off to company headquarters at eleven...

I dismounted for a moment because the sound of the bicycle was getting on my nerves.

In those days, sir, I still believed in what is known as coincidence. I believed that our life was an isolated fragment surrounded by other isolated fragments, each a distinct and a more or less brilliant painting; I believed in the total lack of connection between all things and in the pale, blind futility of our existence. I had as yet no inkling of that mysterious network of innumerable knotted threads, of that vast, all-encompassing fabric into which for each one of us a particular thread has been woven. I reached the highway, got back on my bike, and rode off toward Cadette's tavern.

On opening the door, I was assailed by an unaccustomed racket. Raucous singing and caterwauling. I caught sight of naval and air-force uniforms—near our base there were a lighthouse and an air-force listening post—and the next moment I was surrounded by soldiers who directed my attention to a figure sitting slumped on a bench by the window: glassy-eyed, unseeing, and mumbling incoherent, drunken nonsense. He was from our base, a man called Wiering, normally a quite inconspicuous person who, as far as I could recall the schedule, was nowhere near due for time off. I remembered that he had been due only a few days ago and that he had sold his leave for half a packet of tobacco. I took charge of Wiering, who, without even staggering overmuch, unresistingly let himself be led away. Cadette protested her innocence and accused a few laughing antiaircraft gunners of having got him drunk.

I handed Wiering over to his squad leader, and we agreed to try to say nothing about his absence. Then I entered the bunker, reported my success to your brother, and sat down resignedly at the phone. Kandick had risen from his chair as I came in, then sunk back on his bed; he was already snoring.

I declined your brother's offer to stay awake in my place and for a while sat silently across from him. My silence contained a good deal of hostility. I hated that life, and I was transferring my hatred to your brother as the wearer of a uniform, the possessor of a rank that seemed to justify that life.

Finally he rose to head for his room, turned at the door, and said, "Don't forget that our lives can change at any minute. Nothing is unalterable. Good night." Perhaps he already knew that his words were soon to come true.

VII

Events now followed in such rapid succession that I must first sort them out in my memory if I am to keep them in the right order.

That night I got almost no sleep. Fatigue and despair filled me like an ever-recurring, evil-tasting tide that I had to keep regurgitating; back and forth it flooded, unwilling either to retreat or to utterly engulf me.

Just before two I was wakened by Kandick, who had relieved me at midnight, and I rode off to meet the cook and collect the cow and the sheep: an arduous enterprise accompanied by much frustration and cursing.

It was close to five when, totally exhausted, I was able to start on my way back, and the sky was already growing light as I turned into the avenue at Cadette's tavern. A glorious morning, no doubt, but I was too tired to notice; how pointless and totally irrelevant that grayish-pink light seemed to me as it felt its way up the gray vault of the night sky with delicate, soft rays. There is a stage of fatigue—what soldier is not familiar with it!—that is almost deadly to body and soul. One would commit murder for a single night of unbroken sleep; one is on the verge of tears from exhaustion, indifferent to everything except sleep or oblivion.

When I stepped inside the bunker, Kandick was asleep, sprawled across the table. Even my noisy entrance failed to wake him. I simply flung myself down on my bunk and instantly fell asleep, too tired even to give Kandick a poke in the ribs; besides, I was beyond caring what happened. As far as I was concerned, anybody who liked could come and capture our base.

When I awoke, it was midday: a steaming mess tin was on the table. Your brother was sitting beside it, calmly looking at me. He was about to open his mouth to say something to me when the phone rang. He lifted the receiver, spoke, and the next moment I saw an expression of utter astonishment on his face. Then he repeated several times: "Yes, I understand, yes..." He put down the receiver and burst out laughing.

What had happened was this: our CO had ordered the brain of the cow that had been slaughtered that night to be fried for himself at around 11:00 a.m., had polished it off, and then suddenly been taken so violently ill that it had been necessary to rush him to the field hospital in Abbeville (incidentally, on account of chronic dyspepsia he was considered "unfit for service on the eastern front"). Your brother, being next in seniority, was put in command of the company.

Within an hour your brother and I had to move from Larnton to Pochelet. With our scanty baggage we settled into the CO's quarters, a nice little four-room house, and for the time being were happy to have escaped from Larnton. Two more hours were enough to make ourselves reasonably comfortable in our new quarters and to remove the baggage of the former CO. At four o'clock your brother went over to the orderly room to take charge.

I spent the whole afternoon sitting on our little terrace with a view of the sea, reading the Kierkegaard diaries your brother had lent me.

Since by eight o'clock he hadn't returned, I went to bed and fell asleep at once. I was worn out by the exertions of the previous night and of the day, and the prospect of sleeping the whole night through without interruption seemed irresistible.

The next morning I slept until nearly eight. I barely had time to wake your brother before hurrying off to the drill in which I now had to take part. For the first time in three years I had to endure the ordeal of foot drill. You can't imagine the horror I feel to this day at having merely to write the words "position of attention," those words that form the very foundation of Prussian drill procedure.

At about eight-thirty your brother drove off to take over the command of two bases farther north.

The morning dragged slowly on. At noon I was alone. I listlessly ate my meal, then dozed on my bunk, smoking cigarettes and drinking half a bottle of wine.

Your brother's return awakened me; I heard him come in, go to his room, throw down his belt. Shortly after that he called me in.

He seemed tired and annoyed and at once asked me for a cigarette. We sat facing each other in armchairs, and after a few puffs he surprised me by pulling out a bottle of wine from under the table. He took two glasses from a cupboard, opened the bottle, and poured. We touched glasses and drank.

"Listen," he said finally, after we had sat in silence for a few minutes. "There are people who are born to polish boots. A perfectly unobjectionable, dignified occupation. Perhaps you were not born for that, I don't know. On the other hand, I don't want anyone else around me but you. I think we will be able to talk in greater privacy and at greater length and less in innuendoes. Because I want to *do* something, understand? Not only talk. We have to do something, understand?"

I nodded, although I wasn't very clear about what he meant.

"So," he went on, "it'll be best if we share the boot polishing. Right? One day I do yours and mine, the next you do yours and mine. Is that a deal? Apart from that, you will be on duty in the mornings and have the afternoons off, to which a CO's orderly is entitled. We won't infringe on any regulations. And there's another thing you'll have to take over, something I simply can't do: the cooking."

I gave him a long look. "I have a counterproposal," I said. "Each of us will polish his own boots. I'll be glad to do the cooking and collect our rations."

"Splendid," he cried, "splendid! A good idea. Thanks very much." He shook my hand, raised his glass to me, I raised mine to him. Then he suddenly stood up, walked toward the big portrait of Hitler that hung on the end wall of the room—an ostentatious affair in a heavy gilt frame—and without a word turned it back to front. His hand was still on the frame when the door opened and Schnecker stood on the threshold.

I jumped to my feet, as stipulated. Schnecker looked first at me, then at your brother, who had meanwhile moved back to the table. Then Schnecker said to me in a low voice, "Leave us, please."

I walked to the door, saluted, and left the room.

With heavy steps I walked along the corridor, listening intently, but there was nothing to be heard yet, and I supposed he was waiting for my footsteps to die away. I left the house, but walked around to the rear and lay down in the garden under the open window. There was still no sound.

"Well, then," Captain Schnecker finally said in a calm voice—he had apparently gone over to the wall and turned the picture back to its proper position—"let's begin by correcting this childishness."

"May I ask you," said your brother, his voice just as calm, "whether this is my own living room and whether there is any regulation requiring officers to have portraits of the Führer in their home?"

"No."

I could hear your brother walking over to the wall, and I knew he was turning the picture around again.

"Good," said the captain, "excellent. But with your indisputable intelligence it must be clear to you that there is not much room for doubt when in the presence of his subordinate an officer displays loathing for the portrait of his supreme commander."

"Wrong, my friend. All I loathe is the frame. You know quite well how sensitive I am when it comes to art, and to me it is outright blasphemy to frame the portrait of our modest, simple, soldierly Führer—who has said he won't take off his soldier's tunic as long as the war lasts—to stick his portrait in such a garish frame: to me that's an insult to his person. And, after all, the Führer is also an artist."

"You're as strong as ever in syntax, it seems."

"Stronger, I hope. I've had plenty of time to practice. You fellows saw to that."

They both fell silent, and I knew that your brother was standing there, his hands clasped behind his back, calmly looking Schnecker in the eye.

"Listen to me carefully," Schnecker resumed. "I have been at great pains to clear your name with the regiment and to see that the old affair is forgotten and you're put in command here. That sissy will probably be spending six months in the hospital again and then go on leave and arrive back here with a brand-new stomach ulcer. There were some nasty types who would have liked to see you take orders from a junior lieutenant. I prevented that."

"I wouldn't have cared."

"Why do you think I did that for you?"

"To set a trap for me."

The captain gave a devilish laugh. "There couldn't have been any better trap for you than the mousetrap of Larnton! You could have grown old there. But no"—he raised his voice—"you can't think of anything better to do, on the very first day, the very first day, than to send in almost word for word the same report that was the original reason for your being found unfit to command a company. You can think of nothing better to do than worry about margarine, bread, and sugar for your men. It really does look as if you were out to create difficulties."

"I can't think of anything more important here than the bread, margarine, and sugar for my men. Unfortunately I cannot improve the fortifications at my own expense. That would probably be the next priority."

"You are simply making yourself ridiculous. And, furthermore, on the very first day, another of your requests to be transferred to Russia. Don't worry—the Russian front still needs so many officers that your turn will come."

"What are you going to do with my report about the rations?" your brother asked quietly.

"I shall tear it up."

"No, you won't!" your brother shouted, and I could hear them moving toward each other.

"Then I'll wipe my ass with it!" shouted the captain furiously.

"Here"—there was a brief pause—"here," he cried again, "look at this, read this scrap of paper. It was found yesterday on a carrier pigeon shot down in the sector of our first company. 'The morale of the troops is bad, and the troops are hungry.' Needless to say, it is extremely flattering for me as battalion commander, in the eyes of the regiment and

544   HEINRICH BÖLL

the division, when a carrier pigeon that must have been released in my
sector bears a message of that kind. That is indeed extremely flattering, and on top of that you also produce your idiotic report that"—he
gave his voice a sarcastic undertone and was obviously quoting—"the
troops believe they are constantly being done out of small but regular
quantities of fat, sugar, and bread; that the quartermaster sergeants
declared that, on the basis of the quantities they received, they were
simply unable to issue the prescribed rations; and that"—his voice
became shrill—"this naturally served further to undermine the low
morale of the quartermaster sergeants, for where there was an actual
shortage of one ounce it was easy enough to pilfer two ounces. Oh, all
that's just great for me!"

"The question is whether it's untrue." Your brother's voice was
calm again.

"Untrue! We're not here to seek the truth, which anyway doesn't
exist. We're here to win the war."

"And apparently that can only be done by constantly gypping hungry soldiers, right?"

This was followed by a terrible silence, and they must have moved
even closer together.

"I daresay you believe," came Schnecker's hoarse voice at last, "that
I am eating your men's margarine and sugar myself, don't you?"

Your brother said nothing.

"Do you believe that? I said, Do you believe that?" His voice
seemed to be exploding with rage.

"Not directly, of course."

"Indirectly, then—right?"

"Now you listen to me." Your brother's voice was very calm. "This
paymaster is not only a fool, he's also a bastard. You wouldn't deny that?"

"Of course not. But there's no way I can get rid of the fellow."

"You don't have to. You just have to make him watch his step. And
you can't do that, of course, because you depend on him for your extra
supplies of booze, to which, of course, you're not entitled either. You
see, you need to get drunk every day. I know—on a captain's pay one
can get good and drunk three times a month at the most—I know that
too. And then, of course, you need women. You're a good-looking fellow, a ladies' man, as they say. There you are, then. There's no way you

can get at the paymaster. Those fellows are businessmen; in other words they've covered themselves in every possible direction. And you know I'm right, don't you?"

The terrible part was that I couldn't see anything, and now I couldn't hear anything either, and at that moment, lying out there under the window sill, I realized that eavesdropping is horrible.

What was Schnecker doing, for God's sake? Was he sitting there slumped in his chair, or was he standing, pistol in hand, ready to shoot your brother at any moment? I lay there as if dead, not daring to stir or crawl away...

Again came your brother's voice. "You must try to see my point," he said. "I can't imagine anything worse than cheating a soldier out of his rations or his sleep. After all, we in our officer's uniforms represent the power that compels these men to submit to being killed or being bored to death. That burden is quite enough for me. I wouldn't like the added responsibility of making them suffer more hunger than is provided for by the system." He fell silent again; then after a while his voice continued, heavier and more somber than before. "In a way it's too bad that I'm going to die—otherwise I'd look forward to writing a philosophical treatise on the ounce after the war."

Now I realized that Schnecker had been standing there grinning all the time, his arms folded. He burst into a peal of laughter, as if a pent-up flood were being released.

"Who would have believed it?" he said in a strong, firm voice. "And from the lips of someone wearing the uniform of a German officer! Who would have believed it?" Again that ringing laughter.

"Come now"—I could tell from his voice that he was tightening his belt and straightening up—"let's get back to business. For all I care, the report can go to regimental headquarters. For all I care, make yourself ridiculous, make yourself a laughingstock for the sake of three ounces of margarine, for the sake of three ounces that has to be withheld. And another thing: did you have to pick the rudest bastard in the battalion for your orderly and sit here boozing with him in the afternoon while you were both still on duty?"

Your brother was evidently looking at him in silence; then he laughed. "Oh, of course," he said, "that's right—it was four-thirty when you arrived. I leave it to you to file a counterreport."

After hearing the captain get into his car, I crawled back into the shelter
of some nearby bushes, stood up, and hurried off toward the forest
that blocked the view of the sea. Leaning against the trunk of a fir tree,
I looked out over the waves as they rolled slowly in. It was very quiet,
the air was soft, and there was nothing in sight but the water and the
stretch of sand in front of it that was slowly, very slowly being covered
by the tide; the barbed wire that had been drawn along the tide line was
the only reminder of the war.

A painful sadness, such as I had never known before, welled up
in me. There is no justice, I thought; there is no such thing as an ounce.
The ounce is a fiction, an ounce is nothing, and yet they say: It is an
ounce! And on this nothing, on this ounce, they all grow rich. They
all grow rich solely on the ounce, so it must be something, that ounce.
That's why there have to be so many poor, victimized people, because
an ounce is so little and so many ounces are needed to make a rich man
rich; that's why there have to be all those millions of gray, gaunt figures
obediently marching across Europe with their rifles on their backs, just
so the rats can get fat on their only tasty food—the ounce. There must
be vast numbers of those figures that can be stuffed into a freight car
designed to hold "40 soldiers or 8 horses"—simply because the horses
are bigger than the soldiers, bigger and more valuable.

I was twenty-five at the time, sir. I was no innocent, I was a trooper
like all the rest; I believed in nothing but the sausage on my bread, as
we used to say, in wine and tobacco. At least, I believed that was all I
believed. But where did that unutterable sadness come from, weighing
down my heart like lead, paralyzing me so that I felt too tired even to
put my hand in my pocket to dig out matches and cigarettes?

I had been fifteen when the swastika was suspended like a huge
black spider in the sky over Germany.

Now I wished I could travel across the sea, far, far away to another
world where there were no uniforms, no policemen, no war; but I was
trapped in this cage called Europe. There was no escape: starting from
this coast I could travel eastward for thousands of miles, eastward to
the end of this insane continent, all the way to Vladivostok, and there
would be no life anywhere.

In that hour I would have sold all the rest of my life to sink into
the arms of that girl who had said, "I'm always here"—and who hadn't
been there after all.

As dusk fell, I crept back home, lay down on my bed, and abandoned myself to the sluggish tide of a leaden despair that left no room even for desire. Not a sound was to be heard in our cottage. From the barracks I could hear faint singing. I was incapable of thinking or doing anything, I was at the end of my tether.

VIII

Two days later we were already on our way to Russia.

When I woke up next morning, everything was normal. From the direction of the company kitchen I could hear the men whose job it was to take coffee to their barracks. In your brother's room all was quiet. It was seven o'clock. I got up, went into our own little kitchen, set the frying pan on the electric hotplate, put some fat in it, took the loaf of bread out of the drawer, and began to slice it. As the fat melted, I beat up the eggs in a cup with some cream and stirred them around in the pan. Then I prepared the tray, putting two plates, cups, and knives on it, and went off to the company kitchen.

The mornings were always peaceful. The whole little place had the atmosphere of a somewhat run-down summer camp. That morning the air was already warm, and the soldiers were standing outside their barracks, stripped to the waist and washing.

The topkick was sitting in the kitchen, discussing with the cook how to use up the rest of the cow. He was markedly cooler toward me.

"Please tell the CO," he called out to me while I was filling my mess tin at the coffee urn, "that church services have been scheduled for this afternoon, both denominations, here. The outposts have been notified."

"Yessir," I replied.

The cook also threw me a suspicious glance. He hadn't forgiven me for doing him out of his profit of five hundred francs on the cow, and he probably assumed I'd told your brother about it.

As I left the kitchen, Schmidt called across to me from the orderly room, "We need a dispatch runner for nine o'clock to pick up special orders from the battalion—would you be interested?"

I looked into Schmidt's placid, amiable face. "Yes," I said. All I could see was the pale face of the girl, and I imagined myself pressing my mouth onto her cheeks, her lips, and the little hollow at the base of her neck.

"Yes," I repeated.

As I approached our quarters, I could already see your brother's face, covered with shaving soap, at the window. It was seven-thirty.

Shortly after that, I carried coffee, bread, and eggs into the room and told your brother about the church services and that I had been ordered for nine o'clock to ride over to battalion headquarters.

"Yes," he said as he put on his tunic, "there's something in the air; maybe the cow will be our farewell dinner."

"Do you really think so?" I asked doubtfully.

"Things look bad in Russia."

We sat down. I poured the coffee and we spread scrambled egg on the bread, but first I lit a cigarette. It was the first real breakfast in a long time. The wide, low window toward the north was open, the air, cool yet soft, streamed into the room, and one could see far out over the water.

Your brother, like me, picked up the bread and promptly put it down again, swallowed a mouthful of coffee, and suddenly began to speak in a rapid, almost droning voice:

"I daresay you know that I was considered unfit to lead a company because the very first time I was put in charge of one, I decided to get to the bottom of all those discrepancies in the issuing of rations. You see, my first day as CO, each man was supposed to receive twenty-five ounces of butter. A straightforward calculation: ten men one package, that's all. But oddly enough there was one package for every twelve men. At the time my company, including all subordinate units, consisted of a hundred and eighty men. That meant that, at fifteen times twelve men, somewhere along the line a pound and a half had gone astray. I immediately summoned my quartermaster sergeant, and his excuse was that deliveries had been short. In his presence I phoned the fellow in charge of provisions at battalion headquarters, and he admitted that he had had to short two packages per company because that was all he had received. So my quartermaster sergeant had already kept back one package; at least I had my hands on him—it's always easy to catch the small fry. I still had to clarify how it was possible for the division to have short-shipped five pounds of butter for the five ration-drawing units of our battalion.

"I kept phoning those guys till they almost went out of their minds. I made them spend hours recalculating, and it turned out that each unit had actually had to be shorted three pounds because the butter had turned rancid. Replacements were promised. After a phone bombardment of almost two days I finally had the battalion quartermaster on the hook with a shortage of two pounds. So far so good. Now just figure out how many battalions, sections, ration-drawing units, there are to a division. Oddly enough, for the next three days full rations were issued. Butter and margarine seemed to have lost their tendency to turn rancid. But I persisted. On the fourth day, a shortage again. This time, company and battalion quartermaster sergeants had clean hands. Wherever a shell explodes close by, people are scared, but farther back ... Well, I had a phone. You can imagine how those fellows hated me; I was relentless. If one of the men told me something had gone bad, I contacted his superiors and asked whether this had been reported and whether the facts had been investigated. But I got nowhere. It didn't work. The soldiers never received their full rations for more than four consecutive days. The funny thing was that I also became unpopular in my own company; the topkick and the sergeant were scared and thought I was crazy. Luckily I had won a few officers over to my side. I would phone, or write a report, every day if so much as a single ounce of jam was short. Well, the upshot was that I personally punched the divisional quartermaster in the nose: I need hardly tell you that fellow was fat as a bedbug in an overcrowded barracks. The officers let me down, saying it was futile to fight the administration, it was a clique, and so on."

He swallowed some coffee, picked up the bread again, put it down again.

"Well," he went on, "I was powerless, of course. At the hearing I was accused of being senselessly fanatical, quixotic. The divisional quartermaster emerged from the battle a rosy, innocent lamb. I was duly punished, transferred, and narrowly escaped demotion. But, damn it all, I can think of no more meaningful battle than against the administration, for the administration—*any* administration—is the administration of mindlessness, the administration of the administration. Oh, God! I'd like to take over the administration of life! I'd like to represent the rights of the living against those dead creatures, even if during my next attack I have to throw my insignia in the general's face. I don't want them!" he suddenly shouted, then, embarrassed, began stirring his coffee although it contained neither milk nor sugar. With a sigh he raised his head. "Now it's starting all over again," he said. "You can help me. Do you want to?"

"Sir," I said, blushing, "my conscience isn't sufficiently clear for me to accuse others of filching."

"No?" he merely asked.

I told him about my finaglings in Paris. He listened with lowered head; my confessions clearly embarrassed him.

"You see," I added, after outlining the essentials, "wherever I can cheat the state, I have no scruples. The state has stolen six years of my youth, it has prevented me from learning a trade. I would call that 'getting compensation.'"

"So," he asked quietly, "you wouldn't hesitate to sell a bicycle, for instance, and pocket the proceeds?"

"Absolutely not," I admitted, "although..."

"Although?"

"Although several years of concentration camp seem an excessive price to pay for a bicycle."

"So it's only the punishment that deters you?"

"Yes."

"That's interesting," he cried eagerly. "Most interesting! This is the first time I've heard that put in such classically cynical form. Nevertheless," he went on with a smile, "if you thought there was the slightest chance of somebody being personally harmed, you wouldn't take anything, would you?"

"No," I said.

"We shall see," he said. "I have to go on duty now." It was eight o'clock. He ate his scrambled eggs and bread, swallowed a few more mouthfuls of coffee, and left.

Half a minute later I left the house, without having touched my breakfast.

At eight-fifteen I stopped outside the quiet tavern where, barely a week earlier, I had seen and spoken to the girl. It was so quiet all around that I had to stand still and listen. I think that for the first time in my life I could hear my heart beating—rapidly pounding away, that invisible hammer in my chest...

Very quietly I propped the bicycle against the wall and walked straight through the open gate into the yard, for after dismounting I had heard the gentle sounds of milking. I saw her at once, and she too, having heard my footsteps, had risen and turned around. There she stood: milk dripping from her fingers as they hung, curved inward, by her sides, her hair tied back smooth and tight, her red lips open in surprise, her grubby gray smock slipping off her left shoulder. She recognized me immediately and stood there motionless as I walked toward her.

Without a word I put my arms around her, and for half a second I felt her hair against my cheek and her warm breath on my neck, but when I turned her head toward me to kiss her I realized that her body was cold and stiff in my arms, and her face, which I could now see, registered such resistance and fear that I was shocked.

"Angel," I whispered to her in German, mad with pain, "angel—I love you!"

Her lips grimaced. "*Laisse-moi*," she implored, "*je ne t'aime pas*."

I released her instantly, but she did not step back: she just stood there, and I could see she was on the verge of tears. Tears over me. My face must have expressed intolerable pain.

She pitied me, and when I realized that, could see it in her face, I knew for the first time how much I loved her. Even her pity seemed like a gift.

"Angel," I stammered again, "angel!"

I turned away, but she called me back with a strange, birdlike sound. She was smiling. "Wouldn't you like something to drink?" she asked.

Without waiting for a reply she walked past me, wiped her hands on her smock and, with a gesture of extraordinary grace, pulled her smock up over her shoulder. Dazed, with drooping shoulders, I followed her into the house.

I looked at my watch: twenty past eight. Five minutes had passed, and the world had almost come to an end; a last, soft red glow hung over the horizon—for what lover will ever cease to hope?

She had uncorked a bottle and filled two glasses. "I'm thirsty," she said in a low voice. "The air's so sultry, although it's early yet."

I find it hard to describe her smile: it was affectionate and sad, leaving me no spark of hope, yet not coquettish. It was ineffably human—I know no other word. She raised her glass; I nodded and drank.

The wine was delicious, cool and dry, and her face showed that she found it refreshing.

"Yes," I finally said with an effort, my muteness weighing on me like a heavy burden. "If I could just see you occasionally..."

We put down our glasses, and I followed her as she led the way outside. One more nod from her, and she was gone.

At eight-forty-five I was at battalion headquarters; the other dispatch bearers were already assembled. I sat on the steps outside, surrounded by that know-it-all chatter, and the time passed incredibly fast. Again and again I dug around into my memory, resurrecting the scene in the barn in order to find some tiny hope; but I found nothing, and yet ...

We waited a long time. We smoked, walked up and down, sat down again, and I joined listlessly in the general scuttlebutt; it was almost eleven when we were summoned to the orderly room. We were each handed a dispatch box, flat, locked wooden boxes for each of which there was one key with the battalion and one with the company, thus ensuring that we couldn't discover the contents of the dispatches. Nevertheless, it was obvious we were going to Russia. Normally that would have struck me as the ultimate horror; that day it left me cold. I felt numb. I saw the world and didn't see it. I was aware that the weather had become even more sultry, that the sky was covered with heavy gray clouds. Somehow my will power had also ceased to function. Deep down in a layer of buried consciousness I knew that I must stop, dismount, rest, and try to come to my senses, but I believe I would have gone on riding my bike to the end of the world, on and on, obsessed by the stupefying mechanics of pedaling ... on ... on ... I was dead.

A terrifying clap of thunder roused me. That same instant a warm, heavy rain started coming down in torrents. I looked about me and recognized my surroundings: there was the group of trees, *her* house, and no other shelter in sight. I raced toward the house, dismounted, left my bike lying on the ground, and, carrying the box, burst into the corridor.

I left the door open and stood there without making a sound.

Our bond with nature is closer than we realize. I don't know how long I stood there; I was barely conscious. When I came to again, I realized I was crying.

The beauty of the torrential summer rain, the cosmic power invested in all flowing water, created in my being some sort of parallel; an element of release, of flow, touched me. I wept. The unspeakable, agonizing spasm was relaxed, and I was alive again.

With trembling nostrils I breathed in that marvelous, sweetly moist fragrance that rose like clouds from the meadows.

I wept...

Suddenly I heard the footsteps of two people approaching along the flagstone path that skirted the house. The rain had let up a bit. I winced, as if a long, fine needle had unerringly pierced the very core of my sensitivity: they were your brother's footsteps. We know the people we live with better than we imagine: they were his footsteps. I stood stock still, leaning against the wall in the darkness of the corridor.

With the girl beside him, he entered my field of vision, and it was no surprise to me to see her with him. He was pushing his bicycle, half leaning on it, his face turned toward me; of the girl I could see only her back, her head, slightly bent, and a narrow segment of her soft cheek, and I knew that she was smiling. His face was pale and serious, and there was a kind of blissful pain in it, but the shattering thing was the naturalness with which those two seemed to belong together: uttering not a word, merely exchanging little smiles, that gentle pair simply belonged together.

I can't say I felt jealous. I was breathing heavily, suffused with the pain of being totally excluded. They scarcely moved, they just looked at each other, and there I stood: transfixed to the damp wall of that dilapidated house, thinking that it might feel good to die.

Finally he bent down, kissed her, and said, "*Au revoir, Madeleine.*" He quickly turned away and, pushing his bicycle, walked toward the gate.

"*Au revoir, au revoir!*" she called after him.

Then she took a few steps back, probably so as to gaze after him for as long as possible from the top step, and in doing so she bumped against the closed half of the door, turned slightly, saw me, and gave a little shriek...

Your brother had not yet reached the gate. He rushed back to the door; the girl was still looking at me in horror and disbelief. Now he was quite close, saw me, and instantly grasped the situation.

"Come along," he said to me huskily. I followed him like a condemned man, the dispatch box under my arm, retrieved my bike outside the gate, mounted it, and rode off at his side.

We didn't look back.

IX

Neither of us ever saw her again.

We rode in silence to company headquarters, where we parted without a word. He went to his quarters; I had to deliver the dispatch box, then go to the kitchen to collect our midday meal, having, as always, handed in our mess kits in the morning.

I put my bike in the shed and stopped by the kitchen to receive our two portions of potatoes and stew; then I followed him to our quarters.

He stood up as soon as I entered. He had already brought out the plates from the kitchenette and placed them on the table, also the cutlery, but he tended to do that a bit awkwardly, so I put our two mess kits on the tray and calmly rearranged forks, knives, and plates, straightened the loaf of bread, and removed the wilted stalks from the flowers in the vase.

All this time he was pacing up and down with folded arms.

"We can eat now," I said calmly, when everything was ready.

"All right," he said, and at that moment we looked at each other again for the first time; reluctantly I had to smile. He shook his head, his expression registering bewilderment, then shrugged his shoulders; I was still waiting for him to sit down.

"We don't want to pass over this in complete silence," he said in a low voice, "but it's up to you whether we discuss it or not."

"No," I said, my voice equally subdued, "I'd rather not discuss it."

"Fair enough," he said. We sat down, and I passed him the little ladle we used for serving ourselves from the mess kits. There was a knock at the door. Putting down his spoon, he called out, "Come in!" and the topkick entered. His normally placid face showed agitation.

By next morning we were on the train heading for Russia. The reports and orders I had picked up were already superseded, canceled by telephone instructions. The men to be transferred had to be selected and prepared for departure that same day and wait at the bases for their replacements, which were said to be on their way. The trucks bringing the replacements were then to take the transferred men to an assembly point near Abbeville, where a division had already arrived, been loaded onto the train, and left. But the train had been blown up, casualties had been heavy, and the division was a hundred and twenty men short of combat strength. Your brother and Schnecker were among the officers.

Whereas I had nothing to do but keep an eye on our two packs, your brother didn't have a minute's peace. At the last moment the transferees' clothing and equipment had to be replenished, and men who had suddenly been taken violently ill had to be persuaded that they were in fact fit; men about to go on leave had where feasible to be replaced. Above all, the transferees had to be assembled as soon as possible in Pochelet so they could attend divine service.

The Catholic divisional priest arrived by car shortly before four and, in view of the general chaos, was accommodated in our quarters. I had to endure his company for half an hour, until the arrival of the first penitents, to whom I offered the use of my room while they waited. Meanwhile your brother told me to clear the living room for the celebration of Holy Mass and the administering of the Sacraments. So I found myself alone with the priest for a while. He had the smooth, rosy skin befitting a staff officer in France, and the mild and obliging manners of a wine salesman. When I threw out a few remarks about war, corruption, and officers in general, he gently rotated one hand in the other, felt constrained to remove his cigarette from his lips, and, with a bland expression, said, "Yes, there is much wickedness in the world."

We were interrupted when the first penitent knocked at the door, saluted stiffly, and came in.

I couldn't help muttering to myself, "*Ave, Caesar, morituri...*"

The priest looked at me with a smile. He finally abandoned his cigarette and said, "Well, well, a Latin scholar!"

His gentle look was a signal for me to leave the room.

Out in the garden, all was quiet. Mild autumnal warmth was interspersed with cool air, the sky was blue, and the cottages of Pochelet slept behind their high hedges and fences. Your brother had driven over to Larnton, to try to talk some sense into a young soldier apparently overcome by violent cramps.

Preparations were complete, all the other transferees were ready, and divine service was expected to begin punctually at five. The Protestant clergyman was due any minute.

I strolled slowly along behind the company buildings as far as the crossroads and for the first time entered the Pochelet tavern. It was a single-story, flat-roofed building, a typical outdoor summer restaurant, with its wooden walls and garden chairs. The big room was deserted; through the open door to the kitchen I could see the landlady and her husband at their evening meal. She was a pretty, blonde woman, with a barmaid's cold beauty. Still chewing, she emerged from the kitchen, gave me a friendly smile, and handed me the bottle of white wine I had requested and for which I didn't yet know how to pay.

"Give me another," I said with a laugh. "Then I won't have to bother you again at your supper." She gave a cautionary little smile, hesitated half teasingly, but then, having made up her mind, reached in under the bar and brought out another bottle.

I sat down at one end of the room, aware of that terrible despair in abandoned places of entertainment that creeps toward one from each corner. There was a smell of dust, of summer dust.

I couldn't possibly miss the departure: the road outside the window would bring the men from Larnton and the northern bases right past my nose.

I had a whole hour in which to forget the girl's face, to say good-bye to France, and to drown the soft, pink, well-preserved corpselike face of the priest.

That yellow wine is the most exquisite of all; it is like honey and fire, like light and silk, and it's my belief that God caused it to grow in order to keep alive the memory of Paradise in this depressing den of vice that calls itself human society. The more I drank, the more I became conscious of a serenity such as I had never known, a serenity amounting almost to wisdom. It is wonderful to drink oneself to sleep, to sink into the arms of that kindly brother of Death.

I remember being able to persuade that cool but sweetly smiling woman to let me have two more bottles in exchange for my watch.

I woke up to find myself on a foul-smelling truck, closed my eyes again in horror, and finally became fully awake at the railroad station in Abbeville, beside a troop train on the point of departure. Your brother's laughing face was bent over me.

"He looked," I said, "he looked like a wine salesman..."

"Sure, sure," he said quietly. "Come on, now, get up."

I got to my feet and was assigned by him to a column of fourteen men in the process of being incorporated into a company on the troop train.

We traveled across France, past the shining vineyards of the Rhineland, through central Germany, Saxony, Silesia, Poland. The railroad stations became ever more gray and dismal, the soldiers ever more desperate and cynical. Gradually we started meeting trainloads of wounded, trainloads of prisoners; the ragged population of the occupied territories crowded around our train. The last of our French matches were bartered for eggs, blankets from French houses transformed into butter, parts of equipment exchanged in the darkness of ghostly railroad stations for bacon or tobacco, for even during the transport our rations remained miserably inadequate.

The weather had turned cold, it being now almost the middle of October, and we dragged our long greatcoats through the dirt of Ukrainian stations where tractors were being hurriedly loaded for shipment back to Germany, or where we were held up to allow a transport of severely wounded soldiers to pass along the blocked section.

I didn't see your brother that often. Sometimes, during a brief halt, he would come to our car and chat with us, and on rare occasions, during a longer stop, we found an opportunity to take a stroll together. We never spoke of the past. It was an overcrowded, inadequately locked chamber whose bolts must never be touched.

Sitting side by side next to the buffer stop of a siding or on a damp stack of railroad ties, we tried to feel our way toward the mystery that was awaiting us, that neither of us knew: the front line. For the farther we were hauled into this dark land, the clearer it became that nothing we encountered here would be comparable to the kind of war we had been experiencing in France. Here anything wearing a gray uniform was filled with a frightening urge to get as far to the rear as possible.

This army had never recovered from the shock of that first disastrous winter. The wounded with whom we spoke were waiting tensely for the train to move on, farther back, without stopping. Every minute in this country seemed wasted; all they wanted was to get farther back from the front, not only quickly but also as far back as possible. It was painful to listen to their illusions on the subject of Germany. Would that country, now also dirty, mangled, wretched, and starving, where barracks had become prisons and hospitals had become barracks—would that country live up to their dreams?

A week later we stopped at a fair-sized station said to be not far from the headquarters of Army Group South. Here, after being fed miserable rations (supplied in France) throughout the journey, we were suddenly provided with an excellent meal: there was some good soup, plenty of meat and potatoes, and at the end a distribution of candies, schnapps, and cigarettes.

There was even champagne, and I was lucky enough, when lots were drawn, to win a whole bottle that we had been meant to share. It was very cold, the stove in our car glowed, and I can well remember opening the train door a crack and, while I looked out, drinking up the bottle as I absent-mindedly filled and emptied, filled and emptied, my mug, at the same time breathing in the icy air. I felt stupefied.

Having enjoyed all those delicacies, we suddenly found ourselves being unloaded, and after lining up, we started out on a long, wearisome march to the nearest airfield. That was in the afternoon.

Next morning, while it was still dark, we launched our first attack. What a glorious ring there is to those words: to launch an attack! It sounds like a fanfare, seems to tell of keen young warriors who—in obedience to the stratagems of war—can barely suppress the song on their lips as they attack, attack with exultant hearts.

We, by contrast, had deplaned in early-morning darkness and had to suffer grievously for our premature insobriety. Crammed tightly together in trucks, half suffocated by weapons and packs, we had been driven toward the front line and spent a further two hours in strange houses in a strange village. Each sound coming from the nearby front triggered new fears, it being impossible to relate such sounds to anything one had previously experienced. Thus I was scared over and over again by the sudden high-pitched bark of an antitank cannon that seemed to be positioned right behind our building. Each time I believed that Russian tanks were at our door, and each time I experienced mortal fear.

The light in that little room where we all huddled together had gone out, and when things finally quieted down I simply leaned back in the darkness, searching among shoulders, legs, heads, and weapons for a bit of space, and closed my eyes. A vile stench filled the room. Apparently a barrel of pickled cucumbers had begun to ferment and had burst; the floor was awash with a disgusting, reeking liquid, and our groping hands kept touching the soft, nauseating objects strewn around. I smoked incessantly, if only to keep down my nausea; no one said a word. We had imagined it all quite different, not quite so bad and not so terribly sudden.

It was still dark when we were ordered outside, where to my joy I recognized your brother's voice. The little yard was packed with soldiers, as I could see when the red flash from a cannon briefly illuminated it. A company: that word represents so many living souls, so many destinies, yet how much did a company amount to on this front!

Your brother explained, briefly and seriously, that he would be in command of us, that we had been ordered to seal off a breach. Truly a task for novices! It was appallingly difficult to organize the company in the dark, to hand over the groups and platoons to their respective leaders. I was called out by him and could tell by the grip of his trembling fingers when he grabbed me by the sleeve that he too was scared.

"You stay with me," he said huskily.

Well before dawn we left the village, guided by a sergeant from the staff of the regiment to which we had been assigned. Oh, what a long way we still had to go to reach the actual front! A relief, at least, to have earth under one's feet. In front and behind, seemingly all around us in fact, were gun flares and detonations. It would have been impossible to determine the battle line from these indications. The sergeant knew nothing for certain either. Who did! He told us in a whisper, as we marched along, that a whole battalion had been taken by surprise here, some of them killed, some taken prisoner; a few survivors had managed to escape. It was still uncertain whether the Russians had occupied the position, or whether, surprised by their own success, they had merely withdrawn with booty and prisoners to their own positions.

Strangely enough, those constant detonations didn't bother us much. What was terrible was the dark silence lying ahead of us, and we had to march into that darkness until we met resistance or reached the old positions. It was our job to determine the actual battle line, if possible to reoccupy the old positions and hold them.

There were four of us in the lead: your brother and the sergeant in front, while I followed with a corporal. Sometimes when I think back to those days, I believe that war is an element. When a man falls into water he gets wet, and when a man moves around at the front, where infantrymen and sappers dig themselves into the ground, he is in the war. That atmosphere is an acid test: there are only good fellows and bad; all intermediate categories either fail or rise to the occasion.

My instinct told me: the NCO walking beside me was a bastard. He was a coward, saturated with fear and abandoning himself to it without resistance. The way he flung himself to the ground when your brother or the sergeant softly passed on the command was enough to tell me that he would be capable of anything. There was something uncontrolled, something brutish, about the way he immediately hurled himself down and hugged the earth. The sergeant was very calm; he radiated a quality that can only be called courage, a spiritual aura stronger than fear.

Meeting no resistance, not even from rifle fire, we reached the line; on both sides was a lively exchange of fire, while ahead of us there still seemed to be that dark, silent cotton batting that was going to absorb us.

The sergeant's hearing was fantastically accurate. From among all those sounds, small and large, he pinpointed the one: that of a Very flare pistol being discharged. He dropped instantly to the ground, the signal for us to hiss the command to those behind us so we would no longer be visible in the brilliance of the silver flash.

At each flare I would try to recognize something, but there was only the dark, black earth, with many, many indistinct mounds that could just as well have been plowed furrows as crouching men.

My God, how often have I wondered at the immensity of the power that—despite cowardice and fear—induces millions of men to stagger passively on toward death, as we were doing that night.

We reached the old positions, meeting no resistance and suffering no losses. For the first time we trod in the dark on corpses; for the first time we prepared ourselves for a potential enemy lying in wait for us eighty or a hundred yards away. Everything had to be done incredibly fast. Before daybreak the platoons had to be at their battle stations, the rest of the men in their positions, and contact had to be established with the units on our left and right that had not fallen back.

Perhaps this so-called front is imagined as a straight line, drawn with a ruler on a map by a general-staff officer. Actually it is a very tortuous affair, receding and projecting, a highly irregular snake that adapts to the terrain or is forced by enemy pressure onto unfavorable ground.

How much we had to do in a single hour if daylight was to find our defenses prepared! On the right, no contact could be established. A corporal and two men sent out to look for the nearest German sentry on the right never came back: we never heard or saw anything of them again. Another patrol, accompanied by your brother, moved a bit farther back and discovered that we had advanced much too far on the right. The whole line had to shift and adjust, and all that in total silence, in the dark, in a terrain pockmarked by shell holes. Corpses lay all around—Germans and Russians; weapons, parts of equipment...

The company battle station was located almost in the center of the sector, slightly to the rear. There were two bunkers, each with space for three men. Telephone communication had been cut off. Try to imagine the state of mind of a telephone operator who has been sitting for three years in a hotel room in France, connecting the banal chitchat of the various staffs: now he is in Russia, in a situation fraught with danger, and has been ordered to repair and check the telephone line, half an hour before dawn.

The sergeant was a quiet, slight man, pale and unshaven. The usual decorations dangled casually from his chest. His job done, he stayed on with our group long enough to smoke a cigarette. We hardly spoke, but when he stood up to say goodbye he said with a smile—it sounded almost like an apology—"I'm due to go on leave tonight." He slung his machine pistol on his back, shrugged his shoulders, and shook hands all around; then he drew aside the blanket that shielded the bunker toward the rear.

The next moment he lay dead at our feet.

The shell struck the escarpment of the trench; the dark sky seemed to collapse—the light had gone out. The corporal screamed like a madman; and when, covered with clods of earth and fighting down my fear, I raised myself forcibly, I touched a bleeding body, my hand sank into a foul, wet mass, and I screamed too. Meanwhile your brother had drawn the blanket across again, and switched on his flashlight, revealing a ghastly sight. The legs of the dead sergeant stuck out from under the blanket, into the bunker, and the corporal's right leg had been severed below the knee. Our cigarettes were still alight: your brother held his between his lips.

"Bandage him," he told me, his face pale. He stepped outside.

The artillery barrage continued. We became familiar with the sound of Russian mortars, the horrible whine of the heavy artillery shells that seemed to be driving death before them. While the earth trembled all around us, I bandaged the whimpering corporal. With some vague notion of making a tourniquet, I rashly tore off my suspenders—the next day I would have taken his since by then he no longer needed them, whereas for me there were occasions later when the lack of them almost cost me my life. I made a tourniquet around the stump and wrapped gauze and rags, as many as I could find, over the bleeding wound. When I tried to leave the bunker, the wounded man clung to me, but I had made up my mind to die under the open sky and I pushed him away.

Outside, the darkness was lit up by brief red flames; it looked as if fire were leaping from the earth, fire instantly to be covered by darkness again.

That short barrage seemed to go on forever. I thought the entire eastern front must be in turmoil, a giant offensive under way. Actually it lasted—your brother had checked it on his wristwatch—seven minutes and was comparatively harmless. The company's casualties were four dead and seven wounded.

We were all totally exhausted after the rigors of the train journey, the march, the flight, and again the journey by truck—and now this concentrated encounter with the front. But we were to learn that there was no longer any such thing as sleep, although there were hours when one simply sank into oblivion, slept as if dead, was dragged to one's feet, stood sentry or was sent off to one of the other platoons as a dispatch runner.

In those first nights—during the day it was hardly possible to move outside our sector—I invariably lost my sense of direction. There I would lie, stretched out on the earth, darkness all around, waiting for a flare to go up that would allow me to recognize some landmark that would tell me whether I had to crawl forward, backward, or sideways. Sometimes, when I eventually crawled off, I was aware in that singing, cold silence of something eerie, something indescribable, like an invisible, inaudible, yet palpable breath: the proximity of the enemy. I would know then that I was quite close to the Russian positions, and often a hoarse whisper or call, a terrible, alien laugh, confirmed that I was not mistaken.

Oh, that fear of being taken prisoner by the Russians! It was that fear alone that prevented the war in Russia from ending as early as 1942. Imagine, if you will, what would have happened if our soldiers had been made to fight there for years under the same inhuman conditions, the same incompetent leadership, against the Americans or the British.

We remained in that sector for one week.

X

The attack expected for the morning of the following day did not come until evening. During this attack, something occurred that I would never have believed possible: we repulsed it.

From the moment I saw the first shapeless, muffled-up figures really and truly a hundred yards away from us approaching our sector—from that moment on I stood totally prepared to flee, my whistle at my lips, braced against the rear wall of the trench, one hand poised for the leap. Your brother stood there quite calmly, giving the orders that we had to pass on. Every few seconds we had to duck when a wave of Russian fire seemed to burst right in our faces, and every time that appalling fear when one could raise one's head again: Are they here?

From time to time I would look back to make sure of a retreat under cover, for one of the old soldiers had told me, between two gulps from a bottle of schnapps, "What matters most in this whole war, kiddo, is a retreat under cover."

The Russians came surging forward, forced over and over again by the scythelike action of our machine-gun fire to fling themselves to the ground: the screams of the wounded were already filling the thick gray air. From the rear we were supported by heavy artillery, while the neighboring companies also aimed their fire in front of our sector. Still, it seemed hopeless to try to stem that relentless tide. Just then your brother suddenly gave the order, "Prepare to attack!" Hardly had he uttered the command when a heavy salvo of Russian naval guns forced us to take cover. I ducked, and it flashed through my mind: This is it, you can't go back, by now the Russians are here. But suddenly your brother's voice shouted, "Forward, charge!"

He was the first to go over the top: with a frenzied gesture and another shout, he swept the entire company after him, and charge forward we did. At first the Russians hesitated, but that moment was enough; first a few of them started running, then whole groups turned tail—we could hear the shrill yelling and cursing of their officers while the rest put up their hands. We brought back twenty prisoners, the first living Russians we had seen face to face; their eyes held only one thing—fear.

The evening of the eighth day, I was sitting, for the first time in a long while, alone with your brother in the bunker. While we waited tensely for the ration runners, we drank schnapps and smoked cigarettes. The stretcher bearer had gone back with the ration runners to pick up medicines, bandages, and antitetanus ampules, for if anyone was wounded in the daytime, we had to leave him lying where he was until nightfall. Your brother sat by the phone, and I squatted at his feet on the flattened pile of straw on which we slept.

"The whole secret of attack," he suddenly said, after we had been silent for a long time, "is to imagine how scared the enemy is. Imagine yourself crouching in your hole and you suddenly see some characters charging at you and yelling their heads off! You go crazy with fear; you saw that on Tuesday—we lost all self-control. You have to force the enemy to become passive. Then he's done for."

"You've found the secret of how to win the war," I said dryly. "Sell it for a fortune, and you've got it made."

He gave a quick laugh, then his expression grew serious again, and he lit another cigarette. "But the terrible thing is that one doesn't know which side one wants to win..."

At this moment the stretcher bearer rushed in, shouting, "We're being relieved, sir, we're being relieved!"

What was happening was that the front, whose defense was demanding increasingly pointless sacrifices, was being shortened; the lines were allowed to shrink, and for several days a few units could be saved that were then sent back to the front to reinforce the shortened line. Whatever the reason, it was wonderful to go back to the rear for at least a brief respite. The ration runner hadn't bothered to bring any more rations; we were to have our meal in peace and quiet at the rear. At midnight, when darkness had become solid, we moved off, a sad procession: one week earlier we had moved into position with nearly eighty men, and we were returning with forty-eight.

In the dark it was impossible to make out whether it was the same place. When we actually did reach the village I was filled with a fantastic feeling of life.

Your brother was kept busy for a while, making sure his men were properly accommodated, supervising the distribution of rations. He gave orders that the following day the men would be off duty, attended to a pile of tiresome paperwork in the orderly room, and instructed me to heat up enough water for a thorough wash.

We were billeted in a farm cottage whose rough windows had been nailed up with cardboard and then draped with blankets. I lit four bunker lights, one in each corner, and stoked up the stove with plenty of wood. It was almost November. I had lost all desire for sleep, although an hour earlier I could have collapsed from exhaustion. Slowly savoring every mouthful, I emptied my mess kit, washed down the rich bean soup with generous swigs of schnapps, and stuffed the larger of my two pipes so full of tobacco that the pale yellow shreds hung over the edge. Drawing deeply on my pipe, I would drink another schnapps and watch the roaring flames as they devoured the wood in the stove. From time to time I would dip my hand in the bucket to test the heat of the water. With every pull on my pipe I sucked in something precious, indescribable, something that felt good even as I remembered the dead and the wounded: life.

When the water seemed hot enough, I carefully pulled out my underwear from the bag I had collected from the company baggage, chose a decent civilian shirt—light blue with a proper civilized collar— and sniffed it: it still smelled of Cadette's soap.

Slowly, with an intoxicated sensuousness, I washed myself. Imagine, if you can: you live in the ground and receive every day as much or as little liquid as you need barely to satisfy your most elementary thirst; not a single opportunity to wash even your fingertips, yet still having to spend hours crawling over the wet ground. You become matted with dirt. Fortunately, since we were all newcomers, we had been spared the otherwise inevitable lice, those demoralizing vermin that contributed significantly toward our losing the war. Later I was to become familiar with them.

I kept on washing long enough for the fresh lot of water to have heated up again; then I shaved and put on clean underwear and socks. I was filled with exaltation: never had that rotgut tasted so delicious, never had tobacco tasted so good. Just before two, your brother came back. He greeted me wearily, sat down on the bench by the stove, removed his cap, and, with a sudden gesture, flung it onto the floor in the middle of the room.

While he ate, I set the bucket of water on a low wooden stool, put soap and towel beside it, and laid out the underwear I had taken out of his pack.

Then I lay down on a bed in the corner and watched him. When he began to shave, I said, "You still owe me the solution to a riddle you asked me at the station in Abbeville. About the wine salesman..."

"Yes," he said with a laugh, "that was two weeks ago; it feels as if it had been in another life."

"It was in another life," I said.

"Maybe you're right—I'll give you the solution before the day is out."

The door opened, and in came Schnecker. We were surprised less at the sight of him than of a new decoration on his chest.

I had jumped to my feet and accorded him the mandatory obeisance. With a wave of the hand he said, "Lie down again."

Your brother greeted him silently and, just as silently, offered him a stool.

Schnecker seated himself astride a chair, lit a cigarette, and proceeded to watch your brother shaving.

I had ample time to observe him as he sat turned sideways toward me. He sat extraordinarily still, almost motionless, but when I looked at him more closely I realized that he was completely drunk. He was at that stage when a drunk man is filled with a leaden stability, when an almost idiotic law of gravity keeps him upright. When he started to speak, it became obvious that I had assumed correctly.

"My friend," he began; his voice, very pinched, came from high up in his throat. "I see you're up to some nice little tricks, my friend, hm?"

"What do you mean?" countered your brother, who had finished shaving. He dried his face and put on his shirt.

"I see you're up to some nice little tricks. I haven't heard a thing about there being no duty tomorrow, and you simply go ahead and order it." He laughed.

Your brother laughed too. "If you haven't heard a thing about it, so much the better."

"But now I have heard about it," said the captain, his tone sharpening as he jerked himself to his feet. "And I'm telling you that it's important for the men to go over their weapons and gear tomorrow—the day after that we're being redeployed, assigned to the Seventeenth, a bit farther south, understand?" By now he was almost shouting.

"I understand perfectly, but first I'm going to see that the men get some sleep. Besides..." he hesitated, slowly tied his neckband, ran his hand once more over his hair, looked at Schnecker, and was silent.

"Besides what?" asked the captain.

"Besides," your brother calmly continued, "I would have preferred it if I could have seen you now and then up at the front with me this past week."

"What's that?" A wary look came over the captain's face, and he shot a glance in my direction, but I had closed my eyes and pretended to be asleep. The two men now lowered their voices.

"I would have preferred it if I could have seen you now and then in my sector during this past week. It would have given the men quite a boost, and me too, for that matter. It's dreadful to feel all the time that one is alone. After all, orders are only paper."

"Paper?" asked Schnecker. His expression was now almost maniacal; his voice had slipped too, and he was quite hoarse.

"Yes, paper!" shouted your brother, so loud that I was really startled. "Paper! Paper! A substance inferior even to that gilt tin on your manly chest!"

"Oho!" cried the captain; now he was laughing again. Suddenly he stood stiffly to attention. "I have to inform you, First Lieutenant

Schelling," he said raspingly, "that you have been awarded the Iron Cross, First and Second Class, also the Infantry Assault Medal in Silver. You fought damn well. In fifteen minutes the gentlemen of the battalion will be holding a small celebration in your honor and"—he gave a little bow to himself—"in mine too."

He put on his cap and marched out stiff as a ramrod. It was almost as if he hadn't been there at all. Your brother whistled softly as he cleaned his nails, the cigarette between his lips. I rose and put out two of the lights that had begun to flicker and threatened to burst into flames.

"I don't feel much like sleeping now—how about us looking in on the party?"

"Us?" I asked in surprise.

"Of course you're coming along—you're getting a decoration too, maybe a couple."

"What, me?" I exclaimed.

"Of course," he said, laughing. "Besides, there'll be women there. I'd like to have one more chance to see a woman."

"Girls?" I cried.

"Maybe girls too!" He laughed again. "I've no idea what kind will be there. Anyway, they'll be women, and I'd like the chance to have a glass or two of wine with one of them."

"Jesus!" I cried. "Women!"

He stood up and drew on his greatcoat. I put on my cap and slipped into a padded camouflage jacket.

We stepped out together into the cold night; it was quiet, something resembling peace lay spread under the dark vault of the sky. Headquarters were in a large building, something between a palace and a manor house—I imagine it had been the administrative offices of a kolkhoz.

The sentry let us pass without hindrance, although we didn't know the password. We found ourselves walking along dark corridors and managed to rout out a telephone operator who directed us to the third floor. Raucous singing filled the corridor, which smelled of Russia. A door opened, light and noise streamed out onto the corridor, were immediately swallowed up again, and we soon came upon a figure that was staggering toward a window, apparently to throw up.

"Hello, Piester!" cried your brother. The man turned, recognized your brother, and waved. We went closer. He leaned on a window sill and groaned pitifully. It was the adjutant, an agreeable young lieutenant not much given to talking.

As we stood beside him he said, "I can't take any more, Schelling. He keeps forcing me to drink, I can't take any more, but he threatens to shoot anyone who won't drink. I can't take any more." As he leaned over the sill, I followed him with my eyes; below lay a dark, silent garden that appeared to be planted with vines.

"Where's your room?" asked your brother.

"Why do you ask?"

"Come along."

Your brother took Piester by the arm and steered him ahead down the long corridor. Each time Piester hesitated, your brother gave him another push. Piester opened a door.

"Let's have some light," your brother said to me. I fished out my box of matches, and by the light of the burning match we entered the room. Then I closed the door behind me and ran to the window to fasten the blackout curtain.

The room looked bare. On the floor lay a pack; beside the narrow wooden bed stood an officer's trunk, and on it a half-written letter and a candle stuck to the lid. A piece of broken mirror hung on the wall.

We forced Piester onto the bed; his face was yellow.

"Something terrible is going to happen," mumbled Piester, his eyes closing the moment he lay down. "He's run out of schnapps, and the paymaster won't fork out any more. Something terrible—they're expecting you..."

We went back onto the corridor. All this time I had been listening, almost apprehensively, for a woman's voice, but even now I could hear nothing but that stupid male yowling.

The moment we opened the door, silence fell in the room. It was a scene of utter debauchery: Schnecker was sitting on the table, his legs spread-eagled, his tunic unbuttoned and revealing curly black hair on his broad chest. Beside him stood an artillery officer holding a bottle of cognac upside down over Schnecker's gaping mouth. After a brief pause they both resumed their bestial yowling.

Over in the corner stood the battalion's medical officer, an elderly bourgeois type; beside him a young Russian woman with soft blond hair and a rosy, peasantlike face: she looked like a girl. I assumed her to be the doctor's mistress, a doctor herself, of whom I had heard a good deal when collecting our rations. She was said to be very skillful at bandaging and very kind to the wounded. Now she was watching the scene at the table with a completely dispassionate curiosity, while her lover, looking very nervous, was holding her tightly by the arm.

"Good evening, gentlemen," said your brother.

Schnecker let out a hoarse roar and tried to jump off the table, but he slipped and would have struck it head first if we hadn't caught him in time. The artillery officer smashed the empty bottle onto the floor and looked at us idiotically.

"Good evening," your brother repeated, smiling in the direction of the Russian woman, who bowed slightly and smiled back at us.

We helped Schnecker down from his wedged position on the table. "Not a drop of booze left!" he shouted. "Goddamn it, not a drop left. My good friend Karlemann has just squeezed the last drops out of the bottle for me!" He gratefully patted the artillery officer, who was still laughing idiotically.

"Well!" said your brother. "You're a fine host, I must say. When I arrive there's nothing left!"

Schnecker stared at him. Those bloodshot eyes were hot and ugly.

I could look only at the Russian woman; the mere sight of her soft, rosy skin gave me a pang of happiness, and I trembled as she approached. She kept her eyes firmly on Schnecker as she took her doddering old medical officer by the hand and walked without a sound to the door.

Meanwhile Schnecker had been having an incoherent, raucous dialogue with the artillery officer, but when the Russian woman was almost at the door—I had stepped aside and was close enough to be aware of how crisp and clean she smelled—Schnecker swung around in a flash and, his mouth agape with laughter, shouted, "Stop, my girl—not yet! You have to have another drink with me!" The medical officer had freed his hand and stepped back.

"But you've nothing more to drink!" said the woman, her voice as clear as ringing metal.

"There's more on the way!" He careened around the table, guffawed, dashed to the door, flung it open, and screamed, "Alarm! Alarm! Alarm!"

At first we didn't understand and stood rooted to the spot. Even the artillery officer seemed to have sobered up a bit Schnecker came back and called out to us, "Now he'll have to get out of bed, that stinker—then we'll have some booze!"

Your brother sighed and took a deep breath, flung himself at Schnecker, and thrust him out into the dark corridor. I followed them, the woman screamed, the medical officer shouted, "My God ... my God..." while the artillery officer tried in vain to get around the table, stammering, "Karlemann ... Karlemann..."

Schnecker was now wrestling outside with your brother: he was a muscular fellow, and drunkenness must have doubled his strength. I ran to them, grabbed him from behind, and dragged him over to the window, meanwhile pummeling away at him in my towering rage. Somewhere in the dark the last of his decorations fell with a tinny sound onto the tiled floor. Schnecker groaned, spat, bit, and, whenever he managed to free his mouth, which your brother was clamping shut, screamed like a madman, "Alarm! Alarm!"

When an orderly came up from downstairs and asked what was going on, your brother called out to him, "Nothing, he's drunk." By this time we were pretty close to the window, but now the artillery officer had also slipped through the door and was attacking your brother from behind; furthermore, a staff sergeant came running along the corridor shouting, "What's going on? What is it?"

"Alarm!" yelled Schnecker. "Alarm!"

"Nothing," shouted your brother. "He's drunk!"

He now had Schnecker by the throat, while I had tripped the artillery officer and was preventing him from getting up.

Schnecker had been forced over to the window. He was groaning and seemed to be bleeding somewhere. "Don't you realize, you bastard," your brother said to him, "that the other hundred and twenty men in your battalion can use a few hours' sleep?"

Schnecker, who by this time had freed himself, yelled even louder, "Alarm! I am ordering alarm!" And when your brother, suddenly seized

by a sort of frenzy, punched him right in the face, Schnecker, in a lightning move, drew his pistol, held it to your brother's temple, and pressed
the trigger. Your brother was dead on the spot: he fell to the floor across
the whimpering artillery officer. Schnecker had turned pale; his hand
was still holding the pistol. There was an eerie silence: I was about to
fling myself on him, but at that moment the first Russian tank started
firing outside the building. We stared at each other. Hideous bursts of
firing shattered the sky. Schnecker had already run off down the corridor. I dashed after him but on the way ran into Piester's room and
shouted in his ear, "The Russians are here—move!" Then I ran down
the stairs to the ground-floor corridor and jumped out the window into
the garden.

I managed to escape and from a distance saw that the great building was in flames. I kept running until I was scooped up by another regiment and sent back to the front. Not one man from our unit escaped.
The Russians had overrun the village from three sides and in great
numerical superiority. And although I never saw Schnecker again, or
was ever told, I knew he had managed to get away. He can't die. I
assumed that in some way or other he would inform your mother of
your brother's death. He has done nothing. He just goes on living. All
this I learned during the last few days.

I pass the truth on to you. It belongs to you...

THE CASUALTY

The stories in The Casualty *were written between 1946 and 1952 but only published in 1983, as* Die Verwundung, *by Lamuv Verlag.* The Casualty *was first published in English by Chatto and Windus in 1986; an American edition by Farrar, Straus & Giroux followed in 1987.*

THE EMBRACE

He was looking down on the parting in her hair, a narrow white path; he felt her breasts against his skin, her warm breath in his face, and his gaze fell into the endless distance of that narrow white path. Somewhere on the carpet lay his belt with, clearly visible, the embossed words: GOTT MIT UNS; beside it his tunic with its soiled collarband, and somewhere a clock was ticking.

The window was open, and from outside on the terrace he could hear the tinkle of fine crystal, hear men chuckling and women giggling. The sky was a velvet blue; it was a glorious summer night.

And he could hear her heart beating, very close to his chest, and again his gaze fell into that narrow white path through her hair.

It was dark, but the sky still held that soft summer glow, and he knew he was close to her, as close as he could be, while still so infinitely remote. They didn't say a word. The clock seemed to be ticking him away, the ticking was stronger than the heartbeat against his chest, and he couldn't tell whether it was her heart or his. The message was: you're on leave until reveille; and: one more chance to sleep with a girl, but make a real night of it. They had even given him a bottle of wine.

He could distinctly make out the bottle as it stood on the chest of drawers, a bright band of light. That was the bottle, a bright band of light in the dark. The bottle was empty. The cork must be on the carpet, where his tunic, trousers and belt were lying.

She had lain against his chest, he with one arm round her and smoking with his free hand; they hadn't said a word. All their encounters were marked by silence. He had always thought it might sometimes be possible to talk to a woman, but she never talked.

Outside the sky darkened, the subdued laughter of the guests on the terrace faded away, the women's giggles turned into yawns, and after a while he could hear the glasses clinking louder as the waiter picked up four or five in one hand to carry them away. Then the bottles were being taken away too, making a fuller sound, and finally chairs were upended, tables moved, and he could hear a woman sweeping slowly, thoroughly, conscientiously: the entire night seemed to consist of that sweeping as she swept with a quiet, regular stroke. He could hear the sweep of the broom and the woman's footsteps moving from one end of the terrace to the other; then came a weary, thick voice asking from beyond a door: "Not finished yet?", and the woman's reply, equally weary: "I'll be through in a minute."

Soon after that, complete silence fell; the sky had turned dark blue. Softly and from very far away came the sound of music from behind the heavy curtains of a night club. So they lay side by side, until the empty bottle slowly emerged from the darkness, a band of light growing wider and brighter until the bottle assumed its full, round shape, dark green and empty, and the tunic on the floor with its soiled collarband became visible, and the belt with the embossed words: GOTT MIT UNS.

THE UNKNOWN SOLDIER

Somewhere up ahead was where the front began. He kept thinking they had reached it whenever the truck column slowed down and stopped in a village, where corporals and soldiers with grim, set faces were moving about in dirt and mud. But the journey was always resumed, and he was scared because for a while now they had been hearing shots close by. They must have already moved beyond the emplacements of the heavy artillery since the detonations were now coming from behind, where the column had just come from. But on they went. It was cold, and it was no use to keep trying to pull one's greatcoat closer or tugging at the collar as if it could be made longer. And their gloves were too thin, and he didn't even feel like smoking: he was simply too cold, as well as horribly tired.

His eyes kept closing, but nausea kept him from falling asleep. He was sickened by the exhaust fumes, and it made him uneasy that no one in the truck said a word. Normally their tongues never stopped wagging. Even while they were in the troop train, on their way here, they had talked all day, about their women and their exploits and about their fancy flats back home and their important jobs. There wasn't one of them who didn't have a gorgeous flat and a super job, but now they were all terribly quiet, and he could tell from their breathing that they were shivering with cold. The road was rough, the mud over a foot deep, rutted by tank tracks, with here and there the imprint of a horse's hoof. The poor horses, he thought. And he didn't even think of the infantrymen who had to slog it on foot. It was great to be driven, but it would have been better to walk, it would have warmed them up and they wouldn't have got there so fast.

But now he wanted to get there faster. He really did feel as sick as a dog. With each breath he seemed to inhale new nausea. He could smell not only the stink of the exhaust right under his nose but also the stench of the men sitting behind him, all of whom—including himself—hadn't had a proper wash for a couple of weeks, just hands and faces. A foul miasma of sour, disgusting, dirty, stale sweat came from behind him. Some of the men were smoking; he was ready to throw up and would have welcomed it if someone had taken pity on him, held a service revolver to his head, and pressed the trigger ...

And still they hadn't reached the front. Now he could hear the firing of the machine guns, so close that he felt they must be driving right into it. The village they were passing through looked exactly as he imagined a front-line village to look. Soldiers with muddy boots and the totally deadpan faces of heroes, wearing their decorations and staring straight ahead, and corporals who no longer looked so much like corporals; and some lieutenants, and a field kitchen behind a filthy cottage, in a yard apparently consisting solely of manure and mud. But they were soon through the godforsaken hole and still they hadn't quite reached the front. Goddammit, he thought, where the hell's the infantry?

They stopped beside a small forest that covered a hill. Somewhere up front a voice roared "Everybody out!" and he immediately jumped down from the lorry and began to stamp his feet to get warm. The others tossed out the baggage, and he had to catch not only a machine gun but also the ammunition boxes, which he dropped in the mud. The corporal, pale-faced and shivering, gave him hell for dropping the boxes in the mud. He looked in astonishment at the corporal. What the hell difference did it make? As far as he was concerned they could shoot him on the spot if they felt like it. He simply felt too wretched to care.

He grabbed his rifle, combat pack, and two boxes of ammunition, and stepped into the bushes after hearing the order from up front: "Get off the road!" It was wet in the bushes, some of the men were smoking, and he fished a cigarette out of his pocket. He saw everything and heard everything, yet he heard and saw nothing: the sky was grey all over, without a single dark or light speck, and it must be about five in the afternoon. The soldiers hunkered down on their boxes; some of them were stamping around, but they soon gave up because the ground was too soft and wet, so wet that it splashed when they stamped on it.

Nothing much was said. Somewhere the NCOs were gathered round the lieutenant, and on the path leading into the forest a captain appeared with a list. He was a young captain who for some reason snapped at the lieutenant, and the lieutenant stood to attention. The noise of machine guns started up again: the gunner couldn't have been lying more than ten yards away. Then came the sound of quite a different machine gun, and he knew that that rough, slower, throaty sound must come from the Russian machine guns. For a moment he felt his terrible indifference shot through with something like excitement. The captain in his muddy boots with his incredibly young face was now talking urgently to the lieutenant and the NCOs.

He threw away his cigarette and turned to the man nearest to him. It was cold; he looked at him, and it was some time before he realized that it was Karl—Karl, that quiet, inconspicuous fellow who hadn't had much to say on the journey, an older man wearing a wedding ring who had always seemed a pillar of respectability.

"Karl," he said in a low voice.

"What is it?" Karl answered quietly.

"Got anything to drink?" Karl nodded and fumbled at the canteen hanging from his belt.

He groped for the stopper with one hand, unscrewed it, and lifted the canteen to his mouth, and when the first gulp ran down his throat he was suddenly aware of having a hellish thirst. He groaned with pleasure and drank deeply.

Suddenly their corporal shouted "Fall in!" and Karl hurriedly snatched back his canteen and hooked it on again. All the sections were being called by their corporals, assembled on the forest path, then marched off in rows behind the captain into the forest.

All he could think of was drinking.

His thirst was barbaric: he was tempted to throw himself on the ground and drink the puddle on the path. The forest path seemed familiar. This thin, scrubby growth, these skimpy little beech trees standing far apart, and between them the brown, sodden earth; the grey, endlessly grey sky overhead, and this squelchy path. Up ahead the captain, talking earnestly to the lieutenant, and the corporals beside their sections: just like on the training ground when they used to march off for firing practice ... it was all nonsense, they weren't really in Russia, they hadn't covered all those thousands of kilometres by train to be shot up here or to freeze to death. It was all a dream.

The firing ahead of them sounded regular and familiar: rifles and machine guns, somewhere artillery too.

Suddenly they halted. He looked up to find they were standing in front of a hut hidden in the trees beside the path. Behind it were more huts, and deeper inside the forest he could see holes in the ground, entrances to dug-outs hung with blankets and telephone cables, and somewhere in a dilapidated shed stood a field kitchen. Once again they had to leave the path and step under the scrawny little trees. Troopers emerged from the dug-outs, and some corporals and another lieutenant. They seemed quite unconcerned, and he thought: so it's not Russia after all. Everything was so terribly normal. The trooper who joined them had a machine pistol slung over one shoulder and a pipe stuck in his grey face. He had always imagined that, when they reached the front, the real front, they would be looked at with contempt as being green-horns. But no one looked contemptuously at them; in fact they seemed rather indifferent, if anything a bit sorry for them.

What a marvellous war-game they're having here, he thought. Eve-rything's so incredibly real, I hope the shooting's real too and they'll shoot me dead. His nausea had not subsided; his head ached, and a sour, horrible sick feeling rose from his stomach into his head and seemed to fill all his veins and nerves. He took deep breaths—the fresh air felt good for at least a tenth of a second. They're playing a damn convincing game, he thought, as the trooper who had joined them walked right up to the corporal and said: "To the third."

"Yessir!" replied the corporal, and the trooper gave him an odd look. "Okay, let's go," said the trooper, and he marched off into the for-est, followed by the corporal and the men in single file.

Carrying his ammunition box, he was the last but one. He stag-gered along behind the man in front of him, through that sparse beech wood, feeling miserably cold, sick to his stomach ...

Suddenly their guide, the trooper, threw himself on the ground shouting "Take cover!" and at that very moment some shells burst in front of them. It couldn't be far away: he heard a sickening soft rustling, a rush of wind, then the crash, and one of the little beech trees snapped right off and fell over. He could clearly see a slender tree trunk burst-ing twenty yards away and slowly toppling over, revealing its white, greenish-white, core at the place of impact. Clods of earth rained down, some of them splattering the ground close by. It was wonderful to be lying on the ground. Although he knew very well that this was for real, that they were in Russia, actually in Russia, and almost right up at the very front, all he felt was: how wonderful to be lying on the ground, full length. Although it was wet and the cold and damp quickly penetrated his greatcoat, he simply didn't care.

Dear God, he prayed, let the next shell land right on top of me ... But the trooper was back on his feet, shouting "Let's go!" On they marched and soon they reached the edge of the forest. The trooper waited until they were all there and then explained something to them. He could hear it all quite distinctly, but he couldn't have cared less about any of it; never in his life had he felt so utterly indifferent. Moreover, by this time he was so cold that his teeth were chattering. Before them was a big field, all torn up, and on it a burned-out tank with a Soviet star painted on its side. On either side of the tank were emplacements. It looked exactly like the training area. Proper trenches and dug-out mounds, and he saw which machine gun was firing—it seemed to sound much farther away than it had a while ago when they had been in the lorry. And the machine gun was firing at the remains of a house standing at the end of the field: he saw the impacts, saw the mud spray up from the ruined walls, and from an entirely different direction a throaty-sounding, slower machine gun was now firing at the edge of the forest just where they were standing. The trooper, their leader, threw himself on the ground again, and they didn't wait for him to shout "Take cover!" for one of them had been hit and lay there screaming, screaming horribly, and the machine gun went on firing.

He was about to slide over to his mate, realizing from the voice that it was Willi, but two men were already lying on their stomachs beside Willi, bandaging one leg. He distinctly heard one of the bullets smash into a tender young sapling. A few ricochet bullets buzzed into the void like demented bees.

When he saw the others cautiously crawling backwards, he did the same, although his fatigue and nausea made everything swim before his eyes. It was exhausting work, pushing oneself backwards, and the machine gun was now sawing right above their heads; it was horrifying the way the bullets were slapping into the forest floor behind them or into the soft wood, revealing the young, greenish-white wounds. And then another shell burst, then several more; everything was reduced to noise and a horrible stench, and again a man screamed, then another.

He didn't know who was screaming, all he wanted was to sleep; he closed his eyes and screamed, went on screaming without knowing that he was screaming, until God granted his wish ...

JAK THE TOUT

He arrived one night with the ration runners as a replacement for Gornizek, who lay wounded at battalion headquarters. Those nights were very dark, and fear hung like a thunder cloud over the alien, pitch-black earth. I was up front at a listening post, keeping my eyes and ears open towards the rear, from where the sounds of the ration runners came, just as much as towards the front, towards the dark silence on the Russian side.

It was Gerhard who brought him along, together with my mess-tin and cigarettes.

"D'you want the bread, too?" Gerhard asked, "or shall I keep it for you till tomorrow morning?" I could tell from his voice that he was in a hurry to get back.

"No," I said, "give me the lot, it'll be eaten up right away."

He handed me the bread and the tinned meat in a piece of wax paper, the roll of fruit-drops and some mixed butter and lard on a scrap of cardboard.

All this time the newcomer had been standing there trembling and silent. "And here," said Gerhard, "is the replacement for Gornizek. The lieutenant has sent him out to you, to the listening post."

"Yes," was all I said; it was customary to send newcomers to the most difficult posts. Gerhard crawled back to the rear.

"Come on down," I said quietly. "Not so much noise, for God's sake!" He was making a stupid racket with the stuff hanging from his belt, his spade and gas mask; he stepped clumsily into the hole and almost knocked over my mess-tin. "Idiot," I muttered as I made room for him. I heard rather than saw how he proceeded to unbuckle his belt, place the spade to one side, his gas mask beside it, and his rifle up onto the parapet, pointing at the enemy, and then buckle on his belt again, all strictly according to regulations.

The bean soup was cold by this time, and it was just as well that in the dark I couldn't see all the grubs that must have been boiled out of the beans. There was plenty of meat in the soup, delicious crisp brown bits. Next I ate up the tinned meat from the wax paper and stuffed the bread into the empty mess-tin. He stood perfectly silent beside me, always facing the enemy, and in the blackness of the night I could see a snub-nosed profile. When he turned aside, I could tell from his narrow cheeks that he was still young; his steel helmet looked almost like the shell of a tortoise. These boys had a special something about their cheeks that recalled playing soldiers on a suburban common. "My Redskin brother," they always seemed to be saying, and their lips trembled with fear, and their hearts were stiff with courage. Those poor kids ...

"You might as well sit down," I said in that painstakingly acquired voice that is easily intelligible but scarcely audible a yard away. "Here," I added, pulling at the hem of his greatcoat and almost forcing him down into the hollowed-out seat. "You can't possibly stand all the time."

"But on sentry duty ... " came a feeble voice that cracked like that of a sentimental tenor.

"Shut up!" I hissed at him.

"But on sentry duty," he whispered, "we're not permitted to sit!"

"Nothing's permitted, not even starting a war."

Although I could see him only in outline, I knew that he was now sitting like a pupil in class, hands on knees, bolt upright and ready to jump up any second. I bent forward, drew my greatcoat right over the back of my head, and lit my pipe.

"Want a smoke?"

"No." I was surprised how quickly he had learned to whisper.

"Well, anyway," I said, "have a drink instead."

"No," he repeated, but I grabbed his head and held the neck of the flask to his mouth; as patient as a calf with its first bottle, he swallowed a few times, then made such a violent gesture of disgust that I took away the flask.

"Don't you like it?"

"I do," he stammered, "but I choked."

"Then drink it yourself."

He took the flask out of my hand and swallowed a good gulp.

"Thanks," he murmured. I had a drink, too.

"Feeling better now?"

"Yes—much."

"Not quite so scared, eh?"

He was ashamed to admit that he was scared at all, but they were all like that.

"I'm scared, too," I said, "all the time, that's why I find courage in a bottle."

I felt him jerk towards me, and I leaned over to see his face. All I could see was the bright glint of his eyes, eyes that looked danger-ous, and shadowy dark outlines, but I could smell him. He smelled of army stores, of sweat, storeroom, and leftover soup, and slightly of the schnapps. There was no sound at all; behind us they seemed to have finished doling out the rations. He turned back towards the enemy.

"Is this your first time out?"

Again he was ashamed, I could tell, but he answered: "Yes."

"How long have you been a soldier?"

"Eight weeks."

"And where are you from?"

"From St Avold."

"Where?"

"St Avold. Lorraine, you know ... "

"A long trip?"

"Two weeks."

We fell silent, and I tried to peer through the impenetrable dark-ness ahead. Oh, if only daylight would come, I thought, if one could at least see something, daybreak at least, some fog maybe—see something, see anything, a scrap of light ... but when daylight came I would be wishing that it was dark. If only dusk would fall, or fog would roll in suddenly. It was always the same ...

Up front there was nothing. Off in the distance, the gentle throb-bing of engines. The Russians were being fed, too. Then came the sound of a twittering Russian voice that was abruptly suppressed, as if a hand had been clapped over a mouth. It was nothing ...

"Do you know what our job is?" I asked him. How good it felt not to be alone any more! How wonderful to feel the breath of a human being, to be aware of his stale smell—a human being who was not about to finish one off the very next second!

"Yes," he said, "listening post." Again I was surprised how well he could whisper, almost better than I could. It seemed so effortless. For me it was always an effort, I always wanted to shout, yell, call out, so that the night would collapse like black foam; for me it was a terrible effort, that whispering.

"Fine," I said, "listening post. So we have to be on the look-out for when the Russians come, when they attack. Then we send up a red flare, bang away with our rifles for a bit, and scram, to the rear—got it? But when only a few come, a recce patrol, then we have to keep quiet, let them through, and one of us has to go back and tell the others, tell the lieutenant—you've been in his dug-out, haven't you?"

"Yes," he said, his voice trembling.

"Okay. And if the patrol attacks us both, then we have to finish them off, dead as doornails, right? We mustn't clear out just for a patrol. Got it? Okay?"

"Yes," he said, his voice still trembling, and then I heard a dreadful sound: his teeth were chattering.

"Here," I said, handing him the flask.

I had another drink, too.

"But suppose … suppose …" he stammered, "suppose we can't even see them coming …"

"Then we're done for. But don't worry—we're bound to see them or hear them. And if we suspect something we're allowed to send up a flare, then we'll see everything." He was silent again; it was terrible the way he was never the first to speak.

"But they won't come," I rattled on, "they never come at night. If they come at all, it'll be in the morning, two minutes before dawn …"

"Two minutes before dawn?" he broke in.

"Two minutes before dawn is when they start, then they'll be here by first light …"

"But then surely it's too late."

"Well, then we have to quickly send up a red flare and clear out—don't worry, you'll find you can run like a hare. And don't forget we'll hear it first. What's your name, anyway?" It was a nuisance, every time I wanted to speak to him I had to nudge him, take my hands out of my warm pockets and stuff them back in and wait till they got warm again …

"My name," he said, "my name's Jak."

"English?"

"No," he said, "it's from Jakob … Jak a-k, not Jack—Jak, just Jak."

"Jak," I went on, "what did you do for a living?"

"Me? My last job was as a tout."

"What's that?"

"A tout."

"What did you tout then?"

He jerked his face towards me, and I could tell he was very surprised.

"What did I tout—what did I tout? Well, I was just a tout!"

"What d'you mean? *What* did you tout?"

He was silent for a while, looking straight ahead again; then in the darkness his head turned back towards me.

"Well," he said, "I was touting," and he sighed deeply. "I stood at the railway station, towards the end anyway, and when someone came, came by, in that crowd someone I thought might be interested, most of them were soldiers of course—so when someone came by I'd ask him in a low voice, a very low voice, you know: 'Want a good time, sir?' That's what I'd ask ... " His voice was trembling again, and this time it may not have been fear but recollection.

In my eagerness I forgot to take a drink. "And," I asked hoarsely, "if he did want to have a good time?"

"Then," he said with an effort, and again it seemed to be the recollection that overcame him, "then I'd take him to whichever one of the girls happened to be free."

"To a cathouse, you mean?"

"No," he said matter-of-factly, "I wasn't working for the cathouses, I had a few freelancers, you know, a few loners who kept me going. Three without a license. Irma, Lilli and Amadea ... "

"Amadea?" I broke in.

"Right, that was her name. Funny, eh? She used to tell me that her father had wanted a son and he'd have called him Amadeus so that's why he called her Amadea. Funny, eh?" He actually managed a little laugh.

We had both forgotten why we were sitting in that filthy hole. And now I no longer had to pump him: he rattled away without any help from me.

"Amadea," he went on, "was the nicest. She was always generous and sad and really the prettiest, too, and ... "

"So," I interrupted him, "you were actually a pimp, weren't you?"

"No," he carefully explained, "no," and he sighed again. "Pimps—they're biggies, they're tyrants, they make heaps of money, and they sleep with the girls too."

"And you didn't?"

"No, I was only a tout. It was my job to hook the fish for them to fry and eat, then they'd give me some of the bones to pick ... "

"The bones?"

"Yes." He gave a short laugh. "Just a tip, see? And that's what I lived on after my dad was killed and my mother disappeared. I wasn't fit to work, see, because of my lung. No, the girls I worked for didn't have a pimp, thank God. Otherwise I'd have got beaten up all the time. No, they just worked for themselves, all on their own, no license or anything, and they didn't dare show up in the street like the others—that was too dangerous, so I touted for them." He sighed. "Mind passing me the bottle again?" While I was reaching down to pick up the bottle, he asked: "And what's your name?"

"Hubert," I said, handing him the bottle.

"That feels good," he said, but I couldn't respond because by then I was holding the bottle to my lips. It was empty, and I let it roll gently to one side.

"Hubert," he suddenly said, and now his voice was trembling violently, "look!" He pulled me forward to where he was lying flat on the parapet. "Just look!" If one looked very, very hard one could see very, very far away something like a horizon, a pitch-black line with a suspicion of light over it, and in the lighter darkness above the pitch-black line something was moving like a gentle motion of bushes. It could also be men creeping up, a huge mass of men creeping up without a sound ...

"Why don't you send up a white flare?" he whispered in an expiring voice.

"Listen," I said, placing my hand on his shoulder. "Jak, it's nothing, it's just our fear that's moving out there, it's all that hell, it's the war, it's all that shit that's driving us crazy—it's—it's not real."

"But I can see it, I'm sure it's something—something real—they're coming—they're coming ... " And again I could hear his teeth chattering.

"Yes," I said, "be quiet. It *is* something real. It's sunflower stalks, in the morning you'll see them and laugh, when it's broad daylight you'll see and you'll laugh, it's sunflower stalks, they're about half a mile away, and they look as if they're at the end of the world, don't they? I know them—dried up, black, dirty, some of them shot to pieces, and the Russians have eaten the pods, and it's our fear that's making them move."

"Please—please send up a white flare—send up a flare—I can see them!"

"But I know what they are, Jak!"

"Please send up a flare! Just one single shell ... "

"Come on, Jak," I whispered back, "if they were really coming we could hear them—listen!" We held our breath and listened. There was complete silence, nothing to be heard except those ghastly sounds of silence.

"I hear them," he whispered, and I could tell from his voice that he was deathly pale, "I do hear them—they're coming—they're creeping—they're crawling over the ground—there, a clink! They're coming very silently, and when they're close up it'll be too late ... "

"Jak," I said, "I can't shoot off a flare, I've only two cartridges, understand? And I'll need one in the morning, very early, when the Stukas come, so they know where we are and don't bomb us to hell. And the other one—I'll need that when things really get hot. In the morning you'll be laughing ... "

"In the morning," he said without emotion. "Tomorrow morning I'll be dead." I was so taken aback that I swung round to him. He had spoken firmly and with total conviction.

"Jak," I said, "you're crazy!"

He said nothing, and we leaned back again. I longed to see his face. The face of a real tout, right up close. I had only ever heard them whisper, at street corners and railway stations in all the cities of Europe, and I had always turned away with a sudden hot fear in my heart.

"Jak ... " I started to say.

"*Please* send up a flare!" he whispered, beside himself.

"Jak," I said, "you'll curse me if I do that now. We've another four hours to go, d'you realize? And there'll be a ruckus, I know what to expect. Today's the twenty-first, and that's when they're issued schnapps over there, right now they've been given their schnapps with their rations, understand? And in half an hour they'll start shouting and singing and shooting, and maybe something really will happen. And when the Stukas come in the morning you'll be sweating with fear, they'll drop their bombs that close, and if I don't fire off a white flare we'll be mincemeat, and you'll curse me for sending up a flare now when nothing's happening. Believe me. Tell me some more about yourself. Where did you last do your—touting?"

He sighed deeply. "In Cologne," he said.

"At the main railway station?"

"No," he went on listlessly, "not always. Sometimes at the South station. It made more sense, you see, because the girls lived closer by. Lilli near the opera house, and Irma and Amadea off Barbarossa-Platz. You see," his voice sounding weary as if he were falling asleep, "sometimes when I'd snaffled a fellow at the main station he'd give me the slip on the way, and that was a nuisance; sometimes they got scared on the way or whatever, I don't know, and then they'd give me the slip, without saying a word. It was just too far, from the main station all the way there, and towards the end I often stood at the South station, because a lot of soldiers used to get out there thinking it was Cologne—I mean the main station. And from the South station it was only a stone's throw, it wasn't that easy to give me the slip. First"—now he leaned towards me—"I always went to Amadea, she lived in a building that had a café, later it was destroyed by a fire bomb. Amadea, you know—she was the nicest. She paid me the most, but that wasn't why I went to her first, it really wasn't, you must believe me, truly it wasn't. Oh, you don't believe me, but that really wasn't why I went to her first, just because she paid the most, d'you believe me?" By now he was so intense that I simply had to say yes.

"But Amadea was often busy—funny, wasn't it? She was very often busy. She had a lot of regulars, and sometimes she'd walk the street, too, if business was slow. And when Amadea was busy I was sad, so next I'd go to Lilli. Lilli wasn't bad either, but she drank, and women who drink are terrible, unpredictable, sometimes nasty, sometimes nice, but Lilli was still nicer than Irma. Irma, she was a cold fish, let me tell you. She'd pay ten per cent, and that was it. Ten per cent! There I'd often be running half an hour through the cold night, standing for hours at the station or sitting over some lousy beer in a bar, risking being picked up by the police, and then ten per cent! Shit, I tell you! So Irma was always my last choice. The next day, when I brought her the first customer, she'd give me the money. Sometimes only fifty pfennigs, and once only ten pfennigs—would you believe it? Ten pfennigs!"

"Ten pfennigs?" I asked, horrified.

"Yes," he said. "She'd only been paid one mark. That was all he had on him, the bastard."

"A soldier?"

"No, a civilian, and a really old fellow at that. And she gave me hell as well! Oh, Amadea was different! She always paid me plenty. Never less than two marks. Even when she hadn't been paid anything. And then ... "

"Jak," I asked, "sometimes she charged nothing?"

"That's right, sometimes she charged nothing. Just the opposite, I believe. She'd even give the soldiers cigarettes or sandwiches or just something extra."

"Extra?"

"Yes. Extra. She was very generous. A very, very sad girl, I'm telling you. And she took a bit of an interest in me, too. Wanted to know where I lived and whether I needed any cigarettes and that kind of stuff. And she was pretty, I'd say the prettiest of the lot."

I was about to ask what she looked like, but just at that moment the first Russian started yelling like a madman. A kind of howl went up, gathering other voices, and immediately the first shot was fired. I just managed to grab Jak by the edge of his greatcoat; with one leap he would have been over the top and away, straight into the arms of the Russians. They always run into the arms of the Russians, the fellows who clear out. I pulled the trembling figure back, very close to me. "For God's sake be quiet! It's nothing. They're just a bit drunk, and then they yell and shout blindly over the parapet. And you have to keep your head down, because it's those shots that sometimes find their mark ... "

Now we heard a woman's voice and, although we couldn't understand a word, we knew that they must have yelled and sung something very coarse. Her shrill laughter tore the night to shreds.

"Calm down," I told the struggling, groaning boy, "it won't last long, in a few minutes the commissar will notice and slap them about. They're not allowed to do that, and they're soon cured of what they're not allowed to do, just like us ... "

But the yelling continued, and the wild shouting, and to make matters worse one of our own was firing from behind us. I clung to the boy, who was trying to push me away and clear out. From up ahead came yells, then a shout ... then again yelling ... shots, and once again the horrible voice of the drunk woman. Then total silence, a terrible silence ...

"You see?" I said.

"Now—now they're coming ... "

"No—just listen!"

We listened again, and there was nothing to be heard but the ghastly grinding of silence.

"Do be sensible," I went on, wanting to hear at least my own voice. "Didn't you see the muzzle flashes? They're at least two hundred yards away, and if they come you'll hear, you're bound to hear, I'm telling you."

By this time he seemed to have ceased to care. He just sat there beside me, wordless, rigid.

"Tell me," I asked, "what did she look like, your Amadea?"

He seemed reluctant to answer. "Pretty," he said curtly, "dark hair and shiny bright eyes, and she was very small, terribly small, you know?" He suddenly became talkative again: "... and a bit crazy. That's all you could call it. Every day she used a different name. Inge, Simone, Kathleen, whatever, almost every day a different one ... or Susie Marie. She was a bit crazy, and often she wouldn't accept any money at all."

I grabbed him by the arm. "Jak," I said, "I'll send up a white flare now. I think I hear something."

He held his breath. "Yes," he whispered, "send up a flare, I can hear them, I'll go crazy if you don't ... "

I held onto his arm, grabbed the loaded Very pistol, held it high over my head, and pulled the trigger. There was a whistling roar as if heralding the Last Judgment, and when the light spread out like a gentle, silver liquid—like shimmering Christmas lights—I had no time to look at his face, for I had heard nothing, nothing whatever, and had only sent up the flare in order to see his face, the face of a genuine tout. I had no time, for where that yelling had been before, that shrieking of a drunken woman, there was now a heaving mass of silent figures who ducked to the ground in the light and then suddenly came storming forward with their demented hurrahs. Nor did I have time to send up a red flare, for all around us the terrible furrow of war was opening up and burying us ... I had to drag Jak out of the hole, and after I had somehow managed to pull him out and, screaming with fear, was bending over him to have at least a dying look at his face, he merely whispered, very softly: "Want to have a good time, sir...?" and I was brusquely hurled on top of him by a fierce, terrible hand.

But now my eyes saw nothing but blood, darker than the night, and the face of a crazy prostitute who had given herself for nothing and had even added a little something ...

THE MURDER

"The old man's crazy," I said in a low voice.

"More likely pissed, he's always pissed when he orders an attack. Take it from me, that's how it is." I said nothing, and Heini's voice continued: "He tanks up till he's deaf and blind, and then: Let's go! At 'em! To hell with that kind of courage ... are you asleep?" His hand groped towards me, and he tugged at my belt.

"Stop it," I said, slightly annoyed, "I'm awake. But what I'd like to know is how to get out of this. I don't relish the idea of a hero's death— I can't really say why. And last time, I needn't tell you, we left fifteen men behind; we had to beat it, and the old man was hoarse with rage because he still had a sore throat ... "

"Not a chance—ahead of us the Russians and behind us the Prussians, and us in the middle, on a very narrow black strip; all we can do is try and stay alive."

Somewhere up front a flare shot into the sky, and a kind of pale shimmer flooded the bare, hilly ground ...

"I'll be damned!" Heini suddenly cried, "they're showing a light, those idiots—the shooting'll start any moment, you'll see."

Behind us, where the command posts were located at the top of the slope, someone had apparently pulled away the blanket from a dug-out entrance, a bowed silhouette showed for a moment, then all was dark again; the flare had gone out too ... as if its light had been swallowed up by the infinite darkness ...

"That was the old man's hole, I hope they drop a load right in front of it, or right inside, then there'll be no attack tomorrow ... "

We quickly ducked, for from somewhere ahead came the sound of a gentle crack, then there was a shattering explosion, and behind us on the hilltop a few low, blackish-red flames shot up from the earth. Then all was quiet again, and we listened intently for any noise or shouting to start up behind us. But the silence persisted ...

"Seems they were lucky," Heini muttered angrily. "But it's the truth, isn't it—a nice direct hit on the old man's quarters, and tomorrow we'll have saved the lives of twenty men ... "

We turned back to face the coal-black wall of the night.

"There he sits, the bastard, boozing away and mulling over his plan ... "

"More likely asleep," I said wearily.

"But he had a light!"

"He always has a light, even when he's asleep—I've been there a few times with dispatches. There were two candles burning, and he was asleep. His mouth open, snoring, probably pissed ... "

"I see," Heini said slowly, and something in that "I see" made me take notice. I looked over to where he must be standing and listened to his breathing. "I see," he repeated, and I would have given a lot to be able to see his face: all I could make out, blacker than the black night, were the rough outlines of his figure, and suddenly I heard him start to clamber out of the hole. Small clods of earth trickled from the parapet, and I could hear his hands scrabbling for a grip at the top ...

"What are you up to?" I asked nervously, scared to be alone in this hole.

"I've got to go, and in a hurry, I've got the shits, it may take a while." He had reached the top, and soon I heard his footsteps disappearing off to the right before the darkness swallowed up all sound ...

Alone now, I groped for the bottle of rot-gut and found it in the darkness right under the cold metal of the machine-gun case. I pulled out the stopper, wiped the lip of the bottle with my hand, and drank deeply. The first taste as it touched the roof of my mouth was horrible, but soon a comfortable warmth spread slowly through me. I drank again, and again; then once again, then huddled down onto the bottom of the hole, threw the blanket over me and lit my pipe. All fear had left me. I propped myself on one elbow, covered my face with my hands, leaving just enough room for my pipe, and dozed off ...

I was woken by the weird clatter of the night plane, which concealed cunning and deadly accuracy behind its seeming decrepitude. We had every reason to fear it. I wondered where Heini was and turned round. I was met with an incredible sight: to the rear, along the top of the range of hills where the command posts were, I saw a large, bright spot in the night, an open dug-out entrance, and in the middle of that bright, wavering spot a candle flickering. Agitated voices of scurrying men came alive, the blanket was hastily pulled across, but it was too late: at that very moment the noise of the night plane's engine stopped for a fraction of a second, and just where the light had been a flame shot up that was instantly suffocated by the night. In the absolute silence one could sense everybody ducking, trembling as they flattened themselves on the ground. But the plane flew slowly on. Now from the slope came renewed shouts and the sounds of men digging: picks hacking into the stony soil, and beams were being dragged out...

At last Heini returned from over on the right; clambering back into the hole he cursed: "Goddammit, have I got the shits, I could've gone on for hours! Pass me the bottle, will you?"

His voice was quite calm, but when I passed him the bottle, waiting in the dark for his hand to touch mine so I would know he had hold of the bottle, I could feel him trembling violently. He drank long and deep, and I could hear him panting, and it seemed to me that the night had become even darker and more silent...

"By the way," said Heini a little later, "d'you know the old man is dead? Those were his quarters. Direct hit. I don't imagine he'll have felt a thing—after all, he was pissed ..."

VINGT-ET-UN

I drew an ace, gleefully placed my bet, drew a nine and said "Pass."

Fips turned up his card, a ten; then he smiled at me, for there were a hundred and twenty *pengö* in the kitty. Slowly he took the second card, a queen, then he drew a king and smiled again. And when he picked up the fourth card, I laughed ... but he hadn't even looked at it when we suddenly flung ourselves to the ground: a strange, soft whirring sound was in the air. Our faces were deathly pale. Then from our right came an appalling crash, and immediately afterwards we heard a terrible scream, followed by nothing. There was total silence. Fips was still holding the fourth card face down as he looked at me: "That was Alfred," he said quietly, "go and see what's happened to him." There was still total silence, then we were startled again, this time by the shrill sound of the phone in the next dug-out. Fips jumped across me, threw the rest of the cards down onto the kitty, and flung aside the blanket. I could hear him answering the phone and saying "Yes," and again "Yes," and again, after a brief pause, a third time, "Yes ... "

He emerged, still holding the card. He looked stunned and absent-mindedly tucked the card under his corporal's shoulder strap. "What was it?" I asked calmly.

"Christ!" he shouted at me. "Aren't you going to go and find Alfred?" His eyes held a terrible fear, I forgave him for shouting at me, and I didn't dare ask him who it had been on the phone.

He walked the few steps to the edge of the forest with me and showed me the cable I had to follow to reach Alfred.

Alfred had gone off half an hour earlier to look for a break in the line. I glanced back into the trench and saw Fips standing there with that altogether strange, new fear in his face, saw him lean against the parapet and gaze out over the churned-up terrain. Then I picked up the cable and marched off into the unfamiliar undergrowth. I followed the trail that Alfred's feet had ploughed through the ferns; in some alarm I noticed that the path to the right was moving farther and farther out of sight and that the cable was leading me into totally unknown territory. It was so silent in the forest that my footsteps startled me, that soft, fluttery sound as I brushed against the fern fronds, the grazing of tendrils against my greatcoat, the soft swish of bobbing brambles...

Suddenly I felt the cable in my hands tightening; I pulled at it, but it didn't yield. Somewhere on the ground it must have been caught by a rock, a branch, or some heavy object. I pulled more vigorously and now discovered, just a few paces ahead of me, where it was pinned to the ground. Nervously I went closer, and then I saw him lying there, Alfred's grey figure, his face turned towards me. At the same moment I threw myself to the ground, for I suddenly saw that I was standing in a clearing that opened like a funnel into a hollow. I crawled slowly closer and first looked out across the dead man's body into that unfamiliar, shallow valley that was filled with an oppressive silence. Down there among the meadows flowed a little stream, and beyond it was a steep slope with a bare ridge.

Only then did I look at Alfred. His fixed eyes stared upwards, and involuntarily I followed his gaze into the mute green roof of beech leaves; at that moment I understood why he was smiling and lying there so calmly. His right hand still clasped the receiver of the testing set, and his head was still tilted to the right in a listening pose. I carefully closed his eyelids and released his hand from the set; then, putting my arms round the dead man, I dragged him with me as I crawled slowly back into the forest...

It was as silent as it can only be in war. Those gentle, chirping sounds of a forest in summertime hummed around me; from somewhere up ahead I could hear the good-natured booming of a cannon, but the silence was stronger. I bent down, took Alfred's paybook from his breast pocket and, as I carefully leaned with my left hand on his chest, I heard a strange sound, almost like a sponge being squeezed. Alarmed, I pulled him up and discovered in his back a hole the size of a fist, its edges fringed with shreds of cloth. His whole back was sticky with blood. I lowered him again, removed the steel helmet from his head, and gazed silently at that childish forehead, at that childish mouth which only half an hour ago had laughingly placed his bet. Involuntarily and unknowingly, I called out in a loud, strained voice,

"Alfred, Alfred!" and it seemed to me that he must surely move, but my absorption was penetrated once again by the soft, cruel, menacing sound as of smouldering cotton wool … I threw myself down beside Alfred and this time heard the crash to my left, at the very spot where Fips must have stayed behind. Then all was silent again. I wrenched the testing set from Alfred's shoulder, connected it to the cable, and dialled. "Cherry stone, switchboard," a bored voice responded …

"Cherry stone three, please," I said, and he repeated: "Cherry stone three." I heard him plug in and crank the handle; there followed that typical telephone exchange silence with only a few soft clicks audible. Again I heard him crank, then the voice said: "Cherry stone doesn't answer."

"Is there something wrong with the line?" I asked anxiously.

"No, the connection's all right, there seems to be nobody there."

I hurriedly stuffed Alfred's paybook in my pocket, yanked the set free again and, following my own trail, ran back. After jumping into the trench I first listened for a moment but could hear nothing; then, crouching low, I ran along the trench until I saw Fips lying there…

There wasn't much left of him to recognize, his chest was ripped apart, and blood and bone splinters had swamped his face; only his shoulders were uninjured, and the card was still tucked under his left shoulder strap. I pulled it out: it was a king…

"Twenty-one," I said softly, "you win." I walked back the few paces to where our kitty lay, picked up the notes, tore them into tiny pieces, and scattered the coloured scraps over him like flower petals.

At that moment the phone rang. I stepped across Fips's body into the dug-out, picked up the receiver, and answered. But there was nothing to be heard except for that typical telephone exchange silence and, obeying an obscure urge, I said "Yes!" Now I understood the fear in Fips's eyes. Still no one responded, and again I said, in a loud, mocking voice: "Yes!" And, following the rule of three, I repeated, now obedient and subdued: "Yes." Then I hung up, and I, too, went outside, leaned against the parapet, and waited …

CAUSE OF DEATH: HOOKED NOSE

When Lieutenant Hegemüller returned to his billet, his thin face was trembling with a nervous pallor; his eyes seemed to have gone dead, his face under the flaxen hair was a blank, quivering surface. All day long he had been sitting in the communications room, relaying radio messages to the incessant accompaniment of the chatter of machine pistols as they spewed out their bullets over at the outskirts of the town into the wan afternoon light: over and over again that cackling screech of a new salvo, and knowing that every single link in that rattling chain of sound meant a destroyed or mutilated human life, a body writhing in the dust and tumbling down a slope! And every half hour, with hellish regularity, the thud of a muffled explosion, and knowing that that sound, fading like a retreating thunderstorm, replaced the work of gravediggers, gravedigging in the interests of sanitation; knowing that yet another section of the quarry was at that very moment collapsing over the harvest of the last half hour and burying the living with the dead...

For the thousandth time the lieutenant wiped his pale, sweat-soaked face; then with a curse he kicked open the door to his quarters and stumbled into his room, where with a groan he sat down on his chair. On and on and on rushed the venomous machinery of death—almost as if that ripping, crackling sound were the screech of a monstrous saw splitting the sky so it would collapse when the day's work was done. Often it seemed as though the traces of this destruction must be visible and, his face twitching, he would lean for a moment out of the window to see with his own eyes whether the vast grey vault of the sky were not already tilting like the prow of a foundering ship. He thought he could even hear the gurgling of the black water lying in wait to wash over the wreckage of the world and swallow it up in deadly calm.

Quaking in every limb, he smoked with trembling fingers, knowing that he must do something to fight this madness. For he felt that he was not without guilt, that he had been forced into the stony heart of guilt, a heart that must lie at the centre of this ceaselessly grinding atrocity. Neither the pain he suffered nor the nameless horror and mortal fear could wipe out the consciousness that *he* was shooting and *he* was being shot. Never before had he been so intensely aware of the great cosmic home that embraces all men, the reality of God.

On and on went that biting, grinding, spitting, demented sawing of the machine pistols. There followed a few minutes of a ghastly silence that must make the birds tremble in their hiding-places, and then a detonation: a charge of explosives, drilled into the wall of the quarry, replaced the grim labours of the gravediggers. And again shots, shots, one after the other in an endless chain, each one of them struck Lieutenant Hegemüller in his very heart.

But suddenly he heard a different sound, a subdued sound, the sobbing of a woman. He listened intently, rose to his feet and stepped out into the corridor, listened again for a moment, then flung open the kitchen door and stopped in his tracks: the Russian woman was on her knees, her fists covering her ears, and sobbing, sobbing so that the tears dripped from her blouse onto the floor.

For a moment the lieutenant was gripped by a strange, cold curiosity: tears, he thought, tears, never would I have believed a person could have so many tears. The pain was dripping in great, clear beads out of the elderly woman, collecting in a veritable puddle on the floor between her knees.

Before he had a chance to ask, the woman jumped up and screamed: "They've taken him away, my Piotr, Piotr Stepanovich ... oh sir, sir!"

"But he's not..." the lieutenant shouted back.

"No, sir, he's not a Jew, no. Oh sir, sir!"

The tears gushed from between the fingers that she was pressing against her face as if to staunch a bleeding wound ...

Driven by some overpowering inner force, the lieutenant turned on his heel and, calling out something to the woman, dashed out into the street.

The streets were completely deserted. An eerie tension hung in the air: what hovered over the little town was not only the terror of those crouching in their hiding-places, not only the whip of death. The silence, which filled the streets like pale, grey dust, held a kind of mockery as if one devil were grinning at another.

The lieutenant raced along, sweat dripping from every pore, the terrible sweat that was no release but more like a death sweat poisoned by a bestiality that had been saturated with the killers' vicious lust. A strange burning cold flowed over him from the dead façades of the houses. And yet he was filled with something like joy—no, it actually was joy—what a glorious feeling to run for the life of a human being! In those minutes, racing through the streets at breakneck speed, almost beside himself, his subconscious came to understand many things; a thousand things were revealed to him from out of that nebulous haze he had called his ideology, rising like stars to pierce him with their brilliance and then die away like comets, but their reflection remained within him, as an accumulated source of subdued light.

Panting, covered with dust, he reached the outskirts of the town where the doomed had been herded together at the edge of the steppe. They formed a square surrounded by vehicles mounted with machine guns; in the vehicles, guards lounged behind the slim barrels, smoking their cigarettes.

At first Hegemüller ignored the sentry who tried to stop him, did not react when the man grabbed him by the sleeve. For a second he stared into the man's face, amazed at how close and clear it was. In fact, the faces of the sentry cordon seemed all equally dull-witted and brutish whereas the faces of those inside the cordon seemed in some exquisite manner to have been lifted high above the mass and placed on the pinnacle of humanity. A sombre silence hung over the crowd, something strangely vibrating, fluttering, like the flapping of heavy banners, something solemn, and—Hegemüller felt, as his heart missed a beat— inexplicably comforting, joyful; he felt this joy surge through him, and at that instant he envied the doomed people and was shocked to realize that he was wearing the same uniform as the murderers. Blushing with shame he turned towards the sentry and croaked: "The man whose house I'm billeted in is here. He's not a Jew ..." and since the sentry stood there in apathetic silence he added: "Grimschenko, Piotr ... "

An officer approached the group and raised his eyebrows at the sight of the dusty, sweat-soaked lieutenant, who was wearing neither belt nor cap. Hegemüller now realized that the executioners and their minions were all drunk. With their bloodshot eyes they looked like bulls, and their breath was like steam from a manure heap. Once again

Hegemüller stammered out the name of his host, and the lieutenant in command of the minions scratched his head in a display of gruesome good nature and asked lamely: "Innocent, you mean?"

"Innocent, that too," Hegemüller replied curtly.

The lieutenant seemed taken aback as this little word fell into the pool of his heart. But the word had sunk without trace, without raising ripples, as the lieutenant stepped in front of the doomed figures and shouted: "Grimschenko, Piotr, step forward!" Since nobody moved, and that strangely fluttering silence persisted, he called out the name again, adding: "Can go home!" And when there was still no response he stepped back and said awkwardly: "Gone, maybe already done for, maybe still over there—come with me!"

Hegemüller's eyes followed the finger pointing towards the place of execution.

What he saw was the edge of an enormous quarry that sloped towards the assembly point, and a row of close-ranked soldiers armed with machine pistols. From the assembly point, a procession of the doomed led up to the rim of the quarry, where it flattened out: from this rim the regular, whiplike cracking of the machine pistols sounded through the afternoon air.

And once again, as he followed the drunken lieutenant, it seemed to Hegemüller that the crowd, the doomed crowd, had dissolved into a procession of noble personalities, while the few murderers seemed like brutish clods. Each one of those faces he so anxiously scanned in search of Grimschenko seemed to him calmer, revealing an inexpressibly human gravity. The women with babies in their arms, old people and children, men, girls smeared with faeces who had apparently been pulled out of latrines for the purpose of being murdered; rich and poor, ragged and well-dressed, all were endowed with a sublimity that left Hegemüller speechless. The lieutenant tried to make conversation by throwing out oddly apologetic fragments, not as an excuse for the killings but to gloss over his drunken condition while on duty: "Tough job, this, you know. Couldn't stand it without booze ... hope you understand ... "

But Hegemüller, in whom horror had aroused a strange and sober calm, was nagged by a single question: What do they do with the babies, the tiny ones who can't stand or walk—how is it technically possible? Meanwhile his eyes never left the procession of the doomed, never rose to the rim of the quarry where the pallid afternoon was punctured by the thwacking and spitting of the machine pistols. But on reaching the point where the slope flattened out and he was forced to lift his gaze, he saw the answer to that nagging question. He saw a black boot kicking the bloodied corpse of an infant into the abyss and, averting his eyes in horror and looking along the rim of the quarry, he suddenly saw Grimschenko at the head of the line, saw him collapse under a bullet. With a wild and terrible cry he shouted "Stop, stop!" so loud that the executioners held their fire in alarm. He seized the lieutenant by the arm and dragged him over to where Grimschenko, drenched in blood, was hanging half over the edge. He had not tipped forward into the quarry but, facing away from his killer, had fallen over backwards.

Hegemüller grabbed him and lifted him up, and just then an official voice shouted from somewhere: "Everyone get back—blasting!" Hegemüller did not see the killers running back fifty yards in their panic, or the astonished, bewildered face of the lieutenant in charge of his drunken minions. Hegemüller had grasped Grimschenko's body and hoisted him onto his shoulders; he could feel the flowing blood congealing between his fingers. Behind him the detonation exploded in a cloud of leaden sound into the sky; scarcely a foot or two behind Hegemüller, the rim of the quarry collapsed, and the earth buried both the dead and the half-dead, the infants and the old men who for ninety-four years had borne the burden of life ...

It was no surprise to Hegemüller that the row of killers, waiting with smoking barrels and dull eyes for the next batch, made way for him without resistance. He felt he had the power to force them all onto their knees with a single glance, a single word, those butchers of men in their brand-new uniforms, for in the midst of the red fog of confusion, fear and noise, of stench and anguish, he had felt something that filled him with happiness: Grimschenko's gentle breath that brushed his shoulder like a caress from another world, that tiny breath of the gravely wounded, whose blood had caked his fingers.

Unhindered he passed through the row of murderers, hearing behind him the upsurge of renewed firing. He found a waiting vehicle and shouted at the dozing driver: "Get going—the nearest field hospital!" as he jerked open the door, let Grimschenko slide from his shoulders, and laid him on the back seat.

Suddenly he was dreaming: he was running, running, with a number of others in a mad, gruelling race to a lake in whose waters they wanted to cool off. The heat burned over them, and all round them. The whole world was one pitiless furnace, and they ran and ran, while the sweat flowed from their pores like streams of sour blood. It was an indescribable torture, this race along a dusty road to the lake which they knew lay beyond a curve in the road, yet it was a sensual pleasure, this sweating, a kind of swimming in torture, a dreadful yet in some mysterious way pleasurable torture, while the sweat flowed, flowed, flowed. And then came that curve in the road beyond which must be the lake; with a wild cry he raced round the curve, saw the glittering silver surface of the water, plunged into it with a jubilant shout, knelt down and joyfully dipped his face in the water. Then, just as he was marvelling at how miraculously cool the water was despite the scorching heat, he woke up and opened his eyes.

He was looking into the impassive face of an orderly who was holding an empty jug, and he instantly grasped that he had fainted and been revived with a dash of cold water. He could smell some kind of disinfectant, could hear a typewriter tapping. "Grish, Grimschenko?" he whispered, but the orderly, instead of replying, turned away. "So the Russian's name is Grimschenko—now you can complete the medical report, Sister."

The orderly stepped aside, and Hegemüller felt the cool professional hand of a doctor on his forehead and heard a complacent voice say: "Been overdoing it a bit, eh?" Then the hand slid down his sleeve to his pulse and, while Hegemüller was feeling his own pulse beating irregularly against the doctor's gentle fingers, the complacent voice spoke again: "All right, Sister—got it? Then write down: Cause of death— let's say, hooked nose," and then the complacent voice laughed while the hands belonging to that complacent voice were feeling Hegemüller's pulse almost tenderly. But Hegemüller sat up, took in the white room with a strangely detached expression, then laughed too, and his laughter was as strange as his expression. His eyeballs rolled back as his laughter grew louder and louder; they dimmed and seemed to turn ever further inward, like the closing shutters of a searchlight, taking the whole world inside with them and leaving nothing but a clouded emptiness; Hegemüller laughed, and from then on the only words he ever spoke were: "Cause of death: hooked nose."

VIVE LA FRANCE!

The sentry groped his way across the dark room to the door, opened it and stepped out into the corridor; for half a second he hesitated in the doorway, reluctant to leave the warmth of the room behind him and go out into the cold night. He slowly closed the door and merged with the darkness of the corridor. He could see nothing, he was merely aware that the front door was open, and subconsciously he was surprised to find that the cold which had greeted him in the corridor seemed to be intensified outside: damp, icy, remorseless, it advanced upon him through the open doorway. Then, standing in the entrance, completely enveloped by that damp cold, he was able to distinguish, more or less from memory, the vague outlines of the trees in the park, the furrow of the avenue, on the right the ruined factory whose sinister black wall seemed to rise like a barrier between two underworlds...

A weary, almost desperate voice called out: "Is that you?"

"Yes," he replied, surprised to find he had the strength to utter that one syllable. A deathly fatigue flowed like lead through his limbs, as if dragging him down; his eyelids drooped, and leaning against the front door he fell into a sleep that lasted perhaps for a second, a voluptuous, heavy stupor. To sleep, ah, to sleep.

The sentry he was relieving bumped into him; with a sense of searing pain he was awake again. "It's all yours," said the voice, a voice that contained something like pity.

He couldn't even summon the strength to ask for a cigarette, to open his mouth at all. He was paralyzed by the hopeless deathly fatigue which was suffocating him. His eyes burned like hot coals in their sockets, from his empty stomach rose a sourish, nauseating fluid; his arms and legs were like lumps, numb, leaden. Without knowing it, he uttered muffled, brutish sounds as he collapsed onto stone slabs. But he couldn't sleep: it wasn't the cold that prevented him—he had slept under more difficult conditions and in worse cold—no, he was overstimulated by

606

fatigue. So there he remained, squatting on his heels, wrapped in cold and night, at the top of the wide flight of stone steps—a bundle of misery, with two hours ahead of him, a mountain of agonizing eternity.

Suddenly he realized from the sounds coming from the upper floor of the château that the festivities were not yet over. Laughter, subdued voices, reached him, partly through the corridor, partly through the thickly curtained window. And now something awoke in him, tiny at first yet strong, a raging, minute inner chill, a crystalline chill mounting inside him like a surging spring that froze instantly but continued to grow, a column of ice, rising layer upon layer, and by which he pulled himself up: HATRED. Lost in thought he straightened up, leaned against the wall, and smoked. His fatigue was still there, as well as that nauseating, sour malaise; but now hatred had reared up like a column to support him.

Immediately above his head the door to the little balcony suddenly opened. A lurid light flooded the garden, and the next moment he recognized the conceited voice of the captain; at the same time, someone was pissing from the balcony down onto the steps. He jumped aside in alarm.

Then it was as if the light were being sucked back out of the garden, swallowed up, while the shadows of the two door panels widened; and, just before the last of the light was shut in, he heard that conceited voice saying: "Let's call it a day, gentlemen, it's two o'clock..."

The smell from the puddle on the steps drove him into the garden. With heavy legs, his hands clasped behind him, he plodded as far as the corner of the building.

Then the strident voice of the drunken lieutenant shouted in the corridor "Vive la France!" and burst into peals of laughter over his own wit. In the dimly luminous night the sentry saw the lieutenant staggering down the steps. He remained quite still while with the frantic assurance of the drunk the figure stumbled through the garden parallel to the building, then took the bend too sharply and pitched forward towards the corner.

"What the devil are you doing here?" came the lieutenant's shaky voice.

The sentry's silence hung menacingly in the air. Like a hunter, as he leaned calmly against the wall, he watched the swaying figure as it thrust its corrupted child's face with its torrid breath close to his.

"Can't you hear me? Aren't you at least going to challenge me?"

"Yessir," the sentry replied stoutly.

"And I'm telling you, shoot down anyone who doesn't know the password—anyone, without mercy."

And as if obsessed with that idea, he repeated stubbornly: "Shoot to kill! Shoot to kill!" Without waiting for the sentry's reply, he staggered towards the gate, out into the avenue and, just before turning left into the silent village street, shouted once again: "Vive la France!" His hysterical laughter bounced off the walls of the houses into the park.

With short, quick steps the sentry walked as far as the gate and looked out into the village street; there stood the houses black and silent, and above the outline of their roofs the darkness softened to a watery ink. He could hear the lieutenant's footsteps, hear him kick a stone on the road, follow him in his mind's eye as he turned right into the church square, and could hear muffled knocking on a door. The sentry nodded as if in confirmation when the lieutenant's hoarse, childish voice called out reproachfully, "Yvette! Yvette!"

The church square, opening out to the right beyond the corner, formed an oblique angle with the village street, so that with his last thirty paces the lieutenant had come closer to the sentry again and was standing half-turned towards him. His voice now reached the sentry over the low, dark houses. There was something eerie in the way it seemed to float over the one-storey buildings, always repeating the same words, first reproachfully, "Yvette, Yvette!", then impatiently, in a childish whine, "Open up!" And again reproachfully, "Yvette, damn you!" Next came a strange silence, and the sentry, listening with bated breath, could visualize the door opening soundlessly and white arms pulling the lieutenant inside. But breaking the paralyzing silence the lieutenant suddenly cried out in a shrill voice, "Yvette, you bitch!" Then apparently the door really did open, there was the sound of throaty laughter, and the sentry, standing there in the cold night with eyes closed, his face screwed up with pain, saw quite clearly: the soothing smile on the white face of the girl.

Although he loved neither Yvette nor the lieutenant, he was seized, as he stood shivering beside the gatepost, by an agonizing jealousy, a fierce sense of total desolation, overshadowing even his hatred.

While he tensed to catch every sound, his fatigue had almost evaporated; he turned right and walked down the village street. Since he could never see more than a few paces ahead, the night seemed to be forever retreating. Each step seemed to bring him closer to the dark, black wall that blocked his view; a cruel game, it seemed to him, because even so the distance never diminished. And as a result of this game, the village, that wretched little place of twenty-three houses, a factory, and two run-down châteaux, became boundless, and it seemed an age before he reached the iron fence surrounding the school playground. From the kitchen the smell of stale, watery soup penetrated all the way to the street. Leaning over the low wall that supported the fence he called in a clear, subdued voice, "Hullo there, Willi!"

He heard footsteps coming from the direction of the kitchen; then a dark figure loomed into view. "Here," the sentry called, "I'm over here!" Looking half-asleep, Willi approached the fence, walked along beside it, and stepped through the gate into the street.

"What time is it?"

Willi clumsily rolled up his tunic, fumbled for his watch, pulled it out, and held it close to his face: "Ten past two."

"That's impossible—your watch must have stopped—no, no, that can't be right!"

His voice was trembling dangerously; the sentry waited breathlessly while Willi held the watch to his ear, shook it, then looked at its face again.

"It's going all right, I knew it was, my watch has never stopped yet."

His voice showed no emotion. The sentry stood there without a word; his face was screwed up and withdrawn, hard and tormented.

"Oh, shut up," said Willi, although the sentry hadn't said anything. "Why must you always be so childish? Two hours are two hours, there's nothing you can do about it."

The sentry stood there like a pillar of salt. Ten minutes! he kept thinking, and this single thought pounded away in his brain. Ten minutes, twelve times ten minutes, a hundred and twenty times one minute!

"Look," Willi went on in a complacent tone, "I always think of home, that passes the time for me. One day the war will be over, then we'll go back, take off our tunics, kiss our wives, and go off to work. We've done our duty, see? And we..."

"Shut up!"

The two men looked at each other with hostility, although all they could see of each other was a pale, blurred disc under the black shadow of the steel helmet. Yet each saw the other's face quite plainly, forming it from the sound of the voice and the tension in the air. Willi saw a thin, dark, bitter face with lacklustre eyes, shadowed by grief: the sentry's face. He in turn saw that good-natured, rather cunning, smug face, a bit surprised yet watchful; Willi's face.

"Give me a cigarette," the sentry croaked.

"Hey, listen, you already owe me three. Tell you what, let's make that deal with the watch. For God's sake, a broken watch, what good is it to you! I'll give you twenty-five for it, ten now, that makes thirteen, and the rest the day after tomorrow when the canteen opens—I needn't tell you..."

"Shut up, just hand them over!"

Willi hesitated for a moment, then put his hand in his pocket and pulled out a packet of cigarettes.

"Here—but where..."

The sentry snatched the packet from Willi, opened it, and instantly struck a match. Suddenly the two faces were harshly lit up and looked frighteningly similar: pale, unspeakably weary, slack-mouthed.

"Are you crazy, man?" exclaimed Willi, "and then..."

"Oh, shut up." The sentry's voice now sounded more conciliatory. "They can lick my..."

At that he turned on his heel but swung round again and asked: "What time is it now?"

Again Willi carefully rolled up his tunic, groped for his watch in the little pocket in his waistband, and held it up to his eyes: "Eighteen minutes past—don't forget the watch!"

The sentry strolled down the street as far as the second house and leaned against the door of Madame Sevry's café. He drew deeply and voluptuously on his cigarette, and an extraordinary happiness filled his entire being. The poison radiated a gentle, pleasant vertigo. He closed his eyes. Ten cigarettes, he thought. Now he actually began to feel time slipping between his fingers; that heavy, black, inert, remorseless lump was melting away. It was as if a floodgate had opened and the current was bearing him away.

On either side the road led off into the abyss of darkness; now the silence was released, it too was flowing. For eighteen endless minutes the silence had been like a brake holding back time. Now the silence ran parallel with time, so close to it that the two seemed to be one.

Knowing just where the château was on the right and the school on the left, he imagined he could see them. But the avenue leading from the road to the château—that he really could see. It was like a high, perforated wall, darker than the night and studded with the dim clarity of the sky.

When he carefully tucked away the stub of his cigarette in his pocket, he knew that no more than seven minutes had passed. So it must be twenty-five past two. He decided to take a walk through the factory, that would take care of twelve minutes, and after that to smoke a cigarette. If he then returned slowly to Madame Sevry's door, smoked another cigarette, and walked to the school, it would have to be three o'clock.

Moving away from the door he walked down the gentle slope to the château gates, then slowly on almost to the corner of the church square— sixty-seven paces—where he turned left towards the abandoned gatehouse. From the archway he glanced into the little house from which all the timberwork had been stolen. As he hurried on he suddenly realized he was scared. Yes, without rhyme or reason, he was scared. Who could possibly be looking for anything in this completely looted factory at two thirty in the morning? But he was scared. His footsteps resounded hollowly on the concrete floor, and through the damaged roof he could see scraps of blue-black sky. It seemed to him as if the bare, black room were soaking up the threats of silence through the holes in the roof. The factory had been so radically gutted that it was no longer possible to make out what it had been used for: a big, bare hall where the concrete bases of the machines seemed glued stubbornly to the floor; meaningless iron structures, dirt, torn paper: indescribably cold and dreary.

Rigid with fear, the sentry walked slowly to the end of the great hall where an open doorway led outside. In the blackness of the wall, the open doorway looked like a rectangular piece of dark grey-blue cloth. He headed straight for it, walking softly, for the sound of his footsteps frightened him. Suddenly he stumbled over the rails leading outside, caught himself as he staggered against the wall, and stood with a pounding heart in the doorway. Although here, too, he could see scarcely twenty paces ahead, he believed he must be looking at the wide, open field, for he knew it was there and he could smell it: the sharp sweetness of spring nights above the meadows and fields.

Suddenly his fear flared up and landed right in the middle of his heart. Trembling, he turned round and walked with hesitant steps into the soundless menace, and the farther he went the more he realized that it—his fear—was empty, hollow, and he began to feel almost light-hearted. He even smiled a little as he stepped through the narrow door-way in the black wall into the grounds of the château.

It was like a dream! This round he had made seemed to have taken so long, an entire lifetime, as he mounted the stone stairs again, stepped across the captain's puddle, and stationed himself in the entrance. It was an eerie feeling: time seemed to have passed with ghostly speed yet insane sluggishness, time was disembodied, intangible, contradictory. How terrible to be at its mercy—it was a dream!

The only realities were the puddle, the cold, and the damp. He decided against walking round the château and proceeded to light a cig-arette. His calculations became confused, he had merely a dim notion: one cigarette here and one in Madame Sevry's doorway, then off to Willi, and it would have to be three o'clock. So one hour would have passed. He knew he was deceiving himself, yet, while aware of that, he believed in the deception.

How am I going to tell Willi that I don't even have the watch any more, he thought in desperation, that two evenings ago I drank it away at Madame Sevry's! I have to hold him off till the day after tomorrow and then return the cigarettes to him out of my canteen rations. Franz will have to get twelve, Willi thirteen, so all I'll have left will be seven cigarettes and the tobacco.

And the money he had borrowed! Credit is the worst of all traps for a poor man, he thought bitterly. It was always the same: whenever Marianne's parcels arrived with the money she sent, he would blow it all, it would run through his fingers; after that he would drag himself along over the perilous, seductive bridge of credit, swaying between the abysses of despair and stupor.

And the war stood still! That monster was marking time. Horror without end. Day and night the uniform, and the futility of routine duty, the arrogant, strident bad temper of the officers and the yelling of the

NCOs. They had been driven into the war like a hopeless, vast, grey herd of desperate men. Sometimes the memory of the front, where the monster really had been bare-fanged and bloody, seemed to him easier to endure than the perpetual waiting in this country that vacillated between spiteful muteness and a kindly, gentle irony. Again and again, on the monotonous carousel of the so-called deployment plan, they were shoved for a short time into the dug-outs and then back into this lousy dump, where they knew every single child, every chair and every bar. And the wine was getting worse and worse, the schnapps ever more dubious, cigarettes and rations ever scarcer; it was a cruel game. He tucked the second butt into his little watch pocket, stepped unconcernedly into the captain's puddle, and walked rapidly down the avenue, towards the street, straight to the school.

Good as his word, Willi was standing by the entrance to the building, apparently gently dozing.

"What time is it?" asked the sentry in a hectoring tone. He waited impatiently while Willi completed his fumbling manoeuvre with the watch.

"Quarter to," Willi answered. "Did you bring it along?"

"Bring what along?"

"The watch. You could've just gone to your room to pick it up, couldn't you? I want to send home a parcel tomorrow morning, you see, and ... "

"I left it with the watchmaker in Bechencourt—didn't I tell you? It'll be Monday before I can give it to you."

"Oh, you might've told me. So I s'pose I'll have to pay for the repair, won't I?"

The sentry laughed. "Of course, then you'll have a good watch for twenty-five cigarettes and a few francs—cheap, eh?"

"But we made a deal, and—and are you sure, Monday? Or d'you think...?"

"No, Monday for sure."

The sentry was obsessed with the single thought that it was only a quarter to three. Not even an hour, not even half the time, had gone by! A profound bitterness welled up in him, hatred and rage, a dark fear and, at the same time, despair. All this seemed to choke him, his throat felt bitter and hot and horribly dry, as if from violently suppressed tears.

"Be seeing you," he said in a forced voice as he turned away. He was about to ask the time again, but it was so pointless, it couldn't possibly be more than ten minutes to three.

The street, which he walked along so often during the day and again in the evening to fetch rations—during the day this little bit of street seemed absurdly short and pitiful; now at night it had acquired a mysterious length and breadth. Even the dirty, shabby houses opposite the château grounds were more impressive in the dark. But all he could feel was that desperate bitterness that was almost strangling him. Not even the thought of the cigarettes in his pocket was any comfort, nor was the knowledge that the awkward business of the watch had been postponed for at least two days. He was miserably cold and hungry—a naked, nagging hunger. He put his hands in his pockets, but they were so hopelessly numb that even in there they refused to come to life. His steel helmet suddenly weighed on him like a lump of lead, and at that moment he felt convinced that everything, everything, hatred and torment and despair, was contained in that steel helmet, in that heavy lump on his forehead. He took it off, then stepped into Monsieur Dubuc's gateway, just opposite the entrance to the château.

Now that he was rid of the pressure of the helmet he felt almost light-headed, and unconsciously he was smiling, a gentle, benign smile. He thought: now it *must* be three o'clock! And once the first half had gone by, time passed more quickly: the half-way mark was the ridge that had to be climbed, after that it was downhill all the way. He pictured Marianne's face while closing his eyes, making it appear so close and vivid that he could smell her hair. There would be some mail from her again, he would see her handwriting...

Time flowed, flowed, he could sense it, at breakneck speed it was approaching four o'clock. To sleep, to sleep and dream till six! The thought of tomorrow's duty checked him for a moment like a horse at a hurdle, but then, suddenly, for the first time that night, he heard the striking of the village clock: four strokes and three strokes, relentlessly. Three o'clock! Only three o'clock!

The shock made him duck like a beaten animal; he cringed as if from a cruel blow, gave a groan of animal despair, tried without conviction to kid himself that he'd miscounted. His bare head suddenly felt ice-cold and painful. He jammed on his steel helmet, lit a cigarette,

THE COLLECTED STORIES 615

and in feverish haste, inhaling deeply, smoked two cigarettes, one after another, slavering with hatred, rage and despair.

He even forgot to save up the two butts, flicking them brusquely into the street...

After that, when he walked across to Willi it was eight minutes past three; the next time—it seemed like an eternity of inner torment— it was eleven minutes past three. Those three minutes had been an eternity! Yes, he was done for, that was it; it was all futile. It would never be four o'clock, he would never reach the fourth hour alive, he would be crushed by the hideous millstones of naked time. All comfort and hope had sunk out of sight; not even memory could conjure them up now. There remained nothing but the naked torture of time and the prospect of going on four hours' duty the next day, suffering from hunger and lack of sleep, with the hung-over lieutenant. Rifle drill, about-turn, rifle drill, about-turn, field training, rifle drill, target practice, singing, singing, singing! Four hours: an endless chain of murderous seconds. Four hours! And these two were not even over yet. Time was a cheat, that was it! It cheated him, it destroyed every hope. Two hours! Four hours! Parade-ground duty and sentry duty, hopelessly clamped in this vice! Singing! Singing! Singing songs to satisfy the hung-over lieutenant's sentimental nature.

From the knotted tangle of rage, despair and hatred, hatred now emerged isolated and pure. He embraced that hatred and nursed it; he nurtured it with spiteful phrases about the lieutenant, the pissing captain, and the NCOs. With a ghastly smile he lit his fifth cigarette, standing once again in Madame Sevry's doorway, and looked along the street.

Now he could release that hatred, he no longer needed to nurse and nurture it; it was strong enough to work away independently inside him.

From the sea came a faint wind, damp and cool, that prompted unusual sounds: the groaning of fresh-leaved trees, the creaking of rotting roof-timbers, and the rattle of old, warped doors.

And all at once he knew that time really had passed swiftly; he was not surprised to hear the clock strike a quarter to four.

He hurried back through the avenue and entered the guard-room to rouse his relief. Waking a man is an art, he thought, a soldier's sleep is something sacred, which is why it is kicked around by everyone:

hardly anyone knows how to rouse a soldier from his sleep, the sleep, that costs nothing but is so indescribably precious.

He groped his way across the room and cautiously woke the sentry, not too tentatively and not too brutally—in such a way that the man was immediately awake yet not torn ruthlessly from the profound bliss of sleep. He shook the sentry a few times gently but firmly, and a resigned voice mumbled, "All right, I'm coming."

Pity overwhelmed him; they were all, all of them, clamped into this senseless, cruel system. He waited outside at the entrance to the avenue; he no longer felt cold or hungry, hardly even tired, now that he was sure of his bed.

But suddenly he heard footsteps coming from the church square, strange footsteps, groans, and little yelps of suppressed lust. The staggering was so palpable in the darkness that he could picture the lieutenant, weaving from side to side, sometimes walking briskly, then lurching again. Yvette must have regaled him nicely with her phony liqueurs! Now he was turning into the village street ... For ten paces the lieutenant walked almost normally, humming to himself, then staggered again; and then—then the sentry saw the glowing tip of his cigarette.

Shoot him, shoot him! he thought, and scarcely had the words entered his mind than he released the safety catch of his rifle and aimed it, leaning his left hand on the gatepost and pushing the barrel across it. He was ice-cold and alert, tense with the glorious game of aiming at the lieutenant. And after taking precise aim at the glowing cigarette, he called, keeping his voice down: "Password—who goes there?" He followed the approaching figure with his rifle, and when the voice called back "Vive la France!" he was transfixed by a terrible, savage emotion known only to gamblers who suddenly and compulsively bet everything on a single card: he pressed the trigger. And in the billionth of a second between pressure and discharge, everything within him that was still human, all of it, longed for the bullet to miss, but a sickening, brief, gurgling sound told him otherwise. He was standing there rigid and motionless when the relief sentry grabbed his arm and asked in a scared voice, "What happened?"

"Vive la France," he merely replied and, with chalk-white face and trembling hands, leaned his rifle against the gatepost.

THE CASUALTY

At the point where, half an hour earlier, the dust cloud of the attackers had been, there was now the dust cloud of fleeing men. The dusty haze was drifting over the shimmering steppe towards the military police, confusing them and increasing their fury. Raising their machine pistols they roared: "Stop, you bastards—stop—back to your positions!"

The air was filled with the screams of wounded men left lying on the ground, the shouts of the Russians—a hoarse, frightened barking, and the cries of fleeing men: like a herd of wild horses scenting an obstruction, they halted when confronted by the barrels of the machine pistols, then turned in weary submission and went back.

From behind me I could hear the shouts of the officers as they grouped their men for a new thrust. I could hear the rumbling of tanks, the howling of shells, and still the screams of the badly wounded. Slowly and with a feeling of extraordinary happiness I walked towards the line of military police. They couldn't touch me, I'd been wounded, although there was nothing to show for it in front.

"Stop!" they shouted. "Get back there, you bastard!"

"I've been wounded!" I yelled at them. With suspicious looks they let me approach. I went up to a tense, infuriated lieutenant, turned round and showed him my back. It must have been a pretty big hole, I'd run my hand over it once: damp, sticky blood and shreds of cloth. But I could feel nothing, it was a superb wound, a wound made to order, they couldn't touch me. Actually it must have looked worse than it was. The lieutenant growled something, then said more calmly: "There's a doctor over there."

The valley was empty and silent: half an hour earlier it had contained tanks, artillery, staff officers in their vehicles, the whole hysterical uproar that precedes an attack. Now it was quiet. The doctor was sitting under a tree. Behind me, more wounded men were slowly arriving. I was the first patient of this attack.

"Over here, my friend," said the doctor. He lifted the shreds of cloth. It tickled a bit; then he clucked his tongue and said: "Spit, please." I gagged, my throat was all dry, but I managed to produce a blob.

"Nothing," said the doctor. "You've been lucky, doesn't seem to be anything in your lungs. But, Jesus, that could've been a bad one!" He gave me a tetanus shot. I asked for some water, and he pulled out a flask. I reached out for it, but he held it to my mouth and allowed me only a brief swallow. "Take it easy, lad—d'you have any pain?"

"Yes."

He gave me a pill. I swallowed it. I didn't feel a thing, it was a marvellous wound, made to order, it would take at least four months for the hole to heal, and by that time the war would be over.

"There, you can go now," said the doctor. Next in line stood a man who had been shot in the calf; he was groaning with pain, but he had walked all the way here, using his rifle as a stick.

The valley was magnificent, the loveliest valley I had ever seen. Just bare slopes covered with steppe grass sweltering in the sun. A hazy sky above, nothing else. But it was the most magnificent valley, as glorious as my wound that didn't hurt me and yet was serious. I walked slowly, no longer thirsty and with no back-pack—I'd left that at the front. And I was alone. I sat down somewhere and had a smoke. All this takes time off the war, I thought, they can't touch you, you've been wounded and you're entitled to a bit of a rest. From my vantage point I could look down on the place where the doctor was. There were a lot of men down there, some of them walking along the valley and looking in that barren scene like strollers in the desert. A car was parked there too, right beside the doctor, but I didn't feel like being driven in it, I had plenty of time, they couldn't touch me.

Slowly I walked on. Only now did I realize what a long way we had advanced from Jassy. No matter how often I reached the top of a ridge, there was nothing of the town's white walls to be seen. It was very quiet, apart from a few desultory shots in the distance. Then I saw a forest, and out of the forest came a big, furious car raising a cloud of dust. It was really angry, that car, impatient, irritable, annoyed. It stopped right in front of me. In it sat our general, wearing his steel helmet, and when generals wear their steel helmets something has gone wrong. There was also a colonel, wearing a Knight's Cross, no other decoration. It looked very chic and elegant. The general stood up in the car and yelled at me: "What d'you suppose you're doing?"

"I've been wounded, sir," I replied, and turned round. I almost had to laugh, it was so funny the way I turned my backside to the general.

"It's all right, son." I turned again. His round, red face was still furious, as furious as the car, even though he'd said "son". Generals always say "son"; they don't show much imagination when they speak to you.

"How are things up front?" he asked.

"First they went back, then forward again, I don't really know."

"Where's your rifle, son?"

"Smashed, sir. It was a hand grenade, fell right beside me. My rifle lay on that side and got smashed to pieces."

"Here, have a smoke," he said, handing me a whole packet of cigarettes. Generals usually hand out cigarettes. I thanked him by standing to attention, and off they drove. The colonel touched his cap, which I found quite something considering he had the Knight's Cross and I had nothing on my chest.

On coming out of the forest I saw the town lying all white on its hills and looking magnificent. I felt very happy, they couldn't touch me, I'd been wounded right at the front, ten metres away from the Russians, and maybe I was a hero. They couldn't touch me. I was carrying my haversack, it contained two pairs of socks, and for that I would drink some wine in town, maybe get something to eat, but the idea of eating made me feel quite sick; I'd had nothing to eat or drink for a day and a half. Yet at the thought of the wine I walked faster. I crossed a heath that was all torn up by tank tracks and bombs; a few corpses were lying around, and some dead horses. Beyond this bit of heath the path rose steeply past some houses: I was in town. A tram was waiting in a square. I ran to catch it, like at home. I just made it, and we moved off at once. Maybe the driver had seen me, I thought, and waited for me. The tram was empty. It must have been about noon. It was hot; to right and left the houses slept in the sun. There were only a few dogs running round, and some chickens.

The conductress came towards me with her pouch, wanting money. That's right, I thought, the Romanians are our allies, we're supposed to pay. I shrugged and laughed. But she was quite serious. "Nix," she said firmly. Turning my wound towards her I said: "Kaputt, see?" but that didn't move her. She shrugged her shoulders and rubbed thumb and forefinger. "Nix," she repeated. Digging into my haversack I found some writing paper, a few crushed cigarettes that I intended to smoke in my pipe, the socks, and a pair of nail scissors. I showed her the nail scissors. The driver raced along at breakneck speed. Some other people had got on. The conductress attended to them, then came back. I showed her the scissors. "How many *lei*?" I asked. She wrinkled her nose. She was quite pretty, and I could see that the scissors appealed to her. She snipped her nails with them, smiled at me, and indicated "twenty" with her fingers. I nodded. I was so happy, for they couldn't touch me, maybe I was a hero, I'd been wounded right at the front, ten metres away from the Russians. The conductress gave me a ten-*lei* bill and the ticket for five *lei*. That was all. But I didn't mind. I was happy, they couldn't touch me.

I turned to look out at my surroundings. We passed a café, and I remembered I hadn't had anything to drink for two days and had a raging thirst. The tram stopped at a big square where there was a cinema for the military and some cafés and department stores. It was a busy scene, with soldiers milling round, and whores, and peddlers with their barrows. The whores were fantastically beautiful, with almond eyes and scarlet mouths, but they looked pretty pricey to me.

I got off and went into a café; no one paid any attention to me, no one saw the wound in my back, a superb wound, all bloody, with shreds of cloth and needing at least four months to heal. There was just one soldier in the café, sitting at the back, a corporal, and I could tell at once that he was drunk. To the left sat a man with black hair, coal black, and a fat, pale face, eating a pickled cucumber and smoking a black cigar. To the right sat a woman who smiled at me. She was smoking a cigarette, puffing fiendish smoke rings.

"Lover boy!" she called out, but I didn't like the looks of her, and I was sure she would be very pricey. The corporal at the back called out: "Hey, there!" I walked towards him. His eyes were dim and unfocused. His chest was covered with medals, and he had a large carafe of wine in front of him.

"Help yourself!" he said. My God, how glorious it was to drink! I drank straight from the carafe. My God, how wonderful it was to drink! I could physically feel how parched I was, and it was a cool wine, on the dry side.

"Help yourself!" said the corporal, but the carafe was empty. "Hey, pal!" he called out, and a greasy-looking fellow immediately came from behind a curtain, snatched up the carafe, and carried it off. The black-haired man was now sitting with the woman, who was as blonde as he was dark. He let her take a bite of his pickle and a puff of his cigar; then they both laughed, and the black-haired man called out towards the curtain something that sounded like Latin, a slushy kind of Latin.

The greasy youth arrived with the carafe, a bigger one than the last, and he also brought along another glass.

"Help yourself!" said the corporal.

He poured, and we drank. I drank, I drank, it was glorious, it was wonderful.

"Have a smoke," said the corporal, but I hauled out my general's packet and slapped it onto the table. The blonde woman was laughing with the black-haired man; now they were drinking wine. Wine on top of pickles, I thought, that's asking for trouble, but they seemed to be enjoying it as they blew their fiendish smoke rings in the air.

"Drink away," said the corporal. "I have to go back to the front tonight, for the fifth time, goddammit!"

"Take the tram," I said, "I've just come from there, for the third time."

"Where've you come from?"

"From the front."

"Did you skedaddle?"

"No, I was wounded."

"Oh, come on!"

I showed him my back.

"Goddammit," he exclaimed, "aren't you the lucky one! That's fantastic. Sell it to me!"

"Sell what?"

"That thing there, that red mess on your back—sell it to me!"

He slapped a whole pile of bills on the table, picked up the carafe, and lifted it to his mouth. Then I drank, then he, then I ...

"Hey, pal!" he called.

The greasy youth reappeared and brought another carafe, and we drank.

"Sell it to me, you coward," shouted the corporal. "I'll give you a thousand *lei*, two thousand, three thousand, you can buy yourself the best-looking whores, and tobacco, and wine, and you ..."

"But you can buy wounds right here, they made me an offer at the station."

The corporal suddenly turned sober and grabbed my arm.

"Where?" he asked hoarsely.

"At the station," I said, "they made me an offer right there."

"Hey, pal!" shouted the corporal. "How much?" He slapped some money on the table, grabbed my arm, and said: "Wait here."

He put on his cap, tightened his belt and left.

The greasy youth brought another carafe. "It's paid for," he said with a grin. And I drank. The blonde woman was sitting on the black-haired man's knee, shrieking away. She had a cigar in her mouth and a cold pork chop in her hand. The black-haired man was already quite drunk. I drank and smoked. It was glorious, I was drunk, wonderfully drunk, and I'd been wounded, and they couldn't touch me, maybe I was a hero. Wounded for the third time. The wine was glorious, glorious ...

"Hey, pal!" I called out. The greasy youth came and stood grinning in front of me. I pulled the socks out of my haversack and held them out: "How much wine?" He shrugged and wrinkled his nose, then took the socks and held them up to his face. "Not new," he said, sniffing with his long nose.

"How much?" I asked.

"Give you wine, two like that." He pointed at the carafe.

"Bring it," I said, "bring it here, the wine."

He brought it. Both carafes at once. I drank, I drank, it was glorious, it was wonderful, I was completely drunk, but as sober as only a happy man can be. It was indescribable how cool and dry the wine was, and I paid for it with two pairs of socks. The woman ate a second pork chop as she smoked a cigarette. She was a thin little creature and shrieked like crazy as she sat on the black-haired man's knee. I saw everything clear as clear, drunk though I was. I could see she wasn't wearing either a slip or underpants, and the black-haired man kept pinching her behind; that made her shriek, she shrieked because of that too. Then the black-haired man started yelling his head off, lifted the woman high in the air, and carried her out through the door.

At that moment the corporal walked in again.

"Help yourself!" I called out to him.

"Hey, pal!" shouted the corporal, whereupon the greasy youth appeared at once.

"Wine!" shouted the corporal. "A whole barrel of wine!" and I knew that it had worked. He picked up my second carafe, drank it down at one go, and smashed it against the wall.

"Those fellows," said the corporal, "do a great job. Pistol with silencer. You stand round a corner and stick out your paw, and plop—take a look."

He pulled up his sleeve. They had put a nice clean hole through his forearm, bandaged it, and even supplied him with a casualty certificate.

The greasy youth brought a large carafe. The corporal was beside himself, shouting and drinking, shouting and drinking. And said: "My name's Hubert."

And I drank; it was wonderful.

Then we went off to the first-aid station. Hubert knew all the ropes. As we arrived, a few freight cars were just being loaded with minor casualties. There were two doctors, and in front of each stood a long queue of walking wounded. Since we were drunk, we wanted to come last. We joined the second queue because that doctor looked kinder than the other one. A corporal stood beside him calling out "Next!" Some cases took a long time, and those who had been treated walked through a long corridor leading to a courtyard.

We sat down on a bench, since we were drunk and rather unsteady on our legs. Next to me sat a man who'd had a bullet through the palm of his hand, clear through it, and he was bleeding like a pig onto the bench. He was quite grey in the face.

The doctors were working with the door open, cigarettes between their lips, and sometimes they would take a pull from a bottle. They were slaving away like crazy, and the one I was queuing up for had a nice face, an intelligent face, and I noticed he had skilful, quiet hands. A vehicle arrived with some serious casualties, and we had to wait. The corporal shut the door, and we could hear screams, and there was an even stronger smell of blood and ether. The man with the injured hand had fallen asleep and had stopped bleeding. The blood from his hand had gone all over me, and when I took my paybook out of my left pocket I found it soaked in blood; the first few pages were no longer legible. I was drunk, I didn't care, and they couldn't, they couldn't touch me, they couldn't get at me, I'd been wounded, I'd been wounded right at the front, and maybe I was even a hero.

So now I was the unknown soldier.

I said aloud to myself, "I am the unknown soldier," but the others, sitting on the ground or on the bench, called out "Shut up!" I shut up and looked out onto the street. Hubert had fallen asleep, with his arm stuck out stiffly; it looked very impressive, like a genuine battle injury. They had done a good job; I must be sure and ask him how much it cost. And if the war wasn't over in four months, I'd get them to shoot me through the arm, too, then I'd get the gold badge, then I'd be a proper official hero, and they wouldn't be able to touch me at all. But now he was asleep, they still hadn't finished with the six stretcher cases, and all we could hear was their screaming. I wasn't all that drunk any more. Someone in the queue suddenly asked quietly: "Got a smoke, anyone?" I recognized the man with the leg who had supported himself on his rifle. But he didn't recognize me. He still had his rifle, and his face was the face of a real hero. He was proud. I gave him a few of the general's cigarettes. Hubert was sound asleep and snoring; now his face was quite happy. Then the door opened, and the corporal called out again, "Next!"

After that everything went very fast, and no more vehicles arrived. I was still drunk after all, but I felt fine, with no pain to speak of.

"Hey, next, it's your turn!" the corporal shouted.

I stepped into a classroom where the benches had been piled up and Marshal Antonescu looked down from the wall, together with Crown Prince Michael. There was a disgusting smell of blood and ether. I took off my tunic and shirt, unaided; I was still drunk. "Hurry up!" said the corporal. Crown Prince Michael had a really stupid Hohenzollern face, and he was boss over the black-haired people and the whores and the greasy youths, the onions and the pickles and the wine. But Romania was a real mess, and he'd never bring it off, nor would Antonescu.

At that moment I became perfectly sober, for the doctor was snipping away in my back. I could feel nothing as he had given me a local anaesthetic, but it is a very queer sensation when they snip away in you like that. I could see it all quite clearly: in front of me was a big glass-doored cupboard and behind me a glass instrument-case. And I could see my smooth back and the big hole in it, and the doctor snipping the edges nice and smooth and picking something out of the hole. I felt like a frozen carcass being divided up between two butchers. His snipping was quick and deft; then he dabbed something onto the wound, and I saw that the hole had become much bigger. Go on, make it a little bigger, I thought, then it'll take six months. Maybe the doctor was thinking the same thing. Once again he started snipping and probing. Then came more dabbing, and the corporal, who had been holding me as a matter of routine, went to the door and called out, "Next!"

"Hand grenade, was it, my boy?" the doctor asked as he placed a large wad of cotton wool on the hole in my back.

"I think so," I replied.

"Quite a nice long piece, want to keep it?" He held out a crumpled, bloodied strip of metal.

"No, thanks," I said. He tossed it in the garbage can, and I could see a leg lying there, a real, perfectly good, splendid leg. I was cold sober.

"I'm sure there's a bit of wood in there still, and some shreds of cloth, they'll all have to come out with the pus—just make certain nothing stays behind." He laughed. The corporal bandaged me up, winding all kinds of stuff round me, and now dammit I really did feel like a hero, goddammit, wounded by a hand grenade, right at the front.

The doctor looked at Hubert's clean hole, then at the corporal, and his expression became serious. "Made to order, my friend, just made to order."

I felt hot all over, but Hubert remained cool.

"A really magnificent home-leave shot, that's the fifth today," said the corporal.

"Magnificent," said the doctor, but he didn't touch it, merely glanced at the corporal, and the corporal, who was still bandaging me, went across to have a good look at it; then he too looked at Hubert. "Magnificent," he said.

The doctor, sitting with his legs crossed, was smoking a cigarette. He didn't touch the wound. Hubert was quite calm but no longer drunk.

"What's going on?" he asked in surprise. "May I go now—out that way? Be seeing you, Hans," he said to me. He actually started to leave.

"Hold it," said the doctor. "What d'you think you're doing! Baumüller?" He turned towards the corporal who had bandaged me. I was all through now and put on my belt with the haversack.

"It stinks," said the corporal. "Made to order."

"Coming, Hubert?" I asked.

"You two know each other?" asked the doctor.

"My section leader," I said calmly, "he was lying right beside me ... "

"I see," said the doctor; the corporal who had bandaged me also said, "I see," and they believed me because I had such a splendid hole in my back, a hero's hole. We left.

Hubert pressed my hand.

Standing outside on the railway tracks were three freight cars. In another car men were singing, and there was that authentic smell of railway, of coal and dry wood, as in all railway stations in the world. There was a smell of war. And it was too bad that we were no longer even slightly drunk. Hubert jumped into a car and helped me up, for I was a bit stiff what with all that bandaging; besides, I now had a huge hole in my back. From his left and right pockets he pulled out a bottle, thrust one at me, and shouted triumphantly: "There—drink, drink!" and we drank ... and it was wonderful, they couldn't touch us, we were wounded, properly wounded, maybe we were heroes, and the corporal would get the gold badge, and then they wouldn't be able to touch him at all.

The train started. It would travel through the Carpathians, through the *puszta,* through all of Hungary, all the way to the Vienna Woods.

But first only a few kilometres to the main station, where we received rations: white bread, cheese, and tobacco. Coffee too, but we had no mess-tins. Then blankets were distributed, and we bedded down very comfortably in the freight car. There were only twenty-four of us: it was a French car, and below the inscription: "8 chevaux, 40 hommes" some joker had written: "1/2 elephant, 20,000 white mice." I had to laugh. We were all classified as "minor casualties". I had hoped to be among the so-called "stretcher cases", since those were conveyed home later in white beds in a hospital train. But the doctor at the railway station had said I was a "minor casualty". We were twelve at each end, six a side, and in the middle was an empty space with pots of coffee and mugs. We drank coffee and ate white bread and cheese. Dusk began falling, and the train moved off.

The doctor who had divided us at the station into "minor casualties" and "stretcher cases" had put Hubert in charge of our car. Hubert assigned us our places and distributed the blankets, and before the train left he hauled a keg of wine on board. "Help yourselves!" he cried.

The dusk deepened as we travelled across a grey plain with grazing land and huge herds of cattle. Herdsmen's fires stood out against the flat horizon, and the fires and black smoke from gypsy camps hung in the sky like great banners; the gypsies were singing, we supposed, and we drank. Each man had received a litre of wine, and we were all getting drunk. We were once more in a casualty train, and I was a hero, I would get the silver badge and Hubert the gold; it was his fifth time. One by one the others fell asleep, and I sat alone with Hubert on a wooden crate by the open door, and we drank up the wine, smoked, and didn't say a word.

The sky was grey and beneath it stretched shimmering, cool-green maize fields, and often we were travelling across the steppe and could hear the lowing of the herds, see the quiet fires of the herdsmen. Sometimes we would pass through a station where people were standing waiting for trains going the other way, soldiers and Romanians in colourful costumes, and I thought how terrible it must be for the soldiers to be standing there and going off to the front. It would have been nice if we could have told them where to find the sellers of home-leave shots; then they could immediately have taken the train home again from that station. But no doubt most of them would have been scared. I would have been scared. I know I would have been scared to do something like that, and to me Hubert was a hero. Goddammit, that required courage.

"You're a hero," I said in a low voice.

"Shut up."

Then darkness fell, but the sky was still grey, a soft grey, with the tall poles of the draw-wells outlined against it like black screams of torment. Villages lay silent and patient in their maize fields under the grey sky, and I had no desire to sleep: it was so glorious, it was wonderful, and the most wonderful thing was that they couldn't touch me. We smoked and drank, and neither said a word.

The train stopped at a lighted station, and we could see it was a big one. We halted beside a regular platform that was crowded with people, some of them in rags, but there were also some very smart

Romanian officers with their whores, and Romanian soldiers who got paid in beatings. In a freight car somewhere up front, the stretcher cases were screaming horribly.

The crowd on the platform parted, and two doctors and a corporal approached. Beside me Hubert whistled through his teeth. "We're being screened," he said. Grabbing the empty keg he disappeared behind me, getting down off the train on the side where the tracks were. And I looked right into the solemn faces of the people on the platform and felt myself to be a hero. Up front they were still screaming; I saw from my watch that it was only eleven thirty, and here I'd been thinking the night was almost over.

The doctors entered our car. "On your feet!" one of them shouted, "everybody on their feet!" I felt calm enough but was aware of the tension in the others. I presented myself first. "Right," he said. "Any pain?" "Yes," I said. "A pill, Schwitzkowski." The corporal gave me a pill. The next man was kicked out; he only had a tiny splinter in his arm and hadn't even bled. The doctor shone his flashlight onto each wound. It was dark and silent in the car. Several times he said: "Out!", and those to whom he said "Out!" got out right away and had to wait on the platform. Finally he went over to the corner where a man was lying quite still.

"Get up, damn you!" said the doctor. But the man just lay there and said nothing. Perhaps he's dead, I thought. "What's the matter with you?" shouted the doctor. Now the man said quietly: "Shot in the leg."

"But you're a stretcher case—what are you doing here? Let's have a look." He kneeled down and turned the wounded man onto his stomach. "There?" he asked. "Here?" he asked, and each time the wounded man groaned. "Come on now," said the doctor, "don't be a sissy." Then he said: "Carry him out, put him in with the stretcher cases." Two men picked him up, and the corporal shone his flashlight.

As they carried him past me, I saw that he was already dead. It was quite obvious—he was dead. "But he's dead," I told the corporal. "Shut up," he replied, and they carried him out, and the people on the platform made room. One of the Romanian officers touched his cap. He must have also seen that the man was dead. Back there in the corner, the doctor had poked and prodded him to death.

Someone came and asked how many of us were left. We had to count off, and in the dark I counted off in two different voices. There were still fourteen of us. They brought us some hot milk and a few Romanian cigarettes each. Then we started off again. At the last moment Hubert jumped back on from the far side. There was another man with him who laughed and said there was nothing wrong with him, just that he was almost blind and had broken his glasses. He had a certificate from his lieutenant saying that his glasses had been broken by "enemy action". The half-blind man lay down somewhere in the corner, and Hubert gave him the milk I had been saving for him. We two drank the schnapps he had brought along.

After the hot milk they all needed to go, and for a long time we had no peace on our wooden crate. It was getting chilly, too, and by that time it was quite dark.

In the silent fields we were passing, something seemed to be lying in wait. And the humped villages sleeping among the bushes seemed dangerous.

The apricot brandy was very strong, and when it hit the hot milk I suddenly felt miserably sick. At every rattle, the vomit rose to my throat and slipped down again, and the dark-grey fields became a blur, a whirling mush, before my eyes. I threw up. I grabbed a blanket and lay down on the straw, and Hubert pushed another blanket under my head for a pillow. He said nothing. It was uncannily quiet.

I fell asleep. When I woke up I was shivering.

It was not yet light, and the train had halted in a narrow gorge. Hubert was standing outside smoking a cigarette. "Hallo there!" he called. "Had a good sleep?" I lit a cigarette and got down off the train too. Most of the minor casualties were standing outside. On either side were very steep mountains, and high up, very high up, I saw a young herdsman, a boy, waving his hat. I took off my cap and waved back at him.

The boy shouted something, probably he was very lonely up there and glad when a train passed. I suddenly felt hungry, climbed back into the freight car, and ate up the rest of the white bread and the cheese and drank some cold coffee with it. I wasn't a bit happy any more, I longed to be home. My wound was hurting how, and I could tell that it had begun to fester; I felt very sick. I looked forward to a bed, and I wouldn't have minded a wash. I hadn't washed for three days. We had been marching, attacking, marching, attacking, the food lorry had had a direct hit; then I'd been wounded and since then I'd been boozing: no wonder I was feeling sick. One man stood right beside me and pissed against the inside wall of the car.

"Hey!" I cried. "What d'you think you're doing?"

"I'm pissing," he replied calmly.

"Piss properly, then!"

"I am pissing properly." I was about to get up and show him how to piss, but it was too late—he'd finished and was already buttoning his trousers. Then I saw that it was the half-blind man and thought, he's putting it on.

I picked up my blanket and lay down somewhere else, feeling wretched, and now I wasn't thinking that they couldn't get at me but wondering instead how I could get at them.

The engine whistled, and we crawled over one of those uncomfortably swaying Carpathian bridges; then we came to a station where we were screened all over again. Hubert disappeared as he'd done before. But this time they got the half-blind man, and a few others too. One of them merely had eczema.

"Eczema!" said the doctor. "Are you crazy, to go all the way back to Hungary with eczema?"

By this time there were only eight of us left, and they moved us from three freight cars into one. It was odd that once again we were exactly twenty-four. Maybe all they had was that one car. The man with eczema and the half-blind fellow and all the simple bullet holes had to stay behind just because there was only one car. From among the stretcher cases they carried out those who were no longer fit to be transported. Of one of them there was very little left anyway. He was minus both legs, and it looked like very little when they carried the stretcher past us. He was as white as milk in the face but looked furious, and his bandages were black with blood. They also carried away a body, the man the doctor in our car had poked and prodded to death.

I still felt ghastly, and once again the freight car was crowded. A very stern corporal had been put in charge. He was tall and broad and wore the Cross of Merit, and I was sure he was a schoolteacher and just about to be promoted to sergeant.

"To your places!" he shouted. He suffered from jaundice, and his fat face looked like a bronze statue of Mussolini.

"Sit down!" he shouted.

"Count off!" We counted off.

I simply missed out one number and said "fourteen" instead of "thirteen", and he didn't notice because he forgot to count himself. No one noticed. We were all tired and hungry, and our wounds had begun to hurt.

Then we were given white bread and cheese and some hot coffee. I was worried about Hubert, couldn't see him anywhere, but the engine was there and it looked as if we were going to leave any minute.

I got out, and the stern corporal asked where I was going, saying no one was allowed to get out. I said I had to have a shit; he couldn't do anything about that so he told me to be quick about it.

Walking over to the station building I called out: "Hubert!" I found him in the little bar next to the waiting-room. He was drunk. "I'm changing my money," he called out. "We're going to Hungary, you have to have *pengö* there. Come along, sit down!"

We had a clear view of the train, and I saw the stern corporal sticking his head out of the car several times.

"They've counted off."

"So what?"

"But he's strict, that *Kapo*."

"So what?"

"And the fellow in charge, a doctor, knows exactly how many of us there are."

"So what?"

He was very drunk.

"But what are you going to do? You're one too many!"

"I've already spoken to the doctor."

A girl brought a big hunk of roast pork and some bread; it smelled fantastic and must have cost a lot. We ate, drank some wine, and I thought, well, if he's spoken to the doctor, nothing can happen to him, and I felt fine again. We bought some tobacco and a few more bottles of wine, then walked back to our freight car. Right after that the train left.

The stern corporal asked Hubert: "What are you doing here? You don't belong in here."

"I beg to differ, I've always been in here."

"That's not true."

"Hey, fellows!" Hubert called out. "Haven't I always been in here?"

Most of the men were silent and said nothing, but the eight who had been in our old car called out: "Of course he belongs in here!"

"But we've only reported twenty-four," said the stern corporal.

"That was a mistake."

"We don't make mistakes."

"But it was a mistake."

"We really were twenty-five before," I said.

"Shut up!"

"Because you didn't count yourself," I said.

"You're drunk!" shouted the stern corporal, and now I knew that he really was a schoolteacher.

"This business has to be cleared up," he told Hubert.

"It's been cleared up," Hubert said as he sat down.

"I am responsible."

"You're an arsehole."

"How dare you speak to me like that in front of the troops!"

"Because you are one."

"I'll report it to the doctor."

"I've already reported it to the doctor."

"Reported what?"

"That you're an arsehole."

Everyone laughed, and the stern corporal sat down too. By now it was somewhere round eight or nine in the morning. I felt great, and we drank wine. What I could see of the outside seemed to me already quite Hungarian, but we were still in Romania. There were peasants in the fields, and they waved their hats and called out something that sounded Hungarian.

But then we stopped at a station in a big city, and true enough we were still in Romania. I was appalled at the thought that we might be dropped off here so that I wouldn't even get as far back as Hungary.

Now the doctor will come, I thought, and Hubert hasn't spoken to the doctor of course, and it's all going to come out.

The doctor arrived, quite young. He was laughing—probably glad to have been assigned to this train and so able to travel with us, maybe even as far as the Vienna Woods.

"How's it going, boys?" he called. "Anyone here in pain?" And just as the stern corporal was about to open his mouth, Hubert and

the doctor looked at each other and they both laughed. "Kramer!" the
doctor exclaimed. "What the hell are you doing here? Did you stop
one again?"

"Yes, Berghannes, I did." He jumped off the train and walked up
and down the platform with the doctor. The stern corporal looked
pretty foolish, but then food was delivered which he had to dole out.
White bread and cheese and another roll of fruit-drops, and I ate hungrily. Hubert and the doctor paced up and down the platform until the
train was about to move off.

"Shit," he said. "We'll just barely enter Hungary."

"Who says so?"

"The doctor."

"Shit."

"Right, maybe there's something we can do about it," he said with
a laugh.

"Like what, for instance?"

"We might be able to join the stretcher cases when some of them
have to be unloaded again."

"Then we'll go as far as the Vienna Woods."

"Like hell Vienna Woods—the whole train's only going as far as
Debrecen."

"Okay, so Debrecen's quite near Budapest."

"Let's hope we can work it."

"Is the doctor a good friend of yours?"

"We were at university together."

Christ, I thought, he's been to university. I said no more. He held
out a bottle to me. The train was now moving into the Carpathians,
right into the very heart of them. It was warm, and the schnapps tasted
deliciously of apricots.

"Why so silent?"

"Oh..."

"Come on, what's up?"

"I was just thinking that you're kind of a highbrow if you've been
to university."

"Hell no—don't imagine there's anything so special about universities! What d'you do for a living?"

"I'm a stove-fitter."

"You should be proud you can fit a stove properly so that it draws and people keep warm and can cook on it. I tell you, that's a fine craft, an admirable one, my friend. Here, drink, take a good swig." I took a good swig.

"But at the big universities they learn how to be doctors and judges and teachers, that's a pretty high-class bunch of people," I said.

"Much too high-class. The point is, they're only high-class because they go round with their noses in the air, that's all. To hell with them."

"Are you a doctor or a teacher or a judge?"

"Not me—I never finished, I wanted to be a teacher, but they made me a soldier."

"Well, sure, they can't use the stupidest ones at university ..."

"Don't you believe it—sometimes they like those the best."

"I don't believe it."

He pointed to the stern corporal, saying: "Just look at that fellow: there you have a solid citizen. He believes that everything he does is for the good of the state, but actually all he's concerned with is his citizen's stomach and his arse. He likes to eat well and is a bit of a coward. And likes to bawl people out. The fact is, he's concerned only with himself. He's scared that, because I got into the train, he might be kicked out since he only has jaundice while I've been honourably wounded. Haven't I?"

"Of course."

"There you are, then. The state likes these fellows, although it knows they're concerned only with themselves. It gives them a job where they have something to say but also something to lose, and that takes care of it. To hell with all that. They'll be surprised to see what I'm capable of."

He drank again from the bottle, and I wondered whether he might have been overdoing the booze a bit.

"What d'you think you're doing there?" he called out to the stern corporal, who was working something out on a piece of paper on his knee.

"Counting my assault days and my close-combat days," he said, modestly enough.

"What assault days?"

"*My* assault days."

"Where the hell did you take part in an assault or close combat?"

"Up there near Kishinev—you know."

"Kishinev? Which unit?"

"The tank corps ... "

"And that's where you were in close combat and an assault? You look like a pretty fierce fighter to me, I must say!"

The stern corporal blushed. And I was tempted to feel sorry for him.

"Well," he said, "if you like I can show you. On three assault days I was up at the front, taking round food, bringing back wounded ... "

"You're a bastard, I tell you—you ate up the men's rations and pinched the valuables out of the wounded men's pockets. That's the kind of chap you are."

"How dare you speak to me like that! Cut it out, you're drunk."

"Sure I am, drunks tell the truth. That's the kind of bastard you are. Here," he said suddenly, ripping all the decorations off his chest, "take the Iron Cross and the assault badge and the close-combat badge, I've had it up to here with them."

By now he was totally drunk. I grabbed hold of him and laid him down flat on his blanket.

"You can see he's plastered, can't you?" I said.

The stern corporal said nothing. I picked up the decorations from the floor and put them in my pocket. No one said a word.

We were now travelling through some marvellous scenery, magnificent mountains and picturesque villages and small towns. It was almost noon, and we began to eat our white bread and our tinned cheese, and we were all thirsty. We stopped at a small station, and someone asked the corporal whether we might try and get something to drink.

"I'm not saying another word." He seemed to be still working something out on his knee. "I'm not saying anything any more. I ate up all your rations and pinched your valuables from your pockets. I'm not saying another word."

I almost think he was close to tears, and now I was quite sure he was a schoolteacher.

"Don't be an idiot," someone called out, "he was drunk!"

"Drunks tell the truth ... "

"*Kapo*, don't be such a fool," came another voice, "he was just being mean!"

"No, I'm a bastard."

"Come on, there's a good lad, we don't believe him!"

"I didn't do my duty."

"You did, you did—come on, chin up. Look, he's plastered."

"So can we go and get something to drink?"

"It's against regulations, and if the train suddenly starts to move you'll miss it—but then I'm not responsible. He knows all the doctors intimately, and he sized me up right away."

A few men got off the train, hurried to a nearby house, and came back with some water and some weak coffee. They first let the corporal have a drink. One man wanted to fill up a whole mug for him.

"Hold it," said the corporal, "don't forget your mates."

Then the others got off too, and he said with a laugh: "I'm not responsible any more—it feels good not to be responsible any more! The man responsible is asleep and drunk. He has the right attitude towards duty."

They all looked angrily at the sleeping Hubert. He slept very quietly, but his face showed some stress, and now for the first time I had a good look at him. He was older than I, at least six or seven years older. At least twenty-five. He had very fair hair and a narrow face and didn't look well, but then he'd been drinking pretty heavily the last few days.

Then the young doctor returned and called out: "Kramer!" I pointed at Hubert, and the doctor said: "Let him sleep." Then he told us: "It's all right for you fellows to get off here for a bit, the engine's broken down. It may take a while."

It was a very small station. The station building looked half asleep; it smelled of resin and ripe maize. There were piles of lumber lying around, and stacks of iron and indefinable objects such as seemed to have been left at almost every station. The train stood there without an engine like a snake without a head. Not a soul in sight.

I sniffed the air and suddenly smelled that it was Sunday. There was a smell of inactivity. I walked past the station, where they were all converging like flies onto the bar.

There was such a glorious smell of summer and Sunday, and then I heard sobbing violin music that drove me wild. There wasn't a dog to be seen in the dusty street, not a soul in sight.

Aha, I thought, they've filled their bellies with goulash and now they're sleeping it off, and someone's playing the violin. The music was coming from a tiny bar, and suddenly I realized I was thirsty and went inside.

All I saw there were a few swarthy fellows sitting on dilapidated chairs; they didn't really look in too good shape, they were very thin and sallow, and I thought maybe they hadn't been eating goulash after all. Another man was leaning against the bar producing sobbing sounds from his violin.

I stared in amazement at the violin, surely tears must be pouring down it, but it was quite dry. And the men all looked terribly parched too. Maybe because of all that paprika, I thought. I had never been to Hungary, and I imagined they all ate a lot of paprika and goulash and made their violins sob. Only the mouth of the plump, pretty woman behind the bar was moist, and as I entered and called out "Hallo, comrades!" they laughed and responded with some friendly-sounding Hungarian words; the woman was especially welcoming with her friendly "*Gooter Tak!*"

I walked towards the bar. The fellow went on playing his violin and gave me a pleasant smile.

"Might I please have a glass of water?" I asked very politely, not having a penny in my pocket. The woman laughed, the way we sometimes laugh when someone speaks an incomprehensible language. Then she said, with a cooing sound like a pigeon's in her lovely, smooth throat: "*Bor.*"

But I didn't know what she meant, and I told her so. That made her laugh even more, and delightful dimples appeared in her handsome face. Then she said: "*Birr.*"

I shook my head and said: "No *pengö*," and stubbornly went on asking for water. Meanwhile I had put my hands in my pockets and was listening to the young violinist. The others, too, were listening to him spellbound, smiling only when I caught their eyes. In my pocket, however, I found a brand-new, factory-fresh Wehrmacht handkerchief, one of those olive-green ones, and holding it out to the woman I asked: "How many *pengö* this?"

But she shook her head at once, and I realized I was no longer in Romania. In Romania you could sell anyone anything. A shadow

crossed the woman's face, and I felt sad too because I thought I had
offended her, but she was soon smiling again, set a bottle and glass
on a table, and gestured to me to sit down. "You no *pengö*," she said
encouragingly.

I sat down beside one of the swarthy fellows and listened to the
sobbing violin.

I found it cruelly sad and beautiful; it seemed to smell of passionate kisses and tears shed over a broken heart. I could feel my tears welling up, but then I opened the bottle and poured some wonderful brown
beer into the glass. My mouth watered. At that moment the violinist
paused briefly, and I rose, held up my glass, and called out: "First, my
Hungarian comrades, let me drink to the loveliest of all women," raising my glass to the landlady.

"And then," I went on with a nod towards the violinist: "let me
drink to you, comrade, you who can sob like a god. I'm not making fun
of you, far from it, but keep up the sobbing and to hell with everything
else. And now let me drink to the whole parched Hungarian people—
don't be offended, but I don't know what else to say."

And I drank down the whole huge, glorious glassful, and it tasted
so good that I almost choked with pleasure.

My speech met with loud approval. They seemed to have understood me, and they laughed like children as they raised their glasses to me.

One of them came up and filled my glass; I had to drink it down in
one go. They immediately produced another bottle, and I finished that
off in short order, too. The beer was truly glorious, and it was so warm
outside, and it was summer, and I was in Hungary, and they couldn't
touch me, and I would have no trouble hearing the train whistle and
could quickly run out and jump on. I was soon slightly drunk and sorry
I didn't have any money for treating my Hungarian friends in return.
But they merely smiled when I tried through gestures to indicate my
problem, and the landlady was especially nice to me. I think she liked
me, I liked her, too, although she was much older than I, but she was
kind and generous and she was a handsome woman, a fine figure of a
Hungarian innkeeper ...

After the fourth bottle I began heaping abuse on Hitler. "Comrades," I called out dramatically, "Hitler is an arsehole!" They fully
agreed and stamped their feet in delight. The sobbing violinist was quite

carried away by my speech; he picked up his violin and produced some frantic revolutionary sobbing, his fingers scampering up and down the strings at breakneck speed.

Suddenly one of my new pals grabbed my arm: "Ssh, ssh!" he went, and everyone fell silent. From the direction of the station I could hear loud shouting. I felt a bit sick to my stomach, but then I thought, only bad people are ever in a hurry. I stood up: "Comrades, the hour of farewell has struck. Don't be offended, but the fact is I'd like to get as far as possible to the rear, to a hospital and close to Germany, otherwise I'll be sitting here all summer, drinking beer and listening to the violin. Don't be offended."

They fully understood and urged me to get going. I hurried over to the landlady and tried to kiss her hand, but she gave me a playful shove...

The avenue was lovely and cool, yet there was a smell of summer and Sunday and of Hungary. Dense chestnut trees that looked as rich and thick as that glorious beer. I soon noticed how drunk I was; the avenue seemed to sway ever so slightly.

The train was still there. At first I couldn't see anyone about, but then someone called out, "There he is!" and I saw all the men from the two freight cars lined up, the doctor facing them. The doctor, Hubert's old pal, was angry, angry and upset, and I imagined it was because of me, because I'd been away, but that wasn't it at all. "Where've you been?" he asked sternly, but without waiting for a reply he said: "Fall in!"

I obeyed, and the others laughed because it was obvious that I was good and drunk. The doctor looked at us solemnly, then glanced at a sheet of paper and said somewhat dramatically:

"Men, I have some information that will interest you all. We received it over the radio as a special announcement, and I have no wish to withhold it from you."

He gave us all another solemn look and continued:

"Today, in the early hours of the morning, the joint British–American forces landed on the west coast of France. A battle of the utmost violence is in progress. In this solemn hour, comrades, when the cowardly liars are finally confronting us, we will not fail to utter a threefold 'Sieg Heil!' to our Führer, to whom we owe everything. Comrades— Sieg ..."— "... Heil!" we shouted. He repeated it twice with us. Then you could hear a pin drop, and into that silence Hubert suddenly shouted: "Hurrah, hurrah, hurrah!" We looked up, startled and horrified, including the doctor. Hubert was standing half-asleep by the doorway of the car, deep lines in his face and wisps of straw clinging to his tunic.

"What's that supposed to mean, Kramer?" the doctor shouted furiously.

"Sir, because at least they're confronting us, you see—that's why I'm shouting hurrah. Now we'll defeat them, wipe them out, and then the war will be over—hurrah, hurrah, hurrah!"

He was grinning from ear to ear, and the doctor and the rest of us laughed too.

"Dismiss!" said the doctor, "everyone stay with the train—the engine will be here any minute."

Hubert jumped down from the car and walked over to the doctor; I could see them chatting together. The others crept back into the car; some of them sat down on the stacks of iron, ate their bread and cheese, and drank cold coffee, since they had no *pengö*.

I stayed close to the station exit, waiting for Hubert; my idea was for him to give me some money or come with me so we could treat those parched fellows and the violinist until the landlady was down to the last bottle of that glorious beer.

Hubert slapped me on the shoulder and told me quietly: "Two more hours at least, but I'm not supposed to tell anyone. Are you drunk?"

"Yes."

"What from?"

"Beer."

"Any good?"

"Fantastic," I replied.

"Let's go," said Hubert, "where's this place of yours?"

We slipped away quickly, but as soon as we reached the lovely cool avenue we slowed down. It was warm and summery, and we'd been wounded, and they couldn't touch us, we were in a proper hospital train—oh God, how wonderful it all was.

"Listen," said Hubert as we walked on. "D'you know that we have a genuine, bona fide reason to get drunk?"

"No," I answered.

"Hell," he said, "they've landed, that means the end is near, I tell you—inexorably near. Now at least the end's no longer out of sight."

"The end of the war?" I asked.

"Of course. Now the end is near, just wait and see."

Suddenly Hubert stopped and grabbed my arm. "Quiet!" We could hear the sobbing violin.

"That's in the bar," I said with a laugh.

"In *our* bar?"

"Right!" I said, and Hubert again: "Hurrah, hurrah, hurrah!" Now we were running.

The parched men welcomed us with loud laughter, even the violinist broke off his playing and nodded at me. And the landlady, my plump, handsome landlady, was positively delighted to see me again. I could tell. I made a short speech introducing my friend Hubert, and they all took him to their hearts. Hubert ordered seven bottles of beer for the three parched ones, for the violinist, for the landlady and for the two of us. He slapped a whole bundle of notes onto the table, and I could see from the eyes of the parched ones, those big, shyly glancing eyes, that the men were poor, and I was touched that they had paid for my beer.

Hubert went round filling all the glasses, then jumped onto a chair and raised his own.

"Men," he cried, "and this delightful lady, beg pardon! Is it not a thing of glory that we're all human beings? Is it not wonderful that we are brothers, and is it not disgusting that those pigs started the war in which they want to kill us off? But we're human beings, and we're going to take our revenge by continuing to be brothers, by stealing from them and screwing them—begging your pardon, fair lady—screwing them blind! Mates!" he cried, "Hungarian mates, we're human beings, never forget that. And now let's drink!"

He emptied his glass, and an expression of amazement spread over his face. "I'll be damned!" he exclaimed. "This beer is truly magnificent!"

Everyone got carried away in their enthusiasm. We embraced each other, and I had a notion I might be able to kiss our lovely landlady, but she pushed me away with a laugh, and I saw that she was blushing.

Damn it, I thought, what a bastard you are—she's married and loves her husband, and you young whippersnapper want to kiss her.

And then I stood up and gave another little speech in which I apologized and called myself a bastard. They all understood, including the landlady, who gave me a forgiving smile.

The Hungarians made speeches too, saying that we were brothers and Hitler and Horthy were bastards, and they spat on the floor and sprinkled some beer over it. Each time the landlady brought more beer she chalked seven strokes on a blackboard, and I soon saw that there were quite a lot of strokes. We had a great time, all of us, and told each other the most fantastic stories without understanding a word, and we understood each other famously.

The violinist sobbed out a piece that sounded like wine and silk, dark silk and heavy wine, and when he had finished Hubert suddenly shouted: "Tokay!" But now we noticed that the woman was no longer there. Hubert gently took the violinist's instrument from him and led him to a chair, where he fell asleep at once.

I had a clear view of Hubert slipping a wad of notes into the violinist's pocket. Hubert really did have a fantastic amount of money, and I decided to ask him later on what he had flogged. Hubert picked up the violin and started to play; the parched ones danced in time to his music.

Actually I felt like making another speech, there was so much I wanted to say, but I simply didn't know how to begin.

The landlady returned with a platter of sliced cold meat and bread, and we ate as she watched us with a happy smile. The parched ones tucked in quite nicely, and I realized that they were hungry, really hungry, and it all tasted wonderful, the cold meat and the white bread, and we drank wine as we ate, and meanwhile I learned that *bor* meant wine, the only Hungarian word I knew.

We left some bread and meat on a plate for the violinist, and I spread my new green handkerchief over it to keep away the flies. After our meal, two of the parched ones fell asleep, sinking back into their chairs and closing their eyes; they were gone, sound asleep, and I thought of how hard they must have worked all week, somewhere in the forest, cutting wood or on the farms.

Finally Hubert got up and said: "We have to go now." He went over to the bar, and the woman counted up all the strokes and did a lengthy calculation.

I made another quick trip outside to the back and thought it was

nice of the handsome landlady to follow me. She looked at me sadly
and said some tender words as she stroked my hand; I was sure it was
some kind of nonsense, the kind of thing women say to very small children. And then all of a sudden she kissed me on the lips, and I saw her
blush deeply before she quickly disappeared again into the bar.

I went out through the garden, and I found the avenue more beautiful than ever. Once again I was drunk and the Hungarian woman had
given me a fleeting kiss! I think I must have been in love with her, but
I no longer know whether I was in love with her or with that lovely
fleeting kiss—not that it matters, I was very happy, and I suddenly felt
terribly young because I was drunk and wounded, and now I could feel
my whole back sticky with pus.

The avenue was beautiful, and I wished it would never end. There
was a sweet and slightly dusty smell of Hungary, of summer and Sunday,
and I was as pleased as Punch that my wound was festering, I just didn't
want it to heal quickly! I would go on drinking, for then it wouldn't
heal so fast because the blood goes bad—yes, they'd told me all that
in hospital the first time I was wounded, but in Germany there was no
booze to be had, and that time my wound had healed up quickly.

The train looked horrible, standing there all sober on the rails, in
the heat of the afternoon, and I felt depressed and wanted to go back
and kiss the Hungarian woman all over again.

I was pretty drunk, I realized, when suddenly the engine whistled
and I had to run. In jumping up I stumbled and made a grab for something, and that made my dressing split open. I could feel the warm pus
running down my back into my pants.

They all laughed when I ran my hand down my back and over the
seat of my trousers as if I had shit in my pants. I got out of my tunic
and pulled off my shirt.

I lay face down on a straw pallet. With a flourish, Hubert threw
my shirt out of the train. "*That*'ll fertilize the Hungarian earth!"
he cried.

The other corporal kneeled down beside me and cleaned up the
rest of the goo, then put on a dressing. I had never been so skilfully
bandaged. After packing a thick, clean tampon into the hole in my back,
he wrapped it all up neatly with gauze and finally wound a whole roll
of bandage round me, fastening it on my chest. "That's what we call a

rucksack dressing," he told me.

Hubert looked at him. "Here," he said, "shake, you old arsehole." They shook hands and laughed.

"I'll stand you all some schnapps," my corporal called out, "and we'll have a song."

He passed round the bottle, and a fat infantryman asked: "What are we going to sing?"

"*Come, ye harlots of Damascus!*" Hubert suggested.

So we sang that fine song: "*Come, ye harlots of Damascus!*" It had seventeen verses and a completely unmilitary tune; between verses we drank schnapps.

The soup cauldron in my back was beginning to simmer again, slowly filling up once more with liquid, and—I must admit—it was a pleasant, ticklish feeling.

Out with the goo, I thought, now it's all right for you to get well, as long as that lovely big hole makes you unfit for duty anyway.

Hubert was thrilled by the speed of the train. Standing in the open doorway he kept shouting: "Hurry ... hurry ... all the way to Germany!"

I sat down beside him, dangling my legs and looking out at the smiling Hungarian countryside. It was terrific to see colourfully dressed people standing there sometimes and waving at us.

I had a long Virginia cheroot between my lips, it tasted deliciously bitter and mild, while in my back the goo of pus and blood and shreds of cloth and hand-grenade splinters went on simmering away.

"Mate," the infantryman said to me, "you shouldn't have thrown away your shirt."

"What d'you mean?"

"The thing to do is wash it," he said, "wash it in cold water and flog it—they pay a lot here for underwear."

"Have you been here before?"

He nodded, drew on his pipe, and puffed out the smoke.

"Yes," he replied, "I've been here before, the last time I was wounded, you can buy anything you like here. All you need is *pengö*. And the only way to get hold of *pengö* is by flogging. They've plenty to eat and drink, but they're always on the look-out for underwear and shoes."

He drew again on his pipe.

"Yes," he went on, "for a shirt like that, if it'd been washed, you'd have had no trouble getting twenty or thirty *pengö*, and that means at least two bottles of schnapps—three hundred cigarettes—or three women..."

"Women, too?"

"That's right," he said, "women are expensive here because they're scarce. In the street you won't find any at all." He suddenly perked up, looked out and, leaning forward, said: "What the devil! We're stopping."

So we were. Waiting on the ramp of the freight platform were lorries marked with red crosses. Hubert had come right up close to me. "Now," he said under his breath, "it's now or never."

A sergeant was already running along the platform, shouting: "Everybody out! Everybody out, you're being unloaded here!"

"Oh shit," said the fat infantryman, "we're hardly out of Romania. This place is right close to Kronstadt."

"D'you know it?" someone called out.

"Sure I do," he said, "it's called Siebenheiligegeorge. It used to be Romanian. Piss, I thought we'd be a bit nearer home by now."

We all got out and stood on the platform until the doctor came. As each man filed past him he scribbled something on the casualty slip.

"That means either hospital or casualty assembly point," said the fat infantryman.

Hubert stood in front of me in the queue. When it was our turn the doctor glanced up.

"You're moving on," he told Hubert. "There's no point in leaving you back here with a wound like that. He'll take the place of the double amputee we've unloaded here," he instructed the sergeant.

"He's got to move on too," said Hubert, pointing at me.

"How's that?"

"He's my mate," said the corporal. "We've spent seventeen assault days and twenty-five close-combat days side by side in the shit, and the lad has a huge hole in his back."

The doctor looked at me, and I thought: This is curtains, they're going to unload you here, and the whole mess wasn't worth the effort, you've no more money, can't buy any more booze, and it'll all heal up in no time. Then after two months you'll be up at the front again in some hole, and who knows whether you'll be that lucky next time.

"Hm," went the doctor, his eyes still on me. "Very well then, this man will take the place of the severe abdominal wound—got that?"

The sergeant nodded and indicated where we were to board the train.

I had no other luggage than my hands in my pockets, and it was glorious to saunter over to the train, but I must admit I was too ashamed to look back to where the others were being loaded onto lorries and driven into town.

"Wait a moment," said Hubert as I was about to climb aboard. "There's one catch to it—now we have to stay in bed and won't be able to get hold of any booze. Come with me..."

We walked back across the rails and entered the station bar from the platform. The bar was deserted except for a few empty beer glasses and a lot of flies and heat and the reek of tepid food. He went over and tapped on the zinc counter top.

"Hallo!" he cried. "Anybody at home?"

I had crossed the room and stood looking out into the street. It was a very broad, dusty road; on either side were flat-roofed houses under small, old trees.

All was silent and empty, until suddenly one of the lorries came dashing into the street, making the dust rise in a spreading cloud. The dust covered the whole sky, enveloped the little church spire ... I turned away.

Hubert was standing at the counter negotiating with a neat, elderly woman who couldn't understand a word. They were both laughing. The woman reached under the counter and placed a bottle on it; moving closer I saw that it was a real cherry brandy.

"More," said Hubert with a gesture. Out came the next bottle, apparently some kind of apricot brandy, then some real Scotch whisky.

After lining up six bottles in front of us, the woman wrote a figure with chalk on the kitchen door-frame, then made a quick addition and showed us the total: a hundred and ninety-two *pengö*. Hubert paid with two hundred-*pengö* notes.

"Christ," I asked, "how did you get hold of all that money?"

"God knows!" he said with a laugh. "Maybe it was lying around in the street and I picked it up!"

Inside the hospital train everything looked so superior that I felt like a criminal. White beds and a nice, gentle nurse and background music from a radio.

We each lay on an upper bunk, close enough together for Hubert to be able to pass me the bottle.

"Just to make sure it doesn't heal up," he said. "Cheers!" We drank ... In the bunk below me lay a man who'd had a bullet through his thigh bone; below Hubert lay a man whose left arm had been amputated. We shared our bottle with them. After two cherry brandies the man with the amputated arm grew quite talkative.

"Just imagine," he said, "my arm had been cut right through, like with a knife. A splinter must have sliced its way through, but the arm wasn't quite off. It still hung by a tendon, and I didn't feel a thing. I jumped up, the lieutenant helped me out of the trench, and I ran to the doctor with my arm dangling—you know, like those little balls you used to be able to buy at a fair, and there was masses of blood, but I ran as fast as I could. The doctor went 'snip' with his scissors, just 'snip', the way a barber snips off a single hair—and there lay my arm." He laughed. "I sometimes wonder where they buried it—let's have another drink. The doctor tells me it was all quite straightforward, it would heal up perfectly ... " He paused to drink... "Want another one too?" he asked the fellow lying beneath me.

"No, I don't think it's good for me. I feel sick."

"Seems to me," the one-armed man went on, "I ought to get the gold badge now. What d'you think? I spent three weeks at the front and right the first day I got a graze and lost some blood—that counts, doesn't it? But I had to stay at the front, and a week later I caught another one, on my leg ... I lost some more blood, so that's two wounds, right? And now this one, that makes three, so it seems to me they have to give me the gold, eh? Let's have the bottle again. My sergeant in the Reserve won't believe his eyes when I rejoin his unit with the gold badge plus the Iron Cross—after four weeks the gold plus the Iron Cross, for after all they're bound to give me the Iron Cross, too." He laughed. "He won't believe his eyes and he'll keep his mouth shut—he always said I was a slob, a great big slob, that I was the worst slob he'd ever known. He won't believe his eyes, will he!"

The windows had been blacked out, but you could hear the noise from the platform, and when I pushed aside the blind a bit there it actually was, a big platform.

"See anything?" asked the one-armed man. "On this side there's only rails and freight cars."

"Yes," I said, "a platform, and officers, and Hungarians and Germans, and women—it's dark … a few men are being carried out on stretchers."

"What's the station called?" asked Hubert.

First I took a swig from the bottle, then looked for the sign: it must be somewhere along the platform, but I couldn't find it.

The nurse and an orderly came in, bringing sandwiches and cocoa. The man with the bullet through his thigh began groaning loudly. "Shit!" he shouted at the nurse. "I don't want to be fed—get that filthy metal out of my leg! Shit on your food, shit on your cocoa, I don't want any cocoa, any more than I wanted that metal in my leg!"

The nurse had turned pale. "But," she whispered, "it's not my fault—wait a moment." She put down the tray on a chair and hurried to the middle of the car, to a small white table with medication on it. There was now complete silence: everyone was listening to the thigh casualty's curses.

"Cocoa!" he swore, "cocoa … so they think I'd go overboard with joy because I'm lying here in a white bed and get to drink cocoa! I've never wanted cocoa or this rocking-chair, and I never wanted any metal in my leg—I wanted to stay home, it's all shit, everything is shit…!" By this time he was yelling as if he'd gone out of his mind.

The nurse returned with a syringe.

"Give me a hand," she said to the orderly, who was standing, silent and stupid, beside my bed.

The nurse looked at the temperature chart. "Grolius," she said in a low voice, "do try and be reasonable. You're in pain, aren't you? I … "

"… An injection!" he yelled. "What else, an injection! But … " he suddenly groaned, "don't think I'm going to keel over with joy just because you're gracious enough to give me an injection … give the Führer an injection!"

You could have heard a pin drop. A voice said: "For God's sake, give that arsehole an injection!"

No one spoke, and the nurse murmured: "He's beside himself … really, he's beside himself … "

"Shit," murmured the wounded man, and once more he whispered: "Shit … " I leaned down and saw that he'd fallen asleep. His slack mouth looked bitter and almost black in the reddish stubble of his beard.

"There now!" the nurse said brightly. "Now we'll have supper!"

She began handing round cocoa and sandwiches. The portion for the thigh casualty was placed on the one-armed man's chair. The cocoa was really good, and the sandwiches were spread with tinned fish.

After taking care of everyone, the nurse stood in the doorway holding the empty tray. "Anyone else need anything ... anything urgent?" she asked.

"Pills!" shouted someone from the far end of the car. "Pills! I can't stand the pain!"

"What?" said the nurse. "No, not now, in half an hour you'll all be getting pills for the night anyway."

"Nurse dear," asked Hubert, "where are we here?"

"We're in Nagykaroky," she replied.

"Shit!" Hubert cried. "Oh, goddamn shit!"

"What's matter?" I asked.

"Because we'll only be going as far as Debrecen after all. Half a night more at the most. Then there'll be another fucking hospital where we won't be allowed out."

"But I thought we were going to Vienna, that's what I heard," said the one-armed man. "Aren't we?"

"Balls," someone shouted. "The train's going to Dresden."

"Nonsense ... Vienna Woods ... "

"You'll see, Debrecen's the end of the line."

"Really?" I asked.

"Are you sure?" I asked.

"Yes," he said gloomily. "Here, have a drink, I'm quite sure."

But I didn't want a drink on top of the cocoa, I didn't want to destroy that wonderful sense of well-being. I smoked a cigarette, lay back carefully on my pillows and looked out into the night. I had tucked the blackout curtain slightly to one side and could look into the soft, dark grey night passing by. The train was moving again, everything was quiet except for the groans of the sleeping thigh casualty. Let's hope he sleeps all the way to Debrecen, I thought, let's hope the one-armed fellow keeps his mouth shut about his gold badge and his bloody sarge ... and let's hope no one at either end of the car starts yelling and screaming "shit"; and when the nurse comes I'll ask her to take my pulse so I can feel her gentle hand, and if she has some pills for me I'll let her put them into my mouth, like yesterday, and for a tenth of a second I'll feel her warm, white fingers on my lips.

But after the orderly had collected the dishes, they started playing gramophone records, Beethoven, and that made me cry, simply made me cry, because it reminded me of my mother.

Hell, I thought, never mind, no one's going to see. It was almost dark in the compartment, and we were being rocked from side to side, and I was crying ... I would soon be nineteen, and I'd already been wounded three times, was already a hero, and I was crying because I was reminded of my mother.

In my mind's eye I clearly saw our home in Severin-Strasse, the way it had been before any bombs had fallen. A comfortable living room, very snug and warm and cheerful, and the street full of people, but no one knew who they were or why they were there. My mother was holding my arm, and we were silent, it was a summer evening and we were coming out of a concert ... and my mother said nothing when I suddenly lit a cigarette, although I was only fifteen. There were soldiers in the street too, since it was war and yet not war. We weren't in the least hungry and not at all tired, and when we got home we might even drink a bottle of wine that Alfred had brought from France. I was fifteen and I would never have to be a soldier. And everything about Severin-Strasse felt so good. Beethoven, what a treat a Beethoven concert was.

I could see it all quite clearly. We had passed St Georg's, and a few whores had been standing there in the dark beside the urinal. Now we were passing the charming little square facing St Johann's, the small Romanesque church ...

The street narrowed. We had to walk in the road and sometimes step aside for the tram; then we passed Tietz's, and finally the street widened out: there stood the great bulk of St Severin's tower. I could see everything so clearly: the shops with their displays—cigarettes, chocolate, kitchen spoons and leather soles. I could see it all as clear as day.

It was the nurse's gentle hand that startled me.

"Here we are," came her voice, "here's the Novalgin Quinine for your fever, and there," she said as she handed me the thermometer, "let's have your temperature!"

The mild fever gave me a feeling of contentment. It brought the goo on my back to the boil again, and now I was a hero again, four years older than before, wounded three times, and now an authentic, official hero. Even the sergeant in the Reserve wouldn't be able to touch me, for by the time I was back there again I would have the silver badge, so how could they possibly get at me ...?

By now I really did have a fever: 38.6, and the nurse entered a blue stroke on the curve of my chart that made it look quite alarming.

I had a fever, and from Debrecen it wasn't that far to Vienna, and from Vienna ...

Maybe the front would collapse again at some corner, and there would be a big push, and we would all be moved to the rear, the way I'd heard it told so often—and like a shot we'd be in Vienna or Dresden, and from Dresden ...

"Are you asleep, young fellow?" Hubert asked, "or would you like another drink?"

"No," I said, "I'm asleep, asleep ... "

"Okay, then. Goodnight."

"Goodnight."

But sleep was still a long way off. Somewhere towards the front of the car a man started screaming his head off. Lights were switched on ... people shouted, ran, the nurse arrived and the doctor ... and then all was quiet again.

The thigh casualty groaned and snored softly in his sleep ...

Outside the night was once more totally dark, no longer grey; it was blue-black and silent, and I found I could no longer think of Severin-Strasse. I could think only of Debrecen ... strange, I thought, when we did Hungary in geography you so often put your finger on Debrecen; it lay in the middle of a green patch, but not far away the colour turned to brown, then to very dark brown, that was the Carpathians, and who would ever have thought that one day you'd be swaying so quickly and quietly on your way to Debrecen, in the middle of the night. I tried to imagine the town.

Perhaps there would be some fine cafés there, and lots of things to buy, with *pengö* in your pocket. I glanced across at Hubert, but he had fallen asleep.

It was very quiet, and I longed for the tears to come again, but the image of my mother and of Severin-Strasse was completely wiped out.

THE CAGE

A man stood beside the fence looking pensively through the barbed-wire thicket. He was searching for something human, but all he saw was this tangle, this horribly systematic tangle of wires—then some scarecrow figures staggering through the heat towards the latrines, bare ground and tents, more wire, more scarecrow figures, bare ground and tents stretching away to infinity. At some point there was said to be no more wire, but he couldn't believe it. Equally inhuman was the immaculate, burning, impassive face of the blanched blue sky, where somewhere the sun floated just as pitilessly. The whole world was reduced to motionless scorching heat, held in like the breath of an animal under the spell of noon. The heat weighed on him like some appalling tower of naked fire that seemed to grow and grow and grow ...

His eyes met nothing human; and behind him—he could see it even more clearly, without turning round—was sheer horror. There they lay, those others, round the inviolable football field, packed side by side like rotting fish; next came the meticulously clean latrines, and somewhere a long way behind him was also paradise: the shady, empty tents, guarded by well-fed policemen ...

How quiet it was, how hot!

He suddenly lowered his head, as if his neck were breaking under the fiery hammer-blow, and he saw something that delighted him: the delicate shadows of the barbed wire on the bare ground. They were like the fine tracery of intertwining branches, frail and beautiful, and it seemed to him that they must be infinitely cool, those delicate tracings, all linked with each other; yes, they seemed to be smiling, quietly and soothingly.

He bent down and carefully reached between the wires to pick one of the pretty branches; holding it up to his face he smiled, as if a fan had been gently waved in front of him. Then he reached out with both hands to gather up those sweet shadows. He looked left and right into the thicket, and the quiet happiness in his eyes faded: a wild surge of desire flared up, for there he saw innumerable little tracings which when gathered up must offer a precious, cool eternity of shadow. His pupils dilated as if about to burst out of the prison of his eyeballs: with a shrill cry he plunged into the thicket, and the more he became entangled in the pitiless little barbs the more wildly he flailed, like a fly in a spider's web, while with his hands he tried to grasp the exquisite shadow branches. His flailings were already stilled by the time the well-fed policemen arrived to free him with their wire-cutters.

I CAN'T FORGET HER

I can't forget her; whenever I emerge even for a moment from the vortex of everyday life which with its constant pressure tries to keep me beneath the surface of human reality; whenever I can even for a second turn my back on the ceaseless bustle of the crass pomposity they call life, and pause where their inane shouting cannot reach me: then her image appears before me, as close and distinct and ravishingly beautiful as I saw her years ago, when she was wearing a collarless coat that revealed all of her delicate neck.

At the time they had given up hope for me. The captain had said we were to make a counter-attack, and the lieutenant had made a counter-attack with us. But there was nothing to attack. We ran blindly up a wooded hill one spring evening, but on the expected battleground there was complete silence. We paused on the hill, looked away into the distance, and could see nothing. Then we ran down into the valley, up another hill, and paused again. There was not an enemy in sight. Here and there behind bushes were abandoned holes, half-finished positions of our troops in which the meaningless junk of war had been hastily left behind. It was still quiet; an uncanny silence lay heavily under the great vault of the spring sky that was slowly covering itself with the darker veils of twilight. It was so quiet that the lieutenant's voice startled us: "Carry on!" he ordered. But as we were about to proceed the sky suddenly roared down upon us, and the earth burst open.

The others had quickly dropped to the ground or flung themselves into the abandoned holes; I just caught sight of the sergeant's pipe falling from his mouth, and then it felt as though they had knocked my legs from under my body ...

Five men ran away after the first load had come down. Only the lieutenant and two men stayed behind; they hastily picked me up and ran down the slope with me while up above, where we had been lying, a fresh load came roaring down.

It was only much later, when all was quiet again and they laid me on the forest floor, that I felt any pain. The lieutenant wiped the sweat off his face and looked at me, but I could clearly see that he was not looking at the place where my legs must be. "Don't worry," he said, "we'll get you back all right."

The lieutenant placed a lighted cigarette between my lips, and I can still remember: while the pain increased again I still felt that life was beautiful. I was lying at the bottom of the valley on a forest path beside a little stream; up above, between the tall fir trees, only a narrow strip of sky was visible, a strip that was now silvery, almost white. The birds were singing, and an indescribably soothing silence reigned. I blew the cigarette smoke upward in long blue threads and felt that life was beautiful, and tears came to my eyes ...

"It's all right," said the lieutenant.

They carried me away. But it was a long way, almost two kilometres to the point where the captain had retreated, and I was heavy. I believe all wounded are heavy. The lieutenant carried the front end of the stretcher, and the other two walked behind. We slowly came out of the forest, across meadows and fields, and through another forest, and they had to set me down and wipe off their sweat, while the evening sank lower and lower. When we reached the village, everything was still quiet. They took me into a room where the captain now was. On both sides, school desks had been piled up against the walls, and the teacher's desk was covered with hand grenades. As I was being carried in, they were busy distributing the hand grenades. The captain was shouting into a telephone, threatening someone that he would have him shot. Then he let out a curse and hung up. They set me down behind the teacher's desk, where some other wounded were also lying. One of them was sitting there with his hand shot to pieces; he looked very contented.

The lieutenant gave a report on the counter-attack to the captain, and the captain yelled at the lieutenant that he would have him shot, and the lieutenant said, "Yessir." That made the captain yell even more, and the lieutenant again said, "Yessir," and the captain stopped yelling. They stuck big torches in flowerpots and lit them. By now it was dark, and there seemed to be no electric current. After the hand grenades had been distributed, the room emptied. All that was left were two sergeants, a clerk, the lieutenant and the captain. The captain said to the lieutenant: "See that security sentries are placed all round the village; we'll try to get a few hours' sleep. Tomorrow we'll be starting out early."

"To the rear?" asked the lieutenant quietly.

"Get out!" yelled the captain; the lieutenant left. After he had gone, I looked for the first time at my legs and saw that they were covered with blood, and I couldn't feel them, I felt only pain where normally I would have felt my legs. I was shivering now. Beside me lay a man who must have been shot in the stomach; he was very quiet and pale and scarcely moved; from time to time he merely stroked his hand, very quietly and carefully, across the blanket that covered his stomach. No one paid any attention to us. I imagine the medic had been among the five who had run away. Suddenly the pain reached my stomach and crept higher very quickly; it flowed up like molten lead as far as my heart, and I believe I began to scream and then fainted ...

I woke up and first heard music. I was lying on my side, looking into the face of the fellow with the stomach wound and saw that he was dead. His blanket was all black with congealed blood. And I could hear music, somewhere they must have found a radio. They were playing something quite modern, it must have been a foreign station; then the music was wiped out as if by a wet rag, and they played military marches, then came something classical, and they let that music go on. Then a voice above me said very softly, "Mozart," and I looked up and saw her face and realized at the same moment that it couldn't be Mozart, and I said to that face: "No, it's not Mozart."

She bent over me, and now I saw that she was a doctor or a medical student, she looked so young, but she was holding a stethoscope. Now all I could see was her loose, soft crown of brown hair, for she was bending over my legs, lifting the blanket so that I couldn't see anything. Then she raised her head, looked at me, and said: "It *is* Mozart." She pushed up my sleeve, and I said softly: "No, it can't possibly be Mozart."

The music went on playing, and now I was quite sure that it could never be Mozart. Some of it sounded like real Mozart, but there were other passages that couldn't possibly be Mozart.

My arm was all white. With gentle fingers she felt my pulse, then came a sudden needle prick, and she injected something into my arm.

As she did so, her head came quite close, and I whispered: "Give me a kiss." She blushed deeply, withdrew the needle, and at that moment a voice on the radio said: "Dittersdorf." Suddenly she smiled, and I smiled too, for now I could get a proper look at her because the only torch that was still burning was behind her. "Quick," I said in a louder voice, "give me a kiss." She blushed again and looked even more beautiful; the light from the torch shone on the ceiling and spread in wavering red circles round the walls. She gave a quick glance over her shoulder, then bent over me and kissed me, and at that instant I saw her closed eyelids from very near and felt those soft lips while the torch flung its restless light round the room and the captain's voice bellowed into the telephone again and now some different music was being spewed out of the speaker. Then a voice called out an order, someone picked me up and carried me out into the night and placed me in a cold van, and I had a last glimpse of her standing there, her eyes following me in the torchlight, right among all the school desks that were piled up like the absurd rubble of a collapsing world.

As far as I know, they are all back now in their proper jobs: the captain is an athletics instructor, the lieutenant is dead, and there's nothing I can tell you about the others—after all, I knew them only for a few hours. No doubt the school desks are back in their proper places, the electric light is working again, and torches are lit only on very romantic occasions; and instead of bellowing "I'll have you shot!" the captain is now shouting something harmless such as perhaps: "Idiot!" or "Coward!", when someone can't do a grand circle on the crossbar. My legs have healed up, and I can walk quite well, and they tell me at the Veterans Affairs office that I should be working. But I have a different, much more important occupation: I am looking for her. I can't forget her. People tell me I'm crazy because I make no effort to do a grand circle in the air and land smartly on my feet like a good citizen and then, eager and thirsting for praise, step back in line.

Fortunately they are obliged to give me a pension, and I can afford to wait and search, for I know that I shall find her ...

GREEN ARE THE MEADOWS

The tram was crossing a street whose name—white on blue at the corner under the street-lamp—suddenly seemed familiar to him. He blushed, pulled out his notebook, and found the name of the street, circled in red, on a scribbled page: Bülow-Strasse. He now realized he had always passed over this page, although at heart he hadn't forgotten the name for so much as a single day ...

The tram slowly rounded a curve and stopped. He heard music from a bar, saw gas lamps burning in the dusk; from somewhere beyond a garden fence came the laughter of young girls, and he got off. The suburb was like all the suburbs: pockmarked, dirty, dotted with little gardens and somehow appealing: it had the smell, the sound, the colour and the quite indescribable atmosphere of vulnerability ...

The man heard the tram screeching off and set down his bundle. Although he knew the number by heart, he put his hand into his pocket and once more leafed through his notebook: 14 Bülow-Strasse. Now there was no way of avoiding it. He realized why he had always refused the job of picking up the cigarettes in this particular town. Of course there was many a Bülow-Strasse, every decent town had its Bülow-Strasse, but only in this town was there this house, number 14, where a woman by the name of Gärtner was living, a woman for whom he had a message about something that had happened four years ago and that he should have told her about four years ago ...

The gas lamps lit up the high fence of a lumber yard, and painted on the fence were huge white letters. Through the gaps he saw the light-coloured piles of trim boards, and he wearily deciphered the inscription on the fence: SCHUSTER BROTHERS: then he took a step backwards because the lettering on the fence was so big that his eyes had trouble following it, and much farther along, lit up by another gas lamp, he read: OLDEST LUMBER YARD IN TOWN. At the spot where he could read the final N of this display of integrity there was a large black house in which a few windows shone with a yellow light. The windows were open, he saw lamplight, heard radio music, and somewhere he heard again the girls' bright laughter. Someone was playing a guitar, and a few boys' voices were gently singing, "We lay by the camp fire, Conchita and I ...", other voices joined in, and a second guitar was struck up; the girls' laughter had died away.

The man walked slowly along beside the fence as far as the second gas lamp, which stood exactly between the T and the O. The shining tram rails continued on into a narrow street with closely packed buildings whose façades were almost dead, dark and frightening; the buildings seemed to have been burned out.

The dusk had grown thicker: he now saw those dead façades lit up by a tall, gently swaying lamp, and at the far corner there was another group of young fellows; the tips of their cigarettes glowed in the dusk. That must be the entrance to Bülow-Strasse ...

He was still standing between the T and the O. It was quiet, with only the low, plaintive sounds of the two guitars and the soft voices coming to the end of the song. On the other side of the street were allotment gardens. Just then, a man standing in the dark lit his pipe, and he saw the match light up a fisherman's cap and a pudgy, heavy face, its lips puckered to blow out the match with one puff of smoke. Then all was swallowed up again in the silent darkness. He strolled slowly on, and at the end of the lumber yard's long fence the silence was suddenly broken; from the open doors of a bar came loud male laughter and in the background a frantic male voice yelling from a radio. The first cross-street seemed almost undamaged: loud laughter reached him and shouts and the murmuring conversation of people sitting on chairs outside their doors ...

While walking past this scene as if he were passing an open, crowded living room, he was thinking: I can still go back. I don't have to be in this Bülow-Strasse. But he went on, as if under some compulsion, towards the traffic lights, and he had soon reached the group of young fellows at the street corner. There was some noise coming from Bülow-Strasse, too, but as he quickly turned the corner he saw that these façades also showed great black gaps, and for a moment he wished that number 14 might also have been destroyed. That would solve everything.

At the corner he hesitated. Once I enter the street, there's no going back, he thought. They will recognize me as a stranger, ply me with questions, and I'll have to tell them everything. He made a quick turn to the left and pushed his way through the group of youngsters into the bar. "Evening all," he said, sitting down at the table nearest the door. The landlord behind the counter, tall, thin, dark-complexioned, nodded and called out: "Beer?"

"Yes," said the man.

On a table to his right lay the crutches of an amputee. Beside the fat amputee, who had pushed his hat to the back of his head, sat a man and a woman with troubled expressions, their hands clasped wearily round their beer glasses. Over in a corner some men were playing cards, and on the radio a woman was now singing, "Mamma says it's wrong to kiss, Mamma says it isn't done ... " The landlord brought the beer, and the man said, "Thanks." He put his bundle down on the chair beside him and fumbled in his breast pocket for a crumpled cigarette.

So this is it, he thought, this is the bar. This is where he sang his "Rosemarie" and his "Green are the Meadows"; where he cursed yet proudly showed off his decorations, where he bought cigarettes and stood singing at the counter.

Then all he could see was the man, whose name had been Gärtner, being shot to death by a sergeant called Stevenson. That little, red-haired Stevenson with the cheeky face had shot him right in the stomach with his machine pistol, four shots one above the other, and he had never seen a mouth that had once sung "Rosemarie" so distorted with pain. They had dragged him round the corner of a building, taken off his tunic and ripped open his trousers; a mass of blood and faeces had welled out of his stomach, and the mouth that had once sung "Rosemarie" and "Green are the Meadows" in this very bar had been silenced by pain. They had heard no more shooting, they had taken his paybook from his pocket, and he had jotted down: Gärtner, 14 Bülow-Strasse, with the idea of telling the wife if he should ever find himself in this town. Gärtner hadn't said another word, that horrible mass of blood and faeces came slowly welling out of his stomach, and they—the other man and himself—could only look on helplessly until suddenly a voice behind them shouted "Hands up!" and they discovered that this red-haired sergeant was called Stevenson. The next moment twelve trembling Americans were standing round them, and he had never seen men tremble like that; they trembled so much that he could hear the light tinkling of their machine pistols, and one of the Americans said: "That's one gone, Stevenson ... "

Stevenson made a swift, discarding gesture; he and the other man understood and threw their weapons behind them. The other man—he had never found out his name, they had only known each other for half an hour—had been carrying a machine gun like a big black cat under his arm; now he flung the machine gun behind him into a broad puddle of wet ordure. He heard it splash, just as in the old days their swimming instructor had demonstrated a dive, and in his mind's eye he could still see the bald, yellow globe of the gas lamp. He only came to when one of the Americans in his excitement fired a shot right past his nose, and they saw that Gärtner was dead and heard tanks rumbling towards them ...

He looked at his beer and noticed a little vase of flowers next to his glass—a twig with yellow, plump, but fading pussy-willow, and he realized that spring had come round again, just as it had done so long ago. It must be exactly four years since Stevenson had shot Gärtner in the stomach until blood and faeces poured out. The amputee gave a brutal shrug, and the expressions of the man and woman became still more troubled. The youths outside the door must now have been joined by the girls: he could hear the girls' high laughter, and then they all began to sing, and the man and woman sitting with the fat amputee, their hands still miserably clasping their beer glasses, now looked through the open door and listened to the singing. "Max!" the amputee called out to the landlord. "Bring us three more beers, will you?"

The man could hear that the couple sitting with the amputee were trying to whisper their objections. Outside the young people were singing songs whose words he couldn't make out, soft, soothing, sentimental tunes.

The landlord came past his table, picked up the empty glass, and asked: "Same again?"

"Yes."

The man glanced at the cigarettes he had wrapped in a pair of blue work trousers. Outside the laughing, singing voices of the boys and girls gradually moved away. From the radio now came a talk, and the landlord twiddled the knobs doggedly until music came on again.

"I'd like to pay!" the man called out.

The landlord came over. While putting down the money he asked in a low voice: "Gärtner—didn't Gärtner use to come here quite often?"

"That's right," the landlord said at once, smoothing out the note the man had given him. "Did you know him? Willi Gärtner?"

"Yes. Is he still alive?"

"No, he got killed in the war."

"When?"

"Oh, I don't know—quite late, I think, towards the end. Where did you meet him?"

"We worked together."

"At Plattke's?"

"Yes, at Plattke's ... and his wife, what's she doing?"

The landlord looked at him in surprise: "But she's at Plattke's now! Aren't you there any more?"

"No, I'm not ... "

"I see," said the landlord indifferently. He picked up the empty glass and called out to another customer: "Just a moment—I'm coming!"

The man got up, quietly said, "Goodnight," and, without looking back, left the bar.

Here and there in the unlit, open windows he could see the glow of cigarettes, and he could hear the distant wail of radio sets. The building next door to the bar was number 28. It was a grocery. In the dim half-light he could see the cardboard signs for Maggi and Persil, and in the gloom beyond the shop window a basket of eggs, a pile of cereal packages, and a big glass jar with sour pickles and onions floating around in it. It was like looking through the glass of a neglected aquarium. The objects seemed to float and sway, mollusc-like, slimy creatures carrying on their lecherous existence in the dim half-dark.

So this is it, he thought. This is where his wife bought her vinegar and soup packets and cigarettes, and somewhere round here there'll also be a butcher and a baker ... a stomach like that must, after all, be nourished for a long time before it can be shot up so expertly that blood and faeces come pouring out in a viscous stream. Everything must be done in its proper order. For at least eighteen years a stomach like that must be regularly filled with all those things to be bought for a week's wages from the butcher, the baker and the grocer; and sometimes that stomach must also drink beer and sing, and the mouth belonging to that stomach is also allowed to smoke cigarettes, everything in its proper order ...

The people sitting outside their doors have no idea that somewhere in the world there is an American who shot up their Willi—right through the stomach—flutch ... flutch ... flutch ... flutch ... he would never forget that sound, the demonic mildness, that gentle flopping which had riddled Gärtner's stomach.

The people didn't seem to notice him. He was just someone going home with a pair of blue work trousers under his arm. He stopped and fumbled in his breast pocket for another crumpled cigarette. The crumpled ones were his, that had been agreed. As he stood there he glanced at the next front door and saw that it was number 18. Then came a gap, so the next house must be number 14. He saw lighted windows there and some chairs outside the door.

Glowing ashes had been scattered all over the bomb site, and here and there the remains of briquets were smouldering and there was a smell of rags and potato peelings that had caught fire. In a lighted window he had a fleeting glimpse of a heavy, stout fellow with a cigar in his mouth, and behind his back a woman standing at a stove in front of a smoking frying pan.

Four years ago it had also been spring, it had also been April, everything had turned green again after a terrible winter. They had been aware of that in the chill nights when they had crouched futilely in their holes, guarding bridges over rivers that in many thousands of places could be waded across: they had been aware of it: it was spring. And when the grey dawn came they retreated, attacked and were attacked. The troop units were torn apart, patched together again. Whole regiments cleared out or went over to the enemy; many of the men were caught again at street corners and rounded up, and there was always some officer there to take command. They were posted at street corners or shoved at night into holes just so they could be well and truly shot to pieces. As a result one found oneself with new comrades every day. He had known Gärtner for only half an hour. A lieutenant had arrived and said, "Come with me!" and had stationed him at the intersection beside Gärtner and the man with the machine gun. Gärtner had given him a cigarette, which at that time was worth more than all the decorations put together. Grenades had burst somewhere, tanks had rumbled, there had been some shooting, and suddenly those bullets had flopped into Gärtner's stomach ...

He was still staring at the glowing piles of ashes, breathing in the repulsive stench of scorched rags. Outside number 14 two women were sitting on chairs, dark, stoutish figures in whispered conversation. In the doorway itself stood a young fellow, smoking; he walked towards the youth and said: "Could I have a light, please?"

In silence the fellow casually held his glowing butt against the cigarette, and while the kitchen odours that permeated the youth's clothing rose into the man's nostrils together with the smell of cheap soap, he looked beyond his cigarette into the open, unlit corridor, and then—in that half-second he needed for lighting his cigarette—he heard a couple embracing in there in the dark; he heard those indescribable sounds of wordless tenderness, that gentle groaning that was like suppressed pain; he felt the blood mounting, hot and tormenting, to his head. He hurriedly thanked the youth and walked quickly, very quickly, back, past the glowing ash heaps, past the undamaged houses, the gaps and the grocery. By the time he reached the corner he was almost running because he could hear the tram screeching towards him from behind; and when he glanced over his shoulder and saw its dim yellow lights approaching in the gentle, spring darkness, he broke into a run.

He was so afraid of missing the tram that before reaching the tram stop, where he paused for a moment, he caught only snatches of the young people's singing: the group now seemed to be standing somewhere near the allotment gardens. Now they were singing "Green are the Meadows" so earnestly and meltingly that no more laughter was to be heard between the verses.

The tram came to a stop and he was glad to be able to get on. He wiped away his sweat, had one more passing glimpse of the lumber yard's neatly lettered fence, and wished that the tram could have continued on and on, forever ...

THE RAIN GUTTER

For a long time they lay awake smoking while the wind swept through the house, loosening tiles and tumbling bricks; pieces of plaster sailed down with a crash from the upper floors, shattering below and spreading into rubble.

He saw only a dim sheen of her, a warm, reddish hue when they drew on their cigarettes: the soft outlines of her breasts under her nightgown and her calm profile. The sight of the narrow, firmly closed crease between her lips, that little valley in her face, filled him with tenderness. They tucked the covers in firmly at the sides, nestled close together, and knew that they would keep warm all night long. The shutters rattled, and the wind whistled through the jagged holes in the window panes; above them it howled in the remains of the attic, and somewhere there was the sound of an object slapping noisily and steadily against a wall, something hard, metallic, and she whispered: "That's the gutter, it's been broken for a long time."

She was silent for a moment, then took his hand and softly went on: "The war hadn't started yet, and I was already living here, and whenever I came home I'd see the piece of gutter hanging there, and I'd think: they *must* have it repaired; but they never did. It hung crooked, one of the clamps had come loose, and it always seemed about to fall at any moment. I always heard it when there was a wind, every night when there was a storm and I was lying here. And when the war started it was still hanging there. On the grey house wall you could clearly see where the water had flowed sideways into the wall after every rain: a white path, with a grey border leading down past the window, and on either side there were big round patches with white centres surrounded by darker grey rings. Later on I went far away, I was put to work in Thuringia and Berlin, and when the war was over I came back here, and the gutter was still hanging there: half the building had collapsed—I'd been far away, far, far away, and I'd seen so much pain, death and blood, they had shot at me with machine guns from airplanes, and I'd been scared, so scared—and all that time that piece of galvanized iron had been hanging here, sending the rain into empty space because the wall below was almost completely gone. Roof tiles had fallen off, trees had been toppled, plaster had come crumbling down, bombs had fallen, so many bombs, but that piece of galvanized iron had continued to hang from that one clamp, it had never been hit, its crooked slant had never given way to the blasts."

Her voice became even lower, almost a chant, and she pressed his hand. "So much rain came raining down," she said, "in those six years, so many deaths were died, cathedrals destroyed, but the gutter was still hanging there when I came back. Once again I heard it clattering at night whenever there was a wind. Can you believe that I was happy?"

"I can," he said.

The wind had subsided, it was quiet now, and the cold crept closer. They pulled up the covers and hid their hands inside. In the darkness he could no longer distinguish anything, he couldn't even see her profile, although she was lying so close that he could feel her breath, her calm, regular breathing warm against his skin, and he thought she had fallen asleep. But suddenly he could no longer hear her breathing and he groped for her hands. She moved her hand down and grasped his and held onto it, and he knew they would be warm and he wouldn't have to shiver all night long.

Suddenly he became aware that she was crying. There was nothing to be heard, he just knew from the movements of the bed that she was wiping her face with her left hand. Even that wasn't certain, but he knew she was crying. He sat up, bent over her and felt her breath again: it seemed to spread over his face like a current gently flowing past him. Even when his nose touched her cold cheek, he still could see nothing.

"Lie down," she whispered, "you'll catch cold."

He remained leaning over her, he wanted to see her, but he saw nothing until she suddenly opened her eyes: then he saw the glint of her eyes in the darkness, the shimmering tears.

She cried for a long time. He took her hand, held it, and firmly tucked in the covers again. He held her hand for a long time, until her grip relaxed and her hand slowly slipped out of his—he put his arm round her shoulder, drew her close, and then he too fell asleep, and as they slept their breathing alternated like caresses ...

AUTUMN LONELINESS

How long we spent standing there at the corner I can't tell you. I was filled with a sense of anticipation that was really quite unjustified. It was now autumn, and each time a tram stopped at the corner people came streaming towards us, their footsteps rustling in the dead leaves, and in their steps was joy, the joy of people going home.

We must have stood there for a long time. It had been still quite light when suddenly, without a word, we had stopped, as if to mount guard over the deepening melancholy of autumn, a mood caught in the tops of the plane trees as they slowly shed their leaves.

There was no real reason for it, but each time the tram rang its bell at the corner and people came streaming into the avenue towards us and the tram drove on ringing its bell—each time I was convinced that someone was about to come, someone who knew us, who would ask us to join him, whose homeward steps would force our own weary, aimless footsteps to keep up with the tempo of his happy excitement.

The first ones always came singly and walked very fast; then came the groups, in twos or even threes in animated conversation, and finally another trickle of weary individuals passing us with their heavy burdens before dispersing into the houses scattered among gardens and avenues.

It was a constant suspense that held me spellbound, for after the last person had passed by there was only a brief respite before we heard the distant ping-pinging of the next tram at the previous stop—clanking and screeching its way to the corner.

We stood under the branches of an elderberry tree that reached out over the street far beyond the fence of a neglected garden. Rigid with tension, he had his face turned in the direction of the people approaching through the rustling leaves—the face which, mute and set, had been accompanying me for two months, which I had loved, and also hated, for two months ...

During the time it took four trams to arrive, the tension and anticipation felt wonderful as we stood there in the steadily deepening melancholy of dusk, in the soft, exquisite, damp decay of autumn; but
all of a sudden I knew that no one to whom I might belong would
ever come ...

"I'm leaving," I said huskily, for I had been standing there much
too long as if rooted to the bottom of some swampy bowl that was
about to close imperceptibly over me with a velvety, relentless force.

"Go ahead," he said without looking at me, and for the first time in
two months he forgot to add: "I'll come with you."

His eyes narrowed to slits; without moving, he kept his hard,
metallic gaze fixed on the deserted avenue where now only a few single
leaves were slowly circling to the ground.

All right, I thought, and at that moment something happened to
me, something was released, and I felt my face collapsing, felt sharp,
bitter lines forming round my mouth. It was almost as if my inner tension had been tightly wound up and was now being released as if by a
blow: uncoiling inside me with incredible speed, leaving nothing behind
but that hollow, mournful void that had been there two months ago.
For at that moment it dawned on me: he was standing here waiting for
something quite specific; this spot, this street corner under the spreading branches of the elderberry tree, was his objective, the goal of an
arduous flight, of a journey lasting two months, while for me it was just
another street corner, one of many thousand.

I watched him for a long time, which I could do undisturbed as he
had ceased to notice me. Perhaps he thought I had already left. In his
watchful gaze was something resembling hate, while his shallow, rapid
breathing shook him like the prelude to an explosion ...

If only he would remember, I sighed to myself, to give me one of
the two cigarettes and my share of the bread. I was afraid to ask, for
now the tram was stopping again at the corner. Then I saw, very briefly,
the first and last smile on his face before he rushed forward with a
smothered cry. From among a cluster of people, some of whom he had
thrust aside, I heard a woman's gasp breaking the melancholy silence
of the autumnal evening, and something like a shadow fell across the
astonished void of my heart, for now I knew that I would have to go
on inexorably alone, that I would also have to accept the loss of the

cigarette and the bread and of the two months of shared danger and shared hunger ...

I turned away, dipped my tired feet into the golden waves of dead leaves and walked out of the town, once again towards that Somewhere. The freshness of the falling light was still permeated by the spicy smell of burning potato plants, the smell of childhood and of longing. The sky was starless and drained of colour. Only the grinning face of the moon hung over the horizon, watching me mockingly as I plodded on under the weight of the darkness, towards that Somewhere ...

BESIDE THE RIVER

To tell the truth, I'd never known the meaning of despair. But then, a few days ago, I found out. All of a sudden the whole world seemed grey and wretched; nothing, nothing mattered any more, and I had a bitter lump in my throat, and I thought there was no way out for me, no escape and no help. For I had lost all our ration cards, and at the ration office they would never believe me, they wouldn't replace them, and we had no more money for the black market, and stealing—I really didn't like to steal, and anyway I couldn't steal enough for that many people. For Mother and Father, for Karl and Grete, and for myself, and for our youngest, the baby. And the special mother's card was gone, and Father's manual worker's card—everything, everything was gone, the whole briefcase. I suddenly realized it in the tram, and I didn't bother to look or even ask. It's useless, I thought—who's going to hand over ration cards, and so many, and the mother's card and Father's manual worker's card ...

At that moment I knew the meaning of despair. I got off the tram much earlier and walked straight down to the Rhine; I'll drown myself, I thought. But when I reached the bare, cold avenue and saw the calm, wide, grey river it came to me that it's not so easy to drown oneself; still, I wanted to do it. It must take a long time to die, I thought, and I would have liked a quick, sudden death. Obviously I couldn't go home any more. Mother would simply throw up her hands, and Father would give me a good hiding and say it was a disgrace: a big lout like that, almost seventeen, who's no good for anything anyway, not even for the black market—a big lout like that goes and loses all the ration cards when he's sent out to queue up for the fat rations! And I didn't even get the fat. It was all gone after I had been queuing for about three hours. Still, that might not have lasted too long, that trouble with Father and Mother. But we would have nothing to eat, no one would give us anything. At the ration office they would laugh in our faces because once before we had lost a few coupons; and as for selling or flogging something, we had long ago run out of things, and stealing—you can't steal for so many.

No, I had to drown myself, since I didn't have the nerve to throw myself under some big fat American car. There were many cars driving beside the Rhine, but there wasn't a soul in the avenue. It was bare and cold, and a damp, icy wind blew from the grey, swift-flowing water. I kept walking straight ahead and eventually was surprised at how fast I reached the end of the avenue. The trees seemed to fall away on either side of me, keeling over like poles and disappearing, and I didn't dare look back. So I very quickly reached the end of the avenue where the Rhine widens out a bit and there is a launching ramp for kayaks and a little farther on the ruined bridge. There wasn't a soul there either, only over by the launching ramp an American sat staring into the water. It was odd, the way he was crouching there, sitting on his heels; it was probably too cold to sit on the stones, so there he squatted, throwing precious cigarette butts into the water. Each butt, I thought, is almost half a loaf of bread. Perhaps he isn't smoking at all, but all the Americans just smoke a quarter of a cigarette and throw the rest away. I know it for a fact. He's lucky, I thought, he's not hungry and hasn't lost any coupons, and with every butt he throws three marks and seventy-five pfennigs into the cold grey Rhine. If I were he, I thought, I'd sit down by the stove with a cup of coffee instead of squatting here by the cold Rhine and staring into the dirty water ...

I ran on; yes, I believe I did run. My thoughts about the American had been very brief and fleeting; I had envied him no end, it was terrible how I envied him. So I walked on or ran, I forget now, all the way to the ruined bridge, thinking: if you jump off from up there it's all over, all over in no time. I once read that it is hard to drown yourself by going into the water slowly. You have to plunge in from high up, that's the best way. So I ran towards the ruined bridge. There were no workmen there. Maybe they were on strike, or it's impossible to work out there on the bridges in cold weather. I saw nothing more of the American, I never once looked back.

No, I thought, there's no help and no hope, and no one will replace our ration cards, there are too many of us, Father and Mother, my brother and sister, the baby and I, plus the special mother's card and

Father's manual worker's card. It's hopeless, drown yourself, then at least there'll be one less mouth to feed. It was very, very cold, there in the avenue beside the Rhine; the wind whistled, and bare branches fell from the trees that in summertime are so beautiful.

It was difficult to climb onto the ruined bridge; they had knocked out what remained of the paving, and there was only the skeleton left, and along it ran a kind of little railway, probably for hauling away the rubble.

I climbed very carefully, and I was terribly cold and very much afraid of falling off. I can well remember thinking: how stupid to be scared of falling since you want to drown yourself! If you fall off here, onto the street or onto the rubble, you'll also be dead, and that'll be all right, that's what you want. But it's quite a different thing, I can't explain it. What I wanted was to throw myself into the water and not smash onto the ground, and I thought of all the pain one might suffer and maybe not even be dead. And I didn't want to suffer. So I climbed very carefully over the bare bridge right to the end, the very end where the rails stick out in the air. There I stood, looking into the grey, grey murmuring water, there I stood close to the very end. I felt no fear, only despair, and suddenly I knew that despair is beautiful, it is sweet and nothing, it is nothing, and nothing matters any more.

The Rhine was fairly high, and grey and cold, and for a long time I stared into its face. I also saw the American squatting there, and really did see him throw a precious butt into the water. I was surprised to find him so near, much nearer than I had thought. I looked once again along the whole length of the bare avenue, and then suddenly looked down into the Rhine again, and I became terribly dizzy, and then I fell! All I remember is that my last thought was of Mother, and that it might after all be worse for me to be dead than to have lost the ration cards, the whole lot ... Father's and Mother's and my brother's and sister's and the baby's, plus the special mother's card and Father's manual worker's card, and ... yes, yes, my card too, although I'm a useless mouth, no good even for the black market ...

I guess I must have sat there for an hour beside the murky Rhine, staring into the water. All I could think of was that blonde broad, Gertrud, who was driving me nuts. Hell, I thought, spitting my cigarette into the Rhine: throw yourself in, into that grey brew, and let it carry you down to—to Holland, yes, and still farther, say into the Channel, right down to the bottom of the sea! There wasn't a soul around, and the water was driving me nuts. I know for sure it was the water, and my thinking all the time of that good-looking broad who wouldn't have me. Nope, she wouldn't have me, and I knew for sure that I'd never, never get anywhere with her. And the water wouldn't let go of me, the water was driving me nuts. Hell, I thought, throw yourself in and those goddamn women won't bother you any more, throw yourself in ...

And then I heard someone running along the avenue like a maniac. I've never seen anyone run like that. He's in trouble, I thought, and stared at the water again, but the footsteps in the deserted avenue above made me look up again, and I saw the kid running toward the wrecked bridge, and I thought, I'll bet they're after him and I hope he gets away, never mind if he's been stealing or whatever. A thin, lanky kid, running like a maniac. Again I looked at the water—throw yourself in, a voice kept whispering ... You'll never get her, never, throw yourself in and let the grey brew carry you to Holland, goddammit, and I spat the third cigarette into the water.

For God's sake, I thought, what are you doing here in this country, in this crazy country, where every living soul can think of nothing but cigarettes? In this crazy country where the bridges are all gone and there's no colour, no colour anywhere, dammit, only grey. And everyone chasing after God knows what. And that girl, that crazy, long-legged broad, will never be yours, not for a million cigarettes will she be yours, damn it to hell.

But just then I heard that crazy kid crawling around up there on the bridge. The iron skeleton rang hollow under his boots, and the crazy kid climbed right out to the far end, and there he stood, for the longest time, also looking into the dirty grey water, and all of a sudden I knew that no one was chasing him, but that he ... Goddammit, I thought, he wants to throw himself into the water! And I got a real shock and couldn't take my eyes off the spot where that crazy kid was standing, not moving, not making a sound, up there in the gap of the ruined bridge, and he seemed to sway a little ...

I automatically spat the fourth cigarette into the Rhine and I couldn't take my eyes off that figure up there. I turned cold all over, I was terrified. That boy, that young kid, what kind of troubles can he have, I thought? Girl trouble, and I laughed—at least I think I laughed, I can't be sure. Can this young kid already have girl trouble, I thought? The water said nothing, and it was so quiet that I thought I could hear that kid's breathing as he went on standing there, motionless, silent, in the gap of the ruined bridge. Goddammit, I thought, it mustn't happen, and I was just going to call out when I thought, you'll scare him and then he'll fall for sure. The silence was weird, and we two were all alone in the world with this dirty grey water.

And then, for God's sake, he looked at me, really looked at me, and I was still sitting there, not moving a muscle and Splash! the crazy kid was actually down there in the water!

That really woke me up, and in no time I'd thrown off my jacket and cap. I dived into the cold water and started swimming. It was hard work, but luckily the current carried him toward me. Then suddenly he was gone, gone under, dammit, and my shoes were full of water, they felt like lead on my feet, my shirt was like lead too, and it was cold, icy cold, and not a sign of the kid anywhere ... I paddled on, then trod water for a bit and shouted, yes shouted ... and dammit if the kid didn't come up again, he was already a bit downstream, and I hadn't thought the current was that fast. Now my body seemed to warm up a bit, with panic, at the sight of that lifeless bundle being swept off in that grey dirty water, and me after it, and when I was less than two yards away—I could actually see the blond hair—he was gone again, just gone, dammit ... but I was after him, head down, and Christ Almighty! I'd grabbed hold of him.

Nobody in the world can know how relieved I was when I'd grabbed hold of him. In the middle of the Rhine, and there was only grey, cold, dirty water, and I was as heavy and cold as lead, and yet I felt relieved. It's just that I had no more fear, that's what it must have been ... and I swam slowly across the current with him to the shore and was surprised at how close the shore was.

Jesus, I had no time to shiver or moan, although I'd had a lousy time of it. I'd swallowed a whole lot of water, and the dirty stuff made me feel sick as a dog, but I rested till I got my breath back, then I grabbed his arms and pumped them up and down, up and down, up and down, just like they tell you to, and I got pretty damn hot over it ... There wasn't a living soul up there on the river bank, and no one heard it or saw it. Then the kid opened his eyes, a pair of bright blue child's eyes, for God's sake, and he sicked up water, kept sicking it up ... Dammit, I thought, the kid's got nothing but water in his stomach, and nothing but water came up, and then he felt he had to smile, the kid actually smiled at me ...

By that time I was as cold as hell in those wet things, and I thought, you'll catch your death, and he was shaking like a leaf too.

Then I pulled him up and said: "Go on, boy ... run!" and I just grabbed him by the arm and ran up the ramp with him, he was as limp as a rag doll in my arm, then he stopped again and sicked up some more grey water, dirty grey Rhine water, that was all, then he could run better.

Goddamn, I thought, he has to get warm and you have to get warm, and in the end we ran pretty good, right up to the avenue and then a bit along the avenue. I began to feel quite warm and I sure was panting, but the kid was still shaking like a leaf. Dammit, I thought, he needs to get indoors and then into a bed, but there were no houses there, just a few piles of rubble and some rails, and it was already getting dark. But then one of our vehicles turned up, a Jeep, and I dashed out onto the street and waved my arms. First it drove on, there was a black driving it, but I yelled at the top of my voice: "Hey there, bud ... " and he must have heard from my voice that I was an American—you see, I wasn't wearing a jacket or a cap. So he stopped, and I hauled the kid over, and the black shook his head and said: "Poor kid—almost drowned, did he?"

"Yes," I answered, "let's go, and step on it!" I told him where my billet was.

The boy sat next to me and gave me another of those pathetic smiles, enough to make me feel pretty weird, and I felt his pulse a bit, it seemed okay.

"Hurry!" I shouted to the black. He turned around and grinned and really did speed up, and all the time I was saying: "Make a left, now right, right again," and so on till we actually stopped at my billet.

Pat and Freddie were standing in the hallway and laughed when they saw me coming: "Boy oh boy, is that your charming Gertrud?" But I told them: "Don't laugh, fellows, help me, I've just fished this kid here out of the Rhine." They helped me carry him upstairs to our room, Pat's and my room, and I told Freddie: "Make us some coffee." Then I threw him down on the bed, pulled off his wet things, and rubbed him for a long time with my towel. God, how skinny the kid was, how terribly skinny ... he looked like ... like, hell, like a long, limp, white noodle.

"Pat," I said, for Pat was standing there watching me, "you go on rubbing, I have to get out of these wet things." I was as wet as a drowned rat, too, and scared to death of getting the flu. Then Pat handed me the towel, for the lanky kid on the bed was now red all over like a baby, and he smiled again ... and Pat felt his pulse and said: "Okay, Johnny, he's going to be all right, I guess."

The boys were damn good about it; Freddie brought us some coffee, and Pat scrounged some underwear for the kid, who lay on the bed drinking coffee and smiling, and Pat and I sat on the chairs, and Freddie went off, I guess he went off to the girls again.

Jesus, I thought, what a scramble, but it turned out okay, thank God!

Pat stuck a cigarette between the kid's lips, and you should've seen how he smoked! These Germans, I thought, they all smoke like crazy, they suck on those things as if they contained life itself, their faces go all queer. And then I remembered that my jacket was still lying down there by the water, with the photo, and my cap too, but shit, I thought, why would I still need that photo ...

It was real peaceful and quiet, and the kid was happily chewing away, for Pat had given him some more bread and a can of corned beef and kept refilling his mug with coffee.

"Pat," I said after a while as I lit up too. "Pat, d'you suppose it's all right to ask him why he tried to drown himself?"

"Sure," Pat replied, and asked him.

The lad gave us a wild look and said something to me, and I looked at Pat and Pat shrugged his shoulders. "He's saying something about food, but there's one word I can't understand, I just don't get it ... "

"What word?" I asked.

"*Marken*," Pat said.

"*Marken*?" I asked the boy.

He nodded and said another word, and Pat said: "He's lost them—those things, those *Marken* ... "

"What's that, *Marken*?" I asked Pat. But Pat didn't know.

"*Marken*," I said to the boy. "*Was ist das?*"—that being one phrase I could say properly in German, and I could say *Liebe* too, that's all. That goddamn broad had taught me ...

The boy looked baffled; then with his thin fingers he drew a funny kind of square on the top of the bedside·table and said: "*Papier*."

I can understand *Papier* too, and I thought I knew now what he was trying to say.

"Ah," I said, "pass, you've lost your pass!"

He shook his head: "*Marken*."

"Damn it all, Pat," I said, "this *Marken* is driving me nuts. It must be something pretty special to make him want to drown himself."

Pat refilled our mugs, but that damned *Marken* kept nagging at me. My God, hadn't I seen that youngster standing up there, not moving, not making a sound, in the gap of the ruined bridge, and Splash! goddammit?

"Pat," I said, "look it up, you've got a dictionary."

"Sure," said Pat, jumping up and bringing the dictionary from his locker.

Meanwhile I nodded at the boy and gave him another cigarette, he'd eaten the whole can of corned beef and all the bread, and the coffee must've done him a power of good. And Jesus, the way these guys smoke, it's crazy, they smoke the way we sometimes used to smoke in the war when things got tough. They always smoke as if it was wartime, these Germans.

"Here we are!" Pat cried. "Got it!", and he jumped up, took a letter out of his locker, and showed the kid the stamp on it, but the boy just shook his head and even smiled a bit.

"*Nee*," he said, and he repeated that crazy word that had made him try and drown himself, and I'd never heard it.

"Hold it," Pat said, "I've got it, it's a word that means 'ration cards'," and he quickly turned over the pages of his dictionary.

"Still hungry?" I gestured to the kid. But he shook his head and poured himself another cup of coffee. Jesus, the way they can put away coffee, by the bucket, I thought ...

"Damn it all," Pat cried, "these dictionaries, these crappy dictionaries, these goddamn fucking dictionaries—a kid like that tries to drown himself for some reason or other, and you can't even find it in the dictionary."

"Look," I said to the boy, in English of course, "just tell us what it is, take your time, we're all human, we must be able to understand each other. Tell him, tell Pat," and I pointed to Pat, "just tell this guy." And Pat laughed, but he listened very carefully and the boy told him slowly, very slowly, the poor kid was all embarrassed, taking his time about it, and I understood some of it, and Pat's expression turned very serious.

"I'll be damned!" Pat exclaimed. "How can we be so dumb! They get their food on ration cards, right? They have ration cards, get it? Goddammit, we never thought of it, and that's what he's lost, and that's why he jumped into the Rhine."

"I'll be damned," I muttered. "A kid like that jumps into the river, and we don't know why, can't imagine ... "

We should at least be able to imagine it, I thought, at the very least, even if we can't actually experience it, we should at least be able to imagine it ...

"Pat," I said, "if he's lost them, they'll have to give him some new ones. It's just paper, and they can print them, they simply have to give him some new paper—it's not money, after all. It can happen to anyone, you know, losing them, surely there must be plenty of that printed stuff around ... "

"Balls," Pat replied, "they'll never do it. Because there's some people who just *say* they've lost them, and they sell them or eat twice as much, and the authorities get fed up. Christ, it's like in the war, when you've lost your rifle and suddenly there's a guy coming at you, and you simply can't shoot because you haven't got a rifle. It's just a goddamn war they're carrying on with their paper, that's what it is."

Okay, I thought, but that's terrible, then these folks end up having nothing to eat, nothing, nothing at all, and there's not a thing to be done about it, and that's why he ran like a maniac and threw himself into the Rhine ...

"Yes," Pat said, as if answering my thoughts, "and he's lost them all, the whole lot, for—I believe it's six people, and some other cards too, I just don't get what he means—for a whole month ... "

Jesus, I thought, what are they going to do if that's how it is! They can't do a thing, that kid goes and loses all the ration cards, and I thought to myself I'd drown myself too if I was him. But I still couldn't imagine it ... no, I guess nobody can imagine it.

I stood up, went over to my locker and got two packs of cigarettes for the kid but then I really had a shock, the way he looked at me. He sure gave me a weird look, he's going to go out of his mind on us, I thought, clear out of his mind, that's the kind of face the kid was making.

"Pat," I shouted—yes, I guess I shouted. "Do me a favour and take that boy away, take him away," I shouted. "I can't stand it, that face, those grateful eyes, all for two packs of cigarettes, I can't stand it—I tell you, it's as if I'd given him the whole world. Pat," I shouted, "take him away, and make him a parcel of everything we've got here, pack it all up and give it to him!"

Jesus, was I glad when Pat left with the kid. Pat'll make him a nice big parcel, I thought; and there you sat beside the dirty grey water, chatting a bit with the river all because of some skinny girl's face and thinking: throw yourself in, throw yourself in, let yourself be carried all the way to ... ha, Holland, for Christ's sake! But that child threw himself in, splash! threw himself in because of a few scraps of paper that were worth maybe less than a dollar.

THE GREEN SILK SHIRT

I did exactly as I had been told: without knocking I pushed open the door and walked in. But then it was a shock suddenly to find myself confronting a tall, stout woman whose face had something strange about it, a fantastic complexion: it was healthy, it positively shone with health, calm and confident.

The expression in her eyes was cold; she was standing at the table cleaning vegetables. Beside her was a plate with the remains of a pancake which a big fat cat was sniffing at. The room was cramped and low-ceilinged, the air stale and greasy. A sharp, choking bitterness caught at my throat while my shy gaze roamed restlessly between pancake, cat and the woman's healthy face.

"What d'you want?" she asked without looking up.

With trembling hands I undid the clasp of my briefcase, hitting my head against the low doorframe; finally I brought the object to light: a shirt.

"A shirt," I said huskily, "I thought ... perhaps ... a shirt."

"My husband has enough shirts for ten years!" But then she raised her eyes as if by chance, and her gaze fastened on the soft, rustling, green shirt. When I saw an ungovernable craving flare up in her eyes, I was sure the battle was won. Without wiping her fingers, she grabbed the shirt, holding it up by the shoulders; she turned it round, examined every seam, then muttered something indistinguishable. Impatient and anxious, I watched her go back to her cabbage, cross to the stove, and lift the lid of a sizzling saucepan. The aroma of hot, good-quality fat spread through the room. Meanwhile the cat had been sniffing at the pancake, apparently not finding it good or fresh enough. With a lazy, graceful leap, the cat jumped onto the chair, from the chair onto the floor, and slipped past me through the door.

The fat bubbled, and I thought I could hear the crackling bits of bacon hopping about under the saucepan lid, for by this time some ancient memory had told me that it was bacon, bacon in that saucepan. The woman went on scrubbing her cabbage. Somewhere outside a cow was lowing softly, a cart creaked, and still I stood there at the door while my shirt dangled from a dirty chairback, my beloved, soft, green silk shirt, for whose softness I had been longing for seven years ...

I felt as if I were standing on a red-hot grill while the silence oppressed me unutterably. By now the pancake was covered by a black cloud of sluggish flies: hunger and revulsion, a dreadful revulsion, combined in an acrid bitterness that closed my throat; I began to sweat.

At last I reached out hesitantly for the shirt. "You," I said, my voice even huskier than before, "you ... don't want it?"

"What d'you want for it?" she asked coldly, without looking up. Her quick, deft fingers had finished cleaning the cabbage; she placed the leaves in a colander, ran water over them, stirred them all under the water, then again lifted the lid of the saucepan where the bacon was sizzling. She slid the leaves into the saucepan, and the delicious hiss again revived old memories: memories of a time that might have lain a thousand years in the past, yet I am only twenty-eight ...

"Well, what d'you want for it?" she asked somewhat impatiently.

But I'm no good at bargaining, no, although I have visited every black market between Cap Gris Nez and Krasnodar.

I stammered: "Bacon ... bread ... maybe some flour, I thought ... "

Now for the first time she raised her cold blue eyes and looked at me coolly, and at that moment I knew I was done for ... never, never again in this life would I know the taste of bacon, bacon would forever remain no more than a wave of painful aromatic memory. Nothing mattered any more, her gaze had struck me, transfixed me, and now my whole self was draining out ...

She laughed. "Shirts!" she cried scornfully. "I can have shirts for a few bread ration coupons."

I snatched the shirt from the chair, knotted it round the neck of this virago and strung her up like a drowned cat on the nail beneath the big crucifix that hung black and threatening on the yellow wall above her face ... but I did this only in my imagination. In reality I grabbed my shirt, bundled it up, and stuffed it back into the briefcase, then turned to the door.

The cat was crouching in the hallway over a saucer of milk, greedily lapping it up. As I passed, it lifted its head and nodded as if wanting to acknowledge and comfort me, and in its green, veiled eyes there was something human, something unutterably human …

But because I had been advised to be patient, too, I felt obliged to try again. If only to escape the oppressive brilliance of the sky, I made my way under crippled apple trees, among cowpats and busily pecking chickens, towards a somewhat larger farmhouse situated to one side under the solid shade of some ancient linden trees. The bitterness must have blurred my vision, for it was only at the last moment that I noticed a brawny young farm lad sitting on a bench in front of the house and calling out endearments to two grazing horses. When he saw me he laughed, and called through an open window into the house: "Number eighteen's coming, Ma!" Then he slapped his thigh with glee and began to fill a pipe; his laughter was answered indoors by a throaty chuckle, and the shiny, crimson face of a woman appeared for a second in the window like a dripping pancake. I turned on my heel and ran like a madman, my briefcase tucked tightly under my arm. I didn't slow up until I reached the village street again and walked down the hill that I had climbed half an hour earlier.

I breathed a sigh of relief when I saw the friendly, grey snake of the highway below me, bordered with gentle trees. My pulse slowed down, the bitterness subsided, while I rested at the crossing where the cobbled, neglected, fetid village street emerged into the freedom of the highway.

I was dripping with sweat.

Suddenly I smiled, lit my pipe, pulled off my old, sticky, soiled shirt, and slipped into the cool, soft silk; it flowed gently down my body and right through me, and all my bitterness melted away, all of it, to a mere nothing; and as I walked back along the highway towards the railway station I felt welling up inside me a yearning for the poor, abject face of the city, behind whose contorted features I had so often seen the humanity bred by misery.

THE WAITING-ROOM

At first when I woke up I couldn't believe it—no, it couldn't be true. Once more I stuck my hand out from under the blanket and took it back again. Was I still dreaming? It couldn't be true; could the cold really have broken overnight? It was warm ... and mild; but oh, was I suspicious! I don't know whether you were also born in 1917—we are a very suspicious lot, the survivors of that generation, as rare as cigarettes among so-called honest folk. Well, in the end I had to trust my senses: I got up. Yes, it really was mild, the sunshine was warm and gentle, the windows were entirely free of ice ... they shimmered moistly, like the eyes of young girls who still believe in love.

My heart felt so light while I was dressing—what a relief that the cruel, murderous cold had broken. I looked out of the window: surely people were striding out more freely and happily, although the street was wet, but with a benign wetness, and from between grey clouds shone a moist sun ... and yes, I could almost believe that the trees were turning green! What arrant nonsense, in the middle of January. But you see how little one can trust one's senses and how right I was to be suspicious; oh, careful, careful! You will find it ridiculous, but after walking only a few hundred yards I felt myself sweating ... I really was. You will think: 1917, born during one war and cracked up during another ... No, no, it's really true, I was sweating ...

And I felt so light, the mild air and the sun and the dreamlike certainty that the cold seemed really to have broken made me reckless; at the corner I bought a good cigarette with almost the last of my money, pumped it voluptuously through my lungs, and blew the thin, grey smoke into the springlike air. I responded with a regretful smile to a pretty, red-haired girl who offered me bread-ration coupons and the next moment I had jumped onto a tram passing at full speed. Wasn't there, in spite of all the misery, a gleam of relief in people's eyes that the cruel cold had been conquered by a "warm air front"?

Didn't the sweet, tender air vibrate with sighs of relief? I even found a valid tram ticket in the depths of my coat lining, which meant that I could keep the fifty-pfennig piece intact in my pocket.

I smoked the entire cigarette without pinching it out. That hadn't happened for a long time—how reckless! I calculated in a kind of daze: since April 1945 ... that meant for almost two years, since my first days as a prisoner of war, I hadn't smoked an entire cigarette without pinching it out. Was some fundamental change taking place in me? I spat the butt, which was almost burning my lips, out into the street. The conductress called out cheerfully: "Main station!" I got off deep in thought ...

What bliss, to submerge oneself in the bustle of the huge waiting-room! You will say, or at least think: how can a man who was a soldier for many years, who has had to wait to the point of stupefaction for so many trains in all the waiting-rooms of Europe—how can a man like that enjoy sitting in a waiting-room? Oh, you don't understand. In this swarm of harried, weighed-down fellow creatures who, in the aftermath of war, are travelling—must travel—to somewhere from somewhere—in the midst of this bustle I pursue the secrets of solitude, of that blissful solitude which I was never allowed to find ... Here I can be truly alone, truly, truly alone and dream, dream to my heart's content. Silence is not for us ... silence scares us; with cruel fingers silence rips off the frail blanket of stoicism that we have spread over our memories and thrusts straight into the teeming, bloodied darkness of our brief, pain-fraught life. Silence ... silence is like a great snow-white screen onto which we project the joyless film of our lives. Silence can offer us no rest ...

But here, in this impersonal hum, the ebb and flow of outlandish images, in the midst of sounds I do not hear, of apparitions I do not see ... here there is a kind of peace, that's right, some kind of peace: here I can abandon myself to my dreams.

You will find this very foolish; but I have meanwhile discovered that there is nothing more pleasant than foolishness. Unfortunately we were never given enough time to be foolish ... that was the trouble. We were too young when the horror broke over us, and now we are too old to "learn". Or would you care to tell me what I am supposed to learn? With that mild, warm air, hadn't hope reawakened in those grey, pathetic faces of the homeless?

I idly jingled my fifty-pfennig piece against a bunch of safety pins I carried in my pocket, a habit I had picked up in the army—I always have to carry some safety pins in case buttons are ripped off or fabric gets torn; a cheap little quirk, you must admit, not an expensive indulgence.

I drank my beer straight down; today the insipid stuff tasted marvellous—I was really thirsty; but what had happened to my appetite? I sat down on a chair that had just been vacated and wondered about my appetite, which seemed to have vanished with the cold ... or had the cigarette absorbed it? I was profoundly shocked; where was my hunger, that faithful companion of so many years, that many-headed creature, often searing and vicious, sometimes just gently growling or amiably prompting: that mysterious monster that was second nature to me, fluctuating between wolfish greed and pitiful pleading?

One day, by the grace of God, I shall write a poem, a poem about my hunger. I became very uneasy.

Not only because of my hunger, not only because of this unexpected spring, not only because of my faraway, phantom beloved, perhaps unborn, or perished in the ghastly embrace of the war, for whom I sometimes waited here with a quaking heart ... no, no, I was also here for a purely practical reason. I was waiting for Edi. Edi was to tell me whether the deal would come off; if so, I would be the richer by three hundred marks—if not, well, I wouldn't be. But if it did come off I could buy a violin, which I craved ... it would make me happy, even happier, even freer ... oh, a violin! I love music almost more than I do that faraway, phantom beloved, who, I often believe, will appear any moment in the door of the waiting-room, so that I look tensely and with a trembling heart in that direction ... breathless and intoxicated by the thought that she has now become flesh and blood and will walk towards me with a smile.

So I was waiting for Edi. You may sometimes have wondered what people in waiting-rooms are waiting for! You probably believe that they are all waiting for arriving and departing trains. If you only knew the kind of things a person can wait for. One can wait for anything that exists between Nothing and God. Yes, there are even people waiting for Nothing.

My hair is now considerably thinner; illnesses, usually found only among the aged, plague me according to the season; and if I—please don't be alarmed!—take off my shirt, you can see some scars that might affect you like a painting by Goya; and the scars you could look at if I ... but since you are a lady I will say no more. You won't believe that I finished school ten years ago, by the skin of my teeth incidentally, and that during those ten years I have never been out of uniform, except for the last five months, since my return from P.O.W. camp—and I have never hated anything in my life so totally and profoundly as that uniform! I didn't know what occupation to enter on my release papers. High-school student? High-school graduate? Oh, if only I could have said, with a clear conscience: labourer. But with thinning hair and at almost thirty ... high-school graduate? It didn't seem funny to me—at that moment my eyes were opened...

It was the biggest mistake of my life to listen, against my better judgment, to the advice of so-called sensible older people who told me to "volunteer": because it was inevitable, "then you'll have it over with!" and so on. And the same people give me all kinds of advice today: learn a trade, go to university. Perhaps you will understand that today I am very suspicious of these so-called sensible older people who, after all—I should have thought of that!—are also the voters of those earlier days.

Waiting-room! By the grace of God I may one day write a wonderful poem about you. Not a sonnet. Some formless, ardent, passionate creation, as irrational as love ... O waiting-room, thou art the wellspring of my wisdom, thou art my oasis ... and I have found many a decent cigarette butt in thy depths when my heart was heavy.

I find the relative freedom of a civilian to be extremely pleasant and amusing; it is a glorious thing to be truly free, as free as a person can be without money. With money, of course, this freedom would have an even more golden face.

Don't talk to me about careers! I'll get by ... tramp, you think, gypsy? So what? Do you find that very anti-social? So what? ... I won't go under that easily.

Even in the waiting-room the air was—yes, lighter, I'd say. Hadn't the burden of those terrible hours of waiting been lightened for the travellers now that the icy cold had disappeared overnight as if by magic? And yet there was this waiting, waiting ...

There are even some people who await something—note the difference between waiting and awaiting. Waiting is the condition of a certain impatient hopelessness; awaiting is an expectant certainty: slack sails are filled with the intoxicating breath of hope.

But Edi didn't turn up. I became impatient, restless. Oh, if only I hadn't involved myself in this deal! Time and again I regretted it, and time and again I fell for it; you sell all your freedom when you begin to make deals. Involuntarily, you think of some stupid "compensation", as they call it ... it bores its way, deeper and deeper, gnawing like a worm at the precious peace of dreams and freedom. Always that net you have to slip through. I made up my mind never to get involved in such things again. Why not simply take up begging? How wonderful to be able to rattle off some phrase or other that would yield a modicum of bread and cash.

Of course Edi didn't turn up. Not that he is unreliable: I know him well—we spent many a dark Russian night together in cold and heat, in the dark womb of the earth which is the infantry's element. Edi is quite a smart fellow, although he has been laughing at me for as long as we've known each other, and although he is just a shade too dressy for my taste. But he's loyal. He found me a place when I returned from P.O.W. camp, and he kept my head above water for those first few weeks. And he is reliable. If he doesn't turn up, there must be some good reason ... perhaps they had caught him—who knows?—he's probably involved in all sorts of murky deals I know nothing about; his hands often tremble so strangely, he seems so jittery. And how calm he always used to be! Nothing could faze him or frighten him. But this strange peace in which we children of the war find ourselves has utterly corrupted Edi; he is sinking, I can feel it; he's gradually going under ... the temptation to become unscrupulous is so great that scarcely anyone can resist it. Oh, Edi ... I shall tell him, in a calm and friendly manner, that I won't make any more deals with him, not even the so-called legitimate ones.

Ah, my beloved ... my faraway, faraway darling dove ... if only you were here! Once again I plunged into that beautiful daydream, I cast everything away and went towards her ... that faraway, nameless one, the only one ... towards her, my only true home about whom, by the grace of God, I will some day write one last poem.

Suddenly I felt a rough punch on my right arm and I turned round, startled and annoyed. I looked into the face of an elderly woman who had apparently prodded me on purpose: I awoke to so-called reality, and the "true" face of the waiting-room loomed before me: grimy, musty ... wretched, ugly ... worn-down, worn-out figures, loitering, squatting on bundles that looked as if they couldn't possibly contain objects worth keeping. But the old woman plucked impatiently at my sleeve. "Hey ... young man!" she said. I looked at her squarely; she was sitting on a chair beside me. Grey hair, a coarse, plain face ... a farmer's wife, I thought. A grey-blue kerchief, a wrinkled face, swollen, work-worn hands. I looked up at her expectantly. "Yes?"

She seemed to hesitate a moment, then pointed to the brown hat lying on my right knee: "Wouldn't you like to trade it? I could use it, for my son!"

I was not surprised. When you spend half a day sitting around in waiting-rooms, you get to know the secrets of our so-called modern economy, based on the secret cigarette currency and carried on in the form of barter. I laughed.

"No, I need it myself—it's about the only thing I possess, and after all it's still January."

The old woman shook her head with an exasperating calm. "January!" she said scornfully. "Can't you see that spring has come?" She pointed to the ceiling of the waiting-room as if spring were to be seen there in the flesh.

I looked up involuntarily; the woman had turned away and was digging into some piece of luggage lying half under her chair; in doing so she bumped a youth who was sleeping with his elbows on the table; he opened his eyes in annoyance, swore under his breath, then laid his head down on the table. A young girl sitting opposite me and reading a book glanced up; with a frown she looked at the woman and me and went on reading. The old woman had finally dug out what she was looking for, and her coarse fists placed a big round loaf of bread, brown bread, between us on the table. .

"I'd give you that for it," she said stolidly. I have no doubt the look I gave the bread sealed the fate of my hat. I'm no good at bargaining. I know —I should have pretended to be stand-offish, should have ignored the bread, but I'm no good at bargaining, as I told you before. And besides—at the sight of the crusty brown bread my hunger was back again. In less than no time there it suddenly was beside me, this time wagging its tail and barking with pleasure, like a puppy whimpering expectantly as it sniffs at the housewife's apron; with one astonishing bound it had come back from some distant place where it had gone off for a walk. All that was no doubt to be read in my eyes. The woman knew even before I did that she would get the hat ... oh, that farmer's wife could write a psychology of hunger. How many hungry eyes have hung around her front door!

But I resisted. "No, no ... " I said fervently, and involuntarily grabbed my hat as if to protect it. "No—for a loaf of bread?" My eyes flickered between the bread, my hat, and the woman's cold face. "No," I repeated, trying to give my voice firmness. "Not for a loaf of bread!" The woman seemed somewhat surprised. "Aren't you hungry, then?" What an infamous way to try and snatch my hat from me! For a split second I wondered whether I shouldn't grab the loaf, put on my hat, and make a run for it. But then I would never again be able to enter that waiting-room in a calm frame of mind.

I shook my head vehemently. The woman gave a little smile, a bit more lenient, it seemed to me; then without a word she leaned down and fished out a second loaf from the depths under her chair. "Well?" she asked triumphantly. The light of victory was plain to see in her eyes. The thought that I had only to say the one little word "yes" to gain possession of two fragrant loaves of bread intoxicated me. But had the Devil in the shape of a barterer's soul taken possession of me? "You must ... give me some ... money, too," I stammered, blushing. "You ... I'm unemployed ... " The woman suddenly looked quite angry. "Unemployed?" she repeated, dragging out the word incredulously.

I merely nodded, blushing ever more deeply, for the girl opposite me had once again looked up disapprovingly. "Twenty marks," I said bravely, staking everything on one card, and as if the Devil were really driving me I playfully spun my nice brown hat on one finger ... for all the world like some careless youth. Oh, I knew it was a sort of farewell caress. The woman poked round in an old leather purse, grumpily picked out a few notes, and placed them beside the loaves. "That's it!" she said sternly. Thus I was unwittingly thrust into the role of the person who is to blame for the deal, and the woman looked at me as if I were the most despicable swindler she had ever laid eyes on. Twelve marks I had counted with bated breath ... two loaves and twelve marks, what riches! And how quickly I could calculate: four German or three

Belgian cigarettes ... two American ones! I stuffed the notes into my pocket, drew the loaves towards me, and quickly gave the woman my hat. She turned it round and examined it, her expression indicating that it was absolute rubbish, before it disappeared under the chair into that invisible container. I felt as if I were the lowest of criminals. Then my hunger took a wild leap over everything. I broke off a big chunk from one of the loaves and ordered another glass of beer from the waiter as he rushed past.

After my hunger had been fed its chunk, I was quickly alone again. In fact I even forgot that I had money for cigarettes in my pocket. The sweet grey veil of my dreams had been pulled across again. Ah, wasn't this a day when the beloved might arrive? Wasn't she on her way to me with her golden hair and black eyes, and with a smile that knew everything, everything ... she was coming closer ... closer and closer! Surely she was hungry! Oh, my beloved must be hungry, but I would not face her empty-handed; no doubt she was cold too, but oh, I would wrap her up in the warmth of this springlike day. If she was suffering fear and pain, my heart was open to her. I would give her my room, my bed, and I would sleep on the hard bare floor.

It was dusk outside and getting cold again; there was an icy draught round my feet and head. I looked desperately for my hat ... oh, my hat! You won't believe it, but there was no regret in me, only distress ... no, I did not regret having traded my hat, but it hurt me that it was gone. The cold was cruel, and it was a long way to my room with the bed where I could hide.

How infinitely rich I was in possessing a bed I could crawl into to escape the cruel cold. I would simply stay in bed; nothing and nobody could force me to get up. Mind you, there was silence there. But better to be exposed to silence than to the cold. Believe me, the worst thing is the cold. It crept towards me, across the stone floor and through the ceiling. What a nasty trick, to put on the mild, kindly garment of dusk just to pounce upon me again! I hurried ... hurried out of the station, waited desperately for a few minutes for the tram, and finally walked home.

It was as if my head were gradually freezing solid, as if it were being showered with invisible ice. I had the horrible feeling that it was shrinking, leaving nothing but a tiny button in which a frantic pain was concentrating. What a fool I was to think that spring was here ...

it was January, bitter, stark January. All I could feel was that grinding pain in my head, but then it spread like some crazy turmoil throughout my skull ... spreading, shrinking, taking possession of everything. In the end my whole head consisted only of pain and was growing tinier and tinier ... a glowing, frightful needle-point drilling away at my consciousness, my reason, my whole being.

I believe I was feverish when (I don't know how) I reached home ... I was feverish, haunted by dreams; my beloved was with me, but she was not smiling: instead tears were streaming from her black eyes.

And corpses were piled up round me like ramparts ... ragged, mutilated corpses, some fat, some wizened.

When I woke again to so-called reality, I found myself lying in hospital ...

Several times a day I would see round me those grave faces of the doctors who seemed to know all the secrets of life and death.

I had the dreadful notion that I might have woken up from my dreams wearing a uniform again. What was the difference between this hospital and a field hospital? No, there would be no more fever charts and grey-and-white-striped pyjamas for me. I am sure the urge for freedom made me recover so quickly that the doctors could congratulate themselves. I was well on my way back to health ...

The day soon came when I could say goodbye to the nurse and shake her hand gratefully. I felt compelled to hurry, hurry, as if my beloved had now, at this very moment, arrived and was standing in the entrance to the big waiting-room. I had to hurry ... but the nurse called me back. "Good heavens," she said, shaking her head, "you can't go out in this cold without a hat!" And with a smile she handed me a hat, a blue one, nearly new, that fitted me perfectly ... oh, I have quite a normal head.

Didn't it seem as if Someone were holding a protective hand over my head? Do you understand ...?

AN OPTIMISTIC STORY

Numerous requests to write a truly optimistic story gave me the idea of relating the fate of my friend Franz, a story that is true yet at the same time strange and almost too optimistic, with the result that one has a hard time believing it.

One day my friend Franz was fired from his job as a cub reporter on account of inordinate and insurmountable shyness, and he found himself out on the street almost penniless, hungry, and young enough to be desperate—all this on a sunny spring morning. I hope that the people wanting optimistic stories have no objection to a sunny spring morning, but for the time being, on account of his unemployed condition, I am forced to begin the story on a rather gloomy note. Franz was left with only fifty pfennigs. He gave much thought to what he should do with this. His most fundamental wish was for something to eat, for at all hours of the day and night he felt hungry, and his depression over being fired increased his appetite. Experience, however, had taught him that, to the very hungry, an incomplete meal was worse than no meal at all. Merely to stimulate the taste buds without satisfying them meant—as Franz well knew—worse torment than plain ordinary hunger. He toyed with the idea of appeasing his appetite by smoking, by inducing a kind of mild stupor, but then it occurred to him that smoking in his present condition would probably lead only to nausea.

Brooding over his dilemma, therefore, he walked past the displays in the shop windows. In a chemist's window he saw a display of indigestion pills, fifty pfennigs a package; Franz's digestion was in perfect order: he had none to speak of, in fact couldn't have, since these things do require some physical basis, and for many days Franz had been eating minimal quantities which had been totally consumed in his innards. Franz offered the chemist a mental apology, quickened his pace past a butcher's shop and a bakery, found himself, somewhat calmer, outside a greengrocer's, and wondered whether he shouldn't buy ten pounds of potatoes, boil them, and eat them with their skins. Ten pounds of potatoes in their jackets would certainly not give a mere illusion of satisfied hunger: they would actually satisfy it. But to boil potatoes he needed either wood or coal, as well as matches to light the stove; and since no one had yet thought of selling matches singly (here I permit myself to lay my finger on a sore point in the otherwise blessed and sophisticated state of our economy), the purchase of a box of matches would have meant sacrificing two pounds of potatoes, quite apart from the fact that he possessed neither wood nor coal.

There is really no need to list in detail the number of shops Franz walked past while a plan was taking shape in his head to buy a whole loaf of bread and eat it up on the spot; but a loaf costs fifty-eight pfennigs.

Franz remembered that he still had a tram ticket good for three more trips, with a face value of sixty pfennigs and a resale value of at least thirty. With eighty pfennigs he could easily eat his fill and buy two cigarettes. He therefore decided to make a clean break with his shyness and sell the tram ticket. Luckily he had just reached a tram stop. Studying the waiting passengers, he tried to read from their expressions how they would react to his unusual offer. Then he approached a man with a briefcase and a cigar, braced himself, and said: "Excuse me ... "

"I beg your pardon?" said the man.

"Here," said Franz, presenting his tram ticket. "Unusual circumstances, a temporary embarrassment, oblige me to dispose of this ticket. Could you perhaps ... would you...?"

"No," said the man suspiciously, and with such finality that Franz immediately desisted. Blushing, he left the tram stop, crossed the street, and found himself in front of a newspaper kiosk. Here he stopped and started to read without taking anything in. He made vain efforts to tear himself away from the kiosk, and when the woman inside asked him: "Yes, sir?" he knew he was done for, and with the last vestiges of good sense he named the fattest newspaper he knew, saying huskily and with an unhappy sigh: "*World Echo*." He handed the fifty-pfennig note into the kiosk and received a forty-page packet of paper and printer's ink.

Aware of having committed one of the greatest follies of his life, he decided to go into the park in order at least to read the newspaper. The sun shone very mildly, and it was spring. He asked a passer-by the time and was told it was ten o'clock.

Seated in the park were pensioners, a few young mothers with children, and some unemployed. Noisy children were fighting over places in the sandbox; dogs were scuffling over bits of discarded greasy paper; the young mothers threatened and called out in the general hub-bub. Franz sat down, opened his newspaper with a flourish, and read a bold headline: BRILLIANT POLICE!, followed by: "Our police must recently have perfected some brilliant investigatory methods. They have succeeded in arresting a butcher for black-market activities. In view of the well-known rectitude of this trade ... "

With an angry gesture Franz closed the newspaper and got up, and at that moment an idea came to him of such ingenuity that it may be regarded as the turning point towards the optimistic part of our story. He neatly folded the newspaper, suddenly raised his hitherto shy voice, and called out quite loudly: "*World Echo*! World's Last Echo!"

He was surprised at his own courage and went on shouting, amazed that people took so little notice of him; even more amazed when someone asked him: "How much for the paper?"

Franz replied: "Fifty pfennigs," looked into a disappointed face, and now had enough presence of mind to say: "The latest edition— make it thirty, if you like. Forty pages, an excellent paper ... "

He accepted the tiny ten-pfennig notes and, puffed up with pride, left the park convinced that everything would turn out all right. After briskly crossing a few streets he hopped onto a moving tram and remained surprisingly cool-headed when the conductor came round asking: "Any more fares, please?"

After two stops he got out and walked to the station. Here he bought a cigarette for ten pfennigs, threw ten pfennigs into a beggar's hat, and with his last ten pfennigs bought a platform ticket. Smoking cheerfully, he passed through the barrier and fastened his attention on the Arrivals board. On discovering that a train from Frankfurt was due in one minute, he hurried to that platform. A voice over the loudspeaker said, "Stand back!", and already the train was approaching. And when the train had come to a stop he suddenly had a new idea. Allowing his cigarette to dangle casually from one corner of his mouth, he ran along-side the train shouting: "Hella! Hella dearest! Hella darling!" although he knew nobody of that name. He shouted imploringly, desperately, like a hopeless lover, and eventually, having run all the way from the engine to the tail end of the train, he abandoned his shouting and running with an air of deep resignation. He assured himself of a good exit by wending his way, heavy-hearted and defeated, among the parting couples and grumpy porters. He walked back down the stairs and finally spat out the cigarette butt that had been threatening his lower lip.

Like all shy people who suddenly discover their own courage, he had the feeling that the world was his oyster. From the Arrivals board he took in at a glance that the next train wasn't due for twenty minutes, coming from Dortmund. He decided to go into the station buffet.

Franz wrote me all this in great detail. These days he has plenty of leisure: somewhere in a foreign country he is living with an adorable wife in his own villa. But I must condense his story; I have been charged with writing a brief, optimistic story, for people no longer trust long-winded optimism, so I cannot describe the minutest nuances of every single emotional reaction, the way Franz did.

Let us hurry on, then. He entered the station buffet, buttonholed a waiter, and said hastily, like someone whose time is of inestimable value: "I'm Dr Windheimer. Has Dr Hella Schneekluth been asking for me?" The waiter looked at him sceptically, shook his head, pushed up his glasses, and, disconcerted by the anything-but-shy eyes of my friend, said: "No, sir, I'm sorry."

"Terrible," said Franz, and "Thanks." He sighed, groaned, sat down at a table, pulled out his notebook, which contained nothing, put it back in his pocket, pulled it out again and began to draw girls' profiles in it, until he was interrupted by the waiter saying: "Can I get you anything, sir?"

"No, thanks," Franz calmly replied, "not today. I don't feel like anything today."

The waiter looked at him again over the top of his spectacles and went off with his tray of empty beer glasses. At the next table Franz now spied a peasant woman with a little girl who, with admirable persistence, were eating their way through a basketful of thick sandwiches as if driven by a stubborn, proud, indescribably ennobling sense of duty to fulfil some loathsome task. They had not ordered anything to drink—thrifty folk.

At that moment Franz's hunger announced its presence with such vehemence that he couldn't help laughing, so loudly that everybody

turned towards him—the woman, the child (both of them with a chunk
of white bread in their half-open mouths), the waiter, and all the rest.
Franz looked at a page in his notebook as if he had discovered something outlandishly amusing there. Then he got up, approached the
waiter again, and said in a loud voice: "If anyone should ask for me—
Dr Windheimer—I'll be back in ten minutes," and left.

Outside he studied the Arrivals board again and discovered to his
horror that he had overlooked an arrival from Ostend printed in red.
He raced over to the platform in question, saw the long, luxurious train
standing there, was already opening his mouth, about to call out, when
he remembered that he must use a foreign name, and he called out—no,
he shouted: "Mabel! Mabel dearest! Mabel darling," and the result was
what justifies me in describing this story as optimistic: in the very last
carriage, in the very last compartment, at the last window before the
pessimistically snorting engine, the head of a sweet-looking, fair-haired
girl looked out, and she cried: "Yes!" (in English, of course). Franz
stopped in his tracks, looked her in the face, and said: "Yes, you're the
one," and I must assume that she too, despite his empty pockets, found
him to be the right one; for he ended his really disgustingly detailed letter with: "We understand each other perfectly. Mabel is adorable. Do
you need any money?"

I replied by telegram with the one word: "Yes."

I'M NOT A COMMUNIST

The bus always stops at the same spot. The driver has to be very careful, the street is narrow, and the bay where the bus has to stop is cramped. Each time there is a jolt that wakes me up. I look to my left out of the window and always see the same sign: LADDERS ANY SIZE—THREE MARKS TWENTY PER RUNG. There is no point in looking at my watch to see the time: it is exactly four minutes to six, and if my watch says six or even later, I know my watch is fast. The bus keeps better time than my watch! I look up and see the sign: LADDERS ANY SIZE—THREE MARKS TWENTY PER RUNG; the sign is above the window of a hardware shop, and in the window among the bottling jars, coffee mills, mangles and china a small, three-rung ladder is displayed. At the present time, there are mostly garden chairs in the window, and garden loungers. On one of these a woman reclines, a life-size woman made of papier mâché or wax—I don't know what kind of stuff they use to make mannequins. The mannequin is wearing sunglasses and reading a novel called *A Holiday from Myself*. I can't make out the name of the author, my eyes aren't good enough for that. I look at the mannequin, and the mannequin depresses me, makes me even more depressed than I already am—I ask myself whether such mannequins really have a right to exist. Mannequins made of wax or papier mâché and reading novels called *A Holiday from Myself*. It is all so depressing—to the left of this shop window is a pile of rubble on which mounds of garbage and ashes lie smouldering in the sun. It depresses me to see the mannequin right next to them.

But what interests me most is the ladders. We really should have a ladder. In the cellar we have shelves for our preserves, and the shelves are very high because the cellar is narrow and we have to make the best use of the space. The shelves are poorly made. I nailed them together out of some boards and fastened the whole thing with a piece of thick rope to the gas pipes that run through our cellar. If they were not firmly fastened, I am sure they would collapse under the weight of the jars.

My wife does a lot of bottling. In summer there is a constant smell of freshly boiled cucumbers, cherries, plums and rhubarb. For days on end the smell of hot vinegar permeates our home—it almost makes me ill, but I do see that we need the preserves. The shelves are very high, and on the top shelf are the cherries and peaches we eat on Sundays in winter. On Saturdays my wife always has to climb up there, and she usually stands on an old wooden crate. Last spring my wife fell through a crate like that and had a miscarriage. I wasn't there, of course, and she lay in the cellar bleeding and calling for help until someone found her and took her to hospital.

On Saturday afternoon I went to the hospital and took my wife some flowers: we just looked at each other, and my wife cried—she cried for a long time. It would have been our third, and we had always talked about how we would manage with three children in two rooms. It is bad enough having to live in two rooms with only two children. I know there are worse things—there are people living six or eight to a room. But it is also hard to manage with two children in two rooms on the same floor as three other parties who have no children. That's hard. I don't want to complain—I'm not a Communist, for heaven's sake, but it's really hard.

I'm tired when I come home and I'd like to have half an hour's peace and quiet, only half an hour to eat my supper, but just when I get there they're not quiet and then I smack them—and later, when they're in bed, I feel sorry. Then I sometimes stand beside their bed and look at them, and at such moments I am sometimes a Communist ... Don't tell anyone—it's only for a few moments, you see.

Every evening, when the bus stops, I feel a jolt and look to my left: the suntanned face of the mannequin in the swimsuit is half hidden by the sunglasses, but the title of the book is clearly visible: *A Holiday from Myself*. Maybe one day I'll get off and look for the name of the author. And above the shop window hangs a sign: LADDERS ANY SIZE—THREE MARKS TWENTY PER RUNG. Our ladder would have to have three rungs, that would be nine marks sixty. No matter how much I juggle the figures I can't come up with nine marks sixty. Now it's summer anyway, and it'll be November before my wife begins climbing onto the crate again on Saturdays to bring down a jar of peaches or cherries for Sunday—not till November. So there's plenty of time.

But my wife is expecting again. Don't tell any of our relatives, and please don't tell the people on our floor. There'll be trouble, and I don't want any trouble. All I want is half an hour's peace and quiet a day. The relatives will be angry when they hear that my wife's expecting—and the people on our floor will be even angrier, and I'll start smacking the children again—and then I'll feel sorry again, and at night when they're asleep I'll stand beside their bed and for a few moments be a Communist. It's all so pointless—I'll try not to think about it again till November. I'll look at the mannequin reclining on the lounger reading a novel called *A Holiday from Myself*—that mannequin right beside the pile of rubble and the mounds of ashes from which a dirty yellow stream flows into the gutter whenever it rains.

CONTACTS

Not long ago my wife met the mother of a young girl who cuts the nails of a cabinet minister's daughter. The toenails. There is now great excitement in our family. Formerly we had no contacts whatever, but now we have contacts, contacts that are not to be underestimated. My wife takes this girl's mother flowers and chocolates. The flowers and the chocolates are accepted with thanks although also with some reserve. Since knowing this woman we have been feverishly wondering what position we should propose for me when we reach the point of meeting the girl herself. So far we have never seen her; she is rarely at home, moves of course only in government circles, and has a charming flat in Bonn: two rooms, kitchen, bath, balcony. But nevertheless there is talk that she will soon be available. I am very curious about her and, needless to say, will behave with due humility, though also with determination. It is my belief that in government circles humble determination is appreciated, and it is said that the only people who stand a chance are those who are convinced of their own ability. I am trying to be convinced of my abilities, and I soon will be. Still, wait and see.

To begin with, our credit has improved since it has become known that we have contacts in government circles. The other day I heard a woman in the street say to another: "Here comes Mr B, he has contacts with A." She said it very quietly but so that I should and could hear it, and as I walked past the ladies they smiled sweetly. I nodded condescendingly. Our grocer, who until now had reluctantly allowed us very limited credit and, with a suspicious expression, watched margarine, grey bread and cigarette tobacco disappear into my wife's shopping bag, now smiles when we arrive and offers us delicacies the taste of which we had forgotten: butter, cheese and real coffee. He says: "Now wouldn't you like some of this magnificent Cheddar?" And when my wife hesitates, he says: "Do take some!", then lowers his eyes and grins discreetly. My wife takes some. But yesterday my wife heard him whisper to another woman: "The Bs are related to A!" It's uncanny the way rumours get round. In any event, we eat butter and cheese on our bread—no longer grey bread—and drink real coffee while waiting somewhat tensely for the appearance of the girl who cuts the nails of the cabinet minister's daughter. The toenails. The girl has not turned up yet, and my wife is growing uneasy, although the girl's mother, who meanwhile appears to have developed a fondness for my wife, reassures her and says: "Just be patient." But our patience is wearing thin since we have been making ample use of that tacit credit which has recently been granted us.

The daughter whose toenails our young lady cuts is the minister's favourite daughter. She is studying history of art and is said to be extremely talented. I can believe it. I can believe anything, yet I tremble because the young pedicurist from Bonn still hasn't turned up. We look up encyclopedias and all available biological textbooks in order to gather information on the natural growth rate of toenails, and we discover that it is minimal. So this minister's daughter cannot be the only one. Our young pedicurist probably grasps one toe of Bonn society after another in her adorable hands and removes the burden of dead cells that can pose a threat to nylon stockings and ministerial socks.

I hope her scissors don't slip. I tremble at the thought that she might hurt the minister's daughter. Female art historians have terribly sensitive toenails (I once was in love with an art historian and, on throwing myself at her feet, accidentally leaned my elbow on her toes, without dreaming they could be so sensitive; all was over, and since that day I have known how sensitive are the toes of female art historians). The young girl must be careful; the influence of the daughter on the minister and of the pedicurist on the daughter (who is suspected of social ambitions) is said to be extraordinarily great; and the pedicurist's mother had hinted (everything is hinted) that her daughter has already managed to secure a position for a young man of her acquaintance as clerk in the outer office of a departmental head. "Departmental head" were the magic words for me. The very thing.

Meanwhile the mother of the young lady continues to accept flowers and chocolates with the same kindly smile: we are glad to make this sacrifice on the altar of high society, while we tremble: our credit keeps rising, and people are whispering that I am an illegitimate son of A's.

We have advanced from butter and cheese to pâté and goose-liver sausage; we no longer roll our own but smoke only the better brands. And we are informed: the young lady from Bonn is coming! She actually arrives! She arrives in the car of a secretary of state whose toes she is said to have rid of a whole colony of sinister corns. So be prepared: she is about to appear!

We spent three days in a state of extreme nervousness, and instead of ten-pfennig cigarettes we now smoke fifteen-pfennig cigarettes, since they do a better job of calming our nerves. I shave twice a day, whereas I used to shave twice a week as befits any normal unemployed person. But I have long ceased to be a normal unemployed person. We copy testimonials, over and over again, each one neater and more cogent than the last, type out *curricula vitae* (eighteen copies to be on the safe side), and rush off to have them notarized: a whole stack of paper will supply information on the tremendous capabilities that predestine me for the position of clerk in the outer office of a department head.

Friday and Saturday go by while we consume (on credit, of course) a quarter of a pound of coffee and a package of fifty fifteen-pfennig cigarettes a day. We try to converse in a jargon that might conceivably correspond to government circles. My wife says: "I'm really so down, dahling," and I reply: "Sorry, dahling, must stick it out." And we actually do stick it out until the following Sunday. Sunday afternoon we are invited for tea with the young lady (a reciprocal gesture for those twelve bouquets and five boxes of chocolates). Her mother has assured us that I would spend at least eight minutes alone with her. Eight minutes. I buy two dozen plump pink carnations—three for each minute: magnificent specimens of carnations, so plump and pink they seem about to burst. They look like the essence of rococo ladies. I also buy a delightful box of chocolates and ask my friend to drive us there in his car. We drive to the house, honk like mad, and my wife, who is pale with excitement, keeps whispering: "I'm really so down, dahling, so down."

The young lady looks delightful, slender and self-assured, quite the government pedicurist, yet she is gracious and charming, although a little reserved. She sits enthroned at the head of the table, fussed over by her mother, and I am dismayed to count seven persons at the table: three young scoundrels with their wives and an elderly gentleman who is kind enough audibly to admire my flowers—but our chocolate box is really delightful, it is made of smooth gold cardboard, has a lovely pink pompon on top, and altogether looks more like an exquisite powder box than a box of chocolates: this box, too, is audibly admired by the elderly gentleman (I am deeply grateful to him for this), and during the introductions I notice that the mother says to her daughter: "Mr B and wife," then after a pause, with more emphasis: "Mr B." The young lady throws me a meaningful glance, nods and smiles, and I can feel myself turning pale: I feel that I am the favourite and now accept the presence of those three young scoundrels and their wives with a smile.

The tea party progresses somewhat stiffly: first we discuss the enormous advances in the chocolate industry since the currency reform, a conversation prompted by a chocolate box that seems to have caught the fancy of the elderly gentleman. I have a dark suspicion that he has been invited to the tea party by the mother for tactical reasons. But for my taste the old fellow is too blatant about it, too undiplomatic, and the other three scoundrels, whose chocolate boxes remain ignored, give a bitter-sweet smile and the tea party progresses stiffly until the young lady takes out a cigarette: a ten-pfennig one, and embarks on some delicate government gossip. We spring to our feet, all five of us, to offer her a light, but she accepts only mine. I can feel my chest swelling and begin to have visions of my office in Bonn: red leather armchairs, cinnamon-coloured curtains, fabulous filing cabinets and, as my superior, a retired colonel who for sheer compassion can hardly see straight ...

Suddenly the young lady has vanished, and for a while I fail to notice the signals of her mother who is trying to convey to me that I should leave the room, until my wife nudges me and whispers: "Idiot—out!"

Breathing heavily, I go out of the room. My conversation with the young lady is carried on in a completely down-to-earth, business-like manner. She receives me in the drawing-room, looks with a sigh at her watch, and I realize that some of the eight minutes have already passed—probably half of them. As a result, my speech, which I cautiously begin with "Sorry," turns out to be somewhat confused, but she smiles in spite of it all, accepts my gift of three English pound notes, and finally says: "Please don't overestimate my influence—I'm willing to try simply because I'm convinced of your abilities. You will receive an answer in about three months." A glance she casts at her watch tells

me that it is time for me to leave. I toy briefly with the notion of kissing
her hand, but refrain, whisper my most humble thanks, and stagger out.
Three months. Incidentally, she was pretty.

I return to the tea party and on the faces of the three young scoundrels, whose chocolates were almost totally ignored, I discern poisonous envy. Soon there is an impatient honking outside, and the young
lady's mother announces that her daughter has been summoned back
to Bonn by telegraph in order to relieve the cabinet minister of his calluses; his golf game was to begin at nine tomorrow morning and it was
already five o'clock, and with those calluses he would not be able to
play. We look out into the street to see the minister's car; it is powerful but not particularly elegant. The young lady leaves the house with
a charming little leather case and a briefcase. The tea party breaks up.

When we get home my wife, who has taken careful note of everything, tells me that I was the only one to be alone with "her". The
question as to what "she" is like, I answer with: "Charming, my dear,
quite charming."

I do not tell my wife about the three-month waiting period. Instead
I discuss with her what further courtesies we can show "her". My idea
of offering "her" three months' salary is rejected by my wife as an
appalling lack of good taste. We finally agree on a motor scooter to
be delivered to her anonymously but in such a way that she will know
who sent it. Surely she would find it practical if she were motorized
and would be able to ride from house to house with her charming little
leather case. If she succeeds in treating the cabinet minister successfully
(the fellow seems to have an advanced case of fallen arches), perhaps
my intolerable waiting period of three months will be curtailed. Three
months is more than I can manage, our credit is not all that great—I
hope that the motor scooter, which I shall buy on instalments, will tip
the balance, and that after only one month I will be sitting in those red
leather armchairs. For the time being we both—my wife and I—feel
completely down, and we sincerely regret that there is no such thing
as an eighteen-pfennig cigarette—that would now be the very thing for
our nerves ...

AT THE BORDER

At the time, when I declared my desire to join the Customs service, the whole family was indignant. Only Uncle Jochen was sensible: "Go ahead," he said, "go ahead and join it."

One must make allowances for a certain degree of indignation: I had completed high school, taken a few terms of philosophy, was an ensign first-class in the Reserve—and now merely wished to become a Customs officer.

I have an excellent figure, am healthy and intelligent; moreover, I have always been obedient, so my career was off to a good start. A sense of duty was coupled in me with what I would almost like to call a calm broadmindedness.

By the time I had completed my training period and gone home for a few days' leave, with three shirts, three pairs of underpants, three pairs of socks, a nice uniform and the title "Customs Probationer", the family's indignation had somewhat subsided. My father unbuttoned a bit and was to be heard saying publicly: "My son, you know, the one who was an ensign first-class—my son is now with the Customs."

My first day on duty I guarded the barrier at Bellkerke. It was hot and completely quiet—an afternoon; nothing was happening and, although I was tired and moody, numerous thoughts crossed my mind. After being relieved, I sat down, put those thoughts into some useful order and wrote a short treatise: "Possible Border Incidents During Border Duty", a completely theoretical essay, I must admit, but one which as a modest tract aroused the attention of my superiors. In addition, the essay led to my promotion (out of turn) to Customs Assistant. This proves that my studies in philosophy had not been altogether in vain. I was transferred to the internal Customs service.

By the time I next went on leave, the family was already completely reconciled. In my free time I pondered on a short treatise for which I had as yet no title. In bold moments I almost considered "The

Frontier of Philosophy" but, while I was still uncertain as to the title, the work progressed well. I submitted it for publication in *The Customs Service News Letter*, where, under the title of "The Philosophy of the Frontier", it reinforced my reputation as an analytical Customs officer and resulted in my appointment to full clerk.

Meanwhile I expanded my practical experience and planned to add to my essay an appendix entitled "The Burdens of a Functionary". I had high hopes of this work: it was to show the complexity of our existence at the border as well as in the internal service, and to demonstrate that a uniform does not impair the free flow of thought. I wear the smart green uniform with pride.

Needless to say there is no dearth of envious colleagues, most of whom come from the raw ranks of the mere practitioners, crude types to whom the beauty of the written word cannot be conveyed. There are actually those among them of whom I know for a fact that they have never yet read the literary supplement of a newspaper. Not without a strong inner hesitation I have meanwhile started on a third essay: "Safety of the Frontier, or The Frontier of Safety?" Into this essay, in order to stop the mouths of the envious, I intend to weave much practical knowledge: above all, my experience that it is almost always the diplomats and the riffraff who get away with it, and I have found that the riffraff smuggle so diplomatically and the diplomats so riffraffishly that I will take the liberty of closing my essay with the words: Germans, stay at home and make an honest living! Actually I cannot see why—except in wartime!—one should bother to visit countries other than one's own. French morals and English perfidy infiltrate our country, nothing else.

Under the influence of certain intimate occurrences, my appendix, "The Burdens of a Functionary", became so copious that it almost threatened to turn into a little book of its own. But I persisted and continued my polishing efforts.

My promotion to inspector was made conditional upon demonstration of my practical qualities, and I did not hesitate to report immediately to the front line: I posed as a coffee buyer at a large West German railway station, penetrated the very heart of a gang of which I became a member, and gradually let the current of this gang carry me onward and upward. I slept in extremely dubious dumps, was obliged to consort—in the service of the state—with women as seductive as they were dangerous, drank with thieves, ate with sinners, smoked with criminals and played cards with hard-boiled villains. Stubbornly, patiently, I soldiered on, towards the top, and one day—oh bliss of mission accomplished!—I could give the agreed signal: seventeen men, eleven women, were arrested, and among those captured was the head of the gang.

Although the security of commerce was not completely restored, it was now raised to a higher level. I was given special leave; none of the envious now dared to accuse me of inadequate practical experience. When shortly afterwards I submitted my just completed essay, my triumph was complete: I was promoted to chief inspector and am presumably justified in regarding my career as secure. Moral: let no one be prevented from following the career of his choice!

THE SURFER

After travelling thirty-six hours the young man arrived dead tired in Cologne; it was a hot Sunday afternoon in summer. The station square was crowded; large posters and decorative banners proclaimed a pharmacists' convention. The young man plodded from hotel to hotel, moving farther and farther away from the station, and finally found accommodation at the edge of the old part of the city. The hotel clerk told him he could share a room with another gentleman who had offered to give up the second bed in his room.

The young man climbed up the hot, narrow stairs carrying his only luggage: a briefcase and a bottle of lemonade he had asked for downstairs. On hearing a grumpy "Come in," he opened the door; the first thing he saw was a small white table on which lay many little pieces of paper and a pile of loose, dark-brown tobacco. The room faced the street. The windows were open, the shutters pushed out, and in the wan light the tobacco took on a purplish look. Opposite the door was a mirror; the washbasin had a long, black, yellow-edged crack in it, and in an open wardrobe he first saw only musty darkness but then distinguished a crumpled raincoat and a shabby briefcase from which a leg of some underpants protruded. To the left of the door was an iron bedstead with a white counterpane on which lay a black jacket. He finally made out his roommate lying on the second bed in the shadows of the farthest corner: a stout, unshaven fellow, his blue and white striped shirt arching tautly over his belly. The young man took him for one of the many pharmacists who were filling up all the hotels.

He approached the stout, motionless figure, who from time to time puffed out clouds of smoke, and quietly introduced himself: "My name's Wenk." Without looking up or stirring, the man on the bed mumbled something that sounded like "Welter" and "That's okay," and continued to drowse.

Wenk turned on the tap, placed his briefcase on the bed, hung the man's jacket over a chair and his own over the brass knob of the bedpost, and took off his shirt. He washed slowly and thoroughly, cleaned his teeth and shaved. Welter neither moved nor spoke. His only movement consisted of occasionally opening his thick, swollen-looking lips and puffing out clouds of smoke. On either side of the projecting shutters, the smoke rose into the white triangles of sky.

Wenk felt much refreshed after his wash, lit a cigarette, then lay down on his bed and fell asleep. When he awoke, he found the other man had got up and was shaving. The air had cooled off, and a light breeze gently swayed the shutters. Outside the street was still quiet; somewhere in one of the neighbouring houses a girl was practising an étude, appropriately enough for a Sunday afternoon. She played badly, with many wrong notes, and at one place where the young man expected a cluster of semi-quavers she invariably stumbled or stopped.

Welter was standing in front of the mirror, vigorously swishing his foam-tipped shaving brush around on his face. He still had his pipe clenched between his teeth, but it seemed to have gone out. His shirt sleeves were rolled up, and the movements of his hairy, powerful arms were brisk. Wenk got up, relit his cigarette, and stood by the window. The street was empty, grey and quiet; in the house across the street, a slight, deeply tanned man in a singlet was leaning on the window-sill smoking a black cigar. Farther back in the room he saw a woman in a red petticoat powdering under her arms. The girl at the piano was now playing a folk tune, but that too she played badly, although softly and almost shyly.

"I envy you," Welter said suddenly in a warm, attractive voice, "being able to sleep in this heat."

"When you've been travelling for thirty-six hours ... " said Wenk, turning to Welter, who was just wiping the lather from his razor.

"Pharmacist?" asked Welter.

"No," laughed the young man, "I thought you ... "

"For heaven's sake!" Now Welter was laughing. "Although I've nothing against pharmacists, in fact I wish I were a pharmacist ... By the way," he continued, lighting his pipe, "I've also been travelling thirty-six hours, yet I couldn't sleep—I wish to heaven I were a pharmacist!"

After so many hints Wenk felt obliged to ask, out of politeness: "You mean your job's such a terrible one?"

But Welter was busy rinsing the lather from his face and cleaning his brush. Outside in the street it was growing noisier and, leaning out, Wenk saw what seemed to be a victorious football team in yellow jerseys, surrounded by a crowd of fans, pass by below. Across the street the woman was now leaning out beside the man. She was plump and young, and both she and the man looked bored. Welter had finished now; he was just putting on his tie and asked casually: "Which route did you take?"

"Munich–Hamburg, Hamburg–Cologne." Wenk had meanwhile removed his jacket from the bedpost.

"Good idea. Let's go for a bite to eat, shall we? I hope I'm not intruding … " Welter asked.

The two men spent the whole evening together; they seemed to take to each other. They sat, drank some wine, strolled along the Rhine, and Wenk even persuaded Welter at one point to have an ice cream sundae. But he did not find out about Welter's occupation until later, after they had returned to the hotel. The wind had subsided, and beyond the shutters there was now a heavy, oppressive heat. They were both lying on their beds smoking. From the street came a mild jumble of voices and the sounds of turned-down radios. For a long time they were silent. Wenk smoked his cigarettes quickly one after another, hastily, greedily, until they almost stuck to his lips; then he would toss them across the room into the wash basin. The glow of Welter's pipe swelled from time to time in the dark, then contracted again, covered by ash.

"And why," Welter finally said quietly, "why have you been travelling such a long way?"

Wenk hesitated for a moment, then said: "I've been following a woman … "

"Is she beautiful at least?"

"I think so, yes."

They fell silent again and continued to smoke. From the hot streets and the scorching pavements, the heat rose in oppressive clouds.

"Ah yes," Welter sighed. "You see, I'd say you were twenty-eight years old, fair hair, about six feet tall. What would you do if you had five thousand marks?"

Wenk was silent, but the silence was suddenly different. "Yes," Welter sighed again. "What would you do? The thing is, I'm looking for someone who's about six feet tall, twenty-eight years old, with fair hair. My boss relies on my intuition. 'Welter,' he said, 'go and look for him.

We must have him. Your intuition will help you.' Oh," he gave a scornful laugh, "my own intuition makes me sick. In this heat everything makes me sick. But tell me, what would you do?"

Wenk remained silent for a while. When he began to speak, his voice was subdued, tired, slightly ironic. In the darkness he had flushed and was smiling. From outside still came that gentle, impersonal hum, and Wenk lit another cigarette. He said: "I think I would do as they do in movies. Become a surfer or some such thing ... Riviera ... Florida ... surfing. D'you know about surfing?" Welter didn't answer. Only the glow of his pipe swelled in the dark and subsided again.

"Just for once, to have no worries for three weeks or three hours," Wenk continued, "or three minutes, three seconds, like those rich whores with their johns who go surfing. Can you understand that?"

"Oh yes," Welter said softly.

Again they were silent for a while as they smoked. Then Welter asked suddenly: "You wouldn't take the girl along, the one you've been following?"

Wenk burst out laughing. In the dark he groped for his jacket, threw it across to Welter's bed, and said: "You win, it's been in my breast pocket the whole time—it's all there ... "

Welter did not stir or make any move to pick up or search the jacket. After a minute he merely asked: "Do you think you'll be able to sleep?"

"No," said Wenk.

"Then we might as well get started."

IN FRIEDENSTADT

By the time I reached Friedenstadt, it was too late to phone Sperling. The station was surrounded by darkness, the little square filled with the kind of silence that even in small towns doesn't begin to descend until around eleven. Once again I had miscalculated, just as, while gambling that afternoon, I hadn't won, as I'd expected to, but had lost everything. To look up Sperling at eleven at night would have meant the permanent loss of his favour. That big hunk of a man, almost six foot six, slept at this hour as if pole-axed, while his brutish snoring filled the heavily curtained bedroom.

During the two minutes I stood hesitating on the topmost step outside the station, the few people who had got off the train with me had disappeared. I walked slowly back into the musty, semi-dark hall and looked round for somebody, but there was no one there except the man at the barrier, who seemed to be lost in thought as he stared out at the platform. His shiny cap gave him an air of solidity. I approached him; he raised a peevish face to me.

"Excuse me, sir," I stammered, "I find myself in a predicament. I wonder if you ... "

He interrupted me, coolly waved his ticket punch past my nose, and said in a bored tone of voice: "You're wasting your time—you can take my word for it. I haven't a penny in my pocket." The expression in the fellow's eyes was icy.

"But ... " I tried again.

"You're wasting your time, I tell you. I don't lend money to strangers—even if I had any. Besides ... "

"The fact is ... "

"Besides," he went on imperturbably, pronouncing each syllable like a veritable lead weight, "besides, even if—and you can take my word for it—even if I was a millionaire, I wouldn't give you anything, because ... "

"Good heavens ... "

"... because you've cheated me. No, don't go away!" I turned back and watched him take the used tickets out of his pocket and carefully search through them, as if counting the little bits of pasteboard like money.

"Here," he said, holding up a pale blue object, "a platform ticket, and it came from you."

"Sir!"

"And it came from you! You should be grateful I'm not having you arrested, but instead ... instead you're trying to cadge money from me. Don't go away!" he shouted at me, since I was trying again to sneak off in the dark. "Do you deny it?" he asked in a cold, insistent voice.

"No," I said ...

He put his hand on my shoulder and took off his cap, and now I saw that his face, thank God, wasn't all that brand new.

"Young man," he said, "tell me frankly—what do you live on?"

"On life," I answered.

He looked at me: "Hm. Can one live on that?"

"Certainly," I said, "but it's difficult, there is so little life."

The man put on his cap again, glanced round, then looked down into the black, empty tunnel leading to the platforms. The entire little station was dead. Then he looked at me again, pulled out his tin of tobacco, and asked: "Roll or fill?"

"Roll," I said.

He offered me the open tin and filled his pipe with his broad thumb, while I deftly rolled myself a cigarette.

I sat down at his feet on the floor of the little booth where he usually sits, and we smoked in silence while the clock hand over our heads moved quietly on. The soft sound came to me almost like the purring of a cat ... "Well," he said suddenly, "if you don't mind waiting for the eleven-thirty, you're welcome to sleep at my place. Where are you going anyway?"

"To Sperling."

"Who's that?"

"A man who sometimes gives me money to buy life."

"For nothing?"

"No," I said, "I sell him a piece of my life, and he prints it in his newspaper."

"Oh," he cried, "he has a newspaper?"

"Yes," I said.

"In that case," he said," ... in that case," and he pensively spat out the juice of his pipe, barely missing my head, "... in that case ... "

We were silent again in that semi-dark, musty station hall where the only sound was the gentle, steady purring of the clock hand, until the eleven-thirty arrived. An old woman and a pair of lovers passed through the barrier, then the man closed the iron grille, plucked my sleeve, and helped me up.

By the time we reached his little house, Friedenstadt was enveloped in darkness, and I knew: Sperling's brutish snoring had now reached its climax: it would be roaring through the house, making the windowpanes and the house plants tremble, but I still had a whole night ahead of me ...

UNCOLLECTED STORIES

Many of these stories were collected in Böll's 1979 Du fährst zu oft nach Heidelberg *(Too Many Trips to Heidelberg), which, though never published in English as stand-alone volume, was partially published in English translation as part of the* The Stories of Heinrich Böll, *published by Knopf in 1986.* "Christmas Not Just Once a Year" *was first published in Germany in 1952.*

A number of these stories were first published in translation in American magazines. "The Staech Affair" *and* "No Tears for Schmeck" *were first published in* Encounter. *English translations of* "Rendezvous with Margret or: Happy Ending" *and* "On Being Courteous When Compelled to Break the Law" *both first appeared in* Harper's Magazine, *in the September 1979 and March 1981 issues.* "Confession of a Hijacker" *was first published in English in the October 8, 1978, issue of* The New Yorker.

ADVENTURES OF A HAVERSACK

In September 1914 a man by the name of Joseph Stobski was called up for military service in one of the red brick barracks at Bromberg. Although according to his papers he was a German citizen, he had only a smattering of the mother tongue of his official fatherland. Stobski was twenty-two years old, a watchmaker, and, for reasons of "constitutional debility," had not yet performed any military service. He came from a sleepy little Polish-speaking place called Niestronno, where he had spent his days working in a back room of his father's cottage, tracing designs on gold-plated bracelets—delicate designs—repairing the farmers' watches, and at intervals feeding the pig, milking the cow. In the evenings, when darkness fell over Niestronno, he hadn't gone off to the tavern, hadn't gone to a dance, but had sat stewing over an invention, his oily fingers fiddling with innumerable little wheels and rolling cigarettes—almost all of which he allowed to burn out on the edge of the table—while his mother counted the eggs and complained about the consumption of kerosene.

So now he moved with his cardboard box into the red brick barracks at Bromberg and learned German insofar as it covered the vocabulary of regulations, orders, and rifle parts; he was also familiarized with the trade of infantryman. During instruction, he said "brrett" instead of "bread," "canonn" instead of "cannon"; he cursed in Polish, prayed in Polish; and in the evening he would look gloomily into his dark-brown locker at the little package containing the oily wheels before going off into town to wash down his justified sorrows with schnapps.

He swallowed the sand of Tuchel Heath, wrote postcards to his mother, received bacon from home, managed to get out of regulation church service on Sundays, and would sneak into one of the Polish churches where he could throw himself down onto the tiled floor and weep and pray, although such fervor was ill-suited to anyone wearing the uniform of a Prussian infantryman.

By November 1914 Stobski was considered sufficiently trained to rank as fit to make the journey all across Germany to Flanders. He had thrown sufficient hand grenades into the sand of Tuchel Heath, he had banged away sufficiently often in the rifle ranges, and he sent off the little package containing the oily wheels to his mother, along with a postcard. He was then stuffed into a cattle car and started out on the journey all across his official fatherland, whose mother tongue, insofar as it covered orders, he had learned to master. He allowed rosy-cheeked German girls to pour him coffee and stick flowers into his rifle, he accepted cigarettes, was once even kissed by an elderly woman; and a man wearing a pince-nez who was leaning on a barrier at a railroad crossing called out to him in a very distinct voice a few Latin words of which Stobski understood only *tandem*. For help with this word he turned to his immediate superior, Corporal Habke, who in turn mumbled something about "bicycles," declining any further information. Thus the unwitting Stobski, kissing and being kissed, showered with flowers, chocolate, and cigarettes, crossed the Oder, Elbe, and Rhine rivers, and after ten days was unloaded in the dark at a dingy Belgian railway station. His company assembled in a farmyard, and the captain shouted something in the dark that Stobski didn't understand. Next came stew with noodles to be quickly gulped down from a field kitchen in an ill-lit barn. Sergeant Pilling once again made the rounds and took a brief roll call, and ten minutes later the company marched off in the night toward the west. From that western sky there came the notorious thunderous roar, the sky being intermittently lit up by reddish flashes, and it began to rain. The company left the road, and some hundred and fifty pairs of feet plodded along muddy cart tracks. The artificial thunderstorm came closer and closer, the voices of the officers and sergeants grew hoarse and acquired a disagreeable undertone. Stobski's feet hurt, hurt him very much; besides, he was tired, very tired, but he dragged himself on, through dark villages, along muddy paths, and the closer they came to the thunderstorm the more odious, the more artificial, it sounded. Then the voices of the officers and sergeants became strangely gentle, almost mild, and from left and right came the sound of countless feet tramping along invisible paths and roads.

Stobski realized that they were now in the very heart of that artificial thunderstorm, in fact had actually left some of it behind, for ahead as well as behind them there were reddish flashes. When the order came to fan out, he left the path and ran off to the right, keeping close to Corporal Habke. He could hear shouting, banging, shooting, and now the voices of the officers and sergeants were hoarse again. Stobski's feet still hurt, hurt him very much, and leaving Habke to his own devices he sat down in a wet meadow that smelled of cow dung and thought something that in Polish might have been an approximation of the French word *merde*. He removed his steel helmet, put down his rifle beside him in the grass, unhooked his pack, thought about his beloved oily wheels, and, surrounded by the din of battle, fell asleep. He dreamed of his Polish mother making pancakes in the little warm kitchen, and in his dream it struck him as odd that as soon as the pancakes seemed to be almost ready they exploded in the pan with a bang, and nothing was left of them. His little mother kept ladling dough into the pan, faster and faster; little pancakes would form, bursting an instant before they were ready, and in a sudden rage his little mother—in his dream Stobski had to smile, for his little mother had never really been in a rage—had poured the entire remaining contents of the mixing bowl into the frying pan. Now a great fat yellow pancake lay there, as big as the frying pan, thickened, turned crisp, swelled; Stobski's little mother was already beaming with satisfaction as she picked up the spatula, slid it under the pancake, and—boom!—there was an especially horrible bang, and Stobski had no time to be wakened by it, for he was dead.

A week later, a quarter of a mile from the spot where Stobski had been killed by a direct hit, soldiers from his company found his haversack, together with a piece of his shredded belt, in an English trench: all that was ever found of him on this earth. And when Stobski's haversack containing a piece of homemade hard sausage, his iron rations, and a Polish prayer book were found in this English trench, it was assumed that on the day of the assault Stobski had run with incredible heroism deep into the English lines and been killed there. And so the little Polish mother in Niestronno received a letter from Captain Hummel, informing her of the great heroism of Private Stobski. The little mother had the letter translated by her priest, wept, folded up the letter, laid it between the sheets in her closet, and ordered three Masses for the dead.

But quite suddenly the English reconquered this section of the trench, and Stobski's haversack fell into the hands of the English soldier

Wilkins Grayhead, who ate up the sausage, looked at the Polish prayer book, and with a shake of his head threw it into the Flanders mud. Then he rolled up the haversack and stowed it away in his own pack. Two days later Grayhead lost his left leg; he was transported to London, discharged nine months later from the British army, granted a small pension, and, being no longer able to pursue the honorable occupation of tram driver, found employment as a commissionaire at a London bank.

Now, the wages of a commissionaire are not munificent, and Wilkins Grayhead had brought back two vices from the war: he drank and he smoked, and, since his income was inadequate, he began to sell articles he found superfluous, and he found almost everything superfluous. He sold his furniture, drank up the proceeds, sold his clothes except for a single shabby suit, and, when he had nothing left to sell, bethought himself of the dirty bundle he had put away in the cellar after his discharge. So now he sold the rusting army pistol he had neglected to turn in, a tarpaulin, a pair of shoes, and Stobski's haversack. (As for Wilkins Grayhead, to put it very briefly: he went to the dogs. A hopeless alcoholic, he forfeited respect and job, turned to crime, and, in spite of his lost leg that was reposing in Flanders soil, landed in prison where, corrupt to the marrow, he dragged out the rest of his life as a stool pigeon.)

Stobski's haversack, however, remained in the gloomy vaults of a Soho junk dealer for exactly ten years—until 1926. In the summer of that year, the junk dealer, Luigi Banollo by name, read with close attention a letter from a certain firm called Handsuppers Ltd. which displayed such obvious interest in war surplus of all kinds that Banollo rubbed his hands. Together with his son he searched through his entire inventory and brought to light: 27 army pistols, 58 mess kits, more than 100 tarpaulins, 35 knapsacks, 18 haversacks, and 28 pairs of shoes—all from a wide variety of European armies. For this entire consignment Banollo received a check for 810 pounds sterling drawn on one of the soundest banks in London. Banollo had made a profit of roughly five hundred percent while Banollo junior saw the disappearance of the shoes with a relief that almost defies description, for it had been his responsibility to knead, grease, in short look after those shoes, a responsibility the extent of which is obvious to anyone who has ever had to look after even a single pair of shoes.

Handsuppers Ltd. then proceeded to sell, at a profit of eight hundred and fifty percent (their normal margin), all the items they had bought from Banollo to a South American state that three weeks previously had suddenly realized that it was being threatened by a neighboring state and was now determined to forestall this threat. Private Stobski's haversack, having survived the crossing to South America in the hold of a tramp steamer (the firm of Handsuppers made use of tramp steamers only), fell into the hands of a German by the name of Reinhold von Adams, who had espoused the cause of that South American state for a bounty of forty-five pesetas. Von Adams had spent only twelve of the forty-five pesetas on drink when he was requested to live up to his commitment and, under the command of General Lalango, advance to the border of the neighboring state with the cry of "Victory and loot!" on his lips. But Adams received a bullet smack in the center of his head, and Stobski's haversack passed into the possession of a German called Wilhelm Habke, who, for a bounty of only thirty-five pesetas, had espoused the cause of the other South American state. Habke appropriated the haversack and the remaining thirty-three pesetas and found in addition a piece of bread and half an onion, which had already transferred its odor to the peseta bills. But Habke's ethical and aesthetic scruples were minimal; he added his own bounty and obtained an advance of thirty pesetas after being promoted to corporal in the victorious national army. On opening the flap of the haversack and discovering it to be stamped in black ink with the number "VII/2/II", he remembered his uncle Joachim Habke, who had served in that regiment and been killed. Wilhelm Habke was overcome by violent homesickness. He retired from the army, was presented with a photograph of General Gublanez, and eventually arrived in Berlin. When he took the streetcar from the Zoo station to Spandau, he rode—unwittingly—past the army ordnance department where Stobski's haversack had lain for a week in 1914 before being sent to Bromberg.

Habke was joyously welcomed by his parents and resumed his real occupation, that of a dispatcher; but it soon became apparent that he tended toward political errors. In 1929 he joined the party, with its ugly, dung-colored uniforms, and took down the haversack that he had hung beside the picture of General Gublanez on the wall over his bed to turn it to account for practical purposes: he wore it with his

dung-colored uniform when he went off to Sunday training periods on
the heath. During these exercises Habke shone with his military knowledge: he boasted quite a bit, promoted himself to battalion commander
in that South American war, and explained in detail where, how, and
why he had deployed his heavy weapons at the time. He had totally
forgotten that all he had done was shoot poor von Adams in the head,
rob him of his pesetas, and appropriate his haversack. In 1929 Habke
married, and in 1930 his wife bore him a son, who was given the name
Walter. Walter throve, although his first two years in life were spent
under the sign of the dole; but by the time he was four years old he was
already being given cookies, canned milk, and oranges every morning,
and when he was seven, his father presented him with the faded haversack, saying, "Treat this object with respect. It used to belong to your
great-uncle Joachim Habke, who rose from the ranks to be a captain,
survived eighteen battles, and was executed by Red mutineers in 1918.
I myself wore it in the South American war, in which I was only a lieutenant colonel although I could have become a general if the Fatherland
hadn't had need of me."

Walter venerated the haversack. He wore it with his own dung-
colored uniform from 1936 to 1944, frequently recalled his heroic great-
uncle and his heroic father, and, when he had to spend the night in a
barn, placed the haversack carefully under his head. In it he kept bread,
soft cheese, butter, and his army song book; he brushed it, washed it,
and was happy to see the faded tan gradually turn to soft white. He had
no idea that the legendary heroic great-uncle had died as a corporal on
muddy Flanders soil, not far from the place where a direct hit had killed
Private Stobski.

Walter Habke turned fifteen, laboriously studied English, math,
and Latin at Spandau High School, venerated the haversack, and
believed in heroes until he was forced to be one himself. His father had
departed some time before for Poland, to create some kind of order
somewhere, and shortly after his father had returned, fuming, from
Poland, smoking cigarettes and muttering "Betrayal" as he paced up
and down the cramped Spandau living room—shortly after that, Walter
Habke was forced to be a hero.

One night in March 1945 he lay behind a machine gun on the
outskirts of a Pomeranian village, listening to the dark, thunderous

rumbling that sounded exactly as it had in the movies; he pressed the trigger of the machine gun, shot holes into the dark night, and felt an urge to weep. He heard voices in the night, unfamiliar voices, went on shooting, inserted a new belt, fired, and after emptying the second belt it struck him that everything was very quiet: he was alone. He stood up, adjusted his uniform belt, made sure he had his haversack, and walked slowly off into the night toward the west. He had started to do something that is very injurious to heroism: he had started to think—he thought of the cramped but cozy living room, without knowing that he was thinking of something that no longer existed. By this time young Banollo, who had at one time held Walter's haversack in his hand, was forty, had circled in a bomber over Spandau, opened the bomb hatch, and destroyed the cramped but cozy living room, and now Walter's father was pacing up and down in the cellar of the next-door house, smoking cigarettes, muttering "Betrayal," and feeling uncomfortable at the thought of the order he had created in Poland.

That night, Walter walked on pensively toward the west, finally found an abandoned barn, sat down, pulled the haversack around onto his stomach, opened it up, and ate some army bread, margarine, and a few candies. That was how the Russian soldiers found him: asleep, with tearstained face, a fifteen-year-old boy, empty cartridge belts around his neck, his breath smelling sourly of candy. They shoved him into a column, and Walter Habke marched eastward. Never again was he to see Spandau.

Meanwhile, Niestronno had been German, become Polish, become German again, then Polish again, and Stobski's mother was seventy-five years old. The letter from Captain Hummel still lay in the closet that had long since ceased to contain any linen: Frau Stobski used it to store potatoes; behind the potatoes were a big ham and a china bowl full of eggs, and right at the back, in the darkness, a can of oil. Wood was stacked under the bed, and on the wall an oil lamp spread a reddish glow over the picture of the Madonna of Czestochowa. Back in the stable lolled a thin pig, there was no longer a cow, and the house was filled with the racket of the seven children of the Wolniaks, who had been bombed out of their home in Warsaw. And outside on the road they came trudging by: exhausted, footsore soldiers with pinched faces. They passed by almost every day. At first Wolniak had stood at the roadside, cursing, from time to time picking up a rock, even throwing it; but now he stayed back in his room, where Joseph Stobski had once repaired watches, engraved bracelets, and fiddled around in the evening with his little oily wheels.

In 1939 Polish prisoners of war had trudged past them toward the east, other Polish prisoners toward the west; later, Russian prisoners had trudged past them toward the west, and now for a long time German prisoners had been trudging past them toward the east, and although the nights were still cold and dark, and deep was the sleep of the people of Niestronno, they still woke up at night at the sound of the soft tramping on the roads.

Frau Stobski was one of the first to get up in the morning at Niestronno. She put a coat over her pale-green nightgown, lit the fire in the stove, poured oil into the little lamp in front of the Madonna's picture, carried the ashes to the manure pile, fed the thin pig, then went back into her room to change for Mass. And one morning in April 1945 she found lying outside her front door a very young, fair-haired man with a faded haversack clutched firmly in both hands. Frau Stobski did not scream. She put down the black string bag in which she kept a Polish prayer book, a handkerchief, and a few fragments of thyme—she put down the bag on the window sill, bent down to the young man, and saw immediately that he was dead. Even now she did not scream. It was still dark, with just a faint yellow flicker behind the church windows, and Frau Stobski carefully removed the haversack from the dead man's hands, the haversack that at one time had contained her son's prayer book and a piece of hard sausage from one of her pigs. She dragged the boy inside onto the tiled floor, went into her room, taking along—as if absent-mindedly—the haversack, threw the haversack on the table, and searched through the bundle of dirty, almost worthless zloty bills. Then she set out for the village to rouse the gravedigger.

Later, after the boy had been buried, she found the haversack on her table, picked it up, hesitated—then went to look for a hammer and two nails, banged the nails into the wall, hung up the haversack, and decided to store her onions in it.

If she had only opened the haversack a little wider and raised the flap completely, she would have discovered on it the same number stamped in black ink as had appeared at the top of Captain Hummel's letter.

But she never opened the haversack that wide.

CHRISTMAS NOT JUST ONCE A YEAR

I

Among our relatives, symptoms of disintegration are beginning to show up that for a while we tried silently to ignore but the threat of which we are now determined to face squarely. I do not yet dare use the word "collapse," but the alarming facts are accumulating to the point where they represent a threat and compel me to speak of things that may sound strange to the ears of my contemporaries but whose reality no one can dispute. The mildew of decay has obtained a foothold under the thick, hard veneer of respectability, colonies of deadly parasites heralding the end of the integrity of an entire clan. Today we must regret having ignored the voice of our cousin Franz, who long ago began to draw attention to the terrible consequences of what was on the face of it a harmless event. This event was in itself so trivial that we are now shocked by the extent of its consequences. Franz warned us long ago. Unfortunately he lacked prestige in the family. He had chosen an occupation that had never before been pursued, would never have been permitted to be pursued, by any member of our entire clan: he became a boxer. Of a brooding melancholy even in his youth, and of a piety always described as "a pose of religious zeal," he set out early on paths that caused my Uncle Franz—that kindest of men—deep concern. It was Franz's wont to stay away from school with a frequency that could no longer be described as normal. He met regularly with shady characters in remote parks and dense undergrowth on the outskirts of town, where they practiced the tough rules of fistfighting, showing no concern for the fact that their humanistic heritage was being neglected. Already these young toughs were demonstrating the bad habits of their generation—one that has, needless to say, turned out to be good for nothing. The thrilling intellectual battles of previous centuries did not interest them, so totally were they preoccupied with the dubious thrills of their own century. At first, Franz's piety struck me as being incompatible with these regular exercises in passive and active brutality. But today, certain things are beginning to dawn on me. I shall have to return to this later.

So it was Franz who issued a timely warning, who dissociated himself from certain celebrations, describing it all as affectation and a pain in the neck, above all later refusing to participate in measures deemed necessary to preserve what he called a pain in the neck. However—as I have said—his prestige was not high enough for him to find a hearing among his relatives.

But now things have got so out of hand that we are at a total loss, not knowing how to put a curb on them.

Franz has long since become a famous boxer, yet today he rejects the praise heaped upon him by the family with the same indifference with which he at one time refused to accept any criticism.

His brother, however, my cousin Johannes—a man for whom I would at any time have vouched, a successful attorney, my uncle's favorite son—is said to have become involved with the Communist Party, a rumor I obstinately refuse to believe. My cousin Lucie, until now a normal woman, is said to spend her nights in disreputable places, accompanied by her helpless spouse, at dances for which I can find no other adjective than "existentialist." Even Uncle Franz, that kindest of men, is supposed to have said that he is tired of life—a man who was regarded by the entire clan as a model of vitality and as a paragon of what we have been taught to call a Christian businessman.

Medical bills pile up; psychiatrists, psychologists, are called in. Only my Aunt Milla, who must be cited as the originator of all these phenomena, enjoys the best of health, smiles, is as well and cheerful as she has almost always been. Her bright, cheery manner is now, after our years of heartfelt concern for her well-being, slowly beginning to get on our nerves. For there was a crisis in her life that threatened to become alarming. This is where I will have to go into more detail.

II

It is simple enough with hindsight to discern the origin of a disquieting trend—and, strangely enough, it is only now, when I observe the situation pragmatically, that the things which have been occurring in the family for almost two years seem unusual.

It might have struck us earlier that something was not right. In fact, something wasn't right, and if anything at all has ever been right—which I doubt—here things are occurring that fill me with horror. Throughout the family, Aunt Milla had always been known for her particular fondness for decorating the Christmas tree, a harmless if particular weakness that is fairly widespread in our Fatherland. Her weakness met with smiles all around, and the resistance displayed by Franz from his earliest youth to this "to-do" was always the object of vehement indignation, especially since Franz cut a disquieting figure anyway. He refused to help decorate the tree. Up to a certain point, all this took a normal course. My aunt had become accustomed to Franz's staying away from the pre-Christmas preparations, even from the actual celebration, appearing only for Christmas dinner. It was no longer even discussed.

At the risk of making myself unpopular, I must now mention a fact in defense of which I can only say that it really is one. During the years 1939 to 1945 there was a war on. In wartime there is a lot of singing, shooting, talking, fighting, starving, and dying—and bombs are dropped, all disagreeable things with which I have no intention of boring my contemporaries. I must merely mention them because the war had a bearing on the story I wish to tell. For the war was registered by my Aunt Milla merely as a force that began as early as Christmas 1939 to jeopardize her Christmas tree. Admittedly, her Christmas tree was unusually vulnerable.

The main attractions on my Aunt Milla's Christmas tree were glass dwarfs holding a cork hammer in their uplifted arms with a bell-shaped anvil at their feet. Under the dwarfs' feet, candles were affixed, and upon a certain temperature being reached, a hidden mechanism was set in motion, a hectic agitation was communicated to the dwarfs' arms, with their cork hammers they flailed away like crazy at the bell-shaped anvils, thus, since they were about a dozen in number, producing a concerted elfin tinkling. Furthermore: from the tip of the Christmas tree hung a red-cheeked angel in a silvery dress, and at regular intervals the angel parted its lips to whisper "Peace," and again, "Peace." The mechanical secret of this angel, obstinately guarded, became known to me much later, although at the time I had the opportunity almost every week of admiring it. In addition, of course, my aunt's Christmas tree was also bedecked with sugar rings, cookies, angel hair, marzipan fig- ures, and—last but not least—silver tinsel; and I can still remember that properly attaching the various ornaments took a great deal of effort, requiring the participation of the entire family, so that on Christmas Eve frayed nerves cost us all our appetite, and the mood was then—as one says—dismal, except in the case of my cousin Franz, who, of course, had taken no part in these preparations and was the only one to enjoy the roast and the asparagus, the whipped cream and ice cream.

When we duly arrived, then, for a visit the day after Christmas, and risked the bold assumption that the secret of the talking angel was based on the same mechanism that caused certain dolls to say "Mama" or "Papa," the only response was mocking laughter. Now it is easy to imagine that bombs falling close by posed an extreme hazard to such a vulnerable tree. There were terrible scenes when the dwarfs fell off the tree, and once even the angel toppled to the ground. My aunt was inconsolable. After every air raid she went to endless trouble to restore the tree completely and to maintain it at least over the Christmas holi- days. But even in 1940 it was already a hopeless task. Again at the risk of making myself very unpopular, I must mention in passing that the number of air raids on our city was indeed considerable, to say nothing of their violence. At any rate, my aunt's Christmas tree fell victim—the thread of my narrative forbids my mentioning other victims—to modern warfare; foreign ballistic experts temporarily snuffed out its existence.

We were all genuinely sorry for our aunt, who was a charming, gracious woman. We felt sorry that, after bitter struggles, endless argu- ments, after many tears and scenes, she had to agree to renounce her tree for the duration of the war.

Fortunately—or should I say unfortunately?—that was almost the only impact the war had on her. The shelter built by my uncle was bombproof; moreover, there was always an automobile ready to whisk my Aunt Milla away to areas where nothing was to be seen of the immediate effects of the war. Everything was done to spare her the sight of the appalling destruction. My two cousins were lucky enough not to have to do their war service in its most rigorous form. Johannes quickly joined his uncle's business, which played a crucial role in supplying our city with vegetables. Moreover, he had a chronic gallbladder complaint. Franz, on the other hand, although he became a soldier, was entrusted only with guarding prisoners, an assignment he utilized to render himself unpopular with his military superiors—by treating Russians and Poles as human beings. In those days my cousin Lucie was still unmarried and helped in the business. One afternoon a week she did volunteer war work at a factory that embroidered swastikas. But this is not the place to enumerate the political sins of my relatives.

Anyway, all in all there was no lack of money or food or whatever was necessary for protection, and the only thing my aunt bitterly resented was having to give up her tree. My Uncle Franz, that kindest of men, spent almost fifty years acquiring considerable merit and profit by buying up oranges and lemons in tropical and subtropical countries and selling them with a suitable markup. During the war he expanded his business to include less valuable fruits and vegetables. But after the war the gratifying produce that was his main interest was once again available, and citrus fruit became the object of keenest interest at every level. At this point Uncle Franz succeeded in regaining his former influential position, and he was able to provide the population with the enjoyment of vitamins and himself with that of a respectable fortune.

But he was almost seventy and wanted to retire, to hand over the business to his son-in-law. That is when the event occurred which at the time we smiled at but which today seems to us to have been the cause of the whole wretched sequence of events.

My Aunt Milla started in about the Christmas tree again. That was harmless enough; even the perseverance with which she insisted that everything was to be "like in the old days" merely drew smiles from us. At first there was really no reason to take it all that seriously. Although the war had destroyed so much of which the restoration caused greater concern, why—we said to ourselves—deny a charming old lady this trifling pleasure?

Everyone knows how difficult it was at that time to obtain such things as butter and bacon. But even for my Uncle Franz, who enjoyed the best of connections, it was impossible in 1945 to obtain marzipan figures, chocolate rings, and candles. It was not until 1946 that all these things could be provided. Fortunately, a complete set of dwarfs and anvils as well as an angel had survived.

I well remember the day we were invited to my uncle's home. It was in January 1947, and bitterly cold outside. But indoors it was warm, and there was no shortage of things to eat. And when the lights were put out, the candles lit, when the dwarfs began to hammer, the angel whispered "Peace," and again, "Peace," I felt transported back into an era that I had assumed to be past.

Nevertheless, this experience, although surprising, was not extraordinary. What *was* extraordinary was the experience I had three months later. My mother—it was now the middle of March—had sent me over to find out whether there was anything my Uncle Franz "could do": she was looking for fruit. I strolled through the streets to the part of town where my uncle lived; the air was mild, it was dusk. All unsuspecting, I walked past overgrown piles of rubble and neglected parks and, opening the gate to my uncle's garden, stopped, dumbfounded. In the quiet of the evening, the sound of singing was clearly audible, coming from my uncle's living room. Singing is a good old German custom, and there are many songs about spring, but now I could clearly hear "Holy infant, so tender and mild..."

I must admit to being confused. Slowly I approached the house, waiting for the singing to end. The curtains were drawn shut; I bent down to the keyhole. At that moment the tinkling of the dwarfs' bells reached my ear, and I could clearly hear the whispering of the angel. I didn't have the courage to intrude, and walked slowly back home. In the family, my account produced general merriment. But it was not until Franz appeared and gave us the details that we found out what had happened.

Around Candlemas, the time when in our part of the country the Christmas trees are stripped and then thrown on the garbage pile, where they are picked up by good-for-nothing children to be dragged through ashes and other rubbish, and used for various games—it was around Candlemas that the terrible thing happened. When my cousin Johannes, on Candlemas Eve, after the tree had been lit for the last time, began to detach the dwarfs from their clips, my aunt, until then such a gentle soul, set up a pitiful wail, a wail so violent and sudden that my cousin was startled, and lost control over the gently swaying tree. Then it happened: there was a tinkling and a ringing, dwarfs and bells, anvils and all-surmounting angel—everything crashed to the floor, and my aunt screamed.

She screamed for almost a week. Neurologists were summoned by telegram, psychiatrists came racing up in taxis—but all, even the most famous of them, left the house shrugging their shoulders, although also somewhat alarmed. None of them had been able to put a stop to that shrill, discordant concert. Only the strongest medication yielded a few hours of quiet; however, the dose of Luminal that can be given daily to a sixty-year-old woman without endangering her life is unfortunately rather small. But it is torture to have in the house a woman screaming at the top of her voice; by the second day the family was already totally distraught. Even the comforting words of the priest, who always celebrated Christmas Eve with the family, had no effect: my aunt screamed.

Franz made himself especially unpopular by suggesting a regular exorcism. The priest scolded him, the family was dismayed by his medieval views, and for a few weeks his reputation for brutality outweighed his reputation as a boxer.

Meanwhile everything was being tried to relieve my aunt of her condition. She refused food, did not speak, did not sleep; they tried cold water, hot foot-baths, hot and cold compresses, and the doctors searched through their reference works looking for a name for this neurosis, but could not find it.

And my aunt screamed. She went on screaming until my Uncle Franz—really the kindest of men—hit on the idea of setting up a new Christmas tree.

III

The idea was excellent, but its execution proved to be extremely difficult. By this time it was almost the middle of February, and it is fairly difficult to find an acceptable Christmas tree for sale at that time. The entire business world has long since shifted—with gratifying speed, by the way—to other things. Carnival is approaching: masks and pistols, cowboy hats and crazy headdresses for Czardas princesses fill the store windows where earlier one had been able to admire angels and angel hair, candles and Nativity scenes. The confectionery stores have long since moved their Christmas items back into their storerooms, whereas carnival crackers now adorn their windows. In any event, Christmas trees are not available at this time of year on the regular market.

Eventually an expedition of rapacious grandchildren was equipped with pocket money and a sharp ax. These young people rode out into the state forest and returned late that afternoon, obviously in the best of moods, with a silver fir. But meanwhile it had been discovered that four dwarfs, six bell-shaped anvils, and the all-surmounting angel had been completely destroyed. The marzipan figures and the cookies had fallen victim to the greedy grandchildren. So this generation too, now growing up, is good for nothing; and if ever a generation has been good for something—which I doubt—I have come to the conclusion that it was the generation of our fathers.

Although there was no lack of cash, or of the necessary contacts, it took another four days to assemble all the accessories. Throughout this time, my aunt screamed incessantly. Telegrams to the German toy centers, which were just beginning to get back on their feet, were sent winging through the ether, urgent long-distance calls were made, express packages were delivered during the night by perspiring young postal assistants, bribery ensured an import license from Czechoslovakia at short notice.

Those days will be remembered in the annals of my uncle's family as days of an exceptionally high consumption of coffee, cigarettes, and nerves. Meanwhile my aunt was wasting away: her round face became hard and angular, her mild expression gave way to one of unyielding severity, she did not eat, did not drink, she screamed incessantly, was watched over by two nurses, and the dose of Luminal had to be increased every day.

Franz told us that the entire family was in the grip of a pathological tension when at last, on February 12, the Christmas tree decorations were once again complete. The candles were lit, the curtains drawn, my aunt was brought from her sickroom, and among those assembled only sobs and giggles were to be heard. My aunt's expression began to relax in the light of the candles, and, upon the right degree of warmth being reached, the little glass fellows started hammering away like crazy, and finally the angel whispered "Peace," and again, "Peace," the most beautiful smile lit up my aunt's face, and almost at once the whole family would strike up "O Christmas Tree!" In order to complete the picture, the priest had also been invited, since he normally spent Christmas Eve at Uncle Franz's. He too smiled; he too was relieved and joined in the singing.

No test, no psychologist's expertise, no specialist's disclosure of hidden traumata, had achieved it, but the sensitive heart of my uncle had hit upon the right thing. The Christmas tree therapy of that kindest of men had saved the situation.

My aunt had calmed down and was almost—it was hoped at the time—cured. After a few carols had been sung, a few dishes of cookies emptied, everyone was tired and withdrew for the night, and lo and behold: my aunt fell asleep without any tranquilizer. The two nurses were dismissed, the doctors shrugged their shoulders, everything seemed to be back to normal. My aunt was eating again, drinking again, was once again gracious and gentle. But the following evening, as the twilight hour approached, my uncle was sitting reading the paper beside his wife next to the tree, when she suddenly touched his arm gently and said, "So now let's light the candles and call in the children, I think it's time to begin." Later my uncle admitted to us that he was startled but that he got up to summon his children and grandchildren as quickly as possible and to send word to the priest. The priest arrived, somewhat out of breath and surprised, but the candles were lit, the dwarfs made to hammer, the angel was made to whisper, carols were sung, cookies were eaten—and everything seemed to be back to normal.

IV

Now, all vegetation is subject to certain biological laws, and fir trees, when uprooted from their soil, are known to have the devastating tendency to drop their needles, especially when they are standing in warm rooms, and at my uncle's it was always warm. The life span of the silver fir is somewhat longer than that of the common fir, as has been proved in the well-known treatise *Abies vulgaris and abies nobilis*, by Dr. Hergenring. However, even the life span of the silver fir is not unlimited. With the approach of the carnival season, it became apparent that an attempt must be made to subject my aunt to new distress: the tree was rapidly losing its needles, and during the evening carol singing a slight frown was noticed on my aunt's forehead. At the advice of a really outstanding psychologist, the attempt was now made to speak, in a casual conversational tone, of a possible end to the Christmas season, especially now that trees were beginning to put forth their leaves, something generally acknowledged to be an indication of approaching spring, whereas in our latitudes the word "Christmas" is unquestionably associated with conceptions of winter. My very astute uncle suggested one evening that everyone join in singing the songs "Hark, the birds have all arrived!" and "Come, Lovely May," but even at the very first line of the first of those songs my aunt put on such a grim expression that everyone immediately broke off and intoned "O Christmas Tree!" Three days later, my cousin Johannes was instructed to undertake a mild act of spoliation; but no sooner had he reached out and taken the cork hammer from one of the dwarfs than my aunt started screaming so violently that the dwarf was immediately made whole again, the candles were lit, and, somewhat hastily but very loud, the carol "Silent Night" burst forth.

However, the nights were no longer silent. Loudly singing groups of youthful drunkards roamed through the city with trumpets and drums, everything was covered with streamers and confetti, and children in fancy dress filled the streets during the day, shooting, yelling, some of them singing too. According to private statistics there were at least sixty thousand cowboys and forty thousand Czardas princesses in our city. In short, it was carnival time, a feast we are accustomed to celebrate with a vigor equal to if not surpassing that of Christmas. But my aunt seemed to be blind and deaf: she deplored the carnival costumes that inevitably turn up in the clothes closets of our homes during this time; in a sad voice she complained of the decline of morality since people seemed unable, even during Christmastime, to refrain from these immoral goings-on; and when in my cousin's bedroom she discovered a balloon that, although deflated, still clearly showed a white jester's cap painted on it, she burst into tears and begged my uncle to put a stop to these unholy goings-on.

To its consternation, the family had to conclude that my aunt actually was under the delusion that it was "Christmas Eve." At any rate, my uncle called a family conclave, pleaded for forbearance toward his wife, consideration for her strange mental condition, and proceeded to organize another expedition in order at least to ensure the peace of the evening festivities.

While my aunt was asleep, the decorations were removed from the old tree and installed on the new one, and her condition remained gratifying.

V

But carnival time passed too, and spring really did arrive, and instead of the song "Come, Lovely May," one could have already sung "Lovely May, thou art now come." Then it was June. Four Christmas trees had already withered, and none of the more recently consulted doctors could promise any hope of improvement. My aunt was adamant. Even Dr. Bless, regarded as an international authority, had withdrawn with a shrug of his shoulders to his study after collecting his fee of 1,365 marks, thus supplying further evidence of his unworldliness. A few further, rather vague attempts to curtail or discontinue the celebration met with such screams on the part of my aunt that the family had once and for all to desist from such sacrilege.

The terrible part was that my aunt insisted on all those close to her being present. Among these were also the priest and the grandchildren. It was difficult enough to insist that members of the family turn up regularly, but the case of the priest presented still greater difficulties. For a few weeks, out of consideration for his old penitent, he had stuck it out without grumbling, but the time finally came when, with much hemming and hawing, he tried to explain to my uncle that the situation could not continue. Granted the actual ceremony was brief (it lasted some thirty-eight minutes), but in the long run even this brief ritual was becoming insupportable, the priest maintained. He had other obligations: evening gatherings with his confreres, parochial duties, to say nothing of taking confessions on Saturdays. For several weeks he had put up with having to rearrange his schedule, but toward the end of June he was making vigorous demands for his release. Franz went on the rampage in the family, looking for accomplices to his plan to have his mother placed in an institution, but he was met with rejection on all sides.

In short: problems began to mount. One evening the priest didn't show up, couldn't be reached by either telephone or messenger, and it became apparent that his absence was deliberate. My uncle cursed mightily, and he used the occasion to call the servants of the Church names that I must refuse to repeat. As a last resort, one of the curates, a person of humble origin, was asked to help out. He did so but behaved so appallingly that the result was almost a disaster. However, it must be borne in mind that it was June, in other words—hot; nevertheless, the curtains had been drawn shut in order at least to give the impression of winter darkness, and the candles had been lit. Then the ceremony began. Although the curate had already heard of these strange happenings, he could not really imagine them. With a good deal of trepidation, the family introduced the curate to my aunt, explaining that he was substituting for the priest. To their surprise she accepted this change in the program. So: the dwarfs hammered away, the angel whispered, "O Christmas Tree!" was sung, then cookies were eaten, the carol was sung again, and suddenly the curate was seized with uncontrollable laughter. Later he confessed that he hadn't been able to hear the line "...in winter too, when snowflakes fall," without laughing. He exploded with clerical foolishness, left the room, and was not seen again. Everyone looked breathlessly at my aunt, but in a resigned voice she merely said something about "yokels in priest's clothing," and popped a piece of marzipan into her mouth. At the time we too deplored the incident, but today I am inclined to call it an outburst of natural mirth.

At this point I must—if I am to do justice to the truth—insert that my uncle exploited his connections with the highest ecclesiastical authorities in order to complain about the priest as well as the curate. The matter was handled with the utmost punctiliousness; an action was brought over neglect of parochial duties and was won by both clerics. An appeal is still under consideration.

Fortunately a retired priest was found who lived in the neighborhood. This charming old gentleman graciously and unhesitatingly agreed to put himself at their disposal and complete the regular evening ritual. But I am anticipating. My Uncle Franz, who was sensible enough to realize that the situation was beyond any medical aid, and who also obstinately refused to attempt exorcism, was enough of a businessman to take the long view and to work out the most economical method. He began by putting a stop to the grandchildren's expeditions as early as mid-June, having established that they were costing too much. My ingenious cousin Johannes, who maintains excellent contacts with the business world at all levels, discovered the Fresh Christmas Tree Service provided by Söderbaum's, an efficient company that for the past two years has deserved high praise for relieving the nervous strain of my relatives. After only six months Söderbaum's converted the arrangement into an annual contract at a considerably reduced rate. Further, the company undertook to have the delivery dates precisely established by Dr. Alfast, their specialist in evergreen trees, so that now, three days before the old tree becomes unacceptable, the new one arrives and can be decorated at leisure. Furthermore, as a precautionary measure, two dozen dwarfs are kept in stock and three angels held in reserve. To this day, the confectionery has remained a sore point. It has a devastating tendency to melt and drip down from the tree, faster and more radically than melting wax. At least during the summer months. Every attempt to preserve their seasonal crispness by skillfully camouflaged cooling devices has so far failed, as has a series of experiments designed to test the possibility of embalming the tree. Nevertheless, the family is grateful for and open to any innovative suggestion that might reduce the cost of this permanent festivity.

VI

In the meantime, the evening ceremonies at my uncle's home have acquired an almost professional inflexibility: the family assembles at or around the tree. My aunt comes in, the candles are lit, the dwarfs begin to hammer, and the angel whispers "Peace, peace"; then a few carols are sung, cookies are nibbled, there is some casual conversation, and everyone retires with a yawn and a "Merry Christmas, everyone!"—at which point the young people turn to seasonal diversions while my kindly uncle and Aunt Milla go to bed. Candle smoke remains behind in the room, together with the mild aroma of heated fir branches and the spicy odor of Christmas cookies. The dwarfs, slightly phosphorescent, stand stiffly in the darkness, their arms raised menacingly, and the angel glows in its silvery robe, which is apparently also phosphorescent.

It may be superfluous to remark that the whole family's pleasure in the real Christmas festivities has been greatly diminished. We can, if we so wish, admire a traditional Christmas tree at any time in our uncle's home—and it often happens, when we are sitting on the veranda on a summer evening, after the labors of the day, imbibing Uncle's mild orange punch, that the tinkling of glass bells comes from within, and in the dusk the dwarfs are to be seen hammering away like nimble little devils, while the angel whispers "Peace," and again, "Peace." And we are still taken aback when, in the middle of summer, my uncle suddenly calls out to his children: "Light the tree, please, Mother will be here any minute." At that point, usually right on time, the prelate arrives, a mild old gentleman whom we have all taken to our hearts because he plays his part so beautifully, assuming he even knows he is playing a part and which part. But never mind: he plays it, white-haired, smiling, and the patch of purple below his collar lends the last touch of refinement to his personality. And it is an unusual experience to hear, on warm summer nights, the anxious cry "The candle snuffer—quick, where's the candle snuffer?" It has happened more than once that, during a violent thunderstorm, the dwarfs suddenly felt impelled, without the effect of heat, to raise their arms and swing them wildly, thus providing a kind of unscheduled concert, a fact that the family tried to explain, without much imagination, by the dry word "electricity."

One not wholly inconsiderable aspect of this arrangement is the financial one. Even though, generally speaking, our family is not strapped for cash, such extraordinary expenditures upset all calculations. For, despite every precaution, the wear and tear on dwarfs, anvils, and hammers is, of course, enormous; and the sensitive mechanism enabling the angel to speak requires constant care and maintenance and must from time to time be replaced. Incidentally, I have meanwhile discovered the secret: the angel is connected by a cable to a microphone in the next room, and in front of the mike there is a constantly rotating phonograph record that whispers at intervals "Peace," and again, "Peace." All these items are especially costly in that they are designed for use on only a few days in the year but now have to stand up to hard wear all year round. I was amazed when my uncle told me one day that the dwarfs had actually to be renewed every three months and that a complete set cost no less than a hundred and twenty-eight marks. He had asked an engineer friend of his to reinforce them with a latex coating but without impairing the beauty of their sound. This attempt failed. The consumption of candles, spekulatius, and marzipan, the tree contract, medical bills, and the token of appreciation due every month to the prelate: all that, said my uncle, amounts to a daily average of eleven marks, not to mention the wear and tear on his nerves and other impairments to his health that were then beginning to make themselves felt. But that was in the fall, and these deleterious effects were ascribed to a certain autumnal sensitivity, a matter of quite common observation.

VII

The actual Christmas celebrations went off normally. Something like a sigh of relief went through my uncle's family now that other families were to be seen gathered around Christmas trees, other families had also to sing and eat spekulatius. But the relief lasted only for the duration of the Christmas season. As early as mid-January my cousin Lucie was afflicted by a strange malady: at the sight of the Christmas trees lying around on streets and garbage piles, she would burst into hysterical sobbing. This was followed by a regular attack of madness, which the family tried to pass off as a nervous breakdown. When a friend with whom she was having afternoon coffee smilingly offered her some spekulatius, she knocked the plate out of her hand. It is true, of course, that my cousin is what is known as a temperamental woman; so she knocked the plate out of her friend's hand, walked over to the Christmas tree, ripped it from its stand, and trampled on the glass baubles, artificial mushrooms, candles, and stars, a continuous howl issuing from her lips. The assembled ladies fled, including the hostess, and Lucie was left to rampage while they waited in the hall for the doctor, listening perforce to china being smashed inside the room. I find it difficult, but I must report here that Lucie was taken away in a straitjacket.

Although repeated hypnotic treatments arrested the malady, the actual cure progressed very slowly. Above all, the release from the evening ceremony, on which the doctor insisted, seemed to have a noticeably beneficial effect; after only a few days she began to thrive. After only ten days the doctor could risk at least mentioning spekulatius, but she obstinately refused to eat any. The doctor hit on the brilliant idea of feeding her pickles, offering her salads and hearty meat dishes. That was really poor Lucie's salvation. She laughed again, and she began to spice the endless therapeutic conversations with her doctor by adding ironic comments.

Although the gap caused by Lucie's absence from the evening ceremony was painful for my aunt, it was explained by a circumstance that can be accepted as a valid excuse for all women—pregnancy.

But Lucie had created what is called a precedent: she had proved that, although our aunt suffered when someone was absent, she did not start screaming right away, and my cousin Johannes and his brother-in-law Karl now tried to break out of the strict discipline by pleading illness or business commitments, or offering other more or less transparent reasons. But here my uncle was surprisingly adamant: with relentless severity he stipulated that only in exceptional cases could doctors' certificates be submitted and the briefest of dispensations applied for. My aunt immediately noticed any additional gap and would break into quiet but persistent weeping, giving rise to the most ominous concern.

After a month, Lucie returned and expressed her willingness to rejoin the daily ritual, but her doctor has insisted that a jar of pickles and a plate of hearty sandwiches be kept in readiness for her, her spekulatius trauma having proved to be incurable. Thus for a while all disciplinary problems were resolved by my uncle, who on this point turned out to be surprisingly adamant.

VIII

Soon after the first anniversary of the perpetual Christmas celebration, disturbing rumors began to circulate: my cousin Johannes was said to have obtained an expert opinion from a medical friend as to the foreseeable life span of my aunt—a truly sinister rumor that threw a disquieting light on a peaceful daily family gathering. The expert opinion was said to have been devastating for Johannes. All the vital organs of my aunt, whose life has been a model of sobriety, are completely intact; the life span of her father extended over seventy-eight years, that of her mother over eighty-six. My aunt herself is sixty-two, and there is therefore no reason to prophesy an early and blessed demise for her. Even less, in my opinion, to wish it for her. So when my aunt fell ill during the summer—vomiting and diarrhea plagued the poor woman—there were whisperings that she had been poisoned; but let me expressly declare that this rumor is nothing but a figment on the part of evil-minded relatives. It has been proved beyond a doubt that she suffered from an infection brought in by a grandson. Analyses of my aunt's feces showed not even the slightest trace of poison.

That same summer the first antisocial tendencies showed up in Johannes: he resigned from his choral society, declaring, in writing, that he no longer intended to devote himself to the cultivation of German songs. It is true, of course—if I may interject this here—that, despite his academic degree, he was an uncultured person. For the male choir Virhymnia, being deprived of his bass voice was a great loss.

Lucie's husband, Karl, began secretly to get in touch with emigration offices. The land of his dreams had to have certain qualities: no fir trees must grow there, and their import must be prohibited or made impossible by high tariffs; furthermore—this for his wife's sake—the secret of baking spekulatius must be unknown there and the singing of Christmas carols prohibited. Karl declared his willingness to accept hard manual labor.

Meanwhile his attempts have been released from the curse of secrecy because my uncle has undergone a complete and abrupt change. This took place on such a disagreeable level that we had every reason to be shocked. That respectable man, of whom I can only say that he is as stubborn as he is kind, was observed on paths that are unquestionably immoral and will remain so as long as the world continues to exist. Various things have become known about him, and attested to by witnesses, to which only the word "adultery" can be applied. And the most terrible part about it is that he no longer denies it but claims that he is living under circumstances and conditions that must justify exceptional moral standards. Awkwardly enough, this sudden change came to light at the very time when the appeal against the two clerics of his parish was due to be heard. As a witness, as a crypto-plaintiff, Uncle Franz must have made such an unprepossessing impression that he can be considered solely to blame for the fact that the appeal turned out in favor of the two clerics. But by this time all such things have ceased to interest Uncle Franz: the moral disintegration of Uncle Franz is complete, a *fait accompli.*

He was also the first to hit upon the idea of having an actor represent him at the evening ritual. He had dug up an unemployed bon vivant who imitated him for two weeks so perfectly that not even his wife was aware of the substitution. His children were not aware of it either. It was one of the grandsons who, during a short pause in the singing, suddenly called out, "Grandpa's wearing striped socks!," at the same time triumphantly raising the bon vivant's trouser leg. For the poor artist, this scene must have been terrible. The family too were aghast, and, in order to avert a disaster, they immediately—as already so often in embarrassing situations—struck up a carol. After my aunt had gone to bed, the identity of the artist was quickly established. It was the signal for an almost total collapse.

IX

Still, one must bear in mind that eighteen months is a long time, and that midsummer had arrived again, the season in which my relatives find it hardest to participate in this charade. Listlessly they nibble in the heat at cinnamon stars and gingerbread, smiling fixedly while they crack dry nuts, listening to the tirelessly hammering dwarfs, and flinching when the red-cheeked angel whispers "Peace" above their heads, "Peace." But they carry on while, despite their summer clothing, the perspiration runs down their necks and cheeks and their shirts stick to their bodies. Or, rather, they used to carry on.

For the time being, money is no object—on the contrary, one might say. Now there are whispers that Uncle Franz has been resorting to business methods that virtually no longer permit the description "Christian businessman." He is determined not to allow any appreciable diminution of his fortune, a commitment that both reassures and alarms us.

The unmasking of the bon vivant led to a regular mutiny, the result of which was a compromise: Uncle Franz has undertaken to finance a small ensemble to replace himself, Johannes, my brother-in-law Karl, and Lucie; and an agreement has been reached whereby one of the four takes part in the evening ritual in person, in order to keep an eye on the children. So far the prelate has been quite unaware of this fraud, to which one can by no means apply the adjective "pious." Apart from my aunt and the children, he is the only original character in this charade.

A detailed plan has been worked out, known in the family as the "game plan"; and in view of the fact that one of them always does take part, the actors are also assured of certain free days. Meanwhile the family has noticed that the actors are not at all averse to lending themselves to the ritual and are happy to earn some extra money; consequently their fees have been successfully reduced, there being fortunately no lack of out-of-work actors. Karl has told me that there is a good chance of further reducing this item, and quite considerably, especially since the actors are offered a meal, and, as everybody knows, art doesn't put bread on the table.

X

I have already hinted at the disastrous trend taking place in Lucie: she now spends almost all her time gadding about in night spots, and, especially on days when she has been forced to take part in the ceremony at home, she throws all restraint to the winds. She wears cords, gaudy sweaters, runs around in sandals, and has cut off her glorious hair in favor of a plain square-cut style which, I now learn, has been in vogue more than once as "bangs." Although I have not yet been able to observe any overt immorality on her part, merely a certain exaltation that she herself calls "existentialism," I cannot see my way toward regarding this trend as desirable. I prefer women who are gentle, who move decorously to the rhythm of a waltz, who quote pleasant poetry, and whose diet does not consist exclusively of pickles and goulash overspiced with paprika. Karl's emigration plans seem to be crystallizing: he has discovered a country, not far from the equator, that promises to live up to his conditions, and Lucie is thrilled: in that country people wear clothes not unlike her own, love pungent spices, and dance to rhythms without which she maintains she is no longer able to live. Although it is somewhat shocking that this couple do not seem to cherish the idea of "Home, sweet home," I can understand their desire to get away from it all.

The situation with Johannes is even worse. Unfortunately the nasty rumor has turned out to be true: he has become a Communist. He has broken off all connection with his family, ignores all his obligations, and attends the evening ritual only by proxy: that of his double. His eyes have acquired a fanatical expression; he acts like a dervish at the public functions of his party, neglects his practice, and writes furious articles in appropriate journals. Strangely enough, he now quite often sees Franz, who tries vainly to convert him and whom he tries just as vainly to convert. Despite all spiritual alienation, they have grown somewhat closer on a personal level.

As for Franz, I have not seen him for a long time, only heard of him. He is said to have fallen into a deep depression, spending hours in dim churches, and I believe one is justified in describing his piety as exaggerated. He began to neglect his profession after his family became engulfed in its troubles; and just the other day I saw on the wall of a demolished building a faded poster announcing "Last fight of ex-champion Lenz vs. Lecoq. Lenz retiring from the ring." The poster was dated March, and we are now well into August. Franz is said to be in very poor shape. I believe he finds himself in a situation never before experienced in our family: he is poor. Fortunately he has remained single, so the social consequences of his irresponsible piety affect only himself. With amazing persistence he has been trying to arrange for Lucie's children to be placed under protective guardianship, believing as he does that they are threatened by the evening ritual. But his efforts have been in vain: we can be thankful that the children of well-to-do couples are not exposed to the interference of social institutions.

The one who has removed himself the least from the rest of the family is, in spite of some repulsive traits, Uncle Franz, although it is true that, in spite of his advanced age, he has a mistress, and his commercial practices are of a nature of which, while we may admire them, we can by no means approve. Recently he unearthed an out-of-work stage manager who supervises the evening ritual and sees to it that everything goes like clockwork. And it really does.

XI

Meanwhile almost two years have passed: a long time. And I could not refrain, on one of my evening strolls, from walking past my uncle's house, where normal hospitality is no longer possible, now that unknown artist types are milling around in there every evening and the members of the family indulge in strange-seeming amusements. It was a warm summer's evening when I passed by there, and even as I turned the corner into the chestnut avenue I could hear the words "Christmas glitter decks the forests..." A passing truck rendered the remainder inaudible. I crept slowly up to the house and looked through a gap in the curtains into the room: the resemblance of the playactors to the relatives they were representing was so startling that for a moment I could not make out who actually was in charge—as they call it—that evening. I could not see the dwarfs, but I could hear them. Their chirping tinkle is on wavelengths that penetrate every wall. The whispering of the angel was inaudible. My aunt seemed genuinely happy: she was chatting with the prelate, and it took a while for me to recognize my brother-in-law as the only, if I may so put it, real person. I recognized him by the way he puckered his lips when he blew out a match. There do seem to be unmistakable traits of individuality. It occurred to me that the actors are treated to cigars, cigarettes, and wine; moreover, asparagus is served every evening. If they take advantage of this—and which artist would not?—it means a considerable additional expense for my uncle. The children were playing with dolls and toy wagons in a corner of the room: they looked pale and wan. Perhaps something really should be done about them, after all. It occurred to me that they might be replaced by wax dummies, the kind used in drugstore windows to promote milk powder and skin cream. They always seem very lifelike to me.

So I decide to draw the attention of the family to the possible effects of this unusual daily stimulation on childish minds. Although, of course, a certain amount of discipline can do no harm, it would seem that inordinate demands are being placed upon them in this instance.

I left my observation post when they started to sing "Silent Night." I really couldn't stand that carol. The air was so mild—and for a moment I had the impression of being present at a gathering of ghosts.

I was suddenly seized by a craving for pickles, which gave me an inkling of how greatly Lucie must have suffered.

XII

Meanwhile I have been successful in having the children replaced by wax dummies. The acquisition proved to be expensive—Uncle Franz balked at it for a long time, but it would have been irresponsible to continue to allow the children to be fed marzipan every evening and make them sing carols that may eventually cause psychological damage. The acquisition of the dummies proved fortunate, since Karl and Lucie really did emigrate, and Johannes also withdrew his children from his father's household. Standing amid big steamer trunks, I said goodbye to Karl, Lucie, and the children; they seemed happy, although somewhat apprehensive. Johannes has also moved away from our city. He is busy somewhere reorganizing one of the regional branches of his party.

Uncle Franz is tired of life. In a plaintive voice he recently told me that they keep forgetting to dust the dummies. The servants are giving him enough trouble as it is, and the actors are beginning to get out of hand. They are drinking more than they are entitled to, and some of them have been caught pocketing cigars and cigarettes. I advised my uncle to serve them colored water and to obtain some cardboard cigars.

The only reliable ones are my aunt and the prelate. They chat about the good old days, titter, and seem to be having a good time, and they only break off their conversation when a carol is struck up.

In any event: the ritual is being continued.

My cousin Franz's career has taken a strange turn. He has been accepted as a lay brother in a nearby monastery. The first time I saw him in his monk's habit I got a shock: that tall figure with the broken nose and swollen lips, those brooding eyes—he reminded me more of a convict than of a monk. It almost seemed as if he had divined my thoughts. "Our life is our punishment," he said in a low voice. I followed him into the visitors' room. Our conversation was stiff and halting, and he was obviously relieved when the bell summoned him for prayers in the chapel. I stood there pensively as he left: he was hurrying, and his haste seemed to be genuine.

RECOLLECTIONS OF A YOUNG KING

At the age of thirteen I was proclaimed King of Capota. I happened to be sitting in my room, busy trying to erase the "un" from the "unsatisfactory" at the bottom of one of my essays. My father, Pyg Gy the First of Capota, was off for a month's hunting in the mountains, and I had been told to forward my essay to him by royal express courier. So I was counting on the poor lighting in hunting lodges and busily erasing when I suddenly heard loud cries outside the palace: "Long live Pyg Gy the Second!"

A few minutes later my personal valet came rushing into the room, prostrated himself in the doorway, and whispered devoutly, "May it please Your Majesty not to hold it against me that I once reported Your Majesty to His Excellency the prime minister for smoking."

I found the valet's servility obnoxious, sent him away, and went on erasing. It was my tutor's custom to mark my work with a red indelible pencil. I had just rubbed a hole in the paper when I was interrupted again: the prime minister entered, knelt down by the door, and cried, "Three cheers for Pyg Gy the Second!" He added, "Your Majesty, the people wish to see you."

I was quite bewildered, put down the eraser, dusted off my hands, and asked, "Why do the people wish to see me?"

"Because you are the king."

"Since when?"

"Since half an hour ago. Your most gracious father was fatally shot by a Rasac while hunting." (Rasac is the abbreviation for "Radical Sadists of Capota.")

"Oh, those Rasacs!" I exclaimed. Then I followed the prime minister out onto the balcony and showed myself to the people. I smiled, waved my arms, and felt quite bewildered.

This spontaneous demonstration lasted two hours. It was already beginning to grow dark before the crowd dispersed; a few hours later it came past the palace again in the form of a torchlight procession.

I went back to my rooms, tore up my essays, and threw the scraps into the courtyard of the royal palace. There—as I later found out—they were gathered up by souvenir hunters and sold to foreign countries where today the evidence of my weakness in spelling is displayed under glass.

There now followed some strenuous months. The Rasacs attempted a putsch but were suppressed by the Misacs ("Mild Sadists of Capota") and the army. My father was buried, and I had to attend sessions of Parliament and sign new laws—but on the whole I enjoyed being king because I could now deal differently with my tutor.

When he asked me at lesson time, "May it please Your Majesty to recite the rules regarding improper fractions?" I would say, "No, it does not please me," and he could do nothing about it. When he said, "Would Your Majesty find it intolerable if I were to ask Your Majesty to write down, on about three pages, the motives of William Tell when he murdered Gessler?" I would say, "Yes, I would find it intolerable," and I would require him to enumerate William Tell's motives for my benefit.

Thus, almost effortlessly, I acquired a certain education, burned all my textbooks and copybooks, and devoted myself to my true passions: I played ball, threw my pocketknife at the door panel, read thrillers, and had long conferences with the manager of the royal movie theater. I gave instructions for all my favorite movies to be obtained, and in Parliament I proposed some educational reforms.

It was a glorious time, although I found the parliamentary sessions wearisome. I succeeded in giving an outward impression of the melancholy youthful king and relied entirely on Prime Minister Pelzer, who had been a friend of my father and was a cousin of my deceased mother.

But after three months Pelzer urged me to get married, saying, "You must set an example to the people, Your Majesty." Marriage as such didn't scare me: the bad part was that Pelzer offered me his eleven-year-old daughter Jadwiga, a skinny little girl whom I often saw playing ball in the courtyard. She was considered dumb, was repeating the fifth grade, was pale and looked spiteful. I asked Pelzer for time to think it over and now became genuinely melancholy, spending hours leaning on my windowsill watching Jadwiga playing ball or hopscotch. She was a little more attractively dressed now and from time to time would glance up at me and smile. But her smile seemed to me artificial.

When my decision was due, Pelzer appeared before me in gala uniform: he was a big strapping man with a sallow complexion, black beard, and flashing eyes. "May it please Your Majesty," he said, "to inform me of your decision? Has my child found favor in Your Majesty's eyes?" When I replied with a point-blank "No," something terrible happened: Pelzer ripped the epaulets from his shoulders, the decorations from his chest, threw his portfolio—it was made of synthetic leather—at my feet, tore at his beard, and shouted, "So that is the gratitude of Capotian kings!"

I was in an awkward situation. Without Pelzer, I was lost. Quickly changing my mind, I said, "May I ask you for Jadwiga's hand?"

Pelzer threw himself at my feet, fervently kissed the tips of my shoes, and picked up the epaulets, decorations, and the synthetic-leather portfolio.

We were married in Huldebach Cathedral. There was beer and sausage for the populace as well as eight cigarettes per head and, at my personal suggestion, two free tickets for the carrousel; for a whole week, noise surged around the palace. From now on I helped Jadwiga with her homework, we played ball, played hopscotch, went horseback riding together, and, whenever we felt like it, ordered marzipan from the royal confectioner's or went to the royal movie theater. I still enjoyed being a king; but a serious incident finally put paid to my career.

On reaching the age of fourteen, I was made a colonel and commander in chief of the 8th Cavalry Regiment. Jadwiga was made a major. From time to time we had to inspect the regiment, attend functions at the officers' mess, and on every high holiday pin decorations on the chests of deserving soldiers. I myself received a good many decorations. But then came the Poskopek affair.

Poskopek was a soldier in the fourth squadron of my regiment who deserted one Sunday evening to follow a female circus rider across the border. He was caught, detained, and sentenced to death by a court-martial. As regimental commander it was my job to sign the death warrant, but I simply wrote at the bottom: "Sentence commuted to two weeks' detention, Pyg Gy II."

This note had terrible consequences. The officers of my regiment all ripped their epaulets from their shoulders, the decorations from their chests, and had them scattered about my room by a young lieutenant.

The entire Capotian army joined in the mutiny, and by the evening of that day my entire room was full of epaulets and decorations: it looked a mess.

True, the populace cheered me lustily, but that very night Pelzer informed me that the army had gone over in a body to the Rasacs. There was the crack of rifle shots, and the frantic hammering of machine guns rent the silence around the palace. Although the Misacs had sent me a bodyguard, Pelzer went over to the Rasacs during the night, which meant that I was forced to flee with Jadwiga.

We hastily gathered up clothing, bank notes, and jewelry, the Misacs requisitioned a taxi, and we barely made it to the railway station of the neighboring country, where we sank exhausted into a second-class sleeping compartment and moved off toward the west.

From across the border with Capota came the sound of rifle shots, frantic yelling, the whole terrible music of rebellion.

We traveled for four days and left the train at a city called Wickelheim. Wickelheim—dim memories from my geography lessons told me—was the capital of our neighboring country.

By this time Jadwiga and I had experienced things that we were beginning to appreciate: the smell of the train, acrid and pungent, the taste of sausages at railway stations of which we had never even heard. I could smoke to my heart's content, and Jadwiga began to blossom now that she was relieved of the burden of homework.

On the second day of our stay in Wickelheim, posters appeared everywhere that caught our attention: "Hunke Circus—Hula, the famous equestrienne, with her partner Jürgen Poskopek!" Jadwiga became all excited. "Pyg Gy," she said, "think of our livelihood. Poskopek will help you!"

At our hotel, telegrams were arriving hourly from Capota announcing the victory of the Misacs, the execution of Pelzer, a reorganization of the military.

The new prime minister—he was called Schmidt and was the leader of the Misacs—implored me to return and once again to accept the steel crown of the kings of Capota from the hands of the people.

For a few days I wavered, but ultimately Jadwiga's dread of homework won out. I went to the Hunke Circus, asked for Poskopek, and was welcomed by him ecstatically. "You saved my life!" he cried, standing in the doorway of his trailer. "What can I do for you?"

"Provide me with a livelihood," I said modestly.

Poskopek could not do enough for me: he interceded on my behalf with Herr Hunke, and I began by selling lemonade, then cigarettes, later goulash at the Hunke Circus. I was given a trailer and within a short time was made a cashier. I adopted the name Tückes, Wilhelm Tückes, and from then on ceased to be bothered by telegrams from Capota.

I am regarded as dead, as having disappeared without trace, whereas actually I am roaming the country in Hunke Circus's trailer with my blossoming Jadwiga. I get to sniff the air of foreign lands, to see them, I enjoy the great confidence placed in me by Herr Hunke. And if it were not for Poskopek visiting me now and then and telling me about Capota, if it were not for his wife, Hula, the beautiful equestrienne, assuring me over and over again that her husband owes his life to me, I would never give so much as a thought to having once been a king.

But the other day I came upon actual proof of my former royal life. We were performing in Madrid, and one morning I was strolling with Jadwiga through the city when a big gray building with the inscription "National Museum" caught our eye. "Let's go in," said Jadwiga, so in we went, into one of the large, more remote rooms over whose door hung a sign saying HOLOGRAPHS.

All unsuspecting, we proceeded to look at the handwritings of various heads of state and kings until we came to a glass case discreetly labeled KINGDOM OF CAPOTA—NOW A REPUBLIC. I saw the handwriting of my grandfather Wuck the Fortieth; I saw an excerpt from the famous Capotian Manifesto written in his own hand; I found a sheet from my father's hunting diaries—and finally a scrap from one of my copybooks, a piece of soiled paper on which I read "Helth is Welth." Embarrassed, I turned toward Jadwiga, but she merely smiled and said, "That's all behind you now, forever."

We quickly left the museum, for it was now one o'clock, the performance began at three, and at two I had to open the box office.

A PEACH TREE IN HIS GARDEN STANDS

Special circumstances require me to reveal a secret that I had wanted to preserve to the end of my life: I belong to a club or, rather, a secret society, although I had sworn never to join such an institution. It is most embarrassing, but the problems of the younger generation, as well as the deadly seriousness with which my neighbor guards his peaches, prompt me to make this confession, which I do blushingly. I am a Ribbeckian—and, obedient to the rules of our club, I take pen, ink, and paper, open my old school copybook, and begin to write: "Herr Ribbeck of the Havel lands, / A pear tree in his garden stands…" It feels good to write by hand for a change, it encourages patience, compels me to read the poem slowly and with care, and this in turn compels me to smile, and it certainly does no harm to smile once in a while.

So I slowly copy out the ballad and press down onto the paper the rubber stamp which we—the members of the Society of Ribbeckians—are obliged to keep on hand: "Join our club! Your sole obligation is to copy out the enclosed poem ten times and send it to the owners of fruit trees. You may then call yourself a Ribbeckian, a distinction we trust you will appreciate."

I write my neighbor's address on an envelope, stick on a stamp, and betake myself to the mailbox. It so happens, however, that the mailbox is attached to the garden fence of this very neighbor, and as I lift up the yellow flap of the mailbox I can see him—my neighbor—standing there on a ladder, with outstretched forefinger, lightly touching his peaches one by one. No doubt about it, he is counting them!

Next morning we are standing side by side, my neighbor and I, waiting for the mailman, that grossly underpaid cherub whom not even his obviously flat feet can rob of charm.

My neighbor's face seems even yellower than usual, his lips tremble, and his slightly bloodshot eyes seem to point to a sleepless night.

"It is indescribable," he said to me, "how moral standards are declining. Today's young people: nothing but thieves and robbers. Where is it all going to end?"

"In disaster."

"Precisely. I see you agree."

"Of course, it's inevitable. We are drifting inexorably toward the abyss. All this depravity, this dissipation!"

"No respect for the property of others! One should ... but the police refuse to intervene. Just imagine. Yesterday evening I still had a hundred and thirty-five peaches on my tree—and this morning—care to guess?"

"A hundred and thirty-two?"

"Optimist! A hundred and thirty. Five ripe peaches! Just imagine. I shudder to think of it."

"Sackcloth and ashes—we'll have no alternative. Morality is a thing of the past. I can see there are times ahead of us..."

But the approaching mailman relieves me of having to complete my sentence. The letter that I threw in the mailbox yesterday has gone full circle and now, via the collector, the sorter, and the mailman, has landed in the hands of my neighbor.

There was no mail for me. Who would write to me anyway, since I am not even an active Ribbeckian but merely a passive one? I own no fruit trees, not even a currant bush, and the only person who knows my name is the corner grocer who grudgingly grants me credit and with a sorrowful eye sees gray bread, margarine, and fine-cut tobacco disappear into my shopping bag and stubbornly refuses me any credit for regular cigarettes and red wine. But it is time to observe my neighbor's expression: he has opened the letter, put on his glasses and, with a frown, started to read: he reads, reads, and I am surprised at the length of that ballad. In vain I wait for a smile on his face: nothing, there is nothing. Obviously a person who is not responsive to literature as well as devoid of humor. He takes off his glasses as if he had been reading some trivial bit of printed matter, folds up the letter, opens it again, and hands it to me across the fence, saying, "Listen, aren't you ... er ... what was it again?"

"A writer," I said.

"Of course. Take a look at this, what d'you make of it?"

The sudden sight of my handwriting gives me a bit of a shock. Perhaps, I think, he is a person who can only be reached acoustically, impervious to the charms of the visual. And I begin to read aloud: "Herr Ribbeck of the Havel lands, / A pear tree in his garden stands..."

"Oh, I know what it says!"

"Did you see the stamp at the bottom? There is a stamp there: 'Join our club!...'"

"I know, I know," he says impatiently, and his sallow face turns a shade darker, "but it makes no sense to send me something like that since I only have a peach tree. It's something about pears, isn't it? The way people waste their time!"

Without so much as a nod, he shuffles off to his observation post at the back, where he can keep an eye on his peaches.

I see, I thought, as I folded up my sheet of paper, and now I am wondering whether I should apply for a change in the statutes of our club. Of course the ballad would lose its melody, for there are not that many one-syllable fruits.

PALE ANNA

I didn't get home from the war till the spring of 1950, and there was nobody left in town whom I knew. Luckily for me, my parents had left me some money. I rented a room in town, and there I lay on the bed, smoking and waiting and not knowing what I was waiting for. The idea of a job didn't appeal to me. I gave my landlady money, and she bought what I needed and cooked my meals. Whenever she brought coffee or a meal to my room, she stayed longer than I liked. Her son had been killed at a place called Kalinovka, and after coming into the room she would set the tray down on the table and come over to the darkish corner where my bed was. That's where I dozed away my time, stubbing out my cigarettes against the wall so that the wallpaper around my bed was covered with black smudges. My landlady was pale and skinny, and when her face hung there in the shadows over my bed, I was scared of her. At first I thought she was queer in the head, for her eyes were very bright and large, and she kept on asking me about her son.

"Are you sure you didn't know him? The place was called Kalinovka—weren't you there?"

But I had never heard of a place called Kalinovka, and I would always turn toward the wall saying, "No, really, I can't remember him at all."

My landlady was not queer in the head, she was a very good soul, and I found her questioning painful. She questioned me very often, several times a day, and whenever I went into her kitchen I had to look at the photo of her son, a colored photo hanging over the bench. He had been a laughing, fair-haired boy, and in the photo he was wearing an infantry dress uniform.

"That was taken in the garrison town," said my landlady, "before they were sent to the front."

It was a half-length portrait: he was wearing his steel helmet, and behind him you could see some dummy castle ruins entwined with artificial creepers.

"He was a conductor," my landlady said, "a streetcar conductor. A good worker, my boy was." And then she would reach for the cardboard box of photographs that stood on her sewing table between the scraps of cloth for patching and the skeins of thread. And I had to go through piles of photos of her son: group pictures from his school days, each showing a boy seated in the middle with a slate between his knees, and on the slate a "VI," a "VII," and finally an "VIII." In a separate packet, held together by a red rubber band, were the pictures of his first communion: a smiling little boy in a formal black suit, holding an enormous candle and standing in front of a transparency painted with a golden chalice. Then came pictures of him as a mechanic's apprentice standing by a lathe, grimy-faced, his hands grasping a file.

"That wasn't the right kind of job for him," my landlady would say; "the work was too difficult." And she would show me the last photo taken before he was called up: he was wearing a streetcar conductor's uniform and standing beside a Number 9 streetcar at the terminus, where the tracks curve around in a loop, and I recognized the soda-pop stand where I had so often bought cigarettes, in the days before the war; I recognized the poplars, which are still there now, saw the villa, its gateway flanked by golden lions, which aren't there now, and I would remember the girl I used to think about so often during the war. She had been pretty, with a pale face and almond-shaped eyes, and she had always boarded the streetcar at the Number 9 terminus.

I would stare for a long time at the photo of my landlady's son at the Number 9 terminus and think of many things: of the girl, and the soap factory where I was working in those days; I could hear the screeching of the streetcar, see the pink soda pop I used to drink at the stand in summer, and the green cigarette ads, and again the girl.

"Maybe," the landlady would say, "you did know him after all." I would shake my head and put the picture back in the box: it was a shiny photo and looked like new, although by now it was eight years old.

"No, no," I would say, "and I was never in Kalinovka—really I wasn't."

I often had to go to the kitchen, and she often came to my room, and all day I would think of the thing I wanted to forget—the war— and I would toss my cigarette ash behind the bed and stub the glowing tip out against the wall.

Sometimes, as I lay there in the evening, I could hear a girl's footsteps in the next room, or the Yugoslav who had the room next to the kitchen; I could hear him swearing as he groped for the light switch before going into his room.

It wasn't till I had been living there for three weeks and was holding Karl's picture for what must have been the fiftieth time that I noticed that the streetcar he was standing beside, laughing, with his leather pouch, wasn't empty. For the first time I looked closely at the photo and saw that a girl sitting inside the streetcar, smiling, had got into the snapshot. It was the pretty girl I used to think about so often during the war. The landlady came up to me, studied the look on my face, and said, "Now you recognize him, eh?" Then she stepped behind me and looked over my shoulder at the photo, and from close behind me rose the smell of the fresh peas she was holding in the folds of her apron.

"No," I said quietly, "but the girl."

"The girl?" she said. "That was his fiancée, but maybe it's just as well he never saw her again..."

"Why?" I asked.

She didn't answer but walked away, sat down on her chair by the window, and went on shelling peas. Without looking at me, she said, "Did you know the girl?"

I kept a tight grip on the photo, looked at my landlady, and told her about the soap factory, about the Number 9 terminus, and the pretty girl who always got on there.

"Is that all?"

"Yes," I said. She tipped the peas into a sieve, turned on the faucet, and I could see her thin back.

"When you see her, you'll understand why it's a good thing he never saw her again..."

"See her?" I asked.

She dried her hands on her apron, came over to me, and carefully took away the photo. Her face seemed thinner than ever, her eyes looked past me, but she gently laid her hand on my left arm. "She lives in the room next to yours, Anna does. We always call her our pale Anna because she's got such a white face. You really mean you haven't seen her yet?"

"No," I said, "I haven't, though I guess I've heard her a few times. What's wrong with her, then?"

"I hate to tell you, but it's better for you to know. Her face has been completely destroyed, it's full of scars. She was thrown into a plate-glass window by a bomb blast. You won't recognize her."

That evening I waited a long while before hearing steps in the hall, but the first time I was wrong: it was the tall Yugoslav, who looked at me in astonishment when I dashed out into the hall. Embarrassed, I said "Good evening" and went back into my room.

I tried to imagine her face with scars, but I couldn't, and whenever I saw her face, it was beautiful even with the scars. I thought about the soap factory, about my parents, and about another girl I used to go out with often at that time. Her name was Elizabeth, but she was known as Puss; when I kissed her, she always laughed, and I felt like an idiot. I had written her postcards from the front, and she used to send me little parcels of homemade cookies that were always in crumbs by the time they arrived; she sent me cigarettes and newspapers, and in one of her letters she wrote, "Our boys will win the war all right, and I'm so proud you're one of them."

But I wasn't at all proud to be one of them, and when I was due for leave I didn't write and tell her; I went out with the daughter of a tobacconist who lived in our apartment house. I gave the tobacconist's daughter soap sent me by my firm, and she gave me cigarettes, and we went to the movies together, and we went dancing, and once, when her parents were away, she took me up to her room and I pressed her down onto the couch in the dark; but when I bent over her, she switched on the light and smiled slyly up at me, and in the glare I saw Hitler on the wall, a colored photo, and all around Hitler's picture, arranged in the shape of a heart on the pink wallpaper, was a series of men wearing heroic expressions, postcards thumbtacked to the wall, and men in steel helmets cut out of illustrated weeklies. I left the girl lying there on the couch, lit a cigarette, and went away. Later on, both girls wrote postcards to me at the front telling me I had behaved badly, but I didn't answer...

I waited a long time for Anna, smoked one cigarette after another in the dark, thought of many things, and when the key was thrust into the lock I was too scared to get up and see her face. I heard her open the door to her room, move around in there humming softly to herself, and after a while I got up and waited in the hall. All of a sudden there was silence in her room, she wasn't moving about now or humming, and

I was afraid to knock. I could hear the tall Yugoslav walking up and down in his room, muttering to himself, could hear the water bubbling in my landlady's kitchen. But in Anna's room all was quiet, and through the open door of my own room I could see the black smudges from all those stubbed-out cigarettes on the wallpaper.

The tall Yugoslav was lying on his bed now, there were no more footsteps, I could just hear him muttering; the kettle in my landlady's kitchen had stopped bubbling, and I heard the sound of metal on metal as the landlady put the lid on the coffeepot. Anna's room was still silent, and the thought struck me that later she would tell me everything she had been thinking about while I stood outside her door, and later on she did tell me everything.

I stared at a picture hanging beside the door: the silvery sheen of a lake and a naiad with wet fair hair emerging from it to smile at a young peasant hiding among some very green bushes. I could see part of the naiad's left breast, and her neck was very white and a little too long.

I don't know when it was, but some time later I took hold of the doorknob, and before I turned the knob and slowly pushed open the door, I knew Anna was mine: her face was covered with little scars of a bluish sheen, the smell of mushrooms simmering in a pan came from her room, and I opened the door wide, laid my hand on Anna's shoulder, and tried to smile.

IN SEARCH OF THE READER

My friend Witt has a strange occupation: he is not afraid of calling himself an author, simply because he has some latent knowledge of spelling, vaguely masters a few rules of grammar, and now covers one typed page after another with stylistic exercises that he calls a manuscript as soon as he has enough to make up a bundle.

For years he had to eat the sparse grass of this art on the steppes of culture, until he found a publisher. Soon after the publication of his book, I ran across him in a state of deep depression. His report was indeed depressing: according to his publisher's statement, during the first six months three hundred and fifty copies had been sent out free of charge for reviewing, a few good reviews had appeared, and thirteen copies had actually been sold—resulting in a credit of 5.46 marks for my friend. But he had received an advance of eight hundred marks, and, with sales remaining at that level, this advance would be paid off in roughly a hundred and fifty years.

Now human life expectancy is generally less than that. Disregarding a few, almost legendary Turks, it is estimated at seventy—and, taking into account the memorable hardships imposed upon our lost generation, one can confidently deduct a further ten years from our life span.

I advised my friend to write a second book. Upon publication, it received a warm welcome among experts; the number of review copies rose to more than four hundred; the number of copies sold after six months amounted to twenty-nine. I rolled two cigarettes a day for my friend, patted him on the back, and suggested he now write a third book. But, strangely enough, he took this for sarcasm and withdrew in a huff.

Meanwhile he had passed into literary history as "Standard-Bearer Witt," and a book that had been published about him sold better than his own books.

I didn't see him for almost six months, and imagined him to be putt-ering around again in the purlieus of a lonely genius. Then he turned up at my place and ruefully confessed that he had started a third book after all. I made the suggestion that he offer this work to the book trade in a mimeographed edition of thirty to fifty copies. But he was under the spell of genuine printer's ink; besides, he had accepted another advance, his second child was on the way, and he proclaimed his unwillingness to contribute to the unemployment of sundry compositors, printers, and packers. (His social consciousness has always been very strong!)

Meanwhile nearly a hundred good reviews of his work had appeared and more than ninety copies of his two books had been sold. His publisher had started an action that he called "In Search of the Reader." Handbills had been sent to all bookstores requesting that every Witt purchaser be identified and immediately reported to the publisher with a view to establishing contact between author and reader.

The success of this action was not long in coming. A month after it was launched, a man evidently appeared in the far north who asked for one of my friend's books, bought it, and paid for it. The owner of the bookstore immediately sent off a telegram: WITT PURCHASER HERE— WHAT DO I DO? Meanwhile he kept the customer engaged in conversa-tion, poured coffee, opened packs of cigarettes—behavior to which the customer, albeit astonished, was quite happy to submit himself. Then came the publisher's reply, by top-priority wire: "SEND PURCHASER TO ME, ALL EXPENSES PAID." Fortunately the customer was a high-school teacher, it was a vacation time, and he had no objection to a free trip to southern Germany. The first day he traveled as far as Cologne, where he spent the night in a good hotel, and the next day his train took him south beside the beautiful Rhine, a journey he greatly enjoyed.

By about four o'clock of the second day he had reached his desti-nation, took a taxi from the station to the publishing house, and spent a stimulating hour over coffee and cakes with the publisher's charming wife. Then he was supplied with additional travel funds, taken back to the station, and now traveled second class to that quiet little town where my friend serves the Muses. As the second child had been born some time before, my friend's wife had gone to a movie—a relaxa-tion that, despite all financial embarrassment, should not be denied the wives of authors. So the purchaser happened to find my friend in the process of warming up the children's evening milk and keeping them quiet by singing them a song in which a vulgar word was prominent. This word threw an ugly light on modern German literature...

My friend welcomed his reader enthusiastically, pressed the coffee grinder into his hand, and swiftly disposed of his paternal duties. Before long, the water for the coffee was boiling, and the conversation could have begun. But they were both such shy people that they first regarded each other in mutual, silent admiration for quite a while, until my friend burst out with a cry of "You are a genius—an absolute genius!"

"Oh, no," the guest said diffidently, "I was thinking that of you."

"You're mistaken," said my friend, and finally poured the coffee. "The hallmark of a genius is his rarity, and you belong to a rarer class of human beings than I do."

The visitor tried to put forward some modest objections but was brusquely corrected: "Nothing doing," said my friend. "Writing a book isn't half as bad as it's made out to be. Finding a publisher is child's play, but to buy a book—that I call an act of genius. Do you take milk and sugar?"

The man helped himself, then shyly drew from the right inside pocket of his overcoat the book he had bought in the far north and asked my friend to inscribe it.

"On one condition only," my friend said sternly. "Only on condition that you inscribe my manuscript!"

From a shelf he took down a file, from it removed a stack of typed sheets, placed the stack beside his guest's coffee cup, and said, "Do me the pleasure!"

The guest, a bit flustered, drew out his fountain pen and wrote hesitatingly on the lower edge of the last manuscript page: "In sincere admiration—Günther Schlegel."

But half a minute later, while my friend was still trying to dry the ink by waving his manuscript above the stove, the guest drew from the left inside pocket of his overcoat a bundle of typed sheets and asked my friend to submit this work, which he regarded as his contribution to modern literature, to the publisher for an opinion.

My friend told me that for several minutes he had been speechless with disappointment. His concern for the fate of this man, he said, had filled him with profound bitterness.

So once again they sat silently facing one another for several minutes, until my friend said in a low voice, "I implore you, don't do it—you're forfeiting your originality!"

The guest remained stubbornly silent, clutching his manuscript.

"You will never again receive travel funds," said my friend, "you will never again be served cream cakes. The publisher's wife will put on her sourest expression. For your own sake, I implore you: forget about it!"

But the guest doggedly shook his head, and my friend, in his strenuous efforts to rescue a human being, did not shrink from bringing in his publisher's statements. But all this did not interest Schlegel.

At this point my friend usually broke off his account, and I assume that he simply got into an argument with his visitor. At any rate, a pause ensued while my friend pensively regarded his clenched fists and muttered unintelligibly to himself. But I did learn that Schlegel departed after a curt goodbye, leaving his manuscript behind.

Meanwhile Schlegel's novel, *Woe Unto You, Penelope!*, the story of a returning prisoner of war, has caused quite a stir, and rightly so, among the experts. Schlegel has given up his teaching career—in other words, abandoned a genuine profession in order to devote himself to another profession that I still do not consider to be one...

THE TIDINGS OF BETHLEHEM

The door was not a proper door: it was no more than a few planks loosely nailed together and closed by a wire loop hung over a nail in the doorpost. The man stopped and waited. It's really a disgrace, he thought, that a woman should have to have her child here. He carefully lifted the wire loop off the nail, pushed open the door—and was startled to see the child lying in the straw, the mother, very young, seated on the ground beside it, smiling at the child… Farther back, against the wall, stood someone whom the man didn't dare look at too closely: it might be one of those whom the shepherds had taken for angels. The figure leaning against the wall was wearing a mouse-gray robe and holding flowers in each hand: slender, creamy lilies. The man felt fear mounting in him and thought: Maybe there's some truth after all in the wild tales the shepherds have been telling in town.

The young woman raised her eyes, gave him a friendly, questioning look, and the young man said softly, "Does the master carpenter live here?"

The young woman shook her head. "He's not a master carpenter—just a carpenter."

"Never mind," said the man. "I imagine he'll be able to fix a door if he's brought his tools along."

"He has," said Mary, "and he can fix doors. He used to do that in Nazareth too."

So they really were from Nazareth.

The figure holding the flowers now looked at the man and said, "There's no need to be afraid." The voice was so beautiful that again the man was startled, and he glanced up: the mouse-gray figure looked benevolent but also sad.

"He means Joseph," said the young woman. "I'll go and wake him up. Do you want him to fix a door?"

"Yes, at the inn called the Red Man, just to run the plane over the groove a bit and check the jamb. The door keeps sticking. I'll wait outside, if you wouldn't mind getting him."

"You're welcome to wait in here," said the young woman.

"No, I'd rather wait outside." He glanced across at the mouse-gray figure, who nodded at him with a smile. Then he retreated, walking backward and carefully closing the door by lifting the wire loop over the nail. Men with flowers had always struck him as comical, but the mouse-gray figure didn't look like a man, and not like a woman either, and certainly hadn't struck him as comical.

When Joseph came out with his tool box, the young man took him by the arm, saying, "This way, we have to go around to the left." They went around to the left, and now at last the young man plucked up enough courage to say what he had wanted to say to the young woman but had been afraid to because the figure with the flowers had been standing there. "The shepherds," he said, "have been telling wild tales in town about you people." But Joseph, instead of answering, merely said, "I hope at least you have a chisel—the handle of mine is broken. Is there more than one door?"

"Just the one," said the man, "and we do have a chisel. We need to fix the door in a hurry. We're having some soldiers billeted in our house."

"Billeted? Now? I haven't heard about any maneuvers."

"No, there are no maneuvers, but a whole company of soldiers is coming to Bethlehem. And our house," he said proudly, "our house is getting the captain. The shepherds..." But he broke off, stopped; Joseph stopped too. At the street corner stood the mouse-gray figure with an armful of flowers, white lilies, giving them away to little children who could scarcely toddle: more and more children arrived, as well as mothers with children in arms, and the man who had come for Joseph was much alarmed, for the mouse-gray figure was weeping— the voice, the eyes, had already alarmed him, but the tears were more alarming still. The figure touched the children's mouths, their foreheads, with outstretched hand, kissed their small, dirty hands, and gave each child a lily.

"I was looking for you," Joseph told the mouse-gray figure. "Just now, while I was asleep, I dreamed..."

"I know," said the mouse-gray figure, "we must leave at once."

He waited for a moment until a very small, dirty girl had come up to him.

"Am I not to fix the door for this captain after all?"

"No, we must leave immediately." The figure turned away from the children and took Joseph by the arm, and Joseph said to the man who had come for him, "I'm sorry, it looks as if I won't be able to do it."

"Oh, never mind," said the man. His gaze followed the other two as they walked back to the stable; then he looked down the street where the laughing children were running around with their big white lilies. At that moment he heard the clatter of horses' hooves behind him, turned around, and saw the company riding into town from the highway.

I'll catch it again, he thought, because the door hasn't been fixed.

The children stood by the roadside, waving their flowers at the soldiers. So the soldiers rode into Bethlehem between two lanes of white lilies, and the man who had come for Joseph thought: I believe the shepherds were right in everything they told us...

THE TASTE OF BREAD

At the entrance to the basement he was met by stifling, sour-smelling air. He walked slowly down the slimy steps, groping his way into a yellowish darkness: from somewhere water was dripping, there must be a leak in the roof or a pipe must have burst. The water mingled with dust and rubble, making the steps as slippery as the bottom of a fish tank. He walked on. From a door at the back came some light; in the semidarkness he could make out a sign on his right saying "X-RAY ROOM. DO NOT ENTER." He walked toward the light; it was yellow and soft, and the way it flickered told him that it must be a candle. As he walked on, he looked into dark rooms where he could discern a jumble of chairs, leather sofas, and collapsed cupboards.

The door from which the light came was wide open. Beside the big altar candle stood a nun in a blue habit, tossing some salad in an enamel bowl; the heap of little green leaves had a whitish coating, and he could hear the dressing gently swishing around at the bottom of the bowl. The nun's broad pink hand made the leaves go round and round, and when sometimes a few fell out over the edge, she would calmly pick them up and throw them back in again. Beside the candlestick stood a large saucepan giving off an insipid smell of soup—of hot water, onions, and some kind of bouillon cubes.

In a loud voice he said, "Good evening!"

The nun turned around, alarm on her broad, rosy face, and said softly, "Oh, my goodness—what do you want?" Her hands were dripping with the milky dressing, and a few bits of lettuce leaf were clinging to her soft, childlike arms. "Oh, my goodness," she said, "you did scare me! Do you want something?"

"I'm hungry," he said in a low voice.

But he was no longer looking at the nun. His gaze had shifted to the right, into an open cupboard whose door had been ripped out by air pressure; the jagged remains of the plywood door still hung in the hinges, and the floor was covered with crumbling flakes of paint. The cupboard contained loaves of bread, many loaves. They lay in a careless pile, more than a dozen wrinkled loaves. Instantly his mouth started watering, and, gulping down the surge of saliva, he thought: I'll be eating bread, whatever happens I'll be eating bread... He looked at the nun: her childlike eyes showed compassion and fear. "Hungry?" she said. "You're hungry?" and looked with raised eyebrows at the bowl of salad, the pot of soup, and the pile of bread.

"Bread," he said, "some bread, please."

She went over to the cupboard, took out a loaf, put it on the table, and started looking in a drawer for a knife.

"Thanks," he said softly. "Don't bother, bread can be broken too..."

The nun tucked the bowl of salad under one arm, picked up the pot of soup, and walked out past him.

He hastily broke off a hunk of bread: his chin was trembling, and he could feel the muscles of his mouth and jaws twitching. Then he dug his teeth into the soft, uneven surface of the bread where he had broken it apart. He was eating bread. The bread was stale, must have been a week old, dry rye bread with a red label from some bakery or other. He continued to dig in with his teeth, finishing off even the brown, leathery crust; then he grasped the loaf in both hands and broke off another piece. Eating with his right hand, he clasped the loaf with his left; he went on eating, sat down on the edge of a wooden crate, and, each time he broke off a piece, bit first into the soft center, feeling all around his mouth the touch of the bread like a dry caress, while his teeth went on digging.

MONOLOGUE OF A WAITER

I don't know how it could have happened; after all, I'm no longer a child, I'm almost fifty and should have known what I was doing. Yet I did it, and, to top it all, when I was already off duty and actually nothing more should have happened to me. But it did happen, and so on Christmas Eve I was given notice.

Everything had gone off without a hitch: I had served the guests at dinner without knocking over a glass, without tipping over a gravy boat, without spilling any red wine, had pocketed my tips and withdrawn to my room, thrown jacket and tie onto the bed, slipped my suspenders off my shoulders, opened my bottle of beer, and I was just lifting the lid of the tureen and sniffing—pea soup. That's what I had ordered from the chef, with bacon, without onions, but thickened, well thickened. I'm sure you don't know what "well thickened" means: it would take too long to try and explain this to you—it took my mother three hours to explain what she meant by "well thickened." Well, the soup smelled glorious, and I dipped in the ladle, filled my plate, could feel and see that the soup was thoroughly well thickened— and at that moment my door opened and in came the young rascal I'd noticed at dinner. Small, pale, certainly no older than eight, he had allowed his plate to be piled high and then, without touching any of it, had it all taken away again—turkey and chestnuts, truffles and veal, and not even the dessert, which after all no child ever passes up, he had not so much as touched with a spoon; he'd allowed five pear halves and half a bucket of chocolate sauce to be tipped onto his plate, and he hadn't touched a thing, not a thing, yet all the time not looking as if he were fussy but like someone with a definite plan in mind.

He closed the door quietly behind him, looked at my plate, then at me. "What's that?" he asked.

"That's pea soup," I said.

"There's no such thing," he said with a smile. "That only exists in the fairy tale about the king who lost his way in the forest."

"Well," I said, "one thing's for sure: that's pea soup."

"May I have a taste?"

"Sure, go ahead," I said, "come and sit down."

Well, he ate three plates of pea soup while I sat beside him on my bed, drinking beer and smoking, and I could actually see his little stomach becoming rounder. While I sat on the bed, I thought about a lot of things that I have meanwhile forgotten again—ten minutes, fifteen, quite a long time, time enough to think about many things, about fairy tales, about grown-ups, parents, and suchlike. Finally the little fellow gave up. I took his place and finished off the soup, a plate and a half, while he sat on the bed beside me. Maybe I shouldn't have looked into the empty tureen, for he said, "Oh, dear, I've eaten up all your soup!"

"Never mind," I said, "that was plenty for me. Did you come here to eat pea soup?"

"No, I was just looking for someone to help me find a pit. I thought you might know of one."

Pit, pit ... then it dawned on me—you need one for playing marbles, and I said, "Well, you know, it'll be difficult to find a pit here in this building."

"Can't we make one?" he asked. "Just scoop one on the floor of the room?"

I don't know how it could have happened, but I did it, and when the boss asked me, "How could you do such a thing?" I was at a loss for an answer. Maybe I should have said: Haven't we promised to fulfill our guests' every wish in order to make sure they have a happy and harmonious Christmas? But I didn't, I said nothing. After all, I couldn't have foreseen that the child's mother would trip over the hole in the floor and break her ankle, at night, when she came back drunk from the bar. How could I know that? And that the insurance people would demand an explanation, and so on and so forth? Third-party liability, labor tribunal, and over and over again: incredible, incredible. Should I have explained to them that for three hours, three whole hours, I played marbles with the boy, that he always won, that he even drank some of my beer—until finally, dead tired, he fell into bed? I said nothing; but when they asked me if it was I who had scooped out the hole in the hardwood floor, I couldn't deny it. The pea soup was the only thing they never found out about: that will remain our secret.

Thirty-five years in my profession, always conducted myself impeccably. I don't know how it could have happened; I should have known what I was doing, yet I did it. I took the elevator down to the janitor, borrowed a hammer and chisel, took the elevator up again, chipped a hole in the hardwood floor. After all, I couldn't have foreseen that his mother would trip over it when she came home drunk at four in the morning from the bar. To be quite frank, I'm not all that upset, not even at being fired. Good waiters are always in demand.

UNDINE'S MIGHTY FATHER

I am prepared to believe almost anything of the Rhine, but I have never been able to believe in its carefree summer mood; I have looked for this carefree mood but never found it. Perhaps it is a flaw in my vision or in my character that prevents me from discovering this aspect.

My Rhine is dark and brooding, it is too much a river of merchant cunning for me to be able to believe in its youthful summertime face.

I have traveled on its white ships, have walked over its bordering hills, cycled from Mainz to Cologne, from Rüdesheim to Deutz, from Cologne to Xanten, in fall, spring, and summer; in winter I have stayed at small riverside hotels, and my Rhine was never a summer Rhine.

My Rhine is the one I remember from earliest childhood: a dark, brooding river that I have always feared and loved. I was born three minutes' walk away from it. Before I could talk, when I could barely walk, I was already playing on its banks: we would wade knee-deep in the fallen leaves along the avenue, looking for the paper pinwheels we had entrusted to the east wind, the wind that, too fast for our childish legs, drove the pinwheels westward toward the old moats.

It was fall, the weather was stormy, heavy clouds and the acrid smoke from ships' funnels hung in the air; in the evenings the wind would subside, fog would lie over the Rhine valley, foghorns toot somberly, red and green signal lights at the mastheads float past as if on phantom ships, and we would lean over the bridge railings listening to the strained, high-pitched signal horns of the raftsmen as they traveled downriver.

Winter came: ice floes as big as football fields, white, covered with a thick layer of snow; on such clear days the Rhine was very quiet, the only passengers were the crows being carried by the ice floes toward Holland, calmly riding along on their huge, fantastically elegant taxis.

For many weeks the Rhine remained quiet: only a few narrow, gray channels between the big white floes. Seagulls sailed through the arches of the bridges, ice floes splintered against the piers, and in

February or March we waited breathlessly for the great drifts coming down from the Upper Rhine. Ice masses evoking the Arctic came from upriver, and it was impossible to believe that this was a river on whose banks wine grew, good wine. Layer upon layer of cracking, splintering ice drifted past villages and towns, uprooting trees, crushing houses, less compacted, already less menacing, by the time it reached Cologne.

There is no doubt at all about there being two Rhines: the Upper, the wine drinker's Rhine, and the Lower, the schnapps drinker's Rhine— less well known and on whose behalf I would put in my plea: a Rhine that to this day has never really come to terms with its east bank. Where in bygone times smoke used to rise from the sacrificial fires of Teutonic tribes, now smoke rises from chimney stacks—from Cologne downriver to well north of Duisburg: red, yellow, and green flames, the ghostly silhouette of great industries, while the western, left bank, is more reminiscent of a pastoral riverbank: cows, willows, reeds, and the traces of the Romans' winter encampments. Here they stood, those Roman soldiers, staring at the unreconciled east bank; sacrificing to Venus, to Dionysus, celebrating the birth of Agrippina: a Rhenish girl was the daughter of Germanicus, the granddaughter of Caligula, the mother of Nero, the wife and murderess of Claudius, later murdered by her son, Nero. Rhenish blood in the veins of Nero! She was born in an area of barracks—even in those days, horsemen's barracks, sailors' barracks, legionaries' barracks—and, at the western end of Cologne, the villas of merchants, administrators, officers; bathhouses, swimming baths. Modern times have still not quite caught up with that luxury lying buried beneath the rubble of the centuries, thirty feet below our children's playgrounds.

This river, the old, green Rhine, has seen too many armies— Romans, Teutons, Huns, Cossacks, robber barons, victors and vanquished, and, representing history's most recent heralds, those who came from farthest away: the boys from Wisconsin, Cleveland, or Manila, who carried on the trade started by the Roman mercenaries in the year o. This broad, green-gray, flowing Rhine has seen too much trade, too much history, for me to be able to believe in its youthful summer face. It is easier to believe in its brooding nature, its darkness; the grim ruins of the robber-baron castles on its hills are not the relics of a very joyful interregnum. Here Roman frippery was bartered in the year o for Teutonic feminine favors, and in the year 1947 Zeiss binoculars were bartered for coffee and cigarettes, those little white incense offerings to the transitory nature of life. Not even the Nibelungs, who lived where the wine grows, were a very joyful race; blood was their coin, one side of which was loyalty, the other treachery.

The wine drinker's Rhine ends roughly at Bonn, then passes through a sort of quarantine that reaches as far as Cologne, where the schnapps drinker's Rhine begins. To many this may mean that the Rhine stops here. My Rhine starts here, switches to tranquillity and brooding without forgetting what it had learned and witnessed farther up. It becomes more and more serious toward its mouth until it dies in the North Sea, its waters mingling with those of the open sea. The Rhine of the lovely Middle Rhine madonnas flows toward Rembrandt and is swallowed up by the mists of the North Sea.

My Rhine is the winter Rhine, the Rhine of the crows traveling northwest on their ice floes toward the Lowlands, a Breughel Rhine whose colors are green-gray, black, and white, much gray, and the brown façades of the buildings that wait for the approach of summer before sprucing up again; the quiet Rhine that is still sufficiently elemental to ward off the bustling of the worshipers of Mercury for at least a few weeks, maintaining its own sovereignty, abandoning its old bed to birds, fish, and ice floes. And I am still scared of the Rhine that in spring can become vicious, when household goods come drifting down the river, drowned cattle, uprooted trees, when posters saying WARNING! in red are fixed to the trees along its banks, when the muddy tides rise, when the chains mooring the huge, floating boathouses threaten to snap—scared of the Rhine that murmurs so eerily and so gently through the dreams of children, a dark god bent on showing that it still demands sacrifices. Heathen, pristine Nature, in no way beautiful, it widens out like a sea, thrusts itself, into dwellings, rises greenly in cellars, surges out of canals, roars its way along under bridges: Undine's mighty father.

NO TEARS FOR SCHMECK

I

As Müller's nausea approached the point at which voiding was inevitable, a solemn, reverent silence filled the lecture hall. Professor Schmeck's voice, deliberately unaccentuated, cultured, slightly husky, had now (seventeen minutes before the end of the lecture) advanced to that gentle chant, soothing yet stimulating, which transports a certain type of female student (the hyperintellectual, the kind that used to be known as a bluestocking) to a pitch of excitement bordering on the sexual; at this moment they would have died for him. As for Schmeck, he used—when speaking confidentially—to describe this stage of his lecture as the point at which "the rational element, driven to its outer limits, to the very furthest edge of its possibilities, begins to seem irrational, and," he would add, "my friends, when you consider that any decent church service lasts forty-five minutes, like the sex act—well then, my friends, you'll understand that rhythm and monotony, acceleration and retardation, climax—and relaxation—are an integral part of a church service, the sex act, and—in my opinion, at least—the academic lecture."

At this point, somewhere about the thirty-third minute of the lecture, all indifference vanished from the hall, leaving only adoration and hostility; the adoring listeners could have exploded any minute into inarticulate rhythmic screams, and this would have incited the hostile listeners (who were in the minority) to screams of provocation. But at the very instant when such unacademic behavior appeared imminent, Schmeck broke off in the middle of a sentence and with a prosaic gesture introduced that sobering note which he needed to bring the lecture to a controlled conclusion: he blew his nose with a brightly colored checkered handkerchief, and the compulsive glance with which he briefly inspected it before replacing it in his pocket had a sobering effect on every last female student whose lips may already have been showing traces of light foam. "I need adoration," Schmeck used to say, "but when I get it, I can't take it."

A deep sigh went through the lecture hall, hundreds swore never again to attend a Schmeck lecture—and on Tuesday afternoon they would be crowding round the door, they would stand in line for half an hour, they would miss the lecture given by Livorno, Schmeck's rival, so as to hear Schmeck (who never announced the times of his lectures until Livorno had settled on his; whenever Schmeck was supposed to announce his lecture schedule for the university timetable, he had no compunction about going off to places so remote that he could not be reached even by cable; last semester he had gone on an expedition to the Warrau Indians; for weeks he was hidden in the Orinoco delta, and when his expedition was over, he cabled his lecture schedule from Caracas, and it had been identical with Livorno's—a fact that led someone in the registrar's office to remark, "Obviously he has his spies in Venezuela too").

The deep sigh seemed to Müller to indicate the right moment to do what he ought to have done a quarter of an hour earlier but hadn't had the nerve to: go out and get rid of the contents of his stomach. When he stood up in the front row, his briefcase tucked under his arm, and made his way through the closely packed rows, he was fleetingly aware of the look of indignation, of surprise, on the faces of the students who grudgingly made room for him: even the Schmeck opponents seemed to find it inconceivable that there could be anybody—and an out-and-out Schmeck supporter at that, of whom it was rumored that he was angling for the post of chief assistant lecturer—who would deprive himself even partially of this perfidious brilliance. When Müller at last reached the exit, he heard with half an ear the remainder of the sentence which Schmeck had broken off to blow his nose—"to the heart of the problem: is the mackintosh an accidental or typical manifestation? Is it sociologically significant?"

II

Müller reached the toilet just in time, loosened his tie, ripped open his shirt, heard a shirt button tinkle as it rolled away into the next cubicle, let his briefcase drop to the tiled floor—and vomited. He felt the cold sweat getting even colder on the gradually returning warmth of his face. Keeping his eyes closed, he flushed the toilet by groping for the lever, and was surprised to feel in some definitive way not only liberated but cleansed: what had been flushed away was more than vomit; it was a whole philosophy, a suspicion confirmed, rage—he laughed with relief, wiped his mouth with his handkerchief, hastily pushed up the knot of his tie, picked up his briefcase, and left the cubicle. They had teased him a hundred times, but here was proof of how useful it was always to carry along a towel and soap, a hundred times they had made fun of his "plebeian" soap container. As he opened it now, he could have kissed his mother, for she had urged him to take it with him when he started university three years ago: soap was the very thing he needed now. He pulled uncertainly at his tie, left it the way it was, hung his jacket up on the doorknob, washed his face and hands thoroughly, wiped his neck briefly, and left the washroom as quickly as he could. The corridors were still empty, and if he hurried he could be in his room before Marie. I'll ask her, he thought, whether disgust, which we all know originates in the mind, can have such a drastic effect on the stomach.

III

It was a mild, damp day in early spring. For the first time in three years of university he missed the last, the third, step at the main entrance—he had only reckoned with two—stumbled, and, in catching himself and trying to get back into step, he was conscious of the aftereffects of the appalling quarter of an hour he had just been through. He felt giddy, and he was aware of his surroundings as a pleasant, dreamy blur. The faces of the college girls—majoring in literature, he would imagine—wore a look of impressionistic sensuality; they strolled languidly about under the green trees, carrying their books, and even the Catholic students with their colored caps, who appeared to be holding some kind of meeting in front of the main building, seemed less objectionable than usual: their colored ribbons and caps might have been wisps of a dissolving rainbow. Müller stumbled along, returning greetings mechanically, fighting his way against the stream which now, at half past twelve, was pouring into the university, like a stream of workers at change of shift.

IV

Not until he was in the streetcar, three stops farther on, did he begin to
see properly again, as if he had put on glasses which corrected his vision.
From one suburb to the city center, from the center out again to another
suburb: almost an hour to think things out and "get everything into
proper perspective." It just couldn't be true! Surely Schmeck was the
last man to have to steal from him—Rudolf Müller, third-year student?
Hadn't he told Schmeck he was considering writing a series of essays
to demonstrate "The Sociology of Dress," taking as his first title "On
the Sociology of the Mackintosh," and hadn't Schmeck enthusiastically
agreed, congratulated him, and offered to supervise the whole series?
And hadn't he read the first pages of his "Sociology of the Mackintosh"
aloud to Schmeck in his study, sentences which today he had heard
coming word for word from Schmeck's lips? Müller turned pale again,
tore open his briefcase, and rummaged through it. The soap container
fell to the floor, then a book by Schmeck: *First Principles of Sociology*.
Where was his manuscript? Was it a dream, a memory, or a hallucination that he suddenly found himself looking at—Schmeck's smile as he
stood in the doorway of his study, the white pages of manuscript in
his hand? "Of course, I'll be glad to have a look at your work!" Then
the Easter vacation—first at home, then three weeks in London with a
study group—and today Schmeck's lecture, "Rudiments of a Sociology
of Dress, Part One: On the Sociology of the Mackintosh."

V

Transfer. He automatically got off, on again when his streetcar arrived,
gave a troubled sigh as the elderly conductress sitting on her throne recognized him. Would she make the same joke she had been making ever
since she had seen his student's pass? She made the joke: "Well, well—if
it isn't our gentleman of leisure, all through by eleven-thirty—and now
it's off to the girls, eh?" The passengers laughed, Müller blushed, made
his way to the front, wished he could get out, run faster than the streetcar, and get home and into his room at last, to find out for sure. His
diary would be proof—or would it help to have Marie as a witness? She

had typed his paper for him; he remembered her suggesting she make a carbon copy, he could see her hand holding up the carbon paper, but he had waved it aside, pointing out that it was only a draft, an outline— and he could see Marie's hand putting the carbon paper back into the drawer and starting to type. "Rudolf Müller, philosophy student, 17 Buckwheat Street" ...While he was dictating the heading it struck him one could also write a sociology of food. Buckwheat flour, pancakes, roast beef—in the working-class district where he had grown up this was considered the pinnacle of epicurean delight, on a par in the scale of bliss with sexual pleasures—rice pudding, lentil soup; and before he had even begun dictating his essay to Marie, he already had visions of following up the sociology of the mackintosh with a sociology of french fries. Ideas, ideas, all kinds, in fact—and he knew he had what it took to put these ideas into words.

VI

These endless streets leading out of the city, Roman, Napoleonic— the house numbers were already in the 900s. Fragmented memories: Schmeck's voice—the sudden nausea on first hearing the word "mack-intosh"—eight or nine minutes up there in the front row—the urge to vomit—then the thirty-third minute, Schmeck's handkerchief, his glance at the results of his noisy exertions—at long last the toilet— misty dampness in front of the university—the girls' faces, sensual, blurred—the colored ribbons of the Catholic students like remnants of a dying rainbow—getting onto the Number 12, transferring to the Number 18—the conductress's joke—and already the house numbers on Mainz Street were up to 980, 981. He pulled out one of the three cigarettes he had taken along in his breast pocket as his morning ration, groped for the match.

"Here, son, give us a light too." He stood up, and with a wan smile walked to where the old conductress was squeezing herself down off her throne. He held the burning match to her cigarette butt, then lit his own cigarette, and was pleasantly surprised to find he felt no nausea. "Troubles, son?" He nodded, looked hard at her coarse, red-veined face, dreading the obscenity she might offer as consolation, but she merely nodded and said, "Thank you kindly," clasped his shoulder as the streetcar swung into the terminus loop, got out ahead of him when the streetcar stopped, and waddled along to the front car, where the driver was already unscrewing his Thermos flask.

VII

How small these gray houses were, how narrow the streets. A parked motorcycle was enough to block them; thirty years ago the apostles of progress had not believed that cars would ever become a commonplace. Here visions of the future had become the present, and died; everything that would later claim to be progressive and advanced was regarded with hostility. All the streets were alike, from Acanthus Avenue to Zinnia Road, wintergreen and leek, monkshood (first rejected because it smacked of clericalism but later approved by the Board as being strictly botanical and free of any clericalist taint) and privet—"all growing things" were to be found here in street names, surrounded by a Marx Avenue, at the center an Engels Square (Marx Street and Engels Street had already been appropriated by older working-class districts). The little church had been built later, when it was discovered that the declared atheists were all married to devout wives—when one day (by this time the devout mothers had their grown-up sons and daughters on their side) the polling district had to report more votes for the Catholic Center Party than for the Socialist Party, when old Socialists, crimson with embarrassment, drowned their sorrows in drink and went over in a body to the Communist Party. For years now the little church had been much too small: on Sundays it overflowed, and the model for the new one could be admired at the rectory. Very modern. Beyond Marx Avenue, the neighboring parish of St. Boniface had donated land for the new church of St. Joseph, patron saint of the working class. Construction cranes were already reaching triumphantly into the spring sky.

Müller tried to smile, but couldn't quite, when he thought of his father; it always seemed to him as if the aura of the twenties, that ardent spirit of atheism and enlightenment, still hung in the air here, as if the climate of free love were still present, and, although it was never heard anymore, he seemed to hear echoes in these streets of "Brothers, toward sunlight, toward freedom"; his smile miscarried. Rosemary Street, Tulip Street, Maple Grove—and another cycle of streets in alphabetical order: Acacia Way, and finally Buckwheat Street—"all growing things." There was Number 17; now he could smile as he caught sight of Marie's bicycle: it was propped against the iron railing that Uncle Will had built around the garbage can, the none-too-clean, wobbly bicycle belonging to Baroness von Schlimm (younger branch). His desire to show affection even to the bicycle was manifested in a gentle kick against the back tire. He opened the door, called "Hello, Auntie" into the narrow passageway, which smelled of french fries, picked up the parcel lying on the bottom stair, and rushed upstairs. The staircase was so narrow that his elbow always brushed the reddish-brown hessian wall covering, and Aunt Kate claimed to be able to determine the vehemence and frequency of his ascents from the traces of wear—in the course of the three years a strip had been rubbed almost bare, to a shade resembling a bald head.

VIII

Marie. He never failed to be moved by the intensity of his feelings for her, and each time (by now they had met more than three hundred times; he kept track, so to speak, in his diary), each time she seemed thinner than he remembered her. During the time they were together she seemed to fill out—when he thought of her afterward he remembered her as full—and he was consistently surprised when he saw her again in her original, unaltered thinness. She had taken off her shoes and stockings and was lying on his bed, dark-haired and pale, with a pallor which he still could not help feeling was a sign of consumption.

"Please," she said gently, "don't kiss me. All morning I've been listening to dirty stories about various kinds of love. If you want to be nice, rub my feet." He threw down his briefcase and the parcel, knelt down by the bed, and took her feet in his hands. "How sweet you are," she said. "I only hope you don't get a male-nurse complex—with your kind one has to be so careful—and please," she said, lowering her voice, "let's stay here, I'm too tired to go out to eat. Anyway, our social worker, who looks after employee relations, always regards my absence at lunchtime as antisocial."

"For God's sake," he said, "why don't you quit the whole ghastly business? Those swine."

"Which ones do you mean? My bosses or the other girls?"

"Your bosses," he said, "what you call dirty stories are the outward expression of the only pleasures those girls have; your bourgeois ears..."

"I have feudal ears, in case my ears require a sociological epithet."

"Feudalism succumbed to the bourgeoisie: it married into industry, thereby becoming bourgeois. You are confusing what is accidental in you with what is typical; to attach so much importance to a name by regarding it as valueless as you regard yours is a form of late-bourgeois idealism. Isn't it enough for you that soon—before God and man, as your kind would put it—your name will be Marie Müller?"

"Your hands do feel nice," she said. "When will you be in a position to support a wife and children with them?"

"As soon as you take the trouble to work out how much we'll have to live on when we're married and you go on working."

She sat up and recited in a schoolgirl singsong: "You get two hundred forty-three a month, that's the highest category; as an assistant lecturer you earn two hundred, of which one hundred twenty-five is available because it's earned in conjunction with your university training. That makes three hundred sixty-eight—but your father earns seven hundred ten net, i.e., two hundred sixty more than the free limit, which means that you, since you're an only child, have your income reduced by one hundred thirty. In other words, you're working as an assistant lecturer for nothing—net balance: two hundred thirty-eight. As soon as we get married, half of what I earn above three hundred—i.e., exactly two marks and fifteen pfennigs—will be deducted, so that your total net income will amount to two hundred thirty-five marks and eighty-five pfennigs."

"Congratulations," he said. "So you really got down to it?"

"Yes," she said, "and the most important thing I worked out is that you're working for precisely nothing for this Schmeck-bastard..."

He took his hands off her legs. "Schmeck-bastard—what makes you say that?"

She looked at him, swung her legs round, sat up on the edge of the bed; he pushed his slippers toward her. "What's Schmeck been up to? Something new? Tell me—never mind my feet now—go on, tell me, what's he been up to?"

"Can you wait a moment?" he said; he picked up his briefcase and the parcel from the floor, took the two remaining cigarettes from his breast pocket, lit them both, gave one to Marie, threw briefcase and parcel down beside Marie on the bed, went over to the bookshelf, and pulled out his diary, a fat exercise book standing between Kierkegaard and Kotzebue, sat down at Marie's feet beside the bed.

"Listen," he said. "Here. 'December 13. During a walk with Marie through the park, suddenly struck by the idea of a "Sociology of the Mackintosh."'"

"That's right," said Marie, "you told me about it at the time. Remember my objections?"

"Sure." He turned some more pages. "Here. 'January 2. Began work on it. Outlines, ideas—also viewed material. Went to Meier's Menswear and tried to get a look at their customer list, but no luck...' It goes on— January, February, daily entries about the progress of the work."

"Yes, of course," said Marie, "and at the end of February you dictated the first thirty pages to me."

"Yes, and here, this is what I was looking for: 'March 1. Went to see Schmeck, showed him the first pages of my draft, read parts of it aloud to him. Schmeck asked me to leave the manuscript with him so he could look through it...'"

"That's right, and the next day you went home to your parents."

"And then to England. Came back yesterday—and today was Schmeck's first lecture, and the audience was more interested, more enthralled, more ecstatic than ever, because the subject was so new, so thrilling—at least for the audience. I'll let you guess what Schmeck's lecture was about. Try and guess, my dear baroness."

"If you call me 'baroness' once more, I'll call you—no"—she smiled—"don't worry, I won't call you that, even if you do call me 'baroness.' Would it hurt your feelings if I called you that?"

"If you called me that, no," he said gently. "You can call me what you like. But you have no idea how wonderful it is when they call out after you, whisper as you go by, when they write it after your name on the bulletin board—'Rudolf, Son of the Working Class.' I'm a freak, you see, I'm the great phenomenon, I'm one of those of whom there are only five in every hundred, only fifty in every thousand, and— the higher you go, the more fantastic the ratio—I'm one of those of whom there are only five thousand in every hundred thousand. I am really and truly the son of a working man who is studying at a West German university."

"At the East German universities I guess it's the other way round; ninety-five percent are from working-class families."

"Over there I'd be something absurdly ordinary; here I'm the famous example in discussions, arguments, counterarguments, a real live unadulterated Son of the Working Class—and talented too, very talented. But you still haven't tried to guess what Schmeck was paying homage to today."

"Television, perhaps."

Müller laughed. "No, the big snobs are now in *favor* of television."

"Not"—Marie stubbed out her cigarette in the ashtray Müller was holding—"not the sociology of the mackintosh?"

"What else," said Rudolf in a low voice, "what else?"

"No," said Marie, "he *can't* do that."

"But he has done it, and there were sentences in his lecture that I recognized and remembered how much fun I had had formulating..."

"Too much fun, it seems..."

"Yes, I know—he quoted whole paragraphs."

He got up off the floor and began pacing up and down in the room. "You know how it is when you try to figure out whether you're quoting yourself or someone else—when you hear something you think you've heard or said before, and you try to figure out whether you said it before yourself or whether you only thought it, whether you recognize it or read it—and you go crazy because your memory's not functioning properly?"

"Yes," said Marie, "I always used to worry about whether or not I'd had anything to drink before holy communion. You think you've had a drink of water because so often, so many thousands of times, you have had a drink of water on an empty stomach—but actually you haven't had anything to drink..."

"And yet you can't come up with any convincing proof—that's where a diary is so important."

"You needn't have worried about this particular question: it's obvious that Schmeck's robbed you."

"And done me out of my thesis."

"Oh, my God," said Marie—she stood up next to the bed, put her hand on Rudolf's shoulder, kissed his neck—"oh, my God, you're right, that's true. He's cut the ground from under your feet. Can't you sue him?"

Müller laughed. "Every university on the face of the earth, from Massachusetts to Göttingen to Lima, from Oxford to Nagasaki, will burst out in one united, crazy laugh when a person by the name of Rudolf Müller, Son of the Working Class, gets up and claims to have been robbed by Schmeck. Even the Warraus will join in the derisive laughter, for they know too that the wise white man Schmeck is omniscient in the ways of mankind. But—and this is what would happen if I sued him—if Schmeck got up and said he had been robbed by a person by the name of Müller, they would all nod their heads, even the Hottentots."

"He ought to be exterminated," said Marie.

"At last you're beginning to think in nonbourgeois terms."

"I don't understand how you can still laugh," said Marie.

"There's a very good reason for the fact that I can still laugh," said Müller. He went over to the bed, picked up the parcel, took it over to the table, and began to undo the string. He patiently untied all the knots, so slowly that Marie jerked open the drawer, took out a penknife, and silently held it out to him.

"Exterminated, yes," said Müller, "that might be an idea, but not for anything in the world would I cut this string: that would be cutting right into my mother's heart. When she opens a parcel she carefully unties the string, rolls it up, and puts it aside for future use—the next time she comes here she'll ask me about the string, and if I can't produce it she will predict the imminent end of the world."

Marie snapped the knife shut again, put it back in the drawer, leaned against Müller while he unwrapped the paper from his parcel and carefully folded it up. "You haven't told me yet why you can still laugh," she said. "After all, that was the vilest, filthiest, most disgusting trick that Schmeck could play on you—when you think how he wanted to make you his chief assistant and how he's prophesied a brilliant future for you."

"Well," said Müller, "do you really want to know why?"

She nodded. "Tell me," she said.

He put down the parcel, kissed her. "Damn it all," he murmured, "if it weren't for you I would have done something desperate."

"Do it anyway," she said quietly.

"What?"

"Do something desperate to him," said Marie, "I'll help you."

"What do you want me to do, really kill him?"

"Do something physical to him, not mental—half kill him."

"How?"

"Maybe beat him up—but let's have something to eat first. I'm hungry and I have to go off again in thirty-five minutes."

"I'm not so sure you will go off again."

He carefully folded up a second layer of paper, undid a piece of thinner string tied round the core of the parcel, a shoebox, removed the sheet of notepaper stuck between string and box lid ("Every parcel should contain the address inside as well as out"), and at last, as Marie sighed, he took off the lid of the shoebox: salami, ham, cake, cigarettes, and a package of glutamate. Marie picked up the notepaper from the table and read in a low voice, "My dear boy, I am glad you could make the long journey to England so cheaply. It is wonderful what they are doing these days at the universities. Tell us about London when you come home. Remember how proud we are of you. Now you are really working on your Ph.D. thesis—I just can't believe it. Your loving Mother."

"They really are proud of me," said Müller.

"And they have every reason to be," said Marie. She put away the contents of the parcel in a little cupboard below the bookshelves, took out an opened package of tea. "I'll run down and make us some tea."

IX

"It's funny," said Marie, "but when I propped my bike up against the railing today at noon, I knew that I wouldn't be going back after lunch to that plastics nightmare. One does have premonitions like that. Once when I came home from school I threw my bike against the hedge just like I used to every day; it always sank halfway in, tipped over, the handlebars would get caught in a branch and the front wheel would stick up in the air—and as I threw my bike in there, I knew I wouldn't be going back to school next day, that I would never be going back to any school. It wasn't just that I was fed up with it—there was much more to it than that. I simply knew that it would be wicked for me to go to school for even one more day. Father couldn't get over it; you see, it was exactly four weeks before my graduation, but I said to him: 'Have you ever heard of the sin of gluttony?' 'Yes,' he said, 'I have, but you haven't been guilty of gluttony as far as school's concerned.' 'No,' I said, 'it's just an example—but when you swallow one more mouthful of coffee or one more piece of cake than at a given point you ought to drink or eat, isn't that gluttony?' 'It is,' he said, 'and I can imagine such a thing as spiritual gluttony, only—' but I interrupted him and said, 'There's not room for another thing in me, I already feel like a stuffed goose.' 'It's a pity,' said Father, 'that this has to happen to you four weeks before your graduation. It's such a useful thing to have.' 'Useful for what?' I asked. 'You mean university?' 'Yes,' he said, and I said, 'No, if I'm going to work in a factory, then it's going to be a real one'—and that's what I did. Does it hurt you when I tell you things like this?"

"Yes," said Müller, "it hurts very much to see someone throwing away something that for countless people is the object of all their dreams and aspirations. It's also possible to laugh about clothes, or to despise them, when one has them hanging in the closet or is in a position to buy them any time—it's possible to laugh about anything one has always taken for granted."

"But I didn't laugh about it, and I didn't despise it, and it's true that I preferred to work in a real factory rather than in a university."

"Oh, I believe you," he said. "I do, just as I believe you're really a Catholic."

"By the way, I got a parcel from home yesterday too," said Marie. "Guess what was in it."

"Salami, ham, cake, cigarettes," said Müller, "and no glutamate—and, needless to say, you cut the string with scissors, screwed the paper up into a ball and..."

"Exactly," said Marie, "exactly, only you've forgotten something..."

"No, I haven't," said Müller. "I haven't forgotten anything, you interrupted me, that's all. Then you immediately bit into the salami, then the cake, and right after that you lit a cigarette."

"Come on, let's go to the movies, and then we'll half kill Schmeck this evening."

"Today?" said Müller.

"Of course today," said Marie. "Whenever you think something is right, you should do it at once—and a woman should fight at her man's side."

X

It was dark by the time they came out of the movie, and they found the bicycle-parking attendant in a state of sullen resentment; Marie's ramshackle bicycle was the sole remaining one in his charge. An old man, his coat almost trailing on the ground, rubbing his hands to warm them, walking up and down muttering curses under his breath.

"Give him a tip," whispered Marie. She remained nervously by the chain separating the parking lot from the square in front of the opera house.

"My principles forbid me to give tips except where they form part of the wages. It's an offense against human dignity."

"Perhaps you've got a mistaken idea of human dignity: seven hundred years ago my ancestor, the first Schlimm, was given a whole barony as a tip."

"And maybe that's why you have so little sense of human dignity. Christ," he said, lowering his voice, "what do you give in a case like this?"

"Twenty or thirty pfennigs, I should think, or about the same in cigarettes. Go on, please, you go first. Help your assistant. I'm so embarrassed."

Müller hesitantly approached the attendant, holding out the stub as if it were a pass he didn't quite trust, then, when the old man's furious face was turned toward him, quickly drew the cigarette pack from his pocket, saying, "Sorry, I'm afraid we're a bit late." The old man took the whole pack, stuck it into his coat pocket, gestured in wordless contempt toward the bicycle, and walked past Marie in the direction of the streetcar stop.

"When you're in love with lightweight men," said Marie, "you have the advantage of being able to take them on the luggage carrier." She rode in and out between waiting cars till they got to the front at the red light. "Look out, Müller," she said, "see you don't scratch their paint with your feet, they're very touchy about that, they worry about it more than if their wives get a scratch." And when the driver of the car waiting beside her rolled down his window, she said in a loud voice, "If I were you, I would write a sociology of the various makes of cars. Driving is the training ground of one-upmanship—and the worst ones are the so-called gentlemen behind the wheel. Their false democratic courtesy is positively nauseating; it is hypocrisy par excellence, because it means they expect a medal for something that should be taken for granted."

"Right," said Müller, "and the worst thing about them is, they all think *they* look different from the others, while actually..."

The driver quickly wound up his window again.

"Yellow, Marie," he said.

Marie pushed off, going straight across in front of the cars to the right-hand lane, while Müller conscientiously stuck out his right arm.

"I see I've found a good assistant," he said, as they turned into a dark side street.

"Assistant," said Marie, over her shoulder, "is a weak translation of *adjutorium*—which contains much more: counsel, and some pleasure too. Where does he live?"

"Mommsen Street," said Müller, "Number 37."

"That's wonderful—he's stuck with a street name that must annoy him every time he reads it, says it, writes it—and I hope he has to do each of those things three times a day. I'm sure he hates a classicist like Mommsen."

"He hates him like poison."

"Serves him right that he has to live on Mommsen Street. What's the time?"

"Half past seven."

"A quarter of an hour to go."

She turned into a still darker side street leading to the park, and stopped; Müller jumped off and helped her to guide the bicycle through the barrier. They walked a few yards along the dark path, stopped beside a bush, and Marie threw her bicycle against a shrub; it sank halfway in, got caught on a twig. "Almost like home," said Marie. "There's nothing like shrubbery for bikes."

Müller put his arms around her, kissed her neck, and Marie whispered, "Don't you think I'm a bit too skinny for a woman?"

"Be quiet, assistant," he said.

"You're terribly scared," she said. "I didn't know one could actually feel a person's heart beating—tell me, are you scared?"

"Of course I am," he said. "It's my first assault—and I find it quite incredible that we're really standing here for the purpose of luring Schmeck into a trap, to beat him up. I just can't believe it."

"You see, you have faith in intellectual weapons, in progress and so on, and one has to pay for such mistakes; if there ever were such things as intellectual weapons, they're no use nowadays."

"Try to understand," he whispered, "the mental process: here I am..."

"You poor fellows, you must be schizophrenics. I do wish I weren't so thin. I read somewhere that thin women aren't good for schizoids."

"Your hair actually smells of that filthy plastic, and your hands are quite rough."

"Yes," she whispered. "You see, I'm one of those girls you come across in modern novels. Heading: 'Baroness turns her back on her own class, decides she is really going to *live*.' What's the time now?"

"Almost quarter to."

"He's bound to come soon. It's so satisfactory to be going to trap him in his own vanity. You ought to have heard his voice when he was talking to that radio reporter, 'Regularity, rhythm, that is my principle. A light meal—just a snack, actually, at seven-fifteen—and some strong tea; and at a quarter to eight my evening walk through the park.' You're sure you know what we're going to do?"

"Yes," said Müller. "As soon as he comes round the corner, you lay your bike down right across the path, and when I go 'Psst,' you run and lie down beside it. He'll come running over to you."

"And you come from behind, beat him up thoroughly, hard enough so he needs some time to come to, and we clear off..."

"That doesn't sound quite fair."

"'Fair,'" she said, "that's just one of those mental images."

"And what if he calls for help? Or if he manages to get the upper hand? He weighs at least a hundred pounds more than I do! And, as I say, I don't like the sound of 'from behind.'"

"Of course, people like you always have your mental images. Fair election campaign, and so on—and obviously you always get defeated. Remember I'm coming to help you, that I'll hit him good and hard too—and if we have to we'll just abandon the bike."

"As a corpus delicti? It must be the only bike in town whose appearance is unmistakable."

"Your heart's beating stronger and stronger, faster and faster—you really must be dreadfully scared."

"Aren't you?"

"Sure I am," she said, "but I know we're in the right, and that this is the only way of seeing some kind of justice done, considering the whole world's on his side, including the Hottentots."

"Christ," whispered Müller, "there he is now."

Marie jumped onto the path, snatched her bicycle from the bushes, laid it down in the middle of the damp path. Müller watched Schmeck walking along the lane, hatless, his coat open and flapping. "Damn," he whispered to Marie, "we forgot the dog. Look at that creature, a German shepherd, almost as big as a calf." Marie was standing beside him again, looking over his shoulder toward Schmeck. "Solveig, Solveig," he called hoarsely, fending off the dog who was leaping joyously up at him; then he picked up a stone from the path and threw it toward the bushes, where it dropped scarcely ten yards from Müller.

"Damn," said Marie, "it's useless trying anything with that dog; he's vicious, and trained to attack people—I can tell. We'll get complexes because we didn't do it after all, but it's quite useless." She walked over to the path, picked up her bicycle, nudged Müller, and said softly, "Well, come on, we have to leave, what's the matter?"

"Nothing," said Müller. He took Marie's arm. "I had just forgotten how much I loathe him."

Schmeck was standing under the streetlight stroking the dog, who had laid the stone at his feet; he looked up as the couple entered the circle of light, glanced once more at the dog, then suddenly up again, and walked toward Müller with outstretched hands. "Müller," he said warmly, "my dear Müller, fancy meeting you here"—but Müller succeeded in looking at and yet through Schmeck. Mustn't meet Schmeck's eyes; if I meet them, he thought, I'm lost; I mustn't behave as if he isn't there—he is there, and I'll extinguish him with my eyes—one step, two, three—he felt Marie's firm grasp on his arm, he was panting as if after some enormous exertion.

"Müller," called Schmeck, "it *is* you—can't you take a joke?"

The rest was easy: just keep walking, fast and yet not too fast... They heard Schmeck calling again, "Müller," first loud, then softer, "Müller, Müller, Müller"—and at last they had turned the corner.

Marie's deep sigh startled him; when he turned to her he saw she was crying. He took the bicycle from her, leaned it against a garden fence, wiped her tears away with his finger, put his free hand on her shoulder. "Marie," he said softly, "what's the matter?"

"You scare me," she said, "that wasn't an assault, that was murder. I'm scared he's going to wander around for all eternity in this wretched little park whispering 'Müller, Müller, Müller.' It's like a nightmare: Schmeck's ghost with the dog, in the damp bushes, his beard growing, getting so long that it drags behind him like a frayed belt—and all the time he's whispering 'Müller, Müller, Müller.' Oughtn't I to see if he's all right?"

"No," said Müller, "no, don't, just leave him alone, he's perfectly all right. If you feel sorry for him, give him a mackintosh for his birthday. You can't even begin to think what he's done to me; he turned me into the miracle Son of the Working Class. I was his protégé, as they call it—and no doubt he expects the mackintoshes as a form of tribute—but I'm not going to pay him this tribute, not if I can help it. Tomorrow morning he's going to say casually to Wegelot, his chief assistant, just as he's leaving the room, 'By the way, Müller's gone over into the reactionary camp after all: he's transferred to Livorno. He called me up yesterday saying he wanted to leave the seminar,' and then he'll close the door again, go over to Wegelot, and say, 'Pity about Müller, very talented, but his draft thesis was simply terrible, quite hopeless. I suppose it's difficult for these people who have to fight not only the world around them but their own milieu as well. Pity'—then he'll bite his lip again and leave the room."

"Are you quite sure that's how it's going to be?"

"Quite sure," said Müller. "Come on, let's go home. No tears for Schmeck, Marie."

"The tears weren't for Schmeck," said Marie.

"For me, then?"

"Yes—you're so terribly brave."

"Now that really does sound like a modern novel. Are we going home?"

"Would you think it terrible if I said I would like one (in a word, one) hot meal?"

"All right," Müller said, laughing. "Let's ride to the nearest restaurant."

"We'd better walk. There are a lot of policemen around at this hour—the park, not many lights, spring in the air—attempted rapes—and a summons would cost us as much as two bowls of soup."

Müller wheeled the bicycle. They walked slowly along the lane beside the park; as they stepped out of the light from the next street-lamp they saw a policeman in deep shadow beyond the barrier, leaning against a tree.

"You see," said Marie, loud enough for the policeman to hear, "we've already saved two marks for the summons, but as soon as we get out of sight you can hop up again."

When they had turned the next corner, Marie got up on her bicycle, propping herself against the curb to let Müller get on. She pushed off quickly, leaned back, and called out: "What do you want to do now?"

"How do you mean?"

"I mean, what d'you want to do."

"Now, or generally speaking?"

"Now *and* generally speaking."

"Now I'm going to have something to eat with you, and generally speaking I'm going to see Livorno tomorrow, register for his course, ask for an interview, and offer a suggestion for a thesis."

"On what?"

"'Critical Appreciation of the Collected Works of Schmeck.'"

Marie rode up to the curb, stopped, turned round in the saddle. "On what?"

"I just told you: 'Critical Appreciation of the Collected Works of Schmeck.' I know them almost by heart—and hatred makes good ink."

"Doesn't love?"

"No," said Müller, "love makes the worst ink in the world. Ride on, assistant."

ANECDOTE CONCERNING THE LOWERING OF PRODUCTIVITY

In a harbor on the west coast of Europe, a shabbily dressed man lies dozing in his fishing boat. A smartly dressed tourist is just putting a new roll of color film into his camera to photograph the idyllic picture: blue sky, green sea with peaceful, snowy whitecaps, black boat, red woolen fisherman's cap. Click. Once more: click and, since all good things come in threes and it's better to be safe than sorry, a third time: click. The snapping, almost hostile sound awakens the dozing fisherman, who sleepily sits up, sleepily gropes for his cigarettes, but before he has found what he is looking for the eager tourist is already holding a pack under his nose, not exactly sticking a cigarette between his lips but putting one into his hand, and a fourth click, that of the lighter, completes the overeager courtesy. As a result of that excess of nimble courtesy—scarcely measurable, never verifiable—a certain awkwardness has arisen that the tourist, who speaks the language of the country, tries to bridge by striking up a conversation.

"You'll have a good catch today."

The fisherman shakes his head.

"But I've been told the weather's favorable!"

The fisherman nods.

"So you won't be putting out?"

The fisherman shakes his head, the tourist grows more and more uncomfortable. It is clear that he has the welfare of the shabbily dressed man at heart and that disappointment over the lost opportunity is gnawing at him.

"Oh, I'm sorry—aren't you feeling well?"

At last the fisherman switches from sign language to the spoken word. "I feel fine," he says. "I've never felt better." He stands up, stretches as if to demonstrate his athletic build. "I feel terrific."

The tourist's expression grows steadily more unhappy, and he can no longer suppress the question that threatens, so to speak, to burst his heart: "So why aren't you putting out?"

The reply comes promptly and succinctly. "Because I was already out this morning."

"Was it a good catch?"

"It was so good that I don't need to go out again—I had four lobsters in my traps, and I caught almost two dozen mackerel..."

The fisherman, finally wide awake, now thaws and gives the tourist a reassuring pat on the back. The latter's worried expression strikes him as a sign of touching although unwarranted concern.

"I even have enough for tomorrow and the day after," he says, to put the stranger's mind at rest. "Will you have one of my cigarettes?"

"Thanks, I will."

Cigarettes are placed between lips—a fifth click—the stranger sits down on the edge of the boat, shaking his head, and puts down his camera, for he now needs both hands to give emphasis to his words.

"I don't wish to interfere in your personal affairs," he says, "but just imagine if you were to go out a second, a third, maybe even a fourth time today, and you were to catch three, four, five, maybe even ten dozen mackerel... just imagine that!"

The fisherman nods.

"You would," the tourist continues, "go out not only today but tomorrow, the day after tomorrow, indeed on every favorable day, two, three, maybe four times. Do you know what would happen?"

The fisherman shakes his head.

"In less than a year you would be able to buy a motor, in two years a second boat, in three or four years you might have a small cutter, and with two boats or the cutter you would obviously catch much more. One day you would have two cutters, you would"—from sheer enthusiasm his voice cracks for a few seconds—"you would build a small cold-storage plant, maybe a smokehouse, later a pickling factory, you would fly around in your own helicopter, spot schools of fish, and direct your cutters by radio. You could acquire the salmon rights, open up a fish restaurant, export lobster direct to Paris without a middleman—and then..." Once again words fail the stranger in his enthusiasm. Shaking his head, grieved to the very core of his being, and having lost almost all pleasure in his vacation, he looks out onto the peacefully advancing tide where the uncaught fish are happily leaping around.

"And then..." he says, but again he is speechless in his agitation. The fisherman pats him on the back as if he were a child with a fit of choking. "Then what?" he asks softly.

"Then," says the stranger with restrained enthusiasm, "then, without a care in the world, you could sit here in the harbor, doze in the sun—and look at the glorious sea."

"But I'm already doing that," says the fisherman. "I sit here in the harbor without a care in the world and doze—it was only your clicking that disturbed me."

And so the thus enlightened tourist walked pensively away, for at one time he had believed that he too was working so as someday not to have to work anymore, and no trace of pity for the shabbily dressed fisherman remained in him, only a little envy.

HE CAME AS A BEER-TRUCK DRIVER

I

What he liked best were the slender wine bottles; they fitted so neatly into his coat pocket. He never carried around more than would fit into his coat pockets: a bottle of wine and a piece of cheese in one; bread, tobacco, cigarette papers, matches in the other. No handker-chief, no toothbrush. What soap he needed he found in the toilets on the trains, where he also blew his nose with his fingers and washed his shirts and socks, letting them dry on his warm body. The maximum he would carry in his hands was a paper bag containing some fried chicken, bread, and fruit: after a meal he could toss the remains out the train window.

Whenever he entered a first-class compartment he was aware of that brief hesitation, as if one of the passengers were about to say: Excuse me, but this is first class. He killed this brief hesitation with a laugh. Then, whenever the conductor came along and tickets had to be produced, there was that slight tension followed by two things: surprise and relief when he produced the green-and-white piece of cardboard from his pocket. They didn't even dare look up when he belched. The women either moved away from him or too close to him, neither of which he liked.

What surprised him most was the lipsticks. Whenever a woman took one out of her handbag and put it to her lips, he laughed aloud: he hadn't imagined that this cult had penetrated so far north and become so widespread. This lack of embarrassment on the part of the women and innocence of the men, who failed to recognize their own symbol, amused him. In the course of his long journey he realized that the women made equally innocent use of this obvious symbol, and he laughed even louder. No feeling for signs and wonders. Only the wait-ers seemed aware of something: they served him without venomous

797

servility and, without his having to ask, brought him only food he could eat with his fingers—chicken, bread, fruit—and they weren't even surprised at the generosity of his tips.

Twice, in Vienna and Munich, there had been a lengthy stop during which he had walked to the nearest tavern, sat down at the bar, ordered a beer, kissed the palm of the woman who served him, and stroked her forearms, and each woman had ruffled his hair with her free hand, murmuring, "What are you looking for here?," and each time he had replied, "Europa." One of them—he couldn't remember whether in Vienna or Munich—had murmured, "Europa? Not here!"; the other, "Europa? But surely not here?" And one of them had said when he kissed her palm, "God!," and the other, "Bull!"

He tried out the strange place names as if tasting wine: Munich unpleasant, Ulm pleasant; Stuttgart and Frankfurt unpleasant; Mainz—he nodded. The Rhine was good, very good; he stood at the window while the train traveled beside it; good, he nodded to himself as he smoked. At Koblenz (unpleasant) darkness fell, so he went back into the compartment and slept until he was awakened by a shout that sounded like a shot: Bonn! He laughed and took a long swig from his bottle of wine.

Cologne tasted unpleasant; he had to change trains there. On the train to Ostend he sat across from a white-haired gentleman who smiled at him over newspaper, spectacles, and a purple ascot, put aside the newspaper, and removed his spectacles; then he heard in his own language, "Tell me, where are you from?"

"Don't you know?" he said, and his mouth was filled with a wonderful taste when he could speak his own language.

The old gentleman nodded, no longer smiling. "What are you looking for here?"

"Europa."

"And where are you going?"

"To London."

The old gentleman laughed and shook his head. "But Europa isn't in London."

"Where, then—where is she?"

"Not too far from Aachen."

"And where is Aachen?"

"Next stop but one."

The old gentleman was the first person to accept the proffered bottle of wine and drink from it. "God!" he said, as he lowered it from his lips. "That's some wine." And as he handed back the bottle he asked quietly, "Why are you sad? You'll find her all right."

"It's not sadness you see in my eyes, it's envy."

"Envy? Of what?"

"Of you, because you're all mortal."

"You're mortal, too," said the old gentleman as he tucked his newspaper under his arm, stood up, and lifted a bag down from the rack. The train came to a halt. "Don't forget—the next stop's Aachen."

He stayed out in the corridor, smoking and musing: Had the old gentleman been Death? Purple and white, and spoke his language so beautifully. A young woman with a twitching face hobbled toward him with a cane, tried to pass him; he took her twitching face in his hands like a fruit, it became smooth and soft; passed his hands two or three times along her crooked spine as if it were a musical instrument. He took away her cane and tossed it into the corridor; she groaned, "God, oh God!," tried to kiss his hands. He disengaged himself, ran into the next car, pulled the emergency brake, and jumped off the train before it jerked to a halt.

He lay smiling on his back among beanstalks, heard shouting, saw lanterns swinging; a voice called out, "It was that Greek, that foreign worker!" He tore off a few bean pods, ate the young beans out of their downy shells, drank some wine, waited until the train moved off after much swinging of lanterns. He stood up and, without waiting to brush the earth off his coat and trousers, walked across to the road, toward the next village. What he read on the signpost pleased him greatly: "LANGERWEHE=LONGBORN." At the next tavern he saw behind the glass door the shadow of the landlady, who was about to lock up; he gently pushed open the door, looked into her broad, tired face, and said, "Give me a quick beer, will you?" She locked the door behind him, went to the bar, took a glass from the shelf, and held it under the beer tap.

"You don't happen to be able to drive a car, do you?" she asked.

"Of course I can," he said.

"How about a truck?"

"Sure."

"D'you have a license?"

He fished it out of his pocket, handed it to her, and she studied it carefully.

"Tauros?" she said. "Doesn't that mean 'bull'?"

"My, my!" he said. "Such erudition!"

"I went to a convent school," she said, "you learn a lot there. Okay. You're hired. Let's give it a try."

And that's how he became a beer-truck driver.

II

Not only was her first name unusual; even more so was the fact that she moved in with that fellow Schmitz, an electrician at a paper mill who had inherited a cottage with stable and barn, plus a few acres of land; a bit of a dreamer who to some people seemed morose and somewhat straitlaced because he maintained a stubborn silence in the taverns while others—salesmen, house painters, mailmen—talked about women and sex. He was thought to be a "queer" because he never had anything to do with women or girls, never went to dances—except for that one time with a cousin from Langerwehe who simply dragged him off in her car because she had no escort for the evening. That night at the dance he met her school friend with the unusual name. Suddenly he could actually dance; he danced many times with her, later drew her by the hand through the gaily lit beer garden to the edge of the field, tried to embrace her among the parked cars. "Not here," she said softly.

"Where, then?" he asked.

"In the forest," she said, "far, far away from all these cars. Not where there are cars around."

She drew him away by the hand, deep into the forest.

She gave up her study of engineering and moved in with him in the hamlet of Frauenbroich.

The nuns at the school had expected more of her. "Europa," so her final report had read, "combines intuition and intellectuality in a manner that warrants the expectation of great things from her." The nuns had expected not piety from her but boldness: "The new architectural dimension of a renewed Christian spirit," was how the principal had expressed it. Their annoyance with her was forgotten: that she had usually hidden in the garden to get out of church and prayers, preferring to weed or help with the fruit harvest, and then that affair with the elderly gardener, confessed to not by her but by him. He claimed that she—she was fifteen —had seduced him. She answered all reproaches with the single sentence, "I am a woman, I am a woman, I am a woman." Later with a truck driver who was delivering cement for the new gymnasium, and again the single sentence from her, "I am a woman." Both men were married, scandals just barely avoided. The comment of her home-room teacher, "It is her lack of conscience that makes her so beautiful." High point of her school fame: her meditation on the word "vanish" with its associations of evanescence, thin air, evaporation. The school inspector's comment, "Really worthy of publication." At the same time her astonishing insight into mathematical problems. She did everything "effortlessly": picking fruit, athletics, physics.

Now she was living with that electrician Schmitz, looking after his house, the cow, the chickens, spending days wandering about in the forests collecting berries and mushrooms; putting up preserves, mowing the hay. In Frauenbroich and the surrounding hamlets, people said she also carried on with men in the forest, but no man was ever found who boasted of having carried on with her.

Schmitz was good to her, she was good to him; her origins remained as obscure to him as they had always been to the nuns. Foundling, orphan. Whenever Schmitz asked her about it, she would murmur, "I don't know where I come from." When Schmitz came home and asked her how she was feeling, she would answer as she had answered the nuns when they had asked her the same question, "Like a stranger, but fine."

At night she would often place her right arm under his neck, draw his left arm under her own neck, hum to herself, and say things that to Schmitz's ears sounded odd.

"The loveliest word in your language—vanish."

"Why do you say 'your language'—isn't it yours too?"

He could feel on his arm that she shook her head.

"You know, don't you," she said one night, "that I'm not going to stay with you?"

She could feel in the dark on her arm that he nodded his head.

Schmitz was never afraid, yet he was apprehensive. It seemed to him that she had been with him forever, as if she had always been with him. "Eternity"—the word became for him as long and as broad as it was; time lost its meaning for him: one July morning they had emerged from the forest together, and she had stayed with him; he had taken his vacation, plus some unpaid weeks, and it was early September before he took on the sales depot for bottled beer. He felt as if eternity lay behind him and time lay ahead of him. Even words dropped away, became unfamiliar. "Marry"—he felt as if he had never heard the word; cars—he saw them, yet knew they didn't exist. Europa's presence extinguished words and realities.

"When I have vanished from you," she told him early in September, "take Trude Weihrauch. She is a woman."

III

Next morning at breakfast the landlady scolded him for his manners—for refusing to use a knife, simply tearing the bread into pieces and dipping them into the butter, then into the salt. With a scornful laugh he deigned to use a spoon to scrape the eggs out of their shells. Bread, butter, eggs, salt, and coffee: he enjoyed them all. He studied his route on the map, had her explain the list of agencies to him, where they were located in the hamlets; problems of bottle deposits, and the main principle of the business: "Cash only. After all, they've sold the beer, made their profit, and can pay cash for their new supplies. Only that new fellow, Schmitz in Frauenbroich, you can give him credit for a while." Luckily the truck had already been loaded by his predecessor. "You'll be late getting back," she said as he sat down behind the wheel, "and don't get lost, Bull!"

"Yes," he said, "I'll be late getting back," and drove off with a laugh.

He liked those sleepy hamlets, too small for a tavern or too far away from the next tavern, weary cattle among the fruit trees; unloading full beer crates, loading empty ones, money into the big leather bag; lethargic women with whom he negotiated, lively ones who usually became over-familiar. Toward two in the afternoon, just outside Frauenbroich, he drove off onto a forest path, drank some wine from his bottle, ate some bread and cheese, smoked a cigarette, switched on the motor to back out. He saw her coming along the path toward the truck, put on the brake, let the motor idle in neutral, jumped off, and ran toward her. Brief shyness before he took her in his arms; he was surprised to find that her hair was dark, he had imagined her blond. It bothered her that he smelled of car. "Come," he said softly, "let us vanish."

The truck was found by a pair of lovers that night, the motor still running. Schmitz came back into time, all apprehension fell away from him. No trace of those two. They had vanished in the forests.

THE STAECH AFFAIR

The "ae" in Staech is pronounced like a long, faintly aspirated "a," as in Bach. It bothers the inhabitants of the place—consisting almost entirely of Benedictine monks—to hear the "ae" pronounced as in aerobatics. Hence this preamble. There are some further antagonisms associated with the name "Staech" which I can only mention in passing: a heated dispute among onomatologists, for instance, some maintaining that the "ae" is an unmistakable sign of Germanic origin, while their opponents claim that the final "ch" is an unmistakable sign of Celtic origin. I plead the Celtic cause, knowing only too well how corruptible vowels are; and besides, there is the telltale dialect in and around Staech. Staech is located in the Rhineland. I must dispense with a definition of what constitutes Rhenish, restricting myself to the line of demarcation given to the Rhineland at the time of the Prussian occupation, which has persisted since 1815, and according to this line of demarcation Staech is located in the Rhineland. It is ancient, renowned, beautiful, idyllic; in the midst of tall trees, the incomparable gray of medieval Rhenish romanesque; a robust little river by the name of Brülle provides the landscape's essential ingredient of water. (Brülle is in no way related to the German verb *brüllen*, to roar. Beware of jumping to false etymological conclusions! The name probably derives from *bruhlen*, in turn a local corruption of the amply familiar *buhlen*, to consort illicitly: it has *almost* been established that here, in the midst of these venerable forests, a medieval prelate built an abode for his concubine.)

Staech has two hotels—one luxury, one modest—a youth camp, and a hostel that is used for conferences. The most important feature is the Benedictine abbey. There one can play at being a temporary monk. Tranquillity, Gregorian chants, peace within and without. And then there are the monks in their noble garb, one or other of whom, at any given moment, either at prayer or meditation or in conversation with a guest, embellishes landscape or garden. Everything extremely simple, almost austere; the soil is tilled, orchards are tended. The climate is too harsh for wine.

I can forgo further details and merely point out that Staech is extolled by the protocol officials of the nearby capital as being "a sheer delight." A high-ranking—perhaps even the highest-ranking—official of the protocol department is said to have remarked, "What more can we ask for? The Occident in one of its most cultivated articulations is only fifty Mercedes-minutes away."

Indeed, Staech is virtually irreplaceable. Eleventh (possibly tenth or twelfth) century, gray Rhenish romanesque, Gregorian chants, the opportunity to become a temporary monk or to stay in a luxury hotel and at the same time participate in all the delights of the liturgy and the consolations of *almost* all the sacraments. An area—again I quote a protocol official—abounding in "positively unique opportunities for country rambles" in which, depending on the condition of the heart, lungs, or glands, one can spend half an hour, an entire hour, an hour and a half, three hours, in fact a whole day walking or hiking, equipped with a handy foolproof local map obtainable *free of charge* from the hall porter at the luxury hotel. The fact that in the luxury hotel one can also be a temporary husband or wife is familiar to cynics, who know that the management there is both discreet and broad-minded.

Only the protocol department is in a position to appreciate the invaluable role Staech performs for the benefit of wives of prominent visitors to the nation's capital. While their husbands get down to the nitty-gritty in the capital, the ladies enjoy being driven out to Staech in the protocol Mercedes. Departure is timed for the visitor to arrive in the morning for the Terce or Sext services and thus admire the nobly clad monks both aurally and visually (it is said that there have even been attempts at tactile perception). This is followed by light refreshments or lunch, and then, depending on time, mood, and stamina, a stroll through the truly magnificent woods, and in the afternoon attendance at Nones or Vespers, followed by tea and a drive back, filled with a deep spiritual peace, to the capital. And German as well as foreign politicians find Staech unique as a place of meditation and purification; some very strong-minded men have been seen humbly and tearfully kneeling there. Guests from the United States and Africa are particularly enchanted with Staech, it has even been claimed that spontaneous

conversions have taken place there. And, needless to say, where *Ora*
is demonstrated with such credibility, *Labora* is not forgotten either:
brothers with rough hands, mud on their hands and feet, their habits
sometimes even bespattered with cow dung, are to be seen from time
to time, and the strange part about it is: these working monks are not
merely on show, they are genuine.

One surprising aspect is that the monks are always so willing to leave
this idyllic spot. The travel itch of the monks of Staech has not escaped
the affectionate mockery of the good Rhenish people in the neighborhood: a well-to-do local wag with an unpaid debt of gratitude to the
monks is said to have once presented them with a whole collection of
suitcases for Christmas. The monks really do love to travel; they lecture,
with and without slides, participate in conferences, seminars, panel
discussions; some of them contribute as free-lance writers to the sup-
plements of serious national journals, discussing matters of theology,
religion, and Christianity; and they seize every opportunity of going
off to Hamburg, Munich, or Frankfurt. Yes, they love to go away, these
monks, and they are not always happy to come back. Some are motorized, most are not. Hence the nominal full strength, amounting at present to forty-seven monks and brothers, is seldom achieved.

There have been occasions when only eleven, and once only nine,
were present at afternoon Nones. After one such service a very prominent lady from Thailand apprehensively asked the protocol official
whether there was some contagion in the air and whether—she had
been nourished on early nineteenth-century literature—the reverend
gentlemen were "stricken." The official found himself obliged to seek an
explanation from the abbot and was given the devastating information
that only one was sick, the others were all away on their travels.

Since in this age of technology the number of salaried workers
is perforce steadily increasing (farming, hotel staff, administration),
Staech is not financially self-supporting. It is liberally subsidized by
state and diocese; and, moreover, the fact *that* it is supported is taken
for granted. Not once has this fact been challenged in the finance committee, not even by the most religiously emancipated of its members.
Who would want to see Staech deprived of its subsidies? That would be

like suggesting that Cologne Cathedral be sold as a quarry. Even rabid freethinkers, irreligious Socialists (there are still some of those about), have never thought of withholding approval of the funds earmarked for Staech. Paradoxically enough, in latter years a contrary trend has become noticeable: the representatives of the classic Christian parties are hesitating somewhat longer, whereas the others are consenting with almost embarrassing alacrity. Of one thing there can be no doubt: even the most pettifogging atheist in the capital would not refuse Staech his support. Staech is something it ought not to be: dependent on the state and on the diocese in whose territory it is located. Of course, state and diocese are in a way dependent on Staech, but who could ever plumb the depths of such dialectics of varying interdependence?

One thing is certain: the abbot collects, and not too badly either. But in return state and diocese want to *see* something, or rather: they feel there should *be* something to see and hear. What, after all, is the use of a vast abbey like that, with all its complex economy (which is more complex than its tradition), if, as happened one foggy autumn day during the visit of a (non-Catholic) queen, only fifteen nobly garbed monks were present and the choral singing, even though each one "gave it all he had," sounded thin? Moreover, the participants included two aged bedridden monks who had been pressed somewhat forcibly into service. The queen was disappointed, *very* disappointed. During the ensuing informal lunch at the hotel she looked almost miffed, like a girl who has been done out of a date. After all, Staech *stands* for something. At home the queen had requested a thorough briefing on the history, tradition, and function of Stacch.

As was inevitable, the news of the choir's poor numerical showing reached the ears of the head of state. He—the head of state—was most annoyed and passed on his annoyance to the archbishop, who communicated the incident in a handwritten document beginning "*Scandalum fuisse...*" to the order's abbot general in Rome: the latter took up the matter with Staech and insisted on a list of those present and those absent, with detailed information on the absent monks' reasons for travel. The inquiries were, naturally, somewhat protracted, and even after some pretty massive interpolations the results were meager. Only sixteen of the absent monks could come up with an adequate alibi: eight had been occupied in a completely bona fide pursuit—conducting religious exercises in a convent—and eight had been away on lecture tours for Christian educational projects, some with, some without, colored slides. Five of the younger monks had left to attend a writers' conference ("We must seek contacts with the progressive elements of our own country"), the topic of which had caused both head of state and bishop considerable raising of eyebrows: "Orgasm as Depicted in Contemporary German Literature." It turned out later that four of these young monks had found the topic boring and spent most of their time at the movies, and in the balcony at that, where they could smoke. The alibis for the remaining eleven monks remained obscure. Two had ostensibly gone off to another monastery with which Staech was on friendly terms, to consult some volumes of the *Acta Sanctorum*, those in the Staech library having been stolen during the years of postwar confusion; the two monks had never arrived at the other monastery and, what was more, stubbornly refused to say where they had actually been (as yet unclarified). One monk had gone to Holland, with a purpose but no destination: purpose—to study the changes in Dutch Catholicism. This objective was termed by the bishop "rather vague." The objective of four other monks was given as: the study of Bavarian and Austrian baroque; they may have been traipsing around anywhere between Würzburg and the Hungarian border, but they did bring back an alibi in the form of a pretty good crop of colored slides. One monk had gone to a North German university town ostensibly to encourage an eminent physicist in his desire to convert to Catholicism; what had actually happened (as the physicist himself subsequently told the head of state at a reception) was that the monk tried to prevent the conversion.

Well, there was trouble. The abbot could not be deposed, only voted out of office, and this was something the monks refused to do. They liked their abbot. For a while the abbot managed to curb the monks' travel itch. The next state visitor was a president from Africa, who turned out to be an expert, having been educated by Benedictines. There were thirty-two monks present, but even thirty-two monks do not make the Staech choir seem exactly overcrowded. The effect is roughly that of a hundred and fifty bishops inside St. Peter's: something like a sightseeing group of elderly sacristans. The head of state, amazed at the African

guest's fund of knowledge about the order, expressed distinct annoyance to the head of protocol and raised the question of whether Staech
was still fulfilling its function... The result was a verbal confrontation
between protocol officials and the diocesan secretariat.

The topic remained a secret, but some things inevitably leaked out:
the curbing of travel itch at Staech had been followed by accesses of
kleptomania and exhibitionism. Eleven of the younger monks had had
to be consigned to a private psychiatric clinic. The abbot's request that
notice of important state visits be given well in advance, in order that
he might adjust the monks' travel movements accordingly, was refused.
He was tersely informed that it was up to Staech to be "ready for action"
at all times, since guests, such as journalists from the Eastern European
bloc, often turned up at short notice, eager to see the sights.

What might be called the "Staech affair" ran on for about a year, when
suddenly, one crisp but sunny spring day, head of state *and* bishop
made an unannounced appearance. How these two old codgers had
managed to keep their arrangements a secret was never divulged. Well-
informed circles assume these must have been made during the solemn
reading of the petition for beatification of the nun Huberta Dörffler; the
two men had been seen whispering together. Both men had simply given
orders after breakfast to "harness" their Mercedes 600s and be driven
to Staech, where they had met, and, without first calling on the abbot,
immediately entered the church, Terce having just begun. Present in the
church were fourteen monks.

During the subsequent serving of light refreshments (bread, wine,
olives), the abbot not only seemed relaxed, he *was* relaxed. He said
that, after having managed to achieve almost a full complement during
the visit of an eminent Scandinavian guest—forty-three monks in the
choir!—he had been obliged to reopen the "safety valve." In reply to the
bishop's sarcastic question as to what relevance the words "safety valve"
had to the monastic rule, the abbot responded with a cordial invitation
to have a look at the medical reports of the psychiatric clinic. The two
gentlemen who had come to inflict a defeat on the abbot suffered one
themselves. The abbot declared that he for his part couldn't care less
about state visits, and that he found the politicians who from time to

HEINRICH BÖLL

time fled to Staech in search of consolation and tranquillity a nuisance. He expressed his willingness, in the case of state visits of special importance, to allow alumni and minor orders to take part in choral prayer as guests dressed in monks' habits. Transportation for such auxiliary personnel, as well as the procurement of monks' habits, would be a matter for the Most Reverend Lord Bishop and/or the Right Honorable Herr President to arrange. "And should you wish," he added, with irreverent frankness, "to resort to actors, by all means do so! I decline any further responsibility."

At the next state visit (a Catholic dictator from southwestern Europe), seventy-eight monks could be counted in the Staech choir, by far the majority youthful. In the car, on his way back to the capital, the dictator remarked to his escort, "These Germans! There's no one like them! Even their new generation of ascetic young monks can't be beaten." What he never found out, and what could never be confirmed in the capital, was that sixty of the young monks had been students who had demonstrated there in protest against the dictator's visit and had been arrested; they had been promised release and, in return for a honorarium of forty marks (they had first demanded seventy but finally consented to forty), had been persuaded to have their hair cut.

Meanwhile people have been saying in the capital that the chief of protocol came to a verbal agreement with the chief of police: to be more generous in the arrest of student demonstrators during state visits *and* more generous in their release. Since a relationship exists between state visits and student demonstrations analogous to that between state visits and sightseeing tours of Staech, the Staech problem is regarded as solved. On the occasion of a visit of an Asian statesman, who then evinced an almost churlish lack of interest in monks, eighty-two monks could be counted. It seems there are now also some freeloaders, who obtain more accurate information on the dates of pending state visits than the abbot has as yet been able to do, and who then proceed to demonstrate rather too demonstratively (in the opinion of objective observers)—even investing now and again in a few tomatoes or eggs— in order to be arrested, then released, and acquire a free haircut plus forty marks and a copious lunch at Staech which, at the express wish of the abbot, is charged to diocesan rather than state funds.

Musically speaking, neither freeloaders nor students have so far presented any problem. Gregorian chants seem to come naturally to them. The only problems are those arising between the demonstrating groups, one group denouncing the other as "mercenary consumer-opportunists" and the latter denouncing the former as "abstract fantasists." The abbot of Staech gets along well with both groups, some of the young men—seven so far, apparently—have already entered the monastery as novices, and the fact that now and again during choir practice they slip a Ho Chi Minh into the Gregorian rhythm has so far gone unnoticed, even by a recently converted American statesman who, weary of NATO talk, spent a longer period at Staech than had been provided for by the protocol department. In a farewell communiqué he intimated that his visit to Staech had enriched his image of Germany by an important facet.

TILL DEATH US DO PART

In the draft from the swing door her first match went out, a second one broke on the striking surface, and it was nice of her attorney to offer her his lighter, shielding the flame with his hand. Now at last she could smoke—both felt good, the cigarette and the sunshine. It had taken barely ten minutes, an eternity, and perhaps it was that eternity as well as the permanence of those endless corridors that put the hands of the clock out of action. And the crowds, all those people looking for room numbers, reminded her of a summer clearance sale at Strössel's. What was the difference between divorces and bath towels at a clearance sale? Lineups for both, only that—so it seemed to her—in divorces the final decision was announced more speedily, and speed, after all, was what she had been after. *Schröder* vs. *Schröder*. Divorced. *Naumann* vs. *Naumann*. Divorced. *Blutzger* vs. *Blutzger*. Divorced.

Was the nice lawyer really going to say at this point what he was obliged to say? The only thing he could say? He said it: "Don't take it so hard." Said it although he knew she wasn't taking it hard at all, yet he had to say it, he said it nicely, and it was nice that he said it nicely. And naturally he didn't have much time, had to hurry off to the next case, appear again in court, line up again. *Klotz* vs. *Klotz*. Divorced.

Things had been much the same at the clearance sale: waiting politely, never impatient yet ever attentive until the woman who was too old to wear out even a single new bath towel had decided to take a whole dozen; then on to the next customer, who was clutching three swimsuits. After all, even at Strössel's there was still such a thing as personal service, not like at those discount stores where they unload junk on the customers. After all, the attorney couldn't go on standing beside her forever, there really not being much more to say than "Don't take it so hard." Her position at the top of the steps reminded her acutely of another occasion, seven years ago, when she had stood at the top of the steps leading up to City Hall: parents, witnesses, parents-in-law, photographer, cute little trainbearers—Irmgard's, Ute's, and Oliver's kids; bouquets, the taxi decorated with white roses, the "Till death us do part" still ringing in her ears, and on by taxi to the second ceremony, and once again, this time in church, "Till death us do part."

And here was the bridegroom waiting for her again at the foot of these steps, elated at the successful outcome and a bit embarrassed but also visibly proud of his second success of the day: having managed to find, here at the very foot of the steps, in one of the most hopeless parking areas in town, a spot for his car. Successes of various kinds had played quite a role in the divorce proceedings.

Now it wasn't death but the court that had separated them, and the occasion had lacked all dignity. And if the court, in pronouncing the divorce, had established death, why then wasn't there a funeral? Catafalque, mourners, candles, funeral oration? Or at least the wedding in reverse? Cute little kids, this time maybe Herbert's—Gregor and Marika—who would unfasten her train, lift the bridal wreath off her head, exchange her white dress for a suit: a kind of nuptial striptease performed in public on the steps if there wasn't going to be a funeral?

She had known, of course, that he would be waiting for her here, to start another of those futile discussions, since death had now been established—futile because he couldn't grasp the fact that there was nothing more she wanted from him now that she had moved with their son into a small apartment, neither money, nor her share in the "jointly acquired assets," nor even those six Louis—the how-many-th was it again?—chairs that were indisputably hers, inherited from her grandmother. One day he would probably unload them outside her door because he "simply couldn't stand disputed ownership." She wanted neither the chairs nor the set of Meissen porcelain (thirty-six pieces), nor any kind of a "property settlement." Nothing. After all, she had the boy, for the time being, since he was still living, unmarried, with that other woman—which one was it now, Lotte or Gaby? Not until he married Lotte or Gaby (or was it Connie?) would they have to "share" the boy (and there was no Solomon holding the sword over the child to be shared); all those nasty details about custody had been agreed upon, settled, and so there would be visiting rights, she would hand over the child to be stuffed and spoiled. ("Are you sure you don't want any more whipped cream?" and "Do you really like your new parka?" and "Of course I'll get you the model airplane.") For one day, for two, or a day and a half, and she would pick him up again. ("No, I really can't buy you a new parka, and I can't buy you a color TV for your first communion"—or was it confirmation? "No.")

Another cigarette? Better not. Now that the nice attorney with the chic little lighter no longer stood at her side, that draft from the swing door would force her to light the new cigarette from the old, and little things like that would make her look more of a slut than ever and, when it came to the final decision about the child, would certainly count as a black mark against her. This habit of smoking on the street had already been noted in the divorce files; besides, since she had admitted to being guilty of adultery (before he had, which also had to be admitted), she had anyway been recorded in the court documents as a kind of slut. All that nattering about whether or why women shouldn't, couldn't, mightn't smoke on the street had been described by the opposing attorney as a "pseudo-emancipatory" affectation not appropriate to her "educational level."

A good thing he didn't come up the steps, that he restricted himself to beckoning gestures; a good thing, too, that he shook his head in disapproval when she did, after all, light that second cigarette—not from the first one but with a match that didn't go out, although the clearance sale kept the swing door in constant motion.

Despite the absence of either priest or registry official, of tearful mothers and mothers-in-law, of photographer and cute little kids, at least there might have been an undertaker who would have driven off with something—what?—in a coffin, cremated it, and somewhere—where?—secretly buried it.

Probably he was even missing an appointment for her sake (the merger negotiations with Hocker & Hocker, perhaps, where he had been appointed to solve personnel problems); but would he really miss the Hocker & Hocker negotiations for the sake of a few chairs? He couldn't grasp, simply couldn't, that she didn't hate him at all, that she wanted nothing from him, that he had not merely ceased to matter to her but had become a stranger, someone she had once known, once married, who had become someone else. They had been successful in everything: building a career and building a house. They had failed in only one thing: keeping death at bay. Nor was it only he who had died—she had died too; even her memory of him failed her. And perhaps the clerics and bureaucrats couldn't and wouldn't grasp the fact that this "Till death us do part" didn't mean physical death at all, much less a death before a physical death, that it meant only the entry of a total stranger into the conjugal bedroom insisting on rights he no longer possessed. The role of the court that issued this death certificate and called it a divorce was as irrelevant as that of the priest and the registry official: no one could revive the dead or make death reversible.

She threw down the cigarette, ground it out, and waved him away, finally and firmly. There was nothing further to discuss, and she knew exactly where he was intending to drive her: to the café out in Haydn Park, where at this hour the Turkish waitress would be placing miniature copper vases, each containing one tulip and one hyacinth, on the tables, and straightening the tablecloths; where—at this hour—somewhere in the background a vacuum cleaner was still being used. He had always called it the "Café of Memories," condescendingly pronouncing it "quite good, not high class, certainly not smart." No, she repeated her final dismissive gesture, once, twice, until, shaking his head, he finally did get into his red car, maneuver out of his parking slot and, without waving to her again, drive off, "carefully but self-confidently," in his customary manner.

It was not yet nine-thirty, and now at last she could walk down the steps, buy a newspaper, and enter the café across the street. What a relief that he no longer barred her way down the steps! She was in no hurry, and there were a few things she wanted to think about. At twelve, when her son came home from school, she would give him a big pancake with some canned cherries, and some grilled tomatoes, he loved that. She would play with him, help him with his homework, and maybe go to a movie, maybe even to Haydn Park, to establish the final death of memory. Over canned cherries, pancake, and grilled tomatoes he would naturally ask her whether she was going to get married again. No, she would say, no. One death was enough for her. And would she be going back to work at Strössel's, where he was allowed to sit in the back room, do his homework, play with fabric swatches, and where that nice Mr. Strössel sometimes stroked his head in a friendly way? No. No.

The tablecloth at the café pleased her, felt good under her hands; it actually was pure cotton, old rose with silver stripes, and she thought of the tablecloths at the café in Haydn Park: maize-yellow, coarsely woven, those first ones had been, seven years ago: later came the green ones, with a printed daisy pattern, and finally the bright yellow ones, with no pattern at all but a fringed border, and he had always (and would have done so today) fidgeted with the fringe and tried to persuade her that she really did have a right to some kind of compensation, at least fifteen—maybe twenty—thousand marks that he could (and would) easily raise with a mortgage on the unencumbered house—after all, she had always been a "good although unfaithful spouse, careful and thrifty without being stingy" and had participated "quite positively and productively in the enhancement of their standard of living." As for those Louis chairs and the Meissen porcelain, she really was entitled to those. His fury at her refusal to take any of that had exceeded his fury over her lapse with Strösser; and finally he had (and would have done so today) ripped off some of the cheap fringe and thrown it on the floor—disapproving looks from the Turkish waitress, who was just arriving with tea and coffee, tea for him, coffee for her—further grounds for ominous remarks about her health and a scornful gesture toward the ashtray (which, incidentally, was ugly, dark brown, floor-colored—and which, she must admit, already contained three butts!).

Yes, coffee. Here she was, drinking coffee again, turning over the pages of the newspaper. Here in the café she could also smoke undisturbed, without inviting annoying glances or snide remarks. She thought of the shoving and chasing in the endless corridors of the courthouse, with all those hurrying people who had a sense of injury or had inflicted injury, who were owed rent or hadn't paid rent, where everything was decided and nothing clarified, by nice attorneys and nice judges who couldn't keep death at bay.

Again and again she caught herself smiling at the thought of the timing of the death that had separated them. It had started a year ago, when they were having dinner at the home of his boss, and he suddenly remarked that she was "involved in textiles," which sounded as if she were a carpet or fabric weaver or designer, whereas she had simply been a saleswoman in a dry-goods store—and how happy she had been there, her hands unfolding, refolding, everything pleasing to the hands, the eyes and, when business was quiet, tidying everything up, putting things back into drawers, onto shelves and racks: towels, sheets, handkerchiefs, shirts, and socks, and then one day that nice young man had turned up, the one who had just died, and had asked to see some shirts, although he had no intention of buying one or the money to do so—turned up simply because he was looking for someone to whom he could spill out his excitement over his success: three years after graduating from night school ("I'm involved in electrotechnology," and all he'd been was an electrician) he already had his degree and had been given a subject for his doctoral thesis. And now that phrase, "my wife's involved in textiles," which was supposed to sound at least like applied arts if not art, and how angry, almost sick with rage, it had made him when she said, "Yes, I was a saleswoman in a dry-goods store, and I still help them out sometimes." In the car on the way home not a word, not a syllable, icy silence, hands gripping the steering wheel.

The coffee was surprisingly good, the newspaper boring ("industrial profits too low, wages too high"), and what she picked up from the conversations around her all seemed to be about court cases. ("Facts twisted." "I can prove that the sofa belongs to me." "I'm not going to let them take away my son."). Attorneys' gowns, attorneys' briefcases. An office messenger brought some files that were solemnly opened, carefully scrutinized. And then the young waitress bringing her a second cup of coffee actually put a hand on her shoulder and said, "Don't take it too hard. It'll pass. I cried my eyes out for weeks—weeks, I tell you." She was ready to be angry, but then she smiled and said, "It's already passed." And the waitress went on, "And I was the guilty party too." Too? she thought. Am I the guilty party, and if so how do I show it—because I smoke, maybe? Drink coffee, read the paper, and smile? Yes, of course she was guilty, she had refused to acknowledge the death soon enough and had continued to live out those deadly months with him. Until one day he brought home a new evening dress, bright red, very low-cut, saying, "Wear this to the company dance tonight—I'd like you to dance with my boss and show him everything you've got," but she had worn her old silver-gray with the bead pattern she liked. A month later, when he found out about the affair with Strössel, she remembered his fury when he said, "What you refused to show my boss you've now shown to yours."

Yes, so she had—not long after he had moved out of the bedroom into the guest room, and the next morning had come back into the bedroom with all that porn stuff and a whip and had started a terrible row about his sexual achievements, which she was denying him but which he urgently needed; they were in such stark contrast to his professional achievements that he was developing a neurosis, almost a psychosis; there was no way she could offer him this satisfaction, she had taken away the whip and locked the door after him. The stuff had turned her ice cold, and she blamed herself for still not acknowledging the death, taking the child, ordering a taxi, and driving away. In actual fact she had gone on to share in the remodeling of the house—guest room, guest bathroom, TV room, study, sauna, children's room—and it had been her idea to go to Strössel and ask for a discount, for bath and hand towels, sheets and pillowcases, drapery fabrics. Naturally she had felt a bit uneasy when Strössel looked deep into her eyes and increased the discount from twenty to forty percent; and when his eyes grew misty and he tried to grab her across the counter, she had murmured, "For heaven's sake, not here, not here," and Strössel got the wrong (or right) idea and thought that somewhere else she would be willing. She had actually gone upstairs with him, with that pudgy, bald bachelor who was twenty years older than she and blissful when she lay down with him. And meanwhile he had left the store open and the cash register unattended, and not even the unavoidable unbuttoning and buttoning of clothing had embarrassed her. And later when he packed up her purchases downstairs at the cash desk, he hadn't given her a discount but had made her pay the full retail price, and when he held the door open for her, he hadn't tried to kiss her. The opposing attorney had actually tried to have Strössel attest to her claim of "discount withheld after favors granted," but then her nice attorney had succeeded in keeping Strössel out of it. Yes, she had gone back to Strössel several times. "Not to make purchases?" "No." "How often?" She didn't know, really she didn't. She hadn't counted. Marriage had never been spoken of, the word "love" never mentioned. It was that soft, deeply moved and moving bliss of Strössel's that made her afraid of sinking back onto a rose-colored pillow.

No, she couldn't go back to him, and his old-fashioned store would have been the right place for her, where she knew every case and box, every shelf and drawer, knew the stocks that genuinely did consist of only wool and cotton; she and her hands, that were infallible when it came to spotting any adulteration by even the tiniest synthetic thread. No, she couldn't work in one of those "cheap and nasty" stores either, as Strössel always called them. No, she wouldn't marry again, be present again when a living person died and once again a death separated her. She supposed the time had come when husbands became brutally obscene, and lovers, in an old-fashioned way that was almost too rose-colored, became tender and blissful.

"See?" said the waitress when she paid her bill. "Now we're feeling a bit better, aren't we? After all, you're still a young woman, nice-looking too, and"—here it came—"you've got all your life before you and your son'll stick by you!" She smiled at the waitress again as she left the café.

She would bake her son a hazelnut cake, buy the ingredients on the way home, and if he asked her, "Do I really have to go to that woman?" (Connie, Gaby, Lotte?), she would say, "No." And then there was still the firm of Haunschüder, Kremm & Co., Strössel's old competitors, where the infallibility of her hands would be equally in demand. Only that it was more of a mail-order house, and she wouldn't so often be able to unfold a shirt and smooth it out, as she had done for that attractive young man who had just received his degree and been given the subject for his doctoral thesis. Perhaps instead of cherries she would buy some smoked herring, he liked that just as much, and he would stand beside her while it turned crisp in the pan, while the pancake dough enfolded it and turned golden-brown. She could probably become a buyer at Haunschüder, Kremm & Co.; she knew she could rely on her hands, no adulterating thread would get past them.

ON BEING COURTEOUS WHEN
COMPELLED TO BREAK THE LAW

It would seem idle to extol the obvious forms of courtesy: that naturally one holds the front door open for a child; that one not only refrains from pushing ahead of a child when shopping but steps back for him;

that one allows a tired, stress-ridden schoolchild traveling home on the streetcar, bus, or train to enjoy his seat in peace without disturbing that well-earned peace either verbally or even by so much as staring at him with an expression of moral disapproval.

Further, I take it for granted that one does not allow one's child, one's cat, dog, or bird, to go hungry, that one is prepared, if need be, to go out and steal food for them, and it goes without saying that one must not let one's wife or girlfriend hunger or thirst either;

that none of them should be beaten, even when they ask for it, the courtesy of hands being one of the principal courtesies;

and that one should not pour the honored guest the first, second, or, if at all possible, even the third, but the fourth cup from the teapot, bearing in mind the Chinese proverb: Courtesy lies close to the bottom of the teapot.

Among those courtesies we take for granted is that when dealing with people of either sex who regard themselves as our inferiors—for ESSENTIALLY the concept of "inferior" is, obviously, unacceptable— one must use a slightly more subdued, more restrained tone of voice than when dealing with those who regard themselves as our superiors; of course, the concept of "superior" is also ESSENTIALLY unacceptable, since you cannot simply have a superior served up to you like a bowl of soup, and in dealing with these superiors one should not, need I say, be loud and rude but merely a shade less subdued and a shade less courteous; this behavior might slightly modify the structures.

Moreover, when confronted by a person one dislikes one should not simply make remarks to his face such as "I don't like your mug!"

It is possible to express one's aversion courteously, perhaps as follows, and preferably in writing, since the spoken word always carries with it the risk of rudeness:

"By reason of unfathomable, inscrutable, I will not say cosmic constellations, not wishing to make the stars and their ascendants solely responsible—by reason, therefore, of circumstances that are neither solely responsible nor solely predestined, the—shall we say—strands of sympathetic response between us have unfortunately (I would ask you to interpret this 'unfortunately' as an expression of my regret as well as of my abstract respect for your person) proved incapable of animation. Hence, although 'essentially' you are a most pleasant person and figure, I deem it advisable, indeed necessary, to restrict the number of our encounters to a minimum, to that minimum which compels us, for professional reasons, from time to time to shake hands, discuss details— encounters that are unavoidable in view of the increasing importance of the production of [here the product in question may be inserted, e.g.: novels, bolts, herrings in aspic]. Beyond this necessary minimum I suggest that we eschew the sound of each other's voices, the sight of our skin and hair, the perception of the odors we emanate. It is with some regret that I advise you of this, in the hope that these unfathomable constellations and combinations may change, that the strands of sympathetic response between us may become animated, and that an altered overall situation of sympathetic exchange may possibly enable us to extend the necessary professional contacts to the private domain. Yours most respectfully..."

Such forms of courtesy appear to me too obvious to require more than a passing allusion.

By contrast, however, it seems to me as difficult as it is necessary to point to courtesy in unconventional, indeed illegal, situations. It must be emphasized that ESSENTIALLY the actions I should like to enlarge upon are not merely unconventional or immoral but downright criminal. Let us take, for example, a crime that ESSENTIALLY is as criminal as it is discourteous, such as a bank robbery or a bank holdup, and let us consider that lady, heretofore so law-abiding, respectable, and honorable, who in broad daylight—more precisely, at about 3:29 p.m.—

relieved a savings bank in the suburb of a large German city of seven
thousand marks. Try to imagine the scene: a sixty-one-year-old lady of
the type known as frail, whose appearance calls to mind solitaire or
bridge, the widow of a lieutenant colonel, enters the branch of a savings bank in order to appropriate a sum of money by illegal means! If
this lady became known as the "courteous bank robber," was in fact
described as such in the police files, the use of the adjective "courteous"
was intended to convey her particularly dangerous quality. This lady did
instinctively what the courteous bank robber must do: not even think of
weapons, of violence, or shouting, not even consider such clumsy methods. After all, it is not merely discourteous, it is positively dangerous to
brandish pistols or machine guns and shout, "Hand over the dough, or
I'll shoot!" And of course a lady such as ours does not enter just any old
bank simply out of abstract greed, or because she has suddenly become
unbalanced, but because in her extremity she has regained her balance.
She has carefully considered this action and has her motives!

    The dire plight that forces this lady to this, to put it mildly, uncon-
ventional act must be briefly outlined. She has a son who, having taken
the wrong turn, has served a few minor prison sentences but has now,
discharged once again from jail, found a girlfriend who exerts a stabilizing influence on him. He has a chance of being employed as a pharmaceuticals salesman—his mother has spent a small fortune on telephone
calls and postage, has made use of all her connections (among them two
generals still on active duty) to obtain this chance for him. And now,
like a bolt from the blue and at the last moment, comes the company's
demand: a five-thousand-mark bond! His mother—that very lady who
became known as the courteous bank robber—has found him a small
apartment, developed an affection for his girlfriend, everything is going
splendidly, and now that bombshell: a five-thousand-mark bond! Try
to imagine the scene: the lady's bank credit has already been strained
to the utmost; her pension has shrunk to a bare subsistence level, the
greater part going to pay off the bank; she has borrowed wherever she
could—from bridge friends, her husband's old fellow officers (among
them two colonels and a general), all nice people; she has already eliminated the egg from her breakfast menu, and as she stands there in her
apartment all she can think of is "Beg, borrow, or steal!" and this popular saying turns out to be relatively disastrous for the savings bank.

"Beg, borrow, or steal!"—stealing seems to be the obvious remedy. I should add that the lady is not only frail but proud. Over and over again she has been humiliated, lectured, forced to submit to several thousand well-meant pieces of advice, swallow snide remarks about her beloved son; she has sold most of her furniture, disposed of her collie, to whom she was very attached, and quarreled about this with her best friend, who actually said, "A dog for a dog—that's no bargain!" She has visited her son in a number of jails, paid legal fees, incurred traveling expenses. The only luxury she still permits herself is the telephone: in order that her son can call her at any time, and she him, if he happens to have access to a telephone. There are even moments when she not only *believes* she understands him but actually does. The social experiences of the past four years have pushed her *inwardly* to the verge of becoming a social dropout, but not outwardly: she is always well groomed, looks younger than she is, and now, after her son has raised the alarm over the telephone, the fateful phrase occurs to her "Beg, borrow, or steal!" and its implications take root in her mind in a manner unforeseen by those who spread such sayings. Steal, she thinks, that's the solution, when around two o'clock she remembers that spruce little savings-bank branch situated at the edge of a park in a nearby suburb. Before leaving her apartment she feeds her pretty dwarf finches, tiny birds half the size of a thumb, which she can still afford. The word "steal," so foreign to her, becomes increasingly familiar as she approaches the park in the adjacent suburb, which she reaches by about 3:05. Steal, she thinks, where does one steal bread? In a bakery. Where does one steal sausage? At a butcher's. Where does one steal money? From a till or a bank. The till is immediately rejected, she finds that too *personal*, she does not wish to rob anyone directly; besides, what till would ever contain five thousand marks? And robbing a till seems to her too much of an imposition, almost an importunity.

Her conscience has long since ceased to bother her, she is already preoccupied with tactical and strategic deliberations. Hidden in some bushes, she looks across to the smart little savings bank, knowing that it closes at two-thirty. The bank is empty of customers, and strange things shoot through her mind: naturally she sometimes watches television, she also occasionally goes to the movies, and she thinks—not of weapons, not even of toy weapons, but of the stocking pulled over the face: which had always made her shudder because it was an affront to her aesthetic sense, that deformation of a human face. Moreover, she feels it is beneath her dignity here in the bushes to deprive one of her legs of its stocking; besides, it would provide a clue for possible pursuers. In these deliberations—as the indulgent reader will immediately discern—aesthetics, morals, and tactics come together in unique fashion!

In her handbag is a pair of oversized dark glasses—a gift from her son, who thought they would suit her. She puts on the glasses, ruffles her normally neatly coiffed hair, steps out from the bushes, crosses the street, enters the savings bank: behind the window on the right, a young lady sorting vouchers gives her a polite, slightly forced smile because closing time is only a few minutes away; the center window is closed; behind the one on the left stands a young man of about thirty-four, counting the contents of the cash drawer. He looks up, smiles at her politely, and says the usual, "Can I help you, madam?" At that moment she puts her hand into her bag, pulls it out as a clenched fist, steps closer to the window, and whispers, "Unusually compelling circumstances force me to this, I am sorry to say, unavoidable holdup. My right hand contains a nitrite capsule that can cause great havoc. I very much regret having to threaten you, but I need five thousand marks immediately. Give them to me. Or else..."

The tragic drama of the situation is enhanced by the fact that the teller—like most of his colleagues—is also a courteous person who is not in the least alarmed by the "or else" but instantly grasps the lady's quandary. Furthermore, professional bank robbers never ask for specific amounts, they demand the whole lot. He pauses in his counting—he happens to have just reached the five-hundred-mark bills!—and whispers, "You are putting me in an embarrassing position if you don't use more force. Nobody will ever believe me about the explosive capsule if you don't shout, threaten, put on a convincing scene. After all, there are rules for bank holdups too. You are doing it all wrong."

At that moment the young lady leaves her window, locks the bank from the inside, but leaves the key in the lock. The old lady, no less determined, in fact more determined than ever, recognizes her opportunity. "This capsule," she whispers threateningly. "Nitrite," says the teller,

"is not explosive, merely poisonous. Probably you mean nitroglycerine."
"Not only do I mean it, I have it." It is already clear that the teller, or
rather his money, is doomed. Instead of simply pressing the alarm button, he allows himself to be drawn into an argument; moreover, he
already has little beads of perspiration on his forehead and upper lip
and is puzzling over what the lady might need the money for: Does she
drink? Take dope? Has she gambling debts? A rebellious lover? He puz-
zles too much, fails to make use of his rights, and in this—it is fair to say
strongly meditative—intermezzo, the old lady simply thrusts her hand
through the window (she is smart enough to use her left hand), grabs
as many five-hundred-mark bills as she can, runs to the door, unlocks
it, crosses the street, disappears into the bushes—and only when she is
long out of sight does the teller raise the alarm. It is fairly certain that
this teller would have confronted a discourteous bank robber with far
greater vigor: would have struck the clenched fist, raised the alarm.

Needless to say, the affair had a variety of sequels. Let me allude
to the principal ones: the lady was never caught, the teller was not dismissed, merely transferred to a position where he had no direct contact
with either cash or the public. When the lady discovered that instead
of five thousand marks she had picked up seven thousand marks, she
remitted one thousand nine hundred back to the bank and was clever
enough not to do this by telegram since that might have led to her
identification. She permitted herself a taxi, drove to the railway station,
took the next train to her son: that cost her some ninety marks, the
remaining ten she spent on coffee and a brandy, which she consumed
in the dining car—and felt she had earned. When handing the money
over to her son, she placed her hand over his mouth and said: "Don't
ever ask me where I got it from." Then she phoned her neighbor and
asked her to feed her pretty dwarf finches. Almost superfluous to add
that things turned out well for her son: of course he read in the newspaper about the strange holdup by the "courteous bank robber," and
this act of solidarization by a criminal action on the part of his mother
had a morally stabilizing effect on him, more than several thousand
pieces of good advice, more than his stabilizing girlfriend. He became a
reliable pharmaceuticals salesman with opportunities for advancement,
although it must be added that he could not resist saying to his mother
on more than one occasion: "Imagine you doing *that* for me!" *What*

was never put into words. After much cogitation, the lady fixed the rate of repayment to the bank at one mark a month, her rationale for this low rate being: "Banks can wait." From time to time she sent the teller some flowers, a book, or a theater ticket, and bequeathed him the only valuable piece of furniture she still possessed: a carved medicine chest in neo-Gothic style.

As we see: courtesy pays, for bank employees and bank robbers; and if bank robbers were completely to exclude weapons or explosive capsules, rude language, and rude behavior from their strategy, the day might come when we would no longer speak of bank holdups but only of forced loans, which will merely be a matter of a nonviolent duel between two different manifestations of courtesy.

I must add that bank robbery, when it takes place without violence or physical injury, is quite a popular offense. Every successful bank robbery in which no one is injured releases feelings of joy and even envy among those who would at any time carry out a successful and nonviolent bank robbery if they had the courage.

It is far more difficult even so much as to mention courtesy in the case of an equally punishable offense such as *desertion*. Strangely enough, deserters are considered to be cowardly, an opinion that on closer inspection fails to hold water. The deserter in wartime risks being shot—by either friend or foe, since he never knows into whose hands he will fall, although he thinks he knows from whose hands he is escaping. Whatever national yardsticks one wishes to apply—and oddly enough all nations are agreed on this—the deserter in wartime risks something, and one should respect his risk. But here I wish to speak about the *courteous* deserter *in peacetime*, about that unknown young man who leaves military service without making use of his rights—for instance, the right to conscientious objection; the young man who clears out, disappears—if possible in a foreign country—simply because he has had enough and is fed up with the main burden of a soldier's life—boredom; the man who is not attracted by the more or less enforced camaraderie or by the service as such; who is left cold by money, food, driver's license, educational opportunities, chances of promotion; a nice German boy who—let us say—has read his Eichendorff in school and found him "overwhelming"; a pleasant youth who never finished school because he found it too boring; who became a carpenter, something he enjoyed; who shortly after passing his apprenticeship test was called up for military service, with a total lack of interest in armored vehicles or weapons of any kind, also with no interest in politics but profoundly, although not exclusively, interested in the manufacture of furniture such as he has observed on a number of visits to Italy in the street-level workshops of Rome and Florence, perhaps also of Siena. Moral problems, such as the occasional out-and-out faking of furniture, do not interest him: he wants—he wanted—to go there, and instead now suddenly finds himself in an infantry barracks in—let us say—Neu-Offenbach. Of course, this young man can be seriously reproached on a number of counts: that he lacks civic consciousness, that he should have cleared out to—let us say—Bologna before, rather than after, being called up. He can be reproached for lacking a sense of duty, although this is not the case, since the master carpenter under whom he served his apprenticeship and who has meanwhile fallen victim to structural changes in the economy, gave him an excellent reference. His parents, his teachers, even his friend, have repeatedly tried to persuade him that one must think *realistically*; yet this pleasant young man does think *realistically*, he thinks about seasoned wood, about glue and screws, about workbenches and curved chair legs, and of course he also thinks about girls and wine and things like that. The point is: the army means nothing to him, it says nothing to him, gives nothing to him. There are such cases. It is useless to deplore it, although ESSENTIALLY it is deplorable. That is the way the boy happens to be, and to his credit he did behave in a reasonably fair manner, having faithfully completed his so-called basic training: not that he conceded its necessity, it merely aroused his curiosity. But now he has simply had enough, and he does not turn to some counseling service or other—church, government, nonpartisan—no, he simply clears out; yet, being a courteous person, he does not just sneak off without a word, he writes (from a safe distance and using misleading, i.e., Swiss, stamps) a letter to his captain:

"Dear Sir: The fact that I can find no satisfaction in your profession, which I would have to practice for another year, does not, I trust, hurt your feelings, in the same way that I ask you not to take my desertion personally and certainly not as an insult. It so happens that I am not a soldier and never will be, and nothing could be farther from my mind than to reproach you for not being a carpenter and probably not knowing what a tenon is, let alone how it is made. Of course I am aware—and I would ask you always to bear this in mind—that, although there are laws to force a man to be a soldier for fifteen months, there are no laws to force him to know anything about tenons, and I realize therefore that my comparison of soldier/carpenter is a lame one. So be it, and since there is this law that forces me to spend another year of atrocious boredom, I wish to inform you herewith that I am breaking that law.

"What pains me is the fact that you were such a nice, agreeable, understanding superior, and that naturally I would prefer to inflict on a lousy, beastly officer the pain I may be inflicting on you. More than once you have protected me, who has so little comprehension of absurd army regulations, from punishment; you have smiled understandingly at many a foolishness that aroused the ire of my corporal and even of my comrades—so understandingly that I suspect a crypto-deserter in you, and again you should take that not as an insult but as a compliment. In short: *as* my superior you were even better than my master carpenter, but *what* you—or rather, the army—doled out to me was, quite simply, intolerable, and this does not apply to the food or the allowance but merely to that appalling activity known as 'killing time.' The simple fact is that I do not want to go on killing my time; I want to make it come alive—no more, but no less.

"The only sensible activity, the only one I enjoyed, was the four-day disaster-relief deployment during the floods in Oberduffendorf: it was most enjoyable paddling the rubber dinghy from house to house and bringing the marooned inhabitants of Oberduffendorf hot soup, coffee, bread, and the tabloid—many a face lit up in gratitude! But I ask you, sir, would it not be positively macabre, even wicked, to wait for further disasters in order to find meaning in military service?

"Hoping that you will understand some of my thoughts and not despise my motives, I remain, respectfully yours..."

TOO MANY TRIPS TO HEIDELBERG

*For Klaus Staeck, who knows that the story
is invented from beginning to end, yet true*

That evening, as he sat on the edge of the bed in his pajamas, waiting for the midnight news and smoking one last cigarette, he tried in
retrospect to pinpoint the moment at which this pleasant Sunday had
slipped away from him. The morning had been sunny, fresh, a coolness
of May although it was June, yet the warmth to be expected at noon
was already perceptible: light and temperature had reminded him of
the old days when he had been out training from six to eight before
going to work.

For an hour and a half that morning he had cycled along back
roads between suburbs, between allotment gardens and industrial areas,
past green fields, toolsheds, gardens, the big cemetery, out to where the
forest began far beyond the city limits. On the asphalt stretches he had
speeded up, timing himself and testing his acceleration; he had put on
spurts and found that he was still in good form, might even risk entering
an amateur race again, his legs responding to the joy of having passed
his exam and to his intention of taking up regular training again. What
with his job, night school, earning a living, studying, he hadn't been
able to do much about it these last three years. He would need a new
bike, but that would be no problem provided he could come to terms
with Kronsorgeler tomorrow, and there was no doubt that he would.

After his training spin, a few exercises on the rug in his rented
room, a shower, clean underwear, then by car out to his parents for
breakfast: coffee and toast, fresh eggs and honey, on the terrace Father
had built onto the house; the bright awning—a gift from Karl—and,
as the morning warmed up, the reassuring stereotype utterance of his

parents, "Well, you've almost made it now, you'll soon have made it now." His mother had said "soon," his father "almost," and always the pleasurable harking back to the fear of the last few years, a fear they had never blamed each other for, a fear they had shared: from amateur regional champion and electrician to passing his exam yesterday, erstwhile fear that was beginning to turn into veteran's pride. And they kept asking him what this or that word was in Spanish: carrot or motorcar, Queen of Heaven, bee and busy, breakfast, supper and sundown, and how happy they were when he stayed on for lunch and invited them over to his place next Tuesday to celebrate his success. Father went off to pick up some ice cream for dessert, and he accepted a cup of coffee although an hour later he would have to have coffee again at Carola's parents'. He even had a kirsch and chatted with them about his brother Karl, his sister-in-law Hilda, about Elke and Klaus, the two kids who, they all agreed, were being spoiled, what with their jeans and fringed jackets and cassettes and all that, and constantly there would be those pleasurable sighs: "Well, you'll soon have made it now, you've almost made it now!" That "almost," that "soon," had made him uneasy. He *had* made it! All that remained was the interview with Kronsorgeler, who had been favorably disposed toward him right from the start. Hadn't he done a good job teaching Spanish at the adult education center and German at those evening classes for Spaniards?

Later he helped his father wash the car and his mother weed the garden, and as he was about to leave she brought carrots, spinach, and a bag of cherries from the freezer, packed them in an insulated bag, and insisted that he wait until she had picked some tulips for Carola's mother. Meanwhile his father checked the tires, asked him to start the motor, listened to it suspiciously, then stepped up to the lowered window and asked, "Still making all those trips to Heidelberg—on the autobahn?" It was meant to sound as if he were querying the capability of his old, somewhat decrepit car to cover those fifty miles twice, sometimes three times a week.

"Heidelberg? Yes, I still drive there two or three times a week—it'll be some time before I can afford a Mercedes."

"Oh, yes, Mercedes," said his father. "There's that fellow from the government, the Department of Education, I believe—yesterday he brought in his Mercedes again for a checkup. Insists on my doing the job personally. What's his name again?"

"Kronsorgeler?"

"Yes, that's the one. A very nice fellow. I'd even call him a gentleman, no irony intended."

Just then his mother brought the flowers, saying, "Remember us to Carola, and her parents too, of course. We'll be seeing them on Tuesday anyway." As he was about to drive off, his father came up once more and said, "Don't make too many trips to Heidelberg—with this wreck!"

On his arrival at the Schulte-Bebrungs', Carola hadn't come home yet. She had phoned and left a message that she wasn't quite through with her reports but would come as soon as she could; they were to go ahead with their afternoon coffee.

The terrace was larger, the awning, though faded, more generous, everything more elegant, and even in the barely perceptible shabbiness of the garden furniture, in the grass growing in the cracks between the red tiles, there was something that irritated him like some of those harangues at student demonstrations; things like that, and clothing, were sources of irritation between Carola and himself since she always complained that his clothes were too formal, too bourgeois. With Carola's mother he chatted about growing vegetables, with her father about bicycle races, found the coffee not as good as at his parents', and tried not to let his tension turn into irritation. After all, these were really nice, progressive people who had accepted him without prejudice, officially, even, by sending out engagement announcements. By this time he had become genuinely fond of them, including Carola's mother, whose frequent "charming" had at first got on his nerves.

Eventually Dr. Schulte-Bebrung—a bit embarrassed, so it seemed to him—asked him to come into the garage, where he showed him the newly acquired bicycle that he rode every morning for "a few turns" around the park and the Old Cemetery—a magnificent specimen of a bike. He praised it enthusiastically, quite without envy, mounted it for a test ride around the garden, explained the workings of leg muscles to Schulte-Bebrung (remembering that the senior members of the club had always suffered from cramps!); and after he had dismounted and propped the bike against the wall inside the garage, Schulte-Bebrung asked him, "What do you think—how long would it take me on this magnificent specimen of a bike, as you call it, to get from here to, say, Heidelberg?" It sounded casual enough, innocent, especially as Schulte-Bebrung went on, "You see, I was at university in Heidelberg, had a bike in those days too, and from there to here used to take me—young and strong as I was then—two and a half hours."

He smiled, obviously with no ulterior motive, talked about traffic lights, traffic jams, all the cars that in those days hadn't existed; by car—he'd already tried it out—it took him thirty-five minutes to get to his office, by bicycle only thirty minutes. "And how long does it take you by car to Heidelberg?"

"Half an hour."

The fact that he mentioned the car took away some of the casualness of mentioning Heidelberg, but at that moment Carola arrived, and she was as sweet as ever, as pretty as ever, a bit disheveled, and you could tell she really was dead tired; and now, as he sat on the edge of the bed, a second cigarette still unlit between his fingers, he simply didn't know whether his tension had already turned into irritation and been transferred from him to her, or whether she had been tense and irritable—and this had been transferred from her to him. She kissed him, of course, but whispered in his ear that she wouldn't be going with him today. Then they talked about Kronsorgeler, who had spoken so highly of him, about getting into the civil service, about the boundaries of the regional district, about cycling, tennis, Spanish, and whether he would get an A or only a B. She herself had only scraped through with a C. When invited to stay for supper he pleaded tiredness and work, and no one had particularly urged him to change his mind. The air quickly cooled off again on the terrace; he helped carry chairs and dishes into the house, and when Carola walked with him to the car she kissed him with surprising ardor, put her arms around him, leaned against him, and said, "You know I love you very, very much, and I know you're a splendid fellow, but you do have one little fault: you make too many trips to Heidelberg."

She had run quickly into the house, waved, smiled, blown him kisses, and he could still see her in the rear-view mirror, standing there waving vigorously.

Surely it couldn't be jealousy. After all, she knew he went there to see Diego and Teresa, to help them translate applications, fill out forms and questionnaires; that he drew up petitions, typed the final versions—for the department of aliens, the bureau of social services, the union, the university, the employment office—concerning placing children in schools and kindergartens, bursaries, grants, clothing, holiday camps. She knew what he was doing in Heidelberg, had gone there with him a few times, had done more than her share of typing, and displayed a surprising knowledge of officialese. Once or twice she had even taken Teresa along to a movie and a café, and her father had given her money for a Chilean fund.

Instead of driving home, he had gone to Heidelberg; Diego and Teresa had been out, as had Raoul, Diego's friend. On the way back he had got into a traffic jam, and around nine had looked in on his brother Karl, who went to the fridge for some beer while Hilda fried him some eggs. Together they had watched the Tour de Suisse on TV, in which Eddy Merckx hadn't shown up too well, and, when he left, Hilda had given him a paper bag full of used children's clothing for "that nice gutsy Chilean and his wife."

Now at last the news came on, and he listened with only half an ear: he was thinking of the carrots, the spinach, and the cherries that he still had to put away in the freezer compartment; he lit a second cigarette after all: somewhere—was it in Ireland? there had been an election, a landslide; someone—was it really the Federal President?—had said something very positive about neckties; someone was issuing a denial about something; the stock market was up; still no trace of Idi Amin.

He didn't finish his second cigarette and stubbed it out in a half-empty yogurt tub; he really was dead tired and soon fell asleep, though the word "Heidelberg" kept reverberating in his mind.

He had a frugal breakfast, just milk and bread, tidied up, took a shower, and dressed with care. Putting on his tie he thought of the Federal President—or had it been the Federal Chancellor? Fifteen minutes early for his appointment, he sat on the bench outside Kronsorgeler's outer office, next to him a fat man in trendy, casual clothes; he recognized him from the teacher-training courses but didn't know his name. The fat man whispered, "I'm a Communist, you too?"

"No," he said. "No, I'm not—I hope you don't mind."

The fat man didn't spend long with Kronsorgeler; as he came out he made a gesture that was probably supposed to convey "no dice." Then the secretary asked him to go in; she was pleasant, not exactly young, had always been nice to him—he was surprised when she gave him an encouraging nudge, having always regarded her as too prim for that kind of thing.

Kronsorgeler received him with a smile. He was nice, conservative but nice; objective; not old, in his early forties at most. A bicycle-racing fan, he had given him a lot of encouragement, and they began by discussing the Tour de Suisse: whether Merckx had been bluffing so as to be underrated in the Tour de France or whether he had really lost his form. In Kronsorgeler's opinion, Merckx had been bluffing; he disagreed, feeling that Merckx really was almost finished, there were certain signs of exhaustion that couldn't be faked. Then came the exam: that they had wondered for a long time whether they couldn't give him straight As, the snag had been philosophy. But otherwise: his excellent work at the adult education center, at those evening classes, never taking part in demonstrations ... there was just—Kronsorgeler gave a genuinely warm smile—one tiny little blot.

"Yes, I know," he said. "I make too many trips to Heidelberg."

Kronsorgeler almost blushed; at any rate his embarrassment was obvious. He was a sensitive, reserved person, almost shy; bluntness was not in his nature.

"How do you know?"

"I've been hearing it from all sides. Wherever I go, whoever I talk to. My father, Carola, her father, all I hear is: Heidelberg. Loud and clear, and I wonder whether, if I were to dial the weather bureau or bus information I wouldn't hear: Heidelberg."

For a moment it looked as though Kronsorgeler would rise and place his hands soothingly on his shoulders. He had already risen, then he lowered his hands again, placed them flat on his desk, and said, "I can't tell you how awkward this is for me. I have followed your path, a difficult path, with much sympathy—but there's a report on that

Chilean that isn't very favorable. I can't ignore that report, I simply can't. I have not only rules to follow but also instructions, I've been given not only guidelines but also advice over the phone. Your friend—I take it he is your friend?"

"Yes."

"You'll have plenty of time on your hands during the next few weeks. What are your plans?"

"I'll be training a lot—cycling again, and I'll make lots of trips to Heidelberg."

"By bike?"

"No, by car."

Kronsorgeler sighed. It was obvious he was suffering, genuinely suffering. When he shook hands he whispered, "Don't go to Heidelberg, that's all I can say." Then he smiled and said, "Remember Eddy Merckx."

Even as he closed the door behind him and walked through the outer office, he was thinking of alternatives: translator, interpreter, tour guide, Spanish correspondent for a trading company. He was too old to become a pro, and there were already more than enough electricians. He had forgotten to say goodbye to the secretary, so he turned back and waved to her.

MY FATHER'S COUGH

When my father reached the same age as I am now approaching, he (naturally?) seemed older to me than I feel. Birthdays were not celebrated in our family, that was considered a "Protestant aberration," so I cannot recall any celebration, only a few details of the mood prevailing that October 1930. (My father shared his year of birth, 1870, with Lenin, but that, I believe, was all.)

It was a dismal year. Total financial collapse, not exactly a classic "failure," merely a "compromise with creditors," a procedure I didn't understand, but at any rate it sounded more dignified than "bankruptcy." It was somehow connected with the collapse of an artisans' bank whose manager, if I remember correctly, ended up behind bars. Abuse of confidence, forfeited guarantees, unwise speculations. Our house in the suburbs had to be sold, and not a penny remained of the sales price. Upset and confused, we moved into a large—too large—apartment on Ubier-Ring in Cologne, across from what was then the vocational school.

Bailiffs, bailiffs, affixing seal after seal. We pulled these off while they were still fresh, ignoring this preliminary step to seizure; later we became indifferent and left them in place, and eventually some pieces of furniture (the piano, for instance) bore whole accumulations of seals. We got along fine with the bailiffs. There was irony on both sides, rudeness on neither.

I can remember the appearance of that four-pfennig piece, something to do with political emergency regulations, and the tobacco tax. This four-pfennig piece was a large, attractively designed copper coin, but it may not have appeared until a year or so later, perhaps 1931–32. The Nazis marched triumphantly into the Reichstag. Brüning was chancellor. We read the *Kölnische Volkszeitung*. My older brothers and sisters swore by the *RMV* (*Rhein-Mainische-Volkszeitung*).

I said goodbye to outdoor games. Sadly. Out in the suburb of Raderberg we had still been able to play hockey on the streets (with old umbrella handles and empty condensed-milk cans); rounders often, soccer less often, in Vorgebirg Park. We used to decapitate roses in the park with our "tweakers," known elsewhere in Germany as slings. Our hoop-tossing consisted of flinging old bicycle-wheel rims down a gentle grassy slope; the one whose hoop rolled the farthest was the winner. Records were established, and we rolled our hoops all the way around the block: it wasn't "done" to use bought, wooden hoops. Ping-Pong on the terrace, the swing in the garden; target practice with air rifles on burned-out light bulbs, which in those days were still of the bayonet type. We never found anything military, let alone militaristic, about this target practice. Ten years of freedom and many free games, too numerous for me to list. (St. Martin's torches, building and flying paper kites, marbles.)

In the long corridor of the apartment on Ubier-Ring we continued our target practice, now with regulation targets and bolts that we called "plumets" (the dictionary tells me this comes from the Latin *pluma*: the bolts had little colored tufts attached to them). During target practice, of course, whoever wanted to go into the bathroom, the kitchen, or the bedroom, or happened to be in there, had to be warned. Overall mood: recklessness and fear, not mutually exclusive. Needless to say, not all our income was revealed to the bailiff. There was moonlighting, income from renting out woodworking machinery. Recently I read in Isaac Bashevis Singer's *Enemies, a Love Story*, "If one wanted to live, one had to break the law, because all laws condemned one to death." We wanted to live.

We lived on a modest scale, yet modesty did not become our guiding principle. We had more than enough worries and debts. The rent, food, clothing, books, heating, electricity. The only thing that kept us going was a temporary lightheartedness which, of course, we only achieved temporarily. Somehow, after all, money had also to be found for movies, for cigarettes, for the indispensable coffee: something we didn't always, but did sometimes, achieve. We discovered pawnshops.

It wasn't all as carefree as it may sound. The more modest the scale, the less did modesty become our guiding principle. I gratefully remember the devotion of my older brothers and sisters, who must have made life easier for me, the youngest, by letting me have a little something

from time to time. What scared me most during that period was my
father's cough. He was of slight build (between the ages of twenty and
eighty-five his weight varied by only two or three pounds; only after the
age of eighty-five did he start to lose weight). He was moderate in his
habits but liked to smoke, never inhaled, and he refused to do without
(or at least entirely without!) his "Lundi"—those thin, pungent cigarillos packed in round cans. He was sad in these circumstances, and also
powerless against conditions, and I sometimes think that we children
never paid enough attention to his sadness.

His cough drowned out even the roar of streetcar Number 16, and
we could hear his cough from far away. But the place where I was most
worried by his cough was crowded St. Severin's Church on Sundays. We
never went to Mass en bloc, always individually, rarely did two or three
of us youngsters sit together in one pew, so we waited, each in his own
seat, full of nervous tension, for our father's cough, knowing it would
start up, increase almost to the point of suffocation, and then, as my
father left the church, subside. He would then probably stand outside
and smoke a "Lundi" for his cough.

Now the same age as my father was then, I find that I (and I am
not the only one) have apparently inherited his cough. There are some
people in our household who, as I park outside amid heavy traffic, recognize me through the noise of all those cars by my cough. I hardly ever
have to ring the bell or use my key: someone is opening the front door
before I do either.

My cough must be on a wavelength that penetrates not only traffic
noises and screeching brakes but even police sirens, yet I don't believe
that my cough can be called "penetrating." It consists of variations on
differing forms of hoarseness, usually denotes embarrassment, is seldom
a sign of a cold; and there are some people who know that it is more
than a cough—and less. A granddaughter, for example, who is a year
old, apparently regards it as a form of speech or address; she imitates it,
coughing dialogues develop between us of an ironically amused nature,
dialogues in which we apparently both have something to communicate.
I am reminded of Beuys, who once made a speech consisting only of har-
rumphings and little coughs—and a very clever speech it was, by the way.

Perhaps one should establish harrumphing schools, at least consider
harrumphing as a school subject; anyway, rid it of its silly admonitory

function—to stop someone from making that tactless remark, for instance. *L'art pour l'art* as applied to coughing and harrumphing.

It might also be worth considering whether clever heads shouldn't invent the harrumphing letter-to-the-editor.

RENDEZVOUS WITH MARGRET
OR: HAPPY ENDING

The journey there was pleasant: the Rhine still under early-morning mist; weeping willows, barges, sirens, the trip taking precisely as long as I needed for my breakfast. Coffee and rolls acceptable, eggs fried; no baggage, just cigarettes, newspaper, matches, return ticket, ballpoint pen, wallet, and handkerchief, and the certainty of seeing Margret again. After so many years, after several abortive meetings, after knowing her for more than forty years, I had been surprised and stirred by something I had never seen before: her handwriting, strong yet graceful, and the words, written on the death announcement with surprising firmness: "do come—it would give me so much pleasure to see you again." The small "d" in "do" made me suspect that she had never come to terms with the capital "D"; we all have a letter or two that we stumble over.

On arrival I got rid of my largest piece of baggage, the newspaper. I left it behind in the dining car and reached the cemetery in good time after my own fashion: too late for the *Largo*, the *De Profundis*, and the incense in the chapel, too late also to join the cortège. I was just in time to see the acolytes taking off their vestments and bundling them under their arms as they walked away. The taller one unscrewed the processional cross into three sections, packing it away in a case obviously designed for that purpose, and as they got into the waiting taxi they all lit cigarettes: priest, driver, and acolytes. The driver offered the priest a light, the younger acolyte did the same for the older one, and at that point one of them must have made a joke: I saw them all laugh, saw the older acolyte coughing with laughter and cigarette smoke, and I had to laugh too, when I thought of the sacristy cupboards where in another five minutes they would be putting away their paraphernalia: oak, baroque, three hundred years old, the pride of the parish of St. Francis Xavier, which in 1925 had been renamed St. Peter Canisius; and it wasn't I, it was the deceased who had just been buried, on whose

coffin clods of earth were still falling, he who had saved the day in
1945 by his inspired recollection of the depth of those cupboards where,
behind the neat piles of altar linen and various sacred utensils, we had
hidden cigarettes and coffee stolen from the Americans when they left
their Jeeps unattended or invited us in groups to a kind of Werewolf-
reeducation. It was he, not I, who, with the corrupt cunning of the
European, had correctly sized up the Americans' naïve awe of ecclesiastical institutions, and for years I had wondered why, instead of claiming
credit for this inspiration, he had always ascribed it to me. Much later,
long after I had left home, it dawned on me that a story of that kind
would have done no service to his respectability, whereas it "fitted" me,
although I never really had that idea nor ever would have.

I approached the Zerhoff family grave with circumspection, avoiding
the paths on which I would have encountered men with and without top
hats, ladies with and without Persian lamb coats, former schoolmates
and knights of Catholic orders, schoolmates *as* knights of Catholic
orders. I walked along the familiar path between the rows of graves to
our own family grave, where the last burial—my father's—had taken
place five years ago; it had been insinuated that he had died broken-
hearted because neither of his two sons had begotten a male heir in
any woman's womb; well, he had no female heir either. The burial plot
was well cared for, the lease paid; the gravel was truly snow-white, the
beds of pansies heartshaped, the pansies in turn—nine or eleven to a
bed—planted in the shape of a heart. The names of Mother, Father, and
Josef on the lectern-shaped marble gravestones; above Josef's name, the
inevitable iron cross; the gravestones of long-dead ancestors overgrown
with ivy and, rising above all the graves, the simple, classicistic, vaguely
Puritan cross, to which had later been added a scroll proclaiming in neo-
Gothic script: "Love never endeth." A gravestone was ready for me, too,
the last bearer of the name; the dash after my name and birth date, that
graphic "to," had something ominous about it. Who would continue
to pay the (not inconsiderable) lease when my earthly days were done?
Margret, probably. She was a woman in good health, well off, childless,
a tea drinker, a moderate smoker, and in the melody of her handwriting,
particularly in the small "d," I could perceive a long life for her.

I stood behind the tamarisk hedge, now grown quite dense, that separated the Zerhoff burial plot from ours, and then I saw her: she seemed more attractive than ever, more so than the girl of fifteen with whom I had lain in the grass, more so than the woman of twenty, thirty, and thirty-five with whom I had had those embarrassing and abortive reunions, the last one fifteen years ago in Sinzig when she turned on her heel outside the hotel room and drove away; she hadn't even allowed me to take her to the station. She must be close to fifty now, her thick, rather coarse blond hair had turned an attractive gray, and black suited her.

As children we had often had to come out here on summer evenings to water the flowers: my brother Josef, Margret, myself, and her brother Franzi, into whose grave the last members of the cortège were just then throwing their flowers or their shovelfuls of earth; the familiar drumming of earth on wood, the impact of the bunches of mimosa like the alighting of a bird. Often we had spent our streetcar money on ice cream, setting out on the long homeward journey on foot and, in the summer heat, soon regretting our recklessness, but invariably Josef had produced some hidden "reserves" and paid our fares home, and on the streetcar, relieved and tired, we would argue about whether he had paid for our ice cream or our fares.

I still had to fight back my tears when I thought of Josef, and I still didn't know, after thirty-four years I didn't know, whether it was his death or his last wish that brought tears to my eyes. At the very end of the platform, beyond the station roof, before the arrival of the leave train, we had once again discussed ways and means of not returning to the front, fever, accident, medical certificates—and in the end it was Margret who broke the taboo and spoke of—what do they call it?— "desertion," and Father had stamped his foot in rage and said, "There is no such thing as desertion in our family!" and Josef had laughed and said, "Where to? Am I supposed to swim across the Channel or to Sweden, or across Lake Constance to Switzerland—and Vladivostok, you know, is a pretty long way off," and he was already standing on the steps, the stationmaster had blown his whistle, when he leaned down once more and said clearly, more to me than to my father, "Please, no priests at my grave, no mumbo jumbo at any memorial service." He was nineteen, had given up the study of theology, and Margret was at that time considered almost his fiancée. We never saw him again. We winced,

I more than my father, Margret less, as if whipped by his last words; and of course, when the news of his death arrived, I reminded Father of Josef's last wish, not repeating his words, I was too scared to do that, but simply saying, "You know what he asked for, what his last wish was." But Father had waved me away and, I need hardly say, not done as Josef had asked. They had indeed had their memorial service, with incense, Latin, and catafalque; in solemn pomp they had executed their precise choreography, in their black, gold-embroidered brocade robes, and they had even rounded up a choir of theology students who sang something in Greek. The Eastern Churches were already becoming very fashionable. I have never entered a church since, except as an acolyte and in my later capacity as salesman of devotional supplies; and when Franzi Zerhoff and I had assisted at solemn requiems, they had sometimes reminded me, in their heavy, gold-embroidered brocade robes, of Soviet marshals with their bulky gold shoulder pieces and their chests covered with about a hundred and fifty decorations. Always plenty of Latin, male choir in red-and-white sashes, top hats trembling in their hands, and the air trembling with the vehemence of their chest tones.

Margret's mouth was surprisingly small and still not hard under her austere nose; she was slimmer, only her wrists revealed traces of plumpness. There she stood, dignified, erect, shaking hands, nodding, yet she had kept that swift, ephemeral, springy quality. The gray around her head reminded me of the whitish-gray dust in her hair when we staggered out of the burning house and lay down in the garden on the grass, came together on that June night after saying goodbye to Josef, when so many values and so much that was valuable had been destroyed; and I thought of the dust in her kisses, in her tears, of our irresponsible laughter when Father also came staggering out of the house and saw us lying there, and how our dust-powdered faces screwed up with laughter when he twisted the key to his safe in the air as if it, the air, contained his securities and all that notarized stuff; and of course he didn't know, none of us knew, that in this so charmingly conventional war degrees of heat would build up that venerable safes could not withstand. And in the end, when later they were poking through the debris, he had found nothing but ashes in his molten safe, and it had been Margret, not I (who was of course familiar with such sayings), who told him, "*Memento, quia pulvis es et* ...," but she did not complete the sentence. For a time we were inseparable, but we never came together again, not even with a kiss, not even with a handclasp.

Margret turned toward me and, in a kind of bitter joy, her woman's face changed to the face of that girl who, with me, had scorned accepted values on that June night—or had I then embraced the Margret of today, had I at last caught up with her, she with me? Had Josef's curse at last truly united us? I thought of him, of the whiplash with which he had changed the course of my life, and I realized here, at last, that that was what he had wanted: to change the course of my life, away from gold brocade, male choirs, family graves, real and potential knights of Catholic orders. Perhaps that was the only thing he had learned in that gloriously conventional war, and today, here, facing Margret, I had no reason to bear a grudge against him on that score. I bore no grudge against anyone, not even against my father, who later became very silent, almost humble, and who always looked so expectantly at me when Margret came over from next door. We used to go to the movies, to the theater, for walks, we had long discussions—but we never got as far as even a handclasp, even a flicker of memory. I carried on as an acolyte, regarding it as a job (tips and free meals); I got into the black market, finished high school, left home, and, via the black market, ended up in the devotional-supplies business when I was asked to get hold of a Leonardo da Vinci print for a Moselle vintner's first communion in exchange for butter, and did so. I had a few affairs, and I imagine Margret did, too.

I was standing close enough to be able to read the word "Blackbird," from Margret's lips. I nodded, withdrew, and headed for the "Blackbird," where funeral receptions have been held since time immemorial. I only had to go back to the exit, cross the street, and walk for five minutes through Douglas firs. At the "Blackbird" they were already busy cutting up limp rolls, spreading them with butter, adding slices of sausage or cheese, and decorating them with mayonnaise. I wondered whether Aunt Marga was still alive, she had always insisted on having blood sausage with onion rings, as greedily as if she were starving, although everyone knew that not even she had any idea of the extent of her fortune. The coffee machine was steaming, brandy snifters were being placed on trays, freshly opened bottles beside them (Margret was sure to have firmly insisted on a price "by the bottle"), bottles of mineral water were being snapped open, flowers stuck in little vases. Still the same old, old-fashioned routine.

I recognized the priest, who had arrived without the acolytes and was sitting in a corner smoking a cigar with a contented, off-duty expression. He nodded at me. Not because he recognized me, we had never met. He looked like a nice fellow, I sat down at his table and asked him about the special carrying case for the collapsible cross: in my days as an acolyte we used to have to lug the whole cross around, and it had always been a problem getting it into a car without smashing a window or knocking top hats off heads. And I knew of a few rural communities where the old processional cross was still in use. He told me the name of the company, I jotted it down on my return ticket, then we both speculated as to why people continued to put up with those limp rolls. I told him that even as children we had called those sandwiches "Blackbird pasteboard with mayonnaise," whether we were present as mourners or acolytes or—as frequently happened—as mourning acolytes. They were behind the times, there should be "Hawaiian Toast" or something, and sherry, not brandy, and not Persian lamb coats but mink, and instead of the lousy coffee—why did it always have to be so lousy everywhere?—they should have ordered mocha, which did sometimes turn out like reasonably good coffee.

I glanced at my return ticket, where I had noted the trains: 14:22, 15:17, then none till 17:03; it was now just on eleven, and if I wanted to take Margret along, if I wanted, after thirty-four years, to touch her hair that evening, I supposed I would have to stay on a while and run the risk of encountering a former schoolmate or two among the red-and-white sashes, maybe even among the Catholic knights: one of them was sure to shout the opening lines of *The Odyssey*—in Greek, of course—into my ear, to prove that his classical education had not failed to leave its mark on him. Another, although we had graduated from high school more than thirty years ago and not seen each other since, taking it for granted that I would fully agree, would start moaning about modern times, about his spoiled brats, the Socialists, the general moral decline, and how he was working himself to death in his practice while his third or fourth apartment building was costing him more and more due to this damned inflation. I was prepared to endure this; I knew this kind of talk from funerals I had attended not as a mourner but professionally: I also have an agency for gravestones, and my top hat counts as professional clothing and is tax-deductible. It couldn't take all that long: if we missed the 14:22 we would certainly catch the 15:17.

I was in luck, it was Bertholdi who sat down beside me. I recalled that in eight years of school I hadn't exchanged so much as forty words with him. There had been simply no occasion to do so, and I had reason to regret this now. He was a very nice fellow, without that bitter-sour expression that seems inevitable with successful as well as unsuccessful men at the start of the last third of their lives. Bertholdi asked how my business was going, and when I told him that I had been selling devotional supplies for some years now, he remarked that it must be hard going in this post-Vatican Council era. I agreed that business had taken a beating, but I could also report a certain upswing, and when he mentioned "Lefebvre?" I nodded but also shook my head. His shrewd question could be answered only partially in the affirmative: there was also, I said, independently of the person he had named, a return to the traditional that expressed itself in top hats, bridal trains, elaborate celebrations of first communions, confirmations, and weddings, and in its wake helped the sale of modern devotional supplies, well-crafted icon copies, for instance, in fact anything smacking of the Eastern Churches.

Because he spoke so nicely about his wife and children, I volunteered the information that, together with some business associates, I was engaged in opening up a new market for good icon reproductions: the Soviet Union, which we were supplying—illegally, of course—with excellent reproductions that were mounted over there on old wood panels, preferably worm-eaten, and painted over by skilled craftsmen, and for which there was a good demand. Since artists, craftsmen, and dealers naturally preferred foreign currency, quite a few of these reproductions were finding their way back via the tourist black market. Not exactly sharing in the profits, but doing its best to help, was an organization calling itself "Pictures for the Eastern Churches"; too many Soviet citizens in all the republics had sold off their family icons and now, caught up in the religious wave, found themselves without images.

And, inwardly uneasy because Margret was still moving around and had not yet sat down, I went on to tell Bertholdi the trade's classic story of that long-dead colleague who, putting his trust in the religious currents prevalent during World War I, found himself stuck with some 10,000 portraits of Pope Benedict XV and lacked the financial and mental resources to save his business by profiting from the long reigns of the two Piuses. When asked by Bertholdi whether I would still invest much in Paul VI, I said, "As a contemporary, perhaps; as a dealer in devotional supplies, no," adding that the only pope who had remained in demand after his death was John XXIII.

Bertholdi thanked me for this insight into the "subtleties" of my business and returned the compliment with an autobiographical sketch: he was a senior official in the educational system, complained neither of his children nor of the youth of today, spoke affectionately of his wife, laughingly discussed his pension with all its probable progressions and deductions; he hoped, he was confident, that he would be able to take early retirement so that he would finally have time to read Proust and Henry James. At last Margret came and sat down beside me, beckoned to a waitress to bring me a little pot of mocha, placed her hand on my arm, and said, "I remember how you hate bad coffee, and"—she didn't take away her hand—"just now, when I saw you standing there, it occurred to me, after all these years it occurred to me, that he didn't curse God at all."

"No," I said, "it was only those cursed by God whom he cursed. And that curse was the blessing that he gave us."

Willi Offermann, seated across from us next to the priest, tried to bait me by speaking of Jerusalem and the Holy Sepulcher, and of people who had no religion yet lived very well off it. Did he mean me, or the dealers in devotional supplies in Jerusalem? Do I have no religion and live very well off it? Both questions filled me with doubts. True, I did live off it, but not as well as he seemed to believe, not even my grave-stone agency brought in as much, although I can offer the latest designs and good African stones; and sometimes when I was checking a new shipment of rosaries (for which there was no longer much demand, at least not at the moment, in spite of Lefebvre), I would grasp one and recite the entire rosary. So as not to be looking constantly at Margret, who had got up again to tell a waiter carrying a plate of onion rings and slices of blood sausage to take it over to where Aunt Marga was indeed sitting, I looked at Offermann's wife: she was next to the priest and leaning across him in an effort to calm down her husband on the other side when Offermann suddenly raised his voice and started abusing the "Red scum!"—which was nonsense, because he hadn't seen me for thirty-one years and could have no idea whether I was red or green; besides, a minimum of logic should have told him that no sensible dealer in devotional supplies—and that's what I was—would ever vote for any party without the prefix "Christian." This was so obvious that he could have saved himself his uninformed provocation; I behaved as if he certainly couldn't mean me and smiled at his wife, who looked so nice that he couldn't possibly have deserved her.

Then Margret was beside me again, pouring mocha and remembering that I took whipped cream with it; she had brought over a little dish of it. She smelled of soap, toilet water, and perspiration, a smell that I perceived as familiar—yet it couldn't possibly be familiar to me. It was as if we had spent these thirty-four years together, her years becoming mine, a common tally of the years: some things neglected but nothing missed. I found her much more beautiful than on that June night; actually she had never been a beauty, she had always seemed like a girl who had been bicycling too fast and broken into a sweat, yet she had never been on a bicycle. As I looked at her she became younger and younger, until I could see her playing ball on the path between our two houses, flushed, eager, yet quiet, and she was, after all, the first and only woman from whose lips I had heard the word "desertion."

She kept her hand on my arm, and Offermann grew even angrier, prophesying doom, and seeming to hold me, me personally, responsible for the simultaneous decline in morals and faith; and not even when he spoke of my brother Josef ("Of course, if your brother Josef were still alive, but then the best always get killed!") did I allow myself to be provoked into saying something like You didn't get killed either, nor did Margret—who turned pale and whose hand on my arm was trembling. Finally Offermann attacked the priest, whom he accused of being too passive, and it was I who, in order to calm him down, whispered the opening lines of *The Odyssey* to him across the table. That actually had an effect: his face relaxed, and his wife smiled at me gratefully; the priest was relieved. I had looked at the time and found it was only twelve o'clock and that we would be able to catch the 14:22, and during my Homer recitation I thought of coffee and cakes on the train, thought of the crowded dining car, which was now moving beside the Rhine toward the Lorelei rock, and that probably they still served nothing but that seed cake that was enough to choke a person. But it was a long time since I had last ridden in the dining car in the afternoon, I merely remembered that Margret liked that damn cake. Once, on the train to Sinzig, she had told me it reminded her of a deceased aunt of whom she had been very fond. I beckoned to the waitress and asked her to order me a taxi for a quarter to two.

NOSTALGIA OR: GREASE SPOTS

The night before Erica's wedding I changed my mind and did drive to the hotel to have another talk with Walter. I had known both him and Erica, his fiancée, for a long time; after all, I had lived with Erica for four years, in Mainz, while working on a construction job and at the same time going to night school. Walter had been working on the same construction site and also going to night school. It wasn't a pleasant period. I recall it without nostalgia: the arrogance of our teachers, who were more critical of our accents than of our performance, was so insidious that it was more painful than wordy abuse would have been. Apparently most of them couldn't bear the idea that, with our unabashed dialect, we might eventually acquire a university degree, and they forced us to speak in a way that we used to call "night-school German."

When I came off shift—sometimes at the same time as Walter—the first thing was always a shower, then fresh clothes and a general sprucing up, yet we still had lime under our fingernails, traces of cement in our eyelashes. We slogged away at math, history, Latin even, and when we actually did pass our exams, our teachers behaved as if it were some sort of canonization. After we'd gone on to university there were still—for a while—traces of lime in our hair, of cement behind our ears, sometimes in our nostrils, in spite of Erica's careful inspection of me, after which she would shake her head and whisper in my ear, "You'll never get rid of it, that proletarian background of yours." I felt no regret for my construction job when I won a scholarship and eventually obtained a degree, a B.Comm., with a correct accent, quite good manners, a reasonably decent job in Koblenz, and the prospect of being granted leave of absence to work toward my master's degree.

I was never quite sure whether Erica had left me or I her: I couldn't even remember whether it had been before or after I got my B.Comm. I only remember the bitter half sentences with which she reproached me for having become too stuck up for her, and I reproached her for having remained too vulgar, a word I still regret; over the years her vulgarity had lost its naturalness, it had become deliberate, especially when she came out with details about her job in a lingerie shop, or teased me when I asked her to help me look for traces of cement behind my ears long after I had given up my construction job. To this day, although I haven't set foot on a construction site for eight years (not even on my own—we're building a house, Franziska and I), I sometimes catch myself carefully inspecting my eyelashes and eyebrows in the mirror. This prompts a gentle headshake from Franziska: not knowing the reason for my concern, she ascribes this behavior to an excess of vanity.

In Mainz, Walter had often joined us for supper in our cramming days: on the table a package of margarine, hastily ripped open, potato salad or chips from the store, mayonnaise in a cardboard container; if we were lucky, two fried eggs prepared on the hotplate that never worked properly (Erica was genuinely scared of that hotplate: a thread of egg white had once given her an electric shock); also a loaf of bread from which we hacked off thick slabs—and my perpetual fear of grease spots on books and notebooks lying on the table between mayonnaise and margarine. And I was constantly confusing Ovid with Horace, and of course grease spots did appear on the books, and I happen to loathe grease spots on printed paper, even on newspapers. Even as a child I used to be disgusted when I had to take home pickled or kippered herrings wrapped in newspaper. My father would turn to my mother and say with a note of mockery, "What makes him so fastidious, I wonder? He doesn't get it from me, and certainly not from your family."

It was already quite late, nearly ten, when I reached the hotel. On the eighth floor, as I walked along the corridor looking for Walter's room, I tried to estimate from the distances between doors whether he had a single or a double room: I couldn't face an encounter with Erica. In those seven years I had heard from her only once, a postcard from Marbella on which all she had written was "Boring, boring, boring— and not even any grease spots!"

It was a single room; even before I saw Walter I saw his dark suit on a hanger outside the clothes closet, black shoes underneath, a silver-gray tie on the crossbar of the hanger. My next glance was through the open bathroom door and took in a wet cigarette in a puddle of bathwater: the shreds of tobacco dyed the puddle yellow. Walter had evidently misjudged the size of hotel bathtubs and put in too much bath oil. I saw the glass of whiskey and soda on the plastic stool before I discovered him behind clouds of foam.

"Come right in!" he said. "I imagine you've come to warn me." He wiped the foam from his face and neck and laughed at me.

"Only don't forget our difference in rank: after all, I do have my Ph.D., and you don't—I wonder whether, if it came to a duel, you'd be qualified to challenge me—and don't kid yourself that you can talk me out of marrying her! There's just one thing you should know, just one: in Mainz there was never anything between us, never."

I was glad he didn't laugh as he said that. I closed the bathroom door, sat down on his bed, and looked at the dark suit: that was how, the night before our wedding, my own suit had hung outside a hotel clothes closet in Koblenz, and my tie had also been silver-gray.

I watched Walter come out of the bathroom, rub himself down in his bathrobe, put on his pajamas, throw the bathrobe onto the floor, and, with a laugh, run the silver-gray tie through his hand. "Believe me," he said, "I only met her again a year ago, quite by chance, and—well, now we're getting married. Will you be there tomorrow?"

I shook my head and asked, "In church too?"

"Yes, in church too, because of her parents, who love a good cry at weddings. The civil ceremony alone isn't enough for the tear ducts— and she's still vulgar, but already we're using a butter dish."

"Cut it out," I said, taking the glass of whiskey he held out to me.

"I'm sorry," he said, "I really am. Let's have no old-timers' reminiscences, no explanations, no confessions—and no warnings."

I thought of what I had intended to tell him: what a tramp she really was; that she couldn't handle money; that sometimes I had found hairs in the margarine and always those goddamn grease spots, on books, newspapers, even on photos; how hard it had been to get her out of bed in the morning, and her naïve/proletarian ideas of breakfast-in-bed being the acme of luxury, and the resulting jam spots on the sheets and brown coffee stains on the quilt; yes, and she was lazy, too, and not even clean, I had literally had to force her to wash: sometimes I had actually grabbed hold of her and dumped her in the tub, bathed her the way one bathes a child, with much screaming and spluttering; yes, and that sometimes she had got mad yet had never been in a bad mood, no, never in a bad mood. At that point I remembered the house we were building, to which I never went, leaving it all to Franziska and the architect.

"And just imagine," said Walter, "she doesn't want us to start building a house, and I've always looked for a wife who didn't want that. Now I've found her, at last—she hates building and construction."

I was just about to say, "So do I," but all I said was "Give her my regards. I suppose it's quite final, is it?"

"Final," he said, "in fact, irrevocable if only because of those parental tears. We can't do that to them, we can't deprive them of that."

"As for tears," I said, "they could also shed those if it didn't come off."

"But those wouldn't be the kind of tears they're after, they want the genuine kind, the real kind, with organ music and candles and all that—and they want the barely audible 'I do.' No. And the honeymoon—where d'you think we're going?"

"Venice?"

"Right—gondolas and color photos. Go ahead and cry a bit on your way down in the elevator."

I finished my whiskey, shook his hand, and left, and on my way down in the elevator I cried a bit more than a bit, and I didn't bother to dry my tears as I walked past the concierge out to my car. I had told Franziska I wanted to say hello to an old friend, and that was really all it had been.

IN WHICH LANGUAGE IS ONE
CALLED SCHNECKENRÖDER?

It wasn't at all the way he had imagined it: at worst the white van with the red thing—what was it called?—on it. From the white van into the white bed, from the white bed into the white engine room; green caps, surgical masks, lonely eyes above, red blood in plastic tubes, hurriedly whispered orders, before one was far, far, very far away. Bed? White? Van? Imagined? Ear? Ear? So he did remember something, and he tried to touch them, realized he couldn't find them, couldn't touch them, his ears, yet he could hear: female giggles, male groans, behind a—whatever was it called, what was the word for it?—rectangular, painted sky-blue with a pink border, a bluish light bulb above it, like in an air-raid shelter? Damn it, he knew that all right: air-raid shelter, knew bed, van, white, but what was the word for that rectangular, sky-blue thing with a pink border? Entrance wasn't right, that much he knew, entrance was something that led from the outside to the inside, and this one led from the inside to a still further inside. Could it be *"intrance"*? In this inside there was male laughter now, and female groaning, and damn it, someone was whispering "Paternoster," and clearly, unmistakably, someone else was whispering "Ave Maria." They must be Catholics, that much was certain. Catholics, Protestants, Jews; now he found his ears, they were still there, even his nose, he could feel it as well as his ears, but not his—what were those things called that one used for touching, grasping? He couldn't feel them, didn't know what the red thing on the white van was called. Van. Car. There had been something about a car. His nose even became aware of smells: soups, sauces, he could even hear them gently bubbling, a woman's voice saying *"Los!,"* the "o" in *"Los!"* sounded strange, he had heard that "o" before, it wasn't Russian, or French, or Italian, wasn't—what was the language he couldn't remember?—wasn't English, wasn't Swedish, or Danish, or Dutch—he could think of all the languages, even Arabic—just that one, the one whose name he·was looking for, he couldn't think of that, only the word with that "o" he had heard before popped into his mind—*olvidados*—and that was Spanish. Was he in Spain? The rectangular thing that wasn't an entrance yet led somewhere, the things one grasped with, the red thing on the white van, the language, the language he thought and cursed in—he couldn't think of its name; those other things, the ones one saw with, those he could think of right away: eyes. They wouldn't open, he couldn't raise his—and he even knew that word—eyelids! He couldn't raise his eyelids, he touched them, pushed as he had pushed when trying to lift that damn heavy garage shutter in the house he had once lived in, that damn shutter that always seemed as heavy as lead. Shutter? No, it wasn't a shutter, that sky-blue, rectangular thing with a pink border, it was something one opened yet not a shutter, and not an entrance either. The things one grasped with were finding it hard to hold up his eyelids. And, true enough, he could see: aluminum pans with that pungent brew bubbling in them, spoons, plates, cold stuff beside them: cucumbers, tomatoes, mustard. Yes, it was called mustard, that yellow stuff in the smeared jar with the wooden spatula, all words he knew: soup, mustard, sauce, cucumber—he knew all those words and couldn't remember the things one grasped with and that red thing on the white van he hadn't wanted to be put into; those were spoons, or ladles actually, and a woman, nice, not thin, not old, her hair not smart at all, she was the one who had pronounced the "o" in such a Spanish way. There was also a pot of steaming noodles; did the Spanish eat noodles? The Mexicans— do *they* eat noodles? Whatever were they called, those people who ate such a lot of noodles? Paternoster, Ave Maria—damn it, whatever was going on behind that rectangular sky-blue thing had nothing to do with praying, or were they praying at the same time? Catholics, of course— obviously—how wonderful that he could remember a word like "obviously"!—obviously this was a snack bar—yes, that's what they were called!—and simultaneously—fancy his remembering the word "simultaneously"!—simultaneously one of those places where the same thing went on as behind the entrance that wasn't an entrance. One thing he couldn't do, and that was what the woman was doing when she said *"Los!"*—speak, that's what it was, he couldn't speak—or did the groaning, the giggling, the laughing, the praying have nothing to do with that? Was it a kind of prayer hall or room for confession? Yes, it was called speaking, what the woman did when she said *"Los!"*—he couldn't speak; he had to lower the things one grasps with, his eyelids were growing too heavy, leaden shutters, and on bottles and posters he read those damned "os," so many "os"—and how had he managed to see the sky-blue thing before he pushed up his eyelids? He had seen it before, and the thing one spoke with was called mouth, in the mouth was the tongue: he tried to touch it—nothing, there was nothing to touch, to feel—but smell, hear, see, he could do all that, yet he couldn't speak, and the language spoken by the people who also ate noodles, whatever was that called? Of course: the super-noodle-eaters were the Italians, but the people whose language he spoke, when he could speak, also ate noodles: white noodles, he'd eaten those at home too, white van, white bed, white engine room, green caps, skullcaps actually, lonely eyes; bluish light beyond the sky-blue rectangle, before—before the thing happened that he had imagined so differently. He knew that, before his eyelids fell and his mouth disappeared, he had gone through that sky-blue rectangle—bluish light from loose bulbs, intermittent contacts, that much he knew: intermittent contacts—smiling corpses in bluish intermittent light. He wished he were home in bed—bed? Yellow sheets, blue pillows, the orange reading lamp, and around the bed, who would be standing there? A woman, his wife? Did he have one? He must have one, since there were those whom one had together with a wife, children, so he did have a wife, and children with her, and he also had a—what was it called, what one did when busy earning a living? How did he earn his living? Traveling, a lot of traveling in his—he had just had it, the word for what was revealed on opening the garage; red cross? No, white car, no red cross on it. How had he got to Mexico by car? To this snack bar? Garage shutter—no, not shutter, door, now at last he had it, now he wouldn't have to keep thinking laboriously of the "sky-blue rectangle with a pink border." Door was easier. Here by the door soups and sauces were being ladled out of pans, and all the words on bottles and posters ended in "os." Was he a Spaniard, a Mexican? Then how come the noodles, and what was the name of the woman with whom he had those children? What was she called? He had been with her a long time, after all. One thing was certain: the things one grasped with were fingers, and the fingers were attached to hands. Door, fingers, hands, the red thing on the white van was a cross, and of course he had been beyond that door, someone had pushed him in, someone else had pushed him out. Far away a fragmented word was hovering as if on a celestial course, in lunar spheres, torn shreds flew toward him: Otte-lie-les, that "les" must somehow be related to the "os." Related? That made him laugh, and laughing hurt him around his mouth, the mouth that was no longer there; gone was the mouth along with everything in it, yet it hurt inside and out. Hurt? Everything hurt, everything, his ears, his eyes, his nose, and—what were they called?—his fingers, only his mouth didn't hurt, it wasn't there and only hurt when he laughed about "related"; he could even reverse the "les" and turn it into "sel"—Lie-otte-sel, everything was turning, not turning around, just turning: far, far away everything was rampaging among the pathways of the stars, the glitter of the universe, the shimmer of the moon—the soups and sauces were too spicy, spices, pungent, pathways of the heavens, glitter of the universe, shimmer of the moon, and when he pushed his eyelids up again, with an effort, such an effort, like that damn garage shutter he had once had, he saw the nice woman behind the pans of soups and sauces pushing back one breast into her blue blouse. No more Paternoster, no more Ave Maria, beyond the door, silence, garage, Otte? Clot? Spot? Charlotte? Gavotte? Knot? Charlotte? And then the shreds flew together, linking up like space shuttles, and there it was LIESELOTTE, that was his wife's name; not Spanish, or Mexican, but in a language that contained hardly any words ending in "os." Carlos. *Olvidados.*

What was that language called? What were his children called? Lieselotte was better than the woman behind the counter, and the woman behind the counter was better than the woman beyond the door. Was he soiled, had he soiled himself? With what? With vomit? And the fingers that were attached to his hands couldn't thrust into the inside pocket of his soiled jacket, it was more than his fingers could manage, they couldn't thrust deeply, grasp firmly enough, at where his money and papers and checks had been. Lieselotte, so he had imagined, would have held his hand, and the other younger Lieselotte, his daughter, would have placed her hand on his forehead; it was a good thing to give one's children the names of their parents, two Lieselottes, the older one had black hair but wasn't Spanish, the younger Lieselotte had fair hair, beautiful, yes, with a real golden sheen to it—one Lieselotte should have placed her hand on his forehead, the other should have grasped his hand, or rather his wrist, with one of hers. That was how he had imagined it, if—if—but there were more children there, two more. They were standing around the bed, four of them, two Lieselottes and the boys, young men. What the devil was that language called that he couldn't remember, a language in which there were noodles in a country where noodles were also eaten yet wasn't Italy? No, he wasn't an Italian, nor was he an Austrian, although Austrians ate noodles.

The things you grasped with were fingers; the sky-blue rectangle was a door; the red thing on the white van was a cross. What was revealed behind the garage shutter when you pushed it up was a car. The older Lieselotte had black hair, the younger one fair—she had grown a bit lanky; one boy stood to the left of the older Lieselotte, the other to the right of the younger. Yellow sheets, blue pillows, the reading lamp orange—and on the opposite wall hung the thing that had been red on the white van, hanging there black, plain, crossed at right angles, a cross—and again they came from the glitter of the universe and the shimmer of the moon, came from that crossroads of celestial pathways, the names of the boys: Richard was the one to the left of the older Lieselotte, Heinrich was the one to the right of the younger Lieselotte. Damn it, in which language were you called Heinrich? Chill of the moon, heat of the sun, a circling, or rather a wheeling as with aircraft coming in to land. Aircraft? Surely he'd had his car in the aircraft? Richard was dark-haired and serious, Heinrich blond and cheerful. In which language did that name occur? Veins of the earth—rigid, deep, hard—yet also lava, hot, flowing, rampaging inside and out. As for the younger Lieselotte, she would fill out, that lanky figure, those prominent collarbones, all that would fill out, and one day she would be a stately blonde without hollows; the older Lieselotte was quite a different type, slight yet sturdy, a sturdy woman, with a surprising fullness behind the slightness, a good wife in every situation in life. Not a sturdy fortress, a sturdy wife, not athletic, not the gymnast type—no. Beyond the door it was quiet, as if someone in there were breathing with a gigantic chest. Sturdy fortress, sturdy woman—his laughter brought on a surge of pain, from ear to abdomen, from eye to knee. Everything sore and painful, painful and sore, and nothing below the knee; was there anything below the knee? Knee, that was almost a word like Heinrich. Eyelids pushed up again, heavier than ever, what an effort, how he could see the words on the posters: cigarillos, color photos, corphotolos, Carlos, that was a fellow behind a bull. Was he in Mexico after all, was he a Mexican? Could one be called Heinrich in Mexico? On Sundays, when he had to push up the garage door without help, it had been as heavy as lead and kept sliding down again until finally, with an effort, such an effort, he had pushed it into its catch at the top. The car. He had seldom driven himself, had usually sat in the back, and up front was Schneckenröder, who had an inspired way of driving fast yet phlegmatically. In which language was one called Schneckenröder, who could crawl and race at the same time? Schneckenröder hadn't been driving, nor had he; as usual he had sat in the back. What were those things called that one was driven in but not by Schneckenröder? No, not rental cars, no more than a door could be called a shutter. Those things he had seldom sat in were used only for short distances, from airport to hotel, from hotel to restaurant or movie theater, or to keep appointments. Now he had to laugh again about the sturdy fortress, sturdy woman—he had never called her that, but that's what she was, it had just occurred to him—and he certainly had been in a car, not with Schneckenröder but not driving himself either. Taxis, that's what those things were called, not rental cars, and the fellow had himself taken the money from his pocketbook. Pocket? Jacket pocket? Pocketbook? The fingers refused to go in that far. Color photos, cigarillos, Carlos, *olvidados*, on their way into the pocket the fingers went limp. Laughing was the worst, it hurt, felt sore, made that sloshing lava surge up between the stiff and stony asphalt veins. There was no white, and there was no orange reading lamp, no fair-haired girl with prominent collarbones, no sturdy wife, no mahogany-brown cross on the wall, no serious Richard or cheerful Heinrich; a bit, just a bit of white would have been good, not too much, just a bit, nothing was white here, nothing, not even the breast of the nice woman who had pushed it back into her blouse had been white. There was another "os" on one of the bottles behind the counter, and now, quite clear, quite near, the whispered Paternoster in

his ear, with all the rest of it, all that he supposed went with it, and that
Ave Maria too, that wasn't Spanish, that was Latin, and in the sturdy
fortress—in his, anyway—he hadn't picked up all that much, no, that
really was papist gabble, maybe even combined with a whole lot of
superstitious mumblings. Not a bit of white, not a scrap. Where was
Schneckenröder? Taxis, that's what those things were called, not rental
cars. This lava that was sloshing around in him, this hot, painful, sore
infinity, thinly encased as if in a toy balloon—surely it must soon burst,
pour out, sore, painful, hot? What were corphotolos? And who was
that saying in his ear: "Too late for the doctor, never too late for the
priest"? Surely that was the language in which one was called Heinrich!
He had imagined how it might happen, the best way it would happen
or would have happened; how it might have happened and hadn't happened—not, oh, not like this! Someone reached into the inside pocket
of his jacket, which was more than his fingers had managed, saying,
"We'll find out all right," and that was the language in which one was
called Schneckenröder, and Heinrich, like himself, spoken by someone
who would pronounce the "os" as the woman had in *"Los!,"* and it
was someone else who pushed up his eyelids, and now he could clearly
read what was printed on the bottle—"Calvados"—and was mystified:
since when did anyone drink Calvados in these grubby snack bars with
sky-blue, pink-bordered doors leading to the rear? And still he didn't
know what language it was in which one was called Schneckenröder, or
Heinrich, like himself.

CONFESSION OF A HIJACKER

"Comrade Gospodin, after thorough consultation with the level of control that rules (not always successfully, I must admit) my baser instincts; after close, almost exhausting attention to that inner chamber I would like to call my civic conscience, I have decided to make a confession.

"Yes. I tried to hijack a plane. Yes. I had equipped myself for this purpose with a firearm, and although it was only a fake—a bit of wood, a lot of black shoe polish—it was definitely meant to intimidate. Fortunately, it was wrested from me before I had a chance to employ it. I would ask you, Comrade Gospodin, to note my formulation—'had a chance to employ it'—and not to accuse me of playing formalistic games (how can one seriously employ a fake weapon made of wood and shoe polish?), for I maintain that this formulation does not mean that I would actually have employed or even planned to employ it. To me, the sole function of this weapon was that of a key. No, I will not cast aspersions on such an honorable instrument as a key: to me its function was that of a skeleton key; with it I intended to break into those hallowed regions that are accessible only to foreigners and deserving comrades. Can one commit a more despicable act? Never.

"My motivation in this attempt to hijack a plane—and I claim no mitigating circumstances and request that I be prosecuted to the fullest extent of the law—was something that used to be called longing; moreover, it was—my guilt is hereby doubled, so let the law descend upon me with doubled severity—the longing for a non-socialist country, and yet at this point I must in all fairness set limits to my guilt: I longed for this country not *because* but *although* it is not socialist, and between this 'not because' and 'but although' there lies, of course (as the Prosecutor has correctly established), an 'ideological uncertainty;' there lies (as, with equal correctness, he has established) my 'susceptibility to seduction by capitalist propaganda.' This is quite true.

"The fact is that I did acquire a travel brochure of the city of Copenhagen in an illegal, almost sordid manner. I—forgive me if this squalid deed brings tears to my eyes, and do not, I beg you, hold these tears against me as mere hypocrisy—I fished this brochure out of a trash can on Gorki Street as I leaned over it to toss in my crumpled-up *Pravda* (of which, incidentally, I had read every single word).

"Now, I am well aware that throwing away *Pravda* is enough to make me a suspect, but let me emphasize that I had read it thoroughly, read every single word; I could still recite the contents of the editorial to you. The unforgivable part is that, lured by a photograph of an unclothed female figure which I spied among the garbage, I poked my right hand through the garbage to reach for this female figure.

"I am married, Comrade Gospodin, I have three growing children, I lead a harmonious married life, and I do not want to give the impression that this photograph—this bronze statue of an unclothed woman—was the basic motivation for my attempt at hijacking. No, that woman was merely the skillfully planted capitalist-pornographic bait; actually I—or rather those shady instincts that even my socialist upbringing was unable to eradicate—was disappointed in that woman. I have committed myself to being frank, Comrade Gospodin, and on this point, too, I intend to be frank.

"I am, after all, not without education. I enjoyed excellent instruction in geography, I happen to be a passionate student of maps, and so, starting at Leningrad, I run my finger across the Baltic Sea until I reach city of Copenhagen, and that, Comrade Gospodin, is where my longing awakens: that wonderful city simply fascinates me, and I swear by all that is supposed to be sacred to me I did *not* mean to go there for the sake of pornographic movies and sex shops, no; it was the architectural beauty that attracted me—the canals, the old warehouses that I saw in the brochure after the superficial appeal of the unclothed female figure had quickly faded—and not only the architecture but the philosophy.

"I am only a simple Soviet worker, but I have been attracted time and time again by philosophy—indeed, it has fascinated me—and for that again I have to thank my excellent education. In the library of an acquaintance of my deceased aunt, I once read a tract by this Kierkegaard, who is said to have been a contemporary of the incomparable Karl

THE COLLECTED STORIES   863

Marx; and now you will ask me, with justifiable reproach, why in that case my longing was not directed toward the attractive old town of Trier.

"Here I must make a further confession: I am of Jewish nationality, and certain—or should I say specific—historical events affecting the fate of the Jewish people have considerably lessened my longing to visit a country inhabited by Germans, and I need hardly emphasize—this goes without saying for a Soviet citizen—that I exclude the inhabitants of the German Democratic Republic. But Trier happens not to be situated in the German Democratic Republic, and there are no Germans living in Denmark; besides, Trier is not on the sea, and it does not have the Tivoli, it does not have that wonderful circus of Copenhagen's, and, after all, I wanted to go to Copenhagen not merely for the sake of Kierkegaard but also for the sake of the beauty and gaiety of that city; and if I long for Danish circuses, that is not meant to disparage our glorious Soviet circuses; we have the best clowns, we have wonderful artists, but I simply felt the urge to see a non-Soviet circus, to take a vacation among non-Soviet people.

"I do not deny the beauties of the Crimea or the Caucasus, which I have been privileged to see; I do not deny the beauties of the Baltic among our brother peoples, the Latvians, Lithuanians, and Estonians; I have seen all that, and it drew tears of joy—indeed, of delight—from my sense of beauty. But: I just wanted to go to Denmark, and when all my many attempts to see that beautiful country by legal means, as a Soviet tourist, failed, when all my applications were rejected, I perverted my abilities as a skilled—indeed, prize-winning—mechanic in a criminal manner: out of a chunk of beechwood (secretly, while my family was asleep, under the pretext of furthering my education) I carved a faithful replica of a pistol, using our incomparable first-rate black Soviet shoe polish to give it a metallic sheen. Pretending to be a sightseer, I drove out to the airport, made a note of the departures for Copenhagen, and attempted on the day in question to force my way through the barrier onto an S.A.S. airliner. The attempt was foiled by the vigilance of our militia, to whom I would like at this point to express my thanks.

"I swear, Comrade Gospodin, I swear on the lives of my wife and my children, of all who are dear to me, of all those comrades who are my friends: I would have returned; full of remorse would have given myself up to the authorities and, after serving an appropriate sentence, resumed my occupation as a skilled mechanic; would have spent the rest of my life in this my beloved native land, the land of the workers. I have no illusions but that after a very few days in Copenhagen I would have grown weary of that decadence. After all—and I beg you not to look for any ironic overtures in this—how magnificent is our instruction in geography, how comprehensive ours in philosophy, that such longings should arise!"

Prosecutor Gospodin merely summed up the accused's confession objectively, acknowledging it briefly, so to speak; but, as he went on to explain in detail, he did not attach even the slightest mitigating significance to it. It meant absolutely nothing, he said, if a person confessed to something that had been proved, recorded, and confirmed by the accused's signature. What was shocking about this confession was its references to matters of common knowledge: the advantages of Soviet instruction in geography and philosophy. Praise of such self-evident matters contained an element of toadying, of hypocrisy. What was particularly damning in any assessment of the character of the accused was his praise of Soviet shoe polish, which everyone—Party leaders, government leaders, and, last but not least, the Soviet people—knew was, although not exactly bad, not as good as the accused had maintained; there were reports—and by no means secret, at that—about this shoe polish which stamped the accused as a toadying liar; and (at this point the Prosecutor took the fake pistol out of his briefcase and placed it before the judge) chemical analysis had proved (he placed the expert's report beside the pistol) that this contraption designed for extortion had been treated with an American brand of shoe polish to produce that deceptive metallic sheen. As further proof, here was (once again he fished in his briefcase) a fake pistol that, he said, had been treated with Soviet shoe polish: he pointed out how the wood showed through, how the color was not metallic black but blackish, how the sheen was not steel-gray but grayish.

The accused, he continued, was proved guilty not only by his deed, not only by his needless confession, but by his praise of Soviet shoe polish, his cosmopolitan irony, his subversive mockery; and the court should not allow itself to be deluded by the accused's words of remorse. He, the Prosecutor, asked not for the heaviest sentence but for a heavy one.

THE MAD DOG

The ten stories in The Mad Dog *were written in the late 1930s and the 1940s. The collection, assembled by Böll in 1947, was published posthumously as* Der blasse Hund *by Kiepenheuer & Witsch in 1995. It was published in English by St. Martin's Press in 1997, in a translation by Breon Mitchell, whose introduction to the collection follows below.*

* * *

Early treasures continue to emerge from the literary estate of Heinrich Böll. The sensation created in Germany in 1992 by the publication of the novel *Der Engel schwieg* (*The Silent Angel*, 1994) was due only in part to the obvious interest literary scholars took in the rediscovery of his first sustained work of fiction. More striking was the quality of the work itself. Although no German publisher would take a chance on it in 1950, fearing its vivid portrayal of the harsh realities of the war and its aftermath, the novel found immediate readers in the 1990s. It was not simply that Böll was now a literary icon. The novel spoke directly to the hearts of Germans, with a voice that remained clear, strong, and moving in spite of the intervening decades.

The response to *The Silent Angel* in America quickly reaffirmed that Böll's keen observation and poetic power remained an international affair. The universal themes of human loss and human courage, of spiritual despair and spiritual strength, rang clearly through the pages of the novel. American critics found *The Silent Angel* "a beautiful, urgent novel ... as perfect as anything Böll ever wrote," "a haunting evocation of postwar desolation," and "still pertinent to our own hunger for the bread of meaning amid the rubble of history." The novel was recognized as a key to Böll's entire later development and praised as a magnificent work of art in its own right.

The present collection of hitherto unpublished short stories is of equal importance to readers everywhere. Like *The Silent Angel*, these tales may well have seemed too bleak for German publishers in the immediate aftermath of the war, but they offer powerful and striking insights into the human condition that still touch us today. They range in tone and subject matter from the prewar idealism of "Youth on Fire" to the grim despair of "The Mad Dog," and from scenes of battle to the daily lives of those who struggle to make sense of things when war has ended. Readers will hear echoes of almost every familiar motif from Böll's later work, but, paradoxically, they will be listening to the original source of those very themes.

Perhaps the most surprising story in the collection is "Die Brennenden" ("Youth on Fire"). There is good reason for our surprise: Böll wrote the story when he was nineteen years old, before he had completed the German equivalent of high school. It is thus the earliest of his stories to which we have ever had access, offering a unique, prewar perspective on the young writer. Its striking chords of youthful idealism, the search for spiritual meaning, and the role of the Catholic church already seem familiar, as do a keen eye for telling detail, a deep sympathy for the poor, and an impatience with social conventions and mores. There are also unusual reversals of plot: a young prostitute reveals herself to be a Christian in disguise, a concert pianist takes on a strange lover, a priest performs an unexpected marriage. From the opening scene of contemplated suicide to the closing vision of hope, the story reveals touches of the major writer to come.

"Youth on Fire," written in 1937, reminds us that Heinrich Böll was called to the writer's life from an early age. Although it is difficult to imagine what his stories and novels might have been like without the crucial, formative experience of World War II, it is clear that the war did not create Böll's literary impetus, but only formed and channeled it. In the ten years that intervened between "Youth on Fire" and the earliest of the remaining stories in this collection, Böll's writing was limited almost exclusively to long and detailed letters to his wife.

The spiritual and creative distance covered as Böll absorbed the devastating impact of battle and defeat may be seen in "The Mad Dog," written in 1947, a story that reads like a hopeless cry of pain. Here a young man who might well have been one of the enthusiastic youths listening to Beethoven at the end of "Youth on Fire" is twisted and torn by his country and its fate, impelled toward murderous revenge in a world gone mad. Yet the connecting humanitarian thread remains, unbroken over the years.

The war leaves its imprint on every one of the remaining stories in the volume, from battle scenes to postwar poverty, from senseless destruction to the ruins of love. "The Tale of Berkovo Bridge," printed here for the first time in its original form, offers a powerful metaphor of the conflict of duty and compassion in time of war; "The Fugitive" and "Trapped in Paris" are breathless depictions of soldiers on the run, desperately seeking to avoid the face of death. Several of the stories show men and women searching for remnants of love amid spiritual wreckage, with varying degrees of success. A profound human sympathy permeates this book, a belief that God will forgive us, as we may perhaps one day forgive ourselves.

This collection closes with one of the most moving texts Böll ever wrote: "Paradise Lost." So strong was the hold of the images in this unfinished novel that Böll continued to rework passages from it into both novels and short stories over the next several years. Now at last we have the paradox of the original fragment rendered whole—for the ruined symmetrical garden through which the narrator passes, the mirrored images of memory and present moment, the arrival and departure that frame the tale, create a text of unexpected balance and harmony, a complex aesthetic whole as finished as any reader could desire, a classic story lost but now regained.

—*Breon Mitchell*

THE FUGITIVE

His heart pounding, he watched from his hiding place as the car raced along the country road, its headlights blazing. He jerked back as if struck in the face as the car squealed to a halt, then turned sharply and sent the merciless beam of its searchlight gliding slowly and deliberately back and forth across the fields. Trees flared in unnatural brightness, as if awakened to terrifying life by some magic spell. Bushes were drenched by the harsh, maniacal light before slipping back into darkness; then the beam was stopped short by the wall that hid him. He could almost feel the light damming up against it. Then it flowed across the crumbling top; he shut his eyes, blinded, struck by savage pain as the corrosive beam stabbed at his eyes through a crevice in the wall.

He heard the steady idling of the motor and men's voices; he listened intently as the searchlight was extinguished and the heavy weight of darkness fell over him again. Rising from the cold, damp meadow, he risked raising his head above the wall. The car was standing on the road with its searchlight stowed. He saw the silhouettes of two men, their faces seemingly turned toward him; surely they must sense that he was there ... surely. His eyes bored deeply into the flat darkness, as if forcing it to reveal their faces. He had to know if Germat was there. Germat! His heart skipped a beat. If so, he was lost. Germat was the most cunning bloodhound in the entire zone, a vicious man-eater gifted with nearly supernatural instincts. The men's voices appeared almost apathetic, a steady murmur.

All at once he heard noises to the left and right in the dark field, like someone creeping, dragging his feet, and the unbearable yet unavoidable sucking sound of a boot being pulled from mud that has closed around it. My God ... he had just realized his head must be visible above the wall, like a black oval against the darkened blue of the heavens, even at this distance. He ducked down, panting in brutish fear, and in the next split second, as he tried to bring the dizzying whirl of his thoughts and emotions under control, a bullet whizzed over the wall from the direction of the road, the signal that the hunt was officially on. Had he missed the gunshot in his first moment of panic?

Suddenly he felt totally weightless, strangely light, as if the ice-cold hatred in his heart had crystallized the chaos of fear and peril. He thought quickly yet carefully; now the veil lifted and he saw through their tactics: They had already outflanked him. He heard the sounds of several men to either side, and behind him as well. They probably had a chain of sentries all the way to the road, where Germat waited, directing the hunt with his devilish intellect. It was hopeless. He would be shot a dozen times if he made the slightest move in the darkness. They knew where he was, while he had no idea where they had stationed themselves; he could only head straight into the heart of the trap. Then suddenly he thought of a plan, laughably simple, dazzlingly bold. Hate gave him courage, a savage living hatred that served as well as love. He no longer felt cold, or hungry, or afraid. A deadly enemy stood before him; he had to attack with the strength of an ox and the boldness of genius. He heard the circle close behind him, heard two of the beaters meet behind the orchard wall and establish contact with a few soft words. Then he prayed, a short quick prayer, like a flame flaring up and extinguishing, and he almost felt like smiling, yes, smiling in the darkness, surrounded by hunters, yet almost sure of victory. He raised his hands high above the wall and cried out: "Don't shoot, Germat, I give up!" He heard the startled cries of the men around him, sprang quickly over the wall, and ran toward the road, smiling as he yelled: "Call off your dogs!"

The road was scarcely more than a hundred yards away and he ran quickly, before the troops could recover from their surprise, until he made out the tall figure of Germat through the darkness, standing in his black uniform, blacker than the blue of night. Still holding his hands over his head, he leaped across the ditch. Then, in the glow of the headlights, he had a clear view of Germat's hard, coldly handsome face, his mouth opening to speak with a satisfied smile. Gathering his whole body—his only weapon—he threw himself savagely against Germat with all the crazed fury of his hatred. He felt the impact with a thrill of pleasure, raced around the car, and heard the driver jump out with a yell, just as he had planned; then he lowered himself softly and carefully to the ground and crept slowly, silently, under the car. The low-lying gas tank left just enough space for him to see Germat: He lay two steps away from him on the cold, hard asphalt of the road. It took every ounce of will to suppress the deep, terrible sobbing rising within him. His entire body trembled. He broke out in a nervous sweat as the smell of gas and oil made his empty stomach lurch with nausea.

Almost as a diversion, to break the terrible tension, he looked toward Germat. He lay groaning and cursing on the road, his face twisted in bestial anger. Blood flowed onto the gray, cold, dully gleaming asphalt from a wound on the back of his head. The driver fumbled over him helplessly, managed to lift his head and place a seat cushion beneath it, as the cries of the troops rang out from the darkness.

Germat was now standing. Strickmann had bandaged him and handed him a few pills, which he washed down with brandy; he was leaning against the car. His boots, those elegant soft boots, which poor Gunderland had to polish each morning, stood directly before Joseph's eyes. For an instant he was seized by an insane desire to grab them and jerk backwards, toppling Germat flat on his face again. Yes, he might have risked his life to send that devil flying a second time, but what he heard now occupied his entire attention. Germat cut off the curses and empty threats of the guards in a cold voice and said irritably: "You should have stopped yapping and got right after the bastard ... then we'd have him by now. All right, shine a light over here, Jupp ... "; evidently he'd taken out a map. The men's feet gathered around his beautiful boots. "We're here—at the Breckdorf exit, there's the border; if he wants to cross it, he has to go back down the road we're on now. Damn, my head hurts! If we ever get hold of that swine ... We've got to catch him, I tell you ... that filthy dog." He groaned, stamped his feet, and continued: "All right, Berg and Strickmann, patrol the stretch from here to Eiershagen ... right here, look ... Grosskamp and Strichninski, you cover the stretch between Brickheim and Gordelen. I'll drive back to camp and send reinforcements. Set them up so the entire sector is closed all the way to the border. Okay, you know what to do ... Damn it, pay some attention to the map." He seemed to be holding his head again, groaning and cursing. "Get going," he said. "I'll wait till you've taken your positions. Büttler, get the car turned around ... "

Joseph didn't realize the danger he was in until the engine suddenly revved up and the entire car began to vibrate. He broke out in a cold sweat, a deathly fear. His heart skipped a beat, and with the final ounce of strength in his weakened hands he clutched the rods beneath the car, then lifted his feet and wedged them somewhere between a metal pipe and the car's undercarriage, barely holding on. The car went into reverse to turn around, backed up to the ditch, the tires spun, and his grip slipped as the car lurched. Head down, his legs clamped fast, he dangled helplessly under the car as the tires continued to spin; he held back a scream welling up within him. Almost fainting from weakness, agitation, and terror, he grabbed on tight again, but could no longer suppress the tears. They streamed heavy and hot down his cheeks; he was blinded by the flood...

Somewhere in his subconscious he registered the tilt of the car as Germat jumped onto the running board, but the tears kept flowing, as if the infinite pain of his lost state had broken through the shell of his will and was now pouring into the silence of the night.

He couldn't remember releasing his hands and feet. He felt the wheels race past his head like a final breath of horrible danger; then he found himself battered, dirty, tired and hungry, wet with tears, on the hard, bare road.

In that terrible solitude he almost wished himself back in the company of the hangman's lackeys, caught up in the insane tension of the chase.

The darkness had thickened; a mantle of night lay silent and heavy over the earth. To muffle his footsteps, Joseph left the road, treading on the soft soil of the fields, following the roadway toward Breckdorf. If he could only sit somewhere for just an hour or so, in a house with other people, eat something, clean up, warm himself; my God, just to see a few people other than those he'd been with behind barbed wire for months, in the hangman's clutches. Just one hour, then he could slip past the sentries before reinforcements arrived and reach the border before dawn, and then ... then perhaps freedom...

Holding to the road, his senses tuned to the night, he reached the village, but it must have been late, for there wasn't a light anywhere. The black blocks of the houses rose dimly against the sky, the outline of the trees. He passed a farmyard sunk deep in silence, so close to the hedge that he brushed against the thorns. Then with startling suddenness the huge, uncanny silhouette of a church rose before him, a marvelously peaceful square, surrounded by tall trees, and a house in which a light still burned. He approached it slowly and cautiously; just don't start the dogs barking... Germat's men would be on him like wolves.

His head ached terribly, a piercing pain, like a merciless finger probing his tormented brain. His face was scratched, he was filthy, soaked to the skin, and tired, so tired it took an effort to lift his foot at every step. Finally he was leaning against the dark door, feeling for the bell. It sounded bright and shrill within the hall, startling him. He heard a soft, rapid tread, the light clicked on and seeped under the door. My God, what if he'd dropped in on a hero of the Party by accident? But terror no longer held sway over his exhausted mind, and a sudden wave of nausea seemed to turn his stomach inside out. Dear God, just some rest, rest and a little bread ...

He tumbled through the open door and gathered enough strength to whisper to the dark figure: "Quick ... quick ... shut the door..."

Blinded by the light, overwhelmed by misery, he stood sobbing, pitiful and dirty, leaning against the wall, squinting painfully at the startled chaplain. Music, a fragment of some fading, melancholy melody, reached his ears, and it seemed as if the whole of mankind's dark longing for paradise were concentrated in that one brief phrase of music, sweet and heavy, clouded with sorrow. It struck him like a death blow; he fell as if shot.

When he opened his eyes again, he first saw only books. He stared at an entire wall of them, their bright titles gleaming softly in the dull glow of a desk lamp. He felt the warmth of a stove at his back; he was sitting in a large, soft armchair, with comfortable cushions, to his right a large, flat desk of dark-stained wood. A friendly man's voice asked: "Well?" and as he turned around with a start, he was looking into the narrow, pale face of the chaplain, bending over him. The first thing he noticed was the marvelous fragrance of good tobacco and good soap, mingled with the pleasant neutral odor of the confession box. Large, intelligent gray eyes peered at him from the white planes of the face, veiled by a cool reserve, regarding him with almost impersonal curiosity. Then came the second question: "What now?"

But Joseph was staring at the carpet, lost in dreams, a magnificent, clean, warm, yellow carpet, beautiful, tasteful etchings on the wall. A dream of domesticity and warmth, beauty and security, enveloped the room. The contrast with the sties they lived in at camp was so shocking that tears came to his eyes again. My God, this armchair, soft and human, actually made to sit on! The chaplain's pale face glanced nervously toward the desk, where a few books lay open and various papers were strewn about. "Well?" he asked again, but banished the impatient look from his face at once, as if he were ashamed. Joseph turned slowly to face him.

"Do you have something I could eat? I should wash up, too, and then ... and then ..." He stood up quickly and gestured helplessly at himself. "They're after me... I have to be gone in half an hour... My God, I'm dreaming..." He tightened his hands impatiently into fists and stood trembling.

The chaplain spread his hands at once and said regretfully: "My housekeeper's—" but then interrupted himself, motioned for the pitiful figure to follow him, and stepped out into the hall. Joseph slipped after him.

"You're from the camp?" he asked on the way to the kitchen. Joseph mumbled hoarsely: "Yes." The kitchen was so sparkling clean it looked as if no one had ever cooked there. It seemed meant only for show; everything gleamed in the glow of the glass lamp, not a speck of dust to be seen, not a dish in sight. The cupboards were closed, and the stove was obviously ice cold. The chaplain tugged awkwardly at a cupboard. "For heaven's sake," he said, shaking his head, "she always takes the key with her..." But Joseph had grabbed the poker from the tidy coal box and said tersely, with a strange, almost coldly cynical set to his lips: "If you'll permit me ..." The chaplain turned, startled and concerned, but Joseph pushed him aside, wedged the poker between the doors of the cupboard, and forced it open with a jerk. He regarded the splendors with almost predatory eyes, sighing.

Indignation mixed with a slight disdain showed on the chaplain's face. He watched, clutching his hands nervously behind his back, as the man wolfed down thick slices of bread covered with butter and sausage. The ragged, filthy figure in greasy denim was a bizarre sight, with tousled, dirty hair and ravenous hunger in his large, gray, oddly gleaming eyes. The only sound in the stillness was his noisy chewing and at times a strange snuffling, as if the man had a cold and no handkerchief.

The chaplain couldn't take his eyes off him, but the visitor no longer seemed to notice him.

It seemed as if time had stopped, and that the world consisted only of this kitchen in which he sat trembling beside a vagabond who ate and ate.

Joseph held the loaf of bread in his left hand and the knife in his right, seeming to hesitate; but then he dropped the knife on the table, shoved the bread aside, and stood up. "You could at least have offered me something to drink; you've never eaten a dozen slices like that," he said in genuine irritation, then went over to the sink, fished the soap from a niche in the wall with annoying self-confidence, and began washing his face, puffing noisily. He found the hand towels under a clean cloth behind the oven, as if he knew the layout of the house forward and backward. "Clean underwear, now that would be just fine ... and my feet washed..." he mumbled through the hand towel, drying his face and head roughly, almost relishing it. He hung up the towel and was about to ask for a comb when he looked the chaplain full in the face for the first time. "My God," he said softly, with childlike amazement. "You're not angry with me, are you?"

"No," laughed the chaplain with an annoyed snort. "You're the most charming fellow I've ever met!" He stood waiting by the door. Shaking his head, Joseph walked past him into the hall, heading for the study. He was still shaking his head as he sat down again in the armchair.

The chaplain had turned off the outside lights, relocked the doors, and returned quickly, as if he were afraid to leave the man alone. His face was masked with a strange severity like that of a welfare worker.

"I'll need to ask you for a couple of other things," Joseph said, speaking in an almost businesslike tone. "First a comb; you know how it is, a person feels so unfinished somehow, when he's washed up but hasn't combed his hair ... thanks." He took the black comb and combed his hair contentedly. "And a cigar, if you have one ... and, I'm sorry, a sip of wine ... then I think I'll make it across the border easily. I'm feeling stronger now and I'm not afraid anymore." The chaplain wordlessly handed him a cigar, along with a box of matches. "Now I know why the hangman's men, even though they're stupid, can still lord it over us in camp—because we're always hungry and dirty." He puffed deeply, regarding the cigar and his fingernails in turn. Then he said softly: "Excuse me," and cleaned his nails with a broken matchstick. "There, now I almost feel good … almost." He gazed intently into the chaplain's eyes, and a trace of sympathy appeared on his face. "I really don't know what you're so annoyed about." The chaplain rose with a jerk, as if a fire had started under him; he paced agitatedly in front of the bookcases, his face an odd mixture of fear, sorrow, indignation, and uncertainty.

"In fact," Joseph continued, when he received no answer, "I'm the one who could be offended, since you're not offering me any wine. And viewed objectively, I am a rather charming fellow."

The chaplain paused abruptly before him and stammered: "Are you … are you … a criminal?"

Joseph's eyes narrowed and hardened; he looked at him searchingly. "Of course, I committed a crime against the state, and I think you're about to as well." He glanced at the scattered pages of the manuscript covering the desk. "That is, if you truly represent the ideas that your uniform stands for."

"You let me worry about that." The chaplain laughed, apparently trying to salvage a little humor from the situation. Joseph asked again about wine, but the chaplain merely smiled uncertainly, then paled in fear and nearly cried aloud as Joseph stepped up to him, cowering defensively as Joseph seized him by the top button of his soutane. "All right," he said softly, very softly, "I'll get you some wine."

But Joseph threw his cigar angrily down on the desk and released his hold. "Oh"—he waved him off wearily—"if you only understood what wine it is I want from you. What good do all these treasures do you?" He gestured roughly at the books. "You've learned as little from them as your *confrères* fifty years ago learned from the fulsome pandects we find so contemptible today…" He struck the bookcase dully with his fist. Then he hesitated as he saw the chaplain's tortured face, but his words gushed like a spring released by a drill. "You soak in your certainties like a man in a bathtub of lukewarm water, indecisive, hardly daring to get out and dry off. But you forget that the water is turning cold according to inexorable laws, as cold as reality." His voice had lost its accusatory tone and was almost imploring. He released his gaze from the shocked face of the chaplain and ran his eyes over the book titles. "Here," he said sadly. "You wanted to know my crime."

And he threw the slim brochure onto the desk: "There it is ... and now, goodbye." He took a deep breath and looked around the room a final time, then knelt and said softly: "Bless me, Father, I have a dangerous road ahead." The priest folded his hands and made the sign of the cross over him, and as he tried to hold him back with a helpless smile, Joseph said quietly: "No, forgive me... I have to go now, my life is at stake." And before he left the house, he made the sign of the cross over the figure in black.

It was now totally dark outside, as if the night had rolled itself into a tight ball. The village seemed to cower in darkness, like a flock in a gloomy cave, swallowed by brute silence. It seemed as if loneliness braced itself icily against Joseph as he wended his way cautiously through the dark alleys to the open fields. As if in final farewell, the bells of the church rang in consolation through the night. Four times they sounded from the tower, bright and almost joyful, then twice, dark and heavy, as if God's hammer were falling through all eternity.

In the silent gloom the tones were like a reminder to hold fast to his faith.

Soon he could distinguish the ground's surface and larger obstacles, hedges and bushes and ditches. He could go only by sixth sense, instinctively following the street, which angled away toward the country road. He felt almost nothing, his heart heavy with silence, the infinite silence of one who suffers, for whom there is no answer under the heavens, no answer but God's promise, spanning the earth, wherever any person suffers for the sake of the cross. He was so far, so far from all hate and all bitterness, that prayers formed in him like pure, steady flames rising from the garden of faith, hope, and love, innocent and beautiful as flowers.

He crossed a wooded area, feeling his way cautiously from tree to tree to keep from stumbling in the darkness. Emerging into the open, he saw lights. To the right, ghostly and distant, rose tall structures, illuminated by yellow light, steel-ribbed skeletons. Behind them glowed the red jaws of the blast furnaces, like the gullet of the underworld. My God, those must be the factories at Gordelen! The border lay just beyond them. It couldn't be more than a half hour away. The field fell away before him and was bordered by a line of trees, their silhouette outlined against the distant light, and he saw how the trees ran on ahead, far across the dark, level fields, toward the factory. It must be a road. Everything beyond it lay in darkness; a thick forest seemed to extend into the distance, perhaps even beyond the border.

Nothing could be heard but the strange, distant, grinding murmur from the blast furnaces and pits.

The field before him appeared smooth, a treeless meadow without bushes. He headed to the left, but there was no cover that would allow him to reach the road. He hesitated, saw with increasing clarity the motionless line of trees on the dark base of the road, like an endless row of teeth. Fear overwhelmed him again, tugging violently and mockingly at the cloak of his self-composure. He seemed to see the monstrous grin of a bestial mouth stretched across the face of the night. He pushed off from the tree, almost violently, and began to run. The steep meadow seemed to swallow him; he hadn't realized how abruptly it would fall away.

Suddenly, the heavens seemed to split in two, and the dazzling beam of a searchlight shot out in front of him, as if he had brought it to life. He fell to the ground as if struck by lightning, landing painfully on his chin. His face pressed deep into the bitter, cool damp of the earth while the searchlight sailed back and forth over him like a huge yellow whip. With his face in the soil he failed to hear the sentry's challenge, then a burst of fire raced like an apocalyptic gurgle across the earth in front of him, the bullets thudding into the ground. He lay there, nailed fast by the murderous light, like a target set on the meadow's slope. And before the next series of shots ripped through him he screamed, screamed so loudly in his forsakenness that the heavens would surely collapse. He raised his head again and screamed, blinded by the light, before a final burst from the snarling muzzle extinguished his cries.

All was still as his tormentors surrounded him, shining their flashlights on his torn body, which resembled the earth so closely that it might have been the earth itself that bled. "Yes ... that's him," said an indifferent voice.

YOUTH ON FIRE

Heinrich Perkoning was sixteen years old when, for the first time, he felt like dying. On a gray December day, strolling through the large city he called home, he saw an elderly gentleman he knew follow a bold young prostitute into her house. He was overwhelmed by such infinite pain that he wanted to die. The anguish he felt, which seemed immeasurable, increased with each passing day. He saw so many ugly and evil things, and so few that gave joy to his soul, that he decided to kill himself. He didn't say a word to anyone. He suffered for a year, and no one sensed his pain. He was often on the verge of confiding in someone he thought he could trust but always recoiled at the merely superficial interest they showed, and he closed his heart.

Now he was walking—on yet another December day—along the bank of a broad river, thinking of only one thing: killing himself, taking his own life. Trembling, he slowly descended the stone steps leading to the water. He paused on the bottom step. The water lapped intimately at the stones, as if in gentle encouragement. He'd planned everything carefully in advance: He would drape his coat loosely around his shoulders and sew it up tightly from the inside, preventing any possible swimming motion. He thought again with a shudder of all those who would suffer at the nature and manner of his death. His mother and father, his siblings, and a few others, friends, one or two young women among them, who thought they loved him. They all passed through his mind, slowly and silently. A scarcely perceptible wave of love and longing rose in him yet could not hold him back. He had struggled far too often against such feelings. And he saw the face of a suffering young priest, whispering to him, "The Son of Man knew not where to lay his head, so forsaken was he, so miserable and forsaken among men. Even his disciples deserted him in his hour of need. Only the power of the Holy Spirit could have given them strength to bear the terrible agony and pain, for the sake of God. And yet the Son of Man still loved them.

He knew how ugly and evil the world was, but he was filled with love for a mankind that had strayed—and gave his life for them, and for you. If you believe in him—as you've always claimed—then follow his example and love them all, the bad, those who have lost their way, all those who suffer." Heinrich trembled violently and groaned: "I can't bear it!" But a voice within him, more powerful than he had ever heard, roared: "God's mercy and love flow everywhere; have faith in Him!" And Heinrich turned and ascended the stairs.

He walked along the broad passage beneath the arch of the bridge. Across the street stood a brightly painted wooden pavilion surrounded by shrubs and small trees, a disreputable café. Heinrich reached in his pocket, counted his money, and crossed the street. He entered the grimy place and sat down wordlessly in one of several booths surrounding a small dance floor. An aged, slovenly waitress brought the coffee he ordered. The walls were decorated with stylized red nudes. Lecherous men of various ages sat about with prostitutes. A pretty young girl around seventeen years old, dressed like a prostitute, sat down beside him. She smiled strangely as he waved her away with a tired gesture. Heinrich took out the New Testament he always carried and began to read. The young woman's eyes were so striking he trembled in confusion. He tried to concentrate on the text, but kept glancing into her smiling eyes, which were staring fixedly at him. She propped her elbows on the table and put her chin in her hands. Her brown hair was soft and thick, her face clever and charming, her eyes pure and beautiful, almost childlike. At first Heinrich viewed her with mistrust, but with each glance he grew more surprised. Her large, dark eyes were filled with sorrow; they were pure like those of a child, and sad like those of... But she's a prostitute all the same, he thought, she's trying to seduce me, I must be wrong, she's no good. He returned to his reading. Still, he felt compelled to keep looking up, until, no longer able to bear the terrible uncertainty, he asked in a harsh, brusque voice: "What are you doing here?" She seemed to have been waiting for this question. She loosened a chain with a crucifix from her neck and said in a firm, clear voice, pointing to the cross: "I come in the name of this sign."

Heinrich looked down and blushed in confusion. "I don't really understand, but I believe you." The young woman smiled gently and continued: "Let me explain; it's really quite simple. I've taken a job in this … place … as a prostitute—you know about such things—on a rescue mission. I want to save people, and since I don't think I'm strong enough to battle with lecherous older men, I'm trying to save the young ones. There are countless young men on the verge of ruin. You're not the first I've approached under the mask of sin, but of those I've joined, you're the first who didn't need my help." Heinrich gazed at her speechlessly, as if he couldn't believe his ears. Beneath his almost enraptured gaze, she turned serious and her smile faltered. Now that the sadness in her eyes was no longer muted by her smile, he could see clearly into the bottomless depths of sorrow in her soul.

He wanted to ask if she'd saved anyone yet, but was ashamed to demand an accounting, and waited for her to continue. She sat in mystical beauty, leaning forward slightly, with the suffering visage of an apocalyptic angel. Heinrich could tell that something strange and unexpected was taking place inside her, and in a powerful new rush of shame he covered his face with his hands. All at once he loved this young woman. She continued, her voice now trembling with excitement: "I actually managed to save one of them. He came stumbling in the first week I was here. I could tell he wasn't drunk, but simply weak from hunger. He was as pale as death, his black hair unkempt, and yet he lived. He sat down and shouted almost madly for a woman. I took his arm and led him to my room to save him from scorn, for I could see he was practically insane with misery. I gave him something to eat and let him tell his story. Then he fell asleep.

"I sat beside him for a long time, making sure no one disturbed him. When he awoke he demanded something of me, but fell silent at my look. Then I spoke to him. He was as stunned as a heathen by what I told him. He left early that morning. He visited me often, wanting to hear more about Christ. He hasn't been here for the past four months. He's ashamed of something. I felt it the last time he was here. He wanted to tell me something, but was too ashamed. I know his name, but not his address. I'd like to visit him."

When she finished speaking, she seemed to collapse, sinking down on the table and covering her face with both hands, weeping. Heinrich bent over her. The pain of his love was forgotten; he wanted only to help. "I'll find him, I promise, I… I…" She straightened up and looked at him with a burning, tear-filled gaze. "I think you … you … may have misunderstood me..." She looked at him so strangely that he suddenly knew with utmost clarity that she loved him, not the runaway he had offered to find. He bent down to the weeping girl and whispered: "Don't cry, be happy; help me celebrate the new life I've been granted. I'll serve you, I'll love you more than life itself, please don't cry. We'll leave this squalor and begin a Christian life of poverty. We ...". He felt such joy that words failed him. Language, the most awkward of human mediators, was incapable of expressing what his soul felt. He sank down and kissed the girl's hands. She trembled with joy as he lifted her up and took her in his arms.

That same evening Susanne left her "job." Heinrich sought a place for her to live in the city. She rented a small, clean room where they sat late into the night gazing at each other, but speaking little. They decided to visit Benedikt Tauster, the only person Susanne had managed to save in the torment of her stay at the brothel. Benedikt Tauster was eighteen years old when he first drew public attention. He wrote the infamous essay "Was Napoleon an Erotic Genius as Well?!" subtitled "Meditations on the Well-Known Charmer from Corsica." Even the exclamation mark after the question enraged some readers, although their rage no longer boiled but had now been distilled as steam. Heinrich heard about Benedikt Tauster from one of those readers who had disliked the article. He read his essay and found that its scorn and mockery were directed with almost satanic intelligence against the present situation, for although the text discussed Napoleon's erotic life, it dealt primarily with the contemporary world. The political and social parallels were often so clever that Heinrich laughed till he cried. What impressed him most, however, was the fervent tone that permeated the essay, a wild, intense rapture, which fascinated precisely because it was coupled with irony. The tract concluded like a child apologizing for some naughty deed: "It's too bad that I, Benedikt Tauster, am such a hopeless cripple."

Heinrich discovered Benedikt's whereabouts indirectly, by way of a famous man of letters who had a reputation as a brilliant literary critic. This man had once stated, "Dostoyevsky's greatness lies in the fact that he was a truly gifted disciple of Goethe." As a result of this pronouncement, three shots were fired at his laurel-laden head.

Heinrich learned about him through a prison guard. While paying a pedagogical visit to the man who had made the attempt on his estimable life, the critic whispered in the prison guard's ear: "Unless I'm greatly mistaken—and I doubt that I am—you'll probably be seeing this fellow Benedikt Tauster before long, too." The prison guard, who knew Heinrich, told him about Benedikt Tauster, since he knew that Heinrich had "literary" interests.

Heinrich found Benedikt living in a run-down garret in a bad part of town. He was tall and very thin, with a pale, tormented face. When Heinrich introduced himself as Susanne's fiancé and said they had been looking for him, Benedikt regarded him silently for some time. Then, in a quiet but congenial tone, he said: "So we're friends." Heinrich nodded, and their friendship began. They sat silently for some time, smoking. Then Benedikt looked up and said quietly: "You believe in Christ." Heinrich said: "Yes," although it had not been put as a question. "You've surely read my essay on Napoleon. You know, those swine, those constipated penmen, simply left out the opening. I began: 'May God forgive me if my essay is unworthy. I wrote it in anger at those who make a mockery of His name, yet call themselves Christians.' And they left that out." He looked at Heinrich with flashing eyes.

Benedikt stood and paced the room in thought for some time, then finally came to a stop before Heinrich and said: "I'd like to ask you something." He paused and seemed to be considering whether or not to continue. "In six months a young woman you'll soon meet will bear my child. I met her in a pawnshop. I'd gone there early in the morning, to pawn the only thing I had of value, my watch, because I hadn't eaten for days. I passed it across the counter, the watch was appraised, everything was fine, I was to receive five marks. Then the man asked to see my papers... Embarrassed, I stammered that I didn't have any. He passed the watch back to me and I was about to leave shamefaced when I heard the clear voice of a young woman behind me: 'I'll vouch for the gentleman; here's my identity card.'

"I turned in surprise and looked at her as she handed him her card. She was about my height, with dark hair and a pale face. She regarded me with serious, dark eyes. The man returned her card: 'In the first place you can't offer security for someone else, and secondly you're not an adult yourself, so I can't take your things either.'

"I took her arm and accompanied her home. I was astonished at how naturally everything came to me. I'd never escorted a young woman before. We talked and talked, and were friends at once. I didn't fall in love with her; I simply loved her. As we walked we even cheered up and joked about how hungry we were. But for the most part she walked silently beside me, in melancholy sadness. Only occasionally did she show a spark of joy, saying something with a smile. Her smile was charming, the bright, full-blooded smile of a young woman. We said goodbye on a street corner. I told her where I lived and invited her to come see me. She said nothing, but came that very evening.

"When she arrived, I went straight to her and kissed her. She smiled again. She dropped by every evening, and we would sit and talk. First we recounted our lives, then talked about everything, about God, art, politics—it was wonderful listening to her clever words. And then we prayed together. We revered the good thief crucified at Christ's side, who joined him that very day in paradise.

"My financial affairs were going from bad to worse back then. My only regular income was the twenty-five marks I received each month from the executor of my small inheritance. It had reached a point where I could no longer afford the bare necessities, like clothes and shoes. I started several projects, but the Napoleon essay was the only one I finished. I entrusted it to her, and she carried it around to various houses for almost three weeks, until she found someone willing to publish it. A publisher's representative visited me (a publisher who'd made a fortune with trashy novels). We quickly reached an agreement.

"It was around this time that her father committed suicide. He was a businessman who'd managed to keep his head above water by a series of clever maneuvers, in spite of being deeply in debt. Now his shady deals had been discovered, and he shot himself. She came to me late that afternoon. I longed to see her, for I was sad, even though I had signed a relatively advantageous contract. In the powerful heat of the late summer day, heavy storm clouds were forming on the horizon. The sun had just set, and I gazed from my small window across a city drenched in red. It looked less forlorn than normal ... and yet I felt I could die of sorrow, and knew how much I needed her. Then she arrived, looking half insane. She collapsed into my arms, and gradually I pieced together what had happened from the phrases she stammered out. I could think of nothing to say, and kissed her wordlessly. That night she stayed with me. And that day ... we lost our innocence."

Benedikt talked rapidly, pacing back and forth. Now he broke off and stared out the window. Heinrich wanted to go to him, say something, at least press his hand, when the dark figure of a young woman entered. He recognized her immediately from his description. He greeted her, and Benedikt introduced them. Benedikt gave her his chair and sat beside Heinrich on the bed. In the dim light of the room the two youths could barely make out her silhouette. She began speaking softly in a warm voice: "I've found something for you. A gentleman who runs a private school afternoons is looking for someone to teach grammar-school subjects part time for one mark an hour. You'd have to teach middle-class children who haven't done well in school. The work would be steady, six or seven hours a day. There's a short qualifying exam, but the gentleman waived it. I spoke with him, told him you already have a grammar-school degree. He gets three marks an hour from the parents, by the way." Benedikt looked up slowly, "Thank you, Magdalena.... That means we can get married, that is... if God ... "

All three sat for a long time in the half-darkness. Only once was the silence broken, by Benedikt: "Magdalena, I told you about the young woman in the brothel who taught me the truth about things, you remember... She's to be Heinrich's bride..."

Magdalena sprang up, went over to Heinrich, and fixed her unusually large, dark eyes somberly upon him: "Has she forgiven him ... forgiven us ... for not returning to her? We were too ashamed to face her purity." She turned bright red and stared at the floor. When she looked up again she saw Heinrich smile and nod. She pulled up her chair and joined them.

While Magdalena stayed with Susanne, almost joyful in the aura of the latter's glowing faith, the two youths visited the capitalist schoolmaster. The cold winter rain that murders the poor was still falling. Hatless, clad only in their thin, threadbare coats, they stuck close to the walls of the buildings as they walked along, accepting what little protection they offered. On a broad and elegant suburban avenue, where houses lay in studied reserve behind rows of tall trees and garden parks, they rang

the bell of an almost palatial home. They were led into a reception area
and left waiting for over an hour. After tracing the origin and history
of every picture in the room angrily and in sarcastic detail, they were
almost in a frenzy, and were about to turn their attention to the wallpaper pattern when a "serious" gentleman entered. He was of average
height and portly build, with the smile of a Buddha. They introduced
themselves; he greeted them amiably and within five minutes, without
an exam, Benedikt was hired on the basis of his degree for a probationary period of one month. Heinrich said he would like to teach as well,
and after a quick glance at his credentials he was taken on, in spite of
his youth. "You can start this afternoon," and with these words they
were dismissed. They returned along the same barren route.

"The man is either stupid or crazy," said Heinrich. "He's risking the
entire reputation of his famous school, hiring us just like that."

Benedikt laughed: "He's not crazy, but he is too lazy. But he's not
stupid either. Since he knows Magdalena he probably realizes we're
Catholic, and believers. Catholics, he figures, are afraid to commit a sin,
since they know they'll have to go through the humiliation of confession. They cheat less than those who don't have to slip into a box at
regular intervals to unburden their souls... There are plenty of unbe-
lievers who will only hire Catholic maids, you know, because they think
they won't dare steal anything for fear of having to confess. And he can
toss us out anytime he thinks we're endangering his reputation."

Magdalena was still with Susanne. It was pleasant sitting beside
the warm stove, drinking hot coffee and smoking.

Benedikt and Magdalena soon took their leave, since they still had
to see the priest about their wedding, which was to take place in a week.

Susanne sat beside Heinrich. He stared into her eyes: "Susanne,
I've always hated the sun because I thought its blissful rays were mocking my pain. I found it hard to live, let alone feel any pleasure in life.
Then one day I found the will to live, and that same day I found you,
the joy of my life. The sun hasn't shone since that day, in punishment
for my blasphemy, but it will surely appear again, and I'll greet it joyfully. The days will be filled with wonder for us, Susanne ... Susanne..."
He smiled, the first smile Susanne had seen upon his face, like the simple, clear, godly music of ancient times tentatively settling upon his
young countenance. Susanne was happy to see this gentle outbreak

of joy. They shared something so pure, so far from sin—in an era so constantly near it—that it resembled medieval courtly love, a pleasant, tender breath of blessedness, full of silent jubilation. Heinrich drew her gently closer, kissed her mouth, and the earth seemed to vanish beneath their feet.

The wedding was as sad as a child's funeral. The majestic cathedral, infinitely vast and lofty, had no doubt rarely witnessed a ceremony so forlorn. The few poorly clothed people kneeling before a side altar seemed crushed to pitiful insignificance by the huge room, whose high ceiling of disintegrating gray resembled the cloudy February sky. Magdalena closed her eyes humbly, trembling with joy as she awaited the holy sacrament of marriage, and when, in the course of the ceremony, the priest turned, it was Benedikt's pale, earnest face he confronted. Magdalena's mother and brothers knelt behind them. Her mother's face bore a hint of painful submission, like a violated maiden who, in the purity of her soul, is beginning to forget her body's shame. Something of her brothers' debauchery could still be read in their eyes, masked by their boldness. It was no doubt they who, along with her father, had violated the soul of this woman. From time to time they would sneak a glance at Susanne, kneeling before them at Magdalena's side, her head bowed. The two witnesses, Heinrich and Paul von Sentau, assisted at the mass.

After the benediction the couple stepped forward and knelt on the ancient, plain hassock that had served in many a princely wedding. Both witnesses joined them and the priest began. When the holy ceremony was completed, the young priest spoke. He spoke softly, as if he were afraid of awaking an echo in that vast space, a smile of joy on his face.

"It's customary for the priest to say a few words to a young couple upon uniting them in holy matrimony. Please forgive me, but I can't speak at the moment... We so seldom see true Christian feeling and humbleness before God these days. I hope you understand." He blushed and looked at the floor. "I'm too deeply moved... But permit me to accept your invitation to a small celebration."

Magdalena's brothers took their leave in front of the cathedral. With the disappearance of their greedy, nasty faces, a sense of oppression seemed to lift from the pitifully small party. They walked through the daily life of the great city to their new apartment, situated near the outskirts of the old part of town. The cathedral wasn't actually in their parish, but Benedikt wanted to be married there because that was where his parents had been married, and where he himself had been baptized. The young priest to whom he'd opened his glowing heart six months ago, the night he received the spark of divine truth from Susanne, had gone through old church records and discovered that Danile Tauster had been joined in matrimony with one Adelheid von Sentau in the second year of the Great War. Benedikt's baptism was also recorded. So now they had a fairly long walk from the city center to the suburbs. The young couple led the way, conversing quietly. Magdalena's mother followed with the priest. Susanne walked behind them, between Heinrich and Paul.

Paul, who'd never met Susanne before, was telling her about himself: "I'm the last descendant of a noble Frankish family reduced to middle-class circumstances over a hundred years ago. My cousin Benedikt is my only blood relative. I was born the day my father fell at Langemarck. My mother was barely eighteen. Her young husband's love had rescued her from an orphan's painful life, and she was devastated by his death. Benedikt's mother, my father's sister, only nineteen herself, took me in when I was six months old, although she was expecting a child and deeply concerned about her husband, hospitalized in Romania with a serious head injury. Her husband died three months before Benedikt was born. She bore the sorrow over her husband, her brother, and my mother along with the infinite burden of life. She forced her fiery young soul through the business of everyday life, believing in Christ, the herald of truth and the friend of all those who suffer.

"She received scant pleasure from the boys she raised. She was forced to get a job, and we spent our long morning hours with Veit, a crippled veteran, who lived in a garret next to us. Veit had lost a leg, and had a hard time climbing all those steps on his crutches. He spent a lot of time in bed because his lungs were bad, and he was glad to have us around since he was still young. He was thirty-two years old, and full of energy, and when he learned that our fathers had died in the Great War, he came to love us.

"I was five, Benedikt not quite four, when our friendship with Veit began. Veit believed in nothing. When we entered his room, he would ask with mock solemnity: 'What is the basic rule of life?' and our high-pitched children's voices would respond according to his teaching, 'Everything is shit!' He'd lived through terrible times, and told us horror stories, which we found fascinating. He dripped the poison of unbelief into our childish souls, which remained untouched by the prayers we said each evening when our mother came home, weary and kind. Veit wasn't a bad man, but he had lost touch with God. I think now that the Holy Ghost stirred mysteriously within him, for on one of the final days of his life—I was seven at the time—he said: 'Boys, what do you say in your evening prayers?' 'We pray to Jesus Christ to protect our souls from unbelief, to take our fathers to heaven, to make Veit well again, and to grant our mother happiness.' He smiled uncertainly at us and said: 'That's good, don't forget to say them.' This remark, which ran counter to all his wisdom over the past two years, was to us simply one impression among thousands; we merely absorbed them without differentiating.

"Veit died a few days later. We mourned him deeply for a long time. Mother tried in vain to console us. Time alone healed this wound, and after a period of mourning, the seeds he'd sown began to sprout. We contradicted our mother when she spoke of things in which—as far as we recalled—Veit had not believed, although we did not yet doubt God. That happened much later, when we were exposed to the corrupt wisdom of the streets, and when, after our mother's death, we were despised in high school by the sons of the middle-class and newly wealthy upstarts because we were poor. Increasingly isolated within the realm of our own minds, slowly at first, then with startling suddenness, we denied all things metaphysical, bearing our poverty proudly with bitter, pale faces. We were awash in skepticism, and circumstances and our own short-sightedness conspired to turn us from the cross—repulsed by the cripples who called themselves Christians—long before we knew the first thing about its teachings.

"Our mother died when I was nine, and Benedikt barely eight. The doctors said she died from overwork. She had surely been weakened by the drudgery she undertook out of love for us, but I believe, in fact I'm sure, that she died of sorrow. It had fermented in her for years, and at last dealt her a devastating blow which sent her into the eternal life in which she had always believed. Had she offered us the gentle teachings

of the cross in those decisive early years we surely would have understood, and would not have foundered upon the ignorance and short-
comings of the world around us. Instead we were forced to wander
aimlessly for years on end, groping blindly. We lived on the proceeds of
a tiny house Benedikt's mother had purchased with her scanty income
to offer some small security for the future. People talk about magnificent memorials, documents of love. For me nothing compares to that
tiny, crooked old house in the old city, for which a beautiful, tormented,
lonely young woman suffered long years of hunger.

"One year before my final high school exam, I left Benedikt and
my hometown for the sake of a woman. She had dark brown hair, a
splendid young mouth, and eyes black as night, burning with fire. She
gave a Chopin concert back then... I listened in a trance—moved for
the first time in my life, inspired by the music's magical, melancholy,
seductive sensuality. This young woman, whose profound performance
filled my soul with ecstasy, became my sole desire. The applause still
sounded through the thick curtains as I waited in her dressing room.
Her lackeys had withdrawn under my gaze, the curtain was pulled back,
and she entered with noiseless grace. She was neither startled nor angry.
Without noticing that I was dressed like a beggar, she looked into my
eyes and smiled. She was very young, seventeen. I saw at once that she
was still as innocent as I was. She stood for some time, smiling, while
I waited, pale with pain and joy. She approached and kissed me. I had
never kissed a woman before, and felt the joy of that first kiss from a
woman I loved. In a soft voice that made me tremble, she said: 'I know
you'll laugh, but I love you. You're my first and only love.' We were
united in a night filled with dizzying, sweet pleasure—joyful, but lacking God's blessing.

"I traveled the world with her that year. She gave concerts, was
famous... Never in all that time did I have any clothes other than this
old worn school uniform. She never noticed such things; she was natural
and warm, and I didn't think about them either. We never went to parties. We were always alone, alone with our youth, our love. I could never
bring myself to attend one of her concerts; those thousands of eager
eyes trained on her body, which was mine, would have driven me insane.

"Neither one of us thought about Christ, but a guardian angel
hovered over us, and we were never base. My existence did not remain

unnoticed. The press had discovered me; I know the journalists referred to me among themselves as the great pianist's gigolo. We sinned greatly, but every day was as fresh, glowing, and joyful as the first. And the pleas of my mother, who saw the fruit of her young womb enmeshed in sin, and the entreaties of my second mother at God's throne, were not in vain... I found my way back.

"I was out walking one evening in some small town or other in southern Germany while she was giving a concert, my heart still on fire from our parting, which had taken place before the eyes of the local squire—and all at once it was clear to me that I was taking unfair advantage of her, allowing her to work for me, for I had long since realized that she was miserable playing before the audiences she faced. Only when we were alone, only when she opened her burning heart to me on the piano or violin, was music a joy to her. The realization struck me with terrible force.

"I fled to a nearby church because I knew it was the only place where I could be alone and sat in a back row of the church, shrouded in darkness. The softly murmured prayer reached my ears faintly above the voices of the sparse congregation as they sang. Then I was startled by a loud, clear voice: 'Every sin, every offense against God, begins in pride, even in the slightest arrogance toward a neighbor.' An elderly priest had mounted the pulpit to deliver the sermon, and I was forced to listen, first by his loud, clear voice, and then by what he was saying. My mind followed his words as if entranced, and within a scant fifteen minutes I heard what seemed a strikingly clear overview of the doctrine of the cross. He spoke of humility, of love, of virtue, and when he spoke of ordination, of order, of divine measure, I winced. I realized I had offended against the divine order; it struck me like a bolt of lightning. I was so totally downcast I didn't hear what followed, and remained alone in the church at the conclusion of devotions. I sat for a long time, sweating in agony, and thought I was going to die. I heard footsteps in the silence, looked up, and saw the priest, who, having genuflected before the tabernacle, was preparing to leave. I waved to him like a drowning man. When he stood beside me, regarding me with solemn goodwill, I found I couldn't speak. I saw, believed in, felt God only vaguely, but nonetheless truly. I suffered terribly for my sins, yet I knew as never before that Natalie was a sublime creature of God, and that she was not wicked. I begged God to move her heart as mine had been with the truth and clarity of His being. Then, my voice weak, I spoke to the priest, and told him everything.

"On the way back to the hotel the joy of divine truth burst upon me, and I burned to pass on this treasure, the only one worth possessing, to the person I loved ... still loved. I had no doubt that she would understand. I knew she had natural longings, for I recalled the many hours she wept hot tears because our love remained childless. And her art revealed there was more in her than mere nature. Walking through that late night I seemed to hear again her thousand passionate fantasias, and they were not reduced to vapid meaninglessness when measured by my Christian conscience. I rejoiced in the blissful expectation of showing her the goal. You'll soon learn how things turned out. You'll see a young woman, in many ways still a girl, wearing a plain gold band on her right finger, the symbol of our union. She will be wearing a simple red dress, her only jewelry a rosary, the prayer book of the humble ... the great pianist who married her gigolo and became Natalie von Sentau."

Paul beamed at the two of them, having kept his eyes on the pavement throughout his story. Susanne glowed confusedly over this strange young man, who had no doubt read in her eyes that she would understand him. She saw that Heinrich was smiling.

The small party was received at the door by a slender young woman with brown hair, wearing a simple, dark red dress. The dark beads and gold cross of a rosary were visible about her neck. She had strikingly large, dark eyes, a delicately curved nose. She greeted the young couple first, kissing Magdalena and taking Heinrich's hand firmly. Paul came over quickly and introduced her to the priest and Susanne: "Here she is," he said to Susanne with a laugh.

Natalie had prepared a fine breakfast. The table was tastefully set, there were flowers everywhere, and in the corner a candle burned before a picture of the Virgin Mary.

Natalie smiled as she noticed the surprised looks on their faces: "I discovered it only this morning, in the attic of an old house, looking like a shapeless clump of dust. Who knows how many owners of that tiny house had shoved it aside without noticing it. At first I thought it was a dusty old distaff, but when I lifted it up, it was very heavy, and wherever I touched it gold shimmered through... It must be very old."

A delicious aroma of coffee filled the room. Bread too stood on the table, enticing brown and hearty black, with yellow butter in a brown dish. They sat down happily. February had turned somewhat friendlier, the gray sky at least empty of threatening rain clouds, and a weak glimmer of sun came in through the window from the southwest. It was still cold outside, but here in the room it was pleasantly warm. They spoke little as they ate; something akin to respect for the newly sanctified couple reigned over them.

When they had finished eating, the coffee cups were refilled and tendrils of blue tobacco smoke began to fill the room. Paul said: "We need to think a few things over." Everyone looked at him expectantly. He smiled. "Surely you can see we have to form some sort of club or alliance—something of that kind."

"I agree," Heinrich said, as the others laughed. "Whenever three or more people are in general agreement, something should be set up with membership cards and dues. It would be a strange club, all right: eight members to begin with: a young man crazy enough to get married on a monthly income of less than two hundred marks; the wife of this idiot, who has thereby dropped out of the middle class; the mother of that deranged person; then a great artist who resigned her calling, whose husband, leading a nomadic existence, is the last of his line, a totally degenerate descendant of an ancient noble family; a priest totally enslaved by the Catholic Church; Susanne with her slightly more than shady past; and me..."

"If I can chair the group and compose the club song, I'll join up," said Benedikt, puffing on his pipe with a smile.

The conversation would no doubt have continued in this vein for some time had not the young priest, who had been smiling as he listened, now raised his right hand to stem the tide, speaking softly, almost into the pipe he had just lighted: "In all things truly ridiculous—and of course few of the things people tend to make fun of actually are— one finds something twisted, crooked, or false—and so the ridiculous always has its serious, even satanic, side as well. Clubs, for example, are usually ridiculous, yet still, if they turn truly false and ridiculous, they prove to be no more than one of the thousand various shades of the divine service. I'm convinced many club members who attend church regularly and are 'good Christians' would be far more upset, perhaps even stirred to revolutionary action in spite of their normal apathy, if one of their club rules were broken—or the club funds misused—far more upset than they would be if a sentence were to be struck from the Credo. That's only by way of an example. Whether these things are called current fashion, sports, dance, exercise, or the cinema—or, as is most often the case, money—they are generally nothing more than well-laid, almost comfortably middle-class traps set by Satan. He consumes the still healthy core within them, using them—in nice, decent middle-class fashion (most people are too lazy, tired, and dull to sin wildly)—to divert people gradually from the truth—or better yet, from the tiny residue of truth that would have saved them. And when things have finally reached the point where even those whose duty it is to protect the truth support such traps, then things take their natural course: Beauty is derided, the feeling for beauty is corroded, desire is whipped into a frenzy. It's easy to brew a vile broth from such swamps. So if someone truly wants to found a new club, it should be a 'Club for the Friends of the Absolute.' But that already exists... It's called the Church."

He smiled at his strange conclusion. The others had fallen into thoughtful silence. The young men smoked quietly, thinking to themselves. The young women gazed straight ahead. Magdalena's mother looked at the priest, slightly surprised. Susanne rose and relighted the candle standing before the Madonna, which had somehow gone out. Natalie said softly: "I'd like to play something"—she blushed—"if you ... " Everyone nodded. She stood up and asked Heinrich, who was sitting by the bookcase, to pass her the music. "Beethoven," she said, as he looked at her inquiringly. And while the men laid aside their pipes, and sunlight suddenly streamed through the window, Natalie stepped to the piano, which stood against a white wall unadorned by pictures, bearing only a large black cross.

TRAPPED IN PARIS

Reinhard plundered the paymaster's bullet-riddled car with a soldier's cool indifference. The last stragglers had long since disappeared into the various streets spread out fanlike from the square, and there was no sound or sight of the enemy. The park, ripped and torn by shells, brooded in desolate silence, and the façades of the buildings gaped like an eerily empty stage. Here and there curtains fluttered wildly, almost longingly, from the windows; you could almost hear the frightened breath of people hiding in the cellars, not daring to trust the uncanny stillness in the aftermath of the roar of the attack. The semicircle of the square that adjoined the park—the central portion of the fan from which streets radiated like slender, elegant spokes—was strewn with steel helmets, gas masks, and broken rifles. A bright, smiling heaven arched auspiciously above the incomparably beautiful city, whose brilliance and loveliness beckoned from each of its countless windows. And between scraps of military equipment on the soft, saturated, deep green stretches of grass furrowed with trenches lay corpses, corpses in gray uniforms. It was like a lull in a revolution where the center of action had shifted to some other part of the city, drawing all life along with it. And while the corpses on the meadow clasped the earth as if frozen in eternal lament, the trees that lined the avenue trembled beneath the lighthearted caresses of the soft summer breeze.

Reinhard had slung his weapon and his gear beside the disabled vehicle and was rummaging through a jumble of cardboard boxes, discovering delicacies he had not seen in the long, long years of war. Marvelous cigars and soaps whose mere fragrance could have spelled peace, chocolates and biscuits, the finest linens. With startling rapidity he pulled off his filthy, sweat-soaked shirt and felt the pleasure of a new silk one against his body. He then stuffed his pockets systematically, cramming in as much as he could, intoxicated with happiness, digging through the riches at random, sensing with wild delight that the war, which had seemed so cruel and endless, was beginning to unravel. It was inevitably dissolving, dispersing like a gray, persistent pall of cloud scattered by golden flicks of the sun's lash; the war was unraveling. It seemed to Reinhard as if a huge steel cover screwed down airtight over him had suddenly lifted, releasing him into light and air, and he breathed deeply with a wild, powerful sense of freedom. He drew on his magnificent cigar with a smile, released a blue cloud of smoke into the splendid air, and thought of his wife. Soon he would see her again, soon life would begin, and with a laugh he tossed a couple of packs of cigarettes back in the car to make room for a few bars of expensive soap, fit for a princess, for his sweet love. Then he bent to pick up his sword belt and fasten it around his stuffed and swollen waist. But the next moment he lay flattened against the hot, smelly asphalt, breathing heavily.

From a small grove across the park came a whole column of diminutive, fast-moving cars with soldiers in khaki uniforms, careening madly in a broad front, firing blindly as they approached the square. The last remnant of stillness disappeared as a bullet shattered the car's windshield above him. Gripped suddenly by fear, he was unable to take a calm look to his rear; his confused eyes saw only the merciless smooth surface of the square, across which no flight was possible. The small khaki cars had reached the avenue, gathering on the semicircular square like a pack of small, agile, barking dogs, then dispersing into the streets. One of them passed within a hair's breadth of Reinhard's head, but he had long since assumed the crumpled position he had so often seen among the dead, warding off and embracing in a single gesture. The contented growl of well-maintained tanks approached from the park, and now, risking a quick glance past the flat tire, he saw the advancing columns of infantry and knew it was time to act. The war machine was descending upon him like a cruel curtain and somewhere far beyond it, where the streets opened outward like canyons of deliverance, was the small, beloved face of his wife.

He rose to his knees, concealed behind the bullet-riddled car, and raced toward the nearest street with the improbable, almost grotesque, speed of a madman. But he had failed to notice one of the tanks, followed by a troop of infantry, which had advanced to that very street. He was startled out of the mindless panic of his blind flight by the horrid flutter of a tank shell, winging its way past his head like some terrible bird and exploding against a building with an appalling blast. He threw himself to the ground and crawled on, crazed with fear, while more shells whistled past him like the blows of an enraged man, punching the air. Again and again the rapid flutter above his head, then the detonation, reverberating in the street as if it were a living room. The twelve meters to the street seemed a murderous eternity between life and death. He jumped up and ran, ran toward the street as if into the open arms of life, fluttering curtains, open windows, and the defaced façades of buildings accompanying him as in a dream. The seconds were monstrous waves of fear through which he struggled to make his way. He looked around and saw the barrel of the khaki monster rounding the corner like a silently threatening snout; the soldiers accompanying it, moving soundlessly, struck him as especially cruel as they occupied the nearby doorways, calling out in their nasal language for him to surrender. The next bullet whizzed past his shoulder, so close that he could feel the cold ripple of air, and struck a large store window, which shattered in bright and terrible laughter. Then he was on the ground again, crawling, twisting, changing direction like a wild animal, enveloped by the almost sweet song of the infantry's bullets and the ghastly flutter of bursting tank shells. He reached the edge of the street, sweating, filthy, and totally exhausted. The hideous khaki monster rumbled nearer as soldiers rushed from door to door. Cries and stench, noise, noise. Just as he was about to throw himself with full force against the door of a house, a shot flashed from a basement window directly across the way, grazing his arm, ricocheting off the wall, and angling into infinity with a threatening hum. He lurched in despair, near to surrender, heading up the street again, her dear, small beloved face constantly before him. Suddenly, to the right, a small side street. He threw himself into it as into an abyss, cried out, and the small face grew larger and smiled as, blind with exhaustion, almost feeling his way in spite of the bright, smiling sky, he leaned his shoulder against the first door he came to and it opened easily. He found the bolt to lock it as if he'd known the house for years, then stood silently, leaning against the door, holding his breath, listening. Scarcely a minute had passed since he had leaped from behind the bullet-riddled car to race mindlessly toward the face of his beloved.

He was pale with panic, trembling all over as if he were cold; he heard the tanks rolling closer, several of them, heard shouts from the cellars as the soldiers called back and forth in their crude, chewed-up language, he even thought he could hear the silent fall of their doom-laden rubber soles, but he seemed nailed to the spot by fear, while the street outside seemed to awaken, as if his presence alone had held it in check.

A soft cry of shock, the sort that slips out in moments of greatest danger, released him from paralysis. Startled, he turned and saw a slim, dark-haired young woman in the long, dimly lit hall, her hands stretched forward to ward him off, as delicate and unreal as a fairy tale, dressed in flowing pink.

In the blurred dusk of the hall her hands, face, and dress appeared as an almost flat surface, only the dark ink-spot of her hair stood living and solid in the gray mesh of the air. The frightened gestures relaxed, she approached slowly, and her face emerged, palpable and young, still nervous, in the light passing through the milky glass of the door. Reinhard made an urgent gesture of silence, filled with such need that she instinctively softened her steps. He listened to the sounds outside, tense and alert, as if his fate were to be wrested from that profusion of noise. His eyes searched the charming face of the young woman, and he saw in the human goodness of her gaze that she had no wish to drive him back to ruin.

He quickly surveyed the whole of her face, as if seeking confirmation, the small, delicate mouth, still drawn slightly downward by fear, the sweet, childlike forehead, the fine nose and the sturdy chin, framed and compressed into a small white plane by the raven-black hair. Then he turned his eyes aside, as if trying to see right through the milk glass, and whispered hoarsely, to her astonishment in fluent French: "If you want to help me, find me some clothes." At first she didn't seem to understand, and gazed at him in surprise, then slipped hurriedly back down the hall. He squeezed his hands together, trying to control his violent trembling as he heard them pounding at nearby doors. He worked a cigarette from his pocket with trembling hands, then started in fear at the sound of the flaring match; the silence with which the woman returned along the hall, quickly and quietly, seemed to him a precious caress. He grabbed the bundle she held out to him, walked rapidly into the darkness of the hall, and began changing as quickly as he could. It seemed an act of providence that he already had on the soft white silk shirt, for she had evidently forgotten any linen.

Now rifle butts were pounding at the door, hard and impatient, and he trembled as he remembered how weak the bolt was. But then he heard the woman's voice, and as he heard it, gentle and kind, yet so wonderfully calm and cool, he knew that he was saved; she said indignantly: "Just a moment, sir, I have to get dressed..." She repeated the words in broken English, and received a coarsely muttered reply, which, although unintelligible, sounded like an obscenity delivered with a broad grin. But Reinhard had already changed, and had donned along with his clothes a wonderful, buoyant sense of freedom that intoxicated him. He felt his way toward the cellar door, threw his old stuff down the steps, and went back to the front door in his stocking feet.

The woman regarded him with a smile, and he asked her in a whisper: "Are you really alone here?" When she nodded, he calmly pulled back the bolt on the door. A huge figure, of almost animal perfection in its proportions, a childlike, unhewn face, and the embarrassed yet still threatening question uttered in broken French: "German soldier ... no see?" Since he had addressed his question to the woman, she answered calmly: "No," and shook her head, and, as he turned to scrutinize the man, closely and searchingly, and seemed about to seize him by the shoulder with his massive hand, she added: "This is my husband, he's—" but the word "mute" was cut off amiably by Reinhard, who pulled back the hair at his forehead with a brilliantly acted show of pride and revealed a broad, still pinkly gleaming scar that crossed his brow like the stroke of a sword: "I was wounded, comrade ... up by the canal ... at ... " and he rummaged in his coat pocket as if he meant to produce his papers. "Legionnaire," he added in a murmur, but the giant, had he ever been in doubt, seemed convinced by his fluent French, and touched his cap in smiling salute and apology. There was an incomparable animal elegance in his movements as he turned and shouldered his way out the door. "That's not Europe," the woman said softly. Then the two of them were alone.

Once the peril and the compassion that provided the driving force behind this brief scene had faded, they were overcome by embarrassment. Reinhard mopped his perspiration-soaked brow and took a deep puff of his still-burning cigarette. He still believed he was half dreaming, for eternity had descended upon him, compressed into minutes. With a helpless smile he asked sadly: "What now?" It couldn't have been more than five minutes since he was standing by the car, dreaming of peace, lost in the tranquillity of the afternoon. And now he was standing helpless and destitute in this dim, cool hallway beside a woman he didn't know, astonished by her rare beauty, in misery—drowned in deepest misery...

The face of the woman was cool and reserved, as if she only now realized what she had done in all the excitement. She seemed to be thinking things over as the uncanny silence of the house, heightened by the noise from the street, rippled between them, unfamiliar and oppressive.

Finally, with a gesture of resignation, she rebolted the door, stepped into the hall, and said coldly: "Come this way." There was something almost businesslike in her movements, as if she were conducting a customer into the office of a doctor or lawyer. She opened a door at the end of the hall and entered; depressed, he followed her like a condemned man.

The odor of the dim, tasteful, somewhat overdecorated room engulfed him, delicate and almost gracious, like a true expression of the woman's nature. As if peril and misery were forcing him inexorably to the rim of an abyss, he sensed with dismay that he was becoming increasingly captivated by her beauty. He closed the door softly. She sat in an armchair, her hands propped, while he stood leaning against a sideboard. "Sit down," she said, with what seemed like irritation. He sat down obediently, and as he did so, he was struck by how magnificently the trousers fit. Ridiculous, he thought. The woman's face suddenly lifted toward him like a somber disk. Her large, gray-veiled eyes were sad, and she said softly, without rancor, as if speaking to herself: "You know, I was just thinking, you may be the one who kills my husband at the front."

Reinhard shook his head wearily: "I won't kill any more people in this war, ma'am."

"Are you so sure?" she said quietly, almost imploringly. "How do you know what fate might drive you to, when you might be in a position where it's a matter of life and death to fire in some direction, and might that not be my husband? You want to make it back to Germany, don't you?"

Reinhard blushed. "I want to see my wife."

She glanced briefly at his wedding ring. "The war is far from over, and who can trust a German?" She looked at him searchingly, as if she truly wanted to sound his depths. "I should have turned you in," she continued in a flat voice. "It probably wouldn't even have cost you your life. If Robert doesn't return, I'll feel for the rest of my life that I was his murderer." She smiled suddenly, a beautiful, heartfelt smile. "I love Robert more than my life."

He felt himself turn pale. A wild, unfamiliar, tremendously powerful, seemingly irresistible desire for the woman sitting before him flooded over him, gliding like a secret sorrow. It flowed into him, and it seemed as if his own wife's beautiful face were smiling at him as well, filled with pity and love. He was so miserable, so miserable and forlorn, trapped between obstacles.

"Tell me what to do, ma'am," he said in hoarse agitation, "for all I care, you can lock me up in your cellar like an animal, or I can leave your house now and mix in with the crowd." He rose. He wanted so badly to flee, simply to flee; but then the clamor from the street rose like a tornado twisting into the heavens. Cries could be heard, doors and windows slammed. The woman pulled open the door of the adjoining room, rushed to the window, and peered out past the curtain, breathing rapidly. Khaki figures raced down the street in retreat, and at that same moment a savage burst of fire from a German machine gun swept the roadway like a cruel, invisible broom. The fiendishly rapid spray of bullets gurgled down the canyon of the street like disaster incarnate. All the buildings seemed suddenly desolate, the façades stared emptily, gripped once more by terror. Reinhard shook his head, trembling in agitation. "They really are insane," he murmured in German, without noticing the woman's mistrustful look.

He was deeply shocked as the first gray figure rounded the corner, soiled and dusty. He knew the trooper's cynical face. It was Grote, carrying the slim black machine gun under his arm like a delicate, dangerous animal. Grote, a fine soldier constantly wavering between desertion and the possibility that he might one day wear the highest medals. Yet his face was totally miserable. Reinhard's heart beat wildly, insistently; he'd forgotten everything. He no longer realized he was wearing the soft, lightweight clothing of a civilian. The gray desolation of the army weighed once more upon his shoulders, and without looking toward the woman, he walked slowly, slowly into the hall. A dull pounding at the door awakened him from his dark, brooding mood; he took a few steps, tore open the door, and pulled a totally collapsed body in a khaki uniform inside, a split second before a new troop of gray soldiers darted around the corner and the sound of a savage whip hissed through the narrow street again.

Reinhard bent over the exhausted man, but the woman, who had followed close on his heels, grabbed his shoulder roughly and yelled: "Don't kill him!" Reinhard looked at her, releasing his hands from the fatigued man's chest, and his eyes contained equal measures of unspeakable astonishment and terrible sorrow. He gazed fixedly at her delicate, flushed face with its dark eyes and said softly, as if he could hardly trust his own words: "Do you really take me for a swine, ma'am?" Then he slowly unbuttoned the man's jacket, undid his belt, seized the inert body under the arms, and dragged him into the living room. Slowly, her arms hanging helplessly at her sides, the woman followed. He moved his hands cautiously about the man's body, sensing the silent presence of the woman at his back, pleasing and oppressive at the same time, like a gentle, inexorable wall pushing him nearer and nearer to an abyss. A pale, almost yellowish childlike face, distorted by fear, numb with exhaustion, small, fleshy hands, a shock of touchingly youthful brown hair. He could discover no wound on the body; his pulse was weak, but steady. Perhaps the youngster was only unconscious after all. Reinhard turned slowly, his gaze slipped hurriedly, nervously, past the glowing face. Her youthful, totally transfigured look of sweet shame stirred him strangely, and, his face turned toward the door, he said: "I can't find any wound." But she merely stammered: "Please forgive me..." and now he had to look at her. All that was foreign and cold had fallen from her, and she was so close and familiar and so terribly beautiful that it startled him. Cheerfully, with a smile, he took the hand she offered him, pressed it firmly, so that he wouldn't feel the wild coursing of her blood, this blood a stranger to his own, and then said: "I have nothing to forgive you for, ma'am."

They both regarded this small, poor, unknown soldier as a gift from heaven. What would have happened to them had they been left alone? Outside, in the renewed silence, the heavy tramp of boots in the street, and farther off the rattle of the machine gun. It must be at the park entrance now, near the bullet-riddled car. Reinhard washed the face of the young man while she held the bowl, then made him as comfortable as he could. He could still hear the faint beating of the boy's heart. Now they could look at each other without fear or blushing. Something akin to joy lay in their eyes, a cheerful renunciation, and they knew they needed to wage a fierce battle deep within themselves, for and against each other, to remain faithful. Once again the machine gun gnashed its teeth somewhere in the park, like a file rasping angrily across a thousand tiny, sharp fangs. Reinhard jerked as if the entire burst of gunfire had struck him in the heart. Some uncontrollable urge bound him to the terror and misery outside, and he felt he had to tear himself free, quickly and irrevocably, as from a mysterious umbilical cord. He stretched, put the washcloth aside, and said: "I'd better get rid of my uniform now. You'll be alone for a few minutes." She looked at him in surprise, slightly startled. "And what if the Ger—your countrymen capture you?" Reinhard turned toward the door. "It's not the Germans or Americans I'm running from, ma'am, it's the war. Anyway, I think the Americans are in control this evening."

It was a somber, terrible business, emptying the pockets of the miserable rags in the cellar, with their dangling, half-broken decorations, bundling them together. It seemed gruesome, like looting a corpse, and he tried to do it as quickly and hurriedly as possible, like a necessary yet still nasty task, as if he were secretly burying a murdered man. When he had placed the tangle of clothes in a trash can and concealed it beneath some rubbish, he quickly climbed the stairs again. His hands felt dirty, as if they would never be clean again, and the war, with its cruel necessities, seemed more terrible than ever.

Something akin to jealousy shot through him as he found the woman sitting beside the stranger in the living room, enveloped in the fragrance of aromatic cigarettes, but he was instantly ashamed, as if he had once again defiled himself. She had draped a blue cloak over her pale rose sundress, and he felt he would have to tie his hands to keep from taking her in his arms. He greeted the newly awakened young man with reserve. His curiously childlike and yet depraved eyes responded politely, but with the condescension of the victorious soldier facing a civilian who has remained safely in his home. "*Merci*," he said awkwardly, offering him the pack of cigarettes with a smile, then, turning to the woman, he chewed out an unintelligible sentence in which a few words were clear: *crazy … German … damned animals.* Then he turned abruptly to Reinhard and asked in broken French: "What are they still fighting for, these Germans?" He gestured vaguely outside, where the machine gun again raised its hoarse, threatening bark. Reinhard looked from one to the other uncertainly, but the woman calmed him with a slight shake of her head. This quiet, gentle indication of a bond moved him so deeply that a shiver ran through him.

The whole house was suddenly shaken by a powerful detonation. This was followed by waves of weapon fire in the area. The woman sprang up and leaned against the wall, pale and trembling. Reinhard approached her, placed his hand on her arm, and said calmly: "You're safe, ma'am, that's artillery fire. No, no, believe me, you have nothing to worry about." He watched the stranger's face closely, but a smile triumphed over the young man's initial shock as he cried: "Those are our shells … those are ours!"

Several more shells exploded among the buildings with deafening noise, the dark murmur of advancing tanks could be heard, and the abrupt crack of their cannons, sounding like a sudden blowout, followed by the shattering din of the impact. A few minutes later, from behind the curtain, they again saw the gray figures of the Germans running down the street, a frightening indifference in their gait.

The tanks rolled past the corner again, heading up the street, as the small stranger with the pale child's face smiled, laid a bar of chocolate on the table, shook hands warmly with them both, and left the building. The silence of the house enveloped them again, and now they were alone.

Reinhard went to the door, which the young man had left open, and stuck his head out for an instant before bolting it, feeling the cool, gentle evening air, with its delicate summery smells already offering a foretaste of autumn as it descended upon the beautiful, incomparable city. And perhaps it was the greatest offense of his life, the greatest, that he didn't simply leave the house, but instead turned back, slowly and heavily, into the dusk of the hall, which had become thicker and darker.

The woman stood at the open window, her arms crossed, staring out into the evening at the gardens. Like a piece of bad theater, the sound of voices, high-pitched and somehow tinged with excited joy, arose once more from the street, and it seemed as if these scenes might alternate throughout eternity.

As if wishing to hide even from herself, the woman stood in the recess of the window and did not turn as Reinhard entered. She gazed into the evening sky, its blue now touched with gentle shades of rose and lilac, stretching like a delicate tent above the splendid summer day now coming to a close, a day on which so many men had perished in the cruel arms of war. She seemed to shiver, although the soft breeze was still mild and pleasant. Her shoulders were hunched, she had buttoned the fine blue wool cloak about her, and her pale face, with the small red fruit of the mouth, appeared almost dead. The room was already wrapped in darkness, although it was still bright outside, as bright and friendly and beautiful as Paris, the incomparable city in which the war still raged. Reinhard gazed at her spellbound. Just half a second more, he thought, I'll just look at her, just look, then I'll slip away as quickly and quietly as I can. I'll run and run until the nearness of the distant woman I love extinguishes the terrible, consuming fire within me.

But the woman turned around, suddenly, abruptly, as if she had just awakened, and said softly: "You'll have to leave the house by way of those gardens when it's completely dark. Believe me, a thousand pairs of eyes have seen you enter the house, and any one of them would recognize you again. They don't think you're here anymore, because the house has already been searched."

He protested in a state of shock: "But that means I'll have to wait here several more hours." He felt fear rise within him, wild desires and opposing thoughts, and he was surprised by the joyful smile with which she said: "Do you find it so terrible to be my prisoner until darkness falls?" adding with a wry smile: "But wait a moment ..." She walked past him and he heard her leave the house.

He breathed a sigh of relief. Was he so weak and foolish he couldn't spend two hours beside this beautiful woman without succumbing ineluctably to the terrible sin of betrayal? He had carried the image of his beloved unscathed through all the dangers and temptations, the infinite agonies of war. Was he to give it up now, without wishing to, seduced by the dark, melodious voice of ruin hovering over this city, trapped now in the dusk of this house? Yes, it would be truly stupid to risk his escape for a foolish weakness. Smiling, he lit one of the American's cigarettes and turned on the light. But it seemed as if the dusk, the sweet sense of being lost, couldn't be banished by the warm, bright flood of light, either. It hovered among furniture, in the gaps, even above the reddish lamp shade itself, the sweet fragrance of being lost, drawing him into its spell. Ghastly and sweet, it flowed in, as if the joyful visage of the beautiful city was dissolving into insane caresses, blurred and enticing, as if enveloped by the mists of ruin.

The noise of battle spread steadily throughout the city. From time to time it fell silent, only to burst forth again like the dull blasts of a trumpet. The war's progress could be measured easily by its sounds; it was actually possible to sense the increasing depth and expanse of the blows, to feel the gray soldiers' weakening resistance, and in the streets, as the curtain lifted, the sounds of life swelled forth again.

The evening slowly filled the last bright light of day with blue shadows. It seemed to fall softly, tenderly, friendly and familiar, no more than the darker sister of the cheerful day. Twilight seemed to smile upon this immense and beautiful city, to drape its vast, dark blue cloak around her, as if it couldn't be angry with her, enfolding her in a quiet, loving, and ineffably tender embrace, openly, with no thought for the poor hearts of those who stand aside in misery, weeping, weeping in the arms of longing.

Reinhard turned the light back off. For an instant it seemed completely dark, but then the last gleams of daylight plunged through the open window into the thick dusk of the room. The window was like a benevolent shaft in a prison. Delicate reddish gleams flowed in; they seemed mingled inextricably with the confusing, yet bittersweet smells of the evening, breath and light in one, which wafted beneath the gentle trees of the boulevard. They penetrated to the young man hidden behind the curtains and breathing deeply, brushing him like the terrible caress of a beautiful woman who teases but will not yield. He groaned as if his life's blood were streaming forth, and felt his misery, his total abandonment in this foreign, hostile city, like a single, massive wound, lashed by the inescapable blandishment of his senses. He tore himself away as if he had been anchored to this shadowy play, stumbled through the dusk to the door, pulled it open, and hurried down the hall to the front entrance. But then he paused as if nailed to the spot, for he heard fate itself approaching. The front door opened and the soft steps of the woman came toward him. He saw nothing, nothing at all in the darkness of the hall, as if it were a solid fabric, but never, never in the thousands of seconds that long afternoon had he seen more clearly. He saw her whole, his heart was torn from him, and as the tiny steps approached, he braced himself against the wall, as if forced backward by an invisible power. His eyes closed, his entire being writhed in pain, and he simply reached out, vaguely, as if he were trying to catch a bird flying past, and at the first tender touch he sensed that she too was unable to flee. And as her tears burned upon his cheeks, he longed for the entire darkness of night to crash down around them and bury them in its rubble.

When they awakened, they were so distant ice water might have been flowing between them, distant and cold, lying together a bad dream, while the milky light of the moon streamed mockingly through the open window of the room. She turned her face aside with a shudder and her entire being, mysterious and unfathomable, seemed hidden with her face behind the dark curtain of her hair. Reinhard rose, passed his hand wearily through his hair. He was shivering. Provocative and threatening, the uncanny stillness entered the haze woven of their own confusion within the room, where despairing caresses seemed to have taken hold like poisons.

He slowly pulled on his shoes, which stood beneath the wardrobe as if awaiting him. He shuddered, shuddered again, and a wild fear kept him from turning around; never had he suffered such misery as in this cold night hour, which seemed to mock the tenderness of day and evening, the hour in which, in this deeply foreign city, the myriad dangers of a daring flight ahead, he creeps from the bedroom of a beautiful woman whose sobs express the desolation lodged in his own miserable heart, arid and ineradicable. No, never again in his life could he turn back.

He moved slowly, cautiously, as if fearing to awaken the stillness, to the window; but as he was about to swing over the low sill, the muffled sound of her bare feet froze him in his tracks. He felt the blood flow like ice through his veins and, trembling as if he were about to look directly into the true, naked face of death, he quickly turned his head. And it was strange that this lovely face, sweeter and more beautiful than ever, with its small, smiling bud of a mouth, that this face, like

a gently compelling mirror, forced from him a joyful, open, and innocent smile. There was no longer the slightest fiber of his being that this
woman desired. Her eyes simply compelled him to throw off the entire
burden, and with her small, slender hand, she passed him a slim bundle
of banknotes, which he stuck in his pocket without looking. He seized
her hand unhesitatingly and pressed it. "This may help you," she said in
a small voice, "and don't be sad. The three who love us: God, your wife,
and my husband, may well forgive us," and she kissed him quickly and
lightly on the forehead. Then he swung himself out and walked toward
the cold face of the moon.

THE MAD DOG

The sergeant pushed open the door and said: "Take a look at him. Is he...?" He left his cigarette in his mouth. I approached the motionless figure lying on a bier. Someone perched on a stool beyond the bier rose quickly and said: "Good evening." I recognized the chaplain and nodded. He installed himself at the head of the body.

I turned irritably to the policeman and glanced at his burning cigarette: "Could I have a little more light, please? I can't see a thing." He mounted a chair and arranged the hanging lamp with a cord so that its glow fell directly on the stiffened body. Now that I could see the corpse in full light, I drew back involuntarily. I've seen plenty of dead men, but every time I see one I'm disturbed by the realization that I'm looking at a human being, a person who lived, and suffered, and loved.

I saw at once that he was dead. Not by any medical indication; I sensed it and knew it. But I had been summoned to certify his death officially, so I got down to business. It was my legal duty, after all, to go through the well-rehearsed motions with which human science gropes toward mysteries. The recumbent figure looked ghastly.

His reddish hair was soaked and matted with blood and dirt, practically glued to his head. I made out a few wounds inflicted by blows and cuts. A terrible laceration scored his face, as if a rasp had been pulled across it. His mouth was twisted, the small pale nose flattened; his hands cramped at his sides, still clenched in death; the clothes filthy and smeared with blood. You could sense the infernal rage with which he had been hit, kicked, and gashed; he had been killed with bestial pleasure. I took hold of his jacket resolutely and undid the few buttons that had not been ripped away. Oddly enough his skin was white and tender as a child's; no blood or dirt had penetrated the cloth.

The policeman suddenly bent over me, so near that I could feel his heavy breath, and with a glance at the body, said indifferently: "The party's over, huh?" I stared at him for a few seconds, feeling my face twitch with rage, almost with hate.

My eyes must have said enough. He removed the sweetly stinking cigarette from his mouth with a disconcerted air, then slipped away. At the doorway he added: "Just let me know, Doc." I felt freed somehow. Now I began my examination in earnest. How ridiculous to place a stethoscope upon this chest, to feel this pulse, to carry out the whole helpless charade upon this miserable, flayed body. He couldn't have died from the wounds to his head. Should I take the easy way out medical science offers these days and write on the death certificate: *circulatory failure ... exhaustion ... malnourishment*? I don't know if I laughed. I could discover nothing but the head wounds, which must have been terribly painful, but could scarcely have been fatal, having barely penetrated the outer structure of the skull. They must have been inflicted in blind rage.

Even in this desolate state his uncannily narrow, white face resembled a knife. He must have been a cold, daring fellow, I thought. I slowly rebuttoned his jacket, instinctively brushing the strands of bloody, dirty hair back from his forehead. It seemed as if he were smiling scornfully, mockingly. Then I looked at the chaplain, who had been standing at my side, pallid and silent, a quiet man I knew well. "Murdered?" I asked softly. He simply nodded, then replied in an even softer voice than mine: "A murderer, murdered." I gave a start, then stared once more at the knife-sharp, pale face, which seemed to be laughing, even beneath the agonizing wounds and abuse, cold and arrogant. Horror constricted my throat; it was horrible, this corpse in the gloomy room, drenched by the brutal lamp's harsh circle of light, while everything else lay in darkness. The bare bier ... a few old stools ... the walls with their crumbling plaster ... and this dead body in a tattered gray uniform.

I looked at the chaplain almost imploringly. I was dizzy with exhaustion, fear, and nausea. The policeman's cigarette had finished me off. I had been going all afternoon on an empty stomach, entering miserable dens, powerless, helpless, absurdly at the mercy of circumstances. Although I had seen many things that day, a murdered murderer was still a rarity, even in this city.

"A murderer?" I asked, lost in thought. The chaplain pushed his stool toward me: "Sit down, please," and after I had automatically obeyed him, he continued, leaning on the plank-bed: "You don't know him, then? You really don't?" He looked at me as if he almost doubted that I had my wits about me. "No," I said wearily, "I don't know him." The chaplain shook his head: "You get around so much, I thought you would have heard of the Mad Dog." I jumped up in shock ... my God! "The Mad Dog, here—that face!" I stood beside the chaplain, both of us staring at the pallid, disfigured corpse.

"Did he have time to receive the sacraments?" I asked softly. I waited some time for his response. The chaplain didn't appear to have heard me, and I didn't want to ask again. The silence was nearly stifling, and when the chaplain answered, it seemed as if several minutes had passed: "No ... but he could have. I was with him almost an hour. He was tremendously agitated and alert, before he"—he looked at me—"passed away."

The chaplain stretched his hands out helplessly toward the corpse, as if he wished to caress him. His poor, narrow child's face appeared rigid with emotion—I can think of no other way to put it. He pushed his blond hair back as if in despair, and then blurted in agitation: "You ... you may think I'm crazy, but I'd like to stay with him awhile, until they come to get him, yes, I don't want to leave him alone. He truly loved only one person in his life, and that person betrayed him; you can laugh if you want, but ... aren't we all guilty? And if I stay with him for a while ... perhaps ... " He looked at me with a vague, troubled obstinacy in his eyes. They were blue, with dark circles of hunger clinging beneath them, almost like stigmata. No, the word *crazy* never crossed my mind. And laugh at him, my God! "I'll stay with you," I said.

We were silent for the time it takes to say an Our Father and a Hail Mary. Harsh, strident laughter spilled into our silence from the guard room, women's voices, shrill shrieks. I returned slowly and released the lamp so that it dangled in its former position. The entire room was evenly enveloped in a dull, flat light; the ghastly corpse looked gentler, less rigid, almost more lifelike. Nothing is more merciless than this light, this electric light so appropriate to their cigarettes, their cadaverous faces, their weary lewdness. I hate that electric light.

The laughter from the guard room swelled and receded.

The chaplain started, as if brushed by a private fear, as if some terrible memory had touched him. "Sit down, Doctor," he said quietly. "I want to tell you something about him."

I sat down as asked, while the chaplain sat sideways on the plankbed. We turned our backs to the dead man.

"By strange coincidence," the chaplain began, "he and I were born in the same year, nineteen twenty-eight. He told me everything; you know, I'm not sure whether he was talking to me, or himself, or someone who wasn't here. He stared at the ceiling as he spoke, talking feverishly, in fact he probably had a fever. He never knew his parents, you know, never went to school. He was dragged around various places. His first memories, sometime between the war and the inflation, were of the police dragging off the man he thought of up to then as his father, a crude, cowardly fellow, half tramp, half thief, and half laborer, from some block of flats or other on the outskirts of town.

"Picture a squalid room in which a poor, chronically abused woman lives with a perpetually drunken, lazy, and cowardly brute ... that's the whole of it. You know the situation, Doctor. Once his alleged father was sent off to prison for several years his life settled down somewhat. His aunt—he found out later that this eternally irritable, hateful woman was his aunt—got a job at a factory. The police saw that he was sent to school. And there he stood out because of his unusual intelligence. Can you picture it, Doctor"—the chaplain looked at me—"that knife-sharp face slicing through dull classes at school? Well, he became the top student, but what does that say when in fact he towered so far above the others? And he was ambitious. The teachers recommended that he attend the gymnasium; the minister took an interest in the matter, but this woman, his aunt, opposed the idea angrily; it made her furious. She acted as if they wanted to murder him; she did everything she could to restrict him to her own miserable, crude surroundings. She made all sorts of difficulties, you see, insisting on her rights as his guardian; she harassed him whenever he was home ... he wasn't to try to 'rise' in the world. But she was evidently no match for the combined powers of his teachers and the priest. He was awarded a scholarship to a boarding school, was taken on as a full-time student, and soon exceeded their highest expectations. Everything came easily to him. He learned Latin and Greek as well as mathematics and German ... and he was religious. Yet he wasn't one of those humble types who accepts everything and quietly grinds away at their studies. He was creative, clever, his knowledge in religious instruction was almost that of a theologian. In short, he was a real star. And not once did he recall the milieu he had escaped with anything but horror and disgust; he felt no compassion for it, he shuddered at the thought of it. He even stayed at school during vacations, making himself useful in the library, in the office. There was no doubt that he would follow in the footsteps of his patrons. But he was willful and arrogant, with stubborn self-confidence. 'I think deep down I always felt contempt for all of them, without realizing it,' he said to me. Grinding his teeth in rage, he took whatever punishments his pride occasioned, but was seldom disciplined. He was a star, putting them all to shame. They overlooked things now and then; only when he went too far, or neglected to show the expected humility, was he punished.

"But the older he grew, the more the world tempted him. Riches, fame, power: His heart would speed up when he thought of them; and by the time he was sixteen he had already inwardly abandoned the idea of staying in the order, although he said nothing about it, since he wanted to complete his studies. All genuine religious feeling dissolved in the constant tension caused by this new attitude. The world was so tempting, you see, the whole false blossoming of politics back then, like a communal lust for chaos, the fearful life of unburied corpses; it tempted him. On the other hand, he didn't want to lose his chance to finish school; the misery, the old, terrible domestic misery was still strongly engraved in his memory. He didn't exactly play the hypocrite, but he became calculating. Quite imperceptibly, calculation poisoned him over the months and years. He almost went bad; at any rate he lost what little faith he had.

"When he completed his degree and coldly informed the fathers of his decision, the whole situation was of course somewhat embarrassing, but he turned his back on them without a hint of shame; he 'simply burnt his bridges.' He had his diploma, not a word had been said linking his free education to his entry into the order. He severed all connections with the school and went out into the world, armed only with an excellent education and fierce ambition. He didn't have one decent suit, not a penny to his name, nothing.

"But then one of his schoolmates, a certain Becker, turned out to be a real friend. Becker, whose parents were rich, was studying theology. He supported him financially, talking his parents out of some of the money and providing the rest from his own savings. So Herold left the school... By the way, did you know that he was named Theodor Herold?" The chaplain looked at me inquiringly. How would I know his name? I shook my head.

The noise from the guard room kept threatening to drown us out. Noise ... shouts ... the senseless bellowing of those who voluntarily allow themselves to be incarcerated in the prison of a uniform. The chaplain fell silent, then seemed almost to choke on his words as he said: "What good does it do to tell you all this? We should be praying instead; it's just about the only thing one can do, don't you think?" He gave me a tormented look, as if he were about to collapse beneath an invisible weight. Then he folded his hands. I took him gently by the arm, and I don't know if it was curiosity that impelled me to say: "Go on with your story, please. I want to know everything."

The chaplain looked uneasily at me; he almost seemed mentally disturbed. He stared at me blankly, as if he didn't recognize me, and seemed to be searching his memory to recall who I was; then he took his head in his hands. "Oh, yes," he said in a despairing voice, "Pardon me ... I ... I ... " He gestured helplessly. And then he continued:

"It appears that Becker truly wanted to help Herold. They were studying at a university, and although Becker was somewhat restricted by living in a church hostel, he visited him often, talked with him, and no doubt tried to reawaken his buried religious impulse. But his support was in no way dependent upon this. They argued at times, that's clear, discussing things all young men not yet dead discuss: religion and the concept of the *Volk* and so on, but remained friends through it all. And, although he never said so, he respected Becker, the only person he didn't despise. He loved Becker; and not simply because he supported him, but for the unconditional manner in which he gave the money. Well, no doubt you have some idea of the relationship. Becker must have been an ardent young man who still believed in grace. For the first few semesters all the theology students still believed in grace, which was later often unconsciously replaced by belief in the vicar-general.

"Herold was just as great a phenomenon of intelligence and wit at the university as he had been in school. He not only despised his frivolous and less able fellow students, but his professors too, none of whom, as he put it, could be considered 'a true spiritual guide.' In the meantime he prepared for a possible career in politics. You can imagine how quickly the party absorbed such an intelligent young man.

"But then something terrible happened: He became a soldier, and there was no antidote for that. He hated the military beyond anything he'd known, hated it deeply, for when he tried to make a career there, a strange thing happened: That same officer caste which had welcomed dim-witted criminals from the dankest swamps of society insisted that new recruits meet certain social standards: and of course he failed to meet the conditions of this hierarchy of ignorance. His hatred now firmly established, he made his first declaration of war against society. He saw through the absolute political cowardice of these yes-men. He glowed with white-hot rage and scorn, but of course got nowhere against the well-established clique, and the dull and dreary life in the barracks seemed even more terrible than the misery of his childhood years. War seemed to offer him salvation, and he volunteered for one of those units which, steeped in that spirit which denies all true values, considered the murder conducted behind the lines, known as the destruction of racially inferior types, equivalent to the murder at the front, called war." The chaplain paused in misery and covered his face with his hands, breathing heavily. "Imagine that razor-sharp face among those troops, filled with hate, in that social order which became blinder and more cold-blooded with every passing year under the terrible pressures of war, yoked to the triumphal car of a criminal who denied all values—that gloomy triumphal car whose rotten wheels were soon to crumble, and which collapsed at last in a flood of stinking gasoline fumes.

"Repelled at first by his associates in spite of having volunteered, then increasingly entangled in emotions that bind a bloodthirsty mob, Herold still kept in touch with Becker, who wrote to him, warned him, admonished him. Herold even visited him on leave, congratulating him on his ordination as a priest. Even afterward he maintained contact with Becker, whom he truly loved, a word he never used, given his unusual shyness. He sent Becker packages with items that were scarce back home: cigars, soap, lard, and so on. He wrote letters, sent small packets, but revealed nothing of his spiritual condition. No more discussions on religion and worldviews. He felt irrevocably bound to the gang he had stumbled into, often filled with bitter regret, horrified by the streams of blood mingled with dirt, terrified by bestial cruelties, all these emotions jumbled together with unexamined notions of race, honor, and unconditional obedience, the Fatherland, the master race. He became an officer in those units, was wounded several times, distinguished himself, was decorated. But none of that could expunge the uneasy feeling of guilt. He seemed deeply troubled.

"And in the chaos of anxiety, hatred, and remorse, the worst for him was that Becker ceased writing. He heard nothing from him for over a year. He attributed his silence to the breakdown of communications, the total confusion of an 'incomparable system.' Although he blamed it on these external factors the dark suspicion remained that Becker no longer cared about him. And the closer the end came, the inevitable, disastrous end, the more defiled he felt, burdened with indescribable acts of cruelty.

"Only the thought of Becker, who might perhaps help him, sustained him. A series of clever maneuvers allowed him to avoid capture by the Russians. He managed to smuggle himself through the Russian front lines as a Russian soldier until he reached the area controlled by the Western powers. Here he disappeared, well furnished with money and provisions, somewhere in his devastated hometown, in one of the thousands of hiding places no one would ever discover; and here too he avoided capture. Then he began a careful search for Becker. For him, Becker symbolized salvation. He had no clear idea what sort of help he expected; he was totally broken. The dark water of fear, disgust, and guilt had risen to his chin; he simply wanted to speak with someone who wouldn't threaten him, wouldn't reject him. He saw Becker as the representative of a religion which, contrary to all secular custom, did not judge, did not condemn—the religion that he himself had loved as a child and young boy, whose reflected splendor still shone upon him, without his knowledge.

"Disguised as a disabled soldier, he limped out of his hiding place and began, amid the hopeless chaos, to search for Becker, whom he knew had been a chaplain in a small town. He finally managed to reach the town by hitching a ride in an American military truck. He found the village undamaged, its inhabitants still frightened and confused. And he found Becker. His heart pounding with happiness, he entered the rectory.

"Becker was cold and indifferent. He had broken off the correspondence intentionally. Their entire friendship had died, and Becker acted strangely, treating him as if he'd met him once years ago and had simply run into him again, just another former acquaintance. Herold was shocked by the cool reserve with which his only friend received him, but the dark tumult of torment, blood, and guilt which had gathered within him was too powerful to restrain. He opened his heart to Becker, telling him everything, every single thing, things he could never have written. And when he had finished, and he had nothing more to say or ask, he stared helplessly at Becker. He told me that for the first time in his life, he found himself totally defenseless.

"Becker said nothing. He appeared touched in his professional role as a spiritual adviser, as a paid official of the state, but in human terms, Becker had been completely deadened by everything he had seen, heard, and experienced; by the horrors of the retreat, by hunger, confusion, fear, and bombs. Becker only had a few phrases to offer, you know the sort—ready-made clichés from the spiritual five-and-dime store, the stuff handed out in some confessionals after absolution, one to a customer and on your way ... next, please! Of course he urged him to go to confession, to pray, to become a better man ... imagine!"

The chaplain seized me firmly by the shoulder and forced my weary face in his direction. His eyes flared excitedly, like sparkling blue lights, his poor, pale face was flushed, his mouth twitching. We faced each other almost like combatants, here by the bier bearing the corpse of the Mad Dog! But I was so tired, so very tired. And yet deep, deep within me lay an urgent, passionate interest in this human destiny, and I had to hear how it had ended.

"You see," the chaplain groaned, "I can easily imagine it, because I've done it so many times myself. I can picture it in living detail. Becker no longer had a personal relationship with him. In the face of this terrible torment he produced nothing but a cool, professional response. Perhaps he was worn down, dulled, as may happen to priests in the confessional... My God, nothing but adultery and baseness, year after year! Perhaps, as a doctor, you understand. You find a corpse less gruesome than thousands of others do who've seen far fewer corpses and far less blood, in spite of the war. Unburied bodies are less disturbing and less moving to priests than they are to those who have never peered into the hearts of so-called decent human beings. My God ... that's how it must have been for Becker, you see. The demonic frenzy of the final months of the war had died away and we were in the doldrums, the wind had fallen and everything was still, a becalmed void. Becker was cool toward him. Indifferent, perhaps even dismissive. Herold said: 'He pushed me back into my personal abyss...' And then he plunged into a totally destructive rage.

"He must have been denounced by people who noticed him and found him suspicious. The police were after him; he had to change hiding places several times. They hounded him through the piles of rubble. In the midst of a broad expanse of ruins in the inner city, he finally discovered a bombed-out building with an undamaged cellar, easily accessible and difficult to find, and here, motivated by burning hate, he brooded a few days before emerging as the 'Mad Dog.' He found accomplices easily enough—he couldn't bear to be alone, although he was arrogant and domineering with his henchmen. First they stole enough to make themselves comfortable. Then—planning in cold blood—they amassed a large supply of stolen goods on the black market, stocked their rooms with provisions, and began a hideous game. The whole plan was his; he was the acknowledged leader and judge. He turned up, with a certain aura of mystery, when his henchmen had carried out the burglary and prepared the victim or victims. He declared the method of death according to his mood ... shooting ... stabbing or hanging ... and often simply terrorized them, leaving them quaking under the constant threat." The chaplain paused for a moment. "They killed twenty-three people that way ... twenty-three."

The two of us stared at the motionless body, moved by a deep feeling of horror—cold terror in our veins. The murderer's pale red hair shimmered softly through patches of blood and dirt in the dismal light of the room. The cold, thin-lipped mouth seemed still to be smiling, scornful and cruel, appearing to mock our words, our entire conversation. I turned, trembling, and waited uneasily for the chaplain to turn toward me as well. I felt menaced by doleful spirits, and thought his poor, humane face might offer some consolation. But the chaplain remained silent a long time, staring at the dead man ... a long time. I don't know if he startled me out of my thoughts, or prayers, or merely from a state lost in fear, when he touched me lightly on the shoulder. Now his voice was gentle, almost consoling: "And strangest of all, this man, who was never close to any woman, who lived a life of almost celibate purity, died because of a woman. And it occurred to me he might still be alive, might have been a more humane person, had he found a woman to love, or succumbed only to those vices of all weak men—alcohol and tobacco. In some mysterious sense, he remained chaste. No ruined fragment from paradise could deceive him. And his downfall was brought about by a woman, added to the gang against his will, who wormed her way in, in spite of his objections, his furious outbursts, a woman he could never control, although she committed several murders under his leadership. Worst of all, she was in love with him, and was driven by months of scorn and rejection to murder him. She incited the others, and they fell upon him with a fury more terrible than that reserved for other victims, for it is a diabolical, profoundly shocking enigma that down deep, Hell hates nothing quite so much as itself. They practically tore him to pieces. Yet he was still alive when they found him here at the door with a slip of paper in his breast pocket, on which was written, in a literate hand: *The Mad Dog, for burial by the police.* It was a woman's writing...."

I no longer had the strength to move. Lost, I stared at the dirty ceiling. My God, was I hungry, tired? I was miserable, the absolute horror of it all beyond my grasp, immersed in my own total wretchedness, incapable of prayer. I felt buried beneath the rubble of despair of our entire world by the chaplain's report, and a dull, dark personal fear held me in its rigid, iron claws. Then, as if the words were already dashed to pieces within my mouth, I managed to ask: "Do you think that he...?"

But the chaplain had turned around once more. He seemed to be praying, and—strangely—I too was forced to turn and view the body, the unchanged corpse, smeared with blood and filth. Perhaps I prayed, I don't know... My entire being was a blend of fear and torment and dull foreboding.

But who can describe this state of dull, defensive listlessness in which the mind retains a sharp clarity, a coldness possible only in thought?

Then the door was yanked open so noisily it sounded as if the building was about to be brought down around our heads, and as we turned around, shocked and startled, a harsh voice called out: "All right, let's get the body and—" But then three uniformed figures noticed us and approached more quietly. Things seemed so strangely bright upon their entrance. One of them, a slim, dark-haired man with an impassive face, said quietly: "Good evening," and turned to the other two: "All right now..." But the chaplain, who'd watched in shock all the while, as if lost in thought, finally came to himself. He raised his hands to ward them off and cried out: "No ... no ... let me do that ..." He quickly turned and gathered the frayed human bundle fearlessly, ignoring the shocked cry: "But Father!"

He looked as if he were carrying a dead lover with despairing tenderness.

I followed as in a dream through the warm, terrible brightness of the guard room, out into the damp, dark street, covered with wet patches of dirty snow. A car waited outside, its motor growling, coughing. Slowly, tenderly, the chaplain placed the body on a sack of straw inside the vehicle. There was a smell of gasoline and oil, of war and terror. The darkness, the merciless darkness of winter, lay across the empty façades of the buildings like an unbearable burden.

"But ... no ... you can't do that ..." one of the policemen cried as the chaplain got into the car. But the third made an unambiguous circular motion at his temple—while the dark-haired one stood by quietly, with what seemed to me a pained smile.

The chaplain gestured for me to come closer, and in spite of the swelling roar of the engine, I heard the words he whispered softly to me, as if it were a secret: "He cried in the end, you know ... I wiped away the tears before you came ... because the tears—" But the car suddenly pulled away with a powerful surge, and I saw only a final helpless gesture of the figure in black as he was carried off into the cold, gloomy canyons of the destroyed city.

THE RENDEZVOUS

I went to the quay early to meet her. It had been pouring rain for days. The ground of the promenade had softened, and leaves were rotting in the puddles. Although it was mid-August, the smell of autumn was already in the trees, the café terraces had been cleared, the white chairs and tables stacked and hastily covered with canvas. Nearly all the guests had departed; not a person was in sight. A thick, humid haze floated above the water, almost obscuring the strands of rain. The only other person in view was an employee of the shipping company whose cap was visible behind the small window of his tiny ticket booth.

The waiters stood shivering in the corners of the hotel lobbies, waiting on the few guests seeking afternoon coffee or tea.

A week ago I'd sat down beside her in the cinema. I had arrived early, far too early, and as I walked past the yawning usher into the empty, brightly lit movie house, the first thing I saw was the glare of the projector, its flickering light casting black threads upon the bright rectangle of the screen, gently shifting, tumbling about in the void; and right at the front of the empty hall, near the screen, I saw her, just her delicate neck and green raincoat, and although I had a ticket for one of the better seats, I walked forward and sat down beside her.

I felt the damp rising slowly around me now, leaching itself coolly to me, but I didn't care. My gaze was fixed on the bend in the Rhine where the boat would appear at any moment. The blackboard on which the arrival time had been written in chalk bore only a few smeared, grayish white lines, and water was dripping from the clapper of the bell used to announce arrivals and departures, faster and faster, like a leaky faucet.

A black barge appeared at the far end of the bend, being towed wearily, irritatingly slowly, upstream. I looked at my watch: It was a few minutes to five. If the boat intended to depart again on schedule, ten minutes from now, it had to round the bend at any moment. The man behind the little window of the booth was enjoying a cigarette, his red face veiled now and then by smoke. My coat was already dark from the rain.

The barge had not yet cleared the bend, towing its rear section like a wounded reptile dragging its tail. Just then the fellow opened the booth and his deep voice called out to me: "Pretty boring, isn't it, Doctor?"

I recognized him now. His wife ran a tobacco store somewhere back up the quay, and not an hour ago I'd bought tobacco there and had a long chat with him about the pros and cons of various brands.

"Just recognized you," he said, glancing at my cap. "Come on in for a bit."

He squeezed up against the side of the booth facing the promenade and gestured that I was welcome to take the other side. We stood together like two guards in a sentry box.

"Lousy weather," he resumed, "bloody lousy. Whole season's ruined."

"Yep," I said, and stared out again at the bend in the river. Then I exclaimed, "There!" as a white boat, lighter and faster, pulled alongside and passed the black barge.

"Waiting for someone? Your wife?"

"Yes," I said, and instantly regretted having joined him. It would have been more pleasant to stand in the rain and know that in a quarter of an hour I would be sitting at a table with her, drinking hot tea. The man was so close to me that his curious eyes almost touched my forehead.

I kept my eyes glued on the prow of the white boat, which was now passing under the bridge, still in midstream. It was difficult to see the banks, which were veiled by the vapor of the rain, and the lofty, gloomy mountains floated ghostlike above the haze.

"Ah, love..." the old man said, and shoved his cap back on his head. Staring at the boat, I followed its every move as if I myself were on the river, clasping my hands tightly as I recalled how I had simply reached out in the dark, as the film began. I took her hand and held it, the hand of a stranger who pulled back at first, then gave in, a small hand, hot with shame. Now and then, when the dull shimmer of light from the screen fell upon us, we would glance at one another: I saw a narrow face with pale, serious eyes that seemed to be asking something, and later, when the film had ended, she tried to flee, to lose herself in the crowd, but I spotted her green raincoat again at the tram station.

The boat was now making its way toward the bank from midriver, and only when the man from the booth left and hurried down the smooth gangway did I realize how close the boat was. The motor was clearly audible, and people in raincoats were visible standing by the front exit. The bell was already clanging, its tones ringing out in the rain clouds like signals at sea. I stepped outside, and only then, at that moment, did I realize I felt no touch of joy; only anxiety, restlessness, and the prickling sense of danger that tempts a driver to floor the accelerator on a series of sharp curves.

I tossed my cigarette into a puddle and walked down the gangway. The old man, standing at the bottom, dropped a thick pad between the boat and the piling. A rope was slung over the side of the boat, and the old man wrapped it around an iron stanchion. Then the deckhand slid the gangplank across. I stared blankly at the entrance. Not even her green cape could free me entirely from my trance...

"Good day, Frau Doctor," said the old man, who was now unloading and stacking cases of empty soft-drink bottles.

I took her arm without looking at her and drew her along with me. "Thank you," I said hoarsely.

She sighed deeply, but said nothing.

I squeezed her arm mutely. The bell rang out again behind us, and the motor swelled, then receded as we walked through the puddles on the promenade and entered the hotel.

The lobby was nearly empty. I removed her cape and saw for the first time that she was carrying a small suitcase. "Sorry," I said softly, and took the case, hanging up her cape and freeing myself from my own damp coat and cap. The old art dealer's widow who had forced her company upon me that morning, drinking brandy and regaling me

HEINRICH BÖLL

with cynical anecdotes, was sitting in the lobby. She glanced up at us, then returned to her pastry. The only other person present was an old gentleman who had besieged the newsstand by noon.

"What would you like to drink?" I asked.

"Tea, or something hot." She didn't turn around, and I was offered only the delicate fragrance of her perfume, mingled with the fine haze produced by the rain. I sat down opposite her and called for the waiter, who had been lounging in the corner, keeping an eye on us.

I gave him our order.

We smoked in silence. From time to time we glanced at each other, but whenever our eyes met we would look away. In the stillness we heard only the gentle murmur of the rain, a faint clinking from the table of the art dealer's widow, who was devoting herself wholeheartedly to her torte, and a low conversation between the barmaid and two waiters, which largely drowned itself in the thick carpets and curtains.

I felt my jaw twitch nervously; it was a relief when the waiter arrived. Even the aroma of the strong tea helped. Our hands touched over the sugar bowl; I took her hand firmly and squeezed it, but she pulled away, turning pale, staring in shock at my hand. I followed her startled gaze, and my own hand, with its thick pale fingers, seemed strange to me, strange and uncanny, as if I'd never seen it before. I had forgotten to remove my wedding ring.

"For heaven's sake," I said softly, "aren't you glad to be here?"

"No," she said, shaking her head firmly.

I stirred my tea.

"Are you?" she asked.

I said nothing.

Her skin was white and shining, so cool, and her dark hair gleamed with moisture.

"Did you have a nice trip?"

"Yes," she said quietly, "it was a nice trip, splendid really. On the water like that, properly fogged in, and it smelled so nice. The only bad thing was having to stop here. I would have loved to go on, on up the Rhine in that rain to ... yes, to Basel for all I care. Let me go," she said suddenly. I looked at her: She was pale and her lips were trembling.

"That's crazy," I said quietly. "Why did you come, then?"

"Let me go."

"You probably came just to drive me crazy. Waiter!" I called out loudly.

"Let me go."

The waiter came strolling in from the lobby. "Yes?" he asked.

"Take my wife's suitcase to my room, please."

"Yes, sir."

"Let me go," she said, when the waiter had disappeared with her luggage and cape.

I looked around: The old gentleman was reading his twenty-seventh newspaper, the widow was on her tenth torte, the rain droned down on the skylights, and from the recess by the buffet below came the impersonal murmur of the barmaid with the waiters.

I glanced at her: That beautiful face was totally changed, obstinate and trembling, as she sipped hastily at her scalding tea.

"Come on," I said hoarsely, and took her hand.

"I asked if you were glad."

"No," I cried.

The old gentleman looked up from his paper, and the widow stopped chewing for a moment.

She laughed and followed me.

It was even quieter upstairs. The window in the room opened onto a light shaft, at the bottom of which ashes and rubbish lay soaking beside overflowing trash cans. The only sound was the crazed drone of the rain.

She sat on the bed and smoked, while I paced back and forth with my own cigarette. From time to time we glanced at each other, like people standing at the foot of a mountain, listening to the roar of an onrushing avalanche.

I remembered how I had kissed her in the dark vestibule of a large block of flats on the outskirts of town, where streetcars screeched their way to the end of the line, and in the light of an auto that rounded a corner, I saw her face, white and smiling against the rough brown wall.

"My God," she said suddenly, "why all the moaning? Sit here beside me."
She smiled for the first time that day, then shoved the pillow over and
made room for me.

"Give me your hand."

I did. Her hands were cool and dry, very light. I felt her touch
my wedding ring, then she put my hand back in my lap: My hand was
heavy, almost dead.

"Let me go," she said.

"Go," I said.

Her lips brushed my hand.

I went to the window and waited. The rain was soaking a heap
of ashes that had built up beside the trash can. Beneath the slender
strands of yellowish rain a narrow, dirty channel of water flowed from
the trash can toward a stopped-up drain. Scraps of paper drifted in
a large puddle with peels and crushed cigarette butts, stringy bits of
tobacco floating on the surface like small yellow worms. I flicked my
own stub downward as well, then turned. The room was empty. I had
heard nothing.

THE TRIBE OF ESAU

That heel, the woman thought, he's off again. He's escaped me and this filthy earth. He's gone... She regarded the man with a bitter face. He lay half on his side; she saw his childlike, smiling profile, the mussed hair, and the half-bare arm. He had rolled up his sleeves and was holding a sheet of paper tightly in his right hand.

What a heel, she thought. He *is* a heel. He calls that work, he calls that life, nothing steady, no moderation, a life without order, the heel. Smiling like that.

She attempted to take the sheet of paper from him, but he grumbled angrily in his sleep and she quickly turned away, toward the hotplate. The electric cord was defective, the Bake-lite connection was broken, the prongs stuck in the hot-plate's socket every time as if they'd been glued, and if you pulled hard it damaged the coil, which was constantly going bad. Swearing softly, she repaired the coil, attached it to the hot-plate, and plugged it in. She waited for the coil to glow, holding her breath. It began to glow, and she put on the water. Then she began to straighten the room, rather noisily. It was a mess. He had soaked his feet and shaved before he started drinking; his things lay scattered about, the bowl filled with dirty water, the little mug with dried shaving cream stuck to the rim, his old socks, two hand towels, all scattered about the table, the chair, and the floor between the table and the chair.

Flowers stood on the desk; she removed the wilted ones and tossed them in the washbowl, added the water from the shaving mug, and emptied the whole thing into the rain gutter.

Heel, she thought, almost murmuring now, how long is he going to lie there. He calls that work.

She regarded him more closely. The room was tidy, the water was just starting to simmer, she had time. The look of happiness on his face almost drove her crazy; she hated that happiness. He doesn't get that happiness from me, she thought, he stole it somewhere. He prowls among the fragments of paradise and steals from their substance. And yet I love him…

Abruptly, she tried to imagine him far away, in America or Australia, and her heart convulsed with fear that it might happen. I can't live without him, she thought, it's terrible. Even the pain he causes me makes me happy, the heel.

She pulled the chair over from the desk and sat down by the couch. Her feet hurt; she had walked a long way, looking for a place to borrow more money. No dice again. The last of the tea, she thought, the last of the butter and the last of the bread, and this heel is drunk again. I'd like to know what he wrote…

She tried once more to pull the sheet of paper from his hand, very gently, but he grumbled again, and she was afraid to interrupt the natural course of his sleep. He hated being jerked from sleep. He always said it reminded him of the war: "Jerked from sleep! Sleep, one of God's most precious gifts."

She didn't have a penny, not a bit of credit left anywhere. No money for rent, for electricity—oh, why go over it all again.

She glanced at the hot-plate; the bubbling had subsided. She lifted the kettle with a curse. The coil was no longer glowing. She unplugged it, held her hand over the plate to check the heat, then began poking about on the coil, slowly and systematically, to see where the problem was this time. She cursed softly as she did so. She could feel her throat constricting to cry.

It was driving her crazy. Even if you had money, even if you tried to buy a new coil or a new hot-plate, or a new connection, you couldn't afford it. They asked ridiculous prices for items like that. And yet here you are going nuts over a connection, this shitty little piece of Bake-lite, not worth twenty cents. Sighing, she lifted one tine of the fork—she'd discovered the break, it was hard to see, the coil had darkened and was brittle in several places. Almost every time it was used, it burned through in a new spot. She pulled on both ends of the wire coil and wrapped them around each other, then plugged it back in. It started to glow. She put the water on again.

It just makes me sick, she thought, the way they torment us. If I ever get hold of one of the guys who makes these Bake-lite things or those coils, who drives thousands of men and women nuts, if I ever get hold of him, I'll murder him... The water started bubbling again.

If he would only wake up. His face was so insanely happy it made her sick. She saw nothing of herself in his face. It was horrible to be so alone, to sit by his couch and not know what he had written, or whether it would be published, or if they would get any money for it. Not to know why he was smiling so happily, not to know where he found the money or the credit to get drunk. The bottle had tipped over next to the bed. She picked it up and sniffed at it: Wine, she thought, red wine...

The water seemed to be boiling. She lifted the lid, turned her face quickly from the billowing steam, and poured water in the teapot. Just a bit to warm the pot, then she set it back on the hot-plate. Tea water has to boil like mad, she thought, it has to get just as hot as it can. It has to be almost boiled to death.

She lifted the bottle again, sniffed at it once more, and replaced it carefully beside the couch. I love this heel, she thought... I love him. She returned to the desktop with a sigh and lifted the lid again. The water was bubbling; she filled the pot, unplugged the hot-plate, and set the pot on the plate, which was still warm.

THE TALE OF BERKOVO BRIDGE

The tale of this bridge was a lively topic of discussion at the time. Men cursed and wept over it, some laughed about it, some saw it as one of the countless events forming the general course of war, refusing to accord it any special significance—and indeed in the end the story was forgotten, since it was of no strategic or historic importance.

Yet I now feel obliged to tell what really happened on that decisive day. I've decided to tell things in chronological order, in as much detail as possible, for I suspect I may be the only one still living who played a major role. I know that Schnur and Schneider fell in battle, and I believe that their opposite number, a lieutenant from the staff of the Third Engineer Regiment, fell as well in the final months of the war, for I have sought him in vain. Or he may have wound up in prison, or dropped out of sight, or gone to the dogs, for who can say whether he might not have fallen prey to the general poison of the destruction, eking out a miserable existence, wandering about with no future, and no living connection to the past?

Since I'm going to try to keep things in strict sequence, I'll start with the day I received orders from Southeast Labor Pool Headquarters to take command of the construction—or better, reconstruction—of the bridge at Berkovo. It was a few days after Christmas, and I had been lounging about—with no project, although I longed for one—at KNX Reserve Construction Staff Headquarters. I was delighted finally to have something to do. Having requested and received the materials dealing with the project, I examined them methodically: The Berkovo Bridge had been blown up by a Russian rear-guard commando unit in the course of their retreat in 1941, shortly before the German arrival could prevent its destruction. The idea of rebuilding it was soon abandoned, since the small village of Berkovo had faded into strategic insignificance from both a military and a political point of view, particularly now that the bridge was no longer an important supply point. In the course of battle and the subsequent conquest, a military bridge had been constructed over the Berezina two kilometers to the southeast, which had since been reinforced and widened to serve as a supply line. The commanding officers of Southeast Construction and those of corresponding rank in the army deemed it more sensible at the time to use the materials, which would have been needed to rebuild the bridge at Berkovo, to construct the military bridge instead, particularly since—as I've already said—the market town of Berkovo was insignificant. In the course of the war it served only as a billet for a company of local defense reserves assigned to watch for rear-guard partisan activity.

That, in short, was the prehistory of the Berkovo Bridge.

A few days after Christmas in 1943, I received written orders to rebuild the bridge. I was promised all the men and material necessary for the job—whatever I thought it would take—and on first inspecting the site, I discovered the following: The small river of Berezina is approximately eighty meters wide at that point. The concrete-clad piers were still standing in the river, largely undamaged, while the bridge itself had been completely destroyed in expert fashion; the Berezina River had been washing around it for the past two and a half years. The tiny village of Berkovo consisted of about ten houses, of which five were still occupied or habitable; those remaining had fallen into disrepair over the years through lack of use, and the wood in them had been stripped away by soldiers of the local guard, no doubt for use in lighting the stoves and preparing meals. At the time I was taking my measurements and making the necessary calculations, four of the houses were occupied by the local guard, who were suffering from fatigue and relatively ineffective. An old Russian woman and her daughter lived in the fifth house; the two of them cooked, washed, and cleaned for the soldiers, and kept a tavern too, stocked from mysterious sources with schnapps, wine, and food.

I also came across a small graveyard where soldiers who had died or fallen in the line of duty over the years were buried. An exhumation squad was already in the process of digging up the corpses in order to rebury them in a planned cemetery for heroes of the Fatherland.

Together with my two closest colleagues, Schnur and Schneider, it took me barely three days to make the necessary measurements and calculations. From the time I made my first site inspection, I had devised a plan utilizing the existing concrete piers, bridging them over with an iron and wood superstructure, which, though not permanent, would last for three months or so, and would support even major troop movements with heavy armor. The word from Southeast Construction Headquarters was that the bridge would probably be used in the course of a general retreat, since command expected that the bridge two kilometers to the southeast would be heavily congested.

Of course, building a bridge slated for destruction the moment you've finished it is not a particularly rewarding task. Only the architect's profession places such strong emphasis on an object's durability, while other arts tend toward transience. So we made our measurements and calculations with no great joy, though we were certainly happy to have escaped the dull wait at KNX Reserve Construction Staff Headquarters.

Since my orders included instructions to complete the project within two weeks at the latest, and since I had reckoned on three thousand man-days of labor, I requested two hundred and fifty men, figuring in as usual an extra percentage for high work stoppage, wear and tear, and various other standard imponderables on projects of this nature. And naturally I needed at least fifty additional men as cooks, medics, and guards to handle the workers' mess hall, infirmary, and guard duty. A precondition was the ready availability of sufficient quantities of all the necessary building materials. And lastly, I needed a few explosives experts from the Corps of Engineers during the first two or three days to help blast away the few small remaining portions of the bridge itself.

All these calculations, measurements, and the like had taken the three of us—Schneider, Schnur, and me—roughly three days. During this first stay in Berkovo we had an opportunity to observe the rowdy, one might even say demoralized, behavior of the local reserve, who were under the command of an older second lieutenant and two sergeants. Rumors of the coming general retreat, which could no longer be silenced, had reached this godforsaken village and were running rampant. Morale was sinking daily. Units making for the bridge on the basis of older maps often arrived by mistake, several trucks appeared carrying rations, and troops wandered in who had simply lost their way. The inevitable whispers that passed from man to man carried a message of cynical frankness: It's every man for himself. This was accompanied by a frightening and pernicious maxim: Enjoy the war; peace is going to be hell. These two precepts became standard mottoes of the local guard, who were expecting to be withdrawn any day. There was open prostitution with the tavern keeper's daughter, a coarse, crude blonde, as well as with other women. I myself saw large portions of the clothing depot and items of equipment (including, I presume, weapons) being sold or bartered to Russian vagabonds, who were literally dragging bags of money with them and disposing of the goods in some mysterious manner. There were orgies every night, in which the lieutenant, who raised a few feeble objections now and then, was placated expediently by shoving the best-looking woman present into his bed, after first making sure he'd had plenty to drink.

A certain strange sorrow clung to the soldiers in the midst of these activities, bearing witness to some remnant of decency; and it could perhaps be said that too much was asked of them. I must also add that a fairly large number of soldiers avoided these orgies; but two drunks make more noise than two hundred sober men. None of those who distanced themselves from such goings-on, however, were in a position to oppose them actively. They all suffered from the terrible sickness of resignation.

I reported such incidents the moment I returned to headquarters, as duty required, although I was aware of the difficulty I would have if I were asked, for example, to offer proof of my observations. It was standard practice in the course of a retreat for a unit to keep whatever black-market stock fell into its hands without reporting it.

Immediately upon my return I presented my plans and calculations, which were forwarded at once to the supply depot and labor pool department. Thanks to the admirable energy and high morale of our staff, the requested men and materials were not only made available but loaded and set in motion within the week. They even sent along four transportable barracks to house the men. These proved unnecessary upon arrival, since the local guard had been withdrawn in the meantime, so that the houses were now available. Since it would have been senseless to return the barracks, they simply made things more comfortable in the course of construction.

The South Army Group quickly deployed two panzer units to protect the now suddenly important bridge. These two units were posted approximately two hundred meters to the south and north of us, to protect us from possible surprise attacks from the hinterland as well as possible encroachments by Russian troops breaking through from the other bank of the river. A smaller troop took up position directly behind us, so that, protected by a sort of bridgehead, we were able to begin on schedule and according to plan.

I must add here that my people were extremely nervous, since the withdrawal of the local guard meant that for all practical purposes the area had returned to the status of a battle-field, and in fact based on the sounds of combat we heard over the next few days, at times relatively close, then farther off, we gathered that we were occupying a fairly advanced post.

But everything went according to plan, including the imponderables we had allowed for: work stoppages, loss of materials, unexpected disturbances in the course of construction, rain or extreme cold. The remaining piers had sustained greater damage than expected, for I hadn't been able to examine all of them closely during our initial inspection, no boat having been available. But we had made the necessary allowances, and our work proceeded on schedule. Early on I had the old woman who ran the tavern arrested, along with her daughter and the rest of that bunch, and requested new, supervised prostitutes, who arrived promptly and were billeted in one of the houses. We even managed to have schnapps and tobacco delivered, for over the years we had learned that these items, of relatively minor value in themselves, contributed significantly to the success of any project. After all, you couldn't expect willing and enthusiastic work from forced labor of all nationalities unless certain material advantages were made available to them.

Thus the two-week construction period proceeded according to schedule. The only thing worthy of note were the rumors delivered each day by the men driving the supply trucks: that a general retreat (now and then they even dared to use the word *rout*) was now underway; that a large number of our troops had already evacuated the right bank of the Berezina, which must mean they were planning to allow the main mass of the enemy to advance without resistance; that the bridge to the southeast would probably be sufficient for the retreat after all; all sorts of demoralizing tales to which I naturally closed my ears, even if they weren't truly mutinous enough to call for a military report. I remained in constant contact with headquarters, giving them regular reports on our progress, and it gave me a great deal of satisfaction not to have to make excuses about being behind on the project, since—as I've said—we were right on schedule.

It's true, however—and since I've made it my duty to report the truth, I must add this qualification—that I too was secretly disturbed by the sounds of battle, which had drawn fairly near after the first week and appeared to be approaching steadily ever since, at times coming dangerously close to the right bank of our construction project.

I was also allowing small groups of retreating soldiers to cross over on a footbridge, providing their papers were in order, or if they were accompanied by an officer, since I sympathized with these exhausted men and didn't want to send them two kilometers upstream unnecessarily. But in the case of leaderless and disorderly troops, or individuals who claimed to be stragglers, I was far stricter, insisting that they proceed to the other bridge, since I knew that they would be subjected to careful inspection there and that no one fleeing on his own, or perhaps even planning to desert, would be allowed to cross. The gloomy silence of the officers in these groups, seven or eight of whom I allowed to cross during the first ten days or so, reinforced in me a certain inner pessimism, of which of course I gave no external sign. I was relieved of all personal responsibility by my daily contact with Southeast Construction Headquarters, who constantly emphasized the importance of finishing the bridge on schedule.

Thus everything proceeded according to plan, right up to the final day of construction. Two days before the deadline we were already beginning to affix the thick, treated oak planks to the finished framework of the rebuilt bridge with a special type of threaded rivet. These thick planks could support the heaviest of vehicles and armored weapons. Work progressed well on the final day. Knowing we were near our goal put everyone in a good mood, and the prospect of soon escaping the danger zone—the noise of distant battle from retreating troops could now be heard both night and day—spurred everyone on. I had half the planks we needed carried across the footbridge to the other side of the river—taking responsibility for the risk, having prudently considered the probable success of the measure—so that we could begin laying the planks from both directions on the final day. This introduced a certain healthy competition between the two teams working on the bridge, leaving aside the motivating factors already mentioned above. Over the years I'd often found such competitive situations useful. A total of one hundred and twenty workers were involved, and I had divided them into two teams of sixty each, under the command of Schnur and Schneider. The remaining eighty—the others had dropped out, as predicted—had been ordered to start loading the unused construction supplies, as well as the tools, kitchen utensils, and so on, for my ambition was to inform the Southeast Construction Headquarters of the completion of the bridge and of our total readiness to withdraw in a single call.

Around noon on the final day the teams had drawn so near to one another that I could extend the work break by half an hour with an easy mind (much against the wishes of the men, as I later learned, who would have preferred to work on to the end without a break, in order to escape the increasingly risky situation). The apparent eagerness and exhaustion of the men made me lenient, however. I was filled with the proud knowledge that we were reaching the end of a skillfully calculated project, carried out with equally masterful speed and precision. My commanding officers at headquarters, who had inspected the ongoing project on several occasions in the company of various members of the general's staff, let it be known that I was assured of the Distinguished Service Medal, First Class.

Work continued rapidly after the break, and good progress was being made in loading the supplies. I had already dispatched several trucks.

The noise of battle was constant, and now it came nearer, seeming to concentrate menacingly at a single spot. The sound of heavy cannon reached us like someone pounding steadily and impatiently on a door, trying to break it down, and at times we could hear not only the impact of the shells but also the discharge of the guns. All of these sounds, including infantry fire and the rumble of tanks, accompanied the final hours of our work, but could not prevent it. To be sure, the panzer units deployed for our protection—without having received any orders, as I later learned—made ready to withdraw, and both commanding officers, a lieutenant and a captain, kept a silent eye on the construction site, probably to get some idea as to when their flight might commence.

I was first directly affected when, around three in the afternoon, a young second lieutenant from the engineer brigade drove up in an all-terrain vehicle, accompanied by two soldiers. This very likable and sensible young man told me that he had been ordered to blow up the bridge at four o'clock. He showed me his written orders, and delivered news of recent strategic developments to justify his assignment. The retreat of the troops on the opposite bank was now almost complete. One of the larger units had been left behind to engage the main body of the enemy and give the appearance of major resistance. Of course, the lieutenant told me in confidence, the unit had secretly been given up for lost, and the order had been issued to blow up both bridges at four o'clock, regardless of the situation at the time.

Two enemy army columns were expected to arrive at the respective bridges around four-thirty at the latest, and the Army Command Staff felt they could not afford to leave either bridge open as a line of retreat for the troops who were still fighting, fearing that either bridge might be taken by the enemy and used in their advance. So the order had been given to blow them up by four o'clock at the latest, sooner if necessary. Still, this was not to be done until enemy troops were observed in the immediate vicinity. This would place us in an extremely disadvantageous position, however, since the forest stretched almost to the water along the right bank of the Berezina.

First I inspected the bridge, which was now almost finished, with the young lieutenant, and during this initial inspection, which took place around three-fifteen, he sought out the best locations for the explosives. He was amazed at the state of the bridge. He'd been told it would be at least another week before the bridge at Berkovo would be finished, and he knew the same impression had been conveyed to the officers of the troops battling on the other side. This offered sufficient explanation for the surprising fact that not a single unit of regular troops had tried to cross the bridge up to this point. Even in its present condition it could have served as a crossing, even for motorized units, and I certainly wouldn't have stopped anyone from using it.

I returned at once to my office and, in the presence of the lieutenant, began a fruitless series of phone calls. I called the commanders at Construction Headquarters: They'd heard nothing about blowing up the bridge. I was to continue construction until I received orders to the contrary. Then it took me almost half an hour to reach the Southeast High Command, over lines that had been heavily damaged. The lieutenant's orders were confirmed.

My situation was, as may be imagined, a strange one. Everything the lieutenant said appeared valid, and although I would have given a good deal to complete my project, I had no interest in placing even the least of my men at risk for a single moment longer than my orders required. I therefore phoned again to Construction Headquarters. Like Command Headquarters, they were located approximately two hundred kilometers to the west. The chief himself ordered me rather impatiently to continue construction, as a matter of principle. His exact words were: We mustn't abandon our principles, no matter how much pressure we're under. Then he added that he was expecting to hear from Command Headquarters any minute with confirmation of the lieutenant's orders. He hung up. It was ten minutes to four. The bridge would be finished by four, and an ominous silence reigned on the other side of the river. The bridge was complete except for a remaining gap of about three-quarters of a meter. It would be finished precisely to the minute. Not one of my projects had ever proved untenable. I tested the solidity of the planks and rivet screws one last time. In the meantime all the remaining supplies had been loaded, and only a few empty trucks stood waiting for the workers, their motors running. I had given orders to withdraw at five past four.

Two men from Schneider's team screwed down the last of the rivets a few minutes before four, while the lieutenant was already busy placing the explosives, which were linked by fuses. The lieutenant himself walked to the middle of the bridge at one minute to four, where I was watching the last of the planks being fastened onto the frame. He asked me not to screw down the final plank, since it was a perfect location for a charge of explosives, but I insisted on it, since I had received explicit orders from the chief to stick to our principles. The lieutenant shrugged and walked off. I glanced again at the bridge, then returned to the construction hut with Schnur, Schneider, and the last of the workers to register the completion of the bridge at Berkovo precisely on schedule.

But now something horrifying happened. On the other side, in the breathless silence, fleeing soldiers appeared from the woods, a few carrying wounded men, others racing along singly, in spite of the total exhaustion that could be read in their faces at this short distance; vehicles too emerged from the woods, all in fearful, wild flight. The crowd thickened, streaming from the forest, racing for the bridge, which must have appeared like hope incarnate, since I had ordered a swastika flag attached to its highest point to celebrate its completion.

The lieutenant now rushed from the bridge with his men, shrugged, and showed me his watch, which indicated five seconds to four, pointing with his other hand toward a few Russian tanks firing at the fleeing men and drawing dangerously near to the bridge.

The moment I saw the burning fuse, I too ran to my office and tried to call Southeast Construction Headquarters as quickly as possible. But before my call had gone through, another phone rang. I lifted the receiver and heard the chief's voice: Stop work on the bridge at once. And since he was about to hang up, I cried, "Hold it!" and gave my report according to regulations: construction of the bridge completed on schedule, to the minute, as ordered. But he was no longer listening ... and I was almost deafened by the savage blast with which the bridge now exploded into the air. Then I went to my car and ordered everyone to move out. But I can't tell you what the bridge at Berkovo looked like after the explosion, because I didn't look back, although the shells of the Russian tanks were already landing among the houses of Berkovo. Yet sometimes I think I see those exhausted, fleeing men who fought to the last, protecting us too, as duty demanded, and although I did not actually see them, I see them cursing, the fear of death upon their faces, the fear of capture, and hate for us as well, although we too did nothing but act as duty demanded.

THE DEAD NO LONGER OBEY

The lieutenant told us to take a break and we did. We were at the edge of a forest, the sun was shining, it was springtime, everything was quiet, and we knew the war would soon be coming to an end. Those with tobacco lit up and the rest of us tried to get some sleep. We were tired, having eaten little and carried out several counterattacks over the past three days. It was marvelously peaceful, somewhere birds were singing, and the air was filled with a soft, moist tenderness.

Suddenly the lieutenant starting shouting. He cried out: "Hey!" Then he grew angry and bellowed: "Hey, you!" Finally, becoming furious, his voice broke: "You! You there! You!"

Then we saw who he was yelling at. Someone was sitting on the other side of the woodland road, asleep. It was an ordinary soldier, dressed in gray, leaning back against a tree, asleep. The soldier had a pleasant smile on his freckled face, and we thought the lieutenant would go nuts. We thought the soldier was nuts too, because the lieutenant kept on shouting and the sleeping man kept right on smiling.

The men who had started to smoke stopped, the ones trying to sleep were now wide awake, and some of us were smiling, too. The spring air was fresh and gentle, and we knew that the war would soon be over.

Suddenly the lieutenant stopped shouting and jumped up. He crossed the road in two long strides and struck the sleeping man in the face.

We saw now that the sleeping man was dead. He fell over without a word, no longer smiling. His face was affixed with a terrible grin, and we didn't feel at all sorry for the lieutenant, who came back pale faced, for the sun no longer gave us pleasure. We found no joy in the soft moisture of the mild spring air, and it made little difference to us now whether the war was coming to an end or not. Suddenly we felt we were all dead—the lieutenant too, for he was grinning now, and no longer wore a uniform.

AMERICA

I found Hubert lying in his bed, which he had shoved closer to the stove. He had kindled a pathetic fire from a few old picture frames. Of course it couldn't heat the huge room. A tiny island of a somewhat humane temperature surrounded the stove, but elsewhere the room, with all its paintings, easel, and cupboards, lay cold and poignantly desolate. Hubert was holding a sketch on his knees that he'd just begun, but he was no longer working on it, gazing meditatively instead at some vague spot on the brown bedspread. He greeted me with a smile, laid the drawing aside, and in his sad, large gray eyes, I read for the moment only hunger and scant hope. But I didn't leave him stretched on the rack for long; instead I pulled out some fresh, sweet-smelling, white bread. His eyes gleamed.

"Either you're crazy," he said, "or I am. Or you've stolen this, or I'm dreaming, or..." He made a dismissive gesture and rubbed his eyes. "It's simply not true."

"Look," I said, holding it under his nose, pressing it into his hands, making the crisp crust crackle. "Now you've touched it, experienced it with all your senses. Think you're crazy for all I care, but I certainly didn't steal it. Cut it in two, would you?"

Hubert finally seemed to trust his senses, seized the bread firmly, as if he feared he were reaching into the void, realized that it was real, then pulled the knife from the cupboard with a strange groan. Meanwhile I had pulled the tobacco from my pocket and was cutting the plug into smaller pieces, which I crumbled and placed on the warm stove plate. They call it roasting, I believe. Hubert gazed at me with shining eyes, sniffed greedily, and said: "You've turned into a regular criminal."

We ended up stretched out beside each other on the bed, each of us enjoying our portion of bread, pinching small pieces from the loaf and stuffing them in our mouths, sweet-smelling bread, fresh and still warm, white and delicious. Bread is the best thing there is. Woe unto the man who no longer eats bread because he is full. Woe!

I was happy that Hubert had apparently forgotten the question of where the bread came from. My God, if he'd insisted on knowing. He's so strict about things, a true artist! But he ate silently, happily; ah, happy the man who still has a bit of bread.

"Do you know what I was thinking when you came in?"

I had to admit I didn't. I'm not a psychologist, for God's sake.

"I was wondering, if American universities ran some experiments, I was wondering how many calories they'd find in a genius, in Rembrandt for instance. After all, modern science can tell us anything. What do you think?"

"Maybe they'd discover that a genius lives beyond the norm. That he eats a tremendous amount or starves himself, that his accomplishments are independent of—let's say—his so-called caloric intake."

"But even a genius has a starvation limit. He might starve and freeze all week in a cellar for all I care, and still write a wonderful sonnet. But if you spend your whole life in a cold cellar, it's all over with the sonnet writing, over because you simply no longer have the strength to write sonnets with a pencil stub on some dirty piece of paper."

"But I would claim he might have many, many beautiful unwritten sonnets in his mind, sonnets the world will never see, although they're there, sonnets which might be *immortal* were they known."

Our bread was finished. I reached from the bed and gathered the roasted tobacco from the stove, filled our pipes, and Hubert held out a piece of his drawing as a spill. I lit it at the stove and now we smoked as dusk fell in the large room, creeping in like fog, enveloping everything.

"I'll write to America," said Hubert, "and see if they'll try to figure out Rembrandt's daily calorie intake." He looked at me uneasily. "I have an inferiority complex because I can't work as long as I used to. And I read recently in the newspapers that they've run tests in America showing that at our caloric level a person can't do creative work—at least not two years' worth. This major scientific discovery has depressed me so much I can't paint anymore."

Suddenly he sprang out of bed like a wild man, right past me, raced to the easel, stretched a sheet of paper on the board, and began working like crazy. He dashed off a lively sketch, grabbed the box of watercolors, and was off, with strong, bold strokes, stepping back from time to time to judge the effect. He finished a small painting I couldn't see clearly because it was getting darker and darker in the room. But all at once he turned around and asked me energetically: "Where did you get the bread, you bastard?"

I had to show my colors at last. "I traded my pen for it," I said shyly, "to an American soldier. Here." I pulled the two white cylinders from my pocket. "There's a cigarette for each of us too."

We laid aside our smelly pipes at once and inhaled the marvelous tobacco with deep enjoyment—American cigarettes! Hubert worked boldly on; he had turned on the light.

"The best thing about America, the very best thing of all, are the cigarettes," he said with a laugh.

PARADISE LOST

The former paths were scarcely visible in the tangled shrubbery, in part no longer even recognizable. The broken gaps of the fence admitted one and all, the luxuriant greenery had been trampled flat, wilted, rotted, replaced by new growth, until at last a sort of gauzy jungle had rendered the untended paths impassable. New ones had been ruthlessly flattened, no longer following any plan, but simply the dictates of convenience, and now led to the house from all different directions. Even the old main road, which had bordered the park in a half circle, was scarcely passable. Seams of grass had spread from the sides toward the middle, meeting to form sparse new grassy areas in which stripling elders, box trees, and elder bushes were growing merrily, the decayed banks covered with foliage. The fountain at the upper curve of the path was covered with moss and filled with dirt and tin cans, so that in spite of the wet spring weather, it held scarcely a drop of water. Its iron water spout had been bent by a well-aimed rock, and I discovered signs of children at play, who, digging through the decayed vegetation, had produced a hole at the base of which a thick, greenish fluid was visible. Next I saw that the large, graveled square had been dug up and planted, and that the rocks and gravel had been swept together and dumped into the fountain. A poorly patched fence surrounded a few miserable cabbages, which had been given ample time to rot over the course of the winter. Wilted bean stalks clung to water pipes, and from a few inevitable tin buckets rose the stench of a greenish liquid similar to that which evidently lay hidden beneath the fountain.

At last I came upon a person. Behind some sort of shed, which probably held gardening tools, sat an old man on a crate, a spade propped between his knees, a pipe in his mouth. But even though the gentle, veiled afternoon of my homecoming left me longing for a human face, I was still taken aback when I saw one. I retreated a few steps so that the shed again hid him from view, and only then did I look around.

The former layout of the park could be clearly discerned from this vantage point. The handsome large semicircle, once covered with white gravel, was now traversed by pathetic fences constructed out of narrow strips of stamped tin, warped by rust and ready to break, gas pipes, and box-tree branches. Yet the square still retained the soft, fertile beauty of perfection, even though its once smooth and carefully tended shrub border was now tangled, cut, burned, and trampled. Archaeologists say nothing is more indestructible or more easily found, even centuries later, than a hole, something dug into the earth, and this beautifully designed park was still wholly present in form.

Higher up, at the top of the curve of the clear half circle, lay the round, soiled, but still perfect circle of the fountain, from which the main road led straight to the entrance gate. And in the bearded, greenish, curling undergrowth of the shrubbery the small paths that could scarcely be seen up close were now clearly apparent, indelibly preserved like smooth weals in the foundering, arched backs of the shrubbery, while to the left and right of the main road ran the other two, simple and clear, in the shape of musical clefs.

And now at last I dared to look at the house. I saw it clearly through the gaps in the row of poplars, with their gleaming, thick, fresh-green foliage. I counted the trees; seven of twelve remained, while the willows at either end were still undamaged. The façade of the house, with its gray and intentionally somewhat rough surface, was practically unaltered. A few large patches of plaster had fallen here and there, and large, grayish white water spots appeared in a few places, like the cover of an old, damp-stained book. Only a few of the windows still contained unbroken glass; most were covered instead with mill-board or nailed shut with plywood, while others were partially bricked up and inset with windows too small for the grand casements.

For the moment I was only registering visual impressions. The memories were too numerous, the feelings too powerful, for me to allow them to rise. Although everything—past, memory, youth, and life—bound me to this house and park, I could only stand like a stranger visiting some outlying area of fine homes, who, overcome by simple curiosity, bypasses a gate now rusted shut and steps into the garden through a gap in the fence, to view the traces of destruction.

Painfully we recognize the inner transformations that mark the threshold of maturity. With ineffable sorrow we leave behind the toys and playgrounds of childhood, plunging with fear, sorrow, and desire into that tumult the grown-ups have always called life; more sadly yet do we leave the house of youth, the place of dreams, sensing darkly that our memories are but memories of dreams, already tasting the unspeakable pain we will feel when we are no longer simply adults, but old, and for the first time we glimpse ahead the only moment of which we can be sure, the one in which we cross the threshold of death to enter into another life.

The roof of the house was only partially covered by the old, dark gray tiles. It must have been badly damaged, for large portions were now nailed over with patches of roofing felt or tin, and partly with brightly colored advertising signs, and even outside the tiny attic window I saw a drying rack, from which dismal gray diapers flapped wearily in the slack breeze. At the left corner of the house a section of the gutter was hanging down, just as it had seven years earlier, when I stood at this spot and took my leave. Back then I thought: They'll have to have it repaired; I didn't think: I must leave now, and I don't know if I'll ever return. I thought: They'll have to have it repaired. But they hadn't; it was still hanging there—one of the clamps attaching it to the edge of the roof had come loose, and it hung there at an angle, ready to fall at any moment, and I could see clearly where the water poured at an angle against the gray side of the building each time it rained, rushing down, soaking it, a white path edged in dark gray trailing down past the windows, with large round spots to the left and right, their centers white, with increasingly darker rings about them.

That section of gutter had been dangling there for seven years. Seven years. I had traveled far, I had seen death many times, smelled and felt it. I had lived luxuriously, had hungered, starved to the point where I dreamed of white bread, imagining how I would tear into it, bury my face in it, share it, toss it to the entire starving world. I had starved to the point where I no longer felt hunger, but was wrapped instead in those sweet dreams that make actual eating—when it begins again— seem unspeakably disgusting. I had been shot at thousands of times, by guns, mortars, cannons, ships' artillery, airplanes, bombs, and hand grenades. I'd been hit, I'd tasted my own blood on my lips, flowing stickily from my head, sweet and greasy, quickly thickening. I had marched along dusty roads all over Europe until I could no longer feel my feet, pursued white-throated women through dark suburbs without ever, ever possessing a single one; oh, those white throats in dusky lanes...

So very much had happened to me in that time, and it shocked me to think that this damaged gutter had been hanging here those same seven years, guiding the rain at an angle against the façade of the house. This piece of tin had dangled on what remained of its clamp for seven years, roof tiles had blown off, trees had been uprooted, plaster had crumbled, and bombs had fallen from all sides on the sweet open flanks of the city, in the suburbs, woven about with greenery, but this small piece of tin had never been hit, nor forced by a blast of wind to abandon its angle and fall to the ground. Rain had fallen heavily in those seven years, but it had splashed against the façade of the house, had been absorbed by the porous, sandstone wall, and had emerged again, whitish and gray.

Through the gaps in the row of poplars allowing a clearer view of the house, I could see wash hanging out on windy racks: faded men's shirts, frayed women's linen, sweaters, red and green, dresses, and among them a wet, heavy blanket that seemed to pull down on the rack like a leaden weight. Nothing familiar remained, and I was glad. I had always hated the house, loving only its inhabitants, and although the old forms of the park and house emerged everywhere like the water-mark of eternity, I was most deeply affected by that flimsy piece of tin hanging at an angle above the pockmarked frieze of baby angels supporting the roof.

For some time now I had noticed a shadow at the edge of my vision: the man who was sitting on the bench. Evidently he had risen and walked around the corner of the shed, and I now realized that he must have been standing at the edge of my field of vision for some time—whether for minutes, seconds, or hours I couldn't have said—like a small gray speck of dust when you're too busy looking to wipe it from your eye. I turned around again, taking in the park with a sweeping glance, particularly the shrubbery, deeply and painfully reminded of those two stone benches hidden at the thickest point of the musical-clef paths. Then I turned to the admonishing shadow waiting humbly in my field of vision and advanced a few paces.

Up to that point I had passed through the garden plots wherever there was a gap in a fence without thinking, since I could see no sign of planting or sowing. Now I crossed a tiny field of corn stubble along a narrow path and made my way the few paces to the shed.

It seemed as if I had crossed an acoustic border with those three strides. As soon as I was standing beside the man, who nodded in a friendly fashion and returned my "Good evening" with the same words, I heard the sound of children playing, women calling out, men whistling, all the indescribable sounds of evening leisure in the neighborhood of a crowded house on a spring evening after work. Radios warbled light-heartedly through the air, and at the main entrance to the house, which now lay directly before me, I saw two older girls playing with red balls beside the large sandstone pillars of the door. And now I saw for the first time that the left wing of the house had been hit by a heavy shell, and the hole filled in with ugly, blackish bricks. Small children were playing in a sand pile between the poplar trunks, others were striking each other with sticks, running about and screaming with laughter, and a man had turned his bicycle upside down to work on it with rolled-up sleeves.

The old man beside me had seated himself on a board hastily nailed to two wooden blocks, and I sat down beside him. He was short and thin, and although he was wearing a threadbare sailor's cap, I could see from his bare temples and the completely hairless visible portions of his skull that he must be bald. His narrow face was nicely tanned, and his small, almost colorless eyes regarded me with good-natured curiosity. I had been beside him barely half a second before he seemed to sense that I was eagerly inhaling the aroma of his tobacco. Without a word, he started searching through his pockets, while I immediately felt for my pipe.

"I don't have a paper," he said, holding out a tobacco tin.

"Thanks," I said, took the tin, opened it quickly, and filled my pipe.

"Need a light?" he asked.

I nodded.

"Thanks," I said again, handing the tin back to him.

"You're from…"

"France," I said.

"That's what I was about to say; you can always tell by certain features. Rough time?"

I nodded.

"Right."

It felt good to smoke a pipe with someone, the mutual movements of the lips, a smacking motion, and the gentle, almost inaudible puffs with which, in tandem, the blue clouds of smoke are expelled that come gray from the lungs.

I no longer saw much. I suddenly knew that the old man would ask what they all do, and that I would have to say no. I was worried when he started to speak, but all he said was: "Are you looking for someone?"

"Yes," I said softly.

"Who?"

"Family. Fräulein Maria X."

"Oh," he cried, and although he was sitting so close beside me that I would never forget the smell of his clothes, I felt him withdraw. "The Fräulein!"

He must have sensed the rapid, irregular pounding of my heart, he may have seen the drops of sweat breaking out on my brow, and he was surely astonished to see me remove the pipe from my mouth, hold the bowl in my hand, and sigh deeply. Then he drew nearer and said softly, but more coldly than anything he had said thus far: "Don't worry, she's here."

"Thanks," I said, sticking the pipe back in my mouth. I knew now that I had plenty of time, all the time in the world, and I was surprised myself at the depth of the sigh that emerged from me, without my knowledge or will.

Now I felt the old man scrutinizing my worn and tattered uniform; I sensed him drawing a bit closer and closed my eyes, because I knew what he would ask me now.

"Maybe you know him," he said.

I said nothing.

"He was a corporal. Grittner. Hubert. My son. Western front like you. Maybe you know him."

"Where?" I asked hoarsely.

"Falaise," he said, and I felt him waiting...

"I was there too," I said, and now I looked at him. He had removed his pipe from his mouth, wrapping his right hand around the warm bowl, and in his compressed lips and narrowed eyes stood the certainty that he would learn nothing from me. "No," I said with a sigh, and shook my head. Then I put the pipe back in my mouth and looked toward the house.

"Funny," he said, "so many have come back, and not a single one has known him." I started to say something, but he raised his pipe and cut me off. "Oh, I know," he said. "A name means nothing. At Verdun you seldom knew the person lying a foot away from you, I know all about it."

He interrupted himself, looking up as a young, cheerful voice called from the house: "Dad!"

"Yes," he called out softly, "I'm coming," and he touched the rim of his cap with his pipe stem, said goodbye, and left. I called him back and asked: "Which room is she in?"

He understood me at once and pointed with his pipe toward the room next to the room next to the dangling gutter.

"Thanks," I said, and watched as he headed for the house. He walked, as always, no doubt, slowly and calmly, with a slight stoop. He knocked his pipe on the stone lion, which stood halfway along the row of poplars, then turned and nodded to me once again, and in those few seconds it took him to reach the dark entrance and disappear within it, in those few seconds, I suddenly realized that *we all* are guilty *of everything*. Nothing touches us, for when we're asked about someone, we say no. We always have to say no, and when we say it, our hearts refuse to break, when, in fact, what we are saying is: Am I my brother's keeper?

I knew she wasn't there, but I suddenly stood and followed the old man into the house. I entered without taking a close look, but even in passing through I saw, sensed, and smelled that the house looked as if a company of soldiers had spent three weeks there. The staircase was almost undamaged, missing only a lath here and there, and the upper story was dark. I saw at once that the side windows had been boarded up, the light stood in stiff, silver-gray stripes along the edges of the boards, and the hall gave the impression of a cold, rainy, gray winter day outside, with a leaden sky by evening, followed by a sad and starless night.

And although I knew that she wasn't there, I walked quickly to the end of the hall, knocked, waited, knocked again, and rattled the door handle. Naturally nothing stirred, nor did anything stir within me, and in the half minute I stood there, I kept asking myself why that was. The fact that she had kept this same room said a great deal, said everything. But I felt nothing. Finally I noticed a note attached to the door. I tore it off and read it in the light seeping into the hall through the cracks of the old, musty boards.

It was her handwriting: *Be back at eight. Key next door. M.* I stuck the note in my pocket and knocked at the neighboring door. I had heard nothing before I knocked, but now an oppressive silence weighed upon my heart, as if someone were pumping air into me, pressing tighter and tighter against it. I knocked again, then I heard whispering, someone rose from a bed, a key turned in the lock, and in the flat dimness I saw the head of a pretty blond woman, her hair hanging in her eyes. Although I saw only a small strip of her throat, I knew that she was naked. I could smell it as well.

"Fräulein X," I said, "the key for Fräulein X..."

"Oh," she cried out. "You're the one whose picture is hanging over the bed."

"Yes," I said, "probably so."

She closed the door quickly, I heard more whispers, and then a round, naked, and very pretty arm held out a key to me.

I went back, and during the three steps to the door, in the musty hall, which still looked like winter, I realized that there was no point in holding back the memories any longer, once I was in the room. I stuck the key in the lock, paused for a moment, and crumpled the note in my pocket into a tight, small mass, so that I could feel it between my fingers like a tiny, hard paper ball.

Back then it seemed I could see nothing but the part in her hair. It was below me, straight and neat, white and steep like a very narrow, wonderfully bright pathway between soft, gently rising and falling waves of light brown hair. My gaze fell down that part and was lost forever. That narrow pathway had no end, and I felt the sorrow in my heart for that part in her hair.

He could feel her heart beating against his right side, softly and steadily, and knew it was a good heart, with more love in it for him than he would ever find elsewhere. He knew all these things back then, knew he was so close to her he could never, ever be closer. The window stood half open as the dewy, sweet fragrance of the park, filled with enchanting decay, drifted into the room. The greenish curtain colored the light, dyeing her scattered clothes on the floor a similar green. The carpet and chest of drawers, the chair where his sword belt lay, everything was dusky green, tender and beautiful; even the cheap silver buckle of his belt was tinged with green, and he could read the raised inscription surrounding the national insignia and the laurel-wreath clearly: GOD IS WITH US. At the sight of her linen, the brown skirt and red sweater, an infinite tenderness swept over him. He suddenly understood why men promise to fetch the stars from heaven for a woman. His service jacket lay spread out so that only the inner lining was visible, and part of the shoulder straps, bordered in white, and he saw that the collar-band was soiled. But his happily wandering gaze continued to return to the relentlessly clear and neat part in her hair lying below him, and he knew that this pathway had no end, that he would never come as near to any other human as he had to her. Yet she was as infinitely distant as the pathway of the part in her hair was long.

He felt her warm nose against his chin and her breath on his throat, and he sensed that she would never, ever stir again, if he himself did not stir.

Still holding the key, which was already in the lock, he felt the tiny, wadded note in his hand. He chewed his lower lip as he recalled the voice of the woman next door saying: "Oh, you're the one whose picture is hanging over the bed." She started singing, and he could hear her pause in her song to take a deep breath, and then a man's voice could be heard.

He too wished never to stir again back then, to gaze repeatedly down the ravine of that pathway, at times to strip off his clothes, which lay like the flayed green skins of strange beings on the floor, to hear her heart beating against his right side, softly and steadily, a good heart, a happy heart, a better heart than he could ever hope to find, and to feel her warm nose on his chin and her gentle breath flowing at regular intervals against his throat like the breath of a child.

At times he rested his head upon her forehead, and then he could see, on the dark walls, the large, heavy, beautiful painting attributed to Rubens, the shimmering, bright pink flesh of a woman, overly alive against the dark green walls. But this woman had silver-gray hair, which now looked green as well, and her gracious, slight smile passed over both of them, far into the distance. And when he gazed upward while resting on her forehead, he saw the tops of the poplars, silver-gray and near, smelled their cool, astringent fragrance, and through the gaps he saw in the far, far distance the edge of town, red roofs, the trees' bright foliage, the pale towers of the new churches, the black ones of the old, and recalled that it was autumn, in wartime.

He saw everything and nothing. The pattern in the carpet, an eternally self-renewing meander of colors, crossing, overlapping, recrossing, overlapping again, and at the points of intersection large, brightly colored flowers, the tiny spots of damage on the light brown dressing table, and a small, alluringly bright hole in her stocking, which lay in the middle of the room, a tiny green hole. While he saw everything, he saw nothing but the boundless distance at the end of the part in her hair, inaccessible.

It was so quiet, war seemed impossible. In the halls outside, beyond the pale yellow door, the same warm friendliness reigned that they found in the face of the reclining Rubens. Their gaze passed beyond her to the park outside. The sublime, expansive, luxurious fragrance of autumn gathered at the half-open window, a splendid, total silence hovered in the air, enveloping a room that no one would ever enter or leave again, if such was their wish.

Yet he knew it was not only autumn, but wartime. From the moment reason returned, as his gaze followed the lovely, bright, narrow pathway of the part in her hair, he knew that he would have to rise, leave, and return again, and he feared returning most of all. He knew that the soiled collar-band of his uniform would soon be around his neck, that he would face their snarls, his face impassive, and he had a momentary vision of the distant outline of the city, shaved bare, towerless, flat like the sterile silhouette of a churchless village.

Suddenly he felt the soft touch of her lashes on his cheek, knew that she had opened her eyes, and realized that he was naked. Then he saw her hair close up, the short part in her hair, and beyond it the white pillow. As if he were recovering consciousness, everything drew closer, like a field glass coming into focus. He smelled the garden, redolent and cloud-covered, smelled her skin and heard the soft murmur of voices on the terrace below, heard the clinking of glasses and the full, baroque laughter of a woman. And he realized that all those sitting below knew about them, and that no one would say anything.

He saw in detail what he would be doing in a few minutes. Saw himself dressing, kissing her forehead, quietly leaving the room, disappearing through the rear gate, never to return again.

And in the same instant he realized that he was naked, he pictured her rising that next morning and going downstairs, without a question raised, until one day someone would mention with a smile that the postwoman was certainly bringing a lot of letters, and later he'd seen her a thousand times, running up the stairs with his letters, jerking open the door, leaning back against it, and tearing them open, her hands trembling.

And as he passed through the back entrance, through that rusty, creaking, iron gate, he knew that he would never fear death, but only life.

He released the crumpled note, felt his hands sweating, then turned the key and entered the room.

He walked quickly across the carpet, past the bed, which still stood on the right near the window, and looked toward the window, which opened onto the park: The light entered the room only through the narrow slits of the closed shutters, slicing the space into individual, closely layered planes. The room was saturated with bands of light, separated from each other by thin strata of shadow. Everything he could see was striped light and dark, and there could be no doubt that it was all real. The painting was still on the wall, still too bright and too alive for the dark green wallpaper, the stripes crossing the face, the dresser and bed, and he caught a glimpse of a large glass case overflowing with odds and ends, and a desk between the bed and door. All was dark below the level of the window ledge, illuminated only faintly by the reflection of those stripes of light and shadow, and he gathered from a burning smell the presence of a stove. But he noted all this merely in passing. He had intended to walk over, throw open the window, and take possession of the room, but after the first step he'd sensed something strange, immaterial, insubstantial, ineffable, that reminded him the room was not his. And that it would be equally difficult for him to take possession of either her or the room. Something foreign, unknown, filled him with a jealousy he'd not felt before. The moment he was touched by that shadowy, transitory, but unspeakably real presence, a savage, raging jealousy stabbed deep into his heart, and he knew that far from fearing to have her, he would instead have to fight for her.

He paused for a moment just beyond the threshold, wondering whether to turn on the light, to seek some clue, some concrete object that might possibly explain this sense of strangeness and fright, but he knew at once that it would be nothing tangible or visible, or even connected to tangible, visible objects, and that he had no right to seek such things, even if they existed.

He walked out slowly and relocked the door.

The dialogue of male and female voices next door was louder and clearer now. He even understood a few words, but they rained down like shells falling short.

A door was abruptly opened somewhere in the rear of the house, and for a moment the dimly lit hall filled partially with gray light; other doors opened and shut again, steps faded down a wooden stairway, and now he smelled the distinct odor of fish and sliced onions. He leaned against the door frame. Now he understood what it meant: Her heart had been beating for twenty-five years, but he'd only felt it beat for half a minute, her brain had been thinking for twenty-five years, millions of thoughts, and he'd only known a fraction of them. He'd thought he possessed her, possessed her so thoroughly he could never lose her, so much so, so strongly, that he was afraid to return. Now he understood how senseless and silly he had been to believe that. He knew nothing about her, nothing he could call his own. He might just as well dip a pail in the ocean and claim he owned the sea. He didn't even know what she liked to eat, where she lived or how. He tried to imagine her riding the tram, looking out at passersby, stores, animals, buildings, piles of rubble, flowers and trees, tried to imagine each thought that connected her to all these things, to flowers, trees, animals, people, and stores. Her every thought, dozens every minute, was a world in itself, and there were a million such worlds in her, memories, dreams. He knew so infinitely little of it all that he felt totally miserable, leaning back against the door frame in this dark hall, which smelled increasingly of fish and onions, and now began to reek of vinegar, too.

Jealousy raged like a savage beast that had crept inside him and was now tearing him apart. How he wanted to possess her as he had back then, totally, yet knowing that the smooth pathway of the part in her hair was endless and that he could never travel to its end. How he hated her shoelace; he tried to imagine it: a brown, slightly frayed shoelace, on the end of which some dirt had perhaps dried. She had always been slightly unkempt, in a charming way.

All of it, the terrible intangible strangeness of objects and the thoughts they awakened, struck him the moment he entered the room, and he had recoiled as a thin black wall rose before him, steep and solid, impenetrable, reaching heavenward to the rim of eternity.

He sighed deeply, inhaled as well the reek of vapors now filling the hall with smoke, and felt a quick, strong wave of nausea, suddenly aware of how tired and hungry he was.

He felt his face collapse; his eyes were aching: a gnawing suction deep in the hollows of his eyes, a tormenting, piercing pain he often experienced at the end of a sleepless night. He reinserted the key cautiously in the lock, stumbled into the room, pulled the door closed behind him, and slowly removed the knapsack he carried on his back with a long strap. Then he bent over, felt along the carpet to the left of the door, and slowly slid to the floor. It was wonderful to lie down and stretch out his legs, the knapsack, as so often, under his head.

It must be almost seven. Although he knew her heart beat for him, lovingly and calmly, more lovingly than any other heart ever could, he felt somewhere deep inside that she would not be his, that he would have to relinquish her to something he'd never felt before, something ineffable, stretching from her frayed shoelace to the clouds she sometimes gazed at with thoughts he knew nothing about. He would lose her to the world, that world where it was always so easy to contemplate death, so hard to think of life.

The striped light from the window fell in enlarged form upon the door and wall, a dissolving rectangle, soft and blurred, the white stripes glimmering, the black ones hazy, and he saw that the large black crucifix from the vestibule was now hanging here.

He was oppressed once more by the room's foreignness, a room that wasn't his, by the strange, clean smell of soft soap, clothes, and a hint of cigarette smoke. He rose quickly, picked up his knapsack, and opened the door. As he turned the key in the lock, he wondered for whom the note on the door had been intended. But the thought aroused no hint of jealousy. No, he wasn't jealous of other men. They were all the same, they were all lonely; it was the world he envied so, and the thoughts that filled it.

One of the doors leading into the hall was now standing open, and he could tell by the odor that this was where the fish, onions, and vinegar were being prepared. The vapors filled the room to overflowing and were now seeping into the hall in lukewarm, overpowering waves. He could hear what were apparently raw potatoes being tossed into a pan of sizzling grease; then the bubbling grease gradually subsided to a low, steady crackle as dark gray clouds of vapor billowed from the room, trailing toward the stairwell in soft, slender tendrils. The noise increased, and now and then a door opened. He walked slowly toward the open door and stood for a moment along the opposite wall, watching a short, fat older woman with her left hand stuck in the top of her blouse, slowly turning potatoes in a pan. On an unsanitary-looking table stood a huge porcelain bowl in which gleaming blue fish swam in vinegar, and he could make out the now yellowed sliced onions surrounding them. The entire room was illuminated through a single small pane of glass set in a wooden frame within roughly cemented blocks, which apparently could not be opened. On the kitchen counter—worn, faded, covered with reddish lacquer—stood a bread canister and a scale. He spotted an alarm clock and saw that it was twenty minutes to seven.

He walked back slowly to the stairwell and descended. The white stucco decorations on the ceiling and walls were now defaced islands, scrawled for the most part with all sorts of graffiti.

Descending slowly, step by step, he wondered if he should leave.

Perhaps, he thought, it would be better to go now, before I discover I have no choice; I may spare the menacing angel with the sword the painful duty of driving me out, of watching over my departure with torch and sword. Perhaps I may kneel humbly at the angel's feet, on the threshold, kneel two minutes in his presence, bearing the burden of the last thirty years of my life on my knees.

He paused on a landing and looked through a broken section in the board planks into the back garden. There was the small rusty gate through which he had left back then. It led to a neighboring property, with a well-preserved, well-tended garden; the house, newly roofed and plastered, radiated affluence, security, and serenity. The long, shiny, handsomely painted shutters could close at night or for evening banquets, covering the equally charming, tall and narrow windows. The lawn had been turned and newly seeded. He saw the tiny, deliciously soft shimmer of the first touch of green, the soft down of spring, saw the flower beds with their orderly rows of pansies, and a slender young woman at the side of an equally slender young man, smiling proudly as they strolled slowly along, admiring their garden. The woman was wearing a long, dark brown dress, somewhat darker than the reddish tone of her luxuriantly gleaming hair, with a high-necked yellow sweater, which revealed a narrow strip of her blindingly white throat, like a simple but precious necklace. They looked like clever mechanical dolls, with clever smiles, carefully nuanced, well tempered. Their gestures and steps were so skillfully rehearsed there was no need to note that they were stand-ins in a film that would come to a surprisingly strange end.

He continued slowly to the ground floor and saw that the children were still playing ball at the entrance. It was lovely the way the plump balls flew back and forth so cheerfully in the gray frame of bright light at the door, bouncing softly off the sandstone pilasters, and he heard the bright, eager, unflagging count of the young girls' voices in the contest.

Only now that he was outside did he realize that people must be living in the cellar as well. Rusty brown pipes jutted out of the openings, emitting smoke along with all sorts of cooking odors. Behind the windows, which extended halfway above ground level, he could see a few dismal yellow lights. He heard a radio and voices, and suddenly realized that his hands, seemingly listless within his pockets, were perspiring with fear: He feared the music coming from overbearing mechanical speakers throughout the world, feared the piping, soft, congested voices that undermined the world with their calm, soft security. No place was safe from this so-called music, a steady stream of slime dripping into the ears of humanity from a million speakers. And the smell of onions, fish, vinegar, and fried potatoes permeated the world. He wanted to bury himself deep in the earth and plug his ears, and only now and then, taking a shallow breath, listen to the song of silence, the gentle and lost fragments of paradise.

He wiped his hands on the inner lining of his pockets and walked slowly to the bench where he had been sitting with the old man just a few minutes ago. Having waited years to see her again, the prospect of waiting another hour filled him with a frantic impatience that left him indecisive. He didn't know where to go, the pale wall of her room stood clearly before his eyes, the play of light and shadow from the shutter forming a pattern of silver and black stripes upon it, and over the door the large black crucifix with the white body. He longed to be there on the carpet, the knapsack under his head, looking at the crucifix and waiting, perhaps sleeping as well, but he knew that he would flee from this strange void again, this solid black wall, invisible yet real, thin yet unutterably strong. This wall kept him from entering, throwing open the window, and taking possession of everything, the bed, the view from the window, kept him from gazing out toward the city on the distant horizon, now leveled flat, that he had glimpsed for a moment back then. He had always known the past could never be restored, but actually to experience the fact was frightening. Never, never again... Yet he knew she would never forget him. The trace of his eyes on the things in her room could never be effaced, sharper than the bold and regal line of the firmest brush was the trace of his eyes upon her forehead, upon the painting, the carpet, upon the distant horizon, upon every tiny place on her body.

He saw a man working with a shovel and hoe in another garden plot. He went up to him, looked into a tired, unfriendly face, lit his pipe, still half-filled with tobacco, and sat down on the bench, staring at the ground, which was brown, a dark, moist brown, slightly damp, flecked with traces of the white gravel that had once covered the entire semicircular area. The white specks had turned dark; the gradients of the path had been rolled and flattened. Here and there cornstalks, now rotted black, had been trampled into the path, along with rusty nails, burned matches with blackened heads, and in the center, half of a black trouser button.

His thought about the marble-white benches on the clef-shaped paths through the shrubbery, almost certainly overgrown, now struck him as foolish. He had intended to seek out the bench on the left of the grove, to make his way through the undergrowth and touch its cold, damp surface, but now all he could remember was the fear he'd felt as, leaving that very bench, he had emerged from the grove with Maria and approached the terrace, where laughing guests were drinking wine and chatting softly in the mild humidity of a warm autumn evening.

He had paused at the rim of the fountain, looking up at her room on the upper story by the dangling gutter, already feeling the pain of departure. The house stood quiet and calm, wrapped in twilight; between the rows of poplars he had glimpsed the bright dresses of the women, the glowing tips of cigars, heard the voice of a young woman hired to sing. Only a few people lived in the house back then, it was always quiet, always slightly run-down.

At the fountain's rim he had taken his leave. They'll have to have it repaired, he thought, looking at the dangling gutter. Walking past everyone, he led Maria toward her room. Once inside the door of the building she had walked ahead of him, and in the half darkness of the hall he had seen the long folds of her gray dress, her white throat, and as she turned to step into the room, her soft profile.

Later, in Romania, in a White city, he had entered a shop to barter two handkerchiefs and a pair of socks. It was evening, a lively dark bustle of gray uniforms in the narrow lanes, men in long white coattails, and women. All was quiet and gloomy, filled with the voluptuousness of dissolution and decline. They were near the front, and they could hear the impact of the shells, not the soft, thick sound of dough being pounded in the distance, but close by, strident and savage, as if the earth were a piece of flimsy plywood smashed and splintered by hammers. Sometimes they even heard machine-gun fire, rapid and hopeless, like the grinding of worn-out brakes. In one of those streets that at first seem totally empty and turn out to be teeming with life, he stepped into a store, opened a door that led into the darkness, and found himself in a secondhand shop where musty-smelling clothes dangled on hangers from dismal racks, like corpses hanging their heads, their legs amputated. Cheap knickknacks, utensils, Japanese figurines, and watches

damned to inactivity stood behind the clothes racks on bluish shelves.
He leaned against the low, greasy counter and lit a cigarette.

Suddenly a young Jewish boy emerged silently behind the counter,
pale, his face a mixture of boldness, fear, and nameless sadness. He
laid his brand-new handkerchiefs on the counter along with the pair
of socks. The boy shook his head gently, then was shoved aside by a
woman wearing a wrinkled yellow dress. Her profile reminded him of
Maria's, as she emerged with him from the garden, walking ahead.

The woman greeted him with a silent nod. He watched as she
bent over his things, and her thick hair seemed a dark, dark green. Her
hands fingered the linens and he saw that they were small and surprisingly delicate, like the hands of a child. The linens disappeared quietly
and briskly under the counter and a banknote lay pale blue against the
black wood of the counter. Then she covered the banknote quickly with
one hand, lifted her head, and in her face, pale and pretty, with painted
lips, he read a weary, indifferent offer.

He took the banknote quickly and banged the door behind him,
leaving the clothescorpses swaying slightly on their racks and the Japanese figurines and utensils rattling against one another. He hurried back
to the main street, and although it was almost jammed solid with fleeing people, with tanks, some of them damaged, and with carts, and
although orders were being shouted to awaken a sense of urgency, he
went into a tavern and drank the money up. A crowd of soldiers in the
tavern were saying there was still plenty of time, things weren't so bad,
the Russians didn't have the strength to advance any farther, and he
learned that the front was just two miles off, if it could still be called a
front. Then he turned to wine and schnapps, drowning his fear of the
secondhand shop with its hanging clothescorpses, the boy, and the profile of the woman who smiled at him with lethargic willingness. Later,
because he had a slight leg wound, a medical corps sergeant let him
jump on a train for the wounded as it was leaving a station, steadily
shelled at regular intervals by the Russians.

As he gazed at the tips of his shoes, sharply outlined against the brown
soil mixed with gravel, everything came back to him, how in the dark
train rumbling into the night, someone had given him a piece of sausage

reeking of garlic, and a dry, musty piece of bread. He had been dying of thirst, and only later, much later, after rocking through an interminable night, at a dark and crowded station platform where people were huddled silently for the night, did they receive a little coffee, in a small tin can.

That's how it always was: He would recall Maria's throat, or her profile, and a myriad memories would tumble after them, as if the first small image were simply the initial link in an infinitely long chain that must glide through him whether he wished it or not. But he forced back these thoughts, stared again at the black tips of his English military shoes, and tried to imagine what lay ahead.

Sometimes he tried to imagine he would find some job to earn a little money, enough to lie in that room, on the bed. Now he tried to picture what it would be like on the bed, his gaze fixed on the crucifix that would always be in her field of vision. Maria would be standing at the stove, delicate and slightly helpless, and he would ask her please not to fix fish with vinegar and sliced onions, and perhaps the window would be standing open, and the rain would pour through the broken gutter, and the poplars would shield her room from the echo of countless radios.

But suddenly he realized that another pair of shoes had entered his field of vision. They were beautiful, brown, high-quality men's oxfords, cleaned and polished, looking as if they belonged in a display case, yet standing on the edge of the small path, the heels projecting halfway over the furrow. He had always liked his own shoes, black English military-issue shoes from camp, but now they seemed crude, ugly, and shapeless compared to these handsome, polished, high-quality store-window shoes. But the shoes in a store window lacked socks, nor were they topped by soft, light brown, good-looking trousers that almost matched, with a crease that seemed to have a long, sharp knife hidden inside.

He knocked out his pipe, realizing he couldn't have been smoking more than three minutes on what little tobacco he had left, and he thought how long three minutes could be, how it could last years and years. He lifted his head, looked into a face, and knew that he would never lie on the bed, staring at the black crucifix on the green wall, that Maria would never stand at the stove, that he would never let the rain pour through the damaged gutter. He knew it, even though he realized that short of death, there was nothing that must surely come to pass.

The face was calm and broad, the mouth somewhat thin, the eyes slightly narrow, but the forehead was high and noble; his hair, however, was curly, combed with unnecessary care; he had never liked men with wavy hair...

In the matching hands below, the man carried a brown attaché case, and pressed against the attaché case with the thumb, a soft, light gray hat, with an immaculate sweatband.

The man said to him: "Oh, I see, you're the one over her bed." And he said the same thing he'd said to the pretty woman: "Probably so."

Then he took his hand from his pocket, still clutching the note, which he undid carefully, and held it out, saying: "This must be for you..."

"Oh, yes," said the other, "it's for me. So she'll be back at eight." And he looked at his wristwatch and said: "Over an hour yet."

They looked at each other, the man chewing on his lower lip, and he, on the bench, knew now that she belonged to this man, to him alone, and that nothing and no one in the world could take her from him, just as surely as he knew that he would never lie upon that bed.

Now they looked past each other, and then he looked at the ground again and saw that the man's shoes were tapping restlessly. He kept tapping his toes, and between the tips of the shoes, separated by the regulation distance, the man sitting on the bench saw half of a black trouser button, trampled into the ground.

"Perhaps," the voice now said above him, "we should spend the hour in conversation."

I stood up and followed him, and as I stood, in that tenth of a second, that fractional fraction of the tiniest space of time, I knew that she was lost to me, finally and irrevocably. As long as the garden paths were too narrow to walk side by side he remained in front of me, then he paused for a moment as we reached the broader paths, let me draw up alongside him, and we walked back in silence on the long, straight path that led through the grove toward the entrance, to that rusted gate no one opened anymore. Then we turned left toward one of the gaps in the wall, and I saw a car parked under the thick green roof of the trees, a black, high-quality, solid, and expensive piece of workmanship, reliable, clean, rugged, and sturdy. We slowed down as we approached one of the largest gaps; now we stopped and looked at each other. I saw he was trembling, his lips quivered, the solid, large, well-formed face seemed to come unhinged, and he said to me: "We were married yesterday, no one knows." I simply nodded, looked at the ground, and then at him again.

His eyes spoke a huge truth of which he could not be aware—together with his pain, his poverty, his trembling, all his unknown, repressed pain—the truth that there are things that can't be bought or won, that can only come as a gift, and one of these is love.

I nodded again and walked away. I climbed carefully over the wall, crossed the avenue, and made my way along a rough, treeless road toward the city, where I could catch a train. Behind me the sun stood low on the horizon, casting my shadow so far forward that I could scarcely see the large round dot of my head. Only when I came to some obstacle, a fence, a shed, or a partially collapsed wall, would the shadow of my head pause before me, growing larger and larger, until it flowed beyond the object it had struck, flying from me again, far, far away, so far beyond my flat field of vision that I could no longer see it, and I knew that I would never, never reach it again.

THE TRAIN WAS ON TIME
Translated by Leila Vennewitz / Afterword by William T. Vollmann
978-1-935554-32-5 | $14.95 / $16.95 CAN

"Böll has feelingly symbolized a guilty Germany doing penance for its sins through suffering and death." —*Time*

GROUP PORTRAIT WITH LADY
Translated by Leila Vennewitz
978-1-935554-33-2 | $18.95 / $21.50 CAN

"His most grandly conceived [novel] ... the magnum opus which so far crowns his work."
—The Nobel Prize Committee

WHAT'S TO BECOME OF THE BOY?
OR, SOMETHING TO DO WITH BOOKS
Translated by Leila Vennewitz / Introduction by Anne Applebaum
978-1-61219-001-3 | $14.95 / $16.95 CAN

"The depth of Böll's vision into the human soul can be breathtaking." —*The Washington Post*

THE COLLECTED STORIES
Translated by Leila Vennewitz and Breon Mitchell
978-1-61219-002-0 | $29.95 / $29.95 CAN

"This is a most impressive collection, confirming Böll's standing as one of the best writers of our time. It would form an admirable introduction to his work for those who don't yet know it. It is the work of affirmation, for it proclaims the values of humanity and the unquenchable vitality of the spirit." —*The Scotsman*